HERMAN MELVILLE

PIERRE
or, The Ambiguities

ISRAEL POTTER
His Fifty Years of Exile

THE PIAZZA TALES

THE CONFIDENCE-MAN
His Masquerade

UNCOLLECTED PROSE

BILLY BUDD, SAILOR
(An Inside Narrative)

Distributed to the trade in the United States
and Canada by the Viking Press.

Published outside North America by the Press Syndicate
of the University of Cambridge,
The Pitt Building, Trumpington Street, Cambridge CB21RP, England
ISBN 0 521 30098 3

Library of Congress Catalog Card Number: 84–11249
For Cataloging in Publication Data, see end of *Notes* section.
ISBN 0–940450–24–0

First Printing

Manufactured in the United States of America

HARRISON HAYFORD
WROTE THE NOTES AND SELECTED
THE TEXTS FOR THIS VOLUME

The texts of Pierre, Israel Potter, The Confidence-Man,
The Piazza Tales, and Uncollected Prose are from
The Northwestern-Newberry Edition of the Writings of
Herman Melville edited by Harrison Hayford, Hershel Parker,
and G. Thomas Tanselle and published by Northwestern
University Press and The Newberry Library,
and are printed with the permission of the publishers.
Billy Budd, Sailor, edited by Harrison Hayford and
Merton M. Sealts, Jr., is printed from the
text published by the University of Chicago.

Grateful acknowledgement is made to the National Endowment
for the Humanities and the Ford Foundation for their
generous financial support of this series.

Contents

Each section has its own table of contents.

PIERRE

or

The Ambiguities

Greylock's Most Excellent Majesty

IN OLD TIMES authors were proud of the privilege of dedicating their works to Majesty. A right noble custom, which we of Berkshire must revive. For whether we will or no, Majesty is all around us here in Berkshire, sitting as in a grand Congress of Vienna of majestical hill-tops, and eternally challenging our homage.

But since the majestic mountain, Greylock—my own more immediate sovereign lord and king—hath now, for innumerable ages, been the one grand dedicatee of the earliest rays of all the Berkshire mornings, I know not how his Imperial Purple Majesty (royal-born: Porphyrogenitus) will receive the dedication of my own poor solitary ray.

Nevertheless, forasmuch as I, dwelling with my loyal neighbors, the Maples and the Beeches, in the amphitheater over which his central majesty presides, have received his most bounteous and unstinted fertilizations, it is but meet, that I here devoutly kneel, and render up my gratitude, whether, thereto, The Most Excellent Purple Majesty of Greylock benignantly incline his hoary crown or no.

Pittsfield, Mass.

Contents

Book I

THERE ARE some strange summer mornings in the country, when he who is but a sojourner from the city shall
early walk forth into the fields, and be wonder-smitten with
the trance-like aspect of the green and golden world. Not a
flower stirs; the trees forget to wave; the grass itself seems to
have ceased to grow; and all Nature, as if suddenly become
conscious of her own profound mystery, and feeling no refuge from it but silence, sinks into this wonderful and indescribable repose.

Such was the morning in June, when, issuing from the embowered and high-gabled old home of his fathers, Pierre,
dewily refreshed and spiritualized by sleep, gayly entered the
long, wide, elm-arched street of the village, and half unconsciously bent his steps toward a cottage, which peeped into
view near the end of the vista.

The verdant trance lay far and wide; and through it nothing came but the brindled kine, dreamily wandering to their
pastures, followed, not driven, by ruddy-cheeked, white-
footed boys.

As touched and bewitched by the loveliness of this silence,
Pierre neared the cottage, and lifted his eyes, he swiftly
paused, fixing his glance upon one upper, open casement
there. Why now this impassioned, youthful pause? Why this
enkindled cheek and eye? Upon the sill of the casement, a
snow-white glossy pillow reposes, and a trailing shrub has
softly rested a rich, crimson flower against it.

Well mayst thou seek that pillow, thou odoriferous flower,
thought Pierre; not an hour ago, her own cheek must have
rested there. "Lucy!"

"Pierre!"

As heart rings to heart those voices rang, and for a moment, in the bright hush of the morning, the two stood
silently but ardently eying each other, beholding mutual reflections of a boundless admiration and love.

"Nothing but Pierre," laughed the youth, at last; "thou hast forgotten to bid me good-morning."

"That would be little. Good-mornings, good-evenings, good days, weeks, months, and years to thee, Pierre;—bright Pierre!—Pierre!"

Truly, thought the youth, with a still gaze of inexpressible fondness; truly the skies do ope, and this invoking angel looks down.—"I would return thee thy manifold good-mornings, Lucy, did not that presume thou had'st lived through a night; and by Heaven, thou belong'st to the regions of an infinite day!"

"Fie, now, Pierre; why should ye youths always swear when ye love?"

"Because in us love is profane, since it mortally reaches toward the heaven in ye!"

"There thou fly'st again, Pierre; thou art always circumventing me so. Tell me, why should ye youths ever show so sweet an expertness in turning all trifles of ours into trophies of yours?"

"I know not how that is, but ever was it our fashion to do." And shaking the casement shrub, he dislodged the flower, and conspicuously fastened it in his bosom.—"I must away now, Lucy; see! under these colors I march."

"Bravissimo! oh, my only recruit!"

ii

Pierre was the only son of an affluent, and haughty widow; a lady who externally furnished a singular example of the preservative and beautifying influences of unfluctuating rank, health, and wealth, when joined to a fine mind of medium culture, uncankered by any inconsolable grief, and never worn by sordid cares. In mature age, the rose still miraculously clung to her cheek; litheness had not yet completely uncoiled itself from her waist, nor smoothness unscrolled itself from her brow, nor diamondness departed from her eyes. So that when lit up and bediademed by ball-room lights, Mrs. Glendinning still eclipsed far younger charms, and had she chosen to encourage them, would have been followed by a train of infatuated suitors, little less young than her own son Pierre.

But a reverential and devoted son seemed lover enough for this widow Bloom; and besides all this, Pierre when namelessly annoyed, and sometimes even jealously transported by the too ardent admiration of the handsome youths, who now and then, caught in unintended snares, seemed to entertain some insane hopes of wedding this unattainable being; Pierre had more than once, with a playful malice, openly sworn, that the man—gray-beard, or beardless—who should dare to propose marriage to his mother, that man would by some peremptory unrevealed agency immediately disappear from the earth.

This romantic filial love of Pierre seemed fully returned by the triumphant maternal pride of the widow, who in the clear-cut lineaments and noble air of the son, saw her own graces strangely translated into the opposite sex. There was a striking personal resemblance between them; and as the mother seemed to have long stood still in her beauty, heedless of the passing years; so Pierre seemed to meet her half-way, and by a splendid precocity of form and feature, almost advanced himself to that mature stand-point in Time, where his pedestaled mother so long had stood. In the playfulness of their unclouded love, and with that strange license which a perfect confidence and mutual understanding at all points, had long bred between them, they were wont to call each other brother and sister. Both in public and private this was their usage; nor when thrown among strangers, was this mode of address ever suspected for a sportful assumption; since the amaranthineness of Mrs. Glendinning fully sustained this youthful pretension.—Thus freely and lightsomely for mother and son flowed on the pure joined current of life. But as yet the fair river had not borne its waves to those side-ways repelling rocks, where it was thenceforth destined to be forever divided into two unmixing streams.

An excellent English author of these times enumerating the prime advantages of his natal lot, cites foremost, that he first saw the rural light. So with Pierre. It had been his choice fate to have been born and nurtured in the country, surrounded by scenery whose uncommon loveliness was the perfect mould of a delicate and poetic mind; while the popular names of its finest features appealed to the proudest patriotic and family associations of the historic line of Glendinning. On the meadows which sloped away from the shaded rear of the manorial mansion, far to the winding river, an Indian battle had been fought, in the earlier days of the colony, and in that battle the paternal great-grandfather of Pierre, mortally wounded, had sat unhorsed on his saddle in the grass, with his dying voice, still cheering his men in the fray. This was Saddle-Meadows, a name likewise extended to the mansion and the village. Far beyond these plains, a day's walk for Pierre, rose the storied heights, where in the Revolutionary War his grandfather had for several months defended a rude but all-important stockaded fort, against the repeated combined assaults of Indians, Tories, and Regulars. From before that fort, the gentlemanly, but murderous half-breed, Brandt, had fled, but had survived to dine with General Glendinning, in the amicable times which followed that vindictive war. All the associations of Saddle-Meadows were full of pride to Pierre. The Glendinning deeds by which their estate had so long been held, bore the cyphers of three Indian kings, the aboriginal and only conveyancers of those noble woods and plains. Thus loftily, in the days of his circumscribed youth, did Pierre glance along the background of his race; little recking of that maturer and larger interior development, which should forever deprive these things of their full power of pride in his soul.

But the breeding of Pierre would have been unwisely contracted, had his youth been unintermittingly passed in these rural scenes. At a very early period he had begun to accompany his father and mother—and afterwards his mother alone—in their annual visits to the city; where naturally mingling in a large and polished society, Pierre had insensibly formed himself in the airier graces of life, without enfeebling the vigor derived from a martial race, and fostered in the country's clarion air.

Nor while thus liberally developed in person and manners, was Pierre deficient in a still better and finer culture. Not in vain had he spent long summer afternoons in the deep recesses of his father's fastidiously picked and decorous library; where the Spenserian nymphs had early led him into many a maze of all-bewildering beauty. Thus, with a graceful glow on his limbs, and soft, imaginative flames in his heart, did this Pierre glide toward maturity, thoughtless of that period of remorseless insight, when all these delicate warmths should seem frigid to him, and he should madly demand more ardent fires.

Nor had that pride and love which had so bountifully provided for the youthful nurture of Pierre, neglected his culture in the deepest element of all. It had been a maxim with the father of Pierre, that all gentlemanhood was vain; all claims to it preposterous and absurd, unless the primeval gentleness and golden humanities of religion had been so thoroughly wrought into the complete texture of the character, that he who pronounced himself gentleman, could also rightfully assume the meek, but kingly style of Christian. At the age of sixteen, Pierre partook with his mother of the Holy Sacraments.

It were needless, and more difficult, perhaps, to trace out precisely the absolute motives which prompted these youthful vows. Enough, that as to Pierre had descended the numerous other noble qualities of his ancestors; and as he now stood heir to their forests and farms; so by the same insensible sliding process, he seemed to have inherited their docile homage to a venerable Faith, which the first Glendinning had brought over sea, from beneath the shadow of an English minister. Thus in Pierre was the complete polished steel of the gentleman, girded with Religion's silken sash; and his great-grandfather's soldierly fate had taught him that the generous sash should, in the last bitter trial, furnish its wearer with Glory's shroud; so that what through life had been worn for Grace's sake, in death might safely hold the man. But while thus all alive to the beauty and poesy of his father's faith, Pierre little foresaw that this world hath a secret deeper than beauty, and Life some burdens heavier than death.

So perfect to Pierre had long seemed the illuminated scroll of his life thus far, that only one hiatus was discoverable by him in that sweetly-writ manuscript. A sister had been omitted from the text. He mourned that so delicious a feeling as fraternal love had been denied him. Nor could the fictitious title, which he so often lavished upon his mother, at all supply the absent reality. This emotion was most natural; and the full cause and reason of it even Pierre did not at that time entirely appreciate. For surely a gentle sister is the second best gift to a man; and it is first in point of occurrence; for the wife comes after. He who is sisterless, is as a bachelor before his time. For much that goes to make up the deliciousness of a wife, already lies in the sister.

"Oh, had my father but had a daughter!" cried Pierre; "some one whom I might love, and protect, and fight for, if need be. It must be a glorious thing to engage in a mortal quarrel on a sweet sister's behalf! Now, of all things, would to heaven, I had a sister!"

Thus, ere entranced in the gentler bonds of a lover; thus often would Pierre invoke heaven for a sister; but Pierre did not then know, that if there be any thing a man might well pray against, that thing is the responsive gratification of some of the devoutest prayers of his youth.

It may have been that this strange yearning of Pierre for a sister, had part of its origin in that still stranger feeling of loneliness he sometimes experienced, as not only the solitary head of his family, but the only surnamed male Glendinning extant. A powerful and populous family had by degrees run off into the female branches; so that Pierre found himself surrounded by numerous kinsmen and kinswomen, yet companioned by no surnamed male Glendinning, but the duplicate one reflected to him in the mirror. But in his more wonted natural mood, this thought was not wholly sad to him. Nay, sometimes it mounted into an exultant swell. For in the ruddiness, and flushfulness, and vaingloriousness of his youthful soul, he fondly hoped to have a monopoly of glory in capping the fame-column, whose tall shaft had been erected by his noble sires.

In all this, how unadmonished was our Pierre by that foreboding and prophetic lesson taught, not less by Palmyra's quarries, than by Palmyra's ruins. Among those ruins is a crumbling, uncompleted shaft, and some leagues off, ages ago left in the quarry, is the crumbling corresponding capital, also incomplete. These Time seized and spoiled; these Time crushed in the egg; and the proud stone that should have stood among the clouds, Time left abased beneath the soil.

Oh, what quenchless feud is this, that Time hath with the sons of Men!

iii

It has been said that the beautiful country round about Pierre appealed to very proud memories. But not only through the mere chances of things, had that fine country become ennobled by the deeds of his sires, but in Pierre's eyes, all its hills and swales seemed as sanctified through their very long uninterrupted possession by his race.

That fond ideality which, in the eyes of affection, hallows the least trinket once familiar to the person of a departed love; with Pierre that talisman touched the whole earthly landscape about him; for remembering that on those hills his own fine fathers had gazed; through those woods, over these lawns, by that stream, along these tangled paths, many a grand-dame of his had merrily strolled when a girl; vividly recalling these things, Pierre deemed all that part of the earth a love-token; so that his very horizon was to him as a memorial ring.

The monarchical world very generally imagines, that in demagoguical America the sacred Past hath no fixed statues erected to it, but all things irreverently seethe and boil in the vulgar caldron of an everlasting uncrystalizing Present. This conceit would seem peculiarly applicable to the social condition. With no chartered aristocracy, and no law of entail, how can any family in America imposingly perpetuate itself? Certainly that common saying among us, which declares, that be a family conspicuous as it may, a single half-century shall see it abased; that maxim undoubtedly holds true with the commonalty. In our cities families rise and burst like bubbles in a vat. For indeed the democratic element operates as a subtile acid among us; forever producing new things by corroding the old; as in the south of France verdigris, the primitive material of one kind of green paint, is produced by grape-vinegar poured upon copper plates. Now in general nothing can be more significant of decay than the idea of corrosion; yet on the other hand, nothing can more vividly suggest luxuriance of life, than the idea of green as a color; for green is the peculiar signet of all-fertile Nature herself. Herein by apt analogy we behold the marked anomalousness of America; whose character abroad, we need not be surprised, is misconceived, when we consider how strangely she contradicts all prior notions of human things; and how wonderfully to her, Death itself becomes transmuted into Life. So that political institutions, which in other lands seem above all things intensely artificial, with America seem to possess the divine virtue of a natural law; for the most mighty of nature's laws is this, that out of Death she brings Life.

Still, are there things in the visible world, over which ever-shifting Nature hath not so unbounded a sway. The grass is annually changed; but the limbs of the oak, for a long term of years, defy that annual decree. And if in America the vast mass of families be as the blades of grass, yet some few there are that stand as the oak; which, instead of decaying, annually puts forth new branches; whereby Time, instead of subtracting, is made to capitulate into a multiple virtue.

In this matter we will—not superciliously, but in fair spirit—compare pedigrees with England, and strange as it may seem at the first blush, not without some claim to equality. I dare say, that in this thing the Peerage Book is a good statistical standard whereby to judge her; since the compilers of that work can not be entirely insensible on whose patronage they most rely; and the common intelligence of our own people shall suffice to judge us. But the magnificence of names must not mislead us as to the humility of things. For as the breath in all our lungs is hereditary, and my present breath at this moment, is further descended than the body of the present High Priest of the Jews, so far as he can assuredly trace it; so mere names, which are also but air, do likewise revel in this endless descendedness. But if Richmond, and St. Albans, and Grafton, and Portland, and Buccleugh, be names almost old as England herself, the present Dukes of those names stop in their own genuine pedigrees at Charles II., and there find no very fine fountain; since what we would deem the least glorious parentage under the sun, is precisely the parentage of a Buccleugh, for example; whose ancestress could not well avoid being a mother, it is true, but had accidentally omitted the preliminary rite. Yet a king was the sire. Then only so much the worse; for if it be small insult to be struck by a pauper, but mortal offense to receive a blow from a gentleman, then of all things the bye-blows of kings must be signally unflattering. In England the Peerage is kept alive by incessant restorations and creations. One man, George III., manufactured five hundred and twenty-two peers. An earldom, in abeyance for five centuries, has suddenly been assumed by some commoner, to whom it had not so much descended, as through the art of the lawyers been made flexibly to bend in that direction. For not Thames is so sinuous in his natural course, not the Bridgewater Canal more artificially conducted, than blood in the veins of that winding or manufactured nobility. Perishable as stubble, and fungous as the fungi, those grafted families successively live and die on the eternal soil of a name. In England this day, twenty-five hundred peerages are extinct; but the names survive. So that the empty air of a name is more endurable than a man, or than dynasties of men; the air fills man's lungs and puts life into a man, but man fills not the air, nor puts life into that.

All honor to the names then, and all courtesy to the men; but if St. Albans tell me he is all-honorable and all-eternal, I must still politely refer him to Nell Gwynne.

Beyond Charles II. very few indeed—hardly worthy of note—are the present titled English families which can trace any thing like a direct unvitiated blood-descent from the thief knights of the Norman. Beyond Charles II. their direct genealogies seem vain as though some Jew clothes-man, with a tea-canister on his head, turned over the first chapter of St. Matthew to make out his unmingled participation in the blood of King Saul, who had long died ere the career of the Cæsar began.

Now, not preliminarily to enlarge upon the fact that, while in England an immense mass of state-masonry is brought to bear as a buttress in upholding the hereditary existence of certain houses, while with us nothing of that kind can possibly be admitted; and to omit all mention of the hundreds of unobtrusive families in New England who, nevertheless, might easily trace their uninterrupted English lineage to a time before Charles the Blade: not to speak of the old and oriental-like English planter families of Virginia and the South; the Randolphs for example, one of whose ancestors, in King James' time, married Pocahontas the Indian Princess, and in whose blood therefore an underived aboriginal royalty was flowing over two hundred years ago; consider those most ancient and magnificent Dutch Manors at the North, whose perches are miles—whose meadows overspread adjacent counties—and whose haughty rent-deeds are held by their thousand farmer tenants, so long as grass grows and water runs; which hints of a surprising eternity for a deed, and seems to make lawyer's ink unobliterable as the sea. Some of those manors are two centuries old; and their present patroons or lords will show you stakes and stones on their estates put there—the stones at least—before Nell Gwynne the Duke-mother was born, and genealogies which, like their own river, Hudson, flow somewhat farther and straighter than the Serpentine brooklet in Hyde Park.

These far-descended Dutch meadows lie steeped in a Hindooish haze; an eastern patriarchalness sways its mild crook over pastures, whose tenant flocks shall there feed, long as their own grass grows, long as their own water shall run. Such estates seem to defy Time's tooth, and by conditions which take hold of the indestructible earth seem to cotemporize their fee-simples with eternity. Unimaginable audacity of a worm that but crawls through the soil he so imperially claims!

In midland counties of England they boast of old oaken dining-halls where three hundred men-at-arms could exercise of a rainy afternoon, in the reign of the Plantagenets. But our lords, the Patroons, appeal not to the past, but they point to the present. One will show you that the public census of a county, is but part of the roll of his tenants. Ranges of mountains, high as Ben Nevis or Snowdon, are their walls; and regular armies, with staffs of officers, crossing rivers with artillery, and marching through primeval woods, and threading vast rocky defiles, have been sent out to distrain upon three thousand farmer-tenants of one landlord, at a blow. A fact most suggestive two ways; both whereof shall be nameless here.

But whatever one may think of the existence of such

mighty lordships in the heart of a republic, and however we may wonder at their thus surviving, like Indian mounds, the Revolutionary flood; yet survive and exist they do, and are now owned by their present proprietors, by as good nominal title as any peasant owns his father's old hat, or any duke his great-uncle's old coronet.

For all this, then, we shall not err very widely if we humbly conceive, that—should she choose to glorify herself in that inconsiderable way—our America will make out a good general case with England in this short little matter of large estates, and long pedigrees—pedigrees I mean, wherein is no flaw.

iv

In general terms we have been thus decided in asserting the great genealogical and real-estate dignity of some families in America, because in so doing we poetically establish the richly aristocratic condition of Master Pierre Glendinning, for whom we have before claimed some special family distinction. And to the observant reader the sequel will not fail to show, how important is this circumstance, considered with reference to the singularly developed character and most singular life-career of our hero. Nor will any man dream that the last chapter was merely intended for a foolish bravado, and not with a solid purpose in view.

Now Pierre stands on this noble pedestal; we shall see if he keeps that fine footing; we shall see if Fate hath not just a little bit of a small word or two to say in this world. But it is not laid down here that the Glendinnings dated back beyond Pharaoh, or the deeds of Saddle-Meadows to the Three Magi in the Gospels. Nevertheless, those deeds, as before hinted, did indeed date back to three kings—Indian kings—only so much the finer for that.

But if Pierre did not date back to the Pharaohs, and if the English farmer Hampdens were somewhat the seniors of even the oldest Glendinning; and if some American manors boasted a few additional years and square miles over his, yet think you that it is at all possible, that a youth of nineteen should—merely by way of trial of the thing—strew his ancestral kitchen hearth-stone with wheat in the stalk, and there standing in the chimney thresh out that grain with a flail, whose aerial evolutions had free play among all that masonry; were it not impossible for such a flailer so to thresh wheat in his own ancestral kitchen chimney without feeling just a little twinge or two of what one might call family pride? I should say not.

Or how think you it would be with this youthful Pierre, if every day descending to breakfast, he caught sight of an old tattered British banner or two, hanging over an arched window in his hall; and those banners captured by his grandfather, the general, in fair fight? Or how think you it would be if every time he heard the band of the military company of the village, he should distinctly recognize the peculiar tap of a British kettle-drum also captured by his grandfather in fair fight, and afterwards suitably inscribed on the brass and bestowed upon the Saddle-Meadows Artillery Corps? Or how think you it would be, if sometimes of a mild meditative Fourth of July morning in the country, he carried out with him into the garden by way of ceremonial cane, a long, majestic, silver-tipped staff, a Major-General's baton, once wielded on the plume-nodding and musket-flashing review by the same grandfather several times herein-before mentioned? I should say that considering Pierre was quite young and very unphilosophical as yet, and withal rather high-blooded; and sometimes read the History of the Revolutionary War, and possessed a mother who very frequently made remote social allusions to the epaulettes of the Major-General his grandfather;—I should say that upon all of these occasions, the way it must have been with him, was a very proud, elated sort of way. And if this seem but too fond and foolish in Pierre; and if you tell me that this sort of thing in him showed him no sterling Democrat, and that a truly noble man should never brag of any arm but his own; then I beg you to consider again that this Pierre was but a youngster as yet. And believe me you will pronounce Pierre a thorough-going Democrat in time; perhaps a little too Radical altogether to your fancy.

In conclusion, do not blame me if I here make repetition,

and do verbally quote my own words in saying that *it had been the choice fate of Pierre to have been born and bred in the country*. For to a noble American youth this indeed—more than in any other land—this indeed is a most rare and choice lot. For it is to be observed, that while in other countries, the finest families boast of the country as their home; the more prominent among us, proudly cite the city as their seat. Too often the American that himself makes his fortune, builds him a great metropolitan house, in the most metropolitan street of the most metropolitan town. Whereas a European of the same sort would thereupon migrate into the country. That herein the European hath the better of it, no poet, no philosopher, and no aristocrat will deny. For the country is not only the most poetical and philosophical, but it is the most aristocratic part of this earth, for it is the most venerable, and numerous bards have ennobled it by many fine titles. Whereas the town is the more plebeian portion: which, besides many other things, is plainly evinced by the dirty unwashed face perpetually worn by the town; but the country, like any Queen, is ever attended by scrupulous lady's maids in the guise of the seasons, and the town hath but one dress of brick turned up with stone; but the country hath a brave dress for every week in the year; sometimes she changes her dress twenty-four times in the twenty-four hours; and the country weareth her sun by day as a diamond on a Queen's brow; and the stars by night as necklaces of gold beads; whereas the town's sun is smoky paste, and no diamond, and the town's stars are pinchbeck and not gold.

In the country then Nature planted our Pierre; because Nature intended a rare and original development in Pierre. Never mind if hereby she proved ambiguous to him in the end; nevertheless, in the beginning she did bravely. She blew her wind-clarion from the blue hills, and Pierre neighed out lyrical thoughts, as at the trumpet-blast, a war-horse paws himself into a lyric of foam. She whispered through her deep groves at eve, and gentle whispers of humanness, and sweet whispers of love, ran through Pierre's thought-veins, musical as water over pebbles. She lifted her spangled crest of a thickly-starred night, and forth at that glimpse of their divine

Captain and Lord, ten thousand mailed thoughts of heroicness started up in Pierre's soul, and glared round for some
insulted good cause to defend.

So the country was a glorious benediction to young Pierre;
we shall see if that blessing pass from him as did the divine
blessing from the Hebrews; we shall yet see again, I say,
whether Fate hath not just a little bit of a word or two to say
in this world; we shall see whether this wee scrap of latinity
be very far out of the way—*Nemo contra Deum nisi Deus ipse.*

V

"Sister Mary," said Pierre, returned from his sunrise stroll,
and tapping at his mother's chamber door:—"do you know,
sister Mary, that the trees which have been up all night, are
all abroad again this morning before you?—Do you not smell
something like coffee, my sister?"

A light step moved from within toward the door; which
opened, showing Mrs. Glendinning, in a resplendently cheerful morning robe, and holding a gay wide ribbon in her hand.

"Good morning, madam," said Pierre, slowly, and with a
bow, whose genuine and spontaneous reverence amusingly
contrasted with the sportive manner that had preceded it. For
thus sweetly and religiously was the familiarity of his affections bottomed on the profoundest filial respect.

"Good afternoon to you, Pierre, for I suppose it is afternoon. But come, you shall finish my toilette;—here,
brother—" reaching the ribbon—"now acquit yourself
bravely—" and seating herself away from the glass, she
awaited the good offices of Pierre.

"First Lady in waiting to the Dowager Duchess Glendinning," laughed Pierre, as bowing over before his mother, he
gracefully passed the ribbon round her neck, simply crossing
the ends in front.

"Well, what is to hold it there, Pierre?"

"I am going to try and tack it with a kiss, sister,—there!
—oh, what a pity that sort of fastening won't always hold!—
where's the cameo with the fawns, I gave you last night?—
Ah! on the slab—you were going to wear it then?—Thank
you, my considerate and most politic sister—there!—but

Tartan sailed the seas of fashion, causing all topsails to lower to her; and towing flotillas of young ladies, for all of whom she was bound to find the finest husband harbors in the world.

But does not match-making, like charity, begin at home? Why is her own daughter Lucy without a mate? But not so fast; Mrs. Tartan years ago laid out that sweet programme concerning Pierre and Lucy; but in this case, her programme happened to coincide, in some degree, with a previous one in heaven, and only for that cause did it come to pass, that Pierre Glendinning was the proud elect of Lucy Tartan. Besides, this being a thing so nearly affecting herself, Mrs. Tartan had, for the most part, been rather circumspect and cautious in all her manœuvrings with Pierre and Lucy. Moreover, the thing demanded no manœuvring at all. The two Platonic particles, after roaming in quest of each other, from the time of Saturn and Ops till now; they came together before Mrs. Tartan's own eyes; and what more could Mrs. Tartan do toward making them forever one and indivisible? Once, and only once, had a dim suspicion passed through Pierre's mind, that Mrs. Tartan was a lady thimble-rigger, and slyly rolled the pea.

In their less mature acquaintance, he was breakfasting with Lucy and her mother in the city, and the first cup of coffee had been poured out by Mrs. Tartan, when she declared she smelt matches burning somewhere in the house, and she must see them extinguished. So banning all pursuit, she rose to seek for the burning matches, leaving the pair alone to interchange the civilities of the coffee; and finally sent word to them, from above stairs, that the matches, or something else, had given her a headache, and begged Lucy to send her up some toast and tea, for she would breakfast in her own chamber that morning.

Upon this, Pierre looked from Lucy to his boots, and as he lifted his eyes again, saw Anacreon on the sofa on one side of him, and Moore's Melodies on the other, and some honey on the table, and a bit of white satin on the floor, and a sort of bride's veil on the chandelier.

Never mind though—thought Pierre, fixing his gaze on Lucy—I'm entirely willing to be caught, when the bait is set in Paradise, and the bait is such an angel. Again he glanced at Lucy, and saw a look of infinite subdued vexation, and some unwonted pallor on her cheek. Then willingly he would have kissed the delicious bait, that so gently hated to be tasted in the trap. But glancing round again, and seeing that the music, which Mrs. Tartan, under the pretense of putting in order, had been adjusting upon the piano; seeing that this music was now in a vertical pile against the wall, with—"*Love was once a little boy*," for the outermost and only visible sheet; and thinking this to be a remarkable coincidence under the circumstances; Pierre could not refrain from a humorous smile, though it was a very gentle one, and immediately repented of, especially as Lucy seeing and interpreting it, immediately arose, with an unaccountable, indignant, angelical, adorable, and all-persuasive "Mr. Glendinning?" utterly confounded in him the slightest germ of suspicion as to Lucy's collusion in her mother's imagined artifices.

Indeed, Mrs. Tartan's having any thing whatever to do, or hint, or finesse in this matter of the loves of Pierre and Lucy, was nothing less than immensely gratuitous and sacrilegious. Would Mrs. Tartan doctor lilies when they blow? Would Mrs. Tartan set about match-making between the steel and magnet? Preposterous Mrs. Tartan! But this whole world is a preposterous one, with many preposterous people in it; chief among whom was Mrs. Tartan, match-maker to the nation.

This conduct of Mrs. Tartan, was the more absurd, seeing that she could not but know that Mrs. Glendinning desired the thing. And was not Lucy wealthy?—going to be, that is, very wealthy when her mother died;—(sad thought that for Mrs. Tartan)—and was not her husband's family of the best; and had not Lucy's father been a bosom friend of Pierre's father? And though Lucy might be matched to some one man, where among women was the match for Lucy? Exceedingly preposterous Mrs. Tartan! But when a lady like Mrs. Tartan has nothing positive and useful to do, then she will do just such preposterous things as Mrs. Tartan did.

Well, time went on; and Pierre loved Lucy, and Lucy, Pierre; till at last the two young naval gentlemen, her brothers, happened to arrive in Mrs. Tartan's drawing-room, from their first cruise—a three years' one up the Mediterranean.

They rather stared at Pierre, finding him on the sofa, and Lucy not very remote.

"Pray, be seated, gentlemen," said Pierre. "Plenty of room."

"My darling brothers!" cried Lucy, embracing them.

"My darling brothers and sister!" cried Pierre, folding them together.

"Pray, hold off, sir," said the elder brother, who had served as a passed midshipman for the last two weeks. The younger brother retreated a little, and clapped his hand upon his dirk, saying, "Sir, we are from the Mediterranean. Sir, permit me to say, this is decidedly improper! Who may you be, sir?"

"I can't explain for joy," cried Pierre, hilariously embracing them all again.

"Most extraordinary!" cried the elder brother, extricating his shirt-collar from the embrace, and pulling it up vehemently.

"Draw!" cried the younger, intrepidly.

"Peace, foolish fellows," cried Lucy—"this is your old play-fellow, Pierre Glendinning."

"Pierre? why, Pierre?" cried the lads—"a hug all round again! You've grown a fathom!—who would have known you? But, then—Lucy? I say, Lucy?—what business have you here in this—eh? eh?—hugging-match, I should call it?"

"Oh! Lucy don't mean any thing," cried Pierre—"come, one more all round."

So they all embraced again; and that evening it was publicly known that Pierre was to wed with Lucy.

Whereupon, the young officers took it upon themselves to think—though they by no means presumed to breathe it—that they had authoritatively, though indirectly, accelerated a before ambiguous and highly incommendable state of affairs between the now affianced lovers.

iii

In the fine old robust times of Pierre's grandfather, an American gentleman of substantial person and fortune spent his time in a somewhat different style from the green-house gentlemen of the present day. The grandfather of Pierre measured six feet four inches in height; during a fire in the old manorial mansion, with one dash of his foot, he had smitten down an oaken door, to admit the buckets of his negro slaves; Pierre had often tried on his military vest, which still remained an heirloom at Saddle Meadows, and found the pockets below his knees, and plenty additional room for a fair-sized quarter-cask within its buttoned girth; in a night-scuffle in the wilderness before the Revolutionary War, he had annihilated two Indian savages by making reciprocal bludgeons of their heads. And all this was done by the mildest hearted, and most blue-eyed gentleman in the world, who, according to the patriarchal fashion of those days, was a gentle, white-haired worshiper of all the household gods; the gentlest husband, and the gentlest father; the kindest of masters to his slaves; of the most wonderful unruffledness of temper; a serene smoker of his after-dinner pipe; a forgiver of many injuries; a sweet-hearted, charitable Christian; in fine, a pure, cheerful, child-like, blue-eyed, divine old man; in whose meek, majestic soul, the lion and the lamb embraced—fit image of his God.

Never could Pierre look upon his fine military portrait without an infinite and mournful longing to meet his living aspect in actual life. The majestic sweetness of this portrait was truly wonderful in its effects upon any sensitive and generous-minded young observer. For such, that portrait possessed the heavenly persuasiveness of angelic speech; a glorious gospel framed and hung upon the wall, and declaring to all people, as from the Mount, that man is a noble, god-like being, full of choicest juices; made up of strength and beauty.

Now, this grand old Pierre Glendinning was a great lover of horses; but not in the modern sense, for he was no jockey;—one of his most intimate friends of the masculine gender was a huge, proud, gray horse, of a surprising reserve of manner, his saddle-beast; he had his horses' mangers carved like old trenchers, out of solid maple logs; the key of the corn-bin hung in his library; and no one grained his steeds, but himself; unless his absence from home promoted Moyar, an incorruptible and most punctual old black, to that honorable office. He said that no man loved his horses, unless his own hands grained them. Every Christmas he gave them brimming measures. "I keep Christmas with my horses," said grand old Pierre. This grand old Pierre always rose at sunrise;

washed his face and chest in the open air; and then, returning to his closet, and being completely arrayed at last, stepped forth to make a ceremonious call at his stables, to bid his very honorable friends there a very good and joyful morning. Woe to Cranz, Kit, Douw, or any other of his stable slaves, if grand old Pierre found one horse unblanketed, or one weed among the hay that filled their rack. Not that he ever had Cranz, Kit, Douw, or any of them flogged—a thing unknown in that patriarchal time and country—but he would refuse to say his wonted pleasant word to them; and that was very bitter to them, for Cranz, Kit, Douw, and all of them, loved grand old Pierre, as his shepherds loved old Abraham.

What decorous, lordly, gray-haired steed is this? What old Chaldean rides abroad?—'Tis grand old Pierre; who, every morning before he eats, goes out promenading with his saddle-beast; nor mounts him, without first asking leave. But time glides on, and grand old Pierre grows old: his life's glorious grape now swells with fatness; he has not the conscience to saddle his majestic beast with such a mighty load of manliness. Besides, the noble beast himself is growing old, and has a touching look of meditativeness in his large, attentive eyes. Leg of man, swears grand old Pierre, shall never more bestride my steed; no more shall harness touch him! Then every spring he sowed a field with clover for his steed; and at mid-summer sorted all his meadow grasses, for the choicest hay to winter him; and had his destined grain thrashed out with a flail, whose handle had once borne a flag in a brisk battle, into which this same old steed had pranced with grand old Pierre; one waving mane, one waving sword!

Now needs must grand old Pierre take a morning drive; he rides no more with the old gray steed. He has a phaeton built, fit for a vast General, in whose sash three common men might hide. Doubled, trebled are the huge S shaped leather springs; the wheels seem stolen from some mill; the canopied seat is like a testered bed. From beneath the old archway, not one horse, but two, every morning now draw forth old Pierre, as the Chinese draw their fat god Josh, once every year from out his fane.

But time glides on, and a morning comes, when the phaeton emerges not; but all the yards and courts are full; helmets

line the ways; sword-points strike the stone steps of the
porch; muskets ring upon the stairs; and mournful martial
melodies are heard in all the halls. Grand old Pierre is dead;
and like a hero of old battles, he dies on the eve of another
war; ere wheeling to fire on the foe, his platoons fire over
their old commander's grave; in A.D. 1812, died grand old
Pierre. The drum that beat in brass his funeral march, was a
British kettle-drum, that had once helped beat the vain-glorious march, for the thirty thousand predestined prisoners,
led into sure captivity by that bragging boy, Burgoyne.

Next day the old gray steed turned from his grain; turned
round, and vainly whinnied in his stall. By gracious Moyar's
hand, he refuses to be patted now; plain as horse can speak,
the old gray steed says—"I smell not the wonted hand; where
is grand old Pierre? Grain me not, and groom me not;—
Where is grand old Pierre?"

He sleeps not far from his master now; beneath the field he
cropt, he has softly lain him down; and long ere this, grand
old Pierre and steed have passed through that grass to glory.

But his phaeton—like his plumed hearse, outlives the noble load it bore. And the dark bay steeds that drew grand old
Pierre alive, and by his testament drew him dead, and followed the lordly lead of the led gray horse; those dark bay
steeds are still extant; not in themselves or in their issue; but
in the two descendants of stallions of their own breed. For
on the lands of Saddle Meadows, man and horse are both
hereditary; and this bright morning Pierre Glendinning,
grandson of grand old Pierre, now drives forth with Lucy
Tartan, seated where his own ancestor had sat, and reining
steeds, whose great-great-great-grandfathers grand old Pierre
had reined before.

How proud felt Pierre: In fancy's eye, he saw the horse-
ghosts a-tandem in the van; "These are but wheelers"—cried
young Pierre—"the leaders are the generations."

iv

But Love has more to do with his own possible and probable posterities, than with the once living but now impossible
ancestries in the past. So Pierre's glow of family pride quickly

gave place to a deeper hue, when Lucy bade love's banner blush out from his cheek.

That morning was the choicest drop that Time had in his vase. Ineffable distillations of a soft delight were wafted from the fields and hills. Fatal morning that, to all lovers unbetrothed; "Come to your confessional," it cried. "Behold our airy loves," the birds chirped from the trees; far out at sea, no more the sailors tied their bowline-knots; their hands had lost their cunning; will they, nill they, Love tied love-knots on every spangled spar.

Oh, praised be the beauty of this earth, the beauty, and the bloom, and the mirthfulness thereof! The first worlds made were winter worlds; the second made, were vernal worlds; the third, and last, and perfectest, was this summer world of ours. In the cold and nether spheres, preachers preach of earth, as we of Paradise above. Oh, there, my friends, they say, they have a season, in their language known as summer. Then their fields spin themselves green carpets; snow and ice are not in all the land; then a million strange, bright, fragrant things powder that sward with perfumes; and high, majestic beings, dumb and grand, stand up with outstretched arms, and hold their green canopies over merry angels—men and women— who love and wed, and sleep and dream, beneath the approving glances of their visible god and goddess, glad-hearted sun, and pensive moon!

Oh, praised be the beauty of this earth; the beauty, and the bloom, and the mirthfulness thereof. We lived before, and shall live again; and as we hope for a fairer world than this to come; so we came from one less fine. From each successive world, the demon Principle is more and more dislodged; he is the accursed clog from chaos, and thither, by every new translation, we drive him further and further back again. Hosannahs to this world! so beautiful itself, and the vestibule to more. Out of some past Egypt, we have come to this new Canaan; and from this new Canaan, we press on to some Circassia. Though still the villains, Want and Woe, followed us out of Egypt, and now beg in Canaan's streets: yet Circassia's gates shall not admit them; they, with their sire, the demon Principle, must back to chaos, whence they came.

Love was first begot by Mirth and Peace, in Eden, when

the world was young. The man oppressed with cares, he can not love; the man of gloom finds not the god. So, as youth, for the most part, has no cares, and knows no gloom, therefore, ever since time did begin, youth belongs to love. Love may end in grief and age, and pain and need, and all other modes of human mournfulness; but love begins in joy. Love's first sigh is never breathed, till after love hath laughed. Love laughs first, and then sighs after. Love has not hands, but cymbals; Love's mouth is chambered like a bugle, and the instinctive breathings of his life breathe jubilee notes of joy!

That morning, two bay horses drew two Laughs along the road that led to the hills from Saddle Meadows. Apt time they kept; Pierre Glendinning's young, manly tenor, to Lucy Tartan's girlish treble.

Wondrous fair of face, blue-eyed, and golden-haired, the bright blonde, Lucy, was arrayed in colors harmonious with the heavens. Light blue be thy perpetual color, Lucy; light blue becomes thee best—such the repeated azure counsel of Lucy Tartan's mother. On both sides, from the hedges, came to Pierre the clover bloom of Saddle Meadows, and from Lucy's mouth and cheek came the fresh fragrance of her violet young being.

"Smell I the flowers, or thee?" cried Pierre.

"See I lakes, or eyes?" cried Lucy, her own gazing down into his soul, as two stars gaze down into a tarn.

No Cornwall miner ever sunk so deep a shaft beneath the sea, as Love will sink beneath the floatings of the eyes. Love sees ten million fathoms down, till dazzled by the floor of pearls. The eye is Love's own magic glass, where all things that are not of earth, glide in supernatural light. There are not so many fishes in the sea, as there are sweet images in lovers' eyes. In those miraculous translucencies swim the strange eye-fish with wings, that sometimes leap out, instinct with joy; moist fish-wings wet the lover's cheek. Love's eyes are holy things; therein the mysteries of life are lodged; looking in each other's eyes, lovers see the ultimate secret of the worlds; and with thrills eternally untranslatable, feel that Love is god of all. Man or woman who has never loved, nor once looked deep down into their own lover's eyes, they know not the sweetest and the loftiest religion of this earth.

Love is both Creator's and Saviour's gospel to mankind; a volume bound in rose-leaves, clasped with violets, and by the beaks of humming-birds printed with peach-juice on the leaves of lilies.

Endless is the account of Love. Time and space can not contain Love's story. All things that are sweet to see, or taste, or feel, or hear, all these things were made by Love; and none other things were made by Love. Love made not the Arctic zones, but Love is ever reclaiming them. Say, are not the fierce things of this earth daily, hourly going out? Where now are your wolves of Britain? Where in Virginia now, find you the panther and the pard? Oh, Love is busy everywhere. Everywhere Love hath Moravian missionaries. No Propagandist like to Love. The south wind wooes the barbarous north; on many a distant shore the gentler west wind persuades the arid east.

All this Earth is Love's affianced; vainly the demon Principle howls to stay the banns. Why round her middle wears this world so rich a zone of torrid verdure, if she be not dressing for the final rites? And why provides she orange blossoms and lilies of the valley, if she would not that all men and maids should love and marry? For every wedding where true lovers wed, helps on the march of universal Love. Who are brides here shall be Love's bridemaids in the marriage world to come. So on all sides Love allures; can contain himself what youth who views the wonders of the beauteous woman-world? Where a beautiful woman is, there is all Asia and her Bazars. Italy hath not a sight before the beauty of a Yankee girl; nor heaven a blessing beyond her earthly love. Did not the angelical Lotharios come down to earth, that they might taste of mortal woman's Love and Beauty? even while her own silly brothers were pining after the self-same Paradise they left? Yes, those envying angels did come down; did emigrate; and who emigrates except to be better off?

Love is this world's great redeemer and reformer; and as all beautiful women are her selectest emissaries, so hath Love gifted them with a magnetical persuasiveness, that no youth can possibly repel. The own heart's choice of every youth, seems ever as an inscrutable witch to him; and by ten thousand concentric spells and circling incantations, glides round

and round him, as he turns: murmuring meanings of
unearthly import; and summoning up to him all the subterranean sprites and gnomes; and unpeopling all the sea for
naiads to swim round him; so that mysteries are evoked as in
exhalations by this Love;—what wonder then that Love was
aye a mystic?

V

And this self-same morning Pierre was very mystical; not
continually, though; but most mystical one moment, and
overflowing with mad, unbridled merriment, the next. He
seemed a youthful Magian, and almost a mountebank together. Chaldaic improvisations burst from him, in quick
Golden Verses, on the heel of humorous retort and repartee.
More especially, the bright glance of Lucy was transporting
to him. Now, reckless of his horses, with both arms holding
Lucy in his embrace, like a Sicilian diver he dives deep down
in the Adriatic of her eyes, and brings up some king's-cup of
joy. All the waves in Lucy's eyes seemed waves of infinite glee
to him. And as if, like veritable seas, they did indeed catch
the reflected irradiations of that pellucid azure morning; in
Lucy's eyes, there seemed to shine all the blue glory of the
general day, and all the sweet inscrutableness of the sky. And
certainly, the blue eye of woman, like the sea, is not uninfluenced by the atmosphere. Only in the open air of some divinest, summer day, will you see its ultramarine,—its fluid lapis
lazuli. Then would Pierre burst forth in some screaming
shout of joy; and the striped tigers of his chestnut eyes leaped
in their lashed cages with a fierce delight. Lucy shrank from
him in extreme love; for the extremest top of love, is Fear and
Wonder.

Soon the swift horses drew this fair god and goddess nigh
the wooded hills, whose distant blue, now changed into a
variously-shaded green, stood before them like old Babylonian walls, overgrown with verdure; while here and there, at
regular intervals, the scattered peaks seemed mural towers;
and the clumped pines surmounting them, as lofty archers,
and vast, out-looking watchers of the glorious Babylonian
City of the Day. Catching that hilly air, the prancing horses

neighed; laughed on the ground with gleeful feet. Felt they the gay delightsome spurrings of the day; for the day was mad with excessive joy; and high in heaven you heard the neighing of the horses of the sun; and down dropt their nos-trils' froth in many a fleecy vapor from the hills.

From the plains, the mists rose slowly; reluctant yet to quit so fair a mead. At those green slopings, Pierre reined in his steeds, and soon the twain were seated on the bank, gazing far, and far away; over many a grove and lake; corn-crested uplands, and Herd's-grass lowlands; and long-stretching swales of vividest green, betokening where the greenest bounty of this earth seeks its winding channels; as ever, the most heavenly bounteousness most seeks the lowly places; making green and glad many a humble mortal's breast, and leaving to his own lonely aridness, many a hill-top prince's state.

But Grief, not Joy, is a moralizer; and small moralizing wis-dom caught Pierre from that scene. With Lucy's hand in his, and feeling, softly feeling of its soft tinglingness; he seemed as one placed in linked correspondence with the summer lightnings; and by sweet shock on shock, receiving intimating foretastes of the etherealest delights of earth.

Now, prone on the grass he falls, with his attentive upward glance fixed on Lucy's eyes. "Thou art my heaven, Lucy; and here I lie thy shepherd-king, watching for new eye-stars to rise in thee. Ha! I see Venus' transit now;—lo! a new planet there;—and behind all, an infinite starry nebulousness, as if thy being were backgrounded by some spangled vail of mystery."

Is Lucy deaf to all these ravings of his lyric love? Why looks she down, and vibrates so; and why now from her over-charged lids, drops such warm drops as these? No joy now in Lucy's eyes, and seeming tremor on her lips.

"Ah! thou too ardent and impetuous Pierre!"

"Nay, thou too moist and changeful April! know'st thou not, that the moist and changeful April is followed by the glad, assured, and showerless joy of June? And this, Lucy, this day should be thy June, even as it is the earth's!"

"Ah Pierre! not June to me. But say, are not the sweets of June made sweet by the April tears?"

"Ay, love! but here fall more drops,—more and more;—
these showers are longer than beseem the April, and pertain
not to the June."

"June! June!—thou bride's month of the summer,—following the spring's sweet courtship of the earth,—my June,
my June is yet to come!"

"Oh! yet to come, but fixedly decreed;—good as come,
and better."

"Then no flower that, in the bud, the April showers have
nurtured; no such flower may untimely perish, ere the June
unfolds it? Ye will not swear that, Pierre?"

"The audacious immortalities of divinest love are in me; and
I now swear to thee all the immutable eternities of joyfulness, that ever woman dreamed of, in this dream-house of the
earth. A god decrees to thee unchangeable felicity; and to me,
the unchallenged possession of thee and them, for my inalienable fief.—Do I rave? Look on me, Lucy; think on me, girl."

"Thou art young, and beautiful, and strong; and a joyful
manliness invests thee, Pierre; and thy intrepid heart never yet
felt the touch of fear;—But—"

"But what?"

"Ah, my best Pierre!"

"With kisses I will suck thy secret from thy cheek!—but
what?"

"Let us hie homeward, Pierre. Some nameless sadness,
faintness, strangely comes to me. Foretaste I feel of endless
dreariness. Tell me once more the story of that face, Pierre,—
that mysterious, haunting face, which thou once told'st me,
thou didst thrice vainly try to shun. Blue is the sky, oh, bland
the air, Pierre;—but—tell me the story of the face,—the
dark-eyed, lustrous, imploring, mournful face, that so mystically paled, and shrunk at thine. Ah, Pierre, sometimes I have
thought,—never will I wed with my best Pierre, until the
riddle of that face be known. Tell me, tell me, Pierre;—as a
fixed basilisk, with eyes of steady, flaming mournfulness, that
face this instant fastens me."

"Bewitched! bewitched!—Cursed be the hour I acted on
the thought, that Love hath no reserves. Never should I have
told thee the story of that face, Lucy. I have bared myself too
much to thee. Oh, never should Love know all!"

"Knows not all, then loves not all, Pierre. Never shalt thou so say again;—and Pierre, listen to me. Now,—now, in this inexplicable trepidation that I feel, I do conjure thee, that thou wilt ever continue to do as thou hast done; so that I may ever continue to know all that agitateth thee, the airiest and most transient thought, that ever shall sweep into thee from the wide atmosphere of all things that hem mortality. Did I doubt thee here;—could I ever think, that thy heart hath yet one private nook or corner from me;—fatal disenchanting day for me, my Pierre, would that be. I tell thee, Pierre—and 'tis Love's own self that now speaks through me—only in unbounded confidence and interchangings of all subtlest secrets, can Love possibly endure. Love's self is a secret, and so feeds on secrets, Pierre. Did I only know of thee, what the whole common world may know—what then were Pierre to me?—Thou must be wholly a disclosed secret to me; Love is vain and proud; and when I walk the streets, and meet thy friends, I must still be laughing and hugging to myself the thought,—They know him not;—I only know my Pierre;—none else beneath the circuit of yon sun. Then, swear to me, dear Pierre, that thou wilt never keep a secret from me—no, never, never;—swear!"

"Something seizes me. Thy inexplicable tears, falling, falling on my heart, have now turned it to a stone. I feel icy cold and hard; I will not swear!"

"Pierre! Pierre!"

"God help thee, and God help me, Lucy. I can not think, that in this most mild and dulcet air, the invisible agencies are plotting treasons against our loves. Oh! if ye be now nigh us, ye things I have no name for; then by a name that should be efficacious—by Christ's holy name, I warn ye back from her and me. Touch her not, ye airy devils; hence to your appointed hell! why come ye prowling in these heavenly purlieus? Can not the chains of Love omnipotent bind ye, fiends?"

"Is this Pierre? His eyes glare fearfully; now I see layer on layer deeper in him; he turns round and menaces the air and talks to it, as if defied by the air. Woe is me, that fairy love should raise this evil spell!—Pierre?"

"But now I was infinite distances from thee, oh my Lucy,

wandering baffled in the choking night; but thy voice might find me, though I had wandered to the Boreal realm, Lucy. Here I sit down by thee; I catch a soothing from thee."

"My own, own Pierre! Pierre, into ten trillion pieces I could now be torn for thee; in my bosom would yet hide thee, and there keep thee warm, though I sat down on Arctic ice-floes, frozen to a corpse. My own, best, blessed Pierre! Now, could I plant some poniard in me, that my silly ailings should have power to move thee thus, and pain thee thus. Forgive me, Pierre; thy changed face hath chased the other from me; the fright of thee exceeds all other frights. It does not so haunt me now. Press hard my hand; look hard on me, my love, that its last trace may pass away. Now I feel almost whole again; now, 'tis gone. Up, my Pierre; let us up, and fly these hills, whence, I fear, too wide a prospect meets us. Fly we to the plain. See, thy steeds neigh for thee—they call thee—see, the clouds fly down toward the plain—lo, these hills now seem all desolate to me, and the vale all verdure. Thank thee, Pierre.—See, now, I quit the hills, dry-cheeked; and leave all tears behind to be sucked in by these evergreens, meet emblems of the unchanging love, my own sadness nourishes in me. Hard fate, that Love's best verdure should feed so on tears!"

Now they rolled swiftly down the slopes; nor tempted the upper hills; but sped fast for the plain. Now the cloud hath passed from Lucy's eye; no more the lurid slanting light forks upward from her lover's brow. In the plain they find peace, and love, and joy again.

"It was the merest, idling, wanton vapor, Lucy!"

"An empty echo, Pierre, of a sad sound, long past. Bless thee, my Pierre!"

"The great God wrap thee ever, Lucy. So, now, we are home."

vi

After seeing Lucy into her aunt's most cheerful parlor, and seating her by the honeysuckle that half clambered into the window there; and near to which was her easel for crayon-sketching, upon part of whose frame Lucy had cunningly

trained two slender vines, into whose earth-filled pots two of the three legs of the easel were inserted; and sitting down himself by her, and by his pleasant, lightsome chat, striving to chase the last trace of sadness from her; and not till his object seemed fully gained; Pierre rose to call her good aunt to her, and so take his leave till evening, when Lucy called him back, begging him first to bring her the blue portfolio from her chamber, for she wished to kill her last lingering melancholy—if any indeed did linger now—by diverting her thoughts, in a little pencil sketch, to scenes widely different from those of Saddle Meadows and its hills.

So Pierre went up stairs, but paused on the threshold of the open door. He never had entered that chamber but with feelings of a wonderful reverentialness. The carpet seemed as holy ground. Every chair seemed sanctified by some departed saint, there once seated long ago. Here his book of Love was all a rubric, and said—Bow now, Pierre, bow. But this extreme loyalty to the piety of love, called from him by such glimpses of its most secret inner shrine, was not unrelieved betimes by such quickenings of all his pulses, that in fantasy he pressed the wide beauty of the world in his embracing arms; for all his world resolved itself into his heart's best love for Lucy.

Now, crossing the magic silence of the empty chamber, he caught the snow-white bed reflected in the toilet-glass. This rooted him. For one swift instant, he seemed to see in that one glance the two separate beds—the real one and the reflected one—and an unbidden, most miserable presentiment thereupon stole into him. But in one breath it came and went. So he advanced, and with a fond and gentle joyfulness, his eye now fell upon the spotless bed itself, and fastened on a snow-white roll that lay beside the pillow. Now he started; Lucy seemed coming in upon him; but no—'tis only the foot of one of her little slippers, just peeping into view from under the narrow nether curtains of the bed. Then again his glance fixed itself upon the slender, snow-white, ruffled roll; and he stood as one enchanted. Never precious parchment of the Greek was half so precious in his eyes. Never trembling scholar longed more to unroll the mystic vellum, than Pierre longed to unroll the sacred secrets of that snow-white, ruffled thing. But his hands touched not any object in that chamber, except the one he had gone thither for.

"Here is the blue portfolio, Lucy. See, the key hangs to its silver lock;—were you not fearful I would open it?—'twas tempting, I must confess."

"Open it!" said Lucy—" why, yes, Pierre, yes; what secret thing keep I from thee? Read me through and through. I am entirely thine. See!" and tossing open the portfolio, all manner of rosy things came floating from it, and a most delicate perfume of some invisible essence.

"Ah! thou holy angel, Lucy!"

"Why, Pierre, thou art transfigured; thou now lookest as one who—why, Pierre?"

"As one who had just peeped in at paradise, Lucy; and——"

"Again wandering in thy mind, Pierre; no more—Come, you must leave me, now. I am quite rested again. Quick, call my aunt, and leave me. Stay, this evening we are to look over the book of plates from the city, you know. Be early;—go now, Pierre."

"Well, good-bye, till evening, thou height of all delight."

vii

As Pierre drove through the silent village, beneath the vertical shadows of the noon-day trees, the sweet chamber scene abandoned him, and the mystical face recurred to him, and kept with him. At last, arrived at home, he found his mother absent; so passing straight through the wide middle hall of the mansion, he descended the piazza on the other side, and wandered away in reveries down to the river bank.

Here one primeval pine-tree had been luckily left standing by the otherwise unsparing woodmen, who long ago had cleared that meadow. It was once crossing to this noble pine, from a clump of hemlocks far across the river, that Pierre had first noticed the significant fact, that while the hemlock and the pine are trees of equal growth and stature, and are so similar in their general aspect, that people unused to woods sometimes confound them; and while both trees are proverbially trees of sadness, yet the dark hemlock hath no music in its thoughtful boughs; but the gentle pine-tree drops melodious mournfulness.

At its half-bared roots of sadness, Pierre sat down, and marked the mighty bulk and far out-reaching length of one particular root, which, straying down the bank, the storms and rains had years ago exposed.

"How wide, how strong these roots must spread! Sure, this pine-tree takes powerful hold of this fair earth! Yon bright flower hath not so deep a root. This tree hath outlived a century of that gay flower's generations, and will outlive a century of them yet to come. This is most sad. Hark, now I hear the pyramidical and numberless, flame-like complainings of this Eolean pine;—the wind breathes now upon it:—the wind,—that is God's breath! Is He so sad? Oh, tree! so mighty thou, so lofty, yet so mournful! This is most strange! Hark! as I look up into thy high secrecies, oh, tree, the face, the face, peeps down on me!—'Art thou Pierre? Come to me'—oh, thou mysterious girl,—what an ill-matched pendant thou, to that other countenance of sweet Lucy, which also hangs, and first did hang within my heart! Is grief a pendant then to pleasantness? Is grief a self-willed guest that *will* come in? Yet I have never known thee, Grief;—thou art a legend to me. I have known some fiery broils of glorious frenzy; I have oft tasted of revery; whence comes pensiveness; whence comes sadness; whence all delicious poetic presentiments;—but thou, Grief! art still a ghost-story to me. I know thee not,—do half disbelieve in thee. Not that I would be without my too little cherished fits of sadness now and then; but God keep me from thee, thou other shape of far profounder gloom! I shudder at thee! The face!—the face!— forth again from thy high secrecies, oh, tree! the face steals down upon me. Mysterious girl! who art thou? by what right snatchest thou thus my deepest thoughts? Take thy thin fingers from me;—I am affianced, and not to thee. Leave me!— what share hast thou in me? Surely, thou lovest not me?— that were most miserable for thee, and me, and Lucy. It can not be. What, *who* art thou? Oh! wretched vagueness—too familiar to me, yet inexplicable,—unknown, utterly unknown! I seem to founder in this perplexity. Thou seemest to know somewhat of me, that I know not of myself,—what is

it then? If thou hast a secret in thy eyes of mournful mystery,
out with it; Pierre demands it; what is that thou has veiled in
thee so imperfectly, that I seem to see its motion, but not its
form? It visibly rustles behind the concealing screen. Now,
never into the soul of Pierre, stole there before, a muffledness
like this! If aught really lurks in it, ye sovereign powers that
claim all my leal worshipings, I conjure ye to lift the veil; I
must see it face to face. Tread I on a mine, warn me; advance
I on a precipice, hold me back; but abandon me to an unknown misery, that it shall suddenly seize me, and possess me,
wholly,—that ye will never do; else, Pierre's fond faith in
ye—now clean, untouched—may clean depart; and give me
up to be a railing atheist! Ah, now the face departs. Pray
heaven it hath not only stolen back, and hidden again in thy
high secrecies, oh tree! But 'tis gone—gone—entirely gone;
and I thank God, and I feel joy again; joy, which I also feel
to be my right as man; deprived of joy, I feel I should find
cause for deadly feuds with things invisible. Ha! a coat of
iron-mail seems to grow round, and husk me now; and I have
heard, that the bitterest winters are foretold by a thicker husk
upon the Indian corn; so our old farmers say. But 'tis a dark
similitude. Quit thy analogies; sweet in the orator's mouth,
bitter in the thinker's belly. Now, then, I'll up with my own
joyful will; and with my joy's face scare away all phantoms:—
so, they go; and Pierre is Joy's, and Life's again. Thou pine-
tree!—henceforth I will resist thy too treacherous persuasiveness. Thou'lt not so often woo me to thy airy tent, to ponder
on the gloomy rooted stakes that bind it. Hence now I go;
and peace be with thee, pine! That blessed sereneness which
lurks ever at the heart of sadness—mere sadness—and remains when all the rest has gone;—that sweet feeling is now
mine, and cheaply mine. I am not sorry I was sad, I feel so
blessed now. Dearest Lucy!—well, well;—'twill be a pretty
time we'll have this evening; there's the book of Flemish
prints—that first we must look over; then, second, is Flaxman's Homer—clear-cut outlines, yet full of unadorned barbaric nobleness. Then Flaxman's Dante;—Dante! Night's
and Hell's poet he. No, we will not open Dante. Methinks
now the face—the face—minds me a little of pensive, sweet
Francesca's face—or, rather, as it had been Francesca's

daughter's face—wafted on the sad dark wind, toward observant Virgil and the blistered Florentine. No, we will not open
Flaxman's Dante. Francesca's mournful face is now ideal
to me. Flaxman might evoke it wholly,—make it present in
lines of misery—bewitching power. No! I will not open Flaxman's Dante! Damned be the hour I read in Dante! more
damned than that wherein Paolo and Francesca read in fatal
Launcelot!"

Book III

THE FACE, of which Pierre and Lucy so strangely and fearfully hinted, was not of enchanted air; but its mortal lineaments of mournfulness had been visibly beheld by Pierre. Nor had it accosted him in any privacy; or in any lonely byeway; or beneath the white light of the crescent moon; but in a joyous chamber, bright with candles, and ringing with two score women's gayest voices. Out of the heart of mirthfulness, this shadow had come forth to him. Encircled by bandelets of light, it had still beamed upon him; vaguely historic and prophetic; backward, hinting of some irrevocable sin; forward, pointing to some inevitable ill. One of those faces, which now and then appear to man, and without one word of speech, still reveal glimpses of some fearful gospel. In natural guise, but lit by supernatural light; palpable to the senses, but inscrutable to the soul; in their perfectest impression on us, ever hovering between Tartarean misery and Paradisaic beauty; such faces, compounded so of hell and heaven, overthrow in us all foregone persuasions, and make us wondering children in this world again.

The face had accosted Pierre some weeks previous to his ride with Lucy to the hills beyond Saddle Meadows; and before her arrival for the summer at the village; moreover it had accosted him in a very common and homely scene; but this enhanced the wonder.

On some distant business, with a farmer-tenant, he had been absent from the mansion during the best part of the day, and had but just come home, early of a pleasant moonlight evening, when Dates delivered a message to him from his mother, begging him to come for her about half-past seven that night to Miss Llanyllyn's cottage, in order to accompany her thence to that of the two Miss Pennies. At the mention of that last name, Pierre well knew what he must anticipate. Those elderly and truly pious spinsters, gifted with the most benevolent hearts in the world, and at mid-age deprived by envious nature of their hearing, seemed to have made it a maxim of their charitable lives, that since God had not given them any more the power to hear Christ's gospel preached, they would therefore thenceforth do what they could toward practicing it. Wherefore, as a matter of no possible interest to them now, they abstained from church; and while with prayer-books in their hands the Rev. Mr. Falsgrave's congregation were engaged in worshiping their God, according to the divine behest; the two Miss Pennies, with thread and needle, were hard at work in serving him; making up shirts and gowns for the poor people of the parish. Pierre had heard that they had recently been at the trouble of organizing a regular society, among the neighboring farmers' wives and daughters, to meet twice a month at their own house (the Miss Pennies) for the purpose of sewing in concert for the benefit of various settlements of necessitous emigrants, who had lately pitched their populous shanties further up the river. But though this enterprise had not been started without previously acquainting Mrs. Glendinning of it,—for indeed she was much loved and honored by the pious spinsters,—and their promise of solid assistance from that gracious manorial lady; yet Pierre had not heard that his mother had been officially invited to preside, or be at all present at the semi-monthly meetings; though he supposed, that far from having any scruples against so doing, she would be very glad to associate that way, with the good people of the village.

"Now, brother Pierre"—said Mrs. Glendinning, rising from Miss Llanyllyn's huge cushioned chair—"throw my shawl around me; and good-evening to Lucy's aunt.—There, we shall be late."

As they walked along, she added—"Now, Pierre, I know you are apt to be a little impatient sometimes, of these sewing scenes; but courage; I merely want to peep in on them; so as to get some inkling of what they would indeed be at; and then my promised benefactions can be better selected by me. Besides, Pierre, I could have had Dates escort me, but I preferred you; because I want you to know who they are you live among; how many really pretty, and naturally-refined dames and girls you shall one day be lord of the manor of. I anticipate a rare display of rural red and white."

Cheered by such pleasant promises, Pierre soon found him-

self leading his mother into a room full of faces. The instant
they appeared, a gratuitous old body, seated with her knitting
near the door, squeaked out shrilly—"Ah! dames, dames,—
Madam Glendinning!—Master Pierre Glendinning!"

Almost immediately following this sound, there came a
sudden, long-drawn, unearthly, girlish shriek, from the further corner of the long, double room. Never had human voice
so affected Pierre before. Though he saw not the person from
whom it came, and though the voice was wholly strange to
him, yet the sudden shriek seemed to split its way clean
through his heart, and leave a yawning gap there. For an instant, he stood bewildered; but started at his mother's voice;
her arm being still in his. "Why do you clutch my arm so,
Pierre? You pain me. Pshaw! some one has fainted,—nothing
more."

Instantly Pierre recovered himself, and affecting to mock at
his own trepidation, hurried across the room to offer his services, if such were needed. But dames and maidens had been
all beforehand with him; the lights were wildly flickering in
the air-current made by the flinging open of the casement,
near to where the shriek had come. But the climax of the
tumult was soon past; and presently, upon closing the casement, it subsided almost wholly. The elder of the spinster
Pennies, advancing to Mrs. Glendinning, now gave her to understand, that one of the further crowd of industrious girls
present, had been attacked by a sudden, but fleeting fit,
vaguely imputable to some constitutional disorder or other.
She was now quite well again. And so the company, one and
all, seemingly acting upon their natural good-breeding, which
in any one at bottom, is but delicacy and charity, refrained
from all further curiosity; reminded not the girl of what had
passed; noted her scarce at all; and all needles stitched away
as before.

Leaving his mother to speak with whom she pleased, and
attend alone to her own affairs with the society; Pierre, oblivious now in such a lively crowd, of any past unpleasantness,
after some courtly words to the Miss Pennies,—insinuated
into their understandings through a long coiled trumpet,
which, when not in use, the spinsters wore, hanging like a
powder-horn from their girdles:—and likewise, after mani-

festing the profoundest and most intelligent interest in the mystic mechanism of a huge woolen sock, in course of completion by a spectacled old lady of his more particular acquaintance; after all this had been gone through, and something more too tedious to detail, but which occupied him for nearly half an hour, Pierre, with a slightly blushing, and imperfectly balanced assurance, advanced toward the further crowd of maidens; where, by the light of many a well-snuffed candle, they clubbed all their bright contrasting cheeks, like a dense bed of garden tulips. There were the shy and pretty Maries, Marthas, Susans, Betties, Jennies, Nellies; and forty more fair nymphs, who skimmed the cream, and made the butter of the fat farms of Saddle Meadows.

Assurance is in presence of the assured. Where embarrassments prevail, they affect the most disembarrassed. What wonder, then, that gazing on such a thick array of wreathing, roguish, half-averted, blushing faces—still audacious in their very embarrassment—Pierre, too, should flush a bit, and stammer in his attitudes a little? Youthful love and graciousness were in his heart; kindest words upon his tongue; but there he stood, target for the transfixing glances of those ambushed archers of the eye.

But his abashments last too long; his cheek hath changed from blush to pallor; what strange thing does Pierre Glendinning see? Behind the first close, busy breast-work of young girls, are several very little stands, or circular tables, where sit small groups of twos and threes, sewing in small comparative solitudes, as it were. They would seem to be the less notable of the rural company; or else, for some cause, they have voluntarily retired into their humble banishment. Upon one of these persons engaged at the furthermost and least conspicuous of these little stands, and close by a casement, Pierre's glance is palely fixed.

The girl sits steadily sewing; neither she nor her two companions speak. Her eyes are mostly upon her work; but now and then a very close observer would notice that she furtively lifts them, and moves them sideways and timidly toward Pierre; and then, still more furtively and timidly toward his lady mother, further off. All the while, her preternatural calmness sometimes seems only made to cover the intensest strug-

gle in her bosom. Her unadorned and modest dress is black;
fitting close up to her neck, and clasping it with a plain, velvet
border. To a nice perception, that velvet shows elastically;
contracting and expanding, as though some choked, violent
thing were risen up there within from the teeming region of
her heart. But her dark, olive cheek is without a blush, or sign
of any disquietude. So far as this girl lies upon the common
surface, ineffable composure steeps her. But still, she sideways
steals the furtive, timid glance. Anon, as yielding to the irresistible climax of her concealed emotion, whatever that may
be, she lifts her whole marvelous countenance into the radiant
candlelight, and for one swift instant, that face of supernaturalness unreservedly meets Pierre's. Now, wonderful loveliness, and a still more wonderful loneliness, have with
inexplicable implorings, looked up to him from that henceforth immemorial face. There, too, he seemed to see the fair
ground where Anguish had contended with Beauty, and neither being conqueror, both had laid down on the field.

Recovering at length from his all too obvious emotion,
Pierre turned away still farther, to regain the conscious possession of himself. A wild, bewildering, and incomprehensible
curiosity had seized him, to know something definite of that
face. To this curiosity, at the moment, he entirely surrendered
himself; unable as he was to combat it, or reason with it in
the slightest way. So soon as he felt his outward composure
returned to him, he purposed to chat his way behind the
breastwork of bright eyes and cheeks, and on some parlor
pretense or other, hear, if possible, an audible syllable from
one whose mere silent aspect had so potentially moved him.
But at length, as with this object in mind, he was crossing
the room again, he heard his mother's voice, gayly calling
him away; and turning, saw her shawled and bonneted. He
could now make no plausible stay, and smothering the agitation in him, he bowed a general and hurried adieu to the
company, and went forth with his mother.

They had gone some way homeward, in perfect silence,
when his mother spoke.

"Well, Pierre, what can it possibly be?"

"My God, mother, did you see her then?"

"My son!" cried Mrs. Glendinning, instantly stopping in

terror, and withdrawing her arm from Pierre, " what—what under heaven ails you? This is most strange! I but playfully asked, what you were so steadfastly thinking of; and here you answer me by the strangest question, in a voice that seems to come from under your great-grandfather's tomb! What, in heaven's name, does this mean, Pierre? Why were you so silent, and why now are you so ill-timed in speaking? Answer me;—explain all this;—*she*—*she*—what *she* should you be thinking of but Lucy Tartan?—Pierre, beware, beware! I had thought you firmer in your lady's faith, than such strange behavior as this would seem to hint. Answer me, Pierre, what may this mean? Come, I hate a mystery; speak, my son."

Fortunately, this prolonged verbalized wonder in his mother afforded Pierre time to rally from his double and aggravated astonishment, brought about by first suspecting that his mother also had been struck by the strange aspect of the face, and then, having that suspicion so violently beaten back upon him, by her apparently unaffected alarm at finding him in some region of thought wholly unshared by herself at the time.

"It is nothing—nothing, sister Mary; just nothing at all in the world. I believe I was dreaming—sleep-walking, or something of that sort. They were vastly pretty girls there this evening, sister Mary, were they not? Come, let us walk on—do, sister mine."

"Pierre, Pierre!—but I will take your arm again;—and have you really nothing more to say? were you really wandering, Pierre?"

"I swear to you, my dearest mother, that never before in my whole existence, have I so completely gone wandering in my soul, as at that very moment. But it is all over now." Then in a less earnest and somewhat playful tone, he added: "And sister mine, if you know aught of the physical and sanitary authors, you must be aware, that the only treatment for such a case of harmless temporary aberration, is for all persons to ignore it in the subject. So no more of this foolishness. Talking about it only makes me feel very unpleasantly silly, and there is no knowing that it may not bring it back upon me."

"Then by all means, my dear boy, not another word about it. But it's passing strange—very, very strange indeed. Well,

about that morning business; how fared you? Tell me about
it."

ii

So Pierre, gladly plunging into this welcome current of
talk, was enabled to attend his mother home without furnishing further cause for her concern or wonderment. But not by
any means so readily could he allay his own concern and wonderment. Too really true in itself, however evasive in its effect
at the time, was that earnest answer to his mother, declaring
that never in his whole existence had he been so profoundly
stirred. The face haunted him as some imploring, and beauteous, impassioned, ideal Madonna's haunts the morbidly
longing and enthusiastic, but ever-baffled artist. And ever, as
the mystic face thus rose before his fancy's sight, another
sense was touched in him; the long-drawn, unearthly, girlish
shriek pealed through and through his soul; for now he knew
the shriek came from the face—such Delphic shriek could
only come from such a source. And wherefore that shriek?
thought Pierre. Bodes it ill to the face, or me, or both? How
am I changed, that my appearance on any scene should have
power to work such woe? But it was mostly the face—the
face, that wrought upon him. The shriek seemed as incidentally embodied there.

The emotions he experienced seemed to have taken hold of
the deepest roots and subtlest fibres of his being. And so
much the more that it was so subterranean in him, so much
the more did he feel its weird inscrutableness. What was one
unknown, sad-eyed, shrieking girl to him? There must be sad-
eyed girls somewhere in the world, and this was only one of
them. And what was the most beautiful sad-eyed girl to him?
Sadness might be beautiful, as well as mirth—he lost himself
trying to follow out this tangle. "I will no more of this infatuation," he would cry; but forth from regions of irradiated
air, the divine beauty and imploring sufferings of the face,
stole into his view.

Hitherto I have ever held but lightly, thought Pierre, all
stories of ghostly mysticalness in man; my creed of this world
leads me to believe in visible, beautiful flesh, and audible

breath, however sweet and scented; but only in visible flesh, and audible breath, have I hitherto believed. But now!—now!—and again he would lose himself in the most surprising and preternatural ponderings, which baffled all the introspective cunning of his mind. Himself was too much for himself. He felt that what he had always before considered the solid land of veritable reality, was now being audaciously encroached upon by bannered armies of hooded phantoms, disembarking in his soul, as from flotillas of specter-boats.

The terrors of the face were not those of Gorgon; not by repelling hideousness did it smite him so; but bewilderingly allured him, by its nameless beauty, and its long-suffering, hopeless anguish.

But he was sensible that this general effect upon him, was also special; the face somehow mystically appealing to his own private and individual affections; and by a silent and tyrannic call, challenging him in his deepest moral being, and summoning Truth, Love, Pity, Conscience, to the stand. Apex of all wonders! thought Pierre; this indeed almost unmans me with its wonderfulness. Escape the face he could not. Muffling his own in his bed-clothes—that did not hide it. Flying from it by sunlight down the meadows, was as vain.

Most miraculous of all to Pierre was the vague impression, that somewhere he had seen traits of the likeness of that face before. But where, he could not say; nor could he, in the remotest degree, imagine. He was not unaware—for in one or two instances, he had experienced the fact—that sometimes a man may see a passing countenance in the street, which shall irresistibly and magnetically affect him, for a moment, as wholly unknown to him, and yet strangely reminiscent of some vague face he has previously encountered, in some fancied time, too, of extreme interest to his life. But not so was it now with Pierre. The face had not perplexed him for a few speculative minutes, and then glided from him, to return no more. It stayed close by him; only—and not invariably—could he repel it, by the exertion of all his resolution and self-will. Besides, what of general enchantment lurked in his strange sensations, seemed concentringly condensed, and pointed to a spear-head, that pierced his heart with an inexplicable pang, whenever the specializing emotion—to call it

so—seized the possession of his thoughts, and waved into his
visions, a thousand forms of by-gone times, and many an old
legendary family scene, which he had heard related by his elderly relations, some of them now dead.

Disguising his wild reveries as best he might from the notice of his mother, and all other persons of her household, for
two days Pierre wrestled with his own haunted spirit; and at
last, so effectually purged it of all weirdnesses, and so effectually regained the general mastery of himself, that for a time,
life went with him, as though he had never been stirred so
strangely. Once more, the sweet unconditional thought of
Lucy slid wholly into his soul, dislodging thence all such
phantom occupants. Once more he rode, he walked, he
swam, he vaulted; and with new zest threw himself into the
glowing practice of all those manly exercises, he so dearly
loved. It almost seemed in him, that ere promising forever to
protect, as well as eternally to love, his Lucy, he must first
completely invigorate and embrawn himself into the possession of such a noble muscular manliness, that he might champion Lucy against the whole physical world.

Still—even before the occasional reappearance of the face
to him—Pierre, for all his willful ardor in his gymnasticals
and other diversions, whether in-doors or out, or whether by
book or foil; still, Pierre could not but be secretly annoyed,
and not a little perplexed, as to the motive, which, for the
first time in his recollection, had impelled him, not merely to
conceal from his mother a singular circumstance in his life
(for that, he felt would have been but venial; and besides, as
will eventually be seen, he could find one particular precedent
for it, in his past experience) but likewise, and superaddedly,
to parry, nay, to evade, and, in effect, to return something
alarmingly like a fib, to an explicit question put to him by his
mother;—such being the guise, in which part of the conversation they had had that eventful night, now appeared to his
fastidious sense. He considered also, that his evasive answer
had not pantheistically burst from him in a momentary interregnum of self-command. No; his mother had made quite a
lengthy speech to him; during which he well remembered, he
had been carefully, though with trepidation, turning over in
his mind, how best he might recall her from her unwished-

for and untimely scent. Why had this been so? Was this his wont? What inscrutable thing was it, that so suddenly had seized him, and made him a falsifyer—ay, a falsifyer and nothing less—to his own dearly-beloved, and confiding mother? Here, indeed, was something strange for him; here was stuff for his utmost ethical meditations. But, nevertheless, on strict introspection, he felt, that he would not willingly have it otherwise; not willingly would he now undissemble himself in this matter to his mother. Why was this, too? Was this his wont? Here, again, was food for mysticism. Here, in imperfect inklings, tinglings, presentiments, Pierre began to feel—what all mature men, who are Magians, sooner or later know, and more or less assuredly—that not always in our actions, are we our own factors. But this conceit was very dim in Pierre; and dimness is ever suspicious and repugnant to us; and so, Pierre shrank abhorringly from the infernal catacombs of thought, down into which, this fœtal fancy beckoned him. Only this, though in secret, did he cherish; only this, he felt persuaded of; namely, that not for both worlds would he have his mother made a partner to his sometime mystic mood.

But with this nameless fascination of the face upon him, during those two days that it had first and fully possessed him for its own, did perplexed Pierre refrain from that apparently most natural of all resources,—boldly seeking out, and re-turning to the palpable cause, and questioning her, by look or voice, or both together—the mysterious girl herself? No; not entirely did Pierre here refrain. But his profound curiosity and interest in the matter—strange as it may seem—did not so much appear to be embodied in the mournful person of the olive girl, as by some radiations from her, embodied in the vague conceits which agitated his own soul. *There*, lurked the subtler secret: *that*, Pierre had striven to tear away. From without, no wonderful effect is wrought within ourselves, un-less some interior, responding wonder meets it. That the starry vault shall surcharge the heart with all rapturous mar-velings, is only because we ourselves are greater miracles, and superber trophies than all the stars in universal space. Wonder interlocks with wonder; and then the confounding feeling comes. No cause have we to fancy, that a horse, a dog, a fowl, ever stand transfixed beneath yon skyey load of majesty. But our soul's arches underfit into its; and so, prevent the upper arch from falling on us with unsustainable inscrutableness. "Explain ye my deeper mystery," said the shepherd Chaldean king, smiting his breast, lying on his back upon the plain; "and then, I will bestow all my wonderings upon ye, ye stately stars!" So, in some sort, with Pierre. Explain thou this strange integral feeling in me myself, he thought—turning upon the fancied face—and I will then renounce all other wonders, to gaze wonderingly at thee. But thou hast evoked in me profounder spells than the evoking one, thou face! For me, thou hast uncovered one infinite, dumb, beseeching countenance of mystery, underlying all the surfaces of visible time and space.

But during those two days of his first wild vassalage to his original sensations, Pierre had not been unvisited by less mysterious impulses. Two or three very plain and practical plannings of desirable procedures in reference to some possible homely explication of all this nonsense—so he would momentarily denominate it—now and then flittingly intermitted his pervading mood of semi-madness. Once he had seized his hat, careless of his accustomed gloves and cane, and found himself in the street, walking very rapidly in the direction of the Miss Pennies'. But whither now? he disenchantingly interrogated himself. Where would you go? A million to one, those deaf old spinsters can tell you nothing you burn to know. Deaf old spinsters are not used to be the depositaries of such mystical secrecies. But then, they may reveal her name—where she dwells, and something, however fragmentary and unsatisfactory, of who she is, and whence. Ay; but then, in ten minutes after your leaving them, all the houses in Saddle Meadows would be humming with the gossip of Pierre Glendinning engaged to marry Lucy Tartan, and yet running about the country, in ambiguous pursuit of strange young women. That will never do. You remember, do you not, often seeing the Miss Pennies, hatless and without a shawl, hurrying through the village, like two postmen intent on dropping some tit-bit of precious gossip? What a morsel for them, Pierre, have you, if you now call upon them. Verily, their trumpets are both for use and for significance. Though very deaf, the Miss Pennies are by no means dumb. They blazon very wide.

"Now be sure, and say that it was the Miss Pennies, who left the news—be sure—we—the Miss Pennies—remember—say to Mrs. Glendinning it was we." Such was the message that now half-humorously occurred to Pierre, as having been once confided to him by the sister spinsters, one evening when they called with a choice present of some very *recherche* chit-chat for his mother; but found the manorial lady out; and so charged her son with it; hurrying away to all the inferior houses, so as not to be anywhere forestalled in their disclosure.

Now, I wish it had been any other house than the Miss Pennies; any other house but theirs, and on my soul I believe I should have gone. But not to them—no, that I can not do. It would be sure to reach my mother, and then she would put this and that together—stir a little—let it simmer—and farewell forever to all her majestic notions of my immaculate integrity. Patience, Pierre, the population of this region is not so immense. No dense mobs of Nineveh confound all personal identities in Saddle Meadows. Patience; thou shalt see it soon again; catch it passing thee in some green lane, sacred to thy evening reveries. She that bears it can not dwell remote. Patience, Pierre. Ever are such mysteries best and soonest unraveled by the eventual unraveling of themselves. Or, if you will, go back and get your gloves, and more especially your cane, and begin your own secret voyage of discovery after it. Your cane, I say; because it will probably be a very long and weary walk. True, just now I hinted, that she that bears it can not dwell very remote; but then her nearness may not be at all conspicuous. So, homeward, and put off thy hat, and let thy cane stay still, good Pierre. Seek not to mystify the mystery so.

Thus, intermittingly, ever and anon during those sad two days of deepest sufferance, Pierre would stand reasoning and expostulating with himself; and by such meditative treatment, reassure his own spontaneous impulses. Doubtless, it was wise and right that so he did; doubtless: but in a world so full of all dubieties as this, one can never be entirely certain whether another person, however carefully and cautiously

conscientious, has acted in all respects conceivable for the very
best.

But when the two days were gone by, and Pierre began to
recognize his former self, as restored to him from its mystic
exile, then the thoughts of personally and pointedly seeking
out the unknown, either preliminarily by a call upon the sister
spinsters, or generally by performing the observant lynx-eyed
circuit of the country on foot, and as a crafty inquisitor, dissembling his cause of inquisition; these and all similar intentions completely abandoned Pierre.

He was now diligently striving, with all his mental might,
forever to drive the phantom from him. He seemed to feel
that it begat in him a certain condition of his being, which
was most painful, and every way uncongenial to his natural,
wonted self. It had a touch of he knew not what sort of un-
healthiness in it, so to speak; for, in his then ignorance, he
could find no better term; it seemed to have in it a germ of
somewhat which, if not quickly extirpated, might insidiously
poison and embitter his whole life—that choice, delicious life
which he had vowed to Lucy for his one pure and comprehensive offering—at once a sacrifice and a delight.

Nor in these endeavorings did he entirely fail. For the most
part, he felt now that he had a power over the comings and
the goings of the face; but not on all occasions. Sometimes
the old, original mystic tyranny would steal upon him; the
long, dark, locks of mournful hair would fall upon his soul,
and trail their wonderful melancholy along with them; the
two full, steady, over-brimming eyes of loveliness and anguish
would converge their magic rays, till he felt them kindling he
could not tell what mysterious fires in the heart at which they
aimed.

When once this feeling had him fully, then was the perilous
time for Pierre. For supernatural as the feeling was, and appealing to all things ultramontane to his soul; yet was it a
delicious sadness to him. Some hazy fairy swam above him in
the heavenly ether, and showered down upon him the sweetest pearls of pensiveness. Then he would be seized with a
singular impulse to reveal the secret to some one other individual in the world. Only one, not more; he could not hold
all this strange fullness in himself. It must be shared. In such

an hour it was, that chancing to encounter Lucy (her, whom above all others, he did confidingly adore), she heard the story of the face; nor slept at all that night; nor for a long time freed her pillow completely from wild, Beethoven sounds of distant, waltzing melodies, as of ambiguous fairies dancing on the heath.

iii

This history goes forward and goes backward, as occasion calls. Nimble center, circumference elastic you must have. Now we return to Pierre, wending homeward from his reveries beneath the pine-tree.

His burst of impatience against the sublime Italian, Dante, arising from that poet being the one who, in a former time, had first opened to his shuddering eyes the infinite cliffs and gulfs of human mystery and misery;—though still more in the way of experimental vision, than of sensational presentiment or experience (for as yet he had not seen so far and deep as Dante, and therefore was entirely incompetent to meet the grim bard fairly on his peculiar ground), this ignorant burst of his young impatience,—also arising from that half contemptuous dislike, and sometimes selfish loathing, with which, either naturally feeble or undeveloped minds, regard those dark ravings of the loftier poets, which are in eternal opposition to their own fine-spun, shallow dreams of rapturous or prudential Youth;—this rash, untutored burst of Pierre's young impatience, seemed to have carried off with it, all the other forms of his melancholy—if melancholy it had been—and left him now serene again, and ready for any tranquil pleasantness the gods might have in store. For his, indeed, was true Youth's temperament,—summary with sadness, swift to joyfulness, and long protracting, and detaining with that joyfulness, when once it came fully nigh to him.

As he entered the dining-hall, he saw Dates retiring from another door with his tray. Alone and meditative, by the bared half of the polished table, sat his mother at her dessert; fruit-baskets and a decanter were before her. On the other leaf of the same table, still lay the cloth, folded back upon itself, and set out with one plate and its usual accompaniments.

"Sit down, Pierre; when I came home, I was surprised to hear that the phaeton had returned so early, and here I waited dinner for you, until I could wait no more. But go to the green pantry now, and get what Dates has but just put away for you there. Heigh-ho! too plainly I foresee it—no more regular dinner-hours, or tea-hours, or supper-hours, in Saddle Meadows, till its young lord is wedded. And that puts me in mind of something, Pierre; but I'll defer it till you have eaten a little. Do you know, Pierre, that if you continue these irregular meals of yours, and deprive me so entirely almost of your company, that I shall run fearful risk of getting to be a terrible wine-bibber;—yes, could you unalarmed see me sitting all alone here with this decanter, like any old nurse, Pierre; some solitary, forlorn old nurse, Pierre, deserted by her last friend, and therefore forced to embrace her flask?"

"No, I did not feel any great alarm, sister," said Pierre, smiling, "since I could not but perceive that the decanter was still full to the stopple."

"Possibly it may be only a fresh decanter, Pierre;" then changing her voice suddenly—"but mark me, Mr. Pierre Glendinning!"

"Well, Mrs. Mary Glendinning!"

"Do you know, sir, that you are very shortly to be married,—that indeed the day is all but fixed?"

"How!" cried Pierre, in real joyful astonishment, both at the nature of the tidings, and the earnest tones in which they were conveyed—"dear, dear mother, you have strangely changed your mind then, my dear mother."

"It is even so, dear brother;—before this day month I hope to have a little sister Tartan."

"You talk very strangely, mother," rejoined Pierre, quickly. "I suppose, then, I have next to nothing to say in the matter?"

"Next to nothing, Pierre! What indeed could you say to the purpose? what at all have you to do with it, I should like to know? Do you so much as dream, you silly boy, that men ever have the marrying of themselves? Juxtaposition marries men. There is but one match-maker in the world, Pierre, and that is Mrs. Juxtaposition, a most notorious lady!"

"Very peculiar, disenchanting sort of talk, this, under the circumstances, sister Mary," laying down his fork. "Mrs. Juxtaposition, ah! And in your opinion, mother, does this fine glorious passion only amount to that?"

"Only to that, Pierre; but mark you: according to my creed—though this part of it is a little hazy—Mrs. Juxtaposition moves her pawns only as she herself is moved to so doing by the spirit."

"Ah! that sets it all right again," said Pierre, resuming his fork—"my appetite returns. But what was that about my being married so soon?" he added, vainly striving to assume an air of incredulity and unconcern; "you were joking, I suppose; it seems to me, sister, either you or I was but just now wandering in the mind a little, on that subject. Are you really thinking of any such thing? and have you really vanquished your sagacious scruples by yourself, after I had so long and ineffectually sought to do it for you? Well, I am a million times delighted; tell me quick!"

"I will, Pierre. You very well know, that from the first hour you apprised me—or rather, from a period prior to that— from the moment that I, by my own insight, became aware of your love for Lucy, I have always approved it. Lucy is a delicious girl; of honorable descent, a fortune, well-bred, and the very pattern of all that I think amiable and attractive in a girl of seventeen."

"Well, well, well," cried Pierre rapidly and impetuously; " we both knew that before."

"Well, well, well, Pierre," retorted his mother, mockingly.

"It is not well, well, well; but ill, ill, ill, to torture me so, mother; go on, do!"

"But notwithstanding my admiring approval of your choice, Pierre; yet, as you know, I have resisted your entreaties for my consent to your speedy marriage, because I thought that a girl of scarcely seventeen, and a boy scarcely twenty, should not be in such a hurry;—there was plenty of time, I thought, which could be profitably employed by both."

"Permit me here to interrupt you, mother. Whatever you may have seen in me; she,—I mean Lucy,—has never been in the slightest hurry to be married;—that's all. But I shall regard it as a *lapsus-linguae* in you."

"Undoubtedly, a *lapsus*. But listen to me. I have been care-

fully observing both you and Lucy of late; and that has made
me think further of the matter. Now, Pierre, if you were in
any profession, or in any business at all; nay, if I were a farmer's wife, and you my child, working in my fields; why, then,
you and Lucy should still wait awhile. But as you have nothing to do but to think of Lucy by day, and dream of her by
night, and as she is in the same predicament, I suppose, with
respect to you; and as the consequence of all this begins to
be discernible in a certain, just perceptible, and quite harmless
thinness, so to speak, of the cheek; but a very conspicuous
and dangerous febrileness of the eye; therefore, I choose the
lesser of two evils; and now you have my permission to be
married, as soon as the thing can be done with propriety. I
dare say you have no objection to have the wedding take
place before Christmas, the present month being the first of
summer."

Pierre said nothing; but leaping to his feet, threw his two
arms around his mother, and kissed her repeatedly.

"A most sweet and eloquent answer, Pierre; but sit down
again. I desire now to say a little concerning less attractive,
but quite necessary things connected with this affair. You
know, that by your father's will, these lands and—"

"Miss Lucy, my mistress;" said Dates, throwing open the
door.

Pierre sprang to his feet; but as if suddenly mindful of his
mother's presence, composed himself again, though he still
approached the door.

Lucy entered, carrying a little basket of strawberries.

"Why, how do you do, my dear," said Mrs. Glendinning
affectionately. "This is an unexpected pleasure."

"Yes; and I suppose that Pierre here is a little surprised too;
seeing that he was to call upon me this evening, and not I
upon him before sundown. But I took a sudden fancy for a
solitary stroll,—the afternoon was such a delicious one; and
chancing—it was only chancing—to pass through the Locust
Lane leading hither, I met the strangest little fellow, with this
basket in his hand.—'Yes, buy them, miss'—said he. 'And
how do you know I want to buy them,' returned I, 'I don't
want to buy them.'—'Yes you do, miss; they ought to be
twenty-six cents, but I'll take thirteen cents, that being my

shilling. I always want the odd half cent, I do. Come, I can't wait, I have been expecting you long enough.' "

"A very sagacious little imp," laughed Mrs. Glendinning.

"Impertinent little rascal," cried Pierre.

"And am I not now the silliest of all silly girls, to be telling you my adventures so very frankly," smiled Lucy.

"No; but the most celestial of all innocents," cried Pierre, in a rhapsody of delight. "Frankly open is the flower, that hath nothing but purity to show."

"Now, my dear little Lucy," said Mrs. Glendinning, "let Pierre take off your shawl, and come now and stay to tea with us. Pierre has put back the dinner so, the tea-hour will come now very soon."

"Thank you; but I can not stay this time. Look, I have forgotten my own errand; I brought these strawberries for you, Mrs. Glendinning, and for Pierre;—Pierre is so wonderfully fond of them."

"I was audacious enough to think as much," cried Pierre, "for you *and* me, you see, mother; for you *and* me, you understand that, I hope."

"Perfectly, my dear brother."

Lucy blushed.

"How warm it is, Mrs. Glendinning."

"Very warm, Lucy. So you won't stay to tea?"

"No, I must go now; just a little stroll, that's all; good-bye! Now don't be following me, Pierre. Mrs. Glendinning, will you keep Pierre back? I know you want him; you were talking over some private affair when I entered; you both looked so very confidential."

"And you were not very far from right, Lucy," said Mrs. Glendinning, making no sign to stay her departure.

"Yes, business of the highest importance," said Pierre, fixing his eyes upon Lucy significantly.

At this moment, Lucy just upon the point of her departure, was hovering near the door; the setting sun, streaming through the window, bathed her whole form in golden loveliness and light; that wonderful, and most vivid transparency of her clear Welsh complexion, now fairly glowed like rosy snow. Her flowing, white, blue-ribboned dress, fleecily invested her. Pierre almost thought that she could only depart the house by floating out of the open window, instead of actually stepping from the door. All her aspect to him, was that moment touched with an indescribable gayety, buoyancy, fragility, and an unearthly evanescence.

Youth is no philosopher. Not into young Pierre's heart did there then come the thought, that as the glory of the rose endures but for a day, so the full bloom of girlish airiness and bewitchingness, passes from the earth almost as soon; as jealously absorbed by those frugal elements, which again incorporate that translated girlish bloom, into the first expanding flower-bud. Not into young Pierre, did there then steal that thought of utmost sadness; pondering on the inevitable evanescence of all earthly loveliness; which makes the sweetest things of life only food for ever-devouring and omnivorous melancholy. Pierre's thought was different from this, and yet somehow akin to it.

This to be my wife? I that but the other day weighed an hundred and fifty pounds of solid avoirdupois; — *I* to wed this heavenly fleece? Methinks one husbandly embrace would break her airy zone, and she exhale upward to that heaven whence she hath hither come, condensed to mortal sight. It can not be; I am of heavy earth, and she of airy light. By heaven, but marriage is an impious thing!

Meanwhile, as these things ran through his soul, Mrs. Glendinning also had thinkings of her own.

"A very beautiful tableau," she cried, at last, artistically turning her gay head a little sideways—"very beautiful, indeed; this, I suppose is all premeditated for my entertainment. Orpheus finding his Eurydice; or Pluto stealing Proserpine. Admirable! It might almost stand for either."

"No," said Pierre, gravely; "it is the last. Now, first I see a meaning there." Yes, he added to himself inwardly, I am Pluto stealing Proserpine; and every accepted lover is.

"And you would be very stupid, brother Pierre, if you did not see something there," said his mother, still that way pursuing her own different train of thought. "The meaning thereof is this: Lucy has commanded me to stay you; but in reality she wants you to go along with her. Well, you may go as far as the porch; but then, you must return, for we have not concluded our little affair, you know. Adieu, little lady!"

There was ever a slight degree of affectionate patronizing in the manner of the resplendent, full-blown Mrs. Glendinning, toward the delicate and shrinking girlhood of young Lucy. She treated her very much as she might have treated some surpassingly beautiful and precocious child; and this was precisely what Lucy was. Looking beyond the present period, Mrs. Glendinning could not but perceive, that even in Lucy's womanly maturity, Lucy would still be a child to her; because, she, elated, felt, that in a certain intellectual vigor, so to speak, she was the essential opposite of Lucy, whose sympathetic mind and person had both been cast in one mould of wondrous delicacy. But here Mrs. Glendinning was both right and wrong. So far as she here saw a difference between herself and Lucy Tartan, she did not err; but so far— and that was very far—as she thought she saw her innate superiority to her in the absolute scale of being, here she very widely and immeasurably erred. For what may be artistically styled angelicalness, this is the highest essence compatible with created being; and angelicalness hath no vulgar vigor in it. And that thing which very often prompts to the display of any vigor—which thing, in man or woman, is at bottom nothing but ambition—this quality is purely earthly, and not angelical. It is false, that any angels fell by reason of ambition. Angels never fall; and never feel ambition. Therefore, benevolently, and affectionately, and all-sincerely, as thy heart, oh, Mrs. Glendinning! now standeth affected toward the fleecy Lucy; still, lady, thou dost very sadly mistake it, when the proud, double-arches of the bright breastplate of thy bosom, expand with secret triumph over one, whom thou so sweetly, but still so patronizingly stylest, The Little Lucy.

But ignorant of these further insights, that very superb-looking lady, now waiting Pierre's return from the portico door, sat in a very matronly revery; her eyes fixed upon the decanter of amber-hued wine before her. Whether it was that she somehow saw some lurking analogical similitude between that remarkably slender, and gracefully cut little pint-decanter, brimfull of light, golden wine, or not, there is no absolute telling now. But really, the peculiarly, and reminiscently, and forecastingly complacent expression of her beaming and benevolent countenance, seemed a tell-tale of some conceit very much like the following:—Yes, she's a very pretty little pint-decanter of a girl: a very pretty little Pale Sherry pint-decanter of a girl; and I—I'm a quart decanter of—of—Port—potent Port! Now, Sherry for boys, and Port for men—so I've heard men say; and Pierre is but a boy; but when his father wedded me,—why, his father was turned of five-and-thirty years.

After a little further waiting for him, Mrs. Glendinning heard Pierre's voice—"Yes, before eight o'clock at least, Lucy—no fear;" and then the hall door banged, and Pierre returned to her.

But now she found that this unforeseen visit of Lucy had completely routed all business capacity in her mercurial son; fairly capsizing him again into, there was no telling what sea of pleasant pensiveness.

"Dear me! some other time, sister Mary."

"Not this time; that is very certain, Pierre. Upon my word I shall have to get Lucy kidnapped, and temporarily taken out of the country, and you handcuffed to the table, else there will be no having a preliminary understanding with you, previous to calling in the lawyers. Well, I shall yet manage you, one way or other. Good-bye, Pierre; I see you don't want me now. I suppose I shan't see you till to-morrow morning. Luckily, I have a very interesting book to read. Adieu!"

But Pierre remained in his chair; his gaze fixed upon the stilly sunset beyond the meadows, and far away to the now golden hills. A glorious, softly glorious, and most gracious evening, which seemed plainly a tongue to all humanity, saying: I go down in beauty to rise in joy; Love reigns throughout all worlds that sunsets visit; it is a foolish ghost story; there is no such thing as misery. Would Love, which is omnipotent, have misery in his domain? Would the god of sunlight decree gloom? It is a flawless, speckless, fleckless, beautiful world throughout; joy now, and joy forever!

Then the face, which before had seemed mournfully and reproachfully looking out upon him from the effulgent sunset's heart; the face slid from him; and left alone there with his soul's joy, thinking that that very night he would utter the magic word of marriage to his Lucy; not a happier youth than Pierre Glendinning sat watching that day's sun go down.

iv

After this morning of gayety, this noon of tragedy, and this evening so full of chequered pensiveness; Pierre now possessed his soul in joyful mildness and steadfastness; feeling none of that wild anguish of anticipative rapture, which, in weaker minds, too often dislodges Love's sweet bird from her nest.

The early night was warm, but dark—for the moon was not risen yet—and as Pierre passed on beneath the pendulous canopies of the long arms of the weeping elms of the village, an almost impenetrable blackness surrounded him, but entered not the gently illuminated halls of his heart. He had not gone very far, when in the distance beyond, he noticed a light moving along the opposite side of the road, and slowly approaching. As it was the custom for some of the more elderly, and perhaps timid inhabitants of the village, to carry a lantern when going abroad of so dark a night, this object conveyed no impression of novelty to Pierre; still, as it silently drew nearer and nearer, the one only distinguishable thing before him, he somehow felt a nameless presentiment that the light must be seeking him. He had nearly gained the cottage door, when the lantern crossed over toward him; and as his nimble hand was laid at last upon the little wicket-gate, which he thought was now to admit him to so much delight; a heavy hand was laid upon himself, and at the same moment, the lantern was lifted toward his face, by a hooded and obscure-looking figure, whose half-averted countenance he could but indistinctly discern. But Pierre's own open aspect, seemed to have been quickly scrutinized by the other.

"I have a letter for Pierre Glendinning," said the stranger, "and I believe this is he." At the same moment, a letter was drawn forth, and sought his hand.

"For me!" exclaimed Pierre, faintly, starting at the strangeness of the encounter;—"methinks this is an odd time and place to deliver your mail;—who are you?—Stay!"

But without waiting an answer, the messenger had already turned about, and was re-crossing the road. In the first impulse of the moment, Pierre stept forward, and would have pursued him; but smiling at his own causeless curiosity and trepidation, paused again; and softly turned over the letter in his hand. What mysterious correspondent is this, thought he, circularly moving his thumb upon the seal; no one writes me but from abroad; and their letters come through the office; and as for Lucy—pooh!—when she herself is within, she would hardly have her notes delivered at her own gate. Strange! but I'll in, and read it;—no, not that;—I come to read again in her own sweet heart—that dear missive to me from heaven,—and this impertinent letter would pre-occupy me. I'll wait till I go home.

He entered the gate, and laid his hand upon the cottage knocker. Its sudden coolness caused a slight, and, at any other time, an unaccountable sympathetic sensation in his hand. To his unwonted mood, the knocker seemed to say—"Enter not!—Begone, and first read thy note."

Yielding now, half alarmed, and half bantering with himself, to these shadowy interior monitions, he half-unconsciously quitted the door; repassed the gate; and soon found himself retracing his homeward path.

He equivocated with himself no more; the gloom of the air had now burst into his heart, and extinguished its light; then, first in all his life, Pierre felt the irresistible admonitions and intuitions of Fate.

He entered the hall unnoticed, passed up to his chamber, and hurriedly locking the door in the dark, lit his lamp. As the summoned flame illuminated the room, Pierre, standing before the round center-table, where the lamp was placed, with his hand yet on the brass circle which regulated the wick, started at a figure in the opposite mirror. It bore the outline of Pierre, but now strangely filled with features transformed, and unfamiliar to him; feverish eagerness, fear, and nameless forebodings of ill! He threw himself into a chair, and for a time vainly struggled with the incomprehensible power that possessed him. Then, as he avertedly drew the letter from his bosom, he whispered to himself—Out on thee, Pierre! how sheepish now will ye feel when this tremendous note will turn out to be an invitation to a supper tomorrow night; quick, fool, and write the stereotyped reply: Mr. Pierre Glendinning will be very happy to accept Miss so and so's polite invitation.

Still for the moment he held the letter averted. The messenger had so hurriedly accosted him, and delivered his duty, that Pierre had not yet so much as gained one glance at the superscription of the note. And now the wild thought passed through his mind of what would be the result, should he deliberately destroy the note, without so much as looking at the hand that had addressed it. Hardly had this half-crazy conceit fully made itself legible in his soul, when he was conscious of his two hands meeting in the middle of the sundered note! He leapt from his chair—By heaven! he murmured, unspeakably shocked at the intensity of that mood which had caused him unwittingly as it were, to do for the first time in his whole life, an act of which he was privately ashamed. Though the mood that was on him was none of his own willful seeking; yet now he swiftly felt conscious that he had perhaps a little encouraged it, through that certain strange infatuation of fondness, which the human mind, however vigorous, sometimes feels for any emotion at once novel and mystical. Not willingly, at such times—never mind how fearful we may be—do we try to dissolve the spell which seems, for the time, to admit us, all astonished, into the vague vestibule of the spiritual worlds.

Pierre now seemed distinctly to feel two antagonistic agencies within him; one of which was just struggling into his consciousness, and each of which was striving for the mastery; and between whose respective final ascendencies, he thought he could perceive, though but shadowly, that he himself was to be the only umpire. One bade him finish the selfish destruction of the note; for in some dark way the reading of it would irretrievably entangle his fate. The other bade him dismiss all misgivings; not because there was no possible ground for them, but because to dismiss them was the manlier part, never mind what might betide. This good angel seemed mildly to say—Read, Pierre, though by reading thou may'st entangle thyself, yet may'st thou thereby disentangle others. Read, and feel that best blessedness which, with the sense of all duties discharged, holds happiness indifferent. The bad angel insinuatingly breathed—Read it not, dearest Pierre; but destroy it, and be happy. Then, at the blast of his noble heart, the bad angel shrunk up into nothingness; and the good one defined itself clearer and more clear, and came nigher and more nigh to him, smiling sadly but benignantly; while forth from the infinite distances wonderful harmonies stole into his heart; so that every vein in him pulsed to some heavenly swell.

V

"The name at the end of this letter will be wholly strange to thee. Hitherto my existence has been utterly unknown to thee. This letter will touch thee and pain thee. Willingly would I spare thee, but I can not. My heart bears me witness, that did I think that the suffering these lines would give thee, would, in the faintest degree, compare with what mine has been, I would forever withhold them.

Pierre Glendinning, thou art not the only child of thy father; in the eye of the sun, the hand that traces this is thy sister's; yes, Pierre, Isabel calls thee her brother—her brother! oh, sweetest of words, which so often I have thought to myself, and almost deemed it profanity for an outcast like me to speak or think. Dearest Pierre, my brother, my own father's child! art thou an angel, that thou canst overleap all the heartless usages and fashions of a banded world, that will call thee fool, fool, fool! and curse thee, if thou yieldest to that heavenly impulse which alone can lead thee to respond to the long tyrannizing, and now at last unquenchable yearnings of my bursting heart? Oh, my brother!

But, Pierre Glendinning, I will be proud with thee. Let not my hapless condition extinguish in me, the nobleness which I equally inherit with thee. Thou shalt not be cozened, by my tears and my anguish, into any thing which thy most sober hour will repent. Read no further. If it suit thee, burn this letter; so shalt thou escape the certainty of that knowledge, which, if thou art now cold and selfish, may hereafter, in some maturer, remorseful, and helpless hour, cause thee a poignant upbraiding. No, I shall not, I will not implore thee.—Oh, my brother, my dear, dear Pierre,—help me, fly to me; see, I perish without thee;—pity, pity,—here I freeze in the wide, wide world;—no father, no mother, no sister, no brother, no living thing in the fair form of humanity, that holds me dear. No more, oh no more, dear Pierre, can I endure to be an outcast in the world, for which the dear Savior died. Fly to me, Pierre;—nay, I could tear what I now write,—as I have torn so many other sheets, all written for thy eye, but which never reached thee, because in my distraction, I knew not how to write to thee, nor what to say to thee; and so, behold again how I rave.

Nothing more; I will write no more;—silence becomes this grave;—the heart-sickness steals over me, Pierre, my brother.

Scarce know I what I have written. Yet will I write thee the fatal line, and leave all the rest to thee, Pierre, my brother.— She that is called Isabel Banford dwells in the little red farmhouse, three miles from the village, on the slope toward the lake. To-morrow night-fall—not before—not by day, not by day, Pierre.

THY SISTER, ISABEL."

vi

This letter, inscribed in a feminine, but irregular hand, and in some places almost illegible, plainly attesting the state of the mind which had dictated it;—stained, too, here and there, with spots of tears, which chemically acted upon by the ink, assumed a strange and reddish hue—as if blood and not tears had dropped upon the sheet;—and so completely torn in two by Pierre's own hand, that it indeed seemed the fit scroll of a torn, as well as bleeding heart;—this amazing letter, deprived Pierre for the time of all lucid and definite thought or feeling. He hung half-lifeless in his chair; his hand, clutching the letter, was pressed against his heart, as if some assassin had stabbed him and fled; and Pierre was now holding the dagger in the wound, to stanch the outgushing of the blood.

Ay, Pierre, now indeed art thou hurt with a wound, never to be completely healed but in heaven; for thee, the before undistrusted moral beauty of the world is forever fled; for thee, thy sacred father is no more a saint; all brightness hath gone from thy hills, and all peace from thy plains; and now, now, for the first time, Pierre, Truth rolls a black billow through thy soul! Ah, miserable thou, to whom Truth, in her first tides, bears nothing but wrecks!

The perceptible forms of things; the shapes of thoughts; the pulses of life, but slowly came back to Pierre. And as the mariner, shipwrecked and cast on the beach, has much ado to escape the recoil of the wave that hurled him there; so Pierre long struggled, and struggled, to escape the recoil of that anguish, which had dashed him out of itself, upon the beach of his swoon.

But man was not made to succumb to the villain Woe. Youth is not young and a wrestler in vain. Pierre staggeringly rose to his feet; his wide eyes fixed, and his whole form in a tremble.

"Myself am left, at least," he slowly and half-chokingly murmured. "With myself I front thee! Unhand me all fears, and unlock me all spells! Henceforth I will know nothing but Truth; glad Truth, or sad Truth; I will know what *is*, and do what my deepest angel dictates.—The letter!—Isabel,—sister,—brother,—me, *me*—my sacred father!—This is some accursed dream!—nay, but this paper thing is forged,—a base and malicious forgery, I swear;—Well didst thou hide thy face from me, thou vile lanterned messenger, that didst accost me on the threshold of Joy, with this lying warrant of Woe! Doth Truth come in the dark, and steal on us, and rob us so, and then depart, deaf to all pursuing invocations? If this night, which now wraps my soul, be genuine as that which now wraps this half of the world; then Fate, I have a choice quarrel with thee. Thou art a palterer and a cheat; thou hast lured me on through gay gardens to a gulf. Oh! falsely guided in the days of my Joy, am I now truly led in this night of my grief?—I will be a raver, and none shall stay me! I will lift my hand in fury, for am I not struck? I will be bitter in my breath, for is not this cup of gall? Thou Black Knight, that with visor down, thus confrontest me, and mockest at me; Lo! I strike through thy helm, and will see thy face, be it Gorgon!—Let me go, ye fond affections; all piety leave me;—I will be impious, for piety hath juggled me, and taught me to revere, where I should spurn. From all idols, I tear all veils; henceforth I will see the hidden things; and live right out in my own hidden life!—Now I feel that

nothing but Truth can move me so. This letter is not a forgery. Oh! Isabel, thou art my sister; and I will love thee, and
protect thee, ay, and own thee through all. Ah! forgive me,
ye heavens, for my ignorant ravings, and accept this my
vow.—Here I swear myself Isabel's. Oh! thou poor castaway
girl, that in loneliness and anguish must have long breathed
that same air, which I have only inhaled for delight; thou
who must even now be weeping, and weeping, cast into an
ocean of uncertainty as to thy fate, which heaven hath placed
in my hands; sweet Isabel! would I not be baser than brass,
and harder, and colder than ice, if I could be insensible to
such claims as thine? Thou movest before me, in rainbows
spun of thy tears! I see thee long weeping, and God demands
me for thy comforter; and comfort thee, stand by thee, and
fight for thee, will thy leapingly-acknowledging brother,
whom thy own father named Pierre!"

He could not stay in his chamber: the house contracted to
a nut-shell around him; the walls smote his forehead; bare-
headed he rushed from the place, and only in the infinite air,
found scope for that boundless expansion of his life.

Book IV

I N THEIR PRECISE tracings-out and subtile causations, the strongest and fieriest emotions of life defy all analytical insight. We see the cloud, and feel its bolt; but meteorology only idly essays a critical scrutiny as to how that cloud became charged, and how this bolt so stuns. The metaphysical writers confess, that the most impressive, sudden, and overwhelming event, as well as the minutest, is but the product of an infinite series of infinitely involved and untraceable foregoing occurrences. Just so with every motion of the heart. Why this cheek kindles with a noble enthusiasm; why that lip curls in scorn; these are things not wholly imputable to the immediate apparent cause, which is only one link in the chain; but to a long line of dependencies whose further part is lost in the mid-regions of the impalpable air.

Idle then would it be to attempt by any winding way so to penetrate into the heart, and memory, and inmost life, and nature of Pierre, as to show why it was that a piece of intelligence which, in the natural course of things, many amiable gentlemen, both young and old, have been known to receive with a momentary feeling of surprise, and then a little curiosity to know more, and at last an entire unconcern; idle would it be, to attempt to show how to Pierre it rolled down on his soul like melted lava, and left so deep a deposit of desolation, that all his subsequent endeavors never restored the original temples to the soil, nor all his culture completely revived its buried bloom.

But some random hints may suffice to deprive a little of its strangeness, that tumultuous mood, into which so small a note had thrown him.

There had long stood a shrine in the fresh-foliaged heart of Pierre, up to which he ascended by many tabled steps of remembrance; and around which annually he had hung fresh wreaths of a sweet and holy affection. Made one green bower of at last, by such successive votive offerings of his being; this shrine seemed, and was indeed, a place for the celebration of a chastened joy, rather than for any melancholy rites. But though thus mantled, and tangled with garlands, this shrine was of marble—a niched pillar, deemed solid and eternal, and from whose top radiated all those innumerable sculptured scrolls and branches, which supported the entire one-pillared temple of his moral life; as in some beautiful gothic oratories, one central pillar, trunk-like, upholds the roof. In this shrine, in this niche of this pillar, stood the perfect marble form of his departed father; without blemish, unclouded, snow-white, and serene; Pierre's fond personification of perfect human goodness and virtue. Before this shrine, Pierre poured out the fullness of all young life's most reverential thoughts and beliefs. Not to God had Pierre ever gone in his heart, unless by ascending the steps of that shrine, and so making it the vestibule of his abstractest religion.

Blessed and glorified in his tomb beyond Prince Mausolus is that mortal sire, who, after an honorable, pure course of life, dies, and is buried, as in a choice fountain, in the filial breast of a tender-hearted and intellectually appreciative child. For at that period, the Solomonic insights have not poured their turbid tributaries into the pure-flowing well of the childish life. Rare preservative virtue, too, have those heavenly waters. Thrown into that fountain, all sweet recollections become marbleized; so that things which in themselves were evanescent, thus became unchangeable and eternal. So, some rare waters in Derbyshire will petrify birds'-nests. But if fate preserves the father to a later time, too often the filial obsequies are less profound; the canonization less ethereal. The eye-expanded boy perceives, or vaguely thinks he perceives, slight specks and flaws in the character he once so wholly reverenced.

When Pierre was twelve years old, his father had died, leaving behind him, in the general voice of the world, a marked reputation as a gentleman and a Christian; in the heart of his wife, a green memory of many healthy days of unclouded and joyful wedded life, and in the inmost soul of Pierre, the impression of a bodily form of rare manly beauty and benignity, only rivaled by the supposed perfect mould in which his virtuous heart had been cast. Of pensive evenings, by the wide winter fire, or in summer, in the southern piazza, when that mystical night-silence so peculiar to the country would summon up in the minds of Pierre and his mother, long trains of the images of the past; leading all that spiritual procession, majestically and holily walked the venerated form of the departed husband and father. Then their talk would be reminiscent and serious, but sweet; and again, and again, still deep and deeper, was stamped in Pierre's soul the cherished conceit, that his virtuous father, so beautiful on earth, was now uncorruptibly sainted in heaven. So choicely, and in some degree, secludedly nurtured, Pierre, though now arrived at the age of nineteen, had never yet become so thoroughly initiated into that darker, though truer aspect of things, which an entire residence in the city from the earliest period of life, almost inevitably engraves upon the mind of any keenly observant and reflective youth of Pierre's present years. So that up to this period, in his breast, all remained as it had been; and to Pierre, his father's shrine seemed spotless, and still new as the marble of the tomb of him of Arimathea.

Judge, then, how all-desolating and withering the blast, that for Pierre, in one night, stripped his holiest shrine of all overlaid bloom, and buried the mild statue of the saint beneath the prostrated ruins of the soul's temple itself.

ii

As the vine flourishes, and the grape empurples close up to the very walls and muzzles of cannoned Ehrenbreitstein; so do the sweetest joys of life grow in the very jaws of its perils.

But is life, indeed, a thing for all infidel levities, and we, its misdeemed beneficiaries, so utterly fools and infatuate, that what we take to be our strongest tower of delight, only stands at the caprice of the minutest event—the falling of a leaf, the hearing of a voice, or the receipt of one little bit of paper scratched over with a few small characters by a sharpened feather? Are we so entirely insecure, that that casket, wherein we have placed our holiest and most final joy, and which we have secured by a lock of infinite deftness; can that casket be picked and desecrated at the merest stranger's touch, when we think that we alone hold the only and chosen key?

Pierre! thou art foolish; rebuild—no, not that, for thy shrine still stands; it stands, Pierre, firmly stands; smellest thou not its yet undeparted, embowering bloom? Such a note as thine can be easily enough written, Pierre; impostors are not unknown in this curious world; or the brisk novelist, Pierre, will write thee fifty such notes, and so steal gushing tears from his reader's eyes; even as *thy* note so strangely made thine own manly eyes so arid; so glazed, and so arid, Pierre—foolish Pierre!

Oh! mock not the poniarded heart. The stabbed man knows the steel; prate not to him that it is only a tickling feather. Feels he not the interior gash? What does this blood on my vesture? and what does this pang in my soul?

And here again, not unreasonably, might invocations go up to those Three Weird Ones, that tend Life's loom. Again we might ask them, What threads were those, oh, ye Weird Ones, that ye wove in the years foregone; that now to Pierre, they so unerringly conduct electric presentiments, that his woe is woe, his father no more a saint, and Isabel a sister indeed?

Ah, fathers and mothers! all the world round, be heedful,—give heed! Thy little one may not now comprehend the meaning of those words and those signs, by which, in its innocent presence, thou thinkest to disguise the sinister thing ye would hint. Not now he knows; not very much even of the externals he consciously remarks; but if, in after-life, Fate puts the chemic key of the cipher into his hands; then how swiftly and how wonderfully, he reads all the obscurest and most obliterate inscriptions he finds in his memory; yea, and rummages himself all over, for still hidden writings to read. Oh, darkest lessons of Life have thus been read; all faith in Virtue been murdered, and youth gives itself up to an infidel scorn.

But not thus, altogether, was it now with Pierre; yet so like, in some points, that the above true warning may not misplacedly stand.

His father had died of a fever; and, as is not uncommon in such maladies, toward his end, he at intervals lowly wandered in his mind. At such times, by unobserved, but subtle arts, the devoted family attendants, had restrained his wife from being present at his side. But little Pierre, whose fond, filial love drew him ever to that bed; they heeded not innocent little Pierre, when his father was delirious; and so, one evening, when the shadows intermingled with the curtains; and all the chamber was hushed; and Pierre but dimly saw his father's face; and the fire on the hearth lay in a broken temple of wonderful coals; then a strange, plaintive, infinitely pitiable, low voice, stole forth from the testered bed; and Pierre heard,—"My daughter! my daughter!"

"He wanders again," said the nurse.

"Dear, dear father!" sobbed the child—"thou hast not a daughter, but here is thy own little Pierre."

But again the unregardful voice in the bed was heard; and now in a sudden, pealing wail,—"My daughter!—God! God!—my daughter!"

The child snatched the dying man's hand; it faintly grew to his grasp; but on the other side of the bed, the other hand now also emptily lifted itself, and emptily caught, as if at some other childish fingers. Then both hands dropped on the sheet; and in the twinkling shadows of the evening little Pierre seemed to see, that while the hand which he held wore a faint, feverish flush, the other empty one was ashy white as a leper's.

"It is past," whispered the nurse, "he will wander so no more now till midnight,—that is his wont." And then, in her heart, she wondered how it was, that so excellent a gentleman, and so thoroughly good a man, should wander so ambiguously in his mind; and trembled to think of that mysterious thing in the soul, which seems to acknowledge no human jurisdiction, but in spite of the individual's own innocent self, will still dream horrid dreams, and mutter unmentionable thoughts; and into Pierre's awe-stricken, childish soul, there entered a kindred, though still more nebulous conceit. But it belonged to the spheres of the impalpable ether; and the child soon threw other and sweeter remembrances over it, and covered it up; and at last, it was blended with all other dim things, and imaginings of dimness; and so, seemed to survive to no real life in Pierre. But though through many long years the henbane showed no leaves in his soul; yet the sunken seed was there: and the first glimpse of Isabel's letter caused it to spring forth, as by magic. Then, again, the long-hushed, plaintive and infinitely pitiable voice was heard,—"My daughter! my daughter!" followed by the compunctious "God! God!" And to Pierre, once again the empty hand lifted itself, and once again the ashy hand fell.

iii

In the cold courts of justice the dull head demands oaths, and holy writ proofs; but in the warm halls of the heart one single, untestified memory's spark shall suffice to enkindle such a blaze of evidence, that all the corners of conviction are as suddenly lighted up as a midnight city by a burning building, which on every side whirls its reddened brands.

In a locked, round-windowed closet connecting with the chamber of Pierre, and whither he had always been wont to go, in those sweetly awful hours, when the spirit crieth to the spirit, Come into solitude with me, twin-brother; come away: a secret have I; let me whisper it to thee aside; in this closet, sacred to the Tadmor privacies and repose of the sometimes solitary Pierre, there hung, by long cords from the cornice, a small portrait in oil, before which Pierre had many a time trancedly stood. Had this painting hung in any annual public exhibition, and in its turn been described in print by the casual glancing critics, they would probably have described it thus, and truthfully: "An impromptu portrait of a fine-looking, gay-hearted, youthful gentleman. He is lightly, and, as it were, airily and but grazingly seated in, or rather flittingly tenanting an old-fashioned chair of Malacca. One arm confining his hat and cane is loungingly thrown over the back of the chair, while the fingers of the other hand play with his gold watch-seal and key. The free-templed head is sideways turned, with a peculiarly bright, and care-free, morning expression. He seems as if just dropped in for a visit upon some familiar acquaintance. Altogether, the painting is exceedingly clever and cheerful; with a fine, off-handed expression about it. Undoubtedly a portrait, and no fancy-piece; and, to hazard a vague conjecture, by an amateur."

So bright, and so cheerful then; so trim, and so young; so

singularly healthful, and handsome; what subtile element could so steep this whole portrait, that, to the wife of the original, it was namelessly unpleasant and repelling? The mother of Pierre could never abide this picture which she had always asserted did signally belie her husband. Her fond memories of the departed refused to hang one single wreath around it. It is not he, she would emphatically and almost indignantly exclaim, when more urgently besought to reveal the cause for so unreasonable a dissent from the opinion of nearly all the other connections and relatives of the deceased. But the portrait which she held to do justice to her husband, correctly to convey his features in detail, and more especially their truest, and finest, and noblest combined expression; this portrait was a much larger one, and in the great drawing-room below occupied the most conspicuous and honorable place on the wall.

Even to Pierre these two paintings had always seemed strangely dissimilar. And as the larger one had been painted many years after the other, and therefore brought the original pretty nearly within his own childish recollections; therefore, he himself could not but deem it by far the more truthful and life-like presentation of his father. So that the mere preference of his mother, however strong, was not at all surprising to him, but rather coincided with his own conceit. Yet not for this, must the other portrait be so decidedly rejected. Because, in the first place, there was a difference in time, and some difference of costume to be considered, and the wide difference of the styles of the respective artists, and the wide difference of those respective, semi-reflected, ideal faces, which, even in the presence of the original, a spiritual artist will rather choose to draw from than from the fleshy face, however brilliant and fine. Moreover, while the larger portrait was that of a middle-aged, married man, and seemed to possess all the nameless and slightly portly tranquillities, incident to that condition when a felicitous one; the smaller portrait painted a brisk, unentangled, young bachelor, gayly ranging up and down in the world; light-hearted, and a very little bladish perhaps; and charged to the lips with the first uncloy-ing morning fullness and freshness of life. Here, certainly, large allowance was to be made in any careful, candid estimation of these portraits. To Pierre this conclusion had become well-nigh irresistible, when he placed side by side two portraits of himself; one taken in his early childhood, a frocked and belted boy of four years old; and the other, a grown youth of sixteen. Except an indestructible, all-surviving something in the eyes and on the temples, Pierre could hardly recognize the loud-laughing boy in the tall, and pensively smiling youth. If a few years, then, can have in *me* made all this difference, why not in my father? thought Pierre.

Besides all this, Pierre considered the history, and, so to speak, the family legend of the smaller painting. In his fifteenth year, it was made a present to him by an old maiden aunt, who resided in the city, and who cherished the memory of Pierre's father, with all that wonderful amaranthine devotion which an advanced maiden sister ever feels for the idea of a beloved younger brother, now dead and irrevocably gone. As the only child of that brother, Pierre was an object of the warmest and most extravagant attachment on the part of this lonely aunt, who seemed to see, transformed into youth once again, the likeness, and very soul of her brother, in the fair, inheriting brow of Pierre. Though the portrait we speak of was inordinately prized by her, yet at length the strict canon of her romantic and imaginative love asserted the portrait to be Pierre's—for Pierre was not only his father's only child, but his namesake—so soon as Pierre should be old enough to value aright so holy and inestimable a treasure. She had accordingly sent it to him, trebly boxed, and finally covered with a water-proof cloth; and it was delivered at Saddle Meadows, by an express, confidential messenger, an old gentleman of leisure, once her forlorn, because rejected gallant, but now her contented, and chatty neighbor. Henceforth, before a gold-framed and gold-lidded ivory miniature,—a fraternal gift—aunt Dorothea now offered up her morning and her evening rites, to the memory of the noblest and handsomest of brothers. Yet an annual visit to the far closet of Pierre—no slight undertaking now for one so stricken in years, and every way infirm—attested the earnestness of that strong sense of duty, that painful renunciation of self, which had induced her voluntarily to part with the precious memorial.

iv

"Tell me, aunt," the child Pierre had early said to her, long before the portrait became his—"tell me, aunt, how this chair-portrait, as you call it, was painted;—who painted it?—whose chair was this?—have you the chair now?—I don't see it in your room here;—what is papa looking at so strangely?—I should like to know now, what papa was thinking of, then. Do, now, dear aunt, tell me all about this picture, so that when it is mine, as you promise me, I shall know its whole history."

"Sit down, then, and be very still and attentive, my dear child," said aunt Dorothea; while she a little averted her head, and tremulously and inaccurately sought her pocket, till little Pierre cried—"Why, aunt, the story of the picture is not in any little book, is it, that you are going to take out and read to me?"

"My handkerchief, my child."

"Why, aunt, here it is, at your elbow; here, on the table; here, aunt; take it, do; Oh, don't tell me any thing about the picture, now; I won't hear it."

"Be still, my darling Pierre," said his aunt, taking the handkerchief, "draw the curtain a little, dearest; the light hurts my eyes. Now, go into the closet, and bring me my dark shawl;—take your time.—There; thank you, Pierre; now sit down again, and I will begin.—The picture was painted long ago, my child; you were not born then."

"Not born?" cried little Pierre.

"Not born," said his aunt.

"Well, go on, aunt; but don't tell me again that once upon a time I was not little Pierre at all, and yet my father was alive. Go on, aunt,—do, do!"

"Why, how nervous you are getting, my child;—Be patient; I am very old, Pierre; and old people never like to be hurried."

"Now, my own dear Aunt Dorothea, do forgive me this once, and go on with your story."

"When your poor father was quite a young man, my child, and was on one of his long autumnal visits to his friends in this city, he was rather intimate at times with a cousin of his,

Ralph Winwood, who was about his own age,—a fine youth he was, too, Pierre."

"I never saw him, aunt; pray, where is he now?" interrupted Pierre;—"does he live in the country, now, as mother and I do?"

"Yes, my child; but a far-away, beautiful country, I hope;—he's in heaven, I trust."

"Dead," sighed little Pierre—"go on, aunt."

"Now, cousin Ralph had a great love for painting, my child; and he spent many hours in a room, hung all round with pictures and portraits; and there he had his easel and brushes; and much liked to paint his friends, and hang their faces on his walls; so that when all alone by himself, he yet had plenty of company, who always wore their best expressions to him, and never once ruffled him, by ever getting cross or ill-natured, little Pierre. Often, he had besought your father to sit to him; saying, that his silent circle of friends would never be complete, till your father consented to join them. But in those days, my child, your father was always in motion. It was hard for me to get him to stand still, while I tied his cravat; for he never came to any one but me for that. So he was always putting off, and putting off cousin Ralph. 'Some other time, cousin; not to-day;—to-morrow, perhaps;—or next week;'—and so, at last cousin Ralph began to despair. But I'll catch him yet, cried sly cousin Ralph. So now he said nothing more to your father about the matter of painting him; but every pleasant morning kept his easel and brushes and every thing in readiness; so as to be ready the first moment your father should chance to drop in upon him from his long strolls; for it was now and then your father's wont to pay flying little visits to cousin Ralph in his painting-room.—But, my child, you may draw back the curtain now—it's getting very dim here, seems to me."

"Well, I thought so all along, aunt," said little Pierre, obeying; "but didn't you say the light hurt your eyes."

"But it does not now, little Pierre."

"Well, well; go on, go on, aunt; you can't think how interested I am," said little Pierre, drawing his stool close up to the quilted satin hem of his good Aunt Dorothea's dress.

"I will, my child. But first let me tell you, that about this

time there arrived in the port, a cabin-full of French emigrants of quality;—poor people, Pierre, who were forced to
fly from their native land, because of the cruel, blood-shed-
ding times there. But you have read all that in the little history I gave you, a good while ago."

"I know all about it;—the French Revolution," said little
Pierre.

"What a famous little scholar you are, my dear child,"—
said Aunt Dorothea, faintly smiling—"Among those poor,
but noble emigrants, there was a beautiful young girl, whose
sad fate afterward made a great noise in the city, and made
many eyes to weep, but in vain, for she never was heard of
any more."

"How? how? aunt;—I don't understand;—did she disappear then, aunt?"

"I was a little before my story, child. Yes, she did disappear,
and never was heard of again; but that was afterward, some
time afterward, my child. I am very sure it was; I could take
my oath of that, Pierre."

"Why, dear aunt," said little Pierre, "how earnestly you
talk—after what? your voice is getting very strange; do
now;—don't talk that way; you frighten me so, aunt."

"Perhaps it is this bad cold I have to-day; it makes my voice
a little hoarse, I fear, Pierre. But I will try and not talk so
hoarsely again. Well, my child, some time before this beautiful
young lady disappeared, indeed it was only shortly after the
poor emigrants landed, your father made her acquaintance;
and with many other humane gentlemen of the city, provided
for the wants of the strangers, for they were very poor indeed,
having been stripped of every thing, save a little trifling jew-
elry, which could not go very far. At last, the friends of your
father endeavored to dissuade him from visiting these people
so much; they were fearful that as the young lady was so very
beautiful, and a little inclined to be intriguing—so some
said—your father might be tempted to marry her; which
would not have been a wise thing in him; for though the
young lady might have been very beautiful, and good-
hearted, yet no one on this side of the water certainly knew
her history; and she was a foreigner; and would not have
made so suitable and excellent a match for your father as your

dear mother afterward did, my child. But, for myself, I—who always knew your father very well in all his intentions, and he was very confidential with me, too—I, for my part, never credited that he would do so unwise a thing as marry the strange young lady. At any rate, he at last discontinued his visits to the emigrants; and it was after this that the young lady disappeared. Some said that she must have voluntarily but secretly returned into her own country; and others declared that she must have been kidnapped by French emissaries; for, after her disappearance, rumor began to hint that she was of the noblest birth, and some ways allied to the royal family; and then, again, there were some who shook their heads darkly, and muttered of drownings, and other dark things; which one always hears hinted when people disappear, and no one can find them. But though your father and many other gentlemen moved heaven and earth to find trace of her, yet, as I said before, my child, she never re-appeared."

"The poor French lady!" sighed little Pierre. "Aunt, I'm afraid she was murdered."

"Poor lady, there is no telling," said his aunt. "But listen, for I am coming to the picture again. Now, at the time your father was so often visiting the emigrants, my child, cousin Ralph was one of those who a little fancied that your father was courting her; but cousin Ralph being a quiet young man, and a scholar, not well acquainted with what is wise, or what is foolish in the great world; cousin Ralph would not have been at all mortified had your father really wedded with the refugee young lady. So vainly thinking, as I told you, that your father was courting her, he fancied it would be a very fine thing if he could paint your father as her wooer; that is, paint him just after his coming from his daily visits to the emigrants. So he watched his chance; every thing being ready in his painting-room, as I told you before; and one morning, sure enough, in dropt your father from his walk. But before he came into the room, cousin Ralph had spied him from the window; and when your father entered, cousin Ralph had the sitting-chair ready drawn out, back of his easel, but still fronting toward him, and pretended to be very busy painting. He said to your father—'Glad to see you, cousin Pierre; I am just about something here; sit right down there now, and tell me the news; and I'll sally out with you presently. And tell us something of the emigrants, cousin Pierre,' he slyly added—wishing, you see, to get your father's thoughts running that supposed wooing way, so that he might catch some sort of corresponding expression you see, little Pierre."

"I don't know that I precisely understand, aunt; but go on, I am so interested; do go on, dear aunt."

"Well, by many little cunning shifts and contrivances, cousin Ralph kept your father there sitting, and sitting in the chair, rattling and rattling away, and so self-forgetful too, that he never heeded that all the while sly cousin Ralph was painting and painting just as fast as ever he could; and only making believe laugh at your father's wit; in short, cousin Ralph was stealing his portrait, my child."

"Not *stealing* it, I hope," said Pierre, "that would be very wicked."

"Well, then, we won't call it stealing, since I am sure that cousin Ralph kept your father all the time off from him, and so, could not have possibly picked his pocket, though indeed, he slyly picked his portrait, so to speak. And if indeed it was stealing, or any thing of that sort; yet seeing how much comfort that portrait has been to me, Pierre, and how much it will yet be to you, I hope; I think we must very heartily forgive cousin Ralph, for what he then did."

"Yes, I think we must indeed," chimed in little Pierre, now eagerly eying the very portrait in question, which hung over the mantle.

"Well, by catching your father two or three times more in that way, cousin Ralph at last finished the painting; and when it was all framed, and every way completed, he would have surprised your father by hanging it boldly up in his room among his other portraits, had not your father one morning suddenly come to him—while, indeed, the very picture itself was placed face down on a table and cousin Ralph fixing the cord to it—came to him, and frightened cousin Ralph by quietly saying, that now that he thought of it, it seemed to him that cousin Ralph had been playing tricks with him; but he hoped it was not so. 'What do you mean?' said cousin Ralph, a little flurried. 'You have not been hanging my portrait up here, have you, cousin Ralph?' said your father, glancing along the walls. 'I'm glad I don't see it. It is my whim, cousin Ralph,—and perhaps it is a very silly one,—but if you have been lately painting my portrait, I want you to destroy it; at any rate, don't show it to any one, keep it out of sight. What's that you have there, cousin Ralph?'

"Cousin Ralph was now more and more fluttered; not knowing what to make—as indeed, to this day, I don't completely myself—of your father's strange manner. But he rallied, and said—'This, cousin Pierre, is a secret portrait I have here; you must be aware that we portrait-painters are sometimes called upon to paint such. I, therefore, can not show it to you, or tell you any thing about it.'

" 'Have you been painting my portrait or not, cousin Ralph?' said your father, very suddenly and pointedly.

" 'I have painted nothing that looks as you there look,' said cousin Ralph, evasively, observing in your father's face a fierce-like expression, which he had never seen there before. And more than that, your father could not get from him."

"And what then?" said little Pierre.

"Why not much, my child; only your father never so much as caught one glimpse of that picture; indeed, never knew for certain, whether there was such a painting in the world. Cousin Ralph secretly gave it to me, knowing how tenderly I loved your father; making me solemnly promise never to expose it anywhere where your father could ever see it, or any way hear of it. This promise I faithfully kept; and it was only after your dear father's death, that I hung it in my chamber. There, Pierre, you now have the story of the chair-portrait."

"And a very strange one it is," said Pierre—"and so interesting, I shall never forget it, aunt."

"I hope you never will, my child. Now ring the bell, and we will have a little fruit-cake, and I will take a glass of wine, Pierre;—do you hear, my child?—the bell—ring it. Why, what do you do standing there, Pierre?"

"*Why* did'nt papa want to have cousin Ralph paint his picture, aunt?"

"How these children's minds do run!" exclaimed old aunt Dorothea staring at little Pierre in amazement—"That indeed is more than I can tell you, little Pierre. But cousin Ralph had a foolish fancy about it. He used to tell me, that being in your

father's room some few days after the last scene I described,
he noticed there a very wonderful work on Physiognomy, as
they call it, in which the strangest and shadowiest rules were
laid down for detecting people's innermost secrets by studying their faces. And so, foolish cousin Ralph always flattered
himself, that the reason your father did not want his portrait
taken was, because he was secretly in love with the French
young lady, and did not want his secret published in a portrait; since the wonderful work on Physiognomy had, as it
were, indirectly warned him against running that risk. But
cousin Ralph being such a retired and solitary sort of a youth,
he always had such curious whimsies about things. For my
part, I don't believe your father ever had any such ridiculous
ideas on the subject. To be sure, I myself can not tell you *why*
he did not want his picture taken; but when you get to be as
old as I am, little Pierre, you will find that every one, even
the best of us, at times, is apt to act very queerly and unaccountably; indeed some things we do, we can not entirely
explain the reason of, even to ourselves, little Pierre. But you
will know all about these strange matters by and by."

"I hope I shall, aunt," said little Pierre—"But, dear aunt, I
thought Marten was to bring in some fruit-cake?"

"Ring the bell for him, then, my child."

"Oh! I forgot," said little Pierre, doing her bidding.

By-and-by, while the aunt was sipping her wine; and the
boy eating his cake, and both their eyes were fixed on the
portrait in question; little Pierre, pushing his stool nearer the
picture exclaimed—"Now, aunt, did papa really look exactly
like that? Did you ever see him in that same buff vest, and
huge-figured neckcloth? I remember the seal and key, pretty
well; and it was only a week ago that I saw mamma take them
out of a little locked drawer in her wardrobe—but I don't
remember the queer whiskers; nor the buff vest; nor the huge
white-figured neckcloth; did you ever see papa in that very
neckcloth, aunt?"

"My child, it was I that chose the stuff for that neckcloth;
yes, and hemmed it for him, and worked P.G. in one corner;
but that aint in the picture. It is an excellent likeness, my
child, neckcloth and all; as he looked at that time. Why, little
Pierre, sometimes I sit here all alone by myself, gazing, and

gazing, and gazing at that face, till I begin to think your father is looking at me, and smiling at me, and nodding at me, and saying—Dorothea! Dorothea!"

"How strange," said little Pierre, "I think it begins to look at me now, aunt. Hark! aunt, it's so silent all round in this old-fashioned room, that I think I hear a little jingling in the picture, as if the watch-seal was striking against the key— Hark! aunt."

"Bless me, don't talk so strangely, my child."

"I heard mamma say once—but she did not say so to me— that, for her part, she did not like aunt Dorothea's picture; it was not a good likeness, so she said. Why don't mamma like the picture, aunt?"

"My child, you ask very queer questions. If your mamma don't like the picture, it is for a very plain reason. She has a much larger and finer one at home, which she had painted for herself; yes, and paid I don't know how many hundred dollars for it; and that, too, is an excellent likeness, *that* must be the reason, little Pierre."

And thus the old aunt and the little child ran on; each thinking the other very strange; and both thinking the picture still stranger; and the face in the picture still looked at them frankly, and cheerfully, as if there was nothing kept concealed; and yet again, a little ambiguously and mockingly, as if slyly winking to some other picture, to mark what a very foolish old sister, and what a very silly little son, were growing so monstrously grave and speculative about a huge white-figured neckcloth, a buff vest, and a very gentleman-like and amiable countenance.

And so, after this scene, as usual, one by one, the fleet years ran on; till the little child Pierre had grown up to be the tall Master Pierre, and could call the picture his own; and now, in the privacy of his own little closet, could stand, or lean, or sit before it all day long, if he pleased, and keep thinking, and thinking, and thinking, and thinking, till by-and-by all thoughts were blurred, and at last there were no thoughts at all.

Before the picture was sent to him, in his fifteenth year, it had been only through the inadvertence of his mother, or rather through a casual passing into a parlor by Pierre, that

he had any way learned that his mother did not approve of
the picture. Because, as then Pierre was still young, and the
picture was the picture of his father, and the cherished property of a most excellent, and dearly-beloved, affectionate aunt;
therefore the mother, with an intuitive delicacy, had refrained
from knowingly expressing her peculiar opinion in the presence of little Pierre. And this judicious, though half-unconscious delicacy in the mother, had been perhaps somewhat
singularly answered by a like nicety of sentiment in the child;
for children of a naturally refined organization, and a gentle
nurture, sometimes possess a wonderful, and often undreamed of, daintiness of propriety, and thoughtfulness, and
forbearance, in matters esteemed a little subtile even by their
elders, and self-elected betters. The little Pierre never disclosed to his mother that he had, through another person,
become aware of her thoughts concerning Aunt Dorothea's
portrait; he seemed to possess an intuitive knowledge of the
circumstance, that from the difference of their relationship to
his father, and for other minute reasons, he could in some
things, with the greater propriety, be more inquisitive concerning him, with his aunt, than with his mother, especially
touching the matter of the chair-portrait. And Aunt Dorothea's reasons accounting for his mother's distaste, long continued satisfactory, or at least not unsufficiently explanatory.

And when the portrait arrived at the Meadows, it so
chanced that his mother was abroad; and so Pierre silently
hung it up in his closet; and when after a day or two his
mother returned, he said nothing to her about its arrival,
being still strangely alive to that certain mild mystery which
invested it, and whose sacredness now he was fearful of violating, by provoking any discussion with his mother about
Aunt Dorothea's gift, or by permitting himself to be improp-
erly curious concerning the reasons of his mother's private
and self-reserved opinions of it. But the first time—and it was
not long after the arrival of the portrait—that he knew of his
mother's having entered his closet; then, when he next saw
her, he was prepared to hear what she should voluntarily say
about the late addition to its embellishments; but as she omitted all mention of any thing of that sort, he unobtrusively
scanned her countenance, to mark whether any little clouding

emotion might be discoverable there. But he could discern none. And as all genuine delicacies are by their nature accumulative; therefore this reverential, mutual, but only tacit forbearance of the mother and son, ever after continued uninvaded. And it was another sweet, and sanctified, and sanctifying bond between them. For, whatever some lovers may sometimes say, love does not always abhor a secret, as nature is said to abhor a vacuum. Love is built upon secrets, as lovely Venice upon invisible and incorruptible piles in the sea. Love's secrets, being mysteries, ever pertain to the transcendent and the infinite; and so they are as airy bridges, by which our further shadows pass over into the regions of the golden mists and exhalations; whence all poetical, lovely thoughts are engendered, and drop into us, as though pearls should drop from rainbows.

As time went on, the chasteness and pure virginity of this mutual reservation, only served to dress the portrait in sweeter, because still more mysterious attractions; and to fling, as it were, fresh fennel and rosemary around the revered memory of the father. Though, indeed, as previously recounted, Pierre now and then loved to present to himself for some fanciful solution the penultimate secret of the portrait, in so far, as that involved his mother's distaste; yet the cunning analysis in which such a mental procedure would involve him, never voluntarily transgressed that sacred limit, where his mother's peculiar repugnance began to shade off into ambiguous considerations, touching any unknown possibilities in the character and early life of the original. Not, that he had altogether forbidden his fancy to range in such fields of speculation; but all such imaginings must be contributory to that pure, exalted idea of his father, which, in his soul, was based upon the known acknowledged facts of his father's life.

V

If, when the mind roams up and down in the ever-elastic regions of evanescent invention, any definite form or feature can be assigned to the multitudinous shapes it creates out of the incessant dissolvings of its own prior creations; then might we here attempt to hold and define the least shadowy of those reasons, which about the period of adolescence we now treat of, more frequently occurred to Pierre, whenever he essayed to account for his mother's remarkable distaste for the portrait. Yet will we venture one sketch.

Yes—sometimes dimly thought Pierre—who knows but cousin Ralph, after all, may have been not so very far from the truth, when he surmised that at one time my father did indeed cherish some passing emotion for the beautiful young Frenchwoman. And this portrait being painted at that precise time, and indeed with the precise purpose of perpetuating some shadowy testification of the fact in the countenance of the original: therefore, its expression is not congenial, is not familiar, is not altogether agreeable to my mother: because, not only did my father's features never look so to her (since it was afterward that she first became acquainted with him), but also, that certain womanliness of women; that thing I should perhaps call a tender jealousy, a fastidious vanity, in any other lady, enables her to perceive that the glance of the face in the portrait, is not, in some nameless way, dedicated to herself, but to some other and unknown object; and therefore, is she impatient of it, and it is repelling to her; for she must naturally be intolerant of any imputed reminiscence in my father, which is not in some way connected with her own recollections of him.

Whereas, the larger and more expansive portrait in the great drawing-room, taken in the prime of life; during the best and rosiest days of their wedded union; at the particular desire of my mother; and by a celebrated artist of her own election, and costumed after her own taste; and on all hands considered to be, by those who know, a singularly happy likeness at the period; a belief spiritually reinforced by my own dim infantile remembrances; for all these reasons, this drawing-room portrait possesses an inestimable charm to her; there, she indeed beholds her husband as he had really appeared to her; she does not vacantly gaze upon an unfamiliar phantom called up from the distant, and, to her, well-nigh fabulous days of my father's bachelor life. But in that other portrait, she sees rehearsed to her fond eyes, the latter tales and legends of his devoted wedded love. Yes, I think now that I plainly see it must be so. And yet, ever new conceits come

vaporing up in me, as I look on the strange chair-portrait:
which, though so very much more unfamiliar to me, than it
can possibly be to my mother, still sometimes seems to say—
Pierre, believe not the drawing-room painting; that is not thy
father; or, at least, is not *all* of thy father. Consider in thy
mind, Pierre, whether we two paintings may not make only
one. Faithful wives are ever over-fond to a certain imaginary
image of their husbands; and faithful widows are ever over-
reverential to a certain imagined ghost of that same imagined
image, Pierre. Look again, I am thy father as he more truly
was. In mature life, the world overlays and varnishes us,
Pierre; the thousand proprieties and polished finenesses and
grimaces intervene, Pierre; then, we, as it were, abdicate ourselves, and take unto us another self, Pierre; in youth we *are*,
Pierre, but in age we *seem*. Look again. I am thy real father,
so much the more truly, as thou thinkest thou recognizest me
not, Pierre. To their young children, fathers are not wont to
unfold themselves entirely, Pierre. There are a thousand and
one odd little youthful peccadilloes, that we think we may as
well not divulge to them, Pierre. Consider this strange, ambiguous smile, Pierre; more narrowly regard this mouth. Behold, what is this too ardent and, as it were, unchastened
light in these eyes, Pierre? I am thy father, boy. There was
once a certain, oh, but too lovely young Frenchwoman,
Pierre. Youth is hot, and temptation strong, Pierre; and in the
minutest moment momentous things are irrevocably done,
Pierre; and Time sweeps on, and the thing is not always carried down by its stream, but may be left stranded on its bank;
away beyond, in the young, green countries, Pierre. Look
again. Doth thy mother dislike me for naught? Consider. Do
not all her spontaneous, loving impressions, ever strive to
magnify, and spiritualize, and deify, her husband's memory,
Pierre? Then why doth she cast despite upon me; and never
speak to thee of me; and why dost thou thyself keep silence
before her, Pierre? Consider. Is there no little mystery here?
Probe a little, Pierre. Never fear, never fear. No matter for
thy father now. Look, do I not smile?—yes, and with an unchangeable smile; and thus have I unchangeably smiled for
many long years gone by, Pierre. Oh, it is a permanent smile!
Thus I smiled to cousin Ralph; and thus in thy dear old Aunt

Dorothea's parlor, Pierre; and just so, I smile here to thee,
and even thus in thy father's later life, when his body may
have been in grief, still—hidden away in Aunt Dorothea's
secretary—I thus smiled as before; and just so I'd smile were
I now hung up in the deepest dungeon of the Spanish Inquisition, Pierre; though suspended in outer darkness, still
would I smile with this smile, though then not a soul should
be near. Consider; for a smile is the chosen vehicle for all
ambiguities, Pierre. When we would deceive, we smile; when
we are hatching any nice little artifice, Pierre; only just a little
gratifying our own sweet little appetites, Pierre; then watch
us, and out comes the odd little smile. Once upon a time,
there was a lovely young Frenchwoman, Pierre. Have you
carefully, and analytically, and psychologically, and metaphysically, considered her belongings and surroundings, and all
her incidentals, Pierre? Oh, a strange sort of story, that, thy
dear old Aunt Dorothea once told thee, Pierre. I once knew
a credulous old soul, Pierre. Probe, probe a little—see—
there seems one little crack there, Pierre—a wedge, a wedge.
Something ever comes of all persistent inquiry; we are not so
continually curious for nothing, Pierre; not for nothing, do
we so intrigue and become wily diplomatists, and glozers
with our own minds, Pierre; and afraid of following the Indian trail from the open plain into the dark thickets, Pierre;
but enough; a word to the wise.

   Thus sometimes in the mystical, outer quietude of the long
country nights; either when the hushed mansion was banked
round by the thick-fallen December snows, or banked round
by the immovable white August moonlight; in the haunted
repose of a wide story, tenanted only by himself; and senti-
neling his own little closet; and standing guard, as it were,
before the mystical tent of the picture; and ever watching the
strangely concealed lights of the meanings that so mysteriously moved to and fro within; thus sometimes stood Pierre
before the portrait of his father, unconsciously throwing himself open to all those ineffable hints and ambiguities, and undefined half-suggestions, which now and then people the
soul's atmosphere, as thickly as in a soft, steady snow-storm,
the snow-flakes people the air. Yet as often starting from these

reveries and trances, Pierre would regain the assured element of consciously bidden and self-propelled thought; and then in a moment the air all cleared, not a snow-flake descended, and Pierre, upbraiding himself for his self-indulgent infatuation, would promise never again to fall into a midnight revery before the chair-portrait of his father. Nor did the streams of these reveries seem to leave any conscious sediment in his mind; they were so light and so rapid, that they rolled their own alluvial along; and seemed to leave all Pierre's thought-channels as clean and dry as though never any alluvial stream had rolled there at all.

And so still in his sober, cherishing memories, his father's beatification remained untouched; and all the strangeness of the portrait only served to invest his idea with a fine, legendary romance; the essence whereof was that very mystery, which at other times was so subtly and evilly significant.

But now, *now!*—Isabel's letter read: swift as the first light that slides from the sun, Pierre saw all preceding ambiguities, all mysteries ripped open as if with a keen sword, and forth trooped thickening phantoms of an infinite gloom. Now his remotest infantile reminiscences—the wandering mind of his father—the empty hand, and the ashen—the strange story of Aunt Dorothea—the mystical midnight suggestions of the portrait itself; and, above all, his mother's intuitive aversion, all, all overwhelmed him with reciprocal testimonies.

And now, by irresistible intuitions, all that had been inexplicably mysterious to him in the portrait, and all that had been inexplicably familiar in the face, most magically these now coincided; the merriness of the one not inharmonious with the mournfulness of the other, but by some ineffable correlativeness, they reciprocally identified each other, and, as it were, melted into each other, and thus interpenetratingly uniting, presented lineaments of an added supernaturalness.

On all sides, the physical world of solid objects now slidingly displaced itself from around him, and he floated into an ether of visions; and, starting to his feet with clenched hands and outstaring eyes at the transfixed face in the air, he ejacu-

lated that wonderful verse from Dante, descriptive of the two
mutually absorbing shapes in the Inferno:

> "Ah! how dost thou change,
> Agnello! See! thou art nor double now,
> Nor only one!"

Book V

MISGIVINGS AND PREPARATIONS

IT WAS LONG after midnight when Pierre returned to the house. He had rushed forth in that complete abandonment of soul, which, in so ardent a temperament, attends the first stages of any sudden and tremendous affliction; but now he returned in pallid composure, for the calm spirit of the night, and the then risen moon, and the late revealed stars, had all at last become as a strange subduing melody to him, which, though at first trampled and scorned, yet by degrees had stolen into the windings of his heart, and so shed abroad its own quietude in him. Now, from his height of composure, he firmly gazed abroad upon the charred landscape within him; as the timber man of Canada, forced to fly from the conflagration of his forests, comes back again when the fires have waned, and unblinkingly eyes the immeasurable fields of fire-brands that here and there glow beneath the wide canopy of smoke.

It has been said, that always when Pierre would seek solitude in its material shelter and walled isolation, then the closet communicating with his chamber was his elected haunt. So, going to his room, he took up the now dim-burning lamp he had left there, and instinctively entered that retreat, seating himself, with folded arms and bowed head, in the accustomed dragon-footed old chair. With leaden feet, and heart now changing from iciness to a strange sort of indifference, and a numbing sensation stealing over him, he sat there awhile, till, like the resting traveler in snows, he began to struggle against this inertness as the most treacherous and deadliest of symptoms. He looked up, and found himself fronted by the no longer wholly enigmatical, but still ambiguously smiling picture of his father. Instantly all his consciousness and his anguish returned, but still without power to shake the grim tranquillity which possessed him. Yet endure the smiling portrait he could not; and obeying an irresistible nameless impulse, he rose, and without unhanging it, reversed the picture on the wall.

This brought to sight the defaced and dusty back, with some wrinkled, tattered paper over the joints, which had become loosened from the paste. "Oh, symbol of thy reversed idea in my soul," groaned Pierre; "thou shalt not hang thus. Rather cast thee utterly out, than conspicuously insult thee so. I will no more have a father." He removed the picture wholly from the wall, and the closet; and concealed it in a large chest, covered with blue chintz, and locked it up there. But still, in a square space of slightly discolored wall, the picture still left its shadowy, but vacant and desolate trace. He now strove to banish the least trace of his altered father, as fearful that at present all thoughts concerning him were not only entirely vain, but would prove fatally distracting and incapacitating to a mind, which was now loudly called upon, not only to endure a signal grief, but immediately to act upon it. Wild and cruel case, youth ever thinks; but mistakenly; for Experience well knows, that action, though it seems an aggravation of woe, is really an alleviative; though permanently to alleviate pain, we must first dart some added pangs.

Nor now, though profoundly sensible that his whole previous moral being was overturned, and that for him the fair structure of the world must, in some then unknown way, be entirely rebuilded again, from the lowermost corner stone up; nor now did Pierre torment himself with the thought of that last desolation; and how the desolate place was to be made flourishing again. He seemed to feel that in his deepest soul, lurked an indefinite but potential faith, which could rule in the interregnum of all hereditary beliefs, and circumstantial persuasions; not wholly, he felt, was his soul in anarchy. The indefinite regent had assumed the scepter as its right; and Pierre was not entirely given up to his grief's utter pillage and sack.

To a less enthusiastic heart than Pierre's the foremost question in respect to Isabel which would have presented itself, would have been, *What* must I do? But such a question never presented itself to Pierre; the spontaneous responsiveness of his being left no shadow of dubiousness as to the direct point he must aim at. But if the object was plain, not so the path to it. *How* must I do it? was a problem for which at first there seemed no chance of solution. But without being entirely aware of it himself, Pierre was one of those spirits, which not in a determinate and sordid scrutiny of small pros and cons— but in an impulsive subservience to the god-like dictation of events themselves, find at length the surest solution of perplexities, and the brightest prerogative of command. And as for him, *What* must I do? was a question already answered by the inspiration of the difficulty itself; so now he, as it were, unconsciously discharged his mind, for the present, of all distracting considerations concerning *How* he should do it; assured that the coming interview with Isabel could not but unerringly inspire him there. Still, the inspiration which had thus far directed him had not been entirely mute and undivulging as to many very bitter things which Pierre foresaw in the wide sea of trouble into which he was plunged.

If it be the sacred province and—by the wisest, deemed— the inestimable compensation of the heavier woes, that they both purge the soul of gay-hearted errors and replenish it with a saddened truth; that holy office is not so much accomplished by any covertly inductive reasoning process, whose original motive is received from the particular affliction; as it is the magical effect of the admission into man's inmost spirit of a before unexperienced and wholly inexplicable element, which like electricity suddenly received into any sultry atmosphere of the dark, in all directions splits itself into nimble lances of purifying light; which at one and the same instant discharge all the air of sluggishness and inform it with an illuminating property; so that objects which before, in the uncertainty of the dark, assumed shadowy and romantic outlines, now are lighted up in their substantial realities; so that in these flashing revelations of grief's wonderful fire, we see all things as they are; and though, when the electric element is gone, the shadows once more descend, and the false outlines of objects again return; yet not with their former power to deceive; for now, even in the presence of the falsest aspects, we still retain the impressions of their immovable true ones, though, indeed, once more concealed.

Thus with Pierre. In the joyous young times, ere his great grief came upon him, all the objects which surrounded him were concealingly deceptive. Not only was the long-cherished image of his father now transfigured before him from a green foliaged tree into a blasted trunk, but every other image in his mind attested the universality of that electral light which had darted into his soul. Not even his lovely, immaculate mother, remained entirely untouched, unaltered by the shock. At her changed aspect, when first revealed to him, Pierre had gazed in a panic; and now, when the electrical storm had gone by, he retained in his mind, that so suddenly revealed image, with an infinite mournfulness. She, who in her less splendid but finer and more spiritual part, had ever seemed to Pierre not only as a beautiful saint before whom to offer up his daily orisons, but also as a gentle lady-counsellor and confessor, and her revered chamber as a soft satin-hung cabinet and confessional;—his mother was no longer this all-alluring thing; no more, he too keenly felt, could he go to his mother, as to one who entirely sympathized with him; as to one before whom he could almost unreservedly unbosom himself; as to one capable of pointing out to him the true path where he seemed most beset. Wonderful, indeed, was that electric insight which Fate had now given him into the vital character of his mother. She well might have stood all ordinary tests; but when Pierre thought of the touchstone of his immense strait applied to her spirit; he felt profoundly assured that she would crumble into nothing before it.

She was a noble creature, but formed chiefly for the gilded prosperities of life, and hitherto mostly used to its unruffled serenities; bred and expanded, in all developments, under the sole influence of hereditary forms and world-usages. Not his refined, courtly, loving, equable mother, Pierre felt, could unreservedly, and like a heaven's heroine, meet the shock of his extraordinary emergency, and applaud, to his heart's echo, a sublime resolve, whose execution should call down the astonishment and the jeers of the world.

My mother!—dearest mother!—God hath given me a sister, and unto thee a daughter, and covered her with the world's extremest infamy and scorn, that so I and thou—*thou*, my mother, mightest gloriously own her, and acknowledge her, and,——Nay, nay, groaned Pierre, never, never, could such syllables be one instant tolerated by her. Then, high-up, and towering, and all-forbidding before Pierre grew the before unthought of wonderful edifice of his mother's immense pride;—her pride of birth, her pride of affluence, her pride of purity, and all the pride of high-born, refined, and wealthy Life, and all the Semiramian pride of woman. Then he staggered back upon himself, and only found support in himself. Then Pierre felt that deep in him lurked a divine un-identifiableness, that owned no earthly kith or kin. Yet was this feeling entirely lonesome, and orphan-like. Fain, then, for one moment, would he have recalled the thousand sweet il-lusions of Life; tho' purchased at the price of Life's Truth; so that once more he might not feel himself driven out an infant Ishmael into the desert, with no maternal Hagar to accom-pany and comfort him.

Still, were these emotions without prejudice to his own love for his mother, and without the slightest bitterness re-specting her; and, least of all, there was no shallow disdain toward her of superior virtue. He too plainly saw, that not his mother had made his mother; but the Infinite Haughti-ness had first fashioned her; and then the haughty world had further molded her; nor had a haughty Ritual omitted to fin-ish her.

Wonderful, indeed, we repeat it, was the electrical insight which Pierre now had into the character of his mother, for not even the vivid recalling of her lavish love for him could suffice to gainsay his sudden persuasion. Love me she doth, thought Pierre, but how? Loveth she me with the love past all understanding? that love, which in the loved one's behalf, would still calmly confront all hate? whose most triumphing hymn, triumphs only by swelling above all opposing taunts and despite?—Loving mother, here have I a loved, but world-infamous sister to own;—and if thou lovest me, mother, thy love will love her, too, and in the proudest draw-ing-room take her so much the more proudly by the hand.— And as Pierre thus in fancy led Isabel before his mother; and in fancy led her away, and felt his tongue cleave to the roof of his mouth, with her transfixing look of incredulous, scorn-ful horror; then Pierre's enthusiastic heart sunk in and in, and caved clean away in him, as he so poignantly felt his first feel-ing of the dreary heart-vacancies of the conventional life. Oh heartless, proud, ice-gilded world, how I hate thee, he thought, that thy tyrannous, insatiate grasp, thus now in my

bitterest need—thus doth rob me even of my mother; thus
doth make me now doubly an orphan, without a green grave
to bedew. My tears,—could I weep them,—must now be
wept in the desolate places; now to me is it, as though both
father and mother had gone on distant voyages, and, returning, died in unknown seas.

She loveth me, ay;—but why? Had I been cast in a cripple's mold, how then? Now, do I remember that in her most
caressing love, there ever gleamed some scaly, glittering folds
of pride. Me she loveth with pride's love; in me she thinks
she seeth her own curled and haughty beauty; before my glass
she stands,—pride's priestess—and to her mirrored image,
not to me, she offers up her offerings of kisses. Oh, small
thanks I owe thee, Favorable Goddess, that didst clothe this
form with all the beauty of a man, that so thou mightest hide
from me all the truth of a man. Now I see that in his beauty
a man is snared, and made stone-blind, as the worm within
its silk. Welcome then be Ugliness and Poverty and Infamy,
and all ye other crafty ministers of Truth, that beneath the
hoods and rags of beggars hide yet the belts and crowns of
kings. And dimmed be all beauty that must own the clay; and
dimmed be all wealth, and all delight, and all the annual prosperities of earth, that but gild the links, and stud with diamonds the base rivets and the chains of Lies. Oh, now
methinks I a little see why of old the men of Truth went
barefoot, girded with a rope, and ever moving under mournfulness as underneath a canopy. I remember now those first
wise words, wherewith our Savior Christ first spoke in his
first speech to men:—'Blessed are the poor in spirit, and
blessed they that mourn.' Oh, hitherto I have but piled up
words; bought books, and bought some small experiences,
and builded me in libraries; now I sit down and read. Oh,
now I know the night, and comprehend the sorceries of the
moon, and all the dark persuadings that have their birth in
storms and winds. Oh, not long will Joy abide, when Truth
doth come; nor Grief her laggard be. Well may this head hang
on my breast,—it holds too much; well may my heart knock
at my ribs,—prisoner impatient of his iron bars. Oh, men are
jailers all; jailers of themselves; and in Opinion's world ignorantly hold their noblest part a captive to their vilest; as dis-

guised royal Charles when caught by peasants. The heart! the heart! 'tis God's anointed; let me pursue the heart!

ii

But if the presentiment in Pierre of his mother's pride, as bigotedly hostile to the noble design he cherished; if this feeling was so wretched to him; far more so was the thought of another and a deeper hostility, arising from her more spiritual part. For her pride would not be so scornful, as her wedded memories reject with horror, the unmentionable imputation involved in the mere fact of Isabel's existence. In what galleries of conjecture, among what horrible haunting toads and scorpions, would such a revelation lead her? When Pierre thought of this, the idea of at all divulging his secret to his mother, not only was made repelling by its hopelessness, as an infirm attack upon her citadel of pride, but was made in the last degree inhuman, as torturing her in her tenderest recollections, and desecrating the whitest altar in her sanctuary.

Though the conviction that he must never disclose his secret to his mother was originally an unmeditated, and as it were, an inspired one; yet now he was almost pains-taking in scrutinizing the entire circumstances of the matter, in order that nothing might be overlooked. For already he vaguely felt, that upon the concealment, or the disclosure of this thing, with reference to his mother, hinged his whole future course of conduct, his whole earthly weal, and Isabel's. But the more and the more that he pondered upon it, the more and the more fixed became his original conviction. He considered that in the case of a disclosure, all human probability pointed to his mother's scornful rejection of his suit as a pleader for Isabel's honorable admission into the honorable mansion of the Glendinnings. Then in that case, unconsciously thought Pierre, I shall have given the deep poison of a miserable truth to my mother, without benefit to any, and positive harm to all. And through Pierre's mind there then darted a baleful thought; how that the truth should not always be paraded; how that sometimes a lie is heavenly, and truth infernal. Filially infernal, truly, thought Pierre, if I should by one vile breath of truth, blast my father's blessed

memory in the bosom of my mother, and plant the sharpest
dagger of grief in her soul. I will not do it!

But as this resolution in him opened up so dark and
wretched a background to his view, he strove to think no
more of it now, but postpone it until the interview with Isabel should have in some way more definitely shaped his purposes. For, when suddenly encountering the shock of new
and unanswerable revelations, which he feels must revolution-
ize all the circumstances of his life, man, at first, ever seeks to
shun all conscious definitiveness in his thoughts and purposes; as assured, that the lines that shall precisely define his
present misery, and thereby lay out his future path; these can
only be defined by sharp stakes that cut into his heart.

iii

Most melancholy of all the hours of earth, is that one long,
gray hour, which to the watcher by the lamp intervenes between the night and day; when both lamp and watcher, over-
tasked, grow sickly in the pallid light; and the watcher, seeking for no gladness in the dawn, sees naught but garish
vapors there; and almost invokes a curse upon the public day,
that shall invade his lonely night of sufferance.

The one small window of his closet looked forth upon the
meadow, and across the river, and far away to the distant
heights, storied with the great deeds of the Glendinnings.
Many a time had Pierre sought this window before sunrise,
to behold the blood-red, out-flinging dawn, that would wrap
those purple hills as with a banner. But now the morning
dawned in mist and rain, and came drizzlingly upon his heart.
Yet as the day advanced, and once more showed to him the
accustomed features of his room by that natural light, which,
till this very moment, had never lighted him but to his joy;
now that the day, and not the night, was witness to his woe;
now first the dread reality came appallingly upon him. A
sense of horrible forlornness, feebleness, impotence, and infinite, eternal desolation possessed him. It was not merely mental, but corporeal also. He could not stand; and when he tried
to sit, his arms fell floorwards as tied to leaden weights. Dragging his ball and chain, he fell upon his bed; for when the

mind is cast down, only in sympathetic proneness can the body rest; whence the bed is often Grief's first refuge. Half stupefied, as with opium, he fell into the profoundest sleep.

In an hour he awoke, instantly recalling all the previous night; and now finding himself a little strengthened, and lying so quietly and silently there, almost without bodily consciousness, but his soul unobtrusively alert; careful not to break the spell by the least movement of a limb, or the least turning of his head, Pierre steadfastly faced his grief, and looked deep down into its eyes; and thoroughly, and calmly, and summarily comprehended it now—so at least he thought—and what it demanded from him; and what he must quickly do in its more immediate sequences; and what that course of conduct was, which he must pursue in the coming unevadable breakfast interview with his mother; and what, for the present must be his plan with Lucy. His time of thought was brief. Rising from his bed, he steadied himself upright a moment; and then going to his writing-desk, in a few at first faltering, but at length unlagging lines, traced the following note:

"I must ask pardon of you, Lucy, for so strangely absenting myself last night. But you know me well enough to be very sure that I would not have done so without important cause. I was in the street approaching your cottage, when a message reached me, imperatively calling me away. It is a matter which will take up all my time and attention for, possibly, two or three days. I tell you this, now, that you may be prepared for it. And I know that however unwelcome this may be to you, you will yet bear with it for my sake; for, indeed, and indeed, Lucy dear, I would not dream of staying from you so long, unless irresistibly coerced to it. Do not come to the mansion until I come to you; and do not manifest any curiosity or anxiety about me, should you chance in the interval to see my mother in any other place. Keep just as cheerful as if I were by you all the time. Do this, now, I conjure you; and so farewell!"

He folded the note, and was about sealing it, when he hesitated a moment, and instantly unfolding it, read it to himself. But he could not adequately comprehend his own writing, for a sudden cloud came over him. This passed; and taking his pen hurriedly again, he added the following postscript:

"Lucy, this note may seem mysterious; but if it shall, I did not mean to make it so; nor do I know that I could have helped it. But

the only reason is this, Lucy: the matter which I have alluded to, is
of such a nature, that, for the present I stand virtually pledged not
to disclose it to any person but those more directly involved in it.
But where one can not reveal the thing itself, it only makes it the
more mysterious to write round it this way. So merely know me
entirely unmenaced in person, and eternally faithful to you; and so
be at rest till I see you."

Then sealing the note, and ringing the bell, he gave it in
strict charge to a servant, with directions to deliver it at the
earliest practicable moment, and not wait for any answer. But
as the messenger was departing the chamber, he called him
back, and taking the sealed note again, and hollowing it in
his hand, scrawled inside of it in pencil the following words:
"Don't write me; don't inquire for me;" and then returned it
to the man, who quitted him, leaving Pierre rooted in
thought in the middle of the room.

But he soon roused himself, and left the mansion; and seeking the cool, refreshing meadow stream, where it formed a
deep and shady pool, he bathed; and returning invigorated to
his chamber, changed his entire dress; in the little trifling con-
cernments of his toilette, striving utterly to banish all thought
of that weight upon his soul. Never did he array himself with
more solicitude for effect. It was one of his fond mother's
whims to perfume the lighter contents of his wardrobe; and
it was one of his own little femininenesses—of the sort sometimes curiously observable in very robust-bodied and big-
souled men, as Mohammed, for example—to be very partial
to all pleasant essences. So that when once more he left the
mansion in order to freshen his cheek anew to meet the keen
glance of his mother—to whom the secret of his possible pallor could not be divulged; Pierre went forth all redolent; but
alas! his body only the embalming cerements of his buried
dead within.

iv

His stroll was longer than he meant; and when he returned
up the Linden walk leading to the breakfast-room, and ascended the piazza steps, and glanced into the wide window
there, he saw his mother seated not far from the table; her

face turned toward his own; and heard her gay voice, and peculiarly light and buoyant laugh, accusing him, and not her, of being the morning's laggard now. Dates was busy among some spoons and napkins at a side-stand.

Summoning all possible cheerfulness to his face, Pierre entered the room. Remembering his carefulness in bathing and dressing; and knowing that there is no air so calculated to give bloom to the cheek as that of a damply fresh, cool, and misty morning, Pierre persuaded himself that small trace would now be found on him of his long night of watching.

"Good morning sister;—Such a famous stroll! I have been all the way to"—

"Where? good heavens! where? for such a look as that!— why, Pierre, Pierre? what ails thee? Dates, I will touch the bell presently."

As the good servitor fumbled for a moment among the napkins, as if unwilling to stir so summarily from his accustomed duty, and not without some of a well and long-tried old domestic's vague, intermitted murmuring, at being wholly excluded from a matter of family interest; Mrs. Glendinning kept her fixed eye on Pierre, who, unmindful that the breakfast was not yet entirely ready, seating himself at the table, began helping himself—though but nervously enough—to the cream and sugar. The moment the door closed on Dates, the mother sprang to her feet, and threw her arms around her son; but in that embrace, Pierre miserably felt that their two hearts beat not together in such unison as before.

"What haggard thing possesses thee, my son? Speak, this is incomprehensible! Lucy;—fie!—not she?—no love-quarrel there;—speak, speak, my darling boy!"

"My dear sister," began Pierre.

"Sister me not, now, Pierre;—I am thy mother."

"Well, then, dear mother, thou art quite as incomprehensible to me as I to"—

"Talk faster, Pierre—this calmness freezes me. Tell me; for, by my soul, something most wonderful must have happened to thee. Thou art my son, and I command thee. It is not Lucy; it is something else. Tell me."

"My dear mother," said Pierre, impulsively moving his chair backward from the table, "if thou wouldst only believe

me when I say it, I have really nothing to tell thee. Thou
knowest that sometimes, when I happen to feel very foolishly
studious and philosophical, I sit up late in my chamber; and
then, regardless of the hour, foolishly run out into the air, for
a long stroll across the meadows. I took such a stroll last
night; and had but little time left for napping afterward; and
what nap I had I was none the better for. But I won't be so
silly again, soon; so do, dearest mother, stop looking at me,
and let us to breakfast.—Dates! Touch the bell there, sister."

"Stay, Pierre!—There is a heaviness in this hour. I feel, I
know, that thou art deceiving me;—perhaps I erred in seeking to wrest thy secret from thee; but believe me, my son, I
never thought thou hadst any secret thing from me, except
thy first love for Lucy—and that, my own womanhood tells
me, was most pardonable and right. But now, what can it be?
Pierre, Pierre! consider well before thou determinest upon
withholding confidence from me. I am thy mother. It may
prove a fatal thing. Can that be good and virtuous, Pierre,
which shrinks from a mother's knowledge? Let us not loose
hands so, Pierre; thy confidence from me, mine goes from
thee. Now, shall I touch the bell?"

Pierre, who had thus far been vainly seeking to occupy his
hands with his cup and spoon; he now paused, and unconsciously fastened a speechless glance of mournfulness upon his
mother. Again he felt presentiments of his mother's newly-
revealed character. He foresaw the supposed indignation of
her wounded pride; her gradually estranged affections thereupon; he knew her firmness, and her exaggerated ideas of the
inalienable allegiance of a son. He trembled to think, that
now indeed was come the first initial moment of his heavy
trial. But though he knew all the significance of his mother's
attitude, as she stood before him, intently eying him, with
one hand upon the bell-cord; and though he felt that the
same opening of the door that should now admit Dates,
could not but give eternal exit to all confidence between him
and his mother; and though he felt, too, that this was his
mother's latent thought; nevertheless, he was girded up in his
well-considered resolution.

"Pierre, Pierre! shall I touch the bell?"

"Mother, stay!—yes do, sister."

The bell was rung; and at the summons Dates entered; and looking with some significance at Mrs. Glendinning, said,—"His Reverence has come, my mistress, and is now in the west parlor."

"Show Mr. Falsgrave in here immediately; and bring up the coffee; did I not tell you I expected him to breakfast this morning?"

"Yes, my mistress; but I thought that—that—just then"—glancing alarmedly from mother to son.

"Oh, my good Dates, nothing has happened," cried Mrs. Glendinning, lightly, and with a bitter smile, looking toward her son,—"show Mr. Falsgrave in. Pierre, I did not see thee, to tell thee, last night; but Mr. Falsgrave breakfasts with us by invitation. I was at the parsonage yesterday, to see him about that wretched affair of Delly, and we are finally to settle upon what is to be done this morning. But my mind is made up concerning Ned; no such profligate shall pollute this place; nor shall the disgraceful Delly."

Fortunately, the abrupt entrance of the clergyman, here turned away attention from the sudden pallor of Pierre's countenance, and afforded him time to rally.

"Good morning, madam; good morning, sir;" said Mr. Falsgrave, in a singularly mild, flute-like voice, turning to Mrs. Glendinning and her son; the lady receiving him with answering cordiality, but Pierre too embarrassed just then to be equally polite. As for one brief moment Mr. Falsgrave stood before the pair, ere taking the offered chair from Dates, his aspect was eminently attractive.

There are certain ever-to-be-cherished moments in the life of almost any man, when a variety of little foregoing circumstances all unite to make him temporarily oblivious of whatever may be hard and bitter in his life, and also to make him most amiably and ruddily disposed; when the scene and company immediately before him are highly agreeable; and if at such a time he chance involuntarily to put himself into a scenically favorable bodily posture; then, in that posture, however transient, thou shalt catch the noble stature of his Better Angel; catch a heavenly glimpse of the latent heavenliness of man. It was so with Mr. Falsgrave now. Not a house within a circuit of fifty miles that he preferred entering before the mansion-house of Saddle Meadows; and though the business upon which he had that morning come, was any thing but relishable to him, yet that subject was not in his memory then. Before him stood united in one person, the most exalted lady and the most storied beauty of all the country round; and the finest, most intellectual, and most congenial youth he knew. Before him also, stood the generous foundress and the untiring patroness of the beautiful little marble church, consecrated by the good Bishop, not four years gone by. Before him also, stood—though in polite disguise—the same untiring benefactress, from whose purse, he could not help suspecting, came a great part of his salary, nominally supplied by the rental of the pews. He had been invited to breakfast; a meal, which, in a well-appointed country family, is the most cheerful circumstance of daily life; he smelt all Java's spices in the aroma from the silver coffee-urn; and well he knew, what liquid deliciousness would soon come from it. Besides all this, and many more minutenesses of the kind, he was conscious that Mrs. Glendinning entertained a particular partiality for him (though not enough to marry him, as he ten times knew by very bitter experience), and that Pierre was not behind-hand in his esteem.

And the clergyman was well worthy of it. Nature had been royally bountiful to him in his person. In his happier moments, as the present, his face was radiant with a courtly, but mild benevolence; his person was nobly robust and dignified; while the remarkable smallness of his feet, and the almost infantile delicacy, and vivid whiteness and purity of his hands, strikingly contrasted with his fine girth and stature. For in countries like America, where there is no distinct hereditary caste of gentlemen, whose order is factitiously perpetuated as race-horses and lords are in kingly lands; and especially, in those agricultural districts, where, of a hundred hands, that drop a ballot for the Presidency, ninety-nine shall be of the brownest and the brawniest; in such districts, this daintiness of the fingers, when united with a generally manly aspect, assumes a remarkableness unknown in European nations.

This most prepossessing form of the clergyman lost nothing by the character of his manners, which were polished and unobtrusive, but peculiarly insinuating, without the least appearance of craftiness or affectation. Heaven had given him his fine, silver-keyed person for a flute to play on in this world; and he was nearly the perfect master of it. His graceful motions had the undulatoriness of melodious sounds. You almost thought you heard, not saw him. So much the wonderful, yet natural gentleman he seemed, that more than once Mrs. Glendinning had held him up to Pierre as a splendid example of the polishing and gentlemanizing influences of Christianity upon the mind and manners; declaring, that extravagant as it might seem, she had always been of his father's fancy,—that no man could be a complete gentleman, and preside with dignity at his own table, unless he partook of the church's sacraments. Nor in Mr. Falsgrave's case was this maxim entirely absurd. The child of a poor northern farmer who had wedded a pretty sempstress, the clergyman had no heraldic line of ancestry to show, as warrant and explanation of his handsome person and gentle manners; the first, being the willful partiality of nature; and the second, the consequence of a scholastic life, attempered by a taste for the choicest female society, however small, which he had always regarded as the best relish of existence. If now his manners thus responded to his person, his mind answered to them both, and was their finest illustration. Besides his eloquent persuasiveness in the pulpit, various fugitive papers upon subjects of nature, art, and literature, attested not only his refined affinity to all beautiful things, visible or invisible; but likewise that he possessed a genius for celebrating such things, which in a less indolent and more ambitious nature, would have been sure to have gained a fair poet's name ere now. For this Mr. Falsgrave was just hovering upon his prime of years; a period which, in such a man, is the sweetest, and, to a mature woman, by far the most attractive of manly life. Youth has not yet completely gone with its beauty, grace, and strength; nor has age at all come with its decrepitudes; though the finest undrossed parts of it—its mildness and its wisdom—have gone on before, as decorous chamberlains precede the sedan of some crutched king.

Such was this Mr. Falsgrave, who now sat at Mrs. Glendinning's breakfast table, a corner of one of that lady's generous napkins so inserted into his snowy bosom, that its folds

almost invested him as far down as the table's edge; and he
seemed a sacred priest, indeed, breakfasting in his surplice.

"Pray, Mr. Falsgrave," said Mrs. Glendinning, "break me
off a bit of that roll."

Whether or not his sacerdotal experiences had strangely refined and spiritualized so simple a process as breaking bread;
or whether it was from the spotless aspect of his hands: certain it is that Mr. Falsgrave acquitted himself on this little
occasion, in a manner that beheld of old by Leonardo, might
have given that artist no despicable hint touching his celestial
painting. As Pierre regarded him, sitting there so mild and
meek; such an image of white-browed and white-handed, and
napkined immaculateness; and as he felt the gentle humane
radiations which came from the clergyman's manly and
rounded beautifulness; and as he remembered all the good
that he knew of this man, and all the good that he had heard
of him, and could recall no blemish in his character; and as in
his own concealed misery and forlornness, he contemplated
the open benevolence, and beaming excellent-heartedness of
Mr. Falsgrave, the thought darted through his mind, that if
any living being was capable of giving him worthy counsel in
his strait; and if to any one he could go with Christian propriety and some small hopefulness, that person was the one
before him.

"Pray, Mr. Glendinning," said the clergyman, pleasantly, as
Pierre was silently offering to help him to some tongue—
"don't let me rob you of it—pardon me, but you seem to
have very little yourself this morning, I think. An execrable
pun, I know: but"—turning toward Mrs. Glendinning—
" when one is made to feel very happy, one is somehow apt
to say very silly things. Happiness and silliness—ah, it's a
suspicious coincidence."

"Mr. Falsgrave," said the hostess—"Your cup is empty.
Dates!—We were talking yesterday, Mr. Falsgrave, concerning that vile fellow, Ned."

"Well, Madam," responded the gentleman, a very little
uneasily.

"He shall not stay on any ground of mine; my mind is
made up, sir. Infamous man!—did he not have a wife as virtuous and beautiful now, as when I first gave her away at

your altar?—It was the sheerest and most gratuitous profligacy."

The clergyman mournfully and assentingly moved his head.

"Such men," continued the lady, flushing with the sincerest indignation—"are to my way of thinking more detestable than murderers."

"That is being a little hard upon them, my dear Madam," said Mr. Falsgrave, mildly.

"Do you not think so, Pierre—now," said the lady, turning earnestly upon her son—"is not the man, who has sinned like that Ned, worse than a murderer? Has he not sacrificed one woman completely, and given infamy to another—to both of them—for their portion. If his own legitimate boy should now hate him, I could hardly blame him."

"My dear Madam," said the clergyman, whose eyes having followed Mrs. Glendinning's to her son's countenance, and marking a strange trepidation there, had thus far been earnestly scrutinizing Pierre's not wholly repressible emotion;—"My dear Madam," he said, slightly bending over his stately episcopal-looking person—"Virtue has, perhaps, an over-ardent champion in you; you grow too warm; but Mr. Glendinning, here, he seems to grow too cold. Pray, favor us with your views, Mr. Glendinning?"

"I will not think now of the man," said Pierre, slowly, and looking away from both his auditors—"let us speak of Delly and her infant—she has, or had one, I have loosely heard;—their case is miserable indeed."

"The mother deserves it," said the lady, inflexibly—"and the child—Reverend sir, what are the words of the Bible?"

" 'The sins of the father shall be visited upon the children to the third generation,' " said Mr. Falsgrave, with some slight reluctance in his tones. "But Madam, that does not mean, that the community is in any way to take the infamy of the children into their own voluntary hands, as the conscious delegated stewards of God's inscrutable dispensations. Because it is declared that the infamous consequences of sin shall be hereditary, it does not follow that our personal and active loathing of sin, should descend from the sinful sinner to his sinless child."

"I understand you, sir," said Mrs. Glendinning, coloring

slightly, "you think me too censorious. But if we entirely forget the parentage of the child, and every way receive the child as we would any other, feel for it in all respects the same, and attach no sign of ignominy to it—how then is the Bible dispensation to be fulfilled? Do we not then put ourselves in the way of its fulfilment, and is that wholly free from impiety?"

Here it was the clergyman's turn to color a little, and there was a just perceptible tremor of the under lip.

"Pardon me," continued the lady, courteously, "but if there is any one blemish in the character of the Reverend Mr. Falsgrave, it is that the benevolence of his heart, too much warps in him the holy rigor of our Church's doctrines. For my part, as I loathe the man, I loathe the woman, and never desire to behold the child."

A pause ensued, during which it was fortunate for Pierre, that by the social sorcery of such occasions as the present, the eyes of all three were intent upon the cloth; all three for the moment, giving loose to their own distressful meditations upon the subject in debate, and Mr. Falsgrave vexedly thinking that the scene was becoming a little embarrassing.

Pierre was the first who spoke; as before, he steadfastly kept his eyes away from both his auditors; but though he did not designate his mother, something in the tone of his voice showed that what he said was addressed more particularly to her.

"Since we seem to have been strangely drawn into the ethical aspect of this melancholy matter," said he, "suppose we go further in it; and let me ask, how it should be between the legitimate and the illegitimate child—children of one father—when they shall have passed their childhood?"

Here the clergyman quickly raising his eyes, looked as surprised and searchingly at Pierre, as his politeness would permit.

"Upon my word"—said Mrs. Glendinning, hardly less surprised, and making no attempt at disguising it—"this is an odd question you put; you have been more attentive to the subject than I had fancied. But what do you mean, Pierre? I did not entirely understand you."

"Should the legitimate child shun the illegitimate, when

one father is father to both?" rejoined Pierre, bending his
head still further over his plate.

The clergyman looked a little down again, and was silent;
but still turned his head slightly sideways toward his hostess,
as if awaiting some reply to Pierre from her.

"Ask the world, Pierre"—said Mrs. Glendinning warmly—
"and ask your own heart."

"My own heart? I will, Madam"—said Pierre, now looking
up steadfastly; "but what do *you* think, Mr. Falsgrave?" letting his glance drop again—"should the one shun the other?
should the one refuse his highest sympathy and perfect love
for the other, especially if that other be deserted by all the
rest of the world? What think you would have been our
blessed Savior's thoughts on such a matter? And what was
that he so mildly said to the adulteress?"

A swift color passed over the clergyman's countenance, suf-
fusing even his expanded brow; he slightly moved in his
chair, and looked uncertainly from Pierre to his mother. He
seemed as a shrewd, benevolent-minded man, placed between
opposite opinions—merely opinions—who, with a full, and
doubly-differing persuasion in himself, still refrains from uttering it, because of an irresistible dislike to manifesting an
absolute dissent from the honest convictions of any person,
whom he both socially and morally esteems.

"Well, what do you reply to my son?"—said Mrs. Glendinning at last.

"Madam and sir"—said the clergyman, now regaining his
entire self-possession. "It is one of the social disadvantages
which we of the pulpit labor under, that we are supposed to
know more of the moral obligations of humanity than other
people. And it is a still more serious disadvantage to the
world, that our unconsidered, conversational opinions on the
most complex problems of ethics, are too apt to be considered
authoritative, as indirectly proceeding from the church itself.
Now, nothing can be more erroneous than such notions; and
nothing so embarrasses me, and deprives me of that entire
serenity, which is indispensable to the delivery of a careful
opinion on moral subjects, than when sudden questions of
this sort are put to me in company. Pardon this long pre-

amble, for I have little more to say. It is not every question, however direct, Mr. Glendinning, which can be conscientiously answered with a yes or no. Millions of circumstances modify all moral questions; so that though conscience may possibly dictate freely in any known special case; yet, by one universal maxim, to embrace all moral contingencies,—this is not only impossible, but the attempt, to me, seems foolish."

At this instant, the surplice-like napkin dropped from the clergyman's bosom, showing a minute but exquisitely cut cameo brooch, representing the allegorical union of the serpent and dove. It had been the gift of an appreciative friend, and was sometimes worn on secular occasions like the present.

"I agree with you, sir"—said Pierre, bowing. "I fully agree with you. And now, madam, let us talk of something else."

"You madam me very punctiliously this morning, Mr. Glendinning"—said his mother, half-bitterly smiling, and half-openly offended, but still more surprised at Pierre's frigid demeanor.

" 'Honor thy father and mother;' " said Pierre—"*both* father and mother," he unconsciously added. "And now that it strikes me, Mr. Falsgrave, and now that we have become so strangely polemical this morning, let me say, that as that command is justly said to be the only one with a promise, so it seems to be without any contingency in the application. It would seem—would it not, sir?—that the most deceitful and hypocritical of fathers should be equally honored by the son, as the purest."

"So it would certainly seem, according to the strict letter of the Decalogue—certainly."

"And do you think, sir, that it should be so held, and so applied in actual life? For instance, should I honor my father, if I knew him to be a seducer?"

"Pierre! Pierre!" said his mother, profoundly coloring, and half rising; "there is no need of these argumentative assumptions. You very immensely forget yourself this morning."

"It is merely the interest of the general question, Madam," returned Pierre, coldly. "I am sorry. If your former objection does not apply here, Mr. Falsgrave, will you favor me with an answer to my question?"

"There you are again, Mr. Glendinning," said the clergyman, thankful for Pierre's hint; "that is another question in
morals absolutely incapable of a definite answer, which shall
be universally applicable." Again the surplice-like napkin
chanced to drop.

"I am tacitly rebuked again then, sir," said Pierre, slowly;
"but I admit that perhaps you are again in the right. And
now, Madam, since Mr. Falsgrave and yourself have a little
business together, to which my presence is not necessary, and
may possibly prove quite dispensable, permit me to leave you.
I am going off on a long ramble, so you need not wait dinner
for me. Good morning, Mr. Falsgrave; good morning,
Madam," looking toward his mother.

As the door closed upon him, Mr. Falsgrave spoke—"Mr.
Glendinning looks a little pale to-day: has he been ill?"

"Not that I know of," answered the lady, indifferently, "but
did you ever see young gentleman so stately as he was?
Extraordinary!" she murmured; "what can this mean—
Madam—Madam? But your cup is empty again, sir"—
reaching forth her hand.

"No more, no more, Madam," said the clergyman.

"Madam? pray don't Madam me any more, Mr. Falsgrave;
I have taken a sudden hatred to that title."

"Shall it be Your Majesty, then?" said the clergyman, gallantly; "the May Queens are so styled, and so should be the
Queens of October."

Here the lady laughed. "Come," said she, "let us go into
another room, and settle the affair of that infamous Ned and
that miserable Delly."

v

The swiftness and unrepellableness of the billow which,
with its first shock, had so profoundly whelmed Pierre, had
not only poured into his soul a tumult of entirely new images
and emotions, but, for the time, it almost entirely drove out
of him all previous ones. The things that any way bore directly upon the pregnant fact of Isabel, these things were all
animate and vividly present to him; but the things which bore
more upon himself, and his own personal condition, as now

forever involved with his sister's, these things were not so
animate and present to him. The conjectured past of Isabel
took mysterious hold of his father; therefore, the idea of his
father tyrannized over his imagination; and the possible future of Isabel, as so essentially though indirectly compromis-
able by whatever course of conduct his mother might
hereafter ignorantly pursue with regard to himself, as henceforth, through Isabel, forever altered to her; these considerations brought his mother with blazing prominence before
him.

Heaven, after all, hath been a little merciful to the miserable man; not entirely untempered to human nature are the
most direful blasts of Fate. When on all sides assailed by prospects of disaster, whose final ends are in terror hidden from
it, the soul of man—either, as instinctively convinced that it
can not battle with the whole host at once; or else, benevolently blinded to the larger arc of the circle which menacingly
hems it in;—whichever be the truth, the soul of man, thus
surrounded, can not, and does never intelligently confront the
totality of its wretchedness. The bitter drug is divided into
separate draughts for him: to-day he takes one part of his
woe; to-morrow he takes more; and so on, till the last drop
is drunk.

Not that in the despotism of other things, the thought of
Lucy, and the unconjecturable suffering into which she might
so soon be plunged, owing to the threatening uncertainty of
the state of his own future, as now in great part and at all
hazards dedicated to Isabel; not that this thought had thus far
been alien to him. Icy-cold, and serpent-like, it had overlay-
ingly crawled in upon his other shuddering imaginings; but
those other thoughts would as often upheave again, and absorb it into themselves, so that it would in that way soon
disappear from his cotemporary apprehension. The prevailing
thoughts connected with Isabel he now could front with prepared and open eyes; but the occasional thought of Lucy,
when *that* started up before him, he could only cover his bewildered eyes with his bewildered hands. Nor was this the
cowardice of selfishness, but the infinite sensitiveness of his
soul. He could bear the agonizing thought of Isabel, because

he was immediately resolved to help her, and to assuage a fellow-being's grief; but, as yet, he could not bear the thought of Lucy, because the very resolution that promised balm to Isabel obscurely involved the everlasting peace of Lucy, and therefore aggravatingly threatened a far more than fellow-being's happiness.

Well for Pierre it was, that the penciling presentiments of his mind concerning Lucy as quickly erased as painted their tormenting images. Standing half-befogged upon the mountain of his Fate, all that part of the wide panorama was wrapped in clouds to him; but anon those concealings slid aside, or rather, a quick rent was made in them; disclosing far below, half-vailed in the lower mist, the winding tranquil vale and stream of Lucy's previous happy life; through the swift cloud-rent he caught one glimpse of her expectant and angelic face peeping from the honey-suckled window of her cottage; and the next instant the stormy pinions of the clouds locked themselves over it again; and all was hidden as before; and all went confused in whirling rack and vapor as before. Only by unconscious inspiration, caught from the agencies invisible to man, had he been enabled to write that first obscurely announcing note to Lucy; wherein the collectedness, and the mildness, and the calmness, were but the natural though insidious precursors of the stunning bolts on bolts to follow.

But, while thus, for the most part wrapped from his consciousness and vision, still, the condition of his Lucy, as so deeply affected now, was still more and more disentangling and defining itself from out its nether mist, and even beneath the general upper fog. For when unfathomably stirred, the subtler elements of man do not always reveal themselves in the concocting act; but, as with all other potencies, show themselves chiefly in their ultimate resolvings and results. Strange wild work, and awfully symmetrical and reciprocal, was that now going on within the self-apparently chaotic breast of Pierre. As in his own conscious determinations, the mournful Isabel was being snatched from her captivity of world-wide abandonment; so, deeper down in the more secret chambers of his unsuspecting soul, the smiling Lucy, now as dead and ashy pale, was being bound a ransom for

Isabel's salvation. Eye for eye, and tooth for tooth. Eternally inexorable and unconcerned is Fate, a mere heartless trader in men's joys and woes.

Nor was this general and spontaneous self-concealment of all the most momentous interests of his love, as irretrievably involved with Isabel and his resolution respecting her; nor was this unbidden thing in him unseconded by the prompting of his own conscious judgment, when in the tyranny of the master-event itself, that judgment was permitted some infrequent play. He could not but be aware, that all meditation on Lucy now was worse than useless. How could he now map out his and her young life-chart, when all was yet misty-white with creamy breakers! Still more: divinely dedicated as he felt himself to be; with divine commands upon him to befriend and champion Isabel, through all conceivable contingencies of Time and Chance; how could he insure himself against the insidious inroads of self-interest, and hold intact all his unselfish magnanimities, if once he should permit the distracting thought of Lucy to dispute with Isabel's the pervading possession of his soul?

And if—though but unconsciously as yet—he was almost superhumanly prepared to make a sacrifice of all objects dearest to him, and cut himself away from his last hopes of common happiness, should they cross his grand enthusiast resolution;—if this was so with him; then, how light as gossamer, and thinner and more impalpable than airiest threads of gauze, did he hold all common conventional regardings;— his hereditary duty to his mother, his pledged worldly faith and honor to the hand and seal of his affiancement?

Not that at present all these things did thus present themselves to Pierre; but these things were fœtally forming in him. Impregnations from high enthusiasms he had received; and the now incipient offspring which so stirred, with such painful, vague vibrations in his soul; this, in its mature development, when it should at last come forth in living deeds, would scorn all personal relationship with Pierre, and hold his heart's dearest interests for naught.

Thus, in the Enthusiast to Duty, the heaven-begotten Christ is born; and will not own a mortal parent, and spurns and rends all mortal bonds.

vi

One night, one day, and a small part of the one ensuing evening had been given to Pierre to prepare for the momentous interview with Isabel.

Now, thank God, thought Pierre, the night is past,—the night of Chaos and of Doom; the day only, and the skirt of evening now remain. May heaven new-string my soul, and confirm me in the Christ-like feeling I first felt. May I, in all my least shapeful thoughts still square myself by the inflexible rule of holy right. Let no unmanly, mean temptation cross my path this day; let no base stone lie in it. This day I will forsake the censuses of men, and seek the suffrages of the god-like population of the trees, which now seem to me a nobler race than man. Their high foliage shall drop heavenliness upon me; my feet in contact with their mighty roots, immortal vigor shall so steal into me. Guide me, gird me, guard me, this day, ye sovereign powers! Bind me in bonds I can not break; remove all sinister allurings from me; eternally this day deface in me the detested and distorted images of all the convenient lies and duty-subterfuges of the diving and ducking moralities of this earth. Fill me with consuming fire for them; to my life's muzzle, cram me with your own intent. Let no world-syren come to sing to me this day, and wheedle from me my undauntedness. I cast my eternal die this day, ye powers. On my strong faith in ye Invisibles, I stake three whole felicities, and three whole lives this day. If ye forsake me now,—farewell to Faith, farewell to Truth, farewell to God; exiled for aye from God and man, I shall declare myself an equal power with both; free to make war on Night and Day, and all thoughts and things of mind and matter, which the upper and the nether firmaments do clasp!

vii

But Pierre, though charged with the fire of all divineness, his containing thing was made of clay. Ah, muskets the gods have made to carry infinite combustions, and yet made them of clay!

Save me from being bound to Truth, liege lord, as I am

now. How shall I steal yet further into Pierre, and show how this heavenly fire was helped to be contained in him, by mere contingent things, and things that he knew not. But I shall follow the endless, winding way,—the flowing river in the cave of man; careless whither I be led, reckless where I land.

Was not the face—though mutely mournful—beautiful, bewitchingly? How unfathomable those most wondrous eyes of supernatural light! In those charmed depths, Grief and Beauty plunged and dived together. So beautiful, so mystical, so bewilderingly alluring; speaking of a mournfulness infinitely sweeter and more attractive than all mirthfulness; that face of glorious suffering; that face of touching loveliness; that face was Pierre's own sister's; that face was Isabel's; that face Pierre had visibly seen; into those same supernatural eyes our Pierre had looked. Thus, already, and ere the proposed encounter, he was assured that, in a transcendent degree, womanly beauty, and not womanly ugliness, invited him to champion the right. Be naught concealed in this book of sacred truth. How, if accosted in some squalid lane, a humped, and crippled, hideous girl should have snatched his garment's hem, with—"Save me, Pierre—love me, own me, brother; I am thy sister!"—Ah, if man were wholly made in heaven, why catch we hell-glimpses? Why in the noblest marble pillar that stands beneath the all-comprising vault, ever should we descry the sinister vein? We lie in nature very close to God; and though, further on, the stream may be corrupted by the banks it flows through; yet at the fountain's rim, where mankind stand, there the stream infallibly bespeaks the fountain.

So let no censorious word be here hinted of mortal Pierre. Easy for me to slyly hide these things, and always put him before the eye as immaculate; unsusceptible to the inevitable nature and the lot of common men. I am more frank with Pierre than the best men are with themselves. I am all unguarded and magnanimous with Pierre; therefore you see his weakness, and therefore only. In reserves men build imposing characters; not in revelations. He who shall be wholly honest, though nobler than Ethan Allen; that man shall stand in danger of the meanest mortal's scorn.

Book VI

HALF WISHFUL that the hour would come; half shuddering that every moment it still came nearer and more near to him; dry-eyed, but wet with that dark day's rain; at fall of eve, Pierre emerged from long wanderings in the primeval woods of Saddle Meadows, and for one instant stood motionless upon their sloping skirt.

Where he stood was in the rude wood road, only used by sledges in the time of snow; just where the out-posted trees formed a narrow arch, and fancied gateway leading upon the far, wide pastures sweeping down toward the lake. In that wet and misty eve the scattered, shivering pasture elms seemed standing in a world inhospitable, yet rooted by inscrutable sense of duty to their place. Beyond, the lake lay in one sheet of blankness and of dumbness, unstirred by breeze or breath; fast bound there it lay, with not life enough to reflect the smallest shrub or twig. Yet in that lake was seen the duplicate, stirless sky above. Only in sunshine did that lake catch gay, green images; and these but displaced the imaged muteness of the unfeatured heavens.

On both sides, in the remoter distance, and also far beyond the mild lake's further shore, rose the long, mysterious mountain masses; shaggy with pines and hemlocks, mystical with nameless, vapory exhalations, and in that dim air black with dread and gloom. At their base, profoundest forests lay entranced, and from their far owl-haunted depths of caves and rotted leaves, and unused and unregarded inland overgrowth of decaying wood—for smallest sticks of which, in other climes many a pauper was that moment perishing; from out the infinite inhumanities of those profoundest forests, came a moaning, muttering, roaring, intermitted, changeful sound: rain-shakings of the palsied trees, slidings of rocks undermined, final crashings of long-riven boughs, and devilish gibberish of the forest-ghosts.

But more near, on the mild lake's hither shore, where it

formed a long semi-circular and scooped acclivity of corn-
fields, there the small and low red farm-house lay; its ancient
roof a bed of brightest mosses; its north front (from the
north the moss-wind blows), also moss-incrusted, like the
north side of any vast-trunked maple in the groves. At one
gabled end, a tangled arbor claimed support, and paid for it
by generous gratuities of broad-flung verdure, one viny shaft
of which pointed itself upright against the chimney-bricks, as
if a waving lightning-rod. Against the other gable, you saw
the lowly dairy-shed; its sides close netted with traced Madeira vines; and had you been close enough, peeping through
that imprisoning tracery, and through the light slats barring
the little embrasure of a window, you might have seen the
gentle and contented captives—the pans of milk, and the
snow-white Dutch cheeses in a row, and the molds of golden
butter, and the jars of lily cream. In front, three straight gigantic lindens stood guardians of this verdant spot. A long
way up, almost to the ridge-pole of the house, they showed
little foliage; but then, suddenly, as three huge green bal-
loons, they poised their three vast, inverted, rounded cones
of verdure in the air.

Soon as Pierre's eye rested on the place, a tremor shook
him. Not alone because of Isabel, as there a harborer now,
but because of two dependent and most strange coincidences
which that day's experience had brought to him. He had
gone to breakfast with his mother, his heart charged to overflowing with presentiments of what would probably be her
haughty disposition concerning such a being as Isabel, claiming her maternal love: and lo! the Reverend Mr. Falsgrave
enters, and Ned and Delly are discussed, and that whole sympathetic matter, which Pierre had despaired of bringing before his mother in all its ethic bearings, so as absolutely to
learn her thoughts upon it, and thereby test his own conjectures; all that matter had been fully talked about; so that,
through that strange coincidence, he now perfectly knew his
mother's mind, and had received forewarnings, as if from
heaven, not to make any present disclosure to her. That was
in the morning; and now, at eve catching a glimpse of the
house where Isabel was harboring, at once he recognized it
as the rented farm-house of old Walter Ulver, father to the

self-same Delly, forever ruined through the cruel arts of Ned.

Strangest feelings, almost supernatural, now stole into Pierre. With little power to touch with awe the souls of less susceptible, reflective, and poetic beings, such coincidences, however frequently they may recur, ever fill the finer organization with sensations which transcend all verbal renderings. They take hold of life's subtlest problem. With the lightning's flash, the query is spontaneously propounded—chance, or God? If too, the mind thus influenced be likewise a prey to any settled grief, then on all sides the query magnifies, and at last takes in the all-comprehending round of things. For ever is it seen, that sincere souls in suffering, then most ponder upon final causes. The heart, stirred to its depths, finds correlative sympathy in the head, which likewise is profoundly moved. Before miserable men, when intellectual, all the ages of the world pass as in a manacled procession, and all their myriad links rattle in the mournful mystery.

Pacing beneath the long-skirting shadows of the elevated wood, waiting for the appointed hour to come, Pierre strangely strove to imagine to himself the scene which was destined to ensue. But imagination utterly failed him here; the reality was too real for him; only the face, the face alone now visited him; and so accustomed had he been of late to confound it with the shapes of air, that he almost trembled when he thought that face to face, that face must shortly meet his own.

And now the thicker shadows begin to fall; the place is lost to him; only the three dim, tall lindens pilot him as he descends the hill, hovering upon the house. He knows it not, but his meditative route is sinuous; as if that moment his thought's stream was likewise serpentining: laterally obstructed by insinuated misgivings as to the ultimate utilitarian advisability of the enthusiast resolution that was his. His steps decrease in quickness as he comes more nigh, and sees one feeble light struggling in the rustic double-casement. Infallibly he knows that his own voluntary steps are taking him forever from the brilliant chandeliers of the mansion of Saddle Meadows, to join company with the wretched rush-lights of poverty and woe. But his sublime intuitiveness also paints to him the sun-like glories of god-like truth and virtue; which

though ever obscured by the dense fogs of earth, still shall
shine eventually in unclouded radiance, casting illustrative
light upon the sapphire throne of God.

ii

He stands before the door; the house is steeped in silence;
he knocks; the casement light flickers for a moment, and then
moves away; within, he hears a door creak on its hinges; then
his whole heart beats wildly as the outer latch is lifted; and
holding the light above her supernatural head, Isabel stands
before him. It is herself. No word is spoken; no other soul is
seen. They enter the room of the double casement; and Pierre
sits down, overpowered with bodily faintness and spiritual
awe. He lifts his eyes to Isabel's gaze of loveliness and loneliness; and then a low, sweet, half-sobbing voice of more than
natural musicalness is heard:—

"And so, thou art my brother;—shall I call thee Pierre?"

Steadfastly, with his one first and last fraternal inquisition
of the person of the mystic girl, Pierre now for an instant eyes
her; and in that one instant sees in the imploring face, not
only the nameless touchingness of that of the sewing-girl, but
also the subtler expression of the portrait of his then youthful
father, strangely translated, and intermarryingly blended with
some before unknown, foreign feminineness. In one breath,
Memory and Prophecy, and Intuition tell him—"Pierre, have
no reserves; no minutest possible doubt;—this being is thy
sister; thou gazest on thy father's flesh."

"And so thou art my brother?—shall I call thee Pierre?"

He sprang to his feet, and caught her in his undoubting arms.

"Thou art! thou art!"

He felt a faint struggling within his clasp; her head
drooped against him; his whole form was bathed in the flowing glossiness of her long and unimprisoned hair. Brushing
the locks aside, he now gazed upon the death-like beauty of
the face, and caught immortal sadness from it. She seemed as
dead; as suffocated,—the death that leaves most unimpaired
the latent tranquillities and sweetnesses of the human countenance.

He would have called aloud for succor; but the slow eyes

opened upon him; and slowly he felt the girl's supineness leaving her; and now she recovers herself a little,—and again he feels her faintly struggling in his arms, as if somehow abashed, and incredulous of mortal right to hold her so. Now Pierre repents his overardent and incautious warmth, and feels himself all reverence for her. Tenderly he leads her to a bench within the double casement; and sits beside her; and waits in silence, till the first shock of this encounter shall have left her more composed and more prepared to hold communion with him.

"How feel'st thou now, my sister?"

"Bless thee! bless thee!"

Again the sweet, wild power of the musicalness of the voice, and some soft, strange touch of foreignness in the accent,—so it fancifully seemed to Pierre, thrills through and through his soul. He bent and kissed her brow; and then feels her hand seeking his, and then clasping it without one uttered word.

All his being is now condensed in that one sensation of the clasping hand. He feels it as very small and smooth, but strangely hard. Then he knew that by the lonely labor of her hands, his own father's daughter had earned her living in the same world, where he himself, her own brother, had so idly dwelled. Once more he reverently kissed her brow, and his warm breath against it murmured with a prayer to heaven.

"I have no tongue to speak to thee, Pierre, my brother. My whole being, all my life's thoughts and longings are in endless arrears to thee; then how can I speak to thee? Were it God's will, Pierre, my utmost blessing now, were to lie down and die. Then should I be at peace. Bear with me, Pierre."

"Eternally will I do that, my beloved Isabel! Speak not to me yet awhile, if that seemeth best to thee, if that only is possible to thee. This thy clasping hand, my sister, *this* is now thy tongue to me."

"I know not where to begin to speak to thee, Pierre; and yet my soul o'erbrims in me."

"From my heart's depths, I love and reverence thee; and feel for thee, backward and forward, through all eternity!"

"Oh, Pierre, can'st thou not cure in me this dreaminess, this bewilderingness I feel? My poor head swims and swims, and will not pause. My life can not last long thus; I am too full without discharge. Conjure tears for me, Pierre; that my heart may not break with the present feeling,—more death-like to me than all my grief gone by!"

"Ye thirst-slaking evening skies, ye hilly dews and mists, distil your moisture here! The bolt hath passed; why comes not the following shower?—Make her to weep!"

Then her head sought his support; and big drops fell on him; and anon, Isabel gently slid her head from him, and sat a little composedly beside him.

"If thou feelest in endless arrears of thought to me, my sister; so do I feel toward thee. I too, scarce know what I should speak to thee. But when thou lookest on me, my sister, thou beholdest one, who in his soul hath taken vows immutable, to be to thee, in all respects, and to the uttermost bounds and possibilities of Fate, thy protecting and all-acknowledging brother!"

"Not mere sounds of common words, but inmost tones of my heart's deepest melodies should now be audible to thee. Thou speakest to a human thing, but something heavenly should answer thee;—some flute heard in the air should answer thee; for sure thy most undreamed-of accents, Pierre, sure they have not been unheard on high. Blessings that are imageless to all mortal fancyings, these shall be thine for this."

"Blessing like to thine, doth but recoil and bless homeward to the heart that uttered it. I can not bless thee, my sister, as thou dost bless thyself in blessing my unworthiness. But, Isabel, by still keeping present the first wonder of our meeting, we shall make our hearts all feebleness. Let me then rehearse to thee what Pierre is; what life hitherto he hath been leading; and what hereafter he shall lead;—so thou wilt be prepared."

"Nay, Pierre, that is my office; thou art first entitled to my tale, then, if it suit thee, thou shalt make me the unentitled gift of thine. Listen to me, now. The invisible things will give me strength;—it is not much, Pierre;—nor aught very marvelous. Listen then;—I feel soothed down to utterance now."

During some brief, interluding, silent pauses in their interview thus far, Pierre had heard a soft, slow, sad, to-and-fro, meditative stepping on the floor above; and in the frequent pauses that intermitted the strange story in the following chapter, that same soft, slow, sad, to-and-fro, meditative, and most melancholy stepping, was again and again audible in the silent room.

iii

"I never knew a mortal mother. The farthest stretch of my life's memory can not recall one single feature of such a face. If, indeed, mother of mine hath lived, she is long gone, and cast no shadow on the ground she trod. Pierre, the lips that do now speak to thee, never touched a woman's breast; I seem not of woman born. My first dim life-thoughts cluster round an old, half-ruinous house in some region, for which I now have no chart to seek it out. If such a spot did ever really exist, that too seems to have been withdrawn from all the remainder of the earth. It was a wild, dark house, planted in the midst of a round, cleared, deeply-sloping space, scooped out of the middle of deep stunted pine woods. Ever I shrunk at evening from peeping out of my window, lest the ghostly pines should steal near to me, and reach out their grim arms to snatch me into their horrid shadows. In summer the forest unceasingly hummed with unconjecturable voices of un-known birds and beasts. In winter its deep snows were traced like any paper map, with dotting night-tracks of four-footed creatures, that, even to the sun, were never visible, and never were seen by man at all. In the round open space the dark house stood, without one single green twig or leaf to shelter it; shadeless and shelterless in the heart of shade and shelter. Some of the windows were rudely boarded up, with boards nailed straight up and down; and those rooms were utterly empty, and never were entered, though they were doorless. But often, from the echoing corridor, I gazed into them with fear; for the great fire-places were all in ruins; the lower tier of back-stones were burnt into one white, common crum-bling; and the black bricks above had fallen upon the hearths, heaped here and there with the still falling soot of long-extin-guished fires. Every hearth-stone in that house had one long crack through it; every floor drooped at the corners; and out-side, the whole base of the house, where it rested on the low foundation of greenish stones, was strewn with dull, yellow molderings of the rotting sills. No name; no scrawled or written thing; no book, was in the house; no one memorial speaking of its former occupants. It was dumb as death. No grave-stone, or mound, or any little hillock around the house, betrayed any past burials of man or child. And thus, with no trace then to me of its past history, thus it hath now entirely departed and perished from my slightest knowledge as to where that house so stood, or in what region it so stood. None other house like it have I ever seen. But once I saw plates of the outside of French chateaux which powerfully recalled its dim image to me, especially the two rows of small dormer windows projecting from the inverted hopper-roof. But that house was of wood, and these of stone. Still, sometimes I think that house was not in this country, but somewhere in Europe; perhaps in France; but it is all bewildering to me; and so you must not start at me, for I can not but talk wildly upon so wild a theme.

"In this house I never saw any living human soul, but an old man and woman. The old man's face was almost black with age, and was one purse of wrinkles, his hoary beard always tangled, streaked with dust and earthy crumbs. I think in summer he toiled a little in the garden, or some spot like that, which lay on one side of the house. All my ideas are in uncertainty and confusion here. But the old man and the old woman seemed to have fastened themselves indelibly upon my memory. I suppose their being the only human things around me then, *that* caused the hold they took upon me. They seldom spoke to me; but would sometimes, of dark, gusty nights, sit by the fire and stare at me, and then mumble to each other, and then stare at me again. They were not entirely unkind to me; but, I repeat, they seldom or never spoke to me. What words or language they used to each other, this it is impossible for me to recall. I have often wished to; for then I might at least have some additional idea whether the house was in this country or somewhere beyond the sea. And here I ought to say, that sometimes I have, I know not what sort of vague remembrances of at one time— shortly after the period I now speak of—chattering in two different childish languages; one of which waned in me as the other and latter grew. But more of this anon. It was the woman that gave me my meals; for I did not eat with them. Once they sat by the fire with a loaf between them, and a bottle of some thin sort of reddish wine; and I went up to them, and asked to eat with them, and touched the loaf. But instantly the old man made a motion as if to strike me, but did not, and the woman, glaring at me, snatched the loaf and threw it into the fire before them. I ran frightened from the room; and sought a cat, which I had often tried to coax into some intimacy, but, for some strange cause, without success. But in my frightened loneliness, then, I sought the cat again, and found her up-stairs, softly scratching for some hidden thing among the litter of the abandoned fire-places. I called to her, for I dared not go into the haunted chamber; but she only gazed sideways and unintelligently toward me; and continued her noiseless searchings. I called again, and then she turned round and hissed at me; and I ran down stairs, still stung with the thought of having been driven away there, too. I now knew not where to go to rid myself of my loneliness. At last I went outside of the house, and sat down on a stone, but its coldness went up to my heart, and I rose and stood on my feet. But my head was dizzy; I could not stand; I fell, and knew no more. But next morning I found myself in bed in my uncheerable room, and some dark bread and a cup of water by me.

"It has only been by chance that I have told thee this one particular reminiscence of my early life in that house. I could tell many more like it, but this is enough to show what manner of life I led at that time. Every day that I then lived, I felt all visible sights and all audible sounds growing stranger and stranger, and fearful and more fearful to me. To me the man and the woman were just like the cat; none of them would speak to me; none of them were comprehensible to me. And the man, and the woman, and the cat, were just like the green foundation stones of the house to me; I knew not whence they came, or what cause they had for being there. I say again, no living human soul came to the house but the man and the woman; but sometimes the old man early trudged away to a road that led through the woods, and would not come back till late in the evening; he brought the dark bread, and the thin, reddish wine with him. Though the entrance to the wood was not so very far from the door, yet he came so slowly and infirmly trudging with his little load, that it seemed weary hours on hours between my first descrying him among the trees, and his crossing the splintered threshold.

"Now the wide and vacant blurrings of my early life thicken in my mind. All goes wholly memoryless to me now. It may have been that about that time I grew sick with some fever, in which for a long interval I lost myself. Or it may be true, which I have heard, that after the period of our very earliest recollections, then a space intervenes of entire unknowingness, followed again by the first dim glimpses of the succeeding memory, more or less distinctly embracing all our past up to that one early gap in it.

"However this may be, nothing more can I recall of the house in the wide open space; nothing of how at last I came to leave it; but I must have been still extremely young then. But some uncertain, tossing memory have I of being at last in another round, open space, but immensely larger than the first one, and with no encircling belt of woods. Yet often it seems to me that there were three tall, straight things like pine-trees somewhere there nigh to me at times; and that they fearfully shook and snapt as the old trees used to in the mountain storms. And the floors seemed sometimes to droop at the corners still more steeply than the old floors did; and changefully drooped too, so that I would even seem to feel them drooping under me.

"Now, too, it was that, as it sometimes seems to me, I first and last chattered in the two childish languages I spoke of a little time ago. There seemed people about me, some of whom talked one, and some the other; but I talked both; yet one not so readily as the other; and but beginningly as it were; still this other was the one which was gradually displacing the former. The men who—as it sometimes dreamily seems to me at times—often climbed the three strange tree-like things, they talked—I needs must think—if indeed I have any real thought about so bodiless a phantom as this is—they talked the language which I speak of as at this time gradually waning in me. It was a bonny tongue; oh, seems to me so sparkling-gay and lightsome; just the tongue for a child like me, if the child had not been so sad always. It was pure children's language, Pierre; so twittering—such a chirp.

"In thy own mind, thou must now perceive, that most of these dim remembrances in me, hint vaguely of a ship at sea. But all is dim and vague to me. Scarce know I at any time whether I tell you real things, or the unrealest dreams. Always in me, the solidest things melt into dreams, and dreams into solidities. Never have I wholly recovered from the effects of my strange early life. This it is, that even now—this moment—surrounds thy visible form, my brother, with a mysterious mistiness; so that a second face, and a third face, and a fourth face peep at me from within thy own. Now dim, and more dim, grows in me all the memory of how thou and I did come to meet. I go groping again amid all sorts of shapes, which part to me; so that I seem to advance through the shapes; and yet the shapes have eyes that look at me. I turn round, and they look at me; I step forward, and they look at me.—Let me be silent now; do not speak to me."

iv

Filled with nameless wonderings at this strange being, Pierre sat mute, intensely regarding her half-averted aspect. Her immense soft tresses of the jettiest hair had slantingly fallen over her as though a curtain were half drawn from before some saint enshrined. To Pierre, she seemed half unearthly; but this unearthliness was only her mysteriousness, not any thing that was repelling or menacing to him. And still, the low melodies of her far interior voice hovered in sweet echoes in the room; and were trodden upon, and pressed like gushing grapes, by the steady invisible pacing on the floor above.

She moved a little now, and after some strange wanderings more coherently continued.

"My next memory which I think I can in some degree rely upon, was yet another house, also situated away from human haunts, in the heart of a not entirely silent country. Through this country, and by the house, wound a green and lagging river. That house must have been in some lowland; for the first house I spoke of seems to me to have been somewhere

among mountains, or near to mountains;—the sounds of the
far waterfalls,—I seem to hear them now; the steady up-
pointed cloud-shapes behind the house in the sunset sky—I
seem to see them now. But this other house, this second one,
or third one, I know not which, I say again it was in some
lowland. There were no pines around it; few trees of any sort;
the ground did not slope so steeply as around the first house.
There were cultivated fields about it, and in the distance farm-
houses and out-houses, and cattle, and fowls, and many objects of that familiar sort. This house I am persuaded was in
this country; on this side of the sea. It was a very large house,
and full of people; but for the most part they lived separately.
There were some old people in it, and there were young men,
and young women in it,—some very handsome; and there
were children in it. It seemed a happy place to some of these
people; many of them were always laughing; but it was not a
happy place for me.

"But here I may err, because of my own consciousness I
can not identify in myself—I mean in the memory of my
whole foregoing life,—I say, I can not identify that thing
which is called happiness; that thing whose token is a laugh,
or a smile, or a silent serenity on the lip. I may have been
happy, but it is not in my conscious memory now. Nor do I
feel a longing for it, as though I had never had it; my spirit
seeks different food from happiness; for I think I have a suspicion of what it is. I have suffered wretchedness, but not
because of the absence of happiness, and without praying for
happiness. I pray for peace—for motionlessness—for the
feeling of myself, as of some plant, absorbing life without
seeking it, and existing without individual sensation. I feel
that there can be no perfect peace in individualness. Therefore
I hope one day to feel myself drank up into the pervading
spirit animating all things. I feel I am an exile here. I still go
straying.—Yes; in thy speech, thou smilest.—But let me be
silent again. Do not answer me. When I resume, I will not
wander so, but make short end."

Reverently resolved not to offer the slightest let or hinting
hindrance to the singular tale rehearsing to him, but to sit
passively and receive its marvelous droppings into his soul,
however long the pauses; and as touching less mystical con-

siderations, persuaded that by so doing he should ultimately
derive the least nebulous and imperfect account of Isabel's
history; Pierre still sat waiting her resuming, his eyes fixed
upon the girl's wonderfully beautiful ear, which chancing to
peep forth from among her abundant tresses, nestled in that
blackness like a transparent sea-shell of pearl.

She moved a little now; and after some strange wanderings
more coherently continued; while the sound of the stepping
on the floor above—it seemed to cease.

"I have spoken of the second or rather the third spot in my
memory of the past, as it first appeared to me; I mean, I have
spoken of the people in the house, according to my very earliest recallable impression of them. But I stayed in that house
for several years—five, six, perhaps, seven years—and during
that interval of my stay, all things changed to me, because I
learned more, though always dimly. Some of its occupants
departed; some changed from smiles to tears; some went
moping all the day; some grew as savages and outrageous,
and were dragged below by dumb-like men into deep places,
that I knew nothing of, but dismal sounds came through the
lower floor, groans and clanking fallings, as of iron in straw.
Now and then, I saw coffins silently at noon-day carried into
the house, and in five minutes' time emerge again, seemingly
heavier than they entered; but I saw not who was in them.
Once, I saw an immense-sized coffin, endwise pushed
through a lower window by three men who did not speak;
and watching, I saw it pushed out again, and they drove off
with it. But the numbers of those invisible persons who thus
departed from the house, were made good by other invisible
persons arriving in close carriages. Some in rags and tatters
came on foot, or rather were driven on foot. Once I heard
horrible outcries, and peeping from my window, saw a robust
but squalid and distorted man, seemingly a peasant, tied by
cords with four long ends to them, held behind by as many
ignorant-looking men who with a lash drove the wild squalid
being that way toward the house. Then I heard answering
hand-clappings, shrieks, howls, laughter, blessings, prayers,
oaths, hymns, and all audible confusions issuing from all the
chambers of the house.

"Sometimes there entered the house—though only tran-

siently, departing within the hour they came—people of a
then remarkable aspect to me. They were very composed of
countenance; did not laugh; did not groan; did not weep; did
not make strange faces; did not look endlessly fatigued; were
not strangely and fantastically dressed; in short, did not at all
resemble any people I had ever seen before, except a little like
some few of the persons of the house, who seemed to have
authority over the rest. These people of a remarkable aspect
to me, I thought they were strangely demented people;—
composed of countenance, but wandering of mind; soul-com-
posed and bodily-wandering, and strangely demented people.

"By-and-by, the house seemed to change again, or else my
mind took in more, and modified its first impressions. I was
lodged up-stairs in a little room; there was hardly any furniture in the room; sometimes I wished to go out of it; but the
door was locked. Sometimes the people came and took me
out of the room, into a much larger and very long room, and
here I would collectively see many of the other people of the
house, who seemed likewise brought from distant and separate chambers. In this long room they would vacantly roam
about, and talk vacant talk to each other. Some would stand
in the middle of the room gazing steadily on the floor for
hours together, and never stirred, but only breathed and
gazed upon the floor. Some would sit crouching in the corner, and sit crouching there, and only breathe and crouch in
the corners. Some kept their hands tight on their hearts, and
went slowly promenading up and down, moaning and moaning to themselves. One would say to another—'Feel of it—
here, put thy hand in the break.' Another would mutter—
'Broken, broken, broken'—and would mutter nothing but
that one word *broken*. But most of them were dumb, and
could not, or would not speak, or had forgotten how to
speak. They were nearly all pale people. Some had hair white
as snow, and yet were quite young people. Some were always
talking about Hell, Eternity, and God; and some of all things
as fixedly decreed; others would say nay to this, and then they
would argue, but without much conviction either way. But
once nearly all the people present—even the dumb moping
people, and the sluggish persons crouching in the corners—
nearly all of them laughed once, when after a whole day's

loud babbling, two of these predestinarian opponents, said each to the other—'Thou hast convinced me, friend; but we are quits; for so also, have I convinced thee, the other way; now then, let's argue it all over again; for still, though mutually converted, we are still at odds.' Some harangued the wall; some apostrophized the air; some hissed at the air; some lolled their tongues out at the air; some struck the air; some made motions, as if wrestling with the air, and fell out of the arms of the air, panting from the invisible hug.

"Now, as in the former thing, thou must, ere this, have suspected what manner of place this second or third house was, that I then lived in. But do not speak the word to me. That word has never passed my lips; even now, when I hear the word, I run from it; when I see it printed in a book, I run from the book. The word is wholly unendurable to me. Who brought me to the house; how I came there, I do not know. I lived a long time in the house; that alone I know; I say I know, but still I am uncertain; still Pierre, still the—oh the dreaminess, the bewilderingness—it never entirely leaves me. Let me be still again."

She leaned away from him; she put her small hard hand to her forehead; then moved it down, very slowly, but still hardly over her eyes, and kept it there, making no other sign, and still as death. Then she moved and continued her vague tale of terribleness.

"I must be shorter; I did not mean to turn off into the mere offshootings of my story, here and there; but the dreaminess I speak of leads me sometimes; and I, as impotent then, obey the dreamy prompting. Bear with me; now I will be briefer.

"It came to pass, at last, that there was a contention about me in the house; some contention which I heard in the after rumor only, not at the actual time. Some strangers had arrived; or had come in haste, being sent for to the house. Next day they dressed me in new and pretty, but still plain clothes, and they took me down stairs, and out into the air, and into a carriage with a pleasant-looking woman, a stranger to me; and I was driven off a good way, two days nearly we drove away, stopping somewhere overnight; and on the evening of the second day we came to another house, and went into it, and stayed there.

"This house was a much smaller one than the other, and seemed sweetly quiet to me after that. There was a beautiful infant in it; and this beautiful infant always archly and innocently smiling on me, and strangely beckoning me to come and play with it, and be glad with it; and be thoughtless, and be glad and gleeful with it; this beautiful infant first brought me to my own mind, as it were; first made me sensible that I was something different from stones, trees, cats; first undid in me the fancy that all people were as stones, trees, cats; first filled me with the sweet idea of humanness; first made me aware of the infinite mercifulness, and tenderness, and beautifulness of humanness; and this beautiful infant first filled me with the dim thought of Beauty; and equally, and at the same time, with the feeling of the Sadness; of the immortalness and universalness of the Sadness. I now feel that I should soon have gone,———stop me now; do not let me go that way. I owe all things to that beautiful infant. Oh, how I envied it, lying in its happy mother's breast, and drawing life and gladness, and all its perpetual smilingness from that white and smiling breast. That infant saved me; but still gave me vague desirings. Now I first began to reflect in my mind; to endeavor after the recalling past things; but try as I would, little could I recall, but the bewilderingness;—and the stupor, and the torpor, and the blankness, and the dimness, and the vacant whirlingness of the bewilderingness. Let me be still again."

And the stepping on the floor above,—it then resumed.

V

"I must have been nine, or ten, or eleven years old, when the pleasant-looking woman carried me away from the large house. She was a farmer's wife; and now that was my residence, the farm-house. They taught me to sew, and work with wool, and spin the wool; I was nearly always busy now. This being busy, too, this it must have been, which partly brought to me the power of being sensible of myself as something human. Now I began to feel strange differences. When

I saw a snake trailing through the grass, and darting out the fire-fork from its mouth, I said to myself, That thing is not human, but I am human. When the lightning flashed, and split some beautiful tree, and left it to rot from all its greenness, I said, That lightning is not human, but I am human. And so with all other things. I can not speak coherently here; but somehow I felt that all good, harmless men and women were human things, placed at cross-purposes, in a world of snakes and lightnings, in a world of horrible and inscrutable inhumanities. I have had no training of any sort. All my thoughts well up in me; I know not whether they pertain to the old bewilderings or not; but as they are, they are, and I can not alter them, for I had nothing to do with putting them in my mind, and I never affect any thoughts, and I never adulterate any thoughts; but when I speak, think forth from the tongue, speech being sometimes before the thought; so, often, my own tongue teaches me new things.

"Now as yet I never had questioned the woman, or her husband, or the young girls, their children, why I had been brought to the house, or how long I was to stay in the house. There I was; just as I found myself in the world; there I was; for what cause I had been brought into the world, would have been no stranger question to me, than for what cause I had been brought to the house. I knew nothing of myself, or any thing pertaining to myself; I felt my pulse, my thought; but other things I was ignorant of, except the general feeling of my humanness among the inhumanities. But as I grew older, I expanded in my mind. I began to learn things out of me; to see still stranger, and minuter differences. I called the woman mother, and so did the other girls; yet the woman often kissed them, but seldom me. She always helped them first at table. The farmer scarcely ever spoke to me. Now months, years rolled on, and the young girls began to stare at me. Then the bewilderingness of the old starings of the solitary old man and old woman, by the cracked hearth-stone of the desolate old house, in the desolate, round, open space; the bewilderingness of those old starings now returned to me; and the green starings, and the serpent hissings of the uncompanionable cat, recurred to me, and the feeling of the infinite forlornness of my life rolled over me. But the woman was very kind to me; she taught the girls not to be cruel to me; she would call me to her, and speak cheerfully to me, and I thanked—not God, for I had been taught no God—I thanked the bright human summer, and the joyful human sun in the sky; I thanked the human summer and the sun, that they had given me the woman; and I would sometimes steal away into the beautiful grass, and worship the kind summer and the sun; and often say over to myself the soft words, summer and the sun.

"Still, weeks and years ran on, and my hair began to vail me with its fullness and its length; and now often I heard the word beautiful, spoken of my hair, and beautiful, spoken of myself. They would not say the word openly to me, but I would by chance overhear them whispering it. The word joyed me with the human feeling of it. They were wrong not to say it openly to me; my joy would have been so much the more assured for the openness of their saying beautiful, to me; and I know it would have filled me with all conceivable kindness toward every one. Now I had heard the word beautiful, whispered, now and then, for some months, when a new being came to the house; they called him gentleman. His face was wonderful to me. Something strangely like it, and yet again unlike it, I had seen before, but where, I could not tell. But one day, looking into the smooth water behind the house, there I saw the likeness—something strangely like, and yet unlike, the likeness of his face. This filled me with puzzlings. The new being, the gentleman, he was very gracious to me; he seemed astonished, confounded at me; he looked at me, then at a very little, round picture—so it seemed—which he took from his pocket, and yet concealed from me. Then he kissed me, and looked with tenderness and grief upon me; and I felt a tear fall on me from him. Then he whispered a word into my ear. 'Father,' was the word he whispered; the same word by which the young girls called the farmer. Then I knew it was the word of kindness and of kisses. I kissed the gentleman.

"When he left the house I wept for him to come again. And he did come again. All called him my father now. He came to see me once every month or two; till at last he came not at all; and when I wept and asked for him, they said the word *Dead* to me. Then the bewilderings of the comings and the goings of the coffins at the large and populous house; these bewilderings came over me. What was it to be dead? What is it to be living? Wherein is the difference between the words Death and Life? Had I been ever dead? Was I living? Let me be still again. Do not speak to me."

And the stepping on the floor above; again it did resume.

"Months ran on; and now I somehow learned that my father had every now and then sent money to the woman to keep me with her in the house; and that no more money had come to her after he was dead; the last penny of the former money was now gone. Now the farmer's wife looked troubledly and painfully at me; and the farmer looked unpleasantly and impatiently at me. I felt that something was miserably wrong; I said to myself, I am one too many; I must go away from the pleasant house. Then the bewilderings of all the loneliness and forlornness of all my forlorn and lonely life; all these bewilderings and the whelmings of the bewilderings rolled over me; and I sat down without the house, but could not weep.

"But I was strong, and I was a grown girl now. I said to the woman—Keep me hard at work; let me work all the time, but let me stay with thee. But the other girls were sufficient to do the work; me they wanted not. The farmer looked out of his eyes at me, and the out-lookings of his eyes said plainly to me—Thee we do not want; go from us; thou art one too many; and thou art more than one too many. Then I said to the woman—Hire me out to some one; let me work for some one.—But I spread too wide my little story. I must make an end.

"The woman listened to me, and through her means I went to live at another house, and earned wages there. My work was milking the cows, and making butter, and spinning wool, and weaving carpets of thin strips of cloth. One day there came to this house a pedler. In his wagon he had a guitar, an old guitar, yet a very pretty one, but with broken strings. He had got it slyly in part exchange from the servants of a grand house some distance off. Spite of the broken strings, the thing looked very graceful and beautiful to me; and I knew there was melodiousness lurking in the thing, though I had never seen a guitar before, nor heard of one; but there was a strange humming in my heart that seemed to prophesy of the hummings of the guitar. Intuitively, I knew that the strings were not as they should be. I said to the man—I will buy of thee the thing thou callest a guitar. But thou must put new strings to it. So he went to search for them; and brought the strings, and restringing the guitar, tuned it for me. So with part of my earnings I bought the guitar. Straightway I took it to my little chamber in the gable, and softly laid it on my bed. Then I murmured; sung and murmured to it; very lowly, very softly; I could hardly hear myself. And I changed the modulations of my singings and my murmurings; and still sung, and murmured, lowly, softly,—more and more; and presently I heard a sudden sound: sweet and low beyond all telling was the sweet and sudden sound. I clapt my hands; the guitar was speaking to me; the dear guitar was singing to me; murmuring and singing to me, the guitar. Then I sung and murmured to it with a still different modulation; and once more it answered me from a different string; and once more it murmured to me, and it answered to me with a different string. The guitar was human; the guitar taught me the secret of the guitar; the guitar learned me to play on the guitar. No musicmaster have I ever had but the guitar. I made a loving friend of it; a heart friend of it. It sings to me as I to it. Love is not all on one side with my guitar. All the wonders that are unimaginable and unspeakable; all these wonders are translated in the mysterious melodiousness of the guitar. It knows all my past history. Sometimes it plays to me the mystic visions of the confused large house I never name. Sometimes it brings to me the bird-twitterings in the air; and sometimes it strikes up in me rapturous pulsations of legendary delights eternally unexperienced and unknown to me. Bring me the guitar."

vi

Entranced, lost, as one wandering bedazzled and amazed among innumerable dancing lights, Pierre had motionlessly listened to this abundant-haired, and large-eyed girl of mystery.

"Bring me the guitar!"

Starting from his enchantment, Pierre gazed round the room, and saw the instrument leaning against a corner. Silently he brought it to the girl, and silently sat down again.

"Now listen to the guitar; and the guitar shall sing to thee the sequel of my story; for not in words can it be spoken. So listen to the guitar."

Instantly the room was populous with sounds of melodiousness, and mournfulness, and wonderfulness; the room swarmed with the unintelligible but delicious sounds. The sounds seemed waltzing in the room; the sounds hung pendulous like glittering icicles from the corners of the room; and fell upon him with a ringing silveryness; and were drawn up again to the ceiling, and hung pendulous again, and dropt down upon him again with the ringing silveryness. Fire-flies seemed buzzing in the sounds; summer-lightnings seemed vividly yet softly audible in the sounds.

And still the wild girl played on the guitar; and her long dark shower of curls fell over it, and vailed it; and still, out from the vail came the swarming sweetness, and the utter unintelligibleness, but the infinite significancies of the sounds of the guitar.

"Girl of all-bewildering mystery!" cried Pierre—"Speak to me;—sister, if thou indeed canst be a thing that's mortal—speak to me, if thou be Isabel!"

> "Mystery! Mystery!
> Mystery of Isabel!
> Mystery! Mystery!
> Isabel and Mystery!"

Among the waltzings, and the droppings, and the swarmings of the sounds, Pierre now heard the tones above deftly stealing and winding among the myriad serpentinings of the other melody:—deftly stealing and winding as respected the instrumental sounds, but in themselves wonderfully and abandonedly free and bold—bounding and rebounding as from multitudinous reciprocal walls; while with every syllable the hair-shrouded form of Isabel swayed to and fro with a like abandonment, and suddenness, and wantonness:—then it seemed not like any song; seemed not issuing from any

mouth; but it came forth from beneath the same vail concealing the guitar.

Now a strange wild heat burned upon his brow; he put his
hand to it. Instantly the music changed; and drooped and
changed; and changed and changed; and lingeringly retreated
as it changed; and at last was wholly gone.

Pierre was the first to break the silence.

"Isabel, thou hast filled me with such wonderings; I am so
distraught with thee, that the particular things I had to tell to
thee, when I hither came; these things I can not now recall,
to speak them to thee:—I feel that something is still unsaid
by thee, which at some other time thou wilt reveal. But now
I can stay no longer with thee. Know me eternally as thy
loving, revering, and most marveling brother, who will never
desert thee, Isabel. Now let me kiss thee and depart, till to-
morrow night; when I shall open to thee all my mind, and all
my plans concerning me and thee. Let me kiss thee, and
adieu!"

As full of unquestioning and unfaltering faith in him, the
girl sat motionless and heard him out. Then silently rose, and
turned her boundlessly confiding brow to him. He kissed it
thrice, and without another syllable left the place.

Book VII

NOT IMMEDIATELY, not for a long time, could Pierre fully, or by any approximation, realize the scene which he had just departed. But the vague revelation was now in him, that the visible world, some of which before had seemed but too common and prosaic to him; and but too intelligible; he now vaguely felt, that all the world, and every misconceivedly common and prosaic thing in it, was steeped a million fathoms in a mysteriousness wholly hopeless of solution. First, the enigmatical story of the girl, and the profound sincerity of it, and yet the ever accompanying haziness, obscurity, and almost miraculousness of it;—first, this wonderful story of the girl had displaced all commonness and prosaicness from his soul; and then, the inexplicable spell of the guitar, and the subtleness of the melodious appealings of the few brief words from Isabel sung in the conclusion of the melody—all this had bewitched him, and enchanted him, till he had sat motionless and bending over, as a tree-transformed and mystery-laden visitant, caught and fast bound in some necromancer's garden.

But as now burst from these sorceries, he hurried along the open road, he strove for the time to dispel the mystic feeling, or at least postpone it for a while, until he should have time to rally both body and soul from the more immediate consequences of that day's long fastings and wanderings, and that night's never-to-be-forgotten scene. He now endeavored to beat away all thoughts from him, but of present bodily needs.

Passing through the silent village, he heard the clock tell the mid hour of night. Hurrying on, he entered the mansion by a private door, the key of which hung in a secret outer place. Without undressing, he flung himself upon the bed. But remembering himself again, he rose and adjusted his alarm-clock, so that it would emphatically repeat the hour of five. Then to bed again, and driving off all intrudings of thoughtfulness, and resolutely bending himself to slumber, he by-and-by fell into its at first reluctant, but at last welcoming and hospitable arms. At five he rose; and in the east saw the first spears of the advanced-guard of the day.

It had been his purpose to go forth at that early hour, and so avoid all casual contact with any inmate of the mansion, and spend the entire day in a second wandering in the woods, as the only fit prelude to the society of so wild a being as his new-found sister Isabel. But the familiar home-sights of his chamber strangely worked upon him. For an instant, he almost could have prayed Isabel back into the wonder-world from which she had so slidingly emerged. For an instant, the fond, all-understood blue eyes of Lucy displaced the as tender, but mournful and inscrutable dark glance of Isabel. He seemed placed between them, to choose one or the other; then both seemed his; but into Lucy's eyes there stole half of the mournfulness of Isabel's, without diminishing hers.

Again the faintness, and the long life-weariness benumbed him. He left the mansion, and put his bare forehead against the restoring wind. He re-entered the mansion, and adjusted the clock to repeat emphatically the call of seven; and then lay upon his bed. But now he could not sleep. At seven he changed his dress; and at half-past eight went below to meet his mother at the breakfast table, having a little before overheard her step upon the stair.

ii

He saluted her; but she looked gravely and yet alarmedly, and then in a sudden, illy-repressed panic, upon him. Then he knew he must be wonderfully changed. But his mother spoke not to him, only to return his good-morning. He saw that she was deeply offended with him, on many accounts; moreover, that she was vaguely frightened about him, and finally that notwithstanding all this, her stung pride conquered all apprehensiveness in her; and he knew his mother well enough to be very certain that, though he should unroll a magician's parchment before her now, she would verbally express no interest, and seek no explanation from him. Nevertheless, he could not entirely abstain from testing the power of her reservedness.

"I have been quite an absentee, sister Mary," said he, with ill-affected pleasantness.

"Yes, Pierre. How does the coffee suit you this morning? It is some new coffee."

"It is very nice; very rich and odorous, sister Mary."

"I am glad you find it so, Pierre."

"Why don't you call me brother Pierre?"

"Have I not called you so? Well, then, brother Pierre,—is that better?"

"Why do you look so indifferently and icily upon me, sister Mary?"

"Do I look indifferently and icily? Then I will endeavor to look otherwise. Give me the toast there, Pierre."

"You are very deeply offended at me, my dear mother."

"Not in the slightest degree, Pierre. Have you seen Lucy lately?"

"I have not, my mother."

"Ah! A bit of salmon, Pierre."

"You are too proud to show toward me what you are this moment feeling, my mother."

Mrs. Glendinning slowly rose to her feet, and her full stature of womanly beauty and majesty stood imposingly over him.

"Tempt me no more, Pierre. I will ask no secret from thee; all shall be voluntary between us, as it ever has been, until very lately, or all shall be nothing between us. Beware of me, Pierre. There lives not that being in the world of whom thou hast more reason to beware, so you continue but a little longer to act thus with me."

She reseated herself, and spoke no more. Pierre kept silence; and after snatching a few mouthfuls of he knew not what, silently quitted the table, and the room, and the mansion.

iii

As the door of the breakfast-room closed upon Pierre, Mrs. Glendinning rose, her fork unconsciously retained in her hand. Presently, as she paced the room in deep, rapid thought, she became conscious of something strange in her grasp, and without looking at it, to mark what it was, impulsively flung it from her. A dashing noise was heard, and then a quivering. She turned; and hanging by the side of Pierre's portrait, she saw her own smiling picture pierced through, and the fork, whose silver tines had caught in the painted bosom, vibratingly rankled in the wound.

She advanced swiftly to the picture, and stood intrepidly before it.

"Yes, thou art stabbed! but the wrong hand stabbed thee; this should have been *thy* silver blow," turning to Pierre's portrait face. "Pierre, Pierre, thou hast stabbed me with a poisoned point. I feel my blood chemically changing in me. I, the mother of the only surnamed Glendinning, I feel now as though I had borne the last of a swiftly to be extinguished race. For swiftly to be extinguished is that race, whose only heir but so much as impends upon a deed of shame. And some deed of shame, or something most dubious and most dark, is in thy soul, or else some belying specter, with a cloudy, shame-faced front, sat at yon seat but now! What can it be? Pierre, unbosom. Smile not so lightly upon my heavy grief. Answer; what is it, boy? Can it? can it? no—yes— surely—can it? it can not be! But he was not at Lucy's yesterday; nor was she here; and she would not see me when I called. What can this bode? But not a mere broken match— broken as lovers sometimes break, to mend the break with joyful tears, so soon again—not a mere broken match can break my proud heart so. If that indeed be part, it is not all. But no, no, no; it can not, can not be. He would not, could not, do so mad, so impious a thing. It was a most surprising face, though I confessed it not to him, nor even hinted that I saw it. But no, no, no, it can not be. Such young peerlessness in such humbleness, can not have an honest origin. Lilies are not stalked on weeds, though polluted, they sometimes may stand among them. She must be both poor and vile—some chance-blow of a splendid, worthless rake, doomed to inherit both parts of her infecting portion—vileness and beauty. No, I will not think it of him. But what then? Sometimes I have feared that my pride would work me some woe incurable, by closing both my lips, and varnishing all my front, where I perhaps ought to be wholly in the melted and invoking mood. But who can get at one's own heart, to mend it? Right one's self against another, that, one may sometimes do; but when that other is one's own self, these ribs forbid. Then I will live my nature out. I will stand on pride. I will not budge. Let come what will, I shall not half-way run to meet it, to beat it off. Shall a mother abase herself before her stripling boy? Let him tell me of himself, or let him slide adown!"

iv

Pierre plunged deep into the woods, and paused not for several miles; paused not till he came to a remarkable stone, or rather, smoothed mass of rock, huge as a barn, which, wholly isolated horizontally, was yet sweepingly overarched by beech-trees and chestnuts.

It was shaped something like a lengthened egg, but flattened more; and, at the ends, pointed more; and yet not pointed, but irregularly wedge-shaped. Somewhere near the middle of its under side, there was a lateral ridge; and an obscure point of this ridge rested on a second lengthwise-sharpened rock, slightly protruding from the ground. Beside that one obscure and minute point of contact, the whole enormous and most ponderous mass touched not another object in the wide terraqueous world. It was a breathless thing to see. One broad haunched end hovered within an inch of the soil, all along to the point of teetering contact; but yet touched not the soil. Many feet from that—beneath one part of the opposite end, which was all seamed and half-riven— the vacancy was considerably larger, so as to make it not only possible, but convenient to admit a crawling man; yet no mortal being had ever been known to have the intrepid heart to crawl there.

It might well have been the wonder of all the country round. But strange to tell, though hundreds of cottage hearthstones—where, of long winter-evenings, both old men smoked their pipes and young men shelled their corn—surrounded it, at no very remote distance, yet had the youthful Pierre been the first known publishing discoverer of this stone, which he had thereupon fancifully christened the Memnon Stone. Possibly, the reason why this singular object had so long remained unblazoned to the world, was not so much because it had never before been lighted on—though indeed, both belted and topped by the dense deep luxuriance of the aboriginal forest, it lay like Captain Kidd's sunken hull in the gorge of the river Hudson's Highlands,—its crown being full eight fathoms under high-foliage mark during the great spring-tide of foliage;—and besides this, the cottagers had no special motive for visiting its more immediate vicinity at all; their timber and fuel being obtained from more accessible woodlands—as because, even, if any of the simple people should have chanced to have beheld it, they, in their hood-winked unappreciativeness, would not have accounted it any very marvelous sight, and therefore, would never have thought it worth their while to publish it abroad. So that in real truth, they might have seen it, and yet afterward have forgotten so inconsiderable a circumstance. In short, this wondrous Memnon Stone could be no Memnon Stone to them; nothing but a huge stumbling-block, deeply to be regretted as a vast prospective obstacle in the way of running a handy little cross-road through that wild part of the Manor.

Now one day while reclining near its flank, and intently eying it, and thinking how surprising it was, that in so long-settled a country he should have been the first discerning and appreciative person to light upon such a great natural curiosity, Pierre happened to brush aside several successive layers of old, gray-haired, close cropped, nappy moss, and beneath, to his no small amazement, he saw rudely hammered in the rock some half-obliterate initials—"S. yͤ W." Then he knew, that ignorant of the stone, as all the simple country round might immemorially have been, yet was not himself the only human being who had discovered that marvelous impending spectacle: but long and long ago, in quite another age, the stone had been beheld, and its wonderfulness fully appreciated—as the painstaking initials seemed to testify—by some departed man, who, were he now alive, might possibly wag a beard old as the most venerable oak of centuries' growth. But who,—who in Methuselah's name,—who might have been this "S. yͤ W.?" Pierre pondered long, but could not possibly imagine; for the initials, in their antiqueness, seemed to point to some period before the era of Columbus' discovery of the hemisphere. Happening in the end to mention the strange matter of these initials to a white-haired old gentleman, his city kinsman, who, after a long and richly varied, but unfortunate life, had at last found great solace in the Old Testament, which he was continually studying with ever-increasing admiration; this white-haired old kinsman, after having learnt all the particulars about the stone—its bulk, its height, the precise angle of its critical impendings, and all that,—and then, after much prolonged cogitation upon it, and several long-drawn sighs, and aged looks of hoar significance, and reading certain verses in Ecclesiastes; after all these tedious preliminaries, this not-at-all-to-be-hurried white-haired old kinsman, had laid his tremulous hand upon Pierre's firm young shoulder, and slowly whispered—"Boy; 'tis Solomon the Wise." Pierre could not repress a merry laugh at this; wonderfully diverted by what seemed to him so queer and crotchety a conceit; which he imputed to the alledged dotage of his venerable kinsman, who he well knew had once maintained, that the old Scriptural Ophir was somewhere on our northern sea-coast; so no wonder the old gentleman should fancy that King Solomon might have taken a trip—as a sort of amateur supercargo—of some Tyre or Sidon gold-ship across the water, and happened to light on the Memnon Stone, while rambling about with bow and quiver shooting partridges.

But merriment was by no means Pierre's usual mood when thinking of this stone; much less when seated in the woods, he, in the profound significance of that deep forest silence, viewed its marvelous impendings. A flitting conceit had often crossed him, that he would like nothing better for a headstone than this same imposing pile; in which, at times, during the soft swayings of the surrounding foliage, there seemed to lurk some mournful and lamenting plaint, as for some sweet boy long since departed in the antediluvian time.

Not only might this stone well have been the wonder of the simple country round, but it might well have been its terror. Sometimes, wrought to a mystic mood by contemplating its ponderous inscrutableness, Pierre had called it the Terror Stone. Few could be bribed to climb its giddy height, and crawl out upon its more hovering end. It seemed as if the dropping of one seed from the beak of the smallest flying bird would topple the immense mass over, crashing against the trees.

It was a very familiar thing to Pierre; he had often climbed it, by placing long poles against it, and so creeping up to where it sloped in little crumbling stepping-places; or by climbing high up the neighboring beeches, and then lowering himself down upon the forehead-like summit by the elastic branches. But never had he been fearless enough—or rather fool-hardy enough, it may be, to crawl on the ground beneath the vacancy of the higher end; that spot first menaced by the Terror Stone should it ever really topple.

V

Yet now advancing steadily, and as if by some interior pre-determination, and eying the mass unfalteringly; he then threw himself prone upon the wood's last year's leaves, and slid himself straight into the horrible interspace, and lay there as dead. He spoke not, for speechless thoughts were in him. These gave place at last to things less and less unspeakable; till at last, from beneath the very brow of the beetlings and the menacings of the Terror Stone came the audible words of Pierre:—

"If the miseries of the undisclosable things in me, shall ever unhorse me from my manhood's seat; if to vow myself all Virtue's and all Truth's, be but to make a trembling, dis-trusted slave of me; if Life is to prove a burden I can not bear without ignominious cringings; if indeed our actions are all foreordained, and we are Russian serfs to Fate; if invisible devils do titter at us when we most nobly strive; if Life be a cheating dream, and Virtue as unmeaning and unsequeled with any blessing as the midnight mirth of wine; if by sacri-ficing myself for Duty's sake, my own mother re-sacrifices me; if Duty's self be but a bugbear, and all things are allow-able and unpunishable to man;—then do thou, Mute Mas-siveness, fall on me! Ages thou hast waited; and if these things be thus, then wait no more; for whom better canst thou crush than him who now lies here invoking thee?"

A down-darting bird, all song, swiftly lighted on the un-moved and eternally immovable balancings of the Terror Stone, and cheerfully chirped to Pierre. The tree-boughs bent and waved to the rushes of a sudden, balmy wind; and slowly Pierre crawled forth, and stood haughtily upon his feet, as he owed thanks to none, and went his moody way.

vi

When in his imaginative ruminating moods of early youth, Pierre had christened the wonderful stone by the old resound-ing name of Memnon, he had done so merely from certain associative remembrances of that Egyptian marvel, of which all Eastern travelers speak. And when the fugitive thought had long ago entered him of desiring that same stone for his head-stone, when he should be no more; then he had only yielded to one of those innumerable fanciful notions, tinged with dreamy painless melancholy, which are frequently sug-gested to the mind of a poetic boy. But in after-times, when placed in far different circumstances from those surrounding him at the Meadows, Pierre pondered on the stone, and his young thoughts concerning it, and, later, his desperate act in crawling under it; then an immense significance came to him, and the long-passed unconscious movements of his then youthful heart, seemed now prophetic to him, and allegori-cally verified by the subsequent events.

For, not to speak of the other and subtler meanings which lie crouching behind the colossal haunches of this stone, re-garded as the menacingly impending Terror Stone—hidden to all the simple cottagers, but revealed to Pierre—consider its aspects as the Memnon Stone. For Memnon was that dewey, royal boy, son of Aurora, and born King of Egypt, who, with enthusiastic rashness flinging himself on another's account into a rightful quarrel, fought hand to hand with his overmatch, and met his boyish and most dolorous death be-neath the walls of Troy. His wailing subjects built a monu-ment in Egypt to commemorate his untimely fate. Touched by the breath of the bereaved Aurora, every sunrise that statue gave forth a mournful broken sound, as of a harp-string suddenly sundered, being too harshly wound.

Herein lies an unsummed world of grief. For in this plaintive fable we find embodied the Hamletism of the antique
world; the Hamletism of three thousand years ago: "The
flower of virtue cropped by a too rare mischance." And the
English Tragedy is but Egyptian Memnon, Montaignized and
modernized; for being but a mortal man Shakspeare had his
fathers too.

Now as the Memnon Statue survives down to this present
day, so does that nobly-striving but ever-shipwrecked character in some royal youths (for both Memnon and Hamlet were
the sons of kings), of which that statue is the melancholy
type. But Memnon's sculptured woes did once melodiously
resound; now all is mute. Fit emblem that of old, poetry was
a consecration and an obsequy to all hapless modes of human
life; but in a bantering, barren, and prosaic, heartless age, Aurora's music-moan is lost among our drifting sands, which
whelm alike the monument and the dirge.

vii

As Pierre went on through the woods, all thoughts now
left him but those investing Isabel. He strove to condense her
mysterious haze into some definite and comprehensible shape.
He could not but infer that the feeling of bewilderment,
which she had so often hinted of during their interview, had
caused her continually to go aside from the straight line of
her narration; and finally to end it in an abrupt and enigmatical obscurity. But he also felt assured, that as this was entirely
unintended, and now, doubtless, regretted by herself, so their
coming second interview would help to clear up much of this
mysteriousness; considering that the elapsing interval would
do much to tranquilize her, and rally her into less of wonderfulness to him; he did not therefore so much accuse his un-
thinkingness in naming the postponing hour he had. For,
indeed, looking from the morning down the vista of the day,
it seemed as indefinite and interminable to him. He could not
bring himself to confront any face or house; a plowed field,
any sign of tillage, the rotted stump of a long-felled pine, the
slightest passing trace of man was uncongenial and repelling

to him. Likewise in his own mind all remembrances and imaginings that had to do with the common and general humanity had become, for the time, in the most singular manner distasteful to him. Still, while thus loathing all that was common in the two different worlds—that without, and that within—nevertheless, even in the most withdrawn and subtlest region of his own essential spirit, Pierre could not now find one single agreeable twig of thought whereon to perch his weary soul.

Men in general seldom suffer from this utter pauperism of the spirit. If God hath not blessed them with incurable frivolity, men in general have still some secret thing of self-conceit or virtuous gratulation; men in general have always done some small self-sacrificing deed for some other man; and so, in those now and then recurring hours of despondent lassitude, which must at various and differing intervals overtake almost every civilized human being; such persons straightway bethink them of their one, or two, or three small self-sacrificing things, and suck respite, consolation, and more or less compensating deliciousness from it. But with men of self-disdainful spirits; in whose chosen souls heaven itself hath by a primitive persuasion unindoctrinally fixed that most true Christian doctrine of the utter nothingness of good works; the casual remembrance of their benevolent well-doings, does never distill one drop of comfort for them, even as (in harmony with the correlative Scripture doctrine) the recalling of their outlived errors and misdeeds, conveys to them no slightest pang or shadow of reproach.

Though the clew-defying mysteriousness of Isabel's narration, did now for the time, in this particular mood of his, put on a repelling aspect to our Pierre; yet something must occupy the soul of man; and Isabel was nearest to him then; and Isabel he thought of; at first, with great discomfort and with pain, but anon (for heaven eventually rewards the resolute and duteous thinker) with lessening repugnance, and at last with still-increasing willingness and congenialness. Now he recalled his first impressions, here and there, while she was rehearsing to him her wild tale; he recalled those swift but mystical corroborations in his own mind and memory, which by shedding another twinkling light upon her history, had but increased its mystery, while at the same time remarkably substantiating it.

Her first recallable recollection was of an old deserted chateau-like house in a strange, French-like country, which she dimly imagined to be somewhere beyond the sea. Did not this surprisingly correspond with certain natural inferences to be drawn from his Aunt Dorothea's account of the disappearance of the French young lady? Yes; the French young lady's disappearance on this side the water was only contingent upon her reappearance on the other; then he shuddered as he darkly pictured the possible sequel of her life, and the wresting from her of her infant, and its immurement in the savage mountain wilderness.

But Isabel had also vague impressions of herself crossing the sea;— *re*crossing, emphatically thought Pierre, as he pondered on the unbidden conceit, that she had probably first unconsciously and smuggledly crossed it hidden beneath her sorrowing mother's heart. But in attempting to draw any inferences, from what he himself had ever heard, for a coinciding proof or elucidation of this assumption of Isabel's actual crossing the sea at so tender an age; here Pierre felt all the inadequateness of both his own and Isabel's united knowledge, to clear up the profound mysteriousness of her early life. To the certainty of this irremovable obscurity he bowed himself, and strove to dismiss it from his mind, as worse than hopeless. So, also, in a good degree, did he endeavor to drive out of him, Isabel's reminiscence of the, to her, unnameable large house, from which she had been finally removed by the pleasant woman in the coach. This episode in her life, above all other things, was most cruelly suggestive to him, as possibly involving his father in the privity to a thing, at which Pierre's inmost soul fainted with amazement and abhorrence. Here the helplessness of all further light, and the eternal impossibility of logically exonerating his dead father, in his own mind, from the liability to this, and many other of the blackest self-insinuated suppositions; all this came over Pierre with a power so infernal and intense, that it could only have proceeded from the unretarded malice of the Evil One himself. But subtilly and wantonly as these conceits stole into him,

Pierre as subtilly opposed them; and with the hue-and-cry of his whole indignant soul, pursued them forth again into the wide Tartarean realm from which they had emerged.

The more and the more that Pierre now revolved the story of Isabel in his mind, so much the more he amended his original idea, that much of its obscurity would depart upon a second interview. He saw, or seemed to see, that it was not so much Isabel who had by her wild idiosyncrasies mystified the narration of her history, as it was the essential and unavoidable mystery of her history itself, which had invested Isabel with such wonderful enigmas to him.

viii

The issue of these reconsiderings was the conviction, that all he could now reasonably anticipate from Isabel, in further disclosure on the subject of her life, were some few additional particulars bringing it down to the present moment; and, also, possibly filling out the latter portion of what she had already revealed to him. Nor here, could he persuade himself, that she would have much to say. Isabel had not been so digressive and withholding as he had thought. What more, indeed, could she now have to impart, except by what strange means she had at last come to find her brother out; and the dreary recital of how she had pecuniarily wrestled with her destitute condition; how she had come to leave one place of toiling refuge for another, till now he found her in humble servitude at farmer Ulver's? Is it possible then, thought Pierre, that there lives a human creature in this common world of every-days, whose whole history may be told in little less than two-score words, and yet embody in that smallness a fathomless fountain of ever-welling mystery? Is it possible, after all, that spite of bricks and shaven faces, this world we live in is brimmed with wonders, and I and all mankind, beneath our garbs of common-placeness, conceal enigmas that the stars themselves, and perhaps the highest seraphim can not resolve?

The intuitively certain, however literally unproven fact of Isabel's sisterhood to him, was a link that he now felt binding him to a before unimagined and endless chain of wondering.

His very blood seemed to flow through all his arteries with unwonted subtileness, when he thought that the same tide flowed through the mystic veins of Isabel. All his occasional pangs of dubiousness as to the grand governing thing of all— the reality of the physical relationship—only recoiled back upon him with added tribute of both certainty and insolubleness.

She is my sister—my own father's daughter. Well; why do I believe it? The other day I had not so much as heard the remotest rumor of her existence; and what has since occurred to change me? What so new and incontestable vouchers have I handled? None at all. But I have seen her. Well; grant it; I might have seen a thousand other girls, whom I had never seen before; but for that, I would not own any one among them for my sister. But the portrait, the chair-portrait, Pierre? Think of that. But that was painted before Isabel was born; what can that portrait have to do with Isabel? It is not the portrait of Isabel, it is my father's portrait; and yet my mother swears it is not he.

Now alive as he was to all these searching argumentative itemizings of the minutest known facts any way bearing upon the subject; and yet, at the same time, persuaded, strong as death, that in spite of them, Isabel was indeed his sister; how could Pierre, naturally poetic, and therefore piercing as he was; how could he fail to acknowledge the existence of that all-controlling and all-permeating wonderfulness, which, when imperfectly and isolatedly recognized by the generality, is so significantly denominated The Finger of God? But it is not merely the Finger, it is the whole outspread Hand of God; for doth not Scripture intimate, that He holdeth all of us in the hollow of His hand?—a Hollow, truly!

Still wandering through the forest, his eye pursuing its ever-shifting shadowy vistas; remote from all visible haunts and traces of that strangely wilful race, who, in the sordid traffickings of clay and mud, are ever seeking to denationalize the natural heavenliness of their souls; there came into the mind of Pierre, thoughts and fancies never imbibed within the gates of towns; but only given forth by the atmosphere of primeval forests, which, with the eternal ocean, are the only unchanged general objects remaining to this day, from those that originally met the gaze of Adam. For so it is, that the apparently most inflammable or evaporable of all earthly things, wood and water, are, in this view, immensely the most endurable.

Now all his ponderings, however excursive, wheeled round Isabel as their center; and back to her they came again from every excursion; and again derived some new, small germs for wonderment.

The question of Time occurred to Pierre. How old was Isabel? According to all reasonable inferences from the presumed circumstances of her life, she was his elder, certainly, though by uncertain years; yet her whole aspect was that of more than childlikeness; nevertheless, not only did he feel his muscular superiority to her, so to speak, which made him spontaneously alive to a feeling of elderly protectingness over her; not only did he experience the thoughts of superior world-acquaintance, and general cultured knowledge; but spite of reason's self, and irrespective of all mere computings, he was conscious of a feeling which independently pronounced him her senior in point of Time, and Isabel a child of everlasting youngness. This strange, though strong conceit of his mysterious persuasion, doubtless, had its untraced, and but little-suspected origin in his mind, from ideas born of his devout meditations upon the artless infantileness of her face; which, though profoundly mournful in the general expression, yet did not, by any means, for that cause, lose one whit in its singular infantileness; as the faces of real infants, in their earliest visibleness, do oft-times wear a look of deep and endless sadness. But it was not the sadness, nor indeed, strictly speaking, the infantileness of the face of Isabel which so singularly impressed him with the idea of her original and changeless youthfulness. It was something else; yet something which entirely eluded him.

Imaginatively exalted by the willing suffrages of all mankind into higher and purer realms than men themselves inhabit; beautiful women—those of them at least who are beautiful in soul as well as body—do, notwithstanding the relentless law of earthly fleetingness, still seem, for a long interval, mysteriously exempt from the incantations of decay; for as the outward loveliness touch by touch departs, the interior beauty touch by touch replaces that departing bloom, with charms, which, underivable from earth, possess the ineffaceableness of stars. Else, why at the age of sixty, have some women held in the strongest bonds of love and fealty, men young enough to be their grandsons? And why did all-seducing Ninon unintendingly break scores of hearts at seventy? It is because of the perennialness of womanly sweetness.

Out from the infantile, yet eternal mournfulness of the face of Isabel, there looked on Pierre that angelic childlikeness, which our Savior hints is the one only investiture of translated souls; for of such—even of little children—is the other world.

Now, unending as the wonderful rivers, which once bathed the feet of the primeval generations, and still remain to flow fast by the graves of all succeeding men, and by the beds of all now living; unending, ever-flowing, ran through the soul of Pierre, fresh and fresher, further and still further, thoughts of Isabel. But the more his thoughtful river ran, the more mysteriousness it floated to him; and yet the more certainty that the mysteriousness was unchangeable. In her life there was an unraveled plot; and he felt that unraveled it would eternally remain to him. No slightest hope or dream had he, that what was dark and mournful in her would ever be cleared up into some coming atmosphere of light and mirth. Like all youths, Pierre had conned his novel-lessons; had read more novels than most persons of his years; but their false, inverted attempts at systematizing eternally unsystemizable elements; their audacious, intermeddling impotency, in trying to unravel, and spread out, and classify, the more thin than gossamer threads which make up the complex web of life; these things over Pierre had no power now. Straight through their helpless miserableness he pierced; the one sensational truth in him, transfixed like beetles all the speculative lies in them. He saw that human life doth truly come from that, which all men are agreed to call by the name of *God*; and that it partakes of the unravelable inscrutableness of God. By infallible presentiment he saw, that not always doth life's beginning gloom conclude in gladness; that wedding-bells peal not ever in the last scene of life's fifth act; that while the countless tribes of common novels laboriously spin vails of mystery, only to complacently clear them up at last; and while the countless tribe of common dramas do but repeat the same; yet the profounder emanations of the human mind, intended to illustrate all that can be humanly known of human life; these never unravel their own intricacies, and have no proper endings; but in imperfect, unanticipated, and disappointing sequels (as mutilated stumps), hurry to abrupt intermergings with the eternal tides of time and fate.

So Pierre renounced all thought of ever having Isabel's dark-lantern illuminated to him. Her light was lidded, and the lid was locked. Nor did he feel a pang at this. By posting hither and thither among the reminiscences of his family, and craftily interrogating his remaining relatives on his father's side, he might possibly rake forth some few small grains of dubious and most unsatisfying things, which, were he that way strongly bent, would only serve the more hopelessly to cripple him in his practical resolves. He determined to pry not at all into this sacred problem. For him now the mystery of Isabel possessed all the bewitchingness of the mysterious vault of night, whose very darkness evokes the witchery.

The thoughtful river still ran on in him, and now it floated still another thing to him.

Though the letter of Isabel gushed with all a sister's sacred longings to embrace her brother, and in the most abandoned terms painted the anguish of her life-long estrangement from him; and though, in effect, it took vows to this,—that without his continual love and sympathy, further life for her was only fit to be thrown into the nearest unfathomed pool, or rushing stream; yet when the brother and the sister had encountered, according to the set appointment, none of these impassionedments had been repeated. She had more than thrice thanked God, and most earnestly blessed himself, that now he had come near to her in her loneliness; but no gesture of common and customary sisterly affection. Nay, from his embrace had she not struggled? nor kissed him once; nor had he kissed her, except when the salute was solely sought by him.

Now Pierre began to see mysteries interpierced with mysteries, and mysteries eluding mysteries; and began to seem to see the mere imaginariness of the so supposed solidest principle of human association. Fate had done this thing for them. Fate had separated the brother and the sister, till to each other they somehow seemed so not at all. Sisters shrink not from their brother's kisses. And Pierre felt that never, never would he be able to embrace Isabel with the mere brotherly embrace; while the thought of any other caress, which took hold of any domesticness, was entirely vacant from his uncontaminated soul, for it had never consciously intruded there.

Therefore, forever unsistered for him by the stroke of Fate, and apparently forever, and twice removed from the remotest possibility of that love which had drawn him to his Lucy; yet still the object of the ardentest and deepest emotions of his soul; therefore, to him, Isabel wholly soared out of the realms of mortalness, and for him became transfigured in the highest heaven of uncorrupted Love.

Book VIII

The Second Interview at the Farm-House, and the Second Part of the Story of Isabel • Their Immediate Impulsive Effect upon Pierre

H IS SECOND INTERVIEW with Isabel was more satisfying, but none the less affecting and mystical than the first, though in the beginning, to his no small surprise, it was far more strange and embarrassing.

As before, Isabel herself admitted him into the farm-house, and spoke no word to him till they were both seated in the room of the double casement, and himself had first addressed her. If Pierre had any way predetermined how to deport himself at the moment, it was to manifest by some outward token the utmost affection for his sister; but her rapt silence and that atmosphere of unearthliness which invested her, now froze him to his seat; his arms refused to open, his lips refused to meet in the fraternal kiss; while all the while his heart was overflowing with the deepest love, and he knew full well, that his presence was inexpressibly grateful to the girl. Never did love and reverence so intimately react and blend; never did pity so join with wonder in casting a spell upon the movements of his body, and impeding him in its command.

After a few embarrassed words from Pierre, and a brief reply, a pause ensued, during which not only was the slow, soft stepping overhead quite audible, as at intervals on the night before, but also some slight domestic sounds were heard from the adjoining room; and noticing the unconsciously interrogating expression of Pierre's face, Isabel thus spoke to him:

"I feel, my brother, that thou dost appreciate the peculiarity and the mystery of my life, and of myself, and therefore I am at rest concerning the possibility of thy misconstruing any of my actions. It is only when people refuse to admit the uncommonness of some persons and the circumstances surrounding them, that erroneous conceits are nourished, and their feelings pained. My brother, if ever I shall seem reserved and unembracing to thee, still thou must ever trust the heart of

Isabel, and permit no doubt to cross thee there. My brother, the sounds thou hast just overheard in yonder room, have suggested to thee interesting questions connected with myself. Do not speak; I fervently understand thee. I will tell thee upon what terms I have been living here; and how it is that I, a hired person, am enabled to receive thee in this seemly privacy; for as thou mayest very readily imagine, this room is not my own. And this reminds me also that I have yet some few further trifling things to tell thee respecting the circumstances which have ended in bestowing upon me so angelical a brother."

"I can not retain that word"—said Pierre, with earnest lowness, and drawing a little nearer to her—"of right, it only pertains to thee."

"My brother, I will now go on, and tell thee all that I think thou couldst wish to know, in addition to what was so dimly rehearsed last night. Some three months ago, the people of the distant farm-house, where I was then staying, broke up their household and departed for some Western country. No place immediately presented itself where my services were wanted, but I was hospitably received at an old neighbor's hearth, and most kindly invited to tarry there, till some employ should offer. But I did not wait for chance to help me; my inquiries resulted in ascertaining the sad story of Delly Ulver, and that through the fate which had overtaken her, her aged parents were not only plunged into the most poignant grief, but were deprived of the domestic help of an only daughter, a circumstance whose deep discomfort can not be easily realized by persons who have always been ministered to by servants. Though indeed my natural mood—if I may call it so, for want of a better term—was strangely touched by thinking that the misery of Delly should be the source of benefit to me; yet this had no practically operative effect upon me,—my most inmost and truest thoughts seldom have;— and so I came hither, and my hands will testify that I did not come entirely for naught. Now, my brother, since thou didst leave me yesterday, I have felt no small surprise, that thou didst not then seek from me, how and when I came to learn the name of Glendinning as so closely associated with myself; and how I came to know Saddle Meadows to be the family seat, and how I at last resolved upon addressing thee, Pierre, and none other; and to what may be attributed that very memorable scene in the sewing-circle at the Miss Pennies."

"I have myself been wondering at myself that these things should hitherto have so entirely absented themselves from my mind," responded Pierre;—"but truly, Isabel, thy all-abounding hair falls upon me with some spell which dismisses all ordinary considerations from me, and leaves me only sensible to the Nubian power in thine eyes. But go on, and tell me every thing and any thing. I desire to know all, Isabel, and yet, nothing which thou wilt not voluntarily disclose. I feel that already I know the pith of all; that already I feel toward thee to the very limit of all; and that, whatever remains for thee to tell me, can but corroborate and confirm. So go on, my dearest,—ay, my only sister."

Isabel fixed her wonderful eyes upon him with a gaze of long impassionment; then rose suddenly to her feet, and advanced swiftly toward him; but more suddenly paused, and reseated herself in silence, and continued so for a time, with her head averted from him, and mutely resting on her hand, gazing out of the open casement upon the soft heat-lightning, occasionally revealed there.

She resumed anon.

ii

"My brother, thou wilt remember that certain part of my story which in reference to my more childish years spent remote from here, introduced the gentleman—my—yes, *our* father, Pierre. I can not describe to thee, for indeed, I do not myself comprehend how it was, that though at the time I sometimes called him my father, and the people of the house also called him so, sometimes when speaking of him to me; yet—partly, I suppose, because of the extraordinary secludedness of my previous life—I did not then join in my mind with the word father, all those peculiar associations which the term ordinarily inspires in children. The word father only seemed a word of general love and endearment to me—little or nothing more; it did not seem to involve any claims of any sort, one way or the other. I did not ask the name of my father; for I could have had no motive to hear him named, except to individualize the person who was so peculiarly kind to me; and individualized in that way he already was, since he was generally called by us *the gentleman*, and sometimes *my father*. As I have no reason to suppose that had I then or afterward, questioned the people of the house as to what more particular name my father went by in the world, they would have at all disclosed it to me; and, indeed, since, for certain singular reasons, I now feel convinced that on that point they were pledged to secrecy; I do not know that I ever would have come to learn my father's name,—and by consequence, ever have learned the least shade or shadow of knowledge as to you, Pierre, or any of your kin—had it not been for the merest little accident, which early revealed it to me, though at the moment I did not know the value of that knowledge. The last time my father visited the house, he chanced to leave his handkerchief behind him. It was the farmer's wife who first discovered it. She picked it up, and fumbling at it a moment, as if rapidly examining the corners, tossed it to me, saying, 'Here, Isabel, here is the good gentleman's handkerchief; keep it for him now, till he comes to see little Bell again.' Gladly I caught the handkerchief, and put it into my bosom. It was a white one; and upon closely scanning it, I found a small line of fine faded yellowish writing in the middle of it. At that time I could not read either print or writing, so I was none the wiser then; but still, some secret instinct told me, that the woman would not so freely have given me the handkerchief, had she known there was any writing on it. I forbore questioning her on the subject; I waited till my father should return, to secretly question him. The handkerchief had become dusty by lying on the uncarpeted floor. I took it to the brook and washed it, and laid it out on the grass where none would chance to pass; and I ironed it under my little apron, so that none would be attracted to it, to look at it again. But my father never returned; so, in my grief, the handkerchief became the more and the more endeared to me; it absorbed many of the secret tears I wept in memory of my dear departed friend, whom, in my child-like ignorance, I then equally called *my father* and *the gentleman*. But when the impression of his death became a

fixed thing to me, then again I washed and dried and ironed
the precious memorial of him, and put it away where none
should find it but myself, and resolved never more to soil it
with my tears; and I folded it in such a manner, that the name
was invisibly buried in the heart of it, and it was like opening
a book and turning over many blank leaves before I came to
the mysterious writing, which I knew should be one day read
by me, without direct help from any one. Now I resolved to
learn my letters, and learn to read, in order that of myself I
might learn the meaning of those faded characters. No other
purpose but that only one, did I have in learning then to read.
I easily induced the woman to give me my little teachings,
and being uncommonly quick, and moreover, most eager to
learn, I soon mastered the alphabet, and went on to spelling,
and by-and-by to reading, and at last to the complete deci-
phering of the talismanic word—Glendinning. I was yet very
ignorant. *Glendinning*, thought I, what is that? It sounds
something like *gentleman*;—Glen-din-ning;—just as many
syllables as *gentleman*; and—G—it begins with the same letter; yes, it must mean *my father*. I will think of him by that
word now;—I will not think of the *gentleman*, but of *Glendinning*. When at last I removed from that house and went to
another, and still another, and as I still grew up and thought
more to myself, that word was ever humming in my head, I
saw it would only prove the key to more. But I repressed all
undue curiosity, if any such has ever filled my breast. I would
not ask of any one, who it was that had been Glendinning;
where he had lived; whether, ever any other girl or boy had
called him father as I had done. I resolved to hold myself in
perfect patience, as somehow mystically certain, that Fate
would at last disclose to me, of itself, and at the suitable time,
whatever Fate thought it best for me to know. But now, my
brother, I must go aside a little for a moment.—Hand me
the guitar."

Surprised and rejoiced thus far at the unanticipated newness, and the sweet lucidness and simplicity of Isabel's narrat-
ing, as compared with the obscure and marvelous revelations
of the night before, and all eager for her to continue her story
in the same limpid manner, but remembering into what a
wholly tumultuous and unearthly frame of mind the melodies

of her guitar had formerly thrown him; Pierre now, in handing the instrument to Isabel, could not entirely restrain something like a look of half-regret, accompanied rather strangely
with a half-smile of gentle humor. It did not pass unnoticed
by his sister, who receiving the guitar, looked up into his face
with an expression which would almost have been arch and
playful, were it not for the ever-abiding shadows cast from
her infinite hair into her unfathomed eyes, and redoubledly
shot back again from them.

"Do not be alarmed, my brother; and do not smile at me;
I am not going to play the Mystery of Isabel to thee to-night.
Draw nearer to me now. Hold the light near to me."

So saying she loosened some ivory screws of the guitar, so
as to open a peep lengthwise through its interior.

"Now hold it thus, my brother; thus; and see what thou
wilt see; but wait one instant till I hold the lamp." So saying,
as Pierre held the instrument before him as directed, Isabel
held the lamp so as to cast its light through the round sound-
ing-hole into the heart of the guitar.

"Now, Pierre, now."

Eagerly Pierre did as he was bid; but somehow felt disappointed, and yet surprised at what he saw. He saw the word
Isabel, quite legibly but still fadedly gilded upon a part of one
side of the interior, where it made a projecting curve.

"A very curious place thou hast chosen, Isabel, wherein to
have the ownership of the guitar engraved. How did ever any
person get in there to do it, I should like to know?"

The girl looked surprisedly at him a moment; then took
the instrument from him, and looked into it herself. She put
it down, and continued.

"I see, my brother, thou dost not comprehend. When one
knows every thing about any object, one is too apt to suppose
that the slightest hint will suffice to throw it quite as open to
any other person. *I* did not have the name gilded there, my
brother."

"How?" cried Pierre.

"The name was gilded there when I first got the guitar,
though then I did not know it. The guitar must have been
expressly made for some one by the name of Isabel; because

the lettering could only have been put there before the guitar was put together."

"Go on—hurry," said Pierre.

"Yes, one day, after I had owned it a long time, a strange whim came into me. Thou know'st that it is not at all uncommon for children to break their dearest playthings in order to gratify a half-crazy curiosity to find out what is in the hidden heart of them. So it is with children, sometimes. And, Pierre, I have always been, and feel that I must always continue to be a child, though I should grow to three score years and ten. Seized with this sudden whim, I unscrewed the part I showed thee, and peeped in, and saw 'Isabel.' Now I have not yet told thee, that from as early a time as I can remember, I have nearly always gone by the name of Bell. And at the particular time I now speak of, my knowledge of general and trivial matters was sufficiently advanced to make it quite a familiar thing to me, that Bell was often a diminutive for Isabella, or Isabel. It was therefore no very strange affair, that considering my age, and other connected circumstances at the time, I should have instinctively associated the word Isabel, found in the guitar, with my own abbreviated name, and so be led into all sorts of fancyings. They return upon me now. Do not speak to me."

She leaned away from him, toward the occasionally illuminated casement, in the same manner as on the previous night, and for a few moments seemed struggling with some wild bewilderment. But now she suddenly turned, and fully confronted Pierre with all the wonderfulness of her most surprising face.

"I am called woman, and thou, man, Pierre; but there is neither man nor woman about it. Why should I not speak out to thee? There is no sex in our immaculateness. Pierre, the secret name in the guitar even now thrills me through and through. Pierre, think! think! Oh, canst thou not comprehend? see it?—what I mean, Pierre? The secret name in the guitar thrills me, thrills me, whirls me, whirls me; so secret, wholly hidden, yet constantly carried about in it; unseen, unsuspected, always vibrating to the hidden heart-strings—broken heart-strings; oh, my mother, my mother, my mother!"

As the wild plaints of Isabel pierced into his bosom's core, they carried with them the first inkling of the extraordinary conceit, so vaguely and shrinkingly hinted at in her till now entirely unintelligible words.

She lifted her dry burning eyes of long-fringed fire to him.

"Pierre—I have no slightest proof—but the guitar was *hers*, I know, I feel it was. Say, did I not last night tell thee, how it first sung to me upon the bed, and answered me, without my once touching it? and how it always sung to me and answered me, and soothed and loved me,—Hark now; thou shalt hear my mother's spirit."

She carefully scanned the strings, and tuned them carefully; then placed the guitar in the casement-bench, and knelt before it; and in low, sweet, and changefully modulated notes, so barely audible, that Pierre bent over to catch them; breathed the word *mother, mother, mother!* There was profound silence for a time; when suddenly, to the lowest and least audible note of all, the magical untouched guitar responded with a quick spark of melody, which in the following hush, long vibrated and subsidingly tingled through the room; while to his augmented wonder, he now espied, quivering along the metallic strings of the guitar, some minute scintillations, seemingly caught from the instrument's close proximity to the occasionally irradiated window.

The girl still kept kneeling; but an altogether unwonted expression suddenly overcast her whole countenance. She darted one swift glance at Pierre; and then with a single toss of her hand tumbled her unrestrained locks all over her, so that they tent-wise invested her whole kneeling form close to the floor, and yet swept the floor with their wild redundancy. Never Saya of Limeean girl, at dim mass in St. Dominic's cathedral, so completely muffled the human figure. To Pierre, the deep oaken recess of the double-casement, before which Isabel was kneeling, seemed now the immediate vestibule of some awful shrine, mystically revealed through the obscurely open window, which ever and anon was still softly illumined by the mild heat-lightnings and ground-lightnings, that wove their wonderfulness without, in the unsearchable air of that ebonly warm and most noiseless summer night.

Some unsubduable word was on Pierre's lip, but a sudden voice from out the vail bade him be silent.

"Mother—mother—mother!"

Again, after a preluding silence, the guitar as magically responded as before; the sparks quivered along its strings; and again Pierre felt as in the immediate presence of the spirit.

"Shall I, mother?—Art thou ready? Wilt thou tell me?— Now? Now?"

These words were lowly and sweetly murmured in the same way with the word *mother*, being changefully varied in their modulations, till at the last *now*, the magical guitar again responded; and the girl swiftly drew it to her beneath her dark tent of hair. In this act, as the long curls swept over the strings of the guitar, the strange sparks—still quivering there—caught at those attractive curls; the entire casement was suddenly and wovenly illumined; then waned again; while now, in the succeeding dimness, every downward undulating wave and billow of Isabel's tossed tresses gleamed here and there like a tract of phosphorescent midnight sea; and, simultaneously, all the four winds of the world of melody broke loose; and again as on the previous night, only in a still more subtile, and wholly inexplicable way, Pierre felt himself surrounded by ten thousand sprites and gnomes, and his whole soul was swayed and tossed by supernatural tides; and again he heard the wondrous, rebounding, chanted words:

"Mystery! Mystery!
Mystery of Isabel!
Mystery! Mystery!
Isabel and Mystery!
Mystery!"

iii

Almost deprived of consciousness by the spell flung over him by the marvelous girl, Pierre unknowingly gazed away from her, as on vacancy; and when at last stillness had once more fallen upon the room—all except the stepping—and he recovered his self-possession, and turned to look where he might now be, he was surprised to see Isabel composedly, though avertedly, seated on the bench; the longer and fuller tresses of her now ungleaming hair flung back, and the guitar quietly leaning in the corner.

He was about to put some unconsidered question to her, but she half-anticipated it by bidding him, in a low, but nevertheless almost authoritative tone, not to make any allusion to the scene he had just beheld.

He paused, profoundly thinking to himself, and now felt certain that the entire scene, from the first musical invocation of the guitar, must have unpremeditatedly proceeded from a sudden impulse in the girl, inspired by the peculiar mood into which the preceding conversation, and especially the handling of the guitar under such circumstances, had irresistibly thrown her.

But that certain something of the preternatural in the scene, of which he could not rid his mind: — the, so to speak, voluntary and all but intelligent responsiveness of the guitar — its strangely scintillating strings — the so suddenly glorified head of Isabel; altogether, these things seemed not at the time entirely produced by customary or natural causes. To Pierre's dilated senses Isabel seemed to swim in an electric fluid; the vivid buckler of her brow seemed as a magnetic plate. Now first this night was Pierre made aware of what, in the superstitiousness of his rapt enthusiasm, he could not help believing was an extraordinary physical magnetism in Isabel. And — as it were derived from this marvelous quality thus imputed to her — he now first became vaguely sensible of a certain still more marvelous power in the girl over himself and his most interior thoughts and motions; — a power so hovering upon the confines of the invisible world, that it seemed more inclined that way than this; — a power which not only seemed irresistibly to draw him toward Isabel, but to draw him away from another quarter — wantonly as it were, and yet quite ignorantly and unintendingly; and, besides, without respect apparently to any thing ulterior, and yet again, only under cover of drawing him to her. For over all these things, and interfusing itself with the sparkling electricity in which she seemed to swim, was an ever-creeping and condensing haze of ambiguities. Often, in after-times with her, did he recall this first magnetic night, and would seem to see that she then had bound him to her by an extraordinary atmospheric spell—both physical and spiritual—which henceforth it had become impossible for him to break, but whose full potency he never recognized till long after he had become habituated to its sway. This spell seemed one with that Pantheistic master-spell, which eternally locks in mystery and in muteness the universal subject world, and the physical electricalness of Isabel seemed reciprocal with the heat-lightnings and the ground-lightnings nigh to which it had first become revealed to Pierre. She seemed molded from fire and air, and vivified at some Voltaic pile of August thunder-clouds heaped against the sunset.

The occasional sweet simplicity, and innocence, and humbleness of her story; her often serene and open aspect; her deep-seated, but mostly quiet, unobtrusive sadness, and that touchingness of her less unwonted tone and air;—these only the more signalized and contrastingly emphasized the profounder, subtler, and more mystic part of her. Especially did Pierre feel this, when after another silent interval, she now proceeded with her story in a manner so gently confiding, so entirely artless, so almost peasant-like in its simplicity, and dealing in some details so little sublimated in themselves, that it seemed well nigh impossible that this unassuming maid should be the same dark, regal being who had but just now bade Pierre be silent in so imperious a tone, and around whose wondrous temples the strange electric glory had been playing. Yet not very long did she now thus innocently proceed, ere, at times, some fainter flashes of her electricalness came from her, but only to be followed by such melting, human, and most feminine traits as brought all his soft, enthusiast tears into the sympathetic but still unshedding eyes of Pierre.

iv

"Thou rememberest, my brother, my telling thee last night, how the—the—thou knowest what I mean—*that, there*"—avertedly pointing to the guitar; "thou rememberest how it came into my possession. But perhaps I did not tell thee, that the pedler said he had got it in barter from the servants of a great house some distance from the place where I was then residing."

Pierre signed his acquiescence, and Isabel proceeded.

"Now, at long though stated intervals, that man passed the farm-house in his trading route between the small towns and villages. When I discovered the gilding in the guitar, I kept watch for him; for though I truly felt persuaded that Fate had the dispensing of her own secrets in her own good time; yet I also felt persuaded that in some cases Fate drops us one little hint, leaving our own minds to follow it up, so that we of ourselves may come to the grand secret in reserve. So I kept diligent watch for him; and the next time he stopped, without permitting him at all to guess my motives, I contrived to steal out of him what great house it was from which the guitar had come. And, my brother, it was the mansion of Saddle Meadows."

Pierre started, and the girl went on:

"Yes, my brother, Saddle Meadows; 'old General Glendinning's place,' he said; 'but the old hero's long dead and gone now; and—the more's the pity—so is the young General, his son, dead and gone; but then there is a still younger grandson General left; that family always keep the title and the name a-going; yes, even to the christian name,—Pierre. Pierre Glendinning was the white-haired old General's name, who fought in the old French and Indian wars; and Pierre Glendinning is his young great-grandson's name.' Thou may'st well look at me so, my brother;—yes, he meant thee, *thee*, my brother."

"But the guitar—the guitar!"—cried Pierre—"how came the guitar openly at Saddle Meadows, and how came it to be bartered away by servants? Tell me that, Isabel!"

"Do not put such impetuous questions to me, Pierre; else thou mayst recall the old—may be, it is the evil spell upon me. I can not precisely and knowingly answer thee. I could surmise; but what are surmises worth? Oh, Pierre, better, a million times, and far sweeter are mysteries than surmises: though the mystery be unfathomable, it is still the unfathomableness of fullness; but the surmise, that is but shallow and unmeaning emptiness."

"But this is the most inexplicable point of all. Tell me,

Isabel; surely thou must have thought something about this thing."

"Much, Pierre, very much; but only about the mystery of it—nothing more. Could I, I would not now be fully told, how the guitar came to be at Saddle Meadows, and came to be bartered away by the servants of Saddle Meadows. Enough, that it found me out, and came to me, and spoke and sung to me, and soothed me, and has been every thing to me."

She paused a moment; while vaguely to his secret self Pierre revolved these strange revealings; but now he was all attention again as Isabel resumed.

"I now held in my mind's hand the clew, my brother. But I did not immediately follow it further up. Sufficient to me in my loneliness was the knowledge, that I now knew where my father's family was to be found. As yet not the slightest intention of ever disclosing myself to them, had entered my mind. And assured as I was, that for obvious reasons, none of his surviving relatives could possibly know me, even if they saw me, for what I really was, I felt entire security in the event of encountering any of them by chance. But my unavoidable displacements and migrations from one house to another, at last brought me within twelve miles of Saddle Meadows. I began to feel an increasing longing in me; but side by side with it, a new-born and competing pride,—yes, pride, Pierre. Do my eyes flash? They belie me, if they do not. But it is no common pride, Pierre; for what has Isabel to be proud of in this world? It is the pride of—of—a too, too longing, loving heart, Pierre—the pride of lasting suffering and grief, my brother! Yes, I conquered the great longing with the still more powerful pride, Pierre; and so I would not now be here, in this room,—nor wouldst thou ever have received any line from me; nor, in all worldly probability, ever so much as heard of her who is called Isabel Banford, had it not been for my hearing that at Walter Ulver's, only three miles from the mansion of Saddle Meadows, poor Bell would find people kind enough to give her wages for her work. Feel my hand, my brother."

"Dear divine girl, my own exalted Isabel!" cried Pierre, catching the offered hand with ungovernable emotion, "how most unbeseeming, that this strange hardness, and this still stranger littleness should be united in any human hand. But hard and small, it by an opposite analogy hints of the soft capacious heart that made the hand so hard with heavenly submission to thy most undeserved and martyred lot. Would, Isabel, that these my kisses on the hand, were on the heart itself, and dropt the seeds of eternal joy and comfort there."

He leaped to his feet, and stood before her with such warm, god-like majesty of love and tenderness, that the girl gazed up at him as though he were the one benignant star in all her general night.

"Isabel," cried Pierre, "I stand the sweet penance in my father's stead, thou, in thy mother's. By our earthly acts we shall redeemingly bless both their eternal lots; we will love with the pure and perfect love of angel to an angel. If ever I fall from thee, dear Isabel, may Pierre fall from himself; fall back forever into vacant nothingness and night!"

"My brother, my brother, speak not so to me; it is too much; unused to any love ere now, thine, so heavenly and immense, falls crushing on me! Such love is almost hard to bear as hate. Be still; do not speak to me."

They were both silent for a time; when she went on.

"Yes, my brother, Fate had now brought me within three miles of thee; and—but shall I go straight on, and tell thee all, Pierre? all? every thing? art thou of such divineness, that I may speak straight on, in all my thoughts, heedless whither they may flow, or what things they may float to me?"

"Straight on, and fearlessly," said Pierre.

"By chance I saw thy mother, Pierre, and under such circumstances that I *knew* her to be thy mother; and—but shall I go on?"

"Straight on, my Isabel; thou didst see my mother—well?"

"And when I saw her, though I spake not to her, nor she to me, yet straightway my heart knew that she would love me not."

"Thy heart spake true," muttered Pierre to himself; "go on."

"I re-swore an oath never to reveal myself to thy mother."

"Oath well sworn," again he muttered; "go on."

"But I saw *thee*, Pierre; and, more than ever filled my

mother toward thy father, Pierre, then upheaved in me. Straightway I knew that if ever I should come to be made known to thee, then thy own generous love would open itself to me."

"Again thy heart spake true," he murmured; "go on—and didst thou re-swear again?"

"No, Pierre; but yes, I did. I swore that thou wert my brother; with love and pride I swore, that young and noble Pierre Glendinning was my brother!"

"And only that?"

"Nothing more, Pierre; not to thee even, did I ever think to reveal myself."

"How then? thou *art* revealed to me."

"Yes; but the great God did it, Pierre—not poor Bell. Listen.

"I felt very dreary here; poor, dear Delly—thou must have heard something of her story—a most sorrowful house, Pierre. Hark! that is her seldom-pausing pacing thou hearest from the floor above. So she keeps ever pacing, pacing, pacing; in her track, all thread-bare, Pierre, is her chamber-rug. Her father will not look upon her; her mother, she hath cursed her to her face. Out of yon chamber, Pierre, Delly hath not stept, for now four weeks and more; nor ever hath she once laid upon her bed; it was last made up five weeks ago; but paces, paces, paces, all through the night, till after twelve; and then sits vacant in her chair. Often I would go to her to comfort her; but she says, 'Nay, nay, nay,' to me through the door; says 'Nay, nay, nay,' and only nay to me, through the bolted door; bolted three weeks ago—when I by cunning arts stole her dead baby from her, and with these fingers, alone, by night, scooped out a hollow, and, seconding heaven's own charitable stroke, buried that sweet, wee symbol of her not unpardonable shame far from the ruthless foot of man—yes, bolted three weeks ago, not once unbolted since; her food I must thrust through the little window in her closet. Pierre, hardly these two handfuls has she eaten in a week."

"Curses, wasp-like, cohere on that villain, Ned, and sting him to his death!" cried Pierre, smit by this most piteous tale. "What can be done for her, sweet Isabel; can Pierre do aught?"

"If thou or I do not, then the ever-hospitable grave will prove her quick refuge, Pierre. Father and mother both, are worse than dead and gone to her. They would have turned her forth, I think, but for my own poor petitionings, unceasing in her behalf."

Pierre's deep concern now gave place to a momentary look of benevolent intelligence.

"Isabel, a thought of benefit to Delly has just entered me; but I am still uncertain how best it may be acted on. Resolved I am though to succor her. Do thou still hold her here yet awhile, by thy sweet petitionings, till my further plans are more matured. Now run on with thy story, and so divert me from the pacing;—her every step steps in my soul."

"Thy noble heart hath many chambers, Pierre; the records of thy wealth, I see, are not bound up in the one poor book of Isabel, my brother. Thou art a visible token, Pierre, of the invisible angel-hoods, which in our darker hours we do sometimes distrust. The gospel of thy acts goes very far, my brother. Were all men like to thee, then were there no men at all,—mankind extinct in seraphim!"

"Praises are for the base, my sister, cunningly to entice them to fair Virtue by our ignorings of the ill in them, and our imputings of the good not theirs. So make not my head to hang, sweet Isabel. Praise me not. Go on now with thy tale."

"I have said to thee, my brother, how most dreary I found it here, and from the first. Wonted all my life to sadness—if it be such—still, this house hath such acuteness in its general grief, such hopelessness and despair of any slightest remedy—that even poor Bell could scarce abide it always, without some little going forth into contrasting scenes. So I went forth into the places of delight, only that I might return more braced to minister in the haunts of woe. For continual unchanging residence therein, doth but bring on woe's stupor, and make us as dead. So I went forth betimes; visiting the neighboring cottages; where there were chattering children, and no one place vacant at the cheerful board. Thus at last I chanced to hear of the Sewing Circle to be held at the Miss Pennies'; and how that they were anxious to press into their kind charity all the

maidens of the country round. In various cottages, I was
besought to join; and they at length persuaded me; not that
I was naturally loth to it, and needed such entreaties; but at
first I felt great fear, lest at such a scene I might closely encounter some of the Glendinnings; and that thought was
then namelessly repulsive to me. But by stealthy inquiries I
learned, that the lady of the manorial-house would not be
present;—it proved deceptive information;—but I went;
and all the rest thou knowest."

"I do, sweet Isabel, but thou must tell it over to me; and
all thy emotions there."

V

"Though but one day hath passed, my brother, since we
first met in life, yet thou hast that heavenly magnet in thee,
which draws all my soul's interior to thee. I will go on.—
Having to wait for a neighbor's wagon, I arrived but late at
the Sewing Circle. When I entered, the two joined rooms
were very full. With the farmer's girls, our neighbors, I
passed along to the further corner, where thou didst see me;
and as I went, some heads were turned, and some whisper-
ings I heard, of—'She's the new help at poor Walter
Ulver's—the strange girl they've got—she thinks herself
'mazing pretty, I'll be bound;—but nobody knows her—Oh,
how demure!—but not over-good, I guess;—I wouldn't be
her, not I—mayhap she's some other ruined Delly, run
away;—minx!' It was the first time poor Bell had ever mixed
in such a general crowded company; and knowing little or
nothing of such things, I had thought, that the meeting being
for charity's sweet sake, uncharity could find no harbor there;
but no doubt it was mere thoughtlessness, not malice in
them. Still, it made my heart ache in me sadly; for then I very
keenly felt the dread suspiciousness, in which a strange and
lonely grief invests itself to common eyes; as if grief itself
were not enough, nor innocence any armor to us, but despite
must also come, and icy infamy! Miserable returnings then I
had—even in the midst of bright-budding girls and full-
blown women—miserable returnings then I had of the feeling, the bewildering feeling of the inhumanities I spoke of in

my earlier story. But Pierre, blessed Pierre, do not look so
sadly and half-reproachfully upon me. Lone and lost though
I have been, I love my kind; and charitably and intelligently
pity them, who uncharitably and unintelligently do me despite. And thou, *thou*, blessed brother, hast glorified many
somber places in my soul, and taught me once for all to
know, that my kind are capable of things which would be
glorious in angels. So look away from me, dear Pierre, till
thou hast taught thine eyes more wonted glances."

"They are vile falsifying telegraphs of me, then, sweet Isabel. What my look was I can not tell, but my heart was only
dark with ill-restrained upbraidings against heaven that could
unrelentingly see such innocence as thine so suffer. Go on
with thy too-touching tale."

"Quietly I sat there sewing, not brave enough to look up
at all, and thanking my good star, that had led me to so concealed a nook behind the rest: quietly I sat there, sewing on
a flannel shirt, and with each stitch praying God, that whatever heart it might be folded over, the flannel might hold it
truly warm; and keep out the wide-world-coldness which I
felt myself; and which no flannel, or thickest fur, or any fire
then could keep off from me; quietly I sat there sewing, when
I heard the announcing words—oh, how deep and efface-
ably engraved they are!—'Ah, dames, dames, Madame Glendinning,—Master Pierre Glendinning.' Instantly, my sharp
needle went through my side and stitched my heart; the flannel dropt from my hand; thou heard'st my shriek. But the
good people bore me still nearer to the casement close at
hand, and threw it open wide; and God's own breath
breathed on me; and I rallied; and said it was some merest
passing fit—'twas quite over now—I was used to it—they
had my heart's best thanks—but would they now only leave
me to myself, it were best for me;—I would go on and sew.
And thus it came and passed away; and again I sat sewing on
the flannel, hoping either that the unanticipated persons
would soon depart, or else that some spirit would catch me
away from there; I sat sewing on—till, Pierre! Pierre!—without looking up—for that I dared not do at any time that
evening—only once—without looking up, or knowing aught
but the flannel on my knee, and the needle in my heart, I

felt,—Pierre, *felt*—a glance of magnetic meaning on me.
Long, I, shrinking, sideways turned to meet it, but could not;
till some helping spirit seized me, and all my soul looked up
at thee in my full-fronting face. It was enough. Fate was in
that moment. All the loneliness of my life, all the choked
longings of my soul, now poured over me. I could not away
from them. Then first I felt the complete deplorableness of
my state; that while thou, my brother, had a mother, and
troops of aunts and cousins, and plentiful friends in city and
in country—I, I, Isabel, thy own father's daughter, was
thrust out of all hearts' gates, and shivered in the winter way.
But this was but the least. Not poor Bell can tell thee all the
feelings of poor Bell, or what feelings she felt first. It was all
one whirl of old and new bewilderings, mixed and slanted
with a driving madness. But it was most the sweet, inquisitive, kindly interested aspect of thy face,—so strangely like
thy father's, too—the one only being that I first did love—it
was that which most stirred the distracting storm in me; most
charged me with the immense longings for some one of my
blood to know me, and to own me, though but once, and
then away. Oh, my dear brother—Pierre! Pierre!—could'st
thou take out my heart, and look at it in thy hand, then thou
would'st find it all over written, this way and that, and
crossed again, and yet again, with continual lines of longings,
that found no end but in suddenly calling thee. Call him! Call
him! He will come!—so cried my heart to me; so cried the
leaves and stars to me, as I that night went home. But pride
rose up—the very pride in my own longings,—and as one
arm pulled, the other held. So I stood still, and called thee
not. But Fate will be Fate, and it was fated. Once having met
thy fixed regardful glance; once having seen the full angelicalness in thee, my whole soul was undone by thee; my whole
pride was cut off at the root, and soon showed a blighting in
the bud; which spread deep into my whole being, till I knew,
that utterly decay and die away I must, unless pride let me
go, and I, with the one little trumpet of a pen, blew my
heart's shrillest blast, and called dear Pierre to me. My soul
was full; and as my beseeching ink went tracing o'er the page,
my tears contributed their mite, and made a strange alloy.
How blest I felt that my so bitterly tear-mingled ink—that

last depth of my anguish—would never be visibly known to thee, but the tears would dry upon the page, and all be fair again, ere the so submerged-freighted letter should meet thine eye."

"Ah, there thou wast deceived, poor Isabel," cried Pierre impulsively; "thy tears dried not fair, but dried red, almost like blood; and nothing so much moved my inmost soul as that tragic sight."

"How? how? Pierre, my brother? Dried they red? Oh, horrible! enchantment! most undreamed of!"

"Nay, the ink—the ink! something chemic in it changed thy real tears to seeming blood;—only that, my sister."

"Oh Pierre! thus wonderfully is it—seems to me—that our own hearts do not ever know the extremity of their own sufferings; sometimes we bleed blood, when we think it only water. Of our sufferings, as of our talents, others sometimes are the better judges. But stop me! force me backward to my story! Yet methinks that now thou knowest all;—no, not entirely all. Thou dost not know what planned and winnowed motive I did have in writing thee; nor does poor Bell know that; for poor Bell was too delirious to have planned and winnowed motives then. The impulse in me called thee, not poor Bell. God called thee, Pierre, not poor Bell. Even now, when I have passed one night after seeing thee, and hearkening to all thy full love and graciousness; even now, I stand as one amazed, and feel not what may be coming to me, or what will now befall me, from having so rashly claimed thee for mine. Pierre, now, *now*, this instant a vague anguish fills me. Tell me, by loving me, by owning me, publicly or secretly,—tell me, doth it involve any vital hurt to thee? Speak without reserve; speak honestly; as I do to thee! Speak now, Pierre, and tell me all!"

"Is Love a harm? Can Truth betray to pain? Sweet Isabel, how can hurt come in the path to God? Now, when I know thee all, now did I forget thee, fail to acknowledge thee, and love thee before the wide world's whole brazen width—could I do that; then might'st thou ask thy question reasonably and say—Tell me, Pierre, does not the suffocating in thee of poor Bell's holy claims, does not that involve for thee unending misery? And my truthful soul would echo—Unending misery! Nay, nay, nay. Thou art my sister and I am thy brother; and that part of the world which knows me, shall acknowledge thee; or by heaven I will crush the disdainful world down on its knees to thee, my sweet Isabel!"

"The menacings in thy eyes are dear delights to me; I grow up with thy own glorious stature; and in thee, my brother, I see God's indignant embassador to me, saying—Up, up, Isabel, and take no terms from the common world, but do thou make terms to it, and grind thy fierce rights out of it! Thy catching nobleness unsexes me, my brother; and now I know that in her most exalted moment, then woman no more feels the twin-born softness of her breasts, but feels chain-armor palpitating there!"

Her changed attitude of beautiful audacity; her long scornful hair, that trailed out a disheveled banner; her wonderful transfigured eyes, in which some meteors seemed playing up; all this now seemed to Pierre the work of an invisible enchanter. Transformed she stood before him; and Pierre, bowing low over to her, owned that irrespective, darting majesty of humanity, which can be majestical and menacing in woman as in man.

But her gentler sex returned to Isabel at last; and she sat silent in the casement's niche, looking out upon the soft ground-lightnings of the electric summer night.

vi

Sadly smiling, Pierre broke the pause.

"My sister, thou art so rich, that thou must do me alms; I am very hungry; I have forgotten to eat since breakfast;—and now thou shalt bring me bread and a cup of water, Isabel, ere I go forth from thee. Last night I went rummaging in a pantry, like a bake-house burglar; but to-night thou and I must sup together, Isabel; for as we may henceforth live together, let us begin forthwith to eat in company."

Isabel looked up at him, with sudden and deep emotion, then all acquiescing sweetness, and silently left the room.

As she returned, Pierre, casting his eyes toward the ceiling, said—"She is quiet now, the pacing hath entirely ceased."

"Not the beating, tho'; her foot hath paused, not her unceasing heart. My brother, she is not quiet now; quiet for her hath gone; so that the pivoted stillness of this night is yet a noisy madness to her."

"Give me pen or pencil, and some paper, Isabel."

She laid down her loaf, and plate, and knife, and brought him pen, and ink, and paper.

Pierre took the pen.

"Was this the one, dear Isabel?"

"It is the one, my brother; none other is in this poor cot."

He gazed at it intensely. Then turning to the table, steadily wrote the following note:

"For Delly Ulver: with the deep and true regard and sympathy of Pierre Glendinning.

"Thy sad story—partly known before—hath now more fully come to me, from one who sincerely feels for thee, and who hath imparted her own sincerity to me. Thou desirest to quit this neighborhood, and be somewhere at peace, and find some secluded employ fitted to thy sex and age. With this, I now willingly charge myself, and insure it to thee, so far as my utmost ability can go. Therefore—if consolation be not wholly spurned by thy great grief, which too often happens, though it be but grief's great folly so to feel—therefore, two true friends of thine do here beseech thee to take some little heart to thee, and bethink thee, that all thy life is not yet lived; that Time hath surest healing in his continuous balm. Be patient yet a little while, till thy future lot be disposed for thee, through our best help; and so, know me and Isabel thy earnest friends and true-hearted lovers."

He handed the note to Isabel. She read it silently, and put it down, and spread her two hands over him, and with one motion lifted her eyes toward Delly and toward God.

"Thou think'st it will not pain her to receive the note, Isabel? Thou know'st best. I thought, that ere our help do really reach her, some promise of it now might prove slight comfort. But keep it, and do as thou think'st best."

"Then straightway will I give it her, my brother," said Isabel quitting him.

An infixing stillness, now thrust a long rivet through the night, and fast nailed it to that side of the world. And alone again in such an hour, Pierre could not but listen. He heard Isabel's step on the stair; then it approached him from above;

then he heard a gentle knock, and thought he heard a rustling, as of paper slid over a threshold underneath a door. Then another advancing and opposite step tremblingly met Isabel's; and then both steps stepped from each other, and soon Isabel came back to him.

"Thou did'st knock, and slide it underneath the door?"

"Yes, and she hath it now. Hark! a sobbing! Thank God, long arid grief hath found a tear at last. Pity, sympathy hath done this.—Pierre, for thy dear deed thou art already sainted, ere thou be dead."

"Do saints hunger, Isabel?" said Pierre, striving to call her away from this. "Come, give me the loaf; but no, thou shalt help me, my sister.—Thank thee;—this is twice over the bread of sweetness.—Is this of thine own making, Isabel?"

"My own making, my brother."

"Give me the cup; hand it me with thine own hand. So:— Isabel, my heart and soul are now full of deepest reverence; yet I do dare to call this the real sacrament of the supper.— Eat with me."

They eat together without a single word; and without a single word, Pierre rose, and kissed her pure and spotless brow, and without a single word departed from the place.

vii

We know not Pierre Glendinning's thoughts as he gained the village and passed on beneath its often shrouding trees, and saw no light from man, and heard no sound from man, but only, by intervals, saw at his feet the soft ground-lightnings, snake-like, playing in and out among the blades of grass; and between the trees, caught the far dim light from heaven, and heard the far wide general hum of the sleeping but still breathing earth.

He paused before a detached and pleasant house, with much shrubbery about it. He mounted the portico and knocked distinctly there, just as the village clock struck one. He knocked, but no answer came. He knocked again, and soon he heard a sash thrown up in the second story, and an astonished voice inquired who was there?

"It is Pierre Glendinning, and he desires an instant interview with the Reverend Mr. Falsgrave."

"Do I hear right?—in heaven's name, what is the matter,
young gentleman?"

"Every thing is the matter; the whole world is the matter.
Will you admit me, sir?"

"Certainly—but I beseech thee—nay, stay, I will admit
thee."

In quicker time than could have been anticipated, the door
was opened to Pierre by Mr. Falsgrave in person, holding a
candle, and invested in his very becoming student's wrapper
of Scotch plaid.

"For heaven's sake, what is the matter, Mr. Glendinning?"

"Heaven and earth is the matter, sir! shall we go up to the
study?"

"Certainly, but—but—"

"Well, let us proceed, then."

They went up-stairs, and soon found themselves in the clergyman's retreat, and both sat down; the amazed host still
holding the candle in his hand, and intently eying Pierre, with
an apprehensive aspect.

"Thou art a man of God, sir, I believe."

"I? I? I? upon my word, Mr. Glendinning!"

"Yes, sir, the world calls thee a man of God. Now, what
hast thou, the man of God, decided, with my mother, concerning Delly Ulver?"

"Delly Ulver! why, why—what can this madness mean?"

"It means, sir, what have thou and my mother decided concerning Delly Ulver."

"She?—Delly Ulver? She is to depart the neighborhood;
why, her own parents want her not."

"*How* is she to depart? *Who* is to take her? Art *thou* to take
her? *Where* is she to go? *Who* has food for her? *What* is to
keep her from the pollution to which such as she are every
day driven to contribute, by the detestable uncharitableness
and heartlessness of the world?"

"Mr. Glendinning," said the clergyman, now somewhat
calmly putting down the candle, and folding himself with dignity in his gown; "Mr. Glendinning, I will not now make any
mention of my natural astonishment at this most unusual call,

and the most extraordinary time of it. Thou hast sought information upon a certain point, and I have given it to thee, to the best of my knowledge. All thy after and incidental questions, I choose to have no answer for. I will be most happy to see thee at any other time, but for the present thou must excuse my presence. Good-night, sir."

But Pierre sat entirely still, and the clergyman could not but remain standing still.

"I perfectly comprehend the whole, sir. Delly Ulver, then, is to be driven out to starve or rot; and this, too, by the acquiescence of a man of God. Mr. Falsgrave, the subject of Delly, deeply interesting as it is to me, is only the preface to another, still more interesting to me, and concerning which I once cherished some slight hope that thou wouldst have been able, in thy Christian character, to sincerely and honestly counsel me. But a hint from heaven assures me now, that thou hast no earnest and world-disdaining counsel for me. I must seek it direct from God himself, who, I now know, never delegates his holiest admonishings. But I do not blame thee; I think I begin to see how thy profession is unavoidably entangled by all fleshly alliances, and can not move with godly freedom in a world of benefices. I am more sorry than indignant. Pardon me for my most uncivil call, and know me as not thy enemy. Good-night, sir."

Book IX

More Light, and the Gloom of That Light • More Gloom, and the Light of That Gloom

In those hyperborean regions, to which enthusiastic Truth, and Earnestness, and Independence, will invariably lead a mind fitted by nature for profound and fearless thought, all objects are seen in a dubious, uncertain, and refracting light. Viewed through that rarefied atmosphere the most immemorially admitted maxims of men begin to slide and fluctuate, and finally become wholly inverted; the very heavens themselves being not innocent of producing this confounding effect, since it is mostly in the heavens themselves that these wonderful mirages are exhibited.

But the example of many minds forever lost, like undiscoverable Arctic explorers, amid those treacherous regions, warns us entirely away from them; and we learn that it is not for man to follow the trail of truth too far, since by so doing he entirely loses the directing compass of his mind; for arrived at the Pole, to whose barrenness only it points, there, the needle indifferently respects all points of the horizon alike.

But even the less distant regions of thought are not without their singular introversions. Hardly any sincere man of ordinary reflective powers, and accustomed to exercise them at all, but must have been independently struck by the thought, that, after all, what is so enthusiastically applauded as the march of mind,—meaning the inroads of Truth into Error— which has ever been regarded by hopeful persons as the one fundamental thing most earnestly to be prayed for as the greatest possible Catholic blessing to the world;—almost every thinking man must have been some time or other struck with the idea, that, in certain respects, a tremendous mistake may be lurking here, since all the world does never gregariously advance to Truth, but only here and there some of its individuals do; and by advancing, leave the rest behind; cutting themselves forever adrift from their sympathy, and making themselves always liable to be regarded with distrust, dislike, and often, downright—though, ofttimes, concealed—fear and hate. What wonder, then, that those advanced minds, which in spite of advance, happen still to remain, for the time, ill-regulated, should now and then be goaded into turning round in acts of wanton aggression upon sentiments and opinions now forever left in their rear. Certain it is, that in their earlier stages of advance, especially in youthful minds, as yet untranquilized by long habituation to the world as it inevitably and eternally is; this aggressiveness is almost invariably manifested, and as invariably afterward deplored by themselves.

That amazing shock of practical truth, which in the compass of a very few days and hours had not so much advanced, as magically transplanted the youthful mind of Pierre far beyond all common discernments; it had not been entirely unattended by the lamentable rearward aggressiveness we have endeavored to portray above. Yielding to that unwarrantable mood, he had invaded the profound midnight slumbers of the Reverend Mr. Falsgrave, and most discourteously made war upon that really amiable and estimable person. But as through the strange force of circumstances his advance in insight had been so surprisingly rapid, so also was now his advance in some sort of wisdom, in charitableness; and his concluding words to Mr. Falsgrave, sufficiently evinced that already, ere quitting that gentleman's study, he had begun to repent his ever entering it on such a mission.

And as he now walked on in the profound meditations induced by the hour; and as all that was in him stirred to and fro, intensely agitated by the ever-creative fire of enthusiastic earnestness, he became fully alive to many palliating considerations, which had they previously occurred to him would have peremptorily forbidden his impulsive intrusion upon the respectable clergyman.

But it is through the malice of this earthly air, that only by being guilty of Folly does mortal man in many cases arrive at the perception of Sense. A thought which should forever free us from hasty imprecations upon our ever-recurring intervals of Folly; since though Folly be our teacher, Sense is the lesson she teaches; since if Folly wholly depart from us, Further

Sense will be her companion in the flight, and we will be left
standing midway in wisdom. For it is only the miraculous
vanity of man which ever persuades him, that even for the
most richly gifted mind, there ever arrives an earthly period,
where it can truly say to itself, I have come to the Ultimate
of Human Speculative Knowledge; hereafter, at this present
point I will abide. Sudden onsets of new truth will assail him,
and overturn him as the Tartars did China; for there is no
China Wall that man can build in his soul, which shall permanently stay the irruptions of those barbarous hordes which
Truth ever nourishes in the loins of her frozen, yet teeming
North; so that the Empire of Human Knowledge can never
be lasting in any one dynasty, since Truth still gives new Emperors to the earth.

But the thoughts we here indite as Pierre's are to be very
carefully discriminated from those we indite concerning him.
Ignorant at this time of the ideas concerning the reciprocity
and partnership of Folly and Sense, in contributing to the
mental and moral growth of the mind; Pierre keenly upbraided his thoughtlessness, and began to stagger in his soul;
as distrustful of that radical change in his general sentiments,
which had thus hurried him into a glaring impropriety and
folly; as distrustful of himself, the most wretched distrust of
all. But this last distrust was not of the heart; for heaven itself,
so he felt, had sanctified that with its blessing; but it was the
distrust of his intellect, which in undisciplinedly espousing
the manly enthusiast cause of his heart, seemed to cast a reproach upon that cause itself.

But though evermore hath the earnest heart an eventual
balm for the most deplorable error of the head; yet in the
interval small alleviation is to be had, and the whole man
droops into nameless melancholy. Then it seems as though
the most magnanimous and virtuous resolutions were only
intended for fine spiritual emotions, not as mere preludes to
their bodily translation into acts; since in essaying their embodiment, we have but proved ourselves miserable bunglers,
and thereupon taken ignominious shame to ourselves. Then,
too, the never-entirely repulsed hosts of Commonness, and
Conventionalness, and Worldly Prudent-mindedness return
to the charge; press hard on the faltering soul; and with in-

human hootings deride all its nobleness as mere eccentricity, which further wisdom and experience shall assuredly cure. The man is as seized by arms and legs, and convulsively pulled either way by his own indecisions and doubts. Blackness advances her banner over this cruel altercation, and he droops and swoons beneath its folds.

It was precisely in this mood of mind that, at about two in the morning, Pierre, with a hanging head, now crossed the private threshold of the Mansion of Saddle Meadows.

ii

In the profoundly silent heart of a house full of sleeping serving-men and maids, Pierre now sat in his chamber before his accustomed round table, still tossed with the books and the papers which, three days before, he had abruptly left, for a sudden and more absorbing object. Uppermost and most conspicuous among the books were the Inferno of Dante, and the Hamlet of Shakspeare.

His mind was wandering and vague; his arm wandered and was vague. Soon he found the open Inferno in his hand, and his eye met the following lines, allegorically overscribed within the arch of the outgoings of the womb of human life:

> "Through me you pass into the city of Woe;
>   Through me you pass into eternal pain;
>   Through me, among the people lost for aye.
> *   *   *   *   *   *
>   All hope abandon, ye who enter here."

He dropped the fatal volume from his hand; he dropped his fated head upon his chest.

His mind was wandering and vague; his arm wandered and was vague. Some moments passed, and he found the open Hamlet in his hand, and his eyes met the following lines:

> "The time is out of joint;—Oh cursed spite,
>   That ever I was born to set it right!"

He dropped the too true volume from his hand; his petri-fying heart dropped hollowly within him, as a pebble down Carrisbrook well.

iii

The man Dante Alighieri received unforgivable affronts and insults from the world; and the poet Dante Alighieri be-queathed his immortal curse to it, in the sublime malediction of the Inferno. The fiery tongue whose political forkings lost him the solacements of this world, found its malicious coun-terpart in that muse of fire, which would forever bar the vast bulk of mankind from all solacement in the worlds to come. Fortunately for the felicity of the Dilletante in Literature, the horrible allegorical meanings of the Inferno, lie not on the surface; but unfortunately for the earnest and youthful piercers into truth and reality, those horrible meanings, when first discovered, infuse their poison into a spot pre-viously unprovided with that sovereign antidote of a sense of uncapitulatable security, which is only the possession of the furthest advanced and profoundest souls.

Judge ye, then, ye Judicious, the mood of Pierre, so far as the passage in Dante touched him.

If among the deeper significances of its pervading indefi-niteness, which significances are wisely hidden from all but the rarest adepts, the pregnant tragedy of Hamlet convey any one particular moral at all fitted to the ordinary uses of man, it is this:—that all meditation is worthless, unless it prompt to action; that it is not for man to stand shillyshallying amid the conflicting invasions of surrounding impulses; that in the earliest instant of conviction, the roused man must strike, and, if possible, with the precision and the force of the light-ning-bolt.

Pierre had always been an admiring reader of Hamlet; but neither his age nor his mental experience thus far, had quali-fied him either to catch initiating glimpses into the hopeless gloom of its interior meaning, or to draw from the general story those superficial and purely incidental lessons, wherein the painstaking moralist so complacently expatiates.

The intensest light of reason and revelation combined, can

not shed such blazonings upon the deeper truths in man, as will sometimes proceed from his own profoundest gloom. Utter darkness is then his light, and cat-like he distinctly sees all objects through a medium which is mere blindness to common vision. Wherefore have Gloom and Grief been celebrated of old as the selectest chamberlains to knowledge? Wherefore is it, that not to know Gloom and Grief is not to know aught that an heroic man should learn?

By the light of that gloom, Pierre now turned over the soul of Hamlet in his hand. He knew not—at least, felt not—then, that Hamlet, though a thing of life, was, after all, but a thing of breath, evoked by the wanton magic of a creative hand, and as wantonly dismissed at last into endless halls of hell and night.

It is the not impartially bestowed privilege of the more final insights, that at the same moment they reveal the depths, they do, sometimes, also reveal—though by no means so distinctly—some answering heights. But when only midway down the gulf, its crags wholly conceal the upper vaults, and the wanderer thinks it all one gulf of downward dark.

Judge ye, then, ye Judicious, the mood of Pierre, so far as the passage in Hamlet touched him.

iv

Torn into a hundred shreds the printed pages of Hell and Hamlet lay at his feet, which trampled them, while their vacant covers mocked him with their idle titles. Dante had made him fierce, and Hamlet had insinuated that there was none to strike. Dante had taught him that he had bitter cause of quarrel; Hamlet taunted him with faltering in the fight. Now he began to curse anew his fate, for now he began to see that after all he had been finely juggling with himself, and postponing with himself, and in meditative sentimentalities wasting the moments consecrated to instant action.

Eight-and-forty hours and more had passed. Was Isabel acknowledged? Had she yet hung on his public arm? Who knew yet of Isabel but Pierre? Like a skulking coward he had gone prowling in the woods by day, and like a skulking coward he had stolen to her haunt by night! Like a thief he had sat and stammered and turned pale before his mother, and in the cause of Holy Right, permitted a woman to grow tall and hector over him! Ah! Easy for man to think like a hero; but hard for man to act like one. All imaginable audacities readily enter into the soul; few come boldly forth from it.

Did he, or did he not vitally mean to do this thing? Was the immense stuff to do it his, or was it not his? Why defer? Why put off? What was there to be gained by deferring and putting off? His resolution had been taken, why was it not executed? What more was there to learn? What more which was essential to the public acknowledgment of Isabel, had remained to be learned, after his first glance at her first letter? Had doubts of her identity come over him to stay him?— None at all. Against the wall of the thick darkness of the mystery of Isabel, recorded as by some phosphoric finger was the burning fact, that Isabel was his sister. Why then? How then? Whence then this utter nothing of his acts? Did he stagger at the thought, that at the first announcement to his mother concerning Isabel, and his resolution to own her boldly and lovingly, his proud mother, spurning the reflection on his father, would likewise spurn Pierre and Isabel, and denounce both him and her, and hate them both alike, as unnatural accomplices against the good name of the purest of husbands and parents? Not at all. Such a thought was not in him. For had he not already resolved, that his mother should know nothing of the fact of Isabel?—But how now? What then? How was Isabel to be acknowledged to the world, if his mother was to know nothing of that acknowledgment?— Short-sighted, miserable palterer and huckster, thou hast been playing a most fond and foolish game with thyself! Fool and coward! Coward and fool! Tear thyself open, and read there the confounding story of thy blind dotishness! Thy two grand resolutions—the public acknowledgment of Isabel, and the charitable withholding of her existence from thy own mother,—these are impossible adjuncts.—Likewise, thy so magnanimous purpose to screen thy father's honorable memory from reproach, and thy other intention, the open vindication of thy fraternalness to Isabel,—these also are impossible adjuncts. And the having individually entertained four such resolves, without perceiving that once brought together, they all mutually expire; this, this ineffable folly, Pierre, brands thee in the forehead for an unaccountable infatuate!

Well may'st thou distrust thyself, and curse thyself, and tear thy Hamlet and thy Hell! Oh! fool, blind fool, and a million times an ass! Go, go, thou poor and feeble one! High deeds are not for such blind grubs as thou! Quit Isabel, and go to Lucy! Beg humble pardon of thy mother, and hereafter be a more obedient and good boy to her, Pierre—Pierre, Pierre,—infatuate!

Impossible would it be now to tell all the confusion and confoundings in the soul of Pierre, so soon as the above absurdities in his mind presented themselves first to his combining consciousness. He would fain have disowned the very memory and the mind which produced to him such an immense scandal upon his common sanity. Now indeed did all the fiery floods in the Inferno, and all the rolling gloom in Hamlet suffocate him at once in flame and smoke. The cheeks of his soul collapsed in him: he dashed himself in blind fury and swift madness against the wall, and fell dabbling in the vomit of his loathed identity.

Book X

GLORIFIED BE HIS gracious memory who first said, The deepest gloom precedes the day. We care not whether the saying will prove true to the utmost bounds of things; sufficient that it sometimes does hold true within the bounds of earthly finitude.

Next morning Pierre rose from the floor of his chamber, haggard and tattered in body from his past night's utter misery, but stoically serene and symmetrical in soul, with the foretaste of what then seemed to him a planned and perfect Future. Now he thinks he knows that the wholly unanticipated storm which had so terribly burst upon him, had yet burst upon him for his good; for the place, which in its undetected incipiency, the storm had obscurely occupied in his soul, seemed now clear sky to him; and all his horizon seemed distinctly commanded by him.

His resolution was a strange and extraordinary one; but therefore it only the better met a strange and extraordinary emergency. But it was not only strange and extraordinary in its novelty of mere aspect, but it was wonderful in its unequaled renunciation of himself.

From the first, determined at all hazards to hold his father's fair fame inviolate from any thing he should do in reference to protecting Isabel, and extending to her a brother's utmost devotedness and love; and equally determined not to shake his mother's lasting peace by any useless exposure of unwelcome facts; and yet vowed in his deepest soul some way to embrace Isabel before the world, and yield to her his constant consolation and companionship; and finding no possible mode of unitedly compassing all these ends, without a most singular act of pious imposture, which he thought all heaven would justify in him, since he himself was to be the grand self-renouncing victim; therefore, this was his settled and immovable purpose now; namely: to assume before the world, that by secret rites, Pierre Glendinning was already become the husband of Isabel Banford—an assumption which would entirely warrant his dwelling in her continual company, and upon equal terms, taking her wherever the world admitted him; and at the same time foreclose all sinister inquisitions bearing upon his deceased parent's memory, or any way affecting his mother's lasting peace, as indissolubly linked with that. True, he in embryo, foreknew, that the extraordinary thing he had resolved, would, in another way, indirectly though inevitably, dart a most keen pang into his mother's heart; but this then seemed to him part of the unavoidable vast price of his enthusiastic virtue; and, thus minded, rather would he privately pain his living mother with a wound that might be curable, than cast world-wide and irremediable dishonor—so it seemed to him—upon his departed father.

Probably no other being than Isabel could have produced upon Pierre impressions powerful enough to eventuate in a final resolution so unparalleled as the above. But the wonderful melodiousness of her grief had touched the secret monochord within his breast, by an apparent magic, precisely similar to that which had moved the stringed tongue of her guitar to respond to the heart-strings of her own melancholy plaints. The deep voice of the being of Isabel called to him from out the immense distances of sky and air, and there seemed no veto of the earth that could forbid her heavenly claim.

During the three days that he had personally known her, and so been brought into magnetic contact with her, other persuasions and potencies than those direct ones, involved in her bewildering eyes and marvelous story, had unconsciously left their ineffaceable impressions on him, and perhaps without his privity, had mainly contributed to his resolve. She had impressed him as the glorious child of Pride and Grief, in whose countenance were traceable the divinest lineaments of both her parents. Pride gave to her her nameless nobleness; Grief touched that nobleness with an angelical softness; and again that softness was steeped in a most charitable humility, which was the foundation of her loftiest excellence of all.

Neither by word or letter had Isabel betrayed any spark of those more common emotions and desires which might not unreasonably be ascribed to an ordinary person placed in circumstances like hers. Though almost penniless, she had not invoked the pecuniary bounty of Pierre; and though she was altogether silent on that subject, yet Pierre could not but be strangely sensible of something in her which disdained to voluntarily hang upon the mere bounty even of a brother. Nor, though she by various nameless ways, manifested her consciousness of being surrounded by uncongenial and inferior beings, while yet descended from a generous stock, and personally meriting the most refined companionships which the wide world could yield; nevertheless, she had not demanded of Pierre that he should array her in brocade, and lead her forth among the rare and opulent ladies of the land. But while thus evincing her intuitive, true lady-likeness and nobleness by this entire freedom from all sordid motives, neither had she merged all her feelings in any sickly sentimentalities of sisterly affection toward her so suddenly discovered brother; which, in the case of a naturally unattractive woman in her circumstances, would not have been altogether alluring to Pierre. No. That intense and indescribable longing, which her letter by its very incoherencies had best embodied, proceeded from no base, vain, or ordinary motive whatever; but was the unsuppressible and unmistakable cry of the godhead through her soul, commanding Pierre to fly to her, and do his highest and most glorious duty in the world.

Nor now, as it changedly seemed to Pierre, did that duty consist in stubbornly flying in the marble face of the Past, and striving to reverse the decree which had pronounced that Isabel could never perfectly inherit all the privileges of a legitimate child of her father. And thoroughly now he felt, that even as this would in the present case be both preposterous in itself and cruel in effect to both the living and the dead, so was it entirely undesired by Isabel, who though once yielding to a momentary burst of aggressive enthusiasm, yet in her more wonted mood of mournfulness and sweetness, evinced no such lawless wandering. Thoroughly, now he felt, that Isabel was content to live obscure in her paternal identity, so long as she could any way appease her deep longings for the constant love and sympathy and close domestic contact of some one of her blood. So that Pierre had no slightest misgiving that upon learning the character of his scheme, she would deem it to come short of her natural expectations; while so far as its apparent strangeness was concerned,—a strangeness, perhaps invincible to squeamish and humdrum women—here Pierre anticipated no obstacle in Isabel; for her whole past was strange, and strangeness seemed best befitting to her future.

But had Pierre now reread the opening paragraph of her letter to him, he might have very quickly derived a powerful anticipative objection from his sister, which his own complete disinterestedness concealed from him. Though Pierre had every reason to believe that—owing to her secluded and humble life—Isabel was in entire ignorance of the fact of his precise relation to Lucy Tartan:—an ignorance, whose first indirect and unconscious manifestation in Isabel, had been unspeakably welcome to him;—and though, of course, he had both wisely and benevolently abstained from enlightening her on that point; still, notwithstanding this, was it possible that any true-hearted, noble girl like Isabel, would, to benefit herself, willingly become a participator in an act, which would prospectively and forever bar the blessed boon of marriageable love from one so young and generous as Pierre, and eternally entangle him in a fictitious alliance, which, though in reality but a web of air, yet in effect would prove a wall of iron; for the same powerful motive which induced the thought of forming such an alliance, would always thereafter forbid that tacit exposure of its fictitiousness, which would be consequent upon its public discontinuance, and the real nuptials of Pierre with any other being during the lifetime of Isabel.

But according to what view you take of it, it is either the gracious or the malicious gift of the great gods to man, that on the threshold of any wholly new and momentous devoted enterprise, the thousand ulterior intricacies and emperilings to which it must conduct; these, at the outset, are mostly withheld from sight; and so, through her ever-primeval wilderness Fortune's Knight rides on, alike ignorant of the palaces or the pitfalls in its heart. Surprising, and past all ordinary belief, are those strange oversights and inconsistencies, which the enthu-

siastic meditation upon unique or extreme resolves will sometimes beget in young and over-ardent souls. That all-
comprehending oneness, that calm representativeness, by
which a steady philosophic mind reaches forth and draws to
itself, in their collective entirety, the objects of its contemplations; that pertains not to the young enthusiast. By his eagerness, all objects are deceptively foreshortened; by his intensity
each object is viewed as detached; so that essentially and relatively every thing is misseen by him. Already have we exposed that passing preposterousness in Pierre, which by
reason of the above-named cause which we have endeavored
to portray, induced him to cherish for a time four unitedly
impossible designs. And now we behold this hapless youth all
eager to involve himself in such an inextricable twist of Fate,
that the three dextrous maids themselves could hardly disentangle him, if once he tie the complicating knots about him
and Isabel.

Ah, thou rash boy! are there no couriers in the air to warn
thee away from these emperilings, and point thee to those
Cretan labyrinths, to which thy life's cord is leading thee?
Where now are the high beneficences? Whither fled the sweet
angels that are alledged guardians to man?

Not that the impulsive Pierre wholly overlooked all that
was menacing to him in his future, if now he acted out his
most rare resolve; but eagerly foreshortened by him, they assumed not their full magnitude of menacing; nor, indeed,—
so riveted now his purpose—were they pushed up to his face,
would he for that renounce his self-renunciation; while concerning all things more immediately contingent upon his central resolution; these were, doubtless, in a measure, foreseen
and understood by him. Perfectly, at least, he seemed to foresee and understand, that the present hope of Lucy Tartan
must be banished from his being; that this would carry a terrible pang to her, which in the natural recoil would but redouble his own; that to the world all his heroicness, standing
equally unexplained and unsuspected, therefore the world
would denounce him as infamously false to his betrothed;
reckless of the most binding human vows; a secret wooer and
wedder of an unknown and enigmatic girl; a spurner of all a
loving mother's wisest counselings; a bringer down of lasting

reproach upon an honorable name; a besotted self-exile from a most prosperous house and bounteous fortune; and lastly, that now his whole life would, in the eyes of the wide humanity, be covered with an all-pervading haze of incurable sinisterness, possibly not to be removed even in the concluding hour of death.

Such, oh thou son of man! are the perils and the miseries thou callest down on thee, when, even in a virtuous cause, thou steppest aside from those arbitrary lines of conduct, by which the common world, however base and dastardly, surrounds thee for thy worldly good.

Ofttimes it is very wonderful to trace the rarest and profoundest things, and find their probable origin in something extremely trite or trivial. Yet so strange and complicate is the human soul; so much is confusedly evolved from out itself, and such vast and varied accessions come to it from abroad, and so impossible is it always to distinguish between these two, that the wisest man were rash, positively to assign the precise and incipient origination of his final thoughts and acts. Far as we blind moles can see, man's life seems but an acting upon mysterious hints; it is somehow hinted to us, to do thus or thus. For surely no mere mortal who has at all gone down into himself will ever pretend that his slightest thought or act solely originates in his own defined identity. This preamble seems not entirely unnecessary as usher of the strange conceit, that possibly the latent germ of Pierre's proposed extraordinary mode of executing his proposed extraordinary resolve—namely, the nominal conversion of a sister into a wife—might have been found in the previous conversational conversion of a mother into a sister; for hereby he had habituated his voice and manner to a certain fictitiousness in one of the closest domestic relations of life; and since man's moral texture is very porous, and things assumed upon the surface, at last strike in—hence, this outward habituation to the above-named fictitiousness had insensibly disposed his mind to it as it were; but only innocently and pleasantly as yet. If, by any possibility, this general conceit be so, then to Pierre the times of sportfulness were as pregnant with the hours of earnestness; and in sport he learnt the terms of woe.

ii

If next to that resolve concerning his lasting fraternal succor to Isabel, there was at this present time any determination in Pierre absolutely inflexible, and partaking at once of the sacredness and the indissolubleness of the most solemn oath, it was the enthusiastic, and apparently wholly supererogatory resolution to hold his father's memory untouched; nor to one single being in the world reveal the paternity of Isabel. Unrecallably dead and gone from out the living world, again returned to utter helplessness, so far as this world went; his perished father seemed to appeal to the dutifulness and mercifulness of Pierre, in terms far more moving than though the accents proceeded from his mortal mouth. And what though not through the sin of Pierre, but through his father's sin, that father's fair fame now lay at the mercy of the son, and could only be kept inviolate by the son's free sacrifice of all earthly felicity;—what if this were so? It but struck a still loftier chord in the bosom of the son, and filled him with infinite magnanimities. Never had the generous Pierre cherished the heathenish conceit, that even in the general world, Sin is a fair object to be stretched on the cruelest racks by self-complacent Virtue, that self-complacent Virtue may feed her lily-liveredness on the pallor of Sin's anguish. For perfect Virtue does not more loudly claim our approbation, than repented Sin in its concludedness does demand our utmost tenderness and concern. And as the more immense the Virtue, so should be the more immense our approbation; likewise the more immense the Sin, the more infinite our pity. In some sort, Sin hath its sacredness, not less than holiness. And great Sin calls forth more magnanimity than small Virtue. What man, who is a man, does not feel livelier and more generous emotions toward the great god of Sin—Satan,—than toward yonder haberdasher, who only is a sinner in the small and entirely honorable way of trade?

Though Pierre profoundly shuddered at that impenetrable yet blackly significant nebulousness, which the wild story of Isabel threw around the early life of his father; yet as he recalled the dumb anguish of the invocation of the empty and the ashy hand uplifted from his father's death-bed, he most keenly felt that of whatsoever unknown shade his father's guilt might be, yet in the final hour of death it had been most dismally repented of; by a repentance only the more full of utter wretchedness, that it was a consuming secret in him. Mince the matter how his family would, had not his father died a raver? Whence that raving, following so prosperous a life? Whence, but from the cruelest compunctions?

Touched thus, and strung in all his sinews and his nerves to the holding of his father's memory intact,—Pierre turned his confronting and unfrightened face toward Lucy Tartan, and stilly vowed that not even she should know the whole; no, not know the least.

There is an inevitable keen cruelty in the loftier heroism. It is not heroism only to stand unflinched ourselves in the hour of suffering; but it is heroism to stand unflinched both at our own and at some loved one's united suffering; a united suffering, which we could put an instant period to, if we would but renounce the glorious cause for which ourselves do bleed, and see our most loved one bleed. If he would not reveal his father's shame to the common world, whose favorable opinion for himself, Pierre now despised; how then reveal it to the woman he adored? To her, above all others, would he now uncover his father's tomb, and bid her behold from what vile attaintings he himself had sprung? So Pierre turned round and tied Lucy to the same stake which must hold himself, for he too plainly saw, that it could not be, but that both their hearts must burn.

Yes, his resolve concerning his father's memory involved the necessity of assuming even to Lucy his marriage with Isabel. Here he could not explain himself, even to her. This would aggravate the sharp pang of parting, by self-suggested, though wholly groundless surmising in Lucy's mind, in the most miserable degree contaminating to her idea of him. But on this point, he still fondly trusted that without at all marring his filial bond, he would be enabled by some significant intimations to arrest in Lucy's mind those darker imaginings which might find entrance there; and if he could not set her wholly right, yet prevent her from going wildly wrong.

For his mother Pierre was more prepared. He considered

that by an inscrutable decree, which it was but foolishness to try to evade, or shun, or deny existence to, since he felt it so profoundly pressing on his inmost soul; the family of the Glendinnings was imperiously called upon to offer up a victim to the gods of woe; one grand victim at the least; and that grand victim must be his mother, or himself. If he disclosed his secret to the world, then his mother was made the victim; if at all hazards he kept it to himself, then himself would be the victim. A victim as respecting his mother, because under the peculiar circumstances of the case, the non-disclosure of the secret involved her entire and infamy-engendering misconception of himself. But to this he bowed submissive.

One other thing—and the last to be here named, because the very least in the conscious thoughts of Pierre; one other thing remained to menace him with assured disastrousness. This thing it was, which though but dimly hinted of as yet, still in the apprehension must have exerted a powerful influence upon Pierre, in preparing him for the worst.

His father's last and fatal sickness had seized him suddenly. Both the probable concealed distraction of his mind with reference to his early life as recalled to him in an evil hour, and his consequent mental wanderings; these, with other reasons, had prevented him from framing a new will to supersede one made shortly after his marriage, and ere Pierre was born. By that will which as yet had never been dragged into the courts of law; and which, in the fancied security of her own and her son's congenial and loving future, Mrs. Glendinning had never but once, and then inconclusively, offered to discuss, with a view to a better and more appropriate ordering of things to meet circumstances non-existent at the period the testament was framed; by that will, all the Glendinning property was declared his mother's.

Acutely sensible to those prophetic intimations in him, which painted in advance the haughty temper of his offended mother, as all bitterness and scorn toward a son, once the object of her proudest joy, but now become a deep reproach, as not only rebellious to her, but glaringly dishonorable before the world; Pierre distinctly foresaw, that as she never would have permitted Isabel Banford in her true character to cross her threshold; neither would she now permit Isabel Banford to cross her threshold in any other, and disguised character; least of all, as that unknown and insidious girl, who by some pernicious arts had lured her only son from honor into infamy. But not to admit Isabel, was now to exclude Pierre, if indeed on independent grounds of exasperation against himself, his mother would not cast him out.

Nor did the same interior intimations in him which fore-painted the above bearing of his mother, abstain to trace her whole haughty heart as so unrelentingly set against him, that while she would close her doors against both him and his fictitious wife, so also she would not willingly contribute one copper to support them in a supposed union so entirely abhorrent to her. And though Pierre was not so familiar with the science of the law, as to be quite certain what the law, if appealed to concerning the provisions of his father's will, would decree concerning any possible claims of the son to share with the mother in the property of the sire; yet he prospectively felt an invincible repugnance to dragging his dead father's hand and seal into open Court, and fighting over them with a base mercenary motive, and with his own mother for the antagonist. For so thoroughly did his infallible presentiments paint his mother's character to him, as operated upon and disclosed in all those fiercer traits,—hitherto held in abeyance by the mere chance and felicity of circumstances,—that he felt assured that her exasperation against him would even meet the test of a public legal contention concerning the Glendinning property. For indeed there was a reserved strength and masculineness in the character of his mother, from which on all these points Pierre had every thing to dread. Besides, will the matter how he would, Pierre for nearly two whole years to come, would still remain a minor, an infant in the eye of the law, incapable of personally asserting any legal claim; and though he might sue by his next friend, yet who would be his voluntary next friend, when the execution of his great resolve would, for him, depopulate all the world of friends?

Now to all these things, and many more, seemed the soul of this infatuated young enthusiast braced.

iii

There is a dark, mad mystery in some human hearts, which, sometimes, during the tyranny of a usurper mood, leads them to be all eagerness to cast off the most intense beloved bond, as a hindrance to the attainment of whatever transcendental object that usurper mood so tyrannically suggests. Then the beloved bond seems to hold us to no essential good; lifted to exalted mounts, we can dispense with all the vale; endearments we spurn; kisses are blisters to us; and forsaking the palpitating forms of mortal love, we emptily embrace the boundless and the unbodied air. We think we are not human; we become as immortal bachelors and gods; but again, like the Greek gods themselves, prone we descend to earth; glad to be uxorious once more; glad to hide these god-like heads within the bosoms made of too-seducing clay.

Weary with the invariable earth, the restless sailor breaks from every enfolding arm, and puts to sea in height of tempest that blows off shore. But in long night-watches at the antipodes, how heavily that ocean gloom lies in vast bales upon the deck; thinking that that very moment in his deserted hamlet-home the household sun is high, and many a sun-eyed maiden meridian as the sun. He curses Fate; himself he curses; his senseless madness, which is himself. For whoso once has known this sweet knowledge, and then fled it; in absence, to him the avenging dream will come.

Pierre was now this vulnerable god; this self-upbraiding sailor; this dreamer of the avenging dream. Though in some things he had unjuggled himself, and forced himself to eye the prospect as it was; yet, so far as Lucy was concerned, he was at bottom still a juggler. True, in his extraordinary scheme, Lucy was so intimately interwoven, that it seemed impossible for him at all to cast his future without some way having that heart's love in view. But ignorant of its quantity as yet, or fearful of ascertaining it; like an algebraist, for the real Lucy he, in his scheming thoughts, had substituted but a sign—some empty x—and in the ultimate solution of the problem, that empty x still figured; not the real Lucy.

But now, when risen from the abasement of his chamber-floor, and risen from the still profounder prostration of his soul, Pierre had thought that all the horizon of his dark fate was commanded by him; all his resolutions clearly defined, and immovably decreed; now finally, to top all, there suddenly slid into his inmost heart the living and breathing form of Lucy. His lungs collapsed; his eyeballs glared; for the sweet imagined form, so long buried alive in him, seemed now as gliding on him from the grave; and her light hair swept far adown her shroud.

Then, for the time, all minor things were whelmed in him; his mother, Isabel, the whole wide world; and one only thing remained to him;—this all-including query—Lucy or God?

But here we draw a vail. Some nameless struggles of the soul can not be painted, and some woes will not be told. Let the ambiguous procession of events reveal their own ambiguousness.

Book XI

He Crosses the Rubicon

S UCKED WITHIN the maelstrom, man must go round.
Strike at one end the longest conceivable row of billiard
balls in close contact, and the furthermost ball will start forth,
while all the rest stand still; and yet that last ball was not
struck at all. So, through long previous generations, whether
of births or thoughts, Fate strikes the present man. Idly he
disowns the blow's effect, because he felt no blow, and indeed, received no blow. But Pierre was not arguing Fixed
Fate and Free Will, now; Fixed Fate and Free Will were arguing him, and Fixed Fate got the better in the debate.

The peculiarities of those influences which on the night and
early morning following the last interview with Isabel, persuaded Pierre to the adoption of his final resolve, did now
irresistibly impel him to a remarkable instantaneousness in his
actions, even as before he had proved a lagger.

Without being consciously that way pointed, through the
desire of anticipating any objections on the part of Isabel to
the assumption of a marriage between himself and her; Pierre
was now impetuously hurried into an act, which should have
the effective virtue of such an executed intention, without its
corresponding motive. Because, as the primitive resolve so deplorably involved Lucy, her image was then prominent in his
mind; and hence, because he felt all eagerness to hold her no
longer in suspense, but by a certain sort of charity of cruelty,
at once to pronounce to her her fate; therefore, it was among
his first final thoughts that morning to go to Lucy. And to
this, undoubtedly, so trifling a circumstance as her being
nearer to him, geographically, than Isabel, must have contributed some added, though unconscious influence, in his present fateful frame of mind.

On the previous undetermined days, Pierre had solicitously
sought to disguise his emotions from his mother, by a certain
carefulness and choiceness in his dress. But now, since his
very soul was forced to wear a mask, he would wear no paltry
palliatives and disguisements on his body. He went to the

cottage of Lucy as disordered in his person, as haggard in his face.

ii

She was not risen yet. So, the strange imperious instantaneousness in him, impelled him to go straight to her chamber-door, and in a voice of mild invincibleness, demand immediate audience, for the matter pressed.

Already namelessly concerned and alarmed for her lover, now eight-and-forty hours absent on some mysterious and undisclosable affair; Lucy, at this surprising summons was overwhelmed with sudden terror; and in oblivion of all ordinary proprieties, responded to Pierre's call, by an immediate assent.

Opening the door, he advanced slowly and deliberately toward her; and as Lucy caught his pale determined figure, she gave a cry of groping misery, which knew not the pang that caused it, and lifted herself trembling in her bed; but without uttering one word.

Pierre sat down on the bedside; and his set eyes met her terrified and virgin aspect.

"Decked in snow-white, and pale of cheek, thou indeed art fitted for the altar; but not that one of which thy fond heart did'st dream:—so fair a victim!"

"Pierre!"

" 'Tis the last cruelty of tyrants to make their enemies slay each other."

"My heart! my heart!"

"Nay;——Lucy, I am married."

The girl was no more pale, but white as any leper; the bed-clothes trembled to the concealed shudderings of all her limbs; one moment she sat looking vacantly into the blank eyes of Pierre, and then fell over toward him in a swoon.

Swift madness mounted into the brain of Pierre; all the past seemed as a dream, and all the present an unintelligible horror. He lifted her, and extended her motionless form upon the bed, and stamped for succor. The maid Martha came running into the room, and beholding those two inexplicable figures, shrieked, and turned in terror. But Pierre's repeated cry rallied Martha from this, and darting out of the chamber, she returned with a sharp restorative, which at length brought Lucy back to life.

"Martha! Martha!" now murmured Lucy, in a scarce audible whispering, and shuddering in the maid's own shuddering arms, "quick, quick; come to me—drive it away! wake me! wake me!"

"Nay, pray God to sleep again," cried Martha, bending over her and embracing her, and half-turning upon Pierre with a glance of loathing indignation. "In God's holy name, sir, what may this be? How came you here; accursed!"

"Accursed?—it is well. Is she herself again, Martha?"

"Thou hast somehow murdered her; how then be herself again? My sweet mistress! oh, my young mistress! Tell me! tell me!" and she bent low over her.

Pierre now advanced toward the bed, making a gesture for the maid to leave them; but soon as Lucy re-caught his haggard form, she whisperingly wailed again, "Martha! Martha! drive it away!—there—there! him—him!" and shut her eyes convulsively, with arms abhorrently outstretched.

"Monster! incomprehensible fiend!" cried the anew terror-smitten maid—"depart! See! she dies away at the sight of thee—begone! Wouldst thou murder her afresh? Begone!"

Starched and frozen by his own emotion, Pierre silently turned and quitted the chamber; and heavily descending the stairs, tramped heavily—as a man slowly bearing a great burden—through a long narrow passage leading to a wing in the rear of the cottage, and knocking at Miss Llanyllyn's door, summoned her to Lucy, who, he briefly said, had fainted. Then, without waiting for any response, left the house, and went directly to the mansion.

iii

"Is my mother up yet?" said he to Dates, whom he met in the hall.

"Not yet, sir;—heavens, sir! are you sick?"

"To death! Let me pass."

Ascending toward his mother's chamber, he heard a coming step, and met her on the great middle landing of the stairs, where in an ample niche, a marble group of the temple-polluting Laocoön and his two innocent children, caught in inextricable snarls of snakes, writhed in eternal torments.

"Mother, go back with me to thy chamber."

She eyed his sudden presence with a dark but repressed foreboding; drew herself up haughtily and repellingly, and with a quivering lip, said, "Pierre, thou thyself hast denied me thy confidence, and thou shalt not force me back to it so easily. Speak! what is that now between thee and me?"

"I am married, mother."

"Great God! To whom?"

"Not to Lucy Tartan, mother."

"That thou merely sayest 'tis not Lucy, without saying who indeed it is, this is good proof she is something vile. Does Lucy know thy marriage?"

"I am but just from Lucy's."

Thus far Mrs. Glendinning's rigidity had been slowly relaxing. Now she clutched the balluster, bent over, and trembled, for a moment. Then erected all her haughtiness again, and stood before Pierre in incurious, unappeasable grief and scorn for him.

"My dark soul prophesied something dark. If already thou hast not found other lodgment, and other table than this house supplies, then seek it straight. Beneath my roof, and at my table, he who was once Pierre Glendinning no more puts himself."

She turned from him, and with a tottering step climbed the winding stairs, and disappeared from him; while in the balluster he held, Pierre seemed to feel the sudden thrill running down to him from his mother's convulsive grasp.

He stared about him with an idiot eye; staggered to the floor below, to dumbly quit the house; but as he crossed its threshold, his foot tripped upon its raised ledge; he pitched forward upon the stone portico, and fell. He seemed as jeeringly hurled from beneath his own ancestral roof.

iv

Passing through the broad court-yard's postern, Pierre closed it after him, and then turned and leaned upon it, his eyes fixed upon the great central chimney of the mansion, from which a light blue smoke was wreathing gently into the morning air.

"The hearth-stone from which thou risest, never more, I inly feel, will these feet press. Oh God, what callest thou that which has thus made Pierre a vagabond?"

He walked slowly away, and passing the windows of Lucy, looked up, and saw the white curtains closely drawn, the white cottage profoundly still, and a white saddle-horse tied before the gate.

"I would enter, but again would her abhorrent wails repel; what more can I now say or do to her? I can not explain. She knows all I purposed to disclose. Ay, but thou didst cruelly burst upon her with it; thy impetuousness, thy instantaneousness hath killed her, Pierre!—Nay, nay, nay!—Cruel tidings who can gently break? If to stab be inevitable; then instant be the dagger! Those curtains are close drawn upon her; so let me upon her sweet image draw the curtains of my soul. Sleep, sleep, sleep, sleep, thou angel!—wake no more to Pierre, nor to thyself, my Lucy!"

Passing on now hurriedly and blindly, he jostled against some oppositely-going wayfarer. The man paused amazed; and looking up, Pierre recognized a domestic of the Mansion. That instantaneousness which now impelled him in all his actions, again seized the ascendency in him. Ignoring the dismayed expression of the man at thus encountering his young master, Pierre commanded him to follow him. Going straight to the "Black Swan," the little village Inn, he entered the first vacant room, and bidding the man be seated, sought the keeper of the house, and ordered pen and paper.

If fit opportunity offer in the hour of unusual affliction, minds of a certain temperament find a strange, hysterical relief, in a wild, perverse humorousness, the more alluring from its entire unsuitableness to the occasion; although they seldom manifest this trait toward those individuals more immediately involved in the cause or the effect of their suffering. The cool censoriousness of the mere philosopher would denominate such conduct as nothing short of temporary madness; and perhaps it is, since, in the inexorable and inhuman eye of mere undiluted reason, all grief, whether on our own account, or that of others, is the sheerest unreason and insanity.

The note now written was the following:

"For that Fine Old Fellow, Dates.

"Dates, my old boy, bestir thyself now. Go to my room, Dates, and bring me down my mahogany strong-box and lockup, the thing covered with blue chintz; strap it very carefully, my sweet Dates, it is rather heavy, and set it just without the postern. Then back and bring me down my writing-desk, and set that, too, just without the postern. Then back yet again, and bring me down the old camp-bed (see that all the parts be there), and bind the case well with a cord. Then go to the left corner little drawer in my wardrobe, and thou wilt find my visiting-cards. Tack one on the chest, and the desk, and the camp-bed case. Then get all my clothes together, and pack them in trunks (not forgetting the two old military cloaks, my boy), and tack cards on them also, my good Dates. Then fly round three times indefinitely, my good Dates, and wipe a little of the perspiration off. And then— let me see—then, my good Dates—why what then? Why, this much. Pick up all papers of all sorts that may be lying round my chamber, and see them burned. And then—have old White Hoof put to the lightest farm-wagon, and send the chest, and the desk, and the camp-bed, and the trunks to the 'Black Swan,' where I shall call for them, when I am ready, and not before, sweet Dates. So God bless thee, my fine, old, imperturbable Dates, and adieu!

"Thy old young master,   PIERRE.

"*Nota bene*—Mark well, though, Dates. Should my mother possibly interrupt thee, say that it is my orders, and mention what it is I send for; but on no account show this to thy mistress—D'ye hear?   PIERRE again."

Folding this scrawl into a grotesque shape, Pierre ordered the man to take it forthwith to Dates. But the man, all perplexed, hesitated, turning the billet over in his hand; till Pierre loudly and violently bade him begone; but as the man was then rapidly departing in a panic, Pierre called him back and retracted his rude words; but as the servant now lingered again, perhaps thinking to avail himself of this repentant mood in Pierre, to say something in sympathy or remonstrance to him, Pierre ordered him off with augmented violence, and stamped for him to begone.

Apprising the equally perplexed old landlord that certain things would in the course of that forenoon be left for him, (Pierre,) at the Inn; and also desiring him to prepare a chamber for himself and wife that night; some chamber with a commodious connecting room, which might answer for a dressing-room; and likewise still another chamber for a servant; Pierre departed the place, leaving the old landlord staring vacantly at him, and dumbly marveling what horrible thing had happened to turn the brain of his fine young favorite and old shooting comrade, Master Pierre.

Soon the short old man went out bare-headed upon the low porch of the Inn, descended its one step, and crossed over to the middle of the road, gazing after Pierre. And only as Pierre turned up a distant lane, did his amazement and his solicitude find utterance.

"I taught him—yes, old Casks;—the best shot in all the country round is Master Pierre;—pray God he hits not now the bull's eye in himself.—Married? married? and coming here?—This is pesky strange!"

Book XII

WHEN ON THE previous night Pierre had left the farm-house where Isabel harbored, it will be remembered that no hour, either of night or day, no special time at all had been assigned for a succeeding interview. It was Isabel, who for some doubtlessly sufficient reason of her own, had, for the first meeting, assigned the early hour of darkness.

As now, when the full sun was well up the heavens, Pierre drew near the farm-house of the Ulvers, he descried Isabel, standing without the little dairy-wing, occupied in vertically arranging numerous glittering shield-like milk-pans on a long shelf, where they might purifyingly meet the sun. Her back was toward him. As Pierre passed through the open wicket and crossed the short soft green sward, he unconsciously muffled his footsteps, and now standing close behind his sister, touched her shoulder and stood still.

She started, trembled, turned upon him swiftly, made a low, strange cry, and then gazed rivetedly and imploringly upon him.

"I look rather queerish, sweet Isabel, do I not?" said Pierre at last with a writhed and painful smile.

"My brother, my blessed brother!—speak—tell me—what has happened—what hast thou done? Oh! Oh! I should have warned thee before, Pierre, Pierre; it is my fault—mine, mine!"

"*What* is thy fault, sweet Isabel?"

"Thou hast revealed Isabel to thy mother, Pierre."

"I have not, Isabel. Mrs. Glendinning knows not thy secret at all."

"Mrs. Glendinning?—that's,—that's thine own mother, Pierre! In heaven's name, my brother, explain thyself. Knows not my secret, and yet thou here so suddenly, and with such a fatal aspect? Come, come with me into the house. Quick, Pierre, why dost thou not stir? Oh, my God! if mad myself sometimes, I am to make mad him who loves me best, and

223

who, I fear, has in some way ruined himself for me;—then, let me no more stand upright on this sod, but fall prone beneath it, that I may be hidden! Tell me!" catching Pierre's arms in both her frantic hands—"tell me, do I blast where I look? is my face Gorgon's?"

"Nay, sweet Isabel; but it hath a more sovereign power; that turned to stone; thine might turn white marble into mother's milk."

"Come with me—come quickly."

They passed into the dairy, and sat down on a bench by the honey-suckled casement.

"Pierre, forever fatal and accursed be the day my longing heart called thee to me, if now, in the very spring-time of our related love, thou art minded to play deceivingly with me, even though thou should'st fancy it for my good. Speak to me; oh speak to me, my brother!"

"Thou hintest of deceiving one for one's good. Now supposing, sweet Isabel, that in no case would I affirmatively deceive thee;—in no case whatever;—would'st thou then be willing for thee and me to piously deceive others, for both their and our united good?—Thou sayest nothing. Now, then, is it *my* turn, sweet Isabel, to bid thee speak to me, oh speak to me!"

"That unknown, approaching thing, seemeth ever ill, my brother, which must have unfrank heralds to go before. Oh, Pierre, dear, dear Pierre; be very careful with me! This strange, mysterious, unexampled love between us, makes me all plastic in thy hand. Be very careful with me. I know little out of me. The world seems all one unknown India to me. Look up, look on me, Pierre; say now, thou wilt be very careful; say so, say so, Pierre!"

"If the most exquisite, and fragile filagree of Genoa be carefully handled by its artisan; if sacred nature carefully folds, and warms, and by inconceivable attentivenesses eggs round and round her minute and marvelous embryoes; then, Isabel, do I most carefully and most tenderly egg thee, gentlest one, and the fate of thee! Short of the great God, Isabel, there lives none who will be more careful with thee, more infinitely considerate and delicate with thee."

"From my deepest heart, do I believe thee, Pierre. Yet thou

mayest be very delicate in some point, where delicateness is not all essential, and in some quick impulsive hour, omit thy fullest heedfulness somewhere where heedlessness were most fatal. Nay, nay, my brother; bleach these locks snow-white, thou sun! if I have any thought to reproach thee, Pierre, or betray distrust of thee. But earnestness must sometimes seem suspicious, else it is none. Pierre, Pierre, all thy aspect speaks eloquently of some already executed resolution, born in suddenness. Since I last saw thee, Pierre, some deed irrevocable has been done by thee. My soul is stiff and starched to it; now tell me what it is?"

"Thou, and I, and Delly Ulver, to-morrow morning depart this whole neighborhood, and go to the distant city.—That is it."

"No more?"

"Is it not enough?"

"There is something more, Pierre."

"Thou hast not yet answered a question I put to thee but just now. Bethink thee, Isabel. The deceiving of others by thee and me, in a thing wholly pertaining to ourselves, for their and our united good. Wouldst thou?"

"I would do any thing that does not tend to the marring of thy best lasting fortunes, Pierre. What is it thou wouldst have thee and me to do together? I wait; I wait!"

"Let us go into the room of the double casement, my sister," said Pierre, rising.

"Nay, then; if it can not be said here, then can I not do it anywhere, my brother; for it would harm thee."

"Girl!" cried Pierre, sternly, "if for thee I have lost"—but he checked himself.

"Lost? for me? Now does the very worst blacken on me. Pierre! Pierre!"

"I was foolish, and sought but to frighten thee, my sister. It was very foolish. Do thou now go on with thine innocent work here, and I will come again a few hours hence. Let me go now."

He was turning from her, when Isabel sprang forward to him, caught him with both her arms round him, and held him so convulsively, that her hair sideways swept over him, and half concealed him.

"Pierre, if indeed my soul hath cast on thee the same black shadow that my hair now flings on thee; if thou hast lost aught for me; then eternally is Isabel lost to Isabel, and Isabel will not outlive this night. If I am indeed an accursing thing, I will not act the given part, but cheat the air, and die from it. See; I let thee go, lest some poison I know not of distill upon thee from me."

She slowly drooped, and trembled from him. But Pierre caught her, and supported her.

"Foolish, foolish one! Behold, in the very bodily act of loosing hold of me, thou dost reel and fall;—unanswerable emblem of the indispensable heart-stay, I am to thee, my sweet, sweet Isabel! Prate not then of parting."

"What hast thou lost for me? Tell me!"

"A gainful loss, my sister!"

" 'Tis mere rhetoric! What hast thou lost?"

"Nothing that my inmost heart would now recall. I have bought inner love and glory by a price, which, large or small, I would not now have paid me back, so I must return the thing I bought."

"Is love then cold, and glory white? Thy cheek is snowy, Pierre."

"It should be, for I believe to God that I am pure, let the world think how it may."

"What hast thou lost?"

"Not thee, nor the pride and glory of ever loving thee, and being a continual brother to thee, my best sister. Nay, why dost thou now turn thy face from me?"

"With fine words he wheedles me, and coaxes me, not to know some secret thing. Go, go, Pierre, come to me when thou wilt. I am steeled now to the worst, and to the last. Again I tell thee, I will do any thing—yes, any thing that Pierre commands—for, though outer ill do lower upon us, still, deep within, thou wilt be careful, very careful with me, Pierre?"

"Thou art made of that fine, unshared stuff of which God makes his seraphim. But thy divine devotedness to me, is met by mine to thee. Well mayest thou trust me, Isabel; and whatever strangest thing I may yet propose to thee, thy confidence,—will it not bear me out? Surely thou will not hesitate to plunge, when I plunge first;—already have I plunged! now thou canst not stay upon the bank. Hearken, hearken to me.—I seek not now to gain thy prior assent to a thing as yet undone; but I call to thee now, Isabel, from the depth of a foregone act, to ratify it, backward, by thy consent. Look not so hard upon me. Listen. I will tell all. Isabel, though thou art all fearfulness to injure any living thing, least of all, thy brother; still thy true heart foreknoweth not the myriad alliances and criss-crossings among mankind, the infinite entanglements of all social things, which forbid that one thread should fly the general fabric, on some new line of duty, without tearing itself and tearing others. Listen. All that has happened up to this moment, and all that may be yet to happen, some sudden inspiration now assures me, inevitably proceeded from the first hour I saw thee. Not possibly could it, or can it, be otherwise. Therefore feel I, that I have some patience. Listen. Whatever outer things might possibly be mine; whatever seeming brightest blessings; yet now to live uncomforting and unloving to thee, Isabel; now to dwell domestically away from thee; so that only by stealth, and base connivances of the night, I could come to thee as thy related brother; this would be, and is, unutterably impossible. In my bosom a secret adder of self-reproach and self-infamy would never leave off its sting. Listen. But without gratuitous dishonor to a memory which—for right cause or wrong—is ever sacred and inviolate to me, I can not be an open brother to thee, Isabel. But thou wantest not the openness; for thou dost not pine for empty nominalness, but for vital realness; what thou wantest, is not the occasional openness of my brotherly love; but its continual domestic confidence. Do I not speak thine own hidden heart to thee? say, Isabel? Well, then, still listen to me. One only way presents to this; a most strange way, Isabel; to the world, that never throbbed for thee in love, a most deceitful way; but to all a harmless way; so harmless in its essence, Isabel, that, seems to me, Pierre hath consulted heaven itself upon it, and heaven itself did not say Nay. Still, listen to me; mark me. As thou knowest that thou wouldst now droop and die without me; so would I without thee. We are equal there; mark *that*, too, Isabel. I do not stoop to thee, nor thou to me; but we both reach up alike to a glorious ideal! Now the continualness, the secretness, yet the always present domesticness of our love; how may we best compass that, without jeopardizing the ever-sacred memory I hinted of? One way—one way—only one! A strange way, but most pure. Listen. Brace thyself: here, let me hold thee now; and then whisper it to thee, Isabel. Come, I holding thee, thou canst not fall."

He held her tremblingly; she bent over toward him; his mouth wet her ear; he whispered it.

The girl moved not; was done with all her tremblings; leaned closer to him, with an inexpressible strangeness of an intense love, new and inexplicable. Over the face of Pierre there shot a terrible self-revelation; he imprinted repeated burning kisses upon her; pressed hard her hand; would not let go her sweet and awful passiveness.

Then they changed; they coiled together, and entangledly stood mute.

ii

Mrs. Glendinning walked her chamber; her dress loosened.

"That such accursed vileness should proceed from me! Now will the tongued world say—See the vile boy of Mary Glendinning!—Deceitful! thick with guilt, where I thought it was all guilelessness and gentlest docility to me. It has not happened! It is not day! Were this thing so, I should go mad, and be shut up, and not walk here where every door is open to me.—My own only son married to an unknown—thing! My own only son, false to his holiest plighted public vow— and the wide world knowing to it! He bears my name— Glendinning. I will disown it; were it like this dress, I would tear my name off from me, and burn it till it shriveled to a crisp!—Pierre! Pierre! come back, come back, and swear it is not so! It can not be! Wait: I will ring the bell, and see if it be so."

She rung the bell with violence, and soon heard a responsive knock.

"Come in!—Nay, falter not;" (throwing a shawl over her) "come in. Stand there and tell me if thou darest, that my son was in this house this morning and met me on the stairs. Darest thou say that?"

Dates looked confounded at her most unwonted aspect.

"Say it! find thy tongue! Or I will root mine out and fling it at thee! Say it!"

"My dear mistress!"

"I am not thy mistress! but thou my master; for, if thou sayest it, thou commandest me to madness.—Oh, vile boy!— Begone from me!"

She locked the door upon him, and swiftly and distractedly walked her chamber. She paused, and tossing down the curtains, shut out the sun from the two windows.

Another, but an unsummoned knock, was at the door. She opened it.

"My mistress, his Reverence is below. I would not call you, but he insisted."

"Let him come up."

"Here? Immediately?"

"Didst thou hear me? Let Mr. Falsgrave come up."

As if suddenly and admonishingly made aware, by Dates, of the ungovernable mood of Mrs. Glendinning, the clergyman entered the open door of her chamber with a most deprecating but honest reluctance, and apprehensiveness of he knew not what.

"Be seated, sir; stay, shut the door and lock it."

"Madam!"

"*I* will do it. Be seated. Hast thou seen him?"

"Whom, Madam?—Master Pierre?"

"Him!—quick!"

"It was to speak of him I came, Madam. He made a most extraordinary call upon me last night—midnight."

"And thou marriedst him?—Damn thee!"

"Nay, nay, nay, Madam; there is something here I know not of—I came to tell thee news, but thou hast some o'erwhelming tidings to reveal to me."

"I beg no pardons; but I may be sorry. Mr. Falsgrave, my son, standing publicly plighted to Lucy Tartan, has privately wedded some other girl—some slut!"

"Impossible!"

"True as thou art there. Thou knowest nothing of it then?"

"Nothing, nothing—not one grain till now. Who is it he has wedded?"

"Some *slut*, I tell thee!—I am no lady now, but something deeper,—a woman!—an outraged and pride-poisoned woman!"

She turned from him swiftly, and again paced the room, as frantic and entirely regardless of any presence. Waiting for her to pause, but in vain, Mr. Falsgrave advanced toward her cautiously, and with the profoundest deference, which was almost a cringing, spoke:—

"It is the hour of woe to thee; and I confess my cloth hath no consolation for thee yet awhile. Permit me to withdraw from thee, leaving my best prayers for thee, that thou mayst know some peace, ere this now shut-out sun goes down. Send for me whenever thou desirest me.—May I go now?"

"Begone! and let me not hear thy soft, mincing voice, which is an infamy to a man! Begone, thou helpless, and unhelping one!"

She swiftly paced the room again, swiftly muttering to herself. "Now, now, now, now I see it clearer, clearer—clear now as day! My first dim suspicions pointed right!—too right! Ay—the sewing! it was the sewing!—The shriek!—I saw him gazing rooted at her. He would not speak going home with me. I charged him with his silence; he put me off with lies, lies, lies! Ay, ay, he is married to her, to her;—to her!—perhaps was then. And yet,—and yet,—how can it be?—Lucy, Lucy—I saw him, after that, look on her as if he would be glad to die for her, and go to hell for her, whither he deserves to go!—Oh! oh! oh! Thus ruthlessly to cut off, at one gross sensual dash, the fair succession of an honorable race! Mixing the choicest wine with filthy water from the plebeian pool, and so turning all to undistinguishable rankness!—Oh viper! had I thee now in me, I would be a suicide and a murderer with one blow!"

A third knock was at the door. She opened it.

"My mistress, I thought it would disturb you,—it is so just overhead,—so I have not removed them yet."

"Unravel thy gibberish!—what is it?"

"Pardon, my mistress, I somehow thought you knew it, but you can not."

"What is that writing crumpling in thy hand? Give it me."

"I have promised my young master not to, my mistress."

"I will snatch it, then, and so leave thee blameless.—What? what? what?—He's mad sure!—'Fine old fellow Dates'— what? what?—mad and merry!—chest?—clothes?—trunks? —he wants them?—Tumble them out of his window!—and if he stand right beneath, tumble them out! Dismantle that whole room. Tear up the carpet. I swear, he shall leave no smallest vestige in this house.—Here! this very spot—here, here, where I stand, he may have stood upon;—yes, he tied my shoe-string here; it's slippery! Dates!"

"My mistress."

"Do his bidding. By reflection he has made me infamous to the world; and I will make him infamous to it. Listen, and do not delude thyself that I am crazy. Go up to yonder room" (pointing upward), "and remove every article in it, and where he bid thee set down the chest and trunks, there set down all the contents of that room."

" 'Twas before the house—this house!"

"And if it had not been there, I would order thee to put them there. Dunce! I would have the world know that I dis-own and scorn him! Do my bidding!—Stay. Let the room stand; but take him what he asks for."

"I will, my mistress."

As Dates left the chamber, Mrs. Glendinning again paced it swiftly, and again swiftly muttered: "Now, if I were less a strong and haughty woman, the fit would have gone by ere now. But deep volcanoes long burn, ere they burn out.—Oh, that the world were made of such malleable stuff, that we could recklessly do our fieriest heart's-wish before it, and not falter. Accursed be those four syllables of sound which make up that vile word Propriety. It is a chain and ball to drag;— drag? what sound is that? there's dragging—his trunks—the traveler's—dragging out. Oh would I could so drag my heart, as fishers for the drowned do, as that I might drag up my sunken happiness! Boy! boy! worse than brought in drip-ping drowned to me,—drowned in icy infamy! Oh! oh! oh!"

She threw herself upon the bed, covered her face, and lay motionless. But suddenly rose again, and hurriedly rang the bell.

"Open that desk, and draw the stand to me. Now wait and take this to Miss Lucy."

With a pencil she rapidly traced these lines:—

"My heart bleeds for thee, sweet Lucy. I can not speak—I know it all. Look for me the first hour I regain myself."

Again she threw herself upon the bed, and lay motionless.

iii

Toward sundown that evening, Pierre stood in one of the three bespoken chambers in the Black Swan Inn; the blue chintz-covered chest and the writing-desk before him. His hands were eagerly searching through his pockets.

"The key! the key! Nay, then, I must force it open. It bodes ill, too. Yet lucky is it, some bankers can break into their own vaults, when other means do fail. Not so, ever. Let me see:— yes, the tongs there. Now then for the sweet sight of gold and silver. I never loved it till this day. How long it has been hoarded;—little token pieces, of years ago, from aunts, uncles, cousins innumerable, and from—but I won't mention *them*; dead henceforth to me! Sure there'll be a premium on such ancient gold. There's some broad bits, token pieces to my—I name him not—more than half a century ago. Well, well, I never thought to cast them back into the sordid circulations whence they came. But if they must be spent, now is the time, in this last necessity, and in this sacred cause. 'Tis a most stupid, dunderheaded crowbar. Hoy! so! ah, now for it:—snake's nest!"

Forced suddenly back, the chest-lid had as suddenly revealed to him the chair-portrait lying on top of all the rest, where he had secreted it some days before. Face up, it met him with its noiseless, ever-nameless, and ambiguous, unchanging smile. Now his first repugnance was augmented by an emotion altogether new. That certain lurking lineament in the portrait, whose strange transfer, blended with far other, and sweeter, and nobler characteristics, was visible in the countenance of Isabel; that lineament in the portrait was somehow now detestable; nay, altogether loathsome, ineffably so, to Pierre. He argued not with himself why this was so; he only felt it, and most keenly.

Omitting more subtile inquisition into this deftly-winding theme, it will be enough to hint, perhaps, that possibly one source of this new hatefulness had its primary and unconscious rise in one of those profound ideas, which at times atmospherically, as it were, do insinuate themselves even into very ordinary minds. In the strange relativeness, reciprocalness, and transmittedness, between the long-dead father's portrait, and the living daughter's face, Pierre might have seemed to see reflected to him, by visible and uncontradictable symbols, the tyranny of Time and Fate. Painted before the daughter was conceived or born, like a dumb seer, the portrait still seemed leveling its prophetic finger at that empty air, from which Isabel did finally emerge. There seemed to lurk some mystical intelligence and vitality in the picture; because, since in his own memory of his father, Pierre could not recall any distinct lineament transmitted to Isabel, but vaguely saw such in the portrait; therefore, not Pierre's parent, as any way rememberable by him, but the portrait's painted *self* seemed the real father of Isabel; for, so far as all sense went, Isabel had inherited one peculiar trait nowhither traceable but to it.

And as his father was now sought to be banished from his mind, as a most bitter presence there, but Isabel was become a thing of intense and fearful love for him; therefore, it was loathsome to him, that in the smiling and ambiguous portrait, her sweet mournful image should be so sinisterly becrooked, bemixed, and mutilated to him.

When the first shock, and then the pause were over, he lifted the portrait in his two hands, and held it averted from him.

"It shall not live. Hitherto I have hoarded up mementoes and monuments of the past; been a worshiper of all heirlooms; a fond filer away of letters, locks of hair, bits of ribbon, flowers, and the thousand-and-one minutenesses which love and memory think they sanctify:—but it is forever over now! If to me any memory shall henceforth be dear, I will not mummy it in a visible memorial for every passing beggar's dust to gather on. Love's museum is vain and foolish as the Catacombs, where grinning apes and abject lizards are embalmed, as, forsooth, significant of some imagined charm.

It speaks merely of decay and death, and nothing more; decay and death of endless innumerable generations; it makes of earth one mold. How can lifelessness be fit memorial of life?—So far, for mementoes of the sweetest. As for the rest—now I know this, that in commonest memorials, the twilight fact of death first discloses in some secret way, all the ambiguities of that departed thing or person; obliquely it casts hints, and insinuates surmises base, and eternally incapable of being cleared. Decreed by God Omnipotent it is, that Death should be the last scene of the last act of man's play;—a play, which begin how it may, in farce or comedy, ever hath its tragic end; the curtain inevitably falls upon a corpse. Therefore, never more will I play the vile pigmy, and by small memorials after death, attempt to reverse the decree of death, by essaying the poor perpetuating of the image of the original. Let all die, and mix again! As for this—this!—why longer should I preserve it? Why preserve that on which one can not patient look? If I am resolved to hold his public memory inviolate,—destroy this thing; for here is the one great, condemning, and unsuborned proof, whose mysticalness drives me half mad.—Of old Greek times, before man's brain went into doting bondage, and bleached and beaten in Baconian fulling-mills, his four limbs lost their barbaric tan and beauty; when the round world was fresh, and rosy, and spicy, as a new-plucked apple;—all's wilted now!—in those bold times, the great dead were not, turkey-like, dished in trenchers, and set down all garnished in the ground, to glut the damned Cyclops like a cannibal; but nobly envious Life cheated the glutton worm, and gloriously burned the corpse; so that the spirit up-pointed, and visibly forked to heaven!

"So now will I serve thee. Though that solidity of which thou art the unsolid duplicate, hath long gone to its hideous church-yard account;—and though, God knows! but for one part of thee it may have been fit auditing;—yet will I now a second time see thy obsequies performed, and by now burning thee, urn thee in the great vase of air! Come now!"

A small wood-fire had been kindled on the hearth to purify the long-closed room; it was now diminished to a small pointed heap of glowing embers. Detaching and dismembering the gilded but tarnished frame, Pierre laid the four pieces on the coals; as their dryness soon caught the sparks, he rolled the reversed canvas into a scroll, and tied it, and committed it to the now crackling, clamorous flames. Steadfastly Pierre watched the first crispings and blackenings of the painted scroll, but started as suddenly unwinding from the burnt string that had tied it, for one swift instant, seen through the flame and smoke, the upwrithing portrait tormentedly stared at him in beseeching horror, and then, wrapped in one broad sheet of oily fire, disappeared forever.

Yielding to a sudden ungovernable impulse, Pierre darted his hand among the flames, to rescue the imploring face; but as swiftly drew back his scorched and bootless grasp. His hand was burnt and blackened, but he did not heed it.

He ran back to the chest, and seizing repeated packages of family letters, and all sorts of miscellaneous memorials in paper, he threw them one after the other upon the fire.

"Thus, and thus, and thus! on thy manes I fling fresh spoils; pour out all my memory in one libation!—so, so, so—lower, lower, lower; now all is done, and all is ashes! Henceforth, cast-out Pierre hath no paternity, and no past; and since the Future is one blank to all; therefore, twice-disinherited Pierre stands untrammeledly his ever-present self!—free to do his own self-will and present fancy to whatever end!"

iv

That same sunset Lucy lay in her chamber. A knock was heard at its door, and the responding Martha was met by the now self-controlled and resolute face of Mrs. Glendinning.

"How is your young mistress, Martha? May I come in?"

But waiting for no answer, with the same breath she passed the maid, and determinately entered the room.

She sat down by the bed, and met the open eye, but closed and pallid mouth of Lucy. She gazed rivetedly and inquisitively a moment; then turned a quick aghast look toward Martha, as if seeking warrant for some shuddering thought.

"Miss Lucy"—said Martha—"it is your—it is Mrs. Glendinning. Speak to her, Miss Lucy."

As if left in the last helpless attitude of some spent contortion of her grief, Lucy was not lying in the ordinary posture of one in bed, but lay half cross-wise upon it, with the pale pillows propping her hueless form, and but a single sheet thrown over her, as though she were so heart overladen, that her white body could not bear one added feather. And as in any snowy, marble statue, the drapery clings to the limbs; so as one found drowned, the thin, defining sheet invested Lucy.

"It is Mrs. Glendinning. Will you speak to her, Miss Lucy?"

The thin lips moved and trembled for a moment, and then were still again, and augmented pallor shrouded her.

Martha brought restoratives; and when all was as before, she made a gesture for the lady to depart, and in a whisper, said, "She will not speak to any; she does not speak to me. The doctor has just left—he has been here five times since morning—and says she must be kept entirely quiet." Then pointing to the stand, added, "You see what he has left— mere restoratives. Quiet is her best medicine now, he says. Quiet, quiet, quiet! Oh, sweet quiet, wilt thou now ever come?"

"Has Mrs. Tartan been written to?" whispered the lady. Martha nodded.

So the lady moved to quit the room, saying that once every two hours she would send to know how Lucy fared.

"But where, where is her aunt, Martha?" she exclaimed, lowly, pausing at the door, and glancing in sudden astonishment about the room; "surely, surely, Mrs. Llanyllyn—"

"Poor, poor old lady," weepingly whispered Martha, "she hath caught infection from sweet Lucy's woe; she hurried hither, caught one glimpse of that bed, and fell like dead upon the floor. The Doctor hath two patients now, lady"— glancing at the bed, and tenderly feeling Lucy's bosom, to mark if yet it heaved; "Alack! Alack! oh, reptile! reptile! that could sting so sweet a breast! fire would be too cold for him—accursed!"

"Thy own tongue blister the roof of thy mouth!" cried Mrs. Glendinning, in a half-stifled, whispering scream. " 'Tis not for thee, hired one, to rail at my son, though he were Lucifer, simmering in Hell! Mend thy manners, minx!"

And she left the chamber, dilated with her unconquerable pride, leaving Martha aghast at such venom in such beauty.

Book XIII

They Depart the Meadows

It was just dusk when Pierre approached the Ulver farmhouse, in a wagon belonging to the Black Swan Inn. He met his sister shawled and bonneted in the porch.

"Now then, Isabel, is all ready? Where is Delly? I see two most small and inconsiderable portmanteaux. Wee is the chest that holds the goods of the disowned! The wagon waits, Isabel. Now is all ready? and nothing left?"

"Nothing, Pierre; unless in going hence—but I'll not think of that; all's fated."

"Delly! where is she? Let us go in for her," said Pierre, catching the hand of Isabel, and turning rapidly. As he thus half dragged her into the little lighted entry, and then dropping her hand, placed his touch on the catch of the inner door, Isabel stayed his arm, as if to keep him back, till she should forewarn him against something concerning Delly; but suddenly she started herself; and for one instant, eagerly pointing at his right hand, seemed almost to half shrink from Pierre.

" 'Tis nothing. I am not hurt; a slight burn—the merest accidental scorch this morning. But what's this?" he added, lifting his hand higher; "smoke! soot! this comes of going in the dark; sunlight, and I had seen it. But I have not touched thee, Isabel?"

Isabel lifted her hand and showed the marks.—"But it came from thee, my brother; and I would catch the plague from thee, so that it should make me share thee. Do thou clean thy hand; let mine alone."

"Delly! Delly!"—cried Pierre—" why may I not go to her, to bring her forth?"

Placing her finger upon her lip, Isabel softly opened the door, and showed the object of his inquiry avertedly seated, muffled, on a chair.

"Do not speak to her, my brother," whispered Isabel, "and do not seek to behold her face, as yet. It will pass over now, ere long, I trust. Come, shall we go now? Take Delly forth,

but do not speak to her. I have bidden all good-by; the old
people are in yonder room in the rear; I am glad that they
chose not to come out, to attend our going forth. Come now,
be very quick, Pierre; this is an hour I like not; be it swiftly
past."

Soon all three alighted at the inn. Ordering lights, Pierre
led the way above-stairs, and ushered his two companions
into one of the two outermost rooms of the three adjoining
chambers prepared for all.

"See," said he, to the mute and still self-averting figure of
Delly;—"see, this is thy room, Miss Ulver; Isabel has told
thee all; thou know'st our till now secret marriage; she will
stay with thee now, till I return from a little business down
the street. To-morrow, thou know'st, very early, we take the
stage. I may not see thee again till then, so, be steadfast, and
cheer up a very little, Miss Ulver, and good-night. All will be
well."

ii

Next morning, by break of day, at four o'clock, the four
swift hours were personified in four impatient horses, which
shook their trappings beneath the windows of the inn. Three
figures emerged into the cool dim air and took their places in
the coach.

The old landlord had silently and despondently shaken
Pierre by the hand; the vainglorious driver was on his box,
threadingly adjusting the four reins among the fingers of his
buck-skin gloves; the usual thin company of admiring ostlers
and other early on-lookers were gathered about the porch;
when—on his companions' account—all eager to cut short
any vain delay, at such a painful crisis, Pierre impetuously
shouted for the coach to move. In a moment, the four
meadow-fed young horses leaped forward their own generous
lengths, and the four responsive wheels rolled their complete
circles; while making vast rearward flourishes with his whip,
the elated driver seemed as a bravado-hero signing his ostentatious farewell signature in the empty air. And so, in the dim
of the dawn—and to the defiant crackings of that long and

sharp-resounding whip, the three forever fled the sweet fields of Saddle Meadows.

The short old landlord gazed after the coach awhile, and then re-entering the inn, stroked his gray beard and muttered to himself: — "I have kept this house, now, three-and-thirty years, and have had plenty of bridal-parties come and go; in their long train of wagons, break-downs, buggies, gigs — a gay and giggling train — Ha! — there's a pun! popt out like a cork — ay, and once in ox-carts, all garlanded; ay, and once, the merry bride was bedded on a load of sweet-scented new-cut clover. But such a bridal-party as this morning's — why, it's as sad as funerals. And brave Master Pierre Glendinning is the groom! Well, well, wonders is all the go. I thought I had done with wondering when I passed fifty; but I keep wondering still. Ah, somehow, now, I feel as though I had just come from lowering some old friend beneath the sod, and yet felt the grating cord-marks in my palms. — 'Tis early, but I'll drink. Let's see; cider, — a mug of cider; — 'tis sharp, and pricks like a game-cock's spur, — cider's the drink for grief. Oh, Lord! that fat men should be so thin-skinned, and suffer in pure sympathy on others' account. A thin-skinned, thin man, he don't suffer so, because there ain't so much stuff in him for his thin skin to cover. Well, well, well, well, well; of all colics, save me from the melloncholics; green melons is the greenest thing!"

Book XIV

The Journey and the Pamphlet

ALL PROFOUND THINGS, and emotions of things are preceded and attended by Silence. What a silence is that with which the pale bride precedes the responsive *I will*, to the priest's solemn question, *Wilt thou have this man for thy husband?* In silence, too, the wedded hands are clasped. Yea, in silence the child Christ was born into the world. Silence is the general consecration of the universe. Silence is the invisible laying on of the Divine Pontiff's hands upon the world. Silence is at once the most harmless and the most awful thing in all nature. It speaks of the Reserved Forces of Fate. Silence is the only Voice of our God.

Nor is this so august Silence confined to things simply touching or grand. Like the air, Silence permeates all things, and produces its magical power, as well during that peculiar mood which prevails at a solitary traveler's first setting forth on a journey, as at the unimaginable time when before the world was, Silence brooded on the face of the waters.

No word was spoken by its inmates, as the coach bearing our young Enthusiast, Pierre, and his mournful party, sped forth through the dim dawn into the deep midnight, which still occupied, unrepulsed, the hearts of the old woods through which the road wound, very shortly after quitting the village.

When, first entering the coach, Pierre had pressed his hand upon the cushioned seat to steady his way, some crumpled leaves of paper had met his fingers. He had instinctively clutched them; and the same strange clutching mood of his soul which had prompted that instinctive act, did also prevail in causing him now to retain the crumpled paper in his hand for an hour or more of that wonderful intense silence, which the rapid coach bore through the heart of the general stirless morning silence of the fields and the woods.

His thoughts were very dark and wild; for a space there was rebellion and horrid anarchy and infidelity in his soul. This temporary mood may best be likened to that, which—

according to a singular story once told in the pulpit by a reverend man of God—invaded the heart of an excellent priest. In the midst of a solemn cathedral, upon a cloudy Sunday afternoon, this priest was in the act of publicly administering the bread at the Holy Sacrament of the Supper, when the Evil One suddenly propounded to him the possibility of the mere moonshine of the Christian Religion. Just such now was the mood of Pierre; to him the Evil One propounded the possibility of the mere moonshine of all his self-renouncing Enthusiasm. The Evil One hooted at him, and called him a fool. But by instant and earnest prayer—closing his two eyes, with his two hands still holding the sacramental bread—the devout priest had vanquished the impious Devil. Not so with Pierre. The imperishable monument of his holy Catholic Church; the imperishable record of his Holy Bible; the imperishable intuition of the innate truth of Christianity;— these were the indestructible anchors which still held the priest to his firm Faith's rock, when the sudden storm raised by the Evil One assailed him. But Pierre—where could *he* find the Church, the monument, the Bible, which unequivocally said to him—"Go on; thou art in the Right; I endorse thee all over; go on."—So the difference between the Priest and Pierre was herein:—with the priest it was a matter, whether certain bodiless thoughts of his were true or not true; but with Pierre it was a question whether certain vital acts of his were right or wrong. In this little nut lie germ-like the possible solution of some puzzling problems; and also the discovery of additional, and still more profound problems ensuing upon the solution of the former. For so true is this last, that some men refuse to solve any present problem, for fear of making still more work for themselves in that way.

Now, Pierre thought of the magical, mournful letter of Isabel, he recalled the divine inspiration of that hour when the heroic words burst from his heart—"Comfort thee, and stand by thee, and fight for thee, will thy leapingly-acknowledging brother!" These remembrances unfurled themselves in proud exultations in his soul; and from before such glorious banners of Virtue, the club-footed Evil One limped away in dismay. But now the dread, fateful parting look of his mother came over him; anew he heard the heart-proscribing words—"Be-

neath my roof and at my table, he who was once Pierre Glendinning no more puts himself;"—swooning in her snow-
white bed, the lifeless Lucy lay before him, wrapt as in the
reverberating echoings of her own agonizing shriek: "My
heart! my heart!" Then how swift the recurrence to Isabel,
and the nameless awfulness of his still imperfectly conscious,
incipient, new-mingled emotion toward this mysterious
being. "Lo! I leave corpses wherever I go!" groaned Pierre to
himself—"Can then my conduct be right? Lo! by my conduct
I seem threatened by the possibility of a sin anomalous and
accursed, so anomalous, it may well be the one for which
Scripture says, there is never forgiveness. Corpses behind me,
and the last sin before, how then can my conduct be right?"

In this mood, the silence accompanied him, and the first
visible rays of the morning sun in this same mood found him
and saluted him. The excitement and the sleepless night just
passed, and the strange narcotic of a quiet, steady anguish,
and the sweet quiescence of the air, and the monotonous
cradle-like motion of the coach over a road made firm and
smooth by a refreshing shower over night; these had wrought
their wonted effect upon Isabel and Delly; with hidden faces
they leaned fast asleep in Pierre's sight. Fast asleep—thus unconscious, oh sweet Isabel, oh forlorn Delly, your swift des-
tinies I bear in my own!

Suddenly, as his sad eye fell lower and lower from scanning
their magically quiescent persons, his glance lit upon his own
clutched hand, which rested on his knee. Some paper protruded from that clutch. He knew not how it had got there,
or whence it had come, though himself had closed his own
gripe upon it. He lifted his hand and slowly unfingered and
unbolted the paper, and unrolled it, and carefully smoothed
it, to see what it might be.

It was a thin, tattered, dried-fish-like thing; printed with
blurred ink upon mean, sleazy paper. It seemed the opening
pages of some ruinous old pamphlet—a pamphlet containing
a chapter or so of some very voluminous disquisition. The
conclusion was gone. It must have been accidentally left there
by some previous traveler, who perhaps in drawing out his
handkerchief, had ignorantly extracted his waste paper.

There is a singular infatuation in most men, which leads

them in odd moments, intermitting between their regular occupations, and when they find themselves all alone in some quiet corner or nook, to fasten with unaccountable fondness upon the merest rag of old printed paper—some shred of a long-exploded advertisement perhaps—and read it, and study it, and re-read it, and pore over it, and fairly agonize themselves over this miserable, sleazy paper-rag, which at any other time, or in any other place, they would hardly touch with St. Dunstan's long tongs. So now, in a degree, with Pierre. But notwithstanding that he, with most other human beings, shared in the strange hallucination above mentioned, yet the first glimpse of the title of the dried-fish-like, pamphlet-shaped rag, did almost tempt him to pitch it out of the window. For, be a man's mood what it may, what sensible and ordinary mortal could have patience for any considerable period, to knowingly hold in his conscious hand a printed document (and that too a very blurred one as to ink, and a very sleazy one as to paper), so metaphysically and insufferably entitled as this:—"Chronometricals & Horologicals?"

Doubtless, it was something vastly profound; but it is to be observed, that when a man is in a really profound mood, then all merely verbal or written profundities are unspeakably repulsive, and seem downright childish to him. Nevertheless, the silence still continued; the road ran through an almost unplowed and uninhabited region; the slumberers still slumbered before him; the evil mood was becoming well nigh insupportable to him; so, more to force his mind away from the dark realities of things than from any other motive, Pierre finally tried his best to plunge himself into the pamphlet.

ii

Sooner or later in this life, the earnest, or enthusiastic youth comes to know, and more or less appreciate this startling solecism:—That while, as the grand condition of acceptance to God, Christianity calls upon all men to renounce this world; yet by all odds the most Mammonish part of this world—Europe and America—are owned by none but professed Christian nations, who glory in the owning, and seem to have some reason therefor.

This solecism once vividly and practically apparent; then comes the earnest reperusal of the Gospels: the intense self-absorption into that greatest real miracle of all religions, the Sermon on the Mount. From that divine mount, to all ear-nest-loving youths, flows an inexhaustible soul-melting stream of tenderness and loving-kindness; and they leap exulting to their feet, to think that the founder of their holy religion gave utterance to sentences so infinitely sweet and soothing as these; sentences which embody all the love of the Past, and all the love which can be imagined in any conceivable Future. Such emotions as that Sermon raises in the enthusiastic heart; such emotions all youthful hearts refuse to ascribe to human-ity as their origin. This is of God! cries the heart, and in that cry ceases all inquisition. Now, with this fresh-read sermon in his soul, the youth again gazes abroad upon the world. In-stantly, in aggravation of the former solecism, an overpower-ing sense of the world's downright positive falsity comes over him; the world seems to lie saturated and soaking with lies. The sense of this thing is so overpowering, that at first the youth is apt to refuse the evidence of his own senses; even as he does that same evidence in the matter of the movement of the visible sun in the heavens, which with his own eyes he plainly sees to go round the world, but nevertheless on the authority of other persons,—the Copernican astronomers, whom he never saw—he believes it *not* to go round the world, but the world round it. Just so, too, he hears good and wise people sincerely say: This world only *seems* to be saturated and soaking with lies; but in reality it does not so lie soaking and saturate; along with some lies, there is much truth in this world. But again he refers to his Bible, and there he reads most explicitly, that this world is unconditionally de-praved and accursed; and that at all hazards men must come out of it. But why come out of it, if it be a True World and not a Lying World? Assuredly, then, this world is a lie.

Hereupon then in the soul of the enthusiast youth two ar-mies come to the shock; and unless he prove recreant, or un-less he prove gullible, or unless he can find the talismanic secret, to reconcile this world with his own soul, then there is no peace for him, no slightest truce for him in this life. Now without doubt this Talismanic Secret has never yet been found; and in the nature of human things it seems as though it never can be. Certain philosophers have time and again pretended to have found it; but if they do not in the end discover their own delusion, other people soon discover it for themselves, and so those philosophers and their vain philosophy are let glide away into practical oblivion. Plato, and Spinoza, and Goethe, and many more belong to this guild of self-impostors, with a preposterous rabble of Muggletonian Scots and Yankees, whose vile brogue still the more bestreaks the stripedness of their Greek or German Neoplatonical originals. That profound Silence, that only Voice of our God, which I before spoke of; from that divine thing without a name, those impostor philosophers pretend somehow to have got an answer; which is as absurd, as though they should say they had got water out of stone; for how can a man get a Voice out of Silence?

Certainly, all must admit, that if for any one this problem of the possible reconcilement of this world with our own souls possessed a peculiar and potential interest, that one was Pierre Glendinning at the period we now write of. For in obedience to the loftiest behest of his soul, he had done certain vital acts, which had already lost him his worldly felicity, and which he felt must in the end indirectly work him some still additional and not-to-be-thought-of woe.

Soon then, as after his first distaste at the mystical title, and after his then reading on, merely to drown himself, Pierre at last began to obtain a glimmering into the profound intent of the writer of the sleazy rag pamphlet, he felt a great interest awakened in him. The more he read and re-read, the more this interest deepened, but still the more likewise did his failure to comprehend the writer increase. He seemed somehow to derive some general vague inkling concerning it, but the central conceit refused to become clear to him. The reason whereof is not so easy to be laid down; seeing that the reason-originating heart and mind of man, these organic things themselves are not so easily to be expounded. Something, however, more or less to the point, may be adventured here.

If a man be in any vague latent doubt about the intrinsic correctness and excellence of his general life-theory and practical course of life; then, if that man chance to light on any

other man, or any little treatise, or sermon, which unintendingly, as it were, yet very palpably illustrates to him the intrinsic incorrectness and non-excellence of both the theory
and the practice of his life; then that man will—more or less
unconsciously—try hard to hold himself back from the self-
admitted comprehension of a matter which thus condemns
him. For in this case, to comprehend, is himself to condemn
himself, which is always highly inconvenient and uncomfortable to a man. Again. If a man be told a thing wholly new,
then—during the time of its first announcement to him—it
is entirely impossible for him to comprehend it. For—absurd
as it may seem—men are only made to comprehend things
which they comprehended before (though but in the embryo,
as it were). Things new it is impossible to make them comprehend, by merely talking to them about it. True, sometimes
they pretend to comprehend; in their own hearts they really
believe they do comprehend; outwardly look as though they
did comprehend; wag their bushy tails comprehendingly; but
for all that, they do not comprehend. Possibly, they may afterward come, of themselves, to inhale this new idea from the
circumambient air, and so come to comprehend it; but not
otherwise at all. It will be observed, that neither points of the
above speculations do we, in set terms, attribute to Pierre in
connection with the rag pamphlet. Possibly both might be
applicable; possibly neither. Certain it is, however, that at the
time, in his own heart, he seemed to think that he did not
fully comprehend the strange writer's conceit in all its bearings. Yet was this conceit apparently one of the plainest in the
world; so natural, a child might almost have originated it.
Nevertheless, again so profound, that scarce Jugglarius himself could be the author; and still again so exceedingly trivial,
that Jugglarius' smallest child might well have been ashamed
of it.

Seeing then that this curious paper rag so puzzled Pierre;
foreseeing, too, that Pierre may not in the end be entirely
uninfluenced in his conduct by the torn pamphlet, when afterwards perhaps by other means he shall come to understand
it; or, peradventure, come to know that he, in the first place,
did—seeing too that the author thereof came to be made
known to him by reputation, and though Pierre never spoke

to him, yet exerted a surprising sorcery upon his spirit by the mere distant glimpse of his countenance;—all these reasons I account sufficient apology for inserting in the following chapter the initial part of what seems to me a very fanciful and mystical, rather than philosophical Lecture, from which, I confess, that I myself can derive no conclusion which permanently satisfies those peculiar motions in my soul, to which that Lecture seems more particularly addressed. For to me it seems more the excellently illustrated re-statement of a problem, than the solution of the problem itself. But as such mere illustrations are almost universally taken for solutions (and perhaps they are the only possible human solutions), therefore it may help to the temporary quiet of some inquiring mind; and so not be wholly without use. At the worst, each person can now skip, or read and rail for himself.

iii

"EI,"

BY

PLOTINUS PLINLIMMON,

(*In Three Hundred and Thirty-three Lectures.*)

———

LECTURE FIRST.

CHRONOMETRICALS AND HOROLOGICALS,

(*Being not so much the Portal, as part of the temporary Scaffold to the Portal of this new Philosophy.*)

"Few of us doubt, gentlemen, that human life on this earth is but a state of probation; which among other things implies, that here below, we mortals have only to do with things provisional. Accordingly, I hold that all our so-called wisdom is likewise but provisional.

"This preamble laid down, I begin.

"It seems to me, in my visions, that there is a certain most rare order of human souls, which if carefully carried in the body will almost always and everywhere give Heaven's own Truth, with some small grains of variance. For peculiarly coming from God, the sole source of that heavenly truth, and the great Greenwich hill and tower from which the universal meridians are far out into infinity reckoned; such souls seem as London sea-chronometers (*Greek*, time-namers) which as the London ship floats past Greenwich down the Thames, are accurately adjusted by Greenwich time, and if heedfully kept, will still give that same time, even though carried to the Azores. True, in nearly all cases of long, remote voyages—to China, say—chronometers of the best make, and the most carefully treated, will gradually more or less vary from Greenwich time, without the possibility of the error being corrected by direct comparison with their great standard; but skillful and devout observations of the stars by the sextant will serve materially to lessen such errors. And besides, there is such a thing as *rating* a chronometer; that is, having ascertained its degree of organic inaccuracy, however small, then in all subsequent chronometrical calculations, that ascertained loss or gain can be readily added or deducted, as the case may be. Then again, on these long voyages, the chronometer may be corrected by comparing it with the chronometer of some other ship at sea, more recently from home.

"Now in an artificial world like ours, the soul of man is further removed from its God and the Heavenly Truth, than the chronometer carried to China, is from Greenwich. And, as that chronometer, if at all accurate, will pronounce it to be 12 o'clock high-noon, when the China local watches say, perhaps, it is 12 o'clock midnight; so the chronometric soul, if in this world true to its great Greenwich in the other, will always, in its so-called intuitions of right and wrong, be contradicting the mere local standards and watch-maker's brains of this earth.

"Bacon's brains were mere watch-maker's brains; but Christ was a chronometer; and the most exquisitely adjusted and exact one, and the least affected by all terrestrial jarrings, of any that have ever come to us. And the reason why his teachings seemed folly to the Jews, was because he carried that Heaven's time in Jerusalem, while the Jews carried Jerusalem time there. Did he not expressly say—My wisdom (time) is not of this world? But whatever is really peculiar in the wisdom of Christ seems precisely the same folly to-day as it did 1850 years ago. Because, in all that interval his bequeathed chronometer has still preserved its original Heaven's time, and the general Jerusalem of this world has likewise carefully preserved its own.

"But though the chronometer carried from Greenwich to China, should truly exhibit in China what the time may be at Greenwich at any moment; yet, though thereby it must necessarily contradict China time, it does by no means thence follow, that with respect to China, the China watches are at all out of the way. Precisely the reverse. For the fact of that variance is a presumption that, with respect to China, the Chinese watches must be all right; and consequently as the China watches are right as to China, so the Greenwich chronometers must be wrong as to China. Besides, of what use to the Chinaman would a Greenwich chronometer, keeping Greenwich time, be? Were he thereby to regulate his daily actions, he would be guilty of all manner of absurdities:—going to bed at noon, say, when his neighbors would be sitting down to dinner. And thus, though the earthly wisdom of man be heavenly folly to God; so also, conversely, is the heavenly wisdom of God an earthly folly to man. Literally speaking, this is so. Nor does the God at the heavenly Greenwich expect common men to keep Greenwich wisdom in this remote Chinese world of ours; because such a thing were unprofitable for them here, and, indeed, a falsification of Himself, inasmuch as in that case, China time would be identical with Greenwich time, which would make Greenwich time wrong.

"But why then does God now and then send a heavenly chronometer (as a meteoric stone) into the world, uselessly as it would seem, to give the lie to all the world's time-keepers? Because he is unwilling to leave man without some occasional testimony to this:—that though man's Chinese notions of things may answer well enough here, they are by no means universally applicable, and that the central Greenwich in which He dwells goes by a somewhat different method from this world. And yet it follows not from this, that God's truth is one thing and man's truth another; but—as above hinted, and as will be further elucidated in subsequent lectures—by their very contradictions they are made to correspond.

"By inference it follows, also, that he who finding in himself a chronometrical soul, seeks practically to force that heavenly time upon the earth; in such an attempt he can never succeed, with an absolute and essential success. And as for himself, if he seek to regulate his own daily conduct by it, he will but array all men's earthly time-keepers against him, and thereby work himself woe and death. Both these things are plainly evinced in the character and fate of Christ, and the past and present condition of the religion he taught. But here one thing is to be especially observed. Though Christ encountered woe in both the precept and the practice of his chronometricals, yet did he remain throughout entirely without folly or sin. Whereas, almost invariably, with inferior beings, the absolute effort to live in this world according to the strict letter of the chronometricals is, somehow, apt to involve those inferior beings eventually in strange, *unique* follies and sins, unimagined before. It is the story of the Ephesian matron, allegorized.

"To any earnest man of insight, a faithful contemplation of these ideas concerning Chronometricals and Horologicals, will serve to render provisionally far less dark some few of the otherwise obscurest things which have hitherto tormented the honest-thinking men of all ages. What man who carries a heavenly soul in him, has not groaned to perceive, that unless he committed a sort of suicide as to the practical things of this world, he never can hope to regulate his earthly conduct by that same heavenly soul? And yet by an infallible instinct he knows, that the monitor can not be wrong in itself.

"And where is the earnest and righteous philosopher, gentlemen, who looking right and left, and up and down, through all the ages of the world, the present included; where is there such an one who has not a thousand times been struck with a sort of infidel idea, that whatever other worlds God may be Lord of, he is not the Lord of this; for else this world would seem to give the lie to Him; so utterly repugnant seem its ways to the instinctively known ways of Heaven. But it is not, and can not be so; nor will he who regards this chronometrical conceit aright, ever more be conscious of that horrible idea. For he will then see, or seem to see, that this world's seeming incompatibility with God, absolutely results from its meridianal correspondence with him.

✳   ✳   ✳

"This chronometrical conceit does by no means involve the justification of all the acts which wicked men may perform. For in their wickedness downright wicked men sin as much against their own horologes, as against the heavenly chronometer. That this is so, their spontaneous liability to remorse does plainly evince. No, this conceit merely goes to show, that for the mass of men, the highest abstract heavenly righteousness is not only impossible, but would be entirely out of place, and positively wrong in a world like this. To turn the left cheek if the right be smitten, is chronometrical; hence, no average son of man ever did such a thing. To give *all* that thou hast to the poor, this too is chronometrical; hence no average son of man ever did such a thing. Nevertheless, if a man gives with a certain self-considerate generosity to the poor; abstains from doing downright ill to any man; does his convenient best in a general way to do good to his whole race; takes watchful loving care of his wife and children, relatives, and friends; is perfectly tolerant to all other men's opinions, whatever they may be; is an honest dealer, an honest citizen, and all that; and more especially if he believe that there is a God for infidels, as well as for believers, and acts upon that belief; then, though such a man falls infinitely short of the chronometrical standard, though all his actions are entirely horologic;—yet such a man need never lastingly despond, because he is sometimes guilty of some minor offense:—hasty words, impulsively returning a blow, fits of domestic petulance, selfish enjoyment of a glass of wine while he knows there are those around him who lack a loaf of bread. I say he need never lastingly despond on account of his perpetual liability to these things; because *not* to do them, and their like, would be to be an angel, a chronometer; whereas, he is a man and a horologe.

"Yet does the horologe itself teach, that all liabilities to these things should be checked as much as possible, though it is certain they can never be utterly eradicated. They are only to be checked, then, because, if entirely unrestrained, they would finally run into utter selfishness and human demonism, which, as before hinted, are not by any means justified by the horologe.

"In short, this Chronometrical and Horological conceit, in sum, seems to teach this:—That in things terrestrial (horological) a man must not be governed by ideas celestial (chronometrical); that certain minor self-renunciations in this life his own mere instinct for his own every-day general well-being will teach him to make, but he must by no means make a complete unconditional sacrifice of himself in behalf of any other being, or any cause, or any conceit. (For, does aught else completely and unconditionally sacrifice itself for him? God's own sun does not abate one tittle of its heat in July, however you swoon with that heat in the sun. And if it *did* abate its heat on your behalf, then the wheat and the rye would not ripen; and so, for the incidental benefit of one, a whole population would suffer.)

"A virtuous expediency, then, seems the highest desirable or attainable earthly excellence for the mass of men, and is the only earthly excellence that their Creator intended for them. When they go to heaven, it will be quite another thing. There, they can freely turn the left cheek, because there the right cheek will never be smitten. There they can freely give all to the poor, for *there* there will be no poor to give to. A due appreciation of this matter will do good to man. For, hitherto, being authoritatively taught by his dogmatical teachers that he must, while on earth, aim at heaven, and attain it, too, in all his earthly acts, on pain of eternal wrath; and finding by experience that this is utterly impossible; in his despair, he is too apt to run clean away into all manner of moral abandonment, self-deceit, and hypocrisy (cloaked, however, mostly under an aspect of the most respectable devotion); or else he openly runs, like a mad dog, into atheism. Whereas, let men be taught those Chronometricals and Horologicals, and while still retaining every common-sense incentive to whatever of virtue be practicable and desirable, and having these incentives strengthened, too, by the consciousness of powers to attain their mark; then there would be an end to that fatal despair of becoming all good, which has too often proved the vice-producing

result in many minds of the undiluted chronometrical doctrines hitherto taught to mankind. But if any man say, that such a doctrine as
this I lay down is false, is impious; I would charitably refer that man
to the history of Christendom for the last 1800 years; and ask him,
whether, in spite of all the maxims of Christ, that history is not just
as full of blood, violence, wrong, and iniquity of every kind, as any
previous portion of the world's story? Therefore, it follows, that so
far as practical results are concerned—regarded in a purely earthly
light—the only great original moral doctrine of Christianity (*i.e.* the
chronometrical gratuitous return of good for evil, as distinguished
from the horological forgiveness of injuries taught by some of the
Pagan philosophers), has been found (horologically) a false one; because after 1800 years' inculcation from tens of thousands of pulpits,
it has proved entirely impracticable.

"I but lay down, then, what the best mortal men do daily practice;
and what all really wicked men are very far removed from. I present
consolation to the earnest man, who, among all his human frailties,
is still agonizingly conscious of the beauty of chronometrical excellence. I hold up a practicable virtue to the vicious; and interfere not
with the eternal truth, that, sooner or later, in all cases, downright
vice is downright woe.

"Moreover: if——"

But here the pamphlet was torn, and came to a most untidy
termination.

Book XV

The Cousins

THOUGH RESOLVED to face all out to the last, at whatever desperate hazard, Pierre had not started for the city without some reasonable plans, both with reference to his more immediate circumstances, and his ulterior condition.

There resided in the city a cousin of his, Glendinning Stanly, better known in the general family as Glen Stanly, and by Pierre, as Cousin Glen. Like Pierre, he was an only son; his parents had died in his early childhood; and within the present year he had returned from a protracted sojourn in Europe, to enter, at the age of twenty-one, into the untrammeled possession of a noble property, which in the hands of faithful guardians, had largely accumulated.

In their boyhood and earlier adolescence, Pierre and Glen had cherished a much more than cousinly attachment. At the age of ten, they had furnished an example of the truth, that the friendship of fine-hearted, generous boys, nurtured amid the romance-engendering comforts and elegancies of life, sometimes transcends the bounds of mere boyishness, and revels for a while in the empyrean of a love which only comes short, by one degree, of the sweetest sentiment entertained between the sexes. Nor is this boy-love without the occasional fillips and spicinesses, which at times, by an apparent abatement, enhance the permanent delights of those more advanced lovers who love beneath the cestus of Venus. Jealousies are felt. The sight of another lad too much consorting with the boy's beloved object, shall fill him with emotions akin to those of Othello's; a fancied slight, or lessening of the every-day indications of warm feelings, shall prompt him to bitter upbraidings and reproaches; or shall plunge him into evil moods, for which grim solitude only is congenial.

Nor are the letters of Aphroditean devotees more charged with headlong vows and protestations, more cross-written and crammed with discursive sentimentalities, more undeviating in their semi-weekliness, or dayliness, as the case may be, than are the love-friendship missives of boys. Among those bundles of papers which Pierre, in an ill hour, so frantically destroyed in the chamber of the inn, were two large packages of letters, densely written, and in many cases inscribed cross-wise throughout with red ink upon black; so that the love in those letters was two layers deep, and one pen and one pig-ment were insufficient to paint it. The first package contained the letters of Glen to Pierre, the other those of Pierre to Glen, which, just prior to Glen's departure for Europe, Pierre had obtained from him, in order to re-read them in his absence, and so fortify himself the more in his affection, by reviving reference to the young, ardent hours of its earliest manifesta-tions.

But as the advancing fruit itself extrudes the beautiful blos-som, so in many cases, does the eventual love for the other sex forever dismiss the preliminary love-friendship of boys. The mere outer friendship may in some degree—greater or less—survive; but the singular love in it has perishingly dropped away.

If in the eye of unyielding reality and truth, the earthly heart of man do indeed ever fix upon some one woman, to whom alone, thenceforth eternally to be a devotee, without a single shadow of the misgiving of its faith; and who, to him, does perfectly embody his finest, loftiest dream of feminine loveliness, if this indeed be so—and may Heaven grant that it be—nevertheless, in metropolitan cases, the love of the most single-eyed lover, almost invariably, is nothing more than the ultimate settling of innumerable wandering glances upon some one specific object; as admonished, that the won-derful scope and variety of female loveliness, if too long suf-fered to sway us without decision, shall finally confound all power of selection. The confirmed bachelor is, in America, at least, quite as often the victim of a too profound appreciation of the infinite charmingness of woman, as made solitary for life by the legitimate empire of a cold and tasteless tempera-ment.

Though the peculiar heart-longings pertaining to his age, had at last found their glowing response in the bosom of Lucy; yet for some period prior to that, Pierre had not been insensible to the miscellaneous promptings of the passion. So that even before he became a declarative lover, Love had yet made him her general votary; and so already there had gradually come a cooling over that ardent sentiment which in earlier years he had cherished for Glen.

All round and round does the world lie as in a sharp-shooter's ambush, to pick off the beautiful illusions of youth, by the pitiless cracking rifles of the realities of age. If the general love for women, had in Pierre sensibly modified his particular sentiment toward Glen; neither had the thousand nameless fascinations of the then brilliant paradises of France and Italy, failed to exert their seductive influence on many of the previous feelings of Glen. For as the very best advantages of life are not without some envious drawback, so it is among the evils of enlarged foreign travel, that in young and unsolid minds, it dislodges some of the finest feelings of the home-born nature; replacing them with a fastidious superciliousness, which like the alledged bigoted Federalism of old times would not—according to a political legend—grind its daily coffee in any mill save of European manufacture, and was satirically said to have thought of importing European air for domestic consumption. The mutually curtailed, lessening, long-postponed, and at last altogether ceasing letters of Pierre and Glen were the melancholy attestations of a fact, which perhaps neither of them took very severely to heart, as certainly, concerning it, neither took the other to task.

In the earlier periods of that strange transition from the generous impulsiveness of youth to the provident circumspectness of age, there generally intervenes a brief pause of unpleasant reconsidering; when finding itself all wide of its former spontaneous self, the soul hesitates to commit itself wholly to selfishness; more than repents its wanderings;—yet all this is but transient; and again hurried on by the swift current of life, the prompt-hearted boy scarce longer is to be recognized in matured man,—very slow to feel, deliberate even in love, and statistical even in piety. During the sway of this peculiar period, the boy shall still make some strenuous efforts to retrieve his departing spontaneities; but so alloyed are all such endeavors with the incipiencies of selfishness, that they were best not made at all; since too often they seem but empty and self-deceptive sallies, or still worse, the merest hypocritical assumptions.

Upon the return of Glen from abroad, the commonest
courtesy, not to say the blood-relation between them,
prompted Pierre to welcome him home, with a letter, which
though not over-long, and little enthusiastic, still breathed a
spirit of cousinly consideration and kindness, pervadingly
touched by the then naturally frank and all-attractive spirit of
Pierre. To this, the less earnest and now Europeanized Glen
had replied in a letter all sudden suavity; and in a strain of
artistic artlessness, mourned the apparent decline of their
friendship; yet fondly trusted that now, notwithstanding their
long separation, it would revive with added sincerity. Yet
upon accidentally fixing his glance upon the opening salutation of this delicate missive, Pierre thought he perceived certain, not wholly disguisable chirographic tokens, that the "My
very dear Pierre," with which the letter seemed to have been
begun, had originally been written "Dear Pierre;" but that
when all was concluded, and Glen's signature put to it, then
the ardent words "My very" had been prefixed to the recon-
sidered "Dear Pierre;" a casual supposition, which possibly,
however unfounded, materially retarded any answering
warmth in Pierre, lest his generous flame should only embrace
a flaunted feather. Nor was this idea altogether unreinforced,
when on the reception of a second, and now half-business
letter (of which mixed sort nearly all the subsequent ones
were), from Glen, he found that the "My very dear Pierre"
had already retreated into "My dear Pierre;" and on a third
occasion, into "Dear Pierre;" and on a fourth, had made a
forced and very spirited advanced march up to "My dearest
Pierre." All of which fluctuations augured ill for the determinateness of that love, which, however immensely devoted to
one cause, could yet hoist and sail under the flags of all nations. Nor could he but now applaud a still subsequent letter
from Glen, which abruptly, and almost with apparent indec-
orousness, under the circumstances, commenced the strain of
friendship without any overture of salutation whatever; as if
at last, owing to its infinite delicateness, entirely hopeless of
precisely defining the nature of their mystical love, Glen chose
rather to leave that precise definition to the sympathetical
heart and imagination of Pierre; while he himself would go
on to celebrate the general relation, by many a sugared sen-

tence of miscellaneous devotion. It was a little curious and
rather sardonically diverting, to compare these masterly, yet
not wholly successful, and indeterminate tactics of the accomplished Glen, with the unfaltering stream of *Beloved Pierres*,
which not only flowed along the top margin of all his earlier
letters, but here and there, from their subterranean channel,
flashed out in bright intervals, through all the succeeding
lines. Nor had the chance recollection of these things at all
restrained the reckless hand of Pierre, when he threw the
whole package of letters, both new and old, into that most
honest and summary of all elements, which is neither a respecter of persons, nor a finical critic of what manner of writings it burns; but like ultimate Truth itself, of which it is the
eloquent symbol, consumes all, and only consumes.

When the betrothment of Pierre to Lucy had become an
acknowledged thing, the courtly Glen, besides the customary
felicitations upon that event, had not omitted so fit an opportunity to re-tender to his cousin all his previous jars of honey
and treacle, accompanied by additional boxes of candied
citron and plums. Pierre thanked him kindly; but in certain
little roguish ambiguities begged leave, on the ground of
cloying, to return him inclosed by far the greater portion of
his present; whose non-substantialness was allegorically typi-
fied in the containing letter itself, prepaid with only the usual
postage.

True love, as every one knows, will still withstand many
repulses, even though rude. But whether it was the love or
the politeness of Glen, which on this occasion proved invincible, is a matter we will not discuss. Certain it was, that quite
undaunted, Glen nobly returned to the charge, and in a very
prompt and unexpected answer, extended to Pierre all the
courtesies of the general city, and all the hospitalities of five
sumptuous chambers, which he and his luxurious environ-
ments contrived nominally to occupy in the most fashionable
private hotel of a very opulent town. Nor did Glen rest here;
but like Napoleon, now seemed bent upon gaining the battle
by throwing all his regiments upon one point of attack, and
gaining that point at all hazards. Hearing of some rumor at
the tables of his relatives that the day was being fixed for the
positive nuptials of Pierre; Glen culled all his Parisian port-

folios for his rosiest sheet, and with scented ink, and a pen of gold, indited a most burnished and redolent letter, which, after invoking all the blessings of Apollo and Venus, and the Nine Muses, and the Cardinal Virtues upon the coming event; concluded at last with a really magnificent testimonial to his love.

According to this letter, among his other real estate in the city, Glen had inherited a very charming, little, old house, completely furnished in the style of the last century, in a quarter of the city which, though now not so garishly fashionable as of yore, still in its quiet secludedness, possessed great attractions for the retired billings and cooings of a honeymoon. Indeed he begged leave now to christen it the Cooery, and if after his wedding jaunt, Pierre would deign to visit the city with his bride for a month or two's sojourn, then the Cooery would be but too happy in affording him a harbor. His sweet cousin need be under no apprehension. Owing to the absence of any fit applicant for it, the house had now long been without a tenant, save an old, confidential, bachelor clerk of his father's, who on a nominal rent, and more by way of safe-keeping to the house than any thing else, was now hanging up his well-furbished hat in its hall. This accommodating old clerk would quickly unpeg his beaver at the first hint of new occupants. Glen would charge himself with supplying the house in advance with a proper retinue of servants; fires would be made in the long-unoccupied chambers; the venerable, grotesque, old mahoganies, and marbles, and mirror-frames, and moldings could be very soon dusted and burnished; the kitchen was amply provided with the necessary utensils for cooking; the strong box of old silver immemorially pertaining to the mansion, could be readily carted round from the vaults of the neighboring Bank; while the hampers of old china, still retained in the house, needed but little trouble to unpack; so that silver and china would soon stand assorted in their appropriate closets; at the turning of a faucet in the cellar, the best of the city's water would not fail to contribute its ingredient to the concocting of a welcoming glass of negus before retiring on the first night of their arrival.

The over-fastidiousness of some unhealthily critical minds, as well as the moral pusillanimity of others, equally bars the acceptance of effectually substantial favors from persons whose motive in proffering them, is not altogether clear and unimpeachable; and toward whom, perhaps, some prior coolness or indifference has been shown. But when the acceptance of such a favor would be really convenient and desirable to the one party, and completely unattended with any serious distress to the other; there would seem to be no sensible objection to an immediate embrace of the offer. And when the acceptor is in rank and fortune the general equal of the profferer, and perhaps his superior, so that any courtesy he receives, can be amply returned in the natural course of future events, then all motives to decline are very materially lessened. And as for the thousand inconceivable finicalnesses of small pros and cons about imaginary fitnesses, and proprieties, and self-consistencies; thank heaven, in the hour of heart-health, none such shilly-shallying sail-trimmers ever balk the onward course of a bluff-minded man. He takes the world as it is; and carelessly accommodates himself to its whimsical humors; nor ever feels any compunction at receiving the greatest possible favors from those who are as able to grant, as free to bestow. He himself bestows upon occasion; so that, at bottom, common charity steps in to dictate a favorable consideration for all possible profferings; seeing that the acceptance shall only the more enrich him, indirectly, for new and larger beneficences of his own.

And as for those who noways pretend with themselves to regulate their deportment by considerations of genuine benevolence, and to whom such courteous profferings hypocritically come from persons whom they suspect for secret enemies; then to such minds not only will their own worldly tactics at once forbid the uncivil blank repulse of such offers; but if they are secretly malicious as well as frigid, or if they are at all capable of being fully gratified by the sense of concealed superiority and mastership (which precious few men are) then how delightful for such persons under the guise of mere acquiescence in his own voluntary civilities, to make genteel use of their foe. For one would like to know, what were foes made for except to be used? In the rude ages men hunted and javelined the tiger, because they hated him for a mischief-minded wild-beast; but in these enlightened times,

though we love the tiger as little as ever, still we mostly hunt
him for the sake of his skin. A wise man then will wear his
tiger; every morning put on his tiger for a robe to keep him
warm and adorn him. In this view, foes are far more desirable
than friends; for who would hunt and kill his own faithful
affectionate dog for the sake of his skin? and is a dog's skin
as valuable as a tiger's? Cases there are where it becomes soberly advisable, by direct arts to convert some well-wishers
into foes. It is false that in point of policy a man should never
make enemies. As well-wishers some men may not only be
nugatory but positive obstacles in your peculiar plans; but as
foes you may subordinately cement them into your general
design.

But into these ulterior refinements of cool Tuscan policy,
Pierre as yet had never become initiated; his experiences hitherto not having been varied and ripe enough for that; besides,
he had altogether too much generous blood in his heart. Nevertheless, thereafter, in a less immature hour, though still he
shall not have the heart to practice upon such maxims as the
above, yet shall he have the brain thoroughly to comprehend
their practicability; which is not always the case. And generally, in worldly wisdom, men will deny to one the possession
of all insight, which one does not by his every-day outward
life practically reveal. It is a very common error of some unscrupulously infidel-minded, selfish, unprincipled, or downright knavish men, to suppose that believing men, or
benevolent-hearted men, or good men, do not know enough
to be unscrupulously selfish, do not know enough to be unscrupulous knaves. And thus—thanks to the world!—are
there many spies in the world's camp, who are mistaken for
strolling simpletons. And these strolling simpletons seem to
act upon the principle, that in certain things, we do not so
much learn, by showing that already we know a vast deal, as
by negatively seeming rather ignorant. But here we press
upon the frontiers of that sort of wisdom, which it is very
well to possess, but not sagacious to show that you possess.
Still, men there are, who having quite done with the world,
all its mere worldly contents are become so far indifferent,
that they care little of what mere worldly imprudence they
may be guilty.

Now, if it were not conscious considerations like the really benevolent or neutral ones first mentioned above, it was certainly something akin to them, which had induced Pierre to return a straightforward, manly, and entire acceptance to his cousin of the offer of the house; thanking him, over and over, for his most supererogatory kindness concerning the pre-engagement of servants and so forth, and the setting in order of the silver and china; but reminding him, nevertheless, that he had overlooked all special mention of wines, and begged him to store the bins with a few of the very best brands. He would likewise be obliged, if he would personally purchase at a certain celebrated grocer's, a small bag of undoubted Mocha coffee; but Glen need not order it to be roasted or ground, because Pierre preferred that both those highly important and flavor-deciding operations should be performed instantaneously previous to the final boiling and serving. Nor did he say that he would pay for the wines and the Mocha; he contented himself with merely stating the remissness on the part of his cousin, and pointing out the best way of remedying it.

He concluded his letter by intimating that though the rumor of a set day, and a near one, for his nuptials, was unhappily but ill-founded, yet he would not hold Glen's generous offer as merely based upon that presumption, and consequently falling with it; but on the contrary, would consider it entirely good for whatever time it might prove available to Pierre. He was betrothed beyond a peradventure; and hoped to be married ere death. Meanwhile, Glen would further oblige him by giving the confidential clerk a standing notice to quit.

Though at first quite amazed at this letter,—for indeed, his offer might possibly have proceeded as much from ostentation as any thing else, nor had he dreamed of so unhesitating an acceptance,—Pierre's cousin was too much of a precocious young man of the world, disclosedly to take it in any other than a very friendly, and cousinly, and humorous, and yet practical way; which he plainly evinced by a reply far more sincere and every way creditable, apparently, both to his heart and head, than any letter he had written to Pierre since the days of their boyhood. And thus, by the bluffness and, in some sort, uncompunctuousness of Pierre, this very artificial

youth was well betrayed into an act of effective kindness;
being forced now to drop the empty mask of ostentation, and
put on the solid hearty features of a genuine face. And just
so, are some people in the world to be joked into occasional
effective goodness, when all coyness, and coolness, all resent-
ments, and all solemn preaching, would fail.

ii

But little would we comprehend the peculiar relation between Pierre and Glen—a relation involving in the end the
most serious results—were there not here thrown over the
whole equivocal, preceding account of it, another and more
comprehensive equivocalness, which shall absorb all minor
ones in itself; and so make one pervading ambiguity the only
possible explanation for all the ambiguous details.

It had long been imagined by Pierre, that prior to his own
special devotion to Lucy, the splendid Glen had not been entirely insensible to her surprising charms. Yet this conceit in
its incipiency, he knew not how to account for. Assuredly his
cousin had never in the slightest conceivable hint betrayed it;
and as for Lucy, the same intuitive delicacy which forever forbade Pierre to question her on the subject, did equally close
her own voluntary lips. Between Pierre and Lucy, delicateness
put her sacred signet on this chest of secrecy; which like the
wax of an executor upon a desk, though capable of being
melted into nothing by the smallest candle, for all this, still
possesses to the reverent the prohibitive virtue of inexorable
bars and bolts.

If Pierre superficially considered the deportment of Glen
toward him, therein he could find no possible warrant for
indulging the suspicious idea. Doth jealousy smile so benignantly and offer its house to the bride? Still, on the other
hand, to quit the mere surface of the deportment of Glen, and
penetrate beneath its brocaded vesture; there Pierre sometimes seemed to see the long-lurking and yet unhealed wound
of all a rejected lover's most rankling detestation of a sup-
planting rival, only intensified by their former friendship, and
the unimpairable blood-relation between them. Now, viewed
by the light of this master-solution, all the singular enigmas

in Glen; his capriciousness in the matter of the epistolary—
"Dear Pierres" and "Dearest Pierres;" the mercurial fall from
the fever-heat of cordiality, to below the Zero of indifference;
then the contrary rise to fever-heat; and, above all, his emphatic redundancy of devotion so soon as the positive espous-
als of Pierre seemed on the point of consummation; thus
read, all these riddles apparently found their cunning solution. For the deeper that some men feel a secret and poignant
feeling, the higher they pile the belying surfaces. The friendly
deportment of Glen then was to be considered as in direct
proportion to his hoarded hate; and the climax of that hate
was evinced in throwing open his house to the bride. Yet if
hate was the abstract cause, hate could not be the immediate
motive of the conduct of Glen. Is hate so hospitable? The
immediate motive of Glen then must be the intense desire to
disguise from the wide world, a fact unspeakably humiliating
to his gold-laced and haughty soul: the fact that in the profoundest desire of his heart, Pierre had so victoriously sup-
planted him. Yet was it that very artful deportment in Glen,
which Glen profoundly assumed to this grand end; that con-
summately artful deportment it was, which first obtruded
upon Pierre the surmise, which by that identical method his
cousin was so absorbedly intent upon rendering impossible to
him. Hence we here see that as in the negative way the secrecy of any strong emotion is exceedingly difficult to be kept
lastingly private to one's own bosom by any human being; so
it is one of the most fruitless undertakings in the world, to
attempt by affirmative assumptions to tender to men, the precisely opposite emotion as yours. Therefore the final wisdom
decrees, that if you have aught which you desire to keep a
secret to yourself, be a Quietist there, and do and say nothing
at all about it. For among all the poor chances, this is the
least poor. Pretensions and substitutions are only the recourse
of under-graduates in the science of the world; in which science, on his own ground, my Lord Chesterfield, is the poorest possible preceptor. The earliest instinct of the child, and
the ripest experience of age, unite in affirming simplicity to
be the truest and profoundest part for man. Likewise this simplicity is so universal and all-containing as a rule for human
life, that the subtlest bad man, and the purest good man, as

well as the profoundest wise man, do all alike present it on
that side which they socially turn to the inquisitive and unscrupulous world.

iii

Now the matter of the house had remained in precisely the
above-stated awaiting predicament, down to the time of
Pierre's great life-revolution, the receipt of Isabel's letter. And
though, indeed, Pierre could not but naturally hesitate at still
accepting the use of the dwelling, under the widely different
circumstances in which he now found himself; and though at
first the strongest possible spontaneous objections on the
ground of personal independence, pride, and general scorn,
all clamorously declared in his breast against such a course;
yet, finally, the same uncompunctuous, ever-adaptive sort of
motive which had induced his original acceptation, prompted
him, in the end, still to maintain it unrevoked. It would at
once set him at rest from all immediate tribulations of mere
bed and board; and by affording him a shelter, for an indefinite term, enable him the better to look about him, and consider what could best be done to further the permanent
comfort of those whom Fate had intrusted to his charge.

Irrespective, it would seem, of that wide general awaking
of his profounder being, consequent upon the extraordinary
trials he had so aggregatively encountered of late; the thought
was indignantly suggested to him, that the world must indeed
be organically despicable, if it held that an offer, superfluously
accepted in the hour of his abundance, should now, be rejected in that of his utmost need. And without at all imputing
any singularity of benevolent-mindedness to his cousin, he
did not for a moment question, that under the changed aspect
of affairs, Glen would at least pretend the more eagerly to
welcome him to the house, now that the mere thing of apparent courtesy had become transformed into something like
a thing of positive and urgent necessity. When Pierre also
considered that not himself only was concerned, but likewise
two peculiarly helpless fellow-beings, one of them bound to
him from the first by the most sacred ties, and lately inspiring
an emotion which passed all human precedent in its mixed

and mystical import; these added considerations completely
overthrew in Pierre all remaining dictates of his vague pride
and false independence, if such indeed had ever been his.

Though the interval elapsing between his decision to depart
with his companions for the city, and his actual start in the
coach, had not enabled him to receive any replying word
from his cousin; and though Pierre knew better than to expect it; yet a preparative letter to him he had sent; and did
not doubt that this proceeding would prove well-advised in
the end.

In naturally strong-minded men, however young and inexperienced in some things, those great and sudden emergencies, which but confound the timid and the weak, only serve
to call forth all their generous latentness, and teach them, as
by inspiration, extraordinary maxims of conduct, whose counterpart, in other men, is only the result of a long, variously-
tried and pains-taking life. One of those maxims is, that
when, through whatever cause, we are suddenly translated
from opulence to need, or from a fair fame to a foul; and
straightway it becomes necessary not to contradict the
thing—so far at least as the mere imputation goes,—to some
one previously entertaining high conventional regard for us,
and from whom we would now solicit some genuine helping
offices; then, all explanation or palliation should be scorned;
promptness, boldness, utter gladiatorianism, and a defiant
non-humility should mark every syllable we breathe, and
every line we trace.

The preparative letter of Pierre to Glen, plunged at once
into the very heart of the matter, and was perhaps the briefest
letter he had ever written him. Though by no means are such
characteristics invariable exponents of the predominant mood
or general disposition of a man (since so accidental a thing as
a numb finger, or a bad quill, or poor ink, or squalid paper,
or a rickety desk may produce all sorts of modifications), yet
in the present instance, the handwriting of Pierre happened
plainly to attest and corroborate the spirit of his communication. The sheet was large; but the words were placarded upon
it in heavy though rapid lines, only six or eight to the page.
And as the footman of a haughty visitor—some Count or
Duke—announces the chariot of his lord by a thunderous

knock on the portal; so to Glen did Pierre, in the broad, sweeping, and prodigious superscription of his letter, forewarn him what manner of man was on the road.

In the moment of strong feeling a wonderful condensativeness points the tongue and pen; so that ideas, then enunciated sharp and quick as minute-guns, in some other hour of unruffledness or unstimulatedness, require considerable time and trouble to verbally recall.

Not here and now can we set down the precise contents of Pierre's letter, without a tautology illy doing justice to the ideas themselves. And though indeed the dread of tautology be the continual torment of some earnest minds, and, as such, is surely a weakness in them; and though no wise man will wonder at conscientious Virgil all eager at death to burn his Æniad for a monstrous heap of inefficient superfluity; yet not to dread tautology at times only belongs to those enviable dunces, whom the partial God hath blessed, over all the earth, with the inexhaustible self-riches of vanity, and folly, and a blind self-complacency.

Some rumor of the discontinuance of his betrothment to Lucy Tartan; of his already consummated marriage with a poor and friendless orphan; of his mother's disowning him consequent upon these events; such rumors, Pierre now wrote to his cousin, would very probably, in the parlors of his city-relatives and acquaintances, precede his arrival in town. But he hinted no word of any possible commentary on these things. He simply went on to say, that now, through the fortune of life—which was but the proverbially unreliable fortune of war—he was, for the present, thrown entirely upon his own resources, both for his own support and that of his wife, as well as for the temporary maintenance of a girl, whom he had lately had excellent reason for taking under his especial protection. He proposed a permanent residence in the city; not without some nearly quite settled plans as to the procuring of a competent income, without any ulterior reference to any member of their wealthy and widely ramified family. The house, whose temporary occupancy Glen had before so handsomely proffered him, would now be doubly and trebly desirable to him. But the pre-engaged servants, and the old china, and the old silver, and the old wines, and the

Mocha, were now become altogether unnecessary. Pierre would merely take the place—for a short interval—of the worthy old clerk; and, so far as Glen was concerned, simply stand guardian of the dwelling, till his plans were matured. His cousin had originally made his most bounteous overture, to welcome the coming of the presumed bride of Pierre; and though another lady had now taken her place at the altar, yet Pierre would still regard the offer of Glen as impersonal in that respect, and bearing equal reference to any young lady, who should prove her claim to the possessed hand of Pierre.

Since there was no universal law of opinion in such matters, Glen, on general worldly grounds, might not consider the real Mrs. Glendinning altogether so suitable a match for Pierre, as he possibly might have held numerous other young ladies in his eye: nevertheless, Glen would find her ready to return with sincerity all his cousinly regard and attention. In conclusion, Pierre said, that he and his party meditated an immediate departure, and would very probably arrive in town in eight-and-forty hours after the mailing of the present letter. He therefore begged Glen to see the more indispensable domestic appliances of the house set in some little order against their arrival; to have the rooms aired and lighted; and also forewarn the confidential clerk of what he might soon expect. Then, without any tapering sequel of—"*Yours, very truly and faithfully, my dear Cousin Glen,*" he finished the letter with the abrupt and isolated signature of—"Pierre."

Book XVI

THE STAGE was belated.

The country road they traveled entered the city by a remarkably wide and winding street, a great thoroughfare for its less opulent inhabitants. There was no moon and few stars. It was that preluding hour of the night when the shops are just closing, and the aspect of almost every wayfarer, as he passes through the unequal light reflected from the windows, speaks of one hurrying not abroad, but homeward. Though the thoroughfare was winding, yet no sweep that it made greatly obstructed its long and imposing vista; so that when the coach gained the top of the long and very gradual slope running toward the obscure heart of the town, and the twinkling perspective of two long and parallel rows of lamps was revealed—lamps which seemed not so much intended to dispel the general gloom, as to show some dim path leading through it, into some gloom still deeper beyond—when the coach gained this critical point, the whole vast triangular town, for a moment, seemed dimly and despondently to capitulate to the eye.

And now, ere descending the gradually-sloping declivity, and just on its summit as it were, the inmates of the coach, by numerous hard, painful joltings, and ponderous, dragging trundlings, are suddenly made sensible of some great change in the character of the road. The coach seems rolling over cannon-balls of all calibers. Grasping Pierre's arm, Isabel eagerly and forebodingly demands what is the cause of this most strange and unpleasant transition.

"The pavements, Isabel; this is the town."

Isabel was silent.

But, the first time for many weeks, Delly voluntarily spoke: "It feels not so soft as the green sward, Master Pierre."

"No, Miss Ulver," said Pierre, very bitterly, "the buried hearts of some dead citizens have perhaps come to the surface."

"Sir?" said Delly.

"And are they so hard-hearted here?" asked Isabel.

"Ask yonder pavements, Isabel. Milk dropt from the milk-man's can in December, freezes not more quickly on those stones, than does snow-white innocence, if in poverty, it chance to fall in these streets."

"Then God help my hard fate, Master Pierre," sobbed Delly. "Why didst thou drag hither a poor outcast like me?"

"Forgive me, Miss Ulver," exclaimed Pierre, with sudden warmth, and yet most marked respect; "forgive me; never yet have I entered the city by night, but, somehow, it made me feel both bitter and sad. Come, be cheerful, we shall soon be comfortably housed, and have our comfort all to ourselves; the old clerk I spoke to you about, is now doubtless ruefully eying his hat on the peg. Come, cheer up, Isabel; — 'tis a long ride, but here we are, at last. Come! 'Tis not very far now to our welcome."

"I hear a strange shuffling and clattering," said Delly, with a shudder.

"It does not seem so light as just now," said Isabel.

"Yes," returned Pierre, "it is the shop-shutters being put on; it is the locking, and bolting, and barring of windows and doors; the town's-people are going to their rest."

"Please God they may find it!" sighed Delly.

"They lock and bar out, then, when they rest, do they, Pierre?" said Isabel.

"Yes, and you were thinking that does not bode well for the welcome I spoke of."

"Thou read'st all my soul; yes, I was thinking of that. But whither lead these long, narrow, dismal side-glooms we pass every now and then? What are they? They seem terribly still. I see scarce any body in them; — there's another, now. See how haggardly look its criss-cross, far-separate lamps. — What are these side-glooms, dear Pierre; whither lead they?"

"They are the thin tributaries, sweet Isabel, to the great Oronoco thoroughfare we are in; and like true tributaries, they come from the far-hidden places; from under dark bee-tling secrecies of mortar and stone; through the long marsh-grasses of villainy, and by many a transplanted bough-beam, where the wretched have hung."

"I know nothing of these things, Pierre. But I like not the

town. Think'st thou, Pierre, the time will ever come when all
the earth shall be paved?"

"Thank God, that never can be!"

"These silent side-glooms are horrible;—look! Methinks,
not for the world would I turn into one."

That moment the nigh fore-wheel sharply grated under the
body of the coach.

"Courage!" cried Pierre, " we are in it!—Not so very solitary either; here comes a traveler."

"Hark, what is that?" said Delly, "that keen iron-ringing
sound? It passed us just now."

"The keen traveler," said Pierre, "he has steel plates to his
boot-heels;—some tender-souled elder son, I suppose."

"Pierre," said Isabel, "this silence is unnatural, is fearful.
The forests are never so still."

"Because brick and mortar have deeper secrets than wood
or fell, sweet Isabel. But here we turn again; now if I guess
right, two more turns will bring us to the door. Courage, all
will be well; doubtless he has prepared a famous supper.
Courage, Isabel. Come, shall it be tea or coffee? Some bread,
or crisp toast? We'll have eggs, too; and some cold chicken,
perhaps."—Then muttering to himself—"I hope not that, either; no cold collations! there's too much of that in these paving-stones here, set out for the famishing beggars to eat. No.
I won't have the cold chicken." Then aloud—"But here we
turn again; yes, just as I thought. Ho, driver!" (thrusting his
head out of the window) "to the right! to the right! it should
be on the right! the first house with a light on the right!"

"No lights yet but the street's," answered the surly voice of
the driver.

"Stupid! he has passed it—yes, yes—he has! Ho! ho! stop;
turn back. Have you not passed lighted windows?"

"No lights but the street's," was the rough reply. "What's
the number? the number? Don't keep me beating about here
all night! The number, I say!"

"I do not know it," returned Pierre; "but I well know the
house; you must have passed it, I repeat. You must turn back.
Surely you have passed lighted windows?"

"Then them lights must burn black; there's no lighted windows in the street; I knows the city; old maids lives here, and they are all to bed; rest is warehouses."

"Will you stop the coach, or not?" cried Pierre, now incensed at his surliness in continuing to drive on.

"I obeys orders: the first house with a light; and 'cording to my reck'ning—though to be sure, I don't know nothing of the city where I was born and bred all my life—no, I knows nothing at all about it—'cording to my reck'ning, the first light in this here street will be the watch-house of the ward—yes, there it is—all right! cheap lodgings ye've engaged—nothing to pay, and wictuals in."

To certain temperaments, especially when previously agitated by any deep feeling, there is perhaps nothing more exasperating, and which sooner explodes all self-command, than the coarse, jeering insolence of a porter, cabman, or hackdriver. Fetchers and carriers of the worst city infamy as many of them are; professionally familiar with the most abandoned haunts; in the heart of misery, they drive one of the most mercenary of all the trades of guilt. Day-dozers and sluggards on their lazy boxes in the sunlight, and felinely wakeful and cat-eyed in the dark; most habituated to midnight streets, only trod by sneaking burglars, wantons, and debauchees; often in actual pandering league with the most abhorrent sinks; so that they are equally solicitous and suspectful that every customer they encounter in the dark, will prove a profligate or a knave; this hideous tribe of ogres, and Charon ferry-men to corruption and death, naturally slide into the most practically Calvinistical view of humanity, and hold every man at bottom a fit subject for the coarsest ribaldry and jest; only fine coats and full pockets can whip such mangy hounds into decency. The least impatience, any quickness of temper, a sharp remonstrating word from a customer in a seedy coat, or betraying any other evidence of poverty, however minute and indirect (for in that pecuniary respect they are the most piercing and infallible of all the judgers of men), will be almost sure to provoke, in such cases, their least endurable disdain.

Perhaps it was the unconscious transfer to the stage-driver of some such ideas as these, which now prompted the highly irritated Pierre to an act, which, in a more benignant hour, his better reason would have restrained him from.

He did not see the light to which the driver had referred; and was heedless, in his sudden wrath, that the coach was now going slower in approaching it. Ere Isabel could prevent him, he burst open the door, and leaping to the pavement, sprang ahead of the horses, and violently reined back the leaders by their heads. The driver seized his four-in-hand whip, and with a volley of oaths was about striking out its long, coiling lash at Pierre, when his arm was arrested by a policeman, who suddenly leaping on the stayed coach, commanded him to keep the peace.

"Speak! what is the difficulty here? Be quiet, ladies, nothing serious has happened. Speak you!"

"Pierre! Pierre!" cried the alarmed Isabel. In an instant Pierre was at her side by the window; and now turning to the officer, explained to him that the driver had persisted in passing the house at which he was ordered to stop.

"Then he shall turn to the right about with you, sir;—in double quick time too; do ye hear? I know you rascals well enough. Turn about, you sir, and take the gentleman where he directed."

The cowed driver was beginning a long string of criminating explanations, when turning to Pierre, the policeman calmly desired him to re-enter the coach; he would see him safely at his destination; and then seating himself beside the driver on the box, commanded him to tell the number given him by the gentleman.

"He don't know no numbers—didn't I say he didn't—that's what I got mad about."

"Be still"—said the officer. "Sir"—turning round and addressing Pierre within; "where do you wish to go?"

"I do not know the number, but it is a house in this street; we have passed it; it is, I think, the fourth or fifth house this side of the last corner we turned. It must be lighted up too. It is the small old-fashioned dwelling with stone lion-heads above the windows. But make him turn round, and drive slowly, and I will soon point it out."

"Can't see lions in the dark"—growled the driver—"lions; ha! ha! jackasses more likely!"

"Look you," said the officer, "I shall see you tightly housed this night, my fine fellow, if you don't cease your jabber. Sir," he added, resuming with Pierre, "I am sure there is some mistake here. I perfectly well know now the house you mean. I passed it within the last half-hour; all as quiet there as ever. No one lives there, I think; I never saw a light in it. Are you not mistaken in something, then?"

Pierre paused in perplexity and foreboding. Was it possible that Glen had willfully and utterly neglected his letter? Not possible. But it might not have come to his hand; the mails sometimes delayed. Then again, it was not wholly out of the question, that the house was prepared for them after all, even though it showed no outward sign. But that was not probable. At any rate, as the driver protested, that his four horses and lumbering vehicle could not turn short round in that street; and that if he must go back, it could only be done by driving on, and going round the block, and so retracing his road; and as after such a procedure, on his part, then in case of a confirmed disappointment respecting the house, the driver would seem warranted, at least in some of his unmannerliness; and as Pierre loathed the villain altogether, therefore, in order to run no such risks, he came to a sudden determination on the spot.

"I owe you very much, my good friend," said he to the officer, "for your timely assistance. To be frank, what you have just told me has indeed perplexed me not a little concerning the place where I proposed to stop. Is there no hotel in this neighborhood, where I could leave these ladies while I seek my friend?"

Wonted to all manner of deceitfulness, and engaged in a calling which unavoidably makes one distrustful of mere appearances, however specious, however honest; the really good-hearted officer, now eyed Pierre in the dubious light with a most unpleasant scrutiny; and he abandoned the "Sir," and the tone of his voice sensibly changed, as he replied: — "There is no hotel in this neighborhood; it is too off the thoroughfares."

"Come! come!"—cried the driver, now growing bold again—"though you're an officer, I'm a citizen for all that. You havn't any further right to keep me out of my bed now.

He don't know where he wants to go to, cause he haint got no place at all to go to; so I'll just dump him here, and you dar'n't stay me."

"Don't be impertinent now," said the officer, but not so sternly as before.

"I'll have my rights though, I tell you that! Leave go of my arm; damn ye, get off the box; I've the law now. I say mister, come tramp, here goes your luggage," and so saying he dragged toward him a light trunk on the top of the stage.

"Keep a clean tongue in ye now"—said the officer—"and don't be in quite so great a hurry," then addressing Pierre, who had now re-alighted from the coach—"Well, this can't continue; what do you intend to do?"

"Not to ride further with that man, at any rate," said Pierre; "I will stop right here for the present."

"He! he!" laughed the driver; "he! he! 'mazing 'commodating now—we hitches now, we do—stops right afore the watch-house—he! he!—that's funny!"

"Off with the luggage then, driver," said the policeman—"here hand the small trunk, and now away and unlash there behind."

During all this scene, Delly had remained perfectly silent in her trembling and rustic alarm; while Isabel, by occasional cries to Pierre, had vainly besought some explanation. But though their complete ignorance of city life had caused Pierre's two companions to regard the scene thus far with too much trepidation; yet now, when in the obscurity of night, and in the heart of a strange town, Pierre handed them out of the coach into the naked street, and they saw their luggage piled so near the white light of a watch-house, the same ignorance, in some sort, reversed its effects on them; for they little fancied in what really untoward and wretched circumstances they first touched the flagging of the city.

As the coach lumbered off, and went rolling into the wide murkiness beyond, Pierre spoke to the officer.

"It is a rather strange accident, I confess, my friend, but strange accidents will sometimes happen."

"In the best of families," rejoined the other, a little ironically.

Now, I must not quarrel with this man, thought Pierre to

himself, stung at the officer's tone. Then said:—"Is there any one in your—office?"

"No one as yet—not late enough."

"Will you have the kindness then to house these ladies there for the present, while I make haste to provide them with better lodgment? Lead on, if you please."

The man seemed to hesitate a moment, but finally acquiesced; and soon they passed under the white light, and entered a large, plain, and most forbidding-looking room, with hacked wooden benches and bunks ranged along the sides, and a railing before a desk in one corner. The permanent keeper of the place was quietly reading a paper by the long central double bat's-wing gas-light; and three officers off duty were nodding on a bench.

"Not very liberal accommodations"—said the officer, quietly; "nor always the best of company, but we try to be civil. Be seated, ladies," politely drawing a small bench toward them.

"Hallo, my friends," said Pierre, approaching the nodding three beyond, and tapping them on the shoulder—"Hallo, I say! Will you do me a little favor? Will you help bring some trunks in from the street? I will satisfy you for your trouble, and be much obliged into the bargain."

Instantly the three noddies, used to sudden awakenings, opened their eyes, and stared hard; and being further enlightened by the bat's-wings and first officer, promptly brought in the luggage as desired.

Pierre hurriedly sat down by Isabel, and in a few words gave her to understand, that she was now in a perfectly secure place, however unwelcoming; that the officers would take every care of her, while he made all possible speed in running to the house, and indubitably ascertaining how matters stood there. He hoped to be back in less than ten minutes with good tidings. Explaining his intention to the first officer, and begging him not to leave the girls till he should return, he forthwith sallied into the street. He quickly came to the house, and immediately identified it. But all was profoundly silent and dark. He rang the bell, but no answer; and waiting long enough to be certain, that either the house was indeed deserted, or else the old clerk was unawakeable or absent; and at all events, certain that no slightest preparation had been made for their arrival; Pierre, bitterly disappointed, returned to Isabel with this most unpleasant information.

Nevertheless something must be done, and quickly. Turning to one of the officers, he begged him to go and seek a hack, that the whole party might be taken to some respectable lodging. But the man, as well as his comrades, declined the errand on the score, that there was no stand on their beat, and they could not, on any account, leave their beat. So Pierre himself must go. He by no means liked to leave Isabel and Delly again, on an expedition which might occupy some time. But there seemed no resource, and time now imperiously pressed. Communicating his intention therefore to Isabel, and again entreating the officer's particular services as before, and promising not to leave him unrequited; Pierre again sallied out. He looked up and down the street, and listened; but no sound of any approaching vehicle was audible. He ran on, and turning the first corner, bent his rapid steps toward the greatest and most central avenue of the city, assured that there, if anywhere, he would find what he wanted. It was some distance off; and he was not without hope that an empty hack would meet him ere he arrived there. But the few stray ones he encountered had all muffled fares. He continued on, and at last gained the great avenue. Not habitually used to such scenes, Pierre for a moment was surprised, that the instant he turned out of the narrow, and dark, and death-like bye-street, he should find himself suddenly precipitated into the not-yet-repressed noise and contention, and all the garish night-life of a vast thoroughfare, crowded and wedged by day, and even now, at this late hour, brilliant with occasional illuminations, and echoing to very many swift wheels and footfalls.

ii

"I say, my pretty one! Dear! Dear! young man! Oh, love, you are in a vast hurry, aint you? Can't you stop a bit, now, my dear: do—there's a sweet fellow."

Pierre turned; and in the flashing, sinister, evil cross-lights of a druggist's window, his eye caught the person of a wonderfully beautifully-featured girl; scarlet-cheeked, glaringly-arrayed, and of a figure all natural grace but unnatural vivacity. Her whole form, however, was horribly lit by the green and yellow rays from the druggist's.

"My God!" shuddered Pierre, hurrying forward, "the town's first welcome to youth!"

He was just crossing over to where a line of hacks were drawn up against the opposite curb, when his eye was arrested by a short, gilded name, rather reservedly and aristocratically denominating a large and very handsome house, the second story of which was profusely lighted. He looked up, and was very certain that in this house were the apartments of Glen. Yielding to a sudden impulse, he mounted the single step toward the door, and rang the bell, which was quickly responded to by a very civil black.

As the door opened, he heard the distant interior sound of dancing-music and merriment.

"Is Mr. Stanly in?"

"Mr. Stanly? Yes, but he's engaged."

"How?"

"He is somewhere in the drawing rooms. My mistress is giving a party to the lodgers."

"Ay? Tell Mr. Stanly I wish to see him for one moment if you please; only one moment."

"I dare not call him, sir. He said that possibly some one might call for him to-night—they are calling every night for Mr. Stanly—but I must admit no one, on the plea of the party."

A dark and bitter suspicion now darted through the mind of Pierre; and ungovernably yielding to it, and resolved to prove or falsify it without delay, he said to the black:

"My business is pressing. I must see Mr. Stanly."

"I am sorry, sir, but orders are orders: I am his particular servant here—the one that sees his silver every holyday. I can't disobey him. May I shut the door, sir? for as it is, I can not admit you."

"The drawing-rooms are on the second floor, are they not?" said Pierre quietly.

"Yes," said the black pausing in surprise, and holding the door.

"Yonder are the stairs, I think?"

"That way, sir; but this is yours;" and the now suspicious black was just on the point of closing the portal violently upon him, when Pierre thrust him suddenly aside, and springing up the long stairs, found himself facing an open door, from whence proceeded a burst of combined brilliancy and melody, doubly confusing to one just emerged from the street. But bewildered and all demented as he momentarily felt, he instantly stalked in, and confounded the amazed company with his unremoved slouched hat, pale cheek, and whole dusty, travel-stained, and ferocious aspect.

"Mr. Stanly! where is Mr. Stanly?" he cried, advancing straight through a startled quadrille, while all the music suddenly hushed, and every eye was fixed in vague affright upon him.

"Mr. Stanly! Mr. Stanly!" cried several bladish voices, toward the further end of the further drawing-room, into which the first one widely opened, "Here is a most peculiar fellow after you; who the devil is he?"

"I think I see him," replied a singularly cool, deliberate, and rather drawling voice, yet a very silvery one, and at bottom perhaps a very resolute one; "I think I see him; stand aside, my good fellow, will you; ladies, remove, remove from between me and yonder hat."

The polite compliance of the company thus addressed, now revealed to the advancing Pierre, the tall, robust figure of a remarkably splendid-looking, and brown-bearded young man, dressed with surprising plainness, almost demureness, for such an occasion; but this plainness of his dress was not so obvious at first, the material was so fine, and admirably fitted. He was carelessly lounging in a half side-long attitude upon a large sofa, and appeared as if but just interrupted in some very agreeable chat with a diminutive but vivacious brunette, occupying the other end. The dandy and the man; strength and effeminacy; courage and indolence, were so strangely blended in this superb-eyed youth, that at first sight, it seemed impossible to decide whether there was any genuine mettle in him, or not.

Some years had gone by since the cousins had met; years peculiarly productive of the greatest conceivable changes in the general personal aspect of human beings. Nevertheless, the eye seldom alters. The instant their eyes met, they mutually recognized each other. But both did not betray the recognition.

"Glen!" cried Pierre, and paused a few steps from him.

But the superb-eyed only settled himself lower down in his lounging attitude, and slowly withdrawing a small, unpretending, and unribboned glass from his vest pocket, steadily, yet not entirely insultingly, notwithstanding the circumstances, scrutinized Pierre. Then, dropping his glass, turned slowly round upon the gentlemen near him, saying in the same peculiar, mixed, and musical voice as before:

"I do not know him; it is an entire mistake; why don't the servants take him out, and the music go on?——As I was saying, Miss Clara, the statues you saw in the Louvre are not to be mentioned with those in Florence and Rome. Why, there now is that vaunted *chef d'œuvre*, the Fighting Gladiator of the Louvre——"

"Fighting Gladiator it is!" yelled Pierre, leaping toward him like Spartacus. But the savage impulse in him was restrained by the alarmed female shrieks and wild gestures around him. As he paused, several gentlemen made motions to pinion him; but shaking them off fiercely, he stood erect, and isolated for an instant, and fastening his glance upon his still reclining, and apparently unmoved cousin, thus spoke:—

"Glendinning Stanly, thou disown'st Pierre not so abhorrently as Pierre does thee. By Heaven, had I a knife, Glen, I could prick thee on the spot; let out all thy Glendinning blood, and then sew up the vile remainder. Hound, and base blot upon the general humanity!"

"This is very extraordinary:—remarkable case of combined imposture and insanity; but where are the servants? why don't that black advance? Lead him out, my good Doc, lead him out. Carefully, carefully! stay"—putting his hand in his pocket—"there, take that, and have the poor fellow driven off somewhere."

Bolting his rage in him, as impossible to be sated by any conduct, in such a place, Pierre now turned, sprang down the stairs, and fled the house.

iii

"Hack, sir? Hack, sir? Hack, sir?"

"Cab, sir? Cab, sir? Cab, sir?"

"This way, sir! This way, sir! This way, sir!"

"He's a rogue! Not him! he's a rogue!"

Pierre was surrounded by a crowd of contending hackmen, all holding long whips in their hands; while others eagerly beckoned to him from their boxes, where they sat elevated between their two coach-lamps like shabby, discarded saints. The whip-stalks thickened around him, and several reports of the cracking lashes sharply sounded in his ears. Just bursting from a scene so goading as his interview with the scornful Glen in the dazzling drawing-room, to Pierre, this sudden tumultuous surrounding of him by whip-stalks and lashes, seemed like the onset of the chastising fiends upon Orestes. But, breaking away from them, he seized the first plated door-handle near him, and, leaping into the hack, shouted for whoever was the keeper of it, to mount his box forthwith and drive off in a given direction.

The vehicle had proceeded some way down the great ave-nue when it paused, and the driver demanded whither now; what place?

"The Watch-house of the —— Ward," cried Pierre.

"Hi! hi! Goin' to deliver himself up, hey?" grinned the fel-low to himself—"Well, that's a sort of honest, any way:—g'lang, you dogs!—whist! whee! wha!—g'lang!"

The sights and sounds which met the eye of Pierre on re-entering the watch-house, filled him with inexpressible horror and fury. The before decent, drowsy place, now fairly reeked with all things unseemly. Hardly possible was it to tell what conceivable cause or occasion had, in the comparatively short absence of Pierre, collected such a base congregation. In in-describable disorder, frantic, diseased-looking men and women of all colors, and in all imaginable flaunting, immod-est, grotesque, and shattered dresses, were leaping, yelling, and cursing around him. The torn Madras handkerchiefs of negresses, and the red gowns of yellow girls, hanging in tat-ters from their naked bosoms, mixed with the rent dresses of deep-rouged white women, and the split coats, checkered vests, and protruding shirts of pale, or whiskered, or haggard, or mustached fellows of all nations, some of whom seemed scared from their beds, and others seemingly arrested in the midst of some crazy and wanton dance. On all sides, were heard drunken male and female voices, in English, French, Spanish, and Portuguese, interlarded now and then, with the foulest of all human lingoes, that dialect of sin and death, known as the Cant language, or the Flash.

Running among this combined babel of persons and voices, several of the police were vainly striving to still the tumult; while others were busy handcuffing the more desperate; and here and there the distracted wretches, both men and women, gave downright battle to the officers; and still others already handcuffed struck out at them with their joined ironed arms. Meanwhile, words and phrases unrepeatable in God's sunlight, and whose very existence was utterly unknown, and undreamed of by tens of thousands of the decent people of the city; syllables obscene and accursed were shouted forth in tones plainly evincing that they were the common household breath of their utterers. The thieves'-quarters, and all the brothels, Lock-and-Sin hospitals for incurables, and infirmaries and infernoes of hell seemed to have made one combined sortie, and poured out upon earth through the vile vomitory of some unmentionable cellar.

Though the hitherto imperfect and casual city experiences of Pierre, illy fitted him entirely to comprehend the specific purport of this terrific spectacle; still he knew enough by hearsay of the more infamous life of the town, to imagine from whence, and who, were the objects before him. But all his consciousness at the time was absorbed by the one horrified thought of Isabel and Delly, forced to witness a sight hardly endurable for Pierre himself; or, possibly, sucked into the tumult, and in close personal contact with its loathsomeness. Rushing into the crowd, regardless of the random blows and curses he encountered, he wildly sought for Isabel, and soon descried her struggling from the delirious reaching arms of a half-clad reeling whiskerando. With an immense blow of his mailed fist, he sent the wretch humming, and seizing Isabel, cried out to two officers near, to clear a path for him to

the door. They did so. And in a few minutes the panting
Isabel was safe in the open air. He would have stayed by her,
but she conjured him to return for Delly, exposed to worse
insults than herself. An additional posse of officers now approaching, Pierre committing her to the care of one of them,
and summoning two others to join himself, now re-entered
the room. In another quarter of it, he saw Delly seized on
each hand by two bleared and half-bloody women, who with
fiendish grimaces were ironically twitting her upon her close-
necked dress, and had already stript her handkerchief from
her. She uttered a cry of mixed anguish and joy at the sight
of him; and Pierre soon succeeded in returning with her to
Isabel.

During the absence of Pierre in quest of the hack, and
while Isabel and Delly were quietly awaiting his return, the
door had suddenly burst open, and a detachment of the police
drove in, and caged, the entire miscellaneous night-occupants
of a notorious stew, which they had stormed and carried during the height of some outrageous orgie. The first sight of the
interior of the watch-house, and their being so quickly huddled together within its four blank walls, had suddenly lashed
the mob into frenzy; so that for the time, oblivious of all
other considerations, the entire force of the police was directed to the quelling of the in-door riot; and consequently,
abandoned to their own protection, Isabel and Delly had
been temporarily left to its mercy.

It was no time for Pierre to manifest his indignation at the
officer—even if he could now find him—who had thus falsi-
fied his individual pledge concerning the precious charge
committed to him. Nor was it any time to distress himself
about his luggage, still somewhere within. Quitting all, he
thrust the bewildered and half-lifeless girls into the waiting
hack, which, by his orders, drove back in the direction of the
stand, where Pierre had first taken it up.

When the coach had rolled them well away from the tumult, Pierre stopped it, and said to the man, that he desired
to be taken to the nearest respectable hotel or boarding-house
of any kind, that he knew of. The fellow—maliciously diverted by what had happened thus far—made some ambigu-

ous and rudely merry rejoinder. But warned by his previous rash quarrel with the stage-driver, Pierre passed this unnoticed, and in a controlled, calm, decided manner repeated his directions.

The issue was, that after a rather roundabout drive they drew up in a very respectable side-street, before a large respectable-looking house, illuminated by two tall white lights flanking its portico. Pierre was glad to notice some little remaining stir within, spite of the comparative lateness of the hour. A bare-headed, tidily-dressed, and very intelligent-looking man, with a broom clothes-brush in his hand, appearing, scrutinized him rather sharply at first; but as Pierre advanced further into the light, and his countenance became visible, the man, assuming a respectful but still slightly perplexed air, invited the whole party into a closely adjoining parlor, whose disordered chairs and general dustiness, evinced that after a day's activity it now awaited the morning offices of the housemaids.

"Baggage, sir?"

"I have left my baggage at another place," said Pierre, "I shall send for it to-morrow."

"Ah!" exclaimed the very intelligent-looking man, rather dubiously, "shall I discharge the hack, then?"

"Stay," said Pierre, bethinking him, that it would be well not to let the man know from whence they had last come, "I will discharge it myself, thank you."

So returning to the sidewalk, without debate, he paid the hackman an exorbitant fare, who, anxious to secure such illegal gains beyond all hope of recovery, quickly mounted his box and drove off at a gallop.

"Will you step into the office, sir, now?" said the man, slightly flourishing with his brush—"this way, sir, if you please."

Pierre followed him, into an almost deserted, dimly lit room with a stand in it. Going behind the stand, the man turned round to him a large ledger-like book, thickly inscribed with names, like any directory, and offered him a pen ready dipped in ink.

Understanding the general hint, though secretly irritated at

something in the manner of the man, Pierre drew the book
to him, and wrote in a firm hand, at the bottom of the last-
named column,—

"Mr. and Mrs. Pierre Glendinning, and Miss Ulver."

The man glanced at the writing inquiringly, and then
said—"The other column, sir—where from."

"True," said Pierre, and wrote "Saddle Meadows."

The very intelligent-looking man re-examined the page, and
then slowly stroking his shaven chin, with a fork, made of his
thumb for one tine, and his united four fingers for the other,
said softly and whisperingly—"Anywheres in this country,
sir?"

"Yes, in the country," said Pierre, evasively, and bridling
his ire. "But now show me to two chambers, will you; the
one for myself and wife, I desire to have opening into another, a third one, never mind how small; but I must have a
dressing-room."

"Dressing-room," repeated the man, in an ironically de-
liberative voice—"Dressing-room;—Hem!—You will have
your luggage taken into the dressing-room, then, I suppose.—Oh, I forgot—your luggage aint come yet—ah, yes,
yes, yes—luggage is coming to-morrow—Oh, yes, yes,—
certainly—to-morrow—of course. By the way, sir; I dislike
to seem at all uncivil, and I am sure you will not deem me
so; but—"

"Well," said Pierre, mustering all his self-command for the
coming impertinence.

"When stranger gentlemen come to this house without luggage, we think ourselves bound to ask them to pay their bills
in advance, sir; that is all, sir."

"I shall stay here to-night and the whole of to-morrow, at
any rate," rejoined Pierre, thankful that this was all; "how
much will it be?" and he drew out his purse.

The man's eyes fastened with eagerness on the purse; he
looked from it to the face of him who held it; then seemed
half hesitating an instant; then brightening up, said, with sudden suavity—"Never mind, sir, never mind, sir; though
rogues sometimes be gentlemanly; gentlemen that are gentlemen never go abroad without their diplomas. Their diplomas
are their friends; and their only friends are their dollars; you

have a purse-full of friends.—We have chambers, sir, that will exactly suit you, I think. Bring your ladies and I will show you up to them immediately." So saying, dropping his brush, the very intelligent-looking man lighted one lamp, and taking two unlighted ones in his other hand, led the way down the dusky lead-sheeted hall, Pierre following him with Isabel and Delly.

Book XVII

Young America in Literature

AMONG THE VARIOUS conflicting modes of writing history, there would seem to be two grand practical distinctions, under which all the rest must subordinately range. By the one mode, all contemporaneous circumstances, facts, and events must be set down contemporaneously; by the other, they are only to be set down as the general stream of the narrative shall dictate; for matters which are kindred in time, may be very irrelative in themselves. I elect neither of these; I am careless of either; both are well enough in their way; I write precisely as I please.

In the earlier chapters of this volume, it has somewhere been passingly intimated, that Pierre was not only a reader of the poets and other fine writers, but likewise—and what is a very different thing from the other—a thorough allegorical understander of them, a profound emotional sympathizer with them; in other words, Pierre himself possessed the poetic nature; in himself absolutely, though but latently and floatingly, possessed every whit of the imaginative wealth which he so admired, when by vast pains-takings, and all manner of unrecompensed agonies, systematized on the printed page. Not that as yet his young and immature soul had been accosted by the Wonderful Mutes, and through the vast halls of Silent Truth, had been ushered into the full, secret, eternally inviolable Sanhedrim, where the Poetic Magi discuss, in glorious gibberish, the Alpha and Omega of the Universe. But among the beautiful imaginings of the second and third degree of poets, he freely and comprehendingly ranged.

But it still remains to be said, that Pierre himself had written many a fugitive thing, which had brought him, not only vast credit and compliments from his more immediate acquaintances, but the less partial applauses of the always intelligent, and extremely discriminating public. In short, Pierre had frequently done that, which many other boys have done—published. Not in the imposing form of a book, but in the more modest and becoming way of occasional contributions to magazines and other polite periodicals. His magnificent and victorious *debut* had been made in that delightful love-sonnet, entitled "The Tropical Summer." Not only the public had applauded his gemmed little sketches of thought and fancy, whether in poetry or prose; but the high and mighty Campbell clan of editors of all sorts had bestowed upon him those generous commendations, which, with one instantaneous glance, they had immediately perceived was his due. They spoke in high terms of his surprising command of language; they begged to express their wonder at his euphonious construction of sentences; they regarded with reverence the pervading symmetry of his general style. But transcending even this profound insight into the deep merits of Pierre, they looked infinitely beyond, and confessed their complete inability to restrain their unqualified admiration for the highly judicious smoothness and genteelness of the sentiments and fancies expressed. "This writer," said one,—in an ungovernable burst of admiring fury—"is characterized throughout by Perfect Taste." Another, after endorsingly quoting that sapient, suppressed maxim of Dr. Goldsmith's, which asserts that whatever is new is false, went on to apply it to the excellent productions before him; concluding with this: "He has translated the unruffled gentleman from the drawing-room into the general levee of letters; he never permits himself to astonish; is never betrayed into any thing coarse or new; as assured that whatever astonishes is vulgar, and whatever is new must be crude. Yes, it is the glory of this admirable young author, that vulgarity and vigor— two inseparable adjuncts—are equally removed from him."

A third, perorated a long and beautifully written review, by the bold and startling announcement—"This writer is unquestionably a highly respectable youth."

Nor had the editors of various moral and religious periodicals failed to render the tribute of their severer appreciation, and more enviable, because more chary applause. A renowned clerical and philological conductor of a weekly publication of this kind, whose surprising proficiency in the Greek, Hebrew, and Chaldaic, to which he had devoted by far the greater part of his life, peculiarly fitted him to pronounce unerring judgment upon works of taste in the English, had unhesitatingly delivered himself thus:—"He is blameless in morals, and harmless throughout." Another, had unhesitatingly recom-

mended his effusions to the family-circle. A third, had no reserve in saying, that the predominant end and aim of this
author was evangelical piety.

A mind less naturally strong than Pierre's might well have
been hurried into vast self-complacency, by such eulogy as
this, especially as there could be no possible doubt, that the
primitive verdict pronounced by the editors was irreversible,
except in the highly improbable event of the near approach of
the Millennium, which might establish a different dynasty of
taste, and possibly eject the editors. It is true, that in view
of the general practical vagueness of these panegyrics, and
the circumstance that, in essence, they were all somehow of
the prudently indecisive sort; and, considering that they were
panegyrics, and nothing but panegyrics, without any thing
analytical about them; an elderly friend of a literary turn, had
made bold to say to our hero—"Pierre, this is very high
praise, I grant, and you are a surprisingly young author to
receive it; but I do not see any criticisms as yet."

"Criticisms?" cried Pierre, in amazement; "why, sir, they
are all criticisms! I am the idol of the critics!"

"Ah!" sighed the elderly friend, as if suddenly reminded
that that was true after all—"Ah!" and went on with his inoffensive, non-committal cigar.

Nevertheless, thanks to the editors, such at last became the
popular literary enthusiasm in behalf of Pierre, that two
young men, recently abandoning the ignoble pursuit of tailoring for the more honorable trade of the publisher (probably with an economical view of working up in books, the
linen and cotton shreds of the cutter's counter, after having
been subjected to the action of the paper-mill), had on the
daintiest scolloped-edged paper, and in the neatest possible,
and fine-needle-work hand, addressed him a letter, couched in
the following terms; the general style of which letter will sufficiently evince that, though—thanks to the manufacturer—
their linen and cotton shreds may have been very completely
transmuted into paper, yet the cutters themselves were not yet
entirely out of the metamorphosing mill.

"Hon. Pierre Glendinning,

"Revered Sir,

"The fine cut, the judicious fit of your productions

fill us with amazement. The fabric is excellent—the finest broadcloth of genius. We have just started in business. Your pantaloons—productions, we mean—have never yet been collected. They should be published in the Library form. The tailors—we mean the librarians, demand it. Your fame is now in its finest nap. Now—before the gloss is off—now is the time for the library form. We have recently received an invoice of Chamois——Russia leather. The library form should be a durable form. We respectfully offer to dress your amazing productions in the library form. If you please, we will transmit you a sample of the cloth——we mean a sample-page, with a pattern of the leather. We are ready to give you one tenth of the profits (less discount) for the privilege of arraying your wonderful productions in the library form:—you cashing the seamstresses'——printer's and binder's bills on the day of publication. An answer at your earliest convenience will greatly oblige,—

"Sir, your most obsequious servants,

"WONDER & WEN."

"P.S.—We respectfully submit the enclosed block—— sheet, as some earnest of our intentions to do every thing in your behalf possible to any firm in the trade.

"N.B.—If the list does not comprise all your illustrious wardrobe——works, we mean——, we shall exceedingly regret it. We have hunted through all the drawers——magazines.

"Sample of a coat——title for the works of Glendinning:

THE
COMPLETE WORKS
OF
GLENDINNING
AUTHOR OF
That world-famed production, "The Tropical Summer: a Sonnet."
"The Weather: a Thought." "Life: an Impromptu." "The
late Reverend Mark Graceman: an Obituary." "Honor:
a Stanza." "Beauty: an Acrostic." "Edgar: an
Anagram." "The Pippin: a Paragraph."
&c. &c. &c. &c.
&c. &c. &c.
&c. &c.
&c."

From a designer, Pierre had received the following:

"Sir: I approach you with unfeigned trepidation. For
though you are young in age, you are old in fame and ability.
I can not express to you my ardent admiration of your works;
nor can I but deeply regret that the productions of such
graphic descriptive power, should be unaccompanied by the
humbler illustrative labors of the designer. My services in this
line are entirely at your command. I need not say how proud
I should be, if this hint, on my part, however presuming,
should induce you to reply in terms upon which I could
found the hope of honoring myself and my profession by a
few designs for the works of the illustrious Glendinning. But
the cursory mention of your name here fills me with such
swelling emotions, that I can say nothing more. I would only
add, however, that not being at all connected with the Trade,
my business situation unpleasantly forces me to make cash
down on delivery of each design, the basis of all my professional arrangements. Your noble soul, however, would disdain to suppose, that this sordid necessity, in my merely
business concerns, could ever impair——
                "That profound private veneration and admiration
                    "With which I unmercenarily am,
                        "Great and good Glendinning,
                            "Yours most humbly,
                                "PETER PENCE."

                              ii

These were stirring letters. The Library Form! an Illustrated Edition! His whole heart swelled.
But unfortunately it occurred to Pierre, that as all his writings were not only fugitive, but if put together could not
possibly fill more than a very small duodecimo; therefore the
Library Edition seemed a little premature, perhaps; possibly,
in a slight degree, preposterous. Then, as they were chiefly
made up of little sonnets, brief meditative poems, and moral
essays, the matter for the designer ran some small risk of
being but meager. In his inexperience, he did not know that
such was the great height of invention to which the designer's

art had been carried, that certain gentlemen of that profession had gone to an eminent publishing-house with overtures for an illustrated edition of "Coke upon Lyttleton." Even the City Directory was beautifully illustrated with exquisite engravings of bricks, tongs, and flat-irons.

Concerning the draught for the title-page, it must be confessed, that on seeing the imposing enumeration of his titles—long and magnificent as those preceding the proclamations of some German Prince (*"Hereditary Lord of the back-yard of Crantz Jacobi; Undoubted Proprietor by Seizure of the bedstead of the late Widow Van Lorn; Heir Apparent to the Bankrupt Bakery of Fletz and Flitz; Residuary Legatee of the Confiscated Pin-Money of the Late Dowager Dunker; &c. &c. &c."*) Pierre could not entirely repress a momentary feeling of elation. Yet did he also bow low under the weight of his own ponderosity, as the author of such a vast load of literature. It occasioned him some slight misgivings, however, when he considered, that already in his eighteenth year, his title-page should so immensely surpass in voluminous statisticals the simple page, which in his father's edition prefixed the vast speculations of Plato. Still, he comforted himself with the thought, that as he could not presume to interfere with the bill-stickers of the Gazelle Magazine, who every month covered the walls of the city with gigantic announcements of his name among the other contributors; so neither could he now—in the highly improbable event of closing with the offer of Messrs. Wonder and Wen—presume to interfere with the bill-sticking department of their business concern; for it was plain that they esteemed one's title-page but another unwindowed wall, infinitely more available than most walls, since here was at least one spot in the city where no rival bill-stickers dared to encroach. Nevertheless, resolved as he was to let all such bill-sticking matters take care of themselves, he was sensible of some coy inclination toward that modest method of certain kid-gloved and dainty authors, who scorning the vulgarity of a sounding parade, contented themselves with simply subscribing their name to the title-page; as confident, that that was sufficient guarantee to the notice of all true gentlemen of taste. It was for petty German princes to sound their prolonged titular flourishes. The Czar of Russia contented himself with putting the simple word "NICHOLAS" to his loftiest decrees.

This train of thought terminated at last in various considerations upon the subject of anonymousness in authorship. He regretted that he had not started his literary career under that mask. At present, it might be too late; already the whole universe knew him, and it was in vain at this late day to attempt to hood himself. But when he considered the essential dignity and propriety at all points, of the inviolably anonymous method, he could not but feel the sincerest sympathy for those unfortunate fellows, who, not only naturally averse to any sort of publicity, but progressively ashamed of their own successive productions—written chiefly for the merest cash—were yet cruelly coerced into sounding title-pages by sundry baker's and butcher's bills, and other financial considerations; inasmuch as the placard of the title-page indubitably must assist the publisher in his sales.

But perhaps the ruling, though not altogether conscious motive of Pierre in finally declining—as he did—the services of Messrs. Wonder and Wen, those eager applicants for the privilege of extending and solidifying his fame, arose from the idea that being at this time not very far advanced in years, the probability was, that his future productions might at least equal, if not surpass, in some small degree, those already given to the world. He resolved to wait for his literary canonization until he should at least have outgrown the sophomorean insinuation of the Law; which, with a singular affectation of benignity, pronounced him an "infant." His modesty obscured from him the circumstance, that the greatest lettered celebrities of the time, had, by the divine power of genius, become full graduates in the University of Fame, while yet as legal minors forced to go to their mammas for pennies wherewith to keep them in peanuts.

Not seldom Pierre's social placidity was ruffled by polite entreaties from the young ladies that he would be pleased to grace their Albums with some nice little song. We say that here his social placidity was ruffled; for the true charm of agreeable parlor society is, that there you lose your own sharp individuality and become delightfully merged in that soft social Pantheism, as it were, that rosy melting of all into one, ever prevailing in those drawing-rooms, which pacifically and deliciously belie their own name; inasmuch as there no one draws the sword of his own individuality, but all such ugly weapons are left—as of old—with your hat and cane in the hall. It was very awkward to decline the albums; but somehow it was still worse, and peculiarly distasteful for Pierre to comply. With equal justice apparently, you might either have called this his weakness or his idiosyncrasy. He summoned all his suavity, and refused. And the refusal of Pierre—according to Miss Angelica Amabilia of Ambleside—was sweeter than the compliance of others. But then—prior to the proffer of her album—in a copse at Ambleside, Pierre in a gallant whim had in the lady's own presence voluntarily carved Miss Angelica's initials upon the bark of a beautiful maple. But all young ladies are not Miss Angelicas. Blandly denied in the parlor, they courted repulse in the study. In lovely envelopes they dispatched their albums to Pierre, not omitting to drop a little attar-of-rose in the palm of the domestic who carried them. While now Pierre—pushed to the wall in his gallantry—shilly-shallied as to what he must do, the awaiting albums multiplied upon him; and by-and-by monopolized an entire shelf in his chamber; so that while their combined ornate bindings fairly dazzled his eyes, their excessive redolence all but made him to faint, though indeed, in moderation, he was very partial to perfumes. So that of really chilly afternoons, he was still obliged to drop the upper sashes a few inches.

The simplest of all things it is to write in a lady's album. But Cui Bono? Is there such a dearth of printed reading, that the monkish times must be revived, and ladies books be in manuscript? What could Pierre write of his own on Love or any thing else, that would surpass what divine Hafiz wrote so many long centuries ago? Was there not Anacreon too, and Catullus, and Ovid—all translated, and readily accessible? And then—bless all their souls!—had the dear creatures forgotten Tom Moore? But the handwriting, Pierre,—they want the sight of your hand. Well, thought Pierre, actual feeling is better than transmitted sight, any day. I will give them the actual feeling of my hand, as much as they want. And lips are still better than hands. Let them send their sweet faces to me, and I will kiss *lipographs* upon them forever and a day. This was a felicitous idea. He called Dates, and had the albums carried down by the basket-full into the dining-room. He opened and spread them all out upon the extension-table there; then, modeling himself by the Pope, when His Holiness collectively blesses long crates of rosaries—he waved one devout kiss to the albums; and summoning three servants sent the albums all home, with his best compliments, accompanied with a confectioner's *kiss* for each album, rolled up in the most ethereal tissue.

From various quarters of the land, both town and country, and especially during the preliminary season of autumn, Pierre received various pressing invitations to lecture before Lyceums, Young Men's Associations, and other Literary and Scientific Societies. The letters conveying these invitations possessed quite an imposing and most flattering aspect to the unsophisticated Pierre. One was as follows:—

> "*Urquhartian Club for the Immediate Extension*
> *of the Limits of all Knowledge,*
> *both Human and Divine.*
>
>   "ZADOCKPRATTSVILLE,
>   "*June 11th, 18*—.

"*Author of the 'Tropical Summer,' &c.*

"HONORED AND DEAR SIR:—

"Official duty and private inclination in this present case most delightfully blend. What was the ardent desire of my heart, has now by the action of the *Committee on Lectures* become professionally obligatory upon me. As Chairman of our *Committee on Lectures*, I hereby beg the privilege of entreating that you will honor this Society by lecturing before it on any subject you may choose, and at any day most convenient to yourself. The subject of Human Destiny we would respectfully suggest, without however at all wishing to impede you in your own unbiased selection.

"If you honor us by complying with this invitation, be assured, sir, that the Committee on Lectures will take the best care of you throughout your stay, and endeavor to make

Zadockprattsville agreeable to you. A carriage will be in attendance at the Stage-house to convey yourself and luggage to the Inn, under full escort of the *Committee on Lectures*, with the Chairman at their head.

> "Permit me to join my private homage
>> To my high official consideration for you,
>>> And to subscribe myself
>>>> Very humbly your servant,
>>>>> "DONALD DUNDONALD."

iii

But it was more especially the Lecture invitations coming from venerable, gray-headed metropolitan Societies, and indited by venerable gray-headed Secretaries, which far from elating filled the youthful Pierre with the sincerest sense of humility. Lecture? lecture? such a stripling as I lecture to fifty benches, with ten gray heads on each? five hundred gray heads in all! Shall my one, poor, inexperienced brain presume to lay down the law in a lecture to five hundred life-ripened understandings? It seemed too absurd for thought. Yet the five hundred, through their spokesman, had voluntarily extended this identical invitation to him. Then how could it be otherwise, than that an incipient Timonism should slide into Pierre, when he considered all the disgraceful inferences to be derived from such a fact. He called to mind, how that once upon a time, during a visit of his to the city, the police were called out to quell a portentous riot, occasioned by the vast press and contention for seats at the first lecture of an illustrious lad of nineteen, the author of "A Week at Coney Island."

It is needless to say that Pierre most conscientiously and respectfully declined all polite overtures of this sort.

Similar disenchantments of his cooler judgment did likewise deprive of their full lusciousness several other equally marked demonstrations of his literary celebrity. Applications for autographs showered in upon him; but in sometimes humorously gratifying the more urgent requests of these singular people Pierre could not but feel a pang of regret, that owing to the very youthful and quite unformed character of his handwriting, his signature did not possess that inflexible uniformity, which—for mere prudential reasons, if nothing more—should always mark the hand of illustrious men. His heart thrilled with sympathetic anguish for posterity, which would be certain to stand hopelessly perplexed before so many contradictory signatures of one supereminent name. Alas! posterity would be sure to conclude that they were forgeries all; that no chirographic relic of the sublime poet Glendinning survived to their miserable times.

From the proprietors of the Magazines whose pages were honored by his effusions, he received very pressing epistolary solicitations for the loan of his portrait in oil, in order to take an engraving therefrom, for a frontispiece to their periodicals. But here again the most melancholy considerations obtruded. It had always been one of the lesser ambitions of Pierre, to sport a flowing beard, which he deemed the most noble corporeal badge of the man, not to speak of the illustrious author. But as yet he was beardless; and no cunning compound of Rowland and Son could force a beard which should arrive at maturity in any reasonable time for the frontispiece. Besides, his boyish features and whole expression were daily changing. Would he lend his authority to this unprincipled imposture upon Posterity? Honor forbade.

These epistolary petitions were generally couched in an elaborately respectful style; thereby intimating with what deep reverence his portrait would be handled, while unavoidably subjected to the discipline indispensable to obtain from it the engraved copy they prayed for. But one or two of the persons who made occasional oral requisitions upon him in this matter of his engraved portrait, seemed less regardful of the inherent respect due to every man's portrait, much more, to that of a genius so celebrated as Pierre. They did not even seem to remember that the portrait of any man generally receives, and indeed is entitled to more reverence than the original man himself; since one may freely clap a celebrated friend on the shoulder, yet would by no means tweak his nose in his portrait. The reason whereof may be this: that the portrait is better entitled to reverence than the man; inasmuch as nothing belittling can be imagined concerning the portrait, whereas many unavoidably belittling things can be fancied as touching the man.

Upon one occasion, happening suddenly to encounter a literary acquaintance—a joint editor of the "Captain Kidd Monthly"—who suddenly popped upon him round a corner, Pierre was startled by a rapid—"Good-morning, good-morning;—just the man I wanted:—come, step round now with me, and have your Daguerreotype taken;—get it engraved then in no time;—want it for the next issue."

So saying, this chief mate of Captain Kidd seized Pierre's arm, and in the most vigorous manner was walking him off, like an officer a pickpocket, when Pierre civilly said—"Pray, sir, hold, if you please, I shall do no such thing."—"Pooh, pooh—must have it—public property—come along—only a door or two now."—"Public property!" rejoined Pierre, "that may do very well for the 'Captain Kidd Monthly;'—it's very Captain Kiddish to say so. But I beg to repeat that I do not intend to accede."—"Don't? Really?" cried the other, amazedly staring Pierre full in the countenance;—" why bless your soul, *my* portrait is published—long ago published!"—"Can't help that, sir"—said Pierre. "Oh! come along, come along," and the chief mate seized him again with the most uncompunctious familiarity by the arm. Though the sweetest-tempered youth in the world when but decently treated, Pierre had an ugly devil in him sometimes, very apt to be evoked by the personal profaneness of gentlemen of the Captain Kidd school of literature. "Look you, my good fellow," said he, submitting to his impartial inspection a determinately double fist,—"drop my arm now—or I'll drop you. To the devil with you and your Daguerreotype!"

This incident, suggestive as it was at the time, in the sequel had a surprising effect upon Pierre. For he considered with what infinite readiness now, the most faithful portrait of any one could be taken by the Daguerreotype, whereas in former times a faithful portrait was only within the power of the moneyed, or mental aristocrats of the earth. How natural then the inference, that instead of, as in old times, immortalizing a genius, a portrait now only *dayalized* a dunce. Besides, when every body has his portrait published, true distinction

lies in not having yours published at all. For if you are published along with Tom, Dick, and Harry, and wear a coat of
their cut, how then are you distinct from Tom, Dick, and
Harry? Therefore, even so miserable a motive as downright
personal vanity helped to operate in this matter with Pierre.

Some zealous lovers of the general literature of the age, as
well as declared devotees to his own great genius, frequently
petitioned him for the materials wherewith to frame his biography. They assured him, that life of all things was most
insecure. He might feel many years in him yet; time might go
lightly by him; but in any sudden and fatal sickness, how
would his last hours be embittered by the thought, that he
was about to depart forever, leaving the world utterly unprovided with the knowledge of what were the precise texture
and hue of the first trowsers he wore. These representations
did certainly touch him in a very tender spot, not previously
unknown to the schoolmaster. But when Pierre considered,
that owing to his extreme youth, his own recollections of the
past soon merged into all manner of half-memories and a general vagueness, he could not find it in his conscience to present such materials to the impatient biographers, especially as
his chief verifying authority in these matters of his past career,
was now eternally departed beyond all human appeal. His excellent nurse Clarissa had been dead four years and more. In
vain a young literary friend, the well-known author of two
Indexes and one Epic, to whom the subject happened to be
mentioned, warmly espoused the cause of the distressed biographers; saying that however unpleasant, one must needs pay
the penalty of celebrity; it was no use to stand back; and concluded by taking from the crown of his hat the proof-sheets
of his own biography, which, with the most thoughtful consideration for the masses, was shortly to be published in the
pamphlet form, price only a shilling.

It only the more bewildered and pained him, when still
other and less delicate applicants sent him their regularly
printed *Biographico-Solicito Circulars*, with his name written in
ink; begging him to honor them and the world with a neat
draft of his life, including criticisms on his own writings; the
printed circular indiscriminately protesting, that undoubtedly
he knew more of his own life than any other living man; and

that only he who had put together the great works of Glendinning could be fully qualified thoroughly to analyze them, and cast the ultimate judgment upon their remarkable construction.

Now, it was under the influence of the humiliating emotions engendered by things like the above; it was when thus haunted by publishers, engravers, editors, critics, autograph-collectors, portrait-fanciers, biographers, and petitioning and remonstrating literary friends of all sorts; it was then, that there stole into the youthful soul of Pierre melancholy forebodings of the utter unsatisfactoriness of all human fame; since the most ardent profferings of the most martyrizing demonstrations in his behalf,—these he was sorrowfully obliged to turn away.

And it may well be believed, that after the wonderful vital world-revelation so suddenly made to Pierre at the Meadows—a revelation which, at moments, in some certain things, fairly Timonized him—he had not failed to clutch with peculiar nervous detestation and contempt that ample parcel, containing the letters of his Biographico and other silly correspondents, which, in a less ferocious hour, he had filed away as curiosities. It was with an almost infernal grin, that he saw that particular heap of rubbish eternally quenched in the fire, and felt that as it was consumed before his eyes, so in his soul was forever killed the last and minutest undeveloped microscopic germ of that most despicable vanity to which those absurd correspondents thought to appeal.

Book XVIII

Pierre, as a Juvenile Author, Reconsidered

INASMUCH AS BY various indirect intimations much more than ordinary natural genius has been imputed to Pierre, it may have seemed an inconsistency, that only the merest magazine papers should have been thus far the sole productions of his mind. Nor need it be added, that, in the soberest earnest, those papers contained nothing uncommon; indeed—entirely now to drop all irony, if hitherto any thing like that has been indulged in—those fugitive things of Master Pierre's were the veriest common-place.

It is true, as I long before said, that Nature at Saddle Meadows had very early been as a benediction to Pierre;—had blown her wind-clarion to him from the blue hills, and murmured melodious secrecies to him by her streams and her woods. But while nature thus very early and very abundantly feeds us, she is very late in tutoring us as to the proper methodization of our diet. Or,—to change the metaphor,—there are immense quarries of fine marble; but how to get it out; how to chisel it; how to construct any temple? Youth must wholly quit, then, the quarry, for awhile; and not only go forth, and get tools to use in the quarry, but must go and thoroughly study architecture. Now the quarry-discoverer is long before the stone-cutter; and the stone-cutter is long before the architect; and the architect is long before the temple; for the temple is the crown of the world.

Yes; Pierre was not only very unarchitectural at that time, but Pierre was very young, indeed, at that time. And it is often to be observed, that as in digging for precious metals in the mines, much earthy rubbish has first to be troublesomely handled and thrown out; so, in digging in one's soul for the fine gold of genius, much dullness and common-place is first brought to light. Happy would it be, if the man possessed in himself some receptacle for his own rubbish of this sort: but he is like the occupant of a dwelling, whose refuse can not be clapped into his own cellar, but must be deposited in the street before his own door, for the public functionaries to take care of. No common-place is ever effectually got rid of, except by essentially emptying one's self of it into a book; for once trapped in a book, then the book can be put into the fire, and all will be well. But they are not always put into the fire; and this accounts for the vast majority of miserable books over those of positive merit. Nor will any thoroughly sincere man, who is an author, ever be rash in precisely defining the period, when he has completely ridded himself of his rubbish, and come to the latent gold in his mine. It holds true, in every case, that the wiser a man is, the more misgivings he has on certain points.

It is well enough known, that the best productions of the best human intellects, are generally regarded by those intellects as mere immature freshman exercises, wholly worthless in themselves, except as initiatives for entering the great University of God after death. Certain it is, that if any inferences can be drawn from observations of the familiar lives of men of the greatest mark, their finest things, those which become the foolish glory of the world, are not only very poor and inconsiderable to themselves, but often positively distasteful; they would rather not have the book in the room. In minds comparatively inferior as compared with the above, these surmising considerations so sadden and unfit, that they become careless of what they write; go to their desks with discontent, and only remain there—victims to headache, and pain in the back—by the hard constraint of some social necessity. Equally paltry and despicable to them, are the works thus composed; born of unwillingness and the bill of the baker; the rickety offspring of a parent, careless of life herself, and reckless of the germ-life she contains. Let not the short-sighted world for a moment imagine, that any vanity lurks in such minds; only hired to appear on the stage, not voluntarily claiming the public attention; their utmost life-redness and glow is but rouge, washed off in private with bitterest tears; their laugh only rings because it is hollow; and the answering laugh is no laughter to them.

There is nothing so slipperily alluring as sadness; we become sad in the first place by having nothing stirring to do; we continue in it, because we have found a snug sofa at last. Even so, it may possibly be, that arrived at this quiet retrospective little episode in the career of my hero—this shallowly expansive embayed Tappan Zee of my otherwise deepheady Hudson—I too begin to loungingly expand, and wax harmlessly sad and sentimental.

Now, what has been hitherto presented in reference to Pierre, concerning rubbish, as in some cases the unavoidable first-fruits of genius, is in no wise contradicted by the fact, that the first published works of many meritorious authors have given mature token of genius; for we do not know how many they previously published to the flames; or privately published in their own brains, and suppressed there as quickly. And in the inferior instances of an immediate literary success, in very young writers, it will be almost invariably observable, that for that instant success they were chiefly indebted to some rich and peculiar experience in life, embodied in a book, which because, for that cause, containing original matter, the author himself, forsooth, is to be considered original; in this way, many very original books, being the product of very unoriginal minds. Indeed, man has only to be but a little circumspect, and away flies the last rag of his vanity. The world is forever babbling of originality; but there never yet was an original man, in the sense intended by the world; the first man himself—who according to the Rabbins was also the first author—not being an original; the only original author being God. Had Milton's been the lot of Caspar Hauser, Milton would have been vacant as he. For though the naked soul of man doth assuredly contain one latent element of intellectual productiveness; yet never was there a child born solely from one parent; the visible world of experience being that procreative thing which impregnates the muses; selfreciprocally efficient hermaphrodites being but a fable.

There is infinite nonsense in the world on all of these matters; hence blame me not if I contribute my mite. It is impossible to talk or to write without apparently throwing oneself helplessly open; the Invulnerable Knight wears his visor down. Still, it is pleasant to chat; for it passes the time ere we go to our beds; and speech is further incited, when like strolling improvisatores of Italy, we are paid for our breath. And we are only too thankful when the gapes of the audience dismiss us with the few ducats we earn.

ii

It may have been already inferred, that the pecuniary plans of Pierre touching his independent means of support in the city were based upon his presumed literary capabilities. For what else could he do? He knew no profession, no trade. Glad now perhaps might he have been, if Fate had made him a blacksmith, and not a gentleman, a Glendinning, and a genius. But here he would have been unpardonably rash, had he not already, in some degree, actually tested the fact, in his own personal experience, that it is not altogether impossible for a magazine contributor to Juvenile American literature to receive a few pence in exchange for his ditties. Such cases stand upon imperishable record, and it were both folly and ingratitude to disown them.

But since the fine social position and noble patrimony of Pierre, had thus far rendered it altogether unnecessary for him to earn the least farthing of his own in the world, whether by hand or by brain; it may seem desirable to explain a little here as we go. We shall do so, but always including, the preamble.

Sometimes every possible maxim or thought seems an old one; yet it is among the elder of the things in that unaugmentable stock, that never mind what one's situation may be, however prosperous and happy, he will still be impatient of it; he will still reach out of himself, and beyond every present condition. So, while many a poor be-inked galley-slave, toiling with the heavy oar of a quill, to gain something wherewithal to stave off the cravings of nature; and in his hours of morbid self-reproach, regarding his paltry wages, at all events, as an unavoidable disgrace to him; while this galley-slave of letters would have leaped with delight—reckless of the feeble seams of his pantaloons—at the most distant prospect of inheriting the broad farms of Saddle Meadows, lord of an all-sufficing income, and forever exempt from wearing on his hands those treacherous plague-spots of indigence—videlicet, blots from the inkstand;—Pierre himself, the undoubted and actual possessor of the things only longingly and hopelessly imagined by the other; the then top of Pierre's worldly ambition, was the being able to boast that he had written such matters as publishers would pay something for in the way of a mere business transaction, which they thought would prove profitable. Yet altogether weak and silly as this may seem in Pierre, let us preambillically examine a little further, and see if it be so indeed.

Pierre was proud; and a proud man—proud with the sort of pride now meant—ever holds but lightly those things, however beneficent, which he did not for himself procure. Were such pride carried out to its legitimate end, the man would eat no bread, the seeds whereof he had not himself put into the soil, not entirely without humiliation, that even that seed must be borrowed from some previous planter. A proud man likes to feel himself in himself, and not by reflection in others. He likes to be not only his own Alpha and Omega, but to be distinctly all the intermediate gradations, and then to slope off on his own spine either way, into the endless impalpable ether. What a glory it was then to Pierre, when first in his two gentlemanly hands he jingled the wages of labor! Talk of drums and the fife; the echo of coin of one's own earning is more inspiring than all the trumpets of Sparta. How disdainfully now he eyed the sumptuousness of his hereditary halls—the hangings, and the pictures, and the bragging historic armorials and the banners of the Glendinning renown; confident, that if need should come, he would not be forced to turn resurrectionist, and dig up his grandfather's Indian-chief grave for the ancestral sword and shield, ignominiously to pawn them for a living! He could live on himself. Oh, twice-blessed now, in the feeling of practical capacity, was Pierre.

The mechanic, the day-laborer, has but one way to live; his body must provide for his body. But not only could Pierre in some sort, do that; he could do the other; and letting his body stay lazily at home, send off his soul to labor, and his soul would come faithfully back and pay his body her wages. So, some unprofessional gentlemen of the aristocratic South, who happen to own slaves, give those slaves liberty to go and seek work, and every night return with their wages, which constitute those idle gentlemen's income. Both ambidexter and quadruple-armed is that man, who in a day-laborer's body, possesses a day-laboring soul. Yet let not such an one be over-confident. Our God is a jealous God; He wills not that any man should permanently possess the least shadow of His own self-sufficient attributes. Yoke the body to the soul, and put both to the plough, and the one or the other must in the end assuredly drop in the furrow. Keep, then, thy body effeminate for labor, and thy soul laboriously robust; or else thy soul effeminate for labor, and thy body laboriously robust. Elect! the two will not lastingly abide in one yoke. Thus over the most vigorous and soaring conceits, doth the cloud of Truth come stealing; thus doth the shot, even of a sixty-two-pounder pointed upward, light at last on the earth; for strive we how we may, we can not overshoot the earth's orbit, to receive the attractions of other planets; Earth's law of gravitation extends far beyond her own atmosphere.

In the operative opinion of this world, he who is already fully provided with what is necessary for him, that man shall have more; while he who is deplorably destitute of the same, he shall have taken away from him even that which he hath. Yet the world vows it is a very plain, downright matter-of-fact, plodding, humane sort of world. It is governed only by the simplest principles, and scorns all ambiguities, all transcendentals, and all manner of juggling. Now some imaginatively heterodoxical men are often surprisingly twitted upon their willful inverting of all common-sense notions, their absurd and all-displacing transcendentals, which say three is four, and two and two make ten. But if the eminent Jugglarius himself ever advocated in mere words a doctrine one thousandth part so ridiculous and subversive of all practical sense, as that doctrine which the world actually and eternally practices, of giving unto him who already hath more than enough, still more of the superfluous article, and taking away from him who hath nothing at all, even that which he hath,— then is the truest book in the world a lie.

Wherefore we see that the so-called Transcendentalists are not the only people who deal in Transcendentals. On the contrary, we seem to see that the Utilitarians,—the every-day world's people themselves, far transcend those inferior Transcendentalists by their own incomprehensible worldly maxims. And—what is vastly more—with the one party, their Transcendentals are but theoretic and inactive, and therefore harmless; whereas with the other, they are actually clothed in living deeds.

The highly graveling doctrine and practice of the world, above cited, had in some small degree been manifested in the case of Pierre. He prospectively possessed the fee of several hundred farms scattered over part of two adjoining counties; and now the proprietor of that popular periodical, the Gazelle Magazine, sent him several additional dollars for his sonnets. That proprietor (though in sooth, he never read the sonnets, but referred them to his professional adviser; and was so ignorant, that, for a long time previous to the periodical's actually being started, he insisted upon spelling the Gazelle with a *g* for the *z*, as thus: *Gagelle*; maintaining, that in the Gazelle connection, the *z* was a mere impostor, and that the *g* was soft; for he was a judge of softness, and could speak from experience); that proprietor was undoubtedly a Transcendentalist; for did he not act upon the Transcendental doctrine previously set forth?

Now, the dollars derived from his ditties, these Pierre had always invested in cigars; so that the puffs which indirectly brought him his dollars were again returned, but as perfumed puffs; perfumed with the sweet leaf of Havanna. So that this highly-celebrated and world-renowned Pierre—the great author—whose likeness the world had never seen (for had he not repeatedly refused the world his likeness?), this famous poet, and philosopher, author of "*The Tropical Summer: a Sonnet*;" against whose very life several desperadoes were darkly plotting (for had not the biographers sworn they would have it?); this towering celebrity—there he would sit smoking, and smoking, mild and self-festooned as a vapory mountain. It was very involuntarily and satisfactorily reciprocal. His cigars were lighted in two ways: lighted by the sale of his sonnets, and lighted by the printed sonnets themselves.

For even at that early time in his authorial life, Pierre, however vain of his fame, was not at all proud of his paper. Not only did he make allumettes of his sonnets when published, but was very careless about his discarded manuscripts; they were to be found lying all round the house; gave a great deal of trouble to the housemaids in sweeping; went for kindlings to the fires; and were forever flitting out of the windows, and

under the door-sills, into the faces of people passing the manorial mansion. In this reckless, indifferent way of his, Pierre
himself was a sort of publisher. It is true his more familiar
admirers often earnestly remonstrated with him, against this
irreverence to the primitive vestments of his immortal productions; saying, that whatever had once felt the nib of his
mighty pen, was thenceforth sacred as the lips which had but
once saluted the great toe of the Pope. But hardened as he
was to these friendly censurings, Pierre never forbade that ardent appreciator of "The Tear," who, finding a small fragment
of the original manuscript containing a dot (*tear*), over an *i*
(*eye*), esteemed the significant event providential; and begged
the distinguished favor of being permitted to have it for a
brooch; and ousted a cameo-head of Homer, to replace it
with the more invaluable gem. He became inconsolable, when
being caught in a rain, the dot (*tear*) disappeared from over
the *i* (*eye*); so that the strangeness and wonderfulness of the
sonnet was still conspicuous; in that though the least fragment of it could weep in a drought, yet did it become all
tearless in a shower.

But this indifferent and supercilious amateur—deaf to the
admiration of the world; the enigmatically merry and renowned author of "The Tear;" the pride of the Gazelle Magazine, on whose flaunting cover his name figured at the head
of all contributors—(no small men either; for their lives had
all been fraternally written by each other, and they had
clubbed, and had their likenesses all taken by the aggregate
job, and published on paper, all bought at one shop) this
high-prestiged Pierre—whose future popularity and voluminousness had become so startlingly announced by what he
had already written, that certain speculators came to the
Meadows to survey its water-power, if any, with a view to
start a paper-mill expressly for the great author, and so monopolize his stationery dealings;—this vast being,—spoken
of with awe by all merely youthful aspirants for fame; this
age-neutralizing Pierre;—before whom an old gentleman of
sixty-five, formerly librarian to Congress, on being introduced
to him at the Magazine publishers', devoutly took off his hat,
and kept it so, and remained standing, though Pierre was
socially seated with his hat on;—this wonderful, disdainful

genius—but only life-amateur as yet—is now soon to appear in a far different guise. He shall now learn, and very bitterly learn, that though the world worship Mediocrity and Common Place, yet hath it fire and sword for all contemporary Grandeur; that though it swears that it fiercely assails all Hypocrisy, yet hath it not always an ear for Earnestness.

And though this state of things, united with the ever multiplying freshets of new books, seems inevitably to point to a coming time, when the mass of humanity reduced to one level of dotage, authors shall be scarce as alchymists are to-day, and the printing-press be reckoned a small invention:—yet even now, in the foretaste of this let us hug ourselves, oh, my Aurelian! that though the age of authors be passing, the hours of earnestness shall remain!

Book XIX

The Church of the Apostles

IN THE LOWER old-fashioned part of the city, in a narrow
street—almost a lane—once filled with demure-looking
dwellings, but now chiefly with immense lofty warehouses of
foreign importers; and not far from the corner where the lane
intersected with a very considerable but contracted thoroughfare for merchants and their clerks, and their carmen and porters; stood at this period a rather singular and ancient edifice,
a relic of the more primitive time. The material was a grayish
stone, rudely cut and masoned into walls of surprising thickness and strength; along two of which walls—the side
ones—were distributed as many rows of arched and stately
windows. A capacious, square, and wholly unornamented
tower rose in front to twice the height of the body of the
church; three sides of this tower were pierced with small and
narrow apertures. Thus far, in its external aspect, the building—now more than a century old,—sufficiently attested for
what purpose it had originally been founded. In its rear, was
a large and lofty plain brick structure, with its front to the
rearward street, but its back presented to the back of the
church, leaving a small, flagged, and quadrangular vacancy
between. At the sides of this quadrangle, three stories of
homely brick colonnades afforded covered communication
between the ancient church, and its less elderly adjunct. A
dismantled, rusted, and forlorn old railing of iron fencing in
a small courtyard in front of the rearward building, seemed
to hint, that the latter had usurped an unoccupied space formerly sacred as the old church's burial inclosure. Such a fancy
would have been entirely true. Built when that part of the
city was devoted to private residences, and not to warehouses
and offices as now, the old Church of the Apostles had had
its days of sanctification and grace; but the tide of change and
progress had rolled clean through its broad-aisle and side-
aisles, and swept by far the greater part of its congregation
two or three miles up town. Some stubborn and elderly old
merchants and accountants, lingered awhile among its dusty

pews, listening to the exhortations of a faithful old pastor,
who, sticking to his post in this flight of his congregation,
still propped his half-palsied form in the worm-eaten pulpit,
and occasionally pounded—though now with less vigorous
hand—the moth-eaten covering of its desk. But it came to
pass, that this good old clergyman died; and when the gray-
headed and bald-headed remaining merchants and accountants followed his coffin out of the broad-aisle to see it reverently interred; then that was the last time that ever the old
edifice witnessed the departure of a regular worshiping assembly from its walls. The venerable merchants and accountants
held a meeting, at which it was finally decided, that, hard and
unwelcome as the necessity might be, yet it was now no use
to disguise the fact, that the building could no longer be ef-
ficiently devoted to its primitive purpose. It must be divided
into stores; cut into offices; and given for a roost to the gregarious lawyers. This intention was executed, even to the
making offices high up in the tower; and so well did the thing
succeed, that ultimately the church-yard was invaded for a
supplemental edifice, likewise to be promiscuously rented to
the legal crowd. But this new building very much exceeded
the body of the church in height. It was some seven stories;
a fearful pile of Titanic bricks, lifting its tiled roof almost to
a level with the top of the sacred tower.

In this ambitious erection the proprietors went a few steps,
or rather a few stories, too far. For as people would seldom
willingly fall into legal altercations unless the lawyers were
always very handy to help them; so it is ever an object with
lawyers to have their offices as convenient as feasible to the
street; on the ground-floor, if possible, without a single acclivity of a step; but at any rate not in the seventh story of
any house, where their clients might be deterred from employing them at all, if they were compelled to mount seven
long flights of stairs, one over the other, with very brief landings, in order even to pay their preliminary retaining fees. So,
from some time after its throwing open, the upper stories of
the less ancient attached edifice remained almost wholly without occupants; and by the forlorn echoes of their vacuities,
right over the head of the business-thriving legal gentlemen
below, must—to some few of them at least—have suggested

unwelcome similitudes, having reference to the crowded state of their basement-pockets, as compared with the melancholy condition of their attics;—alas! full purses and empty heads! This dreary posture of affairs, however, was at last much altered for the better, by the gradual filling up of the vacant chambers on high, by scores of those miscellaneous, bread-and-cheese adventures, and ambiguously professional nondescripts in very genteel but shabby black, and unaccountable foreign-looking fellows in blue spectacles; who, previously issuing from unknown parts of the world, like storks in Holland, light on the eaves, and in the attics of lofty old buildings in most large sea-port towns. Here they sit and talk like magpies; or descending in quest of improbable dinners, are to be seen drawn up along the curb in front of the eating-houses, like lean rows of broken-hearted pelicans on a beach; their pockets loose, hanging down and flabby, like the pelican's pouches when fish are hard to be caught. But these poor, penniless devils still strive to make ample amends for their physical forlornness, by resolutely reveling in the region of blissful ideals.

They are mostly artists of various sorts; painters, or sculptors, or indigent students, or teachers of languages, or poets, or fugitive French politicians, or German philosophers. Their mental tendencies, however heterodox at times, are still very fine and spiritual upon the whole; since the vacuity of their exchequers leads them to reject the coarse materialism of Hobbes, and incline to the airy exaltations of the Berkelyan philosophy. Often groping in vain in their pockets, they can not but give in to the Descartian vortices; while the abundance of leisure in their attics (physical and figurative), unites with the leisure in their stomachs, to fit them in an eminent degree for that undivided attention indispensable to the proper digesting of the sublimated Categories of Kant; especially as Kant (can't) is the one great palpable fact in their pervadingly impalpable lives. These are the glorious paupers, from whom I learn the profoundest mysteries of things; since their very existence in the midst of such a terrible precariousness of the commonest means of support, affords a problem on which many speculative nut-crackers have been vainly employed. Yet let me here offer up three locks of my hair, to the memory of all such glorious paupers who have lived and died in this world. Surely, and truly I honor them—noble men often at bottom—and for that very reason I make bold to be gamesome about them; for where fundamental nobleness is, and fundamental honor is due, merriment is never accounted irreverent. The fools and pretenders of humanity, and the impostors and baboons among the gods, these only are offended with raillery; since both those gods and men whose titles to eminence are secure, seldom worry themselves about the seditious gossip of old apple-women, and the skylarkings of funny little boys in the street.

When the substance is gone, men cling to the shadow. Places once set apart to lofty purposes, still retain the name of that loftiness, even when converted to the meanest uses. It would seem, as if forced by imperative Fate to renounce the reality of the romantic and lofty, the people of the present would fain make a compromise by retaining some purely imaginative remainder. The curious effects of this tendency are oftenest evinced in those venerable countries of the old transatlantic world; where still over the Thames one bridge yet retains the monastic title of Blackfriars; though not a single Black Friar, but many a pickpocket, has stood on that bank since a good ways beyond the days of Queen Bess; where still innumerable other historic anomalies sweetly and sadly remind the present man of the wonderful procession that preceded him in his new generation. Nor—though the comparative recentness of our own foundation upon these Columbian shores, excludes any considerable participation in these attractive anomalies,—yet are we not altogether, in our more elderly towns, wholly without some touch of them, here and there. It was thus with the ancient Church of the Apostles—better known, even in its primitive day, under the abbreviative of The Apostles—which, though now converted from its original purpose to one so widely contrasting, yet still retained its majestical name. The lawyer or artist tenanting its chambers, whether in the new building or the old, when asked where he was to be found, invariably replied,—*At the Apostles'*. But because now, at last, in the course of the inevitable transplantations of the more notable localities of the various professions in a thriving and amplifying town, the venerable spot offered not such inducements as before to the legal gentlemen; and as the strange nondescript adventurers and artists, and indigent philosophers of all sorts, crowded in as fast as the others left; therefore, in reference to the metaphysical strangeness of these curious inhabitants, and owing in some sort to the circumstance, that several of them were well-known Teleological Theorists, and Social Reformers, and political propagandists of all manner of heterodoxical tenets; therefore, I say, and partly, peradventure, from some slight waggishness in the public; the immemorial popular name of the ancient church itself was participatingly transferred to the dwellers therein. So it came to pass, that in the general fashion of the day, he who had chambers in the old church was familiarly styled an *Apostle*.

But as every effect is but the cause of another and a subsequent one, so it now happened that finding themselves thus clannishly, and not altogether infelicitously entitled, the occupants of the venerable church began to come together out of their various dens, in more social communion; attracted toward each other by a title common to all. By-and-by, from this, they went further; and insensibly, at last became organized in a peculiar society, which, though exceedingly inconspicuous, and hardly perceptible in its public demonstrations, was still secretly suspected to have some mysterious ulterior object, vaguely connected with the absolute overturning of Church and State, and the hasty and premature advance of some unknown great political and religious Millennium. Still, though some zealous conservatives and devotees of morals, several times left warning at the police-office, to keep a wary eye on the old church; and though, indeed, sometimes an officer would look up inquiringly at the suspicious narrow window-slits in the lofty tower; yet, to say the truth, was the place, to all appearance, a very quiet and decorous one, and its occupants a company of harmless people, whose greatest reproach was efflorescent coats and crack-crowned hats all podding in the sun.

Though in the middle of the day many bales and boxes would be trundled along the stores in front of the Apostles'; and along its critically narrow sidewalk, the merchants would now and then hurry to meet their checks ere the banks should close: yet the street, being mostly devoted to mere warehousing purposes, and not used as a general thoroughfare, it was at all times a rather secluded and silent place. But from an hour or two before sundown to ten or eleven o'clock the next morning, it was remarkably silent and depopulated, except by the Apostles themselves; while every Sunday it presented an aspect of surprising and startling quiescence; showing nothing but one long vista of six or seven stories of inexorable iron shutters on both sides of the way. It was pretty much the same with the other street, which, as before said, intersected with the warehousing lane, not very far from the Apostles'. For though that street was indeed a different one from the latter, being full of cheap refectories for clerks, foreign restaurants, and other places of commercial resort; yet the only hum in it was restricted to business hours; by night it was deserted of every occupant but the lamp-posts; and on Sunday, to walk through it, was like walking through an avenue of sphinxes.

Such, then, was the present condition of the ancient Church of the Apostles; buzzing with a few lingering, equivocal lawyers in the basement, and populous with all sorts of poets, painters, paupers and philosophers above. A mysterious professor of the flute was perched in one of the upper stories of the tower; and often, of silent, moonlight nights, his lofty, melodious notes would be warbled forth over the roofs of the ten thousand warehouses around him—as of yore, the bell had pealed over the domestic gables of a long-departed generation.

ii

On the third night following the arrival of the party in the city, Pierre sat at twilight by a lofty window in the rear building of the Apostles'. The chamber was meager even to meanness. No carpet on the floor, no picture on the wall; nothing but a low, long, and very curious-looking single bedstead, that might possibly serve for an indigent bachelor's pallet, a large, blue, chintz-covered chest, a rickety, rheumatic, and most ancient mahogany chair, and a wide board of the toughest live-oak, about six feet long, laid upon two upright empty flour-barrels, and loaded with a large bottle of ink, an unfastened bundle of quills, a pen-knife, a folder, and a still unbound ream of foolscap paper, significantly stamped, "Ruled; Blue."

There, on the third night, at twilight, sat Pierre by that lofty window of a beggarly room in the rear-building of the Apostles'. He was entirely idle, apparently; there was nothing in his hands; but there might have been something on his heart. Now and then he fixedly gazes at the curious-looking, rusty old bedstead. It seemed powerfully symbolical to him; and most symbolical it was. For it was the ancient dismemberable and portable camp-bedstead of his grandfather, the defiant defender of the Fort, the valiant captain in many an unsuccumbing campaign. On that very camp-bedstead, there, beneath his tent on the field, the glorious old mild-eyed and warrior-hearted general had slept, and but waked to buckle his knight-making sword by his side; for it was noble knighthood to be slain by grand Pierre; in the other world his foes' ghosts bragged of the hand that had given them their passports.

But has that hard bed of War, descended for an inheritance to the soft body of Peace? In the peaceful time of full barns, and when the noise of the peaceful flail is abroad, and the hum of peaceful commerce resounds, is the grandson of two Generals a warrior too? Oh, not for naught, in the time of this seeming peace, are warrior grandsires given to Pierre! For Pierre is a warrior too; Life his campaign, and three fierce allies, Woe and Scorn and Want, his foes. The wide world is banded against him; for lo you! he holds up the standard of Right, and swears by the Eternal and True! But ah, Pierre, Pierre, when thou goest to that bed, how humbling the thought, that thy most extended length measures not the proud six feet four of thy grand John of Gaunt sire! The stature of the warrior is cut down to the dwindled glory of the fight. For more glorious in real tented field to strike down your valiant foe, than in the conflicts of a noble soul with a dastardly world to chase a vile enemy who ne'er will show front.

There, then, on the third night, at twilight, by the lofty window of that beggarly room, sat Pierre in the rear building of the Apostles'. He is gazing out from the window now. But except the donjon form of the old gray tower, seemingly there is nothing to see but a wilderness of tiles, slate, shingles, and tin;—the desolate hanging wildernesses of tiles, slate, shingles and tin, wherewith we modern Babylonians replace the fair hanging-gardens of the fine old Asiatic times when the excellent Nebuchadnezzar was king.

There he sits, a strange exotic, transplanted from the delectable alcoves of the old manorial mansion, to take root in this niggard soil. No more do the sweet purple airs of the hills round about the green fields of Saddle Meadows come revivingly wafted to his cheek. Like a flower he feels the change; his bloom is gone from his cheek; his cheek is wilted and pale.

From the lofty window of that beggarly room, what is it that Pierre is so intently eying? There is no street at his feet; like a profound black gulf the open area of the quadrangle gapes beneath him. But across it, and at the further end of the steep roof of the ancient church, there looms the gray and grand old tower; emblem to Pierre of an unshakable fortitude, which, deep-rooted in the heart of the earth, defied all the howls of the air.

There is a door in Pierre's room opposite the window of Pierre: and now a soft knock is heard in that direction, accompanied by gentle words, asking whether the speaker might enter.

"Yes, always, sweet Isabel"—answered Pierre, rising and approaching the door;—"here: let us drag out the old camp-bed for a sofa; come, sit down now, my sister, and let us fancy ourselves anywhere thou wilt."

"Then, my brother, let us fancy ourselves in realms of everlasting twilight and peace, where no bright sun shall rise, because the black night is always its follower. Twilight and peace, my brother, twilight and peace!"

"It is twilight now, my sister; and surely, this part of the city at least seems still."

"Twilight now, but night soon; then a brief sun, and then another long night. Peace now, but sleep and nothingness soon, and then hard work for thee, my brother, till the sweet twilight come again."

"Let us light a candle, my sister; the evening is deepening."

"For what light a candle, dear Pierre?—Sit close to me, my brother."

He moved nearer to her, and stole one arm around her; her sweet head leaned against his breast; each felt the other's throbbing.

"Oh, my dear Pierre, why should we always be longing for peace, and then be impatient of peace when it comes? Tell me, my brother! Not two hours ago, thou wert wishing for twilight, and now thou wantest a candle to hurry the twilight's last lingering away."

But Pierre did not seem to hear her; his arm embraced her tighter; his whole frame was invisibly trembling. Then suddenly in a low tone of wonderful intensity he breathed:

"Isabel! Isabel!"

She caught one arm around him, as his was around herself; the tremor ran from him to her; both sat dumb.

He rose, and paced the room.

"Well, Pierre; thou camest in here to arrange thy matters, thou saidst. Now what hast thou done? Come, we will light a candle now."

The candle was lighted, and their talk went on.

"How about the papers, my brother? Dost thou find every thing right? Hast thou decided upon what to publish first, while thou art writing the new thing thou didst hint of?"

"Look at that chest, my sister. Seest thou not that the cords are yet untied?"

"Then thou hast not been into it at all as yet?"

"Not at all, Isabel. In ten days I have lived ten thousand years. Forewarned now of the rubbish in that chest, I can not summon the heart to open it. Trash! Dross! Dirt!"

"Pierre! Pierre! what change is this? Didst thou not tell me, ere we came hither, that thy chest not only contained some silver and gold, but likewise far more precious things, readily convertible into silver and gold? Ah, Pierre, thou didst swear we had naught to fear!"

"If I have ever willfully deceived thee, Isabel, may the high gods prove Benedict Arnolds to me, and go over to the devils to reinforce them against me! But to have ignorantly deceived myself and thee together, Isabel; that is a very different thing.

Oh, what a vile juggler and cheat is man! Isabel, in that chest
are things which in the hour of composition, I thought the
very heavens looked in from the windows in astonishment at
their beauty and power. Then, afterward, when days cooled
me down, and again I took them up and scanned them, some
underlying suspicions intruded; but when in the open air, I
recalled the fresh, unwritten images of the bunglingly written
things; then I felt buoyant and triumphant again; as if by that
act of ideal recalling, I had, forsooth, transferred the perfect
ideal to the miserable written attempt at embodying it. This
mood remained. So that afterward how I talked to thee about
the wonderful things I had done; the gold and the silver mine
I had long before sprung for thee and for me, who never were
to come to want in body or mind. Yet all this time, there was
the latent suspicion of folly; but I would not admit it; I shut
my soul's door in its face. Yet now, the ten thousand universal
revealings brand me on the forehead with fool! and like protested notes at the Bankers, all those written things of mine,
are jaggingly cut through and through with the protesting
hammer of Truth!—Oh, I am sick, sick, sick!"

"Let the arms that never were filled but by thee, lure thee
back again, Pierre, to the peace of the twilight, even though
it be of the dimmest!"

She blew out the light, and made Pierre sit down by her;
and their hands were placed in each other's.

"Say, are not thy torments now gone, my brother?"

"But replaced by—by—by—Oh God, Isabel, unhand
me!" cried Pierre, starting up. "Ye heavens, that have hidden
yourselves in the black hood of the night, I call to ye! If to
follow Virtue to her uttermost vista, where common souls
never go; if by that I take hold on hell, and the uttermost
virtue, after all, prove but a betraying pander to the mon-
strousest vice,—then close in and crush me, ye stony walls,
and into one gulf let all things tumble together!"

"My brother! this is some incomprehensible raving," pealed
Isabel, throwing both arms around him;—"my brother, my
brother!"

"Hark thee to thy furthest inland soul"—thrilled Pierre in
a steeled and quivering voice. "Call me brother no more!
How knowest thou I am thy brother? Did thy mother tell

thee? Did my father say so to me?—I am Pierre, and thou
Isabel, wide brother and sister in the common humanity,—
no more. For the rest, let the gods look after their own combustibles. If they have put powder-casks in me—let them
look to it! let them look to it! Ah! now I catch glimpses, and
seem to half-see, somehow, that the uttermost ideal of moral
perfection in man is wide of the mark. The demigods trample
on trash, and Virtue and Vice are trash! Isabel, I will write
such things—I will gospelize the world anew, and show them
deeper secrets than the Apocalypse!—I will write it, I will
write it!"

"Pierre, I am a poor girl, born in the midst of a mystery,
bred in mystery, and still surviving to mystery. So mysterious
myself, the air and the earth are unutterable to me; no word
have I to express them. But these are the circumambient mysteries; thy words, thy thoughts, open other wonder-worlds to
me, whither by myself I might fear to go. But trust to me,
Pierre. With thee, with thee, I would boldly swim a starless
sea, and be buoy to thee, there, when thou the strong swimmer shouldst faint. Thou, Pierre, speakest of Virtue and Vice;
life-secluded Isabel knows neither the one nor the other, but
by hearsay. What are they, in their real selves, Pierre? Tell me
first what is Virtue:—begin!"

"If on that point the gods are dumb, shall a pigmy speak?
Ask the air!"

"Then Virtue is nothing."

"Not that!"

"Then Vice?"

"Look: a nothing is the substance, it casts one shadow one
way, and another the other way; and these two shadows cast
from one nothing; these, seems to me, are Virtue and Vice."

"Then why torment thyself so, dearest Pierre?"

"It is the law."

"What?"

"That a nothing should torment a nothing; for I am a
nothing. It is all a dream—we dream that we dreamed we
dream."

"Pierre, when thou just hovered on the verge, thou wert a
riddle to me; but now, that thou art deep down in the gulf
of the soul,—now, when thou wouldst be lunatic to wise

men, perhaps—now doth poor ignorant Isabel begin to comprehend thee. Thy feeling hath long been mine, Pierre. Long
loneliness and anguish have opened miracles to me. Yes, it is
all a dream!"

Swiftly he caught her in his arms:—"From nothing proceeds nothing, Isabel! How can one sin in a dream?"

"First what is sin, Pierre?"

"Another name for the other name, Isabel."

"For Virtue, Pierre?"

"No, for Vice."

"Let us sit down again, my brother."

"I am Pierre."

"Let us sit down again, Pierre; sit close; thy arm!"

And so, on the third night, when the twilight was gone,
and no lamp was lit, within the lofty window of that beggarly
room, sat Pierre and Isabel hushed.

Book XX

CHARLIE MILLTHORPE

PIERRE HAD BEEN induced to take chambers at the Apostles', by one of the Apostles themselves, an old acquaintance of his, and a native of Saddle Meadows.

Millthorpe was the son of a very respectable farmer—now dead—of more than common intelligence, and whose bowed shoulders and homely garb had still been surmounted by a head fit for a Greek philosopher, and features so fine and regular that they would have well graced an opulent gentleman. The political and social levelings and confoundings of all manner of human elements in America, produce many striking individual anomalies unknown in other lands. Pierre well remembered old farmer Millthorpe:—the handsome, melancholy, calm-tempered, mute, old man; in whose countenance—refinedly ennobled by nature, and yet coarsely tanned and attenuated by many a prolonged day's work in the harvest—rusticity and classicalness were strangely united. The delicate profile of his face, bespoke the loftiest aristocracy; his knobbed and bony hands resembled a beggar's.

Though for several generations the Millthorpes had lived on the Glendinning lands, they loosely and unostentatiously traced their origin to an emigrating English Knight, who had crossed the sea in the time of the elder Charles. But that indigence which had prompted the knight to forsake his courtly country for the howling wilderness, was the only remaining hereditament left to his bedwindled descendants in the fourth and fifth remove. At the time that Pierre first recollected this interesting man, he had, a year or two previous, abandoned an ample farm on account of absolute inability to meet the manorial rent, and was become the occupant of a very poor and contracted little place, on which was a small and half-ruinous house. There, he then harbored with his wife,—a very gentle and retiring person,—his three little daughters, and his only son, a lad of Pierre's own age. The hereditary beauty and youthful bloom of this boy; his sweetness of temper, and something of natural refinement as contrasted with the unrelieved rudeness, and oftentimes sordidness, of his neighbors; these things had early attracted the sympathetic, spontaneous friendliness of Pierre. They were often wont to take their boyish rambles together; and even the severely critical Mrs. Glendinning, always fastidiously cautious as to the companions of Pierre, had never objected to his intimacy with so prepossessing and handsome a rustic as Charles.

Boys are often very swiftly acute in forming a judgment on character. The lads had not long companioned, ere Pierre concluded, that however fine his face, and sweet his temper, young Millthorpe was but little vigorous in mind; besides possessing a certain constitutional, sophomorean presumption and egotism; which, however, having nothing to feed on but his father's meal and potatoes, and his own essentially timid and humane disposition, merely presented an amusing and harmless, though incurable, anomalous feature in his character, not at all impairing the good-will and companionableness of Pierre; for even in his boyhood, Pierre possessed a sterling charity, which could cheerfully overlook all minor blemishes in his inferiors, whether in fortune or mind; content and glad to embrace the good whenever presented, or with whatever conjoined. So, in youth, do we unconsciously act upon those peculiar principles, which in conscious and verbalized maxims shall systematically regulate our maturer lives;—a fact, which forcibly illustrates the necessitarian dependence of our lives, and their subordination, not to ourselves, but to Fate.

If the grown man of taste, possess not only some eye to detect the picturesque in the natural landscape, so also, has he as keen a perception of what may not unfitly be here styled, the *povertiresque* in the social landscape. To such an one, not more picturesquely conspicuous is the dismantled thatch in a painted cottage of Gainsborough, than the time-tangled and want-thinned locks of a beggar, *povertiresquely* diversifying those snug little cabinet-pictures of the world, which, exquisitely varnished and framed, are hung up in the drawing-room minds of humane men of taste, and amiable philosophers of either the "Compensation," or "Optimist" school. They deny that any misery is in the world, except for the purpose of throwing the fine *povertiresque* element into its general picture. Go to! God hath deposited cash in the Bank subject to our gentlemanly order; he hath bounteously blessed the world with a summer carpet of green. Begone, Heraclitus! The lamentations of the rain are but to make us our rainbows!

Not that in equivocal reference to the *povertiresque* old farmer Millthorpe, Pierre is here intended to be hinted at. Still, man can not wholly escape his surroundings. Unconsciously Mrs. Glendinning had always been one of these curious Optimists; and in his boyish life Pierre had not wholly escaped the maternal contagion. Yet often, in calling at the old farmer's for Charles of some early winter mornings, and meeting the painfully embarrassed, thin, feeble features of Mrs. Millthorpe, and the sadly inquisitive and hopelessly half-envious glances of the three little girls; and standing on the threshold, Pierre would catch low, aged, life-weary groans from a recess out of sight from the door; then would Pierre have some boyish inklings of something else than the pure *povertiresque* in poverty: some inklings of what it might be, to be old, and poor, and worn, and rheumatic, with shivering death drawing nigh, and present life itself but a dull and a chill! some inklings of what it might be, for him who in youth had vivaciously leaped from his bed, impatient to meet the earliest sun, and lose no sweet drop of his life, now hating the beams he once so dearly loved; turning round in his bed to the wall to avoid them; and still postponing the foot which should bring him back to the dismal day; when the sun is not gold, but copper; and the sky is not blue, but gray; and the blood, like Rhenish wine, too long unquaffed by Death, grows thin and sour in the veins.

Pierre had not forgotten that the augmented penury of the Millthorpes' was, at the time we now retrospectively treat of, gravely imputed by the gossiping frequenters of the Black Swan Inn, to certain insinuated moral derelictions of the farmer. "The old man tipped his elbow too often," once said in Pierre's hearing an old bottle-necked fellow, performing the identical same act with a half-emptied glass in his hand. But though the form of old Millthorpe was broken, his countenance, however sad and thin, betrayed no slightest sign of the sot, either past or present. He never was publicly known to frequent the inn, and seldom quitted the few acres he cultivated with his son. And though, alas, indigent enough, yet was he most punctually honest in paying his little debts of shillings and pence for his groceries. And though, heaven knows, he had plenty of occasion for all the money he could possibly earn, yet Pierre remembered, that when, one autumn, a hog was bought of him for the servants' hall at the Mansion, the old man never called for his money till the midwinter following; and then, as with trembling fingers he eagerly clutched the silver, he unsteadily said, "I have no use for it now; it might just as well have stood over." It was then, that chancing to overhear this, Mrs. Glendinning had looked at the old man, with a kindly and benignantly interested eye to the *povertiresque*; and murmured, "Ah! the old English Knight is not yet out of his blood. Bravo, old man!"

One day, in Pierre's sight, nine silent figures emerged from the door of old Millthorpe; a coffin was put into a neighbor's farm-wagon; and a procession, some thirty feet long, including the elongated pole and box of the wagon, wound along Saddle Meadows to a hill, where, at last, old Millthorpe was laid down in a bed, where the rising sun should affront him no more. Oh, softest and daintiest of Holland linen is the motherly earth! There, beneath the sublime tester of the infinite sky, like emperors and kings, sleep, in grand state, the beggars and paupers of earth! I joy that Death is this Democrat; and hopeless of all other real and permanent democracies, still hug the thought, that though in life some heads are crowned with gold, and some bound round with thorns, yet chisel them how they will, head-stones are all alike.

This somewhat particular account of the father of young Millthorpe, will better set forth the less immature condition and character of the son, on whom had now descended the maintenance of his mother and sisters. But, though the son of a farmer, Charles was peculiarly averse to hard labor. It was not impossible that by resolute hard labor he might eventually have succeeded in placing his family in a far more comfortable situation than he had ever remembered them. But it was not so fated; the benevolent State had in its great wisdom decreed otherwise.

In the village of Saddle Meadows there was an institution,

half common-school and half academy, but mainly supported
by a general ordinance and financial provision of the government. Here, not only were the rudiments of an English education taught, but likewise some touch of belles lettres, and
composition, and that great American bulwark and bore—
elocution. On the high-raised, stage platform of the Saddle
Meadows Academy, the sons of the most indigent day-laborers were wont to drawl out the fiery revolutionary rhetoric of
Patrick Henry, or gesticulate impetuously through the soft
cadences of Drake's "Culprit Fay." What wonder, then, that
of Saturdays, when there was no elocution and poesy, these
boys should grow melancholy and disdainful over the heavy,
plodding handles of dung-forks and hoes?

At the age of fifteen, the ambition of Charles Millthorpe
was to be either an orator, or a poet; at any rate, a great
genius of one sort or other. He recalled the ancestral Knight,
and indignantly spurned the plow. Detecting in him the first
germ of this inclination, old Millthorpe had very seriously
reasoned with his son; warning him against the evils of his
vagrant ambition. Ambition of that sort was either for undoubted genius, rich boys, or poor boys, standing entirely
alone in the world, with no one relying upon them. Charles
had better consider the case; his father was old and infirm; he
could not last very long; he had nothing to leave behind him
but his plow and his hoe; his mother was sickly; his sisters
pale and delicate; and finally, life was a fact, and the winters
in that part of the country exceedingly bitter and long. Seven
months out of the twelve the pastures bore nothing, and all
cattle must be fed in the barns. But Charles was a boy; advice
often seems the most wantonly wasted of all human breath;
man will not take wisdom on trust; may be, it is well; for
such wisdom is worthless; we must find the true gem for ourselves; and so we go groping and groping for many and many
a day.

Yet was Charles Millthorpe as affectionate and dutiful a boy
as ever boasted of his brain, and knew not that he possessed
a far more excellent and angelical thing in the possession of a
generous heart. His father died; to his family he resolved to
be a second father, and a careful provider now. But not by
hard toil of his hand; but by gentler practices of his mind.

Already he had read many books—history, poetry, romance, essays, and all. The manorial book-shelves had often been honored by his visits, and Pierre had kindly been his librarian. Not to lengthen the tale, at the age of seventeen, Charles sold the horse, the cow, the pig, the plow, the hoe, and almost every movable thing on the premises; and, converting all into cash, departed with his mother and sisters for the city; chiefly basing his expectations of success on some vague representations of an apothecary relative there resident. How he and his mother and sisters battled it out; how they pined and half-starved for a while; how they took in sewing; and Charles took in copying; and all but scantily sufficed for a livelihood; all this may be easily imagined. But some mysterious latent good-will of Fate toward him, had not only thus far kept Charles from the Poor-House, but had really advanced his fortunes in a degree. At any rate, that certain harmless presumption and innocent egotism which have been previously adverted to as sharing in his general character, these had by no means retarded him; for it is often to be observed of the shallower men, that they are the very last to despond. It is the glory of the bladder that nothing can sink it; it is the reproach of a box of treasure, that once overboard it must down.

ii

When arrived in the city, and discovering the heartless neglect of Glen, Pierre,—looking about him for whom to apply to in this strait,—bethought him of his old boy-companion Charlie, and went out to seek him, and found him at last; he saw before him, a tall, well-grown, but rather thin and pale yet strikingly handsome young man of two-and-twenty; occupying a small dusty law-office on the third floor of the older building of the Apostles; assuming to be doing a very large, and hourly increasing business among empty pigeon-holes, and directly under the eye of an unopened bottle of ink; his mother and sisters dwelling in a chamber overhead; and himself, not only following the law for a corporeal living, but likewise interlinked with the peculiar secret, theologico-politico-social schemes of the masonic order of the seedy-coated

Apostles; and pursuing some crude, transcendental Philosophy, for both a contributory means of support, as well as for
his complete intellectual aliment.

Pierre was at first somewhat startled by his exceedingly
frank and familiar manner; all old manorial deference for
Pierre was clean gone and departed; though at the first shock
of their encounter, Charlie could not possibly have known
that Pierre was cast off.

"Ha, Pierre! glad to see you, my boy! Hark ye, next month
I am to deliver an address before the Omega order of the
Apostles. The Grand Master, Plinlimmon, will be there. I
have heard on the best authority that he once said of me—
'That youth has the Primitive Categories in him; he is destined to astonish the world.' Why, lad, I have received propositions from the Editors of the Spinozaist to contribute a
weekly column to their paper, and you know how very few
can understand the Spinozaist; nothing is admitted there but
the Ultimate Transcendentals. Hark now, in your ear; I think
of throwing off the Apostolic disguise and coming boldly
out; Pierre! I think of stumping the State, and preaching our
philosophy to the masses—When did you arrive in town?"

Spite of all his tribulations, Pierre could not restrain a smile
at this highly diverting reception; but well knowing the
youth, he did not conclude from this audacious burst of enthusiastic egotism that his heart had at all corroded; for egotism is one thing, and selfishness another. No sooner did
Pierre intimate his condition to him, than immediately, Charlie was all earnest and practical kindness; recommended the
Apostles as the best possible lodgment for him,—cheap,
snug, and convenient to most public places; he offered to
procure a cart and see himself to the transport of Pierre's luggage; but finally thought it best to mount the stairs and show
him the vacant rooms. But when these at last were decided
upon; and Charlie, all cheerfulness and alacrity, started with
Pierre for the hotel, to assist him in the removal; grasping his
arm the moment they emerged from the great arched door
under the tower of the Apostles; he instantly launched into
his amusing heroics, and continued the strain till the trunks
were fairly in sight.

"Lord! my law-business overwhelms me! I must drive away

some of my clients; I must have my exercise, and this ever-growing business denies it to me. Besides, I owe something to the sublime cause of the general humanity; I must displace some of my briefs for my metaphysical treatises. I can not waste all my oil over bonds and mortgages.—You said you were married, I think?"

But without stopping for any reply, he rattled on. "Well, I suppose it is wise after all. It settles, centralizes, and confirms a man, I have heard.—No, I didn't; it is a random thought of my own, that!—Yes, it makes the world definite to him; it removes his morbid *sub*jectiveness, and makes all things *ob*jective; nine small children, for instance, may be considered *ob*jective. Marriage, hey!—A fine thing, no doubt, no doubt:— domestic—pretty—nice, all round. But I owe something to the world, my boy! By marriage, I might contribute to the population of men, but not to the census of mind. The great men are all bachelors, you know. Their family is the universe: I should say the planet Saturn was their elder son; and Plato their uncle.—So you are married?"

But again, reckless of answers, Charlie went on. "Pierre, a thought, my boy;—a thought for you! You do not say it, but you hint of a low purse. Now I shall help you to fill it— Stump the State on the Kantian Philosophy! A dollar a head, my boy! Pass round your beaver, and you'll get it. I have every confidence in the penetration and magnanimousness of the people! Pierre, hark in your ear;—it's my opinion the world is all wrong. Hist, I say—an entire mistake. Society demands an Avatar,—a Curtius, my boy! to leap into the fiery gulf, and by perishing himself, save the whole empire of men! Pierre, I have long renounced the allurements of life and fashion. Look at my coat, and see how I spurn them! Pierre! but, stop, have you ever a shilling? let's take a cold cut here— it's a cheap place; I go here sometimes. Come, let's in."

Book XXI

PIERRE IMMATURELY ATTEMPTS A MATURE WORK •
TIDINGS FROM THE MEADOWS • PLINLIMMON

W<small>E ARE NOW</small> to behold Pierre permanently lodged in three lofty adjoining chambers of the Apostles. And passing on a little further in time, and overlooking the hundred and one domestic details, of how their internal arrangements were finally put into steady working order; how poor Delly, now giving over the sharper pangs of her grief, found in the lighter occupations of a handmaid and familiar companion to Isabel, the only practical relief from the memories of her miserable past; how Isabel herself in the otherwise occupied hours of Pierre, passed some of her time in mastering the chirographical incoherencies of his manuscripts, with a view to eventually copying them out in a legible hand for the printer; or went below stairs to the rooms of the Millthorpes, and in the modest and amiable society of the three young ladies and their excellent mother, found some little solace for the absence of Pierre; or, when his day's work was done, sat by him in the twilight, and played her mystic guitar till Pierre felt chapter after chapter born of its wondrous suggestiveness; but alas! eternally incapable of being translated into words; for where the deepest words end, there music begins with its supersensuous and all-confounding intimations.

Disowning now all previous exertions of his mind, and burning in scorn even those fine fruits of a care-free fancy, which, written at Saddle Meadows in the sweet legendary time of Lucy and her love, he had jealousy kept from the publishers, as too true and good to be published; renouncing all his foregone self, Pierre was now engaged in a comprehensive compacted work, to whose speedy completion two tremendous motives unitedly impelled;—the burning desire to deliver what he thought to be new, or at least miserably neglected Truth to the world; and the prospective menace of being absolutely penniless, unless by the sale of his book, he could realize money. Swayed to universality of thought by the widely-explosive mental tendencies of the profound events which had lately befallen him, and the unprecedented situation in which he now found himself; and perceiving, by presentiment, that most grand productions of the best human intellects ever are built round a circle, as atolls (*i.e.* the primitive coral islets which, raising themselves in the depths of profoundest seas, rise funnel-like to the surface, and present there a hoop of white rock, which though on the outside everywhere lashed by the ocean, yet excludes all tempests from the quiet lagoon within), digestively including the whole range of all that can be known or dreamed; Pierre was resolved to give the world a book, which the world should hail with surprise and delight. A varied scope of reading, little suspected by his friends, and randomly acquired by a random but lynx-eyed mind, in the course of the multifarious, incidental, bibliographic encounterings of almost any civilized young inquirer after Truth; this poured one considerable contributary stream into that bottomless spring of original thought which the occasion and time had caused to burst out in himself. Now he congratulated himself upon all his cursory acquisitions of this sort; ignorant that in reality to a mind bent on producing some thoughtful thing of absolute Truth, all mere reading is apt to prove but an obstacle hard to overcome; and not an accelerator helpingly pushing him along.

While Pierre was thinking that he was entirely transplanted into a new and wonderful element of Beauty and Power, he was, in fact, but in one of the stages of the transition. That ultimate element once fairly gained, then books no more are needed for buoys to our souls; our own strong limbs support us, and we float over all bottomlessnesses with a jeering impunity. He did not see,—or if he did, he could not yet name the true cause for it,—that already, in the incipiency of his work, the heavy unmalleable element of mere book-knowledge would not congenially weld with the wide fluidness and ethereal airiness of spontaneous creative thought. He would climb Parnassus with a pile of folios on his back. He did not see, that it was nothing at all to him, what other men had written; that though Plato was indeed a transcendently great man in himself, yet Plato must not be transcendently great to him (Pierre), so long as he (Pierre himself) would also do something transcendently great. He did not see that there is no such thing as a standard for the creative spirit; that no one great book must ever be separately regarded, and permitted to domineer with its own uniqueness upon the creative mind; but that all existing great works must be federated in the fancy; and so regarded as a miscellaneous and Pantheistic whole; and then,—without at all dictating to his own mind, or unduly biasing it any way,—thus combined, they would prove simply an exhilarative and provocative to him. He did not see, that even when thus combined, all was but one small mite, compared to the latent infiniteness and inexhaustibility in himself; that all the great books in the world are but the mutilated shadowings-forth of invisible and eternally unembodied images in the soul; so that they are but the mirrors, distortedly reflecting to us our own things; and never mind what the mirror may be, if we would see the object, we must look at the object itself, and not at its reflection.

But, as to the resolute traveler in Switzerland, the Alps do never in one wide and comprehensive sweep, instantaneously reveal their full awfulness of amplitude—their overawing extent of peak crowded on peak, and spur sloping on spur, and chain jammed behind chain, and all their wonderful battalionings of might; so hath heaven wisely ordained, that on first entering into the Switzerland of his soul, man shall not at once perceive its tremendous immensity; lest illy prepared for such an encounter, his spirit should sink and perish in the lowermost snows. Only by judicious degrees, appointed of God, does man come at last to gain his Mont Blanc and take an overtopping view of these Alps; and even then, the tithe is not shown; and far over the invisible Atlantic, the Rocky Mountains and the Andes are yet unbeheld. Appalling is the soul of a man! Better might one be pushed off into the material spaces beyond the uttermost orbit of our sun, than once feel himself fairly afloat in himself!

But not now to consider these ulterior things, Pierre, though strangely and very newly alive to many before unregarded wonders in the general world; still, had he not as yet procured for himself that enchanter's wand of the soul, which but touching the humblest experiences in one's life, straightway it starts up all eyes, in every one of which are endless

significancies. Not yet had he dropped his angle into the well
of his childhood, to find what fish might be there; for who
dreams to find fish in a well? the running stream of the outer
world, there doubtless swim the golden perch and the pick-
erel! Ten million things were as yet uncovered to Pierre. The
old mummy lies buried in cloth on cloth; it takes time to
unwrap this Egyptian king. Yet now, forsooth, because Pierre
began to see through the first superficiality of the world, he
fondly weens he has come to the unlayered substance. But,
far as any geologist has yet gone down into the world, it is
found to consist of nothing but surface stratified on surface.
To its axis, the world being nothing but superinduced super-
ficies. By vast pains we mine into the pyramid; by horrible
gropings we come to the central room; with joy we espy the
sarcophagus; but we lift the lid—and no body is there!—
appallingly vacant as vast is the soul of a man!

ii

He had been engaged some weeks upon his book—in pur-
suance of his settled plan avoiding all contact with any of his
city-connections or friends, even as in his social downfall they
sedulously avoided seeking him out—nor ever once going or
sending to the post-office, though it was but a little round the
corner from where he was, since having dispatched no letters
himself, he expected none; thus isolated from the world, and
intent upon his literary enterprise, Pierre had passed some
weeks, when verbal tidings came to him, of three most momentous events.

First: his mother was dead.

Second: all Saddle Meadows was become Glen Stanly's.

Third: Glen Stanly was believed to be the suitor of Lucy;
who, convalescent from an almost mortal illness, was now
dwelling at her mother's house in town.

It was chiefly the first-mentioned of these events which
darted a sharp natural anguish into Pierre. No letter had come
to him; no smallest ring or memorial been sent him; no
slightest mention made of him in the will; and yet it was
reported that an inconsolable grief had induced his mother's
mortal malady, and driven her at length into insanity, which

suddenly terminated in death; and when he first heard of that event, she had been cold in the ground for twenty-five days.

How plainly did all this speak of the equally immense pride and grief of his once magnificent mother; and how agonizedly now did it hint of her mortally-wounded love for her only and best-beloved Pierre! In vain he reasoned with himself; in vain remonstrated with himself; in vain sought to parade all his stoic arguments to drive off the onslaught of natural passion. Nature prevailed; and with tears that like acid burned and scorched as they flowed, he wept, he raved, at the bitter loss of his parent; whose eyes had been closed by unrelated hands that were hired; but whose heart had been broken, and whose very reason been ruined, by the related hands of her son.

For some interval it almost seemed as if his own heart would snap; his own reason go down. Unendurable grief of a man, when Death itself gives the stab, and then snatches all availments to solacement away. For in the grave is no help, no prayer thither may go, no forgiveness thence come; so that the penitent whose sad victim lies in the ground, for that useless penitent his doom is eternal, and though it be Christmasday with all Christendom, with him it is Hell-day and an eaten liver forever.

With what marvelous precision and exactitude he now went over in his mind all the minutest details of his old joyous life with his mother at Saddle Meadows. He began with his own toilet in the morning; then his mild stroll into the fields; then his cheerful return to call his mother in her chamber; then the gay breakfast—and so on, and on, all through the sweet day, till mother and son kissed, and with light, loving hearts separated to their beds, to prepare themselves for still another day of affectionate delight. This recalling of innocence and joy in the hour of remorsefulness and woe; this is as heating red-hot the pincers that tear us. But in this delirium of his soul, Pierre could not define where that line was, which separated the natural grief for the loss of a parent from that other one which was born of compunction. He strove hard to define it, but could not. He tried to cozen himself into believing that all his grief was but natural, or if there existed any other, that must spring—not from the conscious-

ness of having done any possible wrong—but from the pang
at what terrible cost the more exalted virtues are gained. Nor
did he wholly fail in this endeavor. At last he dismissed his
mother's memory into that same profound vault where hitherto had reposed the swooned form of his Lucy. But, as
sometimes men are coffined in a trance, being thereby mistaken for dead; so it is possible to bury a tranced grief in the
soul, erroneously supposing that it hath no more vitality of
suffering. Now, immortal things only can beget immortality.
It would almost seem one presumptive argument for the endless duration of the human soul, that it is impossible in time
and space to kill any compunction arising from having cruelly
injured a departed fellow-being.

Ere he finally committed his mother to the profoundest
vault of his soul, fain would he have drawn one poor alleviation from a circumstance, which nevertheless, impartially
viewed, seemed equally capable either of soothing or intensifying his grief. His mother's will, which without the least
mention of his own name, bequeathed several legacies to her
friends, and concluded by leaving all Saddle Meadows and its
rent-rolls to Glendinning Stanly; this will bore the date of the
day immediately succeeding his fatal announcement on the
landing of the stairs, of his assumed nuptials with Isabel. It
plausibly pressed upon him, that as all the evidences of his
mother's dying unrelentingness toward him were negative;
and the only positive evidence—so to speak—of even that
negativeness, was the will which omitted all mention of
Pierre; therefore, as that will bore so significant a date, it
must needs be most reasonable to conclude, that it was dictated in the not yet subsided transports of his mother's first
indignation. But small consolation was this, when he considered the final insanity of his mother; for whence that insanity
but from a hate-grief unrelenting, even as his father must have
become insane from a sin-grief irreparable? Nor did this remarkable double-doom of his parents wholly fail to impress
his mind with presentiments concerning his own fate—his
own hereditary liability to madness. Presentiment, I say; but
what is a presentiment? how shall you coherently define a presentiment, or how make any thing out of it which is at all
lucid, unless you say that a presentiment is but a judgment in

disguise? And if a judgment in disguise, and yet possessing this preternaturalness of prophecy, how then shall you escape the fateful conclusion, that you are helplessly held in the six hands of the Sisters? For while still dreading your doom, you foreknow it. Yet how foreknow and dread in one breath, unless with this divine seeming power of prescience, you blend the actual slimy powerlessness of defense?

That his cousin, Glen Stanly, had been chosen by his mother to inherit the domain of the Meadows, was not entirely surprising to Pierre. Not only had Glen always been a favorite with his mother by reason of his superb person and his congeniality of worldly views with herself, but excepting only Pierre, he was her nearest surviving blood relation; and moreover, in his christian name, bore the hereditary syllables, Glendinning. So that if to any one but Pierre the Meadows must descend, Glen, on these general grounds, seemed the appropriate heir.

But it is not natural for a man, never mind who he may be, to see a noble patrimony, rightfully his, go over to a soul-alien, and that alien once his rival in love, and now his heartless, sneering foe; for so Pierre could not but now argue of Glen; it is not natural for a man to see this without singular emotions of discomfort and hate. Nor in Pierre were these feelings at all soothed by the report of Glen's renewed attentions to Lucy. For there is something in the breast of almost every man, which at bottom takes offense at the attentions of any other man offered to a woman, the hope of whose nuptial love he himself may have discarded. Fain would a man self-ishly appropriate all the hearts which have ever in any way confessed themselves his. Besides, in Pierre's case, this resentment was heightened by Glen's previous hypocritical demeanor. For now all his suspicions seemed abundantly verified; and comparing all dates, he inferred that Glen's visit to Europe had only been undertaken to wear off the pang of his rejection by Lucy, a rejection tacitly consequent upon her not denying her affianced relation to Pierre.

But now, under the mask of profound sympathy—in time, ripening into love—for a most beautiful girl, ruffianly deserted by her betrothed, Glen could afford to be entirely open in his new suit, without at all exposing his old scar to the world. So at least it now seemed to Pierre. Moreover, Glen could now approach Lucy under the most favorable possible auspices. He could approach her as a deeply sympathizing friend, all wishful to assuage her sorrow, but hinting nothing, at present, of any selfish matrimonial intent; by enacting this prudent and unclamorous part, the mere sight of such tranquil, disinterested, but indestructible devotedness, could not but suggest in Lucy's mind, very natural comparisons between Glen and Pierre, most deplorably abasing to the latter. Then, no woman—as it would sometimes seem—no woman is utterly free from the influence of a princely social position in her suitor, especially if he be handsome and young. And Glen would come to her now the master of two immense fortunes, and the heir, by voluntary election, no less than by blood propinquity, to the ancestral bannered hall, and the broad manorial meadows of the Glendinnings. And thus, too, the spirit of Pierre's own mother would seem to press Glen's suit. Indeed, situated now as he was Glen would seem all the finest part of Pierre, without any of Pierre's shame; would almost seem Pierre himself—what Pierre had once been to Lucy. And as in the case of a man who has lost a sweet wife, and who long refuses the least consolation; as this man at last finds a singular solace in the companionship of his wife's sister, who happens to bear a peculiar family resemblance to the dead; and as he, in the end, proposes marriage to this sister, merely from the force of such magical associative influences; so it did not seem wholly out of reason to suppose, that the great manly beauty of Glen, possessing a strong related similitude to Pierre's, might raise in Lucy's heart associations, which would lead her at least to seek—if she could not find—solace for one now regarded as dead and gone to her forever, in the devotedness of another, who would notwithstanding almost seem as that dead one brought back to life.

Deep, deep, and still deep and deeper must we go, if we would find out the heart of a man; descending into which is as descending a spiral stair in a shaft, without any end, and where that endlessness is only concealed by the spiralness of the stair, and the blackness of the shaft.

As Pierre conjured up this phantom of Glen transformed into the seeming semblance of himself; as he figured it advancing toward Lucy and raising her hand in devotion; an infinite quenchless rage and malice possessed him. Many commingled emotions combined to provoke this storm. But chief of all was something strangely akin to that indefinable detestation which one feels for any imposter who has dared to assume one's own name and aspect in any equivocal or dishonorable affair; an emotion greatly intensified if this impostor be known for a mean villain at bottom, and also, by the freak of nature to be almost the personal duplicate of the man whose identity he assumes. All these and a host of other distressful and resentful fancies now ran through the breast of Pierre. All his Faith-born, enthusiastic, high-wrought, stoic, and philosophic defenses, were now beaten down by this sudden storm of nature in his soul. For there is no faith, and no stoicism, and no philosophy, that a mortal man can possibly evoke, which will stand the final test of a real impassioned onset of Life and Passion upon him. Then all the fair philosophic or Faith-phantoms that he raised from the mist, slide away and disappear as ghosts at cock-crow. For Faith and philosophy are air, but events are brass. Amidst his gray philosophizings, Life breaks upon a man like a morning.

While this mood was on him, Pierre cursed himself for a heartless villain and an idiot fool;—heartless villain, as the murderer of his mother—idiot fool, because he had thrown away all his felicity; because he had himself, as it were, resigned his noble birthright to a cunning kinsman for a mess of pottage, which now proved all but ashes in his mouth.

Resolved to hide these new, and—as it latently seemed to him—unworthy pangs, from Isabel, as also their cause, he quitted his chamber, intending a long vagabond stroll in the suburbs of the town, to wear off his sharper grief, ere he should again return into her sight.

iii

As Pierre, now hurrying from his chamber, was rapidly passing through one of the higher brick colonnades, connecting the ancient building with the modern, there advanced toward him from the direction of the latter, a very plain, composed, manly figure, with a countenance rather pale if any thing, but quite clear and without wrinkle. Though the brow and the beard, and the steadiness of the head and settledness of the step indicated mature age, yet the blue, bright, but still quiescent eye offered a very striking contrast. In that eye, the gay immortal youth Apollo, seemed enshrined; while on that ivory-throned brow, old Saturn cross-legged sat. The whole countenance of this man, the whole air and look of this man, expressed a cheerful content. Cheerful is the adjective, for it was the contrary of gloom; content—perhaps acquiescence— is the substantive, for it was not Happiness or Delight. But while the personal look and air of this man were thus winning, there was still something latently visible in him which repelled. That something may best be characterized as non-Benevolence. Non-Benevolence seems the best word, for it was neither Malice nor Ill-will; but something passive. To crown all, a certain floating atmosphere seemed to invest and go along with this man. That atmosphere seems only renderable in words by the term Inscrutableness. Though the clothes worn by this man were strictly in accordance with the general style of any unobtrusive gentleman's dress, yet his clothes seemed to disguise this man. One would almost have said, his very face, the apparently natural glance of his very eye disguised this man.

Now, as this person deliberately passed by Pierre, he lifted his hat, gracefully bowed, smiled gently, and passed on. But Pierre was all confusion; he flushed, looked askance, stammered with his hand at his hat to return the courtesy of the other; he seemed thoroughly upset by the mere sight of this hat-lifting, gracefully bowing, gently-smiling, and most miraculously self-possessed, non-benevolent man.

Now who was this man? This man was Plotinus Plinlimmon. Pierre had read a treatise of his in a stage-coach coming to the city, and had heard him often spoken of by Millthorpe and others as the Grand Master of a certain mystic Society among the Apostles. Whence he came, no one could tell. His surname was Welsh, but he was a Tennesseean by birth. He seemed to have no family or blood ties of any sort. He never was known to work with his hands; never to write with his hands (he would not even write a letter); he never was known to open a book. There were no books in his chamber. Never-

theless, some day or other he must have read books, but that
time seemed gone now; as for the sleazy works that went
under his name, they were nothing more than his verbal
things, taken down at random, and bunglingly methodized by
his young disciples.

Finding Plinlimmon thus unfurnished either with books or
pen and paper, and imputing it to something like indigence,
a foreign scholar, a rich nobleman, who chanced to meet him
once, sent him a fine supply of stationery, with a very fine set
of volumes,—Cardan, Epictetus, the Book of Mormon,
Abraham Tucker, Condorcet and the Zend-Avesta. But this
noble foreign scholar calling next day—perhaps in expectation of some compliment for his great kindness—started
aghast at his own package deposited just without the door of
Plinlimmon, and with all fastenings untouched.

"Missent," said Plotinus Plinlimmon placidly: "if any thing,
I looked for some choice Curaçoa from a nobleman like you.
I should be very happy, my dear Count, to accept a few jugs
of choice Curaçoa."

"I thought that the society of which you are the head, excluded all things of that sort"—replied the Count.

"Dear Count, so they do; but Mohammed hath his own
dispensation."

"Ah! I see," said the noble scholar archly.

"I am afraid you do not see, dear Count"—said Plinlimmon; and instantly before the eyes of the Count, the inscrutable atmosphere eddied and eddied roundabout this Plotinus
Plinlimmon.

His chance brushing encounter in the corridor was the first
time that ever Pierre had without medium beheld the form or
the face of Plinlimmon. Very early after taking chambers at
the Apostles', he had been struck by a steady observant blue-
eyed countenance at one of the loftiest windows of the old
gray tower, which on the opposite side of the quadrangular
space, rose prominently before his own chamber. Only
through two panes of glass—his own and the stranger's—
had Pierre hitherto beheld that remarkable face of repose,—
repose neither divine nor human, nor any thing made up of
either or both—but a repose separate and apart—a repose of
a face by itself. One adequate look at that face conveyed to

most philosophical observers a notion of something not before included in their scheme of the Universe.

Now as to the mild sun, glass is no hindrance at all, but he transmits his light and life through the glass; even so through Pierre's panes did the tower face transmit its strange mystery.

Becoming more and more interested in this face, he had questioned Millthorpe concerning it. "Bless your soul"—replied Millthorpe—"that is Plotinus Plinlimmon! our Grand Master, Plotinus Plinlimmon! By gad, you must know Plotinus thoroughly, as I have long done. Come away with me, now, and let me introduce you instanter to Plotinus Plinlimmon."

But Pierre declined; and could not help thinking, that though in all human probability Plotinus well understood Millthorpe, yet Millthorpe could hardly yet have wound himself into Plotinus;—though indeed Plotinus—who at times was capable of assuming a very off-hand, confidential, and simple, sophomorean air—might, for reasons best known to himself, have tacitly pretended to Millthorpe, that he (Millthorpe) had thoroughly wriggled himself into his (Plotinus') innermost soul.

A man will be given a book, and when the donor's back is turned, will carelessly drop it in the first corner; he is not over-anxious to be bothered with the book. But now personally point out to him the author, and ten to one he goes back to the corner, picks up the book, dusts the cover, and very carefully reads that invaluable work. One does not vitally believe in a man till one's own two eyes have beheld him. If then, by the force of peculiar circumstances, Pierre while in the stage, had formerly been drawn into an attentive perusal of the work on "Chronometricals and Horologicals;" how then was his original interest heightened by catching a subsequent glimpse of the author. But at the first reading, not being able—as he thought—to master the pivot-idea of the pamphlet; and as every incomprehended idea is not only a perplexity but a taunting reproach to one's mind, Pierre had at last ceased studying it altogether; nor consciously troubled himself further about it during the remainder of the journey. But still thinking now it might possibly have been mechanically retained by him, he searched all the pockets of his clothes, but without success. He begged Millthorpe to do his best toward procuring him another copy; but it proved impossible to find one. Plotinus himself could not furnish it.

Among other efforts, Pierre in person had accosted a limping half-deaf old book-stall man, not very far from the Apostles'. "Have you the *'Chronometrics,'* my friend?" forgetting the exact title.

"Very bad, very bad!" said the old man, rubbing his back;—"has had the *chronic-rheumatics* ever so long; what's good for 'em?"

Perceiving his mistake, Pierre replied that he did not know what was the infallible remedy.

"Whist! let me tell ye, then, young 'un," said the old cripple, limping close up to him, and putting his mouth in Pierre's ear—"Never catch 'em!—now's the time, while you're young:—never catch 'em!"

By-and-by the blue-eyed, mystic-mild face in the upper window of the old gray tower began to domineer in a very remarkable manner upon Pierre. When in his moods of peculiar depression and despair; when dark thoughts of his miserable condition would steal over him; and black doubts as to the integrity of his unprecedented course in life would most malignantly suggest themselves; when a thought of the vanity of his deep book would glidingly intrude; if glancing at his closet-window that mystic-mild face met Pierre's; under any of these influences the effect was surprising, and not to be adequately detailed in any possible words.

Vain! vain! vain! said the face to him. Fool! fool! fool! said the face to him. Quit! quit! quit! said the face to him. But when he mentally interrogated the face as to why it thrice said Vain! Fool! Quit! to him; here there was no response. For that face did not respond to any thing. Did I not say before that that face was something separate, and apart; a face by itself? Now, any thing which is thus a thing by itself never responds to any other thing. If to affirm, be to expand one's isolated self; and if to deny, be to contract one's isolated self; then to respond is a suspension of all isolation. Though this face in the tower was so clear and so mild; though the gay youth Apollo was enshrined in that eye, and paternal old Saturn sat cross-legged on that ivory brow; yet somehow to

Pierre the face at last wore a sort of malicious leer to him.
But the Kantists might say, that this was a *subjective* sort of
leer in Pierre. Any way, the face seemed to leer upon Pierre.
And now it said to him—*Ass! ass! ass!* This expression was
insufferable. He procured some muslin for his closet-window;
and the face became curtained like any portrait. But this did
not mend the leer. Pierre knew that still the face leered behind
the muslin. What was most terrible was the idea that by some
magical means or other the face had got hold of his secret.
"Ay," shuddered Pierre, "the face knows that Isabel is not my
wife! And that seems the reason it leers."

Then would all manner of wild fancyings float through his
soul, and detached sentences of the "Chronometrics" would
vividly recur to him—sentences before but imperfectly comprehended, but now shedding a strange, baleful light upon
his peculiar condition, and emphatically denouncing it. Again
he tried his best to procure the pamphlet, to read it now by
the commentary of the mystic-mild face; again he searched
through the pockets of his clothes for the stage-coach copy,
but in vain.

And when—at the critical moment of quitting his chambers that morning of the receipt of the fatal tidings—the face
itself—the man himself—this inscrutable Plotinus Plinlimmon himself—did visibly brush by him in the brick corridor,
and all the trepidation he had ever before felt at the mild-
mystic aspect in the tower window, now redoubled upon
him, so that, as before said, he flushed, looked askance, and
stammered with his saluting hand to his hat;—then anew did
there burn in him the desire of procuring the pamphlet.
"Cursed fate that I should have lost it"—he cried;—"more
cursed, that when I did have it, and did read it, I was such a
ninny as not to comprehend; and now it is all too late!"

Yet—to anticipate here—when years after, an old Jew
Clothesman rummaged over a surtout of Pierre's—which by
some means had come into his hands—his lynx-like fingers
happened to feel something foreign between the cloth and the
heavy quilted bombazine lining. He ripped open the skirt,
and found several old pamphlet pages, soft and worn almost
to tissue, but still legible enough to reveal the title—"Chronometricals and Horologicals." Pierre must have ignorantly

thrust it into his pocket, in the stage, and it had worked through a rent there, and worked its way clean down into the skirt, and there helped pad the padding. So that all the time he was hunting for this pamphlet, he himself was wearing the pamphlet. When he brushed past Plinlimmon in the brick corridor, and felt that renewed intense longing for the pamphlet, then his right hand was not two inches from the pamphlet.

Possibly this curious circumstance may in some sort illustrate his self-supposed non-understanding of the pamphlet, as first read by him in the stage. Could he likewise have carried about with him in his mind the thorough understanding of the book, and yet not be aware that he so understood it? I think that—regarded in one light—the final career of Pierre will seem to show, that he *did* understand it. And here it may be randomly suggested, by way of bagatelle, whether some things that men think they do not know, are not for all that thoroughly comprehended by them; and yet, so to speak, though contained in themselves, are kept a secret from themselves? The idea of Death seems such a thing.

Book XXII

THE FLOWER-CURTAIN LIFTED FROM BEFORE A
TROPICAL AUTHOR, WITH SOME REMARKS ON THE
TRANSCENDENTAL FLESH-BRUSH PHILOSOPHY

S OME DAYS PASSED after the fatal tidings from the Meadows, and at length, somewhat mastering his emotions, Pierre again sits down in his chamber; for grieve how he will, yet work he must. And now day succeeds day, and week follows week, and Pierre still sits in his chamber. The long rows of cooled brick-kilns around him scarce know of the change; but from the fair fields of his great-great-great-grandfather's manor, Summer hath flown like a swallow-guest; the perfidious wight, Autumn, hath peeped in at the groves of the maple, and under pretense of clothing them in rich russet and gold, hath stript them at last of the slightest rag, and then ran away laughing; prophetic icicles depend from the arbors round about the old manorial mansion—now locked up and abandoned; and the little, round, marble table in the viny summer-house where, of July mornings, he had sat chatting and drinking negus with his gay mother, is now spread with a shivering napkin of frost; sleety varnish hath encrusted that once gay mother's grave, preparing it for its final cerements of wrapping snow upon snow; wild howl the winds in the woods: it is Winter. Sweet Summer is done; and Autumn is done; but the book, like the bitter winter, is yet to be finished.

That season's wheat is long garnered, Pierre; that season's ripe apples and grapes are in; no crop, no plant, no fruit is out; the whole harvest is done. Oh, woe to that belated winter-overtaken plant, which the summer could not bring to maturity! The drifting winter snows shall whelm it. Think, Pierre, doth not thy plant belong to some other and tropical clime? Though transplanted to northern Maine, the orange-tree of the Floridas will put forth leaves in that parsimonious summer, and show some few tokens of fruitage; yet November will find no golden globes thereon; and the passionate old lumber-man, December, shall peel the whole tree, wrench it off at the ground, and toss it for a fagot to some lime-kiln. Ah, Pierre, Pierre, make haste! make haste! force thy fruitage, lest the winter force thee.

Watch yon little toddler, how long it is learning to stand by itself! First it shrieks and implores, and will not try to stand at all, unless both father and mother uphold it; then a little more bold, it must, at least, feel one parental hand, else again the cry and the tremble; long time is it ere by degrees this child comes to stand without any support. But, by-and-by, grown up to man's estate, it shall leave the very mother that bore it, and the father that begot it, and cross the seas, perhaps, or settle in far Oregon lands. There now, do you see the soul. In its germ on all sides it is closely folded by the world, as the husk folds the tenderest fruit; then it is born from the world-husk, but still now outwardly clings to it; — still clamors for the support of its mother the world, and its father the Deity. But it shall yet learn to stand independent, though not without many a bitter wail, and many a miserable fall.

That hour of the life of a man when first the help of humanity fails him, and he learns that in his obscurity and indigence humanity holds him a dog and no man: that hour is a hard one, but not the hardest. There is still another hour which follows, when he learns that in his infinite comparative minuteness and abjectness, the gods do likewise despise him, and own him not of their clan. Divinity and humanity then are equally willing that he should starve in the street for all that either will do for him. Now cruel father and mother have both let go his hand, and the little soul-toddler, now you shall hear his shriek and his wail, and often his fall.

When at Saddle Meadows, Pierre had wavered and trembled in those first wretched hours ensuing upon the receipt of Isabel's letter; then humanity had let go the hand of Pierre, and therefore his cry; but when at last inured to this, Pierre was seated at his book, willing that humanity should desert him, so long as he thought he felt a far higher support; then, ere long, he began to feel the utter loss of that other support, too; ay, even the paternal gods themselves did now desert Pierre; the toddler was toddling entirely alone, and not without shrieks.

If man must wrestle, perhaps it is well that it should be on the nakedest possible plain.

The three chambers of Pierre at the Apostles' were connecting ones. The first—having a little retreat where Delly slept—was used for the more exacting domestic purposes: here also their meals were taken; the second was the chamber of Isabel; the third was the closet of Pierre. In the first—the dining room, as they called it—there was a stove which boiled the water for their coffee and tea, and where Delly concocted their light repasts. This was their only fire; for, warned again and again to economize to the uttermost, Pierre did not dare to purchase any additional warmth. But by prudent management, a very little warmth may go a great way. In the present case, it went some forty feet or more. A horizontal pipe, after elbowing away from above the stove in the dining-room, pierced the partition wall, and passing straight through Isabel's chamber, entered the closet of Pierre at one corner, and then abruptly disappeared into the wall, where all further caloric—if any—went up through the chimney into the air, to help warm the December sun. Now, the great distance of Pierre's calorical stream from its fountain, sadly impaired it, and weakened it. It hardly had the flavor of heat. It would have had but very inconsiderable influence in raising the depressed spirits of the most mercurial thermometer; certainly it was not very elevating to the spirits of Pierre. Besides, this calorical stream, small as it was, did not flow through the room, but only entered it, to elbow right out of it, as some coquettish maidens enter the heart; moreover, it was in the furthest corner from the only place where, with a judicious view to the light, Pierre's desk-barrels and board could advantageously stand. Often, Isabel insisted upon his having a separate stove to himself; but Pierre would not listen to such a thing. Then Isabel would offer her own room to him; saying it was of no indispensable use to her by day; she could easily spend her time in the dining-room; but Pierre would not listen to such a thing: he would not deprive her of the comfort of a continually accessible privacy; besides, he was now used to his own room, and must sit by that particular window there, and no other. Then Isabel would insist upon keeping her connecting door open while Pierre was employed at his desk, that so the heat of her room might bodily go into his; but Pierre would not listen to such a thing: because he must be religiously locked up while at work; outer love and hate must alike be excluded then. In vain Isabel said she would make not the slightest noise, and muffle the point of the very needle she used. All in vain. Pierre was inflexible here.

Yes, he was resolved to battle it out in his own solitary closet; though a strange, transcendental conceit of one of the more erratic and non-conforming Apostles,—who was also at this time engaged upon a profound work above stairs, and who denied himself his full sufficiency of food, in order to insure an abundant fire;—the strange conceit of this Apostle, I say,—accidentally communicated to Pierre,—that, through all the kingdoms of Nature, caloric was the great universal producer and vivifyer, and could not be prudently excluded from the spot where great books were in the act of creation; and therefore, he (the Apostle) for one, was resolved to plant his head in a hot-bed of stove-warmed air, and so force his brain to germinate and blossom, and bud, and put forth the eventual, crowning, victorious flower;—though indeed this conceit rather staggered Pierre—for in truth, there was no small smack of plausible analogy in it—yet one thought of his purse would wholly expel the unwelcome intrusion, and reinforce his own previous resolve.

However lofty and magnificent the movements of the stars; whatever celestial melodies they may thereby beget; yet the astronomers assure us that they are the most rigidly methodical of all the things that exist. No old housewife goes her daily domestic round with one millionth part the precision of the great planet Jupiter in his stated and unalterable revolutions. He has found his orbit, and stays in it; he has timed himself, and adheres to his periods. So, in some degree with Pierre, now revolving in the troubled orbit of his book.

Pierre rose moderately early; and the better to inure himself to the permanent chill of his room, and to defy and beard to its face, the cruelest cold of the outer air; he would—behind the curtain—throw down the upper sash of his window; and on a square of old painted canvas, formerly wrapping some

bale of goods in the neighborhood, treat his limbs, of those
early December mornings, to a copious ablution, in water
thickened with incipient ice. Nor, in this stoic performance,
was he at all without company,—not present, but adjoiningly
sympathetic; for scarce an Apostle in all those scores and
scores of chambers, but undeviatingly took his daily December bath. Pierre had only to peep out of his pane and glance
round the multi-windowed, inclosing walls of the quadrangle,
to catch plentiful half-glimpses, all round him, of many a lean,
philosophical nudity, refreshing his meager bones with crash-
towel and cold water. "Quick be the play," was their motto:
"Lively our elbows, and nimble all our tenuities." Oh, the
dismal echoings of the raspings of flesh-brushes, perverted to
the filing and polishing of the merest ribs! Oh, the shudder-
some splashings of pails of ice-water over feverish heads, not
unfamiliar with aches! Oh, the rheumatical cracklings of
rusted joints, in that defied air of December! for every thick-
frosted sash was down, and every lean nudity courted the
zephyr!

Among all the innate, hyena-like repellants to the reception
of any set form of a spiritually-minded and pure archetypical
faith, there is nothing so potent in its skeptical tendencies, as
that inevitable perverse ridiculousness, which so often bestreaks some of the essentially finest and noblest aspirations
of those men, who disgusted with the common conventional
quackeries, strive, in their clogged terrestrial humanities, after
some imperfectly discerned, but heavenly ideals: ideals, not
only imperfectly discerned in themselves, but the path to
them so little traceable, that no two minds will entirely agree
upon it.

Hardly a new-light Apostle, but who, in superaddition to
his revolutionary scheme for the minds and philosophies of
men, entertains some insane, heterodoxical notions about the
economy of his body. His soul, introduced by the gentlemanly gods, into the supernal society,—practically rejects
that most sensible maxim of men of the world, who chancing
to gain the friendship of any great character, never make that
the ground of boring him with the supplemental acquaintance of their next friend, who perhaps, is some miserable
ninny. Love me, love my dog, is only an adage for the old

country-women who affectionately kiss their cows. The gods love the soul of a man; often, they will frankly accost it; but they abominate his body; and will forever cut it dead, both here and hereafter. So, if thou wouldst go to the gods, leave thy dog of a body behind thee. And most impotently thou strivest with thy purifying cold baths, and thy diligent scrubbings with flesh-brushes, to prepare it as a meet offering for their altar. Nor shall all thy Pythagorean and Shellian dietings on apple-parings, dried prunes, and crumbs of oat-meal cracker, ever fit thy body for heaven. Feed all things with food convenient for them,—that is, if the food be procurable. The food of thy soul is light and space; feed it then on light and space. But the food of thy body is champagne and oysters; feed it then on champagne and oysters; and so shall it merit a joyful resurrection, if there is any to be. Say, wouldst thou rise with a lantern jaw and a spavined knee? Rise with brawn on thee, and a most royal corporation before thee; so shalt thou in that day claim respectful attention. Know this: that while many a consumptive dietarian has but produced the merest literary flatulencies to the world; convivial authors have alike given utterance to the sublimest wisdom, and created the least gross and most ethereal forms. And for men of demonstrative muscle and action, consider that right royal epitaph which Cyrus the Great caused to be engraved on his tomb—"I could drink a great deal of wine, and it did me a great deal of good." Ah, foolish! to think that by starving thy body, thou shalt fatten thy soul! Is yonder ox fatted because yonder lean fox starves in the winter wood? And prate not of despising thy body, while still thou flourishest thy flesh-brush! The finest houses are most cared for within; the outer walls are freely left to the dust and the soot. Put venison in thee, and so wit shall come out of thee. It is one thing in the mill, but another in the sack.

Now it was the continual, quadrangular example of those forlorn fellows, the Apostles, who, in this period of his half-developments and transitions, had deluded Pierre into the Flesh-Brush Philosophy, and had almost tempted him into the Apple-Parings Dialectics. For all the long wards, corridors, and multitudinous chambers of the Apostles' were

scattered with the stems of apples, the stones of prunes, and
the shells of pea-nuts. They went about huskily muttering
the Kantian Categories through teeth and lips dry and
dusty as any miller's, with the crumbs of Graham crackers.
A tumbler of cold water was the utmost welcome to their
reception rooms; at the grand supposed Sanhedrim presided
over by one of the deputies of Plotinus Plinlimmon, a huge
jug of Adam's Ale, and a bushel-basket of Graham crackers
were the only convivials. Continually bits of cheese were
dropping from their pockets, and old shiny apple parch-
ments were ignorantly exhibited every time they drew out a
manuscript to read you. Some were curious in the vintages
of waters; and in three glass decanters set before you, Fairmount, Croton, and Cochituate; they held that Croton was
the most potent, Fairmount a gentle tonic, and Cochituate
the mildest and least inebriating of all. Take some more
of the Croton, my dear sir! Be brisk with the Fairmount!
Why stops that Cochituate? So on their philosophical tables
went round their Port, their Sherry, and their Claret.

Some, further advanced, rejected mere water in the bath,
as altogether too coarse an element; and so, took to the
Vapor-baths, and steamed their lean ribs every morning.
The smoke which issued from their heads, and overspread
their pages, was prefigured in the mists that issued from under their door-sills and out of their windows. Some could
not sit down of a morning until after first applying the
Vapor-bath outside, and then thoroughly rinsing out their
interiors with five cups of cold Croton. They were as
faithfully replenished fire-buckets; and could they, standing
in one cordon, have consecutively pumped themselves into
each other, then the great fire of 1835 had been far less
wide-spread and disastrous.

Ah! ye poor lean ones! ye wretched Soakites and Vaporites!
have not your niggardly fortunes enough rinsed ye out, and
wizened ye, but ye must still be dragging the hose-pipe, and
throwing still more cold Croton on yourselves and the world?
Ah! attach the screw of your hose-pipe to some fine old butt
of Madeira! pump us some sparkling wine into the world!
see, see, already, from all eternity, two-thirds of it have lain
helplessly soaking!

ii

With cheek rather pale, then, and lips rather blue, Pierre sits down to his plank.

But is Pierre packed in the mail for St. Petersburg this morning? Over his boots are his moccasins; over his ordinary coat is his surtout; and over that, a cloak of Isabel's. Now he is squared to his plank; and at his hint, the affectionate Isabel gently pushes his chair closer to it, for he is so muffled, he can hardly move of himself. Now Delly comes in with bricks hot from the stove; and now Isabel and she with devoted solicitude pack away these comforting stones in the folds of an old blue cloak, a military garment of the grandfather of Pierre, and tenderly arrange it both over and under his feet; but putting the warm flagging beneath. Then Delly brings still another hot brick to put under his inkstand, to prevent the ink from thickening. Then Isabel drags the camp-bedstead nearer to him, on which are the two or three books he may possibly have occasion to refer to that day, with a biscuit or two, and some water, and a clean towel, and a basin. Then she leans against the plank by the elbow of Pierre, a crook-ended stick. Is Pierre a shepherd, or a bishop, or a cripple? No, but he has in effect, reduced himself to the miserable condition of the last. With the crook-ended cane, Pierre—unable to rise without sadly impairing his manifold intrenchments, and admitting the cold air into their innermost nooks,—Pierre, if in his solitude, he should chance to need any thing beyond the reach of his arm, then the crook-ended cane drags it to his immediate vicinity.

Pierre glances slowly all round him; every thing seems to be right; he looks up with a grateful, melancholy satisfaction at Isabel; a tear gathers in her eye; but she conceals it from him by coming very close to him, stooping over, and kissing his brow. 'Tis her lips that leave the warm moisture there; not her tears, she says.

"I suppose I must go now, Pierre. Now don't, don't be so long to-day. I will call thee at half-past four. Thou shalt not strain thine eyes in the twilight."

"We will *see* about that," says Pierre, with an unobserved attempt at a very sad pun. "Come, thou must go. Leave me."

And there he is left.

Pierre is young; heaven gave him the divinest, freshest form of a man; put light into his eye, and fire into his blood, and brawn into his arm, and a joyous, jubilant, overflowing, up-bubbling, universal life in him everywhere. Now look around in that most miserable room, and at that most miserable of all the pursuits of a man, and say if here be the place, and this be the trade, that God intended him for. A rickety chair, two hollow barrels, a plank, paper, pens, and infernally black ink, four leprously dingy white walls, no carpet, a cup of water, and a dry biscuit or two. Oh, I hear the leap of the Texan Camanche, as at this moment he goes crashing like a wild deer through the green underbrush; I hear his glorious whoop of savage and untamable health; and then I look in at Pierre. If physical, practical unreason make the savage, which is he? Civilization, Philosophy, Ideal Virtue! behold your victim!

iii

Some hours pass. Let us peep over the shoulder of Pierre, and see what it is he is writing there, in that most melancholy closet. Here, topping the reeking pile by his side, is the last sheet from his hand, the frenzied ink not yet entirely dry. It is much to our purpose; for in this sheet, he seems to have directly plagiarized from his own experiences, to fill out the mood of his apparent author-hero, Vivia, who thus soliloquizes: "A deep-down, unutterable mournfulness is in me. Now I drop all humorous or indifferent disguises, and all philosophical pretensions. I own myself a brother of the clod, a child of the Primeval Gloom. Hopelessness and despair are over me, as pall on pall. Away, ye chattering apes of a sophomorean Spinoza and Plato, who once didst all but delude me that the night was day, and pain only a tickle. Explain this darkness, exorcise this devil, ye can not. Tell me not, thou inconceivable coxcomb of a Goethe, that the universe can not spare thee and thy immortality, so long as—like a hired waiter—thou makest thyself 'generally useful.' Already the universe gets on without thee, and could still spare a million more of the same identical kidney. Corporations have no souls, and thy Pantheism, what was that? Thou wert but the pretensious, heartless part of a man. Lo! I hold thee in this hand, and thou art crushed in it like an egg from which the meat hath been sucked."

Here is a slip from the floor.

"Whence flow the panegyrical melodies that precede the march of these heroes? From what but from a sounding brass and a tinkling cymbal!"

And here is a second.

"Cast thy eye in there on Vivia; tell me why those four limbs should be clapt in a dismal jail—day out, day in—week out, week in—month out, month in—and himself the voluntary jailer! Is this the end of philosophy? This the larger, and spiritual life? This your boasted empyrean? Is it for this that a man should grow wise, and leave off his most excellent and calumniated folly?"

And here is a third.

"Cast thy eye in there on Vivia; he, who in the pursuit of the highest health of virtue and truth, shows but a pallid cheek! Weigh his heart in thy hand, oh, thou gold-laced, virtuoso Goethe! and tell me whether it does not exceed thy standard weight!"

And here is a fourth.

"Oh God, that man should spoil and rust on the stalk, and be wilted and threshed ere the harvest hath come! And oh God, that men that call themselves men should still insist on a laugh! I hate the world, and could trample all lungs of mankind as grapes, and heel them out of their breath, to think of the woe and the cant,—to think of the Truth and the Lie! Oh! blessed be the twenty-first day of December, and cursed be the twenty-first day of June!"

From these random slips, it would seem, that Pierre is quite conscious of much that is so anomalously hard and bitter in his lot, of much that is so black and terrific in his soul. Yet that knowing his fatal condition does not one whit enable him to change or better his condition. Conclusive proof that he has no power over his condition. For in tremendous extremities human souls are like drowning men; well enough they know they are in peril; well enough they know the causes of that peril;—nevertheless, the sea is the sea, and these drowning men do drown.

iv

From eight o'clock in the morning till half-past four in the evening, Pierre sits there in his room;—eight hours and a half!

From throbbing neck-bands, and swinging belly-bands of gay-hearted horses, the sleigh-bells chimingly jingle;—but Pierre sits there in his room; Thanksgiving comes, with its glad thanks, and crisp turkeys;—but Pierre sits there in his room; soft through the snows, on tinted Indian moccasin, Merry Christmas comes stealing;—but Pierre sits there in his room; it is New-Year's, and like a great flagon, the vast city overbrims at all curb-stones, wharves, and piers, with bubbling jubilations;—but Pierre sits there in his room:—Nor jingling sleigh-bells at throbbing neck-band, or swinging belly-band; nor glad thanks, and crisp turkeys of Thanksgiving; nor tinted Indian moccasin of Merry Christmas softly stealing through the snows; nor New-Year's curb-stones, wharves, and piers, over-brimming with bubbling jubilations:—Nor jingling sleigh-bells, nor glad Thanksgiving, nor Merry Christmas, nor jubilating New Year's:—Nor Bell, Thank, Christ, Year;—none of these are for Pierre. In the midst of the merriments of the mutations of Time, Pierre hath ringed himself in with the grief of Eternity. Pierre is a peak inflexible in the heart of Time, as the isle-peak, Piko, stands unassaultable in the midst of waves.

He will not be called to; he will not be stirred. Sometimes the intent ear of Isabel in the next room, overhears the alternate silence, and then the long lonely scratch of his pen. It is, as if she heard the busy claw of some midnight mole in the ground. Sometimes, she hears a low cough, and sometimes the scrape of his crook-handled cane.

Here surely is a wonderful stillness of eight hours and a half, repeated day after day. In the heart of such silence, surely something is at work. Is it creation, or destruction? Builds Pierre the noble world of a new book? or does the Pale Haggardness unbuild the lungs and the life in him?—Unutterable, that a man should be thus!

When in the meridian flush of the day, we recall the black apex of night; then night seems impossible; this sun can never go down. Oh that the memory of the uttermost gloom as an already tasted thing to the dregs, should be no security against its return. One may be passably well one day, but the next, he may sup at black broth with Pluto.

Is there then all this work to one book, which shall be read in a very few hours; and, far more frequently, utterly skipped in one second; and which, in the end, whatever it be, must undoubtedly go to the worms?

Not so; that which now absorbs the time and the life of Pierre, is not the book, but the primitive elementalizing of the strange stuff, which in the act of attempting that book, has upheaved and upgushed in his soul. Two books are being writ; of which the world shall only see one, and that the bungled one. The larger book, and the infinitely better, is for Pierre's own private shelf. That it is, whose unfathomable cravings drink his blood; the other only demands his ink. But circumstances have so decreed, that the one can not be composed on the paper, but only as the other is writ down in his soul. And the one of the soul is elephantinely sluggish, and will not budget at a breath. Thus Pierre is fastened on by two leeches; —how then can the life of Pierre last? Lo! he is fitting himself for the highest life, by thinning his blood and collapsing his heart. He is learning how to live, by rehearsing the part of death.

Who shall tell all the thoughts and feelings of Pierre in that desolate and shivering room, when at last the idea obtruded, that the wiser and the profounder he should grow, the more and the more he lessened the chances for bread; that could he now hurl his deep book out of the window, and fall to on some shallow nothing of a novel, composable in a month at the longest, then could he reasonably hope for both appreciation and cash. But the devouring profundities, now opened up in him, consume all his vigor; would he, he could not now be entertainingly and profitably shallow in some pellucid and merry romance. Now he sees, that with every accession of the personal divine to him, some great land-slide of the general surrounding divineness slips from him, and falls crashing away. Said I not that the gods, as well as mankind, had unhanded themselves from this Pierre? So now in him you behold the baby toddler I spoke of; forced now to stand and toddle alone.

Now and then he turns to the camp-bed, and wetting his towel in the basin, presses it against his brow. Now he leans back in his chair, as if to give up; but again bends over and plods.

Twilight draws on, the summons of Isabel is heard from the door; the poor, frozen, blue-lipped, soul-shivering traveler for St. Petersburg is unpacked; and for a moment stands toddling on the floor. Then his hat, and his cane, and out he sallies for fresh air. A most comfortless staggering of a stroll! People gaze at him passing, as at some imprudent sick man, willfully burst from his bed. If an acquaintance is met, and would say a pleasant newsmonger's word in his ear, that acquaintance turns from him, affronted at his hard aspect of icy discourtesy. "Bad-hearted," mutters the man, and goes on.

He comes back to his chambers, and sits down at the neat table of Delly; and Isabel soothingly eyes him, and presses him to eat and be strong. But his is the famishing which loathes all food. He can not eat but by force. He has assassinated the natural day; how then can he eat with an appetite? If he lays him down, he can not sleep; he has waked the infinite wakefulness in him; then how can he slumber? Still his book, like a vast lumbering planet, revolves in his aching head. He can not command the thing out of its orbit; fain would be behead himself, to gain one night's repose. At last the heavy hours move on; and sheer exhaustion overtakes him, and he lies still—not asleep as children and day-laborers sleep—but he lies still from his throbbings, and for that interval holdingly sheaths the beak of the vulture in his hand, and lets it not enter his heart.

Morning comes; again the dropt sash, the icy water, the flesh-brush, the breakfast, the hot bricks, the ink, the pen, the from-eight-o'clock-to-half-past-four, and the whole general inclusive hell of the same departed day.

Ah! shivering thus day after day in his wrappers and cloaks, is this the warm lad that once sung to the world of the Tropical Summer?

Book XXIII

A LETTER FOR PIERRE • ISABEL • ARRIVAL OF LUCY'S
EASEL AND TRUNKS AT THE APOSTLES'

IF A FRONTIER man be seized by wild Indians, and carried
far and deep into the wilderness, and there held a captive,
with no slightest probability of eventual deliverance; then the
wisest thing for that man is to exclude from his memory by
every possible method, the least images of those beloved objects now forever reft from him. For the more delicious they
were to him in the now departed possession, so much the
more agonizing shall they be in the present recalling. And
though a strong man may sometimes succeed in strangling
such tormenting memories; yet, if in the beginning permitted
to encroach upon him unchecked, the same man shall, in the
end, become as an idiot. With a continent and an ocean between him and his wife—thus sundered from her, by whatever imperative cause, for a term of long years;—the
husband, if passionately devoted to her, and by nature brood-
ingly sensitive of soul, is wise to forget her till he embrace
her again;—is wise never to remember her if he hear of her
death. And though such complete suicidal forgettings prove
practically impossible, yet is it the shallow and ostentatious
affections alone which are bustling in the offices of obituarian
memories. *The love deep as death*—what mean those five
words, but that such love can not live, and be continually
remembering that the loved one is no more? If it be thus then
in cases where entire unremorsefulness as regards the beloved
absent objects is presumed, how much more intolerable,
when the knowledge of their hopeless wretchedness occurs,
attended by the visitations of before latent upbraidings in the
rememberer as having been any way—even unwillingly—the
producers of their sufferings. There seems no other sane recourse for some moody organizations on whom such things,
under such circumstances intrude, but right and left to flee
them, whatever betide.

If little or nothing hitherto has been said of Lucy Tartan in
reference to the condition of Pierre after his departure from

the Meadows, it has only been because her image did not willingly occupy his soul. He had striven his utmost to banish it thence; and only once—on receiving the tidings of Glen's renewed attentions—did he remit the intensity of those strivings, or rather feel them, as impotent in him in that hour of his manifold and overwhelming prostration.

Not that the pale form of Lucy, swooning on her snow-white bed; not that the inexpressible anguish of the shriek—"My heart! my heart!" would not now at times force themselves upon him, and cause his whole being to thrill with a nameless horror and terror. But the very thrillingness of the phantom made him to shun it, with all remaining might of his spirit.

Nor were there wanting still other, and far more wonderful, though but dimly conscious influences in the breast of Pierre, to meet as repellants the imploring form. Not to speak of his being devoured by the all-exacting theme of his book, there were sinister preoccupations in him of a still subtler and more fearful sort, of which some inklings have already been given.

It was while seated solitary in his room one morning; his flagging faculties seeking a momentary respite; his head sideways turned toward the naked floor, following the seams in it, which, as wires, led straight from where he sat to the connecting door, and disappeared beneath it into the chamber of Isabel; that he started at a tap at that very door, followed by the wonted, low, sweet voice,—

"Pierre! a letter for thee—dost thou hear? a letter,—may I come in?"

At once he felt a dart of surprise and apprehension; for he was precisely in that general condition with respect to the outer world, that he could not reasonably look for any tidings but disastrous, or at least, unwelcome ones. He assented; and Isabel entered, holding out the billet in her hand.

" 'Tis from some lady, Pierre; who can it be?—not thy mother though, of that I am certain;—the expression of her face, as seen by me, not at all answering to the expression of this handwriting here."

"My mother? from my mother?" muttered Pierre, in wild vacancy—"no! no! it can scarce be from her.—Oh, she writes no more, even in her own private tablets now! Death hath stolen the last leaf, and rubbed all out, to scribble his own ineffaceable *hic jacet* there!"

"Pierre!" cried Isabel, in affright.

"Give it me!" he shouted, vehemently, extending his hand. "Forgive me, sweet, sweet Isabel, I have wandered in my mind; this book makes me mad. There; I have it now"—in a tone of indifference—"now, leave me again. It is from some pretty aunt, or cousin, I suppose," carelessly balancing the letter in his hand.

Isabel quitted the room; the moment the door closed upon her, Pierre eagerly split open the letter, and read:—

ii

"This morning I vowed it, my own dearest, dearest Pierre. I feel stronger to-day; for to-day I have still more thought of thine own superhuman, angelical strength; which so, has a very little been transferred to me. Oh, Pierre, Pierre, with what words shall I write thee now;—now, when still knowing nothing, yet something of thy secret I, as a seer, suspect. Grief,—deep, unspeakable grief, hath made me this seer. I could murder myself, Pierre, when I think of my previous blindness; but that only came from my swoon. It was horrible and most murdersome; but now I see thou wert right in being so instantaneous with me, and in never afterward writing to me, Pierre; yes, now I see it, and adore thee the more.

"Ah! thou too noble and angelical Pierre, now I feel that a being like thee, can possibly have no love as other men love; but thou lovest as angels do; not for thyself, but wholly for others. But still are we one, Pierre; thou art sacrificing thyself, and I hasten to re-tie myself to thee, that so I may catch thy fire, and all the ardent multitudinous arms of our common flames may embrace. I will ask of thee nothing, Pierre; thou shalt tell me no secret. Very right wert thou, Pierre, when, in that ride to the hills, thou wouldst not swear the fond, foolish oath I demanded. Very right, very right; now I see it.

"If then I solemnly vow, never to seek from thee any slightest thing which thou wouldst not willingly have me know; if ever I, in all outward actions, shall recognize, just as thou dost, the peculiar position of that mysterious, and ever-sacred

being;—then, may I not come and live with thee? I will be
no encumbrance to thee. I know just where thou art, and
how thou art living; and only just there, Pierre, and only just
so, is any further life endurable, or possible for me. She will
never know—for thus far I am sure thou thyself hast never
disclosed it to her what I once was to thee. Let it seem, as
though I were some nun-like cousin immovably vowed to
dwell with thee in thy strange exile. Show not to me,—never
show more any visible conscious token of love. I will never
to thee. Our mortal lives, oh, my heavenly Pierre, shall henceforth be one mute wooing of each other; with no declaration;
no bridal; till we meet in the pure realms of God's final
blessedness for us;—till we meet where the ever-interrupting
and ever-marring world can not and shall not come; where all
thy hidden, glorious unselfishness shall be gloriously revealed
in the full splendor of that heavenly light; where, no more
forced to these cruelest disguises, she, *she* too shall assume
her own glorious place, nor take it hard, but rather feel the
more blessed, when, there, thy sweet heart, shall be openly
and unreservedly mine. Pierre, Pierre, my Pierre!—only this
thought, this hope, this sublime faith now supports me. Well
was it, that the swoon, in which thou didst leave me, that
long eternity ago—well was it, dear Pierre, that though I
came out of it to stare and grope, yet it was only to stare and
grope, and then I swooned again, and then groped again,
and then again swooned. But all this was vacancy; little I
clutched; nothing I knew; 'twas less than a dream, my Pierre,
I had no conscious thought of thee, love; but felt an utter
blank, a vacancy;—for wert thou not then utterly gone from
me? and what could there then be left of poor Lucy?—But
now, this long, long swoon is past; I come out again into life
and light; but how could I come out, how could I any way
be, my Pierre, if not in thee? So the moment I came out of
the long, long swoon, straightway came to me the immortal
faith in thee, which though it could offer no one slightest
possible argument of mere sense in thy behalf, yet was it only
the more mysteriously imperative for that, my Pierre. Know
then, dearest Pierre, that with every most glaring earthly reason to disbelieve in thy love; I do yet wholly give myself up
to the unshakable belief in it. For I feel, that always is love

love, and can not know change, Pierre; I feel that heaven hath called me to a wonderful office toward thee. By throwing me into that long, long swoon,—during which, Martha tells me, I hardly ate altogether, three ordinary meals,—by that, heaven, I feel now, was preparing me for the superhuman office I speak of; was wholly estranging me from this earth, even while I yet lingered in it; was fitting me for a celestial mission in terrestrial elements. Oh, give to me of thine own dear strength! I am but a poor weak girl, dear Pierre; one that didst once love thee but too fondly, and with earthly frailty. But now I shall be wafted far upward from that; shall soar up to thee, where thou sittest in thine own calm, sublime heaven of heroism.

"Oh seek not to dissuade me, Pierre. Wouldst thou slay me, and slay me a million times more? and never have done with murdering me? I must come! I must come! God himself can not stay me, for it is He that commands me.—I know all that will follow my flight to thee;—my amazed mother, my enraged brothers, the whole taunting and despising world.—But thou art my mother and my brothers, and all the world, and all heaven, and all the universe to me—thou *art* my Pierre. One only being does this soul in me serve—and that is thee, Pierre.—So I am coming to thee, Pierre, and quickly;—to-morrow it shall be, and never more will I quit thee, Pierre. Speak thou immediately to her about me; thou shalt know best what to say. Is there not some connection between our families, Pierre? I have heard my mother sometimes trace such a thing out,—some indirect cousinship. If thou approvest, then, thou shalt say to her, I am thy cousin, Pierre;—thy resolved and immovable nun-like cousin; vowed to dwell with thee forever; to serve thee and her, to guard thee and her without end. Prepare some little corner for me somewhere; but let it be very near. Ere I come, I shall send a few little things,—the tools I shall work by, Pierre, and so contribute to the welfare of all. Look for me then. I am coming! I am coming, my Pierre; for a deep, deep voice assures me, that all noble as thou art, Pierre, some terrible jeopardy involves thee, which my continual presence only can drive away. I am coming! I am coming!"

LUCY.

iii

When surrounded by the base and mercenary crew, man, too long wonted to eye his race with a suspicious disdain, suddenly is brushed by some angelical plume of humanity, and the human accents of superhuman love, and the human eyes of superhuman beauty and glory, suddenly burst on his being; then how wonderful and fearful the shock! It is as if the sky-cope were rent, and from the black valley of Jehosha-phat, he caught upper glimpses of the seraphim in the visible act of adoring.

He held the artless, angelical letter in his unrealizing hand; he started, and gazed round his room, and out at the window, commanding the bare, desolate, all-forbidding quadrangle, and then asked himself whether this was the place that an angel should choose for its visit to earth. Then he felt a vast, out-swelling triumphantness, that the girl whose rare merits his intuitive soul had once so clearly and passionately discerned, should indeed, in this most tremendous of all trials, have ac-quitted herself with such infinite majesty. Then again, he sunk utterly down from her, as in a bottomless gulf, and ran shud-dering through hideous galleries of despair, in pursuit of some vague, white shape, and lo! two unfathomable dark eyes met his, and Isabel stood mutely and mournfully, yet all-ravishingly before him.

He started up from his plank; cast off his manifold wrap-pings, and crossed the floor to remove himself from the spot, where such sweet, such sublime, such terrific revelations had been made him.

Then a timid little rap was heard at the door.

"Pierre, Pierre; now that thou art risen, may I not come in—just for a moment, Pierre."

"Come in, Isabel."

She was approaching him in her wonted most strange and sweetly mournful manner, when he retreated a step from her, and held out his arm, not seemingly to invite, but rather as if to warn.

She looked fixedly in his face, and stood rooted.

"Isabel, another is coming to me. Thou dost not speak, Isabel. She is coming to dwell with us so long as we live, Isabel. Wilt thou not speak?"

The girl still stood rooted; the eyes, which she had first fixed on him, still remained wide-openly riveted.

"Wilt thou not speak, Isabel?" said Pierre, terrified at her frozen, immovable aspect, yet too terrified to manifest his own terror to her; and still coming slowly near her. She slightly raised one arm, as if to grasp some support; then turned her head slowly sideways toward the door by which she had entered; then her dry lips slowly parted—"My bed; lay me; lay me!"

The verbal effort broke her stiffening enchantment of frost; her thawed form sloped sidelong into the air; but Pierre caught her, and bore her into her own chamber, and laid her there on the bed.

"Fan me; fan me!"

He fanned the fainting flame of her life; by-and-by she turned slowly toward him.

"Oh! that feminine word from thy mouth, dear Pierre:—that *she*, that *she!*"

Pierre sat silent, fanning her.

"Oh, I want none in the world but thee, my brother—but thee, but thee! and, oh God! am *I* not enough for thee? Bare earth with my brother were all heaven for me; but all my life, all my full soul, contents not my brother."

Pierre spoke not; he but listened; a terrible, burning curiosity was in him, that made him as heartless. But still all that she had said thus far was ambiguous.

"Had I known—had I but known it before! Oh bitterly cruel to reveal it now. That *she!* That *she!*"

She raised herself suddenly, and almost fiercely confronted him.

"Either thou hast told thy secret, or she is not worthy the commonest love of man! Speak Pierre,—which?"

"The secret is still a secret, Isabel."

"Then is she worthless, Pierre, whoever she be—foolishly, madly fond!—Doth not the world know me for thy wife?—She shall not come! 'Twere a foul blot on thee and me. She shall not come! One look from me shall murder her, Pierre!"

"This is madness, Isabel. Look: now reason with me. Did I not before opening the letter, say to thee, that doubtless it was from some pretty young aunt or cousin?"

"Speak quick!—a cousin?"

"A cousin, Isabel."

"Yet, yet, that is not wholly out of the degree, I have heard. Tell me more, and quicker! more! more!"

"A very strange cousin, Isabel; almost a nun in her notions. Hearing of our mysterious exile, she, without knowing the cause, hath yet as mysteriously vowed herself ours—not so much mine, Isabel, as ours, *ours*—to serve *us*; and by some sweet heavenly fancying, to guide us and guard us here."

"Then, possibly, it may be all very well, Pierre, my brother— my *brother*—I can say that now?"

"Any,—all words are thine, Isabel; words and worlds with all their containings, shall be slaves to thee, Isabel."

She looked eagerly and inquiringly at him; then dropped her eyes, and touched his hand; then gazed again. "Speak so more to me, Pierre! Thou art my brother; art thou not my brother?—But tell me now more of—her; it is all newness, and utter strangeness to me, Pierre."

"I have said, my sweetest sister, that she has this wild, nun-like notion in her. She is willful in it; in this letter she vows she must and will come, and nothing on earth shall stay her. Do not have any sisterly jealousy, then, my sister. Thou wilt find her a most gentle, unobtrusive, ministering girl, Isabel. She will never name the not-to-be-named things to thee; nor hint of them; because she knows them not. Still, without know-ing the secret, she yet hath the vague, unspecializing sensation of the secret—the mystical presentiment, somehow, of the secret. And her divineness hath drowned all womanly curios-ity in her; so that she desires not, in any way, to verify the presentiment; content with the vague presentiment only; for in that, she thinks, the heavenly summons to come to us, lies;—even there, in that, Isabel. Dost thou now comprehend me?"

"I comprehend nothing, Pierre; there is nothing these eyes have ever looked upon, Pierre, that this soul comprehended. Ever, as now, do I go all a-grope amid the wide mysterious-ness of things. Yes, she shall come; it is only one mystery the more. Doth she talk in her sleep, Pierre? Would it be well, if I slept with her, my brother?"

"On thy account; wishful for thy sake; to leave thee incommoded; and—and—not knowing precisely how things really are;—she probably anticipates and desires otherwise, my sister."

She gazed steadfastly at his outwardly firm, but not interiorly unfaltering aspect; and then dropped her glance in silence.

"Yes, she shall come, my brother; she shall come. But it weaves its thread into the general riddle, my brother.—Hath she that which they call the memory, Pierre; the memory? Hath she that?"

"We all have the memory, my sister."

"Not all! not all!—poor Bell hath but very little. Pierre! I have seen her in some dream. She is fair-haired—blue eyes— she is not quite so tall as I, yet a very little slighter."

Pierre started. "Thou hast seen Lucy Tartan, at Saddle Meadows?"

"Is Lucy Tartan the name?—Perhaps, perhaps;—but also, in the dream, Pierre; she came, with her blue eyes turned beseechingly on me; she seemed as if persuading me from thee;— methought she was then more than thy cousin;—methought she was that good angel, which some say, hovers over every human soul; and methought—oh, methought that I was thy other,—thy other angel, Pierre. Look: see these eyes,—this hair—nay, this cheek;—all dark, dark, dark,—and she—the blue-eyed—the fair-haired—oh, once the red-cheeked!"

She tossed her ebon tresses over her; she fixed her ebon eyes on him.

"Say, Pierre; doth not a funerealness invest me? Was ever hearse so plumed?—Oh, God! that I had been born with blue eyes, and fair hair! Those make the livery of heaven! Heard ye ever yet of a good angel with dark eyes, Pierre?— no, no, no—all blue, blue, blue—heaven's own blue—the clear, vivid, unspeakable blue, which we see in June skies, when all clouds are swept by.—But the good angel shall come to thee, Pierre. Then both will be close by thee, my brother; and thou mayest perhaps elect,—elect!—She shall come; she shall come.—When is it to be, dear Pierre?"

"To-morrow, Isabel. So it is here written."

She fixed her eye on the crumpled billet in his hand. "It were vile to ask, but not wrong to suppose the asking.— Pierre,—no, I need not say it,—wouldst thou?"

"No; I would not let thee read it, my sister; I would not; because I have no right to—no right—no right;—that is it; no: I have no right. I will burn it this instant, Isabel."

He stepped from her into the adjoining room; threw the billet into the stove, and watching its last ashes, returned to Isabel.

She looked with endless intimations upon him.

"It is burnt, but not consumed; it is gone, but not lost. Through stove, pipe, and flue, it hath mounted in flame, and gone as a scroll to heaven! It shall appear again, my brother.—Woe is me—woe, woe!—woe is me, oh, woe! Do not speak to me, Pierre; leave me now. She shall come. The Bad angel shall tend the Good; she shall dwell with us, Pierre. Mistrust me not; her considerateness to me, shall be outdone by mine to her.—Let me be alone now, my brother."

iv

Though by the unexpected petition to enter his privacy—a petition he could scarce ever deny to Isabel, since she so religiously abstained from preferring it, unless for some very reasonable cause, Pierre, in the midst of those conflicting, secondary emotions, immediately following the first wonderful effect of Lucy's strange letter, had been forced to put on, toward Isabel, some air of assurance and understanding concerning its contents; yet at bottom, he was still a prey to all manner of devouring mysteries.

Soon, now, as he left the chamber of Isabel, these mysteriousnesses re-mastered him completely; and as he mechanically sat down in the dining-room chair, gently offered him by Delly—for the silent girl saw that some strangeness that sought stillness was in him;—Pierre's mind was revolving how it was possible, or any way conceivable, that Lucy should have been inspired with such seemingly wonderful presentiments of something assumed, or disguising, or non-substantial, somewhere and somehow, in his present most singular apparent position in the eye of the world. The wild words of Isabel yet rang in his ears. It were an outrage upon all womanhood to imagine that Lucy, however yet devoted to him in her hidden heart, should be willing to come to him, so long as she supposed, with the rest of the world, that Pierre was an ordinarily married man. But how—what possible reason—what possible intimation could she have had to suspect the contrary, or to suspect any thing unsound? For neither at this present time, nor at any subsequent period, did Pierre, or could Pierre, possibly imagine that in her marvelous presentiments of Love she had any definite conceit of the precise nature of the secret which so unrevealingly and enchantedly wrapt him. But a peculiar thought passingly recurred to him here.

Within his social recollections there was a very remarkable case of a youth, who, while all but affianced to a beautiful girl—one returning his own throbbings with incipient passion—became somehow casually and momentarily betrayed into an imprudent manifested tenderness toward a second lady; or else, that second lady's deeply-concerned friends caused it to be made known to the poor youth, that such committal tenderness toward her he had displayed, nor had it failed to exert its natural effect upon her; certain it is, this second lady drooped and drooped, and came nigh to dying, all the while raving of the cruel infidelity of her supposed lover; so that those agonizing appeals, from so really lovely a girl, that seemed dying of grief for him, at last so moved the youth, that—morbidly disregardful of the fact, that inasmuch as two ladies claimed him, the prior lady had the best title to his hand—his conscience insanely upbraided him concerning the second lady; he thought that eternal woe would surely overtake him both here and hereafter if he did not renounce his first love—terrible as the effort would be both to him and her—and wed with the second lady; which he accordingly did; while, through his whole subsequent life, delicacy and honor toward his thus wedded wife, forbade that by explaining to his first love how it was with him in this matter, he should tranquilize her heart; and, therefore, in her complete ignorance, she believed that he was willfully and heartlessly false to her; and so came to a lunatic's death on his account.

This strange story of real life, Pierre knew to be also familiar to Lucy; for they had several times conversed upon it; and the first love of the demented youth had been a school-mate of Lucy's, and Lucy had counted upon standing up with her as bridemaid. Now, the passing idea was self-suggested to Pierre, whether into Lucy's mind some such conceit as this, concerning himself and Isabel, might not possibly have stolen. But then again such a supposition proved wholly untenable in the end; for it did by no means suffice for a satisfactory solution of the absolute motive of the extraordinary proposed step of Lucy; nor indeed by any ordinary law of propriety, did it at all seem to justify that step. Therefore, he knew not what to think; hardly what to dream. Wonders, nay, downright miracles and no less were sung about Love; but here was the absolute miracle itself—the out-acted miracle. For infallibly certain he inwardly felt, that whatever her strange conceit; whatever her enigmatical delusion; whatever her most secret and inexplicable motive; still Lucy in her own virgin heart remained transparently immaculate, without shadow of flaw or vein. Nevertheless, what inconceivable conduct this was in her, which she in her letter so passionately proposed! Altogether, it amazed him; it confounded him.

Now, that vague, fearful feeling stole into him, that, rail as all atheists will, there is a mysterious, inscrutable divineness in the world—a God—a Being positively present everywhere;—nay, He is now in this room; the air did part when I here sat down. I displaced the Spirit then—condensed it a little off from this spot. He looked apprehensively around him; he felt overjoyed at the sight of the humanness of Delly.

While he was thus plunged into this mysteriousness, a knock was heard at the door.

Delly hesitatingly rose—"Shall I let any one in, sir?—I think it is Mr. Millthorpe's knock."

"Go and see—go and see"—said Pierre, vacantly.

The moment the door was opened, Millthorpe—for it was he—catching a glimpse of Pierre's seated form, brushed past Delly, and loudly entered the room.

"Ha, ha! well, my boy, how comes on the Inferno? That is it you are writing; one is apt to look black while writing Infernoes; you always loved Dante. My lad! I have finished ten metaphysical treatises; argued five cases before the court; attended all our society's meetings; accompanied our great Professor, Monsieur Volvoon, the lecturer, through his circuit in the philosophical saloons, sharing all the honors of his illustrious triumph; and by the way, let me tell you, Volvoon secretly gives me even more credit than is my due; for 'pon my soul, I did not help write more than one half, at most, of his Lectures; edited—anonymously, though—a learned, scientific work on 'The Precise Cause of the Modifications in the Undulatory Motion in Waves,' a posthumous work of a poor fellow—fine lad he was, too—a friend of mine. Yes, here I have been doing all this, while you still are hammering away at that one poor plaguy Inferno! Oh, there's a secret in dispatching these things; patience! patience! you will yet learn the secret. Time! time! I can't teach it to you, my boy, but Time can: I wish I could, but I can't."

There was another knock at the door.

"Oh!" cried Millthorpe, suddenly turning round to it, "I forgot, my boy. I came to tell you that there is a porter, with some queer things, inquiring for you. I happened to meet him down stairs in the corridors, and I told him to follow me up—I would show him the road; here he is; let him in, let him in, good Delly, my girl."

Thus far, the rattlings of Millthorpe, if producing any effect at all, had but stunned the averted Pierre. But now he started to his feet. A man with his hat on, stood in the door, holding an easel before him.

"Is this Mr. Glendinning's room, gentlemen?"

"Oh, come in, come in," cried Millthorpe, "all right."

"Oh! is that *you*, sir? well, well, then;" and the man set down the easel.

"Well, my boy," exclaimed Millthorpe to Pierre; "you are in the Inferno dream yet. Look; that's what people call an *easel*, my boy. An *easel*, an *easel*—not a *weasel*; you look at it as though you thought it a weasel. Come; wake up, wake up! You ordered it, I suppose, and here it is. Going to paint and illustrate the Inferno, as you go along, I suppose. Well, my friends tell me it is a great pity my own things aint illustrated. But I can't afford it. There now is that Hymn to the Niger, which I threw into a pigeon-hole, a year or two ago—that would be fine for illustrations."

"Is it for Mr. Glendinning you inquire?" said Pierre now, in a slow, icy tone, to the porter.

"Mr. Glendinning, sir; all right, aint it?"

"Perfectly," said Pierre mechanically, and casting another strange, rapt, bewildered glance at the easel. "But something seems strangely wanting here. Ay, now I see, I see it:—Villain!—the vines! Thou hast torn the green heart-strings! Thou hast but left the cold skeleton of the sweet arbor wherein she once nestled! Thou besotted, heartless hind and fiend, dost thou so much as dream in thy shriveled liver of the eternal mischief thou hast done? Restore thou the green vines! untrample them, thou accursed!—Oh my God, my God, trampled vines pounded and crushed in all fibers, how can they live over again, even though they be replanted! Curse thee, thou!—Nay, nay," he added moodily—"I was but wandering to myself." Then rapidly and mockingly— "Pardon, pardon!—porter; I most humbly crave thy most haughty pardon." Then imperiously—"Come, stir thyself, man; thou hast more below: bring all up."

As the astounded porter turned, he whispered to Millthorpe—"Is he safe?—shall I bring 'em?"

"Oh certainly," smiled Millthorpe: "I'll look out for him; he's never really dangerous when I'm present; there, go!"

Two trunks now followed, with "L. T." blurredly marked upon the ends.

"Is that all, my man?" said Pierre, as the trunks were being put down before him; " well, how much?"—that moment his eyes first caught the blurred letters.

"Prepaid, sir; but no objection to more."

Pierre stood mute and unmindful, still fixedly eying the blurred letters; his body contorted, and one side drooping, as though that moment half-way down-stricken with a paralysis, and yet unconscious of the stroke.

His two companions momentarily stood motionless in those respective attitudes, in which they had first caught sight of the remarkable change that had come over him. But, as if ashamed of having been thus affected, Millthorpe summoning a loud, merry voice, advanced toward Pierre, and, tapping his shoulder, cried, "Wake up, wake up, my boy!—He says he is prepaid, but no objection to more."

"Prepaid;—what's that? Go, go, and jabber to apes!"

"A curious young gentleman, is he not?" said Millthorpe

lightly to the porter;—"Look you, my boy, I'll repeat:—He says he's prepaid, but no objection to more."

"Ah?—take that then," said Pierre, vacantly putting something into the porter's hand.

"And what shall I do with this, sir?" said the porter, staring.

"Drink a health; but not mine; that were mockery!"

"With a key, sir? This is a key you gave me."

"Ah!—well, you at least shall not have the thing that unlocks me. Give me the key, and take this."

"Ay, ay!—here's the chink! Thank 'ee sir, thank 'ee. This'll drink. I aint called a porter for nothing; Stout's the word; 2151 is my number; any jobs, call on me."

"Do you ever cart a coffin, my man?" said Pierre.

" 'Pon my soul!" cried Millthorpe, gayly laughing, "if you aint writing an Inferno, then—but never mind. Porter! this gentleman is under medical treatment at present. You had better—ab'—you understand—'squatulate, porter! There, my boy, he is gone; I understand how to manage these fellows; there's a trick in it, my boy—an off-handed sort of what d'ye call it?—you understand—the trick! the trick!—the whole world's a trick. Know the trick of it, all's right; don't know, all's wrong. Ha! ha!"

"The porter is gone then?" said Pierre, calmly. "Well, Mr. Millthorpe, you will have the goodness to follow him."

"Rare joke! admirable!—Good morning, sir. Ha, ha!"

And with his unruffleable hilariousness, Millthorpe quitted the room.

But hardly had the door closed upon him, nor had he yet removed his hand from its outer knob, when suddenly it swung half open again, and thrusting his fair curly head within, Millthorpe cried: "By the way, my boy, I have a word for you. You know that greasy fellow who has been dunning you so of late. Well, be at rest there; he's paid. I was suddenly made flush yesterday:—regular flood-tide. You can return it any day, you know—no hurry; that's all.—But, by the way,—as you look as though you were going to have company here—just send for me in case you want to use me— any bedstead to put up, or heavy things to be lifted about. Don't you and the women do it, now, mind! That's all again. Addios, my boy. Take care of yourself!"

"Stay!" cried Pierre, reaching forth one hand, but moving neither foot—"Stay!"—in the midst of all his prior emotions struck by these singular traits in Millthorpe. But the door was abruptly closed; and singing Fa, la, la: Millthorpe in his seedy coat went tripping down the corridor.

"Plus heart, minus head," muttered Pierre, his eyes fixed on the door. "Now, by heaven! the god that made Millthorpe was both a better and a greater than the god that made Napoleon or Byron.—Plus head, minus heart—Pah! the brains grow maggoty without a heart; but the heart's the preserving salt itself, and can keep sweet without the head.—Delly!"

"Sir?"

"My cousin Miss Tartan is coming here to live with us, Delly. That easel,—those trunks are hers."

"Good heavens!—coming here?—your cousin?—Miss Tartan?"

"Yes, I thought you must have heard of her and me;—but it was broken off, Delly."

"Sir? Sir?"

"I have no explanation, Delly; and from you, I must have no amazement. My cousin,—mind, my *cousin*, Miss Tartan, is coming to live with us. The next room to this, on the other side there, is unoccupied. That room shall be hers. You must wait upon her, too, Delly."

"Certainly sir, certainly; I will do any thing;" said Delly trembling; "but,—but—does Mrs. Glendin-din—does my mistress know this?"

"My wife knows all"—said Pierre sternly. "I will go down and get the key of the room; and you must sweep it out."

"What is to be put into it, sir?" said Delly. "Miss Tartan— why, she is used to all sorts of fine things,—rich carpets— wardrobes—mirrors—curtains;—why, why, why!"

"Look," said Pierre, touching an old rug with his foot;— "here is a bit of carpet; drag that into her room; here is a chair, put that in; and for a bed,—ay, ay," he muttered to himself; "I have made it for her, and she ignorantly lies on it now!—as made—so lie. Oh God!"

"Hark! my mistress is calling"—cried Delly, moving toward the opposite room.

"Stay!"—cried Pierre, grasping her shoulder; "if both

called at one time from these opposite chambers, and both were swooning, which door would you first fly to?"

The girl gazed at him uncomprehendingly and affrighted a moment; and then said,—"This one, sir"—out of mere confusion perhaps, putting her hand on Isabel's latch.

"It is well. Now go."

He stood in an intent unchanged attitude till Delly returned.

"How is my wife, now?"

Again startled by the peculiar emphasis placed on the magical word *wife*, Delly, who had long before this, been occasionally struck with the infrequency of his using that term; she looked at him perplexedly, and said half-unconsciously—

"Your wife, sir?"

"Ay, is she not?"

"God grant that she be—Oh, 'tis most cruel to ask that of poor, poor Delly, sir!"

"Tut for thy tears! Never deny it again then!—I swear to heaven, she is!"

With these wild words, Pierre seized his hat, and departed the room, muttering something about bringing the key of the additional chamber.

As the door closed on him, Delly dropped on her knees. She lifted her head toward the ceiling, but dropped it again, as if tyrannically awed downward, and bent it low over, till her whole form tremulously cringed to the floor.

"God that made me, and that wast not so hard to me as wicked Delly deserved,—God that made me, I pray to thee! ward it off from me, if it be coming to me. Be not deaf to me; these stony walls—Thou canst hear through them. Pity! pity!—mercy, my God!—If they are not married; if I, penitentially seeking to be pure, am now but the servant to a greater sin, than I myself committed: then, pity! pity! pity! pity! pity! Oh God that made me,—See me, see me here—what can Delly do? If I go hence, none will take me in but villains. If I stay, then—for stay I must—and they be not married,—then pity, pity, pity, pity, pity!"

Book XXIV

LUCY AT THE APOSTLES

NEXT MORNING, the recently appropriated room adjoining on the other side of the dining-room, presented a different aspect from that which met the eye of Delly upon first unlocking it with Pierre on the previous evening. Two squares of faded carpeting of different patterns, covered the middle of the floor, leaving, toward the surbase, a wide, blank margin around them. A small glass hung in the pier; beneath that, a little stand, with a foot or two of carpet before it. In one corner was a cot, neatly equipped with bedding. At the outer side of the cot, another strip of carpeting was placed. Lucy's delicate feet should not shiver on the naked floor.

Pierre, Isabel, and Delly were standing in the room; Isabel's eyes were fixed on the cot.

"I think it will be pretty cosy now," said Delly, palely glancing all round, and then adjusting the pillow anew.

"There is no warmth, though," said Isabel. "Pierre, there is no stove in the room. She will be very cold. The pipe—can we not send it this way?" And she looked more intently at him, than the question seemed to warrant.

"Let the pipe stay where it is, Isabel," said Pierre, answering her own pointed gaze. "The dining-room door can stand open. She never liked sleeping in a heated room. Let all be; it is well. Eh! but there is a grate here, I see. I will buy coals. Yes, yes—that can be easily done; a little fire of a morning—the expense will be nothing. Stay, we will have a little fire here now for a welcome. She shall always have fire."

"Better change the pipe, Pierre," said Isabel, "that will be permanent, and save the coals."

"It shall not be done, Isabel. Doth not that pipe and that warmth go into thy room? Shall I rob my wife, good Delly, even to benefit my most devoted and true-hearted cousin?"

"Oh! I should say not, sir; not at all," said Delly hysterically.

A triumphant fire flashed in Isabel's eye; her full bosom arched out; but she was silent.

"She may be here, now, at any moment, Isabel," said Pierre; "come, we will meet her in the dining-room; that is our reception-place, thou knowest."

So the three went into the dining-room.

ii

They had not been there long, when Pierre, who had been pacing up and down, suddenly paused, as if struck by some laggard thought, which had just occurred to him at the eleventh hour. First he looked toward Delly, as if about to bid her quit the apartment, while he should say something private to Isabel; but as if, on a second thought, holding the contrary of this procedure most advisable, he, without preface, at once addressed Isabel, in his ordinary conversational tone, so that Delly could not but plainly hear him, whether she would or no.

"My dear Isabel, though, as I said to thee before, my cousin, Miss Tartan, that strange, and willful, nun-like girl, is at all hazards, mystically resolved to come and live with us, yet it must be quite impossible that her friends can approve in her such a singular step; a step even more singular, Isabel, than thou, in thy unsophisticatedness, can'st at all imagine. I shall be immensely deceived if they do not, to their very utmost, strive against it. Now what I am going to add may be quite unnecessary, but I can not avoid speaking it, for all that."

Isabel with empty hands sat silent, but intently and expectantly eying him; while behind her chair, Delly was bending her face low over her knitting—which she had seized so soon as Pierre had begun speaking—and with trembling fingers was nervously twitching the points of her long needles. It was plain that she awaited Pierre's accents with hardly much less eagerness than Isabel. Marking well this expression in Delly, and apparently not unpleased with it, Pierre continued; but by no slightest outward tone or look seemed addressing his remarks to any one but Isabel.

"Now what I mean, dear Isabel, is this: if that very probable hostility on the part of Miss Tartan's friends to her fulfilling her strange resolution—if any of that hostility should chance to be manifested under thine eye, then thou certainly wilt know how to account for it; and as certainly wilt draw no inference from it in the minutest conceivable degree involving any thing sinister in me. No, I am sure thou wilt not, my dearest Isabel. For, understand me, regarding this strange mood in my cousin as a thing wholly above my comprehension, and indeed regarding my poor cousin herself as a rapt enthusiast in some wild mystery utterly unknown to me; and unwilling ignorantly to interfere in what almost seems some supernatural thing, I shall not repulse her coming, however violently her friends may seek to stay it. I shall not repulse, as certainly as I have not invited. But a neutral attitude sometimes seems a suspicious one. Now what I mean is this: let all such vague suspicions of me, if any, be confined to Lucy's friends; but let not such absurd misgivings come near my dearest Isabel, to give the least uneasiness. Isabel! tell me; have I not now said enough to make plain what I mean? Or, indeed, is not all I have said wholly unnecessary; seeing that when one feels deeply conscientious, one is often apt to seem superfluously, and indeed unpleasantly and unbeseemingly scrupulous? Speak, my own Isabel,"—and he stept nearer to her, reaching forth his arm.

"Thy hand is the caster's ladle, Pierre, which holds me entirely fluid. Into thy forms and slightest moods of thought, thou pourest me; and I there solidify to that form, and take it on, and thenceforth wear it, till once more thou moldest me anew. If what thou tellest me be thy thought, then how can I help its being mine, my Pierre?"

"The gods made thee of a holyday, when all the common world was done, and shaped thee leisurely in elaborate hours, thou paragon!"

So saying, in a burst of admiring love and wonder, Pierre paced the room; while Isabel sat silent, leaning on her hand, and half-vailed with her hair. Delly's nervous stitches became less convulsive. She seemed soothed; some dark and vague conceit seemed driven out of her by something either directly expressed by Pierre, or inferred from his expressions.

iii

"Pierre! Pierre!—Quick! Quick!—They are dragging me back!—oh, quick, dear Pierre!"

"What is that?" swiftly cried Isabel, rising to her feet, and amazedly glancing toward the door leading into the corridor.

But Pierre darted from the room, prohibiting any one from following him.

Half-way down the stairs, a slight, airy, almost unearthly figure was clinging to the balluster; and two young men, one in naval uniform, were vainly seeking to remove the two thin white hands without hurting them. They were Glen Stanly, and Frederic, the elder brother of Lucy.

In a moment, Pierre's hands were among the rest.

"Villain!—Damn thee!" cried Frederic; and letting go the hand of his sister, he struck fiercely at Pierre.

But the blow was intercepted by Pierre.

"Thou hast bewitched, thou damned juggler, the sweetest angel! Defend thyself!"

"Nay, nay," cried Glen, catching the drawn rapier of the frantic brother, and holding him in his powerful grasp; "he is unarmed; this is no time or place to settle our feud with him. Thy sister,—sweet Lucy—let us save her first, and then what thou wilt. Pierre Glendinning—if thou art but the little finger of a man—begone with thee from hence! Thy depravity, thy pollutedness, is that of a fiend!—Thou canst not desire this thing:—the sweet girl is mad!"

Pierre stepped back a little, and looked palely and haggardly at all three.

"I render no accounts: I am what I am. This sweet girl—this angel whom ye two defile by your touches—she is of age by the law:—she is her own mistress by the law. And now, I swear she shall have her will! Unhand the girl! Let her stand alone. See; she will faint; let her go, I say!" And again his hands were among them.

Suddenly, as they all, for the one instant vaguely struggled, the pale girl drooped, and fell sideways toward Pierre; and, unprepared for this, the two opposite champions, unconsciously relinquished their hold, tripped, and stumbled against each other, and both fell on the stairs. Snatching Lucy in his arms, Pierre darted from them; gained the door; drove before him Isabel and Delly,—who, affrighted, had been lingering there;—and bursting into the prepared chamber, laid Lucy on her cot; then swiftly turned out of the room, and locked them all three in: and so swiftly—like lightning—was this whole thing done, that not till the lock clicked, did he find Glen and Frederic fiercely fronting him.

"Gentlemen, it is all over. This door is locked. She is in women's hands.—Stand back!"

As the two infuriated young men now caught at him to hurl him aside, several of the Apostles rapidly entered, having been attracted by the noise.

"Drag them off from me!" cried Pierre. "They are trespassers! drag them off!"

Immediately Glen and Frederic were pinioned by twenty hands; and, in obedience to a sign from Pierre, were dragged out of the room, and dragged down stairs; and given into the custody of a passing officer, as two disorderly youths invading the sanctuary of a private retreat.

In vain they fiercely expostulated; but at last, as if now aware that nothing further could be done without some previous legal action, they most reluctantly and chafingly declared themselves ready to depart. Accordingly they were let go; but not without a terrible menace of swift retribution directed to Pierre.

iv

Happy is the dumb man in the hour of passion. He makes no impulsive threats, and therefore seldom falsifies himself in the transition from choler to calm.

Proceeding into the thoroughfare, after leaving the Apostles', it was not very long ere Glen and Frederic concluded between themselves, that Lucy could not so easily be rescued by threat or force. The pale, inscrutable determinateness, and flinchless intrepidity of Pierre, now began to domineer upon them; for any social unusualness or greatness is sometimes most impressive in the retrospect. What Pierre had said concerning Lucy's being her own mistress in the eye of the law; this now recurred to them. After much tribulation of thought, the more collected Glen proposed, that Frederic's mother should visit the rooms of Pierre; he imagined, that though insensible to their own united intimidations, Lucy might not prove deaf to the maternal prayers. Had Mrs. Tartan been a different woman than she was; had she indeed any disinterested agonies of a generous heart, and not mere match-making mortifications, however poignant; then the hope of Frederic and Glen might have had more likelihood in it. Nevertheless, the experiment was tried, but signally failed.

In the combined presence of her mother, Pierre, Isabel, and Delly; and addressing Pierre and Isabel as Mr. and Mrs. Glendinning; Lucy took the most solemn vows upon herself, to reside with her present host and hostess until they should cast her off. In vain her by turns suppliant, and exasperated mother went down on her knees to her, or seemed almost on the point of smiting her; in vain she painted all the scorn and the loathing; sideways hinted of the handsome and gallant Glen; threatened her that in case she persisted, her entire family would renounce her; and though she should be starving, would not bestow one morsel upon such a recreant, and infinitely worse than dishonorable girl.

To all this, Lucy—now entirely unmenaced in person—replied in the gentlest and most heavenly manner; yet with a collectedness, and steadfastness, from which there was nothing to hope. What she was doing was not of herself; she had been moved to it by all-encompassing influences above, around, and beneath. She felt no pain for her own condition; her only suffering was sympathetic. She looked for no reward; the essence of well-doing was the consciousness of having done well without the least hope of reward. Concerning the loss of worldly wealth and sumptuousness, and all the brocaded applauses of drawing-rooms; these were no loss to her, for they had always been valueless. Nothing was she now renouncing; but in acting upon her present inspiration she was inheriting every thing. Indifferent to scorn, she craved no pity. As to the question of her sanity, that matter she referred to the verdict of angels, and not to the sordid opinions of man. If any one protested that she was defying the sacred counsels of her mother, she had nothing to answer but this: that her mother possessed all her daughterly deference, but her unconditional obedience was elsewhere due. Let all hope of moving her be immediately, and once for all, abandoned. One only thing could move her; and that would only move her, to make her forever immovable;—that thing was death.

Such wonderful strength in such wonderful sweetness; such inflexibility in one so fragile, would have been matter for marvel to any observer. But to her mother it was very much more; for, like many other superficial observers, forming her previous opinion of Lucy upon the slightness of her person, and the dulcetness of her temper, Mrs. Tartan had always imagined that her daughter was quite incapable of any such daring act. As if sterling heavenliness were incompatible with heroicness. These two are never found apart. Nor, though Pierre knew more of Lucy than any one else, did this most singular behavior in her fail to amaze him. Seldom even had the mystery of Isabel fascinated him more, with a fascination partaking of the terrible. The mere bodily aspect of Lucy, as changed by her more recent life, filled him with the most powerful and novel emotions. That unsullied complexion of bloom was now entirely gone, without being any way replaced by sallowness, as is usual in similar instances. And as if her body indeed were the temple of God, and marble indeed were the only fit material for so holy a shrine, a brilliant, supernatural whiteness now gleamed in her cheek. Her head sat on her shoulders as a chiseled statue's head; and the soft, firm light in her eye seemed as much a prodigy, as though a chiseled statue should give token of vision and intelligence.

Isabel also was most strangely moved by this sweet unearthliness in the aspect of Lucy. But it did not so much persuade her by any common appeals to her heart, as irrespectively commend her by the very signet of heaven. In the deference with which she ministered to Lucy's little occasional wants, there was more of blank spontaneousness than compassionate voluntariness. And when it so chanced, that—owing perhaps to some momentary jarring of the distant and lonely guitar—as Lucy was so mildly speaking in the presence of her mother, a sudden, just audible, submissively answering musical, stringed tone, came through the open door from the adjoining chamber; then Isabel, as if seized by some spiritual awe, fell on her knees before Lucy, and made a rapid gesture of homage; yet still, somehow, as it were, without evidence of voluntary will.

Finding all her most ardent efforts ineffectual, Mrs. Tartan now distressedly motioned to Pierre and Isabel to quit the chamber, that she might urge her entreaties and menaces in private. But Lucy gently waved them to stay; and then turned to her mother. Henceforth she had no secrets but those which would also be secrets in heaven. Whatever was publicly known in heaven, should be publicly known on earth. There was no slightest secret between her and her mother.

Wholly confounded by this inscrutableness of her so alienated and infatuated daughter, Mrs. Tartan turned inflamedly upon Pierre, and bade him follow her forth. But again Lucy said nay, there were no secrets between her mother and Pierre. She would anticipate every thing there. Calling for pen and paper, and a book to hold on her knee and write, she traced the following lines, and reached them to her mother:

"I am Lucy Tartan. I have come to dwell during their pleasure with Mr. and Mrs. Pierre Glendinning, of my own unsolicited free-will. If they desire it, I shall go; but no other power shall remove me, except by violence; and against any violence I have the ordinary appeal to the law."

"Read this, madam," said Mrs. Tartan, tremblingly handing it to Isabel, and eying her with a passionate and disdainful significance.

"I have read it," said Isabel, quietly, after a glance, and handing it to Pierre, as if by that act to show, that she had no separate decision in the matter.

"And do you, sir, too, indirectly connive?" said Mrs. Tartan to Pierre, when he had read it.

"I render no accounts, madam. This seems to be the written and final calm will of your daughter. As such, you had best respect it, and depart."

Mrs. Tartan glanced despairingly and incensedly about her; then fixing her eyes on her daughter, spoke.

"Girl! here where I stand, I forever cast thee off. Never more shalt thou be vexed by my maternal entreaties. I shall instruct thy brothers to disown thee; I shall instruct Glen Stanly to banish thy worthless image from his heart, if banished thence it be not already by thine own incredible folly and depravity. For thee, Mr. Monster! the judgment of God will overtake thee for this. And for thee, madam, I have no words for the woman who will connivingly permit her own husband's paramour to dwell beneath her roof. For thee, frail one," (to Delly), "thou needest no amplification.—A nest of vileness! And now, surely, whom God himself hath abandoned forever, a mother may quit, never more to revisit."

This parting maternal malediction seemed to work no visibly corresponding effect upon Lucy; already she was so marble-white, that fear could no more blanch her, if indeed fear was then at all within her heart. For as the highest, and purest, and thinnest ether remains unvexed by all the tumults of the inferior air; so that transparent ether of her cheek, that clear mild azure of her eye, showed no sign of passion, as her terrestrial mother stormed below. Helpings she had from unstirring arms; glimpses she caught of aid invisible; sustained she was by those high powers of immortal Love, that once siding with the weakest reed which the utmost tempest tosses; then that utmost tempest shall be broken down before the irresistible resistings of that weakest reed.

Book XXV

A DAY OR TWO after the arrival of Lucy, when she had quite recovered from any possible ill-effects of recent events,—events conveying such a shock to both Pierre and Isabel,—though to each in a quite different way,—but not, apparently, at least, moving Lucy so intensely—as they were all three sitting at coffee, Lucy expressed her intention to practice her crayon art professionally. It would be so pleasant an employment for her, besides contributing to their common fund. Pierre well knew her expertness in catching likenesses, and judiciously and truthfully beautifying them; not by altering the features so much, as by steeping them in a beautifying atmosphere. For even so, said Lucy, thrown into the Lagoon, and there beheld—as I have heard—the roughest stones, without transformation, put on the softest aspects. If Pierre would only take a little trouble to bring sitters to her room, she doubted not a fine harvest of heads might easily be secured. Certainly, among the numerous inmates of the old Church, Pierre must know many who would have no objections to being sketched. Moreover, though as yet she had had small opportunity to see them; yet among such a remarkable company of poets, philosophers, and mystics of all sorts, there must be some striking heads. In conclusion, she expressed her satisfaction at the chamber prepared for her, inasmuch as having been formerly the studio of an artist, one window had been considerably elevated, while by a singular arrangement of the interior shutters, the light could in any direction be thrown about at will.

Already Pierre had anticipated something of this sort; the first sight of the easel having suggested it to him. His reply was therefore not wholly unconsidered. He said, that so far as she herself was concerned, the systematic practice of her art at present would certainly be a great advantage in supplying her with a very delightful occupation. But since she could hardly hope for any patronage from her mother's fashionable and wealthy associates; indeed, as such a thing must be very far from her own desires; and as it was only from the Apostles she could—for some time to come, at least—reasonably anticipate sitters; and as those Apostles were almost universally a very forlorn and penniless set—though in truth there were some wonderfully rich-looking heads among them—therefore, Lucy must not look for much immediate pecuniary emolument. Ere long she might indeed do something very handsome; but at the outset, it was well to be moderate in her expectations. This admonishment came, modifiedly, from that certain stoic, dogged mood of Pierre, born of his recent life, which taught him never to expect any good from any thing; but always to anticipate ill; however not in unreadiness to meet the contrary; and then, if good came, so much the better. He added that he would that very morning go among the rooms and corridors of the Apostles, familiarly announcing that his cousin, a lady-artist in crayons, occupied a room adjoining his, where she would be very happy to receive any sitters.

"And now, Lucy, what shall be the terms? That is a very important point, thou knowest."

"I suppose, Pierre, they must be very low," said Lucy, looking at him meditatively.

"Very low, Lucy; very low, indeed."

"Well, ten dollars, then."

"Ten Banks of England, Lucy!" exclaimed Pierre. "Why, Lucy, that were almost a quarter's income for some of the Apostles!"

"Four dollars, Pierre."

"I will tell thee now, Lucy—but first, how long does it take to complete one portrait?"

"Two sittings; and two mornings' work by myself, Pierre."

"And let me see; what are thy materials? They are not very costly, I believe. 'Tis not like cutting glass,—thy tools must not be pointed with diamonds, Lucy?"

"See, Pierre!" said Lucy, holding out her little palm, "see; this handful of charcoal, a bit of bread, a crayon or two, and a square of paper:—that is all."

"Well, then, thou shalt charge one-seventy-five for a portrait."

"Only one-seventy-five, Pierre?"

"I am half afraid now we have set it far too high, Lucy. Thou must not be extravagant. Look: if thy terms were ten dollars, and thou didst crayon on trust; then thou wouldst have plenty of sitters, but small returns. But if thou puttest thy terms right-down, and also sayest thou must have thy cash right-down too—don't start so at that *cash*—then not so many sitters to be sure, but more returns. Thou understandest."

"It shall be just as thou say'st, Pierre."

"Well, then, I will write a card for thee, stating thy terms; and put it up conspicuously in thy room, so that every Apostle may know what he has to expect."

"Thank thee, thank thee, cousin Pierre," said Lucy, rising. "I rejoice at thy pleasant and not entirely unhopeful view of my poor little plan. But I must be doing something; I must be earning money. See, I have eaten ever so much bread this morning, but have not earned one penny."

With a humorous sadness Pierre measured the large remainder of the one only piece she had touched, and then would have spoken banteringly to her; but she had slid away into her own room.

He was presently roused from the strange revery into which the conclusion of this scene had thrown him, by the touch of Isabel's hand upon his knee, and her large expressive glance upon his face. During all the foregoing colloquy, she had remained entirely silent; but an unoccupied observer would perhaps have noticed, that some new and very strong emotions were restrainedly stirring within her.

"Pierre!" she said, intently bending over toward him.

"Well, well, Isabel," stammeringly replied Pierre; while a mysterious color suffused itself over his whole face, neck, and brow; and involuntarily he started a little back from her self-proffering form.

Arrested by this movement Isabel eyed him fixedly; then slowly rose, and with immense mournful stateliness, drew herself up, and said: "If thy sister can ever come too nigh to thee, Pierre, tell thy sister so, beforehand; for the September sun draws not up the valley-vapor more jealously from the disdainful earth, than my secret god shall draw me up from thee, if ever I can come too nigh to thee."

Thus speaking, one hand was on her bosom, as if resolutely feeling of something deadly there concealed; but, riveted by her general manner more than by her particular gesture, Pierre, at the instant, did not so particularly note the all-significant movement of the hand upon her bosom, though afterward he recalled it, and darkly and thoroughly comprehended its meaning.

"Too nigh to me, Isabel? Sun or dew, thou fertilizest me! Can sunbeams or drops of dew come too nigh the thing they warm and water? Then sit down by me, Isabel, and sit close; wind in within my ribs,—if so thou canst,—that my one frame may be the continent of two."

"Fine feathers make fine birds, so I have heard," said Isabel, most bitterly—"but do fine sayings always make fine deeds? Pierre, thou didst but just now draw away from me!"

"When we would most dearly embrace, we first throw back our arms, Isabel; I but drew away, to draw so much the closer to thee."

"Well; all words are arrant skirmishers; deeds are the army's self! be it as thou sayest. I yet trust to thee.—Pierre."

"My breath waits thine; what is it, Isabel?"

"I have been more blockish than a block; I am mad to think of it! More mad, that her great sweetness should first remind me of mine own stupidity. But she shall not get the start of me! Pierre, some way I must work for thee! See, I will sell this hair; have these teeth pulled out; but some way I will earn money for thee!"

Pierre now eyed her startledly. Touches of a determinate meaning shone in her; some hidden thing was deeply wounded in her. An affectionate soothing syllable was on his tongue; his arm was out; when shifting his expression, he whisperingly and alarmedly exclaimed—"Hark! she is coming.—Be still."

But rising boldly, Isabel threw open the connecting door, exclaiming half-hysterically—"Look, Lucy; here is the strangest husband; fearful of being caught speaking to his wife!"

With an artist's little box before her—whose rattling, perhaps, had startled Pierre—Lucy was sitting mid-way in her room, opposite the opened door; so that at that moment, both Pierre and Isabel were plainly visible to her. The singular tone of Isabel's voice instantly caused her to look up intently. At once, a sudden irradiation of some subtle intelligence—but whether welcome to her, or otherwise, could not be determined—shot over her whole aspect. She murmured some vague random reply; and then bent low over her box, saying she was very busy.

Isabel closed the door, and sat down again by Pierre. Her countenance wore a mixed and writhing, impatient look. She seemed as one in whom the most powerful emotion of life is caught in inextricable toils of circumstances, and while longing to disengage itself, still knows that all struggles will prove worse than vain; and so, for the moment, grows madly reckless and defiant of all obstacles. Pierre trembled as he gazed upon her. But soon the mood passed from her; her old, sweet mournfulness returned; again the clear unfathomableness was in her mystic eye.

"Pierre, ere now,—ere I ever knew thee—I have done mad things, which I have never been conscious of, but in the dim recalling. I hold such things no things of mine. What I now remember, as just now done, was one of them."

"Thou hast done nothing but shown thy strength, while I have shown my weakness, Isabel;—yes, to the whole world thou art my wife—to her, too, thou art my wife. Have I not told her so, myself? I was weaker than a kitten, Isabel; and thou, strong as those high things angelical, from which utmost beauty takes not strength."

"Pierre, once such syllables from thee, were all refreshing, and bedewing to me; now, though they drop as warmly and as fluidly from thee, yet falling through another and an intercepting zone, they freeze on the way, and clatter on my heart like hail, Pierre.——Thou didst not speak thus to her!"

"She is not Isabel."

The girl gazed at him with a quick and piercing scrutiny; then looked quite calm, and spoke. "My guitar, Pierre: thou know'st how complete a mistress I am of it; now, before thou gettest sitters for the portrait-sketcher, thou shalt get pupils for the music-teacher. Wilt thou?" and she looked at him with a persuasiveness and touchingness, which to Pierre, seemed more than mortal.

"My poor poor, Isabel!" cried Pierre; "thou art the mistress of the natural sweetness of the guitar, not of its invented regulated artifices; and these are all that the silly pupil will pay for learning. And what thou hast can not be taught. Ah, thy sweet ignorance is all transporting to me! my sweet, my sweet!—dear, divine girl!" And impulsively he caught her in his arms.

While the first fire of his feeling plainly glowed upon him, but ere he had yet caught her to him, Isabel had backward glided close to the connecting door; which, at the instant of his embrace, suddenly opened, as by its own volition.

Before the eyes of seated Lucy, Pierre and Isabel stood locked; Pierre's lips upon her cheek.

ii

Notwithstanding the maternal visit of Mrs. Tartan, and the peremptoriness with which it had been closed by her declared departure never to return, and her vow to teach all Lucy's relatives and friends, and Lucy's own brothers, and her suitor, to disown her, and forget her; yet Pierre fancied that he knew too much in general of the human heart, and too much in particular of the character of both Glen and Frederic, to remain entirely untouched by disquietude, concerning what those two fiery youths might now be plotting against him, as the imagined monster, by whose infernal tricks Lucy Tartan was supposed to have been seduced from every earthly seemliness. Not happily, but only so much the more gloomily, did he augur from the fact, that Mrs. Tartan had come to Lucy unattended; and that Glen and Frederic had let eight-and-forty hours and more go by, without giving the slightest hostile or neutral sign. At first he thought, that bridling their impulsive fierceness, they were resolved to take the slower, but perhaps the surer method, to wrest Lucy back to them, by instituting some legal process. But this idea was repulsed by more than one consideration.

Not only was Frederic of that sort of temper, peculiar to military men, which would prompt him, in so closely personal and intensely private and family a matter, to scorn the hireling publicity of the law's lingering arm; and impel him, as by the furiousness of fire, to be his own righter and avenger; for, in him, it was perhaps quite as much the feeling of an outrageous family affront to himself, through Lucy, as her own presumed separate wrong, however black, which stung him to the quick: not only were these things so respecting Frederic; but concerning Glen, Pierre well knew, that be Glen heartless as he might, to do a deed of love, Glen was not heartless to do a deed of hate; that though, on that memorable night of his arrival in the city, Glen had heartlessly closed his door upon him, yet now Glen might heartfully burst Pierre's open, if by that he at all believed, that permanent success would crown the fray.

Besides, Pierre knew this;—that so invincible is the natural, untamable, latent spirit of a courageous manliness in man, that though now socially educated for thousands of years in an arbitrary homage to the Law, as the one only appointed redress for every injured person; yet immemorially and universally, among all gentlemen of spirit, once to have uttered independent personal threats of personal vengeance against your foe, and then, after that, to fall back slinking into a court, and hire with sops a pack of yelping pettifoggers to fight the battle so valiantly proclaimed; this, on the surface, is ever deemed very decorous, and very prudent—a most wise second thought; but, at bottom, a miserably ignoble thing. Frederic was not the watery man for that,—Glen had more grapey blood in him.

Moreover, it seemed quite clear to Pierre, that only by making out Lucy absolutely mad, and striving to prove it by a thousand despicable little particulars, could the law succeed in tearing her from the refuge she had voluntarily sought; a course equally abhorrent to all the parties possibly to be concerned on either side.

What then would those two boiling bloods do? Perhaps they would patrol the streets; and at the first glimpse of lonely Lucy, kidnap her home. Or, if Pierre were with her, then, smite him down by hook or crook, fair play or foul; and then, away with Lucy! Or if Lucy systematically kept her room, then fall on Pierre in the most public way, fell him, and cover him from all decent recognition beneath heaps on heaps of hate and insult; so that broken on the wheel of such dishonor, Pierre might feel himself unstrung, and basely yield the prize.

Not the gibbering of ghosts in any old haunted house; no sulphurous and portentous sign at night beheld in heaven, will so make the hair to stand, as when a proud and honorable man is revolving in his soul the possibilities of some gross public and corporeal disgrace. It is not fear; it is a pridehorror, which is more terrible than any fear. Then, by tremendous imagery, the murderer's mark of Cain is felt burning on the brow, and the already acquitted knife blood-rusts in the clutch of the anticipating hand.

Certain that those two youths must be plotting something furious against him; with the echoes of their scorning curses on the stairs still ringing in his ears—curses, whose swift responses from himself, he, at the time, had had much ado to check;—thoroughly alive to the supernaturalism of that mad frothing hate which a spirited brother forks forth at the insulter of a sister's honor—beyond doubt the most uncompromising of all the social passions known to man—and not blind to the anomalous fact, that if such a brother stab his foe at his own mother's table, all people and all juries would bear him out, accounting every thing allowable to a noble soul made mad by a sweet sister's shame caused by a damned seducer;—imagining to himself his own feelings, if he were actually in the position which Frederic so vividly fancied to be his; remembering that in love matters jealousy is as an adder, and that the jealousy of Glen was double-addered by the extraordinary malice of the apparent circumstances under which Lucy had spurned Glen's arms, and fled to his always successful and now married rival, as if wantonly and shamelessly to nestle there;—remembering all these intense incitements of both those foes of his, Pierre could not but look forward to wild work very soon to come. Nor was the storm of passion in his soul unratified by the decision of his coolest possible hour. Storm and calm both said to him,—Look to thyself, oh Pierre!

Murders are done by maniacs; but the earnest thoughts of murder, these are the collected desperadoes. Pierre was such; fate, or what you will, had made him such. But such he was. And when these things now swam before him; when he thought of all the ambiguities which hemmed him in; the stony walls all round that he could not overleap; the million aggravations of his most malicious lot; the last lingering hope of happiness licked up from him as by flames of fire, and his one only prospect a black, bottomless gulf of guilt, upon whose verge he imminently teetered every hour;—then the utmost hate of Glen and Frederic were jubilantly welcome to him; and murder, done in the act of warding off their ignominious public blow, seemed the one only congenial sequel to such a desperate career.

iii

As a statue, planted on a revolving pedestal, shows now this limb, now that; now front, now back, now side; continually changing, too, its general profile; so does the pivoted, statued soul of man, when turned by the hand of Truth. Lies only never vary; look for no invariableness in Pierre. Nor does any canting showman here stand by to announce his phases as he revolves. Catch his phases as your insight may.

Another day passed on; Glen and Frederic still absenting themselves, and Pierre and Isabel and Lucy all dwelling together. The domestic presence of Lucy had begun to produce a remarkable effect upon Pierre. Sometimes, to the covertly watchful eye of Isabel, he would seem to look upon Lucy with an expression illy befitting their singular and so-supposed merely cousinly relation; and yet again, with another expression still more unaccountable to her,—one of fear and awe, not unmixed with impatience. But his general detailed manner toward Lucy was that of the most delicate and affectionate considerateness—nothing more. He was never alone with her; though, as before, at times alone with Isabel.

Lucy seemed entirely undesirous of usurping any place about him; manifested no slightest unwelcome curiosity as to Pierre, and no painful embarrassment as to Isabel. Nevertheless, more and more did she seem, hour by hour, to be somehow inexplicably sliding between them, without touching them. Pierre felt that some strange heavenly influence was near him, to keep him from some uttermost harm; Isabel was alive to some untraceable displacing agency. Though when all three were together, the marvelous serenity, and sweetness, and utter unsuspectingness of Lucy obviated any thing like a common embarrassment: yet if there was any embarrassment at all beneath that roof, it was sometimes when Pierre was alone with Isabel, after Lucy would innocently quit them.

Meantime Pierre was still going on with his book; every moment becoming still the more sensible of the intensely inauspicious circumstances of all sorts under which that labor was proceeding. And as the now advancing and concentring enterprise demanded more and more compacted vigor from him, he felt that he was having less and less to bring to it. For not only was it the signal misery of Pierre, to be invisibly—though but accidentally—goaded, in the hour of mental immaturity, to the attempt at a mature work,—a circumstance sufficiently lamentable in itself; but also, in the hour of his clamorous pennilessness, he was additionally goaded into an enterprise long and protracted in the execution, and of all things least calculated for pecuniary profit in the end. How these things were so, whence they originated, might be thoroughly and very beneficially explained; but space and time here forbid.

At length, domestic matters—rent and bread—had come to such a pass with him, that whether or no, the first pages must go to the printer; and thus was added still another tribulation; because the printed pages now dictated to the following manuscript, and said to all subsequent thoughts and inventions of Pierre—*Thus and thus; so and so; else an ill match*. Therefore, was his book already limited, bound over, and committed to imperfection, even before it had come to any confirmed form or conclusion at all. Oh, who shall reveal the horrors of poverty in authorship that is high? While the silly Millthorpe was railing against his delay of a few weeks and months; how bitterly did unreplying Pierre feel in his heart, that to most of the great works of humanity, their authors had given, not weeks and months, not years and years, but their wholly surrendered and dedicated lives. On either hand clung to by a girl who would have laid down her life for him; Pierre, nevertheless, in his deepest, highest part, was utterly without sympathy from any thing divine, human, brute, or vegetable. One in a city of hundreds of thousands of human beings, Pierre was solitary as at the Pole.

And the great woe of all was this: that all these things were unsuspected without, and undivulgible from within; the very daggers that stabbed him were joked at by Imbecility, Ignorance, Blockheadedness, Self-Complacency, and the universal Blearedness and Besottedness around him. Now he began to feel that in him, the thews of a Titan were forestallingly cut by the scissors of Fate. He felt as a moose, hamstrung. All things that think, or move, or lie still, seemed as created to mock and torment him. He seemed gifted with loftiness, merely that it might be dragged down to the mud. Still, the profound willfulness in him would not give up. Against the breaking heart, and the bursting head; against all the dismal lassitude, and deathful faintness and sleeplessness, and whirlingness, and craziness, still he like a demigod bore up. His soul's ship foresaw the inevitable rocks, but resolved to sail on, and make a courageous wreck. Now he gave jeer for jeer, and taunted the apes that jibed him. With the soul of an Atheist, he wrote down the godliest things; with the feeling of misery and death in him, he created forms of gladness and life. For the pangs in his heart, he put down hoots on the paper. And every thing else he disguised under the so conveniently adjustable drapery of all-stretchable Philosophy. For the more and the more that he wrote, and the deeper and the deeper that he dived, Pierre saw the everlasting elusiveness of Truth; the universal lurking insincerity of even the greatest and purest written thoughts. Like knavish cards, the leaves of all great books were covertly packed. He was but packing one set the more; and that a very poor jaded set and pack indeed. So that there was nothing he more spurned, than his own aspirations; nothing he more abhorred than the loftiest part of himself. The brightest success, now seemed intolerable to him, since he so plainly saw, that the brightest success could not be the sole offspring of Merit; but of Merit for the one thousandth part, and nine hundred and ninety-nine combining and dovetailing accidents for the rest. So beforehand he despised those laurels which in the very nature of things, can never be impartially bestowed. But while thus all the earth was de-

populated of ambition for him; still circumstances had put
him in the attitude of an eager contender for renown. So
beforehand he felt the unrevealable sting of receiving either
plaudits or censures, equally unsought for, and equally
loathed ere given. So, beforehand he felt the pyramidical
scorn of the genuine loftiness for the whole infinite company of infinitesimal critics. His was the scorn which thinks
it not worth the while to be scornful. Those he most
scorned, never knew it. In that lonely little closet of his,
Pierre foretasted all that this world hath either of praise or
dispraise; and thus foretasting both goblets, anticipatingly
hurled them both in its teeth. All panegyric, all denuncia-
tion, all criticism of any sort, would come too late for
Pierre.

But man does never give himself up thus, a doorless and
shutterless house for the four loosened winds of heaven to
howl through, without still additional dilapidations. Much oftener than before, Pierre laid back in his chair with the deadly
feeling of faintness. Much oftener than before, came staggering home from his evening walk, and from sheer bodily exhaustion economized the breath that answered the anxious
inquiries as to what might be done for him. And as if all the
leagued spiritual inveteracies and malices, combined with his
general bodily exhaustion, were not enough, a special corporeal affliction now descended like a sky-hawk upon him. His
incessant application told upon his eyes. They became so affected, that some days he wrote with the lids nearly closed,
fearful of opening them wide to the light. Through the lashes
he peered upon the paper, which so seemed fretted with
wires. Sometimes he blindly wrote with his eyes turned away
from the paper;—thus unconsciously symbolizing the hostile
necessity and distaste, the former whereof made of him this
most unwilling states-prisoner of letters.

As every evening, after his day's writing was done, the
proofs of the beginning of his work came home for correction, Isabel would read them to him. They were replete with
errors; but preoccupied by the thronging, and undiluted,
pure imaginings of things, he became impatient of such minute, gnat-like torments; he randomly corrected the worst,

and let the rest go; jeering with himself at the rich harvest thus furnished to the entomological critics.

But at last he received a tremendous interior intimation, to hold off—to be still from his unnatural struggle.

In the earlier progress of his book, he had found some relief in making his regular evening walk through the greatest thoroughfare of the city; that so, the utter isolation of his soul, might feel itself the more intensely from the incessant jogglings of his body against the bodies of the hurrying thousands. Then he began to be sensible of more fancying stormy nights, than pleasant ones; for then, the great thoroughfares were less thronged, and the innumerable shop-awnings flapped and beat like schooners' broad sails in a gale, and the shutters banged like lashed bulwarks; and the slates fell hurtling like displaced ship's blocks from aloft. Stemming such tempests through the deserted streets, Pierre felt a dark, triumphant joy; that while others had crawled in fear to their kennels, he alone defied the storm-admiral, whose most vindictive peltings of hail-stones,—striking his iron-framed fiery furnace of a body,—melted into soft dew, and so, harmlessly trickled from off him.

By-and-by, of such howling, pelting nights, he began to bend his steps down the dark, narrow side-streets, in quest of the more secluded and mysterious tap-rooms. There he would feel a singular satisfaction, in sitting down all dripping in a chair, ordering his half-pint of ale before him, and drawing over his cap to protect his eyes from the light, eye the varied faces of the social castaways, who here had their haunts from the bitterest midnights.

But at last he began to feel a distaste for even these; and now nothing but the utter night-desolation of the obscurest warehousing lanes would content him, or be at all sufferable to him. Among these he had now been accustomed to wind in and out every evening; till one night as he paused a moment previous to turning about for home, a sudden, unwonted, and all-pervading sensation seized him. He knew not where he was; he did not have any ordinary life-feeling at all. He could not see; though instinctively putting his hand to his eyes, he seemed to feel that the lids were open. Then he was sensible of a combined blindness, and vertigo, and staggering; before his eyes a million green meteors danced; he felt his foot tottering upon the curb, he put out his hands, and knew no more for the time. When he came to himself he found that he was lying crosswise in the gutter, dabbled with mud and slime. He raised himself to try if he could stand; but the fit was entirely gone. Immediately he quickened his steps homeward, forbearing to rest or pause at all on the way, lest that rush of blood to his head, consequent upon his sudden cessation from walking, should again smite him down. This circumstance warned him away from those desolate streets, lest the repetition of the fit should leave him there to perish by night in unknown and unsuspected loneliness. But if that terrible vertigo had been also intended for another and deeper warning, he regarded such added warning not at all; but again plied heart and brain as before.

But now at last since the very blood in his body had in vain rebelled against his Titanic soul; now the only visible outward symbols of that soul—his eyes—did also turn downright traitors to him, and with more success than the rebellious blood. He had abused them so recklessly, that now they absolutely refused to look on paper. He turned them on paper, and they blinked and shut. The pupils of his eyes rolled away from him in their own orbits. He put his hand up to them, and sat back in his seat. Then, without saying one word, he continued there for his usual term, suspended, motionless, blank.

But next morning—it was some few days after the arrival of Lucy—still feeling that a certain downright infatuation, and no less, is both unavoidable and indispensable in the composition of any great, deep book, or even any wholly unsuccessful attempt at any great, deep book; next morning he returned to the charge. But again the pupils of his eyes rolled away from him in their orbits: and now a general and nameless torpor—some horrible foretaste of death itself—seemed stealing upon him.

iv

During this state of semi-unconsciousness, or rather trance, a remarkable dream or vision came to him. The actual artifi-

cial objects around him slid from him, and were replaced by
a baseless yet most imposing spectacle of natural scenery. But
though a baseless vision in itself, this airy spectacle assumed
very familiar features to Pierre. It was the phantasmagoria of
the Mount of the Titans, a singular height standing quite detached in a wide solitude not far from the grand range of dark
blue hills encircling his ancestral manor.

Say what some poets will, Nature is not so much her own
ever-sweet interpreter, as the mere supplier of that cunning
alphabet, whereby selecting and combining as he pleases, each
man reads his own peculiar lesson according to his own
peculiar mind and mood. Thus a high-aspiring, but most
moody, disappointed bard, chancing once to visit the Meadows and beholding that fine eminence, christened it by the
name it ever after bore; completely extinguishing its former
title—The Delectable Mountain—one long ago bestowed by
an old Baptist farmer, an hereditary admirer of Bunyan and
his most marvelous book. From the spell of that name the
mountain never afterward escaped; for now, gazing upon it
by the light of those suggestive syllables, no poetical observer
could resist the apparent felicity of the title. For as if indeed
the immemorial mount would fain adapt itself to its so recent
name, some people said that it had insensibly changed its pervading aspect within a score or two of winters. Nor was this
strange conceit entirely without foundation, seeing that the
annual displacements of huge rocks and gigantic trees were
continually modifying its whole front and general contour.

On the north side, where it fronted the old Manor-house,
some fifteen miles distant, the height, viewed from the piazza
of a soft haze-canopied summer's noon, presented a long and
beautiful, but not entirely inaccessible-looking purple precipice, some two thousand feet in air, and on each hand sideways sloping down to lofty terraces of pastures.

Those hill-side pastures, be it said, were thickly sown with
a small white amaranthine flower, which, being irreconcilably
distasteful to the cattle, and wholly rejected by them, and yet,
continually multiplying on every hand, did by no means contribute to the agricultural value of those elevated lands. Insomuch, that for this cause, the disheartened dairy tenants of

that part of the Manor, had petitioned their lady-landlord for some abatement in their annual tribute of upland grasses, in the Juny-load; rolls of butter in the October crock; and steers and heifers on the October hoof; with turkeys in the Christmas sleigh.

"The small white flower, it is our bane!" the imploring tenants cried. "The aspiring amaranth, every year it climbs and adds new terraces to its sway! The immortal amaranth, it will not die, but last year's flowers survive to this! The terraced pastures grow glittering white, and in warm June still show like banks of snow:—fit token of the sterileness the amaranth begets! Then free us from the amaranth, good lady, or be pleased to abate our rent!"

Now, on a somewhat nearer approach, the precipice did not belie its purple promise from the manorial piazza;—that sweet imposing purple promise, which seemed fully to vindicate the Bunyanish old title originally bestowed;—but showed the profuse aërial foliage of a hanging forest. Nevertheless, coming still more nigh, long and frequent rents among the mass of leaves revealed horrible glimpses of dark-dripping rocks, and mysterious mouths of wolfish caves. Struck by this most unanticipated view, the tourist now quickened his impulsive steps to verify the change by coming into direct contact with so chameleon a height. As he would now speed on, the lower ground, which from the manor-house piazza seemed all a grassy level, suddenly merged into a very long and weary acclivity, slowly rising close up to the precipice's base; so that the efflorescent grasses rippled against it, as the efflorescent waves of some great swell or long rolling billow ripple against the water-line of a steep gigantic warship on the sea. And, as among the rolling sea-like sands of Egypt, disordered rows of broken Sphinxes lead to the Cheopian pyramid itself; so this long acclivity was thickly strewn with enormous rocky masses, grotesque in shape, and with wonderful features on them, which seemed to express that slumbering intelligence visible in some recumbent beasts—beasts whose intelligence seems struck dumb in them by some sorrowful and inexplicable spell. Nevertheless, round and round those still enchanted rocks, hard by their utmost rims, and in among their cunning crevices, the misanthropic hill-

scaling goat nibbled his sweetest food; for the rocks, so barren in themselves, distilled a subtile moisture, which fed with
greenness all things that grew about their igneous marge.

Quitting those recumbent rocks, you still ascended toward
the hanging forest, and piercing within its lowermost fringe,
then suddenly you stood transfixed, as a marching soldier
confounded at the sight of an impregnable redoubt, where he
had fancied it a practicable vault to his courageous thews.
Cunningly masked hitherto, by the green tapestry of the in-
terlacing leaves, a terrific towering palisade of dark mossy
massiness confronted you; and, trickling with unevaporable
moisture, distilled upon you from its beetling brow slow
thunder-showers of water-drops, chill as the last dews of
death. Now you stood and shivered in that twilight, though
it were high noon and burning August down the meads. All
round and round, the grim scarred rocks rallied and re-rallied
themselves; shot up, protruded, stretched, swelled, and eagerly reached forth; on every side bristlingly radiating with a
hideous repellingness. Tossed, and piled, and indiscriminate
among these, like bridging rifts of logs up-jammed in alluvial-
rushing streams of far Arkansas: or, like great masts and yards
of overwhelmed fleets hurled high and dashed amain, all
splintering together, on hovering ridges of the Atlantic sea,—
you saw the melancholy trophies which the North Wind,
championing the unquenchable quarrel of the Winter, had
wrested from the forests, and dismembered them on their
own chosen battle-ground, in barbarous disdain. 'Mid this
spectacle of wide and wanton spoil, insular noises of falling
rocks would boomingly explode upon the silence and fright
all the echoes, which ran shrieking in and out among the
caves, as wailing women and children in some assaulted town.

Stark desolation; ruin, merciless and ceaseless; chills and
gloom,—all here lived a hidden life, curtained by that cunning purpleness, which, from the piazza of the manor house,
so beautifully invested the mountain once called Delectable,
but now styled Titanic.

Beaten off by such undreamed-of glooms and steeps, you
now sadly retraced your steps, and, mayhap, went skirting the
inferior sideway terraces of pastures; where the multiple and
most sterile inodorous immortalness of the small, white

flower furnished no ailment for the mild cow's meditative cud. But here and there you still might smell from far the sweet aromaticness of clumps of catnip, that dear farm-house herb. Soon you would see the modest verdure of the plant itself; and wheresoever you saw that sight, old foundation stones and rotting timbers of log-houses long extinct would also meet your eye; their desolation illy hid by the green solicitudes of the unemigrating herb. Most fitly named the catnip; since, like the unrunagate cat, though all that's human forsake the place, that plant will long abide, long bask and bloom on the abandoned hearth. Illy hid; for every spring the amaranthine and celestial flower gained on the mortal household herb; for every autumn the catnip died, but never an autumn made the amaranth to wane. The catnip and the amaranth!—man's earthly household peace, and the ever-encroaching appetite for God.

No more now you sideways followed the sad pasture's skirt, but took your way adown the long declivity, fronting the mystic height. In mid field again you paused among the recumbent sphinx-like shapes thrown off from the rocky steep. You paused; fixed by a form defiant, a form of awfulness. You saw Enceladus the Titan, the most potent of all the giants, writhing from out the imprisoning earth;—turbaned with upborne moss he writhed; still, though armless, resisting with his whole striving trunk, the Pelion and the Ossa hurled back at him;—turbaned with upborne moss he writhed; still turning his unconquerable front toward that majestic mount eternally in vain assailed by him, and which, when it had stormed him off, had heaved his undoffable incubus upon him, and deridingly left him there to bay out his ineffectual howl.

To Pierre this wondrous shape had always been a thing of interest, though hitherto all its latent significance had never fully and intelligibly smitten him. In his earlier boyhood a strolling company of young collegian pedestrians had chanced to light upon the rock; and, struck with its remarkableness, had brought a score of picks and spades, and dug round it to unearth it, and find whether indeed it were a demoniac freak of nature, or some stern thing of antediluvian art. Accompanying this eager party, Pierre first beheld that deathless son of Terra. At that time, in its untouched natural state, the statue presented nothing but the turbaned head of igneous rock rising from out the soil, with its unabasable face turned upward toward the mountain, and the bull-like neck clearly defined. With distorted features, scarred and broken, and a black brow mocked by the upborne moss, Enceladus there subterraneously stood, fast frozen into the earth at the junction of the neck. Spades and picks soon heaved part of his Ossa from him, till at last a circular well was opened round him to the depth of some thirteen feet. At that point the wearied young collegians gave over their enterprise in despair. With all their toil, they had not yet come to the girdle of Enceladus. But they had bared good part of his mighty chest, and exposed his mutilated shoulders, and the stumps of his once audacious arms. Thus far uncovering his shame, in that cruel plight they had abandoned him, leaving stark naked his in vain indignant chest to the defilements of the birds, which for untold ages had cast their foulness on his vanquished crest.

Not unworthy to be compared with that leaden Titan, wherewith the art of Marsy and the broad-flung pride of Bourbon enriched the enchanted gardens of Versailles;—and from whose still twisted mouth for sixty feet the waters yet upgush, in elemental rivalry with those Etna flames, of old asserted to be the malicious breath of the borne-down giant;—not unworthy to be compared with that leaden demigod—piled with costly rocks, and with one bent wrenching knee protruding from the broken bronze;—not unworthy to be compared with that bold trophy of high art, this American Enceladus, wrought by the vigorous hand of Nature's self, it did go further than compare;—it did far surpass that fine figure molded by the inferior skill of man. Marsy gave arms to the eternally defenseless; but Nature, more truthful, performed an amputation, and left the impotent Titan without one serviceable ball-and-socket above the thigh.

Such was the wild scenery—the Mount of Titans, and the repulsed group of heaven-assaulters, with Enceladus in their midst shamefully recumbent at its base;—such was the wild scenery, which now to Pierre, in his strange vision, displaced the four blank walls, the desk, and camp-bed, and domineered upon his trance. But no longer petrified in all their ignominious attitudes, the herded Titans now sprung to their feet;

flung themselves up the slope; and anew battered at the precipice's unresounding wall. Foremost among them all, he saw
a moss-turbaned, armless giant, who despairing of any other
mode of wreaking his immitigable hate, turned his vast trunk
into a battering-ram, and hurled his own arched-out ribs
again and yet again against the invulnerable steep.

"Enceladus! it is Enceladus!"—Pierre cried out in his sleep.
That moment the phantom faced him; and Pierre saw Enceladus no more; but on the Titan's armless trunk, his own
duplicate face and features magnifiedly gleamed upon him
with prophetic discomfiture and woe. With trembling frame
he started from his chair, and woke from that ideal horror to
all his actual grief.

V

Nor did Pierre's random knowledge of the ancient fables
fail still further to elucidate the vision which so strangely had
supplied a tongue to muteness. But that elucidation was most
repulsively fateful and foreboding; possibly because Pierre did
not leap the final barrier of gloom; possibly because Pierre
did not willfully wrest some final comfort from the fable;
did not flog this stubborn rock as Moses his, and force even
aridity itself to quench his painful thirst.

Thus smitten, the Mount of Titans seems to yield this following stream:—

Old Titan's self was the son of incestuous Cœlus and Terra,
the son of incestuous Heaven and Earth. And Titan married
his mother Terra, another and accumulatively incestuous
match. And thereof Enceladus was one issue. So Enceladus
was both the son and grandson of an incest; and even thus,
there had been born from the organic blended heavenliness
and earthliness of Pierre, another mixed, uncertain, heaven-
aspiring, but still not wholly earth-emancipated mood; which
again, by its terrestrial taint held down to its terrestrial
mother, generated there the present doubly incestuous Enceladus within him; so that the present mood of Pierre—that
reckless sky-assaulting mood of his, was nevertheless on one
side the grandson of the sky. For it is according to eternal
fitness, that the precipitated Titan should still seek to regain

paternal birthright even by fierce escalade. Wherefore whoso storms the sky gives best proof he came from thither! But whatso crawls contented in the moat before that crystal fort, shows it was born within that slime, and there forever will abide.

Recovered somewhat from the after-spell of this wild vision fixed in his trance, Pierre composed his front as best he might, and straightway left his fatal closet. Concentrating all the remaining stuff in him, he resolved by an entire and violent change, and by a willful act against his own most habitual imaginations, to wrestle with the strange malady of his eyes, this new death-fiend of the trance, and this Inferno of his Titanic vision.

And now, just as he crossed the threshold of the closet, he wishingly strove to assume an expression intended to be not uncheerful—though how indeed his countenance at all looked, he could not tell; for dreading some insupportably dark revealments in his glass, he had of late wholly abstained from appealing to it—and in his mind he rapidly conned over, what indifferent, disguising, or light-hearted gamesome things he should say, when proposing to his companions the little design he cherished.

And even so, to grim Enceladus, the world the gods had ordained for a ball to drag at his o'erfreighted feet;—even so that globe put forth a thousand flowers, whose fragile smiles disguised his ponderous load.

Book XXVI

A Walk: a Foreign Portrait: a Sail: and the End

COME, ISABEL, come, Lucy; we have not had a single walk together yet. It is cold, but clear; and once out of the city, we shall find it sunny. Come: get ready now, and away for a stroll down to the wharf, and then for some of the steamers on the bay. No doubt, Lucy, you will find in the bay scenery some hints for that secret sketch you are so busily occupied with—ere real living sitters do come—and which you so devotedly work at, all alone and behind closed doors."

Upon this, Lucy's original look of pale-rippling pleasantness and surprise—evoked by Pierre's unforeseen proposition to give himself some relaxation—changed into one of infinite, mute, but unrenderable meaning, while her swimming eyes gently, yet all-bewildered, fell to the floor.

"It is finished, then," cried Isabel,—not unmindful of this by-scene, and passionately stepping forward so as to intercept Pierre's momentary rapt glance at the agitated Lucy,—"That vile book, it is finished!—Thank Heaven!"

"Not so," said Pierre; and, displacing all disguisements, a hectic unsummoned expression suddenly came to his face;— "but ere that vile book be finished, I must get on some other element than earth. I have sat on earth's saddle till I am weary; I must now vault over to the other saddle awhile. Oh, seems to me, there should be two ceaseless steeds for a bold man to ride,—the Land and the Sea; and like circus-men we should never dismount, but only be steadied and rested by leaping from one to the other, while still, side by side, they both race round the sun. I have been on the Land steed so long, oh I am dizzy!"

"Thou wilt never listen to me, Pierre," said Lucy lowly; "there is no need of this incessant straining. See, Isabel and I have both offered to be thy amanuenses;—not in mere copying, but in the original writing; I am sure that would greatly assist thee."

"Impossible! I fight a duel in which all seconds are forbid."

"Ah Pierre! Pierre!" cried Lucy, dropping the shawl in her hand, and gazing at him with unspeakable longings of some unfathomable emotion.

Namelessly glancing at Lucy, Isabel slid near to him, seized his hand and spoke.

"I would go blind for thee, Pierre; here, take out these eyes, and use them for glasses." So saying, she looked with a strange momentary haughtiness and defiance at Lucy.

A general half involuntary movement was now made, as if they were about to depart.

"Ye are ready; go ye before"—said Lucy meekly; "I will follow."

"Nay, one on each arm"—said Pierre—"come!"

As they passed through the low arched vestibule into the street, a cheek-burnt, gamesome sailor passing, exclaimed—"Steer small, my lad; 'tis a narrow strait thou art in!"

"What says he?"—said Lucy gently. "Yes, it is a narrow strait of a street indeed."

But Pierre felt a sudden tremble transferred to him from Isabel who whispered something inarticulate in his ear.

Gaining one of the thoroughfares, they drew near to a conspicuous placard over a door, announcing that above stairs was a gallery of paintings, recently imported from Europe, and now on free exhibition preparatory to their sale by auction. Though this encounter had been entirely unforeseen by Pierre, yet yielding to the sudden impulse, he at once proposed their visiting the pictures. The girls assented, and they ascended the stairs.

In the anteroom, a catalogue was put into his hand. He paused to give one hurried, comprehensive glance at it. Among long columns of such names as Rubens, Raphael, Angelo, Domenichino, Da Vinci, all shamelessly prefaced with the words "undoubted," or "testified," Pierre met the following brief line:—"*No. 99. A stranger's head, by an unknown hand.*"

It seemed plain that the whole must be a collection of those wretched imported daubs, which with the incredible effrontery peculiar to some of the foreign picture-dealers in America, are christened by the loftiest names known to Art. But as the most mutilated torsoes of the perfections of antiquity

are not unworthy the student's attention, neither are the most
bungling modern incompletenesses: for both are torsoes; one
of perished perfections in the past; the other, by anticipation,
of yet unfulfilled perfections in the future. Still, as Pierre
walked along by the thickly hung walls, and seemed to detect
the infatuated vanity which must have prompted many of
these utterly unknown artists in the attempted execution by
feeble hand of vigorous themes; he could not repress the most
melancholy foreboding concerning himself. All the walls of
the world seemed thickly hung with the empty and impotent
scope of pictures, grandly outlined, but miserably filled. The
smaller and humbler pictures, representing little familiar
things, were by far the best executed; but these, though
touching him not unpleasingly, in one restricted sense, awoke
no dormant majesties in his soul, and therefore, upon the
whole, were contemptibly inadequate and unsatisfactory.

At last Pierre and Isabel came to that painting of which
Pierre was capriciously in search—No. 99.

"My God! see! see!" cried Isabel, under strong excitement,
"only my mirror has ever shown me that look before! See!
see!"

By some mere hocus-pocus of chance, or subtly designing
knavery, a real Italian gem of art had found its way into this
most hybrid collection of impostures.

No one who has passed through the great galleries of Europe, unbewildered by their wonderful multitudinousness of
surpassing excellence—a redundancy which neutralizes all
discrimination or individualizing capacity in most ordinary
minds—no calm, penetrative person can have victoriously
run that painted gauntlet of the gods, without certain very
special emotions, called forth by some one or more individual
paintings, to which, however, both the catalogues and the
criticisms of the greatest connoisseurs deny any all-transcend-
ing merit, at all answering to the effect thus casually produced. There is no time now to show fully how this is; suffice
it, that in such instances, it is not the abstract excellence always, but often the accidental congeniality, which occasions
this wonderful emotion. Still, the individual himself is apt to
impute it to a different cause; hence, the headlong enthusiastic admiration of some one or two men for things not at all

praised by—or at most, which are indifferent to—the rest of the world—a matter so often considered inexplicable.

But in this Stranger's Head by the Unknown Hand, the abstract general excellence united with the all-surprising, accidental congeniality in producing an accumulated impression of power upon both Pierre and Isabel. Nor was the strangeness of this at all impaired by the apparent uninterestedness of Lucy concerning that very picture. Indeed, Lucy—who, owing to the occasional jolting of the crowd, had loosened her arm from Pierre's, and so, gradually, had gone on along the pictured hall in advance—Lucy had thus passed the strange painting, without the least special pause, and had now wandered round to the precisely opposite side of the hall; where, at this present time, she was standing motionless before a very tolerable copy (the only other good thing in the collection) of that sweetest, most touching, but most awful of all feminine heads—The Cenci of Guido. The wonderfulness of which head consists chiefly, perhaps, in a striking, suggested contrast, half-identical with, and half-analogous to, that almost supernatural one—sometimes visible in the maidens of tropical nations—namely, soft and light blue eyes, with an extremely fair complexion, vailed by funereally jetty hair. But with blue eyes and fair complexion, the Cenci's hair is golden—physically, therefore, all is in strict, natural keeping; which, nevertheless, still the more intensifies the suggested fanciful anomaly of so sweetly and seraphically *blonde* a being, being double-hooded, as it were, by the black crape of the two most horrible crimes (of one of which she is the object, and of the other the agent) possible to civilized humanity—incest and parricide.

Now, this Cenci and "the Stranger" were hung at a good elevation in one of the upper tiers; and, from the opposite walls, exactly faced each other; so that in secret they seemed pantomimically talking over and across the heads of the living spectators below.

With the aspect of the Cenci every one is familiar. "The Stranger" was a dark, comely, youthful man's head, portentously looking out of a dark, shaded ground, and ambiguously smiling. There was no discoverable drapery; the dark head, with its crisp, curly, jetty hair, seemed just disentangling itself from out of curtains and clouds. But to Isabel, in the eye and on the brow, were certain shadowy traces of her own unmistakable likeness; while to Pierre, this face was in part as the resurrection of the one he had burnt at the Inn. Not that the separate features were the same; but the pervading look of it, the subtler interior keeping of the entirety, was almost identical; still, for all this, there was an unequivocal aspect of foreignness, of Europeanism, about both the face itself and the general painting.

"Is it? Is it? Can it be?" whispered Isabel, intensely.

Now, Isabel knew nothing of the painting which Pierre had destroyed. But she solely referred to the living being who—under the designation of her father—had visited her at the cheerful house to which she had been removed during childhood from the large and unnamable one by the pleasant woman in the coach. Without doubt—though indeed she might not have been at all conscious of it in her own mystic mind—she must have somehow vaguely fancied, that this being had always through life worn the same aspect to every body else which he had to her, for so very brief an interval of his possible existence. Solely knowing him—or dreaming of him, it may have been—under that one aspect, she could not conceive of him under any other. Whether or not these considerations touching Isabel's ideas occurred to Pierre at this moment is very improbable. At any rate, he said nothing to her, either to deceive or undeceive, either to enlighten or obscure. For, indeed, he was too much riveted by his own far-interior emotions to analyze now the cotemporary ones of Isabel. So that there here came to pass a not unremarkable thing: for though both were intensely excited by one object, yet their two minds and memories were thereby directed to entirely different contemplations; while still each, for the time—however unreasonably—might have vaguely supposed the other occupied by one and the same contemplation. Pierre was thinking of the chair-portrait: Isabel, of the living face. Yet Isabel's fervid exclamations having reference to the living face, were now, as it were, mechanically responded to by Pierre, in syllables having reference to the chair-portrait. Nevertheless, so subtile and spontaneous was it all, that neither perhaps ever afterward discovered this contradiction; for, events whirled them so rapidly and peremptorily after this, that they had no time for those calm retrospective reveries indispensable perhaps to such a discovery.

"Is it? is it? can it be?" was the intense whisper of Isabel.

"No, it can not be, it is not," replied Pierre; "one of the wonderful coincidences, nothing more."

"Oh, by that word, Pierre, we but vainly seek to explain the inexplicable. Tell me: it is! it must be! it is wonderful!"

"Let us begone; and let us keep eternal silence," said Pierre, quickly; and, seeking Lucy, they abruptly left the place; as before, Pierre, seemingly unwilling to be accosted by any one he knew, or who knew his companions, unconsciously accelerating their steps while forced for a space to tread the thoroughfares.

ii

As they hurried on, Pierre was silent; but wild thoughts were hurrying and shouting in his heart. The most tremendous displacing and revolutionizing thoughts were upheaving in him, with reference to Isabel; nor—though at the time he was hardly conscious of such a thing—were these thoughts wholly unwelcome to him.

How did he know that Isabel was his sister? Setting aside Aunt Dorothea's nebulous legend, to which, in some shadowy points, here and there Isabel's still more nebulous story seemed to fit on,—though but uncertainly enough—and both of which thus blurredly conjoining narrations, regarded in the unscrupulous light of real naked reason, were any thing but legitimately conclusive; and setting aside his own dim reminiscences of his wandering father's death-bed; (for though, in one point of view, those reminiscences might have afforded some degree of presumption as to his father's having been the parent of an unacknowledged daughter, yet were they entirely inconclusive as to that presumed daughter's identity; and the grand point now with Pierre was, not the general question whether his father had had a daughter, but whether, assuming that he had had, *Isabel*, rather than any other living being, *was that daughter*;)—and setting aside all his own manifold and inter-enfolding mystic and transcendental persuasions,—originally born, as he now seemed to feel, purely of an intense procreative enthusiasm:—an enthusiasm no longer so all-potential with him as of yore; setting all these aside, and coming to the plain, palpable facts,—how did he *know* that Isabel was his sister? Nothing that he saw in her face could he remember as having seen in his father's. The chair-portrait, *that* was the entire sum and substance of all possible, rakable, downright presumptive evidence, which peculiarly appealed to his own separate self. Yet here was another portrait of a complete stranger—a European; a portrait imported from across the seas, and to be sold at public auction, which was just as strong an evidence as the other. Then, the original of this second portrait was as much the father of Isabel as the original of the chair-portrait. But perhaps there was no original at all to this second portrait; it might have been a pure fancy piece; to which conceit, indeed, the uncharacterizing style of the filling-up seemed to furnish no small testimony.

With such bewildering meditations as these in him, running up like clasping waves upon the strand of the most latent secrecies of his soul, and with both Isabel and Lucy bodily touching his sides as he walked; the feelings of Pierre were entirely untranslatable into any words that can be used.

Of late to Pierre, much more vividly than ever before, the whole story of Isabel had seemed an enigma, a mystery, an imaginative delirium; especially since he had got so deep into the inventional mysteries of his book. For he who is most practically and deeply conversant with mysticisms and mysteries; he who professionally deals in mysticisms and mysteries himself; often that man, more than any body else, is disposed to regard such things in others as very deceptively bejuggling; and likewise is apt to be rather materialistic in all his own merely personal notions (as in their practical lives, with priests of Eleusinian religions), and more than any other man, is often inclined, at the bottom of his soul, to be uncompromisingly skeptical on all novel visionary hypotheses of any kind. It is only the no-mystics, or the half-mystics, who, properly speaking, are credulous. So that in Pierre, was presented the apparent anomaly of a mind, which by becoming really profound in itself, grew skeptical of all tendered profundities; whereas, the contrary is generally supposed.

By some strange arts Isabel's wonderful story might have been, some way, and for some cause, forged for her, in her childhood, and craftily impressed upon her youthful mind; which so—like a slight mark in a young tree—had now enlargingly grown with her growth, till it had become this immense staring marvel. Tested by any thing real, practical, and reasonable, what less probable, for instance, than that fancied crossing of the sea in her childhood, when upon Pierre's subsequent questioning of her, she did not even know that the sea was salt.

iii

In the midst of all these mental confusions they arrived at the wharf; and selecting the most inviting of the various boats which lay about them in three or four adjacent ferry-slips, and one which was bound for a half-hour's sail across the wide beauty of that glorious bay; they soon found themselves afloat and in swift gliding motion.

They stood leaning on the rail of the guard, as the sharp craft darted out from among the lofty pine-forests of ships'-masts, and the tangled underbrush and cane-brakes of the dwarfed sticks of sloops and scows. Soon, the spires of stone on the land, blent with the masts of wood on the water; the crotch of the twin-rivers pressed the great wedged city almost out of sight. They swept by two little islets distant from the shore; they wholly curved away from the domes of free-stone and marble, and gained the great sublime dome of the bay's wide-open waters.

Small breeze had been felt in the pent city that day, but the fair breeze of naked nature now blew in their faces. The waves began to gather and roll; and just as they gained a point, where—till beyond—between high promontories of fortresses, the wide bay visibly sluiced into the Atlantic, Isabel convulsively grasped the arm of Pierre and convulsively spoke.

"I feel it! I feel it! It is! It is!"

"What feelest thou?—what is it?"

"The motion! the motion!"

"Dost thou not understand, Pierre?" said Lucy, eying with concern and wonder his pale, staring aspect—"The waves: it is the motion of the waves that Isabel speaks of. Look, they are rolling, direct from the sea now."

Again Pierre lapsed into a still stranger silence and revery.

It was impossible altogether to resist the force of this striking corroboration of by far the most surprising and improbable thing in the whole surprising and improbable story of Isabel. Well did he remember her vague reminiscence of the teetering sea, that did not slope exactly as the floors of the unknown, abandoned, old house among the French-like mountains.

While plunged in these mutually neutralizing thoughts of the strange picture and the last exclamations of Isabel, the boat arrived at its destination—a little hamlet on the beach, not very far from the great blue sluice-way into the ocean, which was now yet more distinctly visible than before.

"Don't let us stop here"—cried Isabel. "Look, let us go through there! Bell must go through there! See! see! out there upon the blue! yonder, yonder! far away—out, out!—far, far away, and away, and away, out there! where the two blues meet, and are nothing—Bell must go!"

"Why, Isabel," murmured Lucy, "that would be to go to far England or France; thou wouldst find but few friends in far France, Isabel."

"Friends in far France? And what friends have I here?—Art thou my friend? In thy secret heart dost *thou* wish me well? And for thee, Pierre, what am I but a vile clog to thee; dragging thee back from all thy felicity? Yes, I will go yonder—yonder; out there! I will, I will! Unhand me! Let me plunge!"

For an instant, Lucy looked incoherently from one to the other. But both she and Pierre now mechanically again seized Isabel's frantic arms, as they were thrown again over the outer rail of the boat. They dragged her back; they spoke to her; they soothed her; but though less vehement, Isabel still looked deeply distrustfully at Lucy, and deeply reproachfully at Pierre.

They did not leave the boat as intended; too glad were they all, when it unloosed from its fastenings, and turned about upon the backward trip.

Stepping to shore, Pierre once more hurried his companions through the unavoidable publicity of the thoroughfares; but less rapidly proceeded, soon as they gained the more secluded streets.

iv

Gaining the Apostles', and leaving his two companions to the privacy of their chambers, Pierre sat silent and intent by the stove in the dining-room for a time, and then was on the point of entering his closet from the corridor, when Delly, suddenly following him, said to him, that she had forgotten to mention it before, but he would find two letters in his room, which had been separately left at the door during the absence of the party.

He passed into the closet, and slowly shooting the bolt—which, for want of something better, happened to be an old blunted dagger—walked, with his cap yet unmoved, slowly up to the table, and beheld the letters. They were lying with their sealed sides up; one in either hand, he lifted them; and held them straight out sideways from him.

"I see not the writing; know not yet, by mine own eye, that they are meant for me; yet, in these hands I feel that I now hold the final poniards that shall stab me; and by stabbing me, make *me* too a most swift stabber in the recoil. Which point first?—this!"

He tore open the left-hand letter:—

"SIR:—You are a swindler. Upon the pretense of writing a popular novel for us, you have been receiving cash advances from us, while passing through our press the sheets of a blasphemous rhapsody, filched from the vile Atheists, Lucian and Voltaire. Our great press of publication has hitherto prevented our slightest inspection of our reader's proofs of your book. Send not another sheet to us. Our bill for printing thus far, and also for our cash advances, swindled out of us by you, is now in the hands of our lawyer, who is instructed to proceed with instant rigor.

(Signed) STEEL, FLINT & ASBESTOS."

He folded the left-hand letter, and put it beneath his left heel, and stood upon it so; and then opened the right-hand letter.

"Thou, Pierre Glendinning, art a villainous and perjured liar. It is the sole object of this letter imprintedly to convey the point blank lie to thee; that taken in at thy heart, it may be thence pulsed with thy blood, throughout thy system. We have let some interval pass inactive, to confirm and solidify our hate. Separately, and together, we brand thee, in thy every lung-cell, a liar;—liar, because that is the scornfullest and loathsomest title for a man; which in itself is the compend of all infamous things.

(Signed) GLENDINNING STANLY,
FREDERIC TARTAN."

He folded the right-hand letter, and put it beneath his right heel; then folding his two arms, stood upon both the letters.

"These are most small circumstances; but happening just now to me, become indices to all immensities. For now am I hate-shod! On these I will skate to my acquittal! No longer do I hold terms with aught. World's bread of life, and world's breath of honor, both are snatched from me; but I defy all world's bread and breath. Here I step out before the drawn-up worlds in widest space, and challenge one and all of them to battle! Oh, Glen! oh, Fred! most fraternally do I leap to your rib-crushing hugs! Oh, how I love ye two, that yet can make me lively hate, in a world which elsewise only merits stagnant scorn!—Now, then, where is this swindler's, this coiner's book? Here, on this vile counter, over which the coiner thought to pass it to the world, here will I nail it fast, for a detected cheat! And thus nailed fast now, do I spit upon it, and so get the start of the wise world's worst abuse of it! Now I go out to meet my fate, walking toward me in the street."

As with hat on, and Glen and Frederic's letter invisibly

crumpled in his hand, he—as it were somnambulously—
passed into the room of Isabel, she gave loose to a thin, long
shriek, at his wondrous white and haggard plight; and then,
without the power to stir toward him, sat petrified in her
chair, as one embalmed and glazed with icy varnish.

He heeded her not, but passed straight on through both
intervening rooms, and without a knock unpremeditatedly
entered Lucy's chamber. He would have passed out of that,
also, into the corridor, without one word; but something
stayed him.

The marble girl sat before her easel; a small box of pointed
charcoal, and some pencils by her side; her painter's wand
held out against the frame; the charcoal-pencil suspended in
two fingers, while with the same hand, holding a crust of
bread, she was lightly brushing the portrait-paper, to efface
some ill-considered stroke. The floor was scattered with the
bread-crumbs and charcoal-dust; he looked behind the easel,
and saw his own portrait, in the skeleton.

At the first glimpse of him, Lucy started not, nor stirred;
but as if her own wand had there enchanted her, sat tranced.

"Dead embers of departed fires lie by thee, thou pale girl;
with dead embers thou seekest to relume the flame of all extinguished love! Waste not so that bread; eat it—in bitterness!"

He turned, and entered the corridor, and then, with outstretched arms, paused between the two outer doors of Isabel
and Lucy.

"For ye two, my most undiluted prayer is now, that from
your here unseen and frozen chairs ye may never stir alive;—
the fool of Truth, the fool of Virtue, the fool of Fate, now
quits ye forever!"

As he now sped down the long winding passage, some one
eagerly hailed him from a stair.

"What, what, my boy? where now in such a squally hurry?
Hallo, I say!"

But without heeding him at all, Pierre drove on. Millthorpe
looked anxiously and alarmedly after him a moment, then
made a movement in pursuit, but paused again.

"There was ever a black vein in this Glendinning; and now
that vein is swelled, as if it were just one peg above a tour-

nequet drawn over-tight. I scarce durst dog him now; yet my
heart misgives me that I should.—Shall I go to his rooms
and ask what black thing this is that hath befallen him?—No;
not yet;—might be thought officious—they say I'm given to
that. I'll wait; something may turn up soon. I'll into the front
street, and saunter some; and then—we'll see."

                                        V

Pierre passed on to a remote quarter of the building, and
abruptly entered the room of one of the Apostles whom he
knew. There was no one in it. He hesitated an instant; then
walked up to a book-case, with a chest of drawers in the
lower part.

"Here I saw him put them:—this,—no—here—ay—we'll
try this."

Wrenching open the locked drawer, a brace of pistols, a
powder flask, a bullet-bag, and a round green box of percus-
sion-caps lay before him.

"Ha! what wondrous tools Prometheus used, who knows?
but more wondrous these, that in an instant, can unmake the
topmost three-score-years-and-ten of all Prometheus' mak-
ings. Come: here's two tubes that'll outroar the thousand
pipes of Harlem.—Is the music in 'em?—No?—Well then,
here's powder for the shrill treble; and wadding for the tenor;
and a lead bullet for the concluding bass! And,—and,—
and,—ay; for the top-wadding, I'll send 'em back their lie,
and plant it scorching in their brains!"

He tore off that part of Glen and Fred's letter, which more
particularly gave the lie; and halving it, rammed it home upon
the bullets.

He thrust a pistol into either breast of his coat; and taking
the rearward passages, went down into the back street; directing his rapid steps toward the grand central thoroughfare
of the city.

It was a cold, but clear, quiet, and slantingly sunny day; it
was between four and five of the afternoon; that hour, when
the great glaring avenue was most thronged with haughty-
rolling carriages, and proud-rustling promenaders, both men
and women. But these last were mostly confined to the one

wide pavement to the West; the other pavement was well nigh deserted, save by porters, waiters, and parcel-carriers of the shops. On the west pave, up and down, for three long miles, two streams of glossy, shawled, or broadcloth life unceasingly brushed by each other, as long, resplendent, drooping trains of rival peacocks brush.

Mixing with neither of these, Pierre stalked midway between. From his wild and fatal aspect, one way the people took the wall, the other way they took the curb. Unentangledly Pierre threaded all their host, though in its inmost heart. Bent he was, on a straightforward, mathematical intent. His eyes were all about him as he went; especially he glanced over to the deserted pavement opposite; for that emptiness did not deceive him; he himself had often walked that side, the better to scan the pouring throng upon the other.

Just as he gained a large, open, triangular space, built round with the stateliest public erections;—the very proscenium of the town;—he saw Glen and Fred advancing, in the distance, on the other side. He continued on; and soon he saw them crossing over to him obliquely, so as to take him face-and-face. He continued on; when suddenly running ahead of Fred, who now chafingly stood still (because Fred would not make two, in the direct personal assault upon one) and shouting "Liar! Villain!" Glen leaped toward Pierre from front, and with such lightning-like ferocity, that the simultaneous blow of his cow-hide smote Pierre across the cheek, and left a half-livid and half-bloody brand.

For that one moment, the people fell back on all sides from them; and left them—momentarily recoiled from each other—in a ring of panics.

But clapping both hands to his two breasts, Pierre, on both sides shaking off the sudden white grasp of two rushing girls, tore out both pistols, and rushed headlong upon Glen.

"For thy one blow, take here two deaths! 'Tis speechless sweet to murder thee!"

Spatterings of his own kindred blood were upon the pavement; his own hand had extinguished his house in slaughtering the only unoutlawed human being by the name of Glendinning;—and Pierre was seized by a hundred contending hands.

vi

That sundown, Pierre stood solitary in a low dungeon of the city prison. The cumbersome stone ceiling almost rested on his brow; so that the long tiers of massive cell-galleries above seemed partly piled on him. His immortal, immovable, bleached cheek was dry; but the stone cheeks of the walls were trickling. The pent twilight of the contracted yard, coming through the barred arrow-slit, fell in dim bars upon the granite floor.

"Here, then, is the untimely, timely end;—Life's last chapter well stitched into the middle! Nor book, nor author of the book, hath any sequel, though each hath its last lettering!—It is ambiguous still. Had I been heartless now, disowned, and spurningly portioned off the girl at Saddle Meadows, then had I been happy through a long life on earth, and perchance through a long eternity in heaven! Now, 'tis merely hell in both worlds. Well, be it hell. I will mold a trumpet of the flames, and, with my breath of flame, breathe back my defiance! But give me first another body! I long and long to die, to be rid of this dishonored cheek. *Hung by the neck till thou be dead.*—Not if I forestall you, though!—Oh now to live is death, and now to die is life; now, to my soul, were a sword my midwife!—Hark!—the hangman?—who comes?"

"Thy wife and cousin—so they say;—hope they may be; they may stay till twelve;" wheezingly answered a turnkey, pushing the tottering girls into the cell, and locking the door upon them.

"Ye two pale ghosts, were this the other world, ye were not welcome. Away!—Good Angel and Bad Angel both!—For Pierre is neuter now!"

"Oh, ye stony roofs, and seven-fold stony skies!—not thou art the murderer, but thy sister hath murdered thee, my brother, oh my brother!"

At these wailed words from Isabel, Lucy shrunk up like a scroll, and noiselessly fell at the feet of Pierre.

He touched her heart.—"Dead!—Girl! wife or sister, saint or fiend!"—seizing Isabel in his grasp—"in thy breasts, life for infants lodgeth not, but death-milk for thee and me!—

The drug!" and tearing her bosom loose, he seized the secret vial nesting there.

vii

At night the squat-framed, asthmatic turnkey tramped the dim-lit iron gallery before one of the long honey-combed rows of cells.

"Mighty still there, in that hole, them two mice I let in;—humph!"

Suddenly, at the further end of the gallery, he discerned a shadowy figure emerging from the archway there, and running on before an officer, and impetuously approaching where the turnkey stood.

"More relations coming. These wind-broken chaps are always in before the second death, seeing they always miss the first.—Humph! What a froth the fellow's in!—Wheezes worse than me!"

"Where is she?" cried Fred Tartan, fiercely, to him; "she's not at the murderer's rooms! I sought the sweet girl there, instant upon the blow; but the lone dumb thing I found there only wrung her speechless hands and pointed to the door;—both birds were flown! Where is she, turnkey? I've searched all lengths and breadths but this. Hath any angel swept adown and lighted in your granite hell?"

"Broken his wind, and broken loose, too, aint he?" wheezed the turnkey to the officer who now came up.

"This gentleman seeks a young lady, his sister, someway innocently connected with the prisoner last brought in. Have any females been here to see him?"

"Oh, ay,—two of 'em in there now;" jerking his stumped thumb behind him.

Fred darted toward the designated cell.

"Oh, easy, easy, young gentleman"—jingling at his huge bunch of keys—"easy, easy, till I get the picks—I'm house-wife here.—Hallo, here comes another."

Hurrying through the same archway toward them, there now rapidly advanced a second impetuous figure, running on in advance of a second officer.

"Where is the cell?" demanded Millthorpe.

"He seeks an interview with the last prisoner," explained the second officer.

"Kill 'em both with one stone, then," wheezed the turnkey, gratingly throwing open the door of the cell. "There's his pretty parlor, gentlemen; step in. Reg'lar mouse-hole, arn't it?—Might hear a rabbit burrow on the world's t'other side;—are they all 'sleep?"

"I stumble!" cried Fred, from within; "Lucy! A light! a light!—Lucy!" And he wildly groped about the cell, and blindly caught Millthorpe, who was also wildly groping.

"Blister me not! take off thy bloody touch!—Ho, ho, the light!—Lucy! Lucy!—she's fainted!"

Then both stumbled again, and fell from each other in the cell: and for a moment all seemed still, as though all breaths were held.

As the light was now thrust in, Fred was seen on the floor holding his sister in his arms; and Millthorpe kneeling by the side of Pierre, the unresponsive hand in his; while Isabel, feebly moving, reclined between, against the wall.

"Yes! Yes!—Dead! Dead! Dead!—without one visible wound—her sweet plumage hides it.—Thou hellish carrion, this is thy hellish work! Thy juggler's rifle brought down this heavenly bird! Oh, my God, my God! Thou scalpest me with this sight!"

"The dark vein's burst, and here's the deluge-wreck—all stranded here! Ah, Pierre! my old companion, Pierre;—school-mate—play-mate—friend!—Our sweet boy's walks within the woods!—Oh, I would have rallied thee, and banteringly warned thee from thy too moody ways, but thou wouldst never heed! What scornful innocence rests on thy lips, my friend!—Hand scorched with murderer's powder, yet how woman-soft!—By heaven, these fingers move!—one speechless clasp!—all's o'er!"

"All's o'er, and ye know him not!" came gasping from the wall; and from the fingers of Isabel dropped an empty vial—as it had been a run-out sand-glass—and shivered upon the floor; and her whole form sloped sideways, and she fell upon

Pierre's heart, and her long hair ran over him, and arbored him in ebon vines.

FINIS

ISRAEL POTTER

His Fifty Years of Exile

TO
His Highness
THE
Bunker-Hill Monument

B IOGRAPHY, in its purer form, confined to the ended lives
of the true and brave, may be held the fairest meed of
human virtue—one given and received in entire disinterestedness—since neither can the biographer hope for acknowledgment from the subject, nor the subject at all avail himself
of the biographical distinction conferred.

Israel Potter well merits the present tribute—a private of
Bunker Hill, who for his faithful services was years ago promoted to a still deeper privacy under the ground, with a posthumous pension, in default of any during life, annually paid
him by the spring in ever-new mosses and sward.

I am the more encouraged to lay this performance at the
feet of your Highness, because, with a change in the gram-
matical person, it preserves, almost as in a reprint, Israel Potter's autobiographical story. Shortly after his return in infirm
old age to his native land, a little narrative of his adventures,
forlornly published on sleazy gray paper, appeared among the
peddlers, written, probably, not by himself, but taken down
from his lips by another. But like the crutch-marks of the cripple by the Beautiful Gate, this blurred record is now out of
print. From a tattered copy, rescued by the merest chance
from the rag-pickers, the present account has been drawn,
which, with the exception of some expansions, and additions
of historic and personal details, and one or two shiftings of
scene, may, perhaps, be not unfitly regarded something in the
light of a dilapidated old tombstone retouched.

Well aware that in your Highness' eyes the merit of the
story must be in its general fidelity to the main drift of the
original narrative, I forbore anywhere to mitigate the hard fortunes of my hero; and particularly towards the end, though
sorely tempted, durst not substitute for the allotment of Providence any artistic recompense of poetical justice; so that no
one can complain of the gloom of my closing chapters more
profoundly than myself.

Such is the work, and such the man, that I have the honor
to present to your Highness. That the name here noted should
not have appeared in the volumes of Sparks, may or may not

be a matter for astonishment; but Israel Potter seems purposely to have waited to make his popular advent under the present exalted patronage, seeing that your Highness, according to the definition above, may, in the loftiest sense, be deemed the Great Biographer: the national commemorator of such of the anonymous privates of June 17, 1775, who may never have received other requital than the solid reward of your granite.

Your Highness will pardon me, if, with the warmest ascriptions on this auspicious occasion, I take the liberty to mingle my hearty congratulations on the recurrence of the anniversary day we celebrate, wishing your Highness (though indeed your Highness be somewhat prematurely gray) many returns of the same, and that each of its summer's suns may shine as brightly on your brow as each winter snow shall lightly rest on the grave of Israel Potter.

Your Highness'

Most devoted and obsequious,

THE EDITOR.

JUNE 17th, 1854.

Contents

Chapter 1

THE BIRTHPLACE OF ISRAEL

THE TRAVELLER who at the present day is content to travel in the good old Asiatic style, neither rushed along by a locomotive, nor dragged by a stage-coach; who is willing to enjoy hospitalities at far-scattered farmhouses, instead of paying his bill at an inn; who is not to be frightened by any amount of loneliness, or to be deterred by the roughest roads or the highest hills; such a traveller in the eastern part of Berkshire, Mass., will find ample food for poetic reflection in the singular scenery of a country, which, owing to the ruggedness of the soil and its lying out of the track of all public conveyances, remains almost as unknown to the general tourist as the interior of Bohemia.

Travelling northward from the township of Otis, the road leads for twenty or thirty miles towards Windsor, lengthwise upon that long broken spur of heights which the Green Mountains of Vermont send into Massachusetts. For nearly the whole of the distance, you have the continual sensation of being upon some terrace in the moon. The feeling of the plain or the valley is never yours; scarcely the feeling of the earth. Unless by a sudden precipitation of the road you find yourself plunging into some gorge; you pass on, and on, and on, upon the crests or slopes of pastoral mountains, while far below, mapped out in its beauty, the valley of the Housatonic lies endlessly along at your feet. Often, as your horse gaining some lofty level tract, flat as a table, trots gayly over the almost deserted and sodded road, and your admiring eye sweeps the broad landscape beneath, you seem to be Boótes driving in heaven. Save a potato field here and there, at long intervals, the whole country is either in wood or pasture. Horses, cattle and sheep are the principal inhabitants of these mountains. But all through the year lazy columns of smoke rising from the depths of the forest, proclaim the presence of that half-outlaw, the charcoal-burner; while in early spring added curls of vapor show that the maple sugar-boiler is also at work. But as for farming as a regular vocation, there is not much of it here. At any rate, no man by that means accumulates a fortune from this thin and rocky soil; all whose arable parts have long since been nearly exhausted.

Yet during the first settlement of the country, the region was not unproductive. Here it was that the original settlers came, acting upon the principle well-known to have regulated their choice of site, namely, the high land in preference to the low, as less subject to the unwholesome miasmas generated by breaking into the rich valleys and alluvial bottoms of primeval regions. By degrees, however, they quitted the safety of this sterile elevation, to brave the dangers of richer though lower fields. So that at the present day, some of those mountain townships present an aspect of singular abandonment. Though they have never known aught but peace and health, they, in one lesser aspect at least, look like countries depopulated by plague and war. Every mile or two a house is passed untenanted. The strength of the frame-work of these ancient buildings enables them long to resist the encroachments of decay. Spotted gray and green with the weather-stain, their timbers seem to have lapsed back into their woodland original, forming part now of the general picturesqueness of the natural scene. They are of extraordinary size, compared with modern farm-houses. One peculiar feature is the immense chimney, of light gray stone, perforating the middle of the roof like a tower.

On all sides are seen the tokens of ancient industry. As stone abounds throughout these mountains, that material was, for fences, as ready to the hand as wood, besides being much more durable. Consequently the landscape is intersected in all directions with walls of uncommon neatness and strength.

The number and length of these walls is not more surprising than the size of some of the blocks comprising them. The very Titans seemed to have been at work. That so small an army as the first settlers must needs have been, should have taken such wonderful pains to inclose so ungrateful a soil; that they should have accomplished such herculean undertakings with so slight prospect of reward; this is a consideration which gives us a significant hint of the temper of the men of the Revolutionary era.

Nor could a fitter country be found for the birthplace of the devoted patriot, Israel Potter.

To this day the best stone-wall builders, as the best wood-choppers, come from those solitary mountain towns; a tall, athletic, and hardy race, unerring with the axe as the Indian with the tomahawk; at stone-rolling, patient as Sisyphus, powerful as Samson.

In fine clear June days, the bloom of these mountains is beyond expression delightful. Last visiting these heights ere she vanishes, Spring, like the sunset, flings her sweetest charms upon them. Each tuft of upland grass is musked like a bouquet with perfume. The balmy breeze swings to and fro like a censer. On one side the eye follows for the space of an eagle's flight, the serpentine mountain chains, southwards from the great purple dome of Taconic—the St. Peter's of these hills—northwards to the twin summits of Saddleback, which is the two-steepled natural cathedral of Berkshire; while low down to the west the Housatonic winds on in her watery labyrinth, through charming meadows basking in the reflected rays from the hill-sides. At this season the beauty of every thing around you populates the loneliness of your way. You would not have the country more settled if you could. Content to drink in such loveliness at all your senses, the heart desires no company but nature.

With what rapture you behold, hovering over some vast hollow of the hills, or slowly drifting at an immense height over the far sunken Housatonic valley, some lordly eagle, who in unshared exaltation looks down equally upon plain and mountain. Or you behold a hawk sallying from some crag, like a Rhenish baron of old from his pinnacled castle, and darting down towards the river for his prey. Or perhaps, lazily gliding about in the zenith, this ruffian fowl is suddenly beset by a crow, who with stubborn audacity pecks at him, and spite of all his bravery, finally persecutes him back to his stronghold. The otherwise dauntless bandit, soaring at his topmost height, must needs succumb to this sable image of death. Nor are there wanting many smaller and less famous fowl, who without contributing to the grandeur, yet greatly add to the beauty of the scene. The yellow bird flits like a winged jonquil here and there; like knots of violets the blue birds sport in clusters upon the grass; while hurrying from the pasture to the grove, the red robin seems an incendiary putting torch to the trees. Meanwhile the air is vocal with their hymns, and your own soul joys in the general joy. Like a stranger in an orchestra, you cannot help singing yourself when all around you raise such hosannas.

But in autumn, those gay northerners, the birds, return to their southern plantations. The mountains are left bleak and sere. Solitude settles down upon them in drizzling mists. The traveller is beset, at perilous turns, by dense masses of fog. He emerges for a moment into more penetrable air; and passing some gray, abandoned house, sees the lofty vapors plainly eddy by its desolate door; just as from the plain, you may see it eddy by the pinnacles of distant and lonely heights. Or, dismounting from his frightened horse, he leads him down some scowling glen, where the road steeply dips among grim rocks, only to rise as abruptly again; and as he warily picks his way, uneasy at the menacing scene, he sees some ghost-like object looming through the mist at the roadside; and wending towards it, beholds a rude white stone, uncouthly inscribed, marking the spot where, some fifty or sixty years ago, some farmer was upset in his wood-sled, and perished beneath the load.

In winter this region is blocked up with snow. Inaccessible and impassable, those wild, unfrequented roads, which in August are overgrown with high grass, in December are drifted to the arm-pit with the white fleece from the sky. As if an ocean rolled between man and man, intercommunication is often suspended for weeks and weeks.

Such, at this day, is the country which gave birth to our hero: prophetically styled Israel by the good Puritans, his parents, since for more than forty years, poor Potter wandered in the wild wilderness of the world's extremest hardships and ills.

How little he thought, when, as a boy, hunting after his father's stray cattle among these New England hills, he himself like a beast should be hunted through half of Old England, as a runaway rebel. Or, how could he ever have dreamed, when involved in the autumnal vapors of these mountains, that worse bewilderments awaited him three thousand miles across the sea, wandering forlorn in the coal-fogs of London. But so it was destined to be. This little boy of the hills, born in sight of the sparkling Housatonic, was to linger out the best part of his life a prisoner or a pauper upon the grimy banks of the Thames.

Chapter 2

The Youthful Adventures of Israel

IMAGINATION will easily picture the rural days of the youth of Israel. Let us pass on to a less immature period.

It appears that he began his wanderings very early; moreover, that ere, on just principles throwing off the yoke of his king, Israel, on equally excusable grounds, emancipated himself from his sire. He continued in the enjoyment of parental love till the age of eighteen, when, having formed an attachment for a neighbor's daughter—for some reason, not deemed a suitable match by his father—he was severely reprimanded, warned to discontinue his visits, and threatened with some disgraceful punishment in case he persisted. As the girl was not only beautiful, but amiable—though, as will be seen, rather weak—and her family respectable as any, though unfortunately but poor, Israel deemed his father's conduct unreasonable and oppressive; particularly as it turned out that he had taken secret means to thwart his son with the girl's connections, if not with the girl herself, so as to place almost insurmountable obstacles to an eventual marriage. For it had not been the purpose of Israel to marry at once, but at a future day, when prudence should approve the step. So, oppressed by his father, and bitterly disappointed in his love, the desperate boy formed the determination to quit them both, for another home and other friends.

It was on Sunday, while the family were gone to a farmhouse church near by, that he packed up as much of his clothing as might be contained in a handkerchief, which, with a small quantity of provision, he hid in a piece of woods in the rear of the house. He then returned, and continued in the house till about nine in the evening, when, pretending to go to bed, he passed out of a back door, and hastened to the woods for his bundle.

It was a sultry night in July; and that he might travel with the more ease on the succeeding day, he lay down at the foot of a pine tree, reposing himself till an hour before dawn, when, upon awaking, he heard the soft, prophetic sighing of the pine, stirred by the first breath of the morning. Like the leaflets of that evergreen, all the fibres of his heart trembled within him; tears fell from his eyes. But he thought of the tyranny of his father, and what seemed to him the faithlessness of his love; and shouldering his bundle, arose, and marched on.

His intention was to reach the new countries to the northward and westward, lying between the Dutch settlements on the Hudson, and the Yankee settlements on the Housatonic. This was mainly to elude all search. For the same reason, for the first ten or twelve miles, shunning the public roads, he travelled through the woods; for he knew that he would soon be missed and pursued.

He reached his destination in safety; hired out to a farmer for a month through the harvest; then crossed from the Hudson to the Connecticut. Meeting here with an adventurer to the unknown regions lying about the head waters of the latter river, he ascended with this man in a canoe, paddling and poling for many miles. Here again he hired himself out for three months; at the end of that time to receive for his wages, two hundred acres of land lying in New Hampshire. The cheapness of the land was not alone owing to the newness of the country, but to the perils investing it. Not only was it a wilderness abounding with wild beasts, but the widely scattered inhabitants were in continual dread of being, at some unguarded moment, destroyed or made captive by the Canadian savages, who, ever since the French war, had improved every opportunity to make forays across the defenceless frontier.

His employer proving false to his contract in the matter of the land, and there being no law in the country to force him to fulfil it, Israel,—who however brave-hearted, and even much of a dare-devil upon a pinch, seems, nevertheless, to have evinced, throughout many parts of his career, a singular patience and mildness,—was obliged to look round for other means of livelihood, than clearing out a farm for himself in the wilderness. A party of royal surveyors were at this period surveying the unsettled regions bordering the Connecticut River to its source. At fifteen shillings per month, he engaged himself to this party as assistant chain-bearer, little thinking that the day was to come when he should clank the king's chains in a dungeon, even as now he trailed them a free ranger of the woods. It was midwinter; the land was surveyed upon snow-shoes. At the close of the day, fires were kindled with dry hemlock, a hut thrown up, and the party ate and slept.

Paid off at last, Israel bought a gun and ammunition, and turned hunter. Deer, beaver, &c., were plenty. In two or three months he had many skins to show. I suppose it never entered his mind, that he was thus qualifying himself for a marksman of men. But thus were tutored those wonderful shots who did such execution at Bunker's Hill; these, the hunter-soldiers, whom Putnam bade wait till the white of the enemy's eye was seen.

With the result of his hunting he purchased a hundred acres of land, further down the river, toward the more settled parts; built himself a log hut, and in two summers, with his own hands, cleared thirty acres for sowing. In the winter seasons he hunted and trapped. At the end of the two years, he sold back his land—now much improved—to the original owner, at an advance of fifty pounds. He conveyed his skins and furs to Charlestown, on the Connecticut (sometimes called No. 4), where he trafficked them away for Indian blankets, pigments, and other showy articles adapted to the business of a trader among savages. It was now winter again. Putting his goods on a hand-sled, he started towards Canada, a peddler in the wilderness, stopping at wigwams instead of cottages. One fancies that, had it been summer, Israel would have travelled with a wheelbarrow, and so trundled his wares through the primeval forests, with the same indifference as porters roll their barrows over the flagging of streets. In this way was bred that fearless self-reliance and independence which conducted our forefathers to national freedom.

This Canadian trip proved highly successful. Selling his glittering goods at a great advance, he received in exchange valuable peltries and furs at a corresponding reduction. Returning to Charlestown, he disposed of his return cargo again at a very fine profit. And now, with a light heart and a heavy purse, he resolved to visit his sweetheart and parents, of whom, for three years, he had had no tidings.

They were not less astonished than delighted at his reappearance; he had been numbered with the dead. But his love still seemed strangely coy; willing, but yet somehow mysteriously withheld. The old intrigues were still on foot. Israel soon discovered, that though rejoiced to welcome the return of the prodigal son—so some called him—his father still remained inflexibly determined against the match, and still inexplicably countermined his wooing. With a dolorous heart he mildly yielded to what seemed his fatality; and more intrepid in facing peril for himself, than in endangering others by maintaining his rights (for he was now one-and-twenty), resolved once more to retreat, and quit his blue hills for the bluer billows.

A hermitage in the forest is the refuge of the narrow-minded misanthrope; a hammock on the ocean is the asylum for the generous distressed. The ocean brims with natural griefs and tragedies; and into that watery immensity of terror, man's private grief is lost like a drop.

Travelling on foot to Providence, Rhode Island, Israel shipped on board a sloop, bound with lime to the West Indies. On the tenth day out, the vessel caught fire, from water communicating with the lime. It was impossible to extinguish the flames. The boat was hoisted out, but owing to long exposure to the sun, it needed continual baling to keep it afloat. They had only time to put in a firkin of butter and a ten-gallon keg of water. Eight in number, the crew entrusted themselves to the waves, in a leaky tub, many leagues from land. As the boat swept under the burning bowsprit, Israel caught at a fragment of the flying-jib, which sail had fallen down the stay, owing to the charring, nigh the deck, of the rope which hoisted it. Tanned with the smoke, and its edge blackened with the fire, this bit of canvas helped them bravely on their way. Thanks to kind Providence, on the second day they were picked up by a Dutch ship, bound from Eustatia to Holland. The castaways were humanely received, and supplied with every necessary. At the end of a week, while unsophisticated Israel was sitting in the main-top, thinking what should befall him in Holland, and wondering what sort of unsettled, wild, country it was, and whether there was any deer-shooting or beaver-trapping there; lo! an American brig, bound from Piscataqua to Antigua, comes in sight. The American took them aboard and conveyed them safely to her port. There Israel shipped for Porto Rico; from thence, sailed to Eustatia.

Other rovings ensued; until at last, entering on board a Nantucket ship, he hunted the leviathan off the Western Islands and on the coast of Africa, for sixteen months; returning at length to Nantucket with a brimming hold. From that island he sailed again on another whaling voyage, extending, this time, into the great South Sea. There, promoted to be harpooner, Israel, whose eye and arm had been so improved by practice with his gun in the wilderness, now further intensified his aim, by darting the whale-lance; still, unwittingly, preparing himself for the Bunker Hill rifle.

In this last voyage, our adventurer experienced to the extreme, all the hardships and privations of the whaleman's life on a long voyage to distant and barbarous waters; hardships and privations unknown at the present day, when science has so greatly contributed, in manifold ways, to lessen the sufferings, and add to the comforts of sea-faring men. Heartily sick of the ocean, and longing once more for the bush, Israel, upon receiving his discharge at Nantucket at the end of the voyage, hied straight back for his mountain home.

But if hopes of his sweetheart winged his returning flight, such hopes were not destined to be crowned with fruition. The dear, false girl, was another's.

Chapter 3

ISRAEL GOES TO THE WARS; AND REACHING BUNKER
HILL IN TIME TO BE OF SERVICE THERE, SOON
AFTER IS FORCED TO EXTEND HIS TRAVELS ACROSS
THE SEA INTO THE ENEMY'S LAND

LEFT TO idle lamentations, Israel might now have planted
deep furrows in his brow. But stifling his pain, he chose
rather to plough, than be ploughed. Farming weans man
from his sorrows. That tranquil pursuit tolerates nothing but
tranquil meditations. There, too, in mother earth, you may
plant and reap; not, as in other things, plant and see the
planting torn up by the roots. But if wandering in the wilderness; and wandering upon the waters; if felling trees; and
hunting, and shipwreck; and fighting with whales, and all his
other strange adventures, had not as yet cured poor Israel of
his now hopeless passion; events were at hand for ever to
drown it.

It was the year 1774. The difficulties long pending between
the colonies and England, were arriving at their crisis. Hostilities were certain. The Americans were preparing themselves. Companies were formed in most of the New England
towns; whose members, receiving the name of minute-men,
stood ready to march anywhere at a minute's warning. Israel,
for the last eight months, sojourning as a laborer on a farm
in Windsor, enrolled himself in the regiment of Colonel John
Patterson of Lenox, afterwards General Patterson.

The battle of Lexington was fought on the 18th of April,
1775; news of it arrived in the county of Berkshire on the 20th,
about noon. The next morning at sunrise, Israel swung his
knapsack, shouldered his musket, and with Patterson's regiment, was on the march, quickstep, towards Boston.

Like Putnam, Israel received the stirring tidings at the
plough. But although not less willing than Putnam, to fly to
battle at an instant's notice; yet—only half an acre of the field
remaining to be finished—he whipped up his team and finished it. Before hastening to one duty, he would not leave a

439

prior one undone; and ere helping to whip the British, for a little practice' sake, he applied the gad to his oxen. From the field of the farmer, he rushed to that of the soldier, mingling his blood with his sweat. While we revel in broadcloth, let us not forget what we owe to linsey-woolsey.

With other detachments from various quarters, Israel's regiment remained encamped for several days in the vicinity of Charlestown. On the sixteenth of June, one thousand Americans, including the regiment of Patterson, were set about fortifying Bunker's Hill. Working all through the night, by dawn of the following day, the redoubt was thrown up. But every one knows all about the battle. Suffice it, that Israel was one of those marksmen whom Putnam harangued as touching the enemy's eyes. Forbearing as he was with his oppressive father and unfaithful love, and mild as he was on the farm; Israel was not the same at Bunker Hill. Putnam had enjoined the men to aim at the officers; so Israel aimed between the golden epaulettes, as, in the wilderness, he had aimed between the branching antlers. With dogged disdain of their foes, the English grenadiers marched up the hill with sullen slowness; thus furnishing still surer aims to the muskets which bristled on the redoubt. Modest Israel was used to aver, that considering his practice in the woods, he could hardly be regarded as an inexperienced marksman; hinting, that every shot which the epauletted grenadiers received from his rifle, would, upon a different occasion, have procured him a deer-skin. And like stricken deers the English, rashly brave as they were, fled from the opening fire. But the marksmen's ammunition was expended; a hand-to-hand encounter ensued. Not one American musket in twenty had a bayonet to it. So, wielding the stock right and left, the terrible farmers, with hats and coats off, fought their way among the furred grenadiers; knocking them right and left, as seal hunters on the beach, knock down with their clubs the Shetland seal. In the dense crowd and confusion, while Israel's musket got interlocked, he saw a blade horizontally menacing his feet from the ground. Thinking some fallen enemy sought to strike him at the last gasp, dropping his hold on his musket, he wrenched at the steel, but found that though a brave hand held it, that hand was powerless for ever. It was some British officer's laced sword-arm, cut from the trunk in the act of fighting; refusing to yield up its blade, to the last. At that moment another sword was aimed at Israel's head, by a living officer. In an instant the blow was parried by kindred steel, and the assailant fell by a brother's weapon, wielded by alien hands. But Israel did not come off unscathed. A cut on the right arm near the elbow, received in parrying the officer's blow; a long slit across the chest; a musket-ball buried in his hip, and another mangling him near the ankle of the same leg, were the tokens of intrepidity which our Sicinius Dentatus carried from this memorable field. Nevertheless, with his comrades he succeeded in reaching Prospect Hill, and from thence was conveyed to the hospital at Cambridge. The bullet was extracted, his lesser wounds were dressed, and after much suffering from the fracture of the bone near the ankle, several pieces of which were extracted by the surgeon, ere long, thanks to the high health and pure blood of the farmer, Israel rejoined his regiment when they were throwing up intrenchments on Prospect Hill. Bunker Hill was now in possession of the foe, who in turn had fortified it.

On the third of July, Washington arrived from the South to take the command. Israel witnessed his joyful reception by the huzzaing companies.

The British now quartered in Boston suffered greatly from the scarcity of provisions. Washington took every precaution to prevent their receiving a supply. Inland, all aid could easily be cut off. To guard against their receiving any by water, from tories and other disaffected persons, the general equipped three armed vessels to intercept all traitorous cruisers. Among them was the brigantine Washington, of ten guns, commanded by Captain Martindale. Seamen were hard to be had. The soldiers were called upon to volunteer for these vessels. Israel was one who so did; thinking that as an experienced sailor he should not be backward in a juncture like this, little as he fancied the new service assigned.

Three days out of Boston harbor, the brigantine was captured by the enemy's ship Foy, of twenty guns. Taken prisoner with the rest of the crew, Israel was afterwards put on board the frigate Tartar, with immediate sailing orders for England. Seventy-two were captives in this vessel. Headed by

Israel, these men—half way across the sea—formed a scheme
to take the ship, but were betrayed by a renegade Englishman. As ringleader, Israel was put in irons, and so remained
till the frigate anchored at Portsmouth. There he was brought
on deck; and would have met perhaps some terrible fate, had
it not come out during the examination, that the Englishman
had been a deserter from the army of his native country, ere
proving a traitor to his adopted one. Relieved of his irons,
Israel was placed in the marine hospital on shore, where half
of the prisoners took the small-pox, which swept off a third
of their number. Why talk of Jaffa?

From the hospital the survivors were conveyed to Spithead,
and thrust on board a hulk. And here in the black bowels of
the ship, sunk low in the sunless sea, our poor Israel lay for a
month, like Jonah in the belly of the whale.

But one bright morning, Israel is hailed from the deck. A
bargeman of the commander's boat is sick. Known for a
sailor, Israel for the nonce is appointed to pull the absent
man's oar.

The officers being landed, some of the crew propose, like
merry Englishmen as they are, to hie to a neighboring ale-
house, and have a cosy pot or two together. Agreed. They
start, and Israel with them. As they enter the ale-house door,
our prisoner is suddenly reminded of still more imperative
calls. Unsuspected of any design, he is allowed to leave the
party for a moment. No sooner does Israel see his companions housed, than putting speed into his feet, and letting
grow all his wings, he starts like a deer. He runs four miles
(so he afterwards affirmed) without halting. He sped towards
London; wisely deeming that once in that crowd detection
would be impossible.

Ten miles, as he computed, from where he had left the
bargemen, leisurely passing a public house of a little village
on the road-side, thinking himself now pretty safe—hark,
what is this he hears?—

"Ahoy! what ship?"

"No ship," says Israel, hurrying on.

"Stop."

"If you will attend to your business, I will endeavor to attend to mine," replies Israel coolly. And next minute he lets

grow his wings again; flying, one dare say, at the rate of something less than thirty miles an hour.

"Stop thief!" is now the cry. Numbers rushed from the road-side houses. After a mile's chase, the poor panting deer is caught.

Finding it was no use now to prevaricate, Israel boldly confesses himself a prisoner-of-war. The officer, a good fellow as it turned out, had him escorted back to the inn; where, observing to the landlord, that this must needs be a true-blooded Yankee, he calls for liquors to refresh Israel after his run. Two soldiers are then appointed to guard him for the present. This was towards evening; and up to a late hour at night, the inn was filled with strangers crowding to see the Yankee rebel, as they politely termed him. These honest rustics seemed to think that Yankees were a sort of wild creatures, a species of a 'possum or kangaroo. But Israel is very affable with them. That liquor he drank from the hand of his foe, has perhaps warmed his heart towards all the rest of his enemies. Yet this may not be wholly so. We shall see. At any rate, still he keeps his eye on the main chance—escape. Neither the jokes nor the insults of the mob does he suffer to molest him. He is cogitating a little plot to himself.

It seems that the good officer—not more true to the king his master than indulgent towards the prisoner which that same loyalty made—had left orders that Israel should be supplied with whatever liquor he wanted that night. So, calling for the can again and again, Israel invites the two soldiers to drink and be merry. At length, a wag of the company proposes that Israel should entertain the public with a jig; he (the wag) having heard, that the Yankees were extraordinary dancers. A fiddle is brought in, and poor Israel takes the floor. Not a little cut to think that these people should so unfeelingly seek to be diverted at the expense of an unfortunate prisoner, Israel, while jigging it up and down, still conspires away at his private plot, resolving ere long to give the enemy a touch of certain Yankee steps, as yet undreamed of in their simple philosophy. They would not permit any cessation of his dancing till he had danced himself into a perfect sweat, so that the drops fell from his lank and flaxen hair. But Israel, with much of the gentleness of the dove, is not wholly without the wisdom of the serpent. Pleased to see the flowing bowl, he congratulates himself that his own state of perspiration prevents it from producing any intoxicating effect upon him.

Late at night the company break up. Furnished with a pair of handcuffs, the prisoner is laid on a blanket spread upon the floor at the side of the bed in which his two keepers are to repose. Expressing much gratitude for the blanket, with apparent unconcern, Israel stretches his legs. An hour or two passes. All is quiet without.

The important moment has now arrived. Certain it was, that if this chance were suffered to pass unimproved, a second would hardly present itself. For early, doubtless, on the following morning, if not some way prevented, the two soldiers would convey Israel back to his floating prison, where he would thenceforth remain confined until the close of the war; years and years, perhaps. When he thought of that horrible old hulk, his nerves were restrung for flight. But intrepid as he must be to compass it, wariness too was needed. His keepers had gone to bed pretty well under the influence of the liquor. This was favorable. But still, they were full-grown, strong men; and Israel was handcuffed. So Israel resolved upon strategy first; and if that failed, force afterwards. He eagerly listened. One of the drunken soldiers muttered in his sleep, at first lowly, then louder and louder,—"Catch 'em! Grapple 'em! Have at 'em! Ha—long cutlasses! Take that, runaway!"

"What's the matter with ye, Phil?" hiccoughed the other, who was not yet asleep. "Keep quiet, will ye? Ye ain't at Fontenoy now."

"He's a runaway prisoner, I say. Catch him, catch him!"

"Oh, stush with your drunken dreaming," again hiccoughed his comrade, violently nudging him. "This comes o' carousing."

Shortly after, the dreamer with loud snores fell back into dead sleep. But by something in the sound of the breathing of the other soldier, Israel knew that this man remained uneasily awake. He deliberated a moment what was best to do. At length he determined upon trying his old plea. Calling upon the two soldiers, he informed them that urgent necessity required his immediate presence somewhere in the rear of the house.

"Come, wake up here, Phil," roared the soldier who was awake; "the fellow here says he must step out; cuss these Yankees; no better edication than to be gettin' up on nateral necessities at this time o'night. It ain't nateral; it's unnateral. D—n ye, Yankee, don't ye know no better?"

With many more denunciations, the two now staggered to their feet, and clutching hold of Israel, escorted him down stairs, and through a long, narrow, dark entry, rearward, till they came to a door. No sooner was this unbolted by the foremost guard, then, quick as a flash, manacled Israel, shaking off the grasp of the one behind him, butts him sprawling backwards into the entry; when, dashing in the opposite direction, he bounces the other head over heels into the garden, never using a hand; and then, leaping over the latter's head, darts blindly out into the midnight. Next moment he was at the garden wall. No outlet was discoverable in the gloom. But a fruit-tree grew close to the wall. Springing into it desperately, handcuffed as he was, Israel leaps atop of the barrier, and without pausing to see where he is, drops himself to the ground on the other side, and once more lets grow all his wings. Meantime, with loud outcries, the two baffled drunkards grope deliriously about in the garden.

After running two or three miles, and hearing no sound of pursuit, Israel reins up to rid himself of the handcuffs, which impede him. After much painful labor he succeeds in the attempt. Pressing on again with all speed, day broke, revealing a trim-looking, hedged, and beautiful country, soft, neat, and serene, all colored with the fresh early tints of the spring of 1776.

Bless me, thought Israel, all of a tremble, I shall certainly be caught now; I have broken into some nobleman's park.

But, hurrying forward again, he came to a turnpike road, and then knew that, all comely and shaven as it was, this was simply the open country of England; one bright, broad park, paled in with white foam of the sea. A copse skirting the road was just bursting out into bud. Each unrolling leaf was in very act of escaping from its prison. Israel looked at the budding leaves, and round on the budding sod, and up at the

budding dawn of the day. He was so sad, and these sights
were so gay, that Israel sobbed like a child, while thoughts of
his mountain home rushed like a wind on his heart. But conquering this fit, he marched on, and presently passed nigh a
field, where two figures were working. They had rosy cheeks,
short sturdy legs, showing the blue stocking nearly to the
knee, and were clad in long, coarse, white frocks, and had on
coarse, broad-brimmed straw hats. Their faces were partly
averted.

"Please, ladies," half roguishly says Israel, taking off his hat,
"does this road go to London?"

At this salutation, the two figures turned in a sort of stupid
amazement, causing an almost corresponding expression in
Israel, who now perceived that they were men, and not
women. He had mistaken them, owing to their frocks, and
their wearing no pantaloons, only breeches hidden by their
frocks.

"Beg pardon, lads, but I thought ye were something else,"
said Israel again.

Once more the two figures stared at the stranger, and with
added boorishness of surprise.

"Does this road go to London, gentlemen?"

"Gentlemen—egad!" cried one of the two.

"Egad!" echoed the second.

Putting their hoes before them, the two frocked boors now
took a good long look at Israel, meantime scratching their
heads under their plaited straw hats.

"Does it, gentlemen? Does it go to London? Be kind
enough to tell a poor fellow, do."

"Yees goin' to Lunnun, are yees? Weel—all right—go
along."

And without another word, having now satisfied their rustic curiosity, the two human steers, with wonderful phlegm,
applied themselves to their hoes; supposing, no doubt, that
they had given all requisite information.

Shortly after, Israel passed an old, dark, mossy-looking
chapel, its roof all plastered with the damp yellow dead leaves
of the previous autumn, showered there from a close cluster
of venerable trees, with great trunks, and overstretching
branches. Next moment he found himself entering a village.

The silence of early morning rested upon it. But few figures were seen. Glancing through the window of a now noiseless public-house, Israel saw a table all in disorder, covered with empty flagons, and tobacco-ashes, and long pipes; some of the latter broken.

After pausing here a moment, he moved on, and observed a man over the way standing still and watching him. Instantly Israel was reminded that he had on the dress of an English sailor, and that it was this probably which had arrested the stranger's attention. Well knowing that his peculiar dress exposed him to peril, he hurried on faster to escape the village; resolving at the first opportunity to change his garments. Ere long, in a secluded place about a mile from the village, he saw an old ditcher tottering beneath the weight of a pick-axe, hoe and shovel, going to his work; the very picture of poverty, toil and distress. His clothes were tatters.

Making up to this old man, Israel, after a word or two of salutation, offered to change clothes with him. As his own clothes were prince-like compared to the ditcher's, Israel thought that however much his proposition might excite the suspicion of the ditcher, yet self-interest would prevent his communicating the suspicions. To be brief, the two went behind a hedge, and presently Israel emerged, presenting the most forlorn appearance conceivable; while the old ditcher hobbled off in an opposite direction, correspondingly improved in his aspect; though it was rather ludicrous than otherwise, owing to the immense bagginess of the sailor-trousers flapping about his lean shanks, to say nothing of the spare voluminousness of the pea-jacket. But Israel—how deplorable, how dismal his plight! Little did he ween that these wretched rags he now wore, were but suitable to that long career of destitution before him; one brief career of adventurous wanderings: and then, forty torpid years of pauperism. The coat was all patches. And no two patches were alike, and no one patch was the color of the original cloth. The stringless breeches gaped wide open at the knee; the long woollen stockings looked as if they had been set up at some time for a target. Israel looked suddenly metamorphosed from youth to old age; just like an old man of eighty he looked. But indeed, dull dreary adversity was now in store for him; and adversity, come it at eighteen or eighty, is the true old age of man. The dress befitted the fate.

From the friendly old ditcher, Israel learned the exact course he must steer for London; distant now between seventy and eighty miles. He was also apprised by his venerable friend, that the country was filled with soldiers, on the constant look-out for deserters whether from the navy or army, for the capture of whom a stipulated reward was given, just as in Massachusetts at that time for prowling bears.

Having solemnly enjoined his old friend not to give any information, should any one he meet inquire for such a person as Israel, our adventurer walked briskly on, less heavy of heart, now that he felt comparatively safe in disguise.

Thirty miles were travelled that day. At night Israel stole into a barn, in hopes of finding straw or hay for a bed. But it was spring; all the hay and straw were gone. So after groping about in the dark, he was fain to content himself with an undressed sheep-skin. Cold, hungry, foot-sore, weary, and impatient for the morning dawn, Israel drearily dozed out the night.

By the first peep of day coming through the chinks of the barn, he was up and abroad. Ere long finding himself in the suburbs of a considerable village, the better to guard against detection he supplied himself with a rude crutch, and feigning himself a cripple, hobbled straight through the town, followed by a perverse-minded cur, which kept up a continual, spiteful, suspicious bark. Israel longed to have one good rap at him with his crutch, but thought it would hardly look in character for a poor old cripple to be vindictive.

A few miles further, and he came to a second village. While hobbling through its main street, as through the former one, he was suddenly stopped by a genuine cripple, all in tatters too, who, with a sympathetic air, inquired after the cause of his lameness.

"White swelling," says Israel.

"That's just my ailing," wheezed the other; "but you're lamer than me," he added with a forlorn sort of self-satisfaction, critically eyeing Israel's limp as once more he stumped on his way, not liking to tarry too long.

"But halloo, what's your hurry, friend?" seeing Israel fairly departing—" where 're you going?"

"To London," answered Israel, turning round, heartily wishing the old fellow any where else than present.

"Going to limp to Lunnun, eh? Well, success to ye."

"As much to you, sir," answers Israel politely.

Nigh the opposite suburbs of this village, as good fortune would have it, an empty baggage-wagon bound for the metropolis turned into the main road from a side one. Immediately Israel limps most deplorably, and begs the driver to give a poor cripple a lift. So up he climbs; but after a time, finding the gait of the elephantine draught-horses intolerably slow, Israel craves permission to dismount, when, throwing away his crutch, he takes nimbly to his legs, much to the surprise of his honest friend, the driver.

The only advantage, if any, derived from his trip in the wagon, was, when passing through a third village—but a little distant from the previous one—Israel, by lying down in the wagon, had wholly avoided being seen.

The villages surprised him by their number and proximity. Nothing like this was to be seen at home. Well knowing that in these villages he ran much more risk of detection than in the open country, he henceforth did his best to avoid them, by taking a roundabout course whenever they came in sight from a distance. This mode of travelling not only lengthened his journey, but put unlooked-for obstacles in his path— walls, ditches and streams.

Not half an hour after throwing away his crutch; he leaped a great ditch nineteen feet wide, and of undiscoverable muddy depth. I wonder if the old cripple would think me the lamer one now, thought Israel to himself, arriving on the hither side.

Chapter 4

Further Wanderings of the Refugee, with Some Account of a Good Knight of Brentford Who Befriended Him

AT NIGHTFALL on the third day, Israel had arrived within sixteen miles of the capital. Once more he sought refuge in a barn. This time he found some hay, and flinging himself down procured a tolerable night's rest.

Bright and early he arose refreshed, with the pleasing prospect of reaching his destination ere noon. Encouraged to find himself now so far from his original pursuers, Israel relaxed in his vigilance; and about ten o'clock while passing through the town of Staines suddenly encountered three soldiers. Unfortunately in exchanging clothes with the ditcher, he could not bring himself to include his shirt in the traffic; which shirt was a British navy shirt; a bargeman's shirt; and though hitherto he had crumpled the blue collar out of sight, yet, as it appeared in the present instance, it was not thoroughly concealed. At any rate, keenly on the look-out for deserters, and made acute by hopes of reward for their apprehension, the soldiers spied the fatal collar, and in an instant laid violent hands on the refugee.

"Hey lad!" said the foremost soldier, a corporal, "you are one of his majesty's seamen! come along with ye."

So, unable to give any satisfactory account of himself, he was made prisoner on the spot, and soon after found himself handcuffed and locked up in the Round House of the place, a prison so called, appropriated to runaways, and those convicted of minor offences. Day passed dinnerless and supperless in this dismal durance, and night came on.

Israel had now been three days without food, except one two-penny loaf. The cravings of hunger now became sharper; his spirits, hitherto arming him with fortitude, began to forsake him. Taken captive once again upon the very brink of reaching his goal, poor Israel was on the eve of falling into helpless despair. But he rallied, and considering that grief would only add to his calamity, sought with stubborn patience to habituate himself to misery, but still hold aloof from despondency. He roused himself, and began to bethink him how to be extricated from this labyrinth.

Two hours sawing across the grating of the window, ridded him of his handcuffs. Next came the door, secured luckily with only a hasp and padlock. Thrusting the bolt of his handcuffs through a small window in the door, he succeeded in forcing the hasp and regaining his liberty about three o'clock in the morning.

Not long after sunrise, he passed nigh Brentford, some six or seven miles from the capital. So great was his hunger that downright starvation seemed before him. He chewed grass, and swallowed it. Upon first escaping from the hulk, six English pennies was all the money he had. With two of these he had bought a small loaf the day after fleeing the inn. The other four still remained in his pocket, not having met with a good opportunity to dispose of them for food.

Having torn off the collar of his shirt, and flung it into a hedge, he ventured to accost a respectable carpenter at a pale fence, about a mile this side of Brentford, to whom his deplorable situation now induced him to apply for work. The man did not wish himself to hire, but said that if he (Israel), understood farming or gardening, he might perhaps procure work from Sir John Millet, whose seat, he said, was not remote. He added that the knight was in the habit of employing many men at that season of the year; so he stood a fair chance.

Revived a little by this prospect of relief, Israel starts in quest of the gentleman's seat, agreeably to the directions received. But he mistook his way, and proceeding up a gravelled and beautifully decorated walk, was terrified at catching a glimpse of a number of soldiers thronging a garden. He made an instant retreat before being espied in turn. No wild creature of the American wilderness could have been more panic struck by a fire-brand, than at this period hunted Israel was by a red coat. It afterwards appeared that this garden was the Princess Amelia's.

Taking another path, ere long he came to some laborers shovelling gravel. These proved to be men employed by Sir John. By them he was directed towards the house, when the knight was pointed out to him, walking bareheaded in the inclosure with several guests. Having heard the rich man of

England charged with all sorts of domineering qualities, Israel felt no little misgiving in approaching to an audience with so imposing a stranger. But screwing up his courage, he advanced; while seeing him coming all rags and tatters, the group of gentlemen stood in some wonder awaiting what so singular a phantom might want.

"Mr. Millet," said Israel, bowing towards the bareheaded gentleman.

"Ha,—who are you, pray?"

"A poor fellow, sir, in want of work."

"A wardrobe too, I should say," smiled one of the guests, of a very youthful, prosperous, and dandified air.

"Where's your hoe?" said Sir John.

"I have none, sir."

"Any money to buy one?"

"Only four English pennies, sir."

"*English* pennies. What other sort would you have?"

"Why China pennies to be sure," laughed the youthful gentleman. "See his long, yellow hair behind; he looks like a Chinaman. Some broken-down Mandarin. Pity he's no crown to his old hat; if he had, he might pass it round, and make eight pennies of his four."

"Will you hire me, Mr. Millet?" said Israel.

"Ha! that's queer again," cried the knight.

"Hark ye fellow," said a brisk servant, approaching from the porch, "this is Sir John Millet."

Seeming to take pity on his seeming ignorance, as well as on his undisputable poverty, the good knight now told Israel that if he would come the next morning, he would see him supplied with a hoe, and moreover would hire him.

It would be hard to express the satisfaction of the wanderer, at receiving this encouraging reply. Emboldened by it, he now returns towards a baker's he had spied, and bravely marching in, flings down all four pennies, and demands bread. Thinking he would not have any more food till next morning, Israel resolved to eat only one of the pair of two-penny loaves. But having demolished one, it so sharpened his longing, that yielding to the irresistible temptation, he bolted down the second loaf to keep the other company.

After resting under a hedge, he saw the sun far descended, and so prepared himself for another hard night. Waiting till dark, he crawled into an old carriage-house, finding nothing there but a dismantled old phaeton. Into this he climbed, and curling himself up like a carriage-dog, endeavored to sleep. But unable to endure the constraint of such a bed, got out, and stretched himself on the bare boards of the floor.

No sooner was light in the east, than he hastened to await the commands of one, who, his instinct told him, was destined to prove his benefactor. On his father's farm accustomed to rise with the lark, Israel was surprised to discover as he approached the house, that no soul was astir. It was four o'clock. For a considerable time he walked back and forth before the portal, ere any one appeared. The first riser was a man-servant of the household, who informed Israel that seven o'clock was the hour the people went to their work. Soon after, he met an hostler of the place, who gave him permission to lie on some straw in an outhouse. There he enjoyed a sweet sleep till awakened at seven o'clock, by the sounds of activity around him.

Supplied by the overseer of the men with a large iron fork and a hoe, he followed the hands into the field. He was so weak, he could hardly support his tools. Unwilling to expose his debility, he yet could not succeed in concealing it. At last to avoid worse imputations, he confessed the cause. His companions regarded him with compassion, and exempted him from the severer toil.

About noon, the knight visited his workmen. Noticing that Israel made little progress, he said to him, that though he had long arms and broad shoulders, yet he was feigning himself to be a very weak man, or otherwise must in reality be so.

Hereupon one of the laborers standing by, informed the gentleman how it was with Israel; when immediately the knight put a shilling into his hands, and bade him go to a little road-side inn, which was nearer than the house, and buy him bread and a pot of beer. Thus refreshed he returned to the band, and toiled with them till four o'clock, when the day's work was over.

Arrived at the house, he there again saw his employer, who after attentively eyeing him without speaking, bade a meal be prepared for him; when the maid presenting a smaller supply than her kind master deemed necessary, she was ordered to return and bring out the entire dish. But aware of the danger of sudden repletion of heavy food to one in his condition, Israel, previously recruited by the frugal meal at the inn, partook but sparingly. The repast was spread on the grass, and being over, the good knight again looking inquisitively at Israel, ordered a comfortable bed to be laid in the barn; and here Israel spent a capital night.

After breakfast, next morning, he was proceeding to go with the laborers to their work, when his employer approaching him with a benevolent air, bade him return to his couch, and there remain till he had slept his fill, and was in a better state to resume his labors.

Upon coming forth again a little after noon, he found Sir John walking alone in the grounds. Upon discovering him, Israel would have retreated, fearing that he might intrude; but beckoning him to advance, the knight, as Israel drew nigh, fixed on him such a penetrating glance, that our poor hero quaked to the core. Neither was his dread of detection relieved by the knight's now calling in a loud voice for one from the house. Israel was just on the point of fleeing, when overhearing the words of the master to the servant who now appeared, all dread departed:

"Bring hither some wine!"

It presently came; by order of the knight the salver was set down on a green bank near by, and the servant retired.

"My poor fellow," said Sir John, now pouring out a glass of wine, and handing it to Israel, "I perceive that you are an American; and, if I am not mistaken, you are an escaped prisoner of war. But no fear—drink the wine."

"Mr. Millet," exclaimed Israel aghast, the untasted wine trembling in his hand, "Mr. Millet, I——"

"*Mr.* Millet—there it is again. Why don't you say *Sir John* like the rest?"

"Why, sir—pardon me—but somehow, I can't. I've tried; but I can't. You won't betray me for that?"

"Betray—poor fellow! Hark ye, your history is doubtless a

secret which you would not wish to divulge to a stranger; but whatever happens to you, I pledge you my honor I will never betray you."

"God bless you for that, Mr. Millet."

"Come, come; call me by my right name. I am not Mr. Millet. *You* have said *Sir* to me; and no doubt you have a thousand times said *John* to other people. Now can't you couple the two? Try once. Come. Only *Sir* and then *John*—*Sir John*—that's all."

"John—I can't—Sir, sir!—your pardon. I didn't mean that."

"My good fellow," said the knight looking sharply upon Israel, "tell me, are all your countrymen like you? If so, it's no use fighting them. To that effect, I must write to his Majesty myself. Well, I excuse you from Sir Johnning me. But tell me the truth, are you not a sea-faring man, and lately a prisoner of war?"

Israel frankly confessed it, and told his whole story. The knight listened with much interest; and at its conclusion, warned Israel to beware of the soldiers; for owing to the seats of some of the royal family being in the neighborhood, the red-coats abounded hereabouts.

"I do not wish unnecessarily to speak against my own countrymen," he added, "I but plainly speak for your good. The soldiers you meet prowling on the roads, are not fair specimens of the army. They are a set of mean, dastardly banditti; who, to obtain their fee, would betray their best friends. Once more, I warn you against them. But enough; follow me now to the house, and as you tell me you have exchanged clothes before now, you can do it again. What say you? I will give you coat and breeches for your rags."

Thus generously supplied with clothes, and other comforts by the good knight, and implicitly relying upon the honor of so kind-hearted a man, Israel cheered up, and in the course of two or three weeks had so fattened his flanks, that he was able completely to fill Sir John's old buckskin breeches, which at first had hung but loosely about him.

He was assigned to an occupation which removed him from the other workmen. The strawberry bed was put under his sole charge. And often, of mild, sunny afternoons, the knight, genial and gentle with dinner, would stroll bare-headed to the pleasant strawberry bed, and have nice little confidential chats with Israel; while Israel, charmed by the patriarchal demeanor of this true Abrahamic gentleman, with a smile on his lip, and tears of gratitude in his eyes, offered him, from time to time, the plumpest berries of the bed.

When the strawberry season was over, other parts of the grounds were assigned him. And so six months elapsed, when, at the recommendation of Sir John, Israel procured a good berth in the garden of the Princess Amelia.

So completely now had recent events metamorphosed him in all outward things, that few suspected him of being any other than an Englishman. Not even the knight's domestics. But in the princess's garden, being obliged to work in company with many other laborers, the war was often a topic of discussion among them. And "the d—d Yankee rebels" were not seldom the object of scurrilous remark. Ill could the exile brook in silence such insults upon the country for which he had bled, and for whose honored sake he was that very instant a sufferer. More than once, his indignation came very nigh getting the better of his prudence. He longed for the war to end, that he might but speak a little bit of his mind.

Now the superintendent of the garden was a harsh, overbearing man. The workmen with tame servility endured his worst affronts. But Israel, bred among mountains, found it impossible to restrain himself when made the undeserved object of pitiless epithets. Ere two months went by, he quitted the service of the princess, and engaged himself to a farmer in a small village not far from Brentford. But hardly had he been here three weeks, when a rumor again got afloat, that he was a Yankee prisoner of war. Whence this report arose he could never discover. No sooner did it reach the ears of the soldiers, than they were on the alert. Luckily Israel was apprised of their intentions in time. But he was hard pushed. He was hunted after with a perseverance worthy a less ignoble cause. He had many hairbreadth escapes. Most assuredly he would have been captured, had it not been for the secret good offices of a few individuals, who, perhaps, were not unfriendly to the American side of the question, though they durst not avow it.

Tracked one night by the soldiers to the house of one of these friends, in whose garret he was concealed: he was obliged to force the skuttle, and running along the roof, passed to those of adjoining houses to the number of ten or twelve, finally succeeding in making his escape.

Chapter 5

HARASSED DAY and night, hunted from food and sleep, driven from hole to hole like a fox in the woods; with no chance to earn an hour's wages; he was at last advised by one whose sincerity he could not doubt, to apply, on the good word of Sir John Millet, for a berth as laborer in the King's Gardens at Kew. There, it was said, he would be entirely safe, as no soldier durst approach those premises to molest any soul therein employed. It struck the poor exile as curious, that the very den of the British lion, the private grounds of the British King, should be commended to a refugee as his securest asylum.

His nativity carefully concealed, and being personally introduced to the chief gardener by one who well knew him; armed too with a line from Sir John, and recommended by his introducer as uncommonly expert at horticulture; Israel was soon installed as keeper of certain less private plants and walks of the park.

It was here, to one of his near country retreats, that, coming from perplexities of state—leaving far behind him the dingy old bricks of St. James—George the Third was wont to walk up and down beneath the long arbors formed by the interlockings of lofty trees.

More than once, raking the gravel, Israel through intervening foliage would catch peeps in some private but parallel walk, of that lonely figure, not more shadowy with overhanging leaves than with the shade of royal meditations.

Unauthorized and abhorrent thoughts will sometimes invade the best human heart. Seeing the monarch unguarded before him; remembering that the war was imputed more to the self-will of the King than to the willingness of parliament or the nation; and calling to mind all his own sufferings growing out of that war, with all the calamities of his country; dim impulses, such as those to which the regicide Ravaillac yielded, would shoot balefully across the soul of the exile. But thrusting Satan behind him, Israel vanquished all such temptations. Nor did these ever more disturb him, after his one chance conversation with the monarch.

As he was one day gravelling a little bye-walk; wrapped in thought, the King turning a clump of bushes, suddenly brushed Israel's person.

Immediately Israel touched his hat—but did not remove it—bowed, and was retiring; when something in his air arrested the King's attention.

"You aint an Englishman,—no Englishman—no no."

Pale as death, Israel tried to answer something; but knowing not what to say, stood frozen to the ground.

"You are a Yankee—a Yankee," said the King again in his rapid and half-stammering way.

Again Israel assayed to reply, but could not. What could he say? Could he lie to a King?

"Yes, yes,—you are one of that stubborn race,—that very stubborn race. What brought you here?"

"The fate of war, sir."

"May it please your Majesty," said a low cringing voice, approaching, "this man is in the walk against orders. There is some mistake, may it please your majesty. Quit the walk, blockhead," he hissed at Israel.

It was one of the junior gardeners who thus spoke. It seems that Israel had mistaken his directions that morning.

"Slink, you dog," hissed the gardener again to Israel; then aloud to the king, "A mistake of the man, I assure your majesty."

"Go you away—away with ye, and leave him with me," said the king.

Waiting a moment, till the man was out of hearing, the king again turned upon Israel.

"Were you at Bunker Hill?—that bloody Bunker Hill—eh, eh?"

"Yes, sir."

"Fought like a devil—like a very devil, I suppose?"

"Yes, sir."

"Helped flog—helped flog my soldiers?"

"Yes, sir; but very sorry to do it."

"Eh?—eh?—how's that?"

"I took it to be my sad duty, sir."

"Very much mistaken—very much mistaken indeed. Why do ye sir me?—eh? I'm your king—your king."

"Sir," said Israel firmly, but with deep respect, "I have no king."

The king darted his eye incensedly for a moment; but without quailing, Israel, now that all was out, still stood with mute respect before him. The king, turning suddenly, walked rapidly away from Israel a moment, but presently returning with a less hasty pace, said, "You are rumored to be a spy— a spy, or something of that sort—aint you? But I know you are not—no, no. You are a runaway prisoner-of-war, eh? You have sought this place to be safe from pursuit, eh? eh? Is it not so?—eh? eh? eh?"

"Sir, it is."

"Well, ye're an honest rebel—rebel, yes, rebel. Hark ye, hark. Say nothing of this talk to any one. And hark again. So long as ye remain here at Kew, I shall see that you are safe— safe."

"God bless your majesty!"

"Eh?"

"God bless your noble majesty!"

"Come—come—come," smiled the king in delight, "I thought I could conquer ye—conquer ye."

"Not the king, but the king's kindness, your majesty."

"Join my army—army."

Sadly looking down, Israel silently shook his head.

"You won't? Well, gravel the walk then—gravel away. Very stubborn race—very stubborn race indeed—very—very— very."

And still growling, the magnanimous lion departed.

How the monarch came by his knowledge of so humble an exile, whether through that swift insight into individual character said to form one of the miraculous qualities transmitted with a crown, or whether some of the rumors prevailing outside of the garden had come to his ear, Israel could never determine. Very probably, though, the latter was the case, inasmuch as some vague shadowy report of Israel not being an Englishman, had a little previous to his interview with the king, been communicated to several of the inferior gardeners. Without any impeachment of Israel's fealty to his country, it must still be narrated, that from this his familiar audience with George the Third, he went away with very favorable views of that monarch. Israel now thought that it could not be the warm heart of the king, but the cold heads of his lords in council, that persuaded him so tyrannically to persecute America. Yet hitherto the precise contrary of this had been Israel's opinion, agreeably to the popular prejudice throughout New England.

Thus we see what strange and powerful magic resides in a crown, and how subtly that cheap and easy magnanimity, which in private belongs to most kings, may operate on good-natured and unfortunate souls. Indeed, had it not been for the peculiar disinterested fidelity of our adventurer's patriotism, he would have soon sported the red coat; and perhaps under the immediate patronage of his royal friend, been advanced in time to no mean rank in the army of Britain. Nor in that case would we have had to follow him, as at last we shall, through long, long years of obscure and penurious wandering.

Continuing in the service of the king's gardener at Kew, until a season came when the work of the garden required a less number of laborers; Israel, with several others, was discharged; and the day after, engaged himself for a few months to a farmer in the neighborhood where he had been last employed. But hardly a week had gone by, when the old story of his being a rebel, or a runaway prisoner, or a Yankee! or a spy, began to be revived with added malignity. Like bloodhounds, the soldiers were once more on the track. The houses where he harbored were many times searched; but thanks to the fidelity of a few earnest well-wishers, and to his own unsleeping vigilance and activity, the hunted fox still continued to elude apprehension. To such extremities of harassment, however, did this incessant pursuit subject him, that in a fit of despair he was about to surrender himself, and submit to his fate, when Providence seasonably interposed in his favor.

Chapter 6

Israel Makes the Acquaintance of Certain Secret Friends of America, One of Them Being
the Famous Author of the "Diversions of
Purley." These Despatch Him on a
Sly Errand across the Channel

At this period, though made the victims indeed of British oppression, yet the colonies were not totally without friends in Britain. It was but natural that when Parliament itself held patriotic and gifted men, who not only recommended conciliatory measures, but likewise denounced the war as monstrous; it was but natural that throughout the nation at large there should be many private individuals cherishing similar sentiments; and some who made no scruple clandestinely to act upon them.

Late one night while hiding in a farmer's granary, Israel saw a man with a lantern approaching. He was about to flee, when the man hailed him in a well-known voice, bidding him have no fear. It was the farmer himself. He carried a message to Israel from a gentleman of Brentford, to the effect, that the refugee was earnestly requested to repair on the following evening to that gentleman's mansion.

At first Israel was disposed to surmise that either the farmer was playing him false, or else his honest credulity had been imposed upon by evil-minded persons. At any rate, he regarded the message as a decoy, and for half an hour refused to credit its sincerity. But at length he was induced to think a little better of it. The gentleman giving the invitation was one Squire Woodcock, of Brentford, whose loyalty to the king, had been under suspicion; so at least the farmer averred. This latter information was not without its effect.

At nightfall on the following day, being disguised in strange clothes by the farmer, Israel stole from his retreat, and after a few hours' walk, arrived before the ancient brick house of the Squire; who opening the door in person, and learning who it was that stood there, at once assured Israel in the most solemn manner, that no foul play was intended. So the wanderer suffered himself to enter, and be conducted to a private chamber in the rear of the mansion, where were seated two other gentlemen, attired, in the manner of that age, in long laced coats, with smallclothes, and shoes with silver buckles.

"I am John Woodcock," said the host, "and these gentlemen are Horne Tooke and James Bridges. All three of us are friends to America. We have heard of you for some weeks past, and inferring from your conduct, that you must be a Yankee of the true blue stamp, we have resolved to employ you in a way which you cannot but gladly approve; for surely, though an exile, you are still willing to serve your country; if not as a sailor or soldier, yet as a traveller?"

"Tell me how I may do it?" demanded Israel, not completely at ease.

"At that in good time," smiled the Squire. "The point is now—do you repose confidence in my statements?"

Israel glanced inquiringly upon the Squire; then upon his companions; and meeting the expressive, enthusiastic, candid countenance of Horne Tooke—then in the first honest ardor of his political career—turned to the Squire, and said, "Sir, I believe what you have said. Tell me now what I am to do?"

"Oh, there is just nothing to be done to-night," said the Squire; "nor for some days to come perhaps, but we wanted to have you prepared."

And hereupon he hinted to his guest rather vaguely of his general intention; and that over, begged him to entertain them with some account of his adventures since he first took up arms for his country. To this Israel had no objections in the world, since all men love to tell the tale of hardships endured in a righteous cause. But ere beginning his story, the Squire refreshed him with some cold beef, laid in a snowy napkin, and a glass of Perry, and thrice during the narration of the adventures, pressed him with additional draughts.

But after his second glass, Israel declined to drink more, mild as the beverage was. For he noticed, that not only did the three gentlemen listen with the utmost interest to his story, but likewise interrupted him with questions and cross-questions in the most pertinacious manner. So this led him to be on his guard, not being absolutely certain yet, as to who

they might really be, or what was their real design. But as it
turned out, Squire Woodcock and his friends only sought to
satisfy themselves thoroughly, before making their final disclosures, that the exile was one in whom implicit confidence
might be placed.

And to this desirable conclusion they eventually came; for
upon the ending of Israel's story, after expressing their sympathies for his hardships, and applauding his generous patriotism in so patiently enduring adversity, as well as singing the
praises of his gallant fellow-soldiers of Bunker Hill; they
openly revealed their scheme. They wished to know, whether
Israel would undertake a trip to Paris, to carry an important
message—shortly to be received for transmission through
them—to Doctor Franklin, then in that capital.

"All your expenses shall be paid, not to speak of a compensation besides," said the Squire; " will you go?"

"I must think of it," said Israel, not yet wholly confirmed
in his mind. But once more he cast his glance on Horne
Tooke, and his irresolution was gone.

The Squire now informed Israel that, to avoid suspicions,
it would be necessary for him to remove to another place
until the hour at which he should start for Paris. They enjoined upon him the profoundest secresy; gave him a guinea,
with a letter for a gentleman in White Waltham, a town some
miles from Brentford, which point they begged him to reach
as soon as possible, there to tarry for further instructions.

Having informed him of thus much, Squire Woodcock
asked him to hold out his right foot.

"What for?" said Israel.

"Why, would you not like to have a pair of new boots
against your return?" smiled Horne Tooke.

"Oh yes; no objections at all," said Israel.

"Well then, let the boot-maker measure you," smiled Horne
Tooke.

"Do *you* do it, Mr. Tooke," said the Squire, "you measure
men's parts better than I."

"Hold out your foot, my good friend," said Horne
Tooke—"there—now let's measure your heart."

"For that, measure me round the chest," said Israel.

"Just the man we want," said Mr. Bridges, triumphantly.

"Give him another glass of wine, Squire," said Horne Tooke.

Exchanging the farmer's clothes for still another disguise, Israel now set out immediately, on foot, for his destination, having received minute directions as to his road; and arriving in White Waltham on the following morning, was very cordially received by the gentleman to whom he carried the letter. This person, another of the active English friends of America, possessed a particular knowledge of late events in that land. To him Israel was indebted for much entertaining information. After remaining some ten days at this place, word came from Squire Woodcock, requiring Israel's immediate return, stating the hour at which he must arrive at the house, namely, two o'clock on the following morning. So, after another night's solitary trudge across the country, the wanderer was welcomed by the same three gentlemen as before, seated in the same room.

"The time has now come," said Squire Woodcock. "You must start this morning for Paris. Take off your shoes."

"Am I to steal from here to Paris on my stocking-feet?" said Israel, whose late easy good living at White Waltham had not failed to bring out the good-natured and mirthful part of him, even as his prior experiences had produced, for the most part, something like a contrary result.

"Oh no," smiled Horne Tooke, who always lived well; " we have seven-league-boots for you. Don't you remember my measuring you?"

Hereupon going to the closet, the Squire brought out a pair of new boots. They were fitted with false heels. Unscrewing these, the Squire showed Israel the papers concealed beneath. They were of a fine tissuey fibre, and contained much writing in a very small compass. The boots—it need hardly be said—had been particularly made for the occasion.

"Walk across the room with them," said the Squire, when Israel had pulled them on.

"He'll surely be discovered," smiled Horne Tooke. "Hark, how he creaks."

"Come, come, it's too serious a matter for joking," said the Squire. "Now my fine fellow, be cautious, be sober, be vigilant, and above all things be speedy."

Being furnished now with all requisite directions, and a supply of money, Israel taking leave of Mr. Tooke and Mr. Bridges, was secretly conducted down stairs by the Squire, and in five minutes' time was on his way to Charing Cross in London; where taking the post-coach for Dover, he thence went in a packet to Calais, and in fifteen minutes after landing, was being wheeled over French soil towards Paris. He arrived there in safety, and freely declaring himself an American, the peculiarly friendly relations of the two nations at that period, procured him kindly attentions even from strangers.

Chapter 7

AFTER A CURIOUS ADVENTURE UPON THE PONT
NEUF, ISRAEL ENTERS THE PRESENCE OF THE
RENOWNED SAGE, DR. FRANKLIN, WHOM
HE FINDS RIGHT LEARNEDLY AND
MULTIFARIOUSLY EMPLOYED

FOLLOWING THE directions given him at the place where
the diligence stopped, Israel was crossing the Pont Neuf,
to find Doctor Franklin, when he was suddenly called to by a
man standing on one side of the bridge, just under the eques-
trian statue of Henry IV.

The man had a small, shabby-looking box before him on
the ground, with a box of blacking on one side of it, and
several shoe-brushes upon the other. Holding another brush
in his hand, he politely seconded his verbal invitation by
gracefully flourishing the brush in the air.

"What do you want of me, neighbor?" said Israel, pausing
in somewhat uneasy astonishment.

"Ah Monsieur," exclaimed the man, and with voluble politeness he ran on with a long string of French, which of
course was all Greek to poor Israel. But what his language
failed to convey, his gestures now made very plain. Pointing
to the wet muddy state of the bridge, splashed by a recent
rain, and then to the feet of the wayfarer, and lastly to the
brush in his hand, he appeared to be deeply regretting that a
gentleman of Israel's otherwise imposing appearance, should
be seen abroad with unpolished boots, offering at the same
time to remove their blemishes.

"Ah Monsieur, Monsieur," cried the man, at last running
up to Israel. And with tender violence he forced him towards
the box, and lifting this unwilling customer's right foot
thereon, was proceeding vigorously to work, when suddenly
illuminated by a dreadful suspicion, Israel, fetching the box a
terrible kick, took to his false heels and ran like mad over the
bridge.

Incensed that his politeness should receive such an ungracious return, the man pursued; which but confirming Israel

in his suspicions, he ran all the faster, and thanks to his fleetness, soon succeeded in escaping his pursuer.

Arrived at last at the street and the house, to which he had been directed; in reply to his summons, the gate, very strangely of itself, swung open; and much astonished at this unlooked-for sort of enchantment, Israel entered a wide vaulted passage leading to an open court within. While he was wondering that no soul appeared, suddenly he was hailed from a dark little window, where sat an old man cobbling shoes, while an old woman standing by his side, was thrusting her head into the passage, intently eyeing the stranger. They proved to be the porter and portress; the latter of whom, upon hearing his summons, had invisibly thrust open the gate to Israel, by means of a spring communicating with the little apartment.

Upon hearing the name of Doctor Franklin mentioned, the old woman, all alacrity, hurried out of her den, and with much courtesy showed Israel across the court, up three flights of stairs, to a door in the rear of the spacious building. There she left him while Israel knocked.

"Come in," said a voice.

And immediately Israel stood in the presence of the venerable Doctor Franklin.

Wrapped in a rich dressing-gown—a fanciful present from an admiring Marchesa—curiously embroidered with algebraic figures like a conjuror's robe, and with a skull-cap of black satin on his hive of a head, the man of gravity was seated at a huge claw-footed old table, round as the zodiac. It was covered with printed papers; files of documents; rolls of MSS.; stray bits of strange models in wood and metal; odd-looking pamphlets in various languages; and all sorts of books; including many presentation-copies; embracing history, mechanics, diplomacy, agriculture, political economy, metaphysics, meteorology, and geometry. The walls had a necromantic look; hung round with barometers of different kinds; drawings of surprising inventions; wide maps of far countries in the New World, containing vast empty spaces in the middle, with the word D E S E R T diffusely printed there, so as to span five-and-twenty degrees of longitude with only two syllables,—which printed word however bore a vig-

orous pen-mark, in the Doctor's hand, drawn straight
through it, as if in summary repeal of it; crowded topograph-
ical and trigonometrical charts of various parts of Europe;
with geometrical diagrams, and endless other surprising hangings and upholstery of science.

The chamber itself bore evident marks of antiquity. One
part of the rough-finished wall was sadly cracked; and covered
with dust, looked dim and dark. But the aged inmate, though
wrinkled as well, looked neat and hale. Both wall and sage
were compounded of like materials,—lime and dust; both,
too, were old; but while the rude earth of the wall had no
painted lustre to shed off all fadings and tarnish, and still keep
fresh without, though with long eld its core decayed: the living lime and dust of the sage was frescoed with defensive
bloom of his soul.

The weather was warm; like some old West India hogshead
on the wharf, the whole chamber buzzed with flies. But the
sapient inmate sat still and cool in the midst. Absorbed in
some other world of his occupations and thoughts, these insects, like daily cark and care, did not seem one whit to annoy
him. It was a goodly sight to see this serene, cool and ripe
old philosopher, who by sharp inquisition of man in the
street, and then long meditating upon him, surrounded by all
these queer old implements, charts and books, had grown at
last so wondrous wise. There he sat, quite motionless among
those restless flies; and, with a sound like the low noon murmur of foliage in the woods, turning over the leaves of some
ancient and tattered folio, with a binding dark and shaggy as
the bark of any old oak. It seemed as if supernatural lore must
needs pertain to this gravely ruddy personage; at least far
foresight, pleasant wit, and working wisdom. Old age seemed
in nowise to have dulled him, but to have sharpened; just as
old dinner-knives—so they be of good steel—wax keen,
spear-pointed, and elastic as whale-bone with long usage. Yet
though he was thus lively and vigorous to behold, spite of his
seventy-two years (his exact date at the time) somehow, the
incredible seniority of an antediluvian seemed his. Not the
years of the calendar wholly, but also the years of sapience.
His white hairs and mild brow, spoke of the future as well as
the past. He seemed to be seven score years old; that is, three-

score and ten of prescience added to three score and ten of remembrance, makes just seven score years in all.

But when Israel stepped within the chamber, he lost the complete effect of all this; for the sage's back, not his face, was turned to him.

So, intent on his errand, hurried and heated with his recent run, our courier entered the room, inadequately impressed, for the time, by either it or its occupant.

"Bon jour, bon jour, monsieur," said the man of wisdom, in a cheerful voice, but too busy to turn round just then.

"How do you do, Doctor Franklin," said Israel.

"Ah! I smell Indian corn," said the Doctor, turning round quickly on his chair. "A countryman; sit down, my good sir. Well, what news? Special?"

"Wait a minute, sir," said Israel, stepping across the room towards a chair.

Now there was no carpet on the floor, which was of dark-colored wood, set in lozenges, and slippery with wax, after the usual French style. As Israel walked this slippery floor, his unaccustomed feet slid about very strangely, as if walking on ice, so that he came very near falling.

" 'Pears to me you have rather high heels to your boots," said the grave man of utility, looking sharply down through his spectacles; "Don't you know that it's both wasting leather and endangering your limbs, to wear such high heels? I have thought at my first leisure, to write a little pamphlet against that very abuse. But pray, what are you doing now? Do your boots pinch you, my friend, that you lift one foot from the floor that way?"

At this moment, Israel having seated himself, was just putting his right foot across his left knee.

"How foolish," continued the wise man, "for a rational creature to wear tight boots. Had nature intended rational creatures should so do, she would have made the foot of solid bone, or perhaps of solid iron, instead of bone, muscle, and flesh.—But,—I see. Hold!"

And springing to his own slippered feet, the venerable sage hurried to the door and shot-to the bolt. Then drawing the curtain carefully across the window looking out across the court to various windows on the opposite side, bade Israel proceed with his operations.

"I was mistaken this time," added the Doctor, smiling, as Israel produced his documents from their curious recesses— "your high heels, instead of being idle vanities, seem to be full of meaning."

"Pretty full, Doctor," said Israel, now handing over the papers. "I had a narrow escape with them just now."

"How? How's that?" said the sage, fumbling the papers eagerly.

"Why, crossing the stone bridge there over the *Seen*"—

"*Seine*"—interrupted the Doctor, giving the French pronunciation—"Always get a new word right in the first place, my friend, and you will never get it wrong afterwards."

"Well, I was crossing the bridge there, and who should hail me, but a suspicious looking man, who, under pretence of seeking to polish my boots, wanted slyly to unscrew their heels, and so steal all these precious papers I've brought you."

"My good friend," said the man of gravity, glancing scrutinizingly upon his guest, "have you not in your time, undergone what they call hard times? Been set upon, and persecuted, and very ill entreated by some of your fellow-creatures?"

"That I have, Doctor; yes indeed."

"I thought so. Sad usage has made you sadly suspicious, my honest friend. An indiscriminate distrust of human nature is the worst consequence of a miserable condition, whether brought about by innocence or guilt. And though want of suspicion more than want of sense, sometimes leads a man into harm: yet too much suspicion is as bad as too little sense. The man you met, my friend, most probably, had no artful intention; he knew just nothing about you or your heels; he simply wanted to earn two sous by brushing your boots. Those blacking-men regularly station themselves on the bridge."

"How sorry I am then that I knocked over his box, and then ran away. But he didn't catch me."

"How? surely, my honest friend, you,—appointed to the conveyance of important secret despatches—did not act so imprudently as to kick over an innocent man's box in the public streets of the capital, to which you had been especially sent?"

"Yes, I did, Doctor."

"Never act so unwisely again. If the police had got hold of you, think of what might have ensued."

"Well, it was not very wise of me, that's a fact, Doctor. But, you see, I thought he meant mischief."

"And because you only thought he *meant* mischief, *you* must straightway proceed to *do* mischief. That's poor logic. But think over what I have told you now, while I look over these papers."

In half an hour's time, the Doctor, laying down the documents, again turned towards Israel, and removing his spectacles very placidly, proceeded in the kindest and most familiar manner to read him a paternal detailed lesson upon the ill-advised act he had been guilty of, upon the Pont Neuf; concluding by taking out his purse, and putting three small silver coins into Israel's hands, charging him to seek out the man that very day, and make both apology and restitution for his unlucky mistake.

"All of us, my honest friend," continued the Doctor, "are subject to making mistakes; so that the chief art of life, is to learn how best to remedy mistakes. Now one remedy for mistakes is honesty. So pay the man for the damage done to his box. And now, who are you, my friend? My correspondents here mention your name—Israel Potter—and say you are an American, an escaped prisoner of war, but nothing further. I want to hear your story from your own lips."

Israel immediately began, and related to the Doctor all his adventures up to the present time.

"I suppose," said the Doctor, upon Israel's concluding, "that you desire to return to your friends across the sea?"

"That I do, Doctor," said Israel.

"Well, I think, I shall be able to procure you a passage."

Israel's eyes sparkled with delight. The mild sage noticed it, and added: "But events in these times are uncertain. At the prospect of pleasure never be elated; but, without depression, respect the omens of ill. So much my life has taught me, my honest friend."

Israel felt as though a plum-pudding had been thrust under his nostrils, and then as rapidly withdrawn.

"I think it is probable that in two or three days I shall want you to return with some papers to the persons who sent you to me. In that case you will have to come here once more, and then, my good friend, we will see what can be done towards getting you safely home again."

Israel was pouring out torrents of thanks when the Doctor interrupted him.

"Gratitude, my friend, cannot be too much towards God, but towards man, it should be limited. No man can possibly so serve his fellow, as to merit unbounded gratitude. Over gratitude in the helped person, is apt to breed vanity or arrogance in the helping one. Now in assisting you to get home—if indeed I shall prove able to do so—I shall be simply doing part of my official duty as agent of our common country. So you owe me just nothing at all, but the sum of these coins I put in your hand just now. But that, instead of repaying to me hereafter, you can, when you get home, give to the first soldier's widow you meet. Don't forget it, for it is a debt, a pecuniary liability, owing to me. It will be about a quarter of a dollar, in the Yankee currency. A quarter of a dollar, mind. My honest friend, in pecuniary matters always be exact as a second-hand; never mind with whom it is, father or stranger, peasant or king, be exact to a tick of your honor."

"Well, Doctor," said Israel, "since exactness in these matters is so necessary, let me pay back my debt in the very coins in which it was loaned. There will be no chance of mistake then. Thanks to my Brentford friends, I have enough to spare of my own, to settle damages with the boot-black of the bridge. I only took the money from you, because I thought it would not look well to push it back after being so kindly offered."

"My honest friend" said the Doctor, "I like your straight-forward dealing. I will receive back the money."

"No interest, Doctor, I hope," said Israel.

The sage looked mildly over his spectacles upon Israel, and replied, "My good friend, never permit yourself to be jocose upon pecuniary matters. Never joke at funerals, or during business transactions. The affair between us two, you perhaps deem very trivial, but trifles may involve momentous prin-

ciples. But no more at present. You had better go immediately
and find the boot-black. Having settled with him, return
hither, and you will find a room ready for you near this,
where you will stay during your sojourn in Paris."

"But I thought I would like to have a little look round the
town, before I go back to England," said Israel.

"Business before pleasure, my friend. You must absolutely
remain in your room, just as if you were my prisoner, until
you quit Paris for Calais. Not knowing now at what instant I
shall want you to start, your keeping to your room is indispensable. But when you come back from Brentford again,
then, if nothing happens, you will have a chance to survey
this celebrated capital ere taking ship for America. Now go
directly, and pay the boot-black. Stop, have you the exact
change ready? Don't be taking out all your money in the open
street."

"Doctor," said Israel, "I am not so simple."

"But you knocked over the box."

"That, Doctor, was bravery."

"Bravery in a poor cause, is the height of simplicity, my
friend.—Count out your change. It must be French coin, not
English, that you are to pay the man with.—Ah, that will
do—those three coins will be enough. Put them in a pocket
separate from your other cash. Now go, and hasten to the
bridge."

"Shall I stop to take a meal any where, Doctor, as I return?
I saw several cook-shops as I came hither."

"Cafés and restaurants, they are called here, my honest
friend. Tell me, are you the possessor of a liberal fortune?"

"Not very liberal," said Israel.

"I thought as much. Where little wine is drunk, it is good
to dine out occasionally at a friend's; but where a poor man
dines out at his own charge, it is bad policy. Never dine out
that way, when you can dine in. Do not stop on the way at
all, my honest friend, but come directly back hither, and you
shall dine at home, free of cost, with me."

"Thank you very kindly, Doctor."

And Israel departed for the Pont Neuf. Succeeding in his
errand thither, he returned to Doctor Franklin, and found
that worthy envoy waiting his attendance at a meal, which

according to the Doctor's custom, had been sent from a neighboring restaurant. There were two covers; and without attendance the host and guest sat down. There was only one principal dish, lamb boiled with green peas. Bread and potatoes made up the rest. A decanter-like bottle of uncolored glass, filled with some uncolored beverage, stood at the venerable envoy's elbow.

"Let me fill your glass," said the sage.

"It's white wine, aint it?" said Israel.

"White wine of the very oldest brand; I drink your health in it, my honest friend."

"Why, it's plain water," said Israel, now tasting it.

"Plain water is a very good drink for plain men," replied the wise man.

"Yes," said Israel, "but Squire Woodcock gave me perry, and the other gentleman at White Waltham gave me port, and some other friends have given me brandy."

"Very good, my honest friend; if you like perry and port and brandy, wait till you get back to Squire Woodcock, and the gentleman at White Waltham, and the other friends, and you shall drink perry and port and brandy. But while you are with me, you will drink plain water."

"So it seems, Doctor."

"What do you suppose a glass of port costs?"

"About three pence English, Doctor."

"That must be poor port. But how much good bread will three pence English purchase?"

"Three penny rolls, Doctor."

"How many glasses of port do you suppose a man may drink at a meal?"

"The gentleman at White Waltham drank a bottle at a dinner."

"A bottle contains just thirteen glasses—that's thirty-nine pence, supposing it poor wine. If something of the best, which is the only sort any sane man should drink, as being the least poisonous, it would be quadruple that sum, which is one hundred and fifty-six pence, which is seventy-eight two-penny loaves. Now, do you not think that for one man to swallow down seventy-eight two-penny rolls at one meal is rather extravagant business?"

"But he drank a bottle of wine; he did not eat seventy-eight two-penny rolls, Doctor."

"He drank the money worth of seventy-eight loaves, which is drinking the loaves themselves; for money is bread."

"But he has plenty of money to spare, Doctor."

"To have to spare, is to have to give away. Does the gentleman give much away?"

"Not that I know of, Doctor."

"Then he thinks he has nothing to spare; and thinking he has nothing to spare, and yet prodigally drinking down his money as he does every day, it seems to me that that gentleman stands self-contradicted, and therefore is no good example for plain sensible folks like you and me to follow. My honest friend, if you are poor, avoid wine as a costly luxury; if you are rich, shun it as a fatal indulgence. Stick to plain water. And now, my good friend, if you are through with your meal, we will rise. There is no pastry coming. Pastry is poisoned bread. Never eat pastry. Be a plain man, and stick to plain things. Now, my friend, I shall have to be private until nine o'clock in the evening, when I shall be again at your service. Meantime you may go to your room. I have ordered the one next to this to be prepared for you. But you must not be idle. Here is Poor Richard's Almanac, which in view of our late conversation, I commend to your earnest perusal. And here, too, is a Guide to Paris, an English one, which you can read. Study it well, so that when you come back from England if you should then have an opportunity to travel about Paris, to see its wonders, you will have all the chief places made historically familiar to you. In this world, men must provide knowledge before it is wanted, just as our countrymen in New England get in their winter's fuel one season, to serve them the next."

So saying, this homely sage, and household Plato, showed his humble guest to the door, and standing in the hall, pointed out to him the one which opened into his allotted apartment.

Chapter 8

WHICH HAS SOMETHING TO SAY ABOUT DR. FRANKLIN AND THE LATIN QUARTER

THE FIRST, both in point of time and merit, of American envoys was famous not less for the pastoral simplicity of his manners than for the politic grace of his mind. Viewed from a certain point, there was a touch of primeval orientalness in Benjamin Franklin. Neither is there wanting something like his scriptural parallel. The history of the patriarch Jacob is interesting not less from the unselfish devotion which we are bound to ascribe to him, than from the deep worldly wisdom and polished Italian tact, gleaming under an air of Arcadian unaffectedness. The diplomatist and the shepherd are blended; a union not without warrant; the apostolic serpent and dove. A tanned Machiavelli in tents.

Doubtless, too, notwithstanding his eminence as lord of the moving manor, Jacob's raiment was of homespun; the economic envoy's plain coat and hose, who has not heard of?

Franklin all over is of a piece. He dressed his person as his periods; neat, trim, nothing superfluous, nothing deficient. In some of his works his style is only surpassed by the unimprovable sentences of Hobbes of Malmsbury, the paragon of perspicuity. The mental habits of Hobbes and Franklin in several points, especially in one of some moment, assimilated. Indeed, making due allowance for soil and era, history presents few trios more akin, upon the whole, than Jacob, Hobbes, and Franklin; three labyrinth-minded, but plain-spoken Broadbrims, at once politicians and philosophers; keen observers of the main chance; prudent courtiers; practical magians in linsey woolsey.

In keeping with his general habitudes, Doctor Franklin while at the French Court did not reside in the aristocratical faubourgs. He deemed his worsted hose and scientific tastes more adapted in a domestic way to the other side of the Seine, where the Latin Quarter, at once the haunt of erudition and economy, seemed peculiarly to invite the philosophical Poor Richard to its venerable retreats. Here, of grey,

chilly, drizzly November mornings, in the dark-stoned quadrangle of the time-honored Sorbonne, walked the lean and
slippered metaphysician,—oblivious for the moment that his
sublime thoughts and tattered wardrobe were famous
throughout Europe,—meditating on the theme of his next
lecture; at the same time, in the well-worn chambers overhead, some clayey-visaged chemist in ragged robe-de-
chambre, and with a soiled green flap over his left eye, was
hard at work stooping over retorts and crucibles, discovering
new antipathies in acids, again risking strange explosions similar to that whereby he had already lost the use of one optic;
while in the lofty lodging-houses of the neighboring streets,
indigent young students from all parts of France, were iron-
ing their shabby cocked hats, or inking the whity seams of
their small-clothes, prior to a promenade with their pink-
ribboned little grizzets in the Garden of the Luxembourg.

Long ago the haunt of rank, the Latin Quarter still retains
many old buildings whose imposing architecture singularly
contrasts with the unassuming habits of their present occupants. In some parts its general air is dreary and dim; monastic and theurgic. In those lonely narrow ways—long-drawn
prospectives of desertion—lined with huge piles of silent,
vaulted, old iron-grated buildings of dark grey stone, one almost expects to encounter Paracelsus or Friar Bacon turning
the next corner, with some awful vial of Black-Art elixir in his
hand.

But all the lodging-houses are not so grim. Not to speak of
many of comparatively modern erection, the others of the
better class, however stern in exterior, evince a feminine gayety of taste, more or less, in their furnishings within. The
embellishing, or softening, or screening hand of woman is to
be seen all over the interiors of this metropolis. Like Augustus Cæsar with respect to Rome, the Frenchwoman leaves her
obvious mark on Paris. Like the hand of nature, you know it
can be none else but hers. Yet sometimes she overdoes it, as
nature in the peony; or underdoes it, as nature in the bram-
ble; or—what is still more frequent—is a little slatternly
about it, as nature in the pig-weed.

In this congenial vicinity of the Latin Quarter, and in an
ancient building something like those last alluded to, at a

point midway between the Palais des Beaux Arts and the College of the Sorbonne, the venerable American Envoy pitched his tent when not passing his time at his country retreat at Passy. The frugality of his manner of life did not lose him the good opinion even of the voluptuaries of the showiest of capitals, whose very iron railings are not free from gilt. Franklin was not less a lady's man, than a man's man, a wise man, and an old man. Not only did he enjoy the homage of the choicest Parisian literati, but at the age of seventy-two he was the caressed favorite of the highest born beauties of the Court; who through blind fashion having been originally attracted to him as a famous *savan*, were permanently retained as his admirers by his Plato-like graciousness of good-humor. Having carefully weighed the world, Franklin could act any part in it. By nature turned to knowledge, his mind was often grave, but never serious. At times he had seriousness—extreme seriousness—for others, but never for himself. Tranquillity was to him instead of it. This philosophical levity of tranquillity, so to speak, is shown in his easy variety of pursuits. Printer, postmaster, almanac maker, essayist, chemist, orator, tinker, statesman, humorist, philosopher, parlor-man, political economist, professor of housewifery, ambassador, projector, maxim-monger, herb-doctor, wit:—Jack of all trades, master of each and mastered by none—the type and genius of his land. Franklin was everything but a poet. But since a soul with many qualities, forming of itself a sort of handy index and pocket congress of all humanity, needs the contact of just as many different men, or subjects, in order to the exhibition of its totality; hence very little indeed of the sage's multifariousness will be portrayed in a simple narrative like the present. This casual private intercourse with Israel, but served to manifest him in his far lesser lights; thrifty, domestic, dietarian, and, it may be, didactically waggish. There was much benevolent irony, innocent mischievousness, in the wise man. Seeking here to depict him in his less exalted habitudes, the narrator feels more as if he were playing with one of the sage's worsted hose, then reverentially handling the honored hat which once oracularly sat upon his brow.

So, then, in the Latin Quarter lived Doctor Franklin. And accordingly in the Latin Quarter tarried Israel for the time.

And it was into a room of a house in this same Latin Quarter that Israel had been directed when the sage had requested privacy for a while.

Chapter 9

CLOSING THE DOOR upon himself, Israel advanced to the middle of the chamber, and looked curiously round him.

A dark tessellated floor, but without a rug; two mahogany chairs, with embroidered seats, rather the worse for wear; one mahogany bed, with a gay but tarnished counterpane; a marble wash-stand, cracked, with a china vessel of water, minus the handle. The apartment was very large; this part of the house, which was a very extensive one, embracing the four sides of a quadrangle, having, in a former age, been the hotel of a nobleman. The magnitude of the chamber made its stinted furniture look meagre enough.

But in Israel's eyes, the marble mantel (a comparatively recent addition) and its appurtenances, not only redeemed the rest, but looked quite magnificent and hospitable in the extreme. Because, in the first place, the mantel was graced with an enormous old-fashioned square mirror, of heavy plate glass, set fast, like a tablet, into the wall. And in this mirror was genially reflected the following delicate articles:—First, two bouquets of flowers inserted in pretty vases of porcelain; second, one cake of white soap; third, one cake of rose-colored soap (both cakes very fragrant); fourth, one wax candle; fifth, one china tinder-box; sixth, one bottle of Eau de Cologne; seventh, one paper of loaf sugar, nicely broken into sugar-bowl size; eighth, one silver teaspoon; ninth, one glass tumbler; tenth, one glass decanter of cool pure water; eleventh, one sealed bottle containing a richly hued liquid, and marked "Otard."

"I wonder now what O-t-a-r-d is?" soliloquised Israel, slowly spelling the word. "I have a good mind to step in and ask Dr. Franklin. He knows everything. Let me smell it. No, it's sealed; smell is locked in. Those are pretty flowers. Let's smell them: no smell again. Ah, I see—sort of flowers in women's bonnets—sort of calico flowers. Beautiful soap.

This smells anyhow—regular soap-roses—a white rose and a
red one. That long-necked bottle there looks like a crane. I
wonder what's in that? Hallo! E-a-u—d-e—C-o-l-o-g-n-e. I
wonder if Dr. Franklin understands that? It looks like his
white wine. This is nice sugar. Let's taste. Yes, this is very
nice sugar, sweet as—yes, it's sweet as sugar; better than maple sugar, such as they make at home. But I'm crunching it
too loud, the Doctor will hear me. But here's a teaspoon.
What's this for? There's no tea, nor tea-cup; but here's a tumbler, and here's drinking water. Let me see. Seems to me,
putting this and that and the other thing together, it's a sort
of alphabet that spells something. Spoon, tumbler, water,
sugar,——brandy—that's it. O-t-a-r-d is brandy. Who put
these things here? What does it all mean? Don't put sugar
here for show, don't put a spoon here for ornament, nor a
jug of water. There is only one meaning to it, and that is a
very polite invitation from some invisible person to help myself, if I like, to a glass of brandy and sugar, and if I don't
like, let it alone. That's my reading. I have a good mind to
ask Doctor Franklin about it, though, for there's just a chance
I may be mistaken, and these things here be some other person's private property, not at all meant for me to help myself
from. Co-logne, what's that?—never mind. Soap: soap's to
wash with. I want to use soap, anyway. Let me see—no,
there's no soap on the wash-stand. I see, soap is not given
gratis here in Paris, to boarders. But if you want it, take it
from the marble, and it will be charged in the bill. If you
don't want it let it alone, and no charge. Well, that's fair,
anyway. But then to a man who could not afford to use soap,
such beautiful cakes as these lying before his eyes all the time,
would be a strong temptation. And now that I think of it,
the O-t-a-r-d looks rather tempting too. But if I don't like it
now, I can let it alone. I've a good mind to try it. But it's
sealed. I wonder now if I am right in my understanding of
this alphabet? Who knows? I'll venture one little sip, anyhow.
Come cork. Hark!"

There was a rapid knock at the door.

Clapping down the bottle, Israel said, "Come in."

It was the man of wisdom.

"My honest friend," said the Doctor, stepping with venerable briskness into the room, "I was so busy during your visit to the Pont Neuf, that I did not have time to see that your room was all right. I merely gave the order, and heard that it had been fulfilled. But it just occurred to me, that as the landladies of Paris have some curious customs which might puzzle an entire stranger, my presence here for a moment might explain any little obscurity. Yes, it is as I thought," glancing towards the mantel.

"Oh, Doctor, that reminds me; what is O-t-a-r-d, pray?"

"Otard is poison."

"Shocking."

"Yes, and I think I had best remove it from the room forthwith," replied the sage, in a business-like manner putting the bottle under his arm; "I hope you never use Cologne, do you?"

"What—what is that, Doctor?"

"I see. You never heard of the senseless luxury—a wise ignorance. You smelt flowers upon your mountains. You won't want this, either;" and the Cologne bottle was put under the other arm. "Candle—you'll want that. Soap—you want soap. Use the white cake."

"Is that cheaper, Doctor?"

"Yes, but just as good as the other. You don't ever munch sugar, do you? It's bad for the teeth. I'll take the sugar." So the paper of sugar was likewise dropped into one of the capacious coat pockets.

"Oh, you better take the whole furniture, Doctor Franklin. Here, I'll help you drag out the bedstead."

"My honest friend," said the wise man, pausing solemnly, with the two bottles, like swimmer's bladders under his armpits; "my honest friend, the bedstead you will want; what I propose to remove, you will not want."

"Oh, I was only joking, Doctor."

"I knew that. It's a bad habit, except at the proper time, and with the proper person. The things left on the mantel were there placed by the landlady to be used if wanted; if not, to be left untouched. To-morrow morning, upon the chambermaid's coming in to make your bed, all such articles as remained obviously untouched, would have been removed; the rest would have been charged in the bill, whether you used them up completely or not."

"Just as I thought. Then why not let the bottles stay, Doctor, and save yourself all this trouble?"

"Ah! why indeed. My honest friend, are you not my guest? It were unhandsome in me to permit a third person superfluously to entertain you under what, for the time being, is my own roof."

These words came from the wise man in the most graciously bland and flowing tones. As he ended, he made a sort of conciliatory half bow towards Israel.

Charmed with his condescending affability, Israel, without another word, suffered him to march from the room, bottles and all. Not till the first impression of the venerable envoy's suavity had left him, did Israel begin to surmise the mild superiority of successful strategy which lurked beneath this highly ingratiating air.

"Ah," pondered Israel, sitting gloomily before the rifled mantel, with the empty tumbler and tea-spoon in his hand, "it's sad business to have a Doctor Franklin lodging in the next room. I wonder if he sees to all the boarders this way. How the O-t-a-r-d merchants must hate him, and the pastry-cooks too. I wish I had a good pie to pass the time. I wonder if they ever make pumpkin pies in Paris? So, I've got to stay in this room all the time. Somehow I'm bound to be a prisoner, one way or another. Never mind, I'm an ambassador. That's satisfaction. Hark! The Doctor again.—Come in."

No venerable doctor; but in tripped a young French lass, bloom on her cheek, pink ribbons in her cap, liveliness in all her air, grace in the very tips of her elbows. The most bewitching little chambermaid in Paris. All art, but the picture of artlessness.

"Monsieur! pardon!"

"Oh, I pardong ye freely," said Israel. "Come to call on the Ambassador?"

"Monsieur, is de—de—" but, breaking down at the very threshold in her English, she poured out a long ribbon of sparkling French, the purpose of which was to convey a profusion of fine compliments to the stranger, with many tender inquiries as to whether he was comfortably roomed, and whether there might not be something, however trifling, wanting to his complete accommodation. But Israel understood nothing, at the time, but the exceeding grace, and trim, bewitching figure of the girl.

She stood eyeing him for a few moments more, with a look of pretty theatrical despair; and, after vaguely lingering a while, with another shower of incomprehensible compliments and apologies, tripped like a fairy from the chamber. Directly she was gone, Israel pondered upon a singular glance of the girl. It seemed to him that he had, by his reception, in some way, unaccountably disappointed his beautiful visitor. It struck him very strangely that she had entered all sweetness and friendliness, but had retired as if slighted, with a sort of disdainful and sarcastic levity, all the more stinging from its apparent politeness.

Not long had she disappeared, when a noise in the passage apprised him that, in her hurried retreat, the girl must have stumbled against something. The next moment, he heard a chair scraping in the adjacent apartment, and there was another knock at the door.

It was the man of wisdom this time.

"My honest friend, did you not have a visitor, just now?"

"Yes, Doctor, a very pretty girl called upon me."

"Well, I just stopped in to tell you of another strange custom of Paris. That girl is the chambermaid; but she does not confine herself altogether to one vocation. You must beware of the chambermaids of Paris, my honest friend. Shall I tell the girl, from you, that, unwilling to give her the fatigue of going up and down so many flights of stairs, you will, for the future waive her visits of ceremony?"

"Why, Doctor Franklin, she is a very sweet little girl."

"I know it, my honest friend; the sweeter, the more dangerous. Arsenic is sweeter than sugar. I know you are a very sensible young man; not to be taken in by an artful Ammonite; and so, I think I had better convey your message to the girl forthwith."

So saying, the sage withdrew, leaving Israel once more gloomily seated before the rifled mantel, whose mirror was not again to reflect the form of the charming chambermaid.

"Every time he comes in he robs me," soliloquised Israel, dolefully; " with an air all the time, too, as if he were making me presents. If he thinks me such a very sensible young man, why not let me take care of myself?"

It was growing dusk, and Israel lighting the wax candle, proceeded to read in his Guide-book.

"This is poor sight-seeing," muttered he, at last, "sitting here all by myself, with no company but an empty tumbler, reading about the fine things in Paris, and I, myself, a prisoner in Paris. I wish something extraordinary would turn up now; for instance, a man come in and give me ten thousand pounds. But here's 'Poor Richard;' I am a poor fellow myself; so let's see what comfort he has for a comrade."

Opening the little pamphlet, at random, Israel's eyes fell on the following passages: he read them aloud—

" '*So what signifies wishing and hoping for better times? We may make these times better, if we bestir ourselves. Industry need not wish, and he that lives upon hopes will die fasting, as Poor Richard says. There are no gains, without pains. Then help, hands, for I have no lands, as Poor Richard says.*' Oh confound all this wisdom! It's a sort of insulting to talk wisdom to a man like me. It's wisdom that's cheap, and it's fortune that's dear. That ain't in Poor Richard; but it ought to be," concluded Israel, suddenly slamming down the pamphlet.

He walked across the room, looked at the artificial flowers, and the rose-colored soap, and again went to the table and took up the two books.

"So here is the 'Way to Wealth,' and here is the 'Guide to Paris.' Wonder now whether Paris lies on the Way to Wealth? if so, I am on the road. More likely though, it's a parting-of-the-ways. I shouldn't be surprised if the Doctor meant something sly by putting these two books in my hand. Somehow, the old gentleman has an amazing sly look—a sort of mild slyness—about him, seems to me. His wisdom seems a sort of sly, too. But all in honor, though. I rather think he's one of those old gentlemen who say a vast deal of sense, but hint a world more. Depend upon it, he's sly, sly, sly. Ah, what's this Poor Richard says: 'God helps them that help themselves.' Let's consider that. Poor Richard ain't a Dunker, that's certain, though he has lived in Pennsylvania. 'God helps them that help themselves.' I'll just mark that saw, and leave the pamphlet open to refer to again.—Ah!"

At this point, the Doctor knocked, summoning Israel to his own apartment. Here, after a cup of weak tea, and a little toast, the two had a long, familiar talk together; during which, Israel was delighted with the unpretending talkativeness, serene insight, and benign amiability of the sage. But, for all this, he could hardly forgive him for the Cologne and Otard depredations.

Discovering that, in early life, Israel had been employed on a farm, the man of wisdom at length turned the conversation in that direction; among other things, mentioning to his guest a plan of his (the Doctor's) for yoking oxen, with a yoke to go by a spring instead of a bolt; thus greatly facilitating the operation of hitching on the team to the cart. Israel was very much struck with the improvement; and thought that, if he were home, upon his mountains, he would immediately introduce it among the farmers.

Chapter 10

Another Adventurer Appears upon the Scene

About half-past ten o'clock, as they were thus conversing, Israel's acquaintance, the pretty chambermaid,
rapped at the door, saying, with a titter, that a very rude gentleman in the passage of the court, desired to see Doctor
Franklin.

"A very rude gentleman?" repeated the wise man in French,
narrowly looking at the girl, "that means, a very fine gentleman who has just paid you some energetic compliment. But
let him come up, my girl," he added patriarchically.

In a few moments, a swift coquettish step was heard, followed, as if in chase, by a sharp and manly one. The door
opened. Israel was sitting so that, accidentally his eye pierced
the crevice made by the opening of the door, which, like a
theatrical screen, stood for a moment, between Doctor Franklin, and the just entering visitor. And behind that screen,
through the crack, Israel caught one momentary glimpse of a
little bit of by-play between the pretty chambermaid and the
stranger. The vivacious nymph appeared to have affectedly
run from him on the stairs—doubtless in freakish return for
some liberal advances—but had suffered herself to be overtaken at last ere too late; and on the instant Israel caught sight
of her, was with an insincere air of rosy resentment, receiving
a roguish pinch on the arm, and a still more roguish salute
on the cheek.

The next instant both disappeared from the range of
the crevice; the girl departing whence she had come; the
stranger—transiently invisible as he advanced behind the
door,—entering the room. When Israel now perceived him
again, he seemed, while momentarily hidden, to have undergone a complete transformation.

He was a rather small, elastic, swarthy man, with an aspect
as of a disinherited Indian Chief in European clothes. An
unvanquishable enthusiasm, intensified to perfect sobriety,
couched in his savage, self-possessed eye. He was elegantly
and somewhat extravagantly dressed as a civilian; he carried

488

himself with a rustic, barbaric jauntiness, strangely dashed with a superinduced touch of the Parisian *salon*. His tawny cheek, like a date, spoke of the tropic. A wonderful atmosphere of proud friendlessness and scornful isolation invested him. Yet was there a bit of the poet as well as the outlaw in him, too. A cool solemnity of intrepidity sat on his lip. He looked like one who of purpose sought out harm's way. He looked like one who never had been, and never would be, a subordinate.

Israel thought to himself that seldom before had he seen such a being. Though dressed à-la-mode, he did not seem to be altogether civilized.

So absorbed was our adventurer by the person of the stranger, that a few moments passed ere he began to be aware of the circumstance, that Dr. Franklin and this new visitor having saluted as old acquaintances, were now sitting in earnest conversation together.

"Do as you please; but I will not bide a suitor much longer," said the stranger in bitterness. "Congress gave me to understand that, upon my arrival here, I should be given immediate command of the *Indien*; and now, for no earthly reason that I can see, you Commissioners have presented her, fresh from the stocks at Amsterdam, to the King of France, and not to me. What does the King of France with such a frigate? And what can I *not* do with her? Give me back the 'Indien,' and in less than one month, you shall hear glorious or fatal news of Paul Jones."

"Come, come, Captain," said Doctor Franklin, soothingly, "tell me now, what would you do with her, if you had her?"

"I would teach the British that Paul Jones, though born in Britain, is no subject to the British King, but an untrammelled citizen and sailor of the universe; and I would teach them, too, that if they ruthlessly ravage the American coasts their own coasts are vulnerable as New Holland's. Give me the *Indien*, and I will rain down on wicked England like fire on Sodom."

These words of bravado were not spoken in the tone of a bravo, but a prophet. Erect upon his chair, like an Iroquois, the speaker's look was like that of an unflickering torch.

His air seemed slightly to disturb the old sage's philosophic repose, who, while not seeking to disguise his admiration of the unmistakable spirit of the man, seemed but ill to relish his apparent measureless boasting.

As if both to change the subject a little, as well as put his visitor in better mood—though indeed it might have been but covertly to play with his enthusiasm—the man of wisdom now drew his chair confidentially nearer to the stranger's, and putting one hand in a very friendly, conciliatory way upon his visitor's knee, and rubbing it gently to and fro there, much as a lion-tamer might soothingly manipulate the aggravated king of beasts, said in a winning manner:—"Never mind at present, Captain, about the '*Indien*' affair. Let that sleep a moment. See now, the Jersey privateers do us a great deal of mischief by intercepting our supplies. It has been mentioned to me, that if you had a small vessel—say, even your present ship, the 'Ranger,'—then, by your singular bravery, you might render great service, by following those privateers where larger ships durst not venture their bottoms; or, if but supported by some frigates from Brest at a proper distance, might draw them out, so that the larger vessels could capture them."

"Decoy-duck to French frigates!—Very dignified office, truly!" hissed Paul in a fiery rage. "Doctor Franklin, whatever Paul Jones does for the cause of America, it must be done through unlimited orders: a separate, supreme command; no leader and no counsellor but himself. Have I not already by my services on the American coast shown that I am well worthy all this? Why then do you seek to degrade me below my previous level? I will mount, not sink. I live but for honor and glory. Give me then something honorable and glorious to do, and something famous to do it with. Give me the *Indien*."

The man of wisdom slowly shook his head.

"Everything is lost through this shillyshallying, timidity called prudence," cried Paul Jones, starting to his feet; "to be effectual, war should be carried on like a monsoon; one changeless determination of every particle towards the one unalterable aim. But in vacillating councils, statesmen idle about like the cats' paws in calms. My God, why was I not born a Czar!"

"A Nor-wester rather. Come, come, Captain," added the sage, "sit down; we have a third person present, you see,"— pointing towards Israel, who sat rapt at the volcanic spirit of the stranger.

Paul slightly started, and turned inquiringly upon Israel, who, equally owing to Paul's own earnestness of discourse, and Israel's motionless bearing—had thus far remained undiscovered.

"Never fear, Captain," said the sage, "this man is true blue; a secret courier, and an American born. He is an escaped prisoner of war."

"Ah, captured in a ship?" asked Paul eagerly;—" what ship? None of mine! Paul Jones never was captured."

"No, sir, in the brigantine Washington, out of Boston," replied Israel; "We were cruising to cut off supplies to the English."

"Did your shipmates talk much of me?" demanded Paul, with a look as of a parading Sioux demanding homage to his gew-gaws; " what did they say of Paul Jones?"

"I never heard the name before this evening," said Israel.

"What? Ah—brigantine Washington—let me see; that was before I had outwitted the Solebay frigate, fought the Milford, and captured the Mellish and the rest off Louisbergh. You were long before the news, my lad," he added with a sort of compassionate air.

"Our friend here gave you a rather blunt answer," said the wise man, sagely mischievous, and addressing Paul.

"Yes. And I like him for it. My man, will you go a cruise with Paul Jones? You fellows, so blunt with the tongue, are apt to be sharp with the steel. Come, my lad, return with me to Brest. I go in a few days."

Fired by the contagious spirit of Paul, Israel, forgetting all about his previous desire to reach home, sparkled with response to the summons. But Doctor Franklin interrupted him.

"Our friend here," said he to the Captain, "is at present engaged for very different duty."

Much other conversation followed, during which Paul Jones again and again expressed his impatience at being unemployed, and his resolution to accept of no employ unless it gave him supreme authority; while in answer to all this, Dr. Franklin, not uninfluenced by the uncompromising spirit of his guest, and well knowing that however unpleasant a trait in conversation, or in the transaction of civil affairs, yet in war, this very quality was invaluable, as projectiles and combustibles, finally assured Paul, after many complimentary remarks, that he would immediately exert himself to the utmost to procure for him some enterprise which should come up to his merits.

"Thank you for your frankness," said Paul; "frank myself, I love to deal with a frank man. You, Doctor Franklin, are true, and deep; and so you are frank."

The sage sedately smiled, a queer incredulity just lurking in the corner of his mouth.

"But how about our little scheme for new modelling ships-of-war?" said the Doctor, shifting the subject; "it will be a great thing for our infant navy, if we succeed. Since our last conversation on that subject, Captain, at odds and ends of time, I have thought over the matter, and have begun a little skeleton of the thing here, which I will show you. Whenever one has a new idea in anything mechanical, it is best to clothe it with a body as soon as possible. For you can't improve so well on ideas, as you can on bodies."

With that, going to a little drawer, he produced a small basket, filled with a curious looking unfinished frame-work of wood, and several bits of wood unattached. It looked like a nursery basket containing broken odds and ends of playthings.

"Now look here, Captain, though the thing is but begun at present, yet there is enough to show that *one* idea at least of yours is not feasible."

Paul was all attention, as if having unbounded confidence in whatever the sage might suggest; while Israel looked on, quite as interested as either; his heart swelling with the thought of being privy to the consultations of two such men; consultations, too, having ultimate reference to such momentous affairs as the freeing of nations.

"If," continued the Doctor, taking up some of the loose bits and piling them along on one side of the top of the frame; "if the better to shelter your crew in an engagement,

you construct your rail in the manner proposed—as thus—
then, by the excessive weight of the timber, you will too
much interfere with the ship's centre of gravity. You will have
that too high."

"Ballast in the hold in proportion," said Paul.

"Then you will sink the whole hull too low. But here, to
have less smoke in time of battle, especially on the lower
decks, you proposed a new sort of hatchway. But that won't
do. See here now, I have invented certain ventilating pipes—
they are to traverse the vessel thus"—laying some toilette
pins along—"the current of air to enter here and be discharged there. What do you think of that? But now about the
main things—fast sailing, driving little to leeward, and drawing little water. Look now at this keel. I whittled it only night
before last, just before going to bed. Do you see now
how"—

At this crisis, a knock was heard at the door, and the
chambermaid reappeared, announcing that two gentlemen
were that moment crossing the court below to see Doctor
Franklin.

"The Duke de Chartres, and Count D'Estaing," said the
Doctor, "they appointed for last night but did not come.
Captain, this has something indirectly to do with your affair.
Through the Duke, Count D'Estaing has spoken to the King
about the secret expedition, the design of which you first
threw out. Call early to-morrow, and I will inform you of the
result."

With his tawny hand Paul pulled out his watch, a small,
richly jewelled lady's watch.

"It is so late, I will stay here to-night," he said; "Is there a
convenient room?"

"Quick," said the Doctor, "it might be ill-advised of you to
be seen with me just now. Our friend here will let you share
his chamber. Quick, Israel, and show the Captain thither."

As the door closed upon them in Israel's apartment, Doctor
Franklin's door closed upon the Duke and the Count. Leaving the latter to their discussion of profound plans for the
timely befriending of the American cause, and the crippling
of the power of England on the seas, let us pass the night
with Paul Jones and Israel in the neighboring room.

Chapter 11

Paul Jones in a Reverie

'God helps them that help themselves.' That's a clincher. That's been my experience. But I never saw it in words before. What pamphlet is this? 'Poor Richard,' hey!"

Upon entering Israel's room, Captain Paul, stepping towards the table and spying the open pamphlet there, had taken it up, his eye being immediately attracted to the passage previously marked by our adventurer.

"A rare old gentleman is 'Poor Richard,' " said Israel in response to Paul's observations.

"So he seems, so he seems;" answered Paul, his eye still running over the pamphlet again; " why, 'Poor Richard' reads very much as Doctor Franklin speaks."

"He wrote it," said Israel.

"Aye? Good. So it is, so it is; it's the wise man all over. I must get me a copy of this, and wear it around my neck for a charm. And now about our quarters for the night. I am not going to deprive you of your bed, my man. Do you go to bed and I will doze in the chair here. It's good as dozing in the crosstrees."

"Why not sleep together," said Israel, "see, it is a big bed. Or perhaps you don't fancy your bed-fellow, Captain?"

"When, before the mast, I first sailed out of Whitehaven to Norway," said Paul, coolly, "I had for hammock-mate a full-blooded Congo. We had a white blanket spread in our hammock. Every time I turned in I found the Congo's black wool worked in with the white worsted. By the end of the voyage the blanket was of a pepper-and-salt look, like an old man's turning head. So it's not because I am notional at all, but because I don't care to, my lad. Turn in and go to sleep. Let the lamp burn. I'll see to it. There, go to sleep."

Complying with what seemed as much a command as a request, Israel, though in bed, could not fall into slumber, for thinking of the little circumstance that this strange swarthy man, flaming with wild enterprises, sat in full suit in the chair. He felt an uneasy misgiving sensation, as if he had retired,

494

not only without covering up the fire, but leaving it fiercely burning with spitting faggots of hemlock.

But his natural complaisance induced him at least to feign himself asleep; whereupon Paul, laying down "Poor Richard," rose from his chair, and, withdrawing his boots, began walking rapidly but noiselessly to and fro, in his stockings, in the spacious room, wrapped in Indian meditations. Israel furtively eyed him from beneath the coverlid, and was anew struck by his aspect, now that Paul thought himself unwatched. Stern, relentless purposes, to be pursued to the points of adverse bayonets, and the muzzles of hostile cannon, were expressed in the now rigid lines of his brow. His ruffled right hand was clutched by his side, as if grasping a cutlass. He paced the room as if advancing upon a fortification. Meantime a confused buzz of discussion came from the neighboring chamber. All else was profound midnight tranquillity. Presently, passing the large mirror over the mantel, Paul caught a glimpse of his person. He paused, grimly regarding it, while a dash of pleased coxcombry seemed to mingle with the otherwise savage satisfaction expressed in his face. But the latter predominated. Soon, rolling up his sleeve, with a queer wild smile, Paul lifted his right arm, and stood thus for an interval, eyeing its image in the glass. From where he lay, Israel could not see that side of the arm presented to the mirror, but he saw its reflection, and started at perceiving there, framed in the carved and gilded wood, certain large intertwisted cyphers covering the whole inside of the arm, so far as exposed, with mysterious tatooings. The design was wholly unlike the fanciful figures of anchors, hearts, and cables, sometimes decorating small portions of seamen's bodies. It was a sort of tattooing such as is seen only on thoroughbred savages—deep blue, elaborate, labyrinthine, cabalistic. Israel remembered having beheld, on one of his early voyages, something similar on the arm of a New Zealand warrior, once met, fresh from battle, in his native village. He concluded that on some similar early voyage Paul must have undergone the manipulations of some pagan artist.

Covering his arm again with his laced coat-sleeve, Paul glanced ironically at the hand of the same arm, now again half muffled in ruffles, and ornamented with several Parisian rings.

He then resumed his walking with a prowling air, like one haunting an ambuscade; while a gleam of the consciousness of possessing a character as yet unfathomed, and hidden power to back unsuspected projects, irradiated his cold white brow, which, owing to the shade of his hat in equatorial climates, had been left surmounting his swarthy face, like the snow topping the Andes.

So at midnight, the heart of the metropolis of modern civilization was secretly trod by this jaunty barbarian in broadcloth; a sort of prophetical ghost, glimmering in anticipation upon the advent of those tragic scenes of the French Revolution which levelled the exquisite refinement of Paris with the blood-thirsty ferocity of Borneo; showing that broaches and finger-rings, not less than nose-rings and tattooing, are tokens of the primeval savageness which ever slumbers in human kind, civilised or uncivilised.

Israel slept not a wink that night. The troubled spirit of Paul paced the chamber till morning; when, copiously bathing himself at the wash-stand, Paul looked care-free and fresh as a day-break hawk. After a closeted consultation with Doctor Franklin, he left the place with a light and dandified air, switching his gold-headed cane, and throwing a passing arm round all the pretty chambermaids he encountered, kissing them resoundingly, as if saluting a frigate. All barbarians are rakes.

Chapter 12

O N THE THIRD day, as Israel was walking to and fro in his room, having removed his courier's boots, for fear of disturbing the Doctor, a quick sharp rap at the door announced the American envoy. The man of wisdom entered, with two small wads of paper in one hand, and several crackers and a bit of cheese in the other. There was such an eloquent air of instantaneous dispatch about him, that Israel involuntarily sprang to his boots, and, with two vigorous jerks, hauled them on, and then seizing his hat, like any bird, stood poised for his flight across the channel.

"Well done, my honest friend," said the Doctor; "you have the papers in your heel, I suppose."

"Ah," exclaimed Israel, perceiving the mild irony; and in an instant his boots were off again; when, without another word, the Doctor took one boot, and Israel the other, and forthwith both parties proceeded to secrete the documents.

"I think I could improve the design," said the sage, as, notwithstanding his haste, he critically eyed the screwing apparatus of the boot. "The vacancy should have been in the standing part of the heel, not in the lid. It should go with a spring, too, for better dispatch. I'll draw up a paper on false-heels one of these days, and send it to a private reading, at the Institute. But no time for it now. My honest friend, it is now half-past ten o'clock. At half-past eleven, the diligence starts from the Place-du-Carrousel for Calais. Make all haste till you arrive at Brentford. I have a little provender here for you to eat in the diligence, as you will not have time for a regular meal. A day-and-night courier should never be without a cracker in his pocket. You will probably leave Brentford in a day or two after your arrival there. Be wary, now, my good friend; heed well, that, if you are caught with these papers on British ground, you will involve both yourself and our Brentford friends in fatal calamities. Kick no man's box, never mind whose, in the way. Mind your own box. You can't be too cautious, but don't be too suspicious. God bless you, my honest friend. Go!"

And, flinging the door open for his exit, the Doctor saw Israel dart into the entry, vigorously spring down the stairs, and disappear with all celerity, across the court into the vaulted way.

The man of wisdom stood mildly motionless, a moment, with a look of sagacious, humane meditation on his face, as if pondering upon the chances of the important enterprise: one which, perhaps, might in the sequel affect the weal or woe of nations yet to come. Then suddenly clapping his hand to his capacious coat-pocket, dragged out a bit of cork with some hens' feathers, and hurrying to his room, took out his knife, and proceeded to whittle away at a shuttle-cock of an original scientific construction, which, at some prior time he had promised to send to the young Dutchess D'Abrantes, that very afternoon.

Safely reaching Calais, at night, Israel stepped almost from the diligence into the packet, and, in a few moments, was cutting the water. As on the diligence he took an outside and plebeian seat, so, with the same secret motive of preserving unsuspected the character assumed, he took a deck passage in the packet. It coming on to rain violently, he stole down into the forecastle, dimly lit by a solitary swinging lamp, where were two men industriously smoking, and filling the narrow hole with soporific vapors. These induced strange drowsiness in Israel, and he pondered how best he might indulge it, for a time, without imperilling the precious documents in his custody.

But this pondering in such soporific vapors had the effect of those mathematical devices, whereby restless people cipher themselves to sleep. His languid head fell to his breast. In another moment, he drooped half-lengthwise upon a chest, his legs outstretched before him.

Presently he was awakened by some intermeddlement with his feet. Starting to his elbow, he saw one of the two men in the act of slyly slipping off his right boot, while the left one, already removed, lay on the floor, all ready against the rascal's retreat. Had it not been for the lesson learned on the Pont Neuf, Israel would instantly have inferred that his secret mission was known, and the operator some designed diplomatic knave or other, hired by the British Cabinet, thus to lie in wait for him, fume him into slumber with tobacco, and then rifle him of his momentous despatches. But as it was, he recalled Doctor Franklin's prudent admonitions against the indulgence of premature suspicions.

"Sir," said Israel very civilly, "I will thank you for that boot which lies on the floor, and, if you please, you can let the other stay where it is."

"Excuse me," said the rascal, an accomplished, self-possessed practitioner in his thievish art; "I thought your boots might be pinching you, and only wished to ease you a little."

"Much obliged to ye for your kindness, sir," said Israel; "but they don't pinch me at all. I suppose, though, you think that they wouldn't pinch *you* either; your foot looks rather small. Were you going to try 'em on, just to see how they fitted?"

"No," said the fellow, with sanctimonious seriousness; "but with your permission I should like to try them on, when we get to Dover. I couldn't try them well walking on this tipsy craft's deck, you know."

"No," answered Israel, "and the beach at Dover ain't very smooth either. I guess, upon second thought, you had better not try 'em on at all. Besides, I am a simple sort of a soul,— eccentric they call me,—and don't like my boots to go out of my sight. Ha! ha!"

"What are you laughing at?" said the fellow testily.

"Odd idea! I was just looking at those sad old patched boots there on your feet, and thinking to myself what leaky fire-buckets they would be to pass up a ladder on a burning building. It would hardly be fair now to swop my new boots for those old fire-buckets, would it?"

"By plunko!" cried the fellow, willing now by a bold stroke to change the subject, which was growing slightly annoying; "by plunko, I believe we are getting nigh Dover. Let's see."

And so saying, he sprang up the ladder to the deck. Upon Israel following, he found the little craft half becalmed, rolling on short swells almost in the exact middle of the channel. It was just before the break of the morning; the air clear and fine; the heavens spangled with moistly twinkling stars. The

French and English coasts lay distinctly visible in the strange starlight; the white cliffs of Dover resembling a long gabled block of marble houses. Both shores showed a long straight row of lamps. Israel seemed standing in the middle of the crossing of some wide stately street in London. Presently a breeze sprang up, and ere long our adventurer disembarked at his destined port, and directly posted on for Brentford.

The following afternoon, having gained unobserved admittance into the house, according to preconcerted signals, he was sitting in Squire Woodcock's closet, pulling off his boots and delivering his despatches.

Having looked over the compressed tissuey sheets, and read a line particularly addressed to himself, the Squire turning round upon Israel, congratulated him upon his successful mission; placed some refreshment before him, and apprised him that, owing to certain suspicious symptoms in the neighborhood, he (Israel) must now remain concealed in the house for a day or two, till an answer should be ready for Paris.

It was a venerable mansion, as was somewhere previously stated, of a wide and rambling disorderly spaciousness, built, for the most part, of weather-stained old bricks, in the goodly style called Elizabethan. As without, it was all dark russet bricks; so within, it was nothing but tawny oak panels.

"Now, my good fellow," said the Squire, "my wife has a number of guests, who wander from room to room, having the freedom of the house. So I shall have to put you very snugly away, to guard against any chance of discovery."

So saying, first locking the door, he touched a spring nigh the open fire-place, whereupon one of the black sooty stone jambs of the chimney started ajar, just like the marble gate of a tomb. Inserting one leg of the heavy tongs in the crack, the Squire pried this cavernous gate wide open.

"Why, Squire Woodcock, what is the matter with your chimney?" said Israel.

"Quick, go in."

"Am I to sweep the chimney?" demanded Israel; "I didn't engage for that."

"Pooh, pooh, this is your hiding-place. Come, move in."

"But where does it go to, Squire Woodcock? I don't like the looks of it."

"Follow me. I'll show you."

Pushing his florid corpulence into the mysterious aperture, the elderly Squire led the way up a steep stairs of stone, hardly two feet in width, till they reached a little closet, or rather cell, built into the massive main wall of the mansion, and ventilated and dimly lit by two little sloping slits, ingeniously concealed without, by their forming the sculptured mouths of two griffins cut in a great stone tablet decorating that external part of the dwelling. A mattress lay rolled up in one corner, with a jug of water, a flask of wine, and a wooden trencher containing cold roast beef and bread.

"And I am to be buried alive here?" said Israel, ruefully looking round.

"But your resurrection will soon be at hand," smiled the Squire; "two days at the furthest."

"Though to be sure I was a sort of prisoner in Paris, just as I seem about to be made here," said Israel, "yet Doctor Franklin put me in a better jug than this, Squire Woodcock. It was set out with bouquets and a mirror, and other fine things. Besides, I could step out into the entry whenever I wanted."

"Ah, but my hero, that was in France, and this is in England. There you were in a friendly country: here you are in the enemy's. If you should be discovered in my house, and your connection with me became known, do you know that it would go very hard with me; very hard indeed?"

"Then for your sake, I am willing to stay wherever you think best to put me," replied Israel.

"Well then, you say you want bouquets and a mirror. If those articles will at all help to solace your seclusion, I will bring them to you."

"They really would be company; the sight of my own face particularly."

"Stay here, then. I will be back in ten minutes."

In less than that time, the good old Squire returned, puffing and panting, with a great bunch of flowers, and a small shaving glass.

"There," said he, putting them down; "now keep perfectly quiet; avoid making any undue noise, and on no account descend the stairs, till I come for you again."

"But when will that be?" asked Israel.

"I will try to come twice each day while you are here. But there is no knowing what may happen. If I should not visit you till I come to liberate you—on the evening of the second day, or the morning of the third—you must not be at all surprised, my good fellow. There is plenty of food and water to last you. But mind, on no account descend the stone-stairs, till I come for you."

With that, bidding his guest adieu, he left him.

Israel stood glancing pensively around for a time. By-and-by, moving the rolled mattress under the two air-slits, he mounted, to try if aught were visible beyond. But nothing was to be seen but a very thin slice of blue sky peeping through the lofty foliage of a great tree planted near the side-portal of the mansion; an ancient tree, coeval with the ancient dwelling it guarded.

Sitting down on the mattress, Israel fell into a reverie.

Poverty and liberty, or plenty and a prison, seem to be the two horns of the constant dilemma of my life, thought he. Let's look at the prisoner.

And taking up the shaving glass, he surveyed his lineaments.

"What a pity I didn't think to ask for razors and soap. I want shaving very badly. I shaved last in France. How it would pass the time here. Had I a comb now and a razor, I might shave and curl my hair, and keep making a continual toilet all through the two days, and look spruce as a robin when I get out. I'll ask the squire for the things this very night when he drops in. Hark! ain't that a sort of rumbling in the wall? I hope there ain't any oven next door, if so, I shall be scorched out. Here I am, just like a rat in the wainscot. I wish there was a low window to look out of. I wonder what Doctor Franklin is doing now, and Paul Jones? Hark! there's a bird singing in the leaves. Bell for dinner, that."

And for pastime, he applied himself to the beef and bread, and took a draught of the wine and water.

At last night fell. He was left in utter darkness. No squire.

After an anxious, sleepless night, he saw two long flecks of pale grey light slanted into the cell from the slits, like two long spears. He rose, rolled up his mattress, got upon the roll, and put his mouth to one of the griffins' mouths. He gave a low, just audible whistle, directing it towards the foliage of the tree. Presently there was a slight rustling among the leaves, then one solitary chirrup, and in three minutes a whole chorus of melody burst upon his ear.

"I've waked the first bird" said he to himself, with a smile, "and he's waked all the rest. Now then for breakfast. That over, I dare say the squire will drop in."

But the breakfast was over, and the two flecks of pale light had changed to golden beams, and the golden beams grew less and less slanting, till they straightened themselves up out of sight altogether. It was noon and no squire.

He's gone a hunting before breakfast, and got belated, thought Israel.

The afternoon shadows lengthened. It was sunset; no squire.

He must be very busy trying some sheep-stealer in the hall, mused Israel. I hope he won't forget all about me till to-morrow.

He waited and listened; and listened and waited.

Another restless night; no sleep; morning came. The second day passed like the first, and the night. On the third morning the flowers lay shrunken by his side. Drops of wet oozing through the air-slits, fell dully on the stone floor. He heard the dreary beatings of the tree's leaves against the mouths of the griffins, bedashing them with the spray of the rain-storm without. At intervals a burst of thunder rolled over his head, and lightning flashing down through the slits, lit up the cell with a greenish glare, followed by sharp splashings and rattlings of the redoubled rain-storm.

This is the morning of the third day, murmured Israel to himself; he said he would at the furthest come to me on the morning of the third day. This is it. Patience, he will be here yet. Morning lasts till noon.

But owing to the murkiness of the day, it was very hard to tell when noon came. Israel refused to credit that noon had come and gone, till dusk set plainly in. Dreading he knew not what, he found himself buried in the darkness of still another night. However patient and hopeful hitherto, fortitude now presently left him. Suddenly, as if some contagious fever had seized him, he was afflicted with strange enchantments of misery, undreamed of till now.

He had eaten all the beef, but there was bread and water sufficient to last by economy, for two or three days to come. It was not the pang of hunger then, but a nightmare originating in his mysterious incarceration, which appalled him. All through the long hours of this particular night, the sense of being masoned up in the wall, grew, and grew, and grew upon him, till again and again he lifted himself convulsively from the floor; as if vast blocks of stone had been laid on him; as if he had been digging a deep well, and the stone work with all the excavated earth had caved in upon him, where he burrowed ninety feet beneath the clover. In the blind tomb of the midnight he stretched his two arms sideways, and felt as if coffined at not being able to extend them straight out, on opposite sides, for the narrowness of the cell. He seated himself against one side of the wall, crosswise with the cell, and pushed with his feet at the opposite wall. But still mindful of his promise in this extremity, he uttered no cry. He mutely raved in the darkness. The delirious sense of the absence of light was soon added to his other delirium as to the contraction of space. The lids of his eyes burst with impotent distension. Then he thought the air itself was getting unbearable. He stood up at the griffin slits, pressing his lips far into them till he moulded his lips there, to suck the utmost of the open air possible.

And continually, to heighten his frenzy, there recurred to him again and again what the Squire had told him as to the origin of the cell. It seemed that this part of the old house, or rather this wall of it, was extremely ancient, dating far beyond the era of Elizabeth, having once formed portion of a religious retreat belonging to the Templars. The domestic discipline of this order was rigid and merciless in the extreme. In a side wall of their second-story chapel, horizontal and on a level with the floor, they had an internal vacancy left, exactly of the shape and average size of a coffin. In this place, from time to time, inmates convicted of contumacy were confined; but, strange to say, not till they were penitent. A small hole, of the girth of one's wrist, sunk like a telescope three feet through the masonry into the cell, served at once for ventilation, and to push through food to the prisoner. This hole opening into the chapel also enabled the poor solitaire, as intended, to overhear the religious services at the altar; and, without being present, take part in the same. It was deemed a good sign of the state of the sufferer's soul, if from the gloomy recesses of the wall, was heard the agonized groan of his dismal response. This was regarded in the light of a penitent wail from the dead; because the customs of the order ordained, that when any inmate should be first incarcerated in the wall, he should be committed to it in the presence of all the brethren; the chief reading the burial service as the live body was sepulchred. Sometimes several weeks elapsed ere the disentombment. The penitent being then usually found numb and congealed in all his extremities, like one newly stricken with paralysis.

This coffin-cell of the Templars had been suffered to remain in the demolition of the general edifice, to make way for the erection of the new, in the reign of Queen Elizabeth. It was enlarged somewhat, and altered, and additionally ventilated, to adapt it for a place of concealment in times of civil dissension.

With this history ringing in his solitary brain, it may readily be conceived what Israel's feelings must have been. Here, in this very darkness, centuries ago, hearts, human as his, had mildewed in despair; limbs, robust as his own, had stiffened in immovable torpor.

At length, after what seemed all the prophetic days and years of Daniel, morning broke. The benevolent light entered the cell, soothing his frenzy, as if it had been some smiling human face—nay, the Squire himself, come at last to redeem him from thrall. Soon his dumb ravings entirely left him, and gradually, with a sane, calm mind, he revolved all the circumstances of his condition.

He could not be mistaken; something fatal must have befallen his friend. Israel remembered the Squire's hinting, that in case of the discovery of his clandestine proceedings, it would fare extremely hard with him. Israel was forced to conclude that this same unhappy discovery had been made; that owing to some untoward misadventure, his good friend had been carried off a State-prisoner to London. That prior to his going, the Squire had not apprised any member of his household that he was about to leave behind him a prisoner in the wall; this seemed evident from the circumstance that, thus far, no soul had visited that prisoner. It could not be otherwise. Doubtless, the Squire, having no opportunity to converse in private with his relatives or friends at the moment of his sudden arrest, had been forced to keep his secret, for the present, for fear of involving Israel in still worse calamities. But would he leave him to perish piece-meal in the wall? All surmise was baffled in the unconjecturable possibilities of the case. But some sort of action must speedily be determined upon. Israel would not additionally endanger the Squire, but he could not in such uncertainty consent to perish where he was. He resolved at all hazards to escape: by stealth and noiselessly, if possible; by violence and outcry, if indispensable.

Gliding out of the cell, he descended the stone stairs, and stood before the interior of the jamb. He felt an immovable iron knob; but no more. He groped about gently for some bolt or spring. When before he had passed through the passage with his guide, he had omitted to notice by what precise mechanism the jamb was to be opened from within, or whether, indeed, it could at all be opened except from without.

He was about giving up the search in despair, after sweeping with his two hands every spot of the wall-surface around him, when chancing to turn his whole body a little to one side, he heard a creak, and saw a thin lance of light. His foot had unconsciously pressed some spring laid in the floor. The jamb was ajar. Pushing it open, he stood at liberty in the Squire's closet.

Chapter 13

His Escape from the House, with Various Adventures Following

H E STARTED at the funereal aspect of the room, into which, since he last stood there, undertakers seemed to have stolen. The curtains of the window were festooned with long weepers of crape. The four corners of the red cloth on the round table were knotted with crape.

Knowing nothing of these mournful customs of the country, nevertheless, Israel's instinct whispered him, that Squire Woodcock lived no more on this earth. At once, the whole three days' mystery was made clear. But what was now to be done? His friend must have died very suddenly; most probably, struck down in a fit, from which he never more rose. With him had perished all knowledge of the fact that a stranger was immured in the mansion. If discovered then, prowling here in the inmost privacies of a gentleman's abode, what would befal the wanderer, already not unsuspected in the neighborhood of some underhand guilt as a fugitive? If he adhered to the strict truth, what could he offer in his own defence without convicting himself of acts, which, by English tribunals, would be accounted flagitious crimes? Unless, indeed, by involving the memory of the deceased Squire Woodcock in his own self-acknowledged proceedings, so ungenerous a charge should result in an abhorrent refusal to credit his extraordinary tale, whether as referring to himself or another; and so throw him open to still more grievous suspicions?

While wrapped in these dispiriting reveries, he heard a step not very far off in the passage. It seemed approaching. Instantly he flew to the jamb, which remained unclosed; and disappearing within, drew the stone after him by the iron knob. Owing to his hurried violence, the jamb closed with a dull, dismal and singular noise. A shriek followed from within the room. In a panic, Israel fled up the dark stairs; and near the top, in his eagerness, stumbled, and fell back to the last step with a rolling din, which reverberated by the arch over-

head smote through and through the wall, dying away at last
indistinctly, like low muffled thunder among the clefts of
deep hills. When raising himself instantly, not seriously
bruised by his fall, Israel intently listened;—the echoing
sounds of his descent were mingled with added shrieks from
within the room. They seemed some nervous female's,
alarmed by what must have appeared to her supernatural or
at least unaccountable noises in the wall. Directly he heard
other voices of alarm undistinguishably commingled, and
then, they retreated together, and all again was still.

Recovering from his first amazement, Israel revolved these
occurrences. No creature now in the house knows of the cell,
thought he. Some woman,—the housekeeper, perhaps,—first
entered the room alone. Just as she entered, the jamb closed.
The sudden report made her shriek; then, afterwards, the
noise of my fall prolonging itself, added to her fright, while
her repeated shrieks brought every soul in the house to her;
who, aghast at seeing her lying in a pale faint, it may be, like
a corpse, in a room hung with crape for a man just dead, they
also shrieked out; and then with blended lamentations they
bore the fainting person away. Now this will follow; no
doubt it *has* followed ere now:—they believe that the woman
saw or heard the spirit of Squire Woodcock. Since I seem
then to understand how all these strange events have occurred; since I seem to know that they have plain common
causes; I begin to feel cool and calm again. Let me see. Yes. I
have it. By means of the idea of the ghost prevailing among
the frightened household; by that means, I will this very night
make good my escape. If I can but lay hands on some of the
late Squire's clothing—if but a coat and hat of his—I shall
be certain to succeed. It is not too early to begin now. They
will hardly come back to the room in a hurry. I will return to
it, and see what I can find to serve my purpose. It is the
Squire's private closet; hence it is not unlikely that here some
at least of his clothing will be found.

With these thoughts, he cautiously sprung the iron under
foot, peeped in, and seeing all clear, boldly re-entered the
apartment. He went straight to a high, narrow door in the
opposite wall. The key was in the lock. Opening the door,
there hung several coats, small clothes, pairs of silk stockings,

and hats of the deceased. With little difficulty Israel selected from these the complete suit in which he had last seen his once jovial friend. Carefully closing the door, and carrying the suit with him, he was returning towards the chimney, when he saw the Squire's silver-headed cane leaning against a corner of the wainscot. Taking this also, he stole back to his cell.

Slipping off his own clothing, he deliberately arrayed himself in the borrowed raiment; silk small-clothes and all; then put on the cocked hat, grasped the silver-headed cane in his right hand, and moving his small shaving glass slowly up and down before him, so as by piece-meal to take in his whole figure, felt convinced that he would well pass for Squire Woodcock's genuine phantom. But after the first feeling of self-satisfaction with his anticipated success had left him, it was not without some superstitious embarrassment that Israel felt himself encased in a dead man's broadcloth; nay, in the very coat in which the deceased had no doubt fallen down in his fit. By degrees he began to feel almost as unreal and shadowy as the shade whose part he intended to enact.

Waiting long and anxiously till darkness came, and then till he thought it was fairly midnight, he stole back into the closet, and standing for a moment uneasily in the middle of the floor, thinking over all the risks he might run, he lingered till he felt himself resolute and calm. Then groping for the door, leading into the hall, put his hand on the knob and turned it. But the door refused to budge. Was it locked? The key was not in. Turning the knob once more, and holding it so, he pressed firmly against the door. It did not move. More firmly still, when suddenly it burst open with a loud crackling report. Being cramped, it had stuck in the sill. Less than three seconds passed, when, as Israel was groping his way down the long wide hall towards the large staircase at its opposite end, he heard confused hurrying noises from the neighboring rooms, and in another instant several persons, mostly in night-dresses, appeared at their chamber-doors, thrusting out alarmed faces, lit by a lamp held by one of the number, a rather elderly lady in widow's weeds, who, by her appearance, seemed to have just risen from a sleepless chair, instead of an oblivious couch. Israel's heart beat like a hammer; his face turned like a sheet. But bracing himself, pulling his hat lower down over his eyes, settling his head in the collar of his coat, he advanced along the defile of wildly staring faces. He advanced with a slow and stately step; looked neither to the right nor the left; but went solemnly forward on his now faintly illuminated way, sounding his cane on the floor as he passed. The faces in the doorways curdled his blood, by their rooted looks. Glued to the spot, they seemed incapable of motion. Each one was silent as he advanced towards him or her; but as he left each individual, one after another, behind, each in a frenzy shrieked out, "the Squire, the Squire!" As he passed the lady in the widow's weeds, she fell senseless and crosswise before him. But forced to be immutable in his purpose, Israel solemnly stepping over her prostrate form, marched deliberately on.

In a few minutes more he had reached the main door of the mansion, and withdrawing the chain and bolt, stood in the open air. It was a bright moonlight night. He struck slowly across the open grounds towards the sunken fields beyond. When midway across the grounds, he turned towards the mansion, and saw three of the front windows filled with white faces, gazing in terror at the wonderful spectre. Soon descending a slope, he disappeared from their view.

Presently he came to hilly land in meadow, whose grass having been lately cut, now lay dotting the slope in cocks; a sinuous line of creamy vapor meandered through the lowlands at the base of the hill; while beyond was a dense grove of dwarfish trees, with here and there a tall tapering dead trunk, peeled of the bark, and overpeering the rest. The vapor wore the semblance of a deep stream of water, imperfectly descried; the grove looked like some closely-clustering town on its banks, lorded over by spires of churches.

The whole scene magically reproduced to our adventurer the aspect of Bunker Hill, Charles River, and Boston town, on the well-remembered night of the 16th of June. The same season; the same moon; the same new-mown hay on the shaven sward; hay which was scraped together during the night to help pack into the redoubt so hurriedly thrown up.

Acted on as if by enchantment, Israel sat down on one of the cocks, and gave himself up to reverie. But, worn out by long loss of sleep, his reveries would have soon merged into slumber's still wilder dreams, had he not rallied himself, and departed on his way, fearful of forgetting himself in an emergency like the present. It now occurred to him that, well as his disguise had served him in escaping from the mansion of Squire Woodcock, that disguise might fatally endanger him if he should be discovered in it abroad. He might pass for a ghost at night, and among the relations and immediate friends of the gentleman deceased; but by day, and among indifferent persons, he ran no small risk of being apprehended for an entry-thief. He bitterly lamented his omission in not pulling on the Squire's clothes over his own, so that he might now have reappeared in his former guise.

As meditating over this difficulty, he was passing along, suddenly he saw a man in black standing right in his path, about fifty yards distant, in a field of some growing barley or wheat. The gloomy stranger was standing stock-still; one outstretched arm, with weird intimation pointing towards the deceased Squire's abode. To the brooding soul of the now desolate Israel, so strange a sight roused a supernatural suspicion. His conscience morbidly reproaching him for the terrors he had bred in making his escape from the house; he seemed to see in the fixed gesture of the stranger something more than humanly significant. But somewhat of his intrepidity returned; he resolved to test the apparition. Composing itself to the same deliberate stateliness with which it had paced the hall, the phantom of Squire Woodcock firmly advanced its cane, and marched straight forward towards the mysterious stranger.

As he neared him, Israel shrunk. The dark coat-sleeve flapped on the bony skeleton of the unknown arm. The face was lost in a sort of ghastly blank. It was no living man.

But mechanically continuing his course, Israel drew still nearer and saw—a scarecrow.

An Encounter of Ghosts

Not a little relieved by the discovery, our adventurer paused, more particularly to survey so deceptive an object, which seemed to have been constructed on the most efficient principles; probably by some broken down wax-figure costumer. It comprised the complete wardrobe of a scare-crow, namely: a cocked hat, bunged; tattered coat; old velveteen breeches; and long worsted stockings, full of holes; all stuffed very nicely with straw, and skeletoned by a frame-work of poles. There was a great flapped pocket to the coat—which seemed to have been some laborer's—standing invitingly open. Putting his hands in, Israel drew out the lid of an old tobacco-box, the broken bowl of a pipe, two rusty nails, and a few kernels of wheat. This reminded him of the Squire's pockets. Trying them, he produced a handsome handkerchief, a spectacle-case, with a purse containing some silver and gold, amounting to a little more than five pounds. Such is the difference between the contents of the pockets of scare-crows and the pockets of well-to-do squires. Ere donning his present habiliments, Israel had not omitted to withdraw his own money from his own coat, and put it in the pocket of his own waistcoat, which he had not exchanged.

Looking upon the scare-crow more attentively, it struck him that, miserable as its wardrobe was, nevertheless here was a chance for getting rid of the unsuitable and perilous clothes of the Squire. No other available opportunity might present itself for a time. Before he encountered any living creature by daylight, another suit must somehow be had. His exchange with the old ditcher, after his escape from the inn near Portsmouth, had familiarized him with the most deplorable of wardrobes. Well, too, he knew, and had experienced it, that for a man desirous of avoiding notice, the more wretched the clothes the better. For who does not shun the scurvy wretch, Poverty, advancing in battered hat and lamentable coat?

Without more ado, slipping off the Squire's raiment, he donned the scarecrow's, after carefully shaking out the hay, which, from many alternate soakings and bakings in rain and sun, had become quite broken up, and would have been almost dust, were it not for the mildew which damped it. But sufficient of this wretched old hay remained adhesive to the inside of the breeches and coat sleeves, to produce the most irritating torment.

The grand moral question now came up, what to do with the purse? Would it be dishonest under the circumstances to appropriate that purse? Considering the whole matter, and not forgetting that he had not received from the gentleman deceased the promised reward for his services as courier, Israel concluded that he might justly use the money for his own. To which opinion surely no charitable judge will demur. Besides, what should he do with the purse, if not use it for his own? It would have been insane to have returned it to the relations. Such mysterious honesty would have but resulted in his arrest as a rebel, or rascal. As for the Squire's clothes, handkerchief, and spectacle-case, they must be put out of sight with all despatch. So, going to a morass not remote, Israel sunk them deep down, and heaped tufts of the rank sod upon them. Then returning to the field of corn, sat down under the lee of a rock, about a hundred yards from where the scarecrow had stood, thinking which way he now had best direct his steps. But his late ramble coming after so long a deprivation of rest, soon produced effects not so easy to be shaken off, as when reposing upon the haycock. He felt less anxious too, since changing his apparel. So before he was aware, he fell into deep sleep.

When he awoke, the sun was well up in the sky. Looking around he saw a farm-laborer with a pitch-fork coming at a distance into view, whose steps seemed bent in a direction not far from the spot where he lay. Immediately it struck our adventurer that this man must be familiar with the scarecrow; perhaps had himself fashioned it. Should he miss it then, he might make immediate search, and so discover the thief so imprudently loitering upon the very field of his operations.

Waiting until the man momentarily disappeared in a little hollow, Israel ran briskly to the identical spot where the scarecrow had stood; where, standing stiffly erect, pulling the hat well over his face, and thrusting out his arm, pointed steadfastly towards the Squire's abode, he awaited the event. Soon the man reappeared in sight, and marching right on, paused not far from Israel, and gave him an one earnest look, as if it were his daily wont to satisfy that all was right with the scarecrow. No sooner was the man departed to a reasonable distance, than, quitting his post, Israel struck across the fields towards London. But he had not yet quite quitted the field, when it occurred to him to turn round, and see if the man was completely out of sight; when, to his consternation, he

saw the man returning towards him, evidently by his pace and
gesture in unmixed amazement. The man must have turned
round to look, before Israel had done so. Frozen to the
ground, Israel knew not what to do. But, next moment it
struck him, that this very motionlessness was the least hazardous plan in such a strait. Thrusting out his arm again towards
the house, once more he stood stock-still, and again awaited
the event.

It so happened that this time in pointing towards the
house, Israel unavoidably pointed towards the advancing
man. Hoping that the strangeness of this coincidence might,
by operating on the man's superstition, incline him to beat an
immediate retreat, Israel kept cool as he might. But the man
proved to be of a braver metal than anticipated. In passing
the spot where the scarecrow had stood, and perceiving, beyond the possibility of mistake, that by some unaccountable
agency it had suddenly removed itself to a distance; instead
of being terrified at this verification of his worst apprehensions, the man pushed on for Israel, apparently resolved to
sift this mystery to the bottom.

Seeing him now determinately coming, with pitchfork valiantly presented, Israel, as a last means of practising on the
fellow's fears of the supernatural, suddenly doubled up both
fists, presenting them savagely towards him at a distance of
about twenty paces; at the same time showing his teeth like a
skull's, and demoniacally rolling his eyes. The man paused bewildered; looked all round him; looked at the springing
grain; then across at some trees; then up at the sky; and satisfied at last by those observations, that the world at large had
not undergone a miracle in the last fifteen minutes, resolutely
resumed his advance; the pitchfork like a boarding-pike now
aimed full at the breast of the object. Seeing all his stratagems
vain, Israel now threw himself into the original attitude of the
scarecrow, and once again stood immovable. Abating his pace
by degrees almost to a mere creep, the man at last came
within three feet of him, and pausing, gazed amazed into Israel's eyes. With a stern and terrible expression Israel resolutely returned the glance, but otherwise remained like a
statue; hoping thus to stare his pursuer out of countenance.
At last the man slowly presented one prong of his fork

towards Israel's left eye. Nearer and nearer the sharp point came; till no longer capable of enduring such a test, Israel took to his heels with all speed, his tattered coat-tails streaming behind him. With inveterate purpose the man pursued. Darting blindly on, Israel leaping a gate, suddenly found himself in a field where some dozen laborers were at work; who recognizing the scarecrow—an old acquaintance of theirs, as it would seem—lifted all their hands as the astounding apparition swept by, followed by the man with the pitchfork. Soon all joined in the chase; but Israel proved to have better wind and bottom than any. Outstripping the whole pack, he finally shot out of their sight in an extensive park, heavily timbered in one quarter. He never saw more of these people.

Loitering in the wood till nightfall, he then stole out and made the best of his way towards the house of that good-natured farmer in whose corn-loft he had received his first message from Squire Woodcock. Rousing this man up a little before midnight, he informed him somewhat of his recent adventures, but carefully concealed his having been employed as a secret courier, together with his escape from Squire Woodcock's. All he craved at present was a meal. The meal being over, Israel offered to buy from the farmer his best suit of clothes, and displayed the money on the spot.

"Where did you get so much money?" said his entertainer in a tone of surprise; "your clothes here don't look as if you had seen prosperous times since you left me. Why, you look like a scarecrow."

"That may well be," replied Israel very soberly. "But what do you say? will you sell me your suit?—here's the cash."

"I don't know about it," said the farmer, in doubt; "let me look at the money. Ha!—a silk purse come out of a beggar's pocket!—Quit the house, rascal, you've turned thief."

Thinking that he could not swear to his having come by his money with absolute honesty—since indeed the case was one for the most subtle casuist—Israel knew not what to reply. This honest confusion confirmed the farmer; who with many abusive epithets drove him into the road; telling him that he might thank himself that he did not arrest him on the spot.

In great dolor at this unhappy repulse, Israel trudged on in the moonlight some three miles to the house of another friend, who also had once succored him in extremity. This man proved a very sound sleeper. Instead of succeeding in rousing him by his knocking, Israel but succeeded in rousing his wife, a person not of the greatest amiability. Raising the sash, and seeing so shocking a pauper before her, the woman upbraided him with shameless impropriety in asking charity at dead of night, in a dress so improper too. Looking down at his deplorable velveteens, Israel discovered that his extensive travels had produced a great rent in one loin of the rotten old breeches, through which a whitish fragment protruded.

Remedying this oversight as well as he might, he again implored the woman to wake her husband.

"That I shan't!" said the woman morosely. "Quit the premises, or I'll throw something on ye."

With that, she brought some earthenware to the window, and would have fulfilled her threat, had not Israel prudently retreated some paces. Here he entreated the woman to take mercy on his plight, and since she would not waken her husband, at least throw to him (Israel) her husband's breeches, and he would leave the price of them, with his own breeches to boot, on the sill of the door.

"You behold how sadly I need them," said he; "for heaven's sake befriend me."

"Quit the premises!" reiterated the woman.

"The breeches, the breeches! here is the money," cried Israel, half furious with anxiety.

"Saucy cur," cried the woman, somehow misunderstanding him; "do you cunningly taunt me with *wearing* the breeches? begone!"

Once more, poor Israel decamped, and made for another friend. But here a monstrous bull-dog, indignant that the peace of a quiet family should be disturbed by so outrageous a tatterdemalion, flew at Israel's unfortunate coat, whose rotten skirts the brute tore completely off; leaving the coat razeed to a spencer, which barely came down to the wearer's waist. In attempting to drive the monster away, Israel's hat fell off, upon which the dog pounced with the utmost fierceness, and thrusting both paws into it, rammed out the crown, and went snuffling the wreck before him. Recovering the wretched hat, Israel again beat a retreat, his wardrobe sorely the worse for his visits. Not only was his coat a mere rag, but his breeches, clawed by the dog, were slashed into yawning gaps, while his yellow hair waved over the top of the crownless beaver, like a lonely tuft of heather on the Highlands.

In this plight the morning discovered him dubiously skirmishing on the outskirts of a village.

"Ah! what a true patriot gets for serving his country!" murmured Israel. But soon thinking a little better of his case, and seeing yet another house which had once furnished him with an asylum, he made bold to advance to the door. Luckily he this time met the man himself, just emerging from bed. At first the farmer did not recognize the fugitive; but upon another look, seconded by Israel's plaintive appeal, beckoned him into the barn, where directly our adventurer told him all he thought prudent to disclose of his story; ending by once more offering to negotiate for breeches and coat. Having ere this, emptied and thrown away the purse which had played him so scurvy a trick with the first farmer; he now produced three crown-pieces.

"Three crown-pieces in your pocket, and no crown to your hat!" said the farmer.

"But I assure you, my friend," rejoined Israel, "that a finer hat was never worn, until that confounded bull-dog ruined it."

"True," said the farmer. "I forgot that part of your story. Well, I have a tolerable coat and breeches which I will sell you for your money."

In ten minutes more, Israel was equipped in a grey coat of coarse cloth, not much improved by wear, and breeches to match. For half-a-crown more, he procured a highly respectable-looking hat.

"Now, my kind friend," said Israel, "can you tell me where Horne Tooke, and John Bridges live?"

Our adventurer thought it his best plan to seek out one or other of those gentlemen, both to report proceedings, and learn confirmatory tidings concerning Squire Woodcock, touching whose fate he did not like to inquire of others.

"Horne Tooke? What do you want with Horne Tooke?" said the farmer: "He was Squire Woodcock's friend, wasn't he? The poor Squire! Who would have thought he'd have gone off so suddenly. But apoplexy comes like a bullet."

I was right, thought Israel to himself. "But where does Horne Tooke live?" he demanded again.

"He once lived in Brentford, and wore a cassock there. But I hear he's sold out his living, and gone in his surplice to study law in Lunnon."

This was all news to Israel, who, from various amiable remarks he had heard from Horne Tooke at the Squire's, little dreamed he was an ordained clergyman. Yet a good-natured English clergyman translated Lucian; another, equally good-natured, wrote Tristram Shandy; and a third, an ill-natured appreciator of good-natured Rabelais, died a dean; not to speak of others. Thus ingenious and ingenuous are some of the English clergy.

"You can't tell me, then, where to find Horne Tooke?" said Israel, in perplexity.

"You'll find him, I suppose, in Lunnon."

"What street and number?"

"Don't know. Needle in a haystack."

"Where does Mr. Bridges live?"

"Never heard of any Bridges, except Lunnon bridges, and one Molly Bridges in Bridewell."

So Israel departed; better clothed, but no wiser than before.

What to do next? He reckoned up his money, and concluded he had plenty to carry him back to Doctor Franklin in Paris. Accordingly, taking a turn to avoid the two nearest villages, he directed his steps towards London, where, again taking the post coach for Dover, he arrived on the channel shore just in time to learn that the very coach in which he rode brought the news to the authorities there that all intercourse between the two nations was indefinitely suspended. The characteristic taciturnity and formal stolidity of his fellow-travellers—all Englishmen, mutually unacquainted with each other, and occupying different positions in life—having prevented his sooner hearing the tidings.

Here was another accumulation of misfortunes. All visions but those of eventual imprisonment or starvation vanished from before the present realities of poor Israel Potter. The

Brentford gentleman had flattered him with the prospect of receiving something very handsome for his services as courier. That hope was no more. Doctor Franklin had promised him his good offices in procuring him a passage home to America. Quite out of the question now. The sage had likewise intimated that he might possibly see him some way remunerated for his sufferings in his country's cause. An idea no longer to be harbored. Then Israel recalled the mild man of wisdom's words—"At the prospect of pleasure never be elated; but without depression respect the omens of ill." But he found it as difficult now to comply, in all respects, with the last section of the maxim, as before he had with the first.

While standing wrapped in afflictive reflections on the shore, gazing towards the unattainable coast of France, a pleasant-looking cousinly stranger, in seaman's dress, accosted him, and, after some pleasant conversation, very civilly invited him up a lane into a house of rather secret entertainment. Pleased to be befriended in this his strait, Israel yet looked inquisitively upon the man, not completely satisfied with his good intentions. But the other, with good-humored violence, hurried him up the lane into the inn, when, calling for some spirits, he and Israel very affectionately drank to each other's better health and prosperity.

"Take another glass," said the stranger, affably.

Israel, to drown his heavy-heartedness, complied. The liquor began to take effect.

"Ever at sea?" said the stranger, lightly.

"Oh, yes; been a whaling."

"Ah!" said the other, "happy to hear that, I assure you. Jim! Bill!" And beckoning very quietly to two brawny fellows, in a trice Israel found himself kidnapped into the naval service of the magnanimous old gentleman of Kew Gardens—his Royal Majesty, George III.

"Hands off!" said Israel, fiercely, as the two men pinioned him.

"Reglar game-cock," said the cousinly-looking man. "I must get three guineas for cribbing him. Pleasant voyage to ye, my friend," and, leaving Israel a prisoner, the crimp, buttoning his coat, sauntered leisurely out of the inn.

"I'm no Englishman," roared Israel, in a foam.

"Oh! that's the old story," grinned his gaolers. "Come along. There's no Englishmen in the English fleet. All foreigners. You may take their own word for it."

To be short, in less than a week Israel found himself at Portsmouth, and, ere long, a fore-topman in his majesty's ship of the line, "Unprincipled," scudding before the wind down channel, in company with the "Undaunted," and the "Unconquerable;" all three haughty Dons bound to the East Indian waters as reinforcements to the fleet of Sir Edward Hughes.

And now, we might shortly have to record our adventurer's part in the famous engagement off the coast of Coromandel, between Admiral Suffren's fleet and the English squadron, were it not that fate snatched him on the threshold of events, and, turning him short round whither he had come, sent him back congenially to war against England, instead of on her behalf. Thus repeatedly and rapidly were the fortunes of our wanderer planted, torn up, transplanted, and dropped again, hither and thither, according as the Supreme Disposer of sailors and soldiers saw fit to appoint.

Chapter 14

As running down channel at evening, Israel walked the crowded main-deck of the seventy-four, continually brushed by a thousand hurrying wayfarers, as if he were in some great street in London, jammed with artisans, just returning from their day's labor, novel and painful emotions were his. He found himself dropped into the naval mob without one friend; nay, among enemies, since his country's enemies were his own, and against the kith and kin of these very beings around him, he himself had once lifted a fatal hand. The martial bustle of a great man-of-war, on her first day out of port, was indescribably jarring to his present mood. Those sounds of the human multitude disturbing the solemn natural solitudes of the sea, mysteriously afflicted him. He murmured against that untowardness which, after condemning him to long sorrows on the land, now pursued him with added griefs on the deep. Why should a patriot, leaping for the chance again to attack the oppressor, as at Bunker Hill, now be kidnapped to fight that oppressor's battles on the endless drifts of the Bunker Hills of the billows? But like many other repiners, Israel was perhaps a little premature with upbraidings like these.

Plying on between Scilly and Cape Clear, the Unprincipled—which vessel somewhat outsailed her consorts—fell in, just before dusk, with a large revenue cutter close to, and showing signals of distress. At the moment, no other sail was in sight.

Cursing the necessity of pausing with a strong fair wind at a juncture like this, the officer-of-the-deck shortened sail, and hove to; hailing the cutter, to know what was the matter. As he hailed the small craft from the lofty poop of the bristling seventy-four, this lieutenant seemed standing on the top of Gibraltar, talking to some lowland peasant in a hut. The reply was, that in a sudden flaw of wind, which came nigh capsizing them, not an hour since, the cutter had lost all four fore-

mast men by the violent jibing of a boom. She wanted help
to get back to port.

"You shall have one man," said the officer-of-the-deck,
morosely.

"Let him be a good one then, for heaven's sake," said he in
the cutter; "I ought to have at least two."

During this talk, Israel's curiosity had prompted him to
dart up the ladder from the main-deck, and stand right in the
gangway above, looking out on the strange craft. Meantime
the order had been given to drop a boat. Thinking this a
favorable chance, he stationed himself so that he should be
the foremost to spring into the boat; though crowds of English sailors, eager as himself for the same opportunity to escape from foreign service, clung to the chains of the as yet
imperfectly disciplined man-of-war. As the two men who had
been lowered in the boat hooked her, when afloat, along to
the gangway, Israel dropped like a comet into the stern-
sheets, stumbled forward, and seized an oar. In a moment
more, all the oarsmen were in their places, and with a few
strokes, the boat lay alongside the cutter.

"Take which of them you please," said the lieutenant in
command, addressing the officer in the revenue-cutter, and
motioning with his hand to his boat's crew, as if they were a
parcel of carcasses of mutton, of which the first pick was
offered to some customer. "Quick and choose. Sit down,
men"—to the sailors. "Oh, you are in a great hurry to get rid
of the king's service, ain't you? Brave chaps indeed!—Have
you chosen your man?"

All this while the ten faces of the anxious oarsmen looked
with mute longings and appealings towards the officer of the
cutter; every face turned at the same angle, as if managed by
one machine. And so they were. One motive.

"I take the freckled chap with the yellow hair—him;"
pointing to Israel.

Nine of the upturned faces fell in sullen despair, and ere
Israel could spring to his feet, he felt a violent thrust in his
rear from the toes of one of the disappointed behind him.

"Jump, dobbin!" cried the officer of the boat.

But Israel was already on board. Another moment, and the

boat and cutter parted. Ere long night fell, and the man-of-war and her consorts were out of sight.

The revenue vessel resumed her course towards the nighest port, worked by but four men: the captain, Israel, and two officers. The cabin-boy was kept at the helm. As the only fore-mast man, Israel was put to it pretty hard. Where there is but one man to three masters, woe betide that lonely slave. Be-sides, it was of itself severe work enough to manage the vessel thus short of hands. But to make matters still worse, the cap-tain and his officers were ugly-tempered fellows. The one kicked, and the others cuffed Israel. Whereupon, not sugared with his recent experiences, and maddened by his present hap, Israel seeing himself alone at sea, with only three men, instead of a thousand, to contend against, plucked up a heart, knocked the captain into the lee scuppers, and in his fury was about tumbling the first-officer, a small wash of a fellow, plump overboard, when the captain, jumping to his feet, seized him by his long yellow hair, vowing he would slaugh-ter him. Meantime the cutter flew foaming through the chan-nel, as if in demoniac glee at this uproar on her imperilled deck. While the consternation was at its height, a dark body suddenly loomed at a moderate distance into view, shooting right athwart the stern of the cutter. The next moment a shot struck the water within a boat's length.

"Heave to, and send a boat on board!" roared a voice al-most as loud as the cannon.

"That's a war-ship," cried the captain of the revenue vessel, in alarm; "but she ain't a countryman."

Meantime the officers and Israel stopped the cutter's way.

"Send a boat on board, or I'll sink you," again came roar-ing from the stranger, followed by another shot, striking the water still nearer the cutter.

"For God's sake, don't cannonade us. I haven't got the crew to man a boat," replied the captain of the cutter. "Who are you?"

"Wait till I send a boat to you for that," replied the stranger.

"She's an enemy of some sort, that's plain," said the En-glishman now to his officers; "we ain't at open war with

France; she's some blood-thirsty pirate or other. What d' ye say, men," turning to his officers; "let's outsail her, or be shot to chips. We can beat her at sailing, I know."

With that, nothing doubting that his counsel would be heartily responded to, he ran to the braces to get the cutter before the wind, followed by one officer, while the other, for a useless bravado, hoisted the colors at the stern.

But Israel stood indifferent, or rather all in a fever of conflicting emotions. He thought he recognized the voice from the strange vessel.

"Come, what do ye standing there, fool? Spring to the ropes here!" cried the furious captain.

But Israel did not stir.

Meantime, the confusion on board the stranger, owing to the hurried lowering of her boat, with the cloudiness of the sky darkening the misty sea, united to conceal the bold manœuvre of the cutter. She had almost gained full headway ere an oblique shot, directed by mere chance, struck her stern, tearing the upcurved head of the tiller in the hands of the cabin-boy, and killing him with the splinters. Running to the stump, the captain huzzaed, and steered the reeling ship on. Forced now to hoist back the boat ere giving chase, the stranger was dropped rapidly astern.

All this while storms of maledictions were hurled on Israel. But their exertions at the ropes prevented his shipmates for the time from using personal violence. While observing their efforts, Israel could not but say to himself, "These fellows are as brave as they are brutal."

Soon the stranger was seen dimly wallowing along astern, crowding all sail in chase, while now and then her bow-gun, showing its red tongue, bellowed after them like a mad bull. Two more shots struck the cutter, but without materially damaging her sails, or the ropes immediately upholding them. Several of her less important stays were sundered, however; whose loose tarry ends lashed the air like scorpions. It seemed not improbable that owing to her superior sailing, the keen cutter would yet get clear.

At this juncture, Israel, running towards the captain, who still held the splintered stump of tiller, stood full before him, saying, "I am an enemy, a Yankee; look to yourself."

"Help here, lads, help," roared the captain, "a traitor, a traitor!"

The words were hardly out of his mouth when his voice was silenced for ever. With one prodigious heave of his whole physical force, Israel smote him over the taffrail into the sea, as if the man had fallen backwards over a teetering chair. By this time the two officers were hurrying aft. Ere meeting them midway, Israel, quick as lightning, cast off the two principal halyards, thus letting the large sails all in a tumble of canvass to the deck. Next moment one of the officers was at the helm, to prevent the cutter from capsizing by being without a steersman in such an emergency. The other officer and Israel interlocked. The battle was in the midst of the chaos of blowing canvas. Caught in a rent of the sail, the officer slipped and fell near the sharp iron edge of the hatchway. As he fell, he caught Israel by the most terrible part in which mortality can be grappled. Insane with pain, Israel dashed his adversary's skull against the sharp iron. The officer's hold relaxed; but himself stiffened. Israel made for the helmsman, who as yet knew not the issue of the late tussel. He caught him round the loins, bedding his fingers like grisly claws into his flesh, and hugging him to his heart. The man's ghost, caught like a broken cork in a gurgling bottle's neck, gasped with the embrace. Loosening him suddenly, Israel hurled him from him against the bulwarks. That instant another report was heard, followed by the savage hail—"You down sail at last, do ye? I'm a good mind to sink ye, for your scurvy trick. Pull down that dirty rag there, astern!"

With a loud huzza, Israel hauled down the flag with one hand, while with the other he helped the now slowly gliding craft from falling off before the wind.

In a few moments a boat was alongside. As its commander stepped to the deck, he stumbled against the body of the first-officer, which, owing to the sudden slant of the cutter in coming to the wind, had rolled against the side near the gangway. As he came aft, he heard the moan of the other officer, where he lay under the mizzen shrouds.

"What is all this?" demanded the stranger of Israel.

"It means that I am a Yankee impressed into the king's service; and for their pains I have taken the cutter."

Giving vent to his surprise, the officer looked narrowly at the body by the shrouds, and said, "this man is as good as dead; but we will take him to Captain Paul as a witness in your behalf."

"Captain Paul?—Paul Jones?" cried Israel.

"The same."

"I thought so. I thought that was his voice hailing. It was Captain Paul's voice that somehow put me up to this deed."

"Captain Paul is the devil for putting men up to be tigers. But where are the rest of the crew?"

"Overboard."

"What?" cried the officer; "come on board the Ranger. Captain Paul will use you for a broadside."

Taking the moaning man along with them, and leaving the cutter untenanted by any living soul, the boat now left her for the enemy's ship. But ere they reached it, the man had expired.

Standing foremost on the deck, crowded with three hundred men, as Israel climbed the side, he saw, by the light of battle-lanthorns, a small, swart, brigandish-looking man, wearing a Scotch bonnet, with a gold band to it.

"You rascal," said this person, "why did your paltry smack give me this chase? Where's the rest of your gang?"

"Captain Paul," said Israel, "I believe I remember you. I believe I offered you my bed in Paris some months ago. How is Poor Richard?"

"God! Is this the courier? The Yankee courier? But how now; in an English revenue cutter?"

"Impressed, sir; that's the way."

"But where's the rest of them?" demanded Paul, turning to the officer.

Thereupon the officer very briefly told Paul what Israel had told him.

"Are we to sink the cutter, sir?" said the gunner, now advancing towards Captain Paul. "If it is to be done, now is the time. She is close under us, astern; a few guns pointed downwards, will settle her like a shotted corpse."

"No. Let her drift into Penzance, an anonymous earnest of what the white-squall in Paul Jones intends for the future."

Then giving directions as to the course of the ship, with an order for himself to be called at the first glimpse of a sail, Paul took Israel down with him into his cabin.

"Tell me your story now, my yellow lion. How was it all? Don't stand; sit right down there on the transom. I'm a democratic sort of sea-king. Plump on the wool-sack, I say, and spin the yarn. But hold; you want some grog first."

As Paul handed the flagon, Israel's eye fell upon his hand.

"You don't wear any rings now, Captain, I see. Left them in Paris for safety."

"Aye, with a certain marchioness there," replied Paul, with a dandyish look of sentimental conceit, which sat strangely enough on his otherwise grim and Fejee air.

"I should think rings would be somewhat inconvenient at sea," resumed Israel. "On my first voyage to the West Indies, I wore a girl's ring on my middle finger here, and it wasn't long before, what with hauling wet ropes, and what not, it got a kind of grown down into the flesh, and pained me very bad, let me tell you, it hugged the finger so."

"And did the girl grow as close to your heart, lad?"

"Ah, Captain, girls grow themselves off quicker than we grow them on."

"Some experience with the countesses as well as myself, eh? But the story; wave your yellow mane, my lion—the story."

So Israel went on, and told the story in all particulars.

At its conclusion, Captain Paul eyed him very earnestly. His wild, lonely heart, incapable of sympathizing with cuddled natures made hum-drum by long exemption from pain, was yet drawn towards a being, who in desperation of friendlessness, something like his own, had so fiercely waged battle against tyrannical odds.

"Did you go to sea young, lad?"

"Yes, pretty young."

"I went at twelve, from Whitehaven. Only so high," raising his hand some four feet from the deck. "I was so small, and looked so queer in my little blue jacket, that they called me the monkey. They'll call me something else before long. Did you ever sail out of Whitehaven?"

"No, Captain."

"If you had, you'd have heard sad stories about me. To this

hour they say there that I,—blood-thirsty—coward dog that
I am,—flogged a sailor, one Mungo Maxwell, to death. It's
a lie, by heaven! I flogged him, for he was a mutinous scamp.
But he died naturally, some time afterwards, and on board
another ship. But why talk? They didn't believe the affidavits
of others taken before London courts, triumphantly acquitting me; how then will they credit *my* interested words? If
slander, however much a lie, once gets hold of a man, it will
stick closer than fair fame, as black pitch sticks closer than
white cream. But let 'em slander. I will give the slanderers
matter for curses. When last I left Whitehaven, I swore never
again to set foot on her pier, except, like Cæsar, at Sandwich,
as a foreign invader. Spring under me, good ship; on you I
bound to my vengeance!"

Men with poignant feelings, buried under an air of care-
free self-command, are never proof to the sudden incitements
of passion. Though in the main, they may control themselves,
yet if they but once permit the smallest vent, then they may
bid adieu to all self-restraint, at least for that time. Thus with
Paul on the present occasion. His sympathy with Israel had
prompted this momentary ebullition. When it was gone by,
he seemed not a little to regret it. But he passed it over
lightly, saying, "You see, my fine fellow, what sort of a
bloody cannibal I am. Will you be a sailor of mine? A sailor
of the captain who flogged poor Mungo Maxwell to
death?"

"I will be very happy, Captain Paul, to be sailor under the
man who will yet, I dare say, help flog the British nation to
death."

"You hate 'em, do ye?"

"Like snakes. For months they've hunted me as a dog," half
howled and half wailed Israel, at the memory of all he had
suffered.

"Give me your hand, my lion; wave your wild flax again.
By heaven, you hate so well, I love ye. You shall be my confidential man; stand sentry at my cabin door; sleep in the
cabin; steer my boat; keep by my side whenever I land. What
do you say?"

"I say I'm glad to hear you."

"You are a good, brave soul. You are the first among the

millions of mankind that I ever naturally took to. Come, you are tired. There, go into that state-room for to-night—it's mine. You offered me your bed in Paris."

"But you begged off, Captain, and so must I. Where do you sleep?"

"Lad, I don't sleep half a night out of three. My clothes have not been off now for five days."

"Ah, Captain, you sleep so little and scheme so much, you will die young."

"I know it: I want to: I mean to. Who would live a doddered old stump? What do you think of my Scotch bonnet?"

"It looks well on you, Captain."

"Do you think so? A Scotch bonnet though, ought to look well on a Scotchman. I'm such by birth. Is the gold band too much?"

"I like the gold band, Captain. It looks something as I should think a crown might on a king."

"Aye."

"You would make a better looking king than George III."

"Did you ever see that old granny? Waddles about in farthingales, and carries a peacock fan, don't he? Did you ever see him?"

"Was as close to him as I am to you now, captain. In Kew Gardens it was, where I worked gravelling the walks. I was all alone with him, talking for some ten minutes."

"By Jove, what a chance! Had I but been there! What an opportunity for kidnapping a British king, and carrying him off in a fast-sailing smack to Boston, a hostage for American freedom. But what did you? Didn't you try to do something to him?"

"I had a wicked thought or two, captain; but I got the better of it. Besides, the king behaved handsomely towards me; yes, like a true man. God bless him for it. But it was before that, that I got the better of the wicked thought."

"Ah, meant to stick him, I suppose. Glad you didn't. It would have been very shabby. Never kill a king, but make him captive. He looks better as a fed horse, than a dead carcass. I propose now, this trip, falling on the grounds of the Earl of Selkirk, a privy counsellor, and particular private friend of George III. But I won't hurt a hair of his head.

When I get him on board here, he shall lodge in my best state-room, which I mean to hang with damask for him. I shall drink wine with him, and be very friendly; take him to America, and introduce his lordship into the best circles there; only I shall have him accompanied on his calls by a sentry or two disguised as valets. For the earl's to be on sale, mind; so much ransom; that is, the nobleman, Lord Selkirk, shall have a bodily price pinned on his coat-tail, like any slave up at auction in Charleston. But, my lad with the yellow mane, you very strangely draw out my secrets. And yet you don't talk. Your honesty is a magnet which attracts my sincerity. But I rely on your fidelity."

"I shall be a vice to your plans, Captain Paul. I will receive, but I won't let go, unless you alone loose the screw."

"Well said. To bed now; you ought to. I go on deck. Good-night, ace-of-hearts."

"That is fitter for yourself, Captain Paul; lonely leader of the suit."

"Lonely? Aye, but number one cannot but be lonely, my trump."

"Again I give it back. Ace-of-trumps may it prove to you, Captain Paul; may it be impossible for you ever to be taken. But for me—poor deuce, a trey, that comes in your wake—any king or knave may take me, as before now the knaves have."

"Tut, tut, lad; never be more cheery for another than for yourself. But a fagged body fags the soul. To hammock, to hammock! while I go on deck to clap on more sail to your cradle."

And they separated for that night.

Chapter 15

THEY SAIL AS FAR AS THE CRAG OF AILSA

NEXT MORNING Israel was appointed quarter-master; a subaltern selected from the common seamen, and whose duty mostly stations him in the stern of the ship, where the captain walks. His business is to carry the glass on the look-out for sails; hoist or lower the colors; and keep an eye on the helmsman. Picked out from the crew for their superior respectability and intelligence, as well as for their excellent seamanship, it is not unusual to find the quarter-masters of an armed ship on peculiarly easy terms with the commissioned officers and captain. This berth, therefore, placed Israel in official contiguity to Paul, and without subjecting either to animadversion, made their public intercourse on deck almost as familiar as their unrestrained converse in the cabin.

It was a fine cool day in the beginning of April. They were now off the coast of Wales, whose lofty mountains, crested with snow, presented a Norwegian aspect. The wind was fair, and blew with a strange, bestirring power. The ship—running between Ireland and England, northwards, towards the Irish Sea, the inmost heart of the British waters—seemed, as she snortingly shook the spray from her bow, to be conscious of the dare-devil defiance of the soul which conducted her on this anomalous cruise. Sailing alone from out a naval port of France, crowded with ships-of-the-line, Paul Jones, in his small craft, went forth in single-armed championship against the English host. Armed with but the sling-stones in his one shot-locker, like young David of old, Paul bearded the British giant of Gath. It is not easy, at the present day, to conceive the hardihood of this enterprise. It was a marching up to the muzzle. The act of one who made no compromise with the cannonadings of danger or death; such a scheme as only could have inspired a heart which held at nothing all the prescribed prudence of war, and every obligation of peace; combining in one breast the vengeful indignation and bitter ambition of an outraged hero, with the uncompunctuous desperation of a renegade. In one view, the Coriolanus of the sea; in another, a cross between the gentleman and the wolf.

As Paul stood on the elevated part of the quarter-deck, with none but his confidential quarter-master near him, he yielded to Israel's natural curiosity, to learn something concerning the sailing of the expedition. Paul stood lightly, swaying his body over the sea, by holding on to the mizzen-shrouds, an attitude not inexpressive of his easy audacity; while near by, pacing a few steps to and fro, his long spy glass now under his arm, and now presented at his eye, Israel, looking the very image of vigilant prudence, listened to the warrior's story. It appeared that on the night of the visit of the Duke de Chartres and Count D'Estaing to Doctor Franklin in Paris—the same night that Captain Paul and Israel were joint occupants of the neighboring chamber—the final sanction of the French king to the sailing of an American armament against England, under the direction of the Colonial Commissioner, was made known to the latter functionary. It was a very ticklish affair. Though swaying on the brink of avowed hostilities with England, no verbal declaration had as yet been made by France. Undoubtedly, this enigmatic position of things was highly advantageous to such an enterprise as Paul's.

Without detailing all the steps taken through the united efforts of Captain Paul and Doctor Franklin, suffice it that the determined rover had now attained his wish; the unfettered command of an armed ship in the British waters; a ship legitimately authorized to hoist the American colors; her commander having in his cabin-locker a regular commission as an officer of the American navy. He sailed without any instructions. With that rare insight into rare natures which so largely distinguished the sagacious Franklin, the sage well knew that a prowling *brave*, like Paul Jones, was, like the prowling lion, by nature a solitary warrior. "Let him alone;" was the wise man's answer to some statesman who sought to hamper Paul with a letter of instructions.

Much subtle casuistry has been expended upon the point, whether Paul Jones was a knave or a hero, or a union of both. But war and warriors, like politics and politicians, like religion and religionists, admit of no metaphysics.

On the second day after Israel's arrival on board the

Ranger, as he and Paul were conversing on the deck, Israel suddenly levelling his glass towards the Irish coast, announced a large sail bound in. The Ranger gave chase, and soon, almost within sight of her destination—the port of Dublin—the stranger was taken, manned, and turned round for Brest.

The Ranger then stood over, passed the Isle of Man towards the Cumberland shore, arriving within remote sight of Whitehaven about sunset. At dark she was hovering off the harbor, with a party of volunteers all ready to descend. But the wind shifted and blew fresh, with a violent sea.

"I won't call on old friends in foul weather," said Captain Paul to Israel. "We'll saunter about a little, and leave our cards in a day or two."

Next morning, in Glentinebay, on the south shore of Scotland, they fell in with a revenue wherry. It was the practice of such craft to board merchant vessels. The Ranger was disguised as a merchantman, presenting a broad drab-colored belt all round her hull; under the coat of a Quaker, concealing the intent of a Turk. It was expected that the chartered rover would come alongside the unchartered one. But the former took to flight, her two lug sails staggering under a heavy wind, which the pursuing guns of the Ranger pelted with a hail-storm of shot. The wherry escaped, spite the severe cannonade.

Off the Mull of Galloway, the day following, Paul found himself so nigh a large barley-freighted Scotch coaster, that, to prevent her carrying tidings of him to land, he dispatched her with the news, stern foremost, to Hades; sinking her, and sowing her barley in the sea, broadcast by a broadside. From her crew he learned that there was a fleet of twenty or thirty sail at anchor in Lochryan, with an armed brigantine. He pointed his prow thither; but at the mouth of the loch, the wind turned against him again, in hard squalls. He abandoned the project. Shortly after, he encountered a sloop from Dublin. He sunk her to prevent intelligence.

Thus, seeming as much to bear the elemental commission of Nature, as the military warrant of Congress, swarthy Paul darted hither and thither; hovering like a thunder-cloud off the crowded harbors; then, beaten off by an adverse wind, discharging his lightnings on uncompanioned vessels, whose solitude made them a more conspicuous and easier mark, like lonely trees on the heath. Yet all this while the land was full of garrisons, the embayed waters full of fleets. With the impunity of a Levanter, Paul skimmed his craft in the land-locked heart of the supreme naval power of earth; a torpedo-eel, unknowingly swallowed by Britain in a draught of old ocean, and making sad havoc with her vitals.

Seeing next a large vessel steering for the Clyde, he gave chase, hoping to cut her off. The stranger proving a fast sailer, the pursuit was urged on with vehemence, Paul standing, plank-proud, on the quarter-deck, calling for pulls upon every rope, to stretch each already half-burst sail to the uttermost.

While thus engaged, suddenly a shadow, like that thrown by an eclipse, was seen rapidly gaining along the deck, with a sharp defined line, plain as a seam of the planks. It involved all before it. It was the domineering shadow of the Juan Fernandez-like Crag of Ailsa. The Ranger was in the deep water which makes all round and close up to this great summit of the submarine Grampians.

The crag, more than a mile in circuit, is over a thousand feet high, eight miles from the Ayrshire shore. There stands the cone, lonely as a foundling, proud as Cheops. But, like the battered brains surmounting the Giant of Gath, its haughty summit is crowned by a desolate castle, in and out of whose arches the aerial mists eddy like purposeless phantoms, thronging the soul of some ruinous genius, who, even in overthrow, harbors none but lofty conceptions.

As the Ranger shot nigher under the crag, its height and bulk dwarfed both pursuer and pursued into nut-shells. The main-truck of the Ranger was nine hundred feet below the foundations of the ruin on the crag's top.

While the ship was yet under the shadow, and each seaman's face shared in the general eclipse, a sudden change came over Paul. He issued no more sultanical orders. He did not look so elate as before. At length he gave the command to discontinue the chase. Turning about, they sailed southward.

"Captain Paul," said Israel, shortly afterwards, "you

changed your mind rather queerly about catching that craft. But you thought she was drawing us too far up into the land, I suppose."

"Sink the craft," cried Paul; "it was not any fear of her, nor of King George, which made me turn on my heel; it was yon cock of the walk."

"Cock of the walk?"

"Aye; cock of the walk of the sea; look,—yon Crag of Ailsa."

Chapter 16

They Look in at Carrickfergus, and Descend on Whitehaven

Next day, off Carrickfergus, on the Irish coast, a fishing boat, allured by the Quaker-like look of the incognito craft, came off in full confidence. Her men were seized, their vessel sunk. From them Paul learned that the large ship at anchor in the road, was the ship-of-war Drake, of twenty guns. Upon this he steered away, resolving to return secretly, and attack her that night.

"Surely, Captain Paul," said Israel to his commander, as about sunset they backed and stood in again for the land, "surely, sir, you are not going right in among them this way? Why not wait till she comes out?"

"Because, Yellow-hair, my boy, I am engaged to marry her to-night. The bride's friends won't like the match; and so, this very night, the bride must be carried away. She has a nice tapering waist, hasn't she, through the glass? Ah! I will clasp her to my heart."

He steered straight in like a friend; under easy sail, lounging towards the Drake, with anchor ready to drop, and grapnels to hug. But the wind was high; the anchor was not dropped at the ordered time. The Ranger came to a stand three biscuits' toss off the unmisgiving enemy's quarter, like a peaceful merchantman from the Canadas, laden with harmless lumber.

"I shan't marry her just yet," whispered Paul, seeing his plans for the time frustrated. Gazing in audacious tranquillity upon the decks of the enemy; and amicably answering her hail, with complete self-possession, he commanded the cable to be slipped, and then, as if he had accidentally parted his anchor, turned his prow on the seaward tack, meaning to return again immediately with the same prospect of advantage possessed at first. His plan being to crash suddenly athwart the Drake's bow, so as to have all her decks exposed point-blank to his musketry. But once more the winds interposed. It came on with a storm of snow; he was obliged to give up his project.

Thus, without any warlike appearance, and giving no alarm, Paul, like an invisible ghost, glided by night close to land, actually came to anchor, for an instant, within speaking-distance of an English ship-of-war; and yet came, anchored, answered hail, reconnoitered, debated, decided, and retired, without exciting the least suspicion. His purpose was chain-shot destruction. So easily may the deadliest foe —so he be but dexterous—slide, undreamed of, into human harbors or hearts. And not awakened conscience, but mere prudence, restrain such, if they vanish again without doing harm. At daybreak no soul in Carrickfergus knew that the devil, in a Scotch bonnet, had passed close that way over night.

Seldom has regicidal daring been more strangely coupled with octogenarian prudence, than in many of the predatory enterprises of Paul. It is this combination of apparent incompatibilities which ranks him among extraordinary warriors.

Ere daylight, the storm of the night blew over. The sun saw the Ranger lying midway over channel at the head of the Irish Sea; England, Scotland, and Ireland, with all their lofty cliffs, being simultaneously as plainly in sight beyond the grass-green waters, as the City Hall, St. Paul's, and the Astor House, from the triangular Park in New York. The three kingdoms lay covered with snow, far as the eye could reach.

"Ah, Yellow-hair," said Paul, with a smile, "they show the white flag, the cravens. And, while the white flag stays blanketing yonder heights, we'll make for Whitehaven, my boy. I promised to drop in there a moment ere quitting the country for good. Israel, lad, I mean to step ashore in person, and have a personal hand in the thing. Did you ever drive spikes?"

"I've driven the spike-teeth into harrows before now," replied Israel; "but that was before I was a sailor."

"Well then, driving spikes into harrows is a good introduction to driving spikes into cannon. You are just the man. Put down your glass; go to the carpenter, get a hundred spikes, put them in a bucket with a hammer, and bring all to me."

As evening fell, the great promontory of St. Bees Head, with its lighthouse, not far from Whitehaven, was in distant sight. But the wind became so light, that Paul could not work his ship in close enough at an hour as early as intended. His purpose had been to make the descent and retire ere break of day. But though this intention was frustrated, he did not renounce his plan, for the present would be his last opportunity.

As the night wore on, and the ship with a very light wind glided nigher and nigher the mark, Paul called upon Israel to produce his bucket for final inspection. Thinking some of the spikes too large, he had them filed down a little. He saw to the lanterns and combustibles. Like Peter the Great, he went into the smallest details, while still possessing a genius competent to plan the aggregate. But oversee as one may, it is impossible to guard against carelessness in subordinates. One's sharp eyes can't see behind one's back. It will yet be noted that an important omission was made in the preparations for Whitehaven.

The town contained, at that period, a population of some six or seven thousand inhabitants, defended by forts.

At midnight, Paul Jones, Israel Potter, and twenty-nine others, rowed in two boats to attack the six or seven thousand inhabitants of Whitehaven. There was a long way to pull. This was done in perfect silence. Not a sound was heard except the oars turning in the rowlocks. Nothing was seen except the two lighthouses of the harbor. Through the stilness and the darkness, the two deep-laden boats swam into the haven, like two mysterious whales from the Arctic Sea. As they reached the outer pier, the men saw each other's faces. The day was dawning. The riggers and other artisans of the shipping would before very long be astir. No matter.

The great staple exported from Whitehaven was then, and still is, coal. The town is surrounded by mines; the town is built on mines; its ships moor over mines. The mines honeycomb the land in all directions, and extend in galleries of grottoes for two miles under the sea. By the falling in of the more ancient collieries, numerous houses have been swallowed, as if by an earthquake; and a consternation spread like that of Lisbon, in 1755. So insecure and treacherous was the site of the place now about to be assailed by a desperado, nursed, like the coal, in its vitals.

Now, sailing on the Thames, nigh its mouth, of fair days, when the wind is favorable for inward bound craft, the stranger will sometimes see processions of vessels, all of similar size and rig, stretching for miles and miles, like a long string of horses tied two and two to a rope and driven to market. These are colliers going to London with coal.

About three hundred of these vessels now lay, all crowded together, in one dense mob, at Whitehaven. The tide was out. They lay completely helpless, clear of water, and grounded. They were sooty in hue. Their black yards were deeply canted, like spears, to avoid collision. The three hundred grimy hulls lay wallowing in the mud, like a herd of hippopotami asleep in the alluvium of the Nile. Their sailless, raking masts, and canted yards, resembled a forest of fish-spears thrust into those same hippopotamus hides. Partly flanking one side of the grounded fleet was a fort, whose batteries were raised from the beach. On a little strip of this beach, at the base of the fort, lay a number of small rusty guns, dismounted, heaped together in disorder, as a litter of dogs. Above them projected the mounted cannon.

Paul landed in his own boat at the foot of this fort. He dispatched the other boat to the north side of the haven, with orders to fire the shipping there. Leaving two men at the beach, he then proceeded to get possession of the fort.

"Hold on to the bucket, and give me your shoulder," said he to Israel.

Using Israel for a ladder, in a trice he scaled the wall. The bucket and the men followed. He led the way softly to the guard-house, burst in, and bound the sentinels in their sleep. Then arranging his force, ordered four men to spike the cannon there.

"Now, Israel, your bucket, and follow me to the other fort."

The two went alone about a quarter of a mile.

"Captain Paul," said Israel, on the way, "can we two manage the sentinels?"

"There are none in the fort we go to."

"You know all about the place, captain?"

"Pretty well informed on that subject, I believe. Come along. Yes, lad, I am tolerably well acquainted with Whitehaven. And this morning intend that Whitehaven shall have a slight inkling of *me*. Come on. Here we are."

Scaling the walls, the two involuntarily stood for an instant gazing upon the scene. The gray light of the dawn showed the crowded houses and thronged ships with a haggard distinctness.

"Spike and hammer, lad;—so,—now follow me along, as I go, and give me a spike for every cannon. I'll tongue-tie the thunderers. Speak no more!" and he spiked the first gun. "Be a mute," and he spiked the second. "Dumfounder thee," and he spiked the third. And so, on, and on, and on; Israel following him with the bucket, like a footman, or some charitable gentleman with a basket of alms.

"There, it is done. D'ye see the fire yet, lad, from the north? I don't."

"Not a spark, Captain. But day-sparks come on in the east."

"Forked flames into the hounds! What are they about? Quick, let us back to the first fort; perhaps something has happened, and they are there."

Sure enough, on their return from spiking the cannon Paul and Israel found the other boat back; the crew in confusion; their lantern having burnt out at the very instant they wanted it. By a singular fatality the other lantern, belonging to Paul's boat, was likewise extinguished. No tinder-box had been brought. They had no matches but sulphur matches. Locofocos were not then known.

The day came on apace.

"Captain Paul," said the lieutenant of the second boat, "it is madness to stay longer. See!" and he pointed to the town, now plainly discernible in the grey light.

"Traitor, or coward!" howled Paul, "how came the lanterns out? Israel, my lion, now prove your blood. Get me a light— but one spark!"

"Has any man here a bit of pipe and tobacco in his pocket?" said Israel.

A sailor quickly produced an old stump of a pipe, with tobacco.

"That will do;" and Israel hurried away towards the town.

"What will the loon do with the pipe?" said one. "And where goes he?" cried another.

"Let him alone," said Paul.

The invader now disposed his whole force so as to retreat at an instant's warning. Meantime, the hardy Israel, long experienced in all sorts of shifts and emergencies, boldly ventured to procure, from some inhabitant of Whitehaven, a spark to kindle all Whitehaven's habitations in flames.

There was a lonely house standing somewhat disjoined from the town; some poor laborer's abode. Rapping at the door, Israel, pipe in mouth, begged the inmates for a light for his tobacco.

"What the devil," roared a voice from within; "knock up a man this time of night, to light your pipe? Begone!"

"You are lazy this morning, my friend," replied Israel; "it is daylight. Quick, give me a light. Don't you know your old friend? Shame! open the door."

In a moment a sleepy fellow appeared, let down the bar, and Israel, stalking into the dim room, piloted himself straight to the fire-place, raked away the cinders, lighted his tobacco, and vanished.

All was done in a flash. The man, stupid with sleep, had looked on bewildered. He reeled to the door; but dodging behind a pile of bricks, Israel had already hurried himself out of sight.

"Well done, my lion," was the hail he received from Paul, who, during his absence, had mustered as many pipes as possible, in order to communicate and multiply the fire.

Both boats now pulled to a favorable point of the principal pier of the harbor, crowded close up to a part of which lay one wing of the colliers.

The men began to murmur at persisting in an attempt impossible to be concealed much longer. They were afraid to venture on board the grim colliers, and go groping down into their hulls to fire them. It seemed like a voluntary entrance into dungeons and death.

"Follow me, all of you but ten by the boats," said Paul, without noticing their murmurs. "And now, to put an end to all future burnings in America, by one mighty conflagration of shipping in England. Come on, lads! Pipes and matches in the van!"

He would have distributed the men so as simultaneously to fire different ships at different points, were it not that the

lateness of the hour rendered such a course insanely hazardous. Stationing his party in front of one of the windward
colliers, Paul and Israel sprang on board.

In a twinkling, they had broken open a boatswain's locker,
and, with great bunches of oakum, fine and dry as tinder, had
leaped into the steerage. Here, while Paul made a blaze, Israel
ran to collect the tar-pots, which being presently poured on
the burning matches, oakum and wood, soon increased the
flame.

"It is not a sure thing yet," said Paul, " we must have a
barrel of tar."

They searched about until they found one: knocked out the
head and bottom, and stood it like a martyr in the midst of
the flames. They then retreated up the forward hatchway,
while volumes of smoke were belched from the after one. Not
till this moment did Paul hear the cries of his men, warning
him that the inhabitants were not only actually astir, but
crowds were on their way to the pier.

As he sprang out of the smoke towards the rail of the col-
lier, he saw the sun risen, with thousands of the people. Individuals hurried close to the burning vessel. Leaping to the
ground, Paul, bidding his men stand fast, ran to their front,
and, advancing about thirty feet, presented his own pistol at
now tumultuous Whitehaven.

Those who had rushed to extinguish what they had deemed
but an accidental fire, were now paralyzed into idiotic inaction at the defiance of the incendiary; thinking him some sudden pirate or fiend dropped down from the moon.

While Paul thus stood guarding the incipient conflagration,
Israel, without a weapon, dashed crazily towards the mob on
the shore.

"Come back, come back," cried Paul.

"Not till I start these sheep, as their own wolves many a
time started me!"

As he rushed bare-headed, like a madman, towards the
crowd, the panic spread. They fled from unarmed Israel, further than they had from the pistol of Paul.

The flames now catching the rigging and spiralling around
the masts, the whole ship burned at one end of the harbor,
while the sun, an hour high, burned at the other. Alarm and

amazement, not sleep, now ruled the world. It was time to retreat.

They re-embarked without opposition, first releasing a few prisoners, as the boats could not carry them.

Just as Israel was leaping into the boat, he saw the man at whose house he had procured the fire, staring like a simpleton at him.

"That was good seed you gave me," said Israel, "see what a yield;" pointing to the flames. He then dropped into the boat, leaving only Paul on the pier.

The men cried to their commander, conjuring him not to linger.

But Paul remained for several moments, confronting in silence the clamors of the mob beyond, and waving his solitary hand, like a disdainful tomahawk, towards the surrounding eminences, also covered with the affrighted inhabitants.

When the assailants had rowed pretty well off, the English rushed in great numbers to their forts, but only to find their cannon no better than so much iron in the ore. At length, however, they began to fire, having either brought down some ship's guns, or else mounted the rusty old dogs lying at the foot of the first fort.

In their eagerness they fired with no discretion. The shot fell short; they did not the slightest damage.

Paul's men laughed aloud, and fired their pistols in the air.

Not a splinter was made, not a drop of blood spilled throughout the affair. The intentional harmlessness of the result, as to human life, was only equalled by the desperate courage of the deed. It formed, doubtless, one feature of the compassionate contempt of Paul towards the town, that he took such paternal care of their lives and limbs.

Had it been possible to have landed a few hours earlier, not a ship nor a house could have escaped. But it was the lesson, not the loss, that told. As it was, enough damage had been done to demonstrate—as Paul had declared to the wise man in Paris—that the disasters caused by the wanton fires and assaults on the American coasts, could be easily brought home to the enemy's doors. Though, indeed, if the retaliators

were headed by Paul Jones, the satisfaction would not be
equal to the insult, being abated by the magnanimity of a
chivalrous, however unprincipled a foe.

Chapter 17

THEY CALL AT THE EARL OF SELKIRK'S; AND AFTER-
WARDS FIGHT THE SHIP-OF-WAR DRAKE

THE RANGER now stood over the Solway Frith for the
Scottish shore, and at noon on the same day, Paul, with
twelve men, including two officers and Israel, landed on St.
Mary's Isle, one of the seats of the Earl of Selkirk.

In three consecutive days this elemental warrior either entered the harbors, or landed on the shores of each of the
Three Kingdoms.

The morning was fair and clear. St. Mary's Isle lay shim-
mering in the sun. The light crust of snow had melted, revealing the tender grass and sweet buds of spring mantling
the sides of the cliffs.

At once, upon advancing with his party towards the house,
Paul augured ill for his project from the loneliness of the spot.
No being was seen. But cocking his bonnet at a jaunty angle,
he continued his way. Stationing the men silently round
about the house, followed by Israel, he announced his presence at the porch.

A grey-headed domestic at length responded.

"Is the earl within?"

"He is in Edinburgh, sir."

"Ah—sure?—Is your lady within?"

"Yes, sir—who shall I say it is?"

"A gentleman who calls to pay his respects. Here, take my
card."

And he handed the man his name, as a private gentleman,
superbly engraved at Paris, on gilded paper.

Israel tarried in the hall while the old servant led Paul into
a parlor.

Presently the lady appeared.

"Charming Madame, I wish you a very good morning."

"Who may it be, sir, that I have the happiness to see?" said
the lady, censoriously drawing herself up at the too frank gallantry of the stranger.

"Madame, I sent you my card."

"Which leaves me equally ignorant, sir," said the lady coldly, twirling the gilded pasteboard.

"A courier dispatched to Whitehaven, charming Madame, might bring you more particular tidings as to who has the honor of being your visitor."

Not comprehending what this meant, and deeply displeased, if not vaguely alarmed at the characteristic manner of Paul, the lady, not entirely unembarrassed, replied, that if the gentleman came to view the isle, he was at liberty so to do. She would retire, and send him a guide.

"Countess of Selkirk," said Paul, advancing a step, "I call to see the earl. On business of urgent importance, I call."

"The earl is in Edinburgh," uneasily responded the lady, again about to retire.

"Do you give me your honor as a lady that it is as you say?"

The lady looked at him in dubious resentment.

"Pardon, Madame; I would not lightly impugn a lady's lightest word; but I surmised that, possibly, you might suspect the object of my call; in which case, it would be the most excusable thing in the world for you to seek to shelter from my knowledge the presence of the earl on the isle."

"I do not dream what you mean by all this," said the lady with decided alarm, yet even in her panic courageously maintaining her dignity, as she retired, rather than retreated, nearer the door.

"Madame," said Paul, hereupon waving his hand imploringly, and then tenderly playing with his bonnet with the golden band, while an expression poetically sad and sentimental stole over his tawny face; "it cannot be too poignantly lamented, that in the profession of arms, the officer of fine feelings and genuine sensibility should be sometimes necessitated to public actions which his own private heart cannot approve. This hard case is mine. The earl, Madame, you say is absent.—I believe those words. Far be it from my soul, enchantress, to ascribe a fault to syllables which have proceeded from so faultless a source."

This probably he said in reference to the lady's mouth, which was beautiful in the extreme.

He bowed very lowly, while the lady eyed him with conflicting and troubled emotions, but as yet all in darkness as to his ultimate meaning. But her more immediate alarm had subsided; seeing now, that the sailor-like extravagance of Paul's homage was entirely unaccompanied with any touch of intentional disrespect. Indeed, hyperbolical as were his phrases, his gestures and whole carriage were most heedfully deferential.

Paul continued: "The earl, Madame, being absent, and he being the sole object of my call, you can not labor under the least apprehension, when I now inform you, that I have the honor of being an officer in the American navy, who, having stopped at this isle to secure the person of the Earl of Selkirk as a hostage for the American cause, am, by your assurances, turned away from that intent; pleased, even in disappointment, since that disappointment has served to prolong my interview with the noble lady before me, as well as to leave her domestic tranquillity unimpaired."

"Can you really speak true?" said the lady in undismayed wonderment.

"Madame, through your window you will catch a little peep of the American colonial ship-of-war, Ranger, which I have the honor to command. With my best respects to your lord, and sincere regrets at not finding him at home, permit me to salute your ladyship's hand and withdraw."

But feigning not to notice this Parisian proposition, and artfully entrenching her hand, without seeming to do so, the lady, in a conciliatory tone, begged her visitor to partake of some refreshment ere he departed, at the same time thanking him for his great civility. But declining these hospitalities, Paul bowed thrice, and quitted the room.

In the hall he encountered Israel, standing all agape before a Highland target of steel, with a claymore and foil crossed on top.

"Looks like a pewter platter and knife and fork, Captain Paul."

"So they do, my lion; but come, curse it, the old cock has flown; fine hen, though, left in the nest; no use; we must away empty-handed."

"Why, ain't Mr. Selkirk in?" demanded Israel in roguish concern.

"Mr. Selkirk? Alexander Selkirk, you mean. No, lad, he's not on the Isle of St. Mary's; he's away off, a hermit, on the Isle of Juan Fernandes—the more's the pity; come."

In the porch they encountered the two officers. Paul briefly informed them of the circumstances; saying, nothing remained but to depart forthwith.

"With nothing at all for our pains?" murmured the two officers.

"What, pray, would you have?"

"Some pillage, to be sure—plate."

"Shame. I thought we were three gentlemen."

"So are the English officers in America; but they help themselves to plate whenever they can get it from the private houses of the enemy."

"Come, now, don't be slanderous," said Paul; "these officers you speak of are but one or two out of twenty, mere burglars and light-fingered gentry, using the king's livery but as a disguise to their nefarious trade. The rest are men of honor."

"Captain Paul Jones," responded the two, "we have not come on this expedition in much expectation of regular pay; but we *did* rely upon honorable plunder."

"Honorable plunder! That's something new."

But the officers were not to be turned aside. They were the most efficient in the ship. Seeing them resolute, Paul, for fear of incensing them, was at last, as a matter of policy, obliged to comply. For himself, however, he resolved to have nothing to do with the affair. Charging the officers not to allow the men to enter the house on any pretence, and that no search must be made, and nothing must be taken away, except what the lady should offer them upon making known their demand, he beckoned to Israel and retired indignantly towards the beach. Upon second thoughts, he dispatched Israel back, to enter the house with the officers, as joint receiver of the plate, he being, of course, the most reliable of the seamen.

The lady was not a little disconcerted on receiving the officers. With cool determination they made known their purpose. There was no escape. The lady retired. The butler came; and soon, several silver salvers, and other articles of value, were silently deposited in the parlor in the presence of the officers and Israel.

"Mister Butler," said Israel, "let me go into the dairy and help to carry the milk-pans."

But, scowling upon this rusticity, or roguishness—he knew not which—the butler, in high dudgeon at Israel's republican familiarity, as well as black as a thunder-cloud with the general insult offered to an illustrious household by a party of armed thieves, as he viewed them, declined any assistance. In a quarter of an hour the officers left the house, carrying their booty.

At the porch they were met by a red-cheeked, spiteful-looking lass, who, with her brave lady's compliments, added two child's rattles of silver and coral to their load.

Now, one of the officers was a Frenchman, the other a Spaniard.

The Spaniard dashed his rattle indignantly to the ground. The Frenchman took his very pleasantly, and kissed it, saying to the girl that he would long preserve the coral, as a memento of her rosy cheeks.

When the party arrived on the beach, they found Captain Paul writing with pencil on paper held up against the smooth tableted side of the cliff. Next moment he seemed to be making his signature. With a reproachful glance towards the two officers, he handed the slip to Israel, bidding him hasten immediately with it to the house and place it in Lady Selkirk's own hands.

The note was as follows:—

"MADAME,—

"After so courteous a reception, I am disturbed to make you no better return than you have just experienced from the actions of certain persons under my command. Actions, lady, which my profession of arms obliges me not only to brook, but, in a measure, to countenance. From the bottom of my heart, my dear lady, I deplore this most melancholy necessity of my delicate position. However unhandsome the desire of these men, some complaisance seemed due them from me, for their general good conduct and bravery on former occasions. I had but an instant to consider. I trust, that in unavoidably gratifying them, I have inflicted less injury on your ladyship's property than I have on my own bleeding sensibilities. But my heart will not allow me to say more. Permit me to assure you, dear lady, that when the plate is sold, I shall, at all hazards, become the purchaser, and will be proud to restore it to you, by such conveyance as you may hereafter see fit to appoint.

"From hence I go, Madame, to engage, to-morrow morning, his majesty's ship Drake, of twenty guns, now lying at Carrickfergus. I should meet the enemy with more than wonted resolution, could I flatter myself that, through this unhandsome conduct on the part of my officers, I lie not under the disesteem of the sweet lady of the Isle of St. Mary's. But unconquerable as Mars should I be, could I but dare to dream, that in some green retreat of her charming domain, the Countess of Selkirk offers up a charitable prayer for, my dear lady countess, one, who coming to take a captive, himself has been captivated.

> "Your ladyship's adoring enemy,
> "JOHN PAUL JONES."

How the lady received this super-ardent note, history does not relate. But history has not omitted to record, that after the return of the Ranger to France, through the assiduous efforts of Paul in buying up the booty, piece by piece, from the clutches of those among whom it had been divided, and not without a pecuniary private loss to himself, equal to the total value of the plunder, the plate was punctually restored, even to the silver heads of two pepper-boxes; and, not only this, but the earl, hearing all the particulars, magnanimously wrote Paul a letter, expressing thanks for his politeness. In the opinion of the noble earl, Paul was a man of honor. It were rash to differ in opinion with such high-born authority.

Upon returning to the ship, she was instantly pointed over towards the Irish coast. Next morning Carrickfergus was in sight. Paul would have gone straight in; but Israel, reconnoitering with his glass, informed him that a large ship, probably the Drake, was just coming out.

"What think you, Israel, do they know who we are? Let me have the glass."

"They are dropping a boat now sir," replied Israel, removing the glass from his eye, and handing it to Paul.

"So they are—so they are. They don't know us. I'll decoy that boat alongside. Quick—they are coming for us—take the helm now yourself, my lion, and keep the ship's stern steadily presented towards the advancing boat. Don't let them have the least peep at our broadside."

The boat came on; an officer in its bow all the time eyeing the Ranger through a glass. Presently the boat was within hail.

"Ship ahoy! Who are you?"

"Oh, come alongside," answered Paul through his trumpet, in a rapid off-hand tone, as though he were a gruff sort of friend, impatient at being suspected for a foe.

In a few moments the officer of the boat stepped into the Ranger's gangway. Cocking his bonnet gallantly, Paul advanced towards him, making a very polite bow, saying: "Good morning, sir, good morning; delighted to see you. That's a pretty sword you have; pray, let me look at it."

"I see," said the officer, glancing at the ship's armament, and turning pale. "I am your prisoner."

"No—my guest," responded Paul, winningly. "Pray, let me relieve you of your—your—cane."

Thus humorously he received the officer's delivered sword.

"Now tell me, sir, if you please," he continued; "what brings out his majesty's ship Drake, this fine morning? Going a little airing?"

"She comes out in search of you; but when I left her side half an hour since, she did not know that the ship off the harbor was the one she sought."

"You had news from Whitehaven, I suppose, last night, eh?"

"Aye: express; saying that certain incendiaries had landed there early that morning."

"What?—what sort of men were they, did you say?" said Paul, shaking his bonnet fiercely to one side of his head, and coming close to the officer. "Pardon me," he added derisively,

"I had forgot; you are my *guest*. Israel, see the unfortunate gentleman below, and his men forward."

The Drake was now seen slowly coming out under a light air, attended by five small pleasure-vessels, decorated with flags and streamers, and full of gaily-dressed people, whom motives similar to those which draw visitors to the circus, had induced to embark on their adventurous trip. But they little dreamed how nigh the desperate enemy was.

"Drop the captured boat astern," said Paul; "see what effect that will have on those merry voyagers."

No sooner was the empty boat descried by the pleasure-vessels, than forthwith surmising the truth, they with all diligence turned about and re-entered the harbor. Shortly after, alarm-smokes were seen extending along both sides of the channel.

"They smoke us at last, Captain Paul," said Israel.

"There will be more smoke yet before the day is done," replied Paul gravely.

The wind was right under the land; the tide unfavorable. The Drake worked out very slowly.

Meantime, like some fiery-heated duellist calling on urgent business at frosty daybreak, and long kept waiting at the door by the dilatoriness of his antagonist shrinking at the idea of getting up to be cut to pieces in the cold,—the Ranger, with a better breeze, impatiently tacked to and fro in the channel. At last, when the English vessel had fairly weathered the point, Paul, ranging ahead, courteously led her forth, as a beau might a belle in a ball-room—to mid-channel, and then suffered her to come within hail.

"She is hoisting her colors now, sir," said Israel.

"Give her the stars and stripes, then, my lad."

Joyfully running to the locker, Israel attached the flag to the halyards. The wind freshened. He stood elevated. The bright flag blew around him, a glorified shroud, enveloping him in its red ribbons and spangles, like upspringing tongues, and sparkles of flame.

As the colors rose to their final perch, and streamed in the air, Paul eyed them exultingly.

"I first hoisted that flag on an American ship, and was the first among men to get it saluted. If I perish this night, the name of Paul Jones shall live. Hark! they hail us."

"What ship are you?"

"Your enemy. Come on! What wants the fellow of more prefaces and introductions?"

The sun was now calmly setting over the green land of Ireland. The sky was serene; the sea smooth; the wind just sufficient to waft the two vessels steadily and gently. After the first firing, and a little manœuvering, the two ships glided on freely, side by side; in that mild air exchanging their deadly broadsides, like two friendly horsemen walking their steeds along a plain, chatting as they go. After an hour of this running fight, the conversation ended. The Drake struck. How changed from the big craft of sixty short minutes before! She seemed now, above deck, like a piece of wild western woodland into which choppers had been. Her masts and yards prostrate, and hanging in jack-straws; several of her sails ballooning out, as they dragged in the sea, like great lopped tops of foliage. The black hull and shattered stumps of masts, galled and riddled, looked as if gigantic woodpeckers had been tapping them.

The Drake was the larger ship; more cannon; more men. Her loss in killed and wounded was far the greater. Her brave captain and lieutenant were mortally wounded. The former died as the prize was boarded; the latter, two days after.

It was twilight; the weather still serene. No cannonade, nought that mad man can do, molests the stoical imperturbability of nature, when nature chooses to be still. This weather, holding on all through the following day, greatly facilitated the refitting of the ships. That done, the two vessels, sailing round the north of Ireland, steered towards Brest. They were repeatedly chased by English cruisers; but safely reached their anchorage in the French waters.

"A pretty fair four weeks' yachting, gentlemen," said Paul Jones, as the Ranger swung to her cable, while some French officers boarded her. "I bring two travellers with me, gentlemen," he continued. "Allow me to introduce you to my particular friend, Israel Potter, late of North America; and also to his Britannic Majesty's ship, Drake, late of Carrickfergus, Ireland."

This cruise made loud fame for Paul, especially at the court of France, whose king sent Paul a sword and a medal. But poor Israel, who also had conquered a craft, and all unaided too—what had he?

Chapter 18

THE EXPEDITION THAT SAILED FROM GROIX

THREE MONTHS after anchoring at Brest, through Dr. Franklin's negotiations with the French king, backed by the bestirring ardor of Paul, a squadron of nine vessels of various force were ready in the road of Groix for another descent on the British coasts. These craft were miscellaneously picked up; their crews a mongrel pack; the officers mostly French, unacquainted with each other, and secretly jealous of Paul. The expedition was full of the elements of insubordination and failure. Much bitterness and agony resulted to a spirit like Paul's. But he bore up; and though in many particulars the sequel more than warranted his misgivings, his soul still refused to surrender.

The career of this stubborn adventurer signally illustrates the idea, that since all human affairs are subject to organic disorder; since they are created in, and sustained by, a sort of half-disciplined chaos; hence, he who in great things seeks success, must never wait for smooth water; which never was, and never will be; but with what straggling method he can, dash with all his derangements at his object, leaving the rest to Fortune.

Though nominally commander of the squadron, Paul was not so in effect. Most of his captains conceitedly claimed independent commands. One of them in the end proved a traitor outright; few of the rest were reliable.

As for the ships, that commanded by Paul in person will be a good example of the fleet. She was an old Indiaman, clumsy and crank, smelling strongly of the savor of tea, cloves, and arrack, the cargoes of former voyages. Even at that day, she was, from her venerable grotesqueness, what a cocked hat is, at the present age, among ordinary beavers. Her elephantine bulk was houdahed with a castellated poop like the leaning tower of Pisa. Poor Israel, standing on the top of this poop, spy-glass at his eye, looked more an astronomer than a mariner; having to do, not with the mountains of the billows, but the mountains in the moon. Galileo on Fiesole. She was originally a single-decked ship; that is, carried her armament on one gun-deck. But cutting ports below, in her after part, Paul rammed out there six old eighteen pounders, whose rusty muzzles peered just above the water-line, like a parcel of dirty mulattoes from a cellar-way. Her name was the Duras; but, ere sailing, it was changed to that other appellation, whereby this sad old hulk became afterwards immortal. Though it is not unknown, that a compliment to Doctor Franklin was involved in this change of titles, yet the secret history of the affair will now for the first time be disclosed.

It was evening in the road of Groix. After a fagging day's work, trying to conciliate the hostile jealousy of his officers, and provide, in the face of endless obstacles (for he had to dance attendance on scores of intriguing factors and brokers ashore) the requisite stores for the fleet, Paul sat in his cabin in a half despondent reverie; while Israel, cross-legged at his commander's feet, was patching up some old signals.

"Captain Paul, I don't like our ship's name.—Duras? What's that mean?—Duras? Being cribbed up in a ship named Duras! a sort of makes one feel as if he were in durance vile."

"Gad, I never thought of that before, my lion. Duras—Durance vile. I suppose it's superstition, but I'll change it. Come, Yellow-mane, what shall we call her?"

"Well, Captain Paul, don't you like Doctor Franklin? Hasn't he been the prime man to get this fleet together? Let's call her the Doctor Franklin."

"Oh no, that will too publicly declare him just at present; and Poor Richard wants to be a little shady in this business."

"Poor Richard!—call her Poor Richard, then," cried Israel, suddenly struck by the idea.

"Gad, you have it," answered Paul, springing to his feet, as all trace of his former despondency left him;—"Poor Richard shall be the name, in honor to the saying, that 'God helps them that help themselves,' as Poor Richard says."

Now this was the way the craft came to be called the *Bon Homme Richard*; for it being deemed advisable to have a French rendering of the new title, it assumed the above form.

A few days after, the force sailed. Ere long, they captured several vessels; but the captains of the squadron proving refractory, events took so deplorable a turn, that Paul, for the present, was obliged to return to Groix. Luckily however, at this junction a cartel arrived from England with upwards of a hundred exchanged American seamen, who almost to a man enlisted under the flag of Paul.

Upon the resailing of the force, the old troubles broke out afresh. Most of her consorts insubordinately separated from the Bon Homme Richard. At length Paul found himself in violent storms beating off the rugged southeastern coast of Scotland, with only two accompanying ships. But neither the mutiny of his fleet, nor the chaos of the elements, made him falter in his purpose. Nay, at this crisis, he projected the most daring of all his descents.

The Cheviot Hills were in sight. Sundry vessels had been descried bound in for the Firth of Forth, on whose south shore, well up the Firth, stands Leith, the port of Edinburgh, distant but a mile or two from that capital. He resolved to dash at Leith, and lay it under contribution or in ashes. He called the captains of his two remaining consorts on board his own ship to arrange details. Those worthies had much of fastidious remark to make against the plan. After losing much time in trying to bring to a conclusion their sage deliberations, Paul by addressing their cupidity, achieved that which all appeals to their gallantry could not accomplish. He proclaimed the grand prize of the Leith lottery at no less a figure than £200,000; that being named as the ransom. Enough: the three ships entered the Firth, boldly and freely, as if carrying Quakers to a Peace-Congress.

Along both startled shores the panic of their approach spread like the cholera. The three suspicious crafts had so long lain off and on, that none doubted they were led by the audacious viking, Paul Jones. At five o'clock, on the following morning, they were distinctly seen from the capital of Scotland, quietly sailing up the bay. Batteries were hastily thrown up at Leith, arms were obtained from the castle at Edinburgh, alarm fires were kindled in all directions. Yet with such tranquillity of effrontery did Paul conduct his ships, concealing as much as possible their warlike character, that more than once his vessels were mistaken for merchantmen, and hailed by passing ships as such.

In the afternoon, Israel, at his station on the tower of Pisa, reported a boat with five men coming off to the Richard from the coast of Fife.

"They have hot oat-cakes for us," said Paul, "let 'em come. To encourage them, show them the English ensign, Israel, my lad."

Soon the boat was alongside.

"Well, my good fellows, what can I do for you this afternoon?" said Paul, leaning over the side with a patronizing air.

"Why, captain, we come from the Laird of Crokarky, who wants some powder and ball for his money."

"What would you with powder and ball, pray?"

"Oh! haven't you heard that that bloody pirate, Paul Jones, is somewhere hanging round the coasts?"

"Aye, indeed, but he won't hurt you. He's only going round among the nations, with his old hat, taking up contributions. So, away with ye; ye don't want any powder and ball to give him. He wants contributions of silver, not lead. Prepare yourselves with silver, I say."

"Nay, captain, the Laird ordered us not to return without powder and ball. See, here is the price. It may be the taking of the bloody pirate, if you let us have what we want."

"Well, pass 'em over a keg," said Paul laughing, but modifying his order by a sly whisper to Israel; "Oh, put up your price, it's a gift to ye."

"But ball, captain, what's the use of powder without ball?" roared one of the fellows from the boat's bow, as the keg was lowered in. "We want ball."

"Bless my soul, you bawl loud enough as it is. Away with ye, with what you have. Look to your keg, and hark ye, if ye catch that villain, Paul Jones, give him no quarter."

"But, captain, here," shouted one of the boatmen, "There's a mistake. This is a keg of pickles, not powder. Look," and poking into the bung-hole, he dragged out a green cucumber dripping with brine. "Take this back, and give us the powder."

"Pooh," said Paul, "the powder is at the bottom, pickled powder, best way to keep it. Away with ye, now, and after that bloody embezzler, Paul Jones."

This was Sunday. The ships held on. During the afternoon,

a long tack of the Richard brought her close towards the shores of Fife, near the thriving little port of Kirkaldy.

"There's a great crowd on the beach, captain Paul," said Israel, looking through his glass. "There seems to be an old woman standing on a fish-barrel there, a sort of selling things at auction, to the people, but I can't be certain yet."

"Let me see," said Paul, taking the glass as they came nigher. "Sure enough, it's an old lady—an old quack-doctress, seems to me, in a black gown, too. I must hail her."

Ordering the ship to be kept on towards the port, he shortened sail within easy distance, so as to glide slowly by, and seizing the trumpet, thus spoke:—

"Old lady, ahoy! What are you talking about? What's your text?"

"The righteous shall rejoice when he seeth the vengeance. He shall wash his feet in the blood of the wicked."

"Ah, what a lack of charity. Now hear mine;—God helpeth them that help themselves, as Poor Richard says."

"Reprobate pirate, a gale shall yet come, to drive thee in wrecks from our waters."

"The strong wind of your hate fills my sails well. Adieu," waving his bonnet—"tell us the rest at Leith."

Next morning the ships were almost within cannon-shot of the town. The men to be landed were in the boats. Israel had the tiller of the foremost one, waiting for his commander to enter, when just as Paul's foot was on the gangway, a sudden squall struck all three ships, dashing the boats against them, and creating indiscribable confusion. The squall ended in a violent gale. Getting his men on board with all dispatch, Paul essayed his best to withstand the fury of the wind; but it blew adversely, and with redoubled power. A ship at a distance went down beneath it. The disappointed invader was obliged to turn before the gale, and renounce his project.

To this hour, on the shores of the Firth of Forth, it is the popular persuasion, that the Rev. Mr. Shirra's, of Kirkaldy, powerful intercession, was the direct cause of the elemental repulse experienced off the endangered harbor of Leith.

Through the ill qualities of Paul's associate captains: their timidity, incapable of keeping pace with his daring; their jealousy, blind to his superiority to rivalship—together with the general reduction of his force, now reduced, by desertion, from nine to three ships; and last of all, the enmity of seas and winds, the invader, driven, not by a fleet, but a gale, out of the Scottish waters, had the mortification in prospect of terminating a cruise, so formidable in appearance at the onset, without one added deed to sustain the reputation gained by former exploits. Nevertheless, he was not disheartened. He sought to conciliate fortune, not by despondency, but by resolution. And, as if won by his confident bearing, that fickle power suddenly went over to him from the ranks of the enemy, suddenly as plumed Marshal Ney to the stubborn standard of Napoleon from Elba, marching regenerated on Paris. In a word, luck—that's the word—shortly threw in Paul's way the great action of his life: the most extraordinary of all naval engagements; the unparalleled death-lock with the Serapis.

Chapter 19

THEY FIGHT THE SERAPIS

THE BATTLE between the Bon Homme Richard and the Serapis stands in history as the first signal collision on the sea between the Englishman and the American. For obstinacy, mutual hatred, and courage, it is without precedent or subsequent in the story of ocean. The strife long hung undetermined, but the English flag struck in the end.

There would seem to be something singularly indicatory in this engagement. It may involve at once a type, a parallel, and a prophecy. Sharing the same blood with England, and yet her proved foe in two wars; not wholly inclined at bottom to forget an old grudge: intrepid, unprincipled, reckless, predatory, with boundless ambition, civilized in externals but a savage at heart, America is, or may yet be, the Paul Jones of nations.

Regarded in this indicatory light, the battle between the Bon Homme Richard and the Serapis—in itself so curious—may well enlist our interest.

Never was there a fight so snarled. The intricacy of those incidents which defy the narrator's extrication, is not ill figured in that bewildering intertanglement of all the yards and anchors of the two ships, which confounded them for the time in one chaos of devastation.

Elsewhere than here the reader must go who seeks an elaborate version of the fight, or, indeed, much of any regular account of it whatever. The writer is but brought to mention the battle, because he must needs follow, in all events, the fortunes of the humble adventurer whose life he records. Yet this necessarily involves some general view of each conspicuous incident in which he shares.

Several circumstances of the place and time served to invest the fight with a certain scenic atmosphere, casting a light almost poetic over the wild gloom of its tragic results. The battle was fought between the hours of seven and ten at night; the height of it was under a full harvest moon, in view of thousands of distant spectators crowding the high cliffs of Yorkshire.

From the Tees to the Humber, the eastern coast of Britain, for the most part, wears a savage, melancholy, and Calabrian aspect. It is in course of incessant decay. Every year the isle which repulses nearly all other foes, succumbs to the Attila assaults of the deep. Here and there the base of the cliffs is strewn with masses of rock, undermined by the waves, and tumbled headlong below; where, sometimes, the water completely surrounds them, showing in shattered confusion detached rocks, pyramids, and obelisks, rising half-revealed from the surf,—the Tadmores of the wasteful desert of the sea. Nowhere is this desolation more marked than for those fifty miles of coast between Flamborough Head and the Spurn.

Weathering out the gale which had driven them from Leith, Paul's ships, for a few days, were employed in giving chase to various merchantmen and colliers; capturing some, sinking others, and putting the rest to flight. Off the mouth of the Humber they ineffectually manœuvered with a view of drawing out a king's frigate, reported to be lying at anchor within. At another time a large fleet was encountered, under convoy of some ships of force. But their panic caused the fleet to hug the edge of perilous shoals very nigh the land, where, by reason of his having no competent pilot, Paul durst not approach to molest them. The same night he saw two strangers further out at sea, and chased them until three in the morning; when, getting pretty nigh, he surmised that they must needs be vessels of his own squadron, which, previous to his entering the Firth of Forth, had separated from his command. Daylight proved this supposition correct. Five vessels of the original squadron were now once more in company. About noon, a fleet of forty merchantmen appeared coming round Flamborough Head, protected by two English men-of-war, the Serapis and Countess of Scarborough. Descrying the five cruisers sailing down, the forty sail, like forty chickens, fluttered in a panic under the wing of the shore. Their armed protectors bravely steered from the land, making the disposition for battle. Promptly accepting the challenge, Paul, giving the signal to his consorts, earnestly pressed forward. But, earnest as he was, it was seven in the evening ere the encounter began. Meantime his comrades, heedless of his signals, sailed independently along. Dismissing them from present consideration, we confine ourselves, for a while to the Richard and the Serapis, the grand duellists of the fight.

The Richard carried a motley crew, to keep whom in order one hundred and thirty-five soldiers—themselves a hybrid band—had been put on board, commanded by French officers of inferior rank. Her armament was similarly heterogeneous; guns of all sorts and calibres; but about equal on the whole to those of a thirty-two gun frigate. The spirit of baneful intermixture pervaded this craft throughout.

The Serapis was a frigate of fifty guns, more than half of which individually exceeded in calibre any one gun of the Richard. She had a crew of some three hundred and twenty trained man-of-war's men.

There is something in a naval engagement which radically distinguishes it from one on the land. The ocean, at times, has what is called its *sea* and its *trough of the sea*; but it has neither rivers, woods, banks, towns, nor mountains. In mild weather, it is one hammered plain. Stratagems,—like those of disciplined armies, ambuscades—like those of Indians, are impossible. All is clear, open, fluent. The very element which sustains the combatants, yields at the stroke of a feather. One wind and one tide at one time operate upon all who here engage. This simplicity renders a battle between two men-of-war, with their huge white wings, more akin to the Miltonic contests of archangels than to *the comparatively squalid* tussels of earth.

As the ships neared, a hazy darkness overspread the water. The moon was not yet risen. Objects were perceived with difficulty. Borne by a soft moist breeze over gentle waves, they came within pistol-shot. Owing to the obscurity, and the known neighborhood of other vessels, the Serapis was uncertain who the Richard was. Through the dim mist each ship loomed forth to the other vast, but indistinct, as the ghost of Morven. Sounds of the trampling of resolute men echoed from either hull, whose tight decks dully resounded like drum-heads in a funeral march.

The Serapis hailed. She was answered by a broadside. For half an hour the combatants deliberately manœuvered, continually changing their position, but always within shot fire. The Serapis—the better sailer of the two—kept critically circling the Richard, making lounging advances now and then, and as suddenly steering off; hate causing her to act not unlike a wheeling cock about a hen, when stirred by the contrary passion. Meantime, though within easy speaking distance, no further syllable was exchanged; but an incessant cannonade was kept up.

At this point, a third party, the Scarborough, drew near, seemingly desirous of giving assistance to her consort. But thick smoke was now added to the night's natural obscurity. The Scarborough imperfectly discerned two ships, and plainly saw the common fire they made; but which was which, she could not tell. Eager to befriend the Serapis, she durst not fire a gun, lest she might unwittingly act the part of a foe. As when a hawk and a crow are clawing and beaking high in the air, a second crow flying near, will seek to join the battle, but finding no fair chance to engage, at last flies away to the woods; just so did the Scarborough now. Prudence dictated the step. Because several chance shot—from which of the combatants could not be known—had already struck the Scarborough. So, unwilling uselessly to expose herself, off went for the present this baffled and ineffectual friend.

Not long after, an invisible hand came and set down a great yellow lamp in the east. The hand reached up unseen from below the horizon, and set the lamp down right on the rim of the horizon, as on a threshold; as much as to say, Gentlemen warriors, permit me a little to light up this rather gloomy looking subject. The lamp was the round harvest moon; the one solitary foot-light of the scene. But scarcely did the rays from the lamp pierce that languid haze. Objects before perceived with difficulty, now glimmered ambiguously. Bedded in strange vapors, the great foot-light cast a dubious half demoniac glare across the waters, like the phantasmagoric stream sent athwart a London flagging in a night-rain from an apothecary's blue and green window. Through this sardonical mist, the face of the Man-in-the-Moon—looking right towards the combatants, as if he were standing in a trap-door of the sea, leaning forward leisurely with his arms complacently folded over upon the edge of the horizon,—this queer face wore a serious, apishly self-satisfied leer, as if the Man-in-the-Moon had somehow secretly put up the ships to their contest, and in the depths of his malignant old soul was not unpleased to see how well his charms worked. There stood the grinning Man-in-the-Moon, his head just dodging into view over the rim of the sea:—Mephistopheles prompter of the stage.

Aided now a little by the planet, one of the consorts of the Richard, the Pallas, hovering far outside the fight, dimly discerned the suspicious form of a lonely vessel unknown to her. She resolved to engage it, if it proved a foe. But ere they joined, the unknown ship—which proved to be the Scarborough—received a broadside at long gun's distance from another consort of the Richard, the Alliance. The shot whizzed across the broad interval like shuttlecocks across a great hall. Presently the battledores of both batteries were at work, and rapid compliments of shuttlecocks were very promptly exchanged. The adverse consorts of the two main belligerents fought with all the rage of those fiery seconds who in some desperate duels, make their principal's quarrel their own. Diverted from the Richard and the Serapis by this little by-play, the Man-in-the-Moon, all eager to see what it was, somewhat raised himself from his trap-door with an added grin on his face. By this time, off sneaked the Alliance, and down swept the Pallas, at close quarters engaging the Scarborough; an encounter destined in less than an hour to end in the latter ship's striking her flag.

Compared to the Serapis and the Richard, the Pallas and the Scarborough were as two pages to two knights. In their immature way they showed the same traits as their fully developed superiors.

The Man-in-the-Moon now raised himself still higher to obtain a better view of affairs.

But the Man-in-the-Moon was not the only spectator. From the high cliffs of the shore, and especially from the great promontory of Flamborough Head, the scene was witnessed by crowds of the islanders. Any rustic might be pardoned his curiosity in view of the spectacle presented. Far in the indistinct distance fleets of frightened merchantmen filled the lower air with their sails, as flakes of snow in a snow-storm by night. Hovering undeterminedly, in another direction, were several of the scattered consorts of Paul, taking no part in the fray. Nearer, was an isolated mist, investing the Pallas and Scarborough—a mist slowly adrift on the sea, like a floating isle, and at intervals irradiated with sparkles of fire and resonant with the boom of cannon. Further away, in the deeper water, was a lurid cloud, incessantly torn in shreds of lightning, then fusing together again, once more to be rent. As yet this lurid cloud was neither stationary nor slowly adrift, like the first mentioned one; but, instinct with chaotic vitality, shifted hither and thither, foaming with fire, like a valiant water-spout careering off the coast of Malabar.

To get some idea of the events enacting in that cloud, it will be necessary to enter it; to go and possess it, as a ghost may rush into a body, or the devils into the swine, which running down the steep place perished in the sea; just as the Richard is yet to do.

Thus far the Serapis and the Richard had been manœuvering and chasseing to each other like partners in a cotillon, all the time indulging in rapid repartee.

But finding at last that the superior managableness of the enemy's ship enabled him to get the better of the clumsy old Indiaman, the Richard, in taking position; Paul, with his wonted resolution, at once sought to neutralize this, by hugging him close. But the attempt to lay the Richard right across the head of the Serapis ended quite otherwise, in sending the enemy's jib-boom just over the Richard's great tower of Pisa, where Israel was stationed; who catching it eagerly, stood for an instant holding to the slack of the sail, like one grasping a horse by the mane prior to vaulting into the saddle.

"Aye, hold hard, lad," cried Paul, springing to his side with a coil of rigging. With a few rapid turns he knitted himself to his foe. The wind now acting on the sails of the Serapis forced her, heel and point, her entire length, cheek by jowl, alongside the Richard. The projecting cannon scraped; the yards interlocked; but the hulls did not touch. A long lane of darkling water lay wedged between, like that narrow canal in Venice which dozes between two shadowy piles, and high in air is secretly crossed by the Bridge of Sighs. But where the six yard-arms reciprocally arched overhead, three bridges of sighs were both seen and heard, as the moon and wind kept rising.

Into that Lethean canal,—pond-like in its smoothness as compared with the sea without—fell many a poor soul that night;—fell, for ever forgotten.

As some heaving rent coinciding with a disputed frontier on a volcanic plain, that boundary abyss was the jaws of death to both sides. So contracted was it, that in many cases the gun-rammers had to be thrust into the opposite ports, in order to enter to muzzles of their own cannon. It seemed more an intestine feud, than a fight between strangers. Or, rather, it was as if the Siamese Twins, oblivious of their fraternal bond, should rage in unnatural fight.

Ere long, a horrible explosion was heard, drowning for the instant the cannonade. Two of the old eighteen-pounders— before spoken of, as having been hurriedly set up below the main deck of the Richard—burst all to pieces, killing the sailors who worked them, and shattering all that part of the hull, as if two exploded steam-boilers had shot out of its opposite sides. The effect was like the fall of the walls of a house. Little now upheld the great tower of Pisa but a few naked crow stanchions. Thenceforth, not a few balls from the Serapis must have passed straight through the Richard without grazing her. It was like firing buck-shot through the ribs of a skeleton.

But, further forward, so deadly was the broadside from the heavy batteries of the Serapis,—levelled point-blank, and right down the throat and bowels, as it were, of the Richard—that it cleared everything before it. The men on the Richard's covered gun-deck ran above, like miners from the fire-damp. Collecting on the forecastle, they continued to fight with grenades and muskets. The soldiers also were in the lofty tops, whence they kept up incessant volleys, cascading their fire down as pouring lava from cliffs.

The position of the men in the two ships was now exactly reversed. For while the Serapis was tearing the Richard all to pieces below deck, and had swept that covered part almost of the last man; the Richard's crowd of musketry had complete control of the upper deck of the Serapis, where it was almost impossible for a man to remain unless as a corpse. Though in the beginning, the tops of the Serapis had not been unsupplied with marksmen, yet they had long since been cleared by the overmastering musketry of the Richard. Several, with leg or arm broken by a ball, had been seen going dimly downward from their giddy perch, like falling pigeons shot on the wing.

As busy swallows about barn-eaves and ridge-poles, some of the Richard's marksmen quitting their tops, now went far out on their yard-arms, where they overhung the Serapis. From thence they dropped hand-grenades upon her decks, like apples, which growing in one field fall over the fence into another. Others of their band flung the same sour fruit into the open ports of the Serapis. A hail-storm of aerial combustion descended and slanted on the Serapis, while horizontal thunder-bolts rolled crosswise through the subterranean vaults of the Richard. The belligerents were no longer, in the ordinary sense of things, an English ship, and an American ship. It was a co-partnership and joint-stock combustion-company of both ships; yet divided, even in participation. The two vessels were as two houses, through whose party-wall doors have been cut; one family (the Guelphs) occupying the whole lower story; another family (the Ghibelines) the whole upper story.

Meanwhile determined Paul flew hither and thither like the meteoric corposant-ball, which shiftingly dances on the tips and verges of ships' rigging in storms. Wherever he went, he seemed to cast a pale light on all faces. Blacked and burnt, his Scotch bonnet was compressed to a gun-wad on his head. His Parisian coat, with its gold-laced sleeve laid aside, disclosed to the full the blue tatooing on his arm, which sometimes in fierce gestures streamed in the haze of the cannonade, cabalistically terrific as the charmed standard of Satan. Yet his frenzied manner was less a testimony of his internal commotion than intended to inspirit and madden his men, some of whom seeing him, in transports of intrepidity stripped themselves to their trowsers, exposing their naked bodies to the as naked shot. The same was done on the Serapis, where several guns were seen surrounded by their buff crews as by fauns and satyrs.

At the beginning of the fray, before the ships interlocked, in the intervals of smoke which swept over the ships as mist over mountain-tops, affording open rents here and there—the gun-deck of the Serapis, at certain points, showed, congealed for the instant in all attitudes of dauntlessness, a gallery of marble statues—fighting gladiators.

Stooping low and intent, with one braced leg thrust behind, and one arm thrust forward, curling round towards the muzzle of the gun:—there was seen the *loader*, performing his allotted part; on the other side of the carriage, in the same stooping posture, but with both hands holding his long black pole, pike-wise, ready for instant use—stood the eager *rammer and sponger*; while at the breech, crouched the wary *captain of the gun*, his keen eye, like the watching leopard's, burning along the range; and behind, all tall and erect, the Egyptian symbol of death, stood the *matchman*, immovable for the moment, his long-handled match reversed. Up to their two long death-dealing batteries, the trained men of the Serapis stood and toiled in mechanical magic of discipline. They tended those rows of guns, as Lowell girls the rows of looms in a cotton factory. The Parcæ were not more methodical; Atropos not more fatal; the automaton chess-player not more irresponsible.

"Look, lad; I want a grenade, now, thrown down their main hatch-way. I saw long piles of cartridges there. The powder monkeys have brought them up faster than they can be used. Take a bucket of combustibles, and let's hear from you presently."

These words were spoken by Paul to Israel. Israel did as ordered. In a few minutes, bucket in hand, begrimed with powder, sixty-feet in air, he hung like Apollyon from the extreme tip of the yard over the fated abyss of the hatchway. As he looked down between the eddies of smoke into that slaughterous pit, it was like looking from the verge of a cataract down into the yeasty pool at its base. Watching his chance, he dropped one grenade with such faultless precision, that, striking its mark, an explosion rent the Serapis like a volcano. The long row of heaped cartridges was ignited. The fire ran horizontally, like an express on a railway. More than twenty men were instantly killed: nearly forty wounded. This blow restored the chances of battle, before in favor of the Serapis.

But the drooping spirits of the English were suddenly revived, by an event which crowned the scene by an act on the part of one of the consorts of the Richard, the incredible atrocity of which, has induced all humane minds to impute it rather to some incomprehensible mistake, than to the malignant madness of the perpetrator.

The cautious approach and retreat of a consort of the Serapis, the Scarborough, before the moon rose, has already been mentioned. It is now to be related how that, when the moon was more than an hour high, a consort of the Richard, the Alliance, likewise approached and retreated. This ship, commanded by a Frenchman, infamous in his own navy, and obnoxious in the service to which he at present belonged; this ship, foremost in insurgency to Paul hitherto, and which, for the most part had crept like a poltroon from the fray; the Alliance now was at hand. Seeing her, Paul deemed the battle at an end. But to his horror, the Alliance threw a broadside full into the stern of the Richard, without touching the Serapis. Paul called to her, for God's sake to forbear destroying the Richard. The reply was, a second, a third, a fourth broadside; striking the Richard ahead, astern, and amidships. One of the volleys killed several men and one officer. Meantime, like carpenters' augurs, and the sea-worm called remora, the guns of the Serapis were drilling away at the same doomed hull. After performing her nameless exploit, the Alliance sailed away, and did no more. She was like the great fire of London, breaking out on the heel of the great Plague. By this time, the Richard had received so many shot-holes low down in her hull, that like a sieve she began to settle.

"Do you strike?" cried the English captain.

"I have not yet begun to fight," howled sinking Paul.

This summons and response were whirled on eddies of smoke and flame. Both vessels were now on fire. The men of either knew hardly which to do; strive to destroy the enemy, or save themselves. In the midst of this, one hundred human beings, hitherto invisible strangers, were suddenly added to the rest. Five score English prisoners, till now confined in the Richard's hold, liberated in his consternation, by the master at arms, burst up the hatchways. One of them, the captain of a letter of marque, captured by Paul, off the Scottish coast, crawled through a port, as a burglar through a window, from the one ship to the other, and reported affairs to the English captain.

While Paul and his lieutenants were confronting these prisoners, the gunner, running up from below, and not perceiving his official superiors, and deeming them dead; believing himself now left sole surviving officer, ran to the tower of Pisa to haul down the colors. But they were already shot down and trailing in the water astern, like a sailor's towing shirt. Seeing the gunner there, groping about in the smoke, Israel asked what he wanted.

At this moment, the gunner, rushing to the rail, shouted "quarter! quarter!" to the Serapis.

"I'll quarter ye," yelled Israel, smiting the gunner with the flat of his cutlass.

"Do you strike?" now came from the Serapis.

"Aye, aye, aye!" involuntarily cried Israel, fetching the gunner a shower of blows.

"Do you strike?" again was repeated from the Serapis; whose captain, judging from the augmented confusion on board the Richard, owing to the escape of the prisoners, and also influenced by the report made to him by his late guest of the port-hole, doubted not that the enemy must needs be about surrendering.

"Do you strike?"

"Aye!—I strike *back*," roared Paul, for the first time now hearing the summons.

But judging this frantic response to come, like the others, from some unauthorized source, the English captain directed his boarders to be called; some of whom presently leaped on the Richard's rail; but, throwing out his tatooed arm at them with a sabre at the end of it, Paul showed them how boarders repelled boarders. The English retreated; but not before they had been thinned out again, like spring radishes, by the unfaltering fire from the Richard's tops.

An officer of the Richard, seeing the mass of prisoners delirious with sudden liberty and fright, pricked them with his sword to the pumps; thus keeping the ship afloat by the very blunder which had promised to have been fatal. The vessels now blazed so in the rigging, that both parties desisted from hostilities to subdue the common foe.

When some faint order was again restored upon the Richard, her chances of victory increased, while those of the English, driven under cover, proportionably waned. Early in the contest, Paul, with his own hand, had brought one of his largest guns to bear against the enemy's main-mast. That shot had hit. The mast now plainly tottered. Nevertheless, it seemed as if, in this fight, neither party could be victor. Mutual obliteration from the face of the waters seemed the only natural sequel to hostilities like these. It is, therefore, honor to him as a man, and not reproach to him as an officer, that, to stay such carnage, Captain Pearson, of the Serapis, with his own hands hauled down his colors. But just as an officer from the Richard swung himself on board the Serapis, and accosted the English captain, the first lieutenant of the Serapis came up from below inquiring whether the Richard had struck, since her fire had ceased.

So equal was the conflict that, even after the surrender, it could be, and was, a question to one of the warriors engaged (who had not happened to see the English flag hauled down) whether the Serapis had struck to the Richard, or the Richard to the Serapis. Nay, while the Richard's officer was still amicably conversing with the English captain, a midshipman of the Richard, in act of following his superior on board the surrendered vessel, was run through the thigh by a pike in the hand of an ignorant boarder of the Serapis. While equally ignorant, the cannons below deck were still thundering away at the nominal conqueror from the batteries of the nominally conquered ship.

But though the Serapis had submitted, there were two misanthropical foes on board the Richard which would not so easily succumb,—fire and water. All night the victors were engaged in suppressing the flames. Not until daylight were the flames got under; but though the pumps were kept continually going, the water in the hold still gained. A few hours after sunrise the Richard was deserted for the Serapis and the other vessels of the squadron of Paul. About ten o'clock, the Richard, gorged with slaughter, wallowed heavily, gave a long roll, and blasted by tornadoes of sulphur, slowly sunk, like Gomorrah, out of sight.

The loss of life in the two ships was about equal; one-half of the total number of those engaged being either killed or wounded.

In view of this battle one may well ask—What separates the enlightened man from the savage? Is civilization a thing distinct, or is it an advanced stage of barbarism?

Chapter 20

THE SHUTTLE

F OR A TIME back, across the otherwise blue-jean career of
Israel, Paul Jones flits and re-flits like a crimson thread.
One more brief intermingling of it, and to the plain old
homespun we return.

The battle won, the squadron started for the Texel, where
they arrived in safety. Omitting all mention of intervening
harassments, suffice it, that after some months of inaction as
to anything of a warlike nature, Paul and Israel (both from
different motives, eager to return to America), sailed for that
country in the armed ship Ariel; Paul as commander, Israel as
quarter-master.

Two weeks out, they encountered by night, a frigate-like
craft, supposed to be an enemy. The vessels came within hail,
both showing English colors, with purposes of mutual deception, affecting to belong to the English navy. For an hour,
through their speaking trumpets, the captains equivocally
conversed. A very reserved, adroit, hoodwinking, statesman-
like conversation, indeed. At last, professing some little incredulity as to the truthfulness of the stranger's statement, Paul
intimated a desire that he should put out a boat and come on
board to show his commission, to which the stranger very
affably replied, that unfortunately his boat was exceedingly
leaky. With equal politeness, Paul begged him to consider the
danger attending a refusal, which rejoinder nettled the other,
who suddenly retorted that he would answer for twenty guns,
and that both himself and men were knock-down Englishmen. Upon this, Paul said that he would allow him exactly
five minutes for a sober, second thought. That brief period
passed, Paul, hoisting the American colors, ran close under
the other ship's stern, and engaged her. It was about eight
o'clock at night, that this strange quarrel was picked in the
middle of the ocean. Why cannot men be peaceable on that
great common? Or does nature in those fierce night-brawlers,
the billows, set mankind but a sorry example?

After ten minutes' cannonading, the stranger struck,

shouting out, that half his men were killed. The Ariel's crew hurraed. Boarders were called to take possession. At this juncture, the prize shifting her position so that she headed away, and to leeward of the Ariel, thrust her long spanker boom diagonally over the latter's quarter; when Israel, who was standing close by, instinctively caught hold of it—just as he had grasped the jib-boom of the Serapis—and, at the same moment, hearing the call to take possession, in the valiant excitement of the occasion, he leaped upon the spar, and made a rush for the stranger's deck, thinking, of course, that he would be immediately followed by the regular boarders. But the sails of the strange ship suddenly filled; she began to glide through the sea; her spanker-boom, not having at all entangled itself, offering no hindrance. Israel clinging midway along the boom, soon found himself divided from the Ariel, by a space impossible to be leaped. Meantime, suspecting foul play, Paul set every sail; but the stranger, having already the advantage, contrived to make good her escape, though perseveringly chased by the cheated conqueror.

In the confusion, no eye had observed our hero's spring. But, as the vessels separated more, an officer of the strange ship spying a man on the boom, and taking him for one of his own men, demanded what he did there.

"Clearing the signal halyards, sir," replied Israel, fumbling with the cord which happened to be dangling near by.

"Well, bear a hand and come in, or you will have a bow-chaser at you soon," referring to the bow guns of the Ariel.

"Aye, aye, sir," said Israel, and in a moment he sprang to the deck, and soon found himself mixed in among some two hundred English sailors of a large letter of marque. At once he perceived that the story of half the crew being killed was a mere hoax, played off for the sake of making an escape. Orders were continually being given to pull on this and that rope, as the ship crowded all sail in flight. To these orders Israel with the rest promptly responded, pulling at the rigging stoutly as the best of them; though heaven knows his heart sank deeper and deeper at every pull which thus helped once again to widen the gulf between him and home.

In intervals, he considered with himself what to do. Favored by the obscurity of the night and the number of the crew, and wearing much the same dress as theirs, it was very easy to pass himself off for one of them till morning. But daylight would be sure to expose him, unless some cunning plan could be hit upon. If discovered for what he was, nothing short of a prison awaited him upon the ship's arrival in port.

It was a desperate case; only as desperate a remedy could serve. One thing was sure, he could not hide. Some audacious parade of himself promised the only hope. Marking that the sailors, not being of the regular navy, wore no uniform; and perceiving that his jacket was the only garment on him which bore any distinguishing badge, our adventurer took it off, and privily dropped it overboard, remaining now in his dark blue woollen shirt, and blue cloth waistcoat.

What the more inspirited Israel to the added step now contemplated, was the circumstance, that the ship was not a Frenchman, or other foreigner, but her crew, though enemies, spoke the same language that he did.

So very quietly, at last, he goes aloft into the main-top, and sitting down on an old sail there, beside some eight or ten topmen, in an off-handed way asks one for tobacco.

"Give us a quid, lad," as he settled himself in his seat.

"Halloo," said the strange sailor, "who be you? Get out of the top! The fore and mizzen-top men won't let us go into their tops, and blame me if we'll let any of their gangs come here. So, away ye go."

"You're blind, or crazy, old boy," rejoined Israel. "I'm a top-mate; ain't I, lads?" appealing to the rest.

"There's only ten main-topmen belonging to our watch; if you are one, then there'll be eleven," said a second sailor. "Get out of the top!"

"This is too bad, maties," cried Israel, "to serve an old top-mate this way. Come, come, you are foolish. Give us a quid." And, once more, with the utmost sociability, he addressed the sailor next to him.

"Look ye," returned the other, "if you don't make away with yourself, you skulking spy from the mizzen, we'll drop you to deck like a jewel-block."

Seeing the party thus resolute, Israel, with some affected banter, descended.

The reason why he had tried the scheme—and, spite of the foregoing failure, meant to repeat it—was this: As customary in armed ships, the men were in companies, allotted to particular places and functions. Therefore, to escape final detection, Israel must some way get himself recognized as belonging to some one of those bands; otherwise, as an isolated nondescript, discovery ere long would be certain; especially upon the next general muster. To be sure, the hope in question was a forlorn sort of hope; but it was his sole one, and must therefore be tried.

Mixing in again for a while with the general watch, he at last goes on the forecastle among the sheet-anchor-men there, at present engaged in critically discussing the merits of the late valiant encounter, and expressing their opinion that by daybreak the enemy in chase would be hull-down out of sight.

"To be sure she will," cried Israel, joining in with the group, "old ballyhoo that she is, to be sure. But didn't we pepper her, lads? Give us a chew of tobacco, one of ye? How many have we wounded, do ye know? None killed that I've heard of. Wasn't that a fine hoax we played on 'em? Ha! ha! But give us a chew."

In the prodigal fraternal patriotism of the moment, one of the old worthies freely handed his plug to our adventurer, who, helping himself, returned it, repeating the question as to the killed and wounded.

"Why," said he of the plug, "Jack Jewboy told me, just now, that there's only seven men been carried down to the surgeon, but not a soul killed."

"Good, boys, good!" cried Israel, moving up to one of the gun-carriages, where three or four men were sitting—"slip along, chaps, slip along, and give a watchmate a seat with ye."

"All full here, lad; try the next gun."

"Boys, clear a place here," said Israel, advancing, like one of the family, to that gun.

"Who the devil are *you*, making this row here?" demanded a stern-looking old fellow, captain of the forecastle, "seems to me you make considerable noise. Are you a forecastleman?"

"If the bowsprit belongs here, so do I," rejoined Israel, composedly.

"Let's look at ye, then?" and seizing a battle-lantern, before thrust under a gun, the old veteran came close to Israel before he had time to elude the scrutiny.

"Take that!" said his examiner, and fetching Israel a terrible thump, pushed him ignominiously off the forecastle as some unknown interloper from distant parts of the ship.

With similar perseverance of effrontery, Israel tried other quarters of the vessel. But with equal ill success. Jealous with the spirit of class, no social circle would receive him. As a last resort, he dived down among the *holders*.

A group of them sat round a lantern, in the dark bowels of the ship, like a knot of charcoal burners in a pine forest at midnight.

"Well, boys, what's the good word?" said Israel, advancing very cordially, but keeping as much as possible in the shadow.

"The good word is," rejoined a censorious old *holder*, "that you had best go where you belong—on deck—and not be a skulking down here where you *don't* belong. I suppose this is the way you skulked during the fight."

"Oh, you're growly to-night, shipmate," said Israel, pleasantly—"supper sits hard on your conscience."

"Get out of the hold with ye," roared the other. "On deck, or I'll call the master-at-arms."

Once more Israel decamped.

Sorely against his grain, as a final effort to blend himself openly with the crew, he now went among the *waisters*; the vilest caste of an armed ship's company; mere dregs and settlings—sea-Pariahs; comprising all the lazy, all the inefficient, all the unfortunate and fated, all the melancholy, all the infirm; all the rheumatical scamps, scape-graces, ruined prodigal sons, sooty faces, and swineherds of the crew, not excluding those with dismal wardrobes.

An unhappy, tattered, moping row of them sat along dolefully on the gun-deck, like a parcel of crest-fallen buzzards, exiled from civilized society.

"Cheer up, lads," said Israel, in a jovial tone, "homeward bound, you know. Give us a seat among ye, friends."

"Oh, sit on your head!" answered a sullen fellow in the corner.

"Come, come, no growling; we're homeward-bound. Whoop, my hearties!"

"Work-house bound, you mean," grumbled another sorry chap, in a darned shirt.

"Oh, boys, don't be down-hearted. Let's keep up our spirits. Sing us a song, one of ye, and I'll give the chorus."

"Sing if ye like, but I'll plug my ears for one," said still another sulky varlet, with the toes out of his sea-boots; while all the rest with one roar of misanthropy joined him.

But Israel, not to be daunted, began:

" 'Cease, rude Boreas, cease your growling!' "

"And you cease your squeaking, will ye," cried a fellow in a banged tarpaulin. "Did ye get a ball in the windpipe, that ye cough that way, worse nor a broken-nosed old bellows? Have done with your groaning; it's worse nor the death-rattle."

"Boys, is this the way you treat a watch-mate," demanded Israel reproachfully, "trying to cheer up his friends? Shame on ye, boys. Come, let's be sociable. Spin us a yarn, one of ye. Meantime, rub my back for me, another," and very confidently he leaned against his neighbor.

"Lean off me, will ye?" roared his friend, shoving him away.

"But who *is* this ere singing, leaning, yarn-spinning, chap? Who are ye? Be you a waister, or be you not?"

So saying, one of this peevish, sottish band staggered close up to Israel. But there was a deck above and a deck below, and the lantern swung in the distance. It was too dim to see with critical exactness.

"No such singing chap belongs to our gang, that's flat," he dogmatically exclaimed at last, after an ineffectual scrutiny. "Sail out of this!"

And with a shove, once more poor Israel was rejected.

Black-balled out of every club, he went disheartened on deck. So long, while night screened him at least, as he contented himself with promiscuously circulating, all was safe; it was the endeavor to fraternize with any one set which was sure to endanger him. At last, wearied out, he happened to find himself on the berth deck, where the watch below were slumbering. Some hundred and fifty hammocks were on that deck. Seeing one empty, he leaped in, thinking luck might yet some way befriend him. Here, at last, the sultry confinement put him fast asleep. He was wakened by a savage whiskerando of the other watch, who, seizing him by his waistband, dragged him most indecorously out, furiously denouncing him for a skulker.

Springing to his feet, Israel perceived from the crowd and tumult of the berth deck, now all alive with men leaping into their hammocks, instead of being full of sleepers quietly dosing therein, that the watches were changed. Going above, he renewed in various quarters his offers of intimacy with the fresh men there assembled; but was successively repulsed as before. At length, just as day was breaking, an irascible fellow, whose stubborn opposition our adventurer had long in vain sought to conciliate—this man suddenly perceiving, by the grey morning light, that Israel had somehow an alien sort of general look, very savagely pressed him for explicit information as to who he might be. The answers increased his suspicion. Others began to surround the two. Presently, quite a circle was formed. Sailors from distant parts of the ship drew near. One, and then another, and another, declared that they, in their quarters, too, had been molested by a vagabond claiming fraternity, and seeking to palm himself off upon decent society. In vain Israel protested. The truth, like the day, dawned clearer and clearer. More and more closely he was scanned. At length the hour for having all hands on deck arrived; when the other watch which Israel had first tried, reascending to the deck, and hearing the matter in discussion, they endorsed the charge of molestation and attempted imposture through the night, on the part of some person unknown, but who, likely enough, was the strange man now before them. In the end, the master-at-arms appeared with his bamboo, who, summarily collaring poor Israel, led him as a mysterious culprit to the officer of the deck; which gentleman having heard the charge, examined him in great perplexity, and, saying that he did not at all recognize that countenance, requested the junior officers to contribute their scrutiny. But those officers were equally at fault.

"Who the deuce *are* you?" at last said the officer of the deck, in added bewilderment. "Where did you come from? What's your business? Where are you stationed? What's your name? Who are you, any way? How did you get here? and where are you going?"

"Sir," replied Israel very humbly, "I am going to my regular duty, if you will but let me. I belong to the main top, and ought to be now engaged in preparing the top-gallant stu'n'-sail for hoisting."

"Belong to the main-top? Why, these men here say you have been trying to belong to the fore-top, and the mizen-top, and the forecastle, and the hold, and the waist, and every other part of the ship. This is extraordinary," he added, turning upon the junior officers.

"He must be out of his mind," replied one of them, the sailing-master.

"Out of his mind?" rejoined the officer of the deck. "He's out of all reason; out of all men's knowledge and memories! Why, no one knows him; no one has ever seen him before; no imagination, in the wildest flight of a morbid nightmare, has ever so much as dreamed of him. Who *are* you?" he again added, fierce with amazement. "What's your name? Are you down in the ship's books, or at all in the records of nature?"

"My name, sir, is Peter Perkins," said Israel, thinking it most prudent to conceal his real appellation.

"Certainly, I never heard that name before. Pray, see if Peter Perkins is down on the quarter-bills," he added to a midshipman. "Quick, bring the book here."

Having received it, he ran his fingers along the columns, and dashing down the book, declared that no such name was there.

"You are not down, sir. There is no Peter Perkins here. Tell me at once who are you?"

"It might be, sir," said Israel, gravely, "that seeing I shipped under the effects of liquor, I might, out of absent-mindedness like, have given in some other person's name instead of my own."

"Well, what name have you gone by among your shipmates since you've been aboard?"

"Peter Perkins, sir."

Upon this the officer turned to the men around, inquiring whether the name of Peter Perkins was familiar to them as that of a shipmate. One and all answered no.

"This won't do, sir," now said the officer. "You see it won't do. Who are you?"

"A poor persecuted fellow at your service, sir."

"*Who* persecutes you?"

"Every one, sir. All hands seem to be against me; none of them willing to remember me."

"Tell me," demanded the officer earnestly, "how long do you remember yourself? Do you remember yesterday morning? You must have come into existence by some sort of spontaneous combustion in the hold. Or were you fired aboard from the enemy, last night, in a cartridge? Do you remember yesterday?"

"Oh yes, sir."

"What was you doing yesterday?"

"Well, sir, for one thing, I believe I had the honor of a little talk with yourself."

"With *me*?"

"Yes sir; about nine o'clock in the morning—the sea being smooth and the ship running, as I should think, about seven knots—you came up into the main-top, where I belong, and was pleased to ask my opinion about the best way to set a top gallant stu'n'-sail."

"He's mad! He's mad!" said the officer, with delirious conclusiveness. "Take him away, take him away—put him somewhere, master-at-arms. Stay, one test more. What mess do you belong to?"

"Number 12, sir."

"Mr. Tidds," to a midshipman, "send mess No. 12 to the mast."

Ten sailors replied to the summons, and arranged themselves before Israel.

"Men, does this man belong to your mess?"

"No, sir; never saw him before this morning."

"What are those men's names?" he demanded of Israel.

"Well, sir, I am so intimate with all of them," looking upon them with a kindly glance, "I never call them by their real names, but by nick-names. So, never using their real names, I have forgotten them. The nick-names that I know them by, are Towser, Bowser, Rowser, Snowser."

"Enough. Mad as a March hare. Take him away. Hold," again added the officer, whom some strange fascination still bound to the bootless investigation. "What's *my* name, sir?"

"Why, sir, one of my messmates here called you Lieutenant Williamson, just now, and I never heard you called by any other name."

"There's method in his madness," thought the officer to himself. "What's the captain's name?"

"Why, sir, when we spoke the enemy, last night, I heard him say, through his trumpet, that he was Captain Parker; and very likely he knows his own name."

"I have you now. That ain't the captain's real name."

"He's the best judge himself, sir, of what his name is, I should think."

"Were it not," said the officer, now turning gravely upon his juniors, " were it not, that such a supposition were on other grounds absurd, I should certainly conclude that this man, in some unknown way, got on board here from the enemy last night."

"How could he, sir?" asked the sailing-master.

"Heaven knows. But our spanker-boom geared the other ship, you know, in manœuvering to get headway."

"But supposing he *could* have got here that fashion, which is quite impossible under all the circumstances—what motive could have induced him voluntarily to jump among enemies?"

"Let him answer for himself," said the officer, turning suddenly upon Israel, with the view of taking him off his guard, by the matter of course assumption of the very point at issue.

"Answer, sir. Why did you jump on board here, last night, from the enemy?"

"Jump on board, sir, from the enemy? Why, sir, my station at general quarters is at gun No. 3, of the lower deck, here."

"He's cracked—or else I am turned—or all the world is;—take him away!"

"But where am I to take him, sir?" said the master-at-arms.

"He don't seem to belong anywhere, sir. Where—where am I to take him?"

"Take him out of sight," said the officer, now incensed with his own perplexity. "Take him out of sight, I say."

"Come along, then, my ghost," said the master-at-arms. And, collaring the phantom, he led it hither and thither, not knowing exactly what to do with it.

Some fifteen minutes passed, when the captain coming from his cabin, and observing the master-at-arms leading Israel about in this indefinite style, demanded the reason of that procedure, adding that it was against his express orders for any new and degrading punishments to be invented for his men.

"Come here, master-at-arms. To what end do you lead that man about?"

"To no end in the world, sir. I keep leading him about because he has no final destination."

"Mr. officer of the deck, what does this mean? Who is this strange man? I don't know that I remember him. Who is he? And what is signified by his being led about?"

Hereupon, the officer of the deck, throwing himself into a tragical posture, set forth the entire mystery; much to the captain's astonishment, who at once indignantly turned upon the phantom.

"You rascal—don't try to deceive me. Who are you? and where did you come from last?"

"Sir, my name is Peter Perkins, and I last came from the forecastle, where the master-at-arms last led me, before coming here."

"No joking, sir, no joking."

"Sir, I'm sure it's too serious a business to joke about."

"Do you have the assurance to say, that you, as a regularly shipped man, have been on board this vessel ever since she sailed from Falmouth, ten months ago?"

"Sir, anxious to secure a berth under so good a commander, I was among the first to enlist."

"What ports have we touched at, sir?" said the captain, now in a little softer tone.

"Ports, sir, ports?"

"Yes, sir, *ports*."

Israel began to scratch his yellow hair.

"What *ports*, sir?"

"Well, sir:—Boston, for one."

"Right there," whispered a midshipman.

"What was the next port, sir?"

"Why, sir, I was saying Boston was the *first* port, I believe; wasn't it?—and"—

"The *second* port, sir, is what I want."

"Well—New York."

"Right again," whispered the midshipman.

"And what port are we bound to, now?"

"Let me see—homeward-bound—Falmouth, sir."

"What sort of a place is Boston?"

"Pretty considerable of a place, sir."

"Very straight streets, ain't they?"

"Yes, sir; cow-paths, cut by sheep-walks, and intersected with hen-tracks."

"When did we fire the first gun?"

"Well, sir, just as we were leaving Falmouth, ten months ago—signal-gun, sir."

"Where did we fire the first *shotted* gun, sir?—and what was the name of the privateer we took upon that occasion?"

" 'Pears to me, sir, at that time I was on the sick list. Yes, sir, that must have been the time; I had the brain fever, and lost my mind for a while."

"Master-at-arms, take this man away."

"Where shall I take him, sir?" touching his cap.

"Go, and air him on the forecastle."

So they resumed their devious wanderings. At last, they descended to the berth-deck. It being now breakfast-time, the master-at-arms, a good-humored man, very kindly introduced our hero to his mess, and presented him with breakfast; during which he in vain endeavored, by all sorts of subtle blandishments, to worm out his secret.

At length Israel was set at liberty; and whenever there was an important duty to be done, volunteered to it with such cheerful alacrity, and approved himself so docile and excellent a seaman, that he conciliated the approbation of all the officers, as well as the captain; while his general sociability served in the end, to turn in his favor the suspicious hearts of the mariners. Perceiving his good qualities, both as a sailor and man, the captain of the main-top applied for his admission into that section of the ship; where, still improving upon his former reputation, our hero did duty for the residue of the voyage.

One pleasant afternoon, the last of the passage, when the ship was nearing the Lizard, within a few hours' sail of her port, the officer of the deck, happening to glance upwards towards the main-top, descried Israel there, leaning very leisurely over the rail, looking mildly down where the officer stood.

"Well, Peter Perkins, you seem to belong to the main-top, after all."

"I always told you so, sir," smiled Israel, benevolently down upon him, "though, at first, you remember, sir, you would not believe it."

Chapter 21

SAMSON AMONG THE PHILISTINES

A T LENGTH, as the ship, gliding on past three or four vessels at anchor in the roadstead—one, a man-of-war just furling her sails—came nigh Falmouth town, Israel, from his perch, saw crowds in violent commotion on the shore, while the adjacent roofs were covered with sight-seers. A large man-of-war cutter was just landing its occupants, among whom were a corporal's guard and three officers, besides the naval lieutenant and boat's crew. Some of this company having landed, and formed a sort of lane among the mob, two trim soldiers, armed to the teeth, rose in the stern-sheets; and between them, a martial man of Patagonian stature, their ragged and handcuffed captive, whose defiant head overshadowed theirs, as St. Paul's dome its inferior steeples. Immediately the mob raised a shout, pressing in curiosity towards the colossal stranger; so that, drawing their swords, four of the soldiers had to force a passage for their comrades, who followed on, conducting the giant.

As the letter-of-marque drew still nigher, Israel heard the officer in command of the party ashore shouting, "To the castle! to the castle!" and so, surrounded by shouting throngs, the company moved on, preceded by the four drawn swords, ever and anon flourished at the rioters, towards a large grim pile on a cliff about a mile from the landing. Long as they were in sight, the bulky form of the captive was seen at times swayingly towering over the flashing bayonets and cutlasses, like a great whale breaching amid a hostile retinue of sword-fish. Now and then, too, with barbaric scorn, he taunted them, with cramped gestures of his manacled hands.

When at last the vessel had gained her anchorage, opposite a distant detached warehouse, all was still; and the work of breaking out in the hold immediately commencing, and continuing till nightfall, absorbed all further attention for the present.

Next day was Sunday; and about noon Israel, with others,

was allowed to go ashore for a stroll. The town was quiet. Seeing nothing very interesting there, he passed out, alone, into the fields along shore; and presently found himself climbing the cliff; whereon stood the grim pile before spoken of.

"What place is yon?" he asked of a rustic passing.

"Pendennis Castle."

As he stepped upon the short crisp sward under its walls, he started at a violent sound from within, as of the roar of some tormented lion. Soon the sound became articulate, and he heard the following words bayed out with an amazing vigor:—

"Brag no more, old England; consider you are but an island! Order back your broken battalions! home, and repent in ashes! Long enough have your hired tories across the sea forgotten the Lord their God, and bowed down to Howe and Knyphausen—the Hessian!——Hands off, red-skinned jackall! Wearing the king's plate,* as I do, I have treasures of wrath against you British."

Then came a clanking, as of a chain; many vengeful sounds, all confusedly together; with strugglings. Then again the voice:—

"Ye brought me out here, from my dungeon to this green—affronting yon Sabbath sun—to see how a rebel looks. But I show ye how a true gentleman and Christian can conduct in adversity. Back, dogs! Respect a gentleman and a Christian, though he *be* in rags and smell of bilge-water."

Filled with astonishment at these words, which came from over a massive wall, inclosing what seemed an open parade-space, Israel pressed forward; and soon came to a black archway, leading far within, underneath, to a grassy tract, through a tower. Like two boar's tusks, two sentries stood on guard at either side of the open jaws of the arch. Scrutinizing our adventurer a moment, they signed him permission to enter.

Arrived at the end of the arched-way, where the sun shone, Israel stood transfixed at the scene.

Like some baited bull in the ring, crouched the Patagonian-looking captive, hand-cuffed as before; the grass of the green trampled, and gored up all about him, both by his own move-

---

*Meaning, probably, certain manacles.

ments and those of the people around. Except some soldiers and sailors, these seemed mostly town's-people, collected here out of curiosity. The stranger was outlandishly arrayed in the sorry remains of a half-Indian, half-Canadian sort of a dress, consisting of a fawn-skin jacket—the fur outside and hanging in ragged tufts—a half-rotten, bark-like belt of wampum; aged breeches of sagathy; bedarned worsted stockings to the knee; old moccasins riddled with holes, their metal tags yellow with salt-water rust; a faded red woollen bonnet, not unlike a Russian night-cap, or a portentous, ensanguined full-moon; all soiled, and stuck about with bits of half-rotted straw. He seemed just broken from the dead leaves in David's outlawed Cave of Adullam. Unshaven, beard and hair matted, and profuse as a corn-field beaten down by hail-storms, his whole marred aspect was that of some wild beast; but of a royal sort, and unsubdued by the cage.

"Aye, stare, stare! Though but last night dragged out of a ship's hold, like a smutty tierce; and this morning out of your littered barracks here, like a murderer; for all that, you may well stare at Ethan Ticonderoga Allen, the unconquered soldier, by ——! You Turks never saw a Christian before. Stare on! I am he, who, when your Lord Howe wanted to bribe a patriot to fall down and worship him by an offer of a major-generalship and five thousand acres of choice land in old Vermont—(Hah! three-times-three for glorious old Vermont, and my Green-Mountain-boys! Hurrah! Hurrah! Hurrah!) I am he, I say, who answered your Lord Howe, 'You, *you* offer *our* land? You are like the devil in Scripture, offering all the kingdoms in the world, when the d——d soul had not a corner-lot on earth!' Stare on!"

"Look you, rebel, you had best heed how you talk against General Lord Howe," here said a thin, wasp-waisted, epauleted officer of the castle, coming near and flourishing his sword like a schoolmaster's ferule.

"General Lord Howe? Heed how I talk of that toad-hearted king's lick-spittle of a scarlet poltroon; the vilest wriggler in God's worm-hole below? I tell you, that herds of red-haired devils are impatiently snorting to ladle Lord Howe with all his gang (you included) into the seethingest syrups of tophet's flames!"

At this blast, the wasp-waisted officer was blown backwards as from before the suddenly burst head of a steam-boiler.

Staggering away, with a snapped spine, he muttered something about its being beneath his dignity to bandy further words with a low-lived rebel.

"Come, come, Colonel Allen," here said a mild-looking man in a sort of clerical undress; "respect the day better than to talk thus of what lies beyond. Were you to die this hour, or what is more probable, be hung next week at Tower-wharf, you know not what might become, in eternity, of yourself."

"Reverend Sir," with a mocking bow; "when not better employed braiding my beard, I have a little dabbled in your theologies. And let me tell you, Reverend Sir," lowering and intensifying his voice: "that as to the world of spirits, of which you hint, though I know nothing of the mode or manner of that world, no more than do you, yet I expect when I shall arrive there, to be treated as well as any other gentleman of my merit. That is to say, far better than you British know how to treat an American officer and meek-hearted Christian captured in honorable war, by ——! Every one tells me as you yourself just breathed, and as, crossing the sea, every billow dinned into my ear—that I, Ethan Allen, am to be hung like a thief. If I am, the great Jehovah and the Continental Congress shall avenge me; while I, for my part, shall show you, even on the tree, how a Christian gentleman can die. Meantime, sir, if you are the clergyman you look, act out your consolatory function, by getting an unfortunate Christian gentleman about to die, a bowl of punch."

The good-natured stranger, not to have his religious courtesy appealed to in vain, immediately dispatched his servant, who stood by, to procure the beverage.

At this juncture, a faint rustling sound, as of the advance of an army with banners, was heard. Silks, scarfs, and ribbons fluttered in the background. Presently, a bright squadron of fair ladies drew nigh, escorted by certain outriding gallants of Falmouth.

"Ah," sighed a soft voice; "what a strange sash, and furred vest, and what leopard-like teeth, and what flaxen hair, but all mildewed;—is that he?"

"Yea, is it, lovely charmer," said Allen, like an Ottoman, bowing over his broad, bovine forehead, and breathing the words out like a lute; "it is he—Ethan Allen, the soldier; now, since ladies' eyes visit him, made trebly a captive."

"Why, he talks like a beau in a parlor; this wild, mossed American from the woods," sighed another fair lady to her mate; "but can this be he we came to see? I must have a lock of his hair."

"It is he, adorable Delilah; and fear not, even though incited by the foe, by clipping my locks, to dwindle my strength. Give me your sword, man," turning to an officer;— "Ah! I'm fettered. Clip it yourself, lady."

"No, no—I am"——

"Afraid, would you say? Afraid of the vowed friend and champion of all ladies all round the world? Nay, nay: come hither."

The lady advanced; and soon, overcoming her timidity, her white hand shone like whipped foam amid the matted waves of flaxen hair.

"Ah, this is like clipping tangled tags of gold-lace," cried she; "but see, it is half straw."

"But the wearer is no man-of-straw, lady; were I free, and you had ten thousand foes—horse, foot, and dragoons— how like a friend I could fight for you! Come, you have robbed me of my hair; let me rob your dainty hand of its price. What, afraid again?"

"No, not that; but"——

"I see, lady; I may do it, by your leave, but not by your word; the wonted way of ladies. There, it is done. Sweeter that kiss, than the bitter heart of a cherry."

When at length this lady left, no small talk was had by her with her companions about someway relieving the hard lot of so knightly an unfortunate. Whereupon a worthy, judicious gentleman, of middle-age, in attendance, suggested a bottle of good wine every day, and clean linen once every week. And these, the gentle Englishwoman—too polite and too good to be fastidious—did indeed actually send to Ethan Allen, so long as he tarried a captive in her land.

The withdrawal of this company was followed by a different scene.

A perspiring man in top-boots, a riding whip in his hand, and having the air of a prosperous farmer, brushed in, like a stray bullock, among the rest, for a peep at the giant; having just entered through the arch, as the ladies passed out.

"Hearing that the man who took Ticonderoga was here in Pendennis Castle, I've ridden twenty-five miles to see him; and to-morrow my brother will ride forty for the same purpose. So let me have first look. Sir," he continued, addressing the captive; "will you let me ask you a few plain questions, and be free with you?"

"Be free with me? with all my heart. I love freedom of all things. I'm ready to die for freedom; I expect to. So be free as you please. What is it?"

"Then, sir, permit me to ask what is your occupation in life;—in time of peace, I mean."

"You talk like a tax-gatherer;" rejoined Allen, squinting diabolically at him; "what is my occupation in life? Why, in my younger days I studied divinity, but at present I am a conjuror by profession."

Hereupon everybody laughed, equally at the manner as the words, and the nettled farmer retorted:—

"Conjurer, eh? well, you conjured wrong that time you were taken."

"Not so wrong, though, as you British did, that time I took Ticonderoga, my friend."

At this juncture the servant came with the punch, when his master bade him present it to the captive.

"No!—give it me, sir, with your own hands; and pledge me as gentleman to gentleman."

"I cannot pledge a state-prisoner, Colonel Allen; but I will hand you the punch with my own hands, since you insist upon it."

"Spoken and done like a true gentleman, sir; I am bound to you."

Then receiving the bowl into his gyved hands, the iron ringing against the china, he put it to his lips, and saying, "I hereby give the British nation credit for half a minute's good usage," at one draught emptied it to the bottom.

"The rebel gulps it down like a swilling hog at a trough;" here scoffed a lusty private of the guard, off duty.

"Shame to you!" cried the giver of the bowl.

"Nay, sir; his red coat is a standing blush to him, as it is to the whole scarlet-blushing British army." Then turning derisively upon the private: "you object to my way of taking things, do ye? I fear I shall never please ye. You objected to the way, too, in which I took Ticonderoga, and the way in which I meant to take Montreal. Selah! But, pray, now that I look at you, are not you the hero I caught dodging round, in his shirt, in the cattle-pen, inside the fort? It was the break of day, you remember."

"Come, Yankee," here swore the incensed private; "cease this, or I'll darn your old fawn-skins for ye, with the flat of this sword;" for a specimen, laying it lashwise, but not heavily, across the captive's back.

Turning like a tiger, the giant, catching the steel between his teeth, wrenched it from the private's grasp, and striking it with his manacles, sent it spinning like a juggler's dagger into the air; saying, "Lay your dirty coward's iron on a tied gentleman again, and these," lifting his handcuffed fists, "shall be the beetle of mortality to you!"

The now furious soldier would have struck him with all his force; but several men of the town interposed, reminding him that it were outrageous to attack a chained captive.

"Ah," said Allen, "I am accustomed to that, and therefore I am beforehand with them; and the extremity of what I say against Britain, is not meant for you, kind friends, but for my insulters, present and to come." Then recognizing among the interposers the giver of the bowl, he turned with a courteous bow, saying, "Thank you again and again, my good sir; you may not be the worse for this; ours is an unstable world; so that one gentleman never knows when it may be his turn to be helped of another."

But the soldier still making a riot, and the commotion growing general, a superior officer stepped up, who terminated the scene by remanding the prisoner to his cell, dismissing the towns-people, with all strangers, Israel among the rest, and closing the castle gates after them.

Chapter 22

AMONG THE EPISODES of the Revolutionary War, none is stranger than that of Ethan Allen in England; the event and the man being equally uncommon.

Allen seems to have been a curious combination of a Hercules, a Joe Miller, a Bayard, and a Tom Hyer; had a person like the Belgian giants; mountain music in him like a Swiss; a heart plump as Cœur de Lion's. Though born in New England, he exhibited no trace of her character. He was frank; bluff; companionable as a Pagan; convivial; a Roman; hearty as a harvest. His spirit was essentially western; and herein is his peculiar Americanism; for the western spirit is, or will yet be (for no other is, or can be) the true American one.

For the most part, Allen's manner while in England, was scornful and ferocious in the last degree; however qualified by that wild, heroic sort of levity, which in the hour of oppression or peril, seems inseparable from a nature like his; the mode whereby such a temper best evinces its barbaric disdain of adversity; and how cheaply and waggishly it holds the malice, even though triumphant, of its foes! Aside from that inevitable egotism relatively pertaining to pine trees, spires, and giants, there were, perhaps, two special incidental reasons for the Titanic Vermonter's singular demeanor abroad. Taken captive while heading a forlorn hope before Montreal, he was treated with inexcusable cruelty and indignity; something as if he had fallen into the hands of the Dyaks. Immediately upon his capture he would have been deliberately suffered to have been butchered by the Indian allies, in cold blood on the spot, had he not, with desperate intrepidity, availed himself of his enormous physical strength, by twitching a British officer to him, and using him for a living target, whirling him round and round against the murderous tomahawks of the savages. Shortly afterwards, led into the town, fenced about by bayonets of the guard, the commander of the enemy, one General Prescott, flourished his cane over the captive's head, with brutal insults promising him a rebel's halter at Tyburn. During his passage to England in the same ship wherein went passenger Colonel Guy Johnson, the implacable tory, he was kept heavily ironed in the hold, and in all ways treated as a common mutineer; or, it may be, rather as a lion of Asia; which, though caged, was still too dreadful to behold without fear and trembling; and consequent cruelty. And no wonder, at least for the fear; for on one occasion, when chained hand and foot, he was insulted on shipboard by an officer; with his teeth he twisted off the nail that went through the mortise of his handcuffs, and so, having his arms at liberty, challenged his insulter to combat. Often, as at Pendennis Castle, when no other avengement was at hand, he would hurl on his foes such howling tempests of anathema, as fairly to shock them into retreat. Prompted by somewhat similar motives, both on shipboard and in England, he would often make the most vociferous allusions to Ticonderoga, and the part he played in its capture, well knowing, that of all American names, Ticonderoga was, at that period, by far the most famous and galling to Englishmen.

Parlor-men, dancing-masters, the graduates of the Abbé Bellegarde may shrug their laced shoulders at the boisterousness of Allen in England. True, he stood upon no punctilios with his jailers; for where modest gentlemanhood is all on one side, it is a losing affair; as if my Lord Chesterfield should take off his hat, and smile, and bow, to a mad bull, in hopes of a reciprocation of politeness. When among wild beasts, if they menace you, be a wild beast. Neither is it unlikely that this was the view taken by Allen. For, besides the exasperating tendency to self-assertion which such treatment as his must have bred on a man like him, his experience must have taught him, that by assuming the part of a jocular, reckless, and even braggart barbarian, he would better sustain himself against bullying turnkeys than by submissive quietude. Nor should it be forgotten, that besides the petty details of personal malice, the enemy violated every international usage of right and decency, in treating a distinguished prisoner of war as if he had been a Botany-Bay convict. If, at the present day, in any similar case between the same States, the repetition of such outrages would be more than unlikely, it is only because it is among nations as among individuals: imputed indigence provokes oppression and scorn; but that same indigence being risen to opulence, receives a politic consideration even from its former insulters.

As the event proved, in the course Allen pursued, he was right. Because, though at first nothing was talked of by his captors, and nothing anticipated by himself, but his ignominious execution, or, at the least, prolonged and squalid incarceration; nevertheless, these threats and prospects evaporated, and by his facetious scorn for scorn, under·the extremest sufferings, he finally wrung repentant usage from his foes; and in the end, being liberated from his irons, and walking the quarter-deck where before he had been thrust into the hold, was carried back to America, and in due time at New York, honorably included in a regular exchange of prisoners.

It was not without strange interest that Israel had been an eye-witness of the scenes on the Castle Green. Neither was this interest abated by the painful necessity of concealing, for the present, from his brave countryman and fellow-mountaineer, the fact of a friend being nigh. When at last the throng was dismissed, walking towards the town with the rest, he heard that there were some forty or more other Americans, privates, confined on the cliff. Upon this, inventing a pretence, he turned back, loitering around the walls for any chance glimpse of the captives. Presently, while looking up at a grated embrasure in the tower, he started at a voice from it familiarly hailing him:—

"Potter, is that you? In God's name how came you here?"

At these words, a sentry below had his eye on our astonished adventurer. Bringing his piece to bear, he bade him stand. Next moment Israel was under arrest. Being brought into the presence of the forty prisoners, where they lay in litters of mouldy straw, strewn wtih gnawed bones, as in a kennel, he recognized among them one Singles, now Sergeant Singles, the man who, upon our hero's return home from his last Cape Horn voyage, he had found wedded to his mountain Jenny. Instantly a rush of emotions filled him. Not as when Damon found Pythias. But far stranger, because very different. For not only had this Singles been an alien to Israel (so far as actual intercourse went), but impelled to it by instinct, Israel had all but detested him, as a successful, and perhaps insidious rival. Nor was it altogether unlikely that Singles had reciprocated the feeling. But now, as if the Atlantic rolled, not between two continents, but two worlds—this, and the next—these alien souls, oblivious to hate, melted down into one.

At such a juncture, it was hard to maintain a disguise; especially when it involved the seeming rejection of advances like the sergeant's. Still, converting his real amazement into affected surprise, Israel, in presence of the sentries, declared to Singles that he (Singles) must labor under some unaccountable delusion; for he (Potter) was no Yankee rebel, thank Heaven, but a true man to his king; in short, an honest Englishman, born in Kent, and now serving his country, and doing what damage he might to her foes, by being first captain of a carronade on board a letter-of-marque, that moment in the harbor.

For a moment, the captive stood astounded; but observing Israel more narrowly, detecting his latent look, and bethinking him of the useless peril he had thoughtlessly caused to a countryman, no doubt unfortunate as himself, Singles took his cue, and pretending sullenly to apologize for his error, put on a disappointed and crest-fallen air. Nevertheless, it was not without much difficulty, and after many supplemental scrutinies and inquisitions from a board of officers before whom he was subsequently brought, that our wanderer was finally permitted to quit the cliff.

This luckless adventure not only nipped in the bud a little scheme he had been revolving, for materially befriending Ethan Allen and his comrades, but resulted in making his further stay at Falmouth perilous in the extreme. And as if this were not enough, next day, while hanging over the side, painting the hull, in trepidation of a visit from the castle soldiers, rumor came to the ship that the man-of-war in the haven purposed impressing one-third of the letter of marque's crew; though, indeed, the latter vessel was preparing for a second cruise. Being on board a private armed ship, Israel had little dreamed of its liability to the same governmental hardships with the meanest merchantman. But the system of impressment is no respecter either of pity or person.

His mind was soon determined. Unlike his shipmates, braving immediate and lonely hazard, rather than wait for a collective and ultimate one, he cunningly dropped himself overboard the same night, and after the narrowest risk from the muskets of the man-of-war's sentries (whose gangways he had to pass), succeeded in swimming to shore, where he fell exhausted, but recovering, fled inland; doubly hunted by the thought, that whether as an Englishman, or whether as an American, he would, if caught, be now equally subject to enslavement.

Shortly after the break of day, having gained many miles, he succeeded in ridding himself of his seaman's clothing, having found some mouldy old rags on the banks of a stagnant pond, nigh a rickety building, which looked like a poorhouse,—clothing not improbably, as he surmised, left there, on the bank, by some pauper suicide. Marvel not that he should, with avidity, seize these rags; what the suicides abandon the living hug.

Once more in beggar's garb, the fugitive sped towards London, prompted by the same instinct which impels the hunted fox to the wilderness; for solitudes befriend the endangered wild beast, but crowds are the security, because the true desert of persecuted man. Among the throngs of the capital, Israel for more than forty years was yet to disappear, as one entering at dusk into a thick wood. Nor did ever the German forest, nor Tasso's enchanted one, contain in its depths more things of horror than eventually were revealed in the secret clefts, gulfs, caves and dens of London.

But here we anticipate a page.

Chapter 23

IT WAS a grey, lowering afternoon that, worn-out, half-starved, and haggard, Israel arrived within some ten or fifteen miles of London, and saw scores and scores of forlorn men engaged in a great brick-yard.

For the most part, brick-making is all mud and mire. Where, abroad, the business is carried on largely, as to supply the London Market, hordes of the poorest wretches are employed; their grimy tatters naturally adapting them to an employ where cleanliness is as much out of the question as with a drowned man at the bottom of the lake in the Dismal Swamp.

Desperate with want, Israel resolved to turn brick-maker; nor did he fear to present himself as a stranger; nothing doubting that to such a vocation, his rags would be accounted the best letters-of-introduction.

To be brief, he accosted one of the many surly overseers, or task-masters of the yard, who with no few pompous airs, finally engaged him at six shillings a week; almost equivalent to a dollar and a half. He was appointed to one of the mills for grinding up the ingredients. This mill stood in the open air. It was of a rude, primitive, Eastern aspect; consisting of a sort of hopper, emptying into a barrel-shaped receptacle. In the barrel was a clumsy machine turned round at its axis by a great bent beam, like a well-sweep, only it was horizontal; to this beam, at its outer end, a spavined old horse was attached. The muddy mixture was shovelled into the hopper by spavined-looking old men; while trudging wearily round and round the spavined old horse ground it all up till it slowly squashed out at the bottom of the barrel, in a doughy compound, all ready for the moulds. Where the dough squeezed out of the barrel, a pit was sunken, so as to bring the moulder here stationed down to a level with the trough, into which the dough fell. Israel was assigned to this pit. Men came to him continually, reaching down rude wooden trays, divided into compartments, each of the size and shape of a brick.

With a flat sort of big ladle, Israel slapped the dough into the trays from the trough; then, with a bit of smooth board scraped the top even, and handed it up. Half buried there in the pit, all the time handing those desolate trays, poor Israel seemed some grave-digger, or church-yard man, tucking away dead little innocents in their coffins on one side, and cunningly disinterring them again to resurrectionists stationed on the other.

Twenty of these melancholy old mills were in operation. Twenty heart-broken old horses, rigged out deplorably in cast-off old cart harness, incessantly tugged at twenty great shaggy beams; while from twenty half-burst old barrels, twenty wads of mud, with a lava-like course, gouged out into twenty old troughs, to be slapped by twenty tattered men, into the twenty-times-twenty battered old trays.

Ere entering his pit for the first, Israel had been struck by the dismally devil-may-care gestures of the moulders. But hardly had he himself been a moulder three days, when his previous sedateness of concern at his unfortunate lot, began to conform to the reckless sort of half jolly despair expressed by the others. The truth indeed was, that this continual, violent, helter-skelter slapping of the dough into the moulds, begat a corresponding disposition in the moulder; who, by heedlessly slapping that sad dough, as stuff of little worth, was thereby taught, in his meditations, to slap, with similar heedlessness, his own sadder fortunes, as of still less vital consideration. To these muddy philosophers, men and bricks were equally of clay. What signifies who we be—dukes or ditchers? thought the moulders; all is vanity and clay. So slap, slap, slap; care-free and negligent; with bitter unconcern, these dismal desperadoes flapped down the dough. If this recklessness were vicious of them, be it so; but their vice was like that weed which but grows on barren ground; enrich the soil, and it disappears.

For thirteen weary weeks, lorded over by the taskmasters, Israel toiled in his pit. Though this condemned him to a sort of earthy dungeon, or grave-digger's hole while he worked; yet even when liberated to his meals, naught of a cheery nature greeted him. The yard was encamped, with all its endless rows of tented sheds, and kilns, and mills, upon a wild waste moor, belted round by bogs and fens. The blank horizon, like a rope, coiled round the whole.

Sometimes the air was harsh and bleak; the ridged and mottled sky looked scourged; or cramping fogs set in from sea, for leagues around, ferreting out each rheumatic human bone, and racking it; the sciatic limpers shivered; their aguish rags sponged up the mists. No shelter, though it hailed. The sheds were for the bricks. Unless, indeed, according to the phrase, each man was a "brick," which, in sober scripture, was the case; brick is no bad name for any son of Adam; Eden was but a brick-yard; what is a mortal but a few luckless shovelfuls of clay, moulded in a mould, laid out on a sheet to dry, and ere long quickened into his queer caprices by the sun? Are not men built into communities just like bricks into a wall? Consider the great wall of China: ponder the great populace of Pekin. As man serves bricks, so God him; building him up by billions into the edifices of his purposes. Man attains not to the nobility of a brick, unless taken in the aggregate. Yet is there a difference in brick, whether quick or dead; which, for the last, we now shall see.

All night long, men sat before the mouth of the kilns, feeding them with fuel. A dull smoke—a smoke of their torments—went up from their tops. It was curious to see the kilns under the action of the fire, gradually changing color, like boiling lobsters. When, at last, the fires would be extinguished, the bricks being duly baked, Israel often took a peep into the low vaulted ways at the base, where the flaming faggots had crackled. The bricks immediately lining the vaults would be all burnt to useless scrolls, black as charcoal, and twisted into shapes the most grotesque; the next tier would be a little less withered, but hardly fit for service; and gradually, as you went higher and higher along the successive layers of the kiln, you came to the midmost ones, sound, square, and perfect bricks, bringing the highest prices; from these the contents of the kiln gradually deteriorated in the opposite direction, upward. But the topmost layers, though inferior to the best, by no means presented the distorted look of the furnace-bricks. The furnace-bricks were haggard, with the immediate blistering of the fire—the midmost ones were ruddy with a genial and tempered glow—the summit ones were pale with the languor of too exclusive an exemption from the burden of the blaze.

These kilns were a sort of temporary temples constructed in the yard, each brick being set against its neighbor almost with the care taken by the mason. But as soon as the fire was extinguished, down came the kiln in a tumbled ruin, carted off to London, once more to be set up in ambitious edifices, to a true brick-yard philosopher, little less transient than the kilns.

Sometimes, lading out his dough, Israel could not but bethink him of what seemed enigmatic in his fate. He whom love of country made a hater of her foes—the foreigners among whom he now was thrown—he who, as soldier and sailor, had joined to kill, burn and destroy both them and theirs—here he was at last, serving that very people as a slave, better succeeding in making their bricks than firing their ships. To think that he should be thus helping, with all his strength, to extend the walls of the Thebes of the oppressor, made him half mad. Poor Israel! well-named—bondsman in the English Egypt. But he drowned the thought by still more recklessly spattering with his ladle: "What signifies who we be, or where we are, or what we do?" Slap-dash! "Kings as clowns are codgers—who ain't a nobody?" Splash! "All is vanity and clay."

Chapter 24

In the City of Dis

A T THE END of his brick-making, our adventurer found himself with a tolerable suit of clothes—somewhat darned—on his back, several blood-blisters in his palms, and some verdigris coppers in his pocket. Forthwith, to seek his fortune, he proceeded on foot to the capital, entering, like the king, from Windsor, from the Surrey side.

It was late on a Monday morning, in November—a Blue Monday—a Fifth of November—Guy Fawkes' Day!—very blue, foggy, doleful and gunpowdery, indeed, as shortly will be seen,—that Israel found himself wedged in among the greatest every-day crowd which grimy London presents to the curious stranger. That hereditary crowd—gulf-stream of humanity—which, for continuous centuries, has never ceased pouring, like an endless shoal of herring, over London Bridge.

At the period here written of, the bridge, specifically known by that name, was a singular and sombre pile, built by a cowled monk—Peter of Colechurch—some five hundred years before. Its arches had long been crowded at the sides with strange old rookeries of disproportioned and toppling height, converting the bridge at once into the most densely occupied ward, and most jammed thoroughfare of the town, while, as the skulls of bullocks are hung out for signs to the gateways of shambles, so the withered heads and smoked quarters of traitors, stuck on pikes, long crowned the Southwark entrance.

Though these rookeries, with their grisly heraldry, had been pulled down some twenty years prior to the present visit; still, enough of grotesque and antiquity clung to the structure at large, to render it the most striking of objects, especially to one like our hero, born in a virgin clime, where the only antiquities are the for ever youthful heavens and the earth.

On his route from Brentford to Paris, Israel had passed through the capital, but only as a courier. So that now, for

603

the first, he had time to linger and loiter, and lounge—slowly
absorb what he saw—meditate himself into boundless amazement. For forty years he never recovered from that surprise—
never, till dead, had done with his wondering.

Hung in long, sepulchral arches of stone, the black, be-
smoked bridge seemed a huge scarf of crape, festooning the
river across. Similar funereal festoons spanned it to the west,
while eastward, towards the sea, tiers and tiers of jetty colliers
lay moored, side by side, fleets of black swans.

The Thames, which far away, among the green fields of
Berks, ran clear as a brook, here, polluted by continual vicinity to man, curdled on between rotten wharves, one murky
sheet of sewerage. Fretted by the ill-built piers, awhile it
crested and hissed, then shot balefully through the Erebus
arches, desperate as the lost souls of the harlots, who, every
night, took the same plunge. Meantime, here and there, like
awaiting hearses, the coal-scows drifted along, poled broadside, pell-mell to the current.

And as that tide in the water swept all craft on, so a like
tide seemed hurrying all men, all horses, all vehicles on the
land. As ant-hills, the bridge arches crawled with processions
of carts, coaches, drays, every sort of wheeled, rumbling
thing, the noses of the horses behind touching the backs of
the vehicles in advance, all bespattered with ebon mud, ebon
mud that stuck like Jews' pitch. At times the mass, receiving
some mysterious impulse far in the rear, away among the
coiled thoroughfares out of sight, would start forward with a
spasmodic surge. It seemed as if some squadron of centaurs,
on the thither side of Phlegethon, with charge on charge, was
driving tormented humanity, with all its chattels, across.

Whichever way the eye turned, no tree, no speck of any
green thing was seen; no more than in smithies. All laborers,
of whatsoever sort, were hued like the men in foundries. The
black vistas of streets were as the galleries in coal mines; the
flagging, as flat tomb-stones minus the consecration of moss;
and worn heavily down, by sorrowful tramping, as the vitreous rocks in the cursed Gallipagos, over which the convict
tortoises crawl.

As in eclipses, the sun was hidden; the air darkened; the
whole dull, dismayed aspect of things, as if some neighboring

volcano, belching its premonitory smoke, were about to whelm the great town, as Herculaneum and Pompeii, or the Cities of the Plain. And as they had been upturned in terror towards the mountain, all faces were more or less snowed, or spotted with soot. Nor marble, nor flesh, nor the sad spirit of man, may in this cindery City of Dis abide white.

On they passed; two-and-two, along the packed footpaths of the bridge; long-drawn, methodic, as funerals: some of the faces settled in dry apathy, content with their doom; others seemed mutely raving against it; while still others, like the spirits of Milton and Shelley in the prelatical Hinnom, seemed undeserving their fate, and despising their torture.

As retired at length, midway, in a recess of the bridge, Israel surveyed them, various individual aspects all but frighted him. Knowing not who they were; never destined, it may be, to behold them again; one after the other, they drifted by, uninvoked ghosts in Hades. Some of the wayfarers wore a less serious look; some seemed hysterically merry; but the mournful faces had an earnestness not seen in the others; because man, "poor player," succeeds better in life's tragedy than comedy.

Arrived, in the end, on the Middlesex side, Israel's heart was prophetically heavy; foreknowing, that being of this race, felicity could never be his lot.

For five days he wandered and wandered. Without leaving statelier haunts unvisited, he did not overlook those broader areas; hereditary parks and manors of vice and misery. Not by constitution disposed to gloom, there was a mysteriousness in those impulses which led him at this time to rovings like these. But hereby stoic influences were at work, to fit him at a soon-coming day, for enacting a part in the last extremities here seen; when by sickness, destitution, each busy ill of exile, he was destined to experience a fate, uncommon even to luckless humanity; a fate whose crowning qualities were its remoteness from relief and its depth of obscurity; London, adversity, and the sea, three Armageddons, which, at one and the same time, slay, and secrete their victims.

Chapter 25

FORTY-FIVE YEARS

FOR THE MOST part, what befell Israel during his forty years' wanderings in the London deserts, surpassed the forty years in the natural wilderness of the outcast Hebrews under Moses.

In that London fog, went before him the ever-present cloud by day, but no pillar of fire by the night, except the cold column of the monument; two hundred feet beneath the mocking gilt flames on whose top, at the stone base, the shiverer, of midnight, often laid down.

But these experiences, both from their intensity and his solitude, were necessarily squalid. Best not enlarge upon them. For just as extreme suffering, without hope, is intolerable to the victim, so, to others, is its depiction, without some corresponding delusive mitigation. The gloomiest and truthfulest dramatist seldom chooses for his theme the calamities, however extraordinary, of inferior and private persons; least of all, the pauper's; admonished by the fact, that to the craped palace of the king lying in state, thousands of starers shall throng; but few feel enticed to the shanty, where, like a pealed knuckle-bone, grins the unupholstered corpse of the beggar.

Why at one given stone in the flagging does man after man cross yonder street? What plebeian Lear or Œdipus; what Israel Potter cowers there by the corner they shun? From this turning point then, we too cross over and skim events to the end; omitting the particulars of the starveling's wrangling with rats for prizes in the sewers; or his crawling into an abandoned doorless house in St. Giles', where his hosts were three dead men, one pendant; into another of an alley nigh Houndsditch, where the crazy hovel, in phosphoric rottenness, fell sparkling on him one pitchy midnight, and he received that injury, which excluding activity for no small part of the future, was an added cause of his prolongation of exile; besides not leaving his faculties unaffected by the concussion of one of the rafters on his brain.

But these were some of the incidents not belonging to the beginning of his career. On the contrary, a sort of humble prosperity attended him for a time. Insomuch that once he was not without hopes of being able to buy his homeward passage, so soon as the war should end. But, as stubborn fate would have it, being run over one day at Holborn Bars, and taken into a neighboring bakery, he was there treated with such kindliness by a Kentish lass, the shop-girl, that in the end he thought his debt of gratitude could only be repaid by love. In a word, the money saved up for his ocean voyage was lavished upon a rash embarkation in wedlock.

Originally he had fled to the capital to avoid the dilemma of impressment or imprisonment. In the absence of other motives, the dread of those hardships would have fixed him there till the peace. But now, when hostilities were no more; so was his money. Some period elapsed ere the affairs of the two governments were put on such a footing as to support an American consul at London. Yet, when this came to pass, he could only embrace the facilities for a return here furnished, by deserting a wife and child; wedded and born in the enemy's land.

The peace immediately filled England and more especially London, with hordes of disbanded soldiers; thousands of whom, rather than starve, or turn highwaymen (which no few of their comrades did; stopping coaches at times in the most public streets), would work for such a pittance, as to bring down the wages of all the laboring classes. Neither was our adventurer the least among the sufferers. Driven out of his previous employ—a sort of porter in a river-side warehouse—by this sudden influx of rivals, destitute, honest men like himself, with the ingenuity of his race, he turned his hand to the village art of chair-bottoming. An itinerant, he paraded the streets with the cry of "old chairs to mend!" furnishing a curious illustration of the contradictions of human life; that he who did little but trudge, should be giving cosy seats to all the rest of the world. Meantime, according to another well-known Malthusian enigma in human affairs, his family increased. In all, eleven children were born to him in certain sixpenny garrets in Moorfields. One after the other, ten were buried.

When chair-bottoming would fail, resort was had to match-making. That business being overdone in turn, next came the collecting of old rags, bits of paper, nails, and broken glass. Nor was this the last step. From the gutter, he slid to the sewer. The slope was smooth. In poverty,

——"Facilis descensus Averni."

But many a poor soldier had sloped down there into the boggy canal of Avernus before him. Nay, he had three corporals and a sergeant for company.

But his lot was relieved by two strange things, presently to appear. In 1793 war again broke out; the great French war. This lighted London of some of its superfluous hordes, and lost Israel the subterranean society of his friends, the corporals and sergeant, with whom, wandering forlorn through the black kingdoms of mud, he used to spin yarns about sea prisoners in hulks, and listen to stories of the Black-hole of Calcutta; and often would meet other pairs of poor soldiers, perfect strangers, at the more public corners and intersections of sewers—the Charing-Crosses below; one soldier having the other by his remainder button, earnestly discussing the sad prospects of a rise in bread, or the tide; while through the grating of the gutters overhead, the rusty skylights of the realm, came the hoarse rumblings of bakers' carts, with splashes of the flood whereby these unsuspected gnomes of the city lived.

Encouraged by the exodus of the lost tribes of soldiers, Israel returned to chair-bottoming. And it was in frequenting Covent-Garden market, at early morning, for the purchase of his flags, that he experienced one of the strange alleviations hinted of above. That chatting with the ruddy, aproned, huckster-women, on whose moist cheeks yet trickled the dew of the dawn on the meadows; that being surrounded by bales of hay, as the raker by cocks and ricks in the field; those glimpses of garden produce, the blood-beets, with the damp earth still tufting the roots; that mere handling of his flags, and bethinking him of whence they must have come; the green hedges through which the wagon that brought them had passed; that trudging home with them as a gleaner with his sheaf of wheat; all this was inexpressibly grateful. In want and bitterness, pent in, perforce, between dingy walls, he had rural returns of his boyhood's sweeter days among them; and the hardest stones of his solitary heart (made hard by bare endurance alone), would feel the stir of tender but quenchless memories, like the grass of deserted flagging, upsprouting through its closest seams. Sometimes, when incited by some little incident, however trivial in itself, thoughts of home would—either by gradually working and working upon him, or else by an impetuous rush of recollection—overpower him for a time to a sort of hallucination.

Thus was it:—One fair half-day in the July of 1800, by good luck, he was employed, partly out of charity, by one of the keepers, to trim the sward in an oval inclosure within St. James' Park, a little green, but a three minutes' walk along the gravelled way, from the brick-besmoked and grimy Old Brewery of the palace, which gives its ancient name to the public resort on whose borders it stands. It was a little oval, fenced in with iron palings, between whose bars the imprisoned verdure peered forth, as some wild captive creature of the woods from its cage. And alien Israel there—at times staring dreamily about him—seemed like some amazed runaway steer, or trespassing Pequod Indian, impounded on the shores of Narragansett Bay, long ago; and back to New England our exile was called in his soul. For still working, and thinking of home; and thinking of home, and working amid the verdant quietude of this little oasis, one rapt thought begat another, till at last his mind settled intensely, and yet half humorously, upon the image of Old Huckleberry, his mother's favorite old pillion horse; and, ere long, hearing a sudden scraping noise (some hob-shoe without, against the iron paling), he insanely took it to be Old Huckleberry in his stall, hailing him (Israel) with his shod fore-foot clattering against the planks—his customary trick when hungry—and so, down goes Israel's hook, and with a tuft of white clover, impulsively snatched, he hurries away a few paces in obedience to the imaginary summons. But soon stopping midway, and forlornly gazing round at the inclosure, he bethought him that a far different oval, the great oval of the ocean, must be crossed ere his crazy errand could be done; and even then, Old Huckleberry would

be found long surfeited with clover, since, doubtless, being
dead many a summer, he must be buried beneath it. And
many years after, in a far different part of the town, and in
far less winsome weather too, passing with his bundle of flags
through Red-Cross street, towards Barbican, in a fog so
dense that the dimmed and massed blocks of houses, exaggerated by the loom, seemed shadowy ranges on ranges of midnight hills; he heard a confused pastoral sort of sounds;
tramplings, lowings, halloos, and was suddenly called to by a
voice, to head off certain cattle, bound to Smithfield, bewildered and unruly in the fog. Next instant he saw the white
face—white as an orange blossom—of a black-bodied steer,
in advance of the drove, gleaming ghost-like through the vapors; and presently, forgetting his limp, with rapid shout and
gesture, he was more eager, even than the troubled farmers,
their owners, in driving the riotous cattle back into Barbican.
Monomaniac reminiscences were in him—"To the right, to
the right!" he shouted, as, arrived at the street corner, the
farmers beat the drove to the left, towards Smithfield: "To
the right! you are driving them back to the pastures—to the
right! that way lies the barn-yard!" "Barn-yard?" cried a voice;
"you are dreaming, old man." And so, Israel, now an old
man, was bewitched by the mirage of vapors; he had dreamed
himself home into the mists of the Housatonic mountains;
ruddy boy on the upland pastures again. But how different
the flat, apathetic, dead, London fog now seemed from those
agile mists, which goat-like, climbed the purple peaks, or in
routed armies of phantoms, broke down, pell-mell, dispersed
in flight upon the plain; leaving the cattle-boy loftily alone,
clear-cut as a balloon against the sky.

In 1817, he once more endured extremity; this second peace
again drifting its discharged soldiers on London, so that all
kinds of labor were overstocked. Beggars, too, lighted on the
walks like locusts. Timber-toed cripples stilted along, numerous as French peasants in *sabots*. And, as thirty years before,
on all sides, the exile had heard the supplicatory cry, not addressed to him: "An honorable scar, your honor, received at
Bunker-Hill, or Saratoga, or Trenton, fighting for his most
gracious Majesty, King George!" So now, in presence of the
still-surviving Israel, our Wandering Jew, the amended cry

was anew taken up, by a succeeding generation of unfortunates: "An honorable scar, your honor, received at Corunna, or at Waterloo, or at Trafalgar!" Yet not a few of these petitioners had never been outside of the London Smoke; a sort of crafty aristocracy in their way, who, without having endangered their own persons much if anything, reaped no insignificant share, both of the glory and profit of the bloody battles they claimed; while some of the genuine working heroes, too brave to beg, too cut-up to work, and too poor to live, laid down quietly in corners and died. And here it may be noted, as a fact nationally characteristic, that however desperately reduced at times, even to the sewers, Israel, the American, never sunk below the mud, to actual beggary.

Though henceforth elbowed out of many a chance three-penny job by the added thousands who contended with him against starvation, nevertheless, somehow he continued to subsist, as those tough old oaks of the cliffs, which though hacked at by hail-stones of tempests, and even wantonly maimed by the passing woodman, still, however cramped by rival trees and fettered by rocks, succeed, against all odds, in keeping the vital nerve of the tap-root alive. And even towards the end, in his dismallest December, our veteran could still at intervals feel a momentary warmth in his topmost boughs. In his Moorfields' garret, over a handful of re-ignited cinders (which the night before might have warmed some lord), cinders raked up from the streets, he would drive away dolor, by talking with his one only surviving, and now motherless child—the spared Benjamin of his old age—of the far Canaan beyond the sea; rehearsing to the lad those well-remembered adventures among New-England hills, and painting scenes of nestling happiness and plenty, in which the lowliest shared. And here, shadowy as it was, was the second alleviation hinted of above.

To these tales of the Fortunate Isles of the Free, recounted by one who had been there, the poor enslaved boy of Moorfields listened, night after night, as to the stories of Sinbad the Sailor. When would his father take him there? "Some day to come, my boy;" would be the hopeful response of an unhoping heart. And " would God it were to-morrow!" would be the impassioned reply.

In these talks Israel unconsciously sowed the seeds of his
eventual return. For with added years, the boy felt added
longing to escape his entailed misery, by compassing for his
father and himself, a voyage to the Promised Land. By his
persevering efforts he succeeded at last, against every obstacle,
in gaining credit in the right quarter to his extraordinary
statements. In short, charitably stretching a technical point,
the American Consul finally saw father and son embarked in
the Thames for Boston.

It was the year 1826; half a century since Israel, in early
manhood, had sailed a prisoner in the Tartar frigate from the
same port to which he now was bound. An octogenarian as
he recrossed the brine, he showed locks besnowed as its foam.
White-haired old ocean seemed as a brother.

Chapter 26

Requiescat in Pace

IT HAPPENED that the ship, gaining her port, was moored to the dock on a Fourth-of-July; and half-an-hour after landing, hustled by the riotous crowd near Faneuil Hall, the old man narrowly escaped being run over by a patriotic triumphal car in the procession, flying a broidered banner, inscribed with gilt letters:—

> "BUNKER-HILL.
> 1775.
> GLORY TO THE HEROES THAT FOUGHT!"

It was on Copp's Hill, within the city bounds, one of the enemy's positions during the fight, that our wanderer found his best repose that day. Sitting down here on a mound in the grave-yard, he looked off across Charles River towards the battle-ground, whose incipient monument, at that period, was hard to see, as a struggling sprig of corn in a chilly spring. Upon those heights, fifty years before, his now feeble hands had wielded both ends of the musket. There too he had received that slit upon the chest, which afterwards, in the affair with the Serapis, being traversed by a cutlass wound, made him now the bescarred bearer of a cross.

For a long time he sat mute, gazing blankly about him. The sultry July day was waning. His son sought to cheer him a little ere rising to return to the lodging for the present assigned them by the ship-captain. "Nay," replied the old man, "I shall get no fitter rest than here by the mounds."

But from this true "Potters' Field," the boy at length drew him away; and encouraged next morning by a voluntary purse made up among the reassembled passengers, father and son started by stage for the country of the Housatonic. But the exile's presence in these old mountain townships proved less a return than a resurrection. At first, none knew him, nor could recall having heard of him. Ere long it was found, that more than thirty years previous, the last known survivor of his family in that region, a bachelor, following the example of three-fourths of his neighbors, had sold out and removed to a distant country in the west; where exactly, none could say.

He sought to get a glimpse of his father's homestead. But it had been burnt down long ago. Accompanied by his son, dim-eyed and dim-hearted, he next went to find the site. But the roads had years before been changed. The old road was now broused over by sheep; the new one ran straight through what had formerly been orchards. But new orchards, planted from other suckers, and in time grafted, throve on sunny slopes near by, where blackberries had once been picked by the bushel. At length he came to a field waving with buckwheat. It seemed one of those fields which himself had often reaped. But it turned out, upon inquiry, that but three summers since, a walnut grove had stood there. Then he vaguely remembered that his father had sometimes talked of planting such a grove, to defend the neighboring fields against the cold north wind; yet where precisely that grove was to have been, his shattered mind could not recall. But it seemed not unlikely that during his long exile, the walnut grove had been planted and harvested, as well as the annual crops preceding and succeeding it, on the very same soil.

Ere long, on the mountain side, he passed into an ancient natural wood, which seemed some way familiar, and midway in it, paused to contemplate a strange, mouldy pile, resting at one end against a sturdy beech. Though wherever touched by his staff, however lightly, this pile would crumble, yet here and there, even in powder, it preserved the exact look, each irregularly defined line, of what it had originally been— namely, a half-cord of stout hemlock (one of the woods least affected by exposure to the air), in a foregoing generation chopped and stacked up on the spot, against sledging-time; but, as sometimes happens in such cases, by subsequent oversight, abandoned to oblivious decay. Type now, as it stood there, of for ever arrested intentions, and a long life still rotting in early mishap.

"Do I dream?" mused the bewildered old man, "or what is this vision that comes to me, of a cold, cloudy morning, long, long ago, and I heaving yon elbowed log against the beech, then a sapling? Nay, nay; I can not be so old."

"Come away, father, from this dismal damp wood," said his son, and led him forth.

Blindly ranging to and fro, they next saw a man ploughing. Advancing slowly, the wanderer met him by a little heap of ruinous burnt masonry, like a tumbled chimney, what seemed the jams of the fire-place, now aridly stuck over here and there, with thin, clinging, round prohibitory mosses, like executors' wafers. Just as the oxen were bid stand, the stranger's plough was hitched over sideways, by sudden contact with some sunken stone at the ruin's base.

"There; this is the twentieth year my plough has struck this old hearth-stone. Ah, old man,—sultry day, this."

"Whose house stood here, friend?" said the wanderer, touching the half-buried hearth with his staff, where a fresh furrow overlapped it.

"Don't know; forget the name; gone West, though, I believe. You know 'em?"

But the wanderer made no response; his eye was now fixed on a curious natural bend or wave in one of the bemossed stone jambs.

"What are you looking at so, father?"

" '*Father!*' here," raking with his staff, "*my* father would sit, and here, my mother, and here I, little infant, would totter between, even as now, once again, on the very same spot, but in the unroofed air, I do. The ends meet. Plough away, friend."

Best followed now is this life, by hurrying, like itself, to a close.

Few things remain.

He was repulsed in efforts, after a pension, by certain caprices of law. His scars proved his only medals. He dictated a little book, the record of his fortunes. But long ago it faded out of print—himself out of being—his name out of memory. He died the same day that the oldest oak on his native hills was blown down.

THE PIAZZA TALES

Contents

The Piazza

"With fairest flowers,
Whilst summer lasts, and I live here, Fidele—"

WHEN I REMOVED into the country, it was to occupy an old-fashioned farm-house, which had no piazza—a deficiency the more regretted, because not only did I like piazzas, as somehow combining the coziness of in-doors with the freedom of out-doors, and it is so pleasant to inspect your thermometer there, but the country round about was such a picture, that in berry time no boy climbs hill or crosses vale without coming upon easels planted in every nook, and sunburnt painters painting there. A very paradise of painters. The circle of the stars cut by the circle of the mountains. At least, so looks it from the house; though, once upon the mountains, no circle of them can you see. Had the site been chosen five rods off, this charmed ring would not have been.

The house is old. Seventy years since, from the heart of the Hearth Stone Hills, they quarried the Kaaba, or Holy Stone, to which, each Thanksgiving, the social pilgrims used to come. So long ago, that, in digging for the foundation, the workmen used both spade and axe, fighting the Troglodytes of those subterranean parts—sturdy roots of a sturdy wood, encamped upon what is now a long land-slide of sleeping meadow, sloping away off from my poppy-bed. Of that knit wood, but one survivor stands—an elm, lonely through steadfastness.

Whoever built the house, he builded better than he knew; or else Orion in the zenith flashed down his Damocles' sword to him some starry night, and said, "Build there." For how, otherwise, could it have entered the builder's mind, that, upon the clearing being made, such a purple prospect would be his?—nothing less than Greylock, with all his hills about him, like Charlemagne among his peers.

Now, for a house, so situated in such a country, to have no piazza for the convenience of those who might desire to feast upon the view, and take their time and ease about it, seemed as much of an omission as if a picture-gallery should have no bench; for what but picture-galleries are the marble halls of these same limestone hills?—galleries hung, month after month anew, with pictures ever fading into pictures ever fresh. And beauty is like piety—you cannot run and read it; tranquillity and constancy, with, now-a-days, an easy chair, are needed. For though, of old, when reverence was in vogue, and indolence was not, the devotees of Nature, doubtless, used to stand and adore—just as, in the cathedrals of those ages, the worshipers of a higher Power did—yet, in these times of failing faith and feeble knees, we have the piazza and the pew.

During the first year of my residence, the more leisurely to witness the coronation of Charlemagne (weather permitting, they crown him every sunrise and sunset), I chose me, on the hill-side bank near by, a royal lounge of turf—a green velvet lounge, with long, moss-padded back; while at the head, strangely enough, there grew (but, I suppose, for heraldry) three tufts of blue violets in a field-argent of wild strawberries; and a trellis, with honey-suckle, I set for canopy. Very majestical lounge, indeed. So much so, that here, as with the reclining majesty of Denmark in his orchard, a sly ear-ache invaded me. But, if damps abound at times in Westminster Abbey, because it is so old, why not within this monastery of mountains, which is older?

A piazza must be had.

The house was wide—my fortune narrow; so that, to build a panoramic piazza, one round and round, it could not be— although, indeed, considering the matter by rule and square, the carpenters, in the kindest way, were anxious to gratify my furthest wishes, at I've forgotten how much a foot.

Upon but one of the four sides would prudence grant me what I wanted. Now, which side?

To the east, that long camp of the Hearth Stone Hills, fading far away towards Quito; and every fall, a small white flake of something peering suddenly, of a coolish morning, from the topmost cliff—the season's new-dropped lamb, its earliest fleece; and then the Christmas dawn, draping those dun highlands with red-barred plaids and tartans—goodly sight from your piazza, that. Goodly sight; but, to the north is Charlemagne—can't have the Hearth Stone Hills with Charlemagne.

Well, the south side. Apple-trees are there. Pleasant, of a balmy morning, in the month of May, to sit and see that orchard, white-budded, as for a bridal; and, in October, one green arsenal yard; such piles of ruddy shot. Very fine, I grant; but, to the north is Charlemagne.

The west side, look. An upland pasture, alleying away into a maple wood at top. Sweet, in opening spring, to trace upon the hill-side, otherwise gray and bare—to trace, I say, the oldest paths by their streaks of earliest green. Sweet, indeed, I can't deny; but, to the north is Charlemagne.

So Charlemagne, he carried it. It was not long after 1848; and, somehow, about that time, all round the world, these kings, they had the casting vote, and voted for themselves.

No sooner was ground broken, than all the neighborhood, neighbor Dives, in particular, broke, too—into a laugh. Piazza to the north! Winter piazza! Wants, of winter midnights, to watch the Aurora Borealis, I suppose; hope he's laid in good store of Polar muffs and mittens.

That was in the lion month of March. Not forgotten are the blue noses of the carpenters, and how they scouted at the greenness of the cit, who would build his sole piazza to the north. But March don't last forever; patience, and August comes. And then, in the cool elysium of my northern bower, I, Lazarus in Abraham's bosom, cast down the hill a pitying glance on poor old Dives, tormented in the purgatory of his piazza to the south.

But, even in December, this northern piazza does not repel—nipping cold and gusty though it be, and the north wind, like any miller, bolting by the snow, in finest flour—for then, once more, with frosted beard, I pace the sleety deck, weathering Cape Horn.

In summer, too, Canute-like, sitting here, one is often reminded of the sea. For not only do long ground-swells roll the slanting grain, and little wavelets of the grass ripple over upon the low piazza, as their beach, and the blown down of dandelions is wafted like the spray, and the purple of the mountains is just the purple of the billows, and a still August noon broods upon the deep meadows, as a calm upon the Line; but the vastness and the lonesomeness are so oceanic, and the silence and the sameness, too, that the first peep of a strange house, rising beyond the trees, is for all the world like spying, on the Barbary coast, an unknown sail.

And this recalls my inland voyage to fairy-land. A true voyage; but, take it all in all, interesting as if invented.

From the piazza, some uncertain object I had caught, mysteriously snugged away, to all appearance, in a sort of purpled breast-pocket, high up in a hopper-like hollow, or sunken angle, among the northwestern mountains—yet, whether, really, it was on a mountain-side, or a mountain-top, could not be determined; because, though, viewed from favorable points, a blue summit, peering up away behind the rest, will, as it were, talk to you over their heads, and plainly tell you, that, though he (the blue summit) seems among them, he is not of them (God forbid!), and, indeed, would have you know that he considers himself—as, to say truth, he has good right—by several cubits their superior, nevertheless, certain ranges, here and there double-filed, as in platoons, so shoulder and follow up upon one another, with their irregular shapes and heights, that, from the piazza, a nigher and lower mountain will, in most states of the atmosphere, effacingly shade itself away into a higher and further one; that an object, bleak on the former's crest, will, for all that, appear nested in the latter's flank. These mountains, somehow, they play at hide-and-seek, and all before one's eyes.

But, be that as it may, the spot in question was, at all events, so situated as to be only visible, and then but vaguely, under certain witching conditions of light and shadow.

Indeed, for a year or more, I knew not there was such a spot, and might, perhaps, have never known, had it not been for a wizard afternoon in autumn—late in autumn—a mad poet's afternoon; when the turned maple woods in the broad basin below me, having lost their first vermilion tint, dully smoked, like smouldering towns, when flames expire upon their prey; and rumor had it, that this smokiness in the general air was not all Indian summer—which was not used to be so sick a thing, however mild—but, in great part, was blown from far-off forests, for weeks on fire, in Vermont; so that no wonder the sky was ominous as Hecate's cauldron— and two sportsmen, crossing a red stubble buck-wheat field, seemed guilty Macbeth and foreboding Banquo; and the hermit-sun, hutted in an Adullam cave, well towards the south, according to his season, did little else but, by indirect reflection of narrow rays shot down a Simplon pass among the clouds, just steadily paint one small, round, strawberry mole upon the wan cheek of northwestern hills. Signal as a candle. One spot of radiance, where all else was shade.

Fairies there, thought I; some haunted ring where fairies dance.

Time passed; and the following May, after a gentle shower upon the mountains—a little shower islanded in misty seas of sunshine; such a distant shower—and sometimes two, and three, and four of them, all visible together in different parts—as I love to watch from the piazza, instead of thunder storms, as I used to, which wrap old Greylock, like a Sinai, till one thinks swart Moses must be climbing among scathed hemlocks there; after, I say, that gentle shower, I saw a rainbow, resting its further end just where, in autumn, I had marked the mole. Fairies there, thought I; remembering that rainbows bring out the blooms, and that, if one can but get to the rainbow's end, his fortune is made in a bag of gold. Yon rainbow's end, would I were there, thought I. And none the less I wished it, for now first noticing what seemed some sort of glen, or grotto, in the mountain side; at least, whatever it was, viewed through the rainbow's medium, it glowed like the Potosi mine. But a work-a-day neighbor said, no doubt it was but some old barn—an abandoned one, its broadside beaten in, the acclivity its back-ground. But I, though I had never been there, I knew better.

A few days after, a cheery sunrise kindled a golden sparkle in the same spot as before. The sparkle was of that vividness, it seemed as if it could only come from glass. The building, then—if building, after all, it was—could, at least, not be a barn, much less an abandoned one; stale hay ten years musting in it. No; if aught built by mortal, it must be a cottage; perhaps long vacant and dismantled, but this very spring magically fitted up and glazed.

Again, one noon, in the same direction, I marked, over dimmed tops of terraced foliage, a broader gleam, as of a silver buckler, held sunwards over some croucher's head; which gleam, experience in like cases taught, must come from a roof

newly shingled. This, to me, made pretty sure the recent occupancy of that far cot in fairy land.

Day after day, now, full of interest in my discovery, what
time I could spare from reading the Midsummer Night's
Dream, and all about Titania, wishfully I gazed off towards
the hills; but in vain. Either troops of shadows, an imperial
guard, with slow pace and solemn, defiled along the steeps;
or, routed by pursuing light, fled broadcast from east to
west—old wars of Lucifer and Michael; or the mountains,
though unvexed by these mirrored sham fights in the sky, had
an atmosphere otherwise unfavorable for fairy views. I was
sorry; the more so, because I had to keep my chamber for
some time after—which chamber did not face those hills.

At length, when pretty well again, and sitting out, in the
September morning, upon the piazza, and thinking to myself,
when, just after a little flock of sheep, the farmer's banded
children passed, a-nutting, and said, "How sweet a day"—it
was, after all, but what their fathers call a weather-breeder—
and, indeed, was become so sensitive through my illness, as
that I could not bear to look upon a Chinese creeper of my
adoption, and which, to my delight, climbing a post of the
piazza, had burst out in starry bloom, but now, if you removed the leaves a little, showed millions of strange, canker-
ous worms, which, feeding upon those blossoms, so shared
their blessed hue, as to make it unblessed evermore—worms,
whose germs had doubtless lurked in the very bulb which, so
hopefully, I had planted: in this ingrate peevishness of my
weary convalescence, was I sitting there; when, suddenly
looking off, I saw the golden mountain-window, dazzling like
a deep-sea dolphin. Fairies there, thought I, once more; the
queen of fairies at her fairy-window; at any rate, some glad
mountain-girl; it will do me good, it will cure this weariness,
to look on her. No more; I'll launch my yawl—ho, cheerly,
heart! and push away for fairy-land—for rainbow's end, in
fairy-land.

How to get to fairy-land, by what road, I did not know;
nor could any one inform me; not even one Edmund Spenser,
who had been there—so he wrote me—further than that to
reach fairy-land, it must be voyaged to, and with faith. I took
the fairy-mountain's bearings, and the first fine day, when

strength permitted, got into my yawl—high-pommeled, leather one—cast off the fast, and away I sailed, free voyager as an autumn leaf. Early dawn; and, sallying westward, I sowed the morning before me.

Some miles brought me nigh the hills; but out of present sight of them. I was not lost; for road-side golden-rods, as guide-posts, pointed, I doubted not, the way to the golden window. Following them, I came to a lone and languid region, where the grass-grown ways were traveled but by drowsy cattle, that, less waked than stirred by day, seemed to walk in sleep. Browse, they did not—the enchanted never eat. At least, so says Don Quixote, that sagest sage that ever lived.

On I went, and gained at last the fairy mountain's base, but saw yet no fairy ring. A pasture rose before me. Letting down five mouldering bars—so moistly green, they seemed fished up from some sunken wreck—a wigged old Aries, long-visaged, and with crumpled horn, came snuffing up; and then, retreating, decorously led on along a milky-way of whiteweed, past dim-clustering Pleiades and Hyades, of small forget-me-nots; and would have led me further still his astral path, but for golden flights of yellow-birds—pilots, surely, to the golden window, to one side flying before me, from bush to bush, towards deep woods—which woods themselves were luring—and, somehow, lured, too, by their fence, banning a dark road, which, however dark, led up. I pushed through; when Aries, renouncing me now for some lost soul, wheeled, and went his wiser way. Forbidding and forbidden ground—to him.

A winter wood road, matted all along with winter-green. By the side of pebbly waters—waters the cheerier for their solitude; beneath swaying fir-boughs, petted by no season, but still green in all, on I journeyed—my horse and I; on, by an old saw-mill, bound down and hushed with vines, that his grating voice no more was heard; on, by a deep flume clove through snowy marble, vernal-tinted, where freshet eddies had, on each side, spun out empty chapels in the living rock; on, where Jacks-in-the-pulpit, like their Baptist namesake, preached but to the wilderness; on, where a huge, cross-grain block, fern-bedded, showed where, in forgotten times, man after man had tried to split it, but lost his wedges for his pains—which wedges yet rusted in their holes; on, where, ages past, in step-like ledges of a cascade, skull-hollow pots had been churned out by ceaseless whirling of a flint-stone— ever wearing, but itself unworn; on, by wild rapids pouring into a secret pool, but soothed by circling there awhile, issued forth serenely; on, to less broken ground, and by a little ring, where, truly, fairies must have danced, or else some wheel-tire been heated—for all was bare; still on, and up, and out into a hanging orchard, where maidenly looked down upon me a crescent moon, from morning.

My horse hitched low his head. Red apples rolled before him; Eve's apples; seek-no-furthers. He tasted one, I another; it tasted of the ground. Fairy land not yet, thought I, flinging my bridle to a humped old tree, that crooked out an arm to catch it. For the way now lay where path was none, and none might go but by himself, and only go by daring. Through blackberry brakes that tried to pluck me back, though I but strained towards fruitless growths of mountain-laurel; up slippery steeps to barren heights, where stood none to welcome. Fairy land not yet, thought I, though the morning is here before me.

Foot-sore enough and weary, I gained not then my journey's end, but came ere long to a craggy pass, dipping towards growing regions still beyond. A zigzag road, half overgrown with blueberry bushes, here turned among the cliffs. A rent was in their ragged sides; through it a little track branched off, which, upwards threading that short defile, came breezily out above, to where the mountain-top, part sheltered northward, by a taller brother, sloped gently off a space, ere darkly plunging; and here, among fantastic rocks, reposing in a herd, the foot-track wound, half beaten, up to a little, low-storied, grayish cottage, capped, nun-like, with a peaked roof.

On one slope, the roof was deeply weather-stained, and, nigh the turfy eaves-trough, all velvet-napped; no doubt the snail-monks founded mossy priories there. The other slope was newly shingled. On the north side, doorless and windowless, the clap-boards, innocent of paint, were yet green as the north side of lichened pines, or copperless hulls of Japanese

junks, becalmed. The whole base, like those of the neighboring rocks, was rimmed about with shaded streaks of richest
sod; for, with hearth-stones in fairy land, the natural rock,
though housed, preserves to the last, just as in open fields, its
fertilizing charm; only, by necessity, working now at a remove, to the sward without. So, at least, says Oberon, grave
authority in fairy lore. Though setting Oberon aside, certain
it is, that, even in the common world, the soil, close up to
farm-houses, as close up to pasture rocks, is, even though un-
tended, ever richer than it is a few rods off—such gentle,
nurturing heat is radiated there.

But with this cottage, the shaded streaks were richest in its
front and about its entrance, where the ground-sill, and especially the door-sill had, through long eld, quietly settled
down.

No fence was seen, no inclosure. Near by—ferns, ferns,
ferns; further—woods, woods, woods; beyond—mountains,
mountains, mountains; then—sky, sky, sky. Turned out in
ærial commons, pasture for the mountain moon. Nature, and
but nature, house and all; even a low cross-pile of silver birch,
piled openly, to season; up among whose silvery sticks, as
through the fencing of some sequestered grave, sprang vagrant raspberry bushes—willful assertors of their right of way.

The foot-track, so dainty narrow, just like a sheep-track, led
through long ferns that lodged. Fairy land at last, thought I;
Una and her lamb dwell here. Truly, a small abode—mere
palanquin, set down on the summit, in a pass between two
worlds, participant of neither.

A sultry hour, and I wore a light hat, of yellow sinnet, with
white duck trowsers—both relics of my tropic sea-going.
Clogged in the muffling ferns, I softly stumbled, staining the
knees a sea-green.

Pausing at the threshold, or rather where threshold once
had been, I saw, through the open door-way, a lonely girl,
sewing at a lonely window. A pale-cheeked girl, and fly-
specked window, with wasps about the mended upper panes.
I spoke. She shyly started, like some Tahiti girl, secreted for a
sacrifice, first catching sight, through palms, of Captain Cook.
Recovering, she bade me enter; with her apron brushed off a
stool; then silently resumed her own. With thanks I took the

stool; but now, for a space, I, too, was mute. This, then, is the fairy-mountain house, and here, the fairy queen sitting at her fairy window.

I went up to it. Downwards, directed by the tunneled pass, as through a leveled telescope, I caught sight of a far-off, soft, azure world. I hardly knew it, though I came from it.

"You must find this view very pleasant," said I, at last.

"Oh, sir," tears starting in her eyes, "the first time I looked out of this window, I said 'never, never shall I weary of this.'"

"And what wearies you of it now?"

"I don't know," while a tear fell; "but it is not the view, it is Marianna."

Some months back, her brother, only seventeen, had come hither, a long way from the other side, to cut wood and burn coal, and she, elder sister, had accompanied him. Long had they been orphans, and now, sole inhabitants of the sole house upon the mountain. No guest came, no traveler passed. The zigzag, perilous road was only used at seasons by the coal wagons. The brother was absent the entire day, sometimes the entire night. When at evening, fagged out, he did come home, he soon left his bench, poor fellow, for his bed; just as one, at last, wearily quits that, too, for still deeper rest. The bench, the bed, the grave.

Silent I stood by the fairy window, while these things were being told.

"Do you know," said she at last, as stealing from her story, "do you know who lives yonder?—I have never been down into that country—away off there, I mean; that house, that marble one," pointing far across the lower landscape; "have you not caught it? there, on the long hill-side: the field before, the woods behind; the white shines out against their blue; don't you mark it? the only house in sight."

I looked; and after a time, to my surprise, recognized, more by its position than its aspect, or Marianna's description, my own abode, glimmering much like this mountain one from the piazza. The mirage haze made it appear less a farm-house than King Charming's palace.

"I have often wondered who lives there; but it must be some happy one; again this morning was I thinking so."

"Some happy one," returned I, starting; "and why do you think that? You judge some rich one lives there?"

"Rich or not, I never thought; but it looks so happy, I can't tell how; and it is so far away. Sometimes I think I do but dream it is there. You should see it in a sunset."

"No doubt the sunset gilds it finely; but not more than the sunrise does this house, perhaps."

"This house? The sun is a good sun, but it never gilds this house. Why should it? This old house is rotting. That makes it so mossy. In the morning, the sun comes in at this old window, to be sure—boarded up, when first we came; a window I can't keep clean, do what I may—and half burns, and nearly blinds me at my sewing, besides setting the flies and wasps astir—such flies and wasps as only lone mountain houses know. See, here is the curtain—this apron—I try to shut it out with then. It fades it, you see. Sun gild this house? not that ever Marianna saw."

"Because when this roof is gilded most, then you stay here within."

"The hottest, weariest hour of day, you mean? Sir, the sun gilds not this roof. It leaked so, brother newly shingled all one side. Did you not see it? The north side, where the sun strikes most on what the rain has wetted. The sun is a good sun; but this roof, it first scorches, and then rots. An old house. They went West, and are long dead, they say, who built it. A mountain house. In winter no fox could den in it. That chimney-place has been blocked up with snow, just like a hollow stump."

"Yours are strange fancies, Marianna."

"They but reflect the things."

"Then I should have said, 'These are strange things,' rather than, 'Yours are strange fancies.'"

"As you will;" and took up her sewing.

Something in those quiet words, or in that quiet act, it made me mute again; while, noting, through the fairy window, a broad shadow stealing on, as cast by some gigantic condor, floating at brooding poise on outstretched wings, I marked how, by its deeper and inclusive dusk, it wiped away into itself all lesser shades of rock or fern.

"You watch the cloud," said Marianna.

"No, a shadow; a cloud's, no doubt—though that I cannot see. How did you know it? Your eyes are on your work."

"It dusked my work. There, now the cloud is gone, Tray comes back."

"How?"

"The dog, the shaggy dog. At noon, he steals off, of himself, to change his shape—returns, and lies down awhile, nigh the door. Don't you see him? His head is turned round at you; though, when you came, he looked before him."

"Your eyes rest but on your work; what do you speak of?"

"By the window, crossing."

"You mean this shaggy shadow—the nigh one? And, yes, now that I mark it, it is not unlike a large, black Newfoundland dog. The invading shadow gone, the invaded one returns. But I do not see what casts it."

"For that, you must go without."

"One of those grassy rocks, no doubt."

"You see his head, his face?"

"The shadow's? You speak as if *you* saw it, and all the time your eyes are on your work."

"Tray looks at you," still without glancing up; "this is his hour; I see him."

"Have you, then, so long sat at this mountain-window, where but clouds and vapors pass, that, to you, shadows are as things, though you speak of them as of phantoms; that, by familiar knowledge, working like a second sight, you can, without looking for them, tell just where they are, though, as having mice-like feet, they creep about, and come and go; that, to you, these lifeless shadows are as living friends, who, though out of sight, are not out of mind, even in their faces—is it so?"

"That way I never thought of it. But the friendliest one, that used to soothe my weariness so much, coolly quivering on the ferns, it was taken from me, never to return, as Tray did just now. The shadow of a birch. The tree was struck by lightning, and brother cut it up. You saw the cross-pile outdoors—the buried root lies under it; but not the shadow. That is flown, and never will come back, nor ever anywhere stir again."

Another cloud here stole along, once more blotting out the

dog, and blackening all the mountain; while the stillness was so still, deafness might have forgot itself, or else believed that noiseless shadow spoke.

"Birds, Marianna, singing-birds, I hear none; I hear nothing. Boys and bob-o-links, do they never come a-berrying up here?"

"Birds, I seldom hear; boys, never. The berries mostly ripe and fall—few, but me, the wiser."

"But yellow-birds showed me the way—part way, at least."

"And then flew back. I guess they play about the mountain-side, but don't make the top their home. And no doubt you think that, living so lonesome here, knowing nothing, hearing nothing—little, at least, but sound of thunder and the fall of trees—never reading, seldom speaking, yet ever wakeful, this is what gives me my strange thoughts—for so you call them—this weariness and wakefulness together. Brother, who stands and works in open air, would I could rest like him; but mine is mostly but dull woman's work—sitting, sitting, restless sitting."

"But, do you not go walk at times? These woods are wide."

"And lonesome; lonesome, because so wide. Sometimes, 'tis true, of afternoons, I go a little way; but soon come back again. Better feel lone by hearth, than rock. The shadows hereabouts I know—those in the woods are strangers."

"But the night?"

"Just like the day. Thinking, thinking—a wheel I cannot stop; pure want of sleep it is that turns it."

"I have heard that, for this wakeful weariness, to say one's prayers, and then lay one's head upon a fresh hop pillow——"

"Look!"

Through the fairy window, she pointed down the steep to a small garden patch near by—mere pot of rifled loam, half rounded in by sheltering rocks—where, side by side, some feet apart, nipped and puny, two hop-vines climbed two poles, and, gaining their tip-ends, would have then joined over in an upward clasp, but the baffled shoots, groping awhile in empty air, trailed back whence they sprung.

"You have tried the pillow, then?"

"Yes."

"And prayer?"

"Prayer and pillow."

"Is there no other cure, or charm?"

"Oh, if I could but once get to yonder house, and but look upon whoever the happy being is that lives there! A foolish thought: why do I think it? Is it that I live so lonesome, and know nothing?"

"I, too, know nothing; and, therefore, cannot answer; but, for your sake, Marianna, well could wish that I were that happy one of the happy house you dream you see; for then you would behold him now, and, as you say, this weariness might leave you."

—Enough. Launching my yawl no more for fairy-land, I stick to the piazza. It is my box-royal; and this amphitheatre, my theatre of San Carlo. Yes, the scenery is magical—the illusion so complete. And Madam Meadow Lark, my prima donna, plays her grand engagement here; and, drinking in her sunrise note, which, Memnon-like, seems struck from the golden window, how far from me the weary face behind it.

But, every night, when the curtain falls, truth comes in with darkness. No light shows from the mountain. To and fro I walk the piazza deck, haunted by Marianna's face, and many as real a story.

Bartleby, The Scrivener

A Story of Wall-Street

I AM a rather elderly man. The nature of my avocations for the last thirty years has brought me into more than ordinary contact with what would seem an interesting and somewhat singular set of men, of whom as yet nothing that I know of has ever been written:—I mean the law-copyists or scriveners. I have known very many of them, professionally and privately, and if I pleased, could relate divers histories, at which good-natured gentlemen might smile, and sentimental souls might weep. But I waive the biographies of all other scriveners for a few passages in the life of Bartleby, who was a scrivener the strangest I ever saw or heard of. While of other law-copyists I might write the complete life, of Bartleby nothing of that sort can be done. I believe that no materials exist for a full and satisfactory biography of this man. It is an irreparable loss to literature. Bartleby was one of those beings of whom nothing is ascertainable, except from the original sources, and in his case those are very small. What my own astonished eyes saw of Bartleby, *that* is all I know of him, except, indeed, one vague report which will appear in the sequel.

Ere introducing the scrivener, as he first appeared to me, it is fit I make some mention of myself, my *employés*, my business, my chambers, and general surroundings; because some such description is indispensable to an adequate understanding of the chief character about to be presented.

Imprimis: I am a man who, from his youth upwards, has been filled with a profound conviction that the easiest way of life is the best. Hence, though I belong to a profession proverbially energetic and nervous, even to turbulence, at times, yet nothing of that sort have I ever suffered to invade my peace. I am one of those unambitious lawyers who never addresses a jury, or in any way draws down public applause; but in the cool tranquillity of a snug retreat, do a snug business among rich men's bonds and mortgages and title-deeds. All who know me, consider me an eminently *safe* man. The late

John Jacob Astor, a personage little given to poetic enthusiasm, had no hesitation in pronouncing my first grand point to be prudence; my next, method. I do not speak it in vanity, but simply record the fact, that I was not unemployed in my profession by the late John Jacob Astor; a name which, I admit, I love to repeat, for it hath a rounded and orbicular sound to it, and rings like unto bullion. I will freely add, that I was not insensible to the late John Jacob Astor's good opinion.

Some time prior to the period at which this little history begins, my avocations had been largely increased. The good old office, now extinct in the State of New-York, of a Master in Chancery, had been conferred upon me. It was not a very arduous office, but very pleasantly remunerative. I seldom lose my temper; much more seldom indulge in dangerous indignation at wrongs and outrages; but I must be permitted to be rash here and declare, that I consider the sudden and violent abrogation of the office of Master in Chancery, by the new Constitution, as a —— premature act; inasmuch as I had counted upon a life-lease of the profits, whereas I only received those of a few short years. But this is by the way.

My chambers were up stairs at No. — Wall-street. At one end they looked upon the white wall of the interior of a spacious sky-light shaft, penetrating the building from top to bottom. This view might have been considered rather tame than otherwise, deficient in what landscape painters call "life." But if so, the view from the other end of my chambers offered, at least, a contrast, if nothing more. In that direction my windows commanded an unobstructed view of a lofty brick wall, black by age and everlasting shade; which wall required no spy-glass to bring out its lurking beauties, but for the benefit of all near-sighted spectators, was pushed up to within ten feet of my window panes. Owing to the great height of the surrounding buildings, and my chambers being on the second floor, the interval between this wall and mine not a little resembled a huge square cistern.

At the period just preceding the advent of Bartleby, I had two persons as copyists in my employment, and a promising lad as an office-boy. First, Turkey; second, Nippers; third, Ginger Nut. These may seem names, the like of which are not usually found in the Directory. In truth they were nicknames, mutually conferred upon each other by my three clerks, and were deemed expressive of their respective persons or characters. Turkey was a short, pursy Englishman of about my own age, that is, somewhere not far from sixty. In the morning, one might say, his face was of a fine florid hue, but after twelve o'clock, meridian—his dinner hour—it blazed like a grate full of Christmas coals; and continued blazing—but, as it were, with a gradual wane—till 6 o'clock, P.M. or thereabouts, after which I saw no more of the proprietor of the face, which gaining its meridian with the sun, seemed to set with it, to rise, culminate, and decline the following day, with the like regularity and undiminished glory. There are many singular coincidences I have known in the course of my life, not the least among which was the fact, that exactly when Turkey displayed his fullest beams from his red and radiant countenance, just then, too, at that critical moment, began the daily period when I considered his business capacities as seriously disturbed for the remainder of the twenty-four hours. Not that he was absolutely idle, or averse to business then; far from it. The difficulty was, he was apt to be altogether too energetic. There was a strange, inflamed, flurried, flighty recklessness of activity about him. He would be incautious in dipping his pen into his inkstand. All his blots upon my documents, were dropped there after twelve o'clock, meridian. Indeed, not only would he be reckless and sadly given to making blots in the afternoon, but some days he went further, and was rather noisy. At such times, too, his face flamed with augmented blazonry, as if cannel coal had been heaped on anthracite. He made an unpleasant racket with his chair; spilled his sand-box; in mending his pens, impatiently split them all to pieces, and threw them on the floor in a sudden passion; stood up and leaned over his table, boxing his papers about in a most indecorous manner, very sad to behold in an elderly man like him. Nevertheless, as he was in many ways a most valuable person to me, and all the time before twelve o'clock, meridian, was the quickest, steadiest creature too, accomplishing a great deal of work in a style not easy to be matched—for these reasons, I was willing to overlook his eccentricities, though indeed, occasionally, I remonstrated with him. I did this very gently, however, because, though the civilest, nay, the blandest and most reverential of men in the morning, yet in the afternoon he was disposed, upon provocation, to be slightly rash with his tongue, in fact, insolent. Now, valuing his morning services as I did, and resolved not to lose them; yet, at the same time made uncomfortable by his inflamed ways after twelve o'clock; and being a man of peace, unwilling by my admonitions to call forth unseemly retorts from him; I took upon me, one Saturday noon (he was always worse on Saturdays), to hint to him, very kindly, that perhaps now that he was growing old, it might be well to abridge his labors; in short, he need not come to my chambers after twelve o'clock, but, dinner over, had best go home to his lodgings and rest himself till tea-time. But no; he insisted upon his afternoon devotions. His countenance became intolerably fervid, as he oratorically assured me—gesticulating with a long ruler at the other end of the room—that if his services in the morning were useful, how indispensable, then, in the afternoon?

"With submission, sir," said Turkey on this occasion, "I consider myself your right-hand man. In the morning I but marshal and deploy my columns; but in the afternoon I put myself at their head, and gallantly charge the foe, thus!"— and he made a violent thrust with the ruler.

"But the blots, Turkey," intimated I.

"True,—but, with submission, sir, behold these hairs! I am getting old. Surely, sir, a blot or two of a warm afternoon is not to be severely urged against gray hairs. Old age—even if it blot the page—is honorable. With submission, sir, we *both* are getting old."

This appeal to my fellow-feeling was hardly to be resisted. At all events, I saw that go he would not. So I made up my mind to let him stay, resolving, nevertheless, to see to it, that during the afternoon he had to do with my less important papers.

Nippers, the second on my list, was a whiskered, sallow, and, upon the whole, rather piratical-looking young man of about five and twenty. I always deemed him the victim of two evil powers—ambition and indigestion. The ambition was evinced by a certain impatience of the duties of a mere copyist, an unwarrantable usurpation of strictly professional affairs, such as the original drawing up of legal documents. The indigestion seemed betokened in an occasional nervous testiness and grinning irritability, causing the teeth to audibly grind together over mistakes committed in copying; unnecessary maledictions, hissed, rather than spoken, in the heat of business; and especially by a continual discontent with the height of the table where he worked. Though of a very ingenious mechanical turn, Nippers could never get this table to suit him. He put chips under it, blocks of various sorts, bits of pasteboard, and at last went so far as to attempt an exquisite adjustment by final pieces of folded blotting-paper. But no invention would answer. If, for the sake of easing his back, he brought the table lid at a sharp angle well up towards his chin, and wrote there like a man using the steep roof of a Dutch house for his desk:—then he declared that it stopped the circulation in his arms. If now he lowered the table to his waistbands, and stooped over it in writing, then there was a sore aching in his back. In short, the truth of the matter was, Nippers knew not what he wanted. Or, if he wanted any thing, it was to be rid of a scrivener's table altogether. Among the manifestations of his diseased ambition was a fondness he had for receiving visits from certain ambiguous-looking fellows in seedy coats, whom he called his clients. Indeed I was aware that not only was he, at times, considerable of a ward-politician, but he occasionally did a little business at the Justices' courts, and was not unknown on the steps of the Tombs. I have good reason to believe, however, that one individual who called upon him at my chambers, and who, with a grand air, he insisted was his client, was no other than a dun, and the alleged title-deed, a bill. But with all his failings, and the annoyances he caused me, Nippers, like his compatriot Turkey, was a very useful man to me; wrote a neat, swift hand; and, when he chose, was not deficient in a gentlemanly sort of deportment. Added to this, he always dressed in a gentlemanly sort of way; and so, incidentally, reflected credit upon my chambers. Whereas with respect to Turkey, I had much ado to keep him from being a reproach to me. His clothes were apt to look oily and smell of eating-houses. He wore his pantaloons very loose and baggy in summer. His coats were execrable; his hat not to be handled. But while the hat was a thing of indifference to me, inasmuch as his natural civility and deference, as a dependent Englishman, always led him to doff it the moment he entered the room, yet his coat was another matter. Concerning his coats, I reasoned with him; but with no effect. The truth was, I suppose, that a man with so small an income, could not afford to sport such a lustrous face and a lustrous coat at one and the same time. As Nippers once observed, Turkey's money went chiefly for red ink. One winter day I presented Turkey with a highly-respectable looking coat of my own, a padded gray coat, of a most comfortable warmth, and which buttoned straight up from the knee to the neck. I thought Turkey would appreciate the favor, and abate his rashness and obstreperousness of afternoons. But no. I verily believe that buttoning himself up in so downy and blanket-like a coat had a pernicious effect upon him; upon the same principle that too much oats are bad for horses. In fact, precisely as a rash, restive horse is said to feel his oats, so Turkey felt his coat. It made him insolent. He was a man whom prosperity harmed.

Though concerning the self-indulgent habits of Turkey I had my own private surmises, yet touching Nippers I was well persuaded that whatever might be his faults in other respects, he was, at least, a temperate young man. But indeed, nature herself seemed to have been his vintner, and at his birth charged him so thoroughly with an irritable, brandy-like disposition, that all subsequent potations were needless. When I consider how, amid the stillness of my chambers, Nippers would sometimes impatiently rise from his seat, and stooping over his table, spread his arms wide apart, seize the whole desk, and move it, and jerk it, with a grim, grinding motion on the floor, as if the table were a perverse voluntary agent, intent on thwarting and vexing him; I plainly perceive that for Nippers, brandy and water were altogether super-fluous.

It was fortunate for me that, owing to its peculiar cause—indigestion—the irritability and consequent nervousness of Nippers, were mainly observable in the morning, while in the afternoon he was comparatively mild. So that Turkey's paroxysms only coming on about twelve o'clock, I never had to do with their eccentricities at one time. Their fits relieved each other like guards. When Nippers' was on, Turkey's was off; and *vice versa*. This was a good natural arrangement under the circumstances.

Ginger Nut, the third on my list, was a lad some twelve years old. His father was a carman, ambitious of seeing his son on the bench instead of a cart, before he died. So he sent him to my office as student at law, errand boy, and cleaner and sweeper, at the rate of one dollar a week. He had a little desk to himself, but he did not use it much. Upon inspection, the drawer exhibited a great array of the shells of various sorts of nuts. Indeed, to this quick-witted youth the whole noble science of the law was contained in a nut-shell. Not the least among the employments of Ginger Nut, as well as one which he discharged with the most alacrity, was his duty as cake and apple purveyor for Turkey and Nippers. Copying law papers being proverbially a dry, husky sort of business, my two scriveners were fain to moisten their mouths very often with Spitzenbergs to be had at the numerous stalls nigh the Custom House and Post Office. Also, they sent Ginger Nut very frequently for that peculiar cake—small, flat, round, and very spicy—after which he had been named by them. Of a cold morning when business was but dull, Turkey would gobble up scores of these cakes, as if they were mere wafers—indeed they sell them at the rate of six or eight for a penny—the scrape of his pen blending with the crunching of the crisp particles in his mouth. Of all the fiery afternoon blunders and flurried rashnesses of Turkey, was his once moistening a ginger-cake between his lips, and clapping it on to a mortgage for a seal. I came within an ace of dismissing him then. But he mollified me by making an oriental bow, and saying— "With submission, sir, it was generous of me to find you in stationery on my own account."

Now my original business—that of a conveyancer and title hunter, and drawer-up of recondite documents of all sorts— was considerably increased by receiving the master's office. There was now great work for scriveners. Not only must I push the clerks already with me, but I must have additional help. In answer to my advertisement, a motionless young man one morning, stood upon my office threshold, the door being open, for it was summer. I can see that figure now—pallidly neat, pitiably respectable, incurably forlorn! It was Bartleby.

After a few words touching his qualifications, I engaged him, glad to have among my corps of copyists a man of so singularly sedate an aspect, which I thought might operate beneficially upon the flighty temper of Turkey, and the fiery one of Nippers.

I should have stated before that ground glass folding-doors divided my premises into two parts, one of which was occupied by my scriveners, the other by myself. According to my humor I threw open these doors, or closed them. I resolved to assign Bartleby a corner by the folding-doors, but on my side of them, so as to have this quiet man within easy call, in case any trifling thing was to be done. I placed his desk close up to a small side-window in that part of the room, a window which originally had afforded a lateral view of certain grimy back-yards and bricks, but which, owing to subsequent erections, commanded at present no view at all, though it gave some light. Within three feet of the panes was a wall, and the light came down from far above, between two lofty buildings, as from a very small opening in a dome. Still further to a satisfactory arrangement, I procured a high green folding screen, which might entirely isolate Bartleby from my sight, though not remove him from my voice. And thus, in a manner, privacy and society were conjoined.

At first Bartleby did an extraordinary quantity of writing. As if long famishing for something to copy, he seemed to gorge himself on my documents. There was no pause for digestion. He ran a day and night line, copying by sun-light and by candle-light. I should have been quite delighted with his application, had he been cheerfully industrious. But he wrote on silently, palely, mechanically.

It is, of course, an indispensable part of a scrivener's business to verify the accuracy of his copy, word by word. Where there are two or more scriveners in an office, they assist each other in this examination, one reading from the copy, the other holding the original. It is a very dull, wearisome, and lethargic affair. I can readily imagine that to some sanguine temperaments it would be altogether intolerable. For example, I cannot credit that the mettlesome poet Byron would have contentedly sat down with Bartleby to examine a law document of, say five hundred pages, closely written in a crimpy hand.

Now and then, in the haste of business, it had been my habit to assist in comparing some brief document myself, calling Turkey or Nippers for this purpose. One object I had in placing Bartleby so handy to me behind the screen, was to avail myself of his services on such trivial occasions. It was on the third day, I think, of his being with me, and before any necessity had arisen for having his own writing examined, that, being much hurried to complete a small affair I had in hand, I abruptly called to Bartleby. In my haste and natural expectancy of instant compliance, I sat with my head bent over the original on my desk, and my right hand sideways, and somewhat nervously extended with the copy, so that immediately upon emerging from his retreat, Bartleby might snatch it and proceed to business without the least delay.

In this very attitude did I sit when I called to him, rapidly stating what it was I wanted him to do—namely, to examine a small paper with me. Imagine my surprise, nay, my consternation, when without moving from his privacy, Bartleby in a singularly mild, firm voice, replied, "I would prefer not to."

I sat awhile in perfect silence, rallying my stunned faculties. Immediately it occurred to me that my ears had deceived me, or Bartleby had entirely misunderstood my meaning. I repeated my request in the clearest tone I could assume. But in quite as clear a one came the previous reply, "I would prefer not to."

"Prefer not to," echoed I, rising in high excitement, and crossing the room with a stride. "What do you mean? Are you moon-struck? I want you to help me compare this sheet here—take it," and I thrust it towards him.

"I would prefer not to," said he.

I looked at him steadfastly. His face was leanly composed; his gray eye dimly calm. Not a wrinkle of agitation rippled him. Had there been the least uneasiness, anger, impatience or impertinence in his manner; in other words, had there been any thing ordinarily human about him, doubtless I should have violently dismissed him from the premises. But as it was, I should have as soon thought of turning my pale plaster-of-paris bust of Cicero out of doors. I stood gazing at him awhile, as he went on with his own writing, and then reseated myself at my desk. This is very strange, thought I. What had one best do? But my business hurried me. I concluded to forget the matter for the present, reserving it for my future leisure. So calling Nippers from the other room, the paper was speedily examined.

A few days after this, Bartleby concluded four lengthy documents, being quadruplicates of a week's testimony taken before me in my High Court of Chancery. It became necessary to examine them. It was an important suit, and great accuracy was imperative. Having all things arranged I called Turkey, Nippers and Ginger Nut from the next room, meaning to place the four copies in the hands of my four clerks, while I should read from the original. Accordingly Turkey, Nippers and Ginger Nut had taken their seats in a row, each with his document in hand, when I called to Bartleby to join this interesting group.

"Bartleby! quick, I am waiting."

I heard a slow scrape of his chair legs on the uncarpeted floor, and soon he appeared standing at the entrance of his hermitage.

"What is wanted?" said he mildly.

"The copies, the copies," said I hurriedly. "We are going to examine them. There"—and I held towards him the fourth quadruplicate.

"I would prefer not to," he said, and gently disappeared behind the screen.

For a few moments I was turned into a pillar of salt, standing at the head of my seated column of clerks. Recovering myself, I advanced towards the screen, and demanded the reason for such extraordinary conduct.

"*Why* do you refuse?"

"I would prefer not to."

With any other man I should have flown outright into a dreadful passion, scorned all further words, and thrust him ignominiously from my presence. But there was something about Bartleby that not only strangely disarmed me, but in a wonderful manner touched and disconcerted me. I began to reason with him.

"These are your own copies we are about to examine. It is labor saving to you, because one examination will answer for your four papers. It is common usage. Every copyist is bound to help examine his copy. Is it not so? Will you not speak? Answer!"

"I prefer not to," he replied in a flute-like tone. It seemed to me that while I had been addressing him, he carefully revolved every statement that I made; fully comprehended the meaning; could not gainsay the irresistible conclusion; but, at the same time, some paramount consideration prevailed with him to reply as he did.

"You are decided, then, not to comply with my request— a request made according to common usage and common sense?"

He briefly gave me to understand that on that point my judgment was sound. Yes: his decision was irreversible.

It is not seldom the case that when a man is browbeaten in some unprecedented and violently unreasonable way, he begins to stagger in his own plainest faith. He begins, as it were, vaguely to surmise that, wonderful as it may be, all the justice and all the reason is on the other side. Accordingly, if any disinterested persons are present, he turns to them for some reinforcement for his own faltering mind.

"Turkey," said I, "what do you think of this? Am I not right?"

"With submission, sir," said Turkey, with his blandest tone, "I think that you are."

"Nippers," said I, "what do *you* think of it?"

"I think I should kick him out of the office."

(The reader of nice perceptions will here perceive that, it being morning, Turkey's answer is couched in polite and tranquil terms, but Nippers replies in ill-tempered ones. Or, to repeat a previous sentence, Nippers's ugly mood was on duty, and Turkey's off.)

"Ginger Nut," said I, willing to enlist the smallest suffrage in my behalf, "what do *you* think of it?"

"I think, sir, he's a little *luny*," replied Ginger Nut, with a grin.

"You hear what they say," said I, turning towards the screen, "come forth and do your duty."

But he vouchsafed no reply. I pondered a moment in sore perplexity. But once more business hurried me. I determined again to postpone the consideration of this dilemma to my future leisure. With a little trouble we made out to examine the papers without Bartleby, though at every page or two, Turkey deferentially dropped his opinion that this proceeding was quite out of the common; while Nippers, twitching in his chair with a dyspeptic nervousness, ground out between his set teeth occasional hissing maledictions against the stubborn oaf behind the screen. And for his (Nippers's) part, this was the first and the last time he would do another man's business without pay.

Meanwhile Bartleby sat in his hermitage, oblivious to every thing but his own peculiar business there.

Some days passed, the scrivener being employed upon another lengthy work. His late remarkable conduct led me to regard his ways narrowly. I observed that he never went to dinner; indeed that he never went any where. As yet I had never of my personal knowledge known him to be outside of my office. He was a perpetual sentry in the corner. At about eleven o'clock though, in the morning, I noticed that Ginger Nut would advance toward the opening in Bartleby's screen, as if silently beckoned thither by a gesture invisible to me where I sat. The boy would then leave the office jingling a few pence, and reappear with a handful of ginger-nuts which he delivered in the hermitage, receiving two of the cakes for his trouble.

He lives, then, on ginger-nuts, thought I; never eats a dinner, properly speaking; he must be a vegetarian then; but no; he never eats even vegetables, he eats nothing but ginger-nuts. My mind then ran on in reveries concerning the probable effects upon the human constitution of living entirely on ginger-nuts. Ginger-nuts are so called because they contain ginger as one of their peculiar constituents, and the final flavoring one. Now what was ginger? A hot, spicy thing. Was Bartleby hot and spicy? Not at all. Ginger, then, had no effect upon Bartleby. Probably he preferred it should have none.

Nothing so aggravates an earnest person as a passive resistance. If the individual so resisted be of a not inhumane temper, and the resisting one perfectly harmless in his passivity;

then, in the better moods of the former, he will endeavor charitably to construe to his imagination what proves impossible to be solved by his judgment. Even so, for the most part, I regarded Bartleby and his ways. Poor fellow! thought I, he means no mischief; it is plain he intends no insolence; his aspect sufficiently evinces that his eccentricities are involuntary. He is useful to me. I can get along with him. If I turn him away, the chances are he will fall in with some less indulgent employer, and then he will be rudely treated, and perhaps driven forth miserably to starve. Yes. Here I can cheaply purchase a delicious self-approval. To befriend Bartleby; to humor him in his strange wilfulness, will cost me little or nothing, while I lay up in my soul what will eventually prove a sweet morsel for my conscience. But this mood was not invariable with me. The passiveness of Bartleby sometimes irritated me. I felt strangely goaded on to encounter him in new opposition, to elicit some angry spark from him answerable to my own. But indeed I might as well have essayed to strike fire with my knuckles against a bit of Windsor soap. But one afternoon the evil impulse in me mastered me, and the following little scene ensued:

"Bartleby," said I, " when those papers are all copied, I will compare them with you."

"I would prefer not to."

"How? Surely you do not mean to persist in that mulish vagary?"

No answer.

I threw open the folding-doors near by, and turning upon Turkey and Nippers, exclaimed:

"Bartleby a second time says, he won't examine his papers. What do you think of it, Turkey?"

It was afternoon, be it remembered. Turkey sat glowing like a brass boiler, his bald head steaming, his hands reeling among his blotted papers.

"Think of it?" roared Turkey; "I think I'll just step behind his screen, and black his eyes for him!"

So saying, Turkey rose to his feet and threw his arms into a pugilistic position. He was hurrying away to make good his promise, when I detained him, alarmed at the effect of incautiously rousing Turkey's combativeness after dinner.

"Sit down, Turkey," said I, "and hear what Nippers has to say. What do you think of it, Nippers? Would I not be justified in immediately dismissing Bartleby?"

"Excuse me, that is for you to decide, sir. I think his conduct quite unusual, and indeed unjust, as regards Turkey and myself. But it may only be a passing whim."

"Ah," exclaimed I, "you have strangely changed your mind then—you speak very gently of him now."

"All beer," cried Turkey; "gentleness is effects of beer—Nippers and I dined together to-day. You see how gentle *I* am, sir. Shall I go and black his eyes?"

"You refer to Bartleby, I suppose. No, not to-day, Turkey," I replied; "pray, put up your fists."

I closed the doors, and again advanced towards Bartleby. I felt additional incentives tempting me to my fate. I burned to be rebelled against again. I remembered that Bartleby never left the office.

"Bartleby," said I, "Ginger Nut is away; just step round to the Post Office, won't you? (it was but a three minutes walk,) and see if there is any thing for me."

"I would prefer not to."

"You *will* not?"

"I *prefer* not."

I staggered to my desk, and sat there in a deep study. My blind inveteracy returned. Was there any other thing in which I could procure myself to be ignominiously repulsed by this lean, penniless wight?—my hired clerk? What added thing is there, perfectly reasonable, that he will be sure to refuse to do?

"Bartleby!"

No answer.

"Bartleby," in a louder tone.

No answer.

"Bartleby," I roared.

Like a very ghost, agreeably to the laws of magical invocation, at the third summons, he appeared at the entrance of his hermitage.

"Go to the next room, and tell Nippers to come to me."

"I prefer not to," he respectfully and slowly said, and mildly disappeared.

"Very good, Bartleby," said I, in a quiet sort of serenely severe self-possessed tone, intimating the unalterable purpose of some terrible retribution very close at hand. At the moment I half intended something of the kind. But upon the whole, as it was drawing towards my dinner-hour, I thought it best to put on my hat and walk home for the day, suffering much from perplexity and distress of mind.

Shall I acknowledge it? The conclusion of this whole business was, that it soon became a fixed fact of my chambers, that a pale young scrivener, by the name of Bartleby, had a desk there; that he copied for me at the usual rate of four cents a folio (one hundred words); but he was permanently exempt from examining the work done by him, that duty being transferred to Turkey and Nippers, out of compliment doubtless to their superior acuteness; moreover, said Bartleby was never on any account to be dispatched on the most trivial errand of any sort; and that even if entreated to take upon him such a matter, it was generally understood that he would prefer not to—in other words, that he would refuse point-blank.

As days passed on, I became considerably reconciled to Bartleby. His steadiness, his freedom from all dissipation, his incessant industry (except when he chose to throw himself into a standing revery behind his screen), his great stillness, his unalterableness of demeanor under all circumstances, made him a valuable acquisition. One prime thing was this, —*he was always there*;—first in the morning, continually through the day, and the last at night. I had a singular confidence in his honesty. I felt my most precious papers perfectly safe in his hands. Sometimes to be sure I could not, for the very soul of me, avoid falling into sudden spasmodic passions with him. For it was exceeding difficult to bear in mind all the time those strange peculiarities, privileges, and unheard of exemptions, forming the tacit stipulations on Bartleby's part under which he remained in my office. Now and then, in the eagerness of dispatching pressing business, I would inadvertently summon Bartleby, in a short, rapid tone, to put his finger, say, on the incipient tie of a bit of red tape with which I was about compressing some papers. Of course, from behind the screen the usual answer, "I prefer not to," was sure to come; and then, how could a human creature with the common infirmities of our nature, refrain from bitterly exclaiming upon such perverseness—such unreasonableness. However, every added repulse of this sort which I received only tended to lessen the probability of my repeating the inadvertence.

Here it must be said, that according to the custom of most legal gentlemen occupying chambers in densely-populated law buildings, there were several keys to my door. One was kept by a woman residing in the attic, which person weekly scrubbed and daily swept and dusted my apartments. Another was kept by Turkey for convenience sake. The third I sometimes carried in my own pocket. The fourth I knew not who had.

Now, one Sunday morning I happened to go to Trinity Church, to hear a celebrated preacher, and finding myself rather early on the ground, I thought I would walk round to my chambers for a while. Luckily I had my key with me; but upon applying it to the lock, I found it resisted by something inserted from the inside. Quite surprised, I called out; when to my consternation a key was turned from within; and thrusting his lean visage at me, and holding the door ajar, the apparition of Bartleby appeared, in his shirt sleeves, and otherwise in a strangely tattered dishabille, saying quietly that he was sorry, but he was deeply engaged just then, and—preferred not admitting me at present. In a brief word or two, he moreover added, that perhaps I had better walk round the block two or three times, and by that time he would probably have concluded his affairs.

Now, the utterly unsurmised appearance of Bartleby, tenanting my law-chambers of a Sunday morning, with his cadaverously gentlemanly *nonchalance*, yet withal firm and self-possessed, had such a strange effect upon me, that incontinently I slunk away from my own door, and did as desired. But not without sundry twinges of impotent rebellion against the mild effrontery of this unaccountable scrivener. Indeed, it was his wonderful mildness chiefly, which not only disarmed me, but unmanned me, as it were. For I consider that one, for the time, is a sort of unmanned when he tranquilly permits his hired clerk to dictate to him, and order him away from his own premises. Furthermore, I was full of uneasiness as to what Bartleby could possibly be doing in my office in his shirt sleeves, and in an otherwise dismantled condition of a Sunday morning. Was any thing amiss going on? Nay, that was out of the question. It was not to be thought of for a moment that Bartleby was an immoral person. But what could he be doing there?—copying? Nay again, whatever might be his eccentricities, Bartleby was an eminently decorous person. He would be the last man to sit down to his desk in any state approaching to nudity. Besides, it was Sunday; and there was something about Bartleby that forbade the supposition that he would by any secular occupation violate the proprieties of the day.

Nevertheless, my mind was not pacified; and full of a restless curiosity, at last I returned to the door. Without hindrance I inserted my key, opened it, and entered. Bartleby was not to be seen. I looked round anxiously, peeped behind his screen; but it was very plain that he was gone. Upon more closely examining the place, I surmised that for an indefinite period Bartleby must have ate, dressed, and slept in my office, and that too without plate, mirror, or bed. The cushioned seat of a ricketty old sofa in one corner bore the faint impress of a lean, reclining form. Rolled away under his desk, I found a blanket; under the empty grate, a blacking box and brush; on a chair, a tin basin, with soap and a ragged towel; in a newspaper a few crumbs of ginger-nuts and a morsel of cheese. Yes, thought I, it is evident enough that Bartleby has been making his home here, keeping bachelor's hall all by himself. Immediately then the thought came sweeping across me, What miserable friendlessness and loneliness are here revealed! His poverty is great; but his solitude, how horrible! Think of it. Of a Sunday, Wall-street is deserted as Petra; and every night of every day it is an emptiness. This building too, which of week-days hums with industry and life, at nightfall echoes with sheer vacancy, and all through Sunday is forlorn. And here Bartleby makes his home; sole spectator of a solitude which he has seen all populous—a sort of innocent and transformed Marius brooding among the ruins of Carthage!

For the first time in my life a feeling of overpowering stinging melancholy seized me. Before, I had never experienced aught but a not-unpleasing sadness. The bond of a common humanity now drew me irresistibly to gloom. A fraternal melancholy! For both I and Bartleby were sons of Adam. I remembered the bright silks and sparkling faces I had seen that day, in gala trim, swan-like sailing down the Mississippi of Broadway; and I contrasted them with the pallid copyist, and thought to myself, Ah, happiness courts the light, so we deem the world is gay; but misery hides aloof, so we deem that misery there is none. These sad fancyings—chimeras, doubtless, of a sick and silly brain—led on to other and more special thoughts, concerning the eccentricities of Bartleby. Presentiments of strange discoveries hovered round me. The scrivener's pale form appeared to me laid out, among uncaring strangers, in its shivering winding sheet.

Suddenly I was attracted by Bartleby's closed desk, the key in open sight left in the lock.

I mean no mischief, seek the gratification of no heartless curiosity, thought I; besides, the desk is mine, and its contents too, so I will make bold to look within. Every thing was methodically arranged, the papers smoothly placed. The pigeon holes were deep, and removing the files of documents, I groped into their recesses. Presently I felt something there, and dragged it out. It was an old bandanna handkerchief, heavy and knotted. I opened it, and saw it was a savings' bank.

I now recalled all the quiet mysteries which I had noted in the man. I remembered that he never spoke but to answer; that though at intervals he had considerable time to himself, yet I had never seen him reading—no, not even a newspaper; that for long periods he would stand looking out, at his pale window behind the screen, upon the dead brick wall; I was quite sure he never visited any refectory or eating house; while his pale face clearly indicated that he never drank beer like Turkey, or tea and coffee even, like other men; that he never went any where in particular that I could learn; never went out for a walk, unless indeed that was the case at present; that he had declined telling who he was, or whence he came, or whether he had any relatives in the world; that though so thin and pale, he never complained of ill health. And more than all, I remembered a certain unconscious air of pallid—how shall I call it?—of pallid haughtiness, say, or rather an austere reserve about him, which had positively awed me into my tame compliance with his eccentricities, when I had feared to ask him to do the slightest incidental thing for me, even though I might know, from his long-continued motionlessness, that behind his screen he must be standing in one of those dead-wall reveries of his.

Revolving all these things, and coupling them with the recently discovered fact that he made my office his constant abiding place and home, and not forgetful of his morbid moodiness; revolving all these things, a prudential feeling began to steal over me. My first emotions had been those of pure melancholy and sincerest pity; but just in proportion as the forlornness of Bartleby grew and grew to my imagination, did that same melancholy merge into fear, that pity into repulsion. So true it is, and so terrible too, that up to a certain point the thought or sight of misery enlists our best affections; but, in certain special cases, beyond that point it does not. They err who would assert that invariably this is owing to the inherent selfishness of the human heart. It rather proceeds from a certain hopelessness of remedying excessive and organic ill. To a sensitive being, pity is not seldom pain. And when at last it is perceived that such pity cannot lead to effectual succor, common sense bids the soul be rid of it. What I saw that morning persuaded me that the scrivener was the victim of innate and incurable disorder. I might give alms to his body; but his body did not pain him; it was his soul that suffered, and his soul I could not reach.

I did not accomplish the purpose of going to Trinity Church that morning. Somehow, the things I had seen disqualified me for the time from church-going. I walked homeward, thinking what I would do with Bartleby. Finally, I resolved upon this;—I would put certain calm questions to him the next morning, touching his history, &c., and if he declined to answer them openly and unreservedly (and I supposed he would prefer not), then to give him a twenty dollar bill over and above whatever I might owe him, and tell him his services were no longer required; but that if in any other way I could assist him, I would be happy to do so, especially if he desired to return to his native place, wherever that might be, I would willingly help to defray the expenses. Moreover, if, after reaching home, he found himself at any time in want of aid, a letter from him would be sure of a reply.

The next morning came.

"Bartleby," said I, gently calling to him behind his screen.

No reply.

"Bartleby," said I, in a still gentler tone, "come here; I am not going to ask you to do any thing you would prefer not to do—I simply wish to speak to you."

Upon this he noiselessly slid into view.

"Will you tell me, Bartleby, where you were born?"

"I would prefer not to."

"Will you tell me *any thing* about yourself?"

"I would prefer not to."

"But what reasonable objection can you have to speak to me? I feel friendly towards you."

He did not look at me while I spoke, but kept his glance fixed upon my bust of Cicero, which as I then sat, was directly behind me, some six inches above my head.

"What is your answer, Bartleby?" said I, after waiting a considerable time for a reply, during which his countenance remained immovable, only there was the faintest conceivable tremor of the white attenuated mouth.

"At present I prefer to give no answer," he said, and retired into his hermitage.

It was rather weak in me I confess, but his manner on this occasion nettled me. Not only did there seem to lurk in it a certain calm disdain, but his perverseness seemed ungrateful, considering the undeniable good usage and indulgence he had received from me.

Again I sat ruminating what I should do. Mortified as I was at his behavior, and resolved as I had been to dismiss him when I entered my office, nevertheless I strangely felt something superstitious knocking at my heart, and forbidding me to carry out my purpose, and denouncing me for a villain if I dared to breathe one bitter word against this forlornest of mankind. At last, familiarly drawing my chair behind his screen, I sat down and said: "Bartleby, never mind then about revealing your history; but let me entreat you, as a friend, to comply as far as may be with the usages of this office. Say now you will help to examine papers to-morrow or next day: in short, say now that in a day or two you will begin to be a little reasonable:—say so, Bartleby."

"At present I would prefer not to be a little reasonable," was his mildly cadaverous reply.

Just then the folding-doors opened, and Nippers approached. He seemed suffering from an unusually bad night's rest, induced by severer indigestion than common. He overheard those final words of Bartleby.

"*Prefer not*, eh?" gritted Nippers—"I'd *prefer* him, if I were you, sir," addressing me—"I'd *prefer* him; I'd give him preferences, the stubborn mule! What is it, sir, pray, that he *prefers* not to do now?"

Bartleby moved not a limb.

"Mr. Nippers," said I, "I'd prefer that you would withdraw for the present."

Somehow, of late I had got into the way of involuntarily using this word "prefer" upon all sorts of not exactly suitable occasions. And I trembled to think that my contact with the scrivener had already and seriously affected me in a mental way. And what further and deeper aberration might it not yet produce? This apprehension had not been without efficacy in determining me to summary measures.

As Nippers, looking very sour and sulky, was departing, Turkey blandly and deferentially approached.

"With submission, sir," said he, "yesterday I was thinking about Bartleby here, and I think that if he would but prefer to take a quart of good ale every day, it would do much towards mending him, and enabling him to assist in examining his papers."

"So you have got the word too," said I, slightly excited.

"With submission, what word, sir," asked Turkey, respectfully crowding himself into the contracted space behind the screen, and by so doing, making me jostle the scrivener. "What word, sir?"

"I would prefer to be left alone here," said Bartleby, as if offended at being mobbed in his privacy.

"*That's* the word, Turkey," said I—"*that's* it."

"Oh, *prefer*? oh yes—queer word. I never use it myself. But, sir, as I was saying, if he would but prefer—"

"Turkey," interrupted I, "you will please withdraw."

"Oh certainly, sir, if you prefer that I should."

As he opened the folding-door to retire, Nippers at his desk caught a glimpse of me, and asked whether I would prefer to have a certain paper copied on blue paper or white. He did not in the least roguishly accent the word prefer. It was plain that it involuntarily rolled from his tongue. I thought to myself, surely I must get rid of a demented man, who already has in some degree turned the tongues, if not the heads of myself and clerks. But I thought it prudent not to break the dismission at once.

The next day I noticed that Bartleby did nothing but stand at his window in his dead-wall revery. Upon asking him why he did not write, he said that he had decided upon doing no more writing.

"Why, how now? what next?" exclaimed I, "do no more writing?"

"No more."

"And what is the reason?"

"Do you not see the reason for yourself," he indifferently replied.

I looked steadfastly at him, and perceived that his eyes looked dull and glazed. Instantly it occurred to me, that his unexampled diligence in copying by his dim window for the first few weeks of his stay with me might have temporarily impaired his vision.

I was touched. I said something in condolence with him. I hinted that of course he did wisely in abstaining from writing for a while; and urged him to embrace that opportunity of taking wholesome exercise in the open air. This, however, he did not do. A few days after this, my other clerks being absent, and being in a great hurry to dispatch certain letters by the mail, I thought that, having nothing else earthly to do, Bartleby would surely be less inflexible than usual, and carry these letters to the post-office. But he blankly declined. So, much to my inconvenience, I went myself.

Still added days went by. Whether Bartleby's eyes improved or not, I could not say. To all appearance, I thought they did. But when I asked him if they did, he vouchsafed no answer. At all events, he would do no copying. At last, in reply to my urgings, he informed me that he had permanently given up copying.

"What!" exclaimed I; "suppose your eyes should get entirely well—better than ever before—would you not copy then?"

"I have given up copying," he answered, and slid aside.

He remained as ever, a fixture in my chamber. Nay—if that were possible—he became still more of a fixture than before. What was to be done? He would do nothing in the office: why should he stay there? In plain fact, he had now become a millstone to me, not only useless as a necklace, but afflictive to bear. Yet I was sorry for him. I speak less than truth when I say that, on his own account, he occasioned me uneasiness. If he would but have named a single relative or friend, I would instantly have written, and urged their taking the poor fellow away to some convenient retreat. But he seemed alone, absolutely alone in the universe. A bit of wreck in the mid Atlantic. At length, necessities connected with my business tyrannized over all other considerations. Decently as I could, I told Bartleby that in six days' time he must unconditionally leave the office. I warned him to take measures, in the interval, for procuring some other abode. I offered to assist him in this endeavor, if he himself would but take the first step towards a removal. "And when you finally quit me, Bartleby," added I, "I shall see that you go not away entirely unprovided. Six days from this hour, remember."

At the expiration of that period, I peeped behind the screen, and lo! Bartleby was there.

I buttoned up my coat, balanced myself; advanced slowly towards him, touched his shoulder, and said, "The time has come; you must quit this place; I am sorry for you; here is money; but you must go."

"I would prefer not," he replied, with his back still towards me.

"You *must*."

He remained silent.

Now I had an unbounded confidence in this man's common honesty. He had frequently restored to me sixpences and shillings carelessly dropped upon the floor, for I am apt to be very reckless in such shirt-button affairs. The proceeding then which followed will not be deemed extraordinary.

"Bartleby," said I, "I owe you twelve dollars on account; here are thirty-two; the odd twenty are yours.—Will you take it?" and I handed the bills towards him.

But he made no motion.

"I will leave them here then," putting them under a weight on the table. Then taking my hat and cane and going to the door I tranquilly turned and added—"After you have removed your things from these offices, Bartleby, you will of course lock the door—since every one is now gone for the day but you—and if you please, slip your key underneath the mat, so that I may have it in the morning. I shall not see you again; so good-bye to you. If hereafter in your new place of abode I can be of any service to you, do not fail to advise me by letter. Good-bye, Bartleby, and fare you well."

But he answered not a word; like the last column of some ruined temple, he remained standing mute and solitary in the middle of the otherwise deserted room.

As I walked home in a pensive mood, my vanity got the better of my pity. I could not but highly plume myself on my masterly management in getting rid of Bartleby. Masterly I call it, and such it must appear to any dispassionate thinker. The beauty of my procedure seemed to consist in its perfect quietness. There was no vulgar bullying, no bravado of any sort, no choleric hectoring, and striding to and fro across the apartment, jerking out vehement commands for Bartleby to bundle himself off with his beggarly traps. Nothing of the kind. Without loudly bidding Bartleby depart—as an inferior genius might have done—I *assumed* the ground that depart he must; and upon that assumption built all I had to say. The more I thought over my procedure, the more I was charmed with it. Nevertheless, next morning, upon awakening, I had my doubts,—I had somehow slept off the fumes of vanity. One of the coolest and wisest hours a man has, is just after he awakes in the morning. My procedure seemed as sagacious as ever,—but only in theory. How it would prove in practice—there was the rub. It was truly a beautiful thought to have assumed Bartleby's departure; but, after all, that assumption was simply my own, and none of Bartleby's. The great point was, not whether I had assumed that he would quit me, but whether he would prefer so to do. He was more a man of preferences than assumptions.

After breakfast, I walked down town, arguing the probabilities *pro* and *con*. One moment I thought it would prove a miserable failure, and Bartleby would be found all alive at my office as usual; the next moment it seemed certain that I should find his chair empty. And so I kept veering about. At the corner of Broadway and Canal-street, I saw quite an excited group of people standing in earnest conversation.

"I'll take odds he doesn't," said a voice as I passed.

"Doesn't go?—done!" said I, "put up your money."

I was instinctively putting my hand in my pocket to produce my own, when I remembered that this was an election day. The words I had overheard bore no reference to Bartleby, but to the success or non-success of some candidate for the mayoralty. In my intent frame of mind, I had, as it were, imagined that all Broadway shared in my excitement, and were debating the same question with me. I passed on, very thankful that the uproar of the street screened my momentary absent-mindedness.

As I had intended, I was earlier than usual at my office door. I stood listening for a moment. All was still. He must be gone. I tried the knob. The door was locked. Yes, my procedure had worked to a charm; he indeed must be vanished. Yet a certain melancholy mixed with this: I was almost sorry for my brilliant success. I was fumbling under the door mat for the key, which Bartleby was to have left there for me, when accidentally my knee knocked against a panel, producing a summoning sound, and in response a voice came to me from within—"Not yet; I am occupied."

It was Bartleby.

I was thunderstruck. For an instant I stood like the man who, pipe in mouth, was killed one cloudless afternoon long ago in Virginia, by summer lightning; at his own warm open window he was killed, and remained leaning out there upon the dreamy afternoon, till some one touched him, when he fell.

"Not gone!" I murmured at last. But again obeying that wondrous ascendancy which the inscrutable scrivener had over me, and from which ascendency, for all my chafing, I could not completely escape, I slowly went down stairs and out into the street, and while walking round the block, considered what I should next do in this unheard-of perplexity. Turn the man out by an actual thrusting I could not; to drive him away by calling him hard names would not do; calling in the police was an unpleasant idea; and yet, permit him to enjoy his cadaverous triumph over me,—this too I could not think of. What was to be done? or, if nothing could be done, was there any thing further that I could *assume* in the matter? Yes, as before I had prospectively assumed that Bartleby would depart, so now I might retrospectively assume that departed he was. In the legitimate carrying out of this assumption, I might enter my office in a great hurry, and pretending not to see Bartleby at all, walk straight against him as if he were air. Such a proceeding would in a singular degree have the appearance of a home-thrust. It was hardly possible that Bartleby could withstand such an application of the doctrine of assumptions. But upon second thoughts the success of the plan seemed rather dubious. I resolved to argue the matter over with him again.

"Bartleby," said I, entering the office, with a quietly severe expression, "I am seriously displeased. I am pained, Bartleby. I had thought better of you. I had imagined you of such a gentlemanly organization, that in any delicate dilemma a slight hint would suffice—in short, an assumption. But it appears I am deceived. Why," I added, unaffectedly starting, "you have not even touched that money yet," pointing to it, just where I had left it the evening previous.

He answered nothing.

"Will you, or will you not, quit me?" I now demanded in a sudden passion, advancing close to him.

"I would prefer *not* to quit you," he replied, gently emphasizing the *not*.

"What earthly right have you to stay here? Do you pay any rent? Do you pay my taxes? Or is this property yours?"

He answered nothing.

"Are you ready to go on and write now? Are your eyes recovered? Could you copy a small paper for me this morning? or help examine a few lines? or step round to the post-office? In a word, will you do any thing at all, to give a coloring to your refusal to depart the premises?"

He silently retired into his hermitage.

I was now in such a state of nervous resentment that I thought it but prudent to check myself at present from further demonstrations. Bartleby and I were alone. I remembered the tragedy of the unfortunate Adams and the still more unfortunate Colt in the solitary office of the latter; and how poor Colt, being dreadfully incensed by Adams, and imprudently permitting himself to get wildly excited, was at unawares hurried into his fatal act—an act which certainly no man could possibly deplore more than the actor himself. Often it had occurred to me in my ponderings upon the subject, that had that altercation taken place in the public street, or at a private residence, it would not have terminated as it did. It was the circumstance of being alone in a solitary office, up stairs, of a building entirely unhallowed by humanizing domestic associations—an uncarpeted office, doubtless, of a dusty, haggard sort of appearance;—this it must have been, which greatly helped to enhance the irritable desperation of the hapless Colt.

But when this old Adam of resentment rose in me and tempted me concerning Bartleby, I grappled him and threw him. How? Why, simply by recalling the divine injunction: "A new commandment give I unto you, that ye love one another." Yes, this it was that saved me. Aside from higher considerations, charity often operates as a vastly wise and prudent principle—a great safeguard to its possessor. Men have committed murder for jealousy's sake, and anger's sake, and hatred's sake, and selfishness' sake, and spiritual pride's sake; but no man that ever I heard of, ever committed a diabolical murder for sweet charity's sake. Mere self-interest, then, if no better motive can be enlisted, should, especially with high-tempered men, prompt all beings to charity and philanthropy. At any rate, upon the occasion in question, I strove to drown my exasperated feelings towards the scrivener by benevolently construing his conduct. Poor fellow, poor fellow! thought I, he don't mean any thing; and besides, he has seen hard times, and ought to be indulged.

I endeavored also immediately to occupy myself, and at the same time to comfort my despondency. I tried to fancy that in the course of the morning, at such time as might prove agreeable to him, Bartleby, of his own free accord, would emerge from his hermitage, and take up some decided line of march in the direction of the door. But no. Half-past twelve o'clock came; Turkey began to glow in the face, overturn his inkstand, and become generally obstreperous; Nippers abated down into quietude and courtesy; Ginger Nut munched his noon apple; and Bartleby remained standing at his window in one of his profoundest dead-wall reveries. Will it be credited? Ought I to acknowledge it? That afternoon I left the office without saying one further word to him.

Some days now passed, during which, at leisure intervals I looked a little into "Edwards on the Will," and "Priestley on Necessity." Under the circumstances, those books induced a salutary feeling. Gradually I slid into the persuasion that these troubles of mine touching the scrivener, had been all predestinated from eternity, and Bartleby was billeted upon me for some mysterious purpose of an all-wise Providence, which it was not for a mere mortal like me to fathom. Yes, Bartleby, stay there behind your screen, thought I; I shall persecute you no more; you are harmless and noiseless as any of these old chairs; in short, I never feel so private as when I know you are here. At last I see it, I feel it; I penetrate to the predestinated purpose of my life. I am content. Others may have loftier parts to enact; but my mission in this world, Bartleby, is to furnish you with office-room for such period as you may see fit to remain.

I believe that this wise and blessed frame of mind would have continued with me, had it not been for the unsolicited and uncharitable remarks obtruded upon me by my professional friends who visited the rooms. But this it often is, that the constant friction of illiberal minds wears out at last the best resolves of the more generous. Though to be sure, when I reflected upon it, it was not strange that people entering my office should be struck by the peculiar aspect of the unaccountable Bartleby, and so be tempted to throw out some sinister observations concerning him. Sometimes an attorney having business with me, and calling at my office, and finding no one but the scrivener there, would undertake to obtain some sort of precise information from him touching my whereabouts; but without heeding his idle talk, Bartleby would remain standing immovable in the middle of the room. So after contemplating him in that position for a time, the attorney would depart, no wiser than he came.

Also, when a Reference was going on, and the room full of lawyers and witnesses and business was driving fast; some deeply occupied legal gentleman present, seeing Bartleby wholly unemployed, would request him to run round to his (the legal gentleman's) office and fetch some papers for him. Thereupon, Bartleby would tranquilly decline, and yet remain idle as before. Then the lawyer would give a great stare, and turn to me. And what could I say? At last I was made aware that all through the circle of my professional acquaintance, a whisper of wonder was running round, having reference to the strange creature I kept at my office. This worried me very much. And as the idea came upon me of his possibly turning out a long-lived man, and keep occupying my chambers, and denying my authority; and perplexing my visitors; and scandalizing my professional reputation; and casting a general gloom over the premises; keeping soul and body together to the last upon his savings (for doubtless he spent but half a dime a day), and in the end perhaps outlive me, and claim possession of my office by right of his perpetual occupancy: as all these dark anticipations crowded upon me more and more, and my friends continually intruded their relentless remarks upon the apparition in my room; a great change was wrought in me. I resolved to gather all my faculties together, and for ever rid me of this intolerable incubus.

Ere revolving any complicated project, however, adapted to this end, I first simply suggested to Bartleby the propriety of his permanent departure. In a calm and serious tone, I commended the idea to his careful and mature consideration. But having taken three days to meditate upon it, he apprised me that his original determination remained the same; in short, that he still preferred to abide with me.

What shall I do? I now said to myself, buttoning up my coat to the last button. What shall I do? what ought I to do? what does conscience say I *should* do with this man, or rather ghost? Rid myself of him, I must; go, he shall. But how? You will not thrust him, the poor, pale, passive mortal,—you will not thrust such a helpless creature out of your door? you will not dishonor yourself by such cruelty? No, I will not, I cannot do that. Rather would I let him live and die here, and then mason up his remains in the wall. What then will you do? For all your coaxing, he will not budge. Bribes he leaves under your own paper-weight on your table; in short, it is quite plain that he prefers to cling to you.

Then something severe, something unusual must be done. What! surely you will not have him collared by a constable, and commit his innocent pallor to the common jail? And upon what ground could you procure such a thing to be done?—a vagrant, is he? What! he a vagrant, a wanderer, who refuses to budge? It is because he will *not* be a vagrant, then, that you seek to count him *as* a vagrant. That is too absurd. No visible means of support: there I have him. Wrong again: for indubitably he *does* support himself, and that is the only unanswerable proof that any man can show of his possessing the means so to do. No more then. Since he will not quit me, I must quit him. I will change my offices; I will move elsewhere; and give him fair notice, that if I find him on my new premises I will then proceed against him as a common trespasser.

Acting accordingly, next day I thus addressed him: "I find these chambers too far from the City Hall; the air is unwholesome. In a word, I propose to remove my offices next week, and shall no longer require your services. I tell you this now, in order that you may seek another place."

He made no reply, and nothing more was said.

On the appointed day I engaged carts and men, proceeded to my chambers, and having but little furniture, every thing was removed in a few hours. Throughout, the scrivener remained standing behind the screen, which I directed to be removed the last thing. It was withdrawn; and being folded up like a huge folio, left him the motionless occupant of a naked room. I stood in the entry watching him a moment, while something from within me upbraided me.

I re-entered, with my hand in my pocket—and—and my heart in my mouth.

"Good-bye, Bartleby; I am going—good-bye, and God some way bless you; and take that," slipping something in his hand. But it dropped upon the floor, and then,—strange to say—I tore myself from him whom I had so longed to be rid of.

Established in my new quarters, for a day or two I kept the door locked, and started at every footfall in the passages. When I returned to my rooms after any little absence, I would pause at the threshold for an instant, and attentively listen, ere applying my key. But these fears were needless. Bartleby never came nigh me.

I thought all was going well, when a perturbed looking stranger visited me, inquiring whether I was the person who had recently occupied rooms at No. — Wall-street.

Full of forebodings, I replied that I was.

"Then sir," said the stranger, who proved a lawyer, "you are responsible for the man you left there. He refuses to do any copying; he refuses to do any thing; he says he prefers not to; and he refuses to quit the premises."

"I am very sorry, sir," said I, with assumed tranquillity, but an inward tremor, "but, really, the man you allude to is nothing to me—he is no relation or apprentice of mine, that you should hold me responsible for him."

"In mercy's name, who is he?"

"I certainly cannot inform you. I know nothing about him. Formerly I employed him as a copyist; but he has done nothing for me now for some time past."

"I shall settle him then,—good morning, sir."

Several days passed, and I heard nothing more; and though I often felt a charitable prompting to call at the place and see poor Bartleby, yet a certain squeamishness of I know not what withheld me.

All is over with him, by this time, thought I at last, when through another week no further intelligence reached me. But coming to my room the day after, I found several persons waiting at my door in a high state of nervous excitement.

"That's the man—here he comes," cried the foremost one, whom I recognized as the lawyer who had previously called upon me alone.

"You must take him away, sir, at once," cried a portly person among them, advancing upon me, and whom I knew to be the landlord of No. — Wall-street. "These gentlemen, my tenants, cannot stand it any longer; Mr. B——" pointing to the lawyer, "has turned him out of his room, and he now persists in haunting the building generally, sitting upon the banisters of the stairs by day, and sleeping in the entry by night. Every body is concerned; clients are leaving the offices; some fears are entertained of a mob; something you must do, and that without delay."

Aghast at this torrent, I fell back before it, and would fain have locked myself in my new quarters. In vain I persisted that Bartleby was nothing to me—no more than to any one else. In vain:—I was the last person known to have any thing to do with him, and they held me to the terrible account. Fearful then of being exposed in the papers (as one person present obscurely threatened) I considered the matter, and at length said, that if the lawyer would give me a confidential interview with the scrivener, in his (the lawyer's) own room, I would that afternoon strive my best to rid them of the nuisance they complained of.

Going up stairs to my old haunt, there was Bartleby silently sitting upon the banister at the landing.

"What are you doing here, Bartleby?" said I.

"Sitting upon the banister," he mildly replied.

I motioned him into the lawyer's room, who then left us.

"Bartleby," said I, "are you aware that you are the cause of great tribulation to me, by persisting in occupying the entry after being dismissed from the office?"

No answer.

"Now one of two things must take place. Either you must do something, or something must be done to you. Now what sort of business would you like to engage in? Would you like to re-engage in copying for some one?"

"No; I would prefer not to make any change."

"Would you like a clerkship in a dry-goods store?"

"There is too much confinement about that. No, I would not like a clerkship; but I am not particular."

"Too much confinement," I cried, " why you keep yourself confined all the time!"

"I would prefer not to take a clerkship," he rejoined, as if to settle that little item at once.

"How would a bar-tender's business suit you? There is no trying of the eyesight in that."

"I would not like it at all; though, as I said before, I am not particular."

His unwonted wordiness inspirited me. I returned to the charge.

"Well then, would you like to travel through the country collecting bills for the merchants? That would improve your health."

"No, I would prefer to be doing something else."

"How then would going as a companion to Europe, to entertain some young gentleman with your conversation,—how would that suit you?"

"Not at all. It does not strike me that there is any thing definite about that. I like to be stationary. But I am not particular."

"Stationary you shall be then," I cried, now losing all patience, and for the first time in all my exasperating connection with him fairly flying into a passion. "If you do not go away from these premises before night, I shall feel bound—indeed I *am* bound—to—to—to quit the premises myself!" I rather absurdly concluded, knowing not with what possible threat to try to frighten his immobility into compliance. Despairing of all further efforts, I was precipitately leaving him, when a final thought occurred to me—one which had not been wholly unindulged before.

"Bartleby," said I, in the kindest tone I could assume under such exciting circumstances, "will you go home with me now—not to my office, but my dwelling—and remain there till we can conclude upon some convenient arrangement for you at our leisure? Come, let us start now, right away."

"No: at present I would prefer not to make any change at all."

I answered nothing; but effectually dodging every one by the suddenness and rapidity of my flight, rushed from the building, ran up Wall-street towards Broadway, and jumping into the first omnibus was soon removed from pursuit. As soon as tranquillity returned I distinctly perceived that I had now done all that I possibly could, both in respect to the demands of the landlord and his tenants, and with regard to my own desire and sense of duty, to benefit Bartleby, and shield him from rude persecution. I now strove to be entirely care-free and quiescent; and my conscience justified me in the attempt; though indeed it was not so successful as I could have wished. So fearful was I of being again hunted out by the incensed landlord and his exasperated tenants, that, surrendering my business to Nippers, for a few days I drove about the upper part of the town and through the suburbs, in my rockaway; crossed over to Jersey City and Hoboken, and paid fugitive visits to Manhattanville and Astoria. In fact I almost lived in my rockaway for the time.

When again I entered my office, lo, a note from the landlord lay upon the desk. I opened it with trembling hands. It informed me that the writer had sent to the police, and had Bartleby removed to the Tombs as a vagrant. Moreover, since I knew more about him than any one else, he wished me to appear at that place, and make a suitable statement of the facts. These tidings had a conflicting effect upon me. At first I was indignant; but at last almost approved. The landlord's energetic, summary disposition, had led him to adopt a procedure which I do not think I would have decided upon myself; and yet as a last resort, under such peculiar circumstances, it seemed the only plan.

As I afterwards learned, the poor scrivener, when told that he must be conducted to the Tombs, offered not the slightest obstacle, but in his pale unmoving way, silently acquiesced.

Some of the compassionate and curious bystanders joined the party; and headed by one of the constables arm in arm with Bartleby, the silent procession filed its way through all the noise, and heat, and joy of the roaring thoroughfares at noon.

The same day I received the note I went to the Tombs, or to speak more properly, the Halls of Justice. Seeking the right officer, I stated the purpose of my call, and was informed that the individual I described was indeed within. I then assured the functionary that Bartleby was a perfectly honest man, and greatly to be compassionated, however unaccountably eccentric. I narrated all I knew, and closed by suggesting the idea of letting him remain in as indulgent confinement as possible till something less harsh might be done—though indeed I hardly knew what. At all events, if nothing else could be decided upon, the alms-house must receive him. I then begged to have an interview.

Being under no disgraceful charge, and quite serene and harmless in all his ways, they had permitted him freely to wander about the prison, and especially in the inclosed grass-platted yards thereof. And so I found him there, standing all alone in the quietest of the yards, his face towards a high wall, while all around, from the narrow slits of the jail windows, I thought I saw peering out upon him the eyes of murderers and thieves.

"Bartleby!"

"I know you," he said, without looking round,—"and I want nothing to say to you."

"It was not I that brought you here, Bartleby," said I, keenly pained at his implied suspicion. "And to you, this should not be so vile a place. Nothing reproachful attaches to you by being here. And see, it is not so sad a place as one might think. Look, there is the sky, and here is the grass."

"I know where I am," he replied, but would say nothing more, and so I left him.

As I entered the corridor again, a broad meat-like man, in an apron, accosted me, and jerking his thumb over his shoulder said—"Is that your friend?"

"Yes."

"Does he want to starve? If he does, let him live on the prison fare, that's all."

"Who are you?" asked I, not knowing what to make of such an unofficially speaking person in such a place.

"I am the grub-man. Such gentlemen as have friends here, hire me to provide them with something good to eat."

"Is this so?" said I, turning to the turnkey.

He said it was.

"Well then," said I, slipping some silver into the grub-man's hands (for so they called him). "I want you to give particular attention to my friend there; let him have the best dinner you can get. And you must be as polite to him as possible."

"Introduce me, will you?" said the grub-man, looking at me with an expression which seemed to say he was all impatience for an opportunity to give a specimen of his breeding.

Thinking it would prove of benefit to the scrivener, I acquiesced; and asking the grub-man his name, went up with him to Bartleby.

"Bartleby, this is Mr. Cutlets; you will find him very useful to you."

"Your sarvant, sir, your sarvant," said the grub-man, making a low salutation behind his apron. "Hope you find it pleasant here, sir; nice grounds—cool apartments, sir—hope you'll stay with us some time—try to make it agreeable. May Mrs. Cutlets and I have the pleasure of your company to dinner, sir, in Mrs. Cutlets' private room?"

"I prefer not to dine to-day," said Bartleby, turning away. "It would disagree with me; I am unused to dinners." So saying he slowly moved to the other side of the inclosure, and took up a position fronting the dead-wall.

"How's this?" said the grub-man, addressing me with a stare of astonishment. "He's odd, aint he?"

"I think he is a little deranged," said I, sadly.

"Deranged? deranged is it? Well now, upon my word, I thought that friend of yourn was a gentleman forger; they are always pale and genteel-like, them forgers. I can't help pity 'em—can't help it, sir. Did you know Monroe Edwards?" he added touchingly, and paused. Then, laying his hand pityingly on my shoulder, sighed, "he died of consumption at Sing-Sing. So you weren't acquainted with Monroe?"

"No, I was never socially acquainted with any forgers. But I cannot stop longer. Look to my friend yonder. You will not lose by it. I will see you again."

Some few days after this, I again obtained admission to the Tombs, and went through the corridors in quest of Bartleby; but without finding him.

"I saw him coming from his cell not long ago," said a turnkey, "may be he's gone to loiter in the yards."

So I went in that direction.

"Are you looking for the silent man?" said another turnkey

passing me. "Yonder he lies—sleeping in the yard there. 'Tis not twenty minutes since I saw him lie down."

The yard was entirely quiet. It was not accessible to the common prisoners. The surrounding walls, of amazing thickness, kept off all sounds behind them. The Egyptian character of the masonry weighed upon me with its gloom. But a soft imprisoned turf grew under foot. The heart of the eternal pyramids, it seemed, wherein, by some strange magic, through the clefts, grass-seed, dropped by birds, had sprung.

Strangely huddled at the base of the wall, his knees drawn up, and lying on his side, his head touching the cold stones, I saw the wasted Bartleby. But nothing stirred. I paused; then went close up to him; stooped over, and saw that his dim eyes were open; otherwise he seemed profoundly sleeping. Something prompted me to touch him. I felt his hand, when a tingling shiver ran up my arm and down my spine to my feet.

The round face of the grub-man peered upon me now. "His dinner is ready. Won't he dine to-day, either? Or does he live without dining?"

"Lives without dining," said I, and closed the eyes.

"Eh!—He's asleep, aint he?"

"With kings and counsellors," murmured I.

*   *   *

There would seem little need for proceeding further in this history. Imagination will readily supply the meagre recital of poor Bartleby's interment. But ere parting with the reader, let me say, that if this little narrative has sufficiently interested him, to awaken curiosity as to who Bartleby was, and what manner of life he led prior to the present narrator's making his acquaintance, I can only reply, that in such curiosity I fully share, but am wholly unable to gratify it. Yet here I hardly know whether I should divulge one little item of rumor, which came to my ear a few months after the scrivener's decease. Upon what basis it rested, I could never ascertain; and hence, how true it is I cannot now tell. But inasmuch as this vague report has not been without a certain strange suggestive interest to me, however sad, it may prove the same with some others; and so I will briefly mention it. The report was this: that Bartleby had been a subordinate clerk in the Dead Letter Office at Washington, from which he had been suddenly removed by a change in the administration. When I think over this rumor, hardly can I express the emotions which seize me. Dead letters! does it not sound like dead men? Conceive a man by nature and misfortune prone to a pallid hopelessness, can any business seem more fitted to heighten it than that of continually handling these dead letters, and assorting them for the flames? For by the cart-load they are annually burned. Sometimes from out the folded paper the pale clerk takes a ring:—the finger it was meant for, perhaps, moulders in the grave; a bank-note sent in swiftest charity:—he whom it would relieve, nor eats nor hungers any more; pardon for those who died despairing; hope for those who died unhoping; good tidings for those who died stifled by unrelieved calamities. On errands of life, these letters speed to death.

Ah Bartleby! Ah humanity!

Benito Cereno

IN THE YEAR 1799, Captain Amasa Delano, of Duxbury, in Massachusetts, commanding a large sealer and general trader, lay at anchor, with a valuable cargo, in the harbor of St. Maria—a small, desert, uninhabited island toward the southern extremity of the long coast of Chili. There he had touched for water.

On the second day, not long after dawn, while lying in his berth, his mate came below, informing him that a strange sail was coming into the bay. Ships were then not so plenty in those waters as now. He rose, dressed, and went on deck.

The morning was one peculiar to that coast. Everything was mute and calm; everything gray. The sea, though undulated into long roods of swells, seemed fixed, and was sleeked at the surface like waved lead that has cooled and set in the smelter's mould. The sky seemed a gray surtout. Flights of troubled gray fowl, kith and kin with flights of troubled gray vapors among which they were mixed, skimmed low and fitfully over the waters, as swallows over meadows before storms. Shadows present, foreshadowing deeper shadows to come.

To Captain Delano's surprise, the stranger, viewed through the glass, showed no colors; though to do so upon entering a haven, however, uninhabited in its shores, where but a single other ship might be lying, was the custom among peaceful seamen of all nations. Considering the lawlessness and loneliness of the spot, and the sort of stories, at that day, associated with those seas, Captain Delano's surprise might have deepened into some uneasiness had he not been a person of a singularly undistrustful good nature, not liable, except on extraordinary and repeated incentives, and hardly then, to indulge in personal alarms, any way involving the imputation of malign evil in man. Whether, in view of what humanity is capable, such a trait implies, along with a benevolent heart, more than ordinary quickness and accuracy of intellectual perception, may be left to the wise to determine.

But whatever misgivings might have obtruded on first seeing the stranger, would almost, in any seaman's mind, have been dissipated by observing that, the ship, in navigating into the harbor, was drawing too near the land, for her own safety's sake, owing to a sunken reef making out off her bow. This seemed to prove her a stranger, indeed, not only to the sealer, but the island; consequently, she could be no wonted freebooter on that ocean. With no small interest, Captain Delano continued to watch her—a proceeding not much facilitated by the vapors partly mantling the hull, through which the far matin light from her cabin streamed equivocally enough; much like the sun—by this time hemisphered on the rim of the horizon, and apparently, in company with the strange ship, entering the harbor—which, wimpled by the same low, creeping clouds, showed not unlike a Lima intriguante's one sinister eye peering across the Plaza from the Indian loop-hole of her dusk *saya-y-manta*.

It might have been but a deception of the vapors, but, the longer the stranger was watched, the more singular appeared her maneuvers. Ere long it seemed hard to decide whether she meant to come in or no—what she wanted, or what she was about. The wind, which had breezed up a little during the night, was now extremely light and baffling, which the more increased the apparent uncertainty of her movements.

Surmising, at last, that it might be a ship in distress, Captain Delano ordered his whale-boat to be dropped, and, much to the wary opposition of his mate, prepared to board her, and, at the least, pilot her in. On the night previous, a fishing-party of the seamen had gone a long distance to some detached rocks out of sight from the sealer, and, an hour or two before day-break, had returned, having met with no small success. Presuming that the stranger might have been long off soundings, the good captain put several baskets of the fish, for presents, into his boat, and so pulled away. From her continuing too near the sunken reef, deeming her in danger, calling to his men, he made all haste to apprise those on board of their situation. But, some time ere the boat came up, the wind, light though it was, having shifted, had headed the vessel off, as well as partly broken the vapors from about her.

Upon gaining a less remote view, the ship, when made signally visible on the verge of the leaden-hued swells, with the shreds of fog here and there raggedly furring her, appeared

like a white-washed monastery after a thunder-storm, seen
perched upon some dun cliff among the Pyrenees. But it was
no purely fanciful resemblance which now, for a moment, almost led Captain Delano to think that nothing less than a
ship-load of monks was before him. Peering over the bulwarks were what really seemed, in the hazy distance, throngs
of dark cowls; while, fitfully revealed through the open portholes, other dark moving figures were dimly descried, as of
Black Friars pacing the cloisters.

Upon a still nigher approach, this appearance was modified, and the true character of the vessel was plain—a Spanish
merchantman of the first class; carrying negro slaves, amongst
other valuable freight, from one colonial port to another. A
very large, and, in its time, a very fine vessel, such as in those
days were at intervals encountered along that main; sometimes superseded Acapulco treasure-ships, or retired frigates
of the Spanish king's navy, which, like superannuated Italian
palaces, still, under a decline of masters, preserved signs of
former state.

As the whale-boat drew more and more nigh, the cause of
the peculiar pipe-clayed aspect of the stranger was seen in the
slovenly neglect pervading her. The spars, ropes, and great
part of the bulwarks, looked woolly, from long unacquaint-
ance with the scraper, tar, and the brush. Her keel seemed
laid, her ribs put together, and she launched, from Ezekiel's
Valley of Dry Bones.

In the present business in which she was engaged, the
ship's general model and rig appeared to have undergone no
material change from their original war-like and Froissart pattern. However, no guns were seen.

The tops were large, and were railed about with what had
once been octagonal net-work, all now in sad disrepair. These
tops hung overhead like three ruinous aviaries, in one of
which was seen perched, on a ratlin, a white noddy, a strange
fowl, so called from its lethargic, somnambulistic character,
being frequently caught by hand at sea. Battered and mouldy,
the castellated forecastle seemed some ancient turret, long ago
taken by assault, and then left to decay. Toward the stern, two
high-raised quarter galleries—the balustrades here and there
covered with dry, tindery sea-moss—opening out from the

unoccupied state-cabin, whose dead lights, for all the mild weather, were hermetically closed and calked—these tenant-less balconies hung over the sea as if it were the grand Venetian canal. But the principal relic of faded grandeur was the ample oval of the shield-like stern-piece, intricately carved with the arms of Castile and Leon, medallioned about by groups of mythological or symbolical devices; uppermost and central of which was a dark satyr in a mask, holding his foot on the prostrate neck of a writhing figure, likewise masked.

Whether the ship had a figure-head, or only a plain beak, was not quite certain, owing to canvas wrapped about that part, either to protect it while undergoing a re-furbishing, or else decently to hide its decay. Rudely painted or chalked, as in a sailor freak, along the forward side of a sort of pedestal below the canvas, was the sentence, *"Seguid vuestro jefe,"* (follow your leader); while upon the tarnished head-boards, near by, appeared, in stately capitals, once gilt, the ship's name, "SAN DOMINICK," each letter streakingly corroded with trick-lings of copper-spike rust; while, like mourning weeds, dark festoons of sea-grass slimily swept to and fro over the name, with every hearse-like roll of the hull.

As at last the boat was hooked from the bow along toward the gangway amidship, its keel, while yet some inches separated from the hull, harshly grated as on a sunken coral reef. It proved a huge bunch of conglobated barnacles adhering below the water to the side like a wen; a token of baffling airs and long calms passed somewhere in those seas.

Climbing the side, the visitor was at once surrounded by a clamorous throng of whites and blacks, but the latter out-numbering the former more than could have been expected, negro transportation-ship as the stranger in port was. But, in one language, and as with one voice, all poured out a common tale of suffering; in which the negresses, of whom there were not a few, exceeded the others in their dolorous vehemence. The scurvy, together with a fever, had swept off a great part of their number, more especially the Spaniards. Off Cape Horn, they had narrowly escaped ship-wreck; then, for days together, they had lain tranced without wind; their provisions were low; their water next to none; their lips that moment were baked.

While Captain Delano was thus made the mark of all eager tongues, his one eager glance took in all the faces, with every other object about him.

Always upon first boarding a large and populous ship at sea, especially a foreign one, with a nondescript crew such as Lascars or Manilla men, the impression varies in a peculiar way from that produced by first entering a strange house with strange inmates in a strange land. Both house and ship, the one by its walls and blinds, the other by its high bulwarks like ramparts, hoard from view their interiors till the last moment; but in the case of the ship there is this addition; that the living spectacle it contains, upon its sudden and complete disclosure, has, in contrast with the blank ocean which zones it, something of the effect of enchantment. The ship seems unreal; these strange costumes, gestures, and faces, but a shadowy tableau just emerged from the deep, which directly must receive back what it gave.

Perhaps it was some such influence as above is attempted to be described, which, in Captain Delano's mind, heightened whatever, upon a staid scrutiny, might have seemed unusual; especially the conspicuous figures of four elderly grizzled negroes, their heads like black, doddered willow tops, who, in venerable contrast to the tumult below them, were couched sphynx-like, one on the starboard cat-head, another on the larboard, and the remaining pair face to face on the opposite bulwarks above the main-chains. They each had bits of unstranded old junk in their hands, and, with a sort of stoical self-content, were picking the junk into oakum, a small heap of which lay by their sides. They accompanied the task with a continuous, low, monotonous chant; droning and druling away like so many gray-headed bag-pipers playing a funeral march.

The quarter-deck rose into an ample elevated poop, upon the forward verge of which, lifted, like the oakum-pickers, some eight feet above the general throng, sat along in a row, separated by regular spaces, the cross-legged figures of six other blacks; each with a rusty hatchet in his hand, which, with a bit of brick and a rag, he was engaged like a scullion in scouring; while between each two was a small stack of hatchets, their rusted edges turned forward awaiting a like operation. Though occasionally the four oakum-pickers would briefly address some person or persons in the crowd below, yet the six hatchet-polishers neither spoke to others, nor breathed a whisper among themselves, but sat intent upon their task, except at intervals, when, with the peculiar love in negroes of uniting industry with pastime, two and two they sideways clashed their hatchets together, like cymbals, with a barbarous din. All six, unlike the generality, had the raw aspect of unsophisticated Africans.

But that first comprehensive glance which took in those ten figures, with scores less conspicuous, rested but an instant upon them, as, impatient of the hubbub of voices, the visitor turned in quest of whomsoever it might be that commanded the ship.

But as if not unwilling to let nature make known her own case among his suffering charge, or else in despair of restraining it for the time, the Spanish captain, a gentlemanly, reserved-looking, and rather young man to a stranger's eye, dressed with singular richness, but bearing plain traces of recent sleepless cares and disquietudes, stood passively by, leaning against the main-mast, at one moment casting a dreary, spiritless look upon his excited people, at the next an unhappy glance toward his visitor. By his side stood a black of small stature, in whose rude face, as occasionally, like a shepherd's dog, he mutely turned it up into the Spaniard's, sorrow and affection were equally blended.

Struggling through the throng, the American advanced to the Spaniard, assuring him of his sympathies, and offering to render whatever assistance might be in his power. To which the Spaniard returned, for the present, but grave and ceremonious acknowledgments, his national formality dusked by the saturnine mood of ill health.

But losing no time in mere compliments, Captain Delano returning to the gangway, had his baskets of fish brought up; and as the wind still continued light, so that some hours at least must elapse ere the ship could be brought to the anchorage, he bade his men return to the sealer, and fetch back as much water as the whale-boat could carry, with whatever soft bread the steward might have, all the remaining pumpkins on board, with a box of sugar, and a dozen of his private bottles of cider.

Not many minutes after the boat's pushing off, to the vexation of all, the wind entirely died away, and the tide turning, began drifting back the ship helplessly seaward. But trusting this would not long last, Captain Delano sought with good hopes to cheer up the strangers, feeling no small satisfaction that, with persons in their condition he could—thanks to his frequent voyages along the Spanish main—converse with some freedom in their native tongue.

While left alone with them, he was not long in observing some things tending to heighten his first impressions; but surprise was lost in pity, both for the Spaniards and blacks, alike evidently reduced from scarcity of water and provisions; while long-continued suffering seemed to have brought out the less good-natured qualities of the negroes, besides, at the same time, impairing the Spaniard's authority over them. But, under the circumstances, precisely this condition of things was to have been anticipated. In armies, navies, cities, or families, in nature herself, nothing more relaxes good order than misery. Still, Captain Delano was not without the idea, that had Benito Cereno been a man of greater energy, misrule would hardly have come to the present pass. But the debility, constitutional or induced by the hardships, bodily and mental, of the Spanish captain, was too obvious to be overlooked. A prey to settled dejection, as if long mocked with hope he would not now indulge it, even when it had ceased to be a mock, the prospect of that day or evening at furthest, lying at anchor, with plenty of water for his people, and a brother captain to counsel and befriend, seemed in no perceptible degree to encourage him. His mind appeared unstrung, if not still more seriously affected. Shut up in these oaken walls, chained to one dull round of command, whose unconditionality cloyed him, like some hypochondriac abbot he moved slowly about, at times suddenly pausing, starting, or staring, biting his lip, biting his finger-nail, flushing, paling, twitching his beard, with other symptoms of an absent or moody mind. This distempered spirit was lodged, as before hinted, in as distempered a frame. He was rather tall, but seemed never to have been robust, and now with nervous suffering was almost worn to a skeleton. A tendency to some pulmonary complaint appeared to have been lately confirmed. His voice was like that of one with lungs half gone, hoarsely suppressed, a husky whisper. No wonder that, as in this state he tottered about, his private servant apprehensively followed him. Sometimes the negro gave his master his arm, or took his handkerchief out of his pocket for him; performing these and similar offices with that affectionate zeal which transmutes into something filial or fraternal acts in themselves but menial; and which has gained for the negro the repute of making the most pleasing body servant in the world; one, too, whom a master need be on no stiffly superior terms with, but may treat with familiar trust; less a servant than a devoted companion.

Marking the noisy indocility of the blacks in general, as well as what seemed the sullen inefficiency of the whites, it was not without humane satisfaction that Captain Delano witnessed the steady good conduct of Babo.

But the good conduct of Babo, hardly more than the ill-behavior of others, seemed to withdraw the half-lunatic Don Benito from his cloudy languor. Not that such precisely was the impression made by the Spaniard on the mind of his visitor. The Spaniard's individual unrest was, for the present, but noted as a conspicuous feature in the ship's general affliction. Still, Captain Delano was not a little concerned at what he could not help taking for the time to be Don Benito's unfriendly indifference towards himself. The Spaniard's manner, too, conveyed a sort of sour and gloomy disdain, which he seemed at no pains to disguise. But this the American in charity ascribed to the harassing effects of sickness, since, in former instances, he had noted that there are peculiar natures on whom prolonged physical suffering seems to cancel every social instinct of kindness; as if forced to black bread themselves, they deemed it but equity that each person coming nigh them should, indirectly, by some slight or affront, be made to partake of their fare.

But ere long Captain Delano bethought him that, indulgent as he was at the first, in judging the Spaniard, he might not, after all, have exercised charity enough. At bottom it was Don Benito's reserve which displeased him; but the same reserve was shown towards all but his faithful personal attendant. Even the formal reports which, according to sea-usage, were, at stated times, made to him by some petty underling, either a white, mulatto or black, he hardly had patience enough to listen to, without betraying contemptuous aversion. His manner upon such occasions was, in its degree, not unlike that which might be supposed to have been his imperial countryman's, Charles V., just previous to the anchoritish retirement of that monarch from the throne.

This splenetic disrelish of his place was evinced in almost every function pertaining to it. Proud as he was moody, he condescended to no personal mandate. Whatever special orders were necessary, their delivery was delegated to his body-servant, who in turn transferred them to their ultimate destination, through runners, alert Spanish boys or slave boys, like pages or pilot-fish within easy call continually hovering round Don Benito. So that to have beheld this undemonstrative invalid gliding about, apathetic and mute, no landsman could have dreamed that in him was lodged a dictatorship beyond which, while at sea, there was no earthly appeal.

Thus, the Spaniard, regarded in his reserve, seemed as the involuntary victim of mental disorder. But, in fact, his reserve might, in some degree, have proceeded from design. If so, then here was evinced the unhealthy climax of that icy though conscientious policy, more or less adopted by all commanders of large ships, which, except in signal emergencies, obliterates alike the manifestation of sway with every trace of sociality; transforming the man into a block, or rather into a loaded cannon, which, until there is call for thunder, has nothing to say.

Viewing him in this light, it seemed but a natural token of the perverse habit induced by a long course of such hard self-restraint, that, notwithstanding the present condition of his ship, the Spaniard should still persist in a demeanor, which, however harmless, or, it may be, appropriate, in a well appointed vessel, such as the San Dominick might have been at the outset of the voyage, was anything but judicious now. But the Spaniard perhaps thought that it was with captains as with gods: reserve, under all events, must still be their cue. But more probably this appearance of slumbering dominion might have been but an attempted disguise to conscious imbecility—not deep policy, but shallow device. But be all this as it might, whether Don Benito's manner was designed or not, the more Captain Delano noted its pervading reserve, the less he felt uneasiness at any particular manifestation of that reserve towards himself.

Neither were his thoughts taken up by the captain alone. Wonted to the quiet orderliness of the sealer's comfortable family of a crew, the noisy confusion of the San Dominick's suffering host repeatedly challenged his eye. Some prominent breaches not only of discipline but of decency were observed. These Captain Delano could not but ascribe, in the main, to the absence of those subordinate deck-officers to whom, along with higher duties, is entrusted what may be styled the police department of a populous ship. True, the old oakum-pickers appeared at times to act the part of monitorial constables to their countrymen, the blacks; but though occasionally succeeding in allaying trifling outbreaks now and then between man and man, they could do little or nothing toward establishing general quiet. The San Dominick was in the condition of a transatlantic emigrant ship, among whose multitude of living freight are some individuals, doubtless, as little troublesome as crates and bales; but the friendly remonstrances of such with their ruder companions are of not so much avail as the unfriendly arm of the mate. What the San Dominick wanted was, what the emigrant ship has, stern superior officers. But on these decks not so much as a fourth mate was to be seen.

The visitor's curiosity was roused to learn the particulars of those mishaps which had brought about such absenteeism, with its consequences; because, though deriving some inkling of the voyage from the wails which at the first moment had greeted him, yet of the details no clear understanding had been had. The best account would, doubtless, be given by the captain. Yet at first the visitor was loth to ask it, unwilling to provoke some distant rebuff. But plucking up courage, he at last accosted Don Benito, renewing the expression of his benevolent interest, adding, that did he (Captain Delano) but know the particulars of the ship's misfortunes, he would, perhaps, be better able in the end to relieve them. Would Don Benito favor him with the whole story?

Don Benito faltered; then, like some somnambulist suddenly interfered with, vacantly stared at his visitor, and ended by looking down on the deck. He maintained this posture so long, that Captain Delano, almost equally disconcerted, and involuntarily almost as rude, turned suddenly from him, walking forward to accost one of the Spanish seamen for the desired information. But he had hardly gone five paces, when with a sort of eagerness Don Benito invited him back, regretting his momentary absence of mind, and professing readiness to gratify him.

While most part of the story was being given, the two captains stood on the after part of the main-deck, a privileged spot, no one being near but the servant.

"It is now a hundred and ninety days," began the Spaniard, in his husky whisper, "that this ship, well officered and well manned, with several cabin passengers—some fifty Spaniards in all—sailed from Buenos Ayres bound to Lima, with a general cargo, hardware, Paraguay tea and the like—and," pointing forward, "that parcel of negroes, now not more than a hundred and fifty, as you see, but then numbering over three hundred souls. Off Cape Horn we had heavy gales. In one moment, by night, three of my best officers, with fifteen sailors, were lost, with the main-yard; the spar snapping under them in the slings, as they sought, with heavers, to beat down the icy sail. To lighten the hull, the heavier sacks of mata were thrown into the sea, with most of the water-pipes lashed on deck at the time. And this last necessity it was, combined with the prolonged detentions afterwards experienced, which eventually brought about our chief causes of suffering. When——"

Here there was a sudden fainting attack of his cough, brought on, no doubt, by his mental distress. His servant sustained him, and drawing a cordial from his pocket placed it to his lips. He a little revived. But unwilling to leave him unsupported while yet imperfectly restored, the black with one arm still encircled his master, at the same time keeping his eye fixed on his face, as if to watch for the first sign of complete restoration, or relapse, as the event might prove.

The Spaniard proceeded, but brokenly and obscurely, as one in a dream.

—"Oh, my God! rather than pass through what I have, with joy I would have hailed the most terrible gales; but——"

His cough returned and with increased violence; this subsiding, with reddened lips and closed eyes he fell heavily
against his supporter.

"His mind wanders. He was thinking of the plague that
followed the gales," plaintively sighed the servant; "my poor,
poor master!" wringing one hand, and with the other wiping
the mouth. "But be patient, Señor," again turning to Captain
Delano, "these fits do not last long; master will soon be
himself."

Don Benito reviving, went on; but as this portion of the
story was very brokenly delivered, the substance only will
here be set down.

It appeared that after the ship had been many days tossed
in storms off the Cape, the scurvy broke out, carrying off
numbers of the whites and blacks. When at last they had
worked round into the Pacific, their spars and sails were so
damaged, and so inadequately handled by the surviving mariners, most of whom were become invalids, that, unable to
lay her northerly course by the wind, which was powerful,
the unmanageable ship for successive days and nights was
blown northwestward, where the breeze suddenly deserted
her, in unknown waters, to sultry calms. The absence of the
water-pipes now proved as fatal to life as before their presence
had menaced it. Induced, or at least aggravated, by the more
than scanty allowance of water, a malignant fever followed
the scurvy; with the excessive heat of the lengthened calm,
making such short work of it as to sweep away, as by billows,
whole families of the Africans, and a yet larger number, proportionably, of the Spaniards, including, by a luckless fatality,
every remaining officer on board. Consequently, in the smart
west winds eventually following the calm, the already rent
sails having to be simply dropped, not furled, at need, had
been gradually reduced to the beggar's rags they were now.
To procure substitutes for his lost sailors, as well as supplies
of water and sails, the captain at the earliest opportunity had
made for Baldivia, the southermost civilized port of Chili and
South America; but upon nearing the coast the thick weather
had prevented him from so much as sighting that harbor.
Since which period, almost without a crew, and almost without canvas and almost without water, and at intervals giving

its added dead to the sea, the San Dominick had been battle-dored about by contrary winds, inveigled by currents, or grown weedy in calms. Like a man lost in woods, more than once she had doubled upon her own track.

"But throughout these calamities," huskily continued Don Benito, painfully turning in the half embrace of his servant, "I have to thank those negroes you see, who, though to your inexperienced eyes appearing unruly, have, indeed, conducted themselves with less of restlessness than even their owner could have thought possible under such circumstances."

Here he again fell faintly back. Again his mind wandered: but he rallied, and less obscurely proceeded.

"Yes, their owner was quite right in assuring me that no fetters would be needed with his blacks; so that while, as is wont in this transportation, those negroes have always remained upon deck—not thrust below, as in the Guinea-men—they have, also, from the beginning, been freely per-mitted to range within given bounds at their pleasure."

Once more the faintness returned—his mind roved—but, recovering, he resumed:

"But it is Babo here to whom, under God, I owe not only my own preservation, but likewise to him, chiefly, the merit is due, of pacifying his more ignorant brethren, when at in-tervals tempted to murmurings."

"Ah, master," sighed the black, bowing his face, "don't speak of me; Babo is nothing; what Babo has done was but duty."

"Faithful fellow!" cried Capt. Delano. "Don Benito, I envy you such a friend; slave I cannot call him."

As master and man stood before him, the black upholding the white, Captain Delano could not but bethink him of the beauty of that relationship which could present such a spec-tacle of fidelity on the one hand and confidence on the other. The scene was heightened by the contrast in dress, denoting their relative positions. The Spaniard wore a loose Chili jacket of dark velvet; white small clothes and stockings, with silver buckles at the knee and instep; a high-crowned sombrero, of fine grass; a slender sword, silver mounted, hung from a knot in his sash; the last being an almost invariable adjunct, more for utility than ornament, of a South American gentleman's dress to this hour. Excepting when his occasional nervous contortions brought about disarray, there was a certain precision in his attire, curiously at variance with the unsightly disorder around; especially in the belittered Ghetto, forward of the main-mast, wholly occupied by the blacks.

The servant wore nothing but wide trowsers, apparently, from their coarseness and patches, made out of some old topsail; they were clean, and confined at the waist by a bit of unstranded rope, which, with his composed, deprecatory air at times, made him look something like a begging friar of St. Francis.

However unsuitable for the time and place, at least in the blunt-thinking American's eyes, and however strangely surviving in the midst of all his afflictions, the toilette of Don Benito might not, in fashion at least, have gone beyond the style of the day among South Americans of his class. Though on the present voyage sailing from Buenos Ayres, he had avowed himself a native and resident of Chili, whose inhabitants had not so generally adopted the plain coat and once plebeian pantaloons; but, with a becoming modification, adhered to their provincial costume, picturesque as any in the world. Still, relatively to the pale history of the voyage, and his own pale face, there seemed something so incongruous in the Spaniard's apparel, as almost to suggest the image of an invalid courtier tottering about London streets in the time of the plague.

The portion of the narrative which, perhaps, most excited interest, as well as some surprise, considering the latitudes in question, was the long calms spoken of, and more particularly the ship's so long drifting about. Without communicating the opinion, of course, the American could not but impute at least part of the detentions both to clumsy seamanship and faulty navigation. Eying Don Benito's small, yellow hands, he easily inferred that the young captain had not got into command at the hawse-hole, but the cabin-window; and if so, why wonder at incompetence, in youth, sickness, and gentility united?

But drowning criticism in compassion, after a fresh repetition of his sympathies, Captain Delano having heard out his story, not only engaged, as in the first place, to see Don Benito and his people supplied in their immediate bodily needs, but, also, now further promised to assist him in procuring a large permanent supply of water, as well as some sails and rigging; and, though it would involve no small embarrass-ment to himself, yet he would spare three of his best seamen for temporary deck officers; so that without delay the ship might proceed to Conception, there fully to refit for Lima, her destined port.

Such generosity was not without its effect, even upon the invalid. His face lighted up; eager and hectic, he met the hon-est glance of his visitor. With gratitude he seemed overcome.

"This excitement is bad for master," whispered the servant, taking his arm, and with soothing words gently drawing him aside.

When Don Benito returned, the American was pained to observe that his hopefulness, like the sudden kindling in his cheek, was but febrile and transient.

Ere long, with a joyless mien, looking up towards the poop, the host invited his guest to accompany him there, for the benefit of what little breath of wind might be stirring.

As during the telling of the story, Captain Delano had once or twice started at the occasional cymballing of the hatchet-polishers, wondering why such an interruption should be al-lowed, especially in that part of the ship, and in the ears of an invalid; and moreover, as the hatchets had anything but an attractive look, and the handlers of them still less so, it was, therefore, to tell the truth, not without some lurking reluc-tance, or even shrinking, it may be, that Captain Delano, with apparent complaisance, acquiesced in his host's invitation. The more so, since with an untimely caprice of punctilio, ren-dered distressing by his cadaverous aspect, Don Benito, with Castilian bows, solemnly insisted upon his guest's preceding him up the ladder leading to the elevation; where, one on each side of the last step, sat for armorial supporters and sen-tries two of the ominous file. Gingerly enough stepped good Captain Delano between them, and in the instant of leaving them behind, like one running the gauntlet, he felt an appre-hensive twitch in the calves of his legs.

But when, facing about, he saw the whole file, like so many organ-grinders, still stupidly intent on their work, unmindful of everything beside, he could not but smile at his late fidgeting panic.

Presently, while standing with his host, looking forward upon the decks below, he was struck by one of those instances of insubordination previously alluded to. Three black boys, with two Spanish boys, were sitting together on the hatches, scraping a rude wooden platter, in which some scanty mess had recently been cooked. Suddenly, one of the black boys, enraged at a word dropped by one of his white companions, seized a knife, and though called to forbear by one of the oakum-pickers, struck the lad over the head, inflicting a gash from which blood flowed.

In amazement, Captain Delano inquired what this meant. To which the pale Don Benito dully muttered, that it was merely the sport of the lad.

"Pretty serious sport, truly," rejoined Captain Delano. "Had such a thing happened on board the Bachelor's Delight, instant punishment would have followed."

At these words the Spaniard turned upon the American one of his sudden, staring, half-lunatic looks; then relapsing into his torpor, answered, "Doubtless, doubtless, Señor."

Is it, thought Captain Delano, that this hapless man is one of those paper captains I've known, who by policy wink at what by power they cannot put down? I know no sadder sight than a commander who has little of command but the name.

"I should think, Don Benito," he now said, glancing towards the oakum-picker who had sought to interfere with the boys, "that you would find it advantageous to keep all your blacks employed, especially the younger ones, no matter at what useless task, and no matter what happens to the ship. Why, even with my little band, I find such a course indispensable. I once kept a crew on my quarter-deck thrumming mats for my cabin, when, for three days, I had given up my ship—mats, men, and all—for a speedy loss, owing to the violence of a gale, in which we could do nothing but helplessly drive before it."

"Doubtless, doubtless," muttered Don Benito.

"But," continued Captain Delano, again glancing upon the oakum-pickers and then at the hatchet-polishers, near by, "I see you keep some at least of your host employed."

"Yes," was again the vacant response.

"Those old men there, shaking their pows from their pulpits," continued Captain Delano, pointing to the oakum-pickers, "seem to act the part of old dominies to the rest, little heeded as their admonitions are at times. Is this voluntary on their part, Don Benito, or have you appointed them shepherds to your flock of black sheep?"

"What posts they fill, I appointed them," rejoined the Spaniard, in an acrid tone, as if resenting some supposed satiric reflection.

"And these others, these Ashantee conjurors here," continued Captain Delano, rather uneasily eying the brandished steel of the hatchet-polishers, where in spots it had been brought to a shine, "this seems a curious business they are at, Don Benito?"

"In the gales we met," answered the Spaniard, "what of our general cargo was not thrown overboard was much damaged by the brine. Since coming into calm weather, I have had several cases of knives and hatchets daily brought up for overhauling and cleaning."

"A prudent idea, Don Benito. You are part owner of ship and cargo, I presume; but not of the slaves, perhaps?"

"I am owner of all you see," impatiently returned Don Benito, "except the main company of blacks, who belonged to my late friend, Alexandro Aranda."

As he mentioned this name, his air was heart-broken; his knees shook: his servant supported him.

Thinking he divined the cause of such unusual emotion, to confirm his surmise, Captain Delano, after a pause, said, "And may I ask, Don Benito, whether—since awhile ago you spoke of some cabin passengers—the friend, whose loss so afflicts you at the outset of the voyage accompanied his blacks?"

"Yes."

"But died of the fever?"

"Died of the fever.—Oh, could I but——"

Again quivering, the Spaniard paused.

"Pardon me," said Captain Delano lowly, "but I think that, by a sympathetic experience, I conjecture, Don Benito, what it is that gives the keener edge to your grief. It was once my hard fortune to lose at sea a dear friend, my own brother, then supercargo. Assured of the welfare of his spirit, its departure I could have borne like a man; but that honest eye, that honest hand—both of which had so often met mine— and that warm heart; all, all—like scraps to the dogs—to throw all to the sharks! It was then I vowed never to have for fellow-voyager a man I loved, unless, unbeknown to him, I had provided every requisite, in case of a fatality, for embalming his mortal part for interment on shore. Were your friend's remains now on board this ship, Don Benito, not thus strangely would the mention of his name affect you."

"On board this ship?" echoed the Spaniard. Then, with horrified gestures, as directed against some specter, he unconsciously fell into the ready arms of his attendant, who, with a silent appeal toward Captain Delano, seemed beseeching him not again to broach a theme so unspeakably distressing to his master.

This poor fellow now, thought the pained American, is the victim of that sad superstition which associates goblins with the deserted body of man, as ghosts with an abandoned house. How unlike are we made! What to me, in like case, would have been a solemn satisfaction, the bare suggestion, even, terrifies the Spaniard into this trance. Poor Alexandro Aranda! what would you say could you here see your friend—who, on former voyages, when you for months were left behind, has, I dare say, often longed, and longed, for one peep at you—now transported with terror at the least thought of having you anyway nigh him.

At this moment, with a dreary grave-yard toll, betokening a flaw, the ship's forecastle bell, smote by one of the grizzled oakum-pickers, proclaimed ten o'clock through the leaden calm; when Captain Delano's attention was caught by the moving figure of a gigantic black, emerging from the general crowd below, and slowly advancing towards the elevated poop. An iron collar was about his neck, from which depended a chain, thrice wound round his body; the terminating links padlocked together at a broad band of iron, his girdle.

"How like a mute Atufal moves," murmured the servant.

The black mounted the steps of the poop, and, like a brave prisoner, brought up to receive sentence, stood in unquailing muteness before Don Benito, now recovered from his attack.

At the first glimpse of his approach, Don Benito had started, a resentful shadow swept over his face; and, as with the sudden memory of bootless rage, his white lips glued together.

This is some mulish mutineer, thought Captain Delano, surveying, not without a mixture of admiration, the colossal form of the negro.

"See, he waits your question, master," said the servant.

Thus reminded, Don Benito, nervously averting his glance, as if shunning, by anticipation, some rebellious response, in a disconcerted voice, thus spoke:—

"Atufal, will you ask my pardon now?"

The black was silent.

"Again, master," murmured the servant, with bitter upbraiding eying his countryman, "Again, master; he will bend to master yet."

"Answer," said Don Benito, still averting his glance, "say but the one word *pardon*, and your chains shall be off."

Upon this, the black, slowly raising both arms, let them lifelessly fall, his links clanking, his head bowed; as much as to say, "no, I am content."

"Go," said Don Benito, with inkept and unknown emotion.

Deliberately as he had come, the black obeyed.

"Excuse me, Don Benito," said Captain Delano, "but this scene surprises me; what means it, pray?"

"It means that that negro alone, of all the band, has given me peculiar cause of offense. I have put him in chains; I——"

Here he paused; his hand to his head, as if there were a swimming there, or a sudden bewilderment of memory had come over him; but meeting his servant's kindly glance seemed reassured, and proceeded:—

"I could not scourge such a form. But I told him he must ask my pardon. As yet he has not. At my command, every two hours he stands before me."

"And how long has this been?"

"Some sixty days."

"And obedient in all else? And respectful?"

"Yes."

"Upon my conscience, then," exclaimed Captain Delano, impulsively, "he has a royal spirit in him, this fellow."

"He may have some right to it," bitterly returned Don Benito, "he says he was king in his own land."

"Yes," said the servant, entering a word, "those slits in Atufal's ears once held wedges of gold; but poor Babo here, in his own land, was only a poor slave; a black man's slave was Babo, who now is the white's."

Somewhat annoyed by these conversational familiarities, Captain Delano turned curiously upon the attendant, then glanced inquiringly at his master; but, as if long wonted to these little informalities, neither master nor man seemed to understand him.

"What, pray, was Atufal's offense, Don Benito?" asked Captain Delano; "if it was not something very serious, take a fool's advice, and, in view of his general docility, as well as in some natural respect for his spirit, remit him his penalty."

"No, no, master never will do that," here murmured the servant to himself, "proud Atufal must first ask master's pardon. The slave there carries the padlock, but master here carries the key."

His attention thus directed, Captain Delano now noticed for the first time that, suspended by a slender silken cord, from Don Benito's neck hung a key. At once, from the servant's muttered syllables divining the key's purpose, he smiled and said:—"So, Don Benito—padlock and key—significant symbols, truly."

Biting his lip, Don Benito faltered.

Though the remark of Captain Delano, a man of such native simplicity as to be incapable of satire or irony, had been dropped in playful allusion to the Spaniard's singularly evidenced lordship over the black; yet the hypochondriac seemed in some way to have taken it as a malicious reflection upon his confessed inability thus far to break down, at least, on a verbal summons, the entrenched will of the slave. Deploring this supposed misconception, yet despairing of correcting it, Captain Delano shifted the subject; but finding his companion more than ever withdrawn, as if still sourly digesting the lees of the presumed affront above-mentioned, by-and-by Captain Delano likewise became less talkative, oppressed, against his own will, by what seemed the secret vindictiveness of the morbidly sensitive Spaniard. But the good sailor himself, of a quite contrary disposition, refrained, on his part, alike from the appearance as from the feeling of resentment, and if silent, was only so from contagion.

Presently the Spaniard, assisted by his servant, somewhat discourteously crossed over from his guest; a procedure which, sensibly enough, might have been allowed to pass for idle caprice of ill-humor, had not master and man, lingering round the corner of the elevated skylight, began whispering together in low voices. This was unpleasing. And more: the moody air of the Spaniard, which at times had not been without a sort of valetudinarian stateliness, now seemed anything but dignified; while the menial familiarity of the servant lost its original charm of simple-hearted attachment.

In his embarrassment, the visitor turned his face to the other side of the ship. By so doing, his glance accidentally fell on a young Spanish sailor, a coil of rope in his hand, just stepped from the deck to the first round of the mizzen-rigging. Perhaps the man would not have been particularly noticed, were it not that, during his ascent to one of the yards, he, with a sort of covert intentness, kept his eye fixed on Captain Delano, from whom, presently, it passed, as if by a natural sequence, to the two whisperers.

His own attention thus redirected to that quarter, Captain Delano gave a slight start. From something in Don Benito's manner just then, it seemed as if the visitor had, at least partly, been the subject of the withdrawn consultation going on—a conjecture as little agreeable to the guest as it was little flattering to the host.

The singular alternations of courtesy and ill-breeding in the Spanish captain were unaccountable, except on one of two suppositions—innocent lunacy, or wicked imposture.

But the first idea, though it might naturally have occurred to an indifferent observer, and, in some respect, had not hitherto been wholly a stranger to Captain Delano's mind, yet, now that, in an incipient way, he began to regard the stranger's conduct something in the light of an intentional affront, of course the idea of lunacy was virtually vacated. But if not a lunatic, what then? Under the circumstances, would a gentleman, nay, any honest boor, act the part now acted by his host? The man was an impostor. Some low-born adventurer, masquerading as an oceanic grandee; yet so ignorant of the first requisites of mere gentlemanhood as to be betrayed into the present remarkable indecorum. That strange ceremoniousness, too, at other times evinced, seemed not uncharacteristic of one playing a part above his real level. Benito Cereno—Don Benito Cereno—a sounding name. One, too, at that period, not unknown, in the surname, to supercargoes and sea captains trading along the Spanish Main, as belonging to one of the most enterprising and extensive mercantile families in all those provinces; several members of it having titles; a sort of Castilian Rothschild, with a noble brother, or cousin, in every great trading town of South America. The alleged Don Benito was in early manhood, about twenty-nine or thirty. To assume a sort of roving cadetship in the maritime affairs of such a house, what more likely scheme for a young knave of talent and spirit? But the Spaniard was a pale invalid. Never mind. For even to the degree of simulating mortal disease, the craft of some tricksters had been known to attain. To think that, under the aspect of infantile weakness, the most savage energies might be couched—those velvets of the Spaniard but the silky paw to his fangs.

From no train of thought did these fancies come; not from within, but from without; suddenly, too, and in one throng, like hoar frost; yet as soon to vanish as the mild sun of Captain Delano's good-nature regained its meridian.

Glancing over once more towards his host—whose sideface, revealed above the skylight, was now turned towards him—he was struck by the profile, whose clearness of cut was refined by the thinness incident to ill-health, as well as ennobled about the chin by the beard. Away with suspicion. He was a true off-shoot of a true hidalgo Cereno.

Relieved by these and other better thoughts, the visitor, lightly humming a tune, now began indifferently pacing the poop, so as not to betray to Don Benito that he had at all mistrusted incivility, much less duplicity; for such mistrust would yet be proved illusory, and by the event; though, for the present, the circumstance which had provoked that distrust remained unexplained. But when that little mystery should have been cleared up, Captain Delano thought he might extremely regret it, did he allow Don Benito to become aware that he had indulged in ungenerous surmises. In short, to the Spaniard's black-letter text, it was best, for awhile, to leave open margin.

Presently, his pale face twitching and overcast, the Spaniard, still supported by his attendant, moved over towards his guest, when, with even more than his usual embarrassment, and a strange sort of intriguing intonation in his husky whisper, the following conversation began:—

"Señor, may I ask how long you have lain at this isle?"

"Oh, but a day or two, Don Benito."

"And from what port are you last?"

"Canton."

"And there, Señor, you exchanged your seal-skins for teas and silks, I think you said?"

"Yes. Silks, mostly."

"And the balance you took in specie, perhaps?"

Captain Delano, fidgeting a little, answered—

"Yes; some silver; not a very great deal, though."

"Ah—well. May I ask how many men have you, Señor?"

Captain Delano slightly started, but answered—

"About five-and-twenty, all told."

"And at present, Señor, all on board, I suppose?"

"All on board, Don Benito," replied the Captain, now with satisfaction.

"And will be to-night, Señor?"

At this last question, following so many pertinacious ones, for the soul of him Captain Delano could not but look very earnestly at the questioner, who, instead of meeting the glance, with every token of craven discomposure dropped his eyes to the deck; presenting an unworthy contrast to his servant, who, just then, was kneeling at his feet, adjusting a loose shoe-buckle; his disengaged face meantime, with humble curiosity, turned openly up into his master's downcast one.

The Spaniard, still with a guilty shuffle, repeated his question:—

"And—and will be to-night, Señor?"

"Yes, for aught I know," returned Captain Delano,—"but

nay," rallying himself into fearless truth, "some of them talked
of going off on another fishing party about midnight."

"Your ships generally go—go more or less armed, I believe, Señor?"

"Oh, a six-pounder or two, in case of emergency," was the
intrepidly indifferent reply, " with a small stock of muskets,
sealing-spears, and cutlasses, you know."

As he thus responded, Captain Delano again glanced at
Don Benito, but the latter's eyes were averted; while abruptly
and awkwardly shifting the subject, he made some peevish
allusion to the calm, and then, without apology, once more,
with his attendant, withdrew to the opposite bulwarks, where
the whispering was resumed.

At this moment, and ere Captain Delano could cast a cool
thought upon what had just passed, the young Spanish sailor
before mentioned was seen descending from the rigging. In
act of stooping over to spring inboard to the deck, his voluminous, unconfined frock, or shirt, of coarse woollen, much
spotted with tar, opened out far down the chest, revealing a
soiled under garment of what seemed the finest linen, edged,
about the neck, with a narrow blue ribbon, sadly faded and
worn. At this moment the young sailor's eye was again fixed
on the whisperers, and Captain Delano thought he observed
a lurking significance in it, as if silent signs of some Free-
mason sort had that instant been interchanged.

This once more impelled his own glance in the direction of
Don Benito, and, as before, he could not but infer that himself formed the subject of the conference. He paused. The
sound of the hatchet-polishing fell on his ears. He cast another swift side-look at the two. They had the air of conspir-
ators. In connection with the late questionings and the
incident of the young sailor, these things now begat such return of involuntary suspicion, that the singular guilelessness
of the American could not endure it. Plucking up a gay and
humorous expression, he crossed over to the two rapidly, saying:—"Ha, Don Benito, your black here seems high in your
trust; a sort of privy-counselor, in fact."

Upon this, the servant looked up with a good-natured grin,
but the master started as from a venomous bite. It was a moment or two before the Spaniard sufficiently recovered him-

self to reply; which he did, at last, with cold constraint:—
"Yes, Señor, I have trust in Babo."

Here Babo, changing his previous grin of mere animal humor into an intelligent smile, not ungratefully eyed his master.

Finding that the Spaniard now stood silent and reserved, as if involuntarily, or purposely giving hint that his guest's proximity was inconvenient just then, Captain Delano, unwilling to appear uncivil even to incivility itself, made some trivial remark and moved off; again and again turning over in his mind the mysterious demeanor of Don Benito Cereno.

He had descended from the poop, and, wrapped in thought, was passing near a dark hatchway, leading down into the steerage, when, perceiving motion there, he looked to see what moved. The same instant there was a sparkle in the shadowy hatchway, and he saw one of the Spanish sailors prowling there hurriedly placing his hand in the bosom of his frock, as if hiding something. Before the man could have been certain who it was that was passing, he slunk below out of sight. But enough was seen of him to make it sure that he was the same young sailor before noticed in the rigging.

What was that which so sparkled? thought Captain Delano. It was no lamp—no match—no live coal. Could it have been a jewel? But how come sailors with jewels?—or with silk-trimmed under-shirts either? Has he been robbing the trunks of the dead cabin passengers? But if so, he would hardly wear one of the stolen articles on board ship here. Ah, ah—if now that was, indeed, a secret sign I saw passing between this suspicious fellow and his captain awhile since; if I could only be certain that in my uneasiness my senses did not deceive me, then——

Here, passing from one suspicious thing to another, his mind revolved the point of the strange questions put to him concerning his ship.

By a curious coincidence, as each point was recalled, the black wizards of Ashantee would strike up with their hatchets, as in ominous comment on the white stranger's thoughts. Pressed by such enigmas and portents, it would have been almost against nature, had not, even into the least distrustful heart, some ugly misgivings obtruded.

Observing the ship now helplessly fallen into a current, with enchanted sails, drifting with increased rapidity seaward; and noting that, from a lately intercepted projection of the land, the sealer was hidden, the stout mariner began to quake at thoughts which he barely durst confess to himself. Above all, he began to feel a ghostly dread of Don Benito. And yet when he roused himself, dilated his chest, felt himself strong on his legs, and coolly considered it—what did all these phantoms amount to?

Had the Spaniard any sinister scheme, it must have reference not so much to him (Captain Delano) as to his ship (the Bachelor's Delight). Hence the present drifting away of the one ship from the other, instead of favoring any such possible scheme, was, for the time at least, opposed to it. Clearly any suspicion, combining such contradictions, must need be delusive. Beside, was it not absurd to think of a vessel in distress—a vessel by sickness almost dismanned of her crew—a vessel whose inmates were parched for water—was it not a thousand times absurd that such a craft should, at present, be of a piratical character; or her commander, either for himself or those under him, cherish any desire but for speedy relief and refreshment? But then, might not general distress, and thirst in particular, be affected? And might not that same undiminished Spanish crew, alleged to have perished off to a remnant, be at that very moment lurking in the hold? On heart-broken pretense of entreating a cup of cold water, fiends in human form had got into lonely dwellings, nor retired until a dark deed had been done. And among the Malay pirates, it was no unusual thing to lure ships after them into their treacherous harbors, or entice boarders from a declared enemy at sea, by the spectacle of thinly manned or vacant decks, beneath which prowled a hundred spears with yellow arms ready to upthrust them through the mats. Not that Captain Delano had entirely credited such things. He had heard of them—and now, as stories, they recurred. The present destination of the ship was the anchorage. There she would be near his own vessel. Upon gaining that vicinity, might not the San Dominick, like a slumbering volcano, suddenly let loose energies now hid?

He recalled the Spaniard's manner while telling his story.

There was a gloomy hesitancy and subterfuge about it. It was just the manner of one making up his tale for evil purposes, as he goes. But if that story was not true, what was the truth? That the ship had unlawfully come into the Spaniard's possession? But in many of its details, especially in reference to the more calamitous parts, such as the fatalities among the seamen, the consequent prolonged beating about, the past sufferings from obstinate calms, and still continued suffering from thirst; in all these points, as well as others, Don Benito's story had corroborated not only the wailing ejaculations of the indiscriminate multitude, white and black, but likewise—what seemed impossible to be counterfeit—by the very expression and play of every human feature, which Captain Delano saw. If Don Benito's story was throughout an invention, then every soul on board, down to the youngest negress, was his carefully drilled recruit in the plot: an incredible inference. And yet, if there was ground for mistrusting his veracity, that inference was a legitimate one.

But those questions of the Spaniard. There, indeed, one might pause. Did they not seem put with much the same object with which the burglar or assassin, by day-time, reconnoitres the walls of a house? But, with ill purposes, to solicit such information openly of the chief person endangered, and so, in effect, setting him on his guard; how unlikely a procedure was that? Absurd, then, to suppose that those questions had been prompted by evil designs. Thus, the same conduct, which, in this instance, had raised the alarm, served to dispel it. In short, scarce any suspicion or uneasiness, however apparently reasonable at the time, which was not now, with equal apparent reason, dismissed.

At last he began to laugh at his former forebodings; and laugh at the strange ship for, in its aspect someway siding with them, as it were; and laugh, too, at the odd-looking blacks, particularly those old scissors-grinders, the Ashantees; and those bed-ridden old knitting-women, the oakum-pickers; and almost at the dark Spaniard himself, the central hobgoblin of all.

For the rest, whatever in a serious way seemed enigmatical, was now good-naturedly explained away by the thought that, for the most part, the poor invalid scarcely knew what he was about; either sulking in black vapors, or putting idle questions without sense or object. Evidently, for the present, the man was not fit to be entrusted with the ship. On some benevolent plea withdrawing the command from him, Captain Delano would yet have to send her to Conception, in charge of his second mate, a worthy person and good navigator—a plan not more convenient for the San Dominick than for Don Benito; for, relieved from all anxiety, keeping wholly to his cabin, the sick man, under the good nursing of his servant, would probably, by the end of the passage, be in a measure restored to health, and with that he should also be restored to authority.

Such were the American's thoughts. They were tranquilizing. There was a difference between the idea of Don Benito's darkly pre-ordaining Captain Delano's fate, and Captain Delano's lightly arranging Don Benito's. Nevertheless, it was not without something of relief that the good seaman presently perceived his whale-boat in the distance. Its absence had been prolonged by unexpected detention at the sealer's side, as well as its returning trip lengthened by the continual recession of the goal.

The advancing speck was observed by the blacks. Their shouts attracted the attention of Don Benito, who, with a return of courtesy, approaching Captain Delano, expressed satisfaction at the coming of some supplies, slight and temporary as they must necessarily prove.

Captain Delano responded; but while doing so, his attention was drawn to something passing on the deck below: among the crowd climbing the landward bulwarks, anxiously watching the coming boat, two blacks, to all appearances accidentally incommoded by one of the sailors, flew out against him with horrible curses, which the sailor someway resenting, the two blacks dashed him to the deck and jumped upon him, despite the earnest cries of the oakum-pickers.

"Don Benito," said Captain Delano quickly, "do you see what is going on there? Look!"

But, seized by his cough, the Spaniard staggered, with both hands to his face, on the point of falling. Captain Delano would have supported him, but the servant was more alert, who, with one hand sustaining his master, with the other applied the cordial. Don Benito restored, the black withdrew his support, slipping aside a little, but dutifully remaining within call of a whisper. Such discretion was here evinced as quite wiped away, in the visitor's eyes, any blemish of impropriety which might have attached to the attendant, from the indecorous conferences before mentioned; showing, too, that if the servant were to blame, it might be more the master's fault than his own, since when left to himself he could conduct thus well.

His glance thus called away from the spectacle of disorder to the more pleasing one before him, Captain Delano could not avoid again congratulating his host upon possessing such a servant, who, though perhaps a little too forward now and then, must upon the whole be invaluable to one in the invalid's situation.

"Tell me, Don Benito," he added, with a smile—"I should like to have your man here myself—what will you take for him? Would fifty doubloons be any object?"

"Master wouldn't part with Babo for a thousand doubloons," murmured the black, overhearing the offer, and taking it in earnest, and, with the strange vanity of a faithful slave appreciated by his master, scorning to hear so paltry a valuation put upon him by a stranger. But Don Benito, apparently hardly yet completely restored, and again interrupted by his cough, made but some broken reply.

Soon his physical distress became so great, affecting his mind, too, apparently, that, as if to screen the sad spectacle, the servant gently conducted his master below.

Left to himself, the American, to while away the time till his boat should arrive, would have pleasantly accosted some one of the few Spanish seamen he saw; but recalling something that Don Benito had said touching their ill conduct, he refrained, as a ship-master indisposed to countenance cowardice or unfaithfulness in seamen.

While, with these thoughts, standing with eye directed forward towards that handful of sailors, suddenly he thought that one or two of them returned the glance and with a sort of meaning. He rubbed his eyes, and looked again; but again seemed to see the same thing. Under a new form, but more obscure than any previous one, the old suspicions recurred,

but, in the absence of Don Benito, with less of panic than
before. Despite the bad account given of the sailors, Captain
Delano resolved forthwith to accost one of them. Descending
the poop, he made his way through the blacks, his movement
drawing a queer cry from the oakum-pickers, prompted by
whom, the negroes, twitching each other aside, divided before him; but, as if curious to see what was the object of this
deliberate visit to their Ghetto, closing in behind, in tolerable
order, followed the white stranger up. His progress thus proclaimed as by mounted kings-at-arms, and escorted as by a
Caffre guard of honor, Captain Delano, assuming a good humored, off-handed air, continued to advance; now and then
saying a blithe word to the negroes, and his eye curiously
surveying the white faces, here and there sparsely mixed in
with the blacks, like stray white pawns venturously involved
in the ranks of the chess-men opposed.

While thinking which of them to select for his purpose, he
chanced to observe a sailor seated on the deck engaged in
tarring the strap of a large block, with a circle of blacks squat-
ted round him inquisitively eying the process.

The mean employment of the man was in contrast with
something superior in his figure. His hand, black with continually thrusting it into the tar-pot held for him by a negro,
seemed not naturally allied to his face, a face which would
have been a very fine one but for its haggardness. Whether
this haggardness had aught to do with criminality, could not
be determined; since, as intense heat and cold, though unlike,
produce like sensations, so innocence and guilt, when,
through casual association with mental pain, stamping any
visible impress, use one seal—a hacked one.

Not again that this reflection occurred to Captain Delano
at the time, charitable man as he was. Rather another idea.
Because observing so singular a haggardness combined with
a dark eye, averted as in trouble and shame, and then again
recalling Don Benito's confessed ill opinion of his crew, insensibly he was operated upon by certain general notions
which, while disconnecting pain and abashment from virtue,
invariably link them with vice.

If, indeed, there be any wickedness on board this ship,
thought Captain Delano, be sure that man there has fouled

his hand in it, even as now he fouls it in the pitch. I don't like to accost him. I will speak to this other, this old Jack here on the windlass.

He advanced to an old Barcelona tar, in ragged red breeches and dirty night-cap, cheeks trenched and bronzed, whiskers dense as thorn hedges. Seated between two sleepy-looking Africans, this mariner, like his younger shipmate, was employed upon some rigging—splicing a cable—the sleepy-looking blacks performing the inferior function of holding the outer parts of the ropes for him.

Upon Captain Delano's approach, the man at once hung his head below its previous level; the one necessary for business. It appeared as if he desired to be thought absorbed, with more than common fidelity, in his task. Being addressed, he glanced up, but with what seemed a furtive, diffident air, which sat strangely enough on his weather-beaten visage, much as if a grizzly bear, instead of growling and biting, should simper and cast sheep's eyes. He was asked several questions concerning the voyage, questions purposely referring to several particulars in Don Benito's narrative, not previously corroborated by those impulsive cries greeting the visitor on first coming on board. The questions were briefly answered, confirming all that remained to be confirmed of the story. The negroes about the windlass joined in with the old sailor, but, as they became talkative, he by degrees became mute, and at length quite glum, seemed morosely unwilling to answer more questions, and yet, all the while, this ursine air was somehow mixed with his sheepish one.

Despairing of getting into unembarrassed talk with such a centaur, Captain Delano, after glancing round for a more promising countenance, but seeing none, spoke pleasantly to the blacks to make way for him; and so, amid various grins and grimaces, returned to the poop, feeling a little strange at first, he could hardly tell why, but upon the whole with regained confidence in Benito Cereno.

How plainly, thought he, did that old whiskerando yonder betray a consciousness of ill-desert. No doubt, when he saw me coming, he dreaded lest I, apprised by his Captain of the crew's general misbehavior, came with sharp words for him, and so down with his head. And yet—and yet, now that I think of it, that very old fellow, if I err not, was one of those who seemed so earnestly eying me here awhile since. Ah, these currents spin one's head round almost as much as they do the ship. Ha, there now 's a pleasant sort of sunny sight; quite sociable, too.

His attention had been drawn to a slumbering negress, partly disclosed through the lace-work of some rigging, lying, with youthful limbs carelessly disposed, under the lee of the bulwarks, like a doe in the shade of a woodland rock. Sprawling at her lapped breasts was her wide-awake fawn, stark naked, its black little body half lifted from the deck, crosswise with its dam's; its hands, like two paws, clambering upon her; its mouth and nose ineffectually rooting to get at the mark; and meantime giving a vexatious half-grunt, blending with the composed snore of the negress.

The uncommon vigor of the child at length roused the mother. She started up, at a distance facing Captain Delano. But as if not at all concerned at the attitude in which she had been caught, delightedly she caught the child up, with maternal transports, covering it with kisses.

There's naked nature, now; pure tenderness and love, thought Captain Delano, well pleased.

This incident prompted him to remark the other negresses more particularly than before. He was gratified with their manners; like most uncivilized women, they seemed at once tender of heart and tough of constitution; equally ready to die for their infants or fight for them. Unsophisticated as leopardesses; loving as doves. Ah! thought Captain Delano, these perhaps are some of the very women whom Mungo Park saw in Africa, and gave such a noble account of.

These natural sights somehow insensibly deepened his confidence and ease. At last he looked to see how his boat was getting on; but it was still pretty remote. He turned to see if Don Benito had returned; but he had not.

To change the scene, as well as to please himself with a leisurely observation of the coming boat, stepping over into the mizzen-chains he clambered his way into the starboard quarter-gallery; one of those abandoned Venetian-looking water-balconies previously mentioned; retreats cut off from the deck. As his foot pressed the half-damp, half-dry sea-mosses matting the place, and a chance phantom cats-paw—an islet of breeze, unheralded, unfollowed—as this ghostly cats-paw came fanning his cheek, as his glance fell upon the row of small, round dead-lights, all closed like coppered eyes of the coffined, and the state-cabin door, once connecting with the gallery, even as the dead-lights had once looked out upon it, but now calked fast like a sarcophagus lid, to a purple-black, tarred-over panel, threshold, and post; and he bethought him of the time, when that state-cabin and this state-balcony had heard the voices of the Spanish king's officers, and the forms of the Lima viceroy's daughters had perhaps leaned where he stood—as these and other images flitted through his mind, as the cats-paw through the calm, gradually he felt rising a dreamy inquietude, like that of one who alone on the prairie feels unrest from the repose of the noon.

He leaned against the carved balustrade, again looking off toward his boat; but found his eye falling upon the ribbon grass, trailing along the ship's water-line, straight as a border of green box; and parterres of sea-weed, broad ovals and crescents, floating nigh and far, with what seemed long formal alleys between, crossing the terraces of swells, and sweeping round as if leading to the grottoes below. And overhanging all was the balustrade by his arm, which, partly stained with pitch and partly embossed with moss, seemed the charred ruin of some summer-house in a grand garden long running to waste.

Trying to break one charm, he was but becharmed anew. Though upon the wide sea, he seemed in some far inland country; prisoner in some deserted château, left to stare at empty grounds, and peer out at vague roads, where never wagon or wayfarer passed.

But these enchantments were a little disenchanted as his eye fell on the corroded main-chains. Of an ancient style, massy and rusty in link, shackle and bolt, they seemed even more fit for the ship's present business than the one for which probably she had been built.

Presently he thought something moved nigh the chains. He rubbed his eyes, and looked hard. Groves of rigging were about the chains; and there, peering from behind a great stay, like an Indian from behind a hemlock, a Spanish sailor, a marlingspike in his hand, was seen, who made what seemed an imperfect gesture towards the balcony, but immediately, as if alarmed by some advancing step along the deck within, vanished into the recesses of the hempen forest, like a poacher.

What meant this? Something the man had sought to communicate, unbeknown to any one, even to his captain. Did the secret involve aught unfavorable to his captain? Were those previous misgivings of Captain Delano's about to be verified? Or, in his haunted mood at the moment, had some random, unintentional motion of the man, while busy with the stay, as if repairing it, been mistaken for a significant beckoning?

Not unbewildered, again he gazed off for his boat. But it was temporarily hidden by a rocky spur of the isle. As with some eagerness he bent forward, watching for the first shooting view of its beak, the balustrade gave way before him like charcoal. Had he not clutched an outreaching rope he would have fallen into the sea. The crash, though feeble, and the fall, though hollow, of the rotten fragments, must have been overheard. He glanced up. With sober curiosity peering down upon him was one of the old oakum-pickers, slipped from his perch to an outside boom; while below the old negro, and, invisible to him, reconnoitering from a port-hole like a fox from the mouth of its den, crouched the Spanish sailor again. From something suddenly suggested by the man's air, the mad idea now darted into Captain Delano's mind, that Don Benito's plea of indisposition, in withdrawing below, was but a pretense: that he was engaged there maturing some plot, of which the sailor, by some means gaining an inkling, had a mind to warn the stranger against; incited, it may be, by gratitude for a kind word on first boarding the ship. Was it from foreseeing some possible interference like this, that Don Benito had, beforehand, given such a bad character of his sailors, while praising the negroes; though, indeed, the former seemed as docile as the latter the contrary? The whites, too, by nature, were the shrewder race. A man with some evil design, would he not be likely to speak well of that stupidity which was blind to his depravity, and malign that intelligence from which it might not be hidden? Not unlikely, perhaps. But if the whites had dark secrets concerning Don Benito, could then Don Benito be any way in complicity with the blacks? But they were too stupid. Besides, who ever heard of a white so far a renegade as to apostatize from his very species almost, by leaguing in against it with negroes? These difficulties recalled former ones. Lost in their mazes, Captain Delano, who had now regained the deck, was uneasily advancing along it, when he observed a new face; an aged sailor seated cross-legged near the main hatchway. His skin was shrunk up with wrinkles like a pelican's empty pouch; his hair frosted; his countenance grave and composed. His hands were full of ropes, which he was working into a large knot. Some blacks were about him obligingly dipping the strands for him, here and there, as the exigencies of the operation demanded.

Captain Delano crossed over to him, and stood in silence surveying the knot; his mind, by a not uncongenial transition, passing from its own entanglements to those of the hemp. For intricacy such a knot he had never seen in an American ship, or indeed any other. The old man looked like an Egyptian priest, making gordian knots for the temple of Ammon. The knot seemed a combination of double-bowline-knot, treble-crown-knot, back-handed-well-knot, knot-in-and-out-knot, and jamming-knot.

At last, puzzled to comprehend the meaning of such a knot, Captain Delano addressed the knotter:—

"What are you knotting there, my man?"

"The knot," was the brief reply, without looking up.

"So it seems; but what is it for?"

"For some one else to undo," muttered back the old man, plying his fingers harder than ever, the knot being now nearly completed.

While Captain Delano stood watching him, suddenly the old man threw the knot towards him, saying in broken English,—the first heard in the ship,—something to this effect—"Undo it, cut it, quick." It was said lowly, but with such condensation of rapidity, that the long, slow words in Spanish, which had preceded and followed, almost operated as covers to the brief English between.

For a moment, knot in hand, and knot in head, Captain Delano stood mute; while, without further heeding him, the old man was now intent upon other ropes. Presently there

was a slight stir behind Captain Delano. Turning, he saw the
chained negro, Atufal, standing quietly there. The next moment the old sailor rose, muttering, and, followed by his subordinate negroes, removed to the forward part of the ship,
where in the crowd he disappeared.

An elderly negro, in a clout like an infant's, and with a
pepper and salt head, and a kind of attorney air, now approached Captain Delano. In tolerable Spanish, and with a
good-natured, knowing wink, he informed him that the old
knotter was simple-witted, but harmless; often playing his old
tricks. The negro concluded by begging the knot, for of
course the stranger would not care to be troubled with it.
Unconsciously, it was handed to him. With a sort of congé,
the negro received it, and turning his back, ferreted into it
like a detective Custom House officer after smuggled laces.
Soon, with some African word, equivalent to pshaw, he
tossed the knot overboard.

All this is very queer now, thought Captain Delano, with a
qualmish sort of emotion; but as one feeling incipient sea-
sickness, he strove, by ignoring the symptoms, to get rid of
the malady. Once more he looked off for his boat. To his
delight, it was now again in view, leaving the rocky spur
astern.

The sensation here experienced, after at first relieving his
uneasiness, with unforeseen efficacy, soon began to remove it.
The less distant sight of that well-known boat—showing it,
not as before, half blended with the haze, but with outline
defined, so that its individuality, like a man's, was manifest;
that boat, Rover by name, which, though now in strange
seas, had often pressed the beach of Captain Delano's home,
and, brought to its threshold for repairs, had familiarly lain
there, as a Newfoundland dog; the sight of that household
boat evoked a thousand trustful associations, which, contrasted with previous suspicions, filled him not only with
lightsome confidence, but somehow with half humorous self-
reproaches at his former lack of it.

"What, I, Amasa Delano—Jack of the Beach, as they called
me when a lad—I, Amasa; the same that, duck-satchel in
hand, used to paddle along the waterside to the school-house
made from the old hulk;—I, little Jack of the Beach, that

used to go berrying with cousin Nat and the rest; I to be murdered here at the ends of the earth, on board a haunted pirate-ship by a horrible Spaniard?—Too nonsensical to think of! Who would murder Amasa Delano? His conscience is clean. There is some one above. Fie, fie, Jack of the Beach! you are a child indeed; a child of the second childhood, old boy; you are beginning to dote and drule, I'm afraid."

Light of heart and foot, he stepped aft, and there was met by Don Benito's servant, who, with a pleasing expression, responsive to his own present feelings, informed him that his master had recovered from the effects of his coughing fit, and had just ordered him to go present his compliments to his good guest, Don Amasa, and say that he (Don Benito) would soon have the happiness to rejoin him.

There now, do you mark that? again thought Captain Delano, walking the poop. What a donkey I was. This kind gentleman who here sends me his kind compliments, he, but ten minutes ago, dark-lantern in hand, was dodging round some old grind-stone in the hold, sharpening a hatchet for me, I thought. Well, well; these long calms have a morbid effect on the mind, I've often heard, though I never believed it before. Ha! glancing towards the boat; there's Rover; good dog; a white bone in her mouth. A pretty big bone though, seems to me.—What? Yes, she has fallen afoul of the bubbling tide-rip there. It sets her the other way, too, for the time. Patience.

It was now about noon, though, from the grayness of everything, it seemed to be getting towards dusk.

The calm was confirmed. In the far distance, away from the influence of land, the leaden ocean seemed laid out and leaded up, its course finished, soul gone, defunct. But the current from landward, where the ship was, increased; silently sweeping her further and further towards the tranced waters beyond.

Still, from his knowledge of those latitudes, cherishing hopes of a breeze, and a fair and fresh one, at any moment, Captain Delano, despite present prospects, buoyantly counted upon bringing the San Dominick safely to anchor ere night. The distance swept over was nothing; since, with a good wind, ten minutes' sailing would retrace more than sixty minutes' drifting. Meantime, one moment turning to mark

"Rover" fighting the tide-rip, and the next to see Don Benito approaching, he continued walking the poop.

Gradually he felt a vexation arising from the delay of his boat; this soon merged into uneasiness; and at last, his eye falling continually, as from a stage-box into the pit, upon the strange crowd before and below him, and by and by recognising there the face—now composed to indifference—of the Spanish sailor who had seemed to beckon from the main chains, something of his old trepidations returned.

Ah, thought he—gravely enough—this is like the ague: because it went off, it follows not that it won't come back.

Though ashamed of the relapse, he could not altogether subdue it; and so, exerting his good nature to the utmost, insensibly he came to a compromise.

Yes, this is a strange craft; a strange history, too, and strange folks on board. But—nothing more.

By way of keeping his mind out of mischief till the boat should arrive, he tried to occupy it with turning over and over, in a purely speculative sort of way, some lesser peculiarities of the captain and crew. Among others, four curious points recurred.

First, the affair of the Spanish lad assailed with a knife by the slave boy; an act winked at by Don Benito. Second, the tyranny in Don Benito's treatment of Atufal, the black; as if a child should lead a bull of the Nile by the ring in his nose. Third, the trampling of the sailor by the two negroes; a piece of insolence passed over without so much as a reprimand. Fourth, the cringing submission to their master of all the ship's underlings, mostly blacks; as if by the least inadvertence they feared to draw down his despotic displeasure.

Coupling these points, they seemed somewhat contradictory. But what then, thought Captain Delano, glancing towards his now nearing boat,—what then? Why, Don Benito is a very capricious commander. But he is not the first of the sort I have seen; though it's true he rather exceeds any other. But as a nation—continued he in his reveries—these Spaniards are all an odd set; the very word Spaniard has a curious, conspirator, Guy-Fawkish twang to it. And yet, I dare say, Spaniards in the main are as good folks as any in Duxbury, Massachusetts. Ah good! At last "Rover" has come.

As, with its welcome freight, the boat touched the side, the oakum-pickers, with venerable gestures, sought to restrain the blacks, who, at the sight of three gurried water-casks in its bottom, and a pile of wilted pumpkins in its bow, hung over the bulwarks in disorderly raptures.

Don Benito with his servant now appeared; his coming, perhaps, hastened by hearing the noise. Of him Captain Delano sought permission to serve out the water, so that all might share alike, and none injure themselves by unfair excess. But sensible, and, on Don Benito's account, kind as this offer was, it was received with what seemed impatience; as if aware that he lacked energy as a commander, Don Benito, with the true jealousy of weakness, resented as an affront any interference. So, at least, Captain Delano inferred.

In another moment the casks were being hoisted in, when some of the eager negroes accidentally jostled Captain Delano, where he stood by the gangway; so that, unmindful of Don Benito, yielding to the impulse of the moment, with good-natured authority he bade the blacks stand back; to enforce his words making use of a half-mirthful, half-menacing gesture. Instantly the blacks paused, just where they were, each negro and negress suspended in his or her posture, exactly as the word had found them—for a few seconds continuing so—while, as between the responsive posts of a telegraph, an unknown syllable ran from man to man among the perched oakum-pickers. While the visitor's attention was fixed by this scene, suddenly the hatchet-polishers half rose, and a rapid cry came from Don Benito.

Thinking that at the signal of the Spaniard he was about to be massacred, Captain Delano would have sprung for his boat, but paused, as the oakum-pickers, dropping down into the crowd with earnest exclamations, forced every white and every negro back, at the same moment, with gestures friendly and familiar, almost jocose, bidding him, in substance, not be a fool. Simultaneously the hatchet-polishers resumed their seats, quietly as so many tailors, and at once, as if nothing had happened, the work of hoisting in the casks was resumed, whites and blacks singing at the tackle.

Captain Delano glanced towards Don Benito. As he saw his meager form in the act of recovering itself from reclining in the servant's arms, into which the agitated invalid had fallen, he could not but marvel at the panic by which himself had been surprised on the darting supposition that such a commander, who upon a legitimate occasion, so trivial, too, as it now appeared, could lose all self-command, was, with energetic iniquity, going to bring about his murder.

The casks being on deck, Captain Delano was handed a number of jars and cups by one of the steward's aids, who, in the name of his captain, entreated him to do as he had proposed: dole out the water. He complied, with republican impartiality as to this republican element, which always seeks one level, serving the oldest white no better than the youngest black; excepting, indeed, poor Don Benito, whose condition, if not rank, demanded an extra allowance. To him, in the first place, Captain Delano presented a fair pitcher of the fluid; but, thirsting as he was for it, the Spaniard quaffed not a drop until after several grave bows and salutes. A reciprocation of courtesies which the sight-loving Africans hailed with clapping of hands.

Two of the less wilted pumpkins being reserved for the cabin table, the residue were minced up on the spot for the general regalement. But the soft bread, sugar, and bottled cider, Captain Delano would have given the whites alone, and in chief Don Benito; but the latter objected; which disinterestedness, on his part, not a little pleased the American; and so mouthfuls all around were given alike to whites and blacks; excepting one bottle of cider, which Babo insisted upon setting aside for his master.

Here it may be observed that as, on the first visit of the boat, the American had not permitted his men to board the ship, neither did he now; being unwilling to add to the confusion of the decks.

Not uninfluenced by the peculiar good humor at present prevailing, and for the time oblivious of any but benevolent thoughts, Captain Delano, who from recent indications counted upon a breeze within an hour or two at furthest, dispatched the boat back to the sealer with orders for all the hands that could be spared immediately to set about rafting casks to the watering-place and filling them. Likewise he bade word be carried to his chief officer, that if against present expectation the ship was not brought to anchor by sunset, he need be under no concern, for as there was to be a full moon that night, he (Captain Delano) would remain on board ready to play the pilot, come the wind soon or late.

As the two Captains stood together, observing the departing boat—the servant as it happened having just spied a spot on his master's velvet sleeve, and silently engaged rubbing it out—the American expressed his regrets that the San Dominick had no boats; none, at least, but the unseaworthy old hulk of the long-boat, which, warped as a camel's skeleton in the desert, and almost as bleached, lay pot-wise inverted amidships, one side a little tipped, furnishing a subterraneous sort of den for family groups of the blacks, mostly women and small children; who, squatting on old mats below, or perched above in the dark dome, on the elevated seats, were descried, some distance within, like a social circle of bats, sheltering in some friendly cave; at intervals, ebon flights of naked boys and girls, three or four years old, darting in and out of the den's mouth.

"Had you three or four boats now, Don Benito," said Captain Delano, "I think that, by tugging at the oars, your negroes here might help along matters some.—Did you sail from port without boats, Don Benito?"

"They were stove in the gales, Señor."

"That was bad. Many men, too, you lost then. Boats and men.—Those must have been hard gales, Don Benito."

"Past all speech," cringed the Spaniard.

"Tell me, Don Benito," continued his companion with increased interest, "tell me, were these gales immediately off the pitch of Cape Horn?"

"Cape Horn?—who spoke of Cape Horn?"

"Yourself did, when giving me an account of your voyage," answered Captain Delano with almost equal astonishment at this eating of his own words, even as he ever seemed eating his own heart, on the part of the Spaniard. "You yourself, Don Benito, spoke of Cape Horn," he emphatically repeated.

The Spaniard turned, in a sort of stooping posture, pausing an instant, as one about to make a plunging exchange of elements, as from air to water.

At this moment a messenger-boy, a white, hurried by, in

the regular performance of his function carrying the last expired half hour forward to the forecastle, from the cabin time-
piece, to have it struck at the ship's large bell.

"Master," said the servant, discontinuing his work on the
coat sleeve, and addressing the rapt Spaniard with a sort of
timid apprehensiveness, as one charged with a duty, the discharge of which, it was foreseen, would prove irksome to
the very person who had imposed it, and for whose benefit
it was intended, "master told me never mind where he
was, or how engaged, always to remind him, to a minute,
when shaving-time comes. Miguel has gone to strike the half-
hour afternoon. It is *now*, master. Will master go into the
cuddy?"

"Ah—yes," answered the Spaniard, starting, somewhat as
from dreams into realities; then turning upon Captain Delano, he said that ere long he would resume the conversation.

"Then if master means to talk more to Don Amasa," said
the servant, "why not let Don Amasa sit by master in the
cuddy, and master can talk, and Don Amasa can listen, while
Babo here lathers and strops."

"Yes," said Captain Delano, not unpleased with this sociable plan, "yes, Don Benito, unless you had rather not, I will
go with you."

"Be it so, Señor."

As the three passed aft, the American could not but think
it another strange instance of his host's capriciousness, this
being shaved with such uncommon punctuality in the middle
of the day. But he deemed it more than likely that the servant's anxious fidelity had something to do with the matter;
inasmuch as the timely interruption served to rally his master
from the mood which had evidently been coming upon him.

The place called the cuddy was a light deck-cabin formed
by the poop, a sort of attic to the large cabin below. Part of
it had formerly been the quarters of the officers; but since
their death all the partitionings had been thrown down, and
the whole interior converted into one spacious and airy marine hall; for absence of fine furniture and picturesque disarray, of odd appurtenances, somewhat answering to the wide,
cluttered hall of some eccentric bachelor-squire in the country, who hangs his shooting-jacket and tobacco-pouch on

deer antlers, and keeps his fishing-rod, tongs, and walking-stick in the same corner.

The similitude was heightened, if not originally suggested, by glimpses of the surrounding sea; since, in one aspect, the country and the ocean seem cousins-german.

The floor of the cuddy was matted. Overhead, four or five old muskets were stuck into horizontal holes along the beams. On one side was a claw-footed old table lashed to the deck; a thumbed missal on it, and over it a small, meager crucifix attached to the bulk-head. Under the table lay a dented cutlass or two, with a hacked harpoon, among some melancholy old rigging, like a heap of poor friar's girdles. There were also two long, sharp-ribbed settees of malacca cane, black with age, and uncomfortable to look at as inquisitors' racks, with a large, misshapen arm-chair, which, furnished with a rude barber's crutch at the back, working with a screw, seemed some grotesque, middle-age engine of torment. A flag locker was in one corner, open, exposing various colored bunting, some rolled up, others half unrolled, still others tumbled. Opposite was a cumbrous washstand, of black mahogany, all of one block, with a pedestal, like a font, and over it a railed shelf, containing combs, brushes, and other implements of the toilet. A torn hammock of stained grass swung near; the sheets tossed, and the pillow wrinkled up like a brow, as if whoever slept here slept but illy, with alternate visitations of sad thoughts and bad dreams.

The further extremity of the cuddy, overhanging the ship's stern, was pierced with three openings, windows or port holes, according as men or cannon might peer, socially or unsocially, out of them. At present neither men nor cannon were seen, though huge ring-bolts and other rusty iron fixtures of the wood-work hinted of twenty-four-pounders.

Glancing towards the hammock as he entered, Captain Delano said, "You sleep here, Don Benito?"

"Yes, Señor, since we got into mild weather."

"This seems a sort of dormitory, sitting-room, sail-loft, chapel, armory, and private closet all together, Don Benito," added Captain Delano, looking round.

"Yes, Señor; events have not been favorable to much order in my arrangements."

Here the servant, napkin on arm, made a motion as if wait-ing his master's good pleasure. Don Benito signified his read-iness, when, seating him in the malacca arm-chair, and for the guest's convenience drawing opposite it one of the settees, the servant commenced operations by throwing back his mas-ter's collar and loosening his cravat.

There is something in the negro which, in a peculiar way, fits him for avocations about one's person. Most negroes are natural valets and hair-dressers; taking to the comb and brush congenially as to the castinets, and flourishing them appar-ently with almost equal satisfaction. There is, too, a smooth tact about them in this employment, with a marvelous, noise-less, gliding briskness, not ungraceful in its way, singularly pleasing to behold, and still more so to be the manipulated subject of. And above all is the great gift of good humor. Not the mere grin or laugh is here meant. Those were unsuitable. But a certain easy cheerfulness, harmonious in every glance and gesture; as though God had set the whole negro to some pleasant tune.

When to all this is added the docility arising from the un-aspiring contentment of a limited mind, and that susceptibil-ity of blind attachment sometimes inhering in indisputable inferiors, one readily perceives why those hypochondriacs, Johnson and Byron—it may be something like the hypochon-driac, Benito Cereno—took to their hearts, almost to the ex-clusion of the entire white race, their serving men, the negroes, Barber and Fletcher. But if there be that in the negro which exempts him from the inflicted sourness of the morbid or cynical mind, how, in his most prepossessing aspects, must he appear to a benevolent one? When at ease with respect to exterior things, Captain Delano's nature was not only benign, but familiarly and humorously so. At home, he had often taken rare satisfaction in sitting in his door, watching some free man of color at his work or play. If on a voyage he chanced to have a black sailor, invariably he was on chatty, and half-gamesome terms with him. In fact, like most men of a good, blithe heart, Captain Delano took to negroes, not philanthropically, but genially, just as other men to New-foundland dogs.

Hitherto the circumstances in which he found the San

Dominick had repressed the tendency. But in the cuddy, relieved from his former uneasiness, and, for various reasons,
more sociably inclined than at any previous period of the day,
and seeing the colored servant, napkin on arm, so debonair
about his master, in a business so familiar as that of shaving,
too, all his old weakness for negroes returned.

Among other things, he was amused with an odd instance
of the African love of bright colors and fine shows, in the
black's informally taking from the flag-locker a great piece of
bunting of all hues, and lavishly tucking it under his master's
chin for an apron.

The mode of shaving among the Spaniards is a little different from what it is with other nations. They have a basin,
specifically called a barber's basin, which on one side is
scooped out, so as accurately to receive the chin, against
which it is closely held in lathering; which is done, not with
a brush, but with soap dipped in the water of the basin and
rubbed on the face.

In the present instance salt-water was used for lack of
better; and the parts lathered were only the upper lip, and
low down under the throat, all the rest being cultivated
beard.

The preliminaries being somewhat novel to Captain
Delano, he sat curiously eying them, so that no conversation
took place, nor for the present did Don Benito appear disposed to renew any.

Setting down his basin, the negro searched among the razors, as for the sharpest, and having found it, gave it an additional edge by expertly strapping it on the firm, smooth,
oily skin of his open palm; he then made a gesture as if to
begin, but midway stood suspended for an instant, one hand
elevating the razor, the other professionally dabbling among
the bubbling suds on the Spaniard's lank neck. Not unaffected by the close sight of the gleaming steel, Don Benito
nervously shuddered; his usual ghastliness was heightened by
the lather, which lather, again, was intensified in its hue by
the contrasting sootiness of the negro's body. Altogether the
scene was somewhat peculiar, at least to Captain Delano, nor,
as he saw the two thus postured, could he resist the vagary,
that in the black he saw a headsman, and in the white, a man

at the block. But this was one of those antic conceits, appearing and vanishing in a breath, from which, perhaps, the best
regulated mind is not always free.

Meantime the agitation of the Spaniard had a little loosened the bunting from around him, so that one broad fold
swept curtain-like over the chair-arm to the floor, revealing,
amid a profusion of armorial bars and ground-colors—black,
blue, and yellow—a closed castle in a blood-red field diagonal
with a lion rampant in a white.

"The castle and the lion," exclaimed Captain Delano—
" why, Don Benito, this is the flag of Spain you use here. It's
well it's only I, and not the King, that sees this," he added
with a smile, "but"—turning towards the black,—"it's all
one, I suppose, so the colors be gay;" which playful remark
did not fail somewhat to tickle the negro.

"Now, master," he said, readjusting the flag, and pressing
the head gently further back into the crotch of the chair;
"now master," and the steel glanced nigh the throat.

Again Don Benito faintly shuddered.

"You must not shake so, master.—See, Don Amasa, master
always shakes when I shave him. And yet master knows I
never yet have drawn blood, though it's true, if master will
shake so, I may some of these times. Now master," he continued. "And now, Don Amasa, please go on with your talk
about the gale, and all that, master can hear, and between
times master can answer."

"Ah yes, these gales," said Captain Delano; "but the more
I think of your voyage, Don Benito, the more I wonder, not
at the gales, terrible as they must have been, but at the disastrous interval following them. For here, by your account,
have you been these two months and more getting from Cape
Horn to St. Maria, a distance which I myself, with a good
wind, have sailed in a few days. True, you had calms, and
long ones, but to be becalmed for two months, that is, at
least, unusual. Why, Don Benito, had almost any other gentleman told me such a story, I should have been half disposed
to a little incredulity."

Here an involuntary expression came over the Spaniard,
similar to that just before on the deck, and whether it was the
start he gave, or a sudden gawky roll of the hull in the calm,

or a momentary unsteadiness of the servant's hand; however it was, just then the razor drew blood, spots of which stained the creamy lather under the throat; immediately the black barber drew back his steel, and remaining in his professional attitude, back to Captain Delano, and face to Don Benito, held up the trickling razor, saying, with a sort of half humorous sorrow, "See, master,—you shook so—here's Babo's first blood."

No sword drawn before James the First of England, no assassination in that timid King's presence, could have produced a more terrified aspect than was now presented by Don Benito.

Poor fellow, thought Captain Delano, so nervous he can't even bear the sight of barber's blood; and this unstrung, sick man, is it credible that I should have imagined he meant to spill all my blood, who can't endure the sight of one little drop of his own? Surely, Amasa Delano, you have been beside yourself this day. Tell it not when you get home, sappy Amasa. Well, well, he looks like a murderer, doesn't he? More like as if himself were to be done for. Well, well, this day's experience shall be a good lesson.

Meantime, while these things were running through the honest seaman's mind, the servant had taken the napkin from his arm, and to Don Benito had said—"But answer Don Amasa, please, master, while I wipe this ugly stuff off the razor, and strop it again."

As he said the words, his face was turned half round, so as to be alike visible to the Spaniard and the American, and seemed by its expression to hint, that he was desirous, by getting his master to go on with the conversation, considerately to withdraw his attention from the recent annoying accident. As if glad to snatch the offered relief, Don Benito resumed, rehearsing to Captain Delano, that not only were the calms of unusual duration, but the ship had fallen in with obstinate currents; and other things he added, some of which were but repetitions of former statements, to explain how it came to pass that the passage from Cape Horn to St. Maria had been so exceedingly long, now and then mingling with his words, incidental praises, less qualified than before, to the blacks, for their general good conduct.

These particulars were not given consecutively, the servant, at convenient times, using his razor, and so, between the intervals of shaving, the story and panegyric went on with more than usual huskiness.

To Captain Delano's imagination, now again not wholly at rest, there was something so hollow in the Spaniard's manner, with apparently some reciprocal hollowness in the servant's dusky comment of silence, that the idea flashed across him, that possibly master and man, for some unknown purpose, were acting out, both in word and deed, nay, to the very tremor of Don Benito's limbs, some juggling play before him. Neither did the suspicion of collusion lack apparent support, from the fact of those whispered conferences before mentioned. But then, what could be the object of enacting this play of the barber before him? At last, regarding the notion as a whimsy, insensibly suggested, perhaps, by the theatrical aspect of Don Benito in his harlequin ensign, Captain Delano speedily banished it.

The shaving over, the servant bestirred himself with a small bottle of scented waters, pouring a few drops on the head, and then diligently rubbing; the vehemence of the exercise causing the muscles of his face to twitch rather strangely.

His next operation was with comb, scissors and brush; going round and round, smoothing a curl here, clipping an unruly whisker-hair there, giving a graceful sweep to the temple-lock, with other impromptu touches evincing the hand of a master; while, like any resigned gentleman in barber's hands, Don Benito bore all, much less uneasily, at least, than he had done the razoring; indeed, he sat so pale and rigid now, that the negro seemed a Nubian sculptor finishing off a white statue-head.

All being over at last, the standard of Spain removed, tumbled up, and tossed back into the flag-locker, the negro's warm breath blowing away any stray hair which might have lodged down his master's neck; collar and cravat readjusted; a speck of lint whisked off the velvet lapel; all this being done; backing off a little space, and pausing with an expression of subdued self-complacency, the servant for a moment surveyed his master, as, in toilet at least, the creature of his own tasteful hands.

Captain Delano playfully complimented him upon his achievement; at the same time congratulating Don Benito.

But neither sweet waters, nor shampooing, nor fidelity, nor sociality, delighted the Spaniard. Seeing him relapsing into forbidding gloom, and still remaining seated, Captain Delano, thinking that his presence was undesired just then, withdrew, on pretense of seeing whether, as he had prophecied, any signs of a breeze were visible.

Walking forward to the mainmast, he stood a while thinking over the scene, and not without some undefined misgivings, when he heard a noise near the cuddy, and turning, saw the negro, his hand to his cheek. Advancing, Captain Delano perceived that the cheek was bleeding. He was about to ask the cause, when the negro's wailing soliloquy enlightened him.

"Ah, when will master get better from his sickness; only the sour heart that sour sickness breeds made him serve Babo so; cutting Babo with the razor, because, only by accident, Babo had given master one little scratch; and for the first time in so many a day, too. Ah, ah, ah," holding his hand to his face.

Is it possible, thought Captain Delano; was it to wreak in private his Spanish spite against this poor friend of his, that Don Benito, by his sullen manner, impelled me to withdraw? Ah, this slavery breeds ugly passions in man.—Poor fellow!

He was about to speak in sympathy to the negro, but with a timid reluctance he now reëntered the cuddy.

Presently master and man came forth; Don Benito leaning on his servant as if nothing had happened.

But a sort of love-quarrel, after all, thought Captain Delano.

He accosted Don Benito, and they slowly walked together. They had gone but a few paces, when the steward—a tall, rajah-looking mulatto, orientally set off with a pagoda turban formed by three or four Madras handkerchiefs wound about his head, tier on tier—approaching with a salaam, announced lunch in the cabin.

On their way thither, the two Captains were preceded by the mulatto, who, turning round as he advanced, with continual smiles and bows, ushered them on, a display of elegance which quite completed the insignificance of the small bare-headed Babo, who, as if not unconscious of inferiority, eyed askance the graceful steward. But in part, Captain Delano imputed his jealous watchfulness to that peculiar feeling which the full-blooded African entertains for the adulterated one. As for the steward, his manner, if not bespeaking much dignity of self-respect, yet evidenced his extreme desire to please; which is doubly meritorious, as at once Christian and Chesterfieldian.

Captain Delano observed with interest that while the complexion of the mulatto was hybrid, his physiognomy was European; classically so.

"Don Benito," whispered he, "I am glad to see this usher-of-the-golden-rod of yours; the sight refutes an ugly remark once made to me by a Barbadoes planter; that when a mulatto has a regular European face, look out for him; he is a devil. But see, your steward here has features more regular than King George's of England; and yet there he nods, and bows, and smiles; a king, indeed—the king of kind hearts and polite fellows. What a pleasant voice he has, too!"

"He has, Señor."

"But, tell me, has he not, so far as you have known him, always proved a good, worthy fellow?" said Captain Delano, pausing, while with a final genuflexion the steward disappeared into the cabin; "come, for the reason just mentioned, I am curious to know."

"Francesco is a good man," a sort of sluggishly responded Don Benito, like a phlegmatic appreciator, who would neither find fault nor flatter.

"Ah, I thought so. For it were strange indeed, and not very creditable to us white-skins, if a little of our blood mixed with the African's, should, far from improving the latter's quality, have the sad effect of pouring vitriolic acid into black broth; improving the hue, perhaps, but not the wholesomeness."

"Doubtless, doubtless, Señor, but"—glancing at Babo—"not to speak of negroes, your planter's remark I have heard applied to the Spanish and Indian intermixtures in our provinces. But I know nothing about the matter," he listlessly added.

And here they entered the cabin.

The lunch was a frugal one. Some of Captain Delano's fresh fish and pumpkins, biscuit and salt beef, the reserved bottle of cider, and the San Dominick's last bottle of Canary.

As they entered, Francesco, with two or three colored aids, was hovering over the table giving the last adjustments. Upon perceiving their master they withdrew, Francesco making a smiling congé, and the Spaniard, without condescending to notice it, fastidiously remarking to his companion that he relished not superfluous attendance.

Without companions, host and guest sat down, like a child-less married couple, at opposite ends of the table, Don Benito waving Captain Delano to his place, and, weak as he was, insisting upon that gentleman being seated before himself.

The negro placed a rug under Don Benito's feet, and a cushion behind his back, and then stood behind, not his master's chair, but Captain Delano's. At first, this a little surprised the latter. But it was soon evident that, in taking his position, the black was still true to his master; since by facing him he could the more readily anticipate his slightest want.

"This is an uncommonly intelligent fellow of yours, Don Benito," whispered Captain Delano across the table.

"You say true, Señor."

During the repast, the guest again reverted to parts of Don Benito's story, begging further particulars here and there. He inquired how it was that the scurvy and fever should have committed such wholesale havoc upon the whites, while destroying less than half of the blacks. As if this question reproduced the whole scene of plague before the Spaniard's eyes, miserably reminding him of his solitude in a cabin where before he had had so many friends and officers round him, his hand shook, his face became hueless, broken words escaped; but directly the sane memory of the past seemed replaced by insane terrors of the present. With starting eyes he stared before him at vacancy. For nothing was to be seen but the hand of his servant pushing the Canary over towards him. At length a few sips served partially to restore him. He made random reference to the different constitution of races, enabling one to offer more resistance to certain maladies than another. The thought was new to his companion.

Presently Captain Delano, intending to say something to

his host concerning the pecuniary part of the business he had undertaken for him, especially—since he was strictly accountable to his owners—with reference to the new suit of sails, and other things of that sort; and naturally preferring to conduct such affairs in private, was desirous that the servant should withdraw; imagining that Don Benito for a few minutes could dispense with his attendance. He, however, waited awhile; thinking that, as the conversation proceeded, Don Benito, without being prompted, would perceive the propriety of the step.

But it was otherwise. At last catching his host's eye, Captain Delano, with a slight backward gesture of his thumb, whispered, "Don Benito, pardon me, but there is an interference with the full expression of what I have to say to you."

Upon this the Spaniard changed countenance; which was imputed to his resenting the hint, as in some way a reflection upon his servant. After a moment's pause, he assured his guest that the black's remaining with them could be of no disservice; because since losing his officers he had made Babo (whose original office, it now appeared, had been captain of the slaves) not only his constant attendant and companion, but in all things his confidant.

After this, nothing more could be said; though, indeed, Captain Delano could hardly avoid some little tinge of irritation upon being left ungratified in so inconsiderable a wish, by one, too, for whom he intended such solid services. But it is only his querulousness, thought he; and so filling his glass he proceeded to business.

The price of the sails and other matters was fixed upon. But while this was being done, the American observed that, though his original offer of assistance had been hailed with hectic animation, yet now when it was reduced to a business transaction, indifference and apathy were betrayed. Don Benito, in fact, appeared to submit to hearing the details more out of regard to common propriety, than from any impression that weighty benefit to himself and his voyage was involved.

Soon, this manner became still more reserved. The effort was vain to seek to draw him into social talk. Gnawed by his splenetic mood, he sat twitching his beard, while to little purpose the hand of his servant, mute as that on the wall, slowly pushed over the Canary.

Lunch being over, they sat down on the cushioned transom; the servant placing a pillow behind his master. The long continuance of the calm had now affected the atmosphere. Don Benito sighed heavily, as if for breath.

"Why not adjourn to the cuddy," said Captain Delano; "there is more air there." But the host sat silent and motionless.

Meantime his servant knelt before him, with a large fan of feathers. And Francesco coming in on tiptoes, handed the negro a little cup of aromatic waters, with which at intervals he chafed his master's brow; smoothing the hair along the temples as a nurse does a child's. He spoke no word. He only rested his eye on his master's, as if, amid all Don Benito's distress, a little to refresh his spirit by the silent sight of fidelity.

Presently the ship's bell sounded two o'clock; and through the cabin-windows a slight rippling of the sea was discerned; and from the desired direction.

"There," exclaimed Captain Delano, "I told you so, Don Benito, look!"

He had risen to his feet, speaking in a very animated tone, with a view the more to rouse his companion. But though the crimson curtain of the stern-window near him that moment fluttered against his pale cheek, Don Benito seemed to have even less welcome for the breeze than the calm.

Poor fellow, thought Captain Delano, bitter experience has taught him that one ripple does not make a wind, any more than one swallow a summer. But he is mistaken for once. I will get his ship in for him, and prove it.

Briefly alluding to his weak condition, he urged his host to remain quietly where he was, since he (Captain Delano) would with pleasure take upon himself the responsibility of making the best use of the wind.

Upon gaining the deck, Captain Delano started at the unexpected figure of Atufal, monumentally fixed at the threshold, like one of those sculptured porters of black marble guarding the porches of Egyptian tombs.

But this time the start was, perhaps, purely physical. Atufal's presence, singularly attesting docility even in sullenness, was contrasted with that of the hatchet-polishers, who in patience evinced their industry; while both spectacles showed, that lax as Don Benito's general authority might be, still, whenever he chose to exert it, no man so savage or colossal but must, more or less, bow.

Snatching a trumpet which hung from the bulwarks, with a free step Captain Delano advanced to the forward edge of the poop, issuing his orders in his best Spanish. The few sailors and many negroes, all equally pleased, obediently set about heading the ship towards the harbor.

While giving some directions about setting a lower stu'n'-sail, suddenly Captain Delano heard a voice faithfully repeating his orders. Turning, he saw Babo, now for the time acting, under the pilot, his original part of captain of the slaves. This assistance proved valuable. Tattered sails and warped yards were soon brought into some trim. And no brace or halyard was pulled but to the blithe songs of the inspirited negroes.

Good fellows, thought Captain Delano, a little training would make fine sailors of them. Why see, the very women pull and sing too. These must be some of those Ashantee negresses that make such capital soldiers, I've heard. But who's at the helm. I must have a good hand there.

He went to see.

The San Dominick steered with a cumbrous tiller, with large horizontal pullies attached. At each pully-end stood a subordinate black, and between them, at the tiller-head, the responsible post, a Spanish seaman, whose countenance evinced his due share in the general hopefulness and confidence at the coming of the breeze.

He proved the same man who had behaved with so shame-faced an air on the windlass.

"Ah,—it is you, my man," exclaimed Captain Delano—"well, no more sheep's-eyes now;—look straight forward and keep the ship so. Good hand, I trust? And want to get into the harbor, don't you?"

The man assented with an inward chuckle, grasping the tiller-head firmly. Upon this, unperceived by the American, the two blacks eyed the sailor intently.

Finding all right at the helm, the pilot went forward to the forecastle, to see how matters stood there.

The ship now had way enough to breast the current. With the approach of evening, the breeze would be sure to freshen.

Having done all that was needed for the present, Captain Delano, giving his last orders to the sailors, turned aft to report affairs to Don Benito in the cabin; perhaps additionally incited to rejoin him by the hope of snatching a moment's private chat while his servant was engaged upon deck.

From opposite sides, there were, beneath the poop, two approaches to the cabin; one further forward than the other, and consequently communicating with a longer passage. Marking the servant still above, Captain Delano, taking the nighest entrance—the one last named, and at whose porch Atufal still stood—hurried on his way, till, arrived at the cabin threshold, he paused an instant, a little to recover from his eagerness. Then, with the words of his intended business upon his lips, he entered. As he advanced toward the seated Spaniard, he heard another footstep, keeping time with his. From the opposite door, a salver in hand, the servant was likewise advancing.

"Confound the faithful fellow," thought Captain Delano; "what a vexatious coincidence."

Possibly, the vexation might have been something different, were it not for the brisk confidence inspired by the breeze. But even as it was, he felt a slight twinge, from a sudden indefinite association in his mind of Babo with Atufal.

"Don Benito," said he, "I give you joy; the breeze will hold, and will increase. By the way, your tall man and timepiece, Atufal, stands without. By your order, of course?"

Don Benito recoiled, as if at some bland satirical touch, delivered with such adroit garnish of apparent good-breeding as to present no handle for retort.

He is like one flayed alive, thought Captain Delano; where may one touch him without causing a shrink?

The servant moved before his master, adjusting a cushion; recalled to civility, the Spaniard stiffly replied: "you are right. The slave appears where you saw him, according to my command; which is, that if at the given hour I am below, he must take his stand and abide my coming."

"Ah now, pardon me, but that is treating the poor fellow like an ex-king indeed. Ah, Don Benito," smiling, "for all the license you permit in some things, I fear lest, at bottom, you are a bitter hard master."

Again Don Benito shrank; and this time, as the good sailor thought, from a genuine twinge of his conscience.

Again conversation became constrained. In vain Captain Delano called attention to the now perceptible motion of the keel gently cleaving the sea; with lack-lustre eye, Don Benito returned words few and reserved.

By-and-by, the wind having steadily risen, and still blowing right into the harbor, bore the San Dominick swiftly on. Rounding a point of land, the sealer at distance came into open view.

Meantime Captain Delano had again repaired to the deck, remaining there some time. Having at last altered the ship's course, so as to give the reef a wide berth, he returned for a few moments below.

I will cheer up my poor friend, this time, thought he.

"Better and better, Don Benito," he cried as he blithely reëntered; "there will soon be an end to your cares, at least for awhile. For when, after a long, sad voyage, you know, the anchor drops into the haven, all its vast weight seems lifted from the captain's heart. We are getting on famously, Don Benito. My ship is in sight. Look through this side-light here; there she is; all a-taunt-o! The Bachelor's Delight, my good friend. Ah, how this wind braces one up. Come, you must take a cup of coffee with me this evening. My old steward will give you as fine a cup as ever any sultan tasted. What say you, Don Benito, will you?"

At first, the Spaniard glanced feverishly up, casting a longing look towards the sealer, while with mute concern his servant gazed into his face. Suddenly the old ague of coldness returned, and dropping back to his cushions he was silent.

"You do not answer. Come, all day you have been my host; would you have hospitality all on one side?"

"I cannot go," was the response.

"What? it will not fatigue you. The ships will lie together as near as they can, without swinging foul. It will be little more than stepping from deck to deck; which is but as from room to room. Come, come, you must not refuse me."

"I cannot go," decisively and repulsively repeated Don Benito.

Renouncing all but the last appearance of courtesy, with a sort of cadaverous sullenness, and biting his thin nails to the quick, he glanced, almost glared, at his guest; as if impatient that a stranger's presence should interfere with the full indulgence of his morbid hour. Meantime the sound of the parted waters came more and more gurglingly and merrily in at the windows; as reproaching him for his dark spleen; as telling him that, sulk as he might, and go mad with it, nature cared not a jot; since, whose fault was it, pray?

But the foul mood was now at its depth, as the fair wind at its height.

There was something in the man so far beyond any mere unsociality or sourness previously evinced, that even the forbearing good-nature of his guest could not longer endure it. Wholly at a loss to account for such demeanor, and deeming sickness with eccentricity, however extreme, no adequate excuse, well satisfied, too, that nothing in his own conduct could justify it, Captain Delano's pride began to be roused. Himself became reserved. But all seemed one to the Spaniard. Quitting him, therefore, Captain Delano once more went to the deck.

The ship was now within less than two miles of the sealer. The whale-boat was seen darting over the interval.

To be brief, the two vessels, thanks to the pilot's skill, ere long in neighborly style lay anchored together.

Before returning to his own vessel, Captain Delano had intended communicating to Don Benito the smaller details of the proposed services to be rendered. But, as it was, unwilling anew to subject himself to rebuffs, he resolved, now that he had seen the San Dominick safely moored, immediately to quit her, without further allusion to hospitality or business. Indefinitely postponing his ulterior plans, he would regulate his future actions according to future circumstances. His boat was ready to receive him; but his host still tarried below. Well, thought Captain Delano, if he has little breeding, the more need to show mine. He descended to the cabin to bid a ceremonious, and, it may be, tacitly rebukeful adieu. But to his great satisfaction, Don Benito, as if he began to feel the weight of that treatment with which his slighted guest had, not indecorously, retaliated upon him, now supported by his servant, rose to his feet, and grasping Captain Delano's hand, stood tremulous; too much agitated to speak. But the good augury hence drawn was suddenly dashed, by his resuming all his previous reserve, with augmented gloom, as, with half-averted eyes, he silently reseated himself on his cushions. With a corresponding return of his own chilled feelings, Captain Delano bowed and withdrew.

He was hardly midway in the narrow corridor, dim as a tunnel, leading from the cabin to the stairs, when a sound, as of the tolling for execution in some jail-yard, fell on his ears. It was the echo of the ship's flawed bell, striking the hour, drearily reverberated in this subterranean vault. Instantly, by a fatality not to be withstood, his mind, responsive to the portent, swarmed with superstitious suspicions. He paused. In images far swifter than these sentences, the minutest details of all his former distrusts swept through him.

Hitherto, credulous good-nature had been too ready to furnish excuses for reasonable fears. Why was the Spaniard, so superfluously punctilious at times, now heedless of common propriety in not accompanying to the side his departing guest? Did indisposition forbid? Indisposition had not forbidden more irksome exertion that day. His last equivocal demeanor recurred. He had risen to his feet, grasped his guest's hand, motioned toward his hat; then, in an instant, all was eclipsed in sinister muteness and gloom. Did this imply one brief, repentent relenting at the final moment, from some iniquitous plot, followed by remorseless return to it? His last glance seemed to express a calamitous, yet acquiescent farewell to Captain Delano forever. Why decline the invitation to visit the sealer that evening? Or was the Spaniard less hardened than the Jew, who refrained not from supping at the board of him whom the same night he meant to betray? What imported all those day-long enigmas and contradictions, except they were intended to mystify, preliminary to some stealthy blow? Atufal, the pretended rebel, but punctual shadow, that moment lurked by the threshold without. He seemed a sentry, and more. Who, by his own confession, had stationed him there? Was the negro now lying in wait?

The Spaniard behind—his creature before: to rush from darkness to light was the involuntary choice.

The next moment, with clenched jaw and hand, he passed Atufal, and stood unharmed in the light. As he saw his trim ship lying peacefully at her anchor, and almost within ordinary call; as he saw his household boat, with familiar faces in it, patiently rising and falling on the short waves by the San Dominick's side; and then, glancing about the decks where he stood, saw the oakum-pickers still gravely plying their fingers; and heard the low, buzzing whistle and industrious hum of the hatchet-polishers, still bestirring themselves over their endless occupation; and more than all, as he saw the benign aspect of nature, taking her innocent repose in the evening; the screened sun in the quiet camp of the west shining out like the mild light from Abraham's tent; as charmed eye and ear took in all these, with the chained figure of the black, clenched jaw and hand relaxed. Once again he smiled at the phantoms which had mocked him, and felt something like a tinge of remorse, that, by harboring them even for a moment, he should, by implication, have betrayed an almost atheist doubt of the ever-watchful Providence above.

There was a few minutes' delay, while, in obedience to his orders, the boat was being hooked along to the gangway. During this interval, a sort of saddened satisfaction stole over Captain Delano, at thinking of the kindly offices he had that day discharged for a stranger. Ah, thought he, after good actions one's conscience is never ungrateful, however much so the benefited party may be.

Presently, his foot, in the first act of descent into the boat, pressed the first round of the side-ladder, his face presented inward upon the deck. In the same moment, he heard his name courteously sounded; and, to his pleased surprise, saw Don Benito advancing—an unwonted energy in his air, as if, at the last moment, intent upon making amends for his recent discourtesy. With instinctive good feeling, Captain Delano, withdrawing his foot, turned and reciprocally advanced. As he did so, the Spaniard's nervous eagerness increased, but his vital energy failed; so that, the better to support him, the servant, placing his master's hand on his naked shoulder, and gently holding it there, formed himself into a sort of crutch.

When the two captains met, the Spaniard again fervently took the hand of the American, at the same time casting an earnest glance into his eyes, but, as before, too much overcome to speak.

I have done him wrong, self-reproachfully thought Captain Delano; his apparent coldness has deceived me; in no instance has he meant to offend.

Meantime, as if fearful that the continuance of the scene might too much unstring his master, the servant seemed anxious to terminate it. And so, still presenting himself as a crutch, and walking between the two captains, he advanced with them towards the gangway; while still, as if full of kindly contrition, Don Benito would not let go the hand of Captain Delano, but retained it in his, across the black's body.

Soon they were standing by the side, looking over into the boat, whose crew turned up their curious eyes. Waiting a moment for the Spaniard to relinquish his hold, the now embarrassed Captain Delano lifted his foot, to overstep the threshold of the open gangway; but still Don Benito would not let go his hand. And yet, with an agitated tone, he said, "I can go no further; here I must bid you adieu. Adieu, my dear, dear Don Amasa. Go—go!" suddenly tearing his hand loose, "go, and God guard you better than me, my best friend."

Not unaffected, Captain Delano would now have lingered; but catching the meekly admonitory eye of the servant, with a hasty farewell he descended into his boat, followed by the continual adieus of Don Benito, standing rooted in the gangway.

Seating himself in the stern, Captain Delano, making a last salute, ordered the boat shoved off. The crew had their oars on end. The bowsman pushed the boat a sufficient distance for the oars to be lengthwise dropped. The instant that was done, Don Benito sprang over the bulwarks, falling at the feet of Captain Delano; at the same time, calling towards his ship, but in tones so frenzied, that none in the boat could understand him. But, as if not equally obtuse, three sailors, from three different and distant parts of the ship, splashed into the sea, swimming after their captain, as if intent upon his rescue.

The dismayed officer of the boat eagerly asked what this meant. To which, Captain Delano, turning a disdainful smile upon the unaccountable Spaniard, answered that, for his part, he neither knew nor cared; but it seemed as if Don Benito had taken it into his head to produce the impression among his people that the boat wanted to kidnap him. "Or else— give way for your lives," he wildly added, starting at a clatter- ing hubbub in the ship, above which rang the tocsin of the hatchet-polishers; and seizing Don Benito by the throat he added, "this plotting pirate means murder!" Here, in apparent verification of the words, the servant, a dagger in his hand, was seen on the rail overhead, poised, in the act of leaping, as if with desperate fidelity to befriend his master to the last; while, seemingly to aid the black, the three white sailors were trying to clamber into the hampered bow. Meantime, the whole host of negroes, as if inflamed at the sight of their jeopardized captain, impended in one sooty avalanche over the bulwarks.

All this, with what preceded, and what followed, occurred with such involutions of rapidity, that past, present, and fu- ture seemed one.

Seeing the negro coming, Captain Delano had flung the Spaniard aside, almost in the very act of clutching him, and, by the unconscious recoil, shifting his place, with arms thrown up, so promptly grappled the servant in his descent, that with dagger presented at Captain Delano's heart, the black seemed of purpose to have leaped there as to his mark. But the weapon was wrenched away, and the assailant dashed down into the bottom of the boat, which now, with disentan- gled oars, began to speed through the sea.

At this juncture, the left hand of Captain Delano, on one side, again clutched the half-reclined Don Benito, heedless that he was in a speechless faint, while his right foot, on the other side, ground the prostrate negro; and his right arm pressed for added speed on the after oar, his eye bent for- ward, encouraging his men to their utmost.

But here, the officer of the boat, who had at last succeeded in beating off the towing sailors, and was now, with face turned aft, assisting the bowsman at his oar, suddenly called to Captain Delano, to see what the black was about; while a Portuguese oarsman shouted to him to give heed to what the Spaniard was saying.

Glancing down at his feet, Captain Delano saw the freed hand of the servant aiming with a second dagger—a small one, before concealed in his wool—with this he was snakishly writhing up from the boat's bottom, at the heart of his master, his countenance lividly vindictive, expressing the centred purpose of his soul; while the Spaniard, half-choked, was vainly shrinking away, with husky words, incoherent to all but the Portuguese.

That moment, across the long-benighted mind of Captain Delano, a flash of revelation swept, illuminating in unanticipated clearness his host's whole mysterious demeanor, with every enigmatic event of the day, as well as the entire past voyage of the San Dominick. He smote Babo's hand down, but his own heart smote him harder. With infinite pity he withdrew his hold from Don Benito. Not Captain Delano, but Don Benito, the black, in leaping into the boat, had intended to stab.

Both the black's hands were held, as, glancing up towards the San Dominick, Captain Delano, now with the scales dropped from his eyes, saw the negroes, not in misrule, not in tumult, not as if frantically concerned for Don Benito, but with mask torn away, flourishing hatchets and knives, in ferocious piratical revolt. Like delirious black dervishes, the six Ashantees danced on the poop. Prevented by their foes from springing into the water, the Spanish boys were hurrying up to the topmost spars, while such of the few Spanish sailors, not already in the sea, less alert, were descried, helplessly mixed in, on deck, with the blacks.

Meantime Captain Delano hailed his own vessel, ordering the ports up and the guns run out. But by this time the cable of the San Dominick had been cut; and the fag-end, in lashing out, whipped away the canvas shroud about the beak, suddenly revealing, as the bleached hull swung round towards the open ocean, death for the figure-head, in a human skeleton; chalky comment on the chalked words below, *"Follow your leader."*

At the sight, Don Benito, covering his face, wailed out: " 'Tis he, Aranda! my murdered, unburied friend!"

Upon reaching the sealer, calling for ropes, Captain Delano bound the negro, who made no resistance, and had him hoisted to the deck. He would then have assisted the now almost helpless Don Benito up the side; but Don Benito, wan as he was, refused to move, or be moved, until the negro should have been first put below out of view. When, presently assured that it was done, he no more shrank from the ascent.

The boat was immediately dispatched back to pick up the three swimming sailors. Meantime, the guns were in readiness, though, owing to the San Dominick having glided somewhat astern of the sealer, only the aftermost one could be brought to bear. With this, they fired six times; thinking to cripple the fugitive ship by bringing down her spars. But only a few inconsiderable ropes were shot away. Soon the ship was beyond the gun's range, steering broad out of the bay; the blacks thickly clustering round the bowsprit, one moment with taunting cries towards the whites, the next with upthrown gestures hailing the now dusky moors of ocean— cawing crows escaped from the hand of the fowler.

The first impulse was to slip the cables and give chase. But, upon second thoughts, to pursue with whale-boat and yawl seemed more promising.

Upon inquiring of Don Benito what fire arms they had on board the San Dominick, Captain Delano was answered that they had none that could be used; because, in the earlier stages of the mutiny, a cabin-passenger, since dead, had secretly put out of order the locks of what few muskets there were. But with all his remaining strength, Don Benito entreated the American not to give chase, either with ship or boat; for the negroes had already proved themselves such desperadoes, that, in case of a present assault, nothing but a total massacre of the whites could be looked for. But, regarding this warning as coming from one whose spirit had been crushed by misery, the American did not give up his design.

The boats were got ready and armed. Captain Delano ordered his men into them. He was going himself when Don Benito grasped his arm.

"What! have you saved my life, señor, and are you now
going to throw away your own?"

The officers also, for reasons connected with their interests
and those of the voyage, and a duty owing to the owners,
strongly objected against their commander's going. Weighing
their remonstrances a moment, Captain Delano felt bound to
remain; appointing his chief mate—an athletic and resolute
man, who had been a privateer's-man, and, as his enemies
whispered, a pirate—to head the party. The more to encourage the sailors, they were told, that the Spanish captain considered his ship as good as lost; that she and her cargo,
including some gold and silver, were worth more than a thousand doubloons. Take her, and no small part should be theirs.
The sailors replied with a shout.

The fugitives had now almost gained an offing. It was
nearly night; but the moon was rising. After hard, prolonged
pulling, the boats came up on the ship's quarters, at a suitable
distance laying upon their oars to discharge their muskets.
Having no bullets to return, the negroes sent their yells. But,
upon the second volley, Indian-like, they hurtled their hatchets. One took off a sailor's fingers. Another struck the whale-
boat's bow, cutting off the rope there, and remaining stuck
in the gunwale like a woodman's axe. Snatching it, quivering
from its lodgment, the mate hurled it back. The returned
gauntlet now stuck in the ship's broken quarter-gallery, and
so remained.

The negroes giving too hot a reception, the whites kept a
more respectful distance. Hovering now just out of reach of
the hurtling hatchets, they, with a view to the close encounter
which must soon come, sought to decoy the blacks into entirely disarming themselves of their most murderous weapons
in a hand-to-hand fight, by foolishly flinging them, as mis-
siles, short of the mark, into the sea. But ere long perceiving
the stratagem, the negroes desisted, though not before many
of them had to replace their lost hatchets with handspikes; an
exchange which, as counted upon, proved in the end favorable to the assailants.

Meantime, with a strong wind, the ship still clove the
water; the boats alternately falling behind, and pulling up, to
discharge fresh volleys.

The fire was mostly directed towards the stern, since there, chiefly, the negroes, at present, were clustering. But to kill or maim the negroes was not the object. To take them, with the ship, was the object. To do it, the ship must be boarded; which could not be done by boats while she was sailing so fast.

A thought now struck the mate. Observing the Spanish boys still aloft, high as they could get, he called to them to descend to the yards, and cut adrift the sails. It was done. About this time, owing to causes hereafter to be shown, two Spaniards, in the dress of sailors and conspicuously showing themselves, were killed; not by volleys, but by deliberate marksman's shots; while, as it afterwards appeared, by one of the general discharges, Atufal, the black, and the Spaniard at the helm likewise were killed. What now, with the loss of the sails, and loss of leaders, the ship became unmanageable to the negroes.

With creaking masts, she came heavily round to the wind; the prow slowly swinging, into view of the boats, its skeleton gleaming in the horizontal moonlight, and casting a gigantic ribbed shadow upon the water. One extended arm of the ghost seemed beckoning the whites to avenge it.

"Follow your leader!" cried the mate; and, one on each bow, the boats boarded. Sealing-spears and cutlasses crossed hatchets and hand-spikes. Huddled upon the long-boat amidships, the negresses raised a wailing chant, whose chorus was the clash of the steel.

For a time, the attack wavered; the negroes wedging themselves to beat it back; the half-repelled sailors, as yet unable to gain a footing, fighting as troopers in the saddle, one leg sideways flung over the bulwarks, and one without, plying their cutlasses like carters' whips. But in vain. They were almost overborne, when, rallying themselves into a squad as one man, with a huzza, they sprang inboard; where, entangled, they involuntarily separated again. For a few breaths' space, there was a vague, muffled, inner sound, as of submerged sword-fish rushing hither and thither through shoals of black-fish. Soon, in a reunited band, and joined by the Spanish seamen, the whites came to the surface, irresistibly driving the negroes toward the stern. But a barricade of casks

and sacks, from side to side, had been thrown up by the
mainmast. Here the negroes faced about, and though scorning peace or truce, yet fain would have had a respite. But,
without pause, overleaping the barrier, the unflagging sailors
again closed. Exhausted, the blacks now fought in despair.
Their red tongues lolled, wolf-like, from their black mouths.
But the pale sailors' teeth were set; not a word was spoken;
and, in five minutes more, the ship was won.

Nearly a score of the negroes were killed. Exclusive of those
by the balls, many were mangled; their wounds—mostly inflicted by the long-edged sealing-spears—resembling those
shaven ones of the English at Preston Pans, made by the
poled scythes of the Highlanders. On the other side, none
were killed, though several were wounded; some severely, including the mate. The surviving negroes were temporarily secured, and the ship, towed back into the harbor at midnight,
once more lay anchored.

Omitting the incidents and arrangements ensuing, suffice it
that, after two days spent in refitting, the two ships sailed in
company for Conception, in Chili, and thence for Lima, in
Peru; where, before the vice-regal courts, the whole affair,
from the beginning, underwent investigation.

Though, midway on the passage, the ill-fated Spaniard, relaxed from constraint, showed some signs of regaining health
with free-will; yet, agreeably to his own foreboding, shortly
before arriving at Lima, he relapsed, finally becoming so reduced as to be carried ashore in arms. Hearing of his story
and plight, one of the many religious institutions of the City
of Kings opened an hospitable refuge to him, where both
physician and priest were his nurses, and a member of the
order volunteered to be his one special guardian and consoler,
by night and by day.

The following extracts, translated from one of the official
Spanish documents, will it is hoped, shed light on the preceding narrative, as well as, in the first place, reveal the true port
of departure and true history of the San Dominick's voyage,
down to the time of her touching at the island of St. Maria.

But, ere the extracts come, it may be well to preface them
with a remark.

The document selected, from among many others, for partial translation, contains the deposition of Benito Cereno; the first taken in the case. Some disclosures therein were, at the time, held dubious for both learned and natural reasons. The tribunal inclined to the opinion that the deponent, not undisturbed in his mind by recent events, raved of some things which could never have happened. But subsequent depositions of the surviving sailors, bearing out the revelations of their captain in several of the strangest particulars, gave credence to the rest. So that the tribunal, in its final decision, rested its capital sentences upon statements which, had they lacked confirmation, it would have deemed it but duty to reject.

I, DON JOSE DE ABOS AND PADILLA, His Majesty's Notary for the Royal Revenue, and Register of this Province, and Notary Public of the Holy Crusade of this Bishopric, etc.

Do certify and declare, as much as is requisite in law, that, in the criminal cause commenced the twenty-fourth of the month of September, in the year seventeen hundred and ninety-nine, against the negroes of the ship San Dominick, the following declaration before me was made.

Declaration of the first witness, DON BENITO CERENO.

The same day, and month, and year, His Honor, Doctor Juan Martinez de Rozas, Councilor of the Royal Audience of this Kingdom, and learned in the law of this Intendency, ordered the captain of the ship San Dominick, Don Benito Cereno, to appear; which he did in his litter, attended by the monk Infelez; of whom he received the oath, which he took by God, our Lord, and a sign of the Cross; under which he promised to tell the truth of whatever he should know and should be asked;—and being interrogated agreeably to the tenor of the act commencing the process, he said, that on the twentieth of May last, he set sail with his ship from the port of Valparaiso, bound to that of Callao; loaded with the produce of the country beside thirty cases of hardware and one hundred and sixty blacks, of both sexes, mostly belonging to Don Alexandro Aranda, gentleman, of the city of Mendoza; that the crew of the ship consisted of thirty-six men, beside the persons who went as passengers; that the negroes were in part as follows:

[*Here, in the original, follows a list of some fifty names, descriptions, and ages, compiled from certain recovered documents of Aranda's, and also from recollections of the deponent, from which portions only are extracted.*]

—One, from about eighteen to nineteen years, named José, and this was the man that waited upon his master, Don Alexandro, and who speaks well the Spanish, having served him four or five years; * * * a mulatto, named Francesco, the cabin steward, of a good person and voice, having sung in the Valparaiso churches, native of the province of Buenos Ayres, aged about thirty-five years. * * * A smart negro, named Dago, who had been for many years a grave-digger among the Spaniards, aged forty-six years. * * * Four old negroes, born in Africa, from sixty to seventy, but sound, calkers by trade, whose names are as follows:—the first was named Mure, and he was killed (as was also his son named Diamelo); the second, Natu; the third, Yola, likewise killed; the fourth, Ghofan; and six full-grown negroes, aged from thirty to forty-five, all raw, and born among the Ashantees— Matiluqui, Yau, Lecbe, Mapenda, Yambaio, Akim; four of whom were killed; * * * a powerful negro named Atufal, who, being supposed to have been a chief in Africa, his owners set great store by him. * * * And a small negro of Senegal, but some years among the Spaniards, aged about thirty, which negro's name was Babo; * * * that he does not remember the names of the others, but that still expecting the residue of Don Alexandro's papers will be found, will then take due account of them all, and remit to the court; * * * and thirty-nine women and children of all ages.

[*The catalogue over, the deposition goes on:*]

* * * That all the negroes slept upon deck, as is customary in this navigation, and none wore fetters, because the owner, his friend Aranda, told him that they were all tractable; * * * that on the seventh day after leaving port, at three o'clock in the morning, all the Spaniards being asleep except the two officers on the watch, who were the boatswain, Juan Robles, and the carpenter, Juan Bautista Gayete, and the helmsman and his boy, the negroes revolted suddenly, wounded danger-

ously the boatswain and the carpenter, and successively killed eighteen men of those who were sleeping upon deck, some with hand-spikes and hatchets, and others by throwing them alive overboard, after tying them; that of the Spaniards upon deck, they left about seven, as he thinks, alive and tied, to manœuvre the ship, and three or four more who hid themselves, remained also alive. Although in the act of revolt the negroes made themselves masters of the hatchway, six or seven wounded went through it to the cockpit, without any hindrance on their part; that during the act of revolt, the mate and another person, whose name he does not recollect, attempted to come up through the hatchway, but being quickly wounded, they were obliged to return to the cabin; that the deponent resolved at break of day to come up the companion-way, where the negro Babo was, being the ring-leader, and Atufal, who assisted him, and having spoken to them, exhorted them to cease committing such atrocities, asking them, at the same time, what they wanted and intended to do, offering, himself, to obey their commands; that, notwithstanding this, they threw, in his presence, three men, alive and tied, overboard; that they told the deponent to come up, and that they would not kill him; which having done, the negro Babo asked him whether there were in those seas any negro countries where they might be carried, and he answered them, No; that the negro Babo afterwards told him to carry them to Senegal, or to the neighboring islands of St. Nicolas; and he answered, that this was impossible, on account of the great distance, the necessity involved of rounding Cape Horn, the bad condition of the vessel, the want of provisions, sails, and water; but that the negro Babo replied to him he must carry them in any way; that they would do and conform themselves to everything the deponent should require as to eating and drinking; that after a long conference, being absolutely compelled to please them, for they threatened him to kill all the whites if they were not, at all events, carried to Senegal, he told them that what was most wanting for the voyage was water; that they would go near the coast to take it, and thence they would proceed on their course; that the negro Babo agreed to it; and the deponent steered towards the intermediate ports, hoping to meet some Spanish

or foreign vessel that would save them; that within ten or
eleven days they saw the land, and continued their course by
it in the vicinity of Nasca; that the deponent observed that
the negroes were now restless and mutinous, because he did
not effect the taking in of water, the negro Babo having required, with threats, that it should be done, without fail, the
following day; he told him they saw plainly that the coast was
steep, and the rivers designated in the maps were not to be
found, with other reasons suitable to the circumstances; that
the best way would be to go to the island of Santa Maria,
where they might water and victual easily, it being a solitary
island, as the foreigners did; that the deponent did not go to
Pisco, that was near, nor make any other port of the coast,
because the negro Babo had intimated to him several times,
that he would kill all the whites the very moment he should
perceive any city, town, or settlement of any kind on the
shores to which they should be carried: that having determined to go to the island of Santa Maria, as the deponent
had planned, for the purpose of trying whether, on the passage or near the island itself, they could find any vessel that
should favor them, or whether he could escape from it in a
boat to the neighboring coast of Arauco; to adopt the necessary means he immediately changed his course, steering for
the island; that the negroes Babo and Atufal held daily conferences, in which they discussed what was necessary for their
design of returning to Senegal, whether they were to kill all
the Spaniards, and particularly the deponent; that eight days
after parting from the coast of Nasca, the deponent being on
the watch a little after day-break, and soon after the negroes
had their meeting, the negro Babo came to the place where
the deponent was, and told him that he had determined to
kill his master, Don Alexandro Aranda, both because he and
his companions could not otherwise be sure of their liberty,
and that, to keep the seamen in subjection, he wanted to prepare a warning of what road they should be made to take did
they or any of them oppose him; and that, by means of the
death of Don Alexandro, that warning would best be given;
but, that what this last meant, the deponent did not at the
time comprehend, nor could not, further than that the death
of Don Alexandro was intended; and moreover, the negro

Babo proposed to the deponent to call the mate Raneds, who
was sleeping in the cabin, before the thing was done, for fear,
as the deponent understood it, that the mate, who was a good
navigator, should be killed with Don Alexandro and the rest;
that the deponent, who was the friend, from youth, of Don
Alexandro, prayed and conjured, but all was useless; for the
negro Babo answered him that the thing could not be prevented, and that all the Spaniards risked their death if they
should attempt to frustrate his will in this matter, or any
other; that, in this conflict, the deponent called the mate,
Raneds, who was forced to go apart, and immediately the
negro Babo commanded the Ashantee Matiluqui and the
Ashantee Lecbe to go and commit the murder; that those two
went down with hatchets to the berth of Don Alexandro;
that, yet half alive and mangled, they dragged him on deck;
that they were going to throw him overboard in that state,
but the negro Babo stopped them, bidding the murder be
completed on the deck before him, which was done, when,
by his orders, the body was carried below, forward; that
nothing more was seen of it by the deponent for three days;
* * * that Don Alonzo Sidonia, an old man, long resident at
Valparaiso, and lately appointed to a civil office in Peru,
whither he had taken passage, was at the time sleeping in the
berth opposite Don Alexandro's; that, awakening at his cries,
surprised by them, and at the sight of the negroes with their
bloody hatchets in their hands, he threw himself into the sea
through a window which was near him, and was drowned,
without it being in the power of the deponent to assist or
take him up; * * * that, a short time after killing Aranda,
they brought upon deck his german-cousin, of middle-age,
Don Francisco Masa, of Mendoza, and the young Don Joaquin, Marques de Arambaolaza, then lately from Spain, with
his Spanish servant Ponce, and the three young clerks of
Aranda, José Morairi, Lorenzo Bargas, and Hermenegildo
Gandix, all of Cadiz; that Don Joaquin and Hermenegildo
Gandix, the negro Babo for purposes hereafter to appear, preserved alive; but Don Francisco Masa, José Morairi, and Lo-
renzo Bargas, with Ponce the servant, beside the boatswain,
Juan Robles, the boatswain's mates, Manuel Viscaya and
Roderigo Hurta, and four of the sailors, the negro Babo or-

dered to be thrown alive into the sea, although they made no
resistance, nor begged for anything else but mercy; that the
boatswain, Juan Robles, who knew how to swim, kept the
longest above water, making acts of contrition, and, in the
last words he uttered, charged this deponent to cause mass to
be said for his soul to our Lady of Succor; * * * that, during
the three days which followed, the deponent, uncertain what
fate had befallen the remains of Don Alexandro, frequently
asked the negro Babo where they were, and, if still on board,
whether they were to be preserved for interment ashore, entreating him so to order it; that the negro Babo answered
nothing till the fourth day, when at sunrise, the deponent
coming on deck, the negro Babo showed him a skeleton,
which had been substituted for the ship's proper figure-head,
the image of Christopher Colon, the discoverer of the New
World; that the negro Babo asked him whose skeleton that
was, and whether, from its whiteness, he should not think it
a white's; that, upon his covering his face, the negro Babo,
coming close, said words to this effect: "Keep faith with the
blacks from here to Senegal, or you shall in spirit, as now in
body, follow your leader," pointing to the prow; * * * that
the same morning the negro Babo took by succession each
Spaniard forward, and asked him whose skeleton that was,
and whether, from its whiteness, he should not think it a
white's; that each Spaniard covered his face; that then to each
the negro Babo repeated the words in the first place said to
the deponent; * * * that they (the Spaniards), being then
assembled aft, the negro Babo harangued them, saying that
he had now done all; that the deponent (as navigator for the
negroes) might pursue his course, warning him and all of
them that they should, soul and body, go the way of Don
Alexandro if he saw them (the Spaniards) speak or plot anything against them (the negroes)—a threat which was repeated every day; that, before the events last mentioned, they
had tied the cook to throw him overboard, for it is not
known what thing they heard him speak, but finally the negro
Babo spared his life, at the request of the deponent; that a
few days after, the deponent, endeavoring not to omit any
means to preserve the lives of the remaining whites, spoke to
the negroes peace and tranquillity, and agreed to draw up a

paper, signed by the deponent and the sailors who could write, as also by the negro Babo, for himself and all the blacks, in which the deponent obliged himself to carry them to Senegal, and they not to kill any more, and he formally to make over to them the ship, with the cargo, with which they were for that time satisfied and quieted. * * * But the next day, the more surely to guard against the sailors' escape, the negro Babo commanded all the boats to be destroyed but the long-boat, which was unseaworthy, and another, a cutter in good condition, which, knowing it would yet be wanted for towing the water casks, he had it lowered down into the hold.

* * *

[*Various particulars of the prolonged and perplexed navigation ensuing here follow, with incidents of a calamitous calm, from which portion one passage is extracted, to wit:*]

—That on the fifth day of the calm, all on board suffering much from the heat, and want of water, and five having died in fits, and mad, the negroes became irritable, and for a chance gesture, which they deemed suspicious—though it was harmless—made by the mate, Raneds, to the deponent, in the act of handing a quadrant, they killed him; but that for this they afterwards were sorry, the mate being the only remaining navigator on board, except the deponent.

* * *

—That omitting other events, which daily happened, and which can only serve uselessly to recall past misfortunes and conflicts, after seventy-three days' navigation, reckoned from the time they sailed from Nasca, during which they navigated under a scanty allowance of water, and were afflicted with the calms before mentioned, they at last arrived at the island of Santa Maria, on the seventeenth of the month of August, at about six o'clock in the afternoon, at which hour they cast anchor very near the American ship, Bachelor's Delight, which lay in the same bay, commanded by the generous Captain Amasa Delano; but at six o'clock in the morning, they had already descried the port, and the negroes became uneasy, as soon as at distance they saw the ship, not having expected to see one there; that the negro Babo pacified them, assuring them that no fear need be had; that straightway he ordered the figure on the bow to be covered with canvas, as for repairs, and had the decks a little set in order; that for a time the negro Babo and the negro Atufal conferred; that the negro Atufal was for sailing away, but the negro Babo would not, and, by himself, cast about what to do; that at last he came to the deponent, proposing to him to say and do all that the deponent declares to have said and done to the American captain; * * * * * * that the negro Babo warned him that if he varied in the least, or uttered any word, or gave any look that should give the least intimation of the past events or present state, he would instantly kill him, with all his companions, showing a dagger, which he carried hid, saying something which, as he understood it, meant that that dagger would be alert as his eye; that the negro Babo then announced the plan to all his companions, which pleased them; that he then, the better to disguise the truth, devised many expedients, in some of them uniting deceit and defense; that of this sort was the device of the six Ashantees before named, who were his bravoes; that them he stationed on the break of the poop, as if to clean certain hatchets (in cases, which were part of the cargo), but in reality to use them, and distribute them at need, and at a given word he told them; that, among other devices, was the device of presenting Atufal, his right-hand man, as chained, though in a moment the chains could be dropped; that in every particular he informed the deponent what part he was expected to enact in every device, and what story he was to tell on every occasion, always threatening him with instant death if he varied in the least: that, conscious that many of the negroes would be turbulent, the negro Babo appointed the four aged negroes, who were calkers, to keep what domestic order they could on the decks; that again and again he harangued the Spaniards and his companions, informing them of his intent, and of his devices, and of the invented story that this deponent was to tell, charging them lest any of them varied from that story; that these arrangements were made and matured during the interval of two or three hours, between their first sighting the ship and the arrival on board of Captain Amasa Delano; that this happened about half-past seven o'clock in the morning, Captain Amasa Delano coming in his boat, and all gladly receiving him; that the deponent, as well as he could force himself, acting then the part of principal owner, and a free captain of the ship, told Captain Amasa Delano, when called upon, that he came from Buenos Ayres, bound to Lima, with three hundred negroes; that off Cape Horn, and in a subsequent fever, many negroes had died; that also, by similar casualties, all the sea officers and the greatest part of the crew had died.

*　　　*　　　*

[*And so the deposition goes on, circumstantially recounting the fictitious story dictated to the deponent by Babo, and through the deponent imposed upon Captain Delano; and also recounting the friendly offers of Captain Delano, with other things, but all of which is here omitted. After the fictitious, strange story, etc., the deposition proceeds:*]

—that the generous Captain Amasa Delano remained on board all the day, till he left the ship anchored at six o'clock in the evening, deponent speaking to him always of his pretended misfortunes, under the forementioned principles, without having had it in his power to tell a single word, or give him the least hint, that he might know the truth and state of things; because the negro Babo, performing the office of an officious servant with all the appearance of submission of the humble slave, did not leave the deponent one moment; that this was in order to observe the deponent's actions and words, for the negro Babo understands well the Spanish; and besides, there were thereabout some others who were constantly on the watch, and likewise understood the Spanish; * * * that upon one occasion, while deponent was standing on the deck conversing with Amasa Delano, by a secret sign the negro Babo drew him (the deponent) aside, the act appearing as if originating with the deponent; that then, he being drawn aside, the negro Babo proposed to him to gain from Amasa Delano full particulars about his ship, and crew, and arms; that the deponent asked "For what?" that the negro Babo answered he might conceive; that, grieved at the prospect of what might overtake the generous Captain Amasa

Delano, the deponent at first refused to ask the desired questions, and used every argument to induce the negro Babo to give up this new design; that the negro Babo showed the point of his dagger; that, after the information had been obtained, the negro Babo again drew him aside, telling him that that very night he (the deponent) would be captain of two ships, instead of one, for that, great part of the American's ship's crew being to be absent fishing, the six Ashantees, without any one else, would easily take it; that at this time he said other things to the same purpose; that no entreaties availed; that, before Amasa Delano's coming on board, no hint had been given touching the capture of the American ship: that to prevent this project the deponent was powerless; * * * —that in some things his memory is confused, he cannot distinctly recall every event; * * * —that as soon as they had cast anchor at six of the clock in the evening, as has before been stated, the American Captain took leave to return to his vessel; that upon a sudden impulse, which the deponent believes to have come from God and his angels, he, after the farewell had been said, followed the generous Captain Amasa Delano as far as the gunwale, where he stayed, under pretense of taking leave, until Amasa Delano should have been seated in his boat; that on shoving off, the deponent sprang from the gunwale into the boat, and fell into it, he knows not how, God guarding him; that—

*   *   *

[*Here, in the original, follows the account of what further happened at the escape, and how the San Dominick was retaken, and of the passage to the coast; including in the recital many expressions of "eternal gratitude" to the "generous Captain Amasa Delano." The deposition then proceeds with recapitulatory remarks, and a partial renumeration of the negroes, making record of their individual part in the past events, with a view to furnishing, according to command of the court, the data whereon to found the criminal sentences to be pronounced. From this portion is the following:*]

—That he believes that all the negroes, though not in the first place knowing to the design of revolt, when it was accomplished, approved it. * * * That the negro, José, eighteen years old, and in the personal service of Don Alexandro, was the one who communicated the information to the negro Babo, about the state of things in the cabin, before the revolt; that this is known, because, in the preceding midnights, he used to come from his berth, which was under his master's, in the cabin, to the deck where the ringleader and his associates were, and had secret conversations with the negro Babo, in which he was several times seen by the mate; that, one night, the mate drove him away twice; * * that this same negro José, was the one who, without being commanded to do so by the negro Babo, as Lecbe and Matiluqui were, stabbed his master, Don Alexandro, after he had been dragged half-lifeless to the deck; * * that the mulatto steward, Francesco, was of the first band of revolters, that he was, in all things, the creature and tool of the negro Babo; that, to make his court, he, just before a repast in the cabin, proposed, to the negro Babo, poisoning a dish for the generous Captain Amasa Delano; this is known and believed, because the negroes have said it; but that the negro Babo, having another design, forbade Francesco; * * that the Ashantee Lecbe was one of the worst of them; for that, on the day the ship was retaken, he assisted in the defense of her, with a hatchet in each hand, with one of which he wounded, in the breast, the chief mate of Amasa Delano, in the first act of boarding; this all knew; that, in sight of the deponent, Lecbe struck, with a hatchet, Don Francisco Masa when, by the negro Babo's orders, he was carrying him to throw him overboard, alive; beside participating in the murder, before mentioned, of Don Alexandro Aranda, and others of the cabin-passengers; that, owing to the fury with which the Ashantees fought in the engagement with the boats, but this Lecbe and Yau survived; that Yau was bad as Lecbe; that Yau was the man who, by Babo's command, willingly prepared the skeleton of Don Alexandro, in a way the negroes afterwards told the deponent, but which he, so long as reason is left him, can never divulge; that Yau and Lecbe were the two who, in a calm by night, riveted the skeleton to the bow; this also the negroes told him; that the negro Babo was he who traced the inscription below it; that the negro Babo was the plotter from first to

last; he ordered every murder, and was the helm and keel of
the revolt; that Atufal was his lieutenant in all; but Atufal,
with his own hand, committed no murder; nor did the negro
Babo; * * that Atufal was shot, being killed in the fight with
the boats, ere boarding; * * that the negresses, of age, were
knowing to the revolt, and testified themselves satisfied at the
death of their master, Don Alexandro; that, had the negroes
not restrained them, they would have tortured to death, instead of simply killing, the Spaniards slain by command of
the negro Babo; that the negresses used their utmost influence to have the deponent made away with; that, in the various acts of murder, they sang songs and danced—not gaily,
but solemnly; and before the engagement with the boats, as
well as during the action, they sang melancholy songs to the
negroes, and that this melancholy tone was more inflaming
than a different one would have been, and was so intended;
that all this is believed, because the negroes have said it.

—that of the thirty-six men of the crew exclusive of the passengers, (all of whom are now dead), which the deponent had
knowledge of, six only remained alive, with four cabin-boys
and ship-boys, not included with the crew; * * —that the
negroes broke an arm of one of the cabin-boys and gave him
strokes with hatchets.

[*Then follow various random disclosures referring to various periods of time. The following are extracted:*]

—That during the presence of Captain Amasa Delano on
board, some attempts were made by the sailors, and one by
Hermenegildo Gandix, to convey hints to him of the true
state of affairs; but that these attempts were ineffectual, owing to fear of incurring death, and furthermore owing to the
devices which offered contradictions to the true state of affairs; as well as owing to the generosity and piety of Amasa
Delano incapable of sounding such wickedness; * * * that
Luys Galgo, a sailor about sixty years of age, and formerly of
the king's navy, was one of those who sought to convey tokens to Captain Amasa Delano; but his intent, though undiscovered, being suspected, he was, on a pretense, made to
retire out of sight, and at last into the hold, and there was
made away with. This the negroes have since said; * * * that

one of the ship-boys feeling, from Captain Amasa Delano's presence, some hopes of release, and not having enough prudence, dropped some chance-word respecting his expectations, which being overheard and understood by a slave-boy with whom he was eating at the time, the latter struck him on the head with a knife, inflicting a bad wound, but of which the boy is now healing; that likewise, not long before the ship was brought to anchor, one of the seamen, steering at the time, endangered himself by letting the blacks remark some expression in his countenance, arising from a cause similar to the above; but this sailor, by his heedful after conduct, escaped; * * * that these statements are made to show the court that from the beginning to the end of the revolt, it was impossible for the deponent and his men to act otherwise than they did; * * * —that the third clerk, Hermenegildo Gandix, who before had been forced to live among the seamen, wearing a seaman's habit, and in all respects appearing to be one for the time; he, Gandix, was killed by a musket-ball fired through a mistake from the American boats before boarding; having in his fright ran up the mizzen-rigging, calling to the boats—"don't board," lest upon their boarding the negroes should kill him; that this inducing the Americans to believe he some way favored the cause of the negroes, they fired two balls at him, so that he fell wounded from the rigging, and was drowned in the sea; * * * —that the young Don Joaquin, Marques de Arambaolaza, like Hermenegildo Gandix, the third clerk, was degraded to the office and appearance of a common seaman; that upon one occasion when Don Joaquin shrank, the negro Babo commanded the Ashantee Lecbe to take tar and heat it, and pour it upon Don Joaquin's hands; * * * —that Don Joaquin was killed owing to another mistake of the Americans, but one impossible to be avoided, as upon the approach of the boats, Don Joaquin, with a hatchet tied edge out and upright to his hand, was made by the negroes to appear on the bulwarks; whereupon, seen with arms in his hands and in a questionable attitude, he was shot for a renegade seaman; * * * —that on the person of Don Joaquin was found secreted a jewel, which, by papers that were discovered, proved to have been meant for the shrine of our Lady of Mercy in Lima; a votive offering, beforehand prepared and guarded, to attest his gratitude, when he should have landed in Peru, his last destination, for the safe conclusion of his entire voyage from Spain; * * * —that the jewel, with the other effects of the late Don Joaquin, is in the custody of the brethren of the Hospital de Sacerdotes, awaiting the disposition of the honorable court; * * * —that, owing to the condition of the deponent, as well as the haste in which the boats departed for the attack, the Americans were not forewarned that there were, among the apparent crew, a passenger and one of the clerks disguised by the negro Babo; * * * —that, beside the negroes killed in the action, some were killed after the capture and re-anchoring at night, when shackled to the ring-bolts on deck; that these deaths were committed by the sailors, ere they could be prevented. That so soon as informed of it, Captain Amasa Delano used all his authority, and, in particular with his own hand, struck down Martinez Gola, who, having found a razor in the pocket of an old jacket of his, which one of the shackled negroes had on, was aiming it at the negro's throat; that the noble Captain Amasa Delano also wrenched from the hand of Bartholomew Barlo, a dagger secreted at the time of the massacre of the whites, with which he was in the act of stabbing a shackled negro, who, the same day, with another negro, had thrown him down and jumped upon him; * * * — that, for all the events, befalling through so long a time, during which the ship was in the hands of the negro Babo, he cannot here give account; but that, what he has said is the most substantial of what occurs to him at present, and is the truth under the oath which he has taken; which declaration he affirmed and ratified, after hearing it read to him.

He said that he is twenty-nine years of age, and broken in body and mind; that when finally dismissed by the court, he shall not return home to Chili, but betake himself to the monastery on Mount Agonia without; and signed with his honor, and crossed himself, and, for the time, departed as he came, in his litter, with the monk Infelez, to the Hospital de Sacerdotes.   BENITO CERENO.

DOCTOR ROZAS.

If the Deposition have served as the key to fit into the lock of the complications which precede it, then, as a vault whose door has been flung back, the San Dominick's hull lies open to-day.

Hitherto the nature of this narrative, besides rendering the intricacies in the beginning unavoidable, has more or less required that many things, instead of being set down in the order of occurrence, should be retrospectively, or irregularly given; this last is the case with the following passages, which will conclude the account:

During the long, mild voyage to Lima, there was, as before hinted, a period during which the sufferer a little recovered his health, or, at least in some degree, his tranquillity. Ere the decided relapse which came, the two captains had many cordial conversations—their fraternal unreserve in singular contrast with former withdrawments.

Again and again, it was repeated, how hard it had been to enact the part forced on the Spaniard by Babo.

"Ah, my dear friend," Don Benito once said, "at those very times when you thought me so morose and ungrateful, nay, when, as you now admit, you half thought me plotting your murder, at those very times my heart was frozen; I could not look at you, thinking of what, both on board this ship and your own, hung, from other hands, over my kind benefactor. And as God lives, Don Amasa, I know not whether desire for my own safety alone could have nerved me to that leap into your boat, had it not been for the thought that, did you, unenlightened, return to your ship, you, my best friend, with all who might be with you, stolen upon, that night, in your hammocks, would never in this world have wakened again. Do but think how you walked this deck, how you sat in this cabin, every inch of ground mined into honey-combs under you. Had I dropped the least hint, made the least advance towards an understanding between us, death, explosive death—yours as mine—would have ended the scene."

"True, true," cried Captain Delano, starting, "you have saved my life, Don Benito, more than I yours; saved it, too, against my knowledge and will."

"Nay, my friend," rejoined the Spaniard, courteous even to the point of religion, "God charmed your life, but you saved mine. To think of some things you did—those smilings and chattings, rash pointings and gesturings. For less than these, they slew my mate, Raneds; but you had the Prince of Heaven's safe conduct through all ambuscades."

"Yes, all is owing to Providence, I know; but the temper of my mind that morning was more than commonly pleasant, while the sight of so much suffering, more apparent than real, added to my good nature, compassion, and charity, happily interweaving the three. Had it been otherwise, doubtless, as you hint, some of my interferences might have ended unhappily enough. Besides that, those feelings I spoke of enabled me to get the better of momentary distrust, at times when acuteness might have cost me my life, without saving another's. Only at the end did my suspicions get the better of me, and you know how wide of the mark they then proved."

"Wide, indeed," said Don Benito, sadly; "you were with me all day; stood with me, sat with me, talked with me, looked at me, ate with me, drank with me; and yet, your last act was to clutch for a monster, not only an innocent man, but the most pitiable of all men. To such degree may malign machinations and deceptions impose. So far may even the best man err, in judging the conduct of one with the recesses of whose condition he is not acquainted. But you were forced to it; and you were in time undeceived. Would that, in both respects, it was so ever, and with all men."

"You generalize, Don Benito; and mournfully enough. But the past is passed; why moralize upon it? Forget it. See, yon bright sun has forgotten it all, and the blue sea, and the blue sky; these have turned over new leaves."

"Because they have no memory," he dejectedly replied; "because they are not human."

"But these mild trades that now fan your cheek, do they not come with a human-like healing to you? Warm friends, steadfast friends are the trades."

"With their steadfastness they but waft me to my tomb, señor," was the foreboding response.

"You are saved," cried Captain Delano, more and more astonished and pained; "you are saved; what has cast such a shadow upon you?"

"The negro."

There was silence, while the moody man sat, slowly and

unconsciously gathering his mantle about him, as if it were a pall.

There was no more conversation that day.

But if the Spaniard's melancholy sometimes ended in muteness upon topics like the above, there were others upon which he never spoke at all; on which, indeed, all his old reserves were piled. Pass over the worst, and, only to elucidate, let an item or two of these be cited. The dress so precise and costly, worn by him on the day whose events have been narrated, had not willingly been put on. And that silver-mounted sword, apparent symbol of despotic command, was not, indeed, a sword, but the ghost of one. The scabbard, artificially stiffened, was empty.

As for the black—whose brain, not body, had schemed and led the revolt, with the plot—his slight frame, inadequate to that which it held, had at once yielded to the superior muscular strength of his captor, in the boat. Seeing all was over, he uttered no sound, and could not be forced to. His aspect seemed to say, since I cannot do deeds, I will not speak words. Put in irons in the hold, with the rest, he was carried to Lima. During the passage Don Benito did not visit him. Nor then, nor at any time after, would he look at him. Before the tribunal he refused. When pressed by the judges he fainted. On the testimony of the sailors alone rested the legal identity of Babo.

Some months after, dragged to the gibbet at the tail of a mule, the black met his voiceless end. The body was burned to ashes; but for many days, the head, that hive of subtlety, fixed on a pole in the Plaza, met, unabashed, the gaze of the whites; and across the Plaza looked towards St. Bartholomew's church, in whose vaults slept then, as now, the recovered bones of Aranda; and across the Rimac bridge looked towards the monastery, on Mount Agonia without; where, three months after being dismissed by the court, Benito Cereno, borne on the bier, did, indeed, follow his leader.

The Lightning-Rod Man

WHAT GRAND irregular thunder, thought I, standing on my hearthstone among the Acroceraunian hills, as the scattered bolts boomed overhead and crashed down among the valleys, every bolt followed by zig-zag irradiations, and swift slants of sharp rain, which audibly rang, like a charge of spear-points, on my low shingled roof. I suppose, though, that the mountains hereabouts break and churn up the thunder, so that it is far more glorious here than on the plain. Hark!—some one at the door. Who is this that chooses a time of thunder for making calls? And why don't he, man-fashion, use the knocker, instead of making that doleful undertaker's clatter with his fist against the hollow panel? But let him in. Ah, here he comes. "Good day, sir:" an entire stranger. "Pray be seated." What is that strange-looking walking-stick he carries:—"A fine thunder-storm, sir."

"Fine?—Awful!"

"You are wet. Stand here on the hearth before the fire."

"Not for worlds!"

The stranger still stood in the exact middle of the cottage, where he had first planted himself. His singularity impelled a closer scrutiny. A lean, gloomy figure. Hair dark and lank, mattedly streaked over his brow. His sunken pitfalls of eyes were ringed by indigo halos, and played with an innocuous sort of lightning: the gleam without the bolt. The whole man was dripping. He stood in a puddle on the bare oak floor; his strange walking-stick vertically resting at his side.

It was a polished copper rod, four feet long, lengthwise attached to a neat wooden staff, by insertion into two balls of greenish glass, ringed with copper bands. The metal rod terminated at the top tripodwise, in three keen tines, brightly gilt. He held the thing by the wooden part alone.

"Sir," said I, bowing politely, "have I the honor of a visit from that illustrious god, Jupiter Tonans? So stood he in the Greek statue of old, grasping the lightning-bolt. If you be he, or his viceroy, I have to thank you for this noble storm you have brewed among our mountains. Listen: That was a glorious peal. Ah, to a lover of the majestic, it is a good thing to have the Thunderer himself in one's cottage. The thunder grows finer for that. But pray be seated. This old rush-bottomed arm-chair, I grant, is a poor substitute for your evergreen throne on Olympus; but, condescend to be seated."

While I thus pleasantly spoke, the stranger eyed me, half in wonder and half in a strange sort of horror; but did not move a foot.

"Do, sir, be seated; you need to be dried ere going forth again."

I planted the chair invitingly on the broad hearth, where a little fire had been kindled that afternoon to dissipate the dampness, not the cold; for it was early in the month of September.

But without heeding my solicitation, and still standing in the middle of the floor, the stranger gazed at me portentously and spoke.

"Sir," said he, "excuse me, but instead of my accepting your invitation to be seated on the hearth there, I solemnly warn *you*, that you had best accept *mine*, and stand with me in the middle of the room. Good heavens!" he cried, starting— "there's another of those awful crashes. I warn you, sir, quit the hearth."

"Mr. Jupiter Tonans," said I, quietly rolling my body on the stone, "I stand very well here."

"Are you so horridly ignorant, then," he cried, "as not to know, that by far the most dangerous part of a house during such a terrific tempest as this, is the fire-place?"

"Nay, I did not know that," involuntarily stepping upon the first board next to the stone.

The stranger now assumed such an unpleasant air of successful admonition, that—quite involuntarily again—I stepped back upon the hearth, and threw myself into the erectest, proudest posture I could command. But I said nothing.

"For Heaven's sake," he cried, with a strange mixture of alarm and intimidation—"for Heaven's sake, get off of the hearth! Know you not, that the heated air and soot are conductors;—to say nothing of those immense iron fire-dogs? Quit the spot,—I conjure,—I command you."

"Mr. Jupiter Tonans, I am not accustomed to be commanded in my own house."

"Call me not by that pagan name. You are profane in this time of terror."

"Sir, will you be so good as to tell me your business? If you seek shelter from the storm, you are welcome, so long as you be civil; but if you come on business, open it forthwith. Who are you?"

"I am a dealer in lightning-rods," said the stranger, softening his tone; "my special business is—— Merciful heaven! what a crash!—Have you ever been struck—your premises, I mean? No? It's best to be provided;"—significantly rattling his metallic staff on the floor;—"by nature, there are no castles in thunder-storms; yet, say but the word, and of this cottage I can make a Gibraltar by a few waves of this wand. Hark, what Himmalayas of concussions!"

"You interrupted yourself; your special business you were about to speak of."

"My special business is to travel the country for orders for lightning-rods. This is my specimen-rod;" tapping his staff; "I have the best of references"—fumbling in his pockets. "In Criggan last month, I put up three-and-twenty rods on only five buildings."

"Let me see. Was it not at Criggan last week, about midnight on Saturday, that the steeple, the big elm and the Assembly-room cupola were struck? Any of your rods there?"

"Not on the tree and cupola, but the steeple."

"Of what use is your rod then?"

"Of life-and-death use. But my workman was heedless. In fitting the rod at top to the steeple, he allowed a part of the metal to graze the tin sheeting. Hence the accident. Not my fault, but his. Hark!"

"Never mind. That clap burst quite loud enough to be heard without finger-pointing. Did you hear of the event at Montreal last year? A servant girl struck at her bed-side with a rosary in her hand; the beads being metal. Does your beat extend into the Canadas?"

"No. And I hear that there, iron rods only are in use. They should have *mine*, which are copper. Iron is easily fused. Then they draw out the rod so slender, that it has not body enough to conduct the full electric current. The metal melts; the building is destroyed. My copper rods never act so. Those

Canadians are fools. Some of them knob the rod at the top, which risks a deadly explosion, instead of imperceptibly carrying down the current into the earth, as this sort of rod does. *Mine* is the only true rod. Look at it. Only one dollar a foot."

"This abuse of your own calling in another might make one distrustful with respect to yourself."

"Hark! The thunder becomes less muttering. It is nearing us, and nearing the earth, too. Hark! One crammed crash! All the vibrations made one by nearness. Another flash. Hold!"

"What do you?" I said, seeing him now, instantaneously relinquishing his staff, lean intently forward towards the window, with his right fore and middle fingers on his left wrist.

But ere the words had well escaped me, another exclamation escaped him.

"Crash! only three pulses—less than a third of a mile off—yonder, somewhere in that wood. I passed three stricken oaks there, ripped out new and glittering. The oak draws lightning more than other timber, having iron in solution in its sap. Your floor here seems oak."

"Heart-of-oak. From the peculiar time of your call upon me, I suppose you purposely select stormy weather for your journeys. When the thunder is roaring, you deem it an hour peculiarly favorable for producing impressions favorable to your trade."

"Hark!—Awful!"

"For one who would arm others with fearlessness, you seem unbeseemingly timorous yourself. Common men choose fair weather for their travels: you choose thunder-storms; and yet———"

"That I travel in thunder-storms, I grant; but not without particular precautions, such as only a lightning-rod man may know. Hark! Quick—look at my specimen rod. Only one dollar a foot."

"A very fine rod, I dare say. But what are these particular precautions of yours? Yet first let me close yonder shutters; the slanting rain is beating through the sash. I will bar up."

"Are you mad? Know you not that yon iron bar is a swift conductor? Desist."

"I will simply close the shutters then, and call my boy to bring me a wooden bar. Pray, touch the bell-pull there."

"Are you frantic? That bell-wire might blast you. Never touch bell-wire in a thunder-storm, nor ring a bell of any sort."

"Nor those in belfries? Pray, will you tell me where and how one may be safe in a time like this? Is there any part of my house I may touch with hopes of my life?"

"There is; but not where you now stand. Come away from the wall. The current will sometimes run down a wall, and—a man being a better conductor than a wall—it would leave the wall and run into him. Swoop! *That* must have fallen very nigh. That must have been globular lightning."

"Very probably. Tell me at once, which is, in your opinion, the safest part of this house?"

"This room, and this one spot in it where I stand. Come hither."

"The reasons first."

"Hark!—after the flash the gust—the sashes shiver—the house, the house!—Come hither to me!"

"The reasons, if you please."

"Come hither to me!"

"Thank you again, I think I will try my old stand,—the hearth. And now Mr. Lightning-rod-man, in the pauses of the thunder, be so good as to tell me your reasons for esteeming this one room of the house the safest, and your own one stand-point there the safest spot in it."

There was now a little cessation of the storm for a while. The Lightning-rod man seemed relieved, and replied:—

"Your house is a one-storied house, with an attic and a cellar; this room is between. Hence its comparative safety. Because lightning sometimes passes from the clouds to the earth, and sometimes from the earth to the clouds. Do you comprehend?—and I choose the middle of the room, because, if the lightning should strike the house at all, it would come down the chimney or walls; so, obviously, the further you are from them, the better. Come hither to me, now."

"Presently. Something you just said, instead of alarming me, has strangely inspired confidence."

"What have I said?"

"You said that sometimes lightning flashes from the earth to the clouds."

"Aye, the returning-stroke, as it is called; when the earth, being overcharged with the fluid, flashes its surplus upward."

"The returning-stroke; that is, from earth to sky. Better and better. But come here on the hearth and dry yourself."

"I am better here, and better wet."

"How?"

"It is the safest thing you can do—Hark, again!—to get yourself thoroughly drenched in a thunder-storm. Wet clothes are better conductors than the body; and so, if the lightning strike, it might pass down the wet clothes without touching the body. The storm deepens again. Have you a rug in the house? Rugs are non-conductors. Get one, that I may stand on it here, and you too. The skies blacken—it is dusk at noon. Hark!—the rug, the rug!"

I gave him one; while the hooded mountains seemed closing and tumbling into the cottage.

"And now, since our being dumb will not help us," said I, resuming my place, "let me hear your precautions in travelling during thunder-storms."

"Wait till this one is passed."

"Nay, proceed with the precautions. You stand in the safest possible place according to your own account. Go on."

"Briefly then. I avoid pine-trees, high houses, lonely barns, upland pastures, running water, flocks of cattle and sheep, a crowd of men. If I travel on foot,—as to-day—I do not walk fast; if in my buggy, I touch not its back or sides; if on horseback, I dismount and lead the horse. But of all things, I avoid tall men."

"Do I dream? Man avoid man? and in danger-time too?"

"Tall men in a thunder-storm I avoid. Are you so grossly ignorant as not to know, that the height of a six-footer is sufficient to discharge an electric cloud upon him? Are not lonely Kentuckians, ploughing, smit in the unfinished furrow? Nay, if the six-footer stand by running water, the cloud will sometimes *select* him as its conductor to that running water. Hark! Sure, yon black pinnacle is split. Yes, a man is a good conductor. The lightning goes through and through a man, but only peels a tree. But sir, you have kept me so long answering your questions, that I have not yet come to business. Will you order one of my rods? Look at this specimen one?

See: it is of the best of copper. Copper's the best conductor. Your house is low; but being upon the mountains, that lowness does not one whit depress it. You mountaineers are most exposed. In mountainous countries the lightning-rod man should have most business. Look at the specimen, sir. One rod will answer for a house so small as this. Look over these recommendations. Only one rod, sir; cost, only twenty dollars. Hark! There go all the granite Taconics and Hoosics dashed together like pebbles. By the sound, that must have struck something. An elevation of five feet above the house, will protect twenty feet radius all about the rod. Only twenty dollars, sir—a dollar a foot. Hark!—Dreadful!—Will you order? Will you buy? Shall I put down your name? Think of being a heap of charred offal, like a haltered horse burnt in his stall;—and all in one flash!"

"You pretended envoy extraordinary and minister plenipotentiary to and from Jupiter Tonans," laughed I; "you mere man who come here to put you and your pipestem between clay and sky, do you think that because you can strike a bit of green light from the Leyden jar, that you can thoroughly avert the supernal bolt? Your rod rusts, or breaks, and where are you? Who has empowered you, you Tetzel, to peddle round your indulgences from divine ordinations? The hairs of our heads are numbered, and the days of our lives. In thunder as in sunshine, I stand at ease in the hands of my God. False negotiator, away! See, the scroll of the storm is rolled back; the house is unharmed; and in the blue heavens I read in the rainbow, that the Deity will not, of purpose, make war on man's earth."

"Impious wretch!" foamed the stranger, blackening in the face as the rainbow beamed, "I will publish your infidel notions."

"Begone! move quickly! if quickly you can, you that shine forth into sight in moist times like the worm."

The scowl grew blacker on his face; the indigo-circles enlarged round his eyes as the storm rings round the midnight moon. He sprang upon me; his tri-forked thing at my heart.

I seized it; I snapped it; I dashed it; I trod it; and dragging the dark lightning-king out of my door, flung his elbowed, copper sceptre after him.

But spite of my treatment, and spite of my dissuasive talk of him to my neighbors, the Lightning-rod man still dwells in the land; still travels in storm-time, and drives a brave trade with the fears of man.

The Encantadas, or Enchanted Isles

By Salvator R. Tarnmoor

Sketch First

The Isles at Large

—" That may not be, said then the ferryman,
Least we unweeting hap to be fordonne;
For those same islands seeming now and than,
Are not firme land, nor any certein wonne,
But stragling plots which to and fro do ronne
In the wide waters; therefore are they hight
The Wandering Islands; therefore do them shonne;
For they have oft drawne many a wandring wight
Into most deadly daunger and distressed plight;
For whosoever once hath fastened
His foot thereon may never it recure
But wandreth evermore uncertein and unsure."

*　　　*　　　*　　　*　　　*

"Darke, dolefull, dreary, like a greedy grave,
That still for carrion carcasses doth crave;
On top whereof ay dwelt the ghastly owl,
Shrieking his balefull note, which ever drave
Far from that haunt all other cheerful fowl,
And all about it wandring ghosts did wayle and howl."

TAKE FIVE-AND-TWENTY heaps of cinders dumped here and there in an outside city lot; imagine some of them magnified into mountains, and the vacant lot the sea; and you will have a fit idea of the general aspect of the Encantadas, or Enchanted Isles. A group rather of extinct volcanoes than of isles; looking much as the world at large might, after a penal conflagration.

It is to be doubted whether any spot of earth can, in desolateness, furnish a parallel to this group. Abandoned cemeteries of long ago, old cities by piecemeal tumbling to their ruin, these are melancholy enough; but, like all else which has but once been associated with humanity they still awaken in us some thoughts of sympathy, however sad. Hence, even the

Dead Sea, along with whatever other emotions it may at times inspire, does not fail to touch in the pilgrim some of his less unpleasurable feelings.

And as for solitariness; the great forests of the north, the expanses of unnavigated waters, the Greenland ice-fields, are the profoundest of solitudes to a human observer; still the magic of their changeable tides and seasons mitigates their terror; because, though unvisited by men, those forests are visited by the May; the remotest seas reflect familiar stars even as Lake Erie does; and in the clear air of a fine Polar day, the irradiated, azure ice shows beautifully as malachite.

But the special curse, as one may call it, of the Encantadas, that which exalts them in desolation above Idumea and the Pole, is that to them change never comes; neither the change of seasons nor of sorrows. Cut by the Equator, they know not autumn and they know not spring; while already reduced to the lees of fire, ruin itself can work little more upon them. The showers refresh the deserts, but in these isles, rain never falls. Like split Syrian gourds left withering in the sun, they are cracked by an everlasting drought beneath a torrid sky. "Have mercy upon me," the wailing spirit of the Encantadas seems to cry, "and send Lazarus that he may dip the tip of his finger in water and cool my tongue, for I am tormented in this flame."

Another feature in these isles is their emphatic uninhabitableness. It is deemed a fit type of all-forsaken overthrow, that the jackal should den in the wastes of weedy Babylon; but the Encantadas refuse to harbor even the outcasts of the beasts. Man and wolf alike disown them. Little but reptile life is here found:—tortoises, lizards, immense spiders, snakes, and that strangest anomaly of outlandish nature, the *iguana*. No voice, no low, no howl is heard; the chief sound of life here is a hiss.

On most of the isles where vegetation is found at all, it is more ungrateful than the blankness of Atacama. Tangled thickets of wiry bushes, without fruit and without a name, springing up among deep fissures of calcined rock, and treacherously masking them; or a parched growth of distorted cactus trees.

In many places the coast is rock-bound, or more properly,

clinker-bound; tumbled masses of blackish or greenish stuff like the dross of an iron-furnace, forming dark clefts and caves here and there, into which a ceaseless sea pours a fury of foam; overhanging them with a swirl of gray, haggard mist, amidst which sail screaming flights of unearthly birds heightening the dismal din. However calm the sea without, there is no rest for these swells and those rocks; they lash and are lashed, even when the outer ocean is most at peace with itself. On the oppressive, clouded days, such as are peculiar to this part of the watery Equator, the dark, vitrified masses, many of which raise themselves among white whirlpools and breakers in detached and perilous places off the shore, present a most Plutonian sight. In no world but a fallen one could such lands exist.

Those parts of the strand free from the marks of fire, stretch away in wide level beaches of multitudinous dead shells, with here and there decayed bits of sugar-cane, bamboos, and cocoanuts, washed upon this other and darker world from the charming palm isles to the westward and southward; all the way from Paradise to Tartarus; while mixed with the relics of distant beauty you will sometimes see fragments of charred wood and mouldering ribs of wrecks. Neither will any one be surprised at meeting these last, after observing the conflicting currents which eddy throughout nearly all the wide channels of the entire group. The capriciousness of the tides of air sympathizes with those of the sea. Nowhere is the wind so light, baffling, and every way unreliable, and so given to perplexing calms, as at the Encantadas. Nigh a month has been spent by a ship going from one isle to another, though but ninety miles between; for owing to the force of the current, the boats employed to tow barely suffice to keep the craft from sweeping upon the cliffs, but do nothing towards accelerating her voyage. Sometimes it is impossible for a vessel from afar to fetch up with the group itself, unless large allowances for prospective lee-way have been made ere its coming in sight. And yet, at other times, there is a mysterious indraft, which irresistibly draws a passing vessel among the isles, though not bound to them.

True, at one period, as to some extent at the present day, large fleets of whalemen cruised for Spermaceti upon what some seamen call the Enchanted Ground. But this, as in due place will be described, was off the great outer isle of Albemarle, away from the intricacies of the smaller isles, where there is plenty of sea-room; and hence, to that vicinity, the above remarks do not altogether apply; though even there the current runs at times with singular force, shifting, too, with as singular a caprice. Indeed, there are seasons when currents quite unaccountable prevail for a great distance round about the total group, and are so strong and irregular as to change a vessel's course against the helm, though sailing at the rate of four or five miles the hour. The difference in the reckonings of navigators produced by these causes, along with the light and variable winds, long nourished a persuasion that there existed two distinct clusters of isles in the parallel of the Encantadas, about a hundred leagues apart. Such was the idea of their earlier visitors, the Buccaneers; and as late as 1750, the charts of that part of the Pacific accorded with the strange delusion. And this apparent fleetingness and unreality of the locality of the isles was most probably one reason for the Spaniards calling them the Encantada, or Enchanted Group.

But not uninfluenced by their character, as they now confessedly exist, the modern voyager will be inclined to fancy that the bestowal of this name might have in part originated in that air of spell-bound desertness which so significantly invests the isles. Nothing can better suggest the aspect of once living things malignly crumbled from ruddiness into ashes. Apples of Sodom, after touching, seem these isles.

However wavering their place may seem by reason of the currents, they themselves, at least to one upon the shore, appear invariably the same: fixed, cast, glued into the very body of cadaverous death.

Nor would the appellation, enchanted, seem misapplied in still another sense. For concerning the peculiar reptile inhabitant of these wilds—whose presence gives the group its second Spanish name, Gallipagos—concerning the tortoises found here, most mariners have long cherished a superstition, not more frightful than grotesque. They earnestly believe that all wicked sea-officers, more especially commodores and captains, are at death (and in some cases, before death) transformed into tortoises; thenceforth dwelling upon these hot aridities, sole solitary Lords of Asphaltum.

Doubtless so quaintly dolorous a thought was originally inspired by the woe-begone landscape itself, but more particularly, perhaps, by the tortoises. For apart from their strictly physical features, there is something strangely self-condemned in the appearance of these creatures. Lasting sorrow and penal hopelessness are in no animal form so suppliantly expressed as in theirs; while the thought of their wonderful longevity does not fail to enhance the impression.

Nor even at the risk of meriting the charge of absurdly believing in enchantments, can I restrain the admission that sometimes, even now, when leaving the crowded city to wander out July and August among the Adirondack Mountains, far from the influences of towns and proportionally nigh to the mysterious ones of nature; when at such times I sit me down in the mossy head of some deep-wooded gorge, surrounded by prostrate trunks of blasted pines, and recall, as in a dream, my other and far-distant rovings in the baked heart of the charmed isles; and remember the sudden glimpses of dusky shells, and long languid necks protruded from the leafless thickets; and again have beheld the vitreous inland rocks worn down and grooved into deep ruts by ages and ages of the slow draggings of tortoises in quest of pools of scanty water; I can hardly resist the feeling that in my time I have indeed slept upon evilly enchanted ground.

Nay, such is the vividness of my memory, or the magic of my fancy, that I know not whether I am not the occasional victim of optical delusion concerning the Gallipagos. For often in scenes of social merriment, and especially at revels held by candle-light in old-fashioned mansions, so that shadows are thrown into the further recesses of an angular and spacious room, making them put on a look of haunted undergrowth of lonely woods, I have drawn the attention of my comrades by my fixed gaze and sudden change of air, as I have seemed to see, slowly emerging from those imagined solitudes, and heavily crawling along the floor, the ghost of a gigantic tortoise, with "Memento * * * * " burning in live letters upon his back.

Sketch Second
Two Sides to a Tortoise

"Most ugly shapes and horrible aspects,
Such as Dame Nature selfe mote feare to see,
Or shame, that ever should so fowle defects
From her most cunning hand escaped bee;
All dreadfull pourtraicts of deformitee.
Ne wonder if these do a man appall;
For all that here at home we dreadfull hold
Be but as bugs to fearen babes withall
Compared to the creatures in these isles' entrall.

    *   *   *   *   *

Fear naught, then said the palmer, well avized,
For these same monsters are not these indeed,
But are into these fearful shapes disguized.

    *   *   *   *   *

And lifting up his vertuous staffe on high,
Then all that dreadful armie fast gan flye
Into great Tethys' bosom, where they hidden lye."

In view of the description given, may one be gay upon the Encantadas? Yes: that is, find one the gayety, and he will be gay. And indeed, sackcloth and ashes as they are, the isles are not perhaps unmitigated gloom. For while no spectator can deny their claims to a most solemn and superstitious consideration, no more than my firmest resolutions can decline to behold the spectre-tortoise when emerging from its shadowy recess; yet even the tortoise, dark and melancholy as it is upon the back, still possesses a bright side; its calapee or breast-plate being sometimes of a faint yellowish or golden tinge. Moreover, every one knows that tortoises as well as turtle are of such a make, that if you but put them on their backs you thereby expose their bright sides without the possibility of their recovering themselves, and turning into view the other. But after you have done this, and because you have done this, you should not swear that the tortoise has no dark side. Enjoy the bright, keep it turned up perpetually if you can, but be honest and don't deny the black. Neither should he who cannot turn the tortoise from its natural position so as to hide the darker and expose his livelier aspect, like a great October pumpkin in the sun, for that cause declare the creature to be one total inky blot. The tortoise is both black and bright. But let us to particulars.

Some months before my first stepping ashore upon the group, my ship was cruising in its close vicinity. One noon we found ourselves off the South Head of Albemarle, and not very far from the land. Partly by way of freak, and partly by way of spying out so strange a country, a boat's crew was sent ashore, with orders to see all they could, and besides, bring back whatever tortoises they could conveniently transport.

It was after sunset when the adventurers returned. I looked down over the ship's high side as if looking down over the curb of a well, and dimly saw the damp boat deep in the sea with some unwonted weight. Ropes were dropt over, and presently three huge antediluvian-looking tortoises after much straining were landed on deck. They seemed hardly of the seed of earth. We had been broad upon the waters for five long months, a period amply sufficient to make all things of the land wear a fabulous hue to the dreamy mind. Had three Spanish custom-house officers boarded us then, it is not un-likely that I should have curiously stared at them, felt of them, and stroked them much as savages serve civilized guests. But instead of three custom-house officers, behold these really wondrous tortoises—none of your schoolboy mud-turtles—but black as widower's weeds, heavy as chests of plate, with vast shells medallioned and orbed like shields, and dented and blistered like shields that have breasted a battle, shaggy too, here and there, with dark green moss, and slimy with the spray of the sea. These mystic creatures suddenly translated by night from unutterable solitudes to our peopled deck, af-fected me in a manner not easy to unfold. They seemed newly crawled forth from beneath the foundations of the world. Yea, they seemed the identical tortoises whereon the Hindoo plants this total sphere. With a lantern I inspected them more closely. Such worshipful venerableness of aspect! Such furry greenness mantling the rude peelings and healing the fissures of their shattered shells. I no more saw three tortoises. They expanded—became transfigured. I seemed to see three Roman Coliseums in magnificent decay.

Ye oldest inhabitants of this, or any other isle, said I, pray, give me the freedom of your three walled towns.

The great feeling inspired by these creatures was that of age:—dateless, indefinite endurance. And in fact that any other creature can live and breathe as long as the tortoise of the Encantadas, I will not readily believe. Not to hint of their known capacity of sustaining life, while going without food for an entire year, consider that impregnable armor of their living mail. What other bodily being possesses such a citadel wherein to resist the assaults of Time?

As, lantern in hand, I scraped among the moss and beheld the ancient scars of bruises received in many a sullen fall among the marly mountains of the isle—scars strangely widened, swollen, half obliterate, and yet distorted like those sometimes found in the bark of very hoary trees, I seemed an antiquary of a geologist, studying the bird-tracks and ciphers upon the exhumed slates trod by incredible creatures whose very ghosts are now defunct.

As I lay in my hammock that night, overhead I heard the slow weary draggings of the three ponderous strangers along the encumbered deck. Their stupidity or their resolution was so great, that they never went aside for any impediment. One ceased his movements altogether just before the mid-watch. At sunrise I found him butted like a battering-ram against the immovable foot of the foremast, and still striving, tooth and nail, to force the impossible passage. That these tortoises are the victims of a penal, or malignant, or perhaps a downright diabolical enchanter, seems in nothing more likely than in that strange infatuation of hopeless toil which so often possesses them. I have known them in their journeyings ram themselves heroically against rocks, and long abide there, nudging, wriggling, wedging, in order to displace them, and so hold on their inflexible path. Their crowning curse is their drudging impulse to straightforwardness in a belittered world.

Meeting with no such hinderance as their companion did, the other tortoises merely fell foul of small stumbling-blocks;

buckets, blocks, and coils of rigging; and at times in the act of crawling over them would slip with an astounding rattle to the deck. Listening to these draggings and concussions, I thought me of the haunt from which they came; an isle full of metallic ravines and gulches, sunk bottomlessly into the hearts of splintered mountains, and covered for many miles with inextricable thickets. I then pictured these three straight-forward monsters, century after century, writhing through the shades, grim as blacksmiths; crawling so slowly and ponderously, that not only did toadstools and all fungous things grow beneath their feet, but a sooty moss sprouted upon their backs. With them I lost myself in volcanic mazes; brushed away endless boughs of rotting thickets; till finally in a dream I found myself sitting crosslegged upon the foremost, a Brahmin similarly mounted upon either side, forming a tripod of foreheads which upheld the universal cope.

Such was the wild nightmare begot by my first impression of the Encantadas tortoise. But next evening, strange to say, I sat down with my shipmates, and made a merry repast from tortoise steaks and tortoise stews; and supper over, out knife, and helped convert the three mighty concave shells into three fanciful soup-tureens, and polished the three flat yellowish calapees into three gorgeous salvers.

Sketch Third

Rock Rodondo

> "Forthy this hight the Rock of vile Reproach,
> A dangerous and dreadful place,
> To which nor fish nor fowl did once approach,
> But yelling meaws with sea-gulls hoars and bace
> And cormoyrants with birds of ravenous race,
> Which still sit waiting on that dreadful clift."
>
>   ＊   ＊   ＊   ＊   ＊
>
> "With that the rolling sea resounding soft
> In his big base them fitly answered,
> And on the Rock, the waves breaking aloft,
> A solemn meane unto them measured."

*   *   *   *   *

"Then he the boteman bad row easily,
And let him heare some part of that rare melody."

    *   *   *   *   *

"Suddeinly an innumerable flight
Of harmefull fowles about them fluttering cride,
And with their wicked wings them oft did smight
And sore annoyed, groping in that griesly night."

    *   *   *   *   *

"Even all the nation of unfortunate
And fatal birds about them flocked were."

To go up into a high stone tower is not only a very fine thing in itself, but the very best mode of gaining a comprehensive view of the region round about. It is all the better if this tower stand solitary and alone, like that mysterious Newport one, or else be sole survivor of some perished castle.

Now, with reference to the Enchanted Isles, we are fortunately supplied with just such a noble point of observation in a remarkable rock, from its peculiar figure called of old by the Spaniards, Rock Rodondo, or Round Rock. Some two hundred and fifty feet high, rising straight from the sea ten miles from land, with the whole mountainous group to the south and east, Rock Rodondo occupies, on a large scale, very much the position which the famous Campanile or detached Bell Tower of St. Mark does with respect to the tangled group of hoary edifices around it.

Ere ascending, however, to gaze abroad upon the Encantadas, this sea-tower itself claims attention. It is visible at the distance of thirty miles; and, fully participating in that enchantment which pervades the group, when first seen afar invariably is mistaken for a sail. Four leagues away, of a golden, hazy noon, it seems some Spanish Admiral's ship, stacked up with glittering canvas. Sail ho! Sail ho! Sail ho! from all three masts. But coming nigh, the enchanted frigate is transformed apace into a craggy keep.

My first visit to the spot was made in the gray of the morning. With a view of fishing, we had lowered three boats, and pulling some two miles from our vessel, found ourselves just

before dawn of day close under the moon-shadow of Rodondo. Its aspect was heightened, and yet softened, by the
strange double twilight of the hour. The great full moon
burnt in the low west like a half-spent beacon, casting a soft
mellow tinge upon the sea like that cast by a waning fire of
embers upon a midnight hearth; while along the entire east
the invisible sun sent pallid intimations of his coming. The
wind was light; the waves languid; the stars twinkled with a
faint effulgence; all nature seemed supine with the long night
watch, and half-suspended in jaded expectation of the sun.
This was the critical hour to catch Rodondo in his perfect
mood. The twilight was just enough to reveal every striking
point, without tearing away the dim investiture of wonder.

From a broken, stair-like base, washed, as the steps of a
water-palace, by the waves, the tower rose in entablatures of
strata to a shaven summit. These uniform layers which compose the mass form its most peculiar feature. For at their lines
of junction they project flatly into encircling shelves, from top
to bottom, rising one above another in graduated series. And
as the eaves of any old barn or abbey are alive with swallows,
so were all these rocky ledges with unnumbered sea-fowl.
Eaves upon eaves, and nests upon nests. Here and there were
long birdlime streaks of a ghostly white staining the tower
from sea to air, readily accounting for its sail-like look afar.
All would have been bewitchingly quiescent, were it not for
the demoniac din created by the birds. Not only were the
eaves rustling with them, but they flew densely overhead,
spreading themselves into a winged and continually shifting
canopy. The tower is the resort of aquatic birds for hundreds
of leagues around. To the north, to the east, to the west,
stretches nothing but eternal ocean; so that the man-of-war
hawk coming from the coasts of North America, Polynesia,
or Peru, makes his first land at Rodondo. And yet though
Rodondo be terra-firma, no land-bird ever lighted on it.
Fancy a red-robbin or a canary there! What a falling into the
hands of the Philistines, when the poor warbler should be
surrounded by such locust-flights of strong bandit birds, with
long bills cruel as daggers.

I know not where one can better study the Natural History

of strange sea-fowl than at Rodondo. It is the aviary of Ocean. Birds light here which never touched mast or tree; hermit-birds, which ever fly alone, cloud-birds, familiar with unpierced zones of air.

Let us first glance low down to the lowermost shelf of all, which is the widest too, and but a little space from high-water mark. What outlandish beings are these? Erect as men, but hardly as symmetrical, they stand all round the rock like sculptured caryatides, supporting the next range of eaves above. Their bodies are grotesquely misshapen; their bills short; their feet seemingly legless; while the members at their sides are neither fin, wing, nor arm. And truly neither fish, flesh, nor fowl is the penguin; as an edible, pertaining neither to Carnival nor Lent; without exception the most ambiguous and least lovely creature yet discovered by man. Though dabbling in all three elements, and indeed possessing some rudimental claims to all, the penguin is at home in none. On land it stumps; afloat it sculls; in the air it flops. As if ashamed of her failure, Nature keeps this ungainly child hidden away at the ends of the earth, in the Straits of Magellan, and on the abased sea-story of Rodondo.

But look, what are yon wobegone regiments drawn up on the next shelf above? what rank and file of large strange fowl? what sea Friars of Orders Gray? Pelicans. Their elongated bills, and heavy leathern pouches suspended thereto, give them the most lugubrious expression. A pensive race, they stand for hours together without motion. Their dull, ashy plumage imparts an aspect as if they had been powdered over with cinders. A penitential bird indeed, fitly haunting the shores of the clinkered Encantadas, whereon tormented Job himself might have well sat down and scraped himself with potsherds.

Higher up now we mark the gony, or gray albatross, anomalously so called, an unsightly unpoetic bird, unlike its storied kinsman, which is the snow-white ghost of the haunted Capes of Hope and Horn.

As we still ascend from shelf to shelf, we find the tenants of the tower serially disposed in order of their magnitude:— gannets, black and speckled haglets, jays, sea-hens, sperm-whale-birds, gulls of all varieties:—thrones, princedoms, powers, dominating one above another in senatorial array; while sprinkled over all, like an ever-repeated fly in a great piece of broidery, the stormy petrel or Mother Cary's chicken sounds his continual challenge and alarm. That this mysterious humming-bird of ocean, which had it but brilliancy of hue might from its evanescent liveliness be almost called its butterfly, yet whose chirrup under the stern is ominous to mariners as to the peasant the death-tick sounding from behind the chimney jam—should have its special haunt at the Encantadas, contributes in the seaman's mind, not a little to their dreary spell.

As day advances the dissonant din augments. With ear-splitting cries the wild birds celebrate their matins. Each moment, flights push from the tower, and join the aerial choir hovering overhead, while their places below are supplied by darting myriads. But down through all this discord of commotion, I hear clear silver bugle-like notes unbrokenly falling, like oblique lines of swift slanting rain in a cascading shower. I gaze far up, and behold a snow-white angelic thing, with one long lance-like feather thrust out behind. It is the bright inspiriting chanticleer of ocean, the beauteous bird, from its bestirring whistle of musical invocation, fitly styled the "Boatswain's Mate."

The winged life clouding Rodondo on that well-remembered morning, I saw had its full counterpart in the finny hosts which peopled the waters at its base. Below the water-line, the rock seemed one honey-comb of grottoes, affording labyrinthine lurking places for swarms of fairy fish. All were strange; many exceedingly beautiful; and would have well graced the costliest glass globes in which gold-fish are kept for a show. Nothing was more striking than the complete novelty of many individuals of this multitude. Here hues were seen as yet unpainted, and figures which are unengraved.

To show the multitude, avidity, and nameless fearlessness and tameness of these fish, let me say, that often, marking through clear spaces of water—temporarily made so by the concentric dartings of the fish above the surface—certain larger and less unwary wights, which swam slow and deep; our anglers would cautiously essay to drop their lines down to these last. But in vain; there was no passing the uppermost zone. No sooner did the hook touch the sea, than a hundred infatuates contended for the honor of capture. Poor fish of Rodondo! in your victimized confidence, you are of the number of those who inconsiderately trust, while they do not understand, human nature.

But the dawn is now fairly day. Band after band, the sea-fowl sail away to forage the deep for their food. The tower is left solitary, save the fish caves at its base. Its birdlime gleams in the golden rays like the whitewash of a tall light-house, or the lofty sails of a cruiser. This moment, doubtless, while we know it to be a dead desert rock, other voyagers are taking oaths it is a glad populous ship.

But ropes now, and let us ascend. Yet soft, this is not so easy.

SKETCH FOURTH

A PISGAH VIEW FROM THE ROCK

—"*That done, he leads him to the highest mount,*
From whence, far off he unto him did show:"——

If you seek to ascend Rock Rodondo, take the following prescription. Go three voyages round the world as a main-royal-man of the tallest frigate that floats; then serve a year or two apprenticeship to the guides who conduct strangers up the Peak of Teneriffe; and as many more, respectively, to a rope-dancer, an Indian Juggler, and a chamois. This done, come and be rewarded by the view from our tower. How we get there, we alone know. If we sought to tell others, what the wiser were they? Suffice it, that here at the summit you and I stand. Does any balloonist, does the outlooking man in the moon, take a broader view of space? Much thus, one fancies, looks the universe from Milton's celestial battlements. A boundless watery Kentucky. Here Daniel Boone would have dwelt content.

Never heed for the present yonder Burnt District of the Enchanted Isles. Look edgeways, as it were, past them, to the south. You see nothing; but permit me to point out the direction, if not the place, of certain interesting objects in the vast sea, which kissing this tower's base, we behold unscrolling itself towards the Antarctic Pole.

We stand now ten miles from the Equator. Yonder, to the East, some six hundred miles, lies the continent; this Rock being just about on the parallel of Quito.

Observe another thing here. We are at one of three uninhabited clusters, which, at pretty nearly uniform distances from the main, sentinel, at long intervals from each other, the entire coast of South America. In a peculiar manner, also, they terminate the South American character of country. Of the unnumbered Polynesian chains to the westward, not one partakes of the qualities of the Encantadas or Gallipagos, the isles St. Felix and St. Ambrose, the isles Juan Fernandes and Massafuero. Of the first it needs not here to speak. The second lie a little above the Southern Tropic; lofty, inhospitable, and uninhabitable rocks, one of which, presenting two round hummocks connected by a low reef, exactly resembles a huge double-headed shot. The last lie in the latitude of 33°; high, wild and cloven. Juan Fernandes is sufficiently famous without further description. Massafuero is a Spanish name, expressive of the fact, that the isle so called lies *more without*, that is, further off the main than its neighbor Juan. This isle Massafuero has a very imposing aspect at a distance of eight or ten miles. Approached in one direction, in cloudy weather, its great overhanging height and rugged contour, and more especially a peculiar slope of its broad summits, give it much the air of a vast iceberg drifting in tremendous poise. Its sides are split with dark cavernous recesses, as an old cathedral with its gloomy lateral chapels. Drawing nigh one of these gorges from sea after a long voyage, and beholding some tatterdemallion outlaw, staff in hand, descending its steep rocks toward you, conveys a very queer emotion to a lover of the picturesque.

On fishing parties from ships, at various times, I have chanced to visit each of these groups. The impression they give to the stranger pulling close up in his boat under their grim cliffs is, that surely he must be their first discoverer, such for the most part is the unimpaired . . . . . silence and solitude. And here, by the way, the mode in which these isles were really first lighted upon by Europeans is not unworthy mention, especially as what is about to be said, likewise applies to the original discovery of our Encantadas.

Prior to the year 1563, the voyages made by Spanish ships from Peru to Chili, were full of difficulty. Along this coast the winds from the South most generally prevail; and it had been an invariable custom to keep close in with the land, from a superstitious conceit on the part of the Spaniards, that were they to lose sight of it, the eternal trade wind would waft them into unending waters, from whence would be no return. Here, involved among tortuous capes and headlands, shoals and reefs, beating too against a continual head wind, often light, and sometimes for days and weeks sunk into utter calm, the provincial vessels, in many cases, suffered the extremest hardships, in passages, which at the present day seem to have been incredibly protracted. There is on record in some collections of nautical disasters, an account of one of these ships, which starting on a voyage whose duration was estimated at ten days, spent four months at sea, and indeed never again entered harbor, for in the end she was cast away. Singular to tell, this craft never encountered a gale, but was the vexed sport of malicious calms and currents. Thrice, out of provisions, she put back to an intermediate port, and started afresh, but only yet again to return. Frequent fogs enveloped her; so that no observation could be had of her place, and once, when all hands were joyously anticipating sight of their destination, lo! the vapors lifted and disclosed the mountains from which they had taken their first departure. In the like deceptive vapors she at last struck upon a reef, whence ensued a long series of calamities too sad to detail.

It was the famous pilot, Juan Fernandes, immortalized by the island named after him, who put an end to these coasting tribulations, by boldly venturing the experiment—as Da Gama did before him with respect to Europe—of standing broad out from land. Here he found the winds favorable for getting to the south, and by running westward till beyond the influence of the trades, he regained the coast without difficulty; making the passage which, though in a high degree circuitous, proved far more expeditious than the nominally direct one. Now it was upon these new tracks, and about the year 1670 or thereabouts, that the Enchanted Isles and the rest of the sentinel groups, as they may be called, were discovered. Though I know of no account as to whether any of them were found inhabited or no, it may be reasonably concluded that they have been immemorial solitudes. But let us return to Rodondo.

Southwest from our tower lies all Polynesia, hundreds of leagues away; but straight west, on the precise line of his parallel, no land rises till your keel is beached upon the Kingsmills, a nice little sail of say 5,000 miles.

Having thus by such distant references—with Rodondo the only possible ones—settled our relative place on the sea, let us consider objects not quite so remote. Behold the grim and charred Enchanted Isles. This nearest crater-shaped headland is part of Albemarle, the largest of the group, being some sixty miles or more long, and fifteen broad. Did you ever lay eye on the real genuine Equator? Have you ever, in the largest sense, toed the Line? Well, that identical crater-shaped headland there, all yellow lava, is cut by the Equator exactly as a knife cuts straight through the centre of a pumpkin pie. If you could only see so far, just to one side of that same headland, across yon low dykey ground, you would catch sight of the isle of Narborough, the loftiest land of the cluster; no soil whatever; one seamed clinker from top to bottom; abounding in black caves like smithies; its metallic shore ringing under foot like plates of iron; its central volcanoes standing grouped like a gigantic chimney-stack.

Narborough and Albemarle are neighbors after a quite curious fashion. A familiar diagram will illustrate this strange neighborhood:

Cut a channel at the above letter joint, and the middle transverse limb is Narborough, and all the rest is Albemarle. Volcanic Narborough lies in the black jaws of Albemarle like a wolf's red tongue in his open mouth.

If now you desire the population of Albemarle, I will give you, in round numbers, the statistics, according to the most reliable estimates made upon the spot:

Men, ...	none.
Ant-eaters, ...	unknown.
Man-haters, ...	unknown.
Lizards, ...	500,000.
Snakes, ...	500,000.
Spiders, ...	10,000,000.
Salamanders, ...	unknown.
Devils, ...	do.

Making a clean total of	11,000,000.

exclusive of an incomputable host of fiends, ant-eaters, man-haters, and salamanders.

Albemarle opens his mouth towards the setting sun. His distended jaws form a great bay, which Narborough, his tongue, divides into halves, one whereof is called Weather Bay, the other Lee Bay; while the volcanic promontories terminating his coasts are styled South Head and North Head. I note this, because these Bays are famous in the annals of the Sperm Whale Fishery. The whales come here at certain seasons to calve. When ships first cruised hereabouts, I am told, they used to blockade the entrance of Lee Bay, when their boats going round by Weather Bay, passed through Narborough channel, and so had the Leviathans very neatly in a pen.

The day after we took fish at the base of this Round Tower, we had a fine wind, and shooting round the north headland, suddenly descried a fleet of full thirty sail, all beating to windward like a squadron in line. A brave sight as ever man saw. A most harmonious concord of rushing keels. Their thirty kelsons hummed like thirty harp-strings, and looked as straight whilst they left their parallel traces on the sea. But there proved too many hunters for the game. The fleet broke up, and went their separate ways out of sight, leaving my own ship and two trim gentlemen of London. These last, finding no luck either, likewise vanished; and Lee Bay, with all its appurtenances, and without a rival, devolved to us.

The way of cruising here is this. You keep hovering about the entrance of the bay, in one beat and out the next. But at times—not always, as in other parts of the group—a race-horse of a current sweeps right across its mouth. So, with all sails set, you carefully ply your tacks. How often, standing at the foremast head at sunrise, with our patient prow pointed in between these isles, did I gaze upon that land, not of cakes but of clinkers, not of streams of sparkling water, but arrested torrents of tormented lava.

As the ship runs in from the open sea, Narborough presents its side in one dark craggy mass, soaring up some five or six thousand feet, at which point it hoods itself in heavy clouds, whose lowest level fold is as clearly defined against the rocks, as the snow-line against the Andes. There is dire mischief going on in that upper dark. There toil the demons of fire, who at intervals irradiate the nights with a strange spectral illumination for miles and miles around, but unaccompanied by any further demonstration; or else, suddenly announce themselves by terrific concussions, and the full drama of a volcanic eruption. The blacker that cloud by day, the more may you look for light by night. Often whalemen have found themselves cruising nigh that burning mountain when all aglow with a ball-room blaze. Or, rather, glassworks, you may call this same vitreous isle of Narborough, with its tall chimney-stacks.

Where we still stand, here on Rodondo, we cannot see all the other isles, but it is a good place from which to point out where they lie. Yonder, though, to the E.N.E., I mark a distant dusky ridge. It is Abington Isle, one of the most northerly of the group; so solitary, remote, and blank, it looks like No-Man's Land seen off our northern shore. I doubt whether two human beings ever touched upon that spot. So far as yon Abington Isle is concerned, Adam and his billions of posterity remain uncreated.

Ranging south of Abington, and quite out of sight behind the long spine of Albemarle, lies James's Isle, so called by the early Buccaneers after the luckless Stuart, Duke of York. Observe here, by the way, that, excepting the isles particularized in comparatively recent times, and which mostly received the names of famous Admirals, the Encantadas were first christened by the Spaniards; but these Spanish names were generally effaced on English charts by the subsequent christenings of the Buccaneers, who, in the middle of the seventeenth century, called them after English noblemen and

kings. Of these loyal freebooters and the things which associate their name with the Encantadas, we shall hear anon.
Nay, for one little item, immediately; for between James's Isle
and Albemarle, lies a fantastic islet, strangely known as "Cowley's Enchanted Isle." But as all the group is deemed enchanted, the reason must be given for the spell within a spell
involved by this particular designation. The name was bestowed by that excellent Buccaneer himself, on his first visit
here. Speaking in his published voyages of this spot, he
says—"My fancy led me to call it Cowley's Enchanted Isle,
for we having had a sight of it upon several points of the
compass, it appeared always in so many different forms;
sometimes like a ruined fortification; upon another point like
a great city," &c. No wonder though, that among the Encantadas all sorts of ocular deceptions and mirages should be
met.

That Cowley linked his name with this self-transforming
and bemocking isle, suggests the possibility that it conveyed
to him some meditative image of himself. At least, as is not
impossible, if he were any relative of the mildly thoughtful,
and self-upbraiding poet Cowley, who lived about his time,
the conceit might seem not unwarranted; for that sort of
thing evinced in the naming of this isle runs in the blood, and
may be seen in pirates as in poets.

Still south of James's Isle lie Jervis Isle, Duncan Isle, Crossman's Isle, Brattle Isle, Wood's Isle, Chatham Isle, and various
lesser isles, for the most part an archipelago of aridities, without inhabitant, history, or hope of either in all time to come.
But not far from these are rather notable isles—Barrington,
Charles's, Norfolk, and Hood's. Succeeding chapters will reveal some ground for their notability.

SKETCH FIFTH

THE FRIGATE, AND SHIP FLYAWAY

"Looking far forth into the ocean wide,
A goodly ship with banners bravely dight,
And flag in her top-gallant I espide,
Through the main sea making her merry flight."

Ere quitting Rodondo, it must not be omitted that here, in 1813, the U.S. frigate Essex, Captain David Porter, came near leaving her bones. Lying becalmed one morning with a strong current setting her rapidly towards the rock, a strange sail was descried, which—not out of keeping with alleged enchantments of the neighborhood—seemed to be staggering under a violent wind, while the frigate lay lifeless as if spellbound. But a light air springing up, all sail was made by the frigate in chase of the enemy, as supposed—he being deemed an English whale-ship—but the rapidity of the current was so great, that soon all sight was lost of him; and at meridian the Essex, spite of her drags, was driven so close under the foam-lashed cliffs of Rodondo that for a time all hands gave her up. A smart breeze, however, at last helped her off, though the escape was so critical as to seem almost miraculous.

Thus saved from destruction herself, she now made use of that salvation to destroy the other vessel, if possible. Renewing the chase in the direction in which the stranger had disappeared, sight was caught of him the following morning. Upon being descried he hoisted American colors and stood away from the Essex. A calm ensued; when, still confident that the stranger was an Englishman, Porter despatched a cutter, not to board the enemy, but drive back his boats engaged in towing him. The cutter succeeded. Cutters were subsequently sent to capture him; the stranger now showing English colors in place of American. But when the frigate's boats were within a short distance of their hoped-for prize, another sudden breeze sprang up; the stranger under all sail bore off to the northward, and ere night was hull down ahead of the Essex, which all this time lay perfectly becalmed.

This enigmatic craft—American in the morning, and English in the evening—her sails full of wind in a calm—was never again beheld. An enchanted ship no doubt. So at least the sailors swore.

This cruise of the Essex in the Pacific during the war of 1812, is perhaps the strangest and most stirring to be found in the history of the American navy. She captured the furthest wandering vessels; visited the remotest seas and isles; long hovered in the charmed vicinity of the enchanted group; and finally valiantly gave up the ghost fighting two English frigates in the harbor of Valparaiso. Mention is made of her here for the same reason that the buccaneers will likewise receive record; because, like them, by long cruising among the isles, tortoise-hunting upon their shores, and generally exploring them; for these and other reasons, the Essex is peculiarly associated with the Encantadas.

Here be it said that you have but three eye-witness authorities worth mentioning touching the Enchanted Isles:—Cowley, the buccaneer (1684); Colnett, the whaling-ground explorer (1793); Porter, the post captain (1813). Other than these you have but barren, bootless allusions from some few passing voyagers or compilers.

SKETCH SIXTH

BARRINGTON ISLE AND THE BUCCANEERS

"Let us all servile base subjection scorn,
And as we be sons of the earth so wide,
Let us our father's heritage divide,
And challenge to ourselves our portions dew
Of all the patrimony, which a few
Now hold in hugger-mugger in their hand."

* * * * *

"Lords of the world, and so will wander free,
Where-so us listeth, uncontroll'd of any."

* * * * *

"How bravely now we live, how jocund, how near the first inheritance, without fears, how free from little troubles!"

Near two centuries ago Barrington Isle was the resort of that famous wing of the West Indian buccaneers, which, upon their repulse from the Cuban waters, crossing the Isthmus of Darien, ravaged the Pacific side of the Spanish colonies, and, with the regularity and timing of a modern mail, waylaid the royal treasure ships plying between Manilla and Acapulco. After the toils of piratic war, here they came to say their prayers, enjoy their free-and-easies, count their crackers from the cask, their doubloons from the keg, and measure their silks of Asia with long Toledos for their yard-sticks.

As a secure retreat, an undiscoverable hiding place, no spot in those days could have been better fitted. In the centre of a vast and silent sea, but very little traversed; surrounded by islands, whose inhospitable aspect might well drive away the chance navigator; and yet within a few days' sail of the opulent countries which they made their prey; the unmolested buccaneers found here that tranquillity which they fiercely denied to every civilized harbor in that part of the world. Here, after stress of weather, or a temporary drubbing at the hands of their vindictive foes, or in swift flight with golden booty, those old marauders came, and lay snugly out of all harm's reach. But not only was the place a harbor of safety, and a bower of ease, but for utility in other things it was most admirable.

Barrington Isle is in many respects singularly adapted to careening, refitting, refreshing, and other seamen's purposes. Not only has it good water, and good anchorage, well sheltered from all winds by the high land of Albemarle, but it is the least unproductive isle of the group. Tortoises good for food, trees good for fuel, and long grass good for bedding, abound here, and there are pretty natural walks, and several landscapes to be seen. Indeed, though in its locality belonging to the Enchanted group, Barrington Isle is so unlike most of its neighbors, that it would hardly seem of kin to them.

"I once landed on its western side," says a sentimental voyager long ago, " where it faces the black buttress of Albemarle. I walked beneath groves of trees; not very lofty, and not palm trees, or orange trees, or peach trees, to be sure; but for all that, after long sea-faring very beautiful to walk under, even though they supplied no fruit. And here, in calm spaces at the heads of glades, and on the shaded tops of slopes commanding the most quiet scenery—what do you think I saw? Seats which might have served Brahmins and presidents of peace societies. Fine old ruins of what had once been symmetric lounges of stone and turf; they bore every mark both of artificialness and age, and were undoubtedly made by the buccaneers. One had been a long sofa, with back and arms, just such a sofa as the poet Gray might have loved to throw himself upon, his Crebillon in hand.

"Though they sometimes tarried here for months at a time, and used the spot for a storing-place for spare spars, sails, and casks; yet it is highly improbable that the buccaneers ever erected dwelling-houses upon the isle. They never were here except their ships remained, and they would most likely have slept on board. I mention this, because I cannot avoid the thought, that it is hard to impute the construction of these romantic seats to any other motive than one of pure peacefulness and kindly fellowship with nature. That the buccaneers perpetrated the greatest outrages is very true; that some of them were mere cut-throats is not to be denied; but we know that here and there among their host was a Dampier, a Wafer, and a Cowley, and likewise other men, whose worst reproach was their desperate fortunes; whom persecution, or adversity, or secret and unavengeable wrongs, had driven from Christian society to seek the melancholy solitude or the guilty adventures of the sea. At any rate, long as those ruins of seats on Barrington remain, the most singular monuments are furnished to the fact, that all of the buccaneers were not unmitigated monsters.

"But during my ramble on the isle I was not long in discovering other tokens, of things quite in accordance with those wild traits, popularly, and no doubt truly enough imputed to the freebooters at large. Had I picked up old nails and rusty hoops I would only have thought of the ship's carpenter and cooper. But I found old cutlasses and daggers reduced to mere threads of rust, which doubtless had stuck between Spanish ribs ere now. These were signs of the murderer and robber; the reveller likewise had left his trace. Mixed with shells, fragments of broken jars were lying here and there, high up upon the beach. They were precisely like the jars now used upon the Spanish coast for the wine and Pisco spirits of that country.

"With a rusty dagger-fragment in one hand, and a bit of a wine-jar in another, I sat me down on the ruinous green sofa I have spoken of, and bethought me long and deeply of these same buccaneers. Could it be possible, that they robbed and

murdered one day, revelled the next, and rested themselves by
turning meditative philosophers, rural poets, and seat-builders
on the third? Not very improbable, after all. For consider the
vacillations of a man. Still, strange as it may seem, I must also
abide by the more charitable thought; namely, that among
these adventurers were some gentlemanly, companionable
souls, capable of genuine tranquillity and virtue."

Sketch Seventh

Charles' Isle and the Dog-king

—————————————So with outragious cry,
A thousand villeins round about him swarmed
Out of the rocks and caves adjoining nye;
Vile caitive wretches, ragged, rude, deformed;
All threatning death, all in straunge manner armed;
Some with unweldy clubs, some with long speares,
Some rusty knives, some staves in fier warmd.

  *   *   *   *   *

We will not be of any occupation,
Let such vile vassals, born to base vocation,
Drudge in the world, and for their living droyle,
Which have no wit to live withouten toyle.

Southwest of Barrington lies Charles' Isle. And hereby
hangs a history which I gathered long ago from a shipmate
learned in all the lore of outlandish life.

During the successful revolt of the Spanish provinces from
Old Spain, there fought on behalf of Peru a certain Creole
adventurer from Cuba, who by his bravery and good fortune
at length advanced himself to high rank in the patriot army.
The war being ended, Peru found itself like many valorous
gentlemen, free and independent enough, but with few shot
in the locker. In other words, Peru had not wherewithal to
pay off its troops. But the Creole—I forget his name—volunteered to take his pay in lands. So they told him he might
have his pick of the Enchanted Isles, which were then, as they
still remain, the nominal appanage of Peru. The soldier
straightway embarks thither, explores the group, returns to

Callao, and says he will take a deed of Charles' Isle. Moreover, this deed must stipulate that thenceforth Charles' Isle is not only the sole property of the Creole, but is for ever free of Peru, even as Peru of Spain. To be short, this adventurer procures himself to be made in effect Supreme Lord of the Island, one of the princes of the powers of the earth.*

He now sends forth a proclamation inviting subjects to his as yet unpopulated kingdom. Some eighty souls, men and women, respond; and being provided by their leader with necessaries, and tools of various sorts, together with a few cattle and goats, take ship for the promised land; the last arrival on board, prior to sailing, being the Creole himself, accompanied, strange to say, by a disciplined cavalry company of large grim dogs. These, it was observed on the passage, refusing to consort with the emigrants, remained aristocratically grouped around their master on the elevated quarter-deck, casting disdainful glances forward upon the inferior rabble there; much as from the ramparts, the soldiers of a garrison thrown into a conquered town, eye the inglorious citizen-mob over which they are set to watch.

Now Charles' Isle not only resembles Barrington Isle in being much more inhabitable than other parts of the group; but it is double the size of Barrington; say forty or fifty miles in circuit.

Safely debarked at last, the company under direction of their lord and patron, forthwith proceeded to build their capital city. They make considerable advance in the way of walls of clinkers, and lava floors, nicely sanded with cinders. On the least barren hills they pasture their cattle, while the goats, adventurers by nature, explore the far inland solitudes for a scanty livelihood of lofty herbage. Meantime, abundance of fish and tortoises supply their other wants.

The disorders incident to settling all primitive regions, in the present case were heightened by the peculiarly untoward

---

*The American Spaniards have long been in the habit of making presents of islands to deserving individuals. The pilot Juan Fernandez procured a deed of the isle named after him, and for some years resided there before Selkirk came. It is supposed, however, that he eventually contracted the blues upon his princely property, for after a time he returned to the main, and as report goes, became a very garrulous barber in the city of Lima.

character of many of the pilgrims. His Majesty was forced at last to proclaim martial law, and actually hunted and shot with his own hand several of his rebellious subjects, who, with most questionable intentions, had clandestinely encamped in the interior; whence they stole by night, to prowl barefooted on tiptoe round the precincts of the lava-palace. It is to be remarked, however, that prior to such stern proceedings, the more reliable men had been judiciously picked out for an infantry body-guard, subordinate to the cavalry body-guard of dogs. But the state of politics in this unhappy nation may be somewhat imagined from the circumstance, that all who were not of the body-guard were downright plotters and malignant traitors. At length the death penalty was tacitly abolished, owing to the timely thought, that were strict sportsman's justice to be dispensed among such subjects, ere long the Nimrod King would have little or no remaining game to shoot. The human part of the life-guard was now disbanded, and set to work cultivating the soil, and raising potatoes; the regular army now solely consisting of the dog-regiment. These, as I have heard, were of a singularly ferocious character, though by severe training rendered docile to their master. Armed to the teeth, the Creole now goes in state, surrounded by his canine janizaries, whose terrific bayings prove quite as serviceable as bayonets in keeping down the surgings of revolt.

But the census of the isle, sadly lessened by the dispensation of justice, and not materially recruited by matrimony, began to fill his mind with sad mistrust. Some way the population must be increased. Now, from its possessing a little water, and its comparative pleasantness of aspect, Charles' Isle at this period was occasionally visited by foreign whalers. These His Majesty had always levied upon for port charges, thereby contributing to his revenue. But now he had additional designs. By insidious arts he from time to time cajoles certain sailors to desert their ships and enlist beneath his banner. Soon as missed, their captains crave permission to go and hunt them up. Whereupon His Majesty first hides them very carefully away, and then freely permits the search. In consequence, the delinquents are never found, and the ships retire without them.

Thus, by a two-edged policy of this crafty monarch, foreign nations were crippled in the number of their subjects, and his own were greatly multiplied. He particularly petted these renegado strangers. But alas for the deep-laid schemes of ambitious princes, and alas for the vanity of glory. As the foreign-born Pretorians, unwisely introduced into the Roman state, and still more unwisely made favorites of the Emperors, at last insulted and overturned the throne, even so these lawless mariners, with all the rest of the body-guard and all the populace, broke out into a terrible mutiny, and defied their master. He marched against them with all his dogs. A deadly battle ensued upon the beach. It raged for three hours, the dogs fighting with determined valor, and the sailors reckless of every thing but victory. Three men and thirteen dogs were left dead upon the field, many on both sides were wounded, and the king was forced to fly with the remainder of his canine regiment. The enemy pursued, stoning the dogs with their master into the wilderness of the interior. Discontinuing the pursuit, the victors returned to the village on the shore, stove the spirit-casks, and proclaimed a Republic. The dead men were interred with the honors of war, and the dead dogs ignominiously thrown into the sea. At last, forced by stress of suffering, the fugitive Creole came down from the hills and offered to treat for peace. But the rebels refused it on any other terms than his unconditional banishment. Accordingly, the next ship that arrived carried away the ex-king to Peru.

The history of the king of Charles' Island furnishes another illustration of the difficulty of colonizing barren islands with unprincipled pilgrims.

Doubtless for a long time the exiled monarch, pensively ruralizing in Peru, which afforded him a safe asylum in his calamity, watched every arrival from the Encantadas, to hear news of the failure of the Republic, the consequent penitence of the rebels, and his own recall to royalty. Doubtless he deemed the Republic but a miserable experiment which would soon explode. But no, the insurgents had confederated themselves into a democracy neither Grecian, Roman, nor American. Nay, it was no democracy at all, but a permanent *Riotocracy*, which gloried in having no law but lawlessness.

Great inducements being offered to deserters, their ranks were swelled by accessions of scamps from every ship which touched their shores. Charles' Island was proclaimed the asylum of the oppressed of all navies. Each runaway tar was hailed as a martyr in the cause of freedom, and became immediately installed a ragged citizen of this universal nation. In vain the captains of absconding seamen strove to regain them. Their new compatriots were ready to give any number of ornamental eyes in their behalf. They had few cannon, but their fists were not to be trifled with. So at last it came to pass that no vessels acquainted with the character of that country durst touch there, however sorely in want of refreshment. It became Anathema—a sea Alsatia—the unassailed lurking-place of all sorts of desperadoes, who in the name of liberty did just what they pleased. They continually fluctuated in their numbers. Sailors deserting ships at other islands, or in boats at sea any where in that vicinity, steered for Charles' Isle, as to their sure home of refuge; while sated with the life of the isle, numbers from time to time crossed the water to the neighboring ones, and there presenting themselves to strange captains as shipwrecked seamen, often succeeded in getting on board vessels bound to the Spanish coast; and having a compassionate purse made up for them on landing there.

One warm night during my first visit to the group, our ship was floating along in languid stillness, when some one on the forecastle shouted "Light ho!" We looked and saw a beacon burning on some obscure land off the beam. Our third mate was not intimate with this part of the world. Going to the captain he said, "Sir, shall I put off in a boat? These must be shipwrecked men."

The captain laughed rather grimly, as, shaking his fist towards the beacon, he rapped out an oath, and said—"No, no, you precious rascals, you don't juggle one of my boats ashore this blessed night. You do well, you thieves—you do benevolently to hoist a light yonder as on a dangerous shoal. It tempts no wise man to pull off and see what's the matter, but bids him steer small and keep off shore—that is Charles' Island; brace up, Mr. Mate, and keep the light astern."

Sketch Eighth

Norfolk Isle and the Chola Widow

"At last they in an island did espy
A seemly woman sitting by the shore,
That with great sorrow and sad agony
Seemed some great misfortune to deplore,
And loud to them for succor called evermore."

"Black his eye as the midnight sky,
White his neck as the driven snow,
Red his cheek as the morning light; —
Cold he lies in the ground below.
*   My love is dead,*
*   Gone to his death-bed,*
All under the cactus tree."

"Each lonely scene shall thee restore,
For thee the tear be duly shed;
Belov'd till life can charm no more,
And mourned till Pity's self be dead."

Far to the northeast of Charles' Isle, sequestered from the rest, lies Norfolk Isle; and, however insignificant to most voyagers, to me, through sympathy, that lone island has become a spot made sacred by the strongest trials of humanity.

It was my first visit to the Encantadas. Two days had been spent ashore in hunting tortoises. There was not time to capture many; so on the third afternoon we loosed our sails. We were just in the act of getting under way, the uprooted anchor yet suspended and invisibly swaying beneath the wave, as the good ship gradually turned on her heel to leave the isle behind, when the seaman who heaved with me at the windlass paused suddenly, and directed my attention to something moving on the land, not along the beach, but somewhat back, fluttering from a height.

In view of the sequel of this little story, be it here narrated how it came to pass, that an object which partly from its being so small was quite lost to every other man on board, still caught the eye of my handspike companion. The rest of the crew, myself included, merely stood up to our spikes in heaving; whereas, unwontedly exhilarated at every turn of the ponderous windlass, my belted comrade leaped atop of it, with might and main giving a downward, thewey, perpendicular heave, his raised eye bent in cheery animation upon the slowly receding shore. Being high lifted above all others was the reason he perceived the object, otherwise unperceivable: and this elevation of his eye was owing to the elevation of his spirits; and this again—for truth must out—to a dram of Peruvian pisco, in guerdon for some kindness done, secretly administered to him that morning by our mulatto steward. Now, certainly, pisco does a deal of mischief in the world; yet seeing that, in the present case, it was the means, though indirect, of rescuing a human being from the most dreadful fate, must we not also needs admit that sometimes pisco does a deal of good?

Glancing across the water in the direction pointed out, I saw some white thing hanging from an inland rock, perhaps half a mile from the sea.

"It is a bird; a white-winged bird; perhaps a——no; it is——it is a handkerchief!"

"Aye, a handkerchief!" echoed my comrade, and with a louder shout apprised the captain.

Quickly now—like the running out and training of a great gun—the long cabin spy-glass was thrust through the mizzen rigging from the high platform of the poop; whereupon a human figure was plainly seen upon the inland rock, eagerly waving towards us what seemed to be the handkerchief.

Our captain was a prompt, good fellow. Dropping the glass, he lustily ran forward, ordering the anchor to be dropped again; hands to stand by a boat, and lower away.

In a half-hour's time the swift boat returned. It went with six and came with seven; and the seventh was a woman.

It is not artistic heartlessness, but I wish I could but draw in crayons; for this woman was a most touching sight; and crayons, tracing softly melancholy lines, would best depict the mournful image of the dark-damasked Chola widow.

Her story was soon told, and though given in her own strange language was as quickly understood, for our captain from long trading on the Chilian coast was well versed in the

Spanish. A Chola, or half-breed Indian woman of Payta in Peru, three years gone by, with her young new-wedded husband Felipe, of pure Castilian blood, and her one only Indian brother, Truxill, Hunilla had taken passage on the main in a French whaler, commanded by a joyous man; which vessel, bound to the cruising grounds beyond the Enchanted Isles, proposed passing close by their vicinity. The object of the little party was to procure tortoise oil, a fluid which for its great purity and delicacy is held in high estimation wherever known; and it is well known all along this part of the Pacific coast. With a chest of clothes, tools, cooking utensils, a rude apparatus for trying out the oil, some casks of biscuit, and other things, not omitting two favorite dogs, of which faithful animal all the Cholos are very fond, Hunilla and her companions were safely landed at their chosen place; the Frenchman, according to the contract made ere sailing, engaged to take them off upon returning from a four months' cruise in the westward seas; which interval the three adventurers deemed quite sufficient for their purposes.

On the isle's lone beach they paid him in silver for their passage out, the stranger having declined to carry them at all except upon that condition; though willing to take every means to insure the due fulfilment of his promise. Felipe had striven hard to have this payment put off to the period of the ship's return. But in vain. Still, they thought they had, in another way, ample pledge of the good faith of the Frenchman. It was arranged that the expenses of the passage home should not be payable in silver, but in tortoises; one hundred tortoises ready captured to the returning captain's hand. These the Cholos meant to secure after their own work was done, against the probable time of the Frenchman's coming back; and no doubt in prospect already felt, that in those hundred tortoises—now somewhere ranging the isle's interior—they possessed one hundred hostages. Enough: the vessel sailed; the gazing three on shore answered the loud glee of the singing crew; and ere evening, the French craft was hull down in the distant sea, its masts three faintest lines which quickly faded from Hunilla's eye.

The stranger had given a blithesome promise, and anchored it with oaths; but oaths and anchors equally will drag; nought else abides on fickle earth but unkept promises of joy. Contrary winds from out unstable skies, or contrary moods of his more varying mind, or shipwreck and sudden death in solitary waves; whatever was the cause, the blithe stranger never was seen again.

Yet, however dire a calamity was here in store, misgivings of it ere due time never disturbed the Cholos' busy mind, now all intent upon the toilsome matter which had brought them hither. Nay, by swift doom coming like the thief at night, ere seven weeks went by, two of the little party were removed from all anxieties of land or sea. No more they sought to gaze with feverish fear, or still more feverish hope, beyond the present's horizon line; but into the furthest future their own silent spirits sailed. By persevering labor beneath that burning sun, Felipe and Truxill had brought down to their hut many scores of tortoises, and tried out the oil, when, elated with their good success, and to reward themselves for such hard work, they, too hastily, made a catamaran, or Indian raft, much used on the Spanish main, and merrily started on a fishing trip, just without a long reef with many jagged gaps, running parallel with the shore, about half a mile from it. By some bad tide or hap, or natural negligence of joyfulness (for though they could not be heard, yet by their gestures they seemed singing at the time), forced in deep water against that iron bar, the ill-made catamaran was overset, and came all to pieces; when, dashed by broad-chested swells between their broken logs and the sharp teeth of the reef, both adventurers perished before Hunilla's eyes.

Before Hunilla's eyes they sank. The real woe of this event passed before her sight as some sham tragedy on the stage. She was seated on a rude bower among the withered thickets, crowning a lofty cliff, a little back from the beach. The thickets were so disposed, that in looking upon the sea at large she peered out from among the branches as from the lattice of a high balcony. But upon the day we speak of here, the better to watch the adventure of those two hearts she loved, Hunilla had withdrawn the branches to one side, and held them so. They formed an oval frame, through which the bluely boundless sea rolled like a painted one. And there, the invisible painter painted to her view the wave-tossed and disjointed raft, its once level logs slantingly upheaved, as raking masts, and the four struggling arms undistinguishable among them; and then all subsided into smooth-flowing creamy waters, slowly drifting the splintered wreck; while first and last, no sound of any sort was heard. Death in a silent picture; a dream of the eye; such vanishing shapes as the mirage shows.

So instant was the scene, so trance-like its mild pictorial effect, so distant from her blasted bower and her common sense of things, that Hunilla gazed and gazed, nor raised a finger or a wail. But as good to sit thus dumb, in stupor staring on that dumb show, for all that otherwise might be done. With half a mile of sea between, how could her two enchanted arms aid those four fated ones? The distance long, the time one sand. After the lightning is beheld, what fool shall stay the thunderbolt? Felipe's body was washed ashore, but Truxill's never came; only his gay, braided hat of golden straw—that same sunflower thing he waved to her, pushing from the strand—and now, to the last gallant, it still saluted her. But Felipe's body floated to the marge, with one arm encircling outstretched. Lock-jawed in grim death, the lover-husband, softly clasped his bride, true to her even in death's dream. Ah, Heaven, when man thus keeps his faith, wilt thou be faithless who created the faithful one? But they cannot break faith who never plighted it.

It needs not to be said what nameless misery now wrapped the lonely widow. In telling her own story she passed this almost entirely over, simply recounting the event. Construe the comment of her features, as you might; from her mere words little would you have weened that Hunilla was herself the heroine of her tale. But not thus did she defraud us of our tears. All hearts bled that grief could be so brave.

She but showed us her soul's lid, and the strange ciphers thereon engraved; all within, with pride's timidity, was withheld. Yet was there one exception. Holding out her small olive hand before our captain, she said in mild and slowest Spanish, "Señor, I buried him;" then paused, struggled as against the writhed coilings of a snake, and cringing suddenly, leaped up, repeating in impassioned pain, "I buried him, my life, my soul!"

Doubtless it was by half-unconscious, automatic motions of

her hands, that this heavy-hearted one performed the final offices for Felipe, and planted a rude cross of withered sticks—no green ones might be had—at the head of that lonely grave, where rested now in lasting uncomplaint and quiet haven he whom untranquil seas had overthrown.

But some dull sense of another body that should be interred, of another cross that should hallow another grave—unmade as yet;—some dull anxiety and pain touching her undiscovered brother now haunted the oppressed Hunilla. Her hands fresh from the burial earth, she slowly went back to the beach, with unshaped purposes wandered there, her spell-bound eye bent upon the incessant waves. But they bore nothing to her but a dirge, which maddened her to think that murderers should mourn. As time went by, and these things came less dreamingly to her mind, the strong persuasions of her Romish faith, which sets peculiar store by consecrated urns, prompted her to resume in waking earnest that pious search which had but been begun as in somnambulism. Day after day, week after week, she trod the cindery beach, till at length a double motive edged every eager glance. With equal longing she now looked for the living and the dead; the brother and the captain; alike vanished, never to return. Little accurate note of time had Hunilla taken under such emotions as were hers, and little, outside herself, served for calendar or dial. As to poor Crusoe in the self-same sea, no saint's bell pealed forth the lapse of week or month; each day went by unchallenged; no chanticleer announced those sultry dawns, no lowing herds those poisonous nights. All wonted and steadily recurring sounds, human, or humanized by sweet fellowship with man, but one stirred that torrid trance,—the cry of dogs; save which nought but the rolling sea invaded it, an all pervading monotone; and to the widow that was the least loved voice she could have heard.

No wonder that as her thoughts now wandered to the unreturning ship, and were beaten back again, the hope against hope so struggled in her soul, that at length she desperately said, "Not yet, not yet; my foolish heart runs on too fast." So she forced patience for some further weeks. But to those whom earth's sure indraft draws, patience or impatience is still the same.

Hunilla now sought to settle precisely in her mind, to an hour, how long it was since the ship had sailed; and then, with the same precision, how long a space remained to pass. But this proved impossible. What present day or month it was she could not say. Time was her labyrinth, in which Hunilla was entirely lost.

And now follows——

Against my own purposes a pause descends upon me here. One knows not whether nature doth not impose some secrecy upon him who has been privy to certain things. At least, it is to be doubted whether it be good to blazon such. If some books are deemed most baneful and their sale forbid, how then with deadlier facts, not dreams of doting men? Those whom books will hurt will not be proof against events. Events, not books, should be forbid. But in all things man sows upon the wind, which bloweth just there whither it listeth; for ill or good man cannot know. Often ill comes from the good, as good from ill.

When Hunilla——

Dire sight it is to see some silken beast long dally with a golden lizard ere she devour. More terrible, to see how feline Fate will sometimes dally with a human soul, and by a nameless magic make it repulse a sane despair with a hope which is but mad. Unwittingly I imp this cat-like thing, sporting with the heart of him who reads; for if he feel not, he reads in vain.

—"The ship sails this day, to-day," at last said Hunilla to herself; "this gives me certain time to stand on; without certainty I go mad. In loose ignorance I have hoped and hoped; now in firm knowledge I will but wait. Now I live and no longer perish in bewilderings. Holy Virgin, aid me! Thou wilt waft back the ship. Oh, past length of weary weeks—all to be dragged over—to buy the certainty of to-day, I freely give ye, though I tear ye from me!"

As mariners tossed in tempest on some desolate ledge patch them a boat out of the remnants of their vessel's wreck, and launch it in the self-same waves, see here Hunilla, this lone shipwrecked soul, out of treachery invoking trust. Humanity, thou strong thing, I worship thee, not in the laurelled victor, but in this vanquished one.

Truly Hunilla leaned upon a reed, a real one; no metaphor; a real Eastern reed. A piece of hollow cane, drifted from unknown isles, and found upon the beach, its once jagged ends rubbed smoothly even as by sand-paper; its golden glazing gone. Long ground between the sea and land, upper and nether stone, the unvarnished substance was filed bare, and wore another polish now, one with itself, the polish of its agony. Circular lines at intervals cut all round this surface, divided it into six panels of unequal length. In the first were scored the days, each tenth one marked by a longer and deeper notch; the second was scored for the number of sea-fowl eggs for sustenance, picked out from the rocky nests; the third, how many fish had been caught from the shore; the fourth, how many small tortoises found inland; the fifth, how many days of sun; the sixth, of clouds; which last, of the two, was the greater one. Long night of busy numbering, misery's mathematics, to weary her too-wakeful soul to sleep; yet sleep for that was none.

The panel of the days was deeply worn, the long tenth notches half effaced, as alphabets of the blind. Ten thousand times the longing widow had traced her finger over the bamboo; dull flute, which played on, gave no sound; as if counting birds flown by in air, would hasten tortoises creeping through the woods.

After the one hundred and eightieth day no further mark was seen; that last one was the faintest, as the first the deepest.

"There were more days," said our Captain; "many, many more; why did you not go on and notch them too, Hunilla?"

"Señor, ask me not."

"And meantime, did no other vessel pass the isle?"

"Nay, Señor;—but——"

"You do not speak; but *what*, Hunilla?"

"Ask me not, Señor."

"You saw ships pass, far away; you waved to them; they passed on;—was that it, Hunilla?"

"Señor, be it as you say."

Braced against her woe, Hunilla would not, durst not trust the weakness of her tongue. Then when our Captain asked whether any whale-boats had——

But no, I will not file this thing complete for scoffing souls to quote, and call it firm proof upon their side. The half shall here remain untold. Those two unnamed events which befell Hunilla on this isle, let them abide between her and her God. In nature, as in law, it may be libellous to speak some truths.

Still, how it was that although our vessel had lain three days anchored nigh the isle, its one human tenant should not have discovered us till just upon the point of sailing, never to revisit so lone and far a spot; this needs explaining ere the sequel come.

The place where the French captain had landed the little party was on the farther and opposite end of the isle. There too it was that they had afterwards built their hut. Nor did the widow in her solitude desert the spot where her loved ones had dwelt with her, and where the dearest of the twain now slept his last long sleep, and all her plaints awaked him not, and he of husbands the most faithful during life.

Now, high broken land rises between the opposite extremities of the isle. A ship anchored at one side is invisible from the other. Neither is the isle so small, but a considerable company might wander for days through the wilderness of one side, and never be seen, or their halloos heard, by any stranger holding aloof on the other. Hence Hunilla, who naturally associated the possible coming of ships with her own part of the isle, might to the end have remained quite ignorant of the presence of our vessel, were it not for a mysterious presentiment, borne to her, so our mariners averred, by this isle's enchanted air. Nor did the widow's answer undo the thought.

"How did you come to cross the isle this morning then, Hunilla?" said our Captain.

"Señor, something came flitting by me. It touched my cheek, my heart, Señor."

"What do you say, Hunilla?"

"I have said, Señor; something came through the air."

It was a narrow chance. For when in crossing the isle Hunilla gained the high land in the centre, she must then for the first have perceived our masts, and also marked that their sails were being loosed, perhaps even heard the echoing chorus of the windlass song. The strange ship was about to sail, and she behind. With all haste she now descends the height on the hither side, but soon loses sight of the ship among the sunken jungles at the mountain's base. She struggles on through the withered branches, which seek at every step to bar her path, till she comes to the isolated rock, still some way from the water. This she climbs, to reassure herself. The ship is still in plainest sight. But now worn out with over tension, Hunilla all but faints; she fears to step down from her giddy perch; she is feign to pause, there where she is, and as a last resort catches the turban from her head, unfurls and waves it over the jungles towards us.

During the telling of her story the mariners formed a voiceless circle round Hunilla and the Captain; and when at length the word was given to man the fastest boat, and pull round to the isle's thither side, to bring away Hunilla's chest and the tortoise-oil; such alacrity of both cheery and sad obedience seldom before was seen. Little ado was made. Already the anchor had been recommitted to the bottom, and the ship swung calmly to it.

But Hunilla insisted upon accompanying the boat as indispensable pilot to her hidden hut. So being refreshed with the best the steward could supply, she started with us. Nor did ever any wife of the most famous admiral in her husband's barge receive more silent reverence of respect, than poor Hunilla from this boat's crew.

Rounding many a vitreous cape and bluff, in two hours' time we shot inside the fatal reef; wound into a secret cove, looked up along a green many-gabled lava wall, and saw the island's solitary dwelling.

It hung upon an impending cliff, sheltered on two sides by tangled thickets, and half-screened from view in front by juttings of the rude stairway, which climbed the precipice from the sea. Built of canes, it was thatched with long, mildewed grass. It seemed an abandoned hay-rick whose haymakers were now no more. The roof inclined but one way; the eaves coming to within two feet of the ground. And here was a simple apparatus to collect the dews, or rather doubly-distilled and finest winnowed rains, which, in mercy or in mockery, the night-skies sometimes drop upon these blighted Encantadas. All along beneath the eaves, a spotted sheet, quite weather-stained, was spread, pinned to short, upright stakes, set in the shallow sand. A small clinker, thrown into the cloth, weighed its middle down, thereby straining all moisture into a calabash placed below. This vessel supplied each drop of water ever drunk upon the isle by the Cholos. Hunilla told us the calabash would sometimes, but not often, be half filled over-night. It held six quarts, perhaps. "But," said she, " we were used to thirst. At sandy Payta, where I live, no shower from heaven ever fell; all the water there is brought on mules from the inland vales."

Tied among the thickets were some twenty moaning tortoises, supplying Hunilla's lonely larder; while hundreds of vast tableted black bucklers, like displaced, shattered tombstones of dark slate, were also scattered round. These were the skeleton backs of those great tortoises from which Felipe and Truxill had made their precious oil. Several large calabashes and two goodly kegs were filled with it. In a pot near by were the caked crusts of a quantity which had been permitted to evaporate. "They meant to have strained it off next day," said Hunilla, as she turned aside.

I forgot to mention the most singular sight of all, though the first that greeted us after landing.

Some ten small, soft-haired, ringleted dogs, of a beautiful breed, peculiar to Peru, set up a concert of glad welcomings when we gained the beach, which was responded to by Hunilla. Some of these dogs had, since her widowhood, been born upon the isle, the progeny of the two brought from Payta. Owing to the jagged steeps and pitfalls, tortuous thickets, sunken clefts and perilous intricacies of all sorts in the interior; Hunilla, admonished by the loss of one favorite among them, never allowed these delicate creatures to follow her in her occasional birds'-nests climbs and other wanderings; so that, through long habituation, they offered not to follow, when that morning she crossed the land; and her own soul was then too full of other things to heed their lingering behind. Yet, all along she had so clung to them, that, besides what moisture they lapped up at early daybreak from the small scoop-holes among the adjacent rocks, she had shared the dew of her calabash among them; never laying by any considerable store against those prolonged and utter droughts, which in some disastrous seasons warp these isles.

Having pointed out, at our desire, what few things she would like transported to the ship—her chest, the oil, not omitting the live tortoises which she intended for a grateful present to our Captain—we immediately set to work, carrying them to the boat down the long, sloping stair of deeply-shadowed rock. While my comrades were thus employed, I looked, and Hunilla had disappeared.

It was not curiosity alone, but, it seems to me, something different mingled with it, which prompted me to drop my tortoise, and once more gaze slowly around. I remembered the husband buried by Hunilla's hands. A narrow pathway led into a dense part of the thickets. Following it through many mazes, I came out upon a small, round, open space, deeply chambered there.

The mound rose in the middle; a bare heap of finest sand, like that unverdured heap found at the bottom of an hour-glass run out. At its head stood the cross of withered sticks; the dry, peeled bark still fraying from it; its transverse limb tied up with rope, and forlornly adroop in the silent air.

Hunilla was partly prostrate upon the grave; her dark head bowed, and lost in her long, loosened Indian hair; her hands extended to the cross-foot, with a little brass crucifix clasped between; a crucifix worn featureless, like an ancient graven knocker long plied in vain. She did not see me, and I made no noise, but slid aside, and left the spot.

A few moments ere all was ready for our going, she reappeared among us. I looked into her eyes, but saw no tear. There was something which seemed strangely haughty in her air, and yet it was the air of woe. A Spanish and an Indian grief, which would not visibly lament. Pride's height in vain abased to proneness on the rack; nature's pride subduing nature's torture.

Like pages the small and silken dogs surrounded her, as she slowly descended towards the beach. She caught the two most eager creatures in her arms:—"Mia Teeta! Mia Tomo-teeta!" and fondling them, inquired how many could we take on board.

The mate commanded the boat's crew; not a hard-hearted man, but his way of life had been such that in most things, even in the smallest, simple utility was his leading motive.

"We cannot take them all, Hunilla; our supplies are short; the winds are unreliable; we may be a good many days going to Tombez. So take those you have, Hunilla; but no more."

She was in the boat; the oarsmen too were seated; all save one, who stood ready to push off and then spring himself. With the sagacity of their race, the dogs now seemed aware that they were in the very instant of being deserted upon a barren strand. The gunwales of the boat were high; its prow—presented inland—was lifted; so owing to the water, which they seemed instinctively to shun, the dogs could not well leap into the little craft. But their busy paws hard scraped the prow, as it had been some farmer's door shutting them out from shelter in a winter storm. A clamorous agony of alarm. They did not howl, or whine; they all but spoke.

"Push off! Give way!" cried the mate. The boat gave one heavy drag and lurch, and next moment shot swiftly from the beach, turned on her heel, and sped. The dogs ran howling along the water's marge; now pausing to gaze at the flying boat, then motioning as if to leap in chase, but mysteriously withheld themselves; and again ran howling along the beach. Had they been human beings hardly would they have more vividly inspired the sense of desolation. The oars were plied as confederate feathers of two wings. No one spoke. I looked back upon the beach, and then upon Hunilla, but her face was set in a stern dusky calm. The dogs crouching in her lap vainly licked her rigid hands. She never looked behind her; but sat motionless, till we turned a promontory of the coast and lost all sights and sounds astern. She seemed as one, who having experienced the sharpest of mortal pangs, was henceforth content to have all lesser heart-strings riven, one by one. To Hunilla, pain seemed so necessary, that pain in other beings, though by love and sympathy made her own, was unrepiningly to be borne. A heart of yearning in a frame of steel. A heart of earthly yearning, frozen by the frost which falleth from the sky.

The sequel is soon told. After a long passage, vexed by calms and baffling winds, we made the little port of Tombez in Peru, there to recruit the ship. Payta was not very distant. Our captain sold the tortoise oil to a Tombez merchant; and adding to the silver a contribution from all hands, gave it to our silent passenger, who knew not what the mariners had done.

The last seen of lone Hunilla she was passing into Payta town, riding upon a small gray ass; and before her on the ass's shoulders, she eyed the jointed workings of the beast's armorial cross.

SKETCH NINTH

HOOD'S ISLE AND THE HERMIT OBERLUS

"That darkesome glen they enter, where they find
That cursed man low sitting on the ground,
Musing full sadly in his sullein mind;
His griesly lockes long growen and unbound,
Disordered hong about his shoulders round,
And hid his face, through which his hollow eyne
Lookt deadly dull, and stared as astound;
His raw-bone cheekes, through penurie and pine,
Were shronke into the jawes, as he did never dine.
His garments nought but many ragged clouts,
With thornes together pind and patched was,
The which his naked sides he wrapt abouts."

Southeast of Crossman's Isle lies Hood's Isle, or McCain's Beclouded Isle; and upon its south side is a vitreous cove with a wide strand of dark pounded black lava, called Black Beach, or Oberlus's Landing. It might fitly have been styled Charon's.

It received its name from a wild white creature who spent many years here; in the person of a European bringing into this savage region qualities more diabolical than are to be found among any of the surrounding cannibals.

About half a century ago, Oberlus deserted at the above-named island, then, as now, a solitude. He built himself a den of lava and clinkers, about a mile from the Landing, subsequently called after him, in a vale, or expanded gulch, containing here and there among the rocks about two acres of soil capable of rude cultivation; the only place on the isle not too blasted for that purpose. Here he succeeded in raising a sort of degenerate potatoes and pumpkins, which from time to time he exchanged with needy whalemen passing, for spirits or dollars.

His appearance, from all accounts, was that of the victim of some malignant sorceress; he seemed to have drunk of Circe's cup; beast-like; rags insufficient to hide his nakedness; his befreckled skin blistered by continual exposure to the sun; nose flat; countenance contorted, heavy, earthy; hair and beard unshorn, profuse, and of a fiery red. He struck strangers much as if he were a volcanic creature thrown up by the same convulsion which exploded into sight the isle. All be-patched and coiled asleep in his lonely lava den among the mountains, he looked, they say, as a heaped drift of withered leaves, torn from autumn trees, and so left in some hidden nook by the whirling halt for an instant of a fierce night-wind, which then ruthlessly sweeps on, somewhere else to repeat the capricious act. It is also reported to have been the strangest sight, this same Oberlus, of a sultry, cloudy morning, hidden under his shocking old black tarpaulin hat, hoeing potatoes among the lava. So warped and crooked was his strange nature, that the very handle of his hoe seemed gradually to have shrunk and twisted in his grasp, being a wretched bent stick, elbowed more like a savage's war-sickle than a civilized hoe-handle. It was his mysterious custom upon a first encounter with a stranger ever to present his back; possibly, because that was his better side, since it revealed the least. If the encounter chanced in his garden, as it sometimes did—the new-landed strangers going from the sea-side straight through the gorge, to hunt up the queer green-grocer reported doing business here—Oberlus for a time hoed on, unmindful of all greeting, jovial or bland; as the curious stranger would turn to face him, the recluse, hoe in hand, as diligently would avert himself; bowed over, and sullenly revolving round his murphy hill. Thus far for hoeing. When planting, his whole aspect and all his gestures were so malevolently and uselessly sinister and secret, that he seemed rather in act of dropping poison into wells than potatoes into soil. But among his lesser and more harmless marvels was an idea he ever had, that his visitors came equally as well led by longings to behold the mighty hermit Oberlus in his royal state of solitude, as simply to obtain potatoes, or find whatever company might be upon a barren isle. It seems incredible that such a being should possess such vanity; a misanthrope be conceited; but he really had his notion; and upon the strength of it, often gave himself amusing airs to captains. But after all, this is somewhat of a piece with the well-known eccentricity of some convicts, proud of that very hatefulness which makes them notorious. At other times, another unaccountable whim would seize him, and he would long dodge advancing strangers round the clinkered corners of his hut; sometimes like a stealthy bear, he would slink through the withered thickets up the mountains, and refuse to see the human face.

Except his occasional visitors from the sea, for a long period, the only companions of Oberlus were the crawling tortoises; and he seemed more than degraded to their level, having no desires for a time beyond theirs, unless it were for the stupor brought on by drunkenness. But sufficiently debased as he appeared, there yet lurked in him, only awaiting occasion for discovery, a still further proneness. Indeed the sole superiority of Oberlus over the tortoises was his possession of a larger capacity of degradation; and along with that, something like an intelligent will to it. Moreover, what is about to be revealed, perhaps will show, that selfish ambition, or the love of rule for its own sake, far from being the peculiar infirmity of noble minds, is shared by beings which have no mind at all. No creatures are so selfishly tyrannical as some brutes; as any one who has observed the tenants of the pasture must occasionally have observed.

"This island's mine by Sycorax my mother;" said Oberlus to himself, glaring round upon his haggard solitude. By some means, barter or theft—for in those days ships at intervals still kept touching at his Landing—he obtained an old musket, with a few charges of powder and ball. Possessed of arms, he was stimulated to enterprise, as a tiger that first feels the coming of its claws. The long habit of sole dominion over every object round him, his almost unbroken solitude, his never encountering humanity except on terms of misanthropic independence, or mercantile craftiness, and even such encounters being comparatively but rare; all this must have gradually nourished in him a vast idea of his own importance, together with a pure animal sort of scorn for all the rest of the universe.

The unfortunate Creole, who enjoyed his brief term of royalty at Charles's Isle was perhaps in some degree influenced by not unworthy motives; such as prompt other adventurous spirits to lead colonists into distant regions and assume political pre-eminence over them. His summary execution of many of his Peruvians is quite pardonable, considering the desperate characters he had to deal with; while his offering canine battle to the banded rebels seems under the circumstances altogether just. But for this King Oberlus and what shortly follows, no shade of palliation can be given. He acted out of mere delight in tyranny and cruelty, by virtue of a quality in him inherited from Sycorax his mother. Armed now with that shocking blunderbuss, strong in the thought of being master of that horrid isle, he panted for a chance to prove his potency upon the first specimen of humanity which should fall unbefriended into his hands.

Nor was he long without it. One day he spied a boat upon the beach, with one man, a negro, standing by it. Some distance off was a ship, and Oberlus immediately knew how matters stood. The vessel had put in for wood, and the boat's crew had gone into the thickets for it. From a convenient spot he kept watch of the boat, till presently a straggling company appeared loaded with billets. Throwing these on the beach, they again went into the thickets, while the negro proceeded to load the boat.

Oberlus now makes all haste and accosts the negro, who aghast at seeing any living being inhabiting such a solitude, and especially so horrific a one, immediately falls into a panic, not at all lessened by the ursine suavity of Oberlus, who begs the favor of assisting him in his labors. The negro stands with several billets on his shoulder, in act of shouldering others; and Oberlus, with a short cord concealed in his bosom, kindly proceeds to lift those other billets to their place. In so doing he persists in keeping behind the negro, who rightly suspicious of this, in vain dodges about to gain the front of Oberlus; but Oberlus dodges also; till at last, weary of this bootless attempt at treachery, or fearful of being surprised by

the remainder of the party, Oberlus runs off a little space to
a bush, and fetching his blunderbuss, savagely commands the
negro to desist work and follow him. He refuses. Whereupon,
presenting his piece, Oberlus snaps at him. Luckily the blunderbuss misses fire; but by this time, frightened out of his
wits, the negro, upon a second intrepid summons drops his
billets, surrenders at discretion, and follows on. By a narrow
defile familiar to him, Oberlus speedily removes out of sight
of the water.

On their way up the mountains, he exultingly informs the
negro, that henceforth he is to work for him, and be his slave,
and that his treatment would entirely depend on his future
conduct. But Oberlus, deceived by the first impulsive cowardice of the black, in an evil moment slackens his vigilance. Passing through a narrow way, and perceiving his leader quite off
his guard, the negro, a powerful fellow, suddenly grasps him
in his arms, throws him down, wrests his musketoon from
him, ties his hands with the monster's own cord, shoulders
him, and returns with him down to the boat. When the rest
of the party arrive, Oberlus is carried on board the ship. This
proved an Englishman, and a smuggler; a sort of craft not apt
to be over-charitable. Oberlus is severely whipped, then handcuffed, taken ashore, and compelled to make known his habitation and produce his property. His potatoes, pumpkins,
and tortoises, with a pile of dollars he had hoarded from his
mercantile operations were secured on the spot. But while the
too vindictive smugglers were busy destroying his hut and
garden, Oberlus makes his escape into the mountains, and
conceals himself there in impenetrable recesses, only known
to himself, till the ship sails, when he ventures back, and by
means of an old file which he sticks into a tree, contrives to
free himself from his handcuffs.

Brooding among the ruins of his hut, and the desolate
clinkers and extinct volcanoes of this outcast isle, the insulted
misanthrope now meditates a signal revenge upon humanity,
but conceals his purposes. Vessels still touch the Landing at
times; and by and by Oberlus is enabled to supply them with
some vegetables.

Warned by his former failure in kidnapping strangers, he
now pursues a quite different plan. When seamen come

ashore, he makes up to them like a free-and-easy comrade, invites them to his hut, and with whatever affability his red-haired grimness may assume, entreats them to drink his liquor and be merry. But his guests need little pressing; and so, soon as rendered insensible, are tied hand and foot, and pitched among the clinkers, are there concealed till the ship departs, when finding themselves entirely dependent upon Oberlus, alarmed at his changed demeanor, his savage threats, and above all, that shocking blunderbuss, they willingly enlist under him, becoming his humble slaves, and Oberlus the most incredible of tyrants. So much so, that two or three perish beneath his initiating process. He sets the remainder—four of them—to breaking the caked soil; transporting upon their backs loads of loamy earth, scooped up in moist clefts among the mountains; keeps them on the roughest fare; presents his piece at the slightest hint of insurrection; and in all respects converts them into reptiles at his feet; plebeian garter-snakes to this Lord Anaconda.

At last, Oberlus contrives to stock his arsenal with four rusty cutlasses, and an added supply of powder and ball intended for his blunderbuss. Remitting in good part the labor of his slaves, he now approves himself a man, or rather devil, of great abilities in the way of cajoling or coercing others into acquiescence with his own ulterior designs, however at first abhorrent to them. But indeed, prepared for almost any eventual evil by their previous lawless life, as a sort of ranging Cow-Boys of the sea, which had dissolved within them the whole moral man, so that they were ready to concrete in the first offered mould of baseness now; rotted down from manhood by their hopeless misery on the isle; wonted to cringe in all things to their lord, himself the worst of slaves; these wretches were now become wholly corrupted to his hands. He used them as creatures of an inferior race; in short, he gaffles his four animals, and makes murderers of them; out of cowards fitly manufacturing bravos.

Now, sword or dagger, human arms are but artificial claws and fangs, tied on like false spurs to the fighting cock. So, we repeat, Oberlus, czar of the isle, gaffles his four subjects; that is, with intent of glory, puts four rusty cutlasses into their hands. Like any other autocrat, he had a noble army now.

It might be thought a servile war would hereupon ensue. Arms in the hands of trodden slaves? how indiscreet of Emperor Oberlus! Nay, they had but cutlasses—sad old scythes enough—he a blunderbuss, which by its blind scatterings of all sorts of boulders, clinkers and other scoria would annihilate all four mutineers, like four pigeons at one shot. Besides, at first he did not sleep in his accustomed hut; every lurid sunset, for a time, he might have been seen wending his way among the riven mountains, there to secret himself till dawn in some sulphurous pitfall, undiscoverable to his gang; but finding this at last too troublesome, he now each evening tied his slaves hand and foot, hid the cutlasses, and thrusting them into his barracks, shut to the door, and lying down before it, beneath a rude shed lately added, slept out the night, blunderbuss in hand.

It is supposed that not content with daily parading over a cindery solitude at the head of his fine army, Oberlus now meditated the most active mischief; his probable object being to surprise some passing ship touching at his dominions, massacre the crew, and run away with her to parts unknown. While these plans were simmering in his head, two ships touch in company at the isle, on the opposite side to his; when his designs undergo a sudden change.

The ships are in want of vegetables, which Oberlus promises in great abundance, provided they send their boats round to his landing, so that the crews may bring the vegetables from his garden; informing the two captains, at the same time, that his rascals—slaves and soldiers—had become so abominably lazy and good-for-nothing of late, that he could not make them work by ordinary inducements, and did not have the heart to be severe with them.

The arrangement was agreed to, and the boats were sent and hauled upon the beach. The crews went to the lava hut; but to their surprise nobody was there. After waiting till their patience was exhausted, they returned to the shore, when lo, some stranger—not the Good Samaritan either—seems to have very recently passed that way. Three of the boats were broken in a thousand pieces, and the fourth was missing. By hard toil over the mountains and through the clinkers, some of the strangers succeeded in returning to that side of the isle where the ships lay, when fresh boats are sent to the relief of the rest of the hapless party.

However amazed at the treachery of Oberlus, the two captains afraid of new and still more mysterious atrocities,—and indeed, half imputing such strange events to the enchantments associated with these isles,—perceive no security but in instant flight; leaving Oberlus and his army in quiet possession of the stolen boat.

On the eve of sailing they put a letter in a keg, giving the Pacific Ocean intelligence of the affair, and moored the keg in the bay. Some time subsequent, the keg was opened by another captain chancing to anchor there, but not until after he had dispatched a boat round to Oberlus's Landing. As may be readily surmised, he felt no little inquietude till the boat's return; when another letter was handed him, giving Oberlus's version of the affair. This precious document had been found pinned half-mildewed to the clinker wall of the sulphurous and deserted hut. It ran as follows; showing that Oberlus was at least an accomplished writer, and no mere boor; and what is more, was capable of the most tristful eloquence.

"Sir: I am the most unfortunate ill-treated gentleman that lives. I am a patriot, exiled from my country by the cruel hand of tyranny.

"Banished to these Enchanted Isles, I have again and again besought captains of ships to sell me a boat, but always have been refused, though I offered the handsomest prices in Mexican dollars. At length an opportunity presented of possessing myself of one, and I did not let it slip.

"I have been long endeavoring by hard labor and much solitary suffering to accumulate something to make myself comfortable in a virtuous though unhappy old age; but at various times have been robbed and beaten by men professing to be Christians.

"To-day I sail from the Enchanted group in the good boat Charity bound to the Feejee Isles.   "FATHERLESS OBERLUS.

"*P.S.*—Behind the clinkers, nigh the oven, you will find the old fowl. Do not kill it; be patient; I leave it setting; if it shall have any chicks, I hereby bequeathe them to you, whoever you may be. But don't count your chicks before they are hatched."

The fowl proved a starveling rooster, reduced to a sitting posture by sheer debility.

Oberlus declares that he was bound to the Feejee Isles; but this was only to throw pursuers on a false scent. For after a long time he arrived, alone in his open boat, at Guayaquil. As his miscreants were never again beheld on Hood's Isle, it is supposed, either that they perished for want of water on the passage to Guayaquil, or, what is quite as probable, were thrown overboard by Oberlus, when he found the water growing scarce.

From Guayaquil Oberlus proceeded to Payta; and there, with that nameless witchery peculiar to some of the ugliest animals, wound himself into the affections of a tawny damsel; prevailing upon her to accompany him back to his Enchanted Isle; which doubtless he painted as a Paradise of flowers, not a Tartarus of clinkers.

But unfortunately for the colonization of Hood's Isle with a choice variety of animated nature, the extraordinary and devilish aspect of Oberlus made him to be regarded in Payta as a highly suspicious character. So that being found concealed one night, with matches in his pocket, under the hull of a small vessel just ready to be launched, he was seized and thrown into jail.

The jails in most South American towns are generally of the least wholesome sort. Built of huge cakes of sun-burnt brick, and containing but one room, without windows or yard, and but one door heavily grated with wooden bars, they present both within and without the grimmest aspect. As public edifices they conspicuously stand upon the hot and dusty Plaza, offering to view, through the gratings, their villanous and hopeless inmates, burrowing in all sorts of tragic squalor. And here, for a long time Oberlus was seen; the central figure of a mongrel and assassin band; a creature whom it is religion to detest, since it is philanthropy to hate a misanthrope.

Note.—They who may be disposed to question the possibility of the character above depicted, are referred to the 1st vol. of Porter's Voyage into the Pacific, where they will recognize many sentences, for expedition's sake derived verbatim from thence, and incorporated here; the main difference—save a few passing reflections—between the two accounts being, that the present writer has added to Porter's facts accessory ones picked up in the Pacific from reliable sources;

and where facts conflict, has naturally preferred his own authorities to Porter's. As, for instance, *his* authorities place Oberlus on Hood's Isle: Porter's, on Charles's Isle. The letter found in the hut is also somewhat different, for while at the Encantadas he was informed that not only did it evince a certain clerkliness, but was full of the strangest satiric effrontery which does not adequately appear in Porter's version. I accordingly altered it to suit the general character of its author.

Sketch Tenth

Runaways, Castaways, Solitaries, Grave-stones, etc.

> *"And all about old stocks and stubs of trees,*
> *Whereon nor fruit nor leaf was ever seen,*
> *Did hang upon the ragged knotty knees,*
> *On which had many wretches hanged been."*

Some relics of the hut of Oberlus partially remain to this day at the head of the clinkered valley. Nor does the stranger wandering among other of the Enchanted Isles fail to stumble upon still other solitary abodes, long abandoned to the tortoise and the lizard. Probably few parts of earth have in modern times sheltered so many solitaries. The reason is, that these isles are situated in a distant sea, and the vessels which occasionally visit them are mostly all whalers, or ships bound on dreary and protracted voyages, exempting them in a good degree from both the oversight and the memory of human law. Such is the character of some commanders and some seamen, that under these untoward circumstances, it is quite impossible but that scenes of unpleasantness and discord should occur between them. A sullen hatred of the tyrannic ship will seize the sailor, and he gladly exchanges it for isles, which though blighted as by a continual sirocco and burning breeze, still offer him in their labyrinthine interior, a retreat beyond the possibility of capture. To flee the ship in any Peruvian or Chilian port, even the smallest and most rustical, is not unattended with great risk of apprehension, not to speak of jaguars. A reward of five pesos sends fifty dastardly Spaniards into the woods, who with long knives scour them day and night in eager hopes of securing their prey. Neither is it, in general, much easier to escape pursuit at the isles of Polynesia. Those of them which have felt a civilizing influence present the same difficulty to the runaway with the Peruvian ports, the advanced natives being quite as mercenary and keen of knife and scent, as the retrograde Spaniards; while, owing to the bad odor in which all Europeans lie in the minds of aboriginal savages who have chanced to hear aught of them, to desert the ship among primitive Polynesians, is, in most cases, a hope not unforlorn. Hence the Enchanted Isles become the voluntary tarrying places of all sorts of refugees; some of whom too sadly experience the fact that flight from tyranny does not of itself insure a safe asylum, far less a happy home.

Moreover, it has not seldom happened that hermits have been made upon the isles by the accidents incident to tortoise-hunting. The interior of most of them is tangled and difficult of passage beyond description; the air is sultry and stifling; an intolerable thirst is provoked, for which no running stream offers its kind relief. In a few hours, under an equatorial sun, reduced by these causes to entire exhaustion, woe betide the straggler at the Enchanted Isles! Their extent is such as to forbid an adequate search unless weeks are devoted to it. The impatient ship waits a day or two; when the missing man remaining undiscovered, up goes a stake on the beach, with a letter of regret, and a keg of crackers and another of water tied to it, and away sails the craft.

Nor have there been wanting instances where the inhumanity of some captains has led them to wreak a secure revenge upon seamen who have given their caprice or pride some singular offence. Thrust ashore upon the scorching marl, such mariners are abandoned to perish outright, unless by solitary labors they succeed in discovering some precious dribblets of moisture oozing from a rock or stagnant in a mountain pool.

I was well acquainted with a man, who, lost upon the Isle of Narborough, was brought to such extremes by thirst, that at last he only saved his life by taking that of another being. A large hair-seal came upon the beach. He rushed upon it, stabbed it in the neck, and then throwing himself upon the panting body quaffed at the living wound; the palpitations of the creature's dying heart injecting life into the drinker.

Another seaman thrust ashore in a boat upon an isle at

which no ship ever touched, owing to its peculiar sterility and the shoals about it, and from which all other parts of the group were hidden; this man feeling that it was sure death to remain there, and that nothing worse than death menaced him in quitting it, killed two seals, and inflating their skins, made a float, upon which he transported himself to Charles's Island, and joined the republic there.

But men not endowed with courage equal to such desperate attempts, find their only resource in forthwith seeking for some watering-place, however precarious or scanty; building a hut; catching tortoises and birds; and in all respects preparing for hermit life, till tide or time, or a passing ship arrives to float them off.

At the foot of precipices on many of the isles, small rude basins in the rocks are found, partly filled with rotted rubbish or vegetable decay, or overgrown with thickets, and sometimes a little moist; which, upon examination, reveal plain tokens of artificial instruments employed in hollowing them out, by some poor castaway or still more miserable runaway. These basins are made in places where it was supposed some scanty drops of dew might exude into them from the upper crevices.

The relics of hermitages and stone basins, are not the only signs of vanishing humanity to be found upon the isles. And curious to say, that spot which of all others in settled communities is most animated, at the Enchanted Isles presents the most dreary of aspects. And though it may seem very strange to talk of post-offices in this barren region, yet post-offices are occasionally to be found there. They consist of a stake and bottle. The letters being not only sealed, but corked. They are generally deposited by captains of Nantucketers for the benefit of passing fishermen; and contain statements as to what luck they had in whaling or tortoise-hunting. Frequently, however, long months and months, whole years glide by and no applicant appears. The stake rots and falls, presenting no very exhilarating object.

If now it be added that grave-stones, or rather grave-boards, are also discovered upon some of the isles, the picture will be complete.

Upon the beach of James's Isle for many years, was to be

seen a rude finger-post pointing inland. And perhaps taking it for some signal of possible hospitality in this otherwise desolate spot—some good hermit living there with his maple dish—the stranger would follow on in the path thus indicated, till at last he would come out in a noiseless nook, and find his only welcome, a dead man; his sole greeting the inscription over a grave: "Here, in 1813, fell in a daybreak duel, a Lieutenant of the U.S. frigate Essex, aged twenty-one: attaining his majority in death."

It is but fit that like those old monastic institutions of Europe, whose inmates go not out of their own walls to be inurned, but are entombed there where they die; the Encantadas too should bury their own dead, even as the great general monastery of earth does hers.

It is known that burial in the ocean is a pure necessity of sea-faring life, and that it is only done when land is far astern, and not clearly visible from the bow. Hence to vessels cruising in the vicinity of the Enchanted Isles, they afford a convenient Potter's Field. The interment over, some good-natured forecastle poet and artist seizes his paint-brush, and inscribes a doggerel epitaph. When after a long lapse of time, other good-natured seamen chance to come upon the spot, they usually make a table of the mound, and quaff a friendly can to the poor soul's repose.

As a specimen of these epitaphs, take the following, found in a bleak gorge of Chatham Isle:—

> "Oh Brother Jack, as you pass by,
> As you are now, so once was I.
> Just so game and just so gay,
> But now, alack, they've stopped my pay.
> No more I peep out of my blinkers,
> Here I be—tucked in with clinkers!"

The Bell-Tower

"Like negroes, these powers own man sullenly; mindful of their higher master; while serving, plot revenge."

"The world is apoplectic with high-living of ambition; and apoplexy has its fall."

"Seeking to conquer a larger liberty, man but extends the empire of necessity."

From a Private MS.

IN THE SOUTH of Europe, nigh a once-frescoed capital, now with dank mould cankering its bloom, central in a plain, stands what, at a distance, seems the black mossed stump of some immeasurable pine, fallen, in forgotten days, with Anak and the Titan.

As all along where the pine tree falls, its dissolution leaves a mossy mound—last-flung shadow of the perished trunk; never lengthening, never lessening; unsubject to the fleet falsities of the sun; shade immutable and true gauge which cometh by prostration—so westward from what seems the stump, one steadfast spear of lichened ruin veins the plain.

From that tree-top, what birded chimes of silver throats had rung. A stone pine; a metallic aviary in its crown: the Bell-Tower, built by the great mechanician, the unblest foundling, Bannadonna.

Like Babel's, its base was laid in a high hour of renovated earth, following the second deluge, when the waters of the Dark Ages had dried up, and once more the green appeared. No wonder that, after so long and deep submersion, the jubilant expectation of the race should, as with Noah's sons, soar into Shinar aspiration.

In firm resolve, no man in Europe at that period went beyond Bannadonna. Enriched through commerce with the Levant, the state in which he lived voted to have the noblest Bell-Tower in Italy. His repute assigned him to be architect.

Stone by stone, month by month, the tower rose. Higher, higher; snail-like in pace, but torch or rocket in its pride.

After the masons would depart, the builder, standing alone upon its ever-ascending summit, at close of every day saw that he overtopped still higher walls and trees. He would tarry till a late hour there, wrapped in schemes of other and still loftier piles. Those who of saints' days thronged the spot—hanging to the rude poles of scaffolding, like sailors on yards, or bees on boughs, unmindful of lime and dust, and falling chips of stone—their homage not the less inspirited him to self-esteem.

At length the holiday of the Tower came. To the sound of viols, the climax-stone slowly rose in air, and, amid the firing of ordnance, was laid by Bannadonna's hands upon the final course. Then mounting it, he stood erect, alone, with folded arms; gazing upon the white summits of blue inland Alps, and whiter crests of bluer Alps off-shore—sights invisible from the plain. Invisible, too, from thence was that eye he turned below, when, like the cannon booms, came up to him the people's combustions of applause.

That which stirred them so was, seeing with what serenity the builder stood three hundred feet in air, upon an unrailed perch. This none but he durst do. But his periodic standing upon the pile, in each stage of its growth—such discipline had its last result.

Little remained now but the bells. These, in all respects, must correspond with their receptacle.

The minor ones were prosperously cast. A highly enriched one followed, of a singular make, intended for suspension in a manner before unknown. The purpose of this bell, its rotary motion, and connection with the clock-work, also executed at the time, will, in the sequel, receive mention.

In the one erection, bell-tower and clock-tower were united, though, before that period, such structures had commonly been built distinct; as the Campanile and Torre dell' Orologio of St. Mark to this day attest.

But it was upon the great state-bell that the founder lavished his more daring skill. In vain did some of the less elated magistrates here caution him; saying that though truly the tower was Titanic, yet limit should be set to the dependent weight of its swaying masses. But undeterred, he prepared his mammouth mould, dented with mythological devices; kindled his fires of balsamic firs; melted his tin and copper; and throwing in much plate, contributed by the public spirit of the nobles, let loose the tide.

The unleashed metals bayed like hounds. The workmen shrunk. Through their fright, fatal harm to the bell was dreaded. Fearless as Shadrach, Bannadonna, rushing through the glow, smote the chief culprit with his ponderous ladle. From the smitten part, a splinter was dashed into the seething mass, and at once was melted in.

Next day a portion of the work was heedfully uncovered. All seemed right. Upon the third morning, with equal satisfaction, it was bared still lower. At length, like some old Theban king, the whole cooled casting was disinterred. All was fair except in one strange spot. But as he suffered no one to attend him in these inspections, he concealed the blemish by some preparation which none knew better to devise.

The casting of such a mass was deemed no small triumph for the caster; one, too, in which the state might not scorn to share. The homicide was overlooked. By the charitable that deed was but imputed to sudden transports of esthetic passion, not to any flagitious quality. A kick from an Arabian charger: not sign of vice, but blood.

His felony remitted by the judge, absolution given him by the priest, what more could even a sickly conscience have desired!

Honoring the tower and its builder with another holiday, the republic witnessed the hoisting of the bells and clockwork amid shows and pomps superior to the former.

Some months of more than usual solitude on Bannadonna's part ensued. It was not unknown that he was engaged upon something for the belfry, intended to complete it, and surpass all that had gone before. Most people imagined that the design would involve a casting like the bells. But those who thought they had some further insight, would shake their heads, with hints, that not for nothing did the mechanician keep so secret. Meantime, his seclusion failed not to invest his work with more or less of that sort of mystery pertaining to the forbidden.

Ere long he had a heavy object hoisted to the belfry, wrapped in a dark sack or cloak; a procedure sometimes had in the case of an elaborate piece of sculpture, or statue, which, being intended to grace the front of a new edifice, the architect does not desire exposed to critical eyes, till set up, finished, in its appointed place. Such was the impression now. But, as the object rose, a statuary present observed, or thought he did, that it was not entirely rigid, but was, in a manner, pliant. At last, when the hidden thing had attained its final height, and, obscurely seen from below, seemed almost of itself to step into the belfry, as if with little assistance from the crane, a shrewd old blacksmith present ventured the suspicion that it was but a living man. This surmise was thought a foolish one, while the general interest failed not to augment.

Not without demur from Bannadonna, the chief-magistrate of the town, with an associate—both elderly men—followed what seemed the image up the tower. But, arrived at the belfry, they had little recompense. Plausibly entrenching himself behind the conceded mysteries of his art, the mechanician withheld present explanation. The magistrates glanced toward the cloaked object, which, to their surprise, seemed now to have changed its attitude, or else had before been more perplexingly concealed by the violent muffling action of the wind without. It seemed now seated upon some sort of frame, or chair, contained within the domino. They observed that nigh the top, in a sort of square, the web of the cloth, either from accident or design, had its warp partly withdrawn, and the cross-threads plucked out here and there, so as to form a sort of woven grating. Whether it were the low wind or no, stealing through the stone lattice-work, or only their own perturbed imaginations, is uncertain, but they thought they discerned a slight sort of fitful, spring-like motion, in the domino. Nothing, however incidental or insignificant, escaped their uneasy eyes. Among other things, they pried out, in a corner, an earthen cup, partly corroded and partly encrusted, and one whispered to the other, that this cup was just such a one as might, in mockery, be offered to the lips of some brazen statue, or, perhaps, still worse.

But, being questioned, the mechanician said, that the cup was simply used in his founder's business, and described the purpose; in short, a cup to test the condition of metals in fusion. He added, that it had got into the belfry by the merest chance.

Again, and again, they gazed at the domino, as at some

suspicious incognito—at a Venetian mask. All sorts of vague apprehensions stirred them. They even dreaded lest, when they should descend, the mechanician, though without a flesh and blood companion, for all that, would not be left alone.

Affecting some merriment at their disquietude, he begged to relieve them, by extending a coarse sheet of workman's canvas between them and the object.

Meantime he sought to interest them in his other work; nor, now that the domino was out of sight, did they long remain insensible to the artistic wonders lying round them; wonders hitherto beheld but in their unfinished state; because, since hoisting the bells, none but the caster had entered within the belfry. It was one trait of his, that, even in details, he would not let another do what he could, without too great loss of time, accomplish for himself. So, for several preceding weeks, whatever hours were unemployed in his secret design, had been devoted to elaborating the figures on the bells.

The clock-bell, in particular, now drew attention. Under a patient chisel, the latent beauty of its enrichments, before obscured by the cloudings incident to casting that beauty in its shyest grace, was now revealed. Round and round the bell, twelve figures of gay girls, garlanded, hand-in-hand, danced in a choral ring—the embodied hours.

"Bannadonna," said the chief, "this bell excels all else. No added touch could here improve. Hark!" hearing a sound, " was that the wind?"

"The wind, Eccellenza," was the light response. "But the figures, they are not yet without their faults. They need some touches yet. When those are given, and the——block yonder," pointing towards the canvas screen, " when Haman there, as I merrily call him,—him? it, I mean——when Haman is fixed on this, his lofty tree, then, gentlemen, will I be most happy to receive you here again."

The equivocal reference to the object caused some return of restlessness. However, on their part, the visitors forbore further allusion to it, unwilling, perhaps, to let the foundling see how easily it lay within his plebeian art to stir the placid dignity of nobles.

"Well, Bannadonna," said the chief, "how long ere you are ready to set the clock going, so that the hour shall be sounded? Our interest in you, not less than in the work itself, makes us anxious to be assured of your success. The people, too,—why, they are shouting now. Say the exact hour when you will be ready."

"To-morrow, Eccellenza, if you listen for it,—or should you not, all the same—strange music will be heard. The stroke of one shall be the first from yonder bell," pointing to the bell adorned with girls and garlands, "that stroke shall fall there, where the hand of Una clasps Dua's. The stroke of one shall sever that loved clasp. To-morrow, then, at one o'clock, as struck here, precisely here," advancing and placing his finger upon the clasp, "the poor mechanic will be most happy once more to give you liege audience, in this his littered shop. Farewell till then, illustrious magnificoes, and hark ye for your vassal's stroke."

His still, Vulcanic face hiding its burning brightness like a forge, he moved with ostentatious deference towards the scuttle, as if so far to escort their exit. But the junior magistrate, a kind hearted man, troubled at what seemed to him a certain sardonical disdain, lurking beneath the foundling's humble mien, and in Christian sympathy more distressed at it on his account than on his own, dimly surmising what might be the final fate of such a cynic solitaire, nor perhaps uninfluenced by the general strangeness of surrounding things, this good magistrate had glanced sadly, sideways from the speaker, and thereupon his foreboding eye had started at the expression of the unchanging face of the Hour Una.

"How is this, Bannadonna?" he lowly asked, "Una looks unlike her sisters."

"In Christ's name, Bannadonna," impulsively broke in the chief, his attention, for the first time, attracted to the figure, by his associate's remark, "Una's face looks just like that of Deborah, the prophetess, as painted by the Florentine, Del Fonca."

"Surely, Bannadonna," lowly resumed the milder magistrate, "you meant the twelve should wear the same jocundly abandoned air. But see, the smile of Una seems but a fatal one. 'Tis different."

While his mild associate was speaking, the chief glanced, inquiringly, from him to the caster, as if anxious to mark how the discrepancy would be accounted for. As the chief stood, his advanced foot was on the scuttle's curb.

Bannadonna spoke.

"Eccellenza, now that, following your keener eye, I glance upon the face of Una, I do, indeed, perceive some little variance. But look all round the bell, and you will find no two faces entirely correspond. Because there is a law in art——— but the cold wind is rising more; these lattices are but a poor defense. Suffer me, magnificoes, to conduct you, at least, partly on your way. Those in whose well-being there is a public stake, should be heedfully attended."

"Touching the look of Una, you were saying, Bannadonna, that there was a certain law in art," observed the chief, as the three now descended the stone shaft, "pray, tell me, then———."

"Pardon; another time, Eccellenza;—the tower is damp."

"Nay, I must rest, and hear it now. Here,—here is a wide landing, and through this leeward slit, no wind, but ample light. Tell us of your law; and at large."

"Since, Eccellenza, you insist, know that there is a law in art, which bars the possibility of duplicates. Some years ago, you may remember, I graved a small seal for your republic, bearing, for its chief device, the head of your own ancestor, its illustrious founder. It becoming necessary, for the customs' use, to have innumerable impressions for bales and boxes, I graved an entire plate, containing one hundred of the seals. Now, though, indeed, my object was to have those hundred heads identical, and though, I dare say, people think them so, yet, upon closely scanning an uncut impression from the plate, no two of those five-score faces, side by side, will be found alike. Gravity is the air of all; but, diversified in all. In some, benevolent; in some, ambiguous; in two or three, to a close scrutiny, all but incipiently malign, the variation of less than a hair's breadth in the linear shadings round the mouth sufficing to all this. Now, Eccellenza, transmute that general gravity into joyousness, and subject it to twelve of those variations I have described, and tell me, will you not have my hours here, and Una one of them? But I like———."

"Hark! is that———a footfall above?"

"Mortar, Eccellenza; sometimes it drops to the belfry-floor from the arch where the stone-work was left undressed. I must have it seen to. As I was about to say: for one, I like this law forbidding duplicates. It evokes fine personalities. Yes, Eccellenza, that strange, and—to you—uncertain smile, and those fore-looking eyes of Una, suit Bannadonna very well."

"Hark!—sure we left no soul above?"

"No soul, Eccellenza; rest assured, no *soul*.—Again the mortar."

"It fell not while we were there."

"Ah, in your presence, it better knew its place, Eccellenza," blandly bowed Bannadonna.

"But, Una," said the milder magistrate, "she seemed intently gazing on you; one would have almost sworn that she picked you out from among us three."

"If she did, possibly, it might have been her finer apprehension, Eccellenza."

"How, Bannadonna? I do not understand you."

"No consequence, no consequence, Eccellenza—but the shifted wind is blowing through the slit. Suffer me to escort you on; and then, pardon, but the toiler must to his tools."

"It may be foolish, Signore," said the milder magistrate, as, from the third landing, the two now went down unescorted, "but, somehow, our great mechanician moves me strangely. Why, just now, when he so superciliously replied, his look seemed Sisera's, God's vain foe, in Del Fonca's painting.—And that young, sculptured Deborah, too. Aye, and that——."

"Tush, tush, Signore!" returned the chief. "A passing whim. Deborah?—Where's Jael, pray?"

"Ah," said the other, as they now stepped upon the sod, "Ah, Signore, I see you leave your fears behind you with the chill and gloom; but mine, even in this sunny air, remain. Hark!"

It was a sound from just within the tower door, whence they had emerged. Turning, they saw it closed.

"He has slipped down and barred us out," smiled the chief; "but it is his custom."

Proclamation was now made, that the next day, at one hour after meridian, the clock would strike, and—thanks to the mechanician's powerful art—with unusual accompaniments. But what those should be, none as yet could say. The announcement was received with cheers.

By the looser sort, who encamped about the tower all night, lights were seen gleaming through the topmost blind-work, only disappearing with the morning sun. Strange sounds, too, were heard, or were thought to be, by those whom anxious watching might not have left mentally undisturbed, sounds, not only of some ringing implement, but also—so they said—half-suppressed screams and plainings, such as might have issued from some ghostly engine, over-plied.

Slowly the day drew on; part of the concourse chasing the weary time with songs and games, till, at last, the great blurred sun rolled, like a football, against the plain.

At noon, the nobility and principal citizens came from the town in cavalcade; a guard of soldiers, also, with music, the more to honor the occasion.

Only one hour more. Impatience grew. Watches were held in hands of feverish men, who stood, now scrutinizing their small dial-plates, and then, with neck thrown back, gazing toward the belfry, as if the eye might foretell that which could only be made sensible to the ear, for, as yet, there was no dial to the tower-clock.

The hour-hands of a thousand watches now verged within a hair's breadth of the figure 1. A silence, as of the expectation of some Shiloh, pervaded the swarming plain. Suddenly a dull, mangled sound—naught ringing in it; scarcely audible, indeed, to the outer circles of the people—that dull sound dropped heavily from the belfry. At the same moment, each man stared at his neighbor blankly. All watches were upheld. All hour-hands were at—had passed—the figure 1. No bell-stroke from the tower. The multitude became tumultuous.

Waiting a few moments, the chief magistrate, commanding silence, hailed the belfry, to know what thing unforeseen had happened there.

No response.

He hailed again and yet again.

All continued hushed.

By his order the soldiers burst in the tower-door; when, stationing guards to defend it from the now surging mob, the chief, accompanied by his former associate, climbed the winding stairs. Half-way up, they stopped to listen. No sound.

Mounting faster, they reached the belfry; but, at the threshold, startled at the spectacle disclosed. A spaniel which, unbeknown to them, had followed them thus far, stood shivering as before some unknown monster in a brake: or, rather, as if it snuffed foot-steps leading to some other world.

Bannadonna lay prostrate and bleeding at the base of the bell which was adorned with girls and garlands. He lay at the feet of the hour Una; his head coinciding, in a vertical line, with her left hand, clasped by the hour Dua. With downcast face impending over him, like Jael over nailed Sisera in the tent, was the domino; now no more becloaked.

It had limbs, and seemed clad in a scaly mail, lustrous as a dragon-beetle's. It was manacled, and its clubbed arms were uplifted, as if, with its manacles, once more to smite its already smitten victim. One advanced foot of it was inserted beneath the dead body, as if in the act of spurning it.

Uncertainty falls on what now followed.

It were but natural to suppose that the magistrates would at first shrink from immediate personal contact with what they saw. At the least, for a time, they would stand in involuntary doubt; it may be, in more or less of horrified alarm. Certain it is, that an arquebuss was called for from below. And some add, that its report, followed by a fierce whiz, as of the sudden snapping of a main-spring, with a steely din, as if a stack of sword blades should be dashed upon a pavement, these blended sounds came ringing to the plain, attracting every eye far upward to the belfry, whence, through the lattice-work, thin wreaths of smoke were curling.

Some averred that it was the spaniel, gone mad by fear, which was shot. This, others denied. True it was, the spaniel never more was seen; and, probably, for some unknown reason, it shared the burial now to be related of the domino. For, whatever the preceding circumstances may have been, the first instinctive panic over, or else all ground of reasonable fear removed, the two magistrates, by themselves, quickly re-hooded the figure in the dropped cloak wherein it had been hoisted. The same night, it was secretly lowered to the ground, smuggled to the beach, pulled far out to sea, and sunk. Nor to any after urgency, even in free convivial hours, would the twain ever disclose the full secrets of the belfry.

From the mystery unavoidably investing it, the popular solution of the foundling's fate involved more or less of supernatural agency. But some few less unscientific minds pretended to find little difficulty in otherwise accounting for it. In the chain of circumstantial inferences drawn, there may, or may not, have been some absent or defective links. But, as the explanation in question is the only one which tradition has explicitly preserved, in dearth of better, it will here be given. But, in the first place, it is requisite to present the supposition entertained as to the entire motive and mode, with their origin, of the secret design of Bannadonna; the minds above-mentioned assuming to penetrate as well into his soul as into the event. The disclosure will indirectly involve reference to peculiar matters, none of the clearest, beyond the immediate subject.

At that period, no large bell was made to sound otherwise than as at present, by agitation of a tongue within, by means of ropes, or percussion from without, either from cumbrous machinery, or stalwart watchmen, armed with heavy hammers, stationed in the belfry, or in sentry-boxes on the open roof, according as the bell was sheltered or exposed.

It was from observing these exposed bells, with their watchmen, that the foundling, as was opined, derived the first suggestion of his scheme. Perched on a great mast or spire, the human figure, viewed from below, undergoes such a reduction in its apparent size, as to obliterate its intelligent features. It evinces no personality. Instead of bespeaking volition, its gestures rather resemble the automatic ones of the arms of a telegraph.

Musing, therefore, upon the purely Punchinello aspect of the human figure thus beheld, it had indirectly occurred to Bannadonna to devise some metallic agent, which should strike the hour with its mechanic hand, with even greater precision than the vital one. And, moreover, as the vital watchman on the roof, sallying from his retreat at the given periods, walked to the bell with uplifted mace, to smite it, Bannadonna had resolved that his invention should likewise possess the power of locomotion, and, along with that, the appearance, at least, of intelligence and will.

If the conjectures of those who claimed acquaintance with

the intent of Bannadonna be thus far correct, no unenterprising spirit could have been his. But they stopped not here; intimating that though, indeed, his design had, in the first place, been prompted by the sight of the watchman, and confined to the devising of a subtle substitute for him; yet, as is not seldom the case with projectors, by insensible gradations, proceeding from comparatively pigmy aims to Titanic ones, the original scheme had, in its anticipated eventualities, at last, attained to an unheard of degree of daring. He still bent his efforts upon the locomotive figure for the belfry, but only as a partial type of an ulterior creature, a sort of elephantine Helot, adapted to further, in a degree scarcely to be imagined, the universal conveniences and glories of humanity; supplying nothing less than a supplement to the Six Days' Work; stocking the earth with a new serf, more useful than the ox, swifter than the dolphin, stronger than the lion, more cunning than the ape, for industry an ant, more fiery than serpents, and yet, in patience, another ass. All excellences of all God-made creatures, which served man, were here to receive advancement, and then to be combined in one. Talus was to have been the all-accomplished Helot's name. Talus, iron slave to Bannadonna, and, through him, to man.

Here, it might well be thought that, were these last conjectures as to the foundling's secrets not erroneous, then must he have been hopelessly infected with the craziest chimeras of his age; far outgoing Albert Magnus and Cornelius Agrippa. But the contrary was averred. However marvelous his design, however apparently transcending not alone the bounds of human invention, but those of divine creation, yet the proposed means to be employed were alleged to have been confined within the sober forms of sober reason. It was affirmed that, to a degree of more than sceptic scorn, Bannadonna had been without sympathy for any of the vain-glorious irrationalities of his time. For example, he had not concluded, with the visionaries among the metaphysicians, that between the finer mechanic forces and the ruder animal vitality, some germ of correspondence might prove discoverable. As little did his scheme partake of the enthusiasm of some natural philosophers, who hoped, by physiological and chemical inductions, to arrive at a knowledge of the source of life, and so qualify themselves to manufacture and improve upon it. Much less had he aught in common with the tribe of alchemists, who sought, by a species of incantations, to evoke some surprising vitality from the laboratory. Neither had he imagined with certain sanguine theosophists, that, by faithful adoration of the Highest, unheard-of powers would be vouchsafed to man. A practical materialist, what Bannadonna had aimed at was to have been reached, not by logic, not by crucible, not by conjuration, not by altars; but by plain vice-bench and hammer. In short, to solve nature, to steal into her, to intrigue beyond her, to procure some one else to bind her to his hand;— these, one and all, had not been his objects; but, asking no favors from any element or any being, of himself, to rival her, outstrip her, and rule her. He stooped to conquer. With him, common sense was theurgy; machinery, miracle; Prometheus, the heroic name for machinist; man, the true God.

Nevertheless, in his initial step, so far as the experimental automation for the belfry was concerned, he allowed fancy some little play; or, perhaps, what seemed his fancifulness was but his utilitarian ambition collaterally extended. In figure, the creature for the belfry should not be likened after the human pattern, nor any animal one, nor after the ideals, however wild, of ancient fable, but equally in aspect as in organism be an original production; the more terrible to behold, the better.

Such, then, were the suppositions as to the present scheme, and the reserved intent. How, at the very threshold, so unlooked for a catastrophe overturned all, or, rather, what was the conjecture here, is now to be set forth.

It was thought that on the day preceding the fatality, his visitors having left him, Bannadonna had unpacked the belfry image, adjusted it, and placed it in the retreat provided,—a sort of sentry-box in one corner of the belfry; in short, throughout the night, and for some part of the ensuing morning, he had been engaged in arranging every thing connected with the domino: the issuing from the sentry-box each sixty minutes; sliding along a grooved way, like a railway; advancing to the clock-bell, with uplifted manacles; striking it at one of the twelve junctions of the four-and-twenty hands: then wheeling, circling the bell, and retiring to its post, there to bide for another sixty minutes, when the same process was to be repeated; the bell, by a cunning mechanism, meantime turning on its vertical axis, so as to present, to the descending mace, the clasped hands of the next two figures, when it would strike two, three, and so on, to the end. The musical metal in this time-bell being so managed in the fusion, by some art perishing with its originator, that each of the clasps of the four-and-twenty hands should give forth its own peculiar resonance when parted.

But on the magic metal, the magic and metallic stranger never struck but that one stroke, drove but that one nail, severed but that one clasp, by which Bannadonna clung to his ambitious life. For, after winding up the creature in the sentry-box, so that, for the present, skipping the intervening hours, it should not emerge till the hour of one, but should then infallibly emerge, and, after deftly oiling the grooves whereon it was to slide, it was surmised that the mechanician must then have hurried to the bell, to give his final touches to its sculpture. True artist, he here became absorbed; an absorption still further intensified, it may be, by his striving to abate that strange look of Una; which, though, before others, he had treated with such unconcern, might not, in secret, have been without its thorn.

And so, for the interval, he was oblivious of his creature; which, not oblivious of him, and true to its creation, and true to its heedful winding up, left its post precisely at the given moment; along its well-oiled route, slid noiselessly towards its mark; and aiming at the hand of Una, to ring one clangorous note, dully smote the intervening brain of Bannadonna, turned backwards to it; the manacled arms then instantly upspringing to their hovering poise. The falling body clogged the thing's return; so there it stood, still impending over Bannadonna, as if whispering some post-mortem terror. The chisel lay dropped from the hand, but beside the hand; the oil-flask spilled across the iron track.

In his unhappy end, not unmindful of the rare genius of the mechanician, the republic decreed him a stately funeral. It was resolved that the great bell—the one whose casting had been jeopardized through the timidity of the ill-starred workman—should be rung upon the entrance of the bier into the cathedral. The most robust man of the country round was assigned the office of bell-ringer.

But as the pall-bearers entered the cathedral porch, nought but a broken and disastrous sound, like that of some lone Alpine land-slide, fell from the tower upon their ears. And then, all was hushed.

Glancing backwards, they saw the groined belfry crashed sideways in. It afterwards appeared that the powerful peasant who had the bell-rope in charge, wishing to test at once the full glory of the bell, had swayed down upon the rope with one concentrate jerk. The mass of quaking metal, too ponderous for its frame, and strangely feeble somewhere at its top, loosed from its fastening, tore sideways down, and tumbling in one sheer fall, three hundred feet to the soft sward below, buried itself inverted and half out of sight.

Upon its disinterment, the main fracture was found to have started from a small spot in the ear; which, being scraped, revealed a defect, deceptively minute, in the casting; which defect must subsequently have been pasted over with some unknown compound.

The remolten metal soon reässumed its place in the tower's repaired superstructure. For one year the metallic choir of birds sang musically in its belfry-bough-work of sculptured blinds and traceries. But on the first anniversary of the tower's completion—at early dawn, before the concourse had surrounded it—an earthquake came; one loud crash was heard. The stone-pine, with all its bower of songsters, lay overthrown upon the plain.

So the blind slave obeyed its blinder lord; but, in obedience, slew him. So the creator was killed by the creature. So the bell was too heavy for the tower. So that bell's main weakness was where man's blood had flawed it. And so pride went before the fall.*

*It was not necessary to adhere to the peculiar notation of Italian time. Adherence to it would have impaired the familiar comprehension of the story. Kindred remarks might be offered touching an anachronism or two that occur.

THE CONFIDENCE-MAN

His Masquerade

Contents

Chapter 1

AT SUNRISE on a first of April, there appeared, suddenly as Manco Capac at the lake Titicaca, a man in cream-colors, at the water-side in the city of St. Louis.

His cheek was fair, his chin downy, his hair flaxen, his hat a white fur one, with a long fleecy nap. He had neither trunk, valise, carpet-bag, nor parcel. No porter followed him. He was unaccompanied by friends. From the shrugged shoulders, titters, whispers, wonderings of the crowd, it was plain that he was, in the extremest sense of the word, a stranger.

In the same moment with his advent, he stepped aboard the favorite steamer Fidèle, on the point of starting for New Orleans. Stared at, but unsaluted, with the air of one neither courting nor shunning regard, but evenly pursuing the path of duty, lead it through solitudes or cities, he held on his way along the lower deck until he chanced to come to a placard nigh the captain's office, offering a reward for the capture of a mysterious impostor, supposed to have recently arrived from the East; quite an original genius in his vocation, as would appear, though wherein his originality consisted was not clearly given; but what purported to be a careful description of his person followed.

As if it had been a theatre-bill, crowds were gathered about the announcement, and among them certain chevaliers, whose eyes, it was plain, were on the capitals, or, at least, earnestly seeking sight of them from behind intervening coats; but as for their fingers, they were enveloped in some myth; though, during a chance interval, one of these chevaliers somewhat showed his hand in purchasing from another chevalier, ex-officio a peddler of money-belts, one of his popular safe-guards, while another peddler, who was still another versatile chevalier, hawked, in the thick of the throng, the lives of Meason, the bandit of Ohio, Murrel, the pirate of the Missis-sippi, and the brothers Harpe, the Thugs of the Green River country, in Kentucky—creatures, with others of the sort, one and all exterminated at the time, and for the most part, like the hunted generations of wolves in the same regions, leaving comparatively few successors; which would seem cause for unalloyed gratulation, and is such to all except those who think that in new countries, where the wolves are killed off, the foxes increase.

Pausing at this spot, the stranger so far succeeded in threading his way, as at last to plant himself just beside the placard, when, producing a small slate and tracing some words upon it, he held it up before him on a level with the placard, so that they who read the one might read the other. The words were these:—

"Charity thinketh no evil."

As, in gaining his place, some little perseverance, not to say persistence, of a mildly inoffensive sort, had been unavoidable, it was not with the best relish that the crowd regarded his apparent intrusion; and upon a more attentive survey, perceiving no badge of authority about him, but rather something quite the contrary—he being of an aspect so singularly innocent; an aspect, too, which they took to be somehow inappropriate to the time and place, and inclining to the notion that his writing was of much the same sort: in short, taking him for some strange kind of simpleton, harmless enough, would he keep to himself, but not wholly unobnoxious as an intruder—they made no scruple to jostle him aside; while one, less kind than the rest, or more of a wag, by an unobserved stroke, dexterously flattened down his fleecy hat upon his head. Without readjusting it, the stranger quietly turned, and writing anew upon the slate, again held it up:—

"Charity suffereth long, and is kind."

Illy pleased with his pertinacity, as they thought it, the crowd a second time thrust him aside, and not without epithets and some buffets, all of which were unresented. But, as if at last despairing of so difficult an adventure, wherein one, apparently a non-resistant, sought to impose his presence upon fighting characters, the stranger now moved slowly away, yet not before altering his writing to this:—

"Charity endureth all things."

Shield-like bearing his slate before him, amid stares and jeers he moved slowly up and down, at his turning points again changing his inscription to—

"Charity believeth all things."

and then—

"Charity never faileth."

The word charity, as originally traced, remained throughout uneffaced, not unlike the left-hand numeral of a printed date, otherwise left for convenience in blank.

To some observers, the singularity, if not lunacy, of the stranger was heightened by his muteness, and, perhaps also, by the contrast to his proceedings afforded in the actions— quite in the wonted and sensible order of things—of the barber of the boat, whose quarters, under a smoking-saloon, and over against a bar-room, was next door but two to the captain's office. As if the long, wide, covered deck, hereabouts built up on both sides with shop-like windowed spaces, were some Constantinople arcade or bazaar, where more than one trade is plied, this river barber, aproned and slippered, but rather crusty-looking for the moment, it may be from being newly out of bed, was throwing open his premises for the day, and suitably arranging the exterior. With business-like dispatch, having rattled down his shutters, and at a palm-tree angle set out in the iron fixture his little ornamental pole, and this without overmuch tenderness for the elbows and toes of the crowd, he concluded his operations by bidding people stand still more aside, when, jumping on a stool, he hung over his door, on the customary nail, a gaudy sort of illuminated pasteboard sign, skillfully executed by himself, gilt with the likeness of a razor elbowed in readiness to shave, and also,

for the public benefit, with two words not unfrequently seen
ashore gracing other shops besides barbers': —

"No trust."

An inscription which, though in a sense not less intrusive
than the contrasted ones of the stranger, did not, as it
seemed, provoke any corresponding derision or surprise,
much less indignation; and still less, to all appearances, did it
gain for the inscriber the repute of being a simpleton.

Meanwhile, he with the slate continued moving slowly up
and down, not without causing some stares to change into
jeers, and some jeers into pushes, and some pushes into
punches; when suddenly, in one of his turns, he was hailed
from behind by two porters carrying a large trunk; but as the
summons, though loud, was without effect, they accidentally
or otherwise swung their burden against him, nearly over-
throwing him; when, by a quick start, a peculiar inarticulate
moan, and a pathetic telegraphing of his fingers, he involuntarily betrayed that he was not alone dumb, but also deaf.

Presently, as if not wholly unaffected by his reception thus
far, he went forward, seating himself in a retired spot on the
forecastle, nigh the foot of a ladder there leading to a deck
above, up and down which ladder some of the boatmen, in
discharge of their duties, were occasionally going.

From his betaking himself to this humble quarter, it was
evident that, as a deck-passenger, the stranger, simple though
he seemed, was not entirely ignorant of his place, though his
taking a deck-passage might have been partly for convenience;
as, from his having no luggage, it was probable that his destination was one of the small wayside landings within a few
hours' sail. But, though he might not have a long way to go,
yet he seemed already to have come from a very long distance.

Though neither soiled nor slovenly, his cream-colored suit
had a tossed look, almost linty, as if, traveling night and day
from some far country beyond the prairies, he had long been
without the solace of a bed. His aspect was at once gentle and
jaded, and, from the moment of seating himself, increasing in
tired abstraction and dreaminess. Gradually overtaken by
slumber, his flaxen head drooped, his whole lamb-like figure

relaxed, and, half reclining against the ladder's foot, lay motionless, as some sugar-snow in March, which, softly stealing down over night, with its white placidity startles the brown farmer peering out from his threshold at daybreak.

Chapter 2

"ODD FISH!"

"Poor fellow!"

"Who can he be?"

"Casper Hauser."

"Bless my soul!"

"Uncommon countenance."

"Green prophet from Utah."

"Humbug!"

"Singular innocence."

"Means something."

"Spirit-rapper."

"Moon-calf."

"Piteous."

"Trying to enlist interest."

"Beware of him."

"Fast asleep here, and, doubtless, pick-pockets on board."

"Kind of daylight Endymion."

"Escaped convict, worn out with dodging."

"Jacob dreaming at Luz."

Such the epitaphic comments, conflictingly spoken or thought, of a miscellaneous company, who, assembled on the overlooking, cross-wise balcony at the forward end of the upper deck near by, had not witnessed preceding occurrences.

Meantime, like some enchanted man in his grave, happily oblivious of all gossip, whether chiseled or chatted, the deaf and dumb stranger still tranquilly slept, while now the boat started on her voyage.

The great ship-canal of Ving-King-Ching, in the Flowery Kingdom, seems the Mississippi in parts, where, amply flowing between low, vine-tangled banks, flat as tow-paths, it bears the huge toppling steamers, bedizened and lacquered within like imperial junks.

Pierced along its great white bulk with two tiers of small embrasure-like windows, well above the water-line, the Fidèle, though, might at distance have been taken by strangers for some whitewashed fort on a floating isle.

Merchants on 'change seem the passengers that buzz on her decks, while, from quarters unseen, comes a murmur as of bees in the comb. Fine promenades, domed saloons, long galleries, sunny balconies, confidential passages, bridal chambers, state-rooms plenty as pigeon-holes, and out-of-the-way retreats like secret drawers in an escritoire, present like facilities for publicity or privacy. Auctioneer or coiner, with equal ease, might somewhere here drive his trade.

Though her voyage of twelve hundred miles extends from apple to orange, from clime to clime, yet, like any small ferryboat, to right and left, at every landing, the huge Fidèle still receives additional passengers in exchange for those that disembark; so that, though always full of strangers, she continually, in some degree, adds to, or replaces them with strangers still more strange; like Rio Janeiro fountain, fed from the Corcovado mountains, which is ever overflowing with strange waters, but never with the same strange particles in every part.

Though hitherto, as has been seen, the man in cream-colors had by no means passed unobserved, yet by stealing into retirement, and there going asleep and continuing so, he seemed to have courted oblivion, a boon not often withheld from so humble an applicant as he. Those staring crowds on the shore were now left far behind, seen dimly clustering like swallows on eaves; while the passengers' attention was soon drawn away to the rapidly shooting high bluffs and shottowers on the Missouri shore, or the bluff-looking Missourians and towering Kentuckians among the throngs on the decks.

By-and-by—two or three random stoppages having been made, and the last transient memory of the slumberer vanished, and he himself, not unlikely, waked up and landed ere now—the crowd, as is usual, began in all parts to break up from a concourse into various clusters or squads, which in some cases disintegrated again into quartettes, trios, and couples, or even solitaires; involuntarily submitting to that natural law which ordains dissolution equally to the mass, as in time to the member.

As among Chaucer's Canterbury pilgrims, or those oriental ones crossing the Red Sea towards Mecca in the festival month, there was no lack of variety. Natives of all sorts, and foreigners; men of business and men of pleasure; parlor men and backwoodsmen; farm-hunters and fame-hunters; heiress-hunters, gold-hunters, buffalo-hunters, bee-hunters, happiness-hunters, truth-hunters, and still keener hunters after all these hunters. Fine ladies in slippers, and moccasined squaws; Northern speculators and Eastern philosophers; English, Irish, German, Scotch, Danes; Santa Fé traders in striped blankets, and Broadway bucks in cravats of cloth of gold; fine-looking Kentucky boatmen, and Japanese-looking Mississippi cotton-planters; Quakers in full drab, and United States soldiers in full regimentals; slaves, black, mulatto, quadroon; modish young Spanish Creoles, and old-fashioned French Jews; Mormons and Papists; Dives and Lazarus; jesters and mourners, teetotalers and convivialists, deacons and blacklegs; hard-shell Baptists and clay-eaters; grinning negroes, and Sioux chiefs solemn as high-priests. In short, a piebald parliament, an Anacharsis Cloots congress of all kinds of that multiform pilgrim species, man.

As pine, beech, birch, ash, hackmatack, hemlock, spruce, bass-wood, maple, interweave their foliage in the natural wood, so these varieties of mortals blended their varieties of visage and garb. A Tartar-like picturesqueness; a sort of pagan abandonment and assurance. Here reigned the dashing and all-fusing spirit of the West, whose type is the Mississippi itself, which, uniting the streams of the most distant and opposite zones, pours them along, helter-skelter, in one cosmopolitan and confident tide.

Chapter 3

IN WHICH A VARIETY OF CHARACTERS APPEAR

IN THE FORWARD PART of the boat, not the least attractive object, for a time, was a grotesque negro cripple, in tow-cloth attire and an old coal-sifter of a tamborine in his hand, who, owing to something wrong about his legs, was, in effect, cut down to the stature of a Newfoundland dog; his knotted black fleece and good-natured, honest black face rubbing against the upper part of people's thighs as he made shift to shuffle about, making music, such as it was, and raising a smile even from the gravest. It was curious to see him, out of his very deformity, indigence, and houselessness, so cheerily endured, raising mirth in some of that crowd, whose own purses, hearths, hearts, all their possessions, sound limbs included, could not make gay.

"What is your name, old boy?" said a purple-faced drover, putting his large purple hand on the cripple's bushy wool, as if it were the curled forehead of a black steer.

"Der Black Guinea dey calls me, sar."

"And who is your master, Guinea?"

"Oh sar, I am der dog widout massa."

"A free dog, eh? Well, on your account, I'm sorry for that, Guinea. Dogs without masters fare hard."

"So dey do, sar; so dey do. But you see, sar, dese here legs? What ge'mman want to own dese here legs?"

"But where do you live?"

"All 'long shore, sar; dough now I'se going to see brodder at der landing; but chiefly I libs in der city."

"St. Louis, ah? Where do you sleep there of nights?"

"On der floor of der good baker's oven, sar."

"In an oven? whose, pray? What baker, I should like to know, bakes such black bread in his oven, alongside of his nice white rolls, too. Who is that too charitable baker, pray?"

"Dar he be," with a broad grin lifting his tambourine high over his head.

"The sun is the baker, eh?"

"Yes sar, in der city dat good baker warms der stones for

dis ole darkie when he sleeps out on der pabements o' nights."

"But that must be in the summer only, old boy. How about winter, when the cold Cossacks come clattering and jingling? How about winter, old boy?"

"Den dis poor old darkie shakes werry bad. I tell you, sar. Oh sar, oh! don't speak ob der winter," he added, with a reminiscent shiver, shuffling off into the thickest of the crowd, like a half-frozen black sheep nudging itself a cozy berth in the heart of the white flock.

Thus far not very many pennies had been given him, and, used at last to his strange looks, the less polite passengers of those in that part of the boat began to get their fill of him as a curious object; when suddenly the negro more than revived their first interest by an expedient which, whether by chance or design, was a singular temptation at once to *diversion* and charity, though, even more than his crippled limbs, it put him on a canine footing. In short, as in appearance he seemed a dog, so now, in a merry way, like a dog he began to be treated. Still shuffling among the crowd, now and then he would pause, throwing back his head and opening his mouth like an elephant for tossed apples at a menagerie; when, making a space before him, people would have a bout at a strange sort of pitch-penny game, the cripple's mouth being at once target and purse, and he hailing each expertly-caught copper with a cracked bravura from his tambourine. To be the subject of alms-giving is trying, and to feel in duty bound to appear cheerfully grateful under the trial, must be still more so; but whatever his secret emotions, he swallowed them, while still retaining each copper this side the œsophagus. And nearly always he grinned, and only once or twice did he wince, which was when certain coins, tossed by more playful almoners, came inconveniently nigh to his teeth, an accident whose unwelcomeness was not unedged by the circumstance that the pennies thus thrown proved buttons.

While this game of charity was yet at its height, a limping, gimlet-eyed, sour-faced person—it may be some discharged custom-house officer, who, suddenly stripped of convenient means of support, had concluded to be avenged on government and humanity by making himself miserable for life,

either by hating or suspecting everything and everybody—
this shallow unfortunate, after sundry sorry observations of
the negro, began to croak out something about his deformity
being a sham, got up for financial purposes, which immediately threw a damp upon the frolic benignities of the pitch-
penny players.

But that these suspicions came from one who himself on a
wooden leg went halt, this did not appear to strike anybody
present. That cripples, above all men, should be companionable, or, at least, refrain from picking a fellow-limper to
pieces, in short, should have a little sympathy in common
misfortune, seemed not to occur to the company.

Meantime, the negro's countenance, before marked with
even more than patient good-nature, drooped into a heavy-
hearted expression, full of the most painful distress. So far
abased beneath its proper physical level, that Newfoundland-
dog face turned in passively hopeless appeal, as if instinct told
it that the right or the wrong might not have overmuch to
do with whatever wayward mood superior intelligences might
yield to.

But instinct, though knowing, is yet a teacher set below
reason, which itself says, in the grave words of Lysander in
the comedy, after Puck has made a sage of him with his
spell:—

"The will of man is by his reason swayed."

So that, suddenly change as people may, in their dispositions,
it is not always waywardness, but improved judgment, which,
as in Lysander's case, or the present, operates with them.

Yes, they began to scrutinize the negro curiously enough;
when, emboldened by this evidence of the efficacy of his
words, the wooden-legged man hobbled up to the negro,
and, with the air of a beadle, would, to prove his alleged imposture on the spot, have stripped him and then driven him
away, but was prevented by the crowd's clamor, now taking
part with the poor fellow, against one who had just before
turned nearly all minds the other way. So he with the wooden
leg was forced to retire; when the rest, finding themselves left
sole judges in the case, could not resist the opportunity of

acting the part: not because it is a human weakness to take pleasure in sitting in judgment upon one in a box, as surely this unfortunate negro now was, but that it strangely sharpens human perceptions, when, instead of standing by and having their fellow-feelings touched by the sight of an alleged culprit severely handled by some one justiciary, a crowd suddenly come to be all justiciaries in the same case themselves; as in Arkansas once, a man proved guilty, by law, of murder, but whose condemnation was deemed unjust by the people, so that they rescued him to try him themselves; whereupon, they, as it turned out, found him even guiltier than the court had done, and forthwith proceeded to execution; so that the gallows presented the truly warning spectacle of a man hanged by his friends.

But not to such extremities, or anything like them, did the present crowd come; they, for the time, being content with putting the negro fairly and discreetly to the question; among other things, asking him, had he any documentary proof, any plain paper about him, attesting that his case was not a spurious one.

"No, no, dis poor ole darkie haint none o' dem waloable papers," he wailed.

"But is there not some one who can speak a good word for you?" here said a person newly arrived from another part of the boat, a young Episcopal clergyman, in a long, straight-bodied black coat; small in stature, but manly; with a clear face and blue eye; innocence, tenderness, and good sense triumvirate in his air.

"Oh yes, oh yes, ge'mmen," he eagerly answered, as if his memory, before suddenly frozen up by cold charity, as suddenly thawed back into fluidity at the first kindly word. "Oh yes, oh yes, dar is aboard here a werry nice, good ge'mman wid a weed, and a ge'mman in a gray coat and white tie, what knows all about me; and a ge'mman wid a big book, too; and a yarb-doctor; and a ge'mman in a yaller west; and a ge'mman wid a brass plate; and a ge'mman in a wiolet robe; and a ge'mman as is a sodjer; and ever so many good, kind, honest ge'mmen more aboard what knows me and will speak for me, God bress 'em; yes, and what knows me as well as dis poor old darkie knows hisself, God bress him! Oh, find 'em, find 'em," he earnestly added, "and let 'em come quick, and show you all, ge'mmen, dat dis poor ole darkie is werry well wordy of all you kind ge'mmen's kind confidence."

"But how are we to find all these people in this great crowd?" was the question of a bystander, umbrella in hand; a middle-aged person, a country merchant apparently, whose natural good-feeling had been made at least cautious by the unnatural ill-feeling of the discharged custom-house officer.

"Where are we to find them?" half-rebukefully echoed the young Episcopal clergyman. "I will go find one to begin with," he quickly added, and, with kind haste suiting the action to the word, away he went.

"Wild goose chase!" croaked he with the wooden leg, now again drawing nigh. "Don't believe there's a soul of them aboard. Did ever beggar have such heaps of fine friends? He can walk fast enough when he tries, a good deal faster than I; but he can lie yet faster. He's some white operator, betwisted and painted up for a decoy. He and his friends are all humbugs."

"Have you no charity, friend?" here in self-subdued tones, singularly contrasted with his unsubdued person, said a Methodist minister, advancing; a tall, muscular, martial-looking man, a Tennessean by birth, who in the Mexican war had been volunteer chaplain to a volunteer rifle-regiment.

"Charity is one thing, and truth is another," rejoined he with the wooden leg: "he's a rascal, I say."

"But why not, friend, put as charitable a construction as one can upon the poor fellow?" said the soldier-like Methodist, with increased difficulty maintaining a pacific demeanor towards one whose own asperity seemed so little to entitle him to it: "he looks honest, don't he?"

"Looks are one thing, and facts are another," snapped out the other perversely; "and as to your constructions, what construction can you put upon a rascal, but that a rascal he is?"

"Be not such a Canada thistle," urged the Methodist, with something less of patience than before. "Charity, man, charity."

"To where it belongs with your charity! to heaven with it!" again snapped out the other, diabolically; "here on earth, true charity dotes, and false charity plots. Who betrays a fool with a kiss, the charitable fool has the charity to believe is in love with him, and the charitable knave on the stand gives charitable testimony for his comrade in the box."

"Surely, friend," returned the noble Methodist, with much ado restraining his still waxing indignation—"surely, to say the least, you forget yourself. Apply it home," he continued, with exterior calmness tremulous with inkept emotion. "Suppose, now, I should exercise no charity in judging your own character by the words which have fallen from you; what sort of vile, pitiless man do you think I would take you for?"

"No doubt"—with a grin—"some such pitiless man as has lost his piety in much the same way that the jockey loses his honesty."

"And how is that, friend?" still conscientiously holding back the old Adam in him, as if it were a mastiff he had by the neck.

"Never you mind how it is"—with a sneer; "but all horses aint virtuous, no more than all men kind; and come close to, and much dealt with, some things are catching. When you find me a virtuous jockey, I will find you a benevolent wise man."

"Some insinuation there."

"More fool you that are puzzled by it."

"Reprobate!" cried the other, his indignation now at last almost boiling over; "godless reprobate! if charity did not restrain me, I could call you by names you deserve."

"Could you, indeed?" with an insolent sneer.

"Yea, and teach you charity on the spot," cried the goaded Methodist, suddenly catching this exasperating opponent by his shabby coat-collar, and shaking him till his timber-toe clattered on the deck like a nine-pin. "You took me for a noncombatant did you?—thought, seedy coward that you are, that you could abuse a Christian with impunity. You find your mistake"—with another hearty shake.

"Well said and better done, church militant!" cried a voice.

"The white cravat against the world!" cried another.

"Bravo, bravo!" chorused many voices, with like enthusiasm taking sides with the resolute champion.

"You fools!" cried he with the wooden leg, writhing himself loose and inflamedly turning upon the throng; "you flock of fools, under this captain of fools, in this ship of fools!"

With which exclamations, followed by idle threats against his admonisher, this condign victim to justice hobbled away, as disdaining to hold further argument with such a rabble. But his scorn was more than repaid by the hisses that chased him, in which the brave Methodist, satisfied with the rebuke already administered, was, to omit still better reasons, too magnanimous to join. All he said was, pointing towards the departing recusant, "There he shambles off on his one lone leg, emblematic of his one-sided view of humanity."

"But trust your painted decoy," retorted the other from a distance, pointing back to the black cripple, "and I have my revenge."

"But we aint agoing to trust him!" shouted back a voice.

"So much the better," he jeered back. "Look you," he added, coming to a dead halt where he was; "look you, I have been called a Canada thistle. Very good. And a seedy one: still better. And the seedy Canada thistle has been pretty well shaken among ye: best of all. Dare say some seed has been shaken out; and won't it spring though? And when it does spring, do you cut down the young thistles, and won't they spring the more? It's encouraging and coaxing 'em. Now, when with my thistles your farms shall be well stocked, why then—you may abandon 'em!"

"What does all that mean, now?" asked the country merchant, staring.

"Nothing; the foiled wolf's parting howl," said the Methodist. "Spleen, much spleen, which is the rickety child of his evil heart of unbelief: it has made him mad. I suspect him for one naturally reprobate. Oh, friends," raising his arms as in the pulpit, "oh beloved, how are we admonished by the melancholy spectacle of this raver. Let us profit by the lesson; and is it not this: that if, next to mistrusting Providence, there be aught that man should pray against, it is against mistrusting his fellow-man. I have been in mad-houses full of tragic mopers, and seen there the end of suspicion: the cynic, in the moody madness muttering in the corner; for years a barren fixture there; head lopped over, gnawing his own lip, vulture of himself; while, by fits and starts, from the corner opposite came the grimace of the idiot at him."

"What an example," whispered one.

"Might deter Timon," was the response.

"Oh, oh, good ge'mmen, have you no confidence in dis poor ole darkie?" now wailed the returning negro, who, during the late scene, had stumped apart in alarm.

"Confidence in you?" echoed he who had whispered, with abruptly changed air turning short round; "that remains to be seen."

"I tell you what it is, Ebony," in similarly changed tones said he who had responded to the whisperer, "yonder churl," pointing toward the wooden leg in the distance, "is, no doubt, a churlish fellow enough, and I would not wish to be like him; but that is no reason why you may not be some sort of black Jeremy Diddler."

"No confidence in dis poor ole darkie, den?"

"Before giving you our confidence," said a third, " we will wait the report of the kind gentleman who went in search of one of your friends who was to speak for you."

"Very likely, in that case," said a fourth, " we shall wait here till Christmas. Shouldn't wonder, did we not see that kind gentleman again. After seeking awhile in vain, he will conclude he has been made a fool of, and so not return to us for pure shame. Fact is, I begin to feel a little qualmish about the darkie myself. Something queer about this darkie, depend upon it."

Once more the negro wailed, and turning in despair from the last speaker, imploringly caught the Methodist by the skirt of his coat. But a change had come over that before impassioned intercessor. With an irresolute and troubled air, he mutely eyed the suppliant; against whom, somehow, by what seemed instinctive influences, the distrusts first set on foot were now generally reviving, and, if anything, with added severity.

"No confidence in dis poor ole darkie," yet again wailed the negro, letting go the coat-skirts and turning appealingly all round him.

"Yes, my poor fellow, *I* have confidence in you," now exclaimed the country merchant before named, whom the

negro's appeal, coming so piteously on the heel of pitiless-
ness, seemed at last humanely to have decided in his favor.
"And here, here is some proof of my trust," with which, tucking his umbrella under his arm, and diving down his hand
into his pocket, he fished forth a purse, and, accidentally,
along with it, his business card, which, unobserved, dropped
to the deck. "Here, here, my poor fellow," he continued, extending a half dollar.

Not more grateful for the coin than the kindness, the cripple's face glowed like a polished copper saucepan, and shuffling a pace nigher, with one upstretched hand he received
the alms, while, as unconsciously, his one advanced leather
stump covered the card.

Done in despite of the general sentiment, the good deed of
the merchant was not, perhaps, without its unwelcome return
from the crowd, since that good deed seemed somehow to
convey to them a sort of reproach. Still again, and more pertinaciously than ever, the cry arose against the negro, and still
again he wailed forth his lament and appeal; among other
things, repeating that the friends, of whom already he had
partially run off the list, would freely speak for him, would
anybody go find them.

"Why don't you go find 'em yourself?" demanded a gruff
boatman.

"How can I go find 'em myself? Dis poor ole game-legged
darkie's friends must come to him. Oh, whar, whar is dat
good friend of dis darkie's, dat good man wid de weed?"

At this point, a steward ringing a bell came along, summoning all persons who had not got their tickets to step to
the captain's office; an announcement which speedily thinned
the throng about the black cripple, who himself soon forlornly stumped out of sight, probably on much the same errand as the rest.

Chapter 4

H ow do you do, Mr. Roberts?"

    "Eh?"

"Don't you know me?"

"No, certainly."

The crowd about the captain's office, having in good time melted away, the above encounter took place in one of the side balconies astern, between a man in mourning clean and respectable, but none of the glossiest, a long weed on his hat, and the country-merchant before-mentioned, whom, with the familiarity of an old acquaintance, the former had accosted.

"Is it possible, my dear sir," resumed he with the weed, "that you do not recall my countenance? why yours I recall distinctly as if but half an hour, instead of half an age, had passed since I saw you. Don't you recall me, now? Look harder."

"In my conscience—truly—I protest," honestly bewildered, "bless my soul, sir, I don't know you—really, really. But stay, stay," he hurriedly added, not without gratification, glancing up at the crape on the stranger's hat, "stay—yes—seems to me, though I have not the pleasure of personally knowing you, yet I am pretty sure I have at least *heard* of you, and recently too, quite recently. A poor negro aboard here referred to you, among others, for a character, I think."

"Oh, the cripple. Poor fellow, I know him well. They found me. I have said all I could for him. I think I abated their distrust. Would I could have been of more substantial service. And apropos, sir," he added, "now that it strikes me, allow me to ask, whether the circumstance of one man, however humble, referring for a character to another man, however afflicted, does not argue more or less of moral worth in the latter?"

The good merchant looked puzzled.

"Still you don't recall my countenance?"

"Still does truth compel me to say that I cannot, despite my best efforts," was the reluctantly-candid reply.

"Can I be so changed? Look at me. Or is it I who am mistaken?—Are you not, sir, Henry Roberts, forwarding merchant, of Wheeling, Virginia? Pray, now, if you use the advertisement of business cards, and happen to have one with you, just look at it, and see whether you are not the man I take you for."

"Why," a bit chafed, perhaps, "I hope I know myself."

"And yet self-knowledge is thought by some not so easy. Who knows, my dear sir, but for a time you may have taken yourself for somebody else? Stranger things have happened."

The good merchant stared.

"To come to particulars, my dear sir, I met you, now some six years back, at Brade Brothers & Co.'s office, I think. I was traveling for a Philadelphia house. The senior Brade introduced us, you remember; some business-chat followed, then you forced me home with you to a family tea, and a family time we had. Have you forgotten about the urn, and what I said about Werter's Charlotte, and the bread and butter, and that capital story you told of the large loaf. A hundred times since, I have laughed over it. At least you must recall my name—Ringman, John Ringman."

"Large loaf? Invited you to tea? Ringman? Ringman? Ring? Ring?"

"Ah sir," sadly smiling, "don't ring the changes that way. I see you have a faithless memory, Mr. Roberts. But trust in the faithfulness of mine."

"Well, to tell the truth, in some things my memory aint of the very best," was the honest rejoinder. "But still," he perplexedly added, "still I—"

"Oh sir, suffice it that it is as I say. Doubt not that we are all well acquainted."

"But—but I don't like this going dead against my own memory; I—"

"But didn't you admit, my dear sir, that in some things this memory of yours is a little faithless? Now, those who have faithless memories, should they not have some little confidence in the less faithless memories of others?"

"But, of this friendly chat and tea, I have not the slightest—"

"I see, I see; quite erased from the tablet. Pray, sir," with a sudden illumination, "about six years back, did it happen to you to receive any injury on the head? Surprising effects have arisen from such a cause. Not alone unconsciousness as to events for a greater or less time immediately subsequent to the injury, but likewise—strange to add—oblivion, entire and incurable, as to events embracing a longer or shorter period immediately preceding it; that is, when the mind at the time was perfectly sensible of them, and fully competent also to register them in the memory, and did in fact so do; but all in vain, for all was afterwards bruised out by the injury."

After the first start, the merchant listened with what appeared more than ordinary interest. The other proceeded:

"In my boyhood I was kicked by a horse, and lay insensible for a long time. Upon recovering, what a blank! No faintest trace in regard to how I had come near the horse, or what horse it was, or where it was, or that it was a horse at all that had brought me to that pass. For the knowledge of those particulars I am indebted solely to my friends, in whose statements, I need not say, I place implicit reliance, since particulars of some sort there must have been, and why should they deceive me? You see, sir, the mind is ductile, very much so: but images, ductilely received into it, need a certain time to harden and bake in their impressions, otherwise such a casualty as I speak of will in an instant obliterate them, as though they had never been. We are but clay, sir, potter's clay, as the good book says, clay, feeble, and too-yielding clay. But I will not philosophize. Tell me, was it your misfortune to receive any concussion upon the brain about the period I speak of? If so, I will with pleasure supply the void in your memory by more minutely rehearsing the circumstances of our acquaintance."

The growing interest betrayed by the merchant had not relaxed as the other proceeded. After some hesitation, indeed, something more than hesitation, he confessed that, though he had never received any injury of the sort named, yet, about the time in question, he had in fact been taken with a brain fever, losing his mind completely for a considerable interval. He was continuing, when the stranger with much animation exclaimed:

"There now, you see, I was not wholly mistaken. That brain fever accounts for it all."

"Nay; but—"

"Pardon me, Mr. Roberts," respectfully interrupting him, "but time is short, and I have something private and particular to say to you. Allow me."

Mr. Roberts, good man, could but acquiesce, and the two having silently walked to a less public spot, the manner of the man with the weed suddenly assumed a seriousness almost painful. What might be called a writhing expression stole over him. He seemed struggling with some disastrous necessity inkept. He made one or two attempts to speak, but words seemed to choke him. His companion stood in humane surprise, wondering what was to come. At length, with an effort mastering his feelings, in a tolerably composed tone he spoke:

"If I remember, you are a mason, Mr. Roberts?"

"Yes, yes."

Averting himself a moment, as to recover from a return of agitation, the stranger grasped the other's hand; "and would you not loan a brother a shilling if he needed it?"

The merchant started, apparently, almost as if to retreat.

"Ah, Mr. Roberts, I trust you are not one of those business men, who make a business of never having to do with unfortunates. For God's sake don't leave me, I have something on my heart—on my heart. Under deplorable circumstances thrown among strangers, utter strangers. I want a friend in whom I may confide. Yours, Mr. Roberts, is almost the first known face I've seen for many weeks."

It was so sudden an outburst; the interview offered such a contrast to the scene around, that the merchant, though not used to be very indiscreet, yet, being not entirely inhumane, remained not entirely unmoved.

The other, still tremulous, resumed:

"I need not say, sir, how it cuts me to the soul, to follow up a social salutation with such words as have just been mine. I know that I jeopardize your good opinion. But I can't help it: necessity knows no law, and heeds no risk. Sir, we are masons, one more step aside; I will tell you my story."

In a low, half-suppressed tone, he began it. Judging from his auditor's expression, it seemed to be a tale of singular interest, involving calamities against which no integrity, no forethought, no energy, no genius, no piety, could guard.

At every disclosure, the hearer's commiseration increased. No sentimental pity. As the story went on, he drew from his wallet a bank note, but after a while, at some still more unhappy revelation, changed it for another, probably of a somewhat larger amount; which, when the story was concluded, with an air studiously disclamatory of alms-giving, he put into the stranger's hands; who, on his side, with an air studiously disclamatory of alms-taking, put it into his pocket.

Assistance being received, the stranger's manner assumed a kind and degree of decorum which, under the circumstances, seemed almost coldness. After some words, not over ardent, and yet not exactly inappropriate, he took leave, making a bow which had one knows not what of a certain chastened independence about it; as if misery, however burdensome, could not break down self-respect, nor gratitude, however deep, humiliate a gentleman.

He was hardly yet out of sight, when he paused as if thinking; then with hastened steps returning to the merchant, "I am just reminded that the president, who is also transfer-agent, of the Black Rapids Coal Company, happens to be on board here, and, having been subpœnaed as witness in a stock case on the docket in Kentucky, has his transfer-book with him. A month since, in a panic contrived by artful alarmists, some credulous stock-holders sold out; but, to frustrate the aim of the alarmists, the Company, previously advised of their scheme, so managed it as to get into its own hands those sacrificed shares, resolved that, since a spurious panic must be, the panic-makers should be no gainers by it. The Company, I hear, is now ready, but not anxious, to redispose of those shares; and having obtained them at their depressed value, will now sell them at par, though, prior to the panic, they were held at a handsome figure above. That the readiness of the Company to do this is not generally known, is shown by the fact that the stock still stands on the transfer-book in the Company's name, offering to one in funds a rare chance for investment. For, the panic subsiding more and more every day, it will daily be seen how it originated; confidence will be more than restored; there will be a reaction; from the stock's descent its rise will be higher than from no fall, the holders trusting themselves to fear no second fate."

Having listened at first with curiosity, at last with interest, the merchant replied to the effect, that some time since, through friends concerned with it, he had heard of the company, and heard well of it, but was ignorant that there had latterly been fluctuations. He added that he was no speculator; that hitherto he had avoided having to do with stocks of any sort, but in the present case he really felt something like being tempted. "Pray," in conclusion, "do you think that upon a pinch anything could be transacted on board here with the transfer-agent? Are you acquainted with him?"

"Not personally. I but happened to hear that he was a passenger. For the rest, though it might be somewhat informal, the gentleman might not object to doing a little business on board. Along the Mississippi, you know, business is not so ceremonious as at the East."

"True," returned the merchant, and looked down a moment in thought, then, raising his head quickly, said, in a tone not so benign as his wonted one. "This would seem a rare chance, indeed; why, upon first hearing it, did you not snatch at it? I mean for yourself!"

"I?—would it had been possible!"

Not without some emotion was this said, and not without some embarrassment was the reply. "Ah, yes, I had forgotten."

Upon this, the stranger regarded him with mild gravity, not a little disconcerting; the more so, as there was in it what seemed the aspect not alone of the superior, but, as it were, the rebuker; which sort of bearing, in a beneficiary towards his benefactor, looked strangely enough; none the less, that, somehow, it sat not altogether unbecomingly upon the beneficiary, being free from anything like the appearance of assumption, and mixed with a kind of painful conscientiousness, as though nothing but a proper sense of what he owed to himself swayed him. At length he spoke:

"To reproach a penniless man with remissness in not availing himself of an opportunity for pecuniary investment—but, no, no; it was forgetfulness; and this, charity will impute to some lingering effect of that unfortunate brain-fever, which, as to occurrences dating yet further back, disturbed Mr. Roberts's memory still more seriously."

"As to that," said the merchant, rallying, "I am not—"

"Pardon me, but you must admit, that just now, an unpleasant distrust, however vague, was yours. Ah, shallow as it is, yet, how subtle a thing is suspicion, which at times can invade the humanest of hearts and wisest of heads. But, enough. My object, sir, in calling your attention to this stock, is by way of acknowledgment of your goodness. I but seek to be grateful; if my information leads to nothing, you must remember the motive."

He bowed, and finally retired, leaving Mr. Roberts not wholly without self-reproach, for having momentarily indulged injurious thoughts against one who, it was evident, was possessed of a self-respect which forbade his indulging them himself.

Chapter 5

The man with the weed makes it an even
question whether he be a great sage or a
great simpleton

WELL, THERE IS SORROW in the world, but goodness too; and goodness that is not greenness, either,
no more than sorrow is. Dear good man. Poor beating
heart!"

It was the man with the weed, not very long after quitting
the merchant, murmuring to himself with his hand to his side
like one with the heart-disease.

Meditation over kindness received seemed to have softened
him something, too, it may be, beyond what might, perhaps,
have been looked for from one whose unwonted self-respect
in the hour of need, and in the act of being aided, might have
appeared to some not wholly unlike pride out of place; and
pride, in any place, is seldom very feeling. But the truth, perhaps, is, that those who are least touched with that vice, besides being not unsusceptible to goodness, are sometimes the
ones whom a ruling sense of propriety makes appear cold, if
not thankless, under a favor. For, at such a time, to be full of
warm, earnest words, and heart-felt protestations, is to create
a scene; and well-bred people dislike few things more than
that; which would seem to look as if the world did not relish
earnestness; but, not so; because the world, being earnest itself, likes an earnest scene, and an earnest man, very well, but
only in their place—the stage. See what sad work they make
of it, who, ignorant of this, flame out in Irish enthusiasm and
with Irish sincerity, to a benefactor, who, if a man of sense
and respectability, as well as kindliness, can but be more or
less annoyed by it; and, if of a nervously fastidious nature, as
some are, may be led to think almost as much less favorably
of the beneficiary paining him by his gratitude, as if he had
been guilty of its contrary, instead only of an indiscretion.
But, beneficiaries who know better, though they may feel as
much, if not more, neither inflict such pain, nor are inclined
to run any risk of so doing. And these, being wise, are the

majority. By which one sees how inconsiderate those persons are, who, from the absence of its officious manifestations in the world, complain that there is not much gratitude extant; when the truth is, that there is as much of it as there is of modesty; but, both being for the most part votarists of the shade, for the most part keep out of sight.

What started this was, to account, if necessary, for the changed air of the man with the weed, who, throwing off in private the cold garb of decorum, and so giving warmly loose to his genuine heart, seemed almost transformed into another being. This subdued air of softness, too, was toned with melancholy, melancholy unreserved; a thing which, however at variance with propriety, still the more attested his earnestness; for one knows not how it is, but it sometimes happens that, where earnestness is, there, also, is melancholy.

At the time, he was leaning over the rail at the boat's side, in his pensiveness, unmindful of another pensive figure near—a young gentleman with a swan-neck, wearing a lady-like open shirt collar, thrown back, and tied with a black ribbon. From a square, tableted broach, curiously engraved with Greek characters, he seemed a collegian—not improbably, a sophomore—on his travels; possibly, his first. A small book bound in Roman vellum was in his hand.

Overhearing his murmuring neighbor, the youth regarded him with some surprise, not to say interest. But, singularly for a collegian, being apparently of a retiring nature, he did not speak; when the other still more increased his diffidence by changing from soliloquy to colloquy, in a manner strangely mixed of familiarity and pathos.

"Ah, who is this? You did not hear me, my young friend, did you? Why, you, too, look sad. My melancholy is not catching!"

"Sir, sir," stammered the other.

"Pray, now," with a sort of sociable sorrowfulness, slowly sliding along the rail, "Pray, now, my young friend, what volume have you there? Give me leave," gently drawing it from him. "Tacitus!" Then opening it at random, read: "In general a black and shameful period lies before me." "Dear young sir," touching his arm alarmedly, "don't read this book. It is poison, moral poison. Even were there truth in Tacitus, such truth would have the operation of falsity, and so still be poison, moral poison. Too well I know this Tacitus. In my college-days he came near souring me into cynicism. Yes, I began to turn down my collar, and go about with a disdainfully joyless expression."

"Sir, sir, I—I—"

"Trust me. Now, young friend, perhaps you think that Tacitus, like me, is only melancholy; but he's more—he's ugly. A vast difference, young sir, between the melancholy view and the ugly. The one may show the world still beautiful, not so the other. The one may be compatible with benevolence, the other not. The one may deepen insight, the other shallows it. Drop Tacitus. Phrenologically, my young friend, you would seem to have a well-developed head, and large; but cribbed within the ugly view, the Tacitus view, your large brain, like your large ox in the contracted field, will but starve the more. And don't dream, as some of you students may, that, by taking this same ugly view, the deeper meanings of the deeper books will so alone become revealed to you. Drop Tacitus. His subtlety is falsity. To him, in his double-refined anatomy of human nature, is well applied the Scripture saying—'There is a subtle man, and the same is deceived.' Drop Tacitus. Come, now, let me throw the book overboard."

"Sir, I—I—"

"Not a word; I know just what is in your mind, and that is just what I am speaking to. Yes, learn from me that, though the sorrows of the world are great, its wickedness—that is, its ugliness—is small. Much cause to pity man, little to distrust him. I myself have known adversity, and know it still. But for that, do I turn cynic? No, no: it is small beer that sours. To my fellow-creatures I owe alleviations. So, whatever I may have undergone, it but deepens my confidence in my kind. Now, then" (winningly), "this book—will you let me drown it for you?"

"Really, sir—I—"

"I see, I see. But of course you read Tacitus in order to aid you in understanding human nature—as if truth was ever got at by libel. My young friend, if to know human nature is your object, drop Tacitus and go north to the cemeteries of Auburn and Greenwood."

"Upon my word, I—I—"

"Nay, I foresee all that. But you carry Tacitus, that shallow Tacitus. What do *I* carry? See"—producing a pocket-volume—"Akenside—his 'Pleasures of Imagination.' One of these days you will know it. Whatever our lot, we should read serene and cheery books, fitted to inspire love and trust. But Tacitus! I have long been of opinion that these classics are the bane of colleges; for—not to hint of the immorality of Ovid, Horace, Anacreon, and the rest, and the dangerous theology of Eschylus and others—where will one find views so injurious to human nature as in Thucydides, Juvenal, Lucian, but more particularly Tacitus? When I consider that, ever since the revival of learning, these classics have been the favorites of successive generations of students and studious men, I tremble to think of that mass of unsuspected heresy on every vital topic which for centuries must have simmered unsurmised in the heart of Christendom. But Tacitus—he is the most extraordinary example of a heretic; not one iota of confidence in his kind. What a mockery that such an one should be reputed wise, and Thucydides be esteemed the statesman's manual! But Tacitus—I hate Tacitus; not, though, I trust, with the hate that sins, but a righteous hate. Without confidence himself, Tacitus destroys it in all his readers. Destroys confidence, fraternal confidence, of which God knows that there is in this world none to spare. For, comparatively inexperienced as you are, my dear young friend, did you never observe how little, very little, confidence, there is? I mean between man and man—more particularly between stranger and stranger. In a sad world it is the saddest fact. Confidence! I have sometimes almost thought that confidence is fled; that confidence is the New Astrea—emigrated—vanished—gone." Then softly sliding nearer, with the softest air, quivering down and looking up, "could you now, my dear young sir, under such circumstances, by way of experiment, simply have confidence in *me*?"

From the outset, the sophomore, as has been seen, had struggled with an ever-increasing embarrassment, arising, perhaps, from such strange remarks coming from a stranger—such persistent and prolonged remarks, too. In vain had he more than once sought to break the spell by venturing a deprecatory or leave-taking word. In vain. Somehow, the stranger fascinated him. Little wonder, then, that, when the appeal came, he could hardly speak, but, as before intimated, being apparently of a retiring nature, abruptly retired from the spot, leaving the chagrined stranger to wander away in the opposite direction.

Chapter 6

Y OU—PISH! Why will the captain suffer these begging
fellows on board?"

These pettish words were breathed by a well-to-do gentleman in a ruby-colored velvet vest, and with a ruby-colored
cheek, a ruby-headed cane in his hand, to a man in a gray
coat and white tie, who, shortly after the interview last described, had accosted him for contributions to a Widow and
Orphan Asylum recently founded among the Seminoles.
Upon a cursory view, this last person might have seemed, like
the man with the weed, one of the less unrefined children of
misfortune; but, on a closer observation, his countenance revealed little of sorrow, though much of sanctity.

With added words of touchy disgust, the well-to-do gentleman hurried away. But, though repulsed, and rudely, the man
in gray did not reproach, for a time patiently remaining in the
chilly loneliness to which he had been left, his countenance, however, not without token of latent though chastened reliance.

At length an old gentleman, somewhat bulky, drew nigh,
and from him also a contribution was sought.

"Look, you," coming to a dead halt, and scowling upon
him. "Look, you," swelling his bulk out before him like a
swaying balloon, "look, you, you on others' behalf ask for
money; you, a fellow with a face as long as my arm. Hark ye,
now: there is such a thing as gravity, and in condemned fel-
ons it may be genuine; but of long faces there are three sorts;
that of grief's drudge, that of the lantern-jawed man, and that
of the impostor. You know best which yours is."

"Heaven give you more charity, sir."

"And you less hypocrisy, sir."

With which words, the hard-hearted old gentleman
marched off.

While the other still stood forlorn, the young clergyman,
before introduced, passing that way, catching a chance sight
of him, seemed suddenly struck by some recollection; and,

after a moment's pause, hurried up with: "Your pardon, but shortly since I was all over looking for you."

"For me?" as marveling that one of so little account should be sought for.

"Yes, for you; do you know anything about the negro, apparently a cripple, aboard here? Is he, or is he not, what he seems to be?"

"Ah, poor Guinea! have you, too, been distrusted? you, upon whom nature has placarded the evidence of your claims?"

"Then you do really know him, and he is quite worthy? It relieves me to hear it—much relieves me. Come, let us go find him, and see what can be done."

"Another instance that confidence may come too late. I am sorry to say that at the last landing I myself—just happening to catch sight of him on the gangway-plank—assisted the cripple ashore. No time to talk, only to help. He may not have told you, but he has a brother in that vicinity."

"Really, I regret his going without my seeing him again; regret it, more, perhaps, than you can readily think. You see, shortly after leaving St. Louis, he was on the forecastle, and there, with many others, I saw him, and put trust in him; so much so, that, to convince those who did not, I, at his entreaty, went in search of you, you being one of several individuals he mentioned, and whose personal appearance he more or less described, individuals who he said would willingly speak for him. But, after diligent search, not finding you, and catching no glimpse of any of the others he had enumerated, doubts were at last suggested; but doubts indirectly originating, as I can but think, from prior distrust unfeelingly proclaimed by another. Still, certain it is, I began to suspect."

"Ha, ha, ha!"

A sort of laugh more like a groan than a laugh; and yet, somehow, it seemed intended for a laugh.

Both turned, and the young clergyman started at seeing the wooden-legged man close behind him, morosely grave as a criminal judge with a mustard-plaster on his back. In the present case the mustard-plaster might have been the memory of certain recent biting rebuffs and mortifications.

"Wouldn't think it was I who laughed, would you?"

"But who was it you laughed at? or rather, tried to laugh at?" demanded the young clergyman, flushing, "me?"

"Neither you nor any one within a thousand miles of you. But perhaps you don't believe it."

"If he were of a suspicious temper, he might not," interposed the man in gray calmly, "it is one of the imbecilities of the suspicious person to fancy that every stranger, however absent-minded, he sees so much as smiling or gesturing to himself in any odd sort of way, is secretly making him his butt. In some moods, the movements of an entire street, as the suspicious man walks down it, will seem an express pantomimic jeer at him. In short, the suspicious man kicks himself with his own foot."

"Whoever can do that, ten to one he saves other folks' sole-leather," said the wooden-legged man with a crusty attempt at humor. But with augmented grin and squirm, turning directly upon the young clergyman, "you still think it was *you* I was laughing at, just now. To prove your mistake, I will tell you what I *was* laughing at; a story I happened to call to mind just then."

Whereupon, in his porcupine way, and with sarcastic details, unpleasant to repeat, he related a story, which might, perhaps, in a good-natured version, be rendered as follows:

A certain Frenchman of New Orleans, an old man, less slender in purse than limb, happening to attend the theatre one evening, was so charmed with the character of a faithful wife, as there represented to the life, that nothing would do but he must marry upon it. So, marry he did, a beautiful girl from Tennessee, who had first attracted his attention by her liberal mould, and was subsequently recommended to him through her kin, for her equally liberal education and disposition. Though large, the praise proved not too much. For, ere long, rumor more than corroborated it, by whispering that the lady was liberal to a fault. But though various circumstances, which by most Benedicts would have been deemed all but conclusive, were duly recited to the old Frenchman by his friends, yet such was his confidence that not a syllable would he credit, till, chancing one night to return unexpectedly from a journey, upon entering his apartment, a stranger burst from the alcove: "Begar!" cried he, "now I *begin* to suspec."

His story told, the wooden-legged man threw back his head, and gave vent to a long, gasping, rasping sort of taunting cry, intolerable as that of a high-pressure engine jeering off steam; and that done, with apparent satisfaction hobbled away.

"Who is that scoffer?" said the man in gray, not without warmth. "Who is he, who even were truth on his tongue, his way of speaking it would make truth almost offensive as falsehood? Who is he?"

"He who I mentioned to you as having boasted his suspicion of the negro," replied the young clergyman, recovering from disturbance, "in short; the person to whom I ascribe the origin of my own distrust; he maintained that Guinea was some white scoundrel, betwisted and painted up for a decoy. Yes, these were his very words, I think."

"Impossible! he could not be so wrong-headed. Pray, will you call him back, and let me ask him if he were really in earnest?"

The other complied; and, at length, after no few surly objections, prevailed upon the one-legged individual to return for a moment. Upon which, the man in gray thus addressed him: "This reverend gentleman tells me, sir, that a certain cripple, a poor negro, is by you considered an ingenious impostor. Now, I am not unaware that there are some persons in this world, who, unable to give better proof of being wise, take a strange delight in showing what they think they have sagaciously read in mankind by uncharitable suspicions of them. I hope you are not one of these. In short, would you tell me now, whether you were not merely joking in the notion you threw out about the negro? Would you be so kind?"

"No, I won't be so kind, I'll be so cruel."

"As you please about that."

"Well, he's just what I said he was."

"A white masquerading as a black?"

"Exactly."

The man in gray glanced at the young clergyman a moment, then quietly whispered to him, "I thought you represented your friend here as a very distrustful sort of person, but he appears endued with a singular credulity.—Tell me, sir, do you really think that a white could look the negro so? For one, I should call it pretty good acting."

"Not much better than any other man acts."

"How? Does all the world act? Am *I*, for instance, an actor? Is my reverend friend here, too, a performer?"

"Yes, don't you both perform acts? To do, is to act; so all doers are actors."

"You trifle.—I ask again, if a white, how could he look the negro so?"

"Never saw the negro-minstrels, I suppose?"

"Yes, but they are apt to overdo the ebony; exemplifying the old saying, not more just than charitable, that 'the devil is never so black as he is painted.' But his limbs, if not a cripple, how could he twist his limbs so?"

"How do other hypocritical beggars twist theirs? Easy enough to see how they are hoisted up."

"The sham is evident, then?"

"To the discerning eye," with a horrible screw of his gimlet one.

"Well, where is Guinea?" said the man in gray: " where is he? Let us at once find him, and refute beyond cavil this injurious hypothesis."

"Do so," cried the one-legged man. "I'm just in the humor now for having him found, and leaving the streaks of these fingers on his paint, as the lion leaves the streaks of his nails on a Caffre. They wouldn't let me touch him before. Yes, find him, I'll make wool fly, and him after."

"You forget," here said the young clergyman to the man in gray, "that yourself helped poor Guinea ashore."

"So I did, so I did; how unfortunate. But look now," to the other, "I think that without personal proof I can convince you of your mistake. For I put it to you, is it reasonable to suppose that a man with brains, sufficient to act such a part as you say, would take all that trouble, and run all that hazard, for the mere sake of those few paltry coppers, which, I hear, was all he got for his pains, if pains they were?"

"That puts the case irrefutably," said the young clergyman, with a challenging glance towards the one-legged man.

"You two green-horns! Money, you think, is the sole motive to pains and hazard, deception and deviltry, in this world. How much money did the devil make by gulling Eve?"

Whereupon he hobbled off again with a repetition of his intolerable jeer.

The man in gray stood silently eying his retreat a while, and then, turning to his companion, said: "A bad man, a dangerous man; a man to be put down in any Christian community.—And this was he who was the means of begetting your distrust? Ah, we should shut our ears to distrust, and keep them open only for its opposite."

"You advance a principle, which, if I had acted upon it this morning, I should have spared myself what I now feel.—That but one man, and he with one leg, should have such ill power given him; his one sour word leavening into congenial sourness (as, to my knowledge, it did) the dispositions, before sweet enough, of a numerous company. But, as I hinted, with me at the time his ill words went for nothing; the same as now; only afterwards they had effect; and I confess, this puzzles me."

"It should not. With humane minds, the spirit of distrust works something as certain potions do; it is a spirit which may enter such minds, and yet, for a time, longer or shorter, lie in them quiescent; but only the more deplorable its ultimate activity."

"An uncomfortable solution; for, since that baneful man did but just now anew drop on me his bane, how shall I be sure that my present exemption from its effects will be lasting?"

"You cannot be sure, but you can strive against it."

"How?"

"By strangling the least symptom of distrust, of any sort, which hereafter, upon whatever provocation, may arise in you."

"I will do so." Then added as in soliloquy, "Indeed, indeed, I was to blame in standing passive under such influences as that one-legged man's. My conscience upbraids me.—The poor negro: You see him occasionally, perhaps?"

"No, not often; though in a few days, as it happens, my engagements will call me to the neighborhood of his present retreat; and, no doubt, honest Guinea, who is a grateful soul, will come to see me there."

"Then you have been his benefactor?"

"His benefactor? I did not say that. I have known him."

"Take this mite. Hand it to Guinea when you see him; say it comes from one who has full belief in his honesty, and is sincerely sorry for having indulged, however transiently, in a contrary thought."

"I accept the trust. And, by-the-way, since you are of this truly charitable nature, you will not turn away an appeal in behalf of the Seminole Widow and Orphan Asylum?"

"I have not heard of that charity."

"But recently founded."

After a pause, the clergyman was irresolutely putting his hand in his pocket, when, caught by something in his companion's expression, he eyed him inquisitively, almost uneasily.

"Ah, well," smiled the other wanly, "if that subtle bane, we were speaking of but just now, is so soon beginning to work, in vain my appeal to you. Good-by."

"Nay," not untouched, "you do me injustice; instead of indulging present suspicions, I had rather make amends for previous ones. Here is something for your asylum. Not much; but every drop helps. Of course you have papers?"

"Of course," producing a memorandum book and pencil. "Let me take down name and amount. We publish these names. And now let me give you a little history of our asylum, and the providential way in which it was started."

Chapter 7

A GENTLEMAN WITH GOLD SLEEVE-BUTTONS

AT AN INTERESTING point of the narration, and at the moment when, with much curiosity, indeed, urgency, the narrator was being particularly questioned upon that point, he was, as it happened, altogether diverted both from it and his story, by just then catching sight of a gentleman who had been standing in sight from the beginning, but, until now, as it seemed, without being observed by him.

"Pardon me," said he, rising, "but yonder is one who I know will contribute, and largely. Don't take it amiss if I quit you."

"Go: duty before all things," was the conscientious reply.

The stranger was a man of more than winsome aspect. There he stood apart and in repose, and yet, by his mere look, lured the man in gray from his story, much as, by its graciousness of bearing, some full-leaved elm, alone in a meadow, lures the noon sickleman to throw down his sheaves, and come and apply for the alms of its shade.

But, considering that goodness is no such rare thing among men—the world familiarly know the noun; a common one in every language—it was curious that what so signalized the stranger, and made him look like a kind of foreigner, among the crowd (as to some it make him appear more or less unreal in this portraiture), was but the expression of so prevalent a quality. Such goodness seemed his, allied with such fortune, that, so far as his own personal experience could have gone, scarcely could he have known ill, physical or moral; and as for knowing or suspecting the latter in any serious degree (supposing such degree of it to be), by observation or philosophy; for that, probably, his nature, by its opposition, imperfectly qualified, or from it wholly exempted him. For the rest, he might have been five and fifty, perhaps sixty, but tall, rosy, between plump and portly, with a primy, palmy air, and for the time and place, not to hint of his years, dressed with a strangely festive finish and elegance. The inner-side of his coat-skirts was of white satin, which might have looked es-

pecially inappropriate, had it not seemed less a bit of mere
tailoring than something of an emblem, as it were; an involuntary emblem, let us say, that what seemed so good about
him was not all outside; no, the fine covering had a still finer
lining. Upon one hand he wore a white kid glove, but the
other hand, which was ungloved, looked hardly less white.
Now, as the Fidèle, like most steamboats, was upon deck a
little soot-streaked here and there, especially about the railings, it was a marvel how, under such circumstances, these
hands retained their spotlessness. But, if you watched them a
while, you noticed that they avoided touching anything; you
noticed, in short, that a certain negro body-servant, whose
hands nature had dyed black, perhaps with the same purpose
that millers wear white, this negro servant's hands did most
of his master's handling for him; having to do with dirt on
his account, but not to his prejudice. But if, with the same
undefiledness of consequences to himself, a gentleman could
also sin by deputy, how shocking would that be! But it is not
permitted to be; and even if it were, no judicious moralist
would make proclamation of it.

This gentleman, therefore, there is reason to affirm, was
one who, like the Hebrew governor, knew how to keep his
hands clean, and who never in his life happened to be run
suddenly against by hurrying house-painter, or sweep; in a
word, one whose very good luck it was to be a very good
man.

Not that he looked as if he were a kind of Wilberforce at
all; that superior merit, probably, was not his; nothing in his
manner bespoke him righteous, but only good, and though
to be good is much below being righteous, and though there
is a difference between the two, yet not, it is to be hoped, so
incompatible as that a righteous man can not be a good man;
though, conversely, in the pulpit it has been with much co-
gency urged, that a merely good man, that is, one good
merely by his nature, is so far from thereby being righteous,
that nothing short of a total change and conversion can make
him so; which is something which no honest mind, well read
in the history of righteousness, will care to deny; nevertheless,
since St. Paul himself, agreeing in a sense with the pulpit distinction, though not altogether in the pulpit deduction, and

also pretty plainly intimating which of the two qualities in question enjoys his apostolic preference; I say, since St. Paul has so meaningly said, that, "scarcely for a righteous man will one die, yet peradventure for a good man some would even dare to die;" therefore, when we repeat of this gentleman, that he was only a good man, whatever else by severe censors may be objected to him, it is still to be hoped that his goodness will not at least be considered criminal in him. At all events, no man, not even a righteous man, would think it quite right to commit this gentleman to prison for the crime, extraordinary as he might deem it; more especially, as, until everything could be known, there would be some chance that the gentleman might after all be quite as innocent of it as he himself.

It was pleasant to mark the good man's reception of the salute of the righteous man, that is, the man in gray; his inferior, apparently, not more in the social scale than in stature. Like the benign elm again, the good man seemed to wave the canopy of his goodness over that suitor, not in conceited condescension, but with that even amenity of true majesty, which can be kind to any one without stooping to it.

To the plea in behalf of the Seminole widows and orphans, the gentleman, after a question or two duly answered, responded by producing an ample pocket-book in the good old capacious style, of fine green French morocco and workmanship, bound with silk of the same color, not to omit bills crisp with newness, fresh from the bank, no muckworms' grime upon them. Lucre those bills might be, but as yet having been kept unspotted from the world, not of the filthy sort. Placing now three of those virgin bills in the applicant's hands, he hoped that the smallness of the contribution would be pardoned; to tell the truth, and this at last accounted for his toilet, he was bound but a short run down the river, to attend, in a festive grove, the afternoon wedding of his niece: so did not carry much money with him.

The other was about expressing his thanks when the gentleman in his pleasant way checked him: the gratitude was on the other side. To him, he said, charity was in one sense not an effort, but a luxury; against too great indulgence in which his steward, a humorist, had sometimes admonished him.

In some general talk which followed, relative to organized modes of doing good, the gentleman expressed his regrets that so many benevolent societies as there were, here and there isolated in the land, should not act in concert by coming together, in the way that already in each society the individuals composing it had done, which would result, he thought, in like advantages upon a larger scale. Indeed, such a confederation might, perhaps, be attended with as happy results as politically attended that of the states.

Upon his hitherto moderate enough companion, this suggestion had an effect illustrative in a sort of that notion of Socrates, that the soul is a harmony; for as the sound of a flute, in any particular key, will, it is said, audibly affect the corresponding chord of any harp in good tune, within hearing, just so now did some string in him respond, and with animation.

Which animation, by the way, might seem more or less out of character in the man in gray, considering his unsprightly manner when first introduced, had he not already, in certain after colloquies, given proof, in some degree, of the fact, that, with certain natures, a soberly continent air at times, so far from arguing emptiness of stuff, is good proof it is there, and plenty of it, because unwasted, and may be used the more effectively, too, when opportunity offers. What now follows on the part of the man in gray will still further exemplify, perhaps somewhat strikingly, the truth, or what appears to be such, of this remark.

"Sir," said he eagerly, "I am before you. A project, not dissimilar to yours, was by me thrown out at the World's Fair in London."

"World's Fair? You there? Pray how was that?"

"First, let me—"

"Nay, but first tell me what took you to the Fair?"

"I went to exhibit an invalid's easy-chair I had invented."

"Then you have not always been in the charity business?"

"Is it not charity to ease human suffering? I am, and always have been, as I always will be, I trust, in the charity business, as you call it; but charity is not like a pin, one to make the head, and the other the point; charity is a work to which a good workman may be competent in all its branches. I invented my Protean easy-chair in odd intervals stolen from meals and sleep."

"You call it the Protean easy-chair; pray describe it."

"My Protean easy-chair is a chair so all over bejointed, behinged, and bepadded, everyway so elastic, springy, and docile to the airiest touch, that in some one of its endlessly-changeable accommodations of back, seat, footboard, and arms, the most restless body, the body most racked, nay, I had almost added the most tormented conscience must, somehow and somewhere, find rest. Believing that I owed it to suffering humanity to make known such a chair to the utmost, I scraped together my little means and off to the World's Fair with it."

"You did right. But your scheme; how did you come to hit upon that?"

"I was going to tell you. After seeing my invention duly catalogued and placed, I gave myself up to pondering the scene about me. As I dwelt upon that shining pageant of arts, and moving concourse of nations, and reflected that here was the pride of the world glorying in a glass house, a sense of the fragility of worldly grandeur profoundly impressed me. And I said to myself, I will see if this occasion of vanity cannot supply a hint toward a better profit than was designed. Let some world-wide good to the world-wide cause be now done. In short, inspired by the scene, on the fourth day I issued at the World's Fair my prospectus of the World's Charity."

"Quite a thought. But, pray explain it."

"The World's Charity is to be a society whose members shall comprise deputies from every charity and mission extant; the one object of the society to be the methodization of the world's benevolence; to which end, the present system of voluntary and promiscuous contribution to be done away, and the Society to be empowered by the various governments to levy, annually, one grand benevolence tax upon all mankind; as in Augustus Cæsar's time, the whole world to come up to be taxed; a tax which, for the scheme of it, should be something like the income-tax in England, a tax, also, as before hinted, to be a consolidation-tax of all possible benevolence taxes; as in America here, the state-tax, and the county-tax, and the town-tax, and the poll-tax, are by the assessors rolled into one. This tax, according to my tables, calculated with care, would result in the yearly raising of a fund little short of eight hundred millions; this fund to be annually applied to such objects, and in such modes, as the various charities and missions, in general congress represented, might decree; whereby, in fourteen years, as I estimate, there would have been devoted to good works the sum of eleven thousand two hundred millions; which would warrant the dissolution of the society, as that fund judiciously expended, not a pauper or heathen could remain the round world over."

"Eleven thousand two hundred millions! And all by passing round a *hat*, as it were."

"Yes, I am no Fourier, the projector of an impossible scheme, but a philanthropist and a financier setting forth a philanthropy and a finance which are practicable."

"Practicable?"

"Yes. Eleven thousand two hundred millions; it will frighten none but a retail philanthropist. What is it but eight hundred millions for each of fourteen years? Now eight hundred millions—what is that, to average it, but one little dollar a head for the population of the planet? And who will refuse, what Turk or Dyak even, his own little dollar for sweet charity's sake? Eight hundred millions! More than that sum is yearly expended by mankind, not only in vanities, but miseries. Consider that bloody spendthrift, War. And are mankind so stupid, so wicked, that, upon the demonstration of these things they will not, amending their ways, devote their superfluities to blessing the world instead of cursing it? Eight hundred millions! They have not to make it, it is theirs already; they have but to direct it from ill to good. And to this, scarce a self-denial is demanded. Actually, they would not in the mass be one farthing the poorer for it; as certainly would they be all the better and happier. Don't you see? But admit, as you must, that mankind is not mad, and my project is practicable. For, what creature but a madman would not rather do good than ill, when it is plain that, good or ill, it must return upon himself?"

"Your sort of reasoning," said the good gentleman, adjusting his gold sleeve-buttons, "seems all reasonable enough, but with mankind it wont do."

"Then mankind are not reasoning beings, if reason wont do with them."

"That is not to the purpose. By-the-way, from the manner in which you alluded to the world's census, it would appear that, according to your world-wide scheme, the pauper not less than the nabob is to contribute to the relief of pauperism, and the heathen not less than the Christian to the conversion of heathenism. How is that?"

"Why, that—pardon me—is quibbling. Now, no philanthropist likes to be opposed with quibbling."

"Well, I won't quibble any more. But, after all, if I understand your project, there is little specially new in it, further than the magnifying of means now in operation."

"Magnifying and energizing. For one thing, missions I would thoroughly reform. Missions I would quicken with the Wall street spirit."

"The Wall street spirit?"

"Yes; for if, confessedly, certain spiritual ends are to be gained but through the auxiliary agency of worldly means, then, to the surer gaining of such spiritual ends, the example of worldly policy in worldly projects should not by spiritual projectors be slighted. In brief, the conversion of the heathen, so far, at least, as depending on human effort, would, by the World's Charity, be let out on contract. So much by bid for converting India, so much for Borneo, so much for Africa. Competition allowed, stimulus would be given. There would be no lethargy of monopoly. We should have no mission-house or tract-house of which slanderers could, with any plausibility, say that it had degenerated in its clerkships into a sort of custom-house. But the main point is the Archimedean money-power that would be brought to bear."

"You mean the eight hundred million power?"

"Yes. You see, this doing good to the world by driblets amounts to just nothing. I am for doing good to the world with a will. I am for doing good to the world once for all and having done with it. Do but think, my dear sir, of the eddies and maëlstroms of pagans in China. People here have no conception of it. Of a frosty morning in Hong Kong, pauper pagans are found dead in the streets like so many nipped peas in a bin of peas. To be an immortal being in China is no more distinction than to be a snow-flake in a snow-squall. What are a score or two of missionaries to such a people? A pinch of snuff to the kraken. I am for sending ten thousand missionaries in a body and converting the Chinese *en masse* within six months of the debarkation. The thing is then done, and turn to something else."

"I fear you are too enthusiastic."

"A philanthropist is necessarily an enthusiast; for without enthusiasm what was ever achieved but commonplace? But again: consider the poor in London. To that mob of misery, what is a joint here and a loaf there? I am for voting to them twenty thousand bullocks and one hundred thousand barrels of flour to begin with. They are then comforted, and no more hunger for one while among the poor of London. And so all round."

"Sharing the character of your general project, these things, I take it, are rather examples of wonders that were to be wished, than wonders that will happen."

"And is the age of wonders passed? Is the world too old? Is it barren? Think of Sarah."

"Then I am Abraham reviling the angel (with a smile). But still, as to your design at large, there seems a certain audacity."

"But if to the audacity of the design there be brought a commensurate circumspectness of execution, how then?"

"Why, do you really believe that your World's Charity will ever go into operation?"

"I have confidence that it will."

"But may you not be over-confident?"

"For a Christian to talk so!"

"But think of the obstacles!"

"Obstacles? I have confidence to remove obstacles, though mountains. Yes, confidence in the World's Charity to that degree, that, as no better person offers to supply the place, I have nominated myself provisional treasurer, and will be happy to receive subscriptions, for the present to be devoted to striking off a million more of my prospectuses."

The talk went on; the man in gray revealed a spirit of benevolence which, mindful of the millennial promise, had gone abroad over all the countries of the globe, much as the diligent spirit of the husbandman, stirred by forethought of the coming seed-time, leads him, in March reveries at his fireside, over every field of his farm. The master chord of the man in gray had been touched, and it seemed as if it would never cease vibrating. A not unsilvery tongue, too, was his, with gestures that were a Pentecost of added ones, and persuasiveness before which granite hearts might crumble into gravel.

Strange, therefore, how his auditor, so singularly good-hearted as he seemed, remained proof to such eloquence; though not, as it turned out, to such pleadings. For, after listening a while longer with pleasant incredulity, presently, as the boat touched his place of destination, the gentleman, with a look half humor, half pity, put another bank-note into his hands; charitable to the last, if only to the dreams of enthusiasm.

Chapter 8

A CHARITABLE LADY

IF A DRUNKARD in a sober fit is the dullest of mortals, an enthusiast in a reason-fit is not the most lively. And this, without prejudice to his greatly improved understanding; for, if his elation was the height of his madness, his despondency is but the extreme of his sanity. Something thus now, to all appearance, with the man in gray. Society his stimulus, loneliness was his lethargy. Loneliness, like the sea-breeze, blowing off from a thousand leagues of blankness, he did not find, as veteran solitaires do, if anything, too bracing. In short, left to himself, with none to charm forth his latent lymphatic, he insensibly resumes his original air, a quiescent one, blended of sad humility and demureness.

Ere long he goes laggingly into the ladies' saloon, as in spiritless quest of somebody; but, after some disappointed glances about him, seats himself upon a sofa with an air of melancholy exhaustion and depression.

At the sofa's further end sits a plump and pleasant person, whose aspect seems to hint that, if she have any weak point, it must be anything rather than her excellent heart. From her twilight dress, neither dawn nor dark, apparently she is a widow just breaking the chrysalis of her mourning. A small gilt testament is in her hand, which she has just been reading. Half-relinquished, she holds the book in reverie, her finger inserted at the xiii. of 1st Corinthians, to which chapter possibly her attention might have recently been turned, by witnessing the scene of the monitory mute and his slate.

The sacred page no longer meets her eye; but, as at evening, when for a time the western hills shine on though the sun be set, her thoughtful face retains its tenderness though the teacher is forgotten.

Meantime, the expression of the stranger is such as ere long to attract her glance. But no responsive one. Presently, in her somewhat inquisitive survey, her volume drops. It is restored. No encroaching politeness in the act, but kindness, unadorned. The eyes of the lady sparkle. Evidently, she is not now unprepossessed. Soon, bending over, in a low, sad tone, full of deference, the stranger breathes, "Madam, pardon my freedom, but there is something in that face which strangely draws me. May I ask, are you a sister of the Church?"

"Why—really—you—"

In concern for her embarrassment, he hastens to relieve it, but, without seeming so to do. "It is very solitary for a brother here," eying the showy ladies brocaded in the background. "I find none to mingle souls with. It may be wrong—I *know* it is—but I cannot force myself to be easy with the people of the world. I prefer the company, however silent, of a brother or sister in good standing. By the way, madam, may I ask if you have confidence?"

"Really, sir—why, sir—really—I—"

"Could you put confidence in *me* for instance?"

"Really, sir—as much—I mean, as one may wisely put in a—a—stranger, an entire stranger, I had almost said," rejoined the lady, hardly yet at ease in her affability, drawing aside a little in body, while at the same time her heart might have been drawn as far the other way. A natural struggle between charity and prudence.

"Entire stranger!" with a sigh. "Ah, who would be a stranger? In vain, I wander; no one will have confidence in me."

"You interest me," said the good lady, in mild surprise. "Can I any way befriend you?"

"No one can befriend me, who has not confidence."

"But I—I have—at least to that degree—I mean that—"

"Nay, nay, you have none—none at all. Pardon, I see it. No confidence. Fool, fond fool that I am to seek it!"

"You are unjust, sir," rejoins the good lady with heightened interest; "but it may be that something untoward in your experiences has unduly biased you. Not that I would cast reflections. Believe me, I—yes, yes—I may say—that—that—"

"That you have confidence? Prove it. Let me have twenty dollars."

"Twenty dollars!"

"There, I told you, madam, you had no confidence."

The lady was, in an extraordinary way, touched. She sat in a sort of restless torment, knowing not which way to turn.

She began twenty different sentences, and left off at the first syllable of each. At last, in desperation, she hurried out, "Tell me, sir, for what you want the twenty dollars?"

"And did I not—" then glancing at her half-mourning, "for the widow and the fatherless. I am traveling agent of the Widow and Orphan Asylum, recently founded among the Seminoles."

"And why did you not tell me your object before?" As not a little relieved. "Poor souls—Indians, too—those cruelly-used Indians. Here, here; how could I hesitate? I am so sorry it is no more."

"Grieve not for that, madam," rising and folding up the bank-notes. "This is an inconsiderable sum, I admit, but," taking out his pencil and book, "though I here but register the amount, there is another register, where is set down the motive. Good-bye; you have confidence. Yea, you can say to me as the apostle said to the Corinthians, 'I rejoice that I have confidence in you in all things.' "

Chapter 9

P RAY, SIR, have you seen a gentleman with a weed hereabouts, rather a saddish gentleman? Strange where he can
have gone to. I was talking with him not twenty minutes
since."

By a brisk, ruddy-cheeked man in a tasseled traveling-cap,
carrying under his arm a ledger-like volume, the above words
were addressed to the collegian before introduced, suddenly
accosted by the rail to which not long after his retreat, as in
a previous chapter recounted, he had returned, and there remained.

"Have you seen him, sir?"

Rallied from his apparent diffidence by the genial jauntiness
of the stranger, the youth answered with unwonted promptitude: "Yes, a person with a weed was here not very long
ago."

"Saddish?"

"Yes, and a little cracked, too, I should say."

"It was he. Misfortune, I fear, has disturbed his brain. Now
quick, which way did he go?"

"Why just in the direction from which you came, the gangway yonder."

"Did he? Then the man in the gray coat, whom I just met,
said right: he must have gone ashore. How unlucky!"

He stood vexedly twitching at his cap-tassel, which fell over
by his whisker, and continued: "Well, I am very sorry. In fact,
I had something for him here."—Then drawing nearer, "you
see, he applied to me for relief, no, I do him injustice, not
that, but he began to intimate, you understand. Well, being
very busy just then, I declined; quite rudely, too, in a cold,
morose, unfeeling way, I fear. At all events, not three minutes
afterwards I felt self-reproach, with a kind of prompting, very
peremptory, to deliver over into that unfortunate man's hands
a ten-dollar bill. You smile. Yes, it may be superstition, but I
can't help it; I have my weak side, thank God. Then again,"
he rapidly went on, " we have been so very prosperous lately

in our affairs—by we, I mean the Black Rapids Coal Company—that, really, out of my abundance, associative and individual, it is but fair that a charitable investment or two should be made, don't you think so?"

"Sir," said the collegian without the least embarrassment, "do I understand that you are officially connected with the Black Rapids Coal Company?"

"Yes, I happen to be president and transfer-agent."

"You are?"

"Yes, but what is it to you? You don't want to invest?"

"Why, do you sell the stock?"

"Some might be bought, perhaps; but why do you ask? you don't want to invest?"

"But supposing I did," with cool self-collectedness, "could you do up the thing for me, and here?"

"Bless my soul," gazing at him in amaze, "really, you are quite a business man. Positively, I feel afraid of you."

"Oh, no need of that.—You could sell me some of that stock, then?"

"I don't know, I don't know. To be sure, there are a few shares under peculiar circumstances bought in by the Company; but it would hardly be the thing to convert this boat into the Company's office. I think you had better defer investing. So," with an indifferent air, "you have seen the unfortunate man I spoke of?"

"Let the unfortunate man go his ways.—What is that large book you have with you?"

"My transfer-book. I am subpœnaed with it to court."

"Black Rapids Coal Company," obliquely reading the gilt inscription on the back; "I have heard much of it. Pray do you happen to have with you any statement of the condition of your company?"

"A statement has lately been printed."

"Pardon me, but I am naturally inquisitive. Have you a copy with you?"

"I tell you again, I do not think that it would be suitable to convert this boat into the Company's office.—That unfortunate man, did you relieve him at all?"

"Let the unfortunate man relieve himself.—Hand me the statement."

"Well, you are such a business-man, I can hardly deny you. Here," handing a small, printed pamphlet.

The youth turned it over sagely.

"I hate a suspicious man," said the other, observing him; "but I must say I like to see a cautious one."

"I can gratify you there," languidly returning the pamphlet; "for, as I said before, I am naturally inquisitive; I am also circumspect. No appearances can deceive me. Your statement," he added, "tells a very fine story; but pray, was not your stock a little heavy a while ago? downward tendency? Sort of low spirits among holders on the subject of that stock?"

"Yes, there was a depression. But how came it? who devised it? The 'bears,' sir. The depression of our stock was solely owing to the growling, the hypocritical growling, of the bears."

"How, hypocritical?"

"Why, the most monstrous of all hypocrites are these bears: hypocrites by inversion; hypocrites in the simulation of things dark instead of bright; souls that thrive, less upon depression, than the fiction of depression; professors of the wicked art of manufacturing depressions; spurious Jeremiahs; sham Heraclituses, who, the lugubrious day done, return, like sham Lazaruses among the beggars, to make merry over the gains got by their pretended sore heads—scoundrelly bears!"

"You are warm against these bears?"

"If I am, it is less from the remembrance of their stratagems as to our stock, than from the persuasion that these same destroyers of confidence, and gloomy philosophers of the stock-market, though false in themselves, are yet true types of most destroyers of confidence and gloomy philosophers, the world over. Fellows who, whether in stocks, politics, bread-stuffs, morals, metaphysics, religion—be it what it may—trump up their black panics in the naturally-quiet brightness, solely with a view to some sort of covert advantage. That corpse of calamity which the gloomy philosopher parades, is but his Good-Enough-Morgan."

"I rather like that," knowingly drawled the youth. "I fancy these gloomy souls as little as the next one. Sitting on my sofa after a champagne dinner, smoking my plantation cigar, if a gloomy fellow come to me—what a bore!"

"You tell him it's all stuff, don't you?"

"I tell him it ain't natural. I say to him, you are happy enough, and you know it; and everybody else is as happy as you, and you know that, too; and we shall all be happy after we are no more, and you know that, too; but no, still you must have your sulk."

"And do you know whence this sort of fellow gets his sulk? not from life; for he's often too much of a recluse, or else too young to have seen anything of it. No, he gets it from some of those old plays he sees on the stage, or some of those old books he finds up in garrets. Ten to one, he has lugged home from auction a musty old Seneca, and sets about stuffing himself with that stale old hay; and, thereupon, thinks it looks wise and antique to be a croaker, thinks it's taking a stand 'way above his kind."

"Just so," assented the youth. "I've lived some, and seen a good many such ravens at second hand. By the way, strange how that man with the weed, you were inquiring for, seemed to take me for some soft sentimentalist, only because I kept quiet, and thought, because I had a copy of Tacitus with me, that I was reading him for his gloom, instead of his gossip. But I let him talk. And, indeed, by my manner humored him."

"You shouldn't have done that, now. Unfortunate man, you must have made quite a fool of him."

"His own fault if I did. But I like prosperous fellows, comfortable fellows; fellows that talk comfortably and prosperously, like you. Such fellows are generally honest. And, I say now, I happen to have a superfluity in my pocket, and I'll just—"

"—Act the part of a brother to that unfortunate man?"

"Let the unfortunate man be his own brother. What are you dragging him in for all the time? One would think you didn't care to register any transfers, or dispose of any stock—mind running on something else. I say I will invest."

"Stay, stay, here come some uproarious fellows—this way, this way."

And with off-handed politeness the man with the book

escorted his companion into a private little haven removed from the brawling swells without.

Business transacted, the two came forth, and walked the deck.

"Now tell me, sir," said he with the book, "how comes it that a young gentleman like you, a sedate student at the first appearance, should dabble in stocks and that sort of thing?"

"There are certain sophomorean errors in the world," drawled the sophomore, deliberately adjusting his shirt-collar, "not the least of which is the popular notion touching the nature of the modern scholar, and the nature of the modern scholastic sedateness."

"So it seems, so it seems. Really, this is quite a new leaf in my experience."

"Experience, sir," originally observed the sophomore, "is the only teacher."

"Hence am I your pupil; for it's only when experience speaks, that I can endure to listen to speculation."

"My speculations, sir," dryly drawing himself up, "have been chiefly governed by the maxim of Lord Bacon; I speculate in those philosophies which come home to my business and bosom—pray, do you know of any other good stocks?"

"You wouldn't like to be concerned in the New Jerusalem, would you?"

"New Jerusalem?"

"Yes, the new and thriving city, so called, in northern Minnesota. It was originally founded by certain fugitive Mormons. Hence the name. It stands on the Mississippi. Here, here is the map," producing a roll. "There—there, you see are the public buildings—here the landing—there the park— yonder the botanic gardens—and this, this little dot here, is a perpetual fountain, you understand. You observe there are twenty asterisks. Those are for the lyceums. They have lignum-vitæ rostrums."

"And are all these buildings now standing?"

"All standing—bona fide."

"These marginal squares here, are they the water-lots?"

"Water-lots in the city of New Jerusalem? All terra firma— you don't seem to care about investing, though?"

"Hardly think I should read my title clear, as the law students say," yawned the collegian.

"Prudent—you are prudent. Don't know that you are wholly out, either. At any rate, I would rather have one of your shares of coal stock than two of this other. Still, considering that the first settlement was by two fugitives, who had swum over naked from the opposite shore—it's a surprising place. It is, *bona fide*.—But dear me, I must go. Oh, if by possibility you should come across that unfortunate man—"

"—In that case," with drawling impatience, "I will send for the steward, and have him and his misfortunes consigned overboard."

"Ha ha!—now were some gloomy philosopher here, some theological bear, forever taking occasion to growl down the stock of human nature (with ulterior views, d'ye see, to a fat benefice in the gift of the worshipers of Arimanius), he would pronounce that the sign of a hardening heart and a softening brain. Yes, that would be his sinister construction. But it's nothing more than the oddity of a genial humor—genial but dry. Confess it. Good-bye."

Chapter 10

IN THE CABIN

STOOLS, SETTEES, SOFAS, divans, ottomans; occupying them are clusters of men, old and young, wise and simple; in their hands are cards spotted with diamonds, spades, clubs, hearts; the favorite games are whist, cribbage, and brag. Lounging in arm-chairs or sauntering among the marble-topped tables, amused with the scene, are the comparatively few, who, instead of having hands in the games, for the most part keep their hands in their pockets. These may be the philosophes. But here and there, with a curious expression, one is reading a small sort of handbill of anonymous poetry, rather wordily entitled: —

"ODE

ON THE INTIMATIONS

OF

DISTRUST IN MAN,

UNWILLINGLY INFERRED FROM REPEATED

REPULSES,

IN DISINTERESTED ENDEAVORS

TO PROCURE HIS

CONFIDENCE."

On the floor are many copies, looking as if fluttered down from a balloon. The way they came there was this: A somewhat elderly person, in the quaker dress, had quietly passed through the cabin, and, much in the manner of those railway book-peddlers who precede their proffers of sale by a distribution of puffs, direct or indirect, of the volumes to follow, had, without speaking, handed about the odes, which, for the most part, after a cursory glance, had been disrespectfully tossed aside, as no doubt, the moonstruck production of some wandering rhapsodist.

In due time, book under arm, in trips the ruddy man with the traveling-cap, who, lightly moving to and fro, looks animatedly about him, with a yearning sort of gratulatory affinity and longing, expressive of the very soul of sociality; as much as to say, "Oh, boys, would that I were personally acquainted with each mother's son of you, since what a sweet world, to make sweet acquaintance in, is ours, my brothers; yea, and what dear, happy dogs are we all!"

And just as if he had really warbled it forth, he makes fraternally up to one lounging stranger or another, exchanging with him some pleasant remark.

"Pray, what have you there?" he asked of one newly accosted, a little, dried-up man, who looked as if he never dined.

"A little ode, rather queer, too," was the reply, "of the same sort you see strewn on the floor here."

"I did not observe them. Let me see;" picking one up and looking it over. "Well now, this is pretty; plaintive, especially the opening: —

> 'Alas for man, he hath small sense
> Of genial trust and confidence.'

—If it be so, alas for him, indeed. Runs off very smoothly, sir. Beautiful pathos. But do you think the sentiment just?"

"As to that," said the little dried-up man, "I think it a kind of queer thing altogether, and yet I am almost ashamed to add, it really has set me to thinking; yes and to feeling. Just now, somehow, I feel as it were trustful and genial. I don't know that ever I felt so much so before. I am naturally numb in my sensibilities; but this ode, in its way, works on my numbness not unlike a sermon, which, by lamenting over my lying dead in trespasses and sins, thereby stirs me up to be all alive in well-doing."

"Glad to hear it, and hope you will do well, as the doctors say. But who snowed the odes about here?"

"I cannot say; I have not been here long."

"Wasn't an angel, was it? Come, you say you feel genial, let us do as the rest, and have cards."

"Thank you, I never play cards."

"A bottle of wine?"

"Thank you, I never drink wine."

"Cigars?"

"Thank you, I never smoke cigars."

"Tell stories?"

"To speak truly, I hardly think I know one worth telling."

"Seems to me, then, this geniality you say you feel waked in you, is as water-power in a land without mills. Come, you had better take a genial hand at the cards. To begin, we will play for as small a sum as you please; just enough to make it interesting."

"Indeed, you must excuse me. Somehow I distrust cards."

"What, distrust cards? Genial cards? Then for once I join with our sad Philomel here:—

> 'Alas for man, he hath small sense
> Of genial trust and confidence.'

Good-bye!"

Sauntering and chatting here and there, again, he with the book at length seems fatigued, looks round for a seat, and spying a partly-vacant settee drawn up against the side, drops down there; soon, like his chance neighbor, who happens to be the good merchant, becoming not a little interested in the scene more immediately before him; a party at whist; two cream-faced, giddy, unpolished youths, the one in a red cravat, the other in a green, opposed to two bland, grave, handsome, self-possessed men of middle age, decorously dressed in a sort of professional black, and apparently doctors of some eminence in the civil law.

By-and-by, after a preliminary scanning of the new comer next him the good merchant, sideways leaning over, whispers behind a crumpled copy of the Ode which he holds: "Sir, I don't like the looks of those two, do you?"

"Hardly," was the whispered reply; "those colored cravats are not in the best taste, at least not to mine; but my taste is no rule for all."

"You mistake; I mean the other two, and I don't refer to dress, but countenance. I confess I am not familiar with such gentry any further than reading about them in the papers—but those two are—are sharpers, aint they?"

"Far be from us the captious and fault-finding spirit, my dear sir."

"Indeed, sir, I would not find fault; I am little given that way; but certainly, to say the least, these two youths can hardly be adepts, while the opposed couple may be even more."

"You would not hint that the colored cravats would be so bungling as to lose, and the dark cravats so dextrous as to cheat?—Sour imaginations, my dear sir. Dismiss them. To little purpose have you read the Ode you have there. Years and experience, I trust, have not sophisticated you. A fresh and liberal construction would teach us to regard those four players—indeed, this whole cabin-full of players—as playing at games in which every player plays fair, and not a player but shall win."

"Now, you hardly mean that; because games in which all may win, such games remain as yet in this world uninvented, I think."

"Come, come," luxuriously laying himself back, and casting a free glance upon the players, "fares all paid; digestion sound; care, toil, penury, grief, unknown; lounging on this sofa, with waistband relaxed, why not be cheerfully resigned to one's fate, nor peevishly pick holes in the blessed fate of the world?"

Upon this, the good merchant, after staring long and hard, and then rubbing his forehead, fell into meditation, at first uneasy, but at last composed, and in the end, once more addressed his companion: "Well, I see it's good to out with one's private thoughts now and then. Somehow, I don't know why, a certain misty suspiciousness seems inseparable from most of one's private notions about some men and some things; but once out with these misty notions, and their mere contact with other men's soon dissipates, or, at least, modifies them."

"You think I have done you good, then? may be, I have. But don't thank me, don't thank me. If by words, casually delivered in the social hour, I do any good to right or left, it is but involuntary influence—locust-tree sweetening the herbage under it; no merit at all; mere wholesome accident, of a wholesome nature.—Don't you see?"

Another stare from the good merchant, and both were silent again.

Finding his book, hitherto resting on his lap, rather irksome there, the owner now places it edgewise on the settee, between himself and neighbor; in so doing, chancing to expose the lettering on the back—*"Black Rapids Coal Company"*—which the good merchant, scrupulously honorable, had much ado to avoid reading, so directly would it have fallen under his eye, had he not conscientiously averted it. On a sudden, as if just reminded of something, the stranger starts up, and moves away, in his haste leaving his book; which the merchant observing, without delay takes it up, and, hurrying after, civilly returns it; in which act he could not avoid catching sight by an involuntary glance of part of the lettering.

"Thank you, thank you, my good sir," said the other, receiving the volume, and was resuming his retreat, when the merchant spoke: "Excuse me, but are you not in some way connected with the—the Coal Company I have heard of?"

"There is more than one Coal Company that may be heard of, my good sir," smiled the other, pausing with an expression of painful impatience, disinterestedly mastered.

"But you are connected with one in particular.—The 'Black Rapids,' are you not?"

"How did you find that out?"

"Well, sir, I have heard rather tempting information of your Company."

"Who is your informant, pray?" somewhat coldly.

"A—a person by the name of Ringman."

"Don't know him. But, doubtless, there are plenty who know our Company, whom our Company does not know; in the same way that one may know an individual, yet be unknown to him.—Known this Ringman long? Old friend, I suppose.—But pardon, I must leave you."

"Stay, sir, that—that stock."

"Stock?"

"Yes, it's a little irregular, perhaps, but—"

"Dear me, you don't think of doing any business with me, do you? In my official capacity I have not been authenticated to you. This transfer-book, now," holding it up so as to bring the lettering in sight, "how do you know that it may not be a bogus one? And I, being personally a stranger to you, how can you have confidence in me?"

"Because," knowingly smiled the good merchant, "if you

were other than I have confidence that you are, hardly would you challenge distrust that way."

"But you have not examined my book."

"What need to, if already I believe that it is what it is lettered to be?"

"But you had better. It might suggest doubts."

"Doubts, may be, it might suggest, but not knowledge; for how, by examining the book, should I think I knew any more than I now think I do; since, if it be the true book, I think it so already; and since if it be otherwise, then I have never seen the true one, and don't know what that ought to look like."

"Your logic I will not criticize, but your confidence I admire, and earnestly, too, jocose as was the method I took to draw it out. Enough, we will go to yonder table, and if there be any business which, either in my private or official capacity, I can help you do, pray command me."

Chapter II

ONLY A PAGE OR SO

THE TRANSACTION CONCLUDED, the two still remained seated, falling into familiar conversation, by degrees verging into that confidential sort of sympathetic silence, the last refinement and luxury of unaffected good feeling. A kind of social superstition, to suppose that to be truly friendly one must be saying friendly words all the time, any more than be doing friendly deeds continually. True friendliness, like true religion, being in a sort independent of works.

At length, the good merchant, whose eyes were pensively resting upon the gay tables in the distance, broke the spell by saying that, from the spectacle before them, one would little divine what other quarters of the boat might reveal. He cited the case, accidentally encountered but an hour or two previous, of a shrunken old miser, clad in shrunken old moleskin, stretched out, an invalid, on a bare plank in the emigrants' quarters, eagerly clinging to life and lucre, though the one was gasping for outlet, and about the other he was in torment lest death, or some other unprincipled cut-purse, should be the means of his losing it; by like feeble tenure holding lungs and pouch, and yet knowing and desiring nothing beyond them; for his mind, never raised above mould, was now all but mouldered away. To such a degree, indeed, that he had no trust in anything, not even in his parchment bonds, which, the better to preserve from the tooth of time, he had packed down and sealed up, like brandy peaches, in a tin case of spirits.

The worthy man proceeded at some length with these dispiriting particulars. Nor would his cheery companion wholly deny that there might be a point of view from which such a case of extreme want of confidence might, to the humane mind, present features not altogether welcome as wine and olives after dinner. Still, he was not without compensatory considerations, and, upon the whole, took his companion to task for evincing what, in a good-natured, round-about way, he hinted to be a somewhat jaundiced sentimentality. Nature, he added, in Shakespeare's words, had meal and bran; and, rightly regarded, the bran in its way was not to be condemned.

The other was not disposed to question the justice of Shakespeare's thought, but would hardly admit the propriety of the application in this instance, much less of the comment. So, after some further temperate discussion of the pitiable miser, finding that they could not entirely harmonize, the merchant cited another case, that of the negro cripple. But his companion suggested whether the alleged hardships of that alleged unfortunate might not exist more in the pity of the observer than the experience of the observed. He knew nothing about the cripple, nor had seen him, but ventured to surmise that, could one but get at the real state of his heart, he would be found about as happy as most men, if not, in fact, full as happy as the speaker himself. He added that negroes were by nature a singularly cheerful race; no one ever heard of a native-born African Zimmermann or Torquemada; that even from religion they dismissed all gloom; in their hilarious rituals they danced, so to speak, and, as it were, cut pigeon-wings. It was improbable, therefore, that a negro, however reduced to his stumps by fortune, could be ever thrown off the legs of a laughing philosophy.

Foiled again, the good merchant would not desist, but ventured still a third case, that of the man with the weed, whose story, as narrated by himself, and confirmed and filled out by the testimony of a certain man in a gray coat, whom the merchant had afterwards met, he now proceeded to give; and that, without holding back those particulars disclosed by the second informant, but which delicacy had prevented the unfortunate man himself from touching upon.

But as the good merchant could, perhaps, do better justice to the man than the story, we shall venture to tell it in other words than his, though not to any other effect.

Chapter 12

IT APPEARED that the unfortunate man had had for a wife one of those natures, anomalously vicious, which would almost tempt a metaphysical lover of our species to doubt whether the human form be, in all cases, conclusive evidence of humanity, whether, sometimes, it may not be a kind of unpledged and indifferent tabernacle, and whether, once for all to crush the saying of Thrasea, (an unaccountable one, considering that he himself was so good a man) that "he who hates vice, hates humanity," it should not, in self-defense, be held for a reasonable maxim, that none but the good are human.

Goneril was young, in person lithe and straight, too straight, indeed, for a woman, a complexion naturally rosy, and which would have been charmingly so, but for a certain hardness and bakedness, like that of the glazed colors on stone-ware. Her hair was of a deep, rich chestnut, but worn in close, short curls all round her head. Her Indian figure was not without its impairing effect on her bust, while her mouth would have been pretty but for a trace of moustache. Upon the whole, aided by the resources of the toilet, her appearance at distance was such, that some might have thought her, if anything, rather beautiful, though of a style of beauty rather peculiar and cactus-like.

It was happy for Goneril that her more striking peculiarities were less of the person than of temper and taste. One hardly knows how to reveal, that, while having a natural antipathy to such things as the breast of chicken, or custard, or peach, or grape, Goneril could yet in private make a satisfactory lunch on hard crackers and brawn of ham. She liked lemons, and the only kind of candy she loved were little dried sticks of blue clay, secretly carried in her pocket. Withal she had hard, steady health like a squaw's, with as firm a spirit and resolution. Some other points about her were likewise such as pertain to the women of savage life. Lithe though she was, she loved supineness, but upon occasion could endure like a stoic. She was taciturn, too. From early morning till about three o'clock in the afternoon she would seldom speak—it taking that time to thaw her, by all accounts, into but talking terms with humanity. During the interval she did little but look, and keep looking out of her large, metallic eyes, which her enemies called cold as a cuttle-fish's, but which by her were esteemed gazelle-like; for Goneril was not without vanity. Those who thought they best knew her, often wondered what happiness such a being could take in life, not considering the happiness which is to be had by some natures in the very easy way of simply causing pain to those around them. Those who suffered from Goneril's strange nature, might, with one of those hyperboles to which the resentful incline, have pronounced her some kind of toad; but her worst slanderers could never, with any show of justice, have accused her of being a toady. In a large sense she possessed the virtue of independence of mind. Goneril held it flattery to hint praise even of the absent, and even if merited; but honesty, to fling people's imputed faults into their faces. This was thought malice, but it certainly was not passion. Passion is human. Like an icicle-dagger, Goneril at once stabbed and froze; so at least they said; and when she saw frankness and innocence tyrannized into sad nervousness under her spell, according to the same authority, inly she chewed her blue clay, and you could mark that she chuckled. These peculiarities were strange and unpleasing; but another was alleged, one really incomprehensible. In company she had a strange way of touching, as by accident, the arm or hand of comely young men, and seemed to reap a secret delight from it, but whether from the humane satisfaction of having given the evil-touch, as it is called, or whether it was something else in her, not equally wonderful, but quite as deplorable, remained an enigma.

Needless to say what distress was the unfortunate man's, when, engaged in conversation with company, he would suddenly perceive his Goneril bestowing her mysterious touches, especially in such cases where the strangeness of the thing seemed to strike upon the touched person, notwithstanding good-breeding forbade his proposing the mystery, on the spot, as a subject of discussion for the company. In these cases, too, the unfortunate man could never endure so much as to look upon the touched young gentleman afterwards, fearful of the mortification of meeting in his countenance some kind of more or less quizzingly-knowing expression. He would shudderingly shun the young gentleman. So that here, to the husband, Goneril's touch had the dread operation of the heathen taboo. Now Goneril brooked no chiding. So, at favorable times, he, in a wary manner, and not indelicately, would venture in private interviews gently to make distant allusions to this questionable propensity. She divined him. But, in her cold loveless way, said it was witless to be telling one's dreams, especially foolish ones; but if the unfortunate man liked connubially to rejoice his soul with such chimeras, much connubial joy might they give him. All this was sad—a touching case—but all might, perhaps, have been borne by the unfortunate man—conscientiously mindful of his vow—for better or for worse—to love and cherish his dear Goneril so long as kind heaven might spare her to him—but when, after all that had happened, the devil of jealousy entered her, a calm, clayey, cakey devil, for none other could possess her, and the object of that deranged jealousy, her own child, a little girl of seven, her father's consolation and pet; when he saw Goneril artfully torment the little innocent, and then play the maternal hypocrite with it, the unfortunate man's patient long-suffering gave way. Knowing that she would neither confess nor amend, and might, possibly, become even worse than she was, he thought it but duty as a father, to withdraw the child from her; but, loving it as he did, he could not do so without accompanying it into domestic exile himself. Which, hard though it was, he did. Whereupon the whole female neighborhood, who till now had little enough admired dame Goneril, broke out in indignation against a husband, who, without assigning a cause, could deliberately abandon the wife of his bosom, and sharpen the sting to her, too, by depriving her of the solace of retaining her offspring. To all this, self-respect, with Christian charity towards Goneril, long kept the unfortunate man dumb. And well had it been had he continued so; for when, driven to desperation, he hinted something of the truth of the case, not a soul would credit it; while for Goneril, she pronounced all he said to be a malicious invention. Ere long, at the suggestion of some woman's-rights women, the injured wife began a suit, and, thanks to able counsel and accommodating testimony, succeeded in such a way, as not only to recover custody of the child, but to get such a settlement awarded upon a separation, as to make penniless the unfortunate man (so he averred), besides, through the legal sympathy she enlisted, effecting a judicial blasting of his private reputation. What made it yet more lamentable was, that the unfortunate man, thinking that, before the court, his wisest plan, as well as the most Christian besides, being, as he deemed, not at variance with the truth of the matter, would be to put forth the plea of the mental derangement of Goneril, which done, he could, with less of mortification to himself, and odium to her, reveal in self-defense those eccentricities which had led to his retirement from the joys of wedlock, had much ado in the end to prevent this charge of derangement from fatally recoiling upon himself—especially, when, among other things, he alleged her mysterious touchings. In vain did his counsel, striving to make out the derangement to be where, in fact, if anywhere, it was, urge that, to hold otherwise, to hold that such a being as Goneril was sane, this was constructively a libel upon womankind. Libel be it. And all ended by the unfortunate man's subsequently getting wind of Goneril's intention to procure him to be permanently committed for a lunatic. Upon which he fled, and was now an innocent outcast, wandering forlorn in the great valley of the Mississippi, with a weed on his hat for the loss of his Goneril; for he had lately seen by the papers that she was dead, and thought it but proper to comply with the prescribed form of mourning in such cases. For some days past he had been trying to get money enough to return to his child, and was but now started with inadequate funds.

Now all of this, from the beginning, the good merchant could not but consider rather hard for the unfortunate man.

Chapter 13

THE MAN WITH THE TRAVELING-CAP EVINCES MUCH HUMANITY, AND IN A WAY WHICH WOULD SEEM TO SHOW HIM TO BE ONE OF THE MOST LOGICAL OF OPTIMISTS

YEARS AGO, a grave American savan, being in London, observed at an evening party there, a certain coxcombical fellow, as he thought, an absurd ribbon in his lapel, and full of smart persiflage, whisking about to the admiration of as many as were disposed to admire. Great was the savan's disdain; but, chancing ere long to find himself in a corner with the jackanapes, got into conversation with him, when he was somewhat ill-prepared for the good sense of the jackanapes, but was altogether thrown aback, upon subsequently being whispered by a friend that the jackanapes was almost as great a savan as himself, being no less a personage than Sir Humphrey Davy.

The above anecdote is given just here by way of an anticipative reminder to such readers as, from the kind of jaunty levity, or what may have passed for such, hitherto for the most part appearing in the man with the traveling-cap, may have been tempted into a more or less hasty estimate of him; that such readers, when they find the same person, as they presently will, capable of philosophic and humanitarian discourse—no mere casual sentence or two as heretofore at times, but solidly sustained throughout an almost entire sitting; that they may not, like the American savan, be thereupon betrayed into any surprise incompatible with their own good opinion of their previous penetration.

The merchant's narration being ended, the other would not deny but that it did in some degree affect him. He hoped he was not without proper feeling for the unfortunate man. But he begged to know in what spirit he bore his alleged calamities. Did he despond or have confidence?

The merchant did not, perhaps, take the exact import of the last member of the question; but answered, that, if whether the unfortunate man was becomingly resigned under his affliction or no, was the point, he could say for him that resigned he was, and to an exemplary degree: for not only, so far as known, did he refrain from any one-sided reflections upon human goodness and human justice, but there was observable in him an air of chastened reliance, and at times tempered cheerfulness.

Upon which the other observed, that since the unfortunate man's alleged experience could not be deemed very conciliatory towards a view of human nature better than human nature was, it largely redounded to his fair-mindedness, as well as piety, that under the alleged dissuasives, apparently so, from philanthropy, he had not, in a moment of excitement, been warped over to the ranks of the misanthropes. He doubted not, also, that with such a man his experience would, in the end, act by a complete and beneficent inversion, and so far from shaking his confidence in his kind, confirm it, and rivet it. Which would the more surely be the case, did he (the unfortunate man) at last become satisfied (as sooner or later he probably would be) that in the distraction of his mind his Goneril had not in all respects had fair play. At all events, the description of the lady, charity could not but regard as more or less exaggerated, and so far unjust. The truth probably was that she was a wife with some blemishes mixed with some beauties. But when the blemishes were displayed, her husband, no adept in the female nature, had tried to use reason with her, instead of something far more persuasive. Hence his failure to convince and convert. The act of withdrawing from her, seemed, under the circumstances, abrupt. In brief, there were probably small faults on both sides, more than balanced by large virtues; and one should not be hasty in judging.

When the merchant, strange to say, opposed views so calm and impartial, and again, with some warmth, deplored the case of the unfortunate man, his companion, not without seriousness, checked him, saying, that this would never do; that, though but in the most exceptional case, to admit the existence of unmerited misery, more particularly if alleged to have been brought about by unhindered arts of the wicked, such an admission was, to say the least, not prudent; since, with some, it might unfavorably bias their most important

persuasions. Not that those persuasions were legitimately servile to such influences. Because, since the common occurrences of life could never, in the nature of things, steadily
look one way and tell one story, as flags in the trade-wind;
hence, if the conviction of a Providence, for instance, were in
any way made dependent upon such variabilities as everyday
events, the degree of that conviction would, in thinking
minds, be subject to fluctuations akin to those of the stock-
exchange during a long and uncertain war. Here he glanced
aside at his transfer-book, and after a moment's pause continued. It was of the essence of a right conviction of the divine
nature, as with a right conviction of the human, that, based
less on experience than intuition, it rose above the zones of
weather.

When now the merchant, with all his heart, coincided with
this (as being a sensible, as well as religious person, he could
not but do), his companion expressed satisfaction, that, in an
age of some distrust on such subjects, he could yet meet with
one who shared with him, almost to the full, so sound and
sublime a confidence.

Still, he was far from the illiberality of denying that philosophy duly bounded was permissible. Only he deemed it at
least desirable that, when such a case as that alleged of the
unfortunate man was made the subject of philosophic discussion, it should be so philosophized upon, as not to afford
handles to those unblessed with the true light. For, but to
grant that there was so much as a mystery about such a case,
might by those persons be held for a tacit surrender of the
question. And as for the apparent license temporarily permitted sometimes, to the bad over the good (as was by implication alleged with regard to Goneril and the unfortunate man),
it might be injudicious there to lay too much polemic stress
upon the doctrine of future retribution as the vindication of
present impunity. For though, indeed, to the right-minded
that doctrine was true, and of sufficient solace, yet with the
perverse the polemic mention of it might but provoke the
shallow, though mischievous conceit, that such a doctrine was
but tantamount to the one which should affirm that Providence was not now, but was going to be. In short, with all

sorts of cavilers, it was best, both for them and everybody, that whoever had the true light should stick behind the secure Malakoff of confidence, not be tempted forth to hazardous skirmishes on the open ground of reason. Therefore, he deemed it unadvisable in the good man, even in the privacy of his own mind, or in communion with a congenial one, to indulge in too much latitude of philosophizing, or, indeed, of compassionating, since this might beget an indiscreet habit of thinking and feeling which might unexpectedly betray him upon unsuitable occasions. Indeed, whether in private or public, there was nothing which a good man was more bound to guard himself against than, on some topics, the emotional unreserve of his natural heart; for, that the natural heart, in certain points, was not what it might be, men had been authoritatively admonished.

But he thought he might be getting dry.

The merchant, in his good-nature, thought otherwise, and said that he would be glad to refresh himself with such fruit all day. It was sitting under a ripe pulpit, and better such a seat than under a ripe peach-tree.

The other was pleased to find that he had not, as he feared, been prosing; but would rather not be considered in the formal light of a preacher; he preferred being still received in that of the equal and genial companion. To which end, throwing still more of sociability into his manner, he again reverted to the unfortunate man. Take the very worst view of that case; admit that his Goneril was, indeed, a Goneril; how fortunate to be at last rid of this Goneril, both by nature and by law! If he were acquainted with the unfortunate man, instead of condoling with him, he would congratulate him. Great good fortune had this unfortunate man. Lucky dog, he dared say, after all.

To which the merchant replied, that he earnestly hoped it might be so, and at any rate he tried his best to comfort himself with the persuasion that, if the unfortunate man was not happy in this world, he would, at least, be so in another.

His companion made no question of the unfortunate man's happiness in both worlds; and, presently calling for some champagne, invited the merchant to partake, upon the playful plea that, whatever notions other than felicitous ones he might associate with the unfortunate man, a little champagne would readily bubble away.

At intervals they slowly quaffed several glasses in silence and thoughtfulness. At last the merchant's expressive face flushed, his eye moistly beamed, his lips trembled with an imaginative and feminine sensibility. Without sending a single fume to his head, the wine seemed to shoot to his heart, and begin soothsaying there. "Ah," he cried, pushing his glass from him, "Ah, wine is good, and confidence is good; but can wine or confidence percolate down through all the stony strata of hard considerations, and drop warmly and ruddily into the cold cave of truth? Truth will *not* be comforted. Led by dear charity, lured by sweet hope, fond fancy essays this feat; but in vain; mere dreams and ideals, they explode in your hand, leaving naught but the scorching behind!"

"Why, why, why!" in amaze, at the burst; "bless me, if *In vino veritas* be a true saying, then, for all the fine confidence you professed with me, just now, distrust, deep distrust, underlies it; and ten thousand strong, like the Irish Rebellion, breaks out in you now. That wine, good wine, should do it! Upon my soul," half seriously, half humorously, securing the bottle, "you shall drink no more of it. Wine was meant to gladden the heart, not grieve it; to heighten confidence, not depress it."

Sobered, shamed, all but confounded, by this raillery, the most telling rebuke under such circumstances, the merchant stared about him, and then, with altered mien, stammeringly confessed, that he was almost as much surprised as his companion, at what had escaped him. He did not understand it; was quite at a loss to account for such a rhapsody popping out of him unbidden. It could hardly be the champagne; he felt his brain unaffected; in fact, if anything, the wine had acted upon it something like white of egg in coffee, clarifying and brightening.

"Brightening? brightening it may be, but less like the white of egg in coffee, than like stove-lustre on a stove—black, brightening. Seriously, I repent calling for the champagne. To a temperament like yours, champagne is not to be recommended. Pray, my dear sir, do you feel quite yourself again? Confidence restored?"

"I hope so; I think I may say it is so. But we have had a long talk, and I think I must retire now."

So saying, the merchant rose, and making his adieus, left the table with the air of one, mortified at having been tempted by his own honest goodness, accidentally stimulated into making mad disclosures—to himself as to another—of the queer, unaccountable caprices of his natural heart.

Chapter 14

As THE LAST CHAPTER was begun with a reminder looking forwards, so the present must consist of one glancing backwards.

To some, it may raise a degree of surprise that one so full of confidence, as the merchant has throughout shown himself, up to the moment of his late sudden impulsiveness, should, in that instance, have betrayed such a depth of discontent. He may be thought inconsistent, and even so he is. But for this, is the author to be blamed? True, it may be urged that there is nothing a writer of fiction should more carefully see to, as there is nothing a sensible reader will more carefully look for, than that, in the depiction of any character, its consistency should be preserved. But this, though at first blush, seeming reasonable enough, may, upon a closer view, prove not so much so. For how does it couple with another requirement—equally insisted upon, perhaps—that, while to all fiction is allowed some play of invention, yet, fiction based on fact should never be contradictory to it; and is it not a fact, that, in real life, a consistent character is a *rara avis*? Which being so, the distaste of readers to the contrary sort in books, can hardly arise from any sense of their untrueness. It may rather be from perplexity as to understanding them. But if the acutest sage be often at his wits' ends to understand living character, shall those who are not sages expect to run and read character in those mere phantoms which flit along a page, like shadows along a wall? That fiction, where every character can, by reason of its consistency, be comprehended at a glance, either exhibits but sections of character, making them appear for wholes, or else is very untrue to reality; while, on the other hand, that author who draws a character, even though to common view incongruous in its parts, as the flying-squirrel, and, at different periods, as much at variance with itself as the caterpillar is with the butterfly into which it changes, may yet, in so doing, be not false but faithful to facts.

If reason be judge, no writer has produced such inconsistent characters as nature herself has. It must call for no small sagacity in a reader unerringly to discriminate in a novel between the inconsistencies of conception and those of life. As elsewhere, experience is the only guide here; but as no one man's experience can be coextensive with *what is*, it may be unwise in every case to rest upon it. When the duck-billed beaver of Australia was first brought stuffed to England, the naturalists, appealing to their classifications, maintained that there was, in reality, no such creature; the bill in the specimen must needs be, in some way, artificially stuck on.

But let nature, to the perplexity of the naturalists, produce her duck-billed beavers as she may, lesser authors, some may hold, have no business to be perplexing readers with duck-billed characters. Always, they should represent human nature not in obscurity, but transparency, which, indeed, is the practice with most novelists, and is, perhaps, in certain cases, someway felt to be a kind of honor rendered by them to their kind. But whether it involve honor or otherwise might be mooted, considering that, if these waters of human nature can be so readily seen through, it may be either that they are very pure or very shallow. Upon the whole, it might rather be thought, that he, who, in view of its inconsistencies, says of human nature the same that, in view of its contrasts, is said of the divine nature, that it is past finding out, thereby evinces a better appreciation of it than he who, by always representing it in a clear light, leaves it to be inferred that he clearly knows all about it.

But though there is a prejudice against inconsistent characters in books, yet the prejudice bears the other way, when what seemed at first their inconsistency, afterwards, by the skill of the writer, turns out to be their good keeping. The great masters excel in nothing so much as in this very particular. They challenge astonishment at the tangled web of some character, and then raise admiration still greater at their satisfactory unraveling of it; in this way throwing open, sometimes to the understanding even of school misses, the last complications of that spirit which is affirmed by its Creator to be fearfully and wonderfully made.

At least, something like this is claimed for certain psychological novelists; nor will the claim be here disputed. Yet, as touching this point, it may prove suggestive, that all those sallies of ingenuity, having for their end the revelation of human nature on fixed principles, have, by the best judges, been excluded with contempt from the ranks of the sciences— palmistry, physiognomy, phrenology, psychology. Likewise, the fact, that in all ages such conflicting views have, by the most eminent minds, been taken of mankind, would, as with other topics, seem some presumption of a pretty general and pretty thorough ignorance of it. Which may appear the less improbable if it be considered that, after poring over the best novels professing to portray human nature, the studious youth will still run risk of being too often at fault upon actually entering the world; whereas, had he been furnished with a true delineation, it ought to fare with him something as with a stranger entering, map in hand. Boston town; the streets may be very crooked, he may often pause; but, thanks to his true map, he does not hopelessly lose his way. Nor, to this comparison, can it be an adequate objection, that the twistings of the town are always the same, and those of human nature subject to variation. The grand points of human nature are the same to-day they were a thousand years ago. The only variability in them is in expression, not in feature.

But as, in spite of seeming discouragement, some mathematicians are yet in hopes of hitting upon an exact method of determining the longitude, the more earnest psychologists may, in the face of previous failures, still cherish expectations with regard to some mode of infallibly discovering the heart of man.

But enough has been said by way of apology for whatever may have seemed amiss or obscure in the character of the merchant; so nothing remains but to turn to our comedy, or, rather, to pass from the comedy of thought to that of action.

Chapter 15

THE MERCHANT HAVING withdrawn, the other remained
seated alone for a time, with the air of one who, after
having conversed with some excellent man, carefully ponders
what fell from him, however intellectually inferior it may be,
that none of the profit may be lost; happy if from any honest
word he has heard he can derive some hint, which, besides
confirming him in the theory of virtue, may, likewise, serve
for a finger-post to virtuous action.

Ere long his eye brightened, as if some such hint was now
caught. He rises, book in hand, quits the cabin, and enters
upon a sort of corridor, narrow and dim, a by-way to a retreat
less ornate and cheery than the former; in short, the emigrants' quarters; but which, owing to the present trip being a
down-river one, will doubtless be found comparatively ten-
antless. Owing to obstructions against the side windows, the
whole place is dim and dusky; very much so, for the most
part; yet, by starts, haggardly lit here and there by narrow,
capricious sky-lights in the cornices. But there would seem no
special need for light, the place being designed more to pass
the night in, than the day; in brief, a pine barrens dormitory,
of knotty pine bunks, without bedding. As with the nests in
the geometrical towns of the associate penguin and pelican,
these bunks were disposed with Philadelphian regularity, but,
like the cradle of the oriole, they were pendulous, and, moreover, were, so to speak, three-story cradles; the description of
one of which will suffice for all.

Four ropes, secured to the ceiling, passed downwards
through auger-holes bored in the corners of three rough
planks, which at equal distances rested on knots vertically tied
in the ropes, the lowermost plank but an inch or two from
the floor, the whole affair resembling, on a large scale, rope
book-shelves; only, instead of hanging firmly against a wall,
they swayed to and fro at the least suggestion of motion, but
were more especially lively upon the provocation of a green

emigrant sprawling into one, and trying to lay himself out there, when the cradling would be such as almost to toss him back whence he came. In consequence, one less inexperienced, essaying repose on the uppermost shelf, was liable to serious disturbance, should a raw beginner select a shelf beneath. Sometimes a throng of poor emigrants, coming at night in a sudden rain to occupy these oriole nests, would—through ignorance of their peculiarity—bring about such a rocking uproar of carpentry, joining to it such an uproar of exclamations, that it seemed as if some luckless ship, with all its crew, was being dashed to pieces among the rocks. They were beds devised by some sardonic foe of poor travelers, to deprive them of that tranquillity which should precede, as well as accompany, slumber.—Procrustean beds, on whose hard grain humble worth and honesty writhed, still invoking repose, while but torment responded. Ah, did any one make such a bunk for himself, instead of having it made for him, it might be just, but how cruel, to say, You must lie on it!

But, purgatory as the place would appear, the stranger advances into it; and, like Orpheus in his gay descent to Tartarus, lightly hums to himself an opera snatch.

Suddenly there is a rustling, then a creaking, one of the cradles swings out from a murky nook, a sort of wasted penguin-flipper is supplicatingly put forth, while a wail like that of Dives is heard:—"Water, water!"

It was the miser of whom the merchant had spoken.

Swift as a sister-of-charity, the stranger hovers over him:—"My poor, poor sir, what can I do for you?"

"Ugh, ugh—water!"

Darting out, he procures a glass, returns, and, holding it to the sufferer's lips, supports his head while he drinks: "And did they let you lie here, my poor sir, racked with this parching thirst?"

The miser, a lean old man, whose flesh seemed salted codfish, dry as combustibles; head, like one whittled by an idiot out of a knot; flat, bony mouth, nipped between buzzard nose and chin; expression, flitting between hunks and imbecile—now one, now the other—he made no response. His eyes were closed, his cheek lay upon an old white moleskin coat, rolled under his head, like a wizened apple upon a grimy snow-bank.

Revived at last, he inclined towards his ministrant, and, in a voice disastrous with a cough, said: — "I am old and miserable, a poor beggar, not worth a shoe-string—how can I repay you?"

"By giving me your confidence."

"Confidence!" he squeaked, with changed manner, while the pallet swung, "little left at my age, but take the stale remains, and welcome."

"Such as it is, though, you give it. Very good. Now give me a hundred dollars."

Upon this the miser was all panic. His hands groped towards his waist, then suddenly flew upward beneath his moleskin pillow, and there lay clutching something out of sight. Meantime, to himself he incoherently mumbled: — "Confidence? Cant, gammon! Confidence? hum, bubble! —Confidence? fetch, gouge!—Hundred dollars?—hundred devils!"

Half spent, he lay mute awhile, then feebly raising himself, in a voice for the moment made strong by the sarcasm, said, "A hundred dollars? rather high price to put upon confidence. But don't you see I am a poor, old rat here, dying in the wainscot? You have served me; but, wretch that I am, I can but cough you my thanks,—ugh, ugh, ugh!"

This time his cough was so violent that its convulsions were imparted to the plank, which swung him about like a stone in a sling preparatory to its being hurled.

"Ugh, ugh, ugh!"

"What a shocking cough. I wish my friend the herb-doctor was here now; a box of his Omni-Balsamic Reinvigorator would do you good."

"Ugh, ugh, ugh!"

"I've a good mind to go find him. He's aboard somewhere. I saw his long, snuff-colored surtout. Trust me, his medicines are the best in the world."

"Ugh, ugh, ugh!"

"Oh, how sorry I am."

"No doubt of it," squeaked the other again, "but go, get your charity out on deck. There parade the pursy peacocks;

they don't cough down here in desertion and darkness, like poor old me. Look how scaly a pauper I am, clove with this churchyard cough. Ugh, ugh, ugh!"

"Again, how sorry I feel, not only for your cough, but your poverty. Such a rare chance made unavailable. Did you have but the sum named, how I could invest it for you. Treble profits. But confidence—I fear that, even had you the precious cash, you would not have the more precious confidence I speak of."

"Ugh, ugh, ugh!" flightily raising himself. "What's that? How, how? Then you don't want the money for yourself?"

"My dear, *dear* sir, how could you impute to me such preposterous self-seeking? To solicit out of hand, for my private behoof, an hundred dollars from a perfect stranger? I am not mad, my dear sir."

"How, how?" still more bewildered, "do you, then, go about the world, gratis, seeking to invest people's money for them?"

"My humble profession, sir. I live not for myself; but the world will not have confidence in me, and yet confidence in me were great gain."

"But, but," in a kind of vertigo, " what do—do you do—do with people's money? Ugh, ugh! How is the gain made?"

"To tell that would ruin me. That known, every one would be going into the business, and it would be overdone. A secret, a mystery—all I have to do with you is to receive your confidence, and all you have to do with me is, in due time, to receive it back, thrice paid in trebling profits."

"What, what?" imbecility in the ascendant once more; "but the vouchers, the vouchers," suddenly hunkish again.

"Honesty's best voucher is honesty's face."

"Can't see yours, though," peering through the obscurity.

From this last alternating flicker of rationality, the miser fell back, sputtering, into his previous gibberish, but it took now an arithmetical turn. Eyes closed, he lay muttering to himself—

"One hundred, one hundred—two hundred, two hundred—three hundred, three hundred."

He opened his eyes, feebly stared, and still more feebly said—

"It's a little dim here, ain't it? Ugh, ugh! But, as well as my poor old eyes can see, you look honest."

"I am glad to hear that."

"If—if, now, I should put"—trying to raise himself, but vainly, excitement having all but exhausted him—"if, if now, I should put, put—"

"No ifs. Downright confidence, or none. So help me heaven. I will have no half-confidences."

He said it with an indifferent and superior air, and seemed moving to go.

"Don't, don't leave me, friend; bear with me; age can't help some distrust; it can't, friend, it can't. Ugh, ugh, ugh! Oh, I am so old and miserable. I ought to have a guard*ee*an. Tell me, if—"

"If? No more!"

"Stay! how soon—ugh, ugh!—would my money be trebled? How soon, friend?"

"You won't confide. Good-bye!"

"Stay, stay," falling back now like an infant, "I confide, I confide; help, friend, my distrust!"

From an old buckskin pouch, tremulously dragged forth, ten hoarded eagles, tarnished into the appearance of ten old horn-buttons, were taken, and half-eagerly, half-reluctantly, offered.

"I know not whether I should accept this slack confidence," said the other coldly, receiving the gold, "but an eleventh-hour confidence, a sick-bed confidence, a distempered, death-bed confidence, after all. Give me the healthy confidence of healthy men, with their healthy wits about them. But let that pass. All right. Good-bye!"

"Nay, back, back—receipt, my receipt! Ugh, ugh, ugh! Who are you? What have I done? Where go you? My gold, my gold! Ugh, ugh, ugh!"

But, unluckily for this final flicker of reason, the stranger was now beyond ear-shot, nor was any one else within hearing of so feeble a call.

Chapter 16

A SICK MAN, AFTER SOME IMPATIENCE, IS INDUCED
TO BECOME A PATIENT

T HE SKY SLIDES into blue, the bluffs into bloom; the rapid Mississippi expands; runs sparkling and gurgling, all over in eddies; one magnified wake of a seventy-four. The sun comes out, a golden huzzar, from his tent, flashing his helm on the world. All things, warmed in the landscape, leap. Speeds the dædal boat as a dream.

But, withdrawn in a corner, wrapped about in a shawl, sits an unparticipating man, visited, but not warmed, by the sun—a plant whose hour seems over, while buds are blowing and seeds are astir. On a stool at his left sits a stranger in a snuff-colored surtout, the collar thrown back; his hand waving in persuasive gesture, his eye beaming with hope. But not easily may hope be awakened in one long tranced into hopelessness by a chronic complaint.

To some remark the sick man, by word or look, seemed to have just made an impatiently querulous answer, when, with a deprecatory air, the other resumed:

"Nay, think not I seek to cry up my treatment by crying down that of others. And yet, when one is confident he has truth on his side, and that it is not on the other, it is no very easy thing to be charitable; not that temper is the bar, but conscience; for charity would beget toleration, you know, which is a kind of implied permitting, and in effect a kind of countenancing; and that which is countenanced is so far furthered. But should untruth be furthered? Still, while for the world's good I refuse to further the cause of these mineral doctors, I would fain regard them, not as willful wrong-doers, but good Samaritans erring. And is this— I put it to you, sir—is this the view of an arrogant rival and pretender?"

His physical power all dribbled and gone, the sick man replied not by voice or by gesture; but, with feeble dumb-show of his face, seemed to be saying, "Pray leave me; who was ever cured by talk?"

But the other, as if not unused to make allowances for such despondency, proceeded; and kindly, yet firmly:

"You tell me, that by advice of an eminent physiologist in Louisville, you took tincture of iron. For what? To restore your lost energy. And how? Why, in healthy subjects iron is naturally found in the blood, and iron in the bar is strong; ergo, iron is the source of animal invigoration. But you being deficient in vigor, it follows that the cause is deficiency of iron. Iron, then, must be put into you; and so your tincture. Now as to the theory here, I am mute. But in modesty assuming its truth, and then, as a plain man viewing that theory in practice, I would respectfully question your eminent physiologist: 'Sir,' I would say, 'though by natural processes, lifeless natures taken as nutriment become vitalized, yet is a lifeless nature, under any circumstances, capable of a living transmission, with all its qualities as a lifeless nature unchanged? If, sir, nothing can be incorporated with the living body but by assimilation, and if that implies the conversion of one thing to a different thing (as, in a lamp, oil is assimilated into flame), is it, in this view, likely, that by banqueting on fat, Calvin Edson will fatten? That is, will what is fat on the board prove fat on the bones? If it will, then, sir, what is iron in the vial will prove iron in the vein.' Seems that conclusion too confident?"

But the sick man again turned his dumb-show look, as much as to say, "Pray leave me. Why, with painful words, hint the vanity of that which the pains of this body have too painfully proved?"

But the other, as if unobservant of that querulous look, went on:

"But this notion, that science can play farmer to the flesh, making there what living soil it pleases, seems not so strange as that other conceit—that science is now-a-days so expert that, in consumptive cases, as yours, it can, by prescription of the inhalation of certain vapors, achieve the sublimest act of omnipotence, breathing into all but lifeless dust the breath of life. For did you not tell me, my poor sir, that by order of the great chemist in Baltimore, for three weeks you were never driven out without a respirator, and for a given time of every day sat bolstered up in a sort of gasometer, inspiring vapors generated by the burning of drugs? as if this concocted atmosphere of man were an antidote to the poison of God's natural air. Oh, who can wonder at that old reproach against science, that it is atheistical? And here is my prime reason for opposing these chemical practitioners, who have sought out so many inventions. For what do their inventions indicate, unless it be that kind and degree of pride in human skill, which seems scarce compatible with reverential dependence upon the power above? Try to rid my mind of it as I may, yet still these chemical practitioners with their tinctures, and fumes, and braziers, and occult incantations, seem to me like Pharaoh's vain sorcerers, trying to beat down the will of heaven. Day and night, in all charity, I intercede for them, that heaven may not, in its own language, be provoked to anger with their inventions; may not take vengeance of their inventions. A thousand pities that you should ever have been in the hands of these Egyptians."

But again came nothing but the dumb-show look, as much as to say, "Pray leave me; quacks, and indignation against quacks, both are vain."

But, once more, the other went on: "How different we herb-doctors! who claim nothing, invent nothing; but staff in hand, in glades, and upon hillsides, go about in nature, humbly seeking her cures. True Indian doctors, though not learned in names, we are not unfamiliar with essences—successors of Solomon the Wise, who knew all vegetables, from the cedar of Lebanon, to the hyssop on the wall. Yes, Solomon was the first of herb-doctors. Nor were the virtues of herbs unhonored by yet older ages. Is it not writ, that on a moonlight night,

> 'Medea gathered the enchanted herbs
> That did renew old Æson?'

Ah, would you but have confidence, you should be the new Æson, and I your Medea. A few vials of my Omni-Balsamic Reinvigorator would, I am certain, give you some strength."

Upon this, indignation and abhorrence seemed to work by their excess the effect promised of the balsam. Roused from that long apathy of impotence, the cadaverous man started, and, in a voice that was as the sound of obstructed air gurgling through a maze of broken honey-combs, cried: "Begone! You are all alike. The name of doctor, the dream of helper, condemns you. For years I have been but a gallipot for you experimentizers to rinse your experiments into, and now, in this livid skin, partake of the nature of my contents. Begone! I hate ye."

"I were inhuman, could I take affront at a want of confidence, born of too bitter an experience of betrayers. Yet, permit one who is not without feeling—"

"Begone! Just in that voice talked to me, not six months ago, the German doctor at the water cure, from which I now return, six months and sixty pangs nigher my grave."

"The water-cure? Oh, fatal delusion of the well-meaning Priessnitz!—Sir, trust me—"

"Begone!"

"Nay, an invalid should not always have his own way. Ah, sir, reflect how untimely this distrust in one like you. How weak you are; and weakness, is it not the time for confidence? Yes, when through weakness everything bids despair, then is the time to get strength by confidence."

Relenting in his air, the sick man cast upon him a long glance of beseeching, as if saying, "With confidence must come hope; and how can hope be?"

The herb-doctor took a sealed paper box from his surtout pocket, and holding it towards him, said solemnly, "Turn not away. This may be the last time of health's asking. Work upon yourself; invoke confidence, though from ashes; rouse it; for your life, rouse it, and invoke it, I say."

The other trembled, was silent; and then, a little commanding himself, asked the ingredients of the medicine.

"Herbs."

"What herbs? And the nature of them? And the reason for giving them?"

"It cannot be made known."

"Then I will none of you."

Sedately observant of the juiceless, joyless form before him, the herb-doctor was mute a moment, then said:—"I give up."

"How?"

"You are sick, and a philosopher."

"No, no;—not the last."

"But, to demand the ingredient, with the reason for giving, is the mark of a philosopher; just as the consequence is the penalty of a fool. A sick philosopher is incurable."

"Why?"

"Because he has no confidence."

"How does that make him incurable?"

"Because either he spurns his powder, or, if he take it, it proves a blank cartridge, though the same given to a rustic in like extremity, would act like a charm. I am no materialist; but the mind so acts upon the body, that if the one have no confidence, neither has the other."

Again, the sick man appeared not unmoved. He seemed to be thinking what in candid truth could be said to all this. At length, "You talk of confidence. How comes it that when brought low himself, the herb-doctor, who was most confident to prescribe in other cases, proves least confident to prescribe in his own; having small confidence in himself for himself?"

"But he has confidence in the brother he calls in. And that he does so, is no reproach to him, since he knows that when the body is prostrated, the mind is not erect. Yes, in this hour the herb-doctor does distrust himself, but not his art."

The sick man's knowledge did not warrant him to gainsay this. But he seemed not grieved at it; glad to be confuted in a way tending towards his wish.

"Then you give me hope?" his sunken eye turned up.

"Hope is proportioned to confidence. How much confidence you give me, so much hope do I give you. For this," lifting the box, "if all depended upon this, I should rest. It is nature's own."

"Nature!"

"Why do you start?"

"I know not," with a sort of shudder, "but I have heard of a book entitled 'Nature in Disease.' "

"A title I cannot approve; it is suspiciously scientific. 'Nature in Disease?' As if nature, divine nature, were aught but health; as if through nature disease is decreed! But did I not before hint of the tendency of science, that forbidden tree?

Sir, if despondency is yours from recalling that title, dismiss it. Trust me, nature is health; for health is good, and nature cannot work ill. As little can she work error. Get nature, and you get well. Now, I repeat, this medicine is nature's own."

Again the sick man could not, according to his light, conscientiously disprove what was said. Neither, as before, did he seem over-anxious to do so; the less, as in his sensitiveness it seemed to him, that hardly could he offer so to do without something like the appearance of a kind of implied irreligion; nor in his heart was he ungrateful, that since a spirit opposite to that pervaded all the herb-doctor's hopeful words, therefore, for hopefulness, he (the sick man) had not alone medical warrant, but also doctrinal.

"Then you do really think," hectically, "that if I take this medicine," mechanically reaching out for it, "I shall regain my health?"

"I will not encourage false hopes," relinquishing to him the box, "I will be frank with you. Though frankness is not always the weakness of the mineral practitioner, yet the herb doctor must be frank, or nothing. Now then, sir, in your case, a radical cure—such a cure, understand, as should make you robust—such a cure, sir, I do not and cannot promise."

"Oh, you need not! only restore me the power of being something else to others than a burdensome care, and to myself a droning grief. Only cure me of this misery of weakness; only make me so that I can walk about in the sun and not draw the flies to me, as lured by the coming of decay. Only do that—but that."

"You ask not much; you are wise; not in vain have you suffered. That little you ask, I think, can be granted. But remember, not in a day, nor a week, nor perhaps a month, but sooner or later; I say not exactly when, for I am neither prophet nor charlatan. Still, if, according to the directions in your box there, you take my medicine steadily, without assigning an especial day, near or remote, to discontinue it, then may you calmly look for some eventual result of good. But again I say, you must have confidence."

Feverishly he replied that he now trusted he had, and hourly should pray for its increase. When suddenly relapsing into one of those strange caprices peculiar to some invalids, he added: "But to one like me, it is so hard, so hard. The most confident hopes so often have failed me, and as often have I vowed never, no, never, to trust them again. Oh," feebly wringing his hands, "you do not know, you do not know."

"I know this, that never did a right confidence come to naught. But time is short; you hold your cure, to retain or reject."

"I retain," with a clinch, "and now how much?"

"As much as you can evoke from your heart and heaven."

"How?—the price of this medicine?"

"I thought it was confidence you meant; how much confidence you should have. The medicine,—that is half a dollar a vial. Your box holds six."

The money was paid.

"Now, sir," said the herb-doctor, "my business calls me away, and it may so be that I shall never see you again; if then—"

He paused, for the sick man's countenance fell blank.

"Forgive me," cried the other, "forgive that imprudent phrase 'never see you again.' Though I solely intended it with reference to myself, yet I had forgotten what your sensitiveness might be. I repeat, then, that it may be that we shall not soon have a second interview, so that hereafter, should another of my boxes be needed, you may not be able to replace it except by purchase at the shops; and, in so doing, you may run more or less risk of taking some not salutary mixture. For such is the popularity of the Omni-Balsamic Reinvigorator— thriving not by the credulity of the simple, but the trust of the wise—that certain contrivers have not been idle, though I would not, indeed, hastily affirm of them that they are aware of the sad consequences to the public. Homicides and murderers, some call those contrivers; but I do not; for murder (if such a crime be possible) comes from the heart, and these men's motives come from the purse. Were they not in poverty, I think they would hardly do what they do. Still, the public interests forbid that I should let their needy device for a living succeed. In short, I have adopted precautions. Take the wrapper from any of my vials and hold it to the light, you will see water-marked in capitals the word 'confidence,' which is the countersign of the medicine, as I wish it was of the world. The wrapper bears that mark or else the medicine is counterfeit. But if still any lurking doubt should remain, pray enclose the wrapper to this address," handing a card, "and by return mail I will answer."

At first the sick man listened, with the air of vivid interest, but gradually, while the other was still talking, another strange caprice came over him, and he presented the aspect of the most calamitous dejection.

"How now?" said the herb-doctor.

"You told me to have confidence, said that confidence was indispensable, and here you preach to me distrust. Ah, truth will out!"

"I told you, you must have confidence, unquestioning confidence, I meant confidence in the genuine medicine, and the genuine *me*."

"But in your absence, buying vials purporting to be yours, it seems I cannot have unquestioning confidence."

"Prove all the vials; trust those which are true."

"But to doubt, to suspect, to prove—to have all this wearing work to be doing continually—how opposed to confidence. It is evil!"

"From evil comes good. Distrust is a stage to confidence. How has it proved in our interview? But your voice is husky; I have let you talk too much. You hold your cure; I leave you. But stay—when I hear that health is yours, I will not, like some I know, vainly make boasts; but, giving glory where all glory is due, say, with the devout herb-doctor, Iapis in Virgil, when, in the unseen but efficacious presence of Venus, he with simples healed the wound of Æneas:—

> 'This is no mortal work, no cure of mine,
> Nor art's effect, but done by power divine.' "

Chapter 17

IN A KIND of ante-cabin, a number of respectable looking people, male and female, way-passengers, recently come on board, are listlessly sitting in a mutually shy sort of silence.

Holding up a small, square bottle, ovally labeled with the engraving of a countenance full of soft pity as that of the Romish-painted Madonna, the herb-doctor passes slowly among them, benignly urbane, turning this way and that, saying:—

"Ladies and gentlemen, I hold in my hand here the Samaritan Pain Dissuader, thrice-blessed discovery of that disinterested friend of humanity whose portrait you see. Pure vegetable extract. Warranted to remove the acutest pain within less than ten minutes. Five hundred dollars to be forfeited on failure. Especially efficacious in heart disease and tic-douloureux. Observe the expression of this pledged friend of humanity.—Price only fifty cents."

In vain. After the first idle stare, his auditors—in pretty good health, it seemed—instead of encouraging his politeness, appeared, if anything, impatient of it; and, perhaps, only diffidence, or some small regard for his feelings, prevented them from telling him so. But, insensible to their coldness, or charitably overlooking it, he more wooingly than ever resumed: "May I venture upon a small supposition? Have I your kind leave, ladies and gentlemen?"

To which modest appeal, no one had the kindness to answer a syllable.

"Well," said he, resignedly, "silence is at least not denial, and may be consent. My supposition is this: possibly some lady, here present, has a dear friend at home, a bed-ridden sufferer from spinal complaint. If so, what gift more appropriate to that sufferer than this tasteful little bottle of Pain Dissuader?"

Again he glanced about him, but met much the same reception as before. Those faces, alien alike to sympathy or surprise, seemed patiently to say, "We are travelers; and, as such, must expect to meet, and quietly put up with, many antic fools, and more antic quacks."

"Ladies and gentlemen," (deferentially fixing his eyes upon their now self-complacent faces) "ladies and gentlemen, might I, by your kind leave, venture upon one other small supposition? It is this: that there is scarce a sufferer, this noonday, writhing on his bed, but in his hour he sat satisfactorily healthy and happy; that the Samaritan Pain Dissuader is the one only balm for that to which each living creature—who knows?—may be a draughted victim, present or prospective. In short:—Oh, Happiness on my right hand, and oh, Security on my left, can ye wisely adore a Providence, and not think it wisdom to provide?—Provide!" (Uplifting the bottle.)

What immediate effect, if any, this appeal might have had, is uncertain. For just then the boat touched at a houseless landing, scooped, as by a land-slide, out of sombre forests; back through which led a road, the sole one, which, from its narrowness, and its being walled up with story on story of dusk, matted foliage, presented the vista of some cavernous old gorge in a city, like haunted Cock Lane in London. Issuing from that road, and crossing that landing, there stooped his shaggy form in the door-way, and entered the ante-cabin, with a step so burdensome that shot seemed in his pockets, a kind of invalid Titan in homespun; his beard blackly pendant, like the Carolina-moss, and dank with cypress dew; his countenance tawny and shadowy as an iron-ore country in a clouded day. In one hand he carried a heavy walking-stick of swamp-oak; with the other, led a puny girl, walking in moccasins, not improbably his child, but evidently of alien maternity, perhaps Creole, or even Camanche. Her eye would have been large for a woman, and was inky as the pools of falls among mountain-pines. An Indian blanket, orange-hued, and fringed with bead tassel-work, appeared that morning to have shielded the child from heavy showers. Her limbs were tremulous; she seemed a little Cassandra, in nervousness.

No sooner was the pair spied by the herb-doctor, than with a cheerful air, both arms extended like a host's, he advanced, and taking the child's reluctant hand, said, trippingly: "On your travels, ah, my little May Queen? Glad to see you. What pretty moccasins. Nice to dance in." Then with a half caper sang—

> " 'Hey diddle, diddle, the cat and the fiddle;
> The cow jumped over the moon.'

Come, chirrup, chirrup, my little robin!"

Which playful welcome drew no responsive playfulness from the child, nor appeared to gladden or conciliate the father; but rather, if anything, to dash the dead weight of his heavy-hearted expression with a smile hypochondriacally scornful.

Sobering down now, the herb-doctor addressed the stranger in a manly, business-like way—a transition which, though it might seem a little abrupt, did not appear constrained, and, indeed, served to show that his recent levity was less the habit of a frivolous nature, than the frolic condescension of a kindly heart.

"Excuse me," said he, "but, if I err not, I was speaking to you the other day;—on a Kentucky boat, wasn't it?"

"Never to me," was the reply; the voice deep and lonesome enough to have come from the bottom of an abandoned coal-shaft.

"Ah!—But am I again mistaken, (his eye falling on the swamp-oak stick,) or don't you go a little lame, sir?"

"Never was lame in my life."

"Indeed? I fancied I had perceived not a limp, but a hitch, a slight hitch;—some experience in these things—divined some hidden cause of the hitch—buried bullet, may be—some dragoons in the Mexican war discharged with such, you know.—Hard fate!" he sighed, "little pity for it, for who sees it?—have you dropped anything?"

Why, there is no telling, but the stranger was bowed over, and might have seemed bowing for the purpose of picking up something, were it not that, as arrested in the imperfect posture, he for the moment so remained; slanting his tall stature like a mainmast yielding to the gale, or Adam to the thunder.

The little child pulled him. With a kind of a surge he righted himself, for an instant looked toward the herb-doctor; but, either from emotion or aversion, or both together, withdrew his eyes, saying nothing. Presently, still stooping, he seated himself, drawing his child between his knees, his massy hands tremulous, and still averting his face, while up into the compassionate one of the herb-doctor the child turned a fixed, melancholy glance of repugnance.

The herb-doctor stood observant a moment, then said:

"Surely you have pain, strong pain, somewhere; in strong frames pain is strongest. Try, now, my specific," (holding it up). "Do but look at the expression of this friend of humanity. Trust me, certain cure for any pain in the world. Won't you look?"

"No," choked the other.

"Very good. Merry time to you, little May Queen."

And so, as if he would intrude his cure upon no one, moved pleasantly off, again crying his wares, nor now at last without result. A new-comer, not from the shore, but another part of the boat, a sickly young man, after some questions, purchased a bottle. Upon this, others of the company began a little to wake up as it were; the scales of indifference or prejudice fell from their eyes; now, at last, they seemed to have an inkling that here was something not undesirable which might be had for the buying.

But while, ten times more briskly bland than ever, the herb-doctor was driving his benevolent trade, accompanying each sale with added praises of the thing traded, all at once the dusk giant, seated at some distance, unexpectedly raised his voice with—

"What was that you last said?"

The question was put distinctly, yet resonantly, as when a great clock-bell—stunning admonisher—strikes one; and the stroke, though single, comes bedded in the belfry clamor.

All proceedings were suspended. Hands held forth for the specific were withdrawn, while every eye turned towards the direction whence the question came. But, no way abashed, the herb-doctor, elevating his voice with even more than wonted self-possession, replied—

"I was saying what, since you wish it, I cheerfully repeat, that the Samaritan Pain Dissuader, which I here hold in my hand, will either cure or ease any pain you please, within ten minutes after its application."

"Does it produce insensibility?"

"By no means. Not the least of its merits is, that it is not an opiate. It kills pain without killing feeling."

"You lie! Some pains cannot be eased but by producing insensibility, and cannot be cured but by producing death."

Beyond this the dusk giant said nothing; neither, for impairing the other's market, did there appear much need to. After eying the rude speaker a moment with an expression of mingled admiration and consternation, the company silently exchanged glances of mutual sympathy under unwelcome conviction. Those who had purchased looked sheepish or ashamed; and a cynical-looking little man, with a thin flaggy beard, and a countenance ever wearing the rudiments of a grin, seated alone in a corner commanding a good view of the scene, held a rusty hat before his face.

But, again, the herb-doctor, without noticing the retort, overbearing though it was, began his panegyrics anew, and in a tone more assured than before, going so far now as to say that his specific was sometimes almost as effective in cases of mental suffering as in cases of physical; or rather, to be more precise, in cases when, through sympathy, the two sorts of pain coöperated into a climax of both—in such cases, he said, the specific had done very well. He cited an example: Only three bottles, faithfully taken, cured a Louisiana widow (for three weeks sleepless in a darkened chamber) of neuralgic sorrow for the loss of husband and child, swept off in one night by the last epidemic. For the truth of this, a printed voucher was produced, duly signed.

While he was reading it aloud, a sudden side-blow all but felled him.

It was the giant, who, with a countenance lividly epileptic with hypochondriac mania, exclaimed—

"Profane fiddler on heart-strings! Snake!"

More he would have added, but, convulsed, could not; so, without another word, taking up the child, who had followed him, went with a rocking pace out of the cabin.

"Regardless of decency, and lost to humanity!" exclaimed the herb-doctor, with much ado recovering himself. Then, after a pause, during which he examined his bruise, not omitting to apply externally a little of his specific, and with some success, as it would seem, plained to himself:

"No, no, I won't seek redress; innocence is my redress. But," turning upon them all, "if that man's wrathful blow provokes me to no wrath, should his evil distrust arouse you to distrust? I do devoutly hope," proudly raising voice and arm, "for the honor of humanity—hope that, despite this coward assault, the Samaritan Pain Dissuader stands unshaken in the confidence of all who hear me!"

But, injured as he was, and patient under it, too, somehow his case excited as little compassion as his oratory now did enthusiasm. Still, pathetic to the last, he continued his appeals, notwithstanding the frigid regard of the company, till, suddenly interrupting himself, as if in reply to a quick summons from without, he said hurriedly, "I come, I come," and so, with every token of precipitate dispatch, out of the cabin the herb-doctor went.

Chapter 18

INQUEST INTO THE TRUE CHARACTER OF THE HERB-DOCTOR

S HA'N'T SEE THAT FELLOW again in a hurry," remarked an auburn-haired gentleman, to his neighbor with a hook-nose. "Never knew an operator so completely unmasked."

"But do you think it the fair thing to unmask an operator that way?"

"Fair? It is right."

"Supposing that at high 'change on the Paris Bourse, Asmodeus should lounge in, distributing hand-bills, revealing the true thoughts and designs of all the operators present—would that be the fair thing in Asmodeus? Or, as Hamlet says, were it 'to consider the thing too curiously?' "

"We won't go into that. But since you admit the fellow to be a knave—"

"I don't admit it. Or, if I did, I take it back. Shouldn't wonder if, after all, he is no knave at all, or, but little of one. What can you prove against him?"

"I can prove that he makes dupes."

"Many held in honor do the same; and many, not wholly knaves, do it too."

"How about that last?"

"He is not wholly at heart a knave, I fancy, among whose dupes is himself. Did you not see our quack friend apply to himself his own quackery? A fanatic quack; essentially a fool, though effectively a knave."

Bending over, and looking down between his knees on the floor, the auburn-haired gentleman meditatively scribbled there awhile with his cane, then, glancing up, said:

"I can't conceive how you, in any way, can hold him a fool. How he talked—so glib, so pat, so well."

"A smart fool always talks well; takes a smart fool to be tonguey."

In much the same strain the discussion continued—the hook-nosed gentleman talking at large and excellently, with a view of demonstrating that a smart fool always talks just so.

Ere long he talked to such purpose as almost to convince.

Presently, back came the person of whom the auburn-haired gentleman had predicted that he would not return. Conspicuous in the door-way he stood, saying, in a clear voice, "Is the agent of the Seminole Widow and Orphan Asylum within here?"

No one replied.

"Is there within here any agent or any member of any charitable institution whatever?"

No one seemed competent to answer, or, no one thought it worth while to.

"If there be within here any such person, I have in my hand two dollars for him."

Some interest was manifested.

"I was called away so hurriedly, I forgot this part of my duty. With the proprietor of the Samaritan Pain Dissuader it is a rule, to devote, on the spot, to some benevolent purpose, the half of the proceeds of sales. Eight bottles were disposed of among this company. Hence, four half-dollars remain to charity. Who, as steward, takes the money?"

One or two pair of feet moved upon the floor, as with a sort of itching; but nobody rose.

"Does diffidence prevail over duty? If, I say, there be any gentleman, or any lady, either, here present, who is in any connection with any charitable institution whatever, let him or her come forward. He or she happening to have at hand no certificate of such connection, makes no difference. Not of a suspicious temper, thank God, I shall have confidence in whoever offers to take the money."

A demure-looking woman, in a dress rather tawdry and rumpled, here drew her veil well down and rose; but, marking every eye upon her, thought it advisable, upon the whole, to sit down again.

"Is it to be believed that, in this Christian company, there is no one charitable person? I mean, no one connected with any charity? Well, then, is there no object of charity here?"

Upon this, an unhappy-looking woman, in a sort of mourning, neat, but sadly worn, hid her face behind a meagre bundle, and was heard to sob. Meantime, as not seeing or hearing her, the herb-doctor again spoke, and this time not unpathetically:

"Are there none here who feel in need of help, and who, in accepting such help, would feel that they, in their time, have given or done more than may ever be given or done to them? Man or woman, is there none such here?"

The sobs of the woman were more audible, though she strove to repress them. While nearly every one's attention was bent upon her, a man of the appearance of a day-laborer, with a white bandage across his face, concealing the side of the nose, and who, for coolness' sake, had been sitting in his red-flannel shirt-sleeves, his coat thrown across one shoulder, the darned cuffs drooping behind—this man shufflingly rose, and, with a pace that seemed the lingering memento of the lock-step of convicts, went up for a duly-qualified claimant.

"Poor wounded huzzar!" sighed the herb-doctor, and dropping the money into the man's clam-shell of a hand turned and departed.

The recipient of the alms was about moving after, when the auburn-haired gentleman staid him: "Don't be frightened, you; but I want to see those coins. Yes, yes; good silver, good silver. There, take them again, and while you are about it, go bandage the rest of yourself behind something. D'ye hear? Consider yourself, wholly, the scar of a nose, and be off with yourself."

Being of a forgiving nature, or else from emotion not daring to trust his voice, the man silently, but not without some precipitancy, withdrew.

"Strange," said the auburn-haired gentleman, returning to his friend, "the money was good money."

"Aye, and where your fine knavery now? Knavery to devote the half of one's receipts to charity? He's a fool I say again."

"Others might call him an original genius."

"Yes, being original in his folly. Genius? His genius is a cracked pate, and, as this age goes, not much originality about that."

"May he not be knave, fool, and genius all together?"

"I beg pardon," here said a third person with a gossiping

expression who had been listening, "but you are somewhat puzzled by this man, and well you may be."

"Do you know anything about him?" asked the hooked-nosed gentleman.

"No, but I suspect him for something."

"Suspicion. We want knowledge."

"Well, suspect first and know next. True knowledge comes but by suspicion or revelation. That's my maxim."

"And yet," said the auburn-haired gentleman, "since a wise man will keep even some certainties to himself, much more some suspicions, at least he will at all events so do till they ripen into knowledge."

"Do you hear that about the wise man?" said the hook-nosed gentleman, turning upon the new comer. "Now what is it you suspect of this fellow?"

"I shrewdly suspect him," was the eager response, "for one of those Jesuit emissaries prowling all over our country. The better to accomplish their secret designs, they assume, at times, I am told, the most singular masques; sometimes, in appearance, the absurdest."

This, though indeed for some reason causing a droll smile upon the face of the hook-nosed gentleman, added a third angle to the discussion, which now became a sort of triangular duel, and ended, at last, with but a triangular result.

Chapter 19

A SOLDIER OF FORTUNE

"Mexico? Molino del Rey? Resaca de la Palma?"

"Resaca de la *Tombs*!"

Leaving his reputation to take care of itself, since, as is not seldom the case, he knew nothing of its being in debate, the herb-doctor, wandering towards the forward part of the boat, had there espied a singular character in a grimy old regimental coat, a countenance at once grim and wizened, interwoven paralyzed legs, stiff as icicles, suspended between rude crutches, while the whole rigid body, like a ship's long barometer on gimbals, swung to and fro, mechanically faithful to the motion of the boat. Looking downward while he swung, the cripple seemed in a brown study.

As moved by the sight, and conjecturing that here was some battered hero from the Mexican battle-fields, the herb-doctor had sympathetically accosted him as above, and received the above rather dubious reply. As, with a half moody, half surly sort of air that reply was given, the cripple, by a voluntary jerk, nervously increased his swing (his custom when seized by emotion), so that one would have thought some squall had suddenly rolled the boat and with it the barometer.

"Tombs? my friend," exclaimed the herb-doctor in mild surprise. "You have not descended to the dead, have you? I had imagined you a scarred campaigner, one of the noble children of war, for your dear country a glorious sufferer. But you are Lazarus, it seems."

"Yes, he who had sores."

"Ah, the *other* Lazarus. But I never knew that either of them was in the army," glancing at the dilapidated regimentals.

"That will do now. Jokes enough."

"Friend," said the other reproachfully, "you think amiss. On principle, I greet unfortunates with some pleasant remark, the better to call off their thoughts from their troubles. The physician who is at once wise and humane seldom unreservedly sympathizes with his patient. But come, I am a herb-

939

doctor, and also a natural bone-setter. I may be sanguine, but I think I can do something for you. You look up now. Give me your story. Ere I undertake a cure, I require a full account of the case."

"You can't help me," returned the cripple gruffly. "Go away."

"You seem sadly destitute of—"

"No I ain't destitute; to-day, at least, I can pay my way."

"The Natural Bone-setter is happy, indeed, to hear that. But you were premature. I was deploring your destitution, not of cash, but of confidence. You think the Natural Bone-setter can't help you. Well, suppose he can't, have you any objection to telling him your story? You, my friend, have, in a signal way, experienced adversity. Tell me, then, for my private good, how, without aid from the noble cripple, Epictetus, you have arrived at his heroic sang-froid in misfortune."

At these words the cripple fixed upon the speaker the hard ironic eye of one toughened and defiant in misery, and, in the end, grinned upon him with his unshaven face like an ogre.

"Come, come, be sociable—be human, my friend. Don't make that face; it distresses me."

"I suppose," with a sneer, "you are the man I've long heard of—The Happy Man."

"Happy? my friend. Yes, at least I ought to be. My conscience is peaceful. I have confidence in everybody. I have confidence that, in my humble profession, I do some little good to the world. Yes, I think that, without presumption, I may venture to assent to the proposition that I am the Happy Man—the Happy Bone-setter."

"Then you shall hear my story. Many a month I have longed to get hold of the Happy Man, drill him, drop the powder, and leave him to explode at his leisure."

"What a demoniac unfortunate," exclaimed the herb-doctor retreating. "Regular infernal machine!"

"Look ye," cried the other, stumping after him, and with his horny hand catching him by a horn button, "my name is Thomas Fry. Until my—"

—"Any relation of Mrs. Fry?" interrupted the other. "I still correspond with that excellent lady on the subject of prisons. Tell me, are you anyway connected with *my* Mrs. Fry?"

"Blister Mrs. Fry! What do them sentimental souls know of prisons or any other black fact? I'll tell ye a story of prisons. Ha, ha!"

The herb-doctor shrank, and with reason, the laugh being strangely startling.

"Positively, my friend," said he, "you must stop that; I can't stand that; no more of that. I hope I have the milk of kindness, but your thunder will soon turn it."

"Hold, I haven't come to the milk-turning part yet. My name is Thomas Fry. Until my twenty-third year I went by the nickname of Happy Tom—happy—ha, ha! They called me Happy Tom, d'ye see? because I was so good-natured and laughing all the time, just as I am now—ha, ha!"

Upon this the herb-doctor would, perhaps, have run, but once more the hyæna clawed him. Presently, sobering down, he continued:

"Well, I was born in New York, and there I lived a steady, hard-working man, a cooper by trade. One evening I went to a political meeting in the Park—for you must know, I was in those days a great patriot. As bad luck would have it, there was trouble near, between a gentleman who had been drinking wine, and a pavior who was sober. The pavior chewed tobacco, and the gentleman said it was beastly in him, and pushed him, wanting to have his place. The pavior chewed on and pushed back. Well, the gentleman carried a sword-cane, and presently the pavior was down—skewered."

"How was that?"

"Why you see the pavior undertook something above his strength."

"The other must have been a Samson then. 'Strong as a pavior,' is a proverb."

"So it is, and the gentleman was in body a rather weakly man, but, for all that, I say again, the pavior undertook something above his strength."

"What are you talking about? He tried to maintain his rights, didn't he?"

"Yes; but, for all that, I say again, he undertook something above his strength."

"I don't understand you. But go on."

"Along with the gentleman, I, with other witnesses, was

taken to the Tombs. There was an examination, and, to appear at the trial, the gentleman and witnesses all gave bail—I mean all but me."

"And why didn't you?"

"Couldn't get it."

"Steady, hard-working cooper like you; what was the reason you couldn't get bail?"

"Steady, hard-working cooper hadn't no friends. Well, souse I went into a wet cell, like a canal-boat splashing into the lock; locked up in pickle, d'ye see? against the time of the trial."

"But what had you done?"

"Why, I hadn't got any friends, I tell ye. A worse crime than murder, as ye'll see afore long."

"Murder? Did the wounded man die?"

"Died the third night."

"Then the gentleman's bail didn't help him. Imprisoned now, wasn't he?"

"Had too many friends. No, it was *I* that was imprisoned.—But I was going on: They let me walk about the corridor by day; but at night I must into lock. There the wet and the damp struck into my bones. They doctored me, but no use. When the trial came, I was boosted up and said my say."

"And what was that?"

"My say was that I saw the steel go in, and saw it sticking in."

"And that hung the gentleman."

"Hung him with a gold chain! His friends called a meeting in the Park, and presented him with a gold watch and chain upon his acquittal."

"Acquittal?"

"Didn't I say he had friends?"

There was a pause, broken at last by the herb-doctor's saying: "Well, there is a bright side to everything. If this speak prosaically for justice, it speaks romantically for friendship! But go on, my fine fellow."

"My say being said, they told me I might go. I said I could not without help. So the constables helped me, asking *where* would I go? I told them back to the 'Tombs.' I knew no other place. 'But where are your friends?' said they. 'I have none.'

So they put me into a hand-barrow with an awning to it, and wheeled me down to the dock and on board a boat, and away to Blackwell's Island to the Corporation Hospital. There I got worse—got pretty much as you see me now. Couldn't cure me. After three years, I grew sick of lying in a grated iron bed alongside of groaning thieves and mouldering burglars. They gave me five silver dollars, and these crutches, and I hobbled off. I had an only brother who went to Indiana, years ago. I begged about, to make up a sum to go to him; got to Indiana at last, and they directed me to his grave. It was on a great plain, in a log-church yard with a stump fence, the old gray roots sticking all ways like moose-antlers. The bier, set over the grave, it being the last dug, was of green hickory; bark on, and green twigs sprouting from it. Some one had planted a bunch of violets on the mound, but it was a poor soil (always choose the poorest soils for grave-yards), and they were all dried to tinder. I was going to sit and rest myself on the bier and think about my brother in heaven, but the bier broke down, the legs being only tacked. So, after driving some hogs out of the yard that were rooting there, I came away, and, not to make too long a story of it, here I am, drifting down stream like any other bit of wreck."

The herb-doctor was silent for a time, buried in thought. At last, raising his head, he said: "I have considered your whole story, my friend, and strove to consider it in the light of a commentary on what I believe to be the system of things; but it so jars with all, is so incompatible with all, that you must pardon me, if I honestly tell you, I cannot believe it."

"That don't surprise me."

"How?"

"Hardly anybody believes my story, and so to most I tell a different one."

"How, again?"

"Wait here a bit and I'll show ye."

With that, taking off his rag of a cap, and arranging his tattered regimentals the best he could, off he went stumping among the passengers in an adjoining part of the deck, saying with a jovial kind of air: "Sir, a shilling for Happy Tom, who fought at Buena Vista. Lady, something for General Scott's soldier, crippled in both pins at glorious Contreras."

Now, it so chanced that, unbeknown to the cripple, a prim-looking stranger had overheard part of his story. Beholding him, then, on his present begging adventure, this person, turning to the herb-doctor, indignantly said: "Is it not too bad, sir, that yonder rascal should lie so?"

"Charity never faileth, my good sir," was the reply. "The vice of this unfortunate is pardonable. Consider, he lies not out of wantonness."

"Not out of wantonness. I never heard more wanton lies. In one breath to tell you what would appear to be his true story, and, in the next, away and falsify it."

"For all that, I repeat he lies not out of wantonness. A ripe philosopher, turned out of the great Sorbonne of hard times, he thinks that woes, when told to strangers for money, are best sugared. Though the inglorious lock-jaw of his knee-pans in a wet dungeon is a far more pitiable ill than to have been crippled at glorious Contreras, yet he is of opinion that this lighter and false ill shall attract, while the heavier and real one might repel."

"Nonsense; he belongs to the Devil's regiment; and I have a great mind to expose him."

"Shame upon you. Dare to expose that poor unfortunate, and by heaven—don't you do it, sir."

Noting something in his manner, the other thought it more prudent to retire than retort. By-and-by, the cripple came back, and with glee, having reaped a pretty good harvest.

"There," he laughed, "you know now what sort of soldier I am."

"Aye, one that fights not the stupid Mexican, but a foe worthy your tactics—Fortune!"

"Hi, hi!" clamored the cripple, like a fellow in the pit of a sixpenny theatre, then said, "don't know much what you meant, but it went off well."

This over, his countenance capriciously put on a morose ogreness. To kindly questions he gave no kindly answers. Unhandsome notions were thrown out about "free Ameriky," as he sarcastically called his country. These seemed to disturb and pain the herb-doctor, who, after an interval of thoughtfulness, gravely addressed him in these words:

"You, my worthy friend, to my concern, have reflected upon the government under which you live and suffer. Where is your patriotism? Where your gratitude? True, the charitable may find something in your case, as you put it, partly to account for such reflections as coming from you. Still, be the facts how they may, your reflections are none the less unwarrantable. Grant, for the moment, that your experiences are as you give them; in which case I would admit that government might be thought to have more or less to do with what seems undesirable in them. But it is never to be forgotten that human government, being subordinate to the divine, must needs, therefore, in its degree, partake of the characteristics of the divine. That is, while in general efficacious to happiness, the world's law may yet, in some cases, have, to the eye of reason, an unequal operation, just as, in the same imperfect view, some inequalities may appear in the operations of heaven's law; nevertheless, to one who has a right confidence, final benignity is, in every instance, as sure with the one law as the other. I expound the point at some length, because these are the considerations, my poor fellow, which, weighed as they merit, will enable you to sustain with unimpaired trust the apparent calamities which are yours."

"What do you talk your hog-latin to me for?" cried the cripple, who, throughout the address, betrayed the most illiterate obduracy; and, with an incensed look, anew he swung himself.

Glancing another way till the spasm passed, the other continued:

"Charity marvels not that you should be somewhat hard of conviction, my friend, since you, doubtless, believe yourself hardly dealt by; but forget not that those who are loved are chastened."

"Mustn't chasten them too much, though, and too long, because their skin and heart get hard, and feel neither pain nor tickle."

"To mere reason, your case looks something piteous, I grant. But never despond; many things—the choicest—yet remain. You breathe this bounteous air, are warmed by this gracious sun, and, though poor and friendless, indeed, nor so agile as in your youth, yet, how sweet to roam, day by day, through the groves, plucking the bright mosses and flowers, till forlornness itself becomes a hilarity, and, in your innocent independence, you skip for joy."

"Fine skipping with these 'ere horse-posts—ha ha!"

"Pardon; I forgot the crutches. My mind, figuring you after receiving the benefit of my art, overlooked you as you stand before me."

"Your art? You call yourself a bone-setter—a natural bone-setter, do ye? Go, bone-set the crooked world, and then come bone-set crooked me."

"Truly, my honest friend, I thank you for again recalling me to my original object. Let me examine you," bending down; "ah, I see, I see; much such a case as the negro's. Did you see him? Oh no, you came aboard since. Well, his case was a little something like yours. I prescribed for him, and I shouldn't wonder at all if, in a very short time, he were able to walk almost as well as myself. Now, have you no confidence in my art?"

"Ha, ha!"

The herb-doctor averted himself; but, the wild laugh dying away, resumed:

"I will not force confidence on you. Still, I would fain do the friendly thing by you. Here, take this box; just rub that liniment on the joints night and morning. Take it. Nothing to pay. God bless you. Good-bye."

"Stay," pausing in his swing, not untouched by so unexpected an act; "stay—thank'ee—but will this really do me good? Honor bright, now; will it? Don't deceive a poor fellow," with changed mien and glistening eye.

"Try it. Good-bye."

"Stay, stay! *Sure* it will do me good?"

"Possibly, possibly; no harm in trying. Good-bye."

"Stay, stay; give me three more boxes, and here's the money."

"My friend," returning towards him with a sadly pleased sort of air, "I rejoice in the birth of your confidence and hopefulness. Believe me that, like your crutches, confidence and hopefulness will long support a man when his own legs will not. Stick to confidence and hopefulness, then, since how mad for the cripple to throw his crutches away. You ask for three more boxes of my liniment. Luckily, I have just that number remaining. Here they are. I sell them at half-a-dollar apiece. But I shall take nothing from you. There; God bless you again; good-bye."

"Stay," in a convulsed voice, and rocking himself, "stay, stay! You have made a better man of me. You have borne with me like a good Christian, and talked to me like one, and all that is enough without making me a present of these boxes. Here is the money. I won't take nay. There, there; and may Almighty goodness go with you."

As the herb-doctor withdrew, the cripple gradually subsided from his hard rocking into a gentle oscillation. It expressed, perhaps, the soothed mood of his reverie.

Chapter 20

THE HERB-DOCTOR had not moved far away, when, in advance of him, this spectacle met his eye. A dried-up old man, with the stature of a boy of twelve, was tottering about like one out of his mind, in rumpled clothes of old moleskin, showing recent contact with bedding, his ferret eyes, blinking in the sunlight of the snowy boat, as imbecilely eager, and, at intervals, coughing, he peered hither and thither as if in alarmed search for his nurse. He presented the aspect of one who, bed-rid, has, through overruling excitement, like that of a fire, been stimulated to his feet.

"You seek some one," said the herb-doctor, accosting him. "Can I assist you?"

"Do, do; I am so old and miserable," coughed the old man. "Where is he? This long time I've been trying to get up and find him. But I haven't any friends, and couldn't get up till now. Where is he?"

"Who do you mean?" drawing closer, to stay the further wanderings of one so weakly.

"Why, why, why," now marking the other's dress, " why you, yes you—you, you—ugh, ugh, ugh!"

"I?"

"Ugh, ugh, ugh!—you are the man he spoke of. Who is he?"

"Faith, that is just what I want to know."

"Mercy, mercy!" coughed the old man, bewildered, "ever since seeing him, my head spins round so. I ought to have a guardeean. Is this a snuff-colored surtout of yours, or ain't it? Somehow, can't trust my senses any more, since trusting him—ugh, ugh, ugh!"

"Oh, you have trusted somebody? Glad to hear it. Glad to hear of any instance of that sort. Reflects well upon all men. But you inquire whether this is a snuff-colored surtout. I answer it is; and will add that a herb-doctor wears it."

Upon this the old man, in his broken way, replied that then he (the herb-doctor) was the person he sought—the person spoken of by the other person as yet unknown. He then, with flighty eagerness, wanted to know who this last person was, and where he was, and whether he could be trusted with money to treble it.

"Aye, now, I begin to understand; ten to one you mean my worthy friend, who, in pure goodness of heart, makes people's fortunes for them—their everlasting fortunes, as the phrase goes—only charging his one small commission of confidence. Aye, aye; before intrusting funds with my friend, you want to know about him. Very proper—and, I am glad to assure you, you need have no hesitation; none, none, just none in the world; bona fide, none. Turned me in a trice a hundred dollars the other day into as many eagles."

"Did he? did he? But where is he? Take me to him."

"Pray, take my arm! The boat is large! We may have something of a hunt! Come on! Ah, is that he?"

"Where? where?"

"O, no; I took yonder coat-skirts for his. But no, my honest friend would never turn tail that way. Ah!—"

"Where? where?"

"Another mistake. Surprising resemblance. I took yonder clergyman for him. Come on!"

Having searched that part of the boat without success, they went to another part, and, while exploring that, the boat sided up to a landing, when, as the two were passing by the open guard, the herb-doctor suddenly rushed towards the disembarking throng, crying out: "Mr. Truman, Mr. Truman! There he goes—that's he. Mr. Truman, Mr. Truman!—Confound that steam-pipe. Mr. Truman! for God's sake, Mr. Truman!—No, no.—There, the plank's in—too late—we're off."

With that, the huge boat, with a mighty, walrus wallow, rolled away from the shore, resuming her course.

"How vexatious!" exclaimed the herb-doctor, returning. "Had we been but one single moment sooner.—There he goes, now, towards yon hotel, his portmanteau following. You see him, don't you?"

"Where? where?"

"Can't see him any more. Wheel-house shot between. I am very sorry. I should have so liked you to have let him have a hundred or so of your money. You would have been pleased with the investment, believe me."

"Oh, I *have* let him have some of my money," groaned the old man.

"You have? My dear sir," seizing both the miser's hands in both his own and heartily shaking them. "My dear sir, how I congratulate you. You don't know."

"Ugh, ugh! I fear I don't," with another groan. "His name is Truman, is it?"

"John Truman."

"Where does he live?"

"In St. Louis."

"Where's his office?"

"Let me see. Jones street, number one hundred and—no, no—anyway, it's somewhere or other up-stairs in Jones street."

"Can't you remember the number? Try, now."

"One hundred—two hundred—three hundred—"

"Oh, my hundred dollars! I wonder whether it will be one hundred, two hundred, three hundred, with them! Ugh, ugh! Can't remember the number?"

"Positively, though I once knew, I have forgotten, quite forgotten it. Strange. But never mind. You will easily learn in St. Louis. He is well known there."

"But I have no receipt—ugh, ugh! Nothing to show—don't know where I stand—ought to have a guard*ee*an—ugh, ugh! Don't know anything. Ugh, ugh!"

"Why, you know that you gave him your confidence, don't you?"

"Oh, yes."

"Well, then?"

"But what, what—how, how—ugh, ugh!"

"Why, didn't he tell you?"

"No."

"What! Didn't he tell you that it was a secret, a mystery?"

"Oh—yes."

"Well, then?"

"But I have no bond."

"Don't need any with Mr. Truman. Mr. Truman's word is his bond."

"But how am I to get my profits—ugh, ugh!—and my money back? Don't know anything. Ugh, ugh!"

"Oh, you must have confidence."

"Don't say that word again. Makes my head spin so. Oh, I'm so old and miserable, nobody caring for me, everybody fleecing me, and my head spins so—ugh, ugh!—and this cough racks me so. I say again, I ought to have a guard*ee*an."

"So you ought; and Mr. Truman is your guardian to the extent you invested with him. Sorry we missed him just now. But you'll hear from him, all right. It's imprudent, though, to expose yourself this way. Let me take you to your berth."

Forlornly enough the old miser moved slowly away with him. But, while descending a stairway, he was seized with such coughing that he was fain to pause.

"That is a very bad cough."

"Church-yard—ugh, ugh!—church-yard cough.—Ugh!"

"Have you tried anything for it?"

"Tired of trying. Nothing does me any good—ugh! ugh! Not even the Mammoth Cave. Ugh! ugh! Denned there six months, but coughed so bad the rest of the coughers—ugh! ugh!—black-balled me out. Ugh, ugh! Nothing does me good."

"But have you tried the Omni-Balsamic Reinvigorator, sir?"

"That's what that Truman—ugh, ugh!—said I ought to take. Yarb-medicine; you are that yarb-doctor, too?"

"The same. Suppose you try one of my boxes now. Trust me, from what I know of Mr. Truman, he is not the gentleman to recommend, even in behalf of a friend, anything of whose excellence he is not conscientiously satisfied."

"Ugh!—how much?"

"Only two dollars a box."

"Two dollars? Why don't you say two millions? ugh, ugh! Two dollars, that's two hundred cents; that's eight hundred farthings; that's two thousand mills; and all for one little box of yarb-medicine. My head, my head!—oh, I ought to have a guard*ee*an for my head. Ugh, ugh, ugh, ugh!"

"Well, if two dollars a box seems too much, take a dozen boxes at twenty dollars; and that will be getting four boxes for nothing, and you need use none but those four, the rest you can retail out at a premium, and so cure your cough, and make money by it. Come, you had better do it. Cash down. Can fill an order in a day or two. Here now," producing a box; "pure herbs."

At that moment, seized with another spasm, the miser snatched each interval to fix his half distrustful, half hopeful eye upon the medicine, held alluringly up. "Sure—ugh! Sure it's all nat'ral? Nothing but yarbs? If I only thought it was a purely nat'ral medicine now—all yarbs—ugh, ugh!—oh this cough, this cough—ugh, ugh!—shatters my whole body. Ugh, ugh, ugh!"

"For heaven's sake try my medicine, if but a single box. That it is pure nature you may be confident. Refer you to Mr. Truman."

"Don't know his number—ugh, ugh, ugh, ugh! Oh this cough. He did speak well of this medicine though; said solemnly it would cure me—ugh, ugh, ugh, ugh!—take off a dollar and I'll have a box."

"Can't sir, can't."

"Say a dollar-and-half. Ugh!"

"Can't. Am pledged to the one-price system, only honorable one."

"Take off a shilling—ugh, ugh!"

"Can't."

"Ugh, ugh, ugh—I'll take it.—There."

Grudgingly he handed eight silver coins, but while still in his hand, his cough took him, and they were shaken upon the deck.

One by one, the herb-doctor picked them up, and, examining them, said: "These are not quarters, these are pistareens; and clipped, and sweated, at that."

"Oh don't be so miserly—ugh, ugh!—better a beast than a miser—ugh, ugh!"

"Well, let it go. Anything rather than the idea of your not being cured of such a cough. And I hope, for the credit of humanity, you have not made it appear worse than it is, merely with a view to working upon the weak point of my pity, and so getting my medicine the cheaper. Now, mind, don't take it till night. Just before retiring is the time. There, you can get along now, can't you? I would attend you further, but I land presently, and must go hunt up my luggage."

Chapter 21

A HARD CASE

"Y ARBS, YARBS; natur, natur; you foolish old file you! He diddled you with that hocus-pocus, did he? Yarbs and natur will cure your incurable cough, you think."

It was a rather eccentric-looking person who spoke; somewhat ursine in aspect; sporting a shaggy spencer of the cloth called bear's-skin; a high-peaked cap of raccoon-skin, the long bushy tail switching over behind; raw-hide leggings; grim stubble chin; and to end, a double-barreled gun in hand—a Missouri bachelor, a Hoosier gentleman, of Spartan leisure and fortune, and equally Spartan manners and sentiments; and, as the sequel may show, not less acquainted, in a Spartan way of his own, with philosophy and books, than with woodcraft and rifles.

He must have overheard some of the talk between the miser and the herb-doctor; for, just after the withdrawal of the one, he made up to the other—now at the foot of the stairs leaning against the baluster there—with the greeting above.

"Think it will cure me?" coughed the miser in echo; " why shouldn't it? The medicine is nat'ral yarbs, pure yarbs; yarbs must cure me."

"Because a thing is nat'ral, as you call it, you think it must be good. But who gave you that cough? Was it, or was it not, nature?"

"Sure, you don't think that natur, Dame Natur, will hurt a body, do you?"

"Natur is good Queen Bess; but who's responsible for the cholera?"

"But yarbs, yarbs; yarbs are good?"

"What's deadly-nightshade? Yarb, ain't it?"

"Oh, that a Christian man should speak agin natur and yarbs—ugh, ugh, ugh!—ain't sick men sent out into the country; sent out to natur and grass?"

"Aye, and poets send out the sick spirit to green pastures, like lame horses turned out unshod to the turf to renew their hoofs. A sort of yarb-doctors in their way, poets have it that

953

for sore hearts, as for sore lungs, nature is the grand cure. But who froze to death my teamster on the prairie? And who made an idiot of Peter the Wild Boy?"

"Then you don't believe in these 'ere yarb-doctors?"

"Yarb-doctors? I remember the lank yarb-doctor I saw once on a hospital-cot in Mobile. One of the faculty passing round and seeing who lay there, said with professional triumph, 'Ah, Dr. Green, your yarbs don't help ye now, Dr. Green. Have to come to us and the mercury now, Dr. Green.'—Natur! Y-a-r-b-s!"

"Did I hear something about herbs and herb-doctors?" here said a flute-like voice, advancing.

It was the herb-doctor in person. Carpet-bag in hand, he happened to be strolling back that way.

"Pardon me," addressing the Missourian, "but if I caught your words aright, you would seem to have little confidence in nature; which, really, in my way of thinking, looks like carrying the spirit of distrust pretty far."

"And who of my sublime species may you be?" turning short round upon him, clicking his rifle-lock, with an air which would have seemed half cynic, half wild-cat, were it not for the grotesque excess of the expression, which made its sincerity appear more or less dubious.

"One who has confidence in nature, and confidence in man, with some little modest confidence in himself."

"That's your Confession of Faith, is it? Confidence in man, eh? Pray, which do you think are most, knaves or fools?"

"Having met with few or none of either, I hardly think I am competent to answer."

"I will answer for you. Fools are most."

"Why do you think so?"

"For the same reason that I think oats are numerically more than horses. Don't knaves munch up fools just as horses do oats?"

"A droll, sir; you are a droll. I can appreciate drollery—ha, ha, ha!"

"But I'm in earnest."

"That's the drollery, to deliver droll extravagance with an earnest air—knaves munching up fools as horses oats.— Faith, very droll, indeed, ha, ha, ha! Yes, I think I understand you now, sir. How silly I was to have taken you seriously, in your droll conceits, too, about having no confidence in nature. In reality you have just as much as I have."

"*I* have confidence in nature? *I?* I say again there is nothing I am more suspicious of. I once lost ten thousand dollars by nature. Nature embezzled that amount from me; absconded with ten thousand dollars' worth of my property; a plantation on this stream, swept clean away by one of those sudden shiftings of the banks in a freshet; ten thousand dollars' worth of alluvion thrown broad off upon the waters."

"But have you no confidence that by a reverse shifting that soil will come back after many days?—ah, here is my venerable friend," observing the old miser, "not in your berth yet? Pray, if you *will* keep afoot, don't lean against that baluster; take my arm."

It was taken; and the two stood together; the old miser leaning against the herb-doctor with something of that air of trustful fraternity with which, when standing, the less strong of the Siamese twins habitually leans against the other.

The Missourian eyed them in silence, which was broken by the herb-doctor.

"You look surprised, sir. Is it because I publicly take under my protection a figure like this? But I am never ashamed of honesty, whatever his coat."

"Look you," said the Missourian, after a scrutinizing pause, "you are a queer sort of chap. Don't know exactly what to make of you. Upon the whole though, you somewhat remind me of the last boy I had on my place."

"Good, trustworthy boy, I hope?"

"Oh, very! I am now started to get me made some kind of machine to do the sort of work which boys are supposed to be fitted for."

"Then you have passed a veto upon boys?"

"And men, too."

"But, my dear sir, does not that again imply more or less lack of confidence?—(Stand up a little, just a very little, my venerable friend; you lean rather hard.)—No confidence in boys, no confidence in men, no confidence in nature. Pray, sir, who or what may you have confidence in?"

"I have confidence in distrust; more particularly as applied to you and your herbs."

"Well," with a forbearing smile, "that is frank. But pray, don't forget that when you suspect my herbs you suspect nature."

"Didn't I say that before?"

"Very good. For the argument's sake I will suppose you are in earnest. Now, can you, who suspect nature, deny, that this same nature not only kindly brought you into being, but has faithfully nursed you to your present vigorous and independent condition? Is it not to nature that you are indebted for that robustness of mind which you so unhandsomely use to her scandal? Pray, is it not to nature that you owe the very eyes by which you criticise her?"

"No! for the privilege of vision I am indebted to an oculist, who in my tenth year operated upon me in Philadelphia. Nature made me blind and would have kept me so. My oculist counterplotted her."

"And yet, sir, by your complexion, I judge you live an out-of-door life; without knowing it, you are partial to nature; you fly to nature, the universal mother."

"Very motherly! Sir, in the passion-fits of nature, I've known birds fly from nature to me, rough as I look; yes, sir, in a tempest, refuge here," smiting the folds of his bearskin. "Fact, sir, fact. Come, come, Mr. Palaverer, for all your palavering, did you yourself never shut out nature of a cold, wet night? Bar her out? Bolt her out? Lint her out?"

"As to that," said the herb-doctor calmly, "much may be said."

"Say it, then," ruffling all his hairs. "You can't, sir, can't." Then, as in apostrophe: "Look you, nature! I don't deny but your clover is sweet, and your dandelions don't roar; but whose hailstones smashed my windows?"

"Sir," with unimpaired affability, producing one of his boxes, "I am pained to meet with one who holds nature a dangerous character. Though your manner is refined your voice is rough; in short, you seem to have a sore throat. In the calumniated name of nature, I present you with this box; my venerable friend here has a similar one; but to you, a free gift, sir. Through her regularly-authorized agents, of whom I happen to be one, Nature delights in benefiting those who most abuse her. Pray, take it."

"Away with it! Don't hold it so near. Ten to one there is a torpedo in it. Such things have been. Editors been killed that way. Take it further off, I say."

"Good heavens! my dear sir—"

"I tell you I want none of your boxes," snapping his rifle.

"Oh, take it—ugh, ugh! do take it," chimed in the old miser; "I wish he would give me one for nothing."

"You find it lonely, eh," turning short round; "gulled yourself, you would have a companion."

"How can he find it lonely," returned the herb-doctor, "or how desire a companion, when here I stand by him; I, even I, in whom he has trust? For the gulling, tell me, is it humane to talk so to this poor old man? Granting that his dependence on my medicine is vain, is it kind to deprive him of what, in mere imagination, if nothing more, may help eke out, with hope, his disease? For you, if you have no confidence, and, thanks to your native health, can get along without it, so far, at least, as trusting in my medicine goes; yet, how cruel an argument to use, with this afflicted one here. Is it not for all the world as if some brawny pugilist, aglow in December, should rush in and put out a hospital-fire, because, forsooth, he feeling no need of artificial heat, the shivering patients shall have none? Put it to your conscience, sir, and you will admit, that, whatever be the nature of this afflicted one's trust, you, in opposing it, evince either an erring head or a heart amiss. Come, own, are you not pitiless?"

"Yes, poor soul," said the Missourian, gravely eying the old man—"yes, it *is* pitiless in one like me to speak too honestly to one like you. You are a late sitter-up in this life; past man's usual bed-time; and truth, though with some it makes a wholesome breakfast, proves to all a supper too hearty. Hearty food, taken late, gives bad dreams."

"What, in wonder's name—ugh, ugh!—is he talking about?" asked the old miser, looking up to the herb-doctor.

"Heaven be praised for that!" cried the Missourian.

"Out of his mind, ain't he?" again appealed the old miser.

"Pray, sir," said the herb-doctor to the Missourian, "for what were you giving thanks just now?"

"For this: that, with some minds, truth is, in effect, not so cruel a thing after all, seeing that, like a loaded pistol found by poor devils of savages, it raises more wonder than terror— its peculiar virtue being unguessed, unless, indeed, by indiscreet handling, it should happen to go off of itself."

"I pretend not to divine your meaning there," said the herb-doctor, after a pause, during which he eyed the Missourian with a kind of pinched expression, mixed of pain and curiosity, as if he grieved at his state of mind, and, at the same time, wondered what had brought him to it, "but this much I know," he added, "that the general cast of your thoughts is, to say the least, unfortunate. There is strength in them, but a strength, whose source, being physical, must wither. You will yet recant."

"Recant?"

"Yes, when, as with this old man, your evil days of decay come on, when a hoary captive in your chamber, then will you, something like the dungeoned Italian we read of, gladly seek the breast of that confidence begot in the tender time of your youth, blessed beyond telling if it return to you in age."

"Go back to nurse again, eh? Second childhood, indeed. You are soft."

"Mercy, mercy!" cried the old miser, "what is all this!— ugh, ugh! Do talk sense, my good friends. Ain't you," to the Missourian, "going to buy some of that medicine?"

"Pray, my venerable friend," said the herb-doctor, now trying to straighten himself, "don't lean *quite* so hard; my arm grows numb; abate a little, just a very little."

"Go," said the Missourian, "go lay down in your grave, old man, if you can't stand of yourself. It's a hard world for a leaner."

"As to his grave," said the herb-doctor, "that is far enough off, so he but faithfully take my medicine."

"Ugh, ugh, ugh!—He says true. No, I ain't—ugh! a going to die yet—ugh, ugh, ugh! Many years to live yet, ugh, ugh, ugh!"

"I approve your confidence," said the herb-doctor; "but your coughing distresses me, besides being injurious to you. Pray, let me conduct you to your berth. You are best there. Our friend here will wait till my return, I know."

With which he led the old miser away, and then, coming back, the talk with the Missourian was resumed.

"Sir," said the herb-doctor, with some dignity and more feeling, "now that our infirm friend is withdrawn, allow me, to the full, to express my concern at the words you allowed to escape you in his hearing. Some of those words, if I err not, besides being calculated to beget deplorable distrust in the patient, seemed fitted to convey unpleasant imputations against me, his physician."

"Suppose they did?" with a menacing air.

"Why, then—then, indeed," respectfully retreating, "I fall back upon my previous theory of your general facetiousness. I have the fortune to be in company with a humorist—a wag."

"Fall back you had better, and wag it is," cried the Missourian, following him up, and wagging his raccoon tail almost into the herb-doctor's face, "look you!"

"At what?"

"At this coon. Can you, the fox, catch him?"

"If you mean," returned the other, not unselfpossessed, " whether I flatter myself that I can in any way dupe you, or impose upon you, or pass myself off upon you for what I am not, I, as an honest man, answer that I have neither the inclination nor the power to do aught of the kind."

"Honest man? Seems to me you talk more like a craven."

"You in vain seek to pick a quarrel with me, or put any affront upon me. The innocence in me heals me."

"A healing like your own nostrums. But you are a queer man—a very queer and dubious man; upon the whole, about the most so I ever met."

The scrutiny accompanying this seemed unwelcome to the diffidence of the herb-doctor. As if at once to attest the absence of resentment, as well as to change the subject, he threw a kind of familiar cordiality into his air, and said: "So you are going to get some machine made to do your work? Philanthropic scruples, doubtless, forbid your going as far as New Orleans for slaves?"

"Slaves?" morose again in a twinkling, " won't have 'em! Bad enough to see whites ducking and grinning round for a favor, without having those poor devils of niggers congeeing round for their corn. Though, to me, the niggers are the freer of the two. You are an abolitionist, ain't you?" he added, squaring himself with both hands on his rifle, used for a staff, and gazing in the herb-doctor's face with no more reverence than if it were a target. "You are an abolitionist, ain't you?"

"As to that, I cannot so readily answer. If by abolitionist you mean a zealot, I am none; but if you mean a man, who, being a man, feels for all men, slaves included, and by any lawful act, opposed to nobody's interest, and therefore, rousing nobody's enmity, would willingly abolish suffering (supposing it, in its degree, to exist) from among mankind, irrespective of color, then am I what you say."

"Picked and prudent sentiments. You are the moderate man, the invaluable understrapper of the wicked man. You, the moderate man, may be used for wrong, but are useless for right."

"From all this," said the herb-doctor, still forgivingly, "I infer, that you, a Missourian, though living in a slave-state, are without slave sentiments."

"Aye, but are you? Is not that air of yours, so spiritlessly enduring and yielding, the very air of a slave? Who is your master, pray; or are you owned by a company?"

"*My* master?"

"Aye, for come from Maine or Georgia, you come from a slave-state, and a slave-pen, where the best breeds are to be bought up at any price from a livelihood to the Presidency. Abolitionism, ye gods, but expresses the fellow-feeling of slave for slave."

"The back-woods would seem to have given you rather eccentric notions," now with polite superiority smiled the herb-doctor, still with manly intrepidity forbearing each unmanly thrust, "but to return; since, for your purpose, you will have neither man nor boy, bond nor free, truly, then some sort of machine for you is all there is left. My desires for your success attend you, sir.—Ah!" glancing shoreward, "here is Cape Girardeau; I must leave you."

Chapter 22

"P HILOSOPHICAL Intelligence Office'—novel idea! But
how did you come to dream that I wanted anything in
your absurd line, eh?"

About twenty minutes after leaving Cape Girardeau, the
above was growled out over his shoulder by the Missourian
to a chance stranger who had just accosted him; a round-
backed, baker-kneed man, in a mean five-dollar suit, wearing,
collar-wise by a chain, a small brass plate, inscribed P.I.O.,
and who, with a sort of canine deprecation, slunk obliquely
behind.

"How did you come to dream that I wanted anything in
your line, eh?"

"Oh, respected sir," whined the other, crouching a pace
nearer, and, in his obsequiousness, seeming to wag his very
coat-tails behind him, shabby though they were, "oh, sir,
from long experience, one glance tells me the gentleman who
is in need of our humble services."

"But suppose I did want a boy—what they jocosely call a
good boy—how could your absurd office help me?—Philosophical Intelligence Office?"

"Yes, respected sir, an office founded on strictly philosophical and physio—"

"Look you—come up here—how, by philosophy or phys-
iology either, make good boys to order? Come up here. Don't
give me a crick in the neck. Come up here, come, sir, come,"
calling as if to his pointer. "Tell me, how put the requisite
assortment of good qualities into a boy, as the assorted mince
into the pie?"

"Respected sir, our office—"

"You talk much of that office. Where is it? On board this
boat?"

"Oh no, sir, I just came aboard. Our office—"

"Came aboard at that last landing, eh? Pray, do you know a
herb-doctor there? Smooth scamp in a snuff-colored surtout?"

"Oh, sir, I was but a sojourner at Cape Girardeau. Though, now that you mention a snuff-colored surtout, I think I met such a man as you speak of stepping ashore as I stepped aboard, and 'pears to me I have seen him somewhere before. Looks like a very mild Christian sort of person, I should say. Do you know him, respected sir?"

"Not much, but better than you seem to. Proceed with your business."

With a low, shabby bow, as grateful for the permission, the other began: "Our office—"

"Look you," broke in the bachelor with ire, "have you the spinal complaint? What are you ducking and groveling about? Keep still. Where's your office?"

"The branch one which I represent, is at Alton, sir, in the free state we now pass," (pointing somewhat proudly ashore).

"Free, eh? You a freeman, you flatter yourself? With those coat-tails and that spinal complaint of servility? Free? Just cast up in your private mind who is your master, will you?"

"Oh, oh, oh! I don't understand—indeed—indeed. But, respected sir, as before said, our office, founded on principles wholly new—"

"To the devil with your principles! Bad sign when a man begins to talk of his principles. Hold, come back, sir; back here, back, sir, back! I tell you no more boys for me. Nay, I'm a Mede and Persian. In my old home in the woods I'm pestered enough with squirrels, weasels, chipmunks, skunks. I want no more wild vermin to spoil my temper and waste my substance. Don't talk of boys; enough of your boys; a plague of your boys; chilblains on your boys! As for Intelligence Offices, I've lived in the East, and know 'em. Swindling concerns kept by low-born cynics, under a fawning exterior wreaking their cynic malice upon mankind. You are a fair specimen of 'em."

"Oh dear, dear, dear!"

"Dear? Yes, a thrice dear purchase one of your boys would be to me. A rot on your boys!"

"But, respected sir, if you will not have boys, might we not, in our small way, accommodate you with a man?"

"Accommodate? Pray, no doubt you could accommodate

me with a bosom-friend too, couldn't you? Accommodate! Obliging word accommodate: there's accommodation notes now, where one accommodates another with a loan, and if he don't pay it pretty quickly, accommodates him with a chain to his foot. Accommodate! God forbid that I should ever be accommodated. No, no. Look you, as I told that cousin-german of yours, the herb-doctor, I'm now on the road to get me made some sort of machine to do my work. Machines for me. My cider-mill—does that ever steal my cider? My mowing-machine—does that ever lay a-bed mornings? My corn-husker—does that ever give me insolence? No: cider-mill, mowing-machine, corn-husker—all faithfully attend to their business. Disinterested, too; no board, no wages; yet doing good all their lives long; shining examples that virtue is its own reward—the only practical Christians I know."

"Oh dear, dear, dear, dear!"

"Yes, sir:—boys? Start my soul-bolts, what a difference, in a moral point of view, between a corn-husker and a boy! Sir, a corn-husker, for its patient continuance in well-doing, might not unfitly go to heaven. Do you suppose a boy will?"

"A corn-husker in heaven! (turning up the whites of his eyes). Respected sir, this way of talking as if heaven were a kind of Washington patent-office museum—oh, oh, oh!—as if mere machine-work and puppet-work went to heaven—oh, oh, oh! Things incapable of free agency, to receive the eternal reward of well-doing—oh, oh, oh!"

"You Praise-God-Barebones you, what are you groaning about? Did I say anything of that sort? Seems to me, though you talk so good, you are mighty quick at a hint the other way, or else you want to pick a polemic quarrel with me."

"It may be so or not, respected sir," was now the demure reply; "but if it be, it is only because as a soldier out of honor is quick in taking affront, so a Christian out of religion is quick, sometimes perhaps a little too much so, in spying heresy."

"Well," after an astonished pause, "for an unaccountable pair, you and the herb-doctor ought to yoke together."

So saying, the bachelor was eying him rather sharply, when he with the brass plate recalled him to the discussion by a hint, not unflattering, that he (the man with the brass plate) was all anxiety to hear him further on the subject of servants.

"About that matter," exclaimed the impulsive bachelor, going off at the hint like a rocket, "all thinking minds are, now-a-days, coming to the conclusion—one derived from an immense hereditary experience—see what Horace and others of the ancients say of servants—coming to the conclusion, I say, that boy or man, the human animal is, for most work-purposes, a losing animal. Can't be trusted; less trustworthy than oxen; for conscientiousness a turn-spit dog excels him. Hence these thousand new inventions—carding machines, horse-shoe machines, tunnel-boring machines, reaping machines, apple-paring machines, boot-blacking machines, sewing machines, shaving machines, run-of-errand machines, dumb-waiter machines, and the Lord-only-knows-what machines; all of which announce the era when that refractory animal, the working or serving man, shall be a buried by-gone, a superseded fossil. Shortly prior to which glorious time, I doubt not that a price will be put upon their peltries as upon the knavish 'possums, especially the boys. Yes, sir (ringing his rifle down on the deck), I rejoice to think that the day is at hand, when, prompted to it by law, I shall shoulder this gun and go out a boy-shooting."

"Oh, now! Lord, Lord, Lord!—But *our* office, respected sir, conducted as I ventured to observe—"

"No, sir," bristlingly settling his stubble chin in his coonskins. "Don't try to oil me; the herb-doctor tried that. My experience, carried now through a course—worse than salivation—a course of five and thirty boys, proves to me that boyhood is a natural state of rascality."

"Save us, save us!"

"Yes, sir, yes. My name is Pitch; I stick to what I say. I speak from fifteen years' experience; five and thirty boys; American, Irish, English, German, African, Mulatto; not to speak of that China boy sent me by one who well knew my perplexities, from California; and that Lascar boy from Bombay. Thug! I found him sucking the embryo life from my spring eggs. All rascals, sir, every soul of them; Caucasian or Mongol. Amazing the endless variety of rascality in human nature of the juvenile sort. I remember that, having discharged, one after another, twenty-nine boys—each, too, for some wholly unforeseen species of viciousness peculiar to that one peculiar boy—I remember saying to myself: Now, then, surely, I have got to the end of the list, wholly exhausted it; I have only now to get me a boy, any boy different from those twenty-nine preceding boys, and he infallibly shall be that virtuous boy I have so long been seeking. But, bless me! this thirtieth boy—by the way, having at the time long forsworn your intelligence offices, I had him sent to me from the Commissioners of Emigration, all the way from New York, culled out carefully, in fine, at my particular request, from a standing army of eight hundred boys, the flowers of all nations, so they wrote me, temporarily in barracks on an East River island—I say, this thirtieth boy was in person not ungraceful; his deceased mother a lady's maid, or something of that sort; and in manner, why, in a plebeian way, a perfect Chesterfield; very intelligent, too—quick as a flash. But, such suavity! 'Please sir! please sir!' always bowing and saying, 'Please sir.' In the strangest way, too, combining a filial affection with a menial respect. Took such warm, singular interest in my affairs. Wanted to be considered one of the family— sort of adopted son of mine, I suppose. Of a morning, when I would go out to my stable, with what childlike good nature he would trot out my nag. 'Please sir, I think he's getting fatter and fatter.' 'But, he don't look very clean, does he?' unwilling to be downright harsh with so affectionate a lad; 'and he seems a little hollow inside the haunch there, don't he? or no, perhaps I don't see plain this morning.' 'Oh, please sir, it's just there I think he's gaining so, please.' Polite scamp! I soon found he never gave that wretched nag his oats of nights; didn't bed him either. Was above that sort of chambermaid work. No end to his willful neglects. But the more he abused my service, the more polite he grew."

"Oh, sir, some way you mistook him."

"Not a bit of it. Besides, sir, he was a boy who under a Chesterfieldian exterior hid strong destructive propensities. He cut up my horse-blanket for the bits of leather, for hinges to his chest. Denied it point-blank. After he was gone, found the shreds under his mattress. Would slyly break his hoe-handle, too, on purpose to get rid of hoeing. Then be so gracefully penitent for his fatal excess of industrious strength. Offer to mend all by taking a nice stroll to the nighest settlement—cherry-trees in full bearing all the way—to get the broken thing cobbled. Very politely stole my pears, odd pennies, shillings, dollars, and nuts; regular squirrel at it. But I could prove nothing. Expressed to him my suspicions. Said I, moderately enough, 'A little less politeness, and a little more honesty would suit me better.' He fired up; threatened to sue for libel. I won't say anything about his afterwards, in Ohio, being found in the act of gracefully putting a bar across a railroad track, for the reason that a stoker called him the rogue that he was. But enough: polite boys or saucy boys, white boys or black boys, smart boys or lazy boys, Caucasian boys or Mongol boys—all are rascals."

"Shocking, shocking!" nervously tucking his frayed cravat-end out of sight. "Surely, respected sir, you labor under a deplorable hallucination. Why, pardon again, you seem to have not the slightest confidence in boys. I admit, indeed, that boys, some of them at least, are but too prone to one little foolish foible or other. But, what then, respected sir, when, by natural laws, they finally outgrow such things, and wholly?"

Having until now vented himself mostly in plaintive dissent of canine whines and groans, the man with the brass-plate seemed beginning to summon courage to a less timid encounter. But, upon his maiden essay, was not very encouragingly handled, since the dialogue immediately continued as follows:

"Boys outgrow what is amiss in them? From bad boys spring good men? Sir, 'the child is father of the man;' hence, as all boys are rascals, so are all men. But, God bless me, you must know these things better than I; keeping an intelligence office as you do; a business which must furnish peculiar facilities for studying mankind. Come, come up here, sir; confess you know these things pretty well, after all. Do you not know that all men are rascals, and all boys, too?"

"Sir," replied the other, spite of his shocked feelings seeming to pluck up some spirit, but not to an indiscreet degree, "Sir, heaven be praised, I am far, very far from knowing what you say. True," he thoughtfully continued, " with my associates, I keep an intelligence office, and for ten years, come

October, have, one way or other, been concerned in that line; for no small period in the great city of Cincinnati, too; and though, as you hint, within that long interval, I must have had more or less favorable opportunity for studying mankind—in a business way, scanning not only the faces, but ransacking the lives of several thousands of human beings, male and female, of various nations, both employers and employed, genteel and ungenteel, educated and uneducated; yet—of course, I candidly admit, with some random exceptions, I have, so far as my small observation goes, found that mankind thus domestically viewed, confidentially viewed, I may say; they, upon the whole—making some reasonable allowances for human imperfection—present as pure a moral spectacle as the purest angel could wish. I say it, respected sir, with confidence."

"Gammon! You don't mean what you say. Else you are like a landsman at sea: don't know the ropes, the very things everlastingly pulled before your eyes. Serpent-like, they glide about, traveling blocks too subtle for you. In short, the entire ship is a riddle. Why, you green ones wouldn't know if she were unseaworthy; but still, with thumbs stuck back into your arm-holes, pace the rotten planks, singing, like a fool, words put into your green mouth by the cunning owner, the man who, heavily insuring it, sends his ship to be wrecked—

'A wet sheet and a flowing sea!'—

and, sir, now that it occurs to me, your talk, the whole of it, is but a wet sheet and a flowing sea, and an idle wind that follows fast, offering a striking contrast to my own discourse."

"Sir," exclaimed the man with the brass-plate, his patience now more or less tasked, "permit me with deference to hint that some of your remarks are injudiciously worded. And thus we say to our patrons, when they enter our office full of abuse of us because of some worthy boy we may have sent them— some boy wholly misjudged for the time. Yes, sir, permit me to remark that you do not sufficiently consider that, though a small man, I may have my small share of feelings."

"Well, well, I didn't mean to wound your feelings at all.

And that they are small, very small, I take your word for it. Sorry, sorry. But truth is like a thrashing-machine; tender sensibilities must keep out of the way. Hope you understand me. Don't want to hurt you. All I say is, what I said in the first place, only now I swear it, that all boys are rascals."

"Sir," lowly replied the other, still forbearing like an old lawyer badgered in court, or else like a good-hearted simpleton, the butt of mischievous wags. "Sir, since you come back to the point, will you allow me, in my small, quiet way, to submit to you certain small, quiet views of the subject in hand?"

"Oh, yes!" with insulting indifference, rubbing his chin and looking the other way. "Oh, yes; go on."

"Well, then, respected sir," continued the other, now assuming as genteel an attitude as the irritating set of his pinched five-dollar suit would permit; "well, then, sir, the peculiar principles, the strictly philosophical principles, I may say," guardedly rising in dignity, as he guardedly rose on his toes, "upon which our office is founded, have led me and my associates, in our small, quiet way, to a careful analytical study of man, conducted, too, on a quiet theory, and with an unobtrusive aim wholly our own. That theory I will not now at large set forth. But some of the discoveries resulting from it, I will, by your permission, very briefly mention; such of them, I mean, as refer to the state of boyhood scientifically viewed."

"Then you have studied the thing? expressly studied boys, eh? Why didn't you out with that before?"

"Sir, in my small business way, I have not conversed with so many masters, gentlemen masters, for nothing. I have been taught that in this world there is a precedence of opinions as well as of persons. You have kindly given me your views, I am now, with modesty, about to give you mine."

"Stop flunkying—go on."

"In the first place, sir, our theory teaches us to proceed by analogy from the physical to the moral. Are we right there, sir? Now, sir, take a young boy, a young male infant rather, a man-child in short—what sir, I respectfully ask, do you in the first place remark?"

"A rascal, sir! present and prospective, a rascal!"

"Sir, if passion is to invade, surely science must evacuate. May I proceed? Well, then, what, in the first place, in a general view, do you remark, respected sir, in that male baby or man-child?"

The bachelor privily growled, but this time, upon the whole, better governed himself than before, though not, indeed, to the degree of thinking it prudent to risk an articulate response.

"What do you remark? I respectfully repeat." But, as no answer came, only the low, half-suppressed growl, as of Bruin in a hollow trunk, the questioner continued: "Well, sir, if you will permit me, in my small way, to speak for you, you remark, respected sir, an incipient creation; loose sort of sketchy thing; a little preliminary rag-paper study, or careless cartoon, so to speak, of a man. The idea, you see, respected sir, is there; but, as yet, wants filling out. In a word, respected sir, the man-child is at present but little, every way; I don't pretend to deny it; but, then, he *promises* well, does he not? Yes, promises very well indeed, I may say. (So, too, we say to our patrons in reference to some noble little youngster objected to for being a *dwarf*.) But, to advance one step further," extending his thread-bare leg, as he drew a pace nearer, " we must now drop the figure of the rag-paper cartoon, and borrow one—to use presently, when wanted—from the horticultural kingdom. Some bud, lily-bud, if you please. Now, such points as the new-born man-child has—as yet not all that could be desired, I am free to confess—still, such as they are, there they are, and palpable as those of an adult. But we stop not here," taking another step. "The man-child not only possesses these present points, small though they are, but, likewise—now our horticultural image comes into play—like the bud of the lily, he contains concealed rudiments of others; that is, points at present invisible, with beauties at present dormant."

"Come, come, this talk is getting too horticultural and beautiful altogether. Cut it short, cut it short!"

"Respected sir," with a rustily martial sort of gesture, like a decayed corporal's, " when deploying into the field of discourse the vanguard of an important argument, much more in evolving the grand central forces of a new philosophy of boys, as I may say, surely you will kindly allow scope adequate to the movement in hand, small and humble in its way as that movement may be. Is it worth my while to go on, respected sir?"

"Yes, stop flunkying and go on."

Thus encouraged, again the philosopher with the brass-plate proceeded:

"Supposing, sir, that worthy gentleman (in such terms, to an applicant for service, we allude to some patron we chance to have in our eye), supposing, respected sir, that worthy gentleman, Adam, to have been dropped overnight in Eden, as a calf in the pasture; supposing that, sir—then how could even the learned serpent himself have foreknown that such a downy-chinned little innocent would eventually rival the goat in a beard? Sir, wise as the serpent was, that eventuality would have been entirely hidden from his wisdom."

"I don't know about that. The devil is very sagacious. To judge by the event, he appears to have understood man better even than the Being who made him."

"For God's sake, don't say that, sir! To the point. Can it now with fairness be denied that, in his beard, the man-child prospectively possesses an appendix, not less imposing than patriarchal; and for this goodly beard, should we not by generous anticipation give the man-child, even in his cradle, credit? Should we not now, sir? respectfully I put it."

"Yes, if like pig-weed he mows it down soon as it shoots," porcinely rubbing his stubble-chin against his coon-skins.

"I have hinted at the analogy," continued the other, calmly disregardful of the digression; "now to apply it. Suppose a boy evince no noble quality. Then generously give him credit for his prospective one. Don't you see? So we say to our patrons when they would fain return a boy upon us as unworthy: 'Madam, or sir, (as the case may be) has this boy a beard?' 'No.' 'Has he, we respectfully ask, as yet, evinced any noble quality?' 'No, indeed.' 'Then, madam, or sir, take him back, we humbly beseech; and keep him till that same noble quality sprouts; for, have confidence, it, like the beard, is in him.' "

"Very fine theory," scornfully exclaimed the bachelor, yet in secret, perhaps, not entirely undisturbed by these strange new views of the matter; "but what trust is to be placed in it?"

"The trust of perfect confidence, sir. To proceed. Once more, if you please, regard the man-child."

"Hold!" paw-like thrusting out his bearskin arm, "don't intrude that man-child upon me too often. He who loves not bread, dotes not on dough. As little of your man-child as your logical arrangements will admit."

"Anew regard the man-child," with inspired intrepidity repeated he with the brass-plate, "in the perspective of his developments, I mean. At first the man-child has no teeth, but about the sixth month—am I right, sir?"

"Don't know anything about it."

"To proceed then: though at first deficient in teeth, about the sixth month the man-child begins to put forth in that particular. And sweet those tender little puttings-forth are."

"Very, but blown out of his mouth directly, worthless enough."

"Admitted. And, therefore, we say to our patrons returning with a boy alleged not only to be deficient in goodness, but redundant in ill: 'The lad, madam or sir, evinces very corrupt qualities, does he?' 'No end to them.' 'But, have confidence, there will be; for pray, madam, in this lad's early childhood, were not those frail first teeth, then his, followed by his present sound, even, beautiful and permanent set? And the more objectionable those first teeth became, was not that, madam, we respectfully submit, so much the more reason to look for their speedy substitution by the present sound, even, beautiful and permanent ones?' 'True, true, can't deny that.' 'Then, madam, take him back, we respectfully beg, and wait till, in the now swift course of nature, dropping those transient moral blemishes you complain of, he replacingly buds forth in the sound, even, beautiful and permanent virtues.' "

"Very philosophical again," was the contemptuous reply— the outward contempt, perhaps, proportioned to the inward misgiving. "Vastly philosophical, indeed, but tell me—to continue your analogy—since the second teeth followed—in fact, came from—the first, is there no chance the blemish may be transmitted?"

"Not at all." Abating in humility as he gained in the argument. "The second teeth follow, but do not come from, the first; successors, not sons. The first teeth are not like the germ blossom of the apple, at once the father of, and incorporated into, the growth it foreruns; but they are thrust from their place by the independent undergrowth of the succeeding set—an illustration, by the way, which shows more for me than I meant, though not more than I wish."

"What does it show?" Surly-looking as a thunder-cloud with the inkept unrest of unacknowledged conviction.

"It shows this, respected sir, that in the case of any boy, especially an ill one, to apply unconditionally the saying, that the 'child is father of the man', is, besides implying an uncharitable aspersion of the race, affirming a thing very wide of—"

"—Your analogy," like a snapping turtle.

"Yes, respected sir."

"But is analogy argument? You are a punster."

"Punster, respected sir?" with a look of being aggrieved.

"Yes, you pun with ideas as another man may with words."

"Oh well, sir, whoever talks in that strain, whoever has no confidence in human reason, whoever despises human reason, in vain to reason with him. Still, respected sir," altering his air, "permit me to hint that, had not the force of analogy moved you somewhat, you would hardly have offered to contemn it."

"Talk away," disdainfully; "but pray tell me what has that last analogy of yours to do with your intelligence office business?"

"Everything to do with it, respected sir. From that analogy we derive the reply made to such a patron as, shortly after being supplied by us with an adult servant, proposes to return him upon our hands; not that, while with the patron, said adult has given any cause of dissatisfaction, but the patron has just chanced to hear something unfavorable concerning him from some gentleman who employed said adult long before, while a boy. To which too fastidious patron, we, taking said adult by the hand, and graciously reintroducing him to the patron, say: 'Far be it from you, madam, or sir, to proceed in your censure against this adult, in anything of the spirit of an ex-post-facto law. Madam, or sir, would you visit upon the butterfly the sins of the caterpillar? In the natural advance of all creatures, do they not bury themselves over and over again in the endless resurrection of better and better? Madam, or sir, take back this adult; he may have been a caterpillar, but is now a butterfly.' "

"Pun away; but even accepting your analogical pun, what does it amount to? Was the caterpillar one creature, and is the butterfly another? The butterfly is the caterpillar in a gaudy cloak; stripped of which, there lies the impostor's long spindle of a body, pretty much worm-shaped as before."

"You reject the analogy. To the facts then. You deny that a youth of one character can be transformed into a man of an opposite character. Now then—yes, I have it. There's the founder of La Trappe, and Ignatius Loyola; in boyhood, and someway into manhood, both devil-may-care bloods, and yet, in the end, the wonders of the world for anchoritish self-command. These two examples, by-the-way, we cite to such patrons as would hastily return rakish young waiters upon us. 'Madam, or sir—patience; patience,' we say; 'good madam, or sir, would you discharge forth your cask of good wine, because, while working, it riles more or less? Then discharge not forth this young waiter; the good in him is working.' 'But he is a sad rake.' 'Therein is his promise; the rake being crude material for the saint.' "

"Ah, you are a talking man—what I call a wordy man. You talk, talk."

"And with submission, sir, what is the greatest judge, bishop or prophet, but a talking man? He talks, talks. It is the peculiar vocation of a teacher to talk. What's wisdom itself but table-talk? The best wisdom in this world, and the last spoken by its teacher, did it not literally and truly come in the form of table-talk?"

"You, you, you!" rattling down his rifle.

"To shift the subject, since we cannot agree. Pray, what is your opinion, respected sir, of St. Augustine?"

"St. Augustine? What should I, or you either, know of him? Seems to me, for one in such a business, to say nothing of such a coat, that though you don't know a great deal, indeed, yet you know a good deal more than you ought to know, or than you have a right to know, or than it is safe or expedient for you to know, or than, in the fair course of life, you could have honestly come to know. I am of opinion you should be served like a Jew in the middle ages with his gold; this knowledge of yours, which you haven't enough knowledge to know how to make a right use of, it should be taken from you. And so I have been thinking all along."

"You are merry, sir. But you have a little looked into St. Augustine I suppose."

"St. Augustine on Original Sin is my text book. But you, I ask again, where do you find time or inclination for these out-of-the-way speculations? In fact, your whole talk, the more I think of it, is altogether unexampled and extraordinary."

"Respected sir, have I not already informed you that the quite new method, the strictly philosophical one, on which our office is founded, has led me and my associates to an enlarged study of mankind. It was my fault, if I did not, likewise, hint, that these studies directed always to the scientific procuring of good servants of all sorts, boys included, for the kind gentlemen, our patrons—that these studies, I say, have been conducted equally among all books of all libraries, as among all men of all nations. Then, you rather like St. Augustine, sir?"

"Excellent genius!"

"In some points he was; yet, how comes it that under his own hand, St. Augustine confesses that, until his thirtieth year, he was a very sad dog?"

"A saint a sad dog?"

"Not the saint, but the saint's irresponsible little forerunner—the boy."

"All boys are rascals, and so are all men," again flying off at his tangent; "my name is Pitch; I stick to what I say."

"Ah, sir, permit me—when I behold you on this mild summer's eve, thus eccentrically clothed in the skins of wild beasts, I cannot but conclude that the equally grim and unsuitable habit of your mind is likewise but an eccentric assumption, having no basis in your genuine soul, no more than in nature herself."

"Well, really, now—really," fidgeted the bachelor, not unaffected in his conscience by these benign personalities, "really, really, now, I don't know but that I may have been a little bit too hard upon those five and thirty boys of mine."

"Glad to find you a little softening, sir. Who knows now, but that flexile gracefulness, however questionable at the time of that thirtieth boy of yours, might have been the silky husk of the most solid qualities of maturity. It might have been with him as with the ear of the Indian corn."

"Yes, yes, yes," excitedly cried the bachelor, as the light of this new illustration broke in, "yes, yes; and now that I think of it, how often I've sadly watched my Indian corn in May, wondering whether such sickly, half-eaten sprouts, could ever thrive up into the stiff, stately spear of August."

"A most admirable reflection, sir, and you have only, according to the analogical theory first started by our office, to apply it to that thirtieth boy in question, and see the result. Had you but kept that thirtieth boy—been patient with his sickly virtues, cultivated them, hoed round them, why what a glorious guerdon would have been yours, when at last you should have had a St. Augustine for an ostler."

"Really, really—well, I am glad I didn't send him to jail, as at first I intended."

"Oh that would have been too bad. Grant he was vicious. The petty vices of boys are like the innocent kicks of colts, as yet imperfectly broken. Some boys know not virtue only for the same reason they know not French; it was never taught them. Established upon the basis of parental charity, juvenile asylums exist by law for the benefit of lads convicted of acts which, in adults, would have received other requital. Why? Because, do what they will, society, like our office, at bottom has a Christian confidence in boys. And all this we say to our patrons."

"Your patrons, sir, seem your marines to whom you may say anything," said the other, relapsing. "Why do knowing employers shun youths from asylums, though offered them at the smallest wages? I'll none of your reformado boys."

"Such a boy, respected sir, I would not get for you, but a boy that never needed reform. Do not smile, for as whooping-cough and measles are juvenile diseases, and yet some juveniles never have them, so are there boys equally free from juvenile vices. True, for the best of boys, measles may be contagious, and evil communications corrupt good manners; but a boy with a sound mind in a sound body—such is the boy I would get you. If hitherto, sir, you have struck upon a peculiarly bad vein of boys, so much the more hope now of your hitting a good one."

"That sounds a kind of reasonable, as it were—a little so, really. In fact, though you have said a great many foolish things, very foolish and absurd things, yet, upon the whole, your conversation has been such as might almost lead one less distrustful than I to repose a certain conditional confidence in you, I had almost added in your office, also. Now, for the humor of it, supposing that even I, I myself, really had this sort of conditional confidence, though but a grain, what sort of a boy, in sober fact, could you send me? And what would be your fee?"

"Conducted," replied the other somewhat loftily, rising now in eloquence as his proselyte, for all his pretenses, sunk in conviction, "conducted upon principles involving care, learning, and labor, exceeding what is usual in kindred institutions, the Philosophical Intelligence Office is forced to charges somewhat higher than customary. Briefly, our fee is three dollars in advance. As for the boy, by a lucky chance, I have a very promising little fellow now in my eye—a very likely little fellow, indeed."

"Honest?"

"As the day is long. Might trust him with untold millions. Such, at least, were the marginal observations on the phrenological chart of his head, submitted to me by the mother."

"How old?"

"Just fifteen."

"Tall? Stout?"

"Uncommonly so, for his age, his mother remarked."

"Industrious?"

"The busy bee."

The bachelor fell into a troubled reverie. At last, with much hesitancy, he spoke:

"Do you think now, candidly, that—I say candidly—candidly—could I have some small, limited—some faint, conditional degree of confidence in that boy? Candidly, now?"

"Candidly, you could."

"A sound boy? A good boy?"

"Never knew one more so."

The bachelor fell into another irresolute reverie; then said: "Well, now, you have suggested some rather new views of boys, and men, too. Upon those views in the concrete I at present decline to determine. Nevertheless, for the sake purely of a scientific experiment, I will try that boy. I don't think him an angel, mind. No, no. But I'll try him. There are my three dollars, and here is my address. Send him along this day two weeks. Hold, you will be wanting the money for his passage. There," handing it somewhat reluctantly.

"Ah, thank you. I had forgotten his passage;" then, altering in manner, and gravely holding the bills, continued: "Respected sir, never willingly do I handle money not with perfect willingness, nay, with a certain alacrity, paid. Either tell me that you have a perfect and unquestioning confidence in me (never mind the boy now) or permit me respectfully to return these bills."

"Put 'em up, put 'em up!"

"Thank you. Confidence is the indispensable basis of all sorts of business transactions. Without it, commerce between man and man, as between country and country, would, like a watch, run down and stop. And now, supposing that against present expectation the lad should, after all, evince some little undesirable trait, do not, respected sir, rashly dismiss him. Have but patience, have but confidence. Those transient vices will, ere long, fall out, and be replaced by the sound, firm, even and permanent virtues. Ah," glancing shoreward, towards a grotesquely-shaped bluff, "there's the Devil's Joke, as they call it; the bell for landing will shortly ring. I must go look up the cook I brought for the inn-keeper at Cairo."

Chapter 23

At CAIRO, the old established firm of Fever & Ague is still settling up its unfinished business; that Creole grave-digger, Yellow Jack—his hand at the mattock and spade has not lost its cunning; while Don Saturninus Typhus taking his constitutional with Death, Calvin Edson and three undertakers, in the morass, snuffs up the mephitic breeze with zest.

In the dank twilight, fanned with mosquitoes, and sparkling with fire-flies, the boat now lies before Cairo. She has landed certain passengers, and tarries for the coming of expected ones. Leaning over the rail on the inshore side, the Missourian eyes through the dubious medium that swampy and squalid domain; and over it audibly mumbles his cynical mind to himself, as Apemantus' dog may have mumbled his bone. He bethinks him that the man with the brass-plate was to land on this villainous bank, and for that cause, if no other, begins to suspect him. Like one beginning to rouse himself from a dose of chloroform treacherously given, he half divines, too, that he, the philosopher, had unwittingly been betrayed into being an unphilosophical dupe. To what vicissitudes of light and shade is man subject! He ponders the mystery of human subjectivity in general. He thinks he perceives with Crossbones, his favorite author, that, as one may wake up well in the morning, very well, indeed, and brisk as a buck, I thank you, but ere bed-time get under the weather, there is no telling how—so one may wake up wise, and slow of assent, very wise and very slow, I assure you, and for all that, before night, by like trick in the atmosphere, be left in the lurch a ninny. Health and wisdom equally precious, and equally little as unfluctuating possessions to be relied on.

But where was slipped in the entering wedge? Philosophy, knowledge, experience—were those trusty knights of the castle recreant? No, but unbeknown to them, the enemy stole on the castle's south side, its genial one, where Suspicion, the warder, parleyed. In fine, his too indulgent, too artless and companionable nature betrayed him. Admonished by which, he thinks he must be a little splenetic in his intercourse henceforth.

He revolves the crafty process of sociable chat, by which, as he fancies, the man with the brass-plate wormed into him, and made such a fool of him as insensibly to persuade him to waive, in his exceptional case, that general law of distrust systematically applied to the race. He revolves, but cannot comprehend, the operation, still less the operator. Was the man a trickster, it must be more for the love than the lucre. Two or three dirty dollars the motive to so many nice wiles? And yet how full of mean needs his seeming. Before his mental vision the person of that threadbare Talleyrand, that impoverished Machiavelli, that seedy Rosicrucian—for something of all these he vaguely deems him—passes now in puzzled review. Fain, in his disfavor, would he make out a logical case. The doctrine of analogies recurs. Fallacious enough doctrine when wielded against one's prejudices, but in corroboration of cherished suspicions not without likelihood. Analogically, he couples the slanting cut of the equivocator's coat-tails with the sinister cast in his eye; he weighs slyboot's sleek speech in the light imparted by the oblique import of the smooth slope of his worn boot-heels; the insinuator's undulating flunkyisms dovetail into those of the flunky beast that windeth his way on his belly.

From these uncordial reveries he is roused by a cordial slap on the shoulder, accompanied by a spicy volume of tobacco-smoke, out of which came a voice, sweet as a seraph's:

"A penny for your thoughts, my fine fellow."

Chapter 24

A PHILANTHROPIST UNDERTAKES TO CONVERT A
MISANTHROPE, BUT DOES NOT GET BEYOND
CONFUTING HIM

H ANDS OFF!" cried the bachelor, involuntarily covering
dejection with moroseness.

"Hands off? that sort of label won't do in our Fair.
Whoever in our Fair has fine feelings loves to feel the nap of
fine cloth, especially when a fine fellow wears it."

"And who of my fine-fellow species may you be? From
the Brazils, ain't you? Toucan fowl. Fine feathers on foul
meat."

This ungentle mention of the toucan was not improbably
suggested by the parti-hued, and rather plumagy aspect of the
stranger, no bigot it would seem, but a liberalist, in dress, and
whose wardrobe, almost anywhere than on the liberal Mississippi, used to all sorts of fantastic informalities, might, even
to observers less critical than the bachelor, have looked, if
anything, a little out of the common; but not more so perhaps, than, considering the bear and raccoon costume, the
bachelor's own appearance. In short, the stranger sported a
vesture barred with various hues, that of the cochineal pre-
dominating, in style participating of a Highland plaid, Emir's
robe, and French blouse; from its plaited sort of front peeped
glimpses of a flowered regatta-shirt, while, for the rest, white
trowsers of ample duck flowed over maroon-colored slippers,
and a jaunty smoking-cap of regal purple crowned him off at
top; king of traveled good-fellows, evidently. Grotesque as all
was, nothing looked stiff or unused; all showed signs of easy
service, the least wonted thing setting like a wonted glove.
That genial hand, which had just been laid on the ungenial
shoulder, was now carelessly thrust down before him, sailor-
fashion, into a sort of Indian belt, confining the redundant
vesture; the other held, by its long bright cherry-stem, a Nu-
remburgh pipe in blast, its great porcelain bowl painted in
miniature with linked crests and arms of interlinked nations—
a florid show. As by subtle saturations of its mellowing

essence the tobacco had ripened the bowl, so it looked as if something similar of the interior spirit came rosily out on the cheek. But rosy pipe-bowl, or rosy countenance, all was lost on that unrosy man, the bachelor, who, waiting a moment till the commotion, caused by the boat's renewed progress, had a little abated, thus continued:

"Hark ye," jeeringly eying the cap and belt, "did you ever see Signor Marzetti in the African pantomime?"

"No;—good performer?"

"Excellent; plays the intelligent ape till he seems it. With such naturalness can a being endowed with an immortal spirit enter into that of a monkey. But where's your tail? In the pantomime, Marzetti, no hypocrite in his monkery, prides himself on that."

The stranger, now at rest, sideways and genially, on one hip, his right leg cavalierly crossed before the other, the toe of his vertical slipper pointed easily down on the deck, whiffed out a long, leisurely sort of indifferent and charitable puff, betokening him more or less of the mature man of the world, a character which, like its opposite, the sincere Christian's, is not always swift to take offense; and then, drawing near, still smoking, again laid his hand, this time with mild impressiveness, on the ursine shoulder, and not unamiably said: "That in your address there is a sufficiency of the *fortiter in re* few unbiased observers will question; but that this is duly attempered with the *suaviter in modo* may admit, I think, of an honest doubt. My dear fellow," beaming his eyes full upon him, "what injury have I done you, that you should receive my greeting with a curtailed civility?"

"Off hands;" once more shaking the friendly member from him. "Who in the name of the great chimpanzee, in whose likeness, you, Marzetti, and the other chatterers are made, who in thunder are you?"

"A cosmopolitan, a catholic man; who, being such, ties himself to no narrow tailor or teacher, but federates, in heart as in costume, something of the various gallantries of men under various suns. Oh, one roams not over the gallant globe in vain. Bred by it, is a fraternal and fusing feeling. No man is a stranger. You accost anybody. Warm and confiding, you wait not for measured advances. And though, indeed, mine, in this instance, have met with no very hilarious encouragement, yet the principle of a true citizen of the world is still to return good for ill.—My dear fellow, tell me how I can serve you."

"By dispatching yourself, Mr. Popinjay-of-the-world, into the heart of the Lunar Mountains. You are another of them. Out of my sight!"

"Is the sight of humanity so very disagreeable to you then? Ah, I may be foolish, but for my part, in all its aspects, I love it. Served up à la Pole, or à la Moor, à la Ladrone, or à la Yankee, that good dish, man, still delights me; or rather is man a wine I never weary of comparing and sipping; wherefore am I a pledged cosmopolitan, a sort of London-Dock-Vault connoisseur, going about from Teheran to Natchitoches, a taster of races; in all his vintages, smacking my lips over this racy creature, man, continually. But as there are teetotal palates which have a distaste even for Amontillado, so I suppose there may be teetotal souls which relish not even the very best brands of humanity. Excuse me, but it just occurs to me that you, my dear fellow, possibly lead a solitary life."

"Solitary?" starting as at a touch of divination.

"Yes: in a solitary life one insensibly contracts oddities,—talking to one's self now."

"Been eaves-dropping, eh?"

"Why, a soliloquist in a crowd can hardly but be overheard, and without much reproach to the hearer."

"You are an eaves-dropper."

"Well. Be it so."

"Confess yourself an eaves-dropper?"

"I confess that when you were muttering here I, passing by, caught a word or two, and, by like chance, something previous of your chat with the Intelligence-office man;—a rather sensible fellow, by the way; much of my style of thinking; would, for his own sake, he were of my style of dress. Grief to good minds, to see a man of superior sense forced to hide his light under the bushel of an inferior coat.—Well, from what little I heard, I said to myself, Here now is one with the unprofitable philosophy of disesteem for man. Which disease, in the main, I have observed—excuse me—to spring from a certain lowness, if not sourness, of spirits inseparable from sequestration. Trust me, one had better mix in, and do like others. Sad business, this holding out against having a good time. Life is a pic-nic *en costume*; one must take a part, assume a character, stand ready in a sensible way to play the fool. To come in plain clothes, with a long face, as a wise-acre, only makes one a discomfort to himself, and a blot upon the scene. Like your jug of cold water among the wine-flasks, it leaves you unelated among the elated ones. No, no. This austerity won't do. Let me tell you too— *en confiance*— that while revelry may not always merge into ebriety, soberness, in too deep potations, may become a sort of sottishness. Which sober sottishness, in my way of thinking, is only to be cured by beginning at the other end of the horn, to tipple a little."

"Pray, what society of vintners and old topers are you hired to lecture for?"

"I fear I did not give my meaning clearly. A little story may help. The story of the worthy old woman of Goshen, a very moral old woman, who wouldn't let her shoats eat fattening apples in fall, for fear the fruit might ferment upon their brains, and so make them swinish. Now, during a green Christmas, inauspicious to the old, this worthy old woman fell into a moping decline, took to her bed, no appetite, and refused to see her best friends. In much concern her good man sent for the doctor, who, after seeing the patient and putting a question or two, beckoned the husband out, and said: 'Deacon, do you want her cured?' 'Indeed I do.' 'Go directly, then, and buy a jug of Santa Cruz.' 'Santa Cruz? my wife drink Santa Cruz?' 'Either that or die.' 'But how much?' 'As much as she can get down.' 'But she'll get drunk!' 'That's the cure.' Wise men, like doctors, must be obeyed. Much against the grain, the sober deacon got the unsober medicine, and, equally against her conscience, the poor old woman took it; but, by so doing, ere long recovered health and spirits, famous appetite, and glad again to see her friends; and having by this experience broken the ice of arid abstinence, never afterwards kept herself a cup too low."

This story had the effect of surprising the bachelor into interest, though hardly into approval.

"If I take your parable right," said he, sinking no little of

his former churlishness, "the meaning is, that one cannot enjoy life with gusto unless he renounce the too-sober view of
life. But since the too-sober view is, doubtless, nearer true
than the too-drunken; I, who rate truth, though cold water,
above untruth, though Tokay, will stick to my earthen jug."

"I see," slowly spirting upward a spiral staircase of lazy
smoke, "I see; you go in for the lofty."

"How?"

"Oh, nothing! but if I wasn't afraid of prosing, I might tell
another story about an old boot in a pieman's loft, contracting there between sun and oven an unseemly, dry-seasoned
curl and warp. You've seen such leathery old garretteers,
haven't you? Very high, sober, solitary, philosophic, grand,
old boots, indeed; but I, for my part, would rather be the
pieman's trodden slipper on the ground. Talking of piemen,
humble-pie before proud-cake for me. This notion of being
lone and lofty is a sad mistake. Men I hold in this respect to
be like roosters; the one that betakes himself to a lone and
lofty perch is the hen-pecked one, or the one that has the
pip."

"You are abusive!" cried the bachelor, evidently touched.

"Who is abused? You, or the race? You won't stand by and
see the human race abused? Oh, then, you have some respect
for the human race."

"I have some respect for *myself*," with a lip not so firm as
before.

"And what race may *you* belong to? now don't you see, my
dear fellow, in what inconsistencies one involves himself by
affecting disesteem for men? To a charm, my little stratagem
succeeded. Come, come, think better of it, and, as a first step
to a new mind, give up solitude. I fear, by the way, you have
at some time been reading Zimmermann, that old Mr. Me-
grims of a Zimmermann, whose book on Solitude is as vain
as Hume's on Suicide, as Bacon's on Knowledge; and, like
these, will betray him who seeks to steer soul and body by it,
like a false religion. All they, be they what boasted ones you
please, who, to the yearning of our kind after a founded rule
of content, offer aught not in the spirit of fellowly gladness
based on due confidence in what is above, away with them
for poor dupes, or still poorer impostors."

His manner here was so earnest that scarcely any auditor, perhaps, but would have been more or less impressed by it, while, possibly, nervous opponents might have a little quailed under it. Thinking within himself a moment, the bachelor replied: "Had you experience, you would know that your tippling theory, take it in what sense you will, is poor as any other. And Rabelais's pro-wine Koran no more trustworthy than Mahomet's anti-wine one."

"Enough," for a finality knocking the ashes from his pipe, "we talk and keep talking, and still stand where we did. What do you say for a walk? My arm, and let's a turn. They are to have dancing on the hurricane-deck to-night. I shall fling them off a Scotch jig, while, to save the pieces, you hold my loose change; and following that, I propose that you, my dear fellow, stack your gun, and throw your bearskins in a sailor's hornpipe—I holding your watch. What do you say?"

At this proposition the other was himself again, all raccoon.

"Look you," thumping down his rifle, "are you Jeremy Diddler No. 3?"

"Jeremy Diddler? I have heard of Jeremy the prophet, and Jeremy Taylor the divine, but your other Jeremy is a gentleman I am unacquainted with."

"You are his confidential clerk, ain't you?"

"*Whose*, pray? Not that I think myself unworthy of being confided in, but I don't understand."

"You are another of them. Somehow I meet with the most extraordinary metaphysical scamps to-day. Sort of visitation of them. And yet that herb-doctor Diddler somehow takes off the raw edge of the Diddlers that come after him."

"Herb-doctor? who is he?"

"Like you—another of them."

"*Who?*" Then drawing near, as if for a good long explanatory chat, his left hand spread, and his pipe-stem coming crosswise down upon it like a ferule, "You think amiss of me. Now to undeceive you, I will just enter into a little argument and—"

"No you don't. No more little arguments for me. Had too many little arguments to-day."

"But put a case. Can you deny—I dare you to deny—that

the man leading a solitary life is peculiarly exposed to the sorriest misconceptions touching strangers?"

"Yes, I *do* deny it," again, in his impulsiveness, snapping at the controversial bait, "and I will confute you there in a trice. Look, you—"

"Now, now, now, my dear fellow," thrusting out both vertical palms for double shields, "you crowd me too hard. You don't give one a chance. Say what you will, to shun a social proposition like mine, to shun society in any way, evinces a churlish nature—cold, loveless; as, to embrace it, shows one warm and friendly, in fact, sunshiny."

Here the other, all agog again, in his perverse way, launched forth into the unkindest references to deaf old worldlings keeping in the deafening world; and gouty gluttons limping to their gouty gormandizings; and corseted coquets clasping their corseted cavaliers in the waltz, all for disinterested society's sake; and thousands, bankrupt through lavishness, ruining themselves out of pure love of the sweet company of man—no envies, rivalries, or other unhandsome motive to it.

"Ah, now," deprecating with his pipe, "irony is so unjust; never could abide irony; something Satanic about irony. God defend me from Irony, and Satire, his bosom friend."

"A right knave's prayer, and a right fool's, too," snapping his rifle-lock.

"Now be frank. Own that was a little gratuitous. But, no, no, you didn't mean it; any way, I can make allowances. Ah, did you but know it, how much pleasanter to puff at this philanthropic pipe, than still to keep fumbling at that misanthropic rifle. As for your worldling, glutton, and coquette, though, doubtless, being such, they may have their little foibles—as who has not?—yet not one of the three can be reproached with that awful sin of shunning society; awful I call it, for not seldom it presupposes a still darker thing than itself—remorse."

"Remorse drives man away from man? How came your fellow-creature, Cain, after the first murder, to go and build the first city? And why is it that the modern Cain dreads nothing so much as solitary confinement?"

"My dear fellow, you get excited. Say what you will, I for

one must have my fellow-creatures round me. Thick, too—I must have them thick."

"The pick-pocket, too, loves to have his fellow-creatures round him. Tut, man! no one goes into the crowd but for his end; and the end of too many is the same as the pick-pocket's—a purse."

"Now, my dear fellow, how can you have the conscience to say that, when it is as much according to natural law that men are social as sheep gregarious. But grant that, in being social, each man has his end, do you, upon the strength of that, do you yourself, I say, mix with man, now, immediately, and be your end a more genial philosophy. Come, let's take a turn."

Again he offered his fraternal arm; but the bachelor once more flung it off, and, raising his rifle in energetic invocation, cried: "Now the high-constable catch and confound all knaves in towns and rats in grain-bins, and if in this boat, which is a human grain-bin for the time, any sly, smooth, philandering rat be dodging now, pin him, thou high rat-catcher, against this rail."

"A noble burst! shows you at heart a trump. And when a card's that, little matters it whether it be spade or diamond. You are good wine that, to be still better, only needs a shaking up. Come, let's agree that we'll to New Orleans, and there embark for London—I staying with my friends nigh Primrose-hill, and you putting up at the Piazza, Covent Garden—Piazza, Covent Garden; for tell me—since you will not be a disciple to the full—tell me, was not that humor, of Diogenes, which led him to live, a merry-andrew, in the flower-market, better than that of the less wise Athenian, which made him a skulking scare-crow in pine-barrens? An injudicious gentleman, Lord Timon."

"Your hand!" seizing it.

"Bless me, how cordial a squeeze. It is agreed we shall be brothers, then?"

"As much so as a brace of misanthropes can be," with another and terrific squeeze. "I had thought that the moderns had degenerated beneath the capacity of misanthropy. Rejoiced, though but in one instance, and that disguised, to be undeceived."

The other stared in blank amaze.

"Won't do. You are Diogenes, Diogenes in disguise. I say—Diogenes masquerading as a cosmopolitan."

With ruefully altered mien, the stranger still stood mute awhile. At length, in a pained tone, spoke: "How hard the lot of that pleader who, in his zeal conceding too much, is taken to belong to a side which he but labors, however ineffectually, to convert!" Then with another change of air: "To you, an Ishmael, disguising in sportiveness my intent, I came ambassador from the human race, charged with the assurance that for your mislike they bore no answering grudge, but sought to conciliate accord between you and them. Yet you take me not for the honest envoy, but I know not what sort of unheard-of spy. Sir," he less lowly added, "this mistaking of your man should teach you how you may mistake all men. For God's sake," laying both hands upon him, "get you confidence. See how distrust has duped you. I, Diogenes? I he who, going a step beyond misanthropy, was less a man-hater than a man-hooter? Better were I stark and stiff!"

With which the philanthropist moved away less lightsome than he had come, leaving the discomfited misanthrope to the solitude he held so sapient.

Chapter 25

The Cosmopolitan makes an acquaintance

IN THE ACT of retiring, the cosmopolitan was met by a passenger, who, with the bluff *abord* of the West, thus addressed him, though a stranger.

"Queer 'coon, your friend. Had a little skrimmage with him myself. Rather entertaining old 'coon, if he wasn't so deuced analytical. Reminded me somehow of what I've heard about Colonel John Moredock, of Illinois, only your friend ain't quite so good a fellow at bottom, I should think."

It was in the semicircular porch of a cabin, opening a recess from the deck, lit by a zoned lamp swung overhead, and sending its light vertically down, like the sun at noon. Beneath the lamp stood the speaker, affording to any one disposed to it no unfavorable chance for scrutiny; but the glance now resting on him betrayed no such rudeness.

A man neither tall nor stout, neither short nor gaunt; but with a body fitted, as by measure, to the service of his mind. For the rest, one less favored perhaps in his features than his clothes; and of these the beauty may have been less in the fit than the cut; to say nothing of the fineness of the nap, seeming out of keeping with something the reverse of fine in the skin; and the unsuitableness of a violet vest, sending up sunset hues to a countenance betokening a kind of bilious habit.

But, upon the whole, it could not be fairly said that his appearance was unprepossessing; indeed, to the congenial, it would have been doubtless not uncongenial; while to others, it could not fail to be at least curiously interesting, from the warm air of florid cordiality, contrasting itself with one knows not what kind of aguish sallowness of saving discretion lurking behind it. Ungracious critics might have thought that the manner flushed the man, something in the same fictitious ways that the vest flushed the cheek. And though his teeth were singularly good, those same ungracious ones might have hinted that they were too good to be true; or rather, were not so good as they might be; since the best false teeth are those made with at least two or three blemishes, the more to look like life. But fortunately for better constructions, no such critics had the stranger now in eye; only the cosmopolitan, who, after, in the first place, acknowledging his advances with a mute salute—in which acknowledgment, if there seemed less of spirit than in his way of accosting the Missourian, it was probably because of the saddening sequel of that late interview—thus now replied: "Colonel John Moredock," repeating the words abstractedly; "that surname recalls reminiscences. Pray," with enlivened air, "was he anyway connected with the Moredocks of Moredock Hall, Northamptonshire, England?"

"I know no more of the Moredocks of Moredock Hall than of the Burdocks of Burdock Hut," returned the other, with the air somehow of one whose fortunes had been of his own making; "all I know is, that the late Colonel John Moredock was a famous one in his time; eye like Lochiel's; finger like a trigger; nerve like a catamount's; and with but two little oddities—seldom stirred without his rifle, and hated Indians like snakes."

"Your Moredock, then, would seem a Moredock of Misanthrope Hall—the Woods. No very sleek creature, the colonel, I fancy."

"Sleek or not, he was no uncombed one, but silky bearded and curly headed, and to all but Indians juicy as a peach. But Indians—how the late Colonel John Moredock, Indian-hater of Illinois, did hate Indians, to be sure!"

"Never heard of such a thing. Hate Indians? Why should he or anybody else hate Indians? *I* admire Indians. Indians I have always heard to be one of the finest of the primitive races, possessed of many heroic virtues. Some noble women, too. When I think of Pocahontas, I am ready to love Indians. Then there's Massasoit, and Philip of Mount Hope, and Tecumseh, and Red-Jacket, and Logan—all heroes; and there's the Five Nations, and Araucanians—federations and communities of heroes. God bless me; hate Indians? Surely the late Colonel John Moredock must have wandered in his mind."

"Wandered in the woods considerably, but never wandered elsewhere, that I ever heard."

"Are you in earnest? Was there ever one who so made it his

particular mission to hate Indians that, to designate him, a special word has been coined—Indian-hater?"

"Even so."

"Dear me, you take it very calmly.—But really, I would like to know something about this Indian-hating. I can hardly believe such a thing to be. Could you favor me with a little history of the extraordinary man you mentioned?"

"With all my heart," and immediately stepping from the porch, gestured the cosmopolitan to a settee near by, on deck. "There, sir, sit you there, and I will sit here beside you—you desire to hear of Colonel John Moredock. Well, a day in my boyhood is marked with a white stone—the day I saw the colonel's rifle, powder-horn attached, hanging in a cabin on the West bank of the Wabash river. I was going westward a long journey through the wilderness with my father. It was high noon, and we had stopped at the cabin to unsaddle and bait. The man at the cabin pointed out the rifle, and told whose it was, adding that the colonel was that moment sleeping on wolf-skins in the corn-loft above, so we must not talk very loud, for the colonel had been out all night hunting (Indians, mind), and it would be cruel to disturb his sleep. Curious to see one so famous, we waited two hours over, in hopes he would come forth; but he did not. So, it being necessary to get to the next cabin before nightfall, we had at last to ride off without the wished-for satisfaction. Though, to tell the truth, I, for one, did not go away entirely ungratified, for, while my father was watering the horses, I slipped back into the cabin, and stepping a round or two up the ladder, pushed my head through the trap, and peered about. Not much light in the loft; but off, in the further corner, I saw what I took to be the wolf-skins, and on them a bundle of something, like a drift of leaves; and at one end, what seemed a moss-ball; and over it, deer-antlers branched; and close by, a small squirrel sprang out from a maple-bowl of nuts, brushed the moss-ball with his tail, through a hole, and vanished, squeaking. That bit of woodland scene was all I saw. No Colonel Moredock there, unless that moss-ball was his curly head, seen in the back view. I would have gone clear up, but the man below had warned me, that though, from his camping habits, the colonel could sleep through thunder, he was for the same cause amazing quick to waken at the sound of footsteps, however soft, and especially if human."

"Excuse me," said the other, softly laying his hand on the narrator's wrist, "but I fear the colonel was of a distrustful nature—little or no confidence. He *was* a little suspicious-minded, wasn't he?"

"Not a bit. Knew too much. Suspected nobody, but was not ignorant of Indians. Well: though, as you may gather, I never fully saw the man, yet, have I, one way and another, heard about as much of him as any other; in particular, have I heard his history again and again from my father's friend, James Hall, the judge, you know. In every company being called upon to give this history, which none could better do, the judge at last fell into a style so methodic, you would have thought he spoke less to mere auditors than to an invisible amanuensis; seemed talking for the press; very impressive way with him indeed. And I, having an equally impressible memory, think that, upon a pinch, I can render you the judge upon the colonel almost word for word."

"Do so, by all means," said the cosmopolitan, well pleased.

"Shall I give you the judge's philosophy, and all?"

"As to that," rejoined the other gravely, pausing over the pipe-bowl he was filling, "the desirableness, to a man of a certain mind, of having another man's philosophy given, depends considerably upon what school of philosophy that other man belongs to. Of what school or system was the judge, pray?"

"Why, though he knew how to read and write, the judge never had much schooling. But, I should say he belonged, if anything, to the free-school system. Yes, a true patriot, the judge went in strong for free-schools."

"In philosophy? The man of a certain mind, then, while respecting the judge's patriotism, and not blind to the judge's capacity for narrative, such as he may prove to have, might, perhaps, with prudence, waive an opinion of the judge's probable philosophy. But I am no rigorist; proceed, I beg; his philosophy or not, as you please."

"Well, I would mostly skip that part, only, to begin, some reconnoitering of the ground in a philosophical way the judge always deemed indispensable with strangers. For you must know that Indian-hating was no monopoly of Colonel More-dock's; but a passion, in one form or other, and to a degree, greater or less, largely shared among the class to which he belonged. And Indian-hating still exists; and, no doubt, will continue to exist, so long as Indians do. Indian-hating, then, shall be my first theme, and Colonel Moredock, the Indian-hater, my next and last."

With which the stranger, settling himself in his seat, com-menced—the hearer paying marked regard, slowly smoking, his glance, meanwhile, steadfastly abstracted towards the deck, but his right ear so disposed towards the speaker that each word came through as little atmospheric intervention as possible. To intensify the sense of hearing, he seemed to sink the sense of sight. No complaisance of mere speech could have been so flattering, or expressed such striking politeness as this mute eloquence of thoroughly digesting attention.

Chapter 26

CONTAINING THE METAPHYSICS OF INDIAN-HATING,
ACCORDING TO THE VIEWS OF ONE EVIDENTLY NOT
SO PREPOSSESSED AS ROUSSEAU IN FAVOR OF
SAVAGES

THE JUDGE ALWAYS began in these words: 'The back-woodsman's hatred of the Indian has been a topic for some remark. In the earlier times of the frontier the passion was thought to be readily accounted for. But Indian rapine having mostly ceased through regions where it once prevailed, the philanthropist is surprised that Indian-hating has not in like degree ceased with it. He wonders why the backwoodsman still regards the red man in much the same spirit that a jury does a murderer, or a trapper a wild cat—a creature, in whose behalf mercy were not wisdom; truce is vain; he must be executed.

" 'A curious point,' the judge would continue, ' which perhaps not everybody, even upon explanation, may fully understand; while, in order for any one to approach to an understanding, it is necessary for him to learn, or if he already know, to bear in mind, what manner of man the backwoodsman is; as for what manner of man the Indian is, many know, either from history or experience.

" 'The backwoodsman is a lonely man. He is a thoughtful man. He is a man strong and unsophisticated. Impulsive, he is what some might call unprincipled. At any rate, he is self-willed; being one who less hearkens to what others may say about things, than looks for himself, to see what are things themselves. If in straits, there are few to help; he must depend upon himself; he must continually look to himself. Hence self-reliance, to the degree of standing by his own judgment, though it stand alone. Not that he deems himself infallible; too many mistakes in following trails prove the contrary; but he thinks that nature destines such sagacity as she has given him, as she destines it to the 'possum. To these fellow-beings of the wilds their untutored sagacity is their best dependence. If with either it prove faulty, if the 'possum's betray it to the trap, or the backwoodsman's mislead him into ambuscade, there are consequences to be undergone, but no self-blame. As with the 'possum, instincts prevail with the backwoodsman over precepts. Like the 'possum, the backwoodsman presents the spectacle of a creature dwelling exclusively among the works of God, yet these, truth must confess, breed little in him of a godly mind. Small bowing and scraping is his, further than when with bent knee he points his rifle, or picks its flint. With few companions, solitude by necessity his lengthened lot, he stands the trial—no slight one, since, next to dying, solitude, rightly borne, is perhaps of fortitude the most rigorous test. But not merely is the backwoodsman content to be alone, but in no few cases is anxious to be so. The sight of smoke ten miles off is provocation to one more remove from man, one step deeper into nature. Is it that he feels that whatever man may be, man is not the universe? that glory, beauty, kindness, are not all engrossed by him? that as the presence of man frights birds away, so, many bird-like thoughts? Be that how it will, the backwoodsman is not without some fineness to his nature. Hairy Orson as he looks, it may be with him as with the Shetland seal—beneath the bristles lurks the fur.

" 'Though held in a sort a barbarian, the backwoodsman would seem to America what Alexander was to Asia—captain in the vanguard of conquering civilization. Whatever the nation's growing opulence or power, does it not lackey his heels? Pathfinder, provider of security to those who come after him, for himself he asks nothing but hardship. Worthy to be compared with Moses in the Exodus, or the Emperor Julian in Gaul, who on foot, and bare-browed, at the head of covered or mounted legions, marched so through the elements, day after day. The tide of emigration, let it roll as it will, never overwhelms the backwoodsman into itself; he rides upon advance, as the Polynesian upon the comb of the surf.

" 'Thus, though he keep moving on through life, he maintains with respect to nature much the same unaltered relation throughout; with her creatures, too, including panthers and Indians. Hence, it is not unlikely that, accurate as the theory of the Peace Congress may be with respect to those two

varieties of beings, among others, yet the backwoodsman
might be qualified to throw out some practical suggestions.

" 'As the child born to a backwoodsman must in turn lead
his father's life—a life which, as related to humanity, is related mainly to Indians—it is thought best not to mince matters, out of delicacy; but to tell the boy pretty plainly what an
Indian is, and what he must expect from him. For however
charitable it may be to view Indians as members of the Society of Friends, yet to affirm them such to one ignorant of
Indians, whose lonely path lies a long way through their
lands, this, in the event, might prove not only injudicious but
cruel. At least something of this kind would seem the maxim
upon which backwoods' education is based. Accordingly, if in
youth the backwoodsman incline to knowledge, as is generally the case, he hears little from his schoolmasters, the old
chroniclers of the forest, but histories of Indian lying, Indian
theft, Indian double-dealing, Indian fraud and perfidy, Indian
want of conscience, Indian blood-thirstiness, Indian diabo-
lism—histories which, though of wild woods, are almost as
full of things unangelic as the Newgate Calendar or the Annals of Europe. In these Indian narratives and traditions the
lad is thoroughly grounded. "As the twig is bent the tree's
inclined." The instinct of antipathy against an Indian grows
in the backwoodsman with the sense of good and bad, right
and wrong. In one breath he learns that a brother is to be
loved, and an Indian to be hated.

" 'Such are the facts,' the judge would say, 'upon which, if
one seek to moralize, he must do so with an eye to them. It
is terrible that one creature should so regard another, should
make it conscience to abhor an entire race. It is terrible; but
is it surprising? Surprising, that one should hate a race which
he believes to be red from a cause akin to that which makes
some tribes of garden insects green? A race whose name is
upon the frontier a *memento mori*; painted to him in every
evil light; now a horse-thief like those in Moyamensing; now
an assassin like a New York rowdy; now a treaty-breaker like
an Austrian; now a Palmer with poisoned arrows; now a judicial murderer and Jeffries, after a fierce farce of trial condemning his victim to bloody death; or a Jew with hospitable
speeches cozening some fainting stranger into ambuscade,

there to burke him, and account it a deed grateful to Mani-
tou, his god.

" 'Still, all this is less advanced as truths of the Indians than
as examples of the backwoodsman's impression of them—in
which the charitable may think he does them some injustice.
Certain it is, the Indians themselves think so; quite unani-
mously, too. The Indians, indeed, protest against the backwoodsman's view of them; and some think that one cause of
their returning his antipathy so sincerely as they do, is their
moral indignation at being so libeled by him, as they really
believe and say. But whether, on this or any point, the Indians should be permitted to testify for themselves, to the exclusion of other testimony, is a question that may be left to the
Supreme Court. At any rate, it has been observed that when
an Indian becomes a genuine proselyte to Christianity (such
cases, however, not being very many; though, indeed, entire
tribes are sometimes nominally brought to the true light,) he
will not in that case conceal his enlightened conviction, that
his race's portion by nature is total depravity; and, in that
way, as much as admits that the backwoodsman's worst idea
of it is not very far from true; while, on the other hand, those
red men who are the greatest sticklers for the theory of Indian
virtue, and Indian loving-kindness, are sometimes the arrant-
est horse-thieves and tomahawkers among them. So, at least,
avers the backwoodsman. And though, knowing the Indian
nature, as he thinks he does, he fancies he is not ignorant that
an Indian may in some points deceive himself almost as effectually as in bush-tactics he can another, yet his theory and his
practice as above contrasted seem to involve an inconsistency
so extreme, that the backwoodsman only accounts for it on
the supposition that when a tomahawking red-man advances
the notion of the benignity of the red race, it is but part and
parcel with that subtle strategy which he finds so useful in
war, in hunting, and the general conduct of life.'

"In further explanation of that deep abhorrence with which
the backwoodsman regards the savage, the judge used to
think it might perhaps a little help, to consider what kind of
stimulus to it is furnished in those forest histories and traditions before spoken of. In which behalf, he would tell the
story of the little colony of Wrights and Weavers, originally

seven cousins from Virginia, who, after successive removals with their families, at last established themselves near the southern frontier of the Bloody Ground, Kentucky: 'They were strong, brave men; but, unlike many of the pioneers in those days, theirs was no love of conflict for conflict's sake. Step by step they had been lured to their lonely resting-place by the ever-beckoning seductions of a fertile and virgin land, with a singular exemption, during the march, from Indian molestation. But clearings made and houses built, the bright shield was soon to turn its other side. After repeated persecutions and eventual hostilities, forced on them by a dwindled tribe in their neighborhood—persecutions resulting in loss of crops and cattle; hostilities in which they lost two of their number, illy to be spared, besides others getting painful wounds—the five remaining cousins made, with some serious concessions, a kind of treaty with Mocmohoc, the chief—being to this induced by the harryings of the enemy, leaving them no peace. But they were further prompted, indeed, first incited, by the suddenly changed ways of Mocmohoc, who, though hitherto deemed a savage almost perfidious as Cæsar Borgia, yet now put on a seeming the reverse of this, engaging to bury the hatchet, smoke the pipe, and be friends forever; not friends in the mere sense of renouncing enmity, but in the sense of kindliness, active and familiar.

" 'But what the chief now seemed, did not wholly blind them to what the chief had been; so that, though in no small degree influenced by his change of bearing, they still distrusted him enough to covenant with him, among other articles on their side, that though friendly visits should be exchanged between the wigwams and the cabins, yet the five cousins should never, on any account, be expected to enter the chief's lodge together. The intention was, though they reserved it, that if ever, under the guise of amity, the chief should mean them mischief, and effect it, it should be but partially; so that some of the five might survive, not only for their families' sake, but also for retribution's. Nevertheless, Mocmohoc did, upon a time, with such fine art and pleasing carriage win their confidence, that he brought them all together to a feast of bear's meat, and there, by stratagem, ended them. Years after, over their calcined bones and those of all their families, the chief, reproached for his treachery by a proud hunter whom he had made captive, jeered out, "Treachery? pale face! 'Twas they who broke their covenant first, in coming all together; they that broke it first, in trusting Mocmohoc." '

"At this point the judge would pause, and lifting his hand, and rolling his eyes, exclaim in a solemn enough voice, 'Circling wiles and bloody lusts. The acuteness and genius of the chief but make him the more atrocious.'

"After another pause, he would begin an imaginary kind of dialogue between a backwoodsman and a questioner:

" 'But are all Indians like Mocmohoc?—Not all have proved such; but in the least harmful may lie his germ. There is an Indian nature. "Indian blood is in me," is the half-breed's threat.—But are not some Indians kind?—Yes, but kind Indians are mostly lazy, and reputed simple—at all events, are seldom chiefs; chiefs among the red men being taken from the active, and those accounted wise. Hence, with small promotion, kind Indians have but proportionate influence. And kind Indians may be forced to do unkind biddings. So "beware the Indian, kind or unkind," said Daniel Boone, who lost his sons by them.—But, have all you backwoodsmen been some way victimized by Indians?—No.—Well, and in certain cases may not at least some few of you be favored by them?—Yes, but scarce one among us so self-important, or so selfish-minded, as to hold his personal exemption from Indian outrage such a set-off against the contrary experience of so many others, as that he must needs, in a general way, think well of Indians; or, if he do, an arrow in his flank might suggest a pertinent doubt.

" 'In short,' according to the judge, 'if we at all credit the backwoodsman, his feeling against Indians, to be taken aright, must be considered as being not so much on his own account as on others', or jointly on both accounts. True it is, scarce a family he knows but some member of it, or connection, has been by Indians maimed or scalped. What avails, then, that some one Indian, or some two or three, treat a backwoodsman friendly-like? He fears me, he thinks. Take my rifle from me, give him motive, and what will come? Or if not so, how know I what involuntary preparations may be going on in him for things as unbeknown in present time to him as me—a sort of chemical preparation in the soul for malice, as chemical preparation in the body for malady.'

"Not that the backwoodsman ever used those words, you see, but the judge found him expression for his meaning. And this point he would conclude with saying, that, 'what is called a "friendly Indian" is a very rare sort of creature; and well it was so, for no ruthlessness exceeds that of a "friendly Indian" turned enemy. A coward friend, he makes a valiant foe.

" 'But, thus far the passion in question has been viewed in a general way as that of a community. When to his due share of this the backwoodsman adds his private passion, we have then the stock out of which is formed, if formed at all, the Indian-hater *par excellence*.'

"The Indian-hater *par excellence* the judge defined to be one 'who, having with his mother's milk drank in small love for red men, in youth or early manhood, ere the sensibilities become osseous, receives at their hand some signal outrage, or, which in effect is much the same, some of his kin have, or some friend. Now, nature all around him by her solitudes wooing or bidding him muse upon this matter, he accordingly does so, till the thought develops such attraction, that much as straggling vapors troop from all sides to a storm-cloud, so straggling thoughts of other outrages troop to the nucleus thought, assimilate with it, and swell it. At last, taking counsel with the elements, he comes to his resolution. An intenser Hannibal, he makes a vow, the hate of which is a vortex from whose suction scarce the remotest chip of the guilty race may reasonably feel secure. Next, he declares himself and settles his temporal affairs. With the solemnity of a Spaniard turned monk, he takes leave of his kin; or rather, these leave-takings have something of the still more impressive finality of death-bed adieus. Last, he commits himself to the forest primeval; there, so long as life shall be his, to act upon a calm, cloistered scheme of strategical, implacable, and lonesome vengeance. Ever on the noiseless trail; cool, collected, patient; less seen than felt; snuffing, smelling—a Leather-stocking Nemesis. In the settlements he will not be seen again; in eyes of old companions tears may start at some chance thing that speaks of him; but they never look for him, nor call; they know he will not come. Suns and seasons fleet; the tiger-lily blows and falls; babes are born and leap in their mothers' arms; but, the Indian-hater is good as gone to his long home, and "Terror" is his epitaph.'

"Here the judge, not unaffected, would pause again, but presently resume: 'How evident that in strict speech there can be no biography of an Indian-hater *par excellence*, any more than one of a sword-fish, or other deep-sea denizen; or, which is still less imaginable, one of a dead man. The career of the Indian-hater *par excellence* has the impenetrability of the fate of a lost steamer. Doubtless, events, terrible ones, have happened, must have happened; but the powers that be in nature have taken order that they shall never become news.

" 'But, luckily for the curious, there is a species of diluted Indian-hater, one whose heart proves not so steely as his brain. Soft enticements of domestic life too often draw him from the ascetic trail; a monk who apostatizes to the world at times. Like a mariner, too, though much abroad, he may have a wife and family in some green harbor which he does not forget. It is with him as with the Papist converts in Senegal; fasting and mortification prove hard to bear.'

"The judge, with his usual judgment, always thought that the intense solitude to which the Indian-hater consigns himself, has, by its overawing influence, no little to do with relaxing his vow. He would relate instances where, after some months' lonely scoutings, the Indian-hater is suddenly seized with a sort of calenture; hurries openly towards the first smoke, though he knows it is an Indian's, announces himself as a lost hunter, gives the savage his rifle, throws himself upon his charity, embraces him with much affection, imploring the privilege of living a while in his sweet companionship. What is too often the sequel of so distempered a procedure may be best known by those who best know the Indian. Upon the whole, the judge, by two and thirty good and sufficient reasons, would maintain that there was no known vocation whose consistent following calls for such self-containings as that of the Indian-hater *par excellence*. In the highest view, he considered such a soul one peeping out but once an age.

"For the diluted Indian-hater, although the vacations he permits himself impair the keeping of the character, yet, it should not be overlooked that this is the man who, by his very infirmity, enables us to form surmises, however inadequate, of what Indian-hating in its perfection is."

"One moment," gently interrupted the cosmopolitan here, "and let me refill my calumet."

Which being done, the other proceeded:—

Chapter 27

COMING TO MENTION the man to whose story all thus far said was but the introduction, the judge, who, like you, was a great smoker, would insist upon all the company taking cigars, and then lighting a fresh one himself, rise in his place, and, with the solemnest voice, say—'Gentlemen, let us smoke to the memory of Colonel John Moredock;' when, after several whiffs taken standing in deep silence and deeper reverie, he would resume his seat and his discourse, something in these words:

" 'Though Colonel John Moredock was not an Indian-hater *par excellence*, he yet cherished a kind of sentiment towards the red man, and in that degree, and so acted out his sentiment as sufficiently to merit the tribute just rendered to his memory.

" 'John Moredock was the son of a woman married thrice, and thrice widowed by a tomahawk. The three successive husbands of this woman had been pioneers, and with them she had wandered from wilderness to wilderness, always on the frontier. With nine children, she at last found herself at a little clearing, afterwards Vincennes. There she joined a company about to remove to the new country of Illinois. On the eastern side of Illinois there were then no settlements; but on the west side, the shore of the Mississippi, there were, near the mouth of the Kaskaskia, some old hamlets of French. To the vicinity of those hamlets, very innocent and pleasant places, a new Arcadia, Mrs. Moredock's party was destined; for thereabouts, among the vines, they meant to settle. They embarked upon the Wabash in boats, proposing descending that stream into the Ohio, and the Ohio into the Mississippi, and so, northwards, towards the point to be reached. All went well till they made the rock of the Grand Tower on the Mississippi, where they had to land and drag their boats round a point swept by a strong current. Here a party of Indians, lying in wait, rushed out and murdered nearly all of them. The widow was among the victims with her children, John excepted, who, some fifty miles distant, was following with a second party.

" 'He was just entering upon manhood, when thus left in nature sole survivor of his race. Other youngsters might have turned mourners; he turned avenger. His nerves were electric wires—sensitive, but steel. He was one who, from self-possession, could be made neither to flush nor pale. It is said that when the tidings were brought him, he was ashore sitting beneath a hemlock eating his dinner of venison—and as the tidings were told him, after the first start he kept on eating, but slowly and deliberately, chewing the wild news with the wild meat, as if both together, turned to chyle, together should sinew him to his intent. From that meal he rose an Indian-hater. He rose; got his arms, prevailed upon some comrades to join him, and without delay started to discover who were the actual transgressors. They proved to belong to a band of twenty renegades from various tribes, outlaws even among Indians, and who had formed themselves into a marauding crew. No opportunity for action being at the time presented, he dismissed his friends; told them to go on, thanking them, and saying he would ask their aid at some future day. For upwards of a year, alone in the wilds, he watched the crew. Once, what he thought a favorable chance having occurred—it being midwinter, and the savages encamped, apparently to remain so—he anew mustered his friends, and marched against them; but, getting wind of his coming, the enemy fled, and in such panic that everything was left behind but their weapons. During the winter, much the same thing happened upon two subsequent occasions. The next year he sought them at the head of a party pledged to serve him for forty days. At last the hour came. It was on the shore of the Mississippi. From their covert, Moredock and his men dimly described the gang of Cains in the red dusk of evening, paddling over to a jungled island in midstream, there the more securely to lodge; for Moredock's retributive spirit in the wilderness spoke ever to their trepidations now, like the voice calling through the garden. Waiting until dead of night, the whites swam the river, towing after them a raft laden with their arms. On landing, Moredock cut the fastenings of the enemy's canoes, and turned them, with his own raft, adrift; resolved that there should be neither escape for the Indians, nor safety, except in victory, for the whites. Victorious the whites were; but three of the Indians saved themselves by taking to the stream. Moredock's band lost not a man.

" 'Three of the murderers survived. He knew their names and persons. In the course of three years each successively fell by his own hand. All were now dead. But this did not suffice. He made no avowal, but to kill Indians had become his passion. As an athlete, he had few equals; as a shot, none; in single combat, not to be beaten. Master of that woodland-cunning enabling the adept to subsist where the tyro would perish, and expert in all those arts by which an enemy is pursued for weeks, perhaps months, without once suspecting it, he kept to the forest. The solitary Indian that met him, died. When a number was descried, he would either secretly pursue their track for some chance to strike at least one blow; or if, while thus engaged, he himself was discovered, he would elude them by superior skill.

" 'Many years he spent thus; and though after a time he was, in a degree, restored to the ordinary life of the region and period, yet it is believed that John Moredock never let pass an opportunity of quenching an Indian. Sins of commission in that kind may have been his, but none of omission.

" 'It were to err to suppose,' the judge would say, 'that this gentleman was naturally ferocious, or peculiarly possessed of those qualities, which, unhelped by provocation of events, tend to withdraw man from social life. On the contrary, Moredock was an example of something apparently self-contradicting, certainly curious, but, at the same time, undeniable: namely, that nearly all Indian-haters have at bottom loving hearts; at any rate, hearts, if anything, more generous than the average. Certain it is, that, to the degree in which he mingled in the life of the settlements. Moredock showed himself not without humane feelings. No cold husband or colder father, he; and, though often and long away from his household, bore its needs in mind, and provided for them. He could be very convivial; told a good story (though never of his more private exploits), and sung a capital song. Hospitable, not backward to help a neighbor; by report, benevolent, as retributive, in secret; while, in a general manner, though sometimes grave—as is not unusual with men of his complexion, a sultry and tragical brown—yet with nobody, Indians excepted, otherwise than courteous in a manly fashion; a moccasined gentleman, admired and loved. In fact, no one more popular, as an incident to follow may prove.

" 'His bravery, whether in Indian fight or any other, was unquestionable. An officer in the ranging service during the war of 1812, he acquitted himself with more than credit. Of his soldierly character, this anecdote is told: Not long after Hull's dubious surrender at Detroit, Moredock with some of his rangers rode up at night to a log-house, there to rest till morning. The horses being attended to, supper over, and sleeping-places assigned the troop, the host showed the colonel his best bed, not on the ground like the rest, but a bed that stood on legs. But out of delicacy, the guest declined to monopolize it, or, indeed, to occupy it at all; when, to increase the inducement, as the host thought, he was told that a general officer had once slept in that bed. "Who, pray?" asked the colonel. "General Hull." "Then you must not take offense," said the colonel, buttoning up his coat, "but, really, no coward's bed, for me, however comfortable." Accordingly he took up with valor's bed—a cold one on the ground.

" 'At one time the colonel was a member of the territorial council of Illinois, and at the formation of the state government, was pressed to become candidate for governor, but begged to be excused. And, though he declined to give his reasons for declining, yet by those who best knew him the cause was not wholly unsurmised. In his official capacity he might be called upon to enter into friendly treaties with Indian tribes, a thing not to be thought of. And even did no such contingency arise, yet he felt there would be an impropriety in the Governor of Illinois stealing out now and then, during a recess of the legislative bodies, for a few days' shooting at human beings, within the limits of his paternal chief-magistracy. If the governorship offered large honors, from

Moredock it demanded larger sacrifices. These were incompatibles. In short, he was not unaware that to be a consistent Indian-hater involves the renunciation of ambition, with its objects—the pomps and glories of the world; and since religion, pronouncing such things vanities, accounts it merit to renounce them, therefore, so far as this goes, Indian-hating, whatever may be thought of it in other respects, may be regarded as not wholly without the efficacy of a devout sentiment.' "

Here the narrator paused. Then, after his long and irksome sitting, started to his feet, and regulating his disordered shirt-frill, and at the same time adjustingly shaking his legs down in his rumpled pantaloons, concluded: "There, I have done; having given you, not my story, mind, or my thoughts, but another's. And now, for your friend Coonskins, I doubt not, that, if the judge were here, he would pronounce him a sort of comprehensive Colonel Moredock, who, too much spreading his passion, shallows it."

CHARITY, CHARITY!" exclaimed the cosmopolitan, "never a sound judgment without charity. When man judges man, charity is less a bounty from our mercy than just allowance for the insensible lee-way of human fallibility. God forbid that my eccentric friend should be what you hint. You do not know him, or but imperfectly. His outside deceived you; at first it came near deceiving even me. But I seized a chance, when, owing to indignation against some wrong, he laid himself a little open; I seized that lucky chance, I say, to inspect his heart, and found it an inviting oyster in a forbidding shell. His outside is but put on. Ashamed of his own goodness, he treats mankind as those strange old uncles in romances do their nephews—snapping at them all the time and yet loving them as the apple of their eye."

"Well, my words with him were few. Perhaps he is not what I took him for. Yes, for aught I know, you may be right."

"Glad to hear it. Charity, like poetry, should be cultivated, if only for its being graceful. And now, since you have renounced your notion, I should be happy would you, so to speak, renounce your story, too. That story strikes me with even more incredulity than wonder. To me some parts don't hang together. If the man of hate, how could John Moredock be also the man of love? Either his lone campaigns are fabulous as Hercules'; or else, those being true, what was thrown in about his geniality is but garnish. In short, if ever there was such a man as Moredock, he, in my way of thinking, was either misanthrope or nothing; and his misanthropy the more intense from being focused on one race of men. Though, like suicide, man-hatred would seem peculiarly a Roman and a Grecian passion—that is, Pagan; yet, the annals of neither Rome nor Greece can produce the equal in man-hatred of Colonel Moredock, as the judge and you have painted him. As for this Indian-hating in general, I can only say of it what

Dr. Johnson said of the alleged Lisbon earthquake: 'Sir, I don't believe it.' "

"Didn't believe it? Why not? Clashed with any little prejudice of his?"

"Doctor Johnson had no prejudice; but, like a certain other person," with an ingenuous smile, "he had sensibilities, and those were pained."

"Dr. Johnson was a good Christian, wasn't he?"

"He was."

"Suppose he had been something else."

"Then small incredulity as to the alleged earthquake."

"Suppose he had been also a misanthrope?"

"Then small incredulity as to the robberies and murders alleged to have been perpetrated under the pall of smoke and ashes. The infidels of the time were quick to credit those reports and worse. So true is it that, while religion, contrary to the common notion, implies, in certain cases, a spirit of slow reserve as to assent, infidelity, which claims to despise credulity, is sometimes swift to it."

"You rather jumble together misanthropy and infidelity."

"I do not jumble them; they are coördinates. For misanthropy, springing from the same root with disbelief of religion, is twin with that. It springs from the same root, I say; for, set aside materialism, and what is an atheist, but one who does not, or will not, see in the universe a ruling principle of love; and what a misanthrope, but one who does not, or will not, see in man a ruling principle of kindness? Don't you see? In either case the vice consists in a want of confidence."

"What sort of a sensation is misanthropy?"

"Might as well ask me what sort of sensation is hydrophobia. Don't know; never had it. But I have often wondered what it can be like. Can a misanthrope feel warm, I ask myself; take ease? be companionable with himself? Can a misanthrope smoke a cigar and muse? How fares he in solitude? Has the misanthrope such a thing as an appetite? Shall a peach refresh him? The effervescence of champagne, with what eye does he behold it? Is summer good to him? Of long winters how much can he sleep? What are his dreams? How feels he, and what does he, when suddenly awakened, alone, at dead of night, by fusilades of thunder?"

"Like you," said the stranger, "I can't understand the misanthrope. So far as my experience goes, either mankind is worthy one's best love, or else I have been lucky. Never has it been my lot to have been wronged, though but in the smallest degree. Cheating, backbiting, superciliousness, disdain, hard-heartedness, and all that brood, I know but by report. Cold regards tossed over the sinister shoulder of a former friend, ingratitude in a beneficiary, treachery in a confidant—such things may be; but I must take somebody's word for it. Now the bridge that has carried me so well over, shall I not praise it?"

"Ingratitude to the worthy bridge not to do so. Man is a noble fellow, and in an age of satirists, I am not displeased to find one who has confidence in him, and bravely stands up for him."

"Yes, I always speak a good word for man; and what is more, am always ready to do a good deed for him."

"You are a man after my own heart," responded the cosmopolitan, with a candor which lost nothing by its calmness. "Indeed," he added, "our sentiments agree so, that were they written in a book, whose was whose, few but the nicest critics might determine."

"Since we are thus joined in mind," said the stranger, " why not be joined in hand?"

"My hand is always at the service of virtue," frankly extending it to him as to virtue personified.

"And now," said the stranger, cordially retaining his hand, "you know our fashion here at the West. It may be a little low, but it is kind. Briefly, we being newly-made friends must drink together. What say you?"

"Thank you; but indeed, you must excuse me."

"Why?"

"Because, to tell the truth, I have to-day met so many old friends, all free-hearted, convivial gentlemen, that really, really, though for the present I succeed in mastering it, I am at bottom almost in the condition of a sailor who, stepping ashore after a long voyage, ere night reels with loving welcomes, his head of less capacity than his heart."

At the allusion to old friends, the stranger's countenance a little fell, as a jealous lover's might at hearing from his sweetheart of former ones. But rallying, he said: "No doubt they treated you to something strong; but wine—surely, that gentle creature, wine; come, let us have a little gentle wine at one of these little tables here. Come, come." Then essaying to roll about like a full pipe in the sea, sang in a voice which had had more of good-fellowship, had there been less of a latent squeak to it:

> "Let us drink of the wine of the vine benign,
> That sparkles warm in Sansovine."

The cosmopolitan, with longing eye upon him, stood as sorely tempted and wavering a moment; then, abruptly stepping towards him, with a look of dissolved surrender, said: "When mermaid songs move figure-heads, then may glory, gold, and women try their blandishments on me. But a good fellow, singing a good song, he woos forth my every spike, so that my whole hull, like a ship's, sailing by a magnetic rock, caves in with acquiescence. Enough: when one has a heart of a certain sort, it is in vain trying to be resolute."

Chapter 29

The boon companions

THE WINE, port, being called for, and the two seated at the little table, a natural pause of convivial expectancy ensued; the stranger's eye turned towards the bar near by, watching the red-cheeked, white-aproned man there, blithely dusting the bottle, and invitingly arranging the salver and glasses; when, with a sudden impulse turning round his head towards his companion, he said, "Ours is friendship at first sight, ain't it?"

"It is," was the placidly pleased reply: "and the same may be said of friendship at first sight as of love at first sight: it is the only true one, the only noble one. It bespeaks confidence. Who would go sounding his way into love or friendship, like a strange ship by night, into an enemy's harbor?"

"Right. Boldly in before the wind. Agreeable, how we always agree. By-the-way, though but a formality, friends should know each other's names. What is yours, pray?"

"Francis Goodman. But those who love me, call me Frank. And yours?"

"Charles Arnold Noble. But do you call me Charlie."

"I will, Charlie; nothing like preserving in manhood the fraternal familiarities of youth. It proves the heart a rosy boy to the last."

"My sentiments again. Ah!"

It was a smiling waiter, with the smiling bottle, the cork drawn; a common quart bottle, but for the occasion fitted at bottom into a little bark basket, braided with porcupine quills, gayly tinted in the Indian fashion. This being set before the entertainer, he regarded it with affectionate interest, but seemed not to understand, or else to pretend not to, a handsome red label pasted on the bottle, bearing the capital letters, P. W.

"P. W.," said he at last, perplexedly eying the pleasing poser, "now what does P. W. mean?"

"Shouldn't wonder," said the cosmopolitan gravely, "if it stood for port wine. You called for port wine, didn't you?"

"Why so it is, so it is!"

"I find some little mysteries not very hard to clear up," said the other, quietly crossing his legs.

This commonplace seemed to escape the stranger's hearing, for, full of his bottle, he now rubbed his somewhat sallow hands over it, and with a strange kind of cackle, meant to be a chirrup, cried: "Good wine, good wine; is it not the peculiar bond of good feeling?" Then brimming both glasses, pushed one over, saying, with what seemed intended for an air of fine disdain: "Ill betide those gloomy skeptics who maintain that now-a-days pure wine is unpurchasable; that almost every variety on sale is less the vintage of vineyards than laboratories; that most bar-keepers are but a set of male Brinvillierses, with complaisant arts practicing against the lives of their best friends, their customers."

A shade passed over the cosmopolitan. After a few minutes' down-cast musing, he lifted his eyes and said: "I have long thought, my dear Charlie, that the spirit in which wine is regarded by too many in these days is one of the most painful examples of want of confidence. Look at these glasses. He who could mistrust poison in this wine would mistrust consumption in Hebe's cheek. While, as for suspicions against the dealers in wine and sellers of it, those who cherish such suspicions can have but limited trust in the human heart. Each human heart they must think to be much like each bottle of port, not such port as this, but such port as they hold to. Strange traducers, who see good faith in nothing, however sacred. Not medicines, not the wine in sacraments, has escaped them. The doctor with his phial, and the priest with his chalice, they deem equally the unconscious dispensers of bogus cordials to the dying."

"Dreadful!"

"Dreadful indeed," said the cosmopolitan solemnly. "These distrusters stab at the very soul of confidence. If this wine," impressively holding up his full glass, "if this wine with its bright promise be not true, how shall man be, whose promise can be no brighter? But if wine be false, while men are true, whither shall fly convivial geniality? To think of sincerely-genial souls drinking each other's health at unawares in perfidious and murderous drugs!"

"Horrible!"

"Much too much so to be true, Charlie. Let us forget it. Come, you are my entertainer on this occasion, and yet you don't pledge me. I have been waiting for it."

"Pardon, pardon," half confusedly and half ostentatiously lifting his glass. "I pledge you, Frank, with my whole heart, believe me," taking a draught too decorous to be large, but which, small though it was, was followed by a slight involuntary wryness to the mouth.

"And I return you the pledge, Charlie, heart-warm as it came to me, and honest as this wine I drink it in," reciprocated the cosmopolitan with princely kindliness in his gesture, taking a generous swallow, concluding in a smack, which, though audible, was not so much so as to be unpleasing.

"Talking of alleged spuriousness of wines," said he, tranquilly setting down his glass, and then sloping back his head and with friendly fixedness eying the wine, "perhaps the strangest part of those allegings is, that there is, as claimed, a kind of man who, while convinced that on this continent most wines are shams, yet still drinks away at them; accounting wine so fine a thing, that even the sham article is better than none at all. And if the temperance people urge that, by this course, he will sooner or later be undermined in health, he answers, 'And do you think I don't know that? But health without cheer I hold a bore; and cheer, even of the spurious sort, has its price, which I am willing to pay.'"

"Such a man, Frank, must have a disposition ungovernably bacchanalian."

"Yes, if such a man there be, which I don't credit. It is a fable, but a fable from which I once heard a person of less genius than grotesqueness draw a moral even more extravagant than the fable itself. He said that it illustrated, as in a parable, how that a man of a disposition ungovernably good-natured might still familiarly associate with men, though, at the same time, he believed the greater part of men false-hearted—accounting society so sweet a thing that even the spurious sort was better than none at all. And if the Rochefoucaultites urge that, by this course, he will sooner or later be undermined in security, he answers, 'And do you think I don't know that? But security without society I hold a bore;

and society, even of the spurious sort, has its price, which I am willing to pay.' "

"A most singular theory," said the stranger with a slight fidget, eying his companion with some inquisitiveness, "indeed, Frank, a most slanderous thought," he exclaimed in sudden heat and with an involuntary look almost of being personally aggrieved.

"In one sense it merits all you say, and more," rejoined the other with wonted mildness, "but, for a kind of drollery in it, charity might, perhaps, overlook something of the wickedness. Humor is, in fact, so blessed a thing, that even in the least virtuous product of the human mind, if there can be found but nine good jokes, some philosophers are clement enough to affirm that those nine good jokes should redeem all the wicked thoughts, though plenty as the populace of Sodom. At any rate, this same humor has something, there is no telling what, of beneficence in it, it is such a catholicon and charm—nearly all men agreeing in relishing it, though they may agree in little else—and in its way it undeniably does such a deal of familiar good in the world, that no wonder it is almost a proverb, that a man of humor, a man capable of a good loud laugh—seem how he may in other things—can hardly be a heartless scamp."

"Ha, ha, ha!" laughed the other, pointing to the figure of a pale pauper-boy on the deck below, whose pitiableness was touched, as it were, with ludicrousness by a pair of monstrous boots, apparently some mason's discarded ones, cracked with drouth, half eaten by lime, and curled up about the toe like a bassoon. "Look—ha, ha, ha!"

"I see," said the other, with what seemed quiet appreciation, but of a kind expressing an eye to the grotesque, without blindness to what in this case accompanied it, "I see; and the way in which it moves you, Charlie, comes in very apropos to point the proverb I was speaking of. Indeed, had you intended this effect, it could not have been more so. For who that heard that laugh, but would as naturally argue from it a sound heart as sound lungs? True, it is said that a man may smile, and smile, and smile, and be a villain; but it is not said that a man may laugh, and laugh, and laugh, and be one, is it, Charlie?"

"Ha, ha, ha!—no no, no no."

"Why Charlie, your explosions illustrate my remarks almost as aptly as the chemist's imitation volcano did his lectures. But even if experience did not sanction the proverb, that a good laugher cannot be a bad man, I should yet feel bound in confidence to believe it, since it is a saying current among the people, and I doubt not originated among them, and hence *must* be true; for the voice of the people is the voice of truth. Don't you think so?"

"Of course I do. If Truth don't speak through the people, it never speaks at all; so I heard one say."

"A true saying. But we stray. The popular notion of humor, considered as index to the heart, would seem curiously confirmed by Aristotle—I think, in his 'Politics,' (a work, by-the-by, which, however it may be viewed upon the whole, yet, from the tenor of certain sections, should not, without precaution, be placed in the hands of youth)—who remarks that the least lovable men in history seem to have had for humor not only a disrelish, but a hatred; and this, in some cases, along with an extraordinary dry taste for practical punning. I remember it is related of Phalaris, the capricious tyrant of Sicily, that he once caused a poor fellow to be beheaded on a horse-block, for no other cause than having a horse-laugh."

"Funny Phalaris!"

"Cruel Phalaris!"

As after fire-crackers, there was a pause, both looking downward on the table as if mutually struck by the contrast of exclamations, and pondering upon its significance, if any. So, at least, it seemed; but on one side it might have been otherwise: for presently glancing up, the cosmopolitan said: "In the instance of the moral, drolly cynic, drawn from the queer bacchanalian fellow we were speaking of, who had his reasons for still drinking spurious wine, though knowing it to be such—there, I say, we have an example of what is certainly a wicked thought, but conceived in humor. I will now give you one of a wicked thought conceived in wickedness. You shall compare the two, and answer, whether in the one case the sting is not neutralized by the humor, and whether in the other the absence of humor does not leave the sting free play. I once heard a wit, a mere wit, mind, an irreligious Parisian wit, say, with regard to the temperance movement, that none, to their personal benefit, joined it sooner than niggards and knaves; because, as he affirmed, the one by it saved money and the other made money, as in ship-owners cutting off the spirit ration without giving its equivalent, and gamblers and all sorts of subtle tricksters sticking to cold water, the better to keep a cool head for business."

"A wicked thought, indeed!" cried the stranger, feelingly.

"Yes," leaning over the table on his elbow and genially gesturing at him with his forefinger: "yes, and, as I said, you don't remark the sting of it?"

"I do, indeed. Most calumnious thought, Frank!"

"No humor in it?"

"Not a bit!"

"Well now, Charlie," eying him with moist regard, "let us drink. It appears to me you don't drink freely."

"Oh, oh—indeed, indeed—I am not backward there. I protest, a freer drinker than friend Charlie you will find nowhere," with feverish zeal snatching his glass, but only in the sequel to dally with it. "By-the-way, Frank," said he, perhaps, or perhaps not, to draw attention from himself, "by-the-way, I saw a good thing the other day; capital thing; a panegyric on the press. It pleased me so, I got it by heart at two readings. It is a kind of poetry, but in a form which stands in something the same relation to blank verse which that does to rhyme. A sort of free-and-easy chant with refrains to it. Shall I recite it?"

"Anything in praise of the press I shall be happy to hear," rejoined the cosmopolitan, "the more so," he gravely proceeded, "as of late I have observed in some quarters a disposition to disparage the press."

"Disparage the press?"

"Even so; some gloomy souls affirming that it is proving with that great invention as with brandy or eau-de-vie, which, upon its first discovery, was believed by the doctors to be, as its French name implies, a panacea—a notion which experience, it may be thought, has not fully verified."

"You surprise me, Frank. Are there really those who so decry the press? Tell me more. Their reasons."

"Reasons they have none, but affirmations they have many; among other things affirming that, while under dynastic despotisms, the press is to the people little but an improvisatore, under popular ones it is too apt to be their Jack Cade. In fine, these sour sages regard the press in the light of a Colt's revolver, pledged to no cause but his in whose chance hands it may be; deeming the one invention an improvement upon the pen, much akin to what the other is upon the pistol; involving, along with the multiplication of the barrel, no consecration of the aim. The term 'freedom of the press' they consider on a par with *freedom of Colt's revolver*. Hence, for truth and the right, they hold, to indulge hopes from the one is little more sensible than for Kossuth and Mazzini to indulge hopes from the other. Heart-breaking views enough, you think; but their refutation is in every true reformer's contempt. Is it not so?"

"Without doubt. But go on, go on. I like to hear you," flatteringly brimming up his glass for him.

"For one," continued the cosmopolitan, grandly swelling his chest, "I hold the press to be neither the people's improvisatore, nor Jack Cade; neither their paid fool, nor conceited drudge. I think interest never prevails with it over duty. The press still speaks for truth though impaled, in the teeth of lies though intrenched. Disdaining for it the poor name of cheap diffuser of news, I claim for it the independent apostleship of Advancer of Knowledge:—the iron Paul! Paul, I say; for not only does the press advance knowledge, but righteousness. In the press, as in the sun, resides, my dear Charlie, a dedicated principle of beneficent force and light. For the Satanic press, by its coappearance with the apostolic, it is no more an aspersion to that, than to the true sun is the coappearance of the mock one. For all the baleful-looking parhelion, god Apollo dispenses the day. In a word, Charlie, what the sovereign of England is titularly, I hold the press to be actually—Defender of the Faith!—defender of the faith in the final triumph of truth over error, metaphysics over superstition, theory over falsehood, machinery over nature, and the good man over the bad. Such are my views, which, if stated at some length, you, Charlie, must pardon, for it is a theme upon which I cannot speak with cold brevity. And now I am impatient for your panegyric, which, I doubt not, will put mine to the blush."

"It is rather in the blush-giving vein," smiled the other; "but such as it is, Frank, you shall have it."

"Tell me when you are about to begin," said the cosmopolitan, "for, when at public dinners the press is toasted, I always drink the toast standing, and shall stand while you pronounce the panegyric."

"Very good, Frank; you may stand up now."

He accordingly did so, when the stranger likewise rose, and uplifting the ruby wine-flask, began.

Chapter 30

"PRAISE BE UNTO the press, not Faust's, but Noah's; let us extol and magnify the press, the true press of Noah, from which breaketh the true morning. Praise be unto the press, not the black press but the red; let us extol and magnify the press, the red press of Noah, from which cometh inspiration. Ye pressmen of the Rhineland and the Rhine, join in with all ye who tread out the glad tidings on isle Madeira or Mitylene.—Who giveth redness of eyes by making men long to tarry at the fine print?—Praise be unto the press, the rosy press of Noah, which giveth rosiness of hearts, by making men long to tarry at the rosy wine.—Who hath babblings and contentions? Who, without cause, inflicteth wounds? Praise be unto the press, the kindly press of Noah, which knitteth friends, which fuseth foes.—Who may be bribed?—Who may be bound?—Praise be unto the press, the free press of Noah, which will not lie for tyrants, but make tyrants speak the truth.—Then praise be unto the press, the frank old press of Noah; then let us extol and magnify the press, the brave old press of Noah; then let us with roses garland and enwreath the press, the grand old press of Noah, from which flow streams of knowledge which give man a bliss no more unreal than his pain.' "

"You deceived me," smiled the cosmopolitan, as both now resumed their seats; "you roguishly took advantage of my simplicity; you archly played upon my enthusiasm. But never mind; the offense, if any, was so charming, I almost wish you would offend again. As for certain poetic left-handers in your panegyric, those I cheerfully concede to the indefinite privileges of the poet. Upon the whole, it was quite in the lyric style—a style I always admire on account of that spirit of Sibyllic confidence and assurance which is, perhaps, its prime ingredient. But come," glancing at his companion's glass, "for a lyrist, you let the bottle stay with you too long."

"The lyre and the vine forever!" cried the other in his rapture, or what seemed such, heedless of the hint, "the vine, the vine! is it not the most graceful and bounteous of all growths? And, by its being such, is not something meant—divinely meant? As I live, a vine, a Catawba vine, shall be planted on my grave!"

"A genial thought; but your glass there."

"Oh, oh," taking a moderate sip, "but you, why don't you drink?"

"You have forgotten, my dear Charlie, what I told you of my previous convivialities to-day."

"Oh," cried the other, now in manner quite abandoned to the lyric mood, not without contrast to the easy sociability of his companion. "Oh, one can't drink too much of good old wine—the genuine, mellow old port. Pooh, pooh! drink away."

"Then keep me company."

"Of course," with a flourish, taking another sip—"suppose we have cigars. Never mind your pipe there; a pipe is best when alone. I say, waiter, bring some cigars—your best."

They were brought in a pretty little bit of western pottery, representing some kind of Indian utensil, mummy-colored, set down in a mass of tobacco leaves, whose long, green fans, fancifully grouped, formed with peeps of red the sides of the receptacle.

Accompanying it were two accessories, also bits of pottery, but smaller, both globes; one in guise of an apple flushed with red and gold to the life, and, through a cleft at top, you saw it was hollow. This was for the ashes. The other, gray, with wrinkled surface, in the likeness of a wasp's nest, was the match-box.

"There," said the stranger, pushing over the cigar-stand, "help yourself, and I will touch you off," taking a match. "Nothing like tobacco," he added, when the fumes of the cigar began to wreathe, glancing from the smoker to the pottery, "I will have a Virginia tobacco-plant set over my grave beside the Catawba vine."

"Improvement upon your first idea, which by itself was good—but you don't smoke."

"Presently, presently—let me fill your glass again. You don't drink."

"Thank you; but no more just now. Fill *your* glass."

"Presently, presently; do you drink on. Never mind me. Now that it strikes me, let me say, that he who, out of super-fine gentility or fanatic morality, denies himself tobacco, suffers a more serious abatement in the cheap pleasures of life than the dandy in his iron boot, or the celibate on his iron cot. While for him who would fain revel in tobacco, but cannot, it is a thing at which philanthropists must weep, to see such an one, again and again, madly returning to the cigar, which, for his incompetent stomach, he cannot enjoy, while still, after each shameful repulse, the sweet dream of the impossible good goads him on to his fierce misery once more—poor eunuch!"

"I agree with you," said the cosmopolitan, still gravely social, "but you don't smoke."

"Presently, presently, do you smoke on. As I was saying about—"

"But *why* don't you smoke—come. You don't think that tobacco, when in league with wine, too much enhances the latter's vinous quality—in short, with certain constitutions tends to impair self-possession, do you?"

"To think that, were treason to good fellowship," was the warm disclaimer. "No, no. But the fact is, there is an unpropitious flavor in my mouth just now. Ate of a diabolical ragout at dinner, so I shan't smoke till I have washed away the lingering memento of it with wine. But smoke away, you, and pray, don't forget to drink. By-the-way, while we sit here so companionably, giving loose to any companionable nothing, your uncompanionable friend, Coonskins, is, by pure contrast, brought to recollection. If he were but here now, he would see how much of real heart-joy he denies himself by not hob-a-nobbing with his kind."

"Why," with loitering emphasis, slowly withdrawing his cigar, "I thought I had undeceived you there. I thought you had come to a better understanding of my eccentric friend."

"Well, I thought so, too; but first impressions will return, you know. In truth, now that I think of it, I am led to conjecture from chance things which dropped from Coonskins, during the little interview I had with him, that he is not a Missourian by birth, but years ago came West here, a young misanthrope from the other side of the Alleghanies, less to make his fortune, than to flee man. Now, since they say trifles sometimes effect great results, I shouldn't wonder, if his history were probed, it would be found that what first indirectly gave his sad bias to Coonskins was his disgust at reading in boyhood the advice of Polonius to Laertes—advice which, in the selfishness it inculcates, is almost on a par with a sort of ballad upon the economies of money-making, to be occasionally seen pasted against the desk of small retail traders in New England."

"I do hope now, my dear fellow," said the cosmopolitan with an air of bland protest, "that, in my presence at least, you will throw out nothing to the prejudice of the sons of the Puritans."

"Hey-day and high times indeed," exclaimed the other, nettled, "sons of the Puritans forsooth! And who be Puritans, that I, an Alabamaian, must do them reverence? A set of sourly conceited old Malvolios, whom Shakespeare laughs his fill at in his comedies."

"Pray, what were you about to suggest with regard to Polonius," observed the cosmopolitan with quiet forbearance, expressive of the patience of a superior mind at the petulance of an inferior one; "how do you characterize his advice to Laertes?"

"As false, fatal, and calumnious," exclaimed the other, with a degree of ardor befitting one resenting a stigma upon the family escutcheon, "and for a father to give his son—monstrous. The case you see is this: The son is going abroad, and for the first. What does the father? Invoke God's blessing upon him? Put the blessed Bible in his trunk? No. Crams him with maxims smacking of my Lord Chesterfield, with maxims of France, with maxims of Italy."

"No, no, be charitable, not that. Why, does he not among other things say:—

> 'The friends thou hast, and their adoption tried,
> Grapple them to thy soul with hooks of steel'?

Is that compatible with maxims of Italy?"

"Yes it is, Frank. Don't you see? Laertes is to take the best

of care of his friends—his proved friends, on the same principle that a wine-corker takes the best of care of his proved
bottles. When a bottle gets a sharp knock and don't break, he
says, 'Ah, I'll keep that bottle.' Why? Because he loves it? No,
he has particular use for it."

"Dear, dear!" appealingly turning in distress, "that—that
kind of criticism is—is—in fact—it won't do."

"Won't truth do, Frank? You are so charitable with everybody, do but consider the tone of the speech. Now I put it
to you, Frank; is there anything in it hortatory to high, heroic, disinterested effort? Anything like 'sell all thou hast and
give to the poor?' And, in other points, what desire seems
most in the father's mind, that his son should cherish nobleness for himself, or be on his guard against the contrary thing
in others? An irreligious warner, Frank—no devout coun-
selor, is Polonius. I hate him. Nor can I bear to hear your veterans of the world affirm, that he who steers through life by
the advice of old Polonius will not steer among the breakers."

"No, no—I hope nobody affirms that," rejoined the cosmopolitan, with tranquil abandonment; sideways reposing his
arm at full length upon the table. "I hope nobody affirms
that; because, if Polonius' advice be taken in your sense, then
the recommendation of it by men of experience would appear
to involve more or less of an unhandsome sort of reflection
upon human nature. And yet," with a perplexed air, "your
suggestions have put things in such a strange light to me as
in fact a little to disturb my previous notions of Polonius and
what he says. To be frank, by your ingenuity you have unsettled me there, to that degree that were it not for our coincidence of opinion in general, I should almost think I was now
at length beginning to feel the ill effect of an immature mind,
too much consorting with a mature one, except on the
ground of first principles in common."

"Really and truly," cried the other with a kind of tickled
modesty and pleased concern, "mine is an understanding too
weak to throw out grapnels and hug another to it. I have
indeed heard of some great scholars in these days, whose
boast is less that they have made disciples than victims. But
for me, had I the power to do such things, I have not the
heart to desire."

"I believe you, my dear Charlie. And yet, I repeat, by your commentaries on Polonius you have, I know not how, unsettled me; so that now I don't exactly see how Shakespeare meant the words he puts in Polonius' mouth."

"Some say that he meant them to open people's eyes; but I don't think so."

"Open their eyes?" echoed the cosmopolitan, slowly expanding his; " what is there in this world for one to open his eyes to? I mean in the sort of invidious sense you cite?"

"Well, others say he meant to corrupt people's morals; and still others, that he had no express intention at all, but in effect opens their eyes and corrupts their morals in one operation. All of which I reject."

"Of course you reject so crude an hypothesis; and yet, to confess, in reading Shakespeare in my closet, struck by some passage, I have laid down the volume, and said: 'This Shakespeare is a queer man.' At times seeming irresponsible, he does not always seem reliable. There appears to be a certain— what shall I call it?—hidden sun, say, about him, at once enlightening and mystifying. Now, I should be afraid to say what I have sometimes thought that hidden sun might be."

"Do you think it was the true light?" with clandestine geniality again filling the other's glass.

"I would prefer to decline answering a categorical question there. Shakespeare has got to be a kind of deity. Prudent minds, having certain latent thoughts concerning him, will reserve them in a condition of lasting probation. Still, as touching avowable speculations, we are permitted a tether. Shakespeare himself is to be adored, not arraigned; but, so we do it with humility, we may a little canvass his characters. There's his Autolycus now, a fellow that always puzzled me. How is one to take Autolycus? A rogue so happy, so lucky, so triumphant, of so almost captivatingly vicious a career that a virtuous man reduced to the poor-house (were such a contingency conceivable), might almost long to change sides with him. And yet, see the words put into his mouth: 'Oh,' cries Autolycus, as he comes galloping, gay as a buck, upon the stage, 'oh,' he laughs, 'oh what a fool is Honesty, and Trust, his sworn brother, a very simple gentleman.' Think of that. Trust, that is, confidence—that is, the thing in this uni-

verse the sacredest—is rattlingly pronounced just the simplest. And the scenes in which the rogue figures seem
purposely devised for verification of his principles. Mind,
Charlie, I do not say it *is* so, far from it; but I *do* say it seems
so. Yes, Autolycus would seem a needy varlet acting upon the
persuasion that less is to be got by invoking pockets than
picking them, more to be made by an expert knave than a
bungling beggar; and for this reason, as he thinks, that the
soft heads outnumber the soft hearts. The devil's drilled recruit, Autolycus is joyous as if he wore the livery of heaven.
When disturbed by the character and career of one thus
wicked and thus happy, my sole consolation is in the fact that
no such creature ever existed, except in the powerful imagination which evoked him. And yet, a creature, a living creature, he is, though only a poet was his maker. It may be, that
in that paper-and-ink investiture of his, Autolycus acts more
effectively upon mankind than he would in a flesh-and-blood
one. Can his influence be salutary? True, in Autolycus there
is humor; but though, according to my principle, humor is in
general to be held a saving quality, yet the case of Autolycus
is an exception; because it is his humor which, so to speak,
oils his mischievousness. The bravadoing mischievousness of
Autolycus is slid into the world on humor, as a pirate
schooner, with colors flying, is launched into the sea on
greased ways."

"I approve of Autolycus as little as you," said the stranger,
who, during his companion's commonplaces, had seemed less
attentive to them than to maturing within his own mind the
original conceptions destined to eclipse them. "But I cannot
believe that Autolycus, mischievous as he must prove upon
the stage, can be near so much so as such a character as
Polonius."

"I don't know about that," bluntly, and yet not impolitely,
returned the cosmopolitan; "to be sure, accepting your view
of the old courtier, then if between him and Autolycus you
raise the question of unprepossessingness, I grant you the latter comes off best. For a moist rogue may tickle the midriff,
while a dry worldling may but wrinkle the spleen."

"But Polonius is not dry," said the other excitedly; "he
drules. One sees the fly-blown old fop drule and look wise.

His vile wisdom is made the viler by his vile rheuminess. The bowing and cringing, time-serving old sinner—is such an one to give manly precepts to youth? The discreet, decorous, old dotard-of-state; senile prudence; fatuous soullessness! The ribanded old dog is paralytic all down one side, and that the side of nobleness. His soul is gone out. Only nature's automatonism keeps him on his legs. As with some old trees, the bark survives the pith, and will still stand stiffly up, though but to rim round punk, so the body of old Polonius has outlived his soul."

"Come, come," said the cosmopolitan with serious air, almost displeased; "though I yield to none in admiration of earnestness, yet, I think, even earnestness may have limits. To humane minds, strong language is always more or less distressing. Besides, Polonius is an old man—as I remember him upon the stage—with snowy locks. Now charity requires that such a figure—think of it how you will—should at least be treated with civility. Moreover, old age is ripeness, and I once heard say, 'Better ripe than raw.' "

"But not better rotten than raw!" bringing down his hand with energy on the table.

"Why, bless me," in mild surprise contemplating his heated comrade, "how you fly out against this unfortunate Polonius—a being that never was, nor will be. And yet, viewed in a Christian light," he added pensively, "I don't know that anger against this man of straw is a whit less wise than anger against a man of flesh. Madness, to be mad with anything."

"That may be, or may not be," returned the other, a little testily, perhaps; "but I stick to what I said, that it is better to be raw than rotten. And what is to be feared on that head, may be known from this: that it is with the best of hearts as with the best of pears—a dangerous experiment to linger too long upon the scene. This did Polonius. Thank fortune, Frank, I am young, every tooth sound in my head, and if good wine can keep me where I am, long shall I remain so."

"True," with a smile. "But wine, to do good, must be drunk. You have talked much and well, Charlie; but drunk little and indifferently—fill up."

"Presently, presently," with a hasty and preoccupied air. "If I remember right, Polonius hints as much as that one should, under no circumstances, commit the indiscretion of aiding in a pecuniary way an unfortunate friend. He drules out some stale stuff about 'loan losing both itself and friend,' don't he? But our bottle; is it glued fast? Keep it moving, my dear Frank. Good wine, and upon my soul I begin to feel it, and through me old Polonius—yes, this wine, I fear, is what excites me so against that detestable old dog without a tooth."

Upon this, the cosmopolitan, cigar in mouth, slowly raised the bottle, and brought it slowly to the light, looking at it steadfastly, as one might at a thermometer in August, to see not how low it was, but how high. Then whiffing out a puff, set it down, and said: "Well, Charlie, if what wine you have drunk came out of this bottle, in that case I should say that if—supposing a case—that if one fellow had an object in getting another fellow fuddled, and this fellow to be fuddled was of your capacity, the operation would be comparatively inexpensive. What do you think, Charlie?"

"Why, I think I don't much admire the supposition," said Charlie, with a look of resentment; "it ain't safe, depend upon it, Frank, to venture upon too jocose suppositions with one's friends."

"Why, bless you, Charlie, my supposition wasn't personal, but general. You mustn't be so touchy."

"If I am touchy it is the wine. Sometimes, when I freely drink it, it has a touchy effect on me, I have observed."

"Freely drink? you haven't drunk the perfect measure of one glass, yet. While for me, this must be my fourth or fifth, thanks to your importunity; not to speak of all I drank this morning, for old acquaintance' sake. Drink, drink; you must drink."

"Oh, I drink while you are talking," laughed the other; "you have not noticed it, but I have drunk my share. Have a queer way I learned from a sedate old uncle, who used to tip off his glass unperceived. Do you fill up, and my glass, too. There! Now away with that stump, and have a new cigar. Good fellowship forever!" again in the lyric mood. "Say, Frank, are we not men? I say are we not human? Tell me, were they not human who engendered us, as before heaven I believe they shall be whom we shall engender? Fill up, up, up, my friend. Let the ruby tide aspire, and all ruby aspirations with it! Up, fill up! Be we convivial. And conviviality, what is it? The word, I mean; what expresses it? A living together. But bats live together, and did you ever hear of convivial bats?"

"If I ever did," observed the cosmopolitan, "it has quite slipped my recollection."

"But *why* did you never hear of convivial bats, nor anybody else? Because bats, though they live together, live not together genially. Bats are not genial souls. But men are; and how delightful to think that the word which among men signifies the highest pitch of geniality, implies, as indispensable auxiliary, the cheery benediction of the bottle. Yes, Frank, to live together in the finest sense, we must drink together. And so, what wonder that he who loves not wine, that sober wretch has a lean heart—a heart like a wrung-out old bluing-bag, and loves not his kind? Out upon him, to the rag-house with him, hang him—the ungenial soul!"

"Oh, now, now, can't you be convivial without being censorious? I like easy, unexcited conviviality. For the sober man, really, though for my part I naturally love a cheerful glass, I will not prescribe my nature as the law to other natures. So don't abuse the sober man. Conviviality is one good thing, and sobriety is another good thing. So don't be one-sided."

"Well, if I am one-sided, it is the wine. Indeed, indeed, I have indulged too genially. My excitement upon slight provocation shows it. But yours is a stronger head; drink you. By the way, talking of geniality, it is much on the increase in these days, ain't it?"

"It is, and I hail the fact. Nothing better attests the advance of the humanitarian spirit. In former and less humanitarian ages—the ages of amphitheatres and gladiators—geniality was mostly confined to the fireside and table. But in our age—the age of joint-stock companies and free-and-easies—it is with this precious quality as with precious gold in old Peru, which Pizarro found making up the scullion's sauce-pot as the Inca's crown. Yes, we golden boys, the moderns, have geniality everywhere—a bounty broadcast like noonlight."

"True, true; my sentiments again. Geniality has invaded each department and profession. We have genial senators, genial authors, genial lecturers, genial doctors, genial clergymen, genial surgeons, and the next thing we shall have genial hangmen."

"As to the last-named sort of person," said the cosmopolitan, "I trust that the advancing spirit of geniality will at last enable us to dispense with him. No murderers—no hangmen. And surely, when the whole world shall have been genialized, it will be as out of place to talk of murderers, as in a Christianized world to talk of sinners."

"To pursue the thought," said the other, "every blessing is attended with some evil, and—"

"Stay," said the cosmopolitan, "that may be better let pass for a loose saying, than for hopeful doctrine."

"Well, assuming the saying's truth, it would apply to the future supremacy of the genial spirit, since then it will fare with the hangman as it did with the weaver when the spinning-jenny whizzed into the ascendant. Thrown out of employment, what could Jack Ketch turn his hand to? Butchering?"

"That he could turn his hand to it seems probable; but that, under the circumstances, it would be appropriate, might in some minds admit of a question. For one, I am inclined to think—and I trust it will not be held fastidiousness—that it would hardly be suitable to the dignity of our nature, that an individual, once employed in attending the last hours of human unfortunates, should, that office being extinct, transfer himself to the business of attending the last hours of unfortunate cattle. I would suggest that the individual turn valet— a vocation to which he would, perhaps, appear not wholly inadapted by his familiar dexterity about the person. In particular, for giving a finishing tie to a gentleman's cravat, I know few who would, in all likelihood, be, from previous occupation, better fitted than the professional person in question."

"Are you in earnest?" regarding the serene speaker with unaffected curiosity; "are you really in earnest?"

"I trust I am never otherwise," was the mildly earnest reply; "but talking of the advance of geniality, I am not without hopes that it will eventually exert its influence even upon so difficult a subject as the misanthrope."

"A genial misanthrope! I thought I had stretched the rope

pretty hard in talking of genial hangmen. A genial misanthrope is no more conceivable than a surly philanthropist."

"True," lightly depositing in an unbroken little cylinder the ashes of his cigar, "true, the two you name are well opposed."

"Why, you talk as if there *was* such a being as a surly philanthropist."

"I do. My eccentric friend, whom you call Coonskins, is an example. Does he not, as I explained to you, hide under a surly air a philanthropic heart? Now, the genial misanthrope, when, in the process of eras, he shall turn up, will be the converse of this; under an affable air, he will hide a misanthropical heart. In short, the genial misanthrope will be a new kind of monster, but still no small improvement upon the original one, since, instead of making faces and throwing stones at people, like that poor old crazy man, Timon, he will take steps, fiddle in hand, and set the tickled world a dancing. In a word, as the progress of Christianization mellows those in manner whom it cannot mend in mind, much the same will it prove with the progress of genialization. And so, thanks to geniality, the misanthrope, reclaimed from his boorish address, will take on refinement and softness—to so genial a degree, indeed, that it may possibly fall out that the misanthrope of the coming century will be almost as popular as, I am sincerely sorry to say, some philanthropists of the present time would seem not to be, as witness my eccentric friend named before."

"Well," cried the other, a little weary, perhaps, of a speculation so abstract, " well, however it may be with the century to come, certainly in the century which is, whatever else one may be, he must be genial or he is nothing. So fill up, fill up, and be genial!"

"I am trying my best," said the cosmopolitan, still calmly companionable. "A moment since, we talked of Pizarro, gold, and Peru; no doubt, now, you remember that when the Spaniard first entered Atahalpa's treasure-chamber, and saw such profusion of plate stacked up, right and left, with the wantonness of old barrels in a brewer's yard, the needy fellow felt a twinge of misgiving, of want of confidence, as to the genuineness of an opulence so profuse. He went about rapping the shining vases with his knuckles. But it was all gold, pure gold, good gold, sterling gold, which how cheerfully would have been stamped such at Goldsmiths' Hall. And just so those needy minds, which, through their own insincerity, having no confidence in mankind, doubt lest the liberal geniality of this age be spurious. They are small Pizarros in their way—by the very princeliness of men's geniality stunned into distrust of it."

"Far be such distrust from you and me, my genial friend," cried the other fervently; "fill up, fill up!"

"Well, this all along seems a division of labor," smiled the cosmopolitan. "I do about all the drinking, and you do about all—the genial. But yours is a nature competent to do that to a large population. And now, my friend," with a peculiarly grave air, evidently foreshadowing something not unimportant, and very likely of close personal interest; "wine, you know, opens the heart, and—"

"Opens it!" with exultation, "it thaws it right out. Every heart is ice-bound till wine melt it, and reveal the tender grass and sweet herbage budding below, with every dear secret, hidden before like a dropped jewel in a snow-bank, lying there unsuspected through winter till spring."

"And just in that way, my dear Charlie, is one of my little secrets now to be shown forth."

"Ah!" eagerly moving round his chair, "what is it?"

"Be not so impetuous, my dear Charlie. Let me explain. You see, naturally, I am a man not overgifted with assurance; in general, I am, if anything, diffidently reserved; so, if I shall presently seem otherwise, the reason is, that you, by the geniality you have evinced in all your talk, and especially the noble way in which, while affirming your good opinion of men, you intimated that you never could prove false to any man, but most by your indignation at a particularly illiberal passage in Polonius' advice—in short, in short," with extreme embarrassment, "how shall I express what I mean, unless I add that by your whole character you impel me to throw myself upon your nobleness; in one word, put confidence in you, a generous confidence?"

"I see, I see," with heightened interest, "something of moment you wish to confide. Now, what is it, Frank? Love affair?"

"No, not that."

"What, then, my *dear* Frank? Speak—depend upon me to the last. Out with it."

"Out it shall come, then," said the cosmopolitan. "I am in want, urgent want, of money."

Chapter 31

A METAMORPHOSIS MORE SURPRISING THAN
ANY IN OVID

"IN WANT of money!" pushing back his chair as from a suddenly-disclosed man-trap or crater.

"Yes," naïvely assented the cosmopolitan, "and you are going to loan me fifty dollars. I could almost wish I was in need of more, only for your sake. Yes, my dear Charlie, for your sake; that you might the better prove your noble kindliness, my dear Charlie."

"None of your dear Charlies," cried the other, springing to his feet, and buttoning up his coat, as if hastily to depart upon a long journey.

"Why, why, why?" painfully looking up.

"None of your why, why, whys!" tossing out a foot, "go to the devil, sir! Beggar, impostor!—never so deceived in a man in my life."

Chapter 32

WHILE SPEAKING or rather hissing those words, the boon companion underwent much such a change as one reads of in fairy-books. Out of old materials sprang a new creature. Cadmus glided into the snake.

The cosmopolitan rose, the traces of previous feeling vanished; looked steadfastly at his transformed friend a moment, then, taking ten half-eagles from his pocket, stooped down, and laid them, one by one, in a circle round him; and, retiring a pace, waved his long tasseled pipe with the air of a necromancer, an air heightened by his costume, accompanying each wave with a solemn murmur of cabalistical words.

Meantime, he within the magic-ring stood suddenly rapt, exhibiting every symptom of a successful charm—a turned cheek, a fixed attitude, a frozen eye; spellbound, not more by the waving wand than by the ten invincible talismans on the floor.

"Reappear, reappear, reappear, oh, my former friend! Replace this hideous apparition with thy blest shape, and be the token of thy return the words, 'My dear Frank.'"

"My dear Frank," now cried the restored friend, cordially stepping out of the ring, with regained self-possession regaining lost identity, "My dear Frank, what a funny man you are; full of fun as an egg of meat. How could you tell me that absurd story of your being in need? But I relish a good joke too well to spoil it by letting on. Of course, I humored the thing; and, on my side, put on all the cruel airs you would have me. Come, this little episode of fictitious estrangement will but enhance the delightful reality. Let us sit down again, and finish our bottle."

"With all my heart," said the cosmopolitan, dropping the necromancer with the same facility with which he had assumed it. "Yes," he added, soberly picking up the gold pieces, and returning them with a chink to his pocket, "yes, I am something of a funny man now and then; while for you,

Charlie," eying him in tenderness, " what you say about your humoring the thing is true enough; never did man second a joke better than you did just now. You played your part better than I did mine; you played it, Charlie, to the life."

"You see, I once belonged to an amateur play company; that accounts for it. But come, fill up, and let's talk of something else."

"Well," acquiesced the cosmopolitan, seating himself, and quietly brimming his glass, " what shall we talk about?"

"Oh, anything you please," a sort of nervously accommodating.

"Well, suppose we talk about Charlemont?"

"Charlemont? What's Charlemont? Who's Charlemont?"

"You shall hear, my dear Charlie," answered the cosmopolitan. "I will tell you the story of Charlemont, the gentleman-madman."

Chapter 33

WHICH MAY PASS FOR WHATEVER IT MAY PROVE TO BE WORTH

BUT ERE BE GIVEN the rather grave story of Charlemont, a reply must in civility be made to a certain voice which methinks I hear, that, in view of past chapters, and more particularly the last, where certain antics appear, exclaims: How unreal all this is! Who did ever dress or act like your cosmopolitan? And who, it might be returned, did ever dress or act like harlequin?

Strange, that in a work of amusement, this severe fidelity to real life should be exacted by any one, who, by taking up such a work, sufficiently shows that he is not unwilling to drop real life, and turn, for a time, to something different. Yes, it is, indeed, strange that any one should clamor for the thing he is weary of; that any one, who, for any cause, finds real life dull, should yet demand of him who is to divert his attention from it, that he should be true to that dullness.

There is another class, and with this class we side, who sit down to a work of amusement tolerantly as they sit at a play, and with much the same expectations and feelings. They look that fancy shall evoke scenes different from those of the same old crowd round the custom-house counter, and same old dishes on the boarding-house table, with characters unlike those of the same old acquaintances they meet in the same old way every day in the same old street. And as, in real life, the proprieties will not allow people to act out themselves with that unreserve permitted to the stage; so, in books of fiction, they look not only for more entertainment, but, at bottom, even for more reality, than real life itself can show. Thus, though they want novelty, they want nature, too; but nature unfettered, exhilarated, in effect transformed. In this way of thinking, the people in a fiction, like the people in a play, must dress as nobody exactly dresses, talk as nobody exactly talks, act as nobody exactly acts. It is with fiction as with religion: it should present another world, and yet one to which we feel the tie.

If, then, something is to be pardoned to well-meant endeavor, surely a little is to be allowed to that writer who, in all his scenes, does but seek to minister to what, as he understands it, is the implied wish of the more indulgent lovers of entertainment, before whom harlequin can never appear in a coat too parti-colored, or cut capers too fantastic.

One word more. Though every one knows how bootless it is to be in all cases vindicating one's self, never mind how convinced one may be that he is never in the wrong; yet, so precious to man is the approbation of his kind, that to rest, though but under an imaginary censure applied to but a work of imagination, is no easy thing. The mention of this weakness will explain why all such readers as may think they perceive something inharmonious between the boisterous hilarity of the cosmopolitan with the bristling cynic, and his restrained good-nature with the boon-companion, are now referred to that chapter where some similar apparent inconsistency in another character is, on general principles, modestly endeavored to be apologized for.

Chapter 34

CHARLEMONT was a young merchant of French descent, living in St. Louis—a man not deficient in mind, and possessed of that sterling and captivating kindliness, seldom in perfection seen but in youthful bachelors, united at times to a remarkable sort of gracefully devil-may-care and witty good-humor. Of course, he was admired by everybody, and loved, as only mankind can love, by not a few. But in his twenty-ninth year a change came over him. Like one whose hair turns gray in a night, so in a day Charlemont turned from affable to morose. His acquaintances were passed without greeting; while, as for his confidential friends, them he pointedly, unscrupulously, and with a kind of fierceness, cut dead.

"One, provoked by such conduct, would fain have resented it with words as disdainful; while another, shocked by the change, and, in concern for a friend, magnanimously overlooking affronts, implored to know what sudden, secret grief had distempered him. But from resentment and from tenderness Charlemont alike turned away.

"Ere long, to the general surprise, the merchant Charlemont was gazetted, and the same day it was reported that he had withdrawn from town, but not before placing his entire property in the hands of responsible assignees for the benefit of creditors.

"Whither he had vanished, none could guess. At length, nothing being heard, it was surmised that he must have made away with himself—a surmise, doubtless, originating in the remembrance of the change some months previous to his bankruptcy—a change of a sort only to be ascribed to a mind suddenly thrown from its balance.

"Years passed. It was spring-time, and lo, one bright morning, Charlemont lounged into the St. Louis coffee-houses— gay, polite, humane, companionable, and dressed in the height of costly elegance. Not only was he alive, but he was himself again. Upon meeting with old acquaintances, he made the first advances, and in such a manner that it was impossible not to meet him half-way. Upon other old friends, whom he did not chance casually to meet, he either personally called, or left his card and compliments for them; and to several, sent presents of game or hampers of wine.

"They say the world is sometimes harshly unforgiving, but it was not so to Charlemont. The world feels a return of love for one who returns to it as he did. Expressive of its renewed interest was a whisper, an inquiring whisper, how now, exactly, so long after his bankruptcy, it fared with Charlemont's purse. Rumor, seldom at a loss for answers, replied that he had spent nine years in Marseilles in France, and there acquiring a second fortune, had returned with it, a man devoted henceforth to genial friendships.

"Added years went by, and the restored wanderer still the same; or rather, by his noble qualities, grew up like golden maize in the encouraging sun of good opinions. But still the latent wonder was, what had caused that change in him at a period when, pretty much as now, he was, to all appearance, in the possession of the same fortune, the same friends, the same popularity. But nobody thought it would be the thing to question him here.

"At last, at a dinner at his house, when all the guests but one had successively departed; this remaining guest, an old acquaintance, being just enough under the influence of wine to set aside the fear of touching upon a delicate point, ventured, in a way which perhaps spoke more favorably for his heart than his tact, to beg of his host to explain the one enigma of his life. Deep melancholy overspread the before cheery face of Charlemont; he sat for some moments tremulously silent; then pushing a full decanter towards the guest, in a choked voice, said: 'No, no! when by art, and care, and time, flowers are made to bloom over a grave, who would seek to dig all up again only to know the mystery?—The wine.' When both glasses were filled, Charlemont took his, and lifting it, added lowly: 'If ever, in days to come, you shall see ruin at hand, and, thinking you understand mankind, shall tremble for your friendships, and tremble for your pride; and, partly through love for the one and fear for the other, shall resolve to be beforehand with the world, and save it from a sin by prospectively taking that sin to yourself, then will you do as one I now dream of once did, and like him will you suffer; but how fortunate and how grateful should you be, if like him, after all that had happened, you could be a little happy again.'

"When the guest went away, it was with the persuasion, that though outwardly restored in mind as in fortune, yet, some taint of Charlemont's old malady survived, and that it was not well for friends to touch one dangerous string."

Chapter 35

WELL, WHAT do you think of the story of Charlemont?" mildly asked he who had told it.

"A very strange one," answered the auditor, who had been such not with perfect ease, "but is it true?"

"Of course not; it is a story which I told with the purpose of every story-teller—to amuse. Hence, if it seem strange to you, that strangeness is the romance; it is what contrasts it with real life; it is the invention, in brief, the fiction as opposed to the fact. For do but ask yourself, my dear Charlie," lovingly leaning over towards him, "I rest it with your own heart now, whether such a forereaching motive as Charlemont hinted he had acted on in his change—whether such a motive, I say, were a sort of one at all justified by the nature of human society? Would you, for one, turn the cold shoulder to a friend—a convivial one, say, whose pennilessness should be suddenly revealed to you?"

"How can you ask me, my dear Frank? You know I would scorn such meanness." But rising somewhat disconcerted— "really, early as it is, I think I must retire; my head," putting up his hand to it, "feels unpleasantly; this confounded elixir of logwood, little as I drank of it, has played the deuce with me."

"Little as you drank of this elixir of logwood? Why, Charlie, you are losing your mind. To talk so of the genuine, mellow old port. Yes, I think that by all means you had better away, and sleep it off. There—don't apologize—don't explain—go, go—I understand you exactly. I will see you to-morrow."

Chapter 36

In which the Cosmopolitan is accosted by a mystic, whereupon ensues pretty much such talk as might be expected

As, not without some haste, the boon companion withdrew, a stranger advanced, and touching the cosmopolitan, said: "I think I heard you say you would see that man again. Be warned; don't you do so."

He turned, surveying the speaker; a blue-eyed man, sandy-haired, and Saxon-looking; perhaps five and forty; tall, and, but for a certain angularity, well made; little touch of the drawing-room about him, but a look of plain propriety of a Puritan sort, with a kind of farmer dignity. His age seemed betokened more by his brow, placidly thoughtful, than by his general aspect, which had that look of youthfulness in maturity, peculiar sometimes to habitual health of body, the original gift of nature, or in part the effect or reward of steady temperance of the passions, kept so, perhaps, by constitution as much as morality. A neat, comely, almost ruddy cheek, coolly fresh, like a red clover-blossom at coolish dawn—the color of warmth preserved by the virtue of chill. Toning the whole man, was one-knows-not-what of shrewdness and mythiness, strangely jumbled; in that way, he seemed a kind of cross between a Yankee peddler and a Tartar priest, though it seemed as if, at a pinch, the first would not in all probability play second fiddle to the last.

"Sir," said the cosmopolitan, rising and bowing with slow dignity, "if I cannot with unmixed satisfaction hail a hint pointed at one who has just been clinking the social glass with me, on the other hand, I am not disposed to underrate the motive which, in the present case, could alone have prompted such an intimation. My friend, whose seat is still warm, has retired for the night, leaving more or less in his bottle here. Pray, sit down in his seat, and partake with me; and then, if you choose to hint aught further unfavorable to the man, the genial warmth of whose person in part passes into yours, and whose genial hospitality meanders through you—be it so."

"Quite beautiful conceits," said the stranger, now scholastically and artistically eying the picturesque speaker, as if he were a statue in the Pitti Palace; "very beautiful:" then with the gravest interest, "yours, sir, if I mistake not, must be a beautiful soul—one full of all love and truth; for where beauty is, there must those be."

"A pleasing belief," rejoined the cosmopolitan, beginning with an even air, "and to confess, long ago it pleased me. Yes, with you and Schiller, I am pleased to believe that beauty is at bottom incompatible with ill, and therefore am so eccentric as to have confidence in the latent benignity of that beautiful creature, the rattle-snake, whose lithe neck and burnished maze of tawny gold, as he sleekly curls aloft in the sun, who on the prairie can behold without wonder?"

As he breathed these words, he seemed so to enter into their spirit—as some earnest descriptive speakers will—as unconsciously to wreathe his form and sidelong crest his head, till he all but seemed the creature described. Meantime, the stranger regarded him with little surprise, apparently, though with much contemplativeness of a mystical sort, and presently said: "When charmed by the beauty of that viper, did it never occur to you to change personalities with him? to feel what it was to be a snake? to glide unsuspected in grass? to sting, to kill at a touch; your whole beautiful body one iridescent scabbard of death? In short, did the wish never occur to you to feel yourself exempt from knowledge, and conscience, and revel for a while in the care-free, joyous life of a perfectly instinctive, unscrupulous, and irresponsible creature?"

"Such a wish," replied the other, not perceptibly disturbed, "I must confess, never consciously was mine. Such a wish, indeed, could hardly occur to ordinary imaginations, and mine I cannot think much above the average."

"But now that the idea is suggested," said the stranger, with infantile intellectuality, "does it not raise the desire?"

"Hardly. For though I do not think I have any uncharitable prejudice against the rattle-snake, still, I should not like to be one. If I were a rattle-snake now, there would be no such thing as being genial with men—men would be afraid of me, and then I should be a very lonesome and miserable rattlesnake."

"True, men would be afraid of you. And why? Because of your rattle, your hollow rattle—a sound, as I have been told, like the shaking together of small, dry skulls in a tune of the Waltz of Death. And here we have another beautiful truth. When any creature is by its make inimical to other creatures, nature in effect labels that creature, much as an apothecary does a poison. So that whoever is destroyed by a rattle-snake, or other harmful agent, it is his own fault. He should have respected the label. Hence that significant passage in Scripture, 'Who will pity the charmer that is bitten with a serpent?'"

"*I* would pity him," said the cosmopolitan, a little bluntly, perhaps.

"But don't you think," rejoined the other, still maintaining his passionless air, "don't you think, that for a man to pity where nature is pitiless, is a little presuming?"

"Let casuists decide the casuistry, but the compassion the heart decides for itself. But, sir," deepening in seriousness, "as I now for the first realize, you but a moment since introduced the word irresponsible in a way I am not used to. Now, sir, though, out of a tolerant spirit, as I hope, I try my best never to be frightened at any speculation, so long as it is pursued in honesty, yet, for once, I must acknowledge that you do really, in the point cited, cause me uneasiness; because a proper view of the universe, that view which is suited to breed a proper confidence, teaches, if I err not, that since all things are justly presided over, not very many living agents but must be some way accountable."

"Is a rattle-snake accountable?" asked the stranger with such a preternaturally cold, gemmy glance out of his pellucid blue eye, that he seemed more a metaphysical merman than a feeling man; "is a rattle-snake accountable?"

"If I will not affirm that it is," returned the other, with the caution of no inexperienced thinker, "neither will I deny it. But if we suppose it so, I need not say that such accountability is neither to you, nor me, nor the Court of Common Pleas, but to something superior."

He was proceeding, when the stranger would have interrupted him; but as reading his argument in his eye, the cosmopolitan, without waiting for it to be put into words, at once spoke to it: "You object to my supposition, for but such it is, that the rattle-snake's accountability is not by nature manifest; but might not much the same thing be urged against man's? A *reductio ad absurdum*, proving the objection vain. But if now," he continued, "you consider what capacity for mischief there is in a rattle-snake (observe, I do not charge it with being mischievous, I but say it has the capacity), could you well avoid admitting that that would be no symmetrical view of the universe which should maintain that, while to man it is forbidden to kill, without judicial cause, his fellow, yet the rattle-snake has an implied permit of unaccountability to murder any creature it takes capricious umbrage at—man included?—But," with a wearied air, "this is no genial talk; at least it is not so to me. Zeal at unawares embarked me in it. I regret it. Pray, sit down, and take some of this wine."

"Your suggestions are new to me," said the other, with a kind of condescending appreciativeness, as of one who, out of devotion to knowledge, disdains not to appropriate the least crumb of it, even from a pauper's board; "and, as I am a very Athenian in hailing a new thought, I cannot consent to let it drop so abruptly. Now, the rattle-snake—"

"Nothing more about rattle-snakes, I beseech," in distress; "I must positively decline to reënter upon that subject. Sit down, sir, I beg, and take some of this wine."

"To invite me to sit down with you is hospitable," collectedly acquiescing now in the change of topics; "and hospitality being fabled to be of oriental origin, and forming, as it does, the subject of a pleasing Arabian romance, as well as being a very romantic thing in itself—hence I always hear the expressions of hospitality with pleasure. But, as for the wine, my regard for that beverage is so extreme, and I am so fearful of letting it sate me, that I keep my love for it in the lasting condition of an untried abstraction. Briefly, I quaff immense draughts of wine from the page of Hafiz, but wine from a cup I seldom as much as sip."

The cosmopolitan turned a mild glance upon the speaker, who, now occupying the chair opposite him, sat there purely and coldly radiant as a prism. It seemed as if one could almost hear him vitreously chime and ring. That moment a waiter passed, whom, arresting with a sign, the cosmopolitan bid go bring a goblet of ice-water. "Ice it well, waiter," said he; "and now," turning to the stranger, " will you, if you please, give me your reason for the warning words you first addressed to me?"

"I hope they were not such warnings as most warnings are," said the stranger; " warnings which do not forewarn, but in mockery come after the fact. And yet something in you bids me think now, that whatever latent design your impostor friend might have had upon you, it as yet remains unaccomplished. You read his label."

"And what did it say? 'This is a genial soul.' So you see you must either give up your doctrine of labels, or else your prejudice against my friend. But tell me," with renewed earnestness, " what do you take him for? What is he?"

"What are you? What am I? Nobody knows who anybody is. The data which life furnishes, towards forming a true estimate of any being, are as insufficient to that end as in geometry one side given would be to determine the triangle."

"But is not this doctrine of triangles someway inconsistent with your doctrine of labels?"

"Yes, but what of that? I seldom care to be consistent. In a philosophical view, consistency is a certain level at all times, maintained in all the thoughts of one's mind. But, since nature is nearly all hill and dale, how can one keep naturally advancing in knowledge without submitting to the natural inequalities in the progress? Advance into knowledge is just like advance upon the grand Erie canal, where, from the character of the country, change of level is inevitable; you are locked up and locked down with perpetual inconsistencies, and yet all the time you get on; while the dullest part of the whole route is what the boatmen call the 'long level'—a consistently-flat surface of sixty miles through stagnant swamps."

"In one particular," rejoined the cosmopolitan, "your simile is, perhaps, unfortunate. For, after all these weary lockings-up and lockings-down, upon how much of a higher plain do you finally stand? Enough to make it an object? Having from youth been taught reverence for knowledge, you must pardon me if, on but this one account, I reject your analogy. But really you someway bewitch me with your tempting discourse, so that I keep straying from my point unawares. You tell me you cannot certainly know who or what my friend is; pray, what do you conjecture him to be?"

"I conjecture him to be what, among the ancient Egyptians, was called a —— " using some unknown word.

"A ——! And what is that?"

"A —— is what Proclus, in a little note to his third book on the theology of Plato, defines as —— —— " coming out with a sentence of Greek.

Holding up his glass, and steadily looking through its transparency, the cosmopolitan rejoined: "That, in so defining the thing, Proclus set it to modern understandings in the most crystal light it was susceptible of, I will not rashly deny; still, if you could put the definition in words suited to perceptions like mine, I should take it for a favor."

"A favor!" slightly lifting his cool eyebrows; "a bridal favor I understand, a knot of white ribands, a very beautiful type of the purity of true marriage; but of other favors I am yet to learn; and still, in a vague way, the word, as you employ it, strikes me as unpleasingly significant in general of some poor, unheroic submission to being done good to."

Here the goblet of iced-water was brought, and, in compliance with a sign from the cosmopolitan, was placed before the stranger, who, not before expressing acknowledgments, took a draught, apparently refreshing—its very coldness, as with some is the case, proving not entirely uncongenial.

At last, setting down the goblet, and gently wiping from his lips the beads of water freshly clinging there as to the valve of a coral-shell upon a reef, he turned upon the cosmopolitan, and, in a manner the most cool, self-possessed, and matter-of-fact possible, said: "I hold to the metempsychosis; and whoever I may be now, I feel that I was once the stoic Arrian, and have inklings of having been equally puzzled by a word in the current language of that former time, very probably answering to your word *favor*."

"Would you favor me by explaining?" said the cosmopolitan, blandly.

"Sir," responded the stranger, with a very slight degree of severity, "I like lucidity, of all things, and am afraid I shall hardly be able to converse satisfactorily with you, unless you bear it in mind."

The cosmopolitan ruminatingly eyed him awhile, then said: "The best way, as I have heard, to get out of a labyrinth, is to retrace one's steps. I will accordingly retrace mine, and beg you will accompany me. In short, once again to return to the point: for what reason did you warn me against my friend?"

"Briefly, then, and clearly, because, as before said, I conjecture him to be what, among the ancient Egyptians—"

"Pray, now," earnestly deprecated the cosmopolitan, "pray, now, why disturb the repose of those ancient Egyptians? What to us are their words or their thoughts? Are we pauper Arabs, without a house of our own, that, with the mummies, we must turn squatters among the dust of the Catacombs?"

"Pharaoh's poorest brick-maker lies proudlier in his rags than the Emperor of all the Russias in his hollands," oracularly said the stranger; "for death, though in a worm, is majestic; while life, though in a king, is contemptible. So talk not against mummies. It is a part of my mission to teach mankind a due reverence for mummies."

Fortunately, to arrest these incoherencies, or rather, to vary them, a haggard, inspired-looking man now approached—a crazy beggar, asking alms under the form of peddling a rhapsodical tract, composed by himself, and setting forth his claims to some rhapsodical apostleship. Though ragged and dirty, there was about him no touch of vulgarity; for, by nature, his manner was not unrefined, his frame slender, and appeared the more so from the broad, untanned frontlet of his brow, tangled over with a disheveled mass of raven curls, throwing a still deeper tinge upon a complexion like that of a shriveled berry. Nothing could exceed his look of picturesque Italian ruin and dethronement, heightened by what seemed just one glimmering peep of reason, insufficient to do him any lasting good, but enough, perhaps, to suggest a torment of latent doubts at times, whether his addled dream of glory were true.

Accepting the tract offered him, the cosmopolitan glanced over it, and, seeming to see just what it was, closed it, put it in his pocket, eyed the man a moment, then, leaning over and presenting him with a shilling, said to him, in tones kind and considerate: "I am sorry, my friend, that I happen to be engaged just now; but, having purchased your work, I promise myself much satisfaction in its perusal at my earliest leisure."

In his tattered, single-breasted frock-coat, buttoned meagerly up to his chin, the shatter-brain made him a bow, which, for courtesy, would not have misbecome a viscount, then turned with silent appeal to the stranger. But the stranger sat more like a cold prism than ever, while an expression of keen Yankee cuteness, now replacing his former mystical one, lent added icicles to his aspect. His whole air said: "Nothing from me." The repulsed petitioner threw a look full of resentful pride and cracked disdain upon him, and went his way.

"Come, now," said the cosmopolitan, a little reproachfully, "you ought to have sympathized with that man; tell me, did you feel no fellow-feeling? Look at his tract here, quite in the transcendental vein."

"Excuse me," said the stranger, declining the tract, "I never patronize scoundrels."

"Scoundrels?"

"I detected in him, sir, a damning peep of sense—damning, I say; for sense in a seeming madman is scoundrelism. I take him for a cunning vagabond, who picks up a vagabond living by adroitly playing the madman. Did you not remark how he flinched under my eye?"

"Really," drawing a long, astonished breath, "I could hardly have divined in you a temper so subtlely distrustful. Flinched? to be sure he did, poor fellow; you received him with so lame a welcome. As for his adroitly playing the madman, invidious critics might object the same to some one or two strolling magi of these days. But that is a matter I know nothing about. But, once more, and for the last time, to return to the point: why sir, did you warn me against my friend? I shall rejoice, if, as I think it will prove, your want of confidence in my friend rests upon a basis equally slender with your distrust of the lunatic. Come, why did you warn me? Put it, I beseech, in few words, and those English."

"I warned you against him because he is suspected for what on these boats is known—so they tell me—as a Mississippi operator."

"An operator, ah? he operates, does he? My friend, then, is

something like what the Indians call a Great Medicine, is he? He operates, he purges, he drains off the repletions."

"I perceive, sir," said the stranger, constitutionally obtuse to the pleasant drollery, "that your notion, of what is called a Great Medicine, needs correction. The Great Medicine among the Indians is less a bolus than a man in grave esteem for his politic sagacity."

"And is not my friend politic? Is not my friend sagacious? By your own definition, is not my friend a Great Medicine?"

"No, he is an operator, a Mississippi operator; an equivocal character. That he is such, I little doubt, having had him pointed out to me as such by one desirous of initiating me into any little novelty of this western region, where I never before traveled. And, sir, if I am not mistaken, you also are a stranger here (but, indeed, where in this strange universe is not one a stranger?) and that is a reason why I felt moved to warn you against a companion who could not be otherwise than perilous to one of a free and trustful disposition. But I repeat the hope, that, thus far at least, he has not succeeded with you, and trust that, for the future, he will not."

"Thank you for your concern; but hardly can I equally thank you for so steadily maintaining the hypothesis of my friend's objectionableness. True, I but made his acquaintance for the first to-day, and know little of his antecedents; but that would seem no just reason why a nature like his should not of itself inspire confidence. And since your own knowledge of the gentleman is not, by your account, so exact as it might be, you will pardon me if I decline to welcome any further suggestions unflattering to him. Indeed, sir," with friendly decision, "let us change the subject."

Chapter 37

The mystical master introduces the practical disciple

B OTH, THE SUBJECT and the interlocutor," replied the stranger rising, and waiting the return towards him of a promenader, that moment turning at the further end of his walk.

"Egbert!" said he, calling.

Egbert, a well-dressed, commercial-looking gentleman of about thirty, responded in a way strikingly deferential, and in a moment stood near, in the attitude less of an equal companion apparently than a confidential follower.

"This," said the stranger, taking Egbert by the hand and leading him to the cosmopolitan, "this is Egbert, a disciple. I wish you to know Egbert. Egbert was the first among mankind to reduce to practice the principles of Mark Winsome — principles previously accounted as less adapted to life than the closet. Egbert," turning to the disciple, who, with seeming modesty, a little shrank under these compliments, "Egbert, this," with a salute towards the cosmopolitan, "is, like all of us, a stranger. I wish you, Egbert, to know this brother stranger; be communicative with him. Particularly if, by anything hitherto dropped, his curiosity has been roused as to the precise nature of my philosophy, I trust you will not leave such curiosity ungratified. You, Egbert, by simply setting forth your practice, can do more to enlighten one as to my theory, than I myself can by mere speech. Indeed, it is by you that I myself best understand myself. For to every philosophy are certain rear parts, very important parts, and these, like the rear of one's head, are best seen by reflection. Now, as in a glass, you, Egbert, in your life, reflect to me the more important part of my system. He, who approves you, approves the philosophy of Mark Winsome."

Though portions of this harangue may, perhaps, in the phraseology seem self-complaisant, yet no trace of self-complacency was perceptible in the speaker's manner, which, throughout was plain, unassuming, dignified, and manly; the teacher and prophet seemed to lurk more in the idea, so to speak, than in the mere bearing of him who was the vehicle of it.

"Sir," said the cosmopolitan, who seemed not a little interested in this new aspect of matters, "you speak of a certain philosophy, and a more or less occult one it may be, and hint of its bearing upon practical life; pray, tell me, if the study of this philosophy tends to the same formation of character with the experiences of the world?"

"It does; and that is the test of its truth; for any philosophy that, being in operation contradictory to the ways of the world, tends to produce a character at odds with it, such a philosophy must necessarily be but a cheat and a dream."

"You a little surprise me," answered the cosmopolitan; "for, from an occasional profundity in you, and also from your allusions to a profound work on the theology of Plato, it would seem but natural to surmise that, if you are the originator of any philosophy, it must needs so partake of the abstruse, as to exalt it above the comparatively vile uses of life."

"No uncommon mistake with regard to me," rejoined the other. Then meekly standing like a Raphael: "If still in golden accents old Memnon murmurs his riddle, none the less does the balance-sheet of every man's ledger unriddle the profit or loss of life. Sir," with calm energy, "man came into this world, not to sit down and muse, not to befog himself with vain subtleties, but to gird up his loins and to work. Mystery is in the morning, and mystery in the night, and the beauty of mystery is everywhere; but still the plain truth remains, that mouth and purse must be filled. If, hitherto, you have supposed me a visionary, be undeceived. I am no one-ideaed one, either; no more than the seers before me. Was not Seneca a usurer? Bacon a courtier? and Swedenborg, though with one eye on the invisible, did he not keep the other on the main chance? Along with whatever else it may be given me to be, I am a man of serviceable knowledge, and a man of the world. Know me for such. And as for my disciple here," turning towards him, "if you look to find any soft Utopianisms and last year's sunsets in him, I smile to think how he will set you right. The doctrines I have taught him will, I trust, lead him neither to the mad-house nor the poor-house, as so many other doctrines have served credulous sticklers. Furthermore," glancing upon him paternally, "Egbert is both my disciple and my poet. For poetry is not a thing of ink and rhyme, but of thought and act, and, in the latter way, is by any one to be found anywhere, when in useful action sought. In a word, my disciple here is a thriving young merchant, a practical poet in the West India trade. There," presenting Egbert's hand to the cosmopolitan, "I join you, and leave you." With which words, and without bowing, the master withdrew.

Chapter 38

IN THE MASTER'S presence the disciple had stood as one not ignorant of his place; modesty was in his expression, with a sort of reverential depression. But the presence of the superior withdrawn, he seemed lithely to shoot up erect from beneath it, like one of those wire men from a toy snuff-box.

He was, as before said, a young man of about thirty. His countenance of that neuter sort, which, in repose, is neither prepossessing nor disagreeable; so that it seemed quite uncertain how he would turn out. His dress was neat, with just enough of the mode to save it from the reproach of originality; in which general respect, though with a readjustment of details, his costume seemed modeled upon his master's. But, upon the whole, he was, to all appearances, the last person in the world that one would take for the disciple of any transcendental philosophy; though, indeed, something about his sharp nose and shaved chin seemed to hint that if mysticism, as a lesson, ever came in his way, he might, with the characteristic knack of a true New-Englander, turn even so profitless a thing to some profitable account.

"Well," said he, now familiarly seating himself in the vacated chair, "what do you think of Mark? Sublime fellow, ain't he?"

"That each member of the human guild is worthy respect, my friend," rejoined the cosmopolitan, "is a fact which no admirer of that guild will question; but that, in view of higher natures, the word sublime, so frequently applied to them, can, without confusion, be also applied to man, is a point which man will decide for himself; though, indeed, if he decide it in the affirmative, it is not for me to object. But I am curious to know more of that philosophy of which, at present, I have but inklings. You, its first disciple among men, it seems, are peculiarly qualified to expound it. Have you any objections to begin now?"

"None at all," squaring himself to the table. "Where shall I begin? At first principles?"

"You remember that it was in a practical way that you were represented as being fitted for the clear exposition. Now, what you call first principles, I have, in some things, found to be more or less vague. Permit me, then, in a plain way, to suppose some common case in real life, and that done, I would like you to tell me how you, the practical disciple of the philosophy I wish to know about, would, in that case, conduct."

"A business-like view. Propose the case."

"Not only the case, but the persons. The case is this: There are two friends, friends from childhood, bosom-friends; one of whom, for the first time, being in need, for the first time seeks a loan from the other, who, so far as fortune goes, is more than competent to grant it. And the persons are to be you and I: you, the friend from whom the loan is sought— I, the friend who seeks it; you, the disciple of the philosophy in question—I, a common man, with no more philosophy than to know that when I am comfortably warm I don't feel cold, and when I have the ague I shake. Mind, now, you must work up your imagination, and, as much as possible, talk and behave just as if the case supposed were a fact. For brevity, you shall call me Frank, and I will call you Charlie. Are you agreed?"

"Perfectly. You begin."

The cosmopolitan paused a moment, then, assuming a serious and care-worn air, suitable to the part to be enacted, addressed his hypothesized friend.

Chapter 39

THE HYPOTHETICAL FRIENDS

"CHARLIE, I am going to put confidence in you."
"You always have, and with reason. What is it, Frank?"
"Charlie, I am in want—urgent want of money."
"That's not well."

"But it *will* be well, Charlie, if you loan me a hundred dollars. I would not ask this of you, only my need is sore, and you and I have so long shared hearts and minds together, however unequally on my side, that nothing remains to prove our friendship than, with the same inequality on my side, to share purses. You will do me the favor, won't you?"

"Favor? What do you mean, by asking me to do you a favor?"

"Why, Charlie, you never used to talk so."

"Because, Frank, you on your side, never used to talk so."

"But won't you loan me the money?"

"No, Frank."

"Why?"

"Because my rule forbids. I give away money, but never loan it; and of course the man who calls himself my friend is above receiving alms. The negotiation of a loan is a business transaction. And I will transact no business with a friend. What a friend is, he is socially and intellectually; and I rate social and intellectual friendship too high to degrade it on either side into a pecuniary make-shift. To be sure there are, and I have, what is called business friends; that is, commercial acquaintances, very convenient persons. But I draw a red-ink line between them and my friends in the true sense—my friends social and intellectual. In brief, a true friend has nothing to do with loans; he should have a soul above loans. Loans are such unfriendly accommodations as are to be had from the soulless corporation of a bank, by giving the regular security and paying the regular discount."

"An *unfriendly* accommodation? Do those words go together handsomely?"

"Like the poor farmer's team, of an old man and a

1057

cow—not handsomely, but to the purpose. Look, Frank, a loan of money on interest is a sale of money on credit. To sell a thing on credit may be an accommodation, but where is the friendliness? Few men in their senses, except operators, borrow money on interest, except upon a necessity akin to starvation. Well, now, where is the friendliness of my letting a starving man have, say, the money's worth of a barrel of flour upon the condition that, on a given day, he shall let me have the money's worth of a barrel and a half of flour; especially if I add this further proviso, that if he fail so to do, I shall then, to secure to myself the money's worth of my barrel and his half barrel, put his heart up at public auction, and, as it is cruel to part families, throw in his wife's and children's?"

"I understand," with a pathetic shudder; "but even did it come to that, such a step on the creditor's part, let us, for the honor of human nature, hope, were less the intention than the contingency."

"But, Frank, a contingency not unprovided for in the taking beforehand of due securities."

"Still, Charlie, was not the loan in the first place a friend's act?"

"And the auction in the last place an enemy's act. Don't you see? The enmity lies couched in the friendship, just as the ruin in the relief."

"I must be very stupid to-day, Charlie, but really, I can't understand this. Excuse me, my dear friend, but it strikes me that in going into the philosophy of the subject, you go somewhat out of your depth."

"So said the incautious wader-out to the ocean; but the ocean replied: 'It is just the other way, my wet friend,' and drowned him."

"That, Charlie, is a fable about as unjust to the ocean, as some of Æsop's are to the animals. The ocean is a magnanimous element, and would scorn to assassinate a poor fellow, let alone taunting him in the act. But I don't understand what you say about enmity couched in friendship, and ruin in relief."

"I will illustrate, Frank. The needy man is a train slipped

off the rail. He who loans him money on interest is the one who, by way of accommodation, helps get the train back where it belongs; but then, by way of making all square, and a little more, telegraphs to an agent, thirty miles a-head by a precipice, to throw just there, on his account, a beam across the track. Your needy man's principal-and-interest friend is, I say again, a friend with an enmity in reserve. No, no, my dear friend, no interest for me. I scorn interest."

"Well, Charlie, none need you charge. Loan me without interest."

"That would be alms again."

"Alms, if the sum borrowed is returned?"

"Yes: an alms, not of the principal, but the interest."

"Well, I am in sore need, so I will not decline the alms. Seeing that it is you, Charlie, gratefully will I accept the alms of the interest. No humiliation between friends."

"Now, how in the refined view of friendship can you suffer yourself to talk so, my dear Frank? It pains me. For though I am not of the sour mind of Solomon, that, in the hour of need, a stranger is better than a brother; yet, I entirely agree with my sublime master, who, in his Essay on Friendship, says so nobly, that if he want a terrestrial convenience, not to his friend celestial (or friend social and intellectual) would he go; no: for his terrestrial convenience, to his friend terrestrial (or humbler business-friend) he goes. Very lucidly he adds the reason: Because, for the superior nature, which on no account can ever descend to do good, to be annoyed with requests to do it, when the inferior one, which by no instruction can ever rise above that capacity, stands always inclined to it—this is unsuitable."

"Then I will not consider you as my friend celestial, but as the other."

"It racks me to come to that; but, to oblige you, I'll do it. We are business friends; business is business. You want to negotiate a loan. Very good. On what paper? Will you pay three per cent. a month? Where is your security?"

"Surely, you will not exact those formalities from your old schoolmate—him with whom you have so often sauntered down the groves of Academe, discoursing of the beauty of virtue, and the grace that is in kindliness—and all for so paltry a sum. Security? Our being fellow-academics, and friends from childhood up, is security."

"Pardon me, my dear Frank, our being fellow-academics is the worst of securities; while, our having been friends from childhood up is just no security at all. You forget we are now business friends."

"And you, on your side, forget, Charlie, that as your business friend I can give you no security; my need being so sore that I cannot get an indorser."

"No indorser, then, no business loan."

"Since then, Charlie, neither as the one nor the other sort of friend you have defined, can I prevail with you; how if, combining the two, I sue as both?"

"Are you a centaur?"

"When all is said then, what good have I of your friendship, regarded in what light you will?"

"The good which is in the philosophy of Mark Winsome, as reduced to practice by a practical disciple."

"And why don't you add, much good may the philosophy of Mark Winsome do me? Ah," turning invokingly, " what is friendship, if it be not the helping hand and the feeling heart, the good Samaritan pouring out at need the purse as the vial!"

"Now, my dear Frank, don't be childish. Through tears never did man see his way in the dark. I should hold you unworthy that sincere friendship I bear you, could I think that friendship in the ideal is too lofty for you to conceive. And let me tell you, my dear Frank, that you would seriously shake the foundations of our love, if ever again you should repeat the present scene. The philosophy, which is mine in the strongest way, teaches plain-dealing. Let me, then, now, as at the most suitable time, candidly disclose certain circumstances you seem in ignorance of. Though our friendship began in boyhood, think not that, on my side at least, it began injudiciously. Boys are little men, it is said. You, I juvenilely picked out for my friend, for your favorable points at the time; not the least of which were your good manners, handsome dress, and your parents' rank and repute of wealth. In short, like any grown man, boy though I was, I went into the market and chose me my mutton, not for its leanness, but its fatness. In other words, there seemed in you, the schoolboy who always had silver in his pocket, a reasonable probability that you would never stand in lean need of fat succor; and if my early impression has not been verified by the event, it is only because of the caprice of fortune producing a fallibility of human expectations, however discreet."

"Oh, that I should listen to this cold-blooded disclosure!"

"A little cold blood in your ardent veins, my dear Frank, wouldn't do you any harm, let me tell you. Cold-blooded? You say that, because my disclosure seems to involve a vile prudence on my side. But not so. My reason for choosing you in part for the points I have mentioned, was solely with a view of preserving inviolate the delicacy of the connection. For—do but think of it—what more distressing to delicate friendship, formed early, than your friend's eventually, in manhood, dropping in of a rainy night for his little loan of five dollars or so? Can delicate friendship stand that? And, on the other side, would delicate friendship, so long as it retained its delicacy, do that? Would you not instinctively say of your dripping friend in the entry, 'I have been deceived, fraudulently deceived, in this man; he is no true friend that, in platonic love to demand love-rites?' "

"And rites, doubly rights, they are, cruel Charlie!"

"Take it how you will, heed well how, by too importunately claiming those rights, as you call them, you shake those foundations I hinted of. For though, as it turns out, I, in my early friendship, built me a fair house on a poor site; yet such pains and cost have I lavished on that house, that, after all, it is dear to me. No, I would not lose the sweet boon of your friendship, Frank. But beware."

"And of what? Of being in need? Oh, Charlie! you talk not to a god, a being who in himself holds his own estate, but to a man who, being a man, is the sport of fate's wind and wave, and who mounts towards heaven or sinks towards hell, as the billows roll him in trough or on crest."

"Tut! Frank. Man is no such poor devil as that comes to— no poor drifting sea-weed of the universe. Man has a soul;

which, if he will, puts him beyond fortune's finger and the future's spite. Don't whine like fortune's whipped dog, Frank, or by the heart of a true friend, I will cut ye."

"Cut me you have already, cruel Charlie, and to the quick. Call to mind the days we went nutting, the times we walked in the woods, arms wreathed about each other, showing trunks invined like the trees:—oh, Charlie!"

"Pish! we were boys."

"Then lucky the fate of the first-born of Egypt, cold in the grave ere maturity struck them with a sharper frost.— Charlie?"

"Fie! you're a girl."

"Help, help, Charlie, I want help!"

"Help? to say nothing of the friend, there is something wrong about the man who wants help. There is somewhere a defect, a want, in brief, a need, a crying need, somewhere about that man."

"So there is, Charlie.—Help, Help!"

"How foolish a cry, when to implore help, is itself the proof of undesert of it."

"Oh, this, all along, is not you, Charlie, but some ventriloquist who usurps your larynx. It is Mark Winsome that speaks, not Charlie."

"If so, thank heaven, the voice of Mark Winsome is not alien but congenial to my larynx. If the philosophy of that illustrious teacher find little response among mankind at large, it is less that they do not possess teachable tempers, than because they are so unfortunate as not to have natures predisposed to accord with him."

"Welcome, that compliment to humanity," exclaimed Frank with energy, "the truer because unintended. And long in this respect may humanity remain what you affirm it. And long it will; since humanity, inwardly feeling how subject it is to straits, and hence how precious is help, will, for selfishness' sake, if no other, long postpone ratifying a philosophy that banishes help from the world. But Charlie, Charlie! speak as you used to; tell me you will help me. Were the case reversed, not less freely would I loan you the money than you would ask me to loan it."

"*I* ask? *I* ask a loan? Frank, by this hand, under no circumstances would I accept a loan, though without asking pressed on me. The experience of China Aster might warn me."

"And what was that?"

"Not very unlike the experience of the man that built himself a palace of moon-beams, and when the moon set was surprised that his palace vanished with it. I will tell you about China Aster. I wish I could do so in my own words, but unhappily the original story-teller here has so tyrannized over me, that it is quite impossible for me to repeat his incidents without sliding into his style. I forewarn you of this, that you may not think me so maudlin as, in some parts, the story would seem to make its narrator. It is too bad that any intellect, especially in so small a matter, should have such power to impose itself upon another, against its best exerted will, too. However, it is satisfaction to know that the main moral, to which all tends, I fully approve. But, to begin."

Chapter 40

In which the story of China Aster is at
second-hand told by one who, while not
disapproving the moral, disclaims the spirit
of the style

CHINA ASTER was a young candle-maker of Marietta, at
the mouth of the Muskingum—one whose trade would
seem a kind of subordinate branch of that parent craft and
mystery of the hosts of heaven, to be the means, effectively or
otherwise, of shedding some light through the darkness of a
planet benighted. But he made little money by the business.
Much ado had poor China Aster and his family to live; he
could, if he chose, light up from his stores a whole street, but
not so easily could he light up with prosperity the hearts of
his household.

"Now, China Aster, it so happened, had a friend, Orchis, a
shoemaker; one whose calling it is to defend the understandings of men from naked contact with the substance of things:
a very useful vocation, and which, spite of all the wiseacres
may prophesy, will hardly go out of fashion so long as rocks
are hard and flints will gall. All at once, by a capital prize in
a lottery, this useful shoemaker was raised from a bench to a
sofa. A small nabob was the shoemaker now, and the understandings of men, let them shift for themselves. Not that Orchis was, by prosperity, elated into heartlessness. Not at all.
Because, in his fine apparel, strolling one morning into the
candlery, and gayly switching about at the candle-boxes with
his gold-headed cane—while poor China Aster, with his
greasy paper cap and leather apron, was selling one candle for
one penny to a poor orange-woman, who, with the patronizing coolness of a liberal customer, required it to be carefully
rolled up and tied in a half sheet of paper—lively Orchis, the
woman being gone, discontinued his gay switchings and said:
'This is poor business for you, friend China Aster; your capital is too small. You must drop this vile tallow and hold up
pure spermaceti to the world. I tell you what it is, you shall
have one thousand dollars to extend with. In fact, you must

make money, China Aster. I don't like to see your little boy paddling about without shoes, as he does.'

" 'Heaven bless your goodness, friend Orchis,' replied the candle-maker, 'but don't take it illy if I call to mind the word of my uncle, the blacksmith, who, when a loan was offered him, declined it, saying: "To ply my own hammer, light though it be, I think best, rather than piece it out heavier by welding to it a bit off a neighbor's hammer, though that may have some weight to spare; otherwise, were the borrowed bit suddenly wanted again, it might not split off at the welding, but too much to one side or the other." '

" 'Nonsense, friend China Aster, don't be so honest; your boy is barefoot. Besides, a rich man lose by a poor man? Or a friend be the worse by a friend? China Aster, I am afraid that, in leaning over into your vats here, this morning, you have spilled out your wisdom. Hush! I won't hear any more. Where's your desk? Oh, here.' With that, Orchis dashed off a check on his bank, and off-handedly presenting it, said: 'There, friend China Aster, is your one thousand dollars; when you make it ten thousand, as you soon enough will (for experience, the only true knowledge, teaches me that, for every one, good luck is in store), then, China Aster, why, then you can return me the money or not, just as you please. But, in any event, give yourself no concern, for I shall never demand payment.'

"Now, as kind heaven will so have it that to a hungry man bread is a great temptation, and, therefore, he is not too harshly to be blamed, if, when freely offered, he take it, even though it be uncertain whether he shall ever be able to reciprocate; so, to a poor man, proffered money is equally enticing, and the worst that can be said of him, if he accept it, is just what can be said in the other case of the hungry man. In short, the poor candle-maker's scrupulous morality succumbed to his unscrupulous necessity, as is now and then apt to be the case. He took the check, and was about carefully putting it away for the present, when Orchis, switching about again with his gold-headed cane, said: 'By-the-way, China Aster, it don't mean anything, but suppose you make a little memorandum of this; won't do any harm, you know.' So China Aster gave Orchis his note for one thousand dollars on demand. Orchis took it, and looked at it a moment, 'Pooh, I told you, friend China Aster, I wasn't going ever to make any *demand*.' Then tearing up the note, and switching away again at the candle-boxes, said, carelessly; 'Put it at four years.' So China Aster gave Orchis his note for one thousand dollars at four years. 'You see I'll never trouble you about this,' said Orchis, slipping it in his pocket-book, 'give yourself no further thought, friend China Aster, than how best to invest your money. And don't forget my hint about spermaceti. Go into that, and I'll buy all my light of you,' with which encouraging words, he, with wonted, rattling kindness, took leave.

"China Aster remained standing just where Orchis had left him; when, suddenly, two elderly friends, having nothing better to do, dropped in for a chat. The chat over, China Aster, in greasy cap and apron, ran after Orchis, and said: 'Friend Orchis, heaven will reward you for your good intentions, but here is your check, and now give me my note.'

" 'Your honesty is a bore, China Aster,' said Orchis, not without displeasure. 'I won't take the check from you.'

" 'Then you must take it from the pavement, Orchis,' said China Aster; and, picking up a stone, he placed the check under it on the walk.

" 'China Aster,' said Orchis, inquisitively eying him, 'after my leaving the candlery just now, what asses dropped in there to advise with you, that now you hurry after me, and act so like a fool? Shouldn't wonder if it was those two old asses that the boys nickname Old Plain Talk and Old Prudence.'

" 'Yes, it was those two, Orchis, but don't call them names.'

" 'A brace of spavined old croakers. Old Plain Talk had a shrew for a wife, and that's made him shrewish; and Old Prudence, when a boy, broke down in an apple-stall, and that discouraged him for life. No better sport for a knowing spark like me than to hear Old Plain Talk wheeze out his sour old saws, while Old Prudence stands by, leaning on his staff, wagging his frosty old pow, and chiming in at every clause.'

" 'How can you speak so, friend Orchis, of those who were my father's friends?'

" 'Save me from my friends, if those old croakers were Old Honesty's friends. I call your father so, for every one used to.

Why did they let him go in his old age on the town? Why, China Aster, I've often heard from my mother, the chronicler, that those two old fellows, with Old Conscience—as the boys called the crabbed old quaker, that's dead now—they three used to go to the poor-house when your father was there, and get round his bed, and talk to him for all the world as Eliphaz, Bildad, and Zophar did to poor old pauper Job. Yes, Job's comforters were Old Plain Talk, and Old Prudence, and Old Conscience, to your poor old father. Friends? I should like to know who you call foes? With their everlasting croaking and reproaching they tormented poor Old Honesty, your father, to death.'

"At these words, recalling the sad end of his worthy parent, China Aster could not restrain some tears. Upon which Orchis said: 'Why, China Aster, you are the dolefulest creature. Why don't you, China Aster, take a bright view of life? You will never get on in your business or anything else, if you don't take the bright view of life. It's the ruination of a man to take the dismal one.' Then, gayly poking at him with his gold-headed cane, 'Why don't you, then? Why don't you be bright and hopeful, like me? Why don't you have confidence, China Aster?'

" 'I'm sure I don't know, friend Orchis,' soberly replied China Aster, 'but may be my not having drawn a lottery-prize, like you, may make some difference.'

" 'Nonsense! before I knew anything about the prize I was gay as a lark, just as gay as I am now. In fact, it has always been a principle with me to hold to the bright view.'

"Upon this, China Aster looked a little hard at Orchis, because the truth was, that until the lucky prize came to him, Orchis had gone under the nickname of Doleful Dumps, he having been beforetimes of a hypochondriac turn, so much so as to save up and put by a few dollars of his scanty earnings against that rainy day he used to groan so much about.

" 'I tell you what it is, now, friend China Aster,' said Orchis, pointing down to the check under the stone, and then slapping his pocket, 'the check shall lie there if you say so, but your note shan't keep it company. In fact, China Aster, I am too sincerely your friend to take advantage of a passing fit of

the blues in you. You *shall* reap the benefit of my friendship.'
With which, buttoning up his coat in a jiffy, away he ran,
leaving the check behind.

"At first, China Aster was going to tear it up, but thinking
that this ought not to be done except in the presence of the
drawer of the check, he mused a while, and picking it up,
trudged back to the candlery, fully resolved to call upon Orchis soon as his day's work was over, and destroy the check
before his eyes. But it so happened that when China Aster
called, Orchis was out, and, having waited for him a weary
time in vain, China Aster went home, still with the check, but
still resolved not to keep it another day. Bright and early next
morning he would a second time go after Orchis, and would,
no doubt, make a sure thing of it, by finding him in his bed;
for since the lottery-prize came to him, Orchis, besides becoming more cheery, had also grown a little lazy. But as destiny would have it, that same night China Aster had a dream,
in which a being in the guise of a smiling angel, and holding
a kind of cornucopia in her hand, hovered over him, pouring
down showers of small gold dollars, thick as kernels of corn.
'I am Bright Future, friend China Aster,' said the angel, 'and
if you do what friend Orchis would have you do, just see
what will come of it.' With which Bright Future, with another swing of her cornucopia, poured such another shower
of small gold dollars upon him, that it seemed to bank him
up all round, and he waded about in it like a maltster in malt.

"Now, dreams are wonderful things, as everybody
knows—so wonderful, indeed, that some people stop not
short of ascribing them directly to heaven; and China Aster,
who was of a proper turn of mind in everything, thought that
in consideration of the dream, it would be but well to wait a
little, ere seeking Orchis again. During the day, China Aster's
mind dwelling continually upon the dream, he was so full of
it, that when Old Plain Talk dropped in to see him, just before dinner-time, as he often did, out of the interest he took
in Old Honesty's son, China Aster told all about his vision,
adding that he could not think that so radiant an angel could
deceive; and, indeed, talked at such a rate that one would
have thought he believed the angel some beautiful human
philanthropist. Something in this sort Old Plain Talk under-

stood him, and, accordingly, in his plain way, said: 'China Aster, you tell me that an angel appeared to you in a dream. Now, what does that amount to but this, that you dreamed an angel appeared to you? Go right away, China Aster, and return the check, as I advised you before. If friend Prudence were here, he would say just the same thing.' With which words Old Plain Talk went off to find friend Prudence, but not succeeding, was returning to the candlery himself, when, at distance mistaking him for a dun who had long annoyed him, China Aster in a panic barred all his doors, and ran to the back part of the candlery, where no knock could be heard.

"By this sad mistake, being left with no friend to argue the other side of the question, China Aster was so worked upon at last, by musing over his dream, that nothing would do but he must get the check cashed, and lay out the money the very same day in buying a good lot of spermaceti to make into candles, by which operation he counted upon turning a better penny than he ever had before in his life; in fact, this he believed would prove the foundation of that famous fortune which the angel had promised him.

"Now, in using the money, China Aster was resolved punctually to pay the interest every six months till the principal should be returned, howbeit not a word about such a thing had been breathed by Orchis; though, indeed, according to custom, as well as law, in such matters, interest would legitimately accrue on the loan, nothing to the contrary having been put in the bond. Whether Orchis at the time had this in mind or not, there is no sure telling; but, to all appearance, he never so much as cared to think about the matter, one way or other.

"Though the spermaceti venture rather disappointed China Aster's sanguine expectations, yet he made out to pay the first six months' interest, and though his next venture turned out still less prosperously, yet by pinching his family in the matter of fresh meat, and, what pained him still more, his boys' schooling, he contrived to pay the second six months' interest, sincerely grieved that integrity, as well as its opposite, though not in an equal degree, costs something, sometimes.

"Meanwhile, Orchis had gone on a trip to Europe by advice of a physician; it so happening that, since the lottery-prize came to him, it had been discovered to Orchis that his health was not very firm, though he had never complained of anything before but a slight ailing of the spleen, scarce worth talking about at the time. So Orchis, being abroad, could not help China Aster's paying his interest as he did, however much he might have been opposed to it; for China Aster paid it to Orchis's agent, who was too business-like a turn to decline interest regularly paid in on a loan.

"But overmuch to trouble the agent on that score was not again to be the fate of China Aster; for, not being of that skeptical spirit which refuses to trust customers, his third venture resulted, through bad debts, in almost a total loss—a bad blow for the candle-maker. Neither did Old Plain Talk and Old Prudence neglect the opportunity to read him an uncheerful enough lesson upon the consequences of his disregarding their advice in the matter of having nothing to do with borrowed money. 'It's all just as I predicted,' said Old Plain Talk, blowing his old nose with his old bandana. 'Yea, indeed is it,' chimed in Old Prudence, rapping his staff on the floor, and then leaning upon it, looking with solemn forebodings upon China Aster. Low-spirited enough felt the poor candle-maker; till all at once who should come with a bright face to him but his bright friend, the angel, in another dream. Again the cornucopia poured out its treasure, and promised still more. Revived by the vision, he resolved not to be downhearted, but up and at it once more—contrary to the advice of Old Plain Talk, backed as usual by his crony, which was to the effect, that, under present circumstances, the best thing China Aster could do, would be to wind up his business, settle, if he could, all his liabilities, and then go to work as a journeyman, by which he could earn good wages, and give up, from that time henceforth, all thoughts of rising above being a paid subordinate to men more able than himself, for China Aster's career thus far plainly proved him the legitimate son of Old Honesty, who, as every one knew, had never shown much business-talent, so little, in fact, that many said of him that he had no business to be in business. And just this plain saying Plain Talk now plainly applied to China Aster, and Old Prudence never disagreed with him. But the angel in the dream did, and, maugre Plain Talk, put quite other notions into the candle-maker.

"He considered what he should do towards reëstablishing himself. Doubtless, had Orchis been in the country, he would have aided him in this strait. As it was, he applied to others; and as in the world, much as some may hint to the contrary, an honest man in misfortune still can find friends to stay by him and help him, even so it proved with China Aster, who at last succeeded in borrowing from a rich old farmer the sum of six hundred dollars, at the usual interest of money-lenders, upon the security of a secret bond signed by China Aster's wife and himself, to the effect that all such right and title to any property that should be left her by a well-to-do childless uncle, an invalid tanner, such property should, in the event of China Aster's failing to return the borrowed sum on the given day, be the lawful possession of the money-lender. True, it was just as much as China Aster could possibly do to induce his wife, a careful woman, to sign this bond; because she had always regarded her promised share in her uncle's estate as an anchor well to windward of the hard times in which China Aster had always been more or less involved, and from which, in her bosom, she never had seen much chance of his freeing himself. Some notion may be had of China Aster's standing in the heart and head of his wife, by a short sentence commonly used in reply to such persons as happened to sound her on the point. 'China Aster,' she would say, 'is a good husband, but a bad business man!' Indeed, she was a connection on the maternal side of Old Plain Talk's. But had not China Aster taken good care not to let Old Plain Talk and Old Prudence hear of his dealings with the old farmer, ten to one they would, in some way, have interfered with his success in that quarter.

"It has been hinted that the honesty of China Aster was what mainly induced the money-lender to befriend him in his misfortune, and this must be apparent; for, had China Aster been a different man, the money-lender might have dreaded lest, in the event of his failing to meet his note, he might some way prove slippery—more especially as, in the hour of distress, worked upon by remorse for so jeopardizing his wife's money, his heart might prove a traitor to his bond, not to hint that it was more than doubtful how such a secret security and claim, as in the last resort would be the old farmer's, would stand in a court of law. But though one inference from all this may be, that had China Aster been something else than what he was, he would not have been trusted, and, therefore, he would have been effectually shut out from running his own and wife's head into the usurer's noose; yet those who, when everything at last came out, maintained that, in this view and to this extent, the honesty of the candle-maker was no advantage to him, in so saying, such persons said what every good heart must deplore, and no prudent tongue will admit.

"It may be mentioned, that the old farmer made China Aster take part of his loan in three old dried-up cows and one lame horse, not improved by the glanders. These were thrown in at a pretty high figure, the old money-lender having a singular prejudice in regard to the high value of any sort of stock raised on his farm. With a great deal of difficulty, and at more loss, China Aster disposed of his cattle at public auction, no private purchaser being found who could be prevailed upon to invest. And now, raking and scraping in every way, and working early and late, China Aster at last started afresh, nor without again largely and confidently extending himself. However, he did not try his hand at the spermaceti again, but, admonished by experience, returned to tallow. But, having bought a good lot of it, by the time he got it into candles, tallow fell so low, and candles with it, that his candles per pound barely sold for what he had paid for the tallow. Meantime, a year's unpaid interest had accrued on Orchis' loan, but China Aster gave himself not so much concern about that as about the interest now due to the old farmer. But he was glad that the principal there had yet some time to run. However, the skinny old fellow gave him some trouble by coming after him every day or two on a scraggy old white horse, furnished with a musty old saddle, and goaded into his shambling old paces with a withered old raw hide. All the neighbors said that surely Death himself on the pale horse was after poor China Aster now. And something so it proved; for, ere long, China Aster found himself involved in troubles mortal enough.

"At this juncture Orchis was heard of. Orchis, it seemed, had returned from his travels, and clandestinely married, and, in a kind of queer way, was living in Pennsylvania among his wife's relations, who, among other things, had induced him to join a church, or rather semi-religious school, of Come-Outers; and what was still more, Orchis, without coming to the spot himself, had sent word to his agent to dispose of some of his property in Marietta, and remit him the proceeds. Within a year after, China Aster received a letter from Orchis, commending him for his punctuality in paying the first year's interest, and regretting the necessity that he (Orchis) was now under of using all his dividends; so he relied upon China Aster's paying the next six months' interest, and of course with the back interest. Not more surprised than alarmed, China Aster thought of taking steamboat to go and see Orchis, but he was saved that expense by the unexpected arrival in Marietta of Orchis in person, suddenly called there by that strange kind of capriciousness lately characterizing him. No sooner did China Aster hear of his old friend's arrival than he hurried to call upon him. He found him curiously rusty in dress, sallow in cheek, and decidedly less gay and cordial in manner, which the more surprised China Aster, because, in former days, he had more than once heard Orchis, in his light rattling way, declare that all he (Orchis) wanted to make him a perfectly happy, hilarious, and benignant man, was a voyage to Europe and a wife, with a free development of his inmost nature.

"Upon China Aster's stating his case, his rusted friend was silent for a time; then, in an odd way, said that he would not crowd China Aster, but still his (Orchis') necessities were urgent. Could not China Aster mortgage the candlery? He was honest, and must have moneyed friends; and could he not press his sales of candles? Could not the market be forced a little in that particular? The profits on candles must be very great. Seeing, now, that Orchis had the notion that the candle-making business was a very profitable one, and knowing sorely enough what an error was here, China Aster tried to undeceive him. But he could not drive the truth into Orchis—Orchis being very obtuse here, and, at the same time, strange to say, very melancholy. Finally, Orchis glanced off

from so unpleasing a subject into the most unexpected reflections, taken from a religious point of view, upon the unsta-
bleness and deceitfulness of the human heart. But having, as
he thought, experienced something of that sort of thing,
China Aster did not take exception to his friend's observations, but still refrained from so doing, almost as much for
the sake of sympathetic sociality as anything else. Presently,
Orchis, without much ceremony, rose, and saying he must
write a letter to his wife, bade his friend good-bye, but without warmly shaking him by the hand as of old.

"In much concern at the change, China Aster made earnest
inquiries in suitable quarters, as to what things, as yet unheard of, had befallen Orchis, to bring about such a revolution; and learned at last that, besides traveling, and getting
married, and joining the sect of Come-Outers, Orchis had
somehow got a bad dyspepsia, and lost considerable property
through a breach of trust on the part of a factor in New York.
Telling these things to Old Plain Talk, that man of some
knowledge of the world shook his old head, and told China
Aster that, though he hoped it might prove otherwise, yet it
seemed to him that all he had communicated about Orchis
worked together for bad omens as to his future forbearance—
especially, he added with a grim sort of smile, in view of his
joining the sect of Come-Outers; for, if some men knew what
was their inmost natures, instead of coming out with it, they
would try their best to keep it in, which, indeed, was the way
with the prudent sort. In all which sour notions Old Prudence, as usual, chimed in.

"When interest-day came again, China Aster, by the utmost
exertions, could only pay Orchis' agent a small part of what
was due, and a part of that was made up by his children's gift
money (bright tenpenny pieces and new quarters, kept in
their little money-boxes), and pawning his best clothes, with
those of his wife and children, so that all were subjected to
the hardship of staying away from church. And the old
usurer, too, now beginning to be obstreperous, China Aster
paid him his interest and some other pressing debts with
money got by, at last, mortgaging the candlery.

"When next interest-day came round for Orchis, not a
penny could be raised. With much grief of heart, China Aster

so informed Orchis' agent. Meantime, the note to the old usurer fell due, and nothing from China Aster was ready to meet it; yet, as heaven sends its rain on the just and unjust alike, by a coincidence not unfavorable to the old farmer, the well-to-do uncle, the tanner, having died, the usurer entered upon possession of such part of his property left by will to the wife of China Aster. When still the next interest-day for Orchis came round, it found China Aster worse off than ever; for, besides his other troubles, he was now weak with sickness. Feebly dragging himself to Orchis' agent, he met him in the street, told him just how it was; upon which the agent, with a grave enough face, said that he had instructions from his employer not to crowd him about the interest at present, but to say to him that about the time the note would mature, Orchis would have heavy liabilities to meet, and therefore the note must at that time be certainly paid, and, of course, the back interest with it; and not only so, but, as Orchis had had to allow the interest for good part of the time, he hoped that, for the back interest, China Aster would, in reciprocation, have no objections to allowing interest on the interest annually. To be sure, this was not the law; but, between friends who accommodate each other, it was the custom.

"Just then, Old Plain Talk with Old Prudence turned the corner, coming plump upon China Aster as the agent left him; and whether it was a sun-stroke, or whether they accidentally ran against him, or whether it was his being so weak, or whether it was everything together, or how it was exactly, there is no telling, but poor China Aster fell to the earth, and, striking his head sharply, was picked up senseless. It was a day in July; such a light and heat as only the midsummer banks of the inland Ohio know. China Aster was taken home on a door; lingered a few days with a wandering mind, and kept wandering on, till at last, at dead of night, when nobody was aware, his spirit wandered away into the other world.

"Old Plain Talk and Old Prudence, neither of whom ever omitted attending any funeral, which, indeed, was their chief exercise—these two were among the sincerest mourners who followed the remains of the son of their ancient friend to the grave.

"It is needless to tell of the executions that followed; how that the candlery was sold by the mortgagee; how Orchis never got a penny for his loan; and how, in the case of the poor widow, chastisement was tempered with mercy; for, though she was left penniless, she was not left childless. Yet, unmindful of the alleviation, a spirit of complaint, at what she impatiently called the bitterness of her lot and the hardness of the world, so preyed upon her, as ere long to hurry her from the obscurity of indigence to the deeper shades of the tomb.

"But though the straits in which China Aster had left his family had, besides apparently dimming the world's regard, likewise seemed to dim its sense of the probity of its deceased head, and though this, as some thought, did not speak well for the world, yet it happened in this case, as in others, that, though the world may for a time seem insensible to that merit which lies under a cloud, yet, sooner or later, it always renders honor where honor is due; for, upon the death of the widow, the freemen of Marietta, as a tribute of respect for China Aster, and an expression of their conviction of his high moral worth, passed a resolution, that, until they attained maturity, his children should be considered the town's guests. No mere verbal compliment, like those of some public bodies; for, on the same day, the orphans were officially installed in that hospitable edifice where their worthy grandfather, the town's guest before them, had breathed his last breath.

"But sometimes honor may be paid to the memory of an honest man, and still his mound remain without a monument. Not so, however, with the candle-maker. At an early day, Plain Talk had procured a plain stone, and was digesting in his mind what pithy word or two to place upon it, when there was discovered, in China Aster's otherwise empty wallet, an epitaph, written, probably, in one of those disconsolate hours, attended with more or less mental aberration, perhaps, so frequent with him for some months prior to his end. A memorandum on the back expressed the wish that it might be placed over his grave. Though with the sentiment of the epitaph Plain Talk did not disagree, he himself being at times of a hypochondriac turn—at least, so many said—yet the language struck him as too much drawn out; so, after consultation with Old Prudence, he decided upon making use of the epitaph, yet not without verbal retrenchments. And though, when these were made, the thing still appeared wordy to him, nevertheless, thinking that, since a dead man was to be spoken about, it was but just to let him speak for himself, especially when he spoke sincerely, and when, by so doing, the more salutary lesson would be given, he had the retrenched inscription chiseled as follows upon the stone:

'HERE LIE
THE REMAINS OF
CHINA ASTER THE CANDLE-MAKER,
WHOSE CAREER
WAS AN EXAMPLE OF THE TRUTH OF SCRIPTURE, AS FOUND
IN THE
SOBER PHILOSOPHY
OF
SOLOMON THE WISE;
FOR HE WAS RUINED BY ALLOWING HIMSELF TO BE PERSUADED,
AGAINST HIS BETTER SENSE,
INTO THE FREE INDULGENCE OF CONFIDENCE,
AND
AN ARDENTLY BRIGHT VIEW OF LIFE,
TO THE EXCLUSION
OF
THAT COUNSEL WHICH COMES BY HEEDING
THE
OPPOSITE VIEW.'

"This inscription raised some talk in the town, and was rather severely criticised by the capitalist—one of a very cheerful turn—who had secured his loan to China Aster by the mortgage; and though it also proved obnoxious to the man who, in town-meeting, had first moved for the compliment to China Aster's memory, and, indeed, was deemed by him a sort of slur upon the candle-maker, to that degree that he refused to believe that the candle-maker himself had composed it, charging Old Plain Talk with the authorship, alleging that the internal evidence showed that none but that veteran old croaker could have penned such a jeremiade—yet, for all this, the stone stood. In everything, of course, Old Plain Talk was seconded by Old Prudence; who, one day going to the grave-yard, in great-coat and over-shoes—for, though it was a sunshiny morning, he thought that, owing to heavy dews, dampness might lurk in the ground—long stood before the stone, sharply leaning over on his staff, spectacles on nose, spelling out the epitaph word by word; and, afterwards meeting Old Plain Talk in the street, gave a great rap with his stick, and said: 'Friend Plain Talk, that epitaph will do very well. Nevertheless, one short sentence is wanting.' Upon which, Plain Talk said it was too late, the chiseled words being so arranged, after the usual manner of such inscriptions, that nothing could be interlined. 'Then,' said Old Prudence, 'I will put it in the shape of a postscript.' Accordingly, with the approbation of Old Plain Talk, he had the following words chiseled at the left-hand corner of the stone, and pretty low down:

'The root of all was a friendly loan.' "

Chapter 41

"WITH WHAT HEART," cried Frank, still in character, "have you told me this story? A story I can no way approve; for its moral, if accepted, would drain me of all reliance upon my last stay, and, therefore, of my last courage in life. For, what was that bright view of China Aster but a cheerful trust that, if he but kept up a brave heart, worked hard, and ever hoped for the best, all at last would go well? If your purpose, Charlie, in telling me this story, was to pain me, and keenly, you have succeeded; but, if it was to destroy my last confidence, I praise God you have not."

"Confidence?" cried Charlie, who, on his side, seemed with his whole heart to enter into the spirit of the thing, "what has confidence to do with the matter? That moral of the story, which I am for commending to you, is this: the folly, on both sides, of a friend's helping a friend. For was not that loan of Orchis to China Aster the first step towards their estrangement? And did it not bring about what in effect was the enmity of Orchis? I tell you, Frank, true friendship, like other precious things, is not rashly to be meddled with. And what more meddlesome between friends than a loan? A regular marplot. For how can you help that the helper must turn out a creditor? And creditor and friend, can they ever be one? no, not in the most lenient case; since, out of lenity to forego one's claim, is less to be a friendly creditor than to cease to be a creditor at all. But it will not do to rely upon this lenity, no, not in the best man; for the best man, as the worst, is subject to all mortal contingencies. He may travel, he may marry, he may join the Come-Outers, or some equally untoward school or sect, not to speak of other things that more or less tend to new-cast the character. And were there nothing else, who shall answer for his digestion, upon which so much depends?"

"But Charlie, dear Charlie—"

"Nay, wait.—You have hearkened to my story in vain, if you do not see that, however indulgent and right-minded I may seem to you now, that is no guarantee for the future. And into the power of that uncertain personality which, through the mutability of my humanity, I may hereafter become, should not common sense dissuade you, my dear Frank, from putting yourself? Consider. Would you, in your present need, be willing to accept a loan from a friend, securing him by a mortgage on your homestead, and do so, knowing that you had no reason to feel satisfied that the mortgage might not eventually be transferred into the hands of a foe? Yet the difference between this man and that man is not so great as the difference between what the same man be to-day and what he may be in days to come. For there is no bent of heart or turn of thought which any man holds by virtue of an unalterable nature or will. Even those feelings and opinions deemed most identical with eternal right and truth, it is not impossible but that, as personal persuasions, they may in reality be but the result of some chance tip of Fate's elbow in throwing her dice. For, not to go into the first seeds of things, and passing by the accident of parentage predisposing to this or that habit of mind, descend below these, and tell me, if you change this man's experiences or that man's books, will wisdom go surety for his unchanged convictions? As particular food begets particular dreams, so particular experiences or books particular feelings or beliefs. I will hear nothing of that fine babble about development and its laws; there is no development in opinion and feeling but the developments of time and tide. You may deem all this talk idle, Frank; but conscience bids me show you how fundamental the reasons for treating you as I do."

"But Charlie, dear Charlie, what new notions are these? I thought that man was no poor drifting weed of the universe, as you phrased it; that, if so minded, he could have a will, a way, a thought, and a heart of his own. But now you have turned everything upside down again, with an inconsistency that amazes and shocks me."

"Inconsistency? Bah!"

"There speaks the ventriloquist again," sighed Frank, in bitterness.

Illy pleased, it may be, by this repetition of an allusion little flattering to his originality, however much so to his docility, the disciple sought to carry it off by exclaiming: "Yes, I turn over day and night, with indefatigable pains, the sublime pages of my master, and unfortunately for you, my dear friend, I find nothing *there* that leads me to think otherwise than I do. But enough: in this matter the experience of China Aster teaches a moral more to the point than anything Mark Winsome can offer, or I either."

"I cannot think so, Charlie; for neither am I China Aster, nor do I stand in his position. The loan to China Aster was to extend his business with; the loan I seek is to relieve my necessities."

"Your dress, my dear Frank, is respectable; your cheek is not gaunt. Why talk of necessities when nakedness and starvation beget the only real necessities?"

"But I need relief, Charlie; and so sorely, that I now conjure you to forget that I was ever your friend, while I apply to you only as a fellow-being, whom, surely, you will not turn away."

"That I will not. Take off your hat, bow over to the ground, and supplicate an alms of me in the way of London streets, and you shall not be a sturdy beggar in vain. But no man drops pennies into the hat of a friend, let me tell you. If you turn beggar, then, for the honor of noble friendship, I turn stranger."

"Enough," cried the other, rising, and with a toss of his shoulders seeming disdainfully to throw off the character he had assumed. "Enough. I have had my fill of the philosophy of Mark Winsome as put into action. And moonshiny as it in theory may be, yet a very practical philosophy it turns out in effect, as he himself engaged I should find. But, miserable for my race should I be, if I thought he spoke truth when he claimed, for proof of the soundness of his system, that the study of it tended to much the same formation of character with the experiences of the world.—Apt disciple! Why wrinkle the brow, and waste the oil both of life and the lamp, only to turn out a head kept cool by the under ice of the heart? What your illustrious magian has taught you, any poor, old, broken-down, heart-shrunken dandy might have lisped. Pray, leave me, and with you take the last dregs of your inhuman philosophy. And here, take this shilling, and at the first wood-landing buy yourself a few chips to warm the frozen natures of you and your philosopher by."

With these words and a grand scorn the cosmopolitan turned on his heel, leaving his companion at a loss to determine where exactly the fictitious character had been dropped, and the real one, if any, resumed. If any, because, with pointed meaning, there occurred to him, as he gazed after the cosmopolitan, these familiar lines:

> "All the world's a stage,
> And all the men and women merely players,
> Who have their exits and their entrances,
> And one man in his time plays many parts."

Chapter 42

BLESS YOU, barber!"

Now, owing to the lateness of the hour, the barber had been all alone until within the ten minutes last passed; when, finding himself rather dullish company to himself, he thought he would have a good time with Souter John and Tam O'Shanter, otherwise called Somnus and Morpheus, two very good fellows, though one was not very bright, and the other an arrant rattle-brain, who, though much listened to by some, no wise man would believe under oath.

In short, with back presented to the glare of his lamps, and so to the door, the honest barber was taking what are called cat-naps, and dreaming in his chair; so that, upon suddenly hearing the benediction above, pronounced in tones not un-angelic, starting up, half awake, he stared before him, but saw nothing, for the stranger stood behind. What with cat-naps, dreams, and bewilderments, therefore, the voice seemed a sort of spiritual manifestation to him; so that, for the moment, he stood all agape, eyes fixed, and one arm in the air.

"Why, barber, are you reaching up to catch birds there with salt?"

"Ah!" turning round disenchanted, "it is only a man, then."

"*Only* a man? As if to be but man were nothing. But don't be too sure what I am. You call me *man*, just as the townsfolk called the angels who, in man's form, came to Lot's house; just as the Jew rustics called the devils who, in man's form, haunted the tombs. You can conclude nothing absolute from the human form, barber."

"But I can conclude something from that sort of talk, with that sort of dress," shrewdly thought the barber, eying him with regained self-possession, and not without some latent touch of apprehension at being alone with him. What was passing in his mind seemed divined by the other, who now, more rationally and gravely, and as if he expected it should be attended to, said: "Whatever else you may conclude upon, it is my desire that you conclude to give me a good shave," at the same time loosening his neck-cloth. "Are you competent to a good shave, barber?"

"No broker more so, sir," answered the barber, whom the business-like proposition instinctively made confine to business-ends his views of the visitor.

"Broker? What has a broker to do with lather? A broker I have always understood to be a worthy dealer in certain papers and metals."

"He, he!" taking him now for some dry sort of joker, whose jokes, he being a customer, it might be as well to appreciate, "he, he! You understand well enough, sir. Take this seat, sir," laying his hand on a great stuffed chair, high-backed and high-armed, crimson-covered, and raised on a sort of dais, and which seemed but to lack a canopy and quarterings, to make it in aspect quite a throne, "take this seat, sir."

"Thank you," sitting down; "and now, pray, explain that about the broker. But look, look—what's this?" suddenly rising, and pointing, with his long pipe, towards a gilt notification swinging among colored fly-papers from the ceiling, like a tavern sign, *"No Trust?"* "No trust means distrust; distrust means no confidence. Barber," turning upon him excitedly, " what fell suspiciousness prompts this scandalous confession? My life!" stamping his foot, "if but to tell a dog that you have no confidence in him be matter for affront to the dog, what an insult to take that way the whole haughty race of man by the beard! By my heart, sir! but at least you are valiant; backing the spleen of Thersites with the pluck of Agamemnon."

"Your sort of talk, sir, is not exactly in my line," said the barber, rather ruefully, being now again hopeless of his customer, and not without return of uneasiness; "not in my line, sir," he emphatically repeated.

"But the taking of mankind by the nose is; a habit, barber, which I sadly fear has insensibly bred in you a disrespect for man. For how, indeed, may respectful conceptions of him co-exist with the perpetual habit of taking him by the nose? But, tell me, though I, too, clearly see the import of your notification, I do not, as yet, perceive the object. What is it?"

"Now you speak a little in my line, sir," said the barber, not unrelieved at this return to plain talk; "that notification I find very useful, sparing me much work which would not pay. Yes, I lost a good deal, off and on, before putting that up," gratefully glancing towards it.

"But what is its object? Surely, you don't mean to say, in so many words, that you have no confidence? For instance, now," flinging aside his neck-cloth, throwing back his blouse, and reseating himself on the tonsorial throne, at sight of which proceeding the barber mechanically filled a cup with hot water from a copper vessel over a spirit-lamp, "for instance, now, suppose I say to you, 'Barber, my dear barber, unhappily I have no small change by me to-night, but shave me, and depend upon your money to-morrow'—suppose I should say that now, you would put trust in me, wouldn't you? You would have confidence?"

"Seeing that it is you, sir," with complaisance replied the barber, now mixing the lather, "seeing that it is *you*, sir, I won't answer that question. No need to."

"Of course, of course—in that view. But, as a supposition—you would have confidence in me, wouldn't you?"

"Why—yes, yes."

"Then why that sign?"

"Ah, sir, all people ain't like you," was the smooth reply, at the same time, as if smoothly to close the debate, beginning smoothly to apply the lather, which operation, however, was, by a motion, protested against by the subject, but only out of a desire to rejoin, which was done in these words:

"All people ain't like me. Then I must be either better or worse than most people. Worse, you could not mean; no, barber, you could not mean that; hardly that. It remains, then, that you think me better than most people. But that I ain't vain enough to believe; though, from vanity, I confess, I could never yet, by my best wrestlings, entirely free myself; nor, indeed, to be frank, am I at bottom over anxious to— this same vanity, barber, being so harmless, so useful, so comfortable, so pleasingly preposterous a passion."

"Very true, sir; and upon my honor, sir, you talk very well. But the lather is getting a little cold, sir."

"Better cold lather, barber, than a cold heart. Why that cold sign? Ah, I don't wonder you try to shirk the confession. You feel in your soul how ungenerous a hint is there. And yet, barber, now that I look into your eyes—which somehow speak to me of the mother that must have so often looked into them before me—I dare say, though you may not think it, that the spirit of that notification is not one with your nature. For look now, setting business views aside, regarding the thing in an abstract light; in short, supposing a case, barber; supposing, I say, you see a stranger, his face accidentally averted, but his visible part very respectable-looking; what now, barber—I put it to your conscience, to your charity— what would be your impression of that man, in a moral point of view? Being in a signal sense a stranger, would you, for that, signally set him down for a knave?"

"Certainly not, sir; by no means," cried the barber, humanely resentful.

"You would upon the face of him—"

"Hold, sir," said the barber, "nothing about the face; you remember, sir, that is out of sight."

"I forgot that. Well then, you would, upon the *back* of him, conclude him to be, not improbably, some worthy sort of person; in short, an honest man; wouldn't you?"

"Not unlikely I should, sir."

"Well now—don't be so impatient with your brush, barber—suppose that honest man meet you by night in some dark corner of the boat where his face would still remain unseen, asking you to trust him for a shave—how then?"

"Wouldn't trust him, sir."

"But is not an honest man to be trusted?"

"Why—why—yes, sir."

"There! don't you see, now?"

"See what?" asked the disconcerted barber, rather vexedly.

"Why, you stand self-contradicted, barber; don't you?"

"No," doggedly.

"Barber," gravely, and after a pause of concern, "the enemies of our race have a saying that insincerity is the most universal and inveterate vice of man—the lasting bar to real amelioration, whether of individuals or of the world. Don't you now, barber, by your stubbornness on this occasion, give color to such a calumny?"

"Hity-tity!" cried the barber, losing patience, and with it respect; "stubbornness?" Then clattering round the brush in the cup, "Will you be shaved, or won't you?"

"Barber, I will be shaved, and with pleasure; but, pray, don't raise your voice that way. Why, now, if you go through life gritting your teeth in that fashion, what a comfortless time you will have."

"I take as much comfort in this world as you or any other man," cried the barber, whom the other's sweetness of temper seemed rather to exasperate than soothe.

"To resent the imputation of anything like unhappiness I have often observed to be peculiar to certain orders of men," said the other pensively, and half to himself, "just as to be indifferent to that imputation, from holding happiness but for a secondary good and inferior grace, I have observed to be equally peculiar to other kinds of men. Pray, barber," innocently looking up, " which think you is the superior creature?"

"All this sort of talk," cried the barber, still unmollified, "is, as I told you once before, not in my line. In a few minutes I shall shut up this shop. Will you be shaved?"

"Shave away, barber. What hinders?" turning up his face like a flower.

The shaving began, and proceeded in silence, till at length it became necessary to prepare to relather a little—affording an opportunity for resuming the subject, which, on one side, was not let slip.

"Barber," with a kind of cautious kindliness, feeling his way, "barber, now have a little patience with me; do; trust me, I wish not to offend. I have been thinking over that supposed case of the man with the averted face, and I cannot rid my mind of the impression that, by your opposite replies to my questions at the time, you showed yourself much of a piece with a good many other men—that is, you have confidence, and then again, you have none. Now, what I would ask is, do you think it sensible standing for a sensible man, one foot on confidence and the other on suspicion? Don't you think, barber, that you ought to elect? Don't you think consistency requires that you should either say 'I have confidence in all men,' and take down your notification; or else say, 'I suspect all men,' and keep it up?"

This dispassionate, if not deferential, way of putting the case, did not fail to impress the barber, and proportionately conciliate him. Likewise, from its pointedness, it served to make him thoughtful; for, instead of going to the copper vessel for more water, as he had purposed, he halted half-way towards it, and, after a pause, cup in hand, said: "Sir, I hope you would not do me injustice. I don't say, and can't say, and wouldn't say, that I suspect all men; but I *do* say that strangers are not to be trusted, and so," pointing up to the sign, "no trust."

"But look, now, I beg, barber," rejoined the other deprecatingly, not presuming too much upon the barber's changed temper; "look, now; to say that strangers are not to be trusted, does not that imply something like saying that mankind is not to be trusted; for the mass of mankind, are they not necessarily strangers to each individual man? Come, come, my friend," winningly, "you are no Timon to hold the mass of mankind untrustworthy. Take down your notification; it is misanthropical; much the same sign that Timon traced with charcoal on the forehead of a skull stuck over his cave. Take it down, barber; take it down to-night. Trust men. Just try the experiment of trusting men for this one little trip. Come now, I'm a philanthropist, and will insure you against losing a cent."

The barber shook his head dryly, and answered, "Sir, you must excuse me. I have a family."

Chapter 43

Very charming

"S O YOU ARE a philanthropist, sir," added the barber with an illuminated look; "that accounts, then, for all. Very odd sort of man the philanthropist. You are the second one, sir, I have seen. Very odd sort of man, indeed, the philanthropist. Ah, sir," again meditatively stirring in the shaving-cup, "I sadly fear, lest you philanthropists know better what goodness is, than what men are." Then, eying him as if he were some strange creature behind cage-bars, "So you are a philanthropist, sir."

"I am Philanthropos, and love mankind. And, what is more than you do, barber, I trust them."

Here the barber, casually recalled to his business, would have replenished his shaving-cup, but finding now that on his last visit to the water-vessel he had not replaced it over the lamp, he did so now; and, while waiting for it to heat again, became almost as sociable as if the heating water were meant for whisky-punch; and almost as pleasantly garrulous as the pleasant barbers in romances.

"Sir," said he, taking a throne beside his customer (for in a row there were three thrones on the dais, as for the three kings of Cologne, those patron saints of the traveler), "sir, you say you trust men. Well, I suppose I might share some of your trust, were it not for this trade, that I follow, too much letting me in behind the scenes."

"I think I understand," with a saddened look; "and much the same thing I have heard from persons in pursuits different from yours—from the lawyer, from the congressman, from the editor, not to mention others, each, with a strange kind of melancholy vanity, claiming for his vocation the distinction of affording the surest inlets to the conviction that man is no better than he should be. All of which testimony, if reliable, would, by mutual corroboration, justify some disturbance in a good man's mind. But no, no; it is a mistake—all a mistake."

"True, sir, very true," assented the barber.

"Glad to hear that," brightening up.

"Not so fast, sir," said the barber; "I agree with you in thinking that the lawyer, and the congressman, and the editor, are in error, but only in so far as each claims peculiar facilities for the sort of knowledge in question; because, you see, sir, the truth is, that every trade or pursuit which brings one into contact with the facts, sir, such trade or pursuit is equally an avenue to those facts."

"*How* exactly is that?"

"Why, sir, in my opinion—and for the last twenty years I have, at odd times, turned the matter over some in my mind—he who comes to know man, will not remain in ignorance of man. I think I am not rash in saying that; am I, sir?"

"Barber, you talk like an oracle—obscurely, barber, obscurely."

"Well, sir," with some self-complacency, "the barber has always been held an oracle, but as for the obscurity, that I don't admit."

"But pray, now, by your account, what precisely may be this mysterious knowledge gained in your trade? I grant you, indeed, as before hinted, that your trade, imposing on you the necessity of functionally tweaking the noses of mankind, is, in that respect, unfortunate, very much so; nevertheless, a well-regulated imagination should be proof even to such a provocation to improper conceits. But what I want to learn from you, barber, is, how does the mere handling of the outside of men's heads lead you to distrust the inside of their hearts?"

"What, sir, to say nothing more, can one be forever dealing in macassar oil, hair dyes, cosmetics, false moustaches, wigs, and toupees, and still believe that men are wholly what they look to be? What think you, sir, are a thoughtful barber's reflections, when, behind a careful curtain, he shaves the thin, dead stubble off a head, and then dismisses it to the world, radiant in curling auburn? To contrast the shamefaced air behind the curtain, the fearful looking forward to being possibly discovered there by a prying acquaintance, with the cheerful assurance and challenging pride with which the same man steps forth again, a gay deception, into the street, while some honest, shock-headed fellow humbly gives him the wall. Ah, sir, they may talk of the courage of truth, but my trade teaches me that truth sometimes is sheepish. Lies, lies, sir, brave lies are the lions!"

"You twist the moral, barber; you sadly twist it. Look, now; take it this way: A modest man thrust out naked into the street, would he not be abashed? Take him in and clothe him; would not his confidence be restored? And in either case, is any reproach involved? Now, what is true of the whole, holds proportionably true of the part. The bald head is a nakedness which the wig is a coat to. To feel uneasy at the possibility of the exposure of one's nakedness at top, and to feel comforted by the consciousness of having it clothed— these feelings, instead of being dishonorable to a bald man, do, in fact, but attest a proper respect for himself and his fellows. And as for the deception, you may as well call the fine roof of a fine chateau a deception, since, like a fine wig, it also is an artificial cover to the head, and equally, in the common eye, decorates the wearer.—I have confuted you, my dear barber; I have confounded you."

"Pardon," said the barber, "but I do not see that you have. His coat and his roof no man pretends to palm off as a part of himself, but the bald man palms off hair, not his, for his own."

"Not *his*, barber? If he have fairly purchased his hair, the law will protect him in its ownership, even against the claims of the head on which it grew. But it cannot be that you believe what you say, barber; you talk merely for the humor. I could not think so of you as to suppose that you would contentedly deal in the impostures you condemn."

"Ah, sir, I must live."

"And can't you do that without sinning against your conscience, as you believe? Take up some other calling."

"Wouldn't mend the matter much, sir."

"Do you think, then, barber, that, in a certain point, all the trades and callings of men are much on a par? Fatal, indeed," raising his hand, "inexpressibly dreadful, the trade of the barber, if to such conclusions it necessarily leads. Barber," eying him not without emotion, "you appear to me not so much a misbeliever, as a man misled. Now, let me set you on the right track; let me restore you to trust in human nature, and by no other means than the very trade that has brought you to suspect it."

"You mean, sir, you would have me try the experiment of taking down that notification," again pointing to it with his brush; "but, dear me, while I sit chatting here, the water boils over."

With which words, and such a well-pleased, sly, snug, expression, as they say some men have when they think their little stratagem has succeeded, he hurried to the copper vessel, and soon had his cup foaming up with white bubbles, as if it were a mug of new ale.

Meantime, the other would have fain gone on with the discourse; but the cunning barber lathered him with so generous a brush, so piled up the foam on him, that his face looked like the yeasty crest of a billow, and vain to think of talking under it, as for a drowning priest in the sea to exhort his fellow-sinners on a raft. Nothing would do, but he must keep his mouth shut. Doubtless, the interval was not, in a meditative way, unimproved; for, upon the traces of the operation being at last removed, the cosmopolitan rose, and, for added refreshment, washed his face and hands; and having generally readjusted himself, began, at last, addressing the barber in a manner different, singularly so, from his previous one. Hard to say exactly what the manner was, any more than to hint it was a sort of magical; in a benign way, not wholly unlike the manner, fabled or otherwise, of certain creatures in nature, which have the power of persuasive fascination—the power of holding another creature by the button of the eye, as it were, despite the serious disinclination, and, indeed, earnest protest, of the victim. With this manner the conclusion of the matter was not out of keeping; for, in the end, all argument and expostulation proved vain, the barber being irresistibly persuaded to agree to try, for the remainder of the present trip, the experiment of trusting men, as both phrased it. True, to save his credit as a free agent, he was loud in averring that it was only for the novelty of the thing that he so agreed, and he required the other, as before volunteered, to go security to him against any loss that might ensue; but still the fact remained, that he engaged to trust men, a thing he had before said he would not do, at least not unreservedly. Still the more to save his credit, he now insisted upon it, as a last point, that the agreement should be put in black and white, especially the security part. The other made no demur; pen, ink, and paper were provided, and grave as any notary the cosmopolitan sat down, but, ere taking the pen, glanced up at the notification, and said: "First down with that sign, barber— Timon's sign, there; down with it."

This, being in the agreement, was done—though a little reluctantly—with an eye to the future, the sign being carefully put away in a drawer.

"Now, then, for the writing," said the cosmopolitan, squaring himself. "Ah," with a sigh, "I shall make a poor lawyer, I fear. Ain't used, you see, barber, to a business which, ignoring the principle of honor, holds no nail fast till clinched. Strange, barber," taking up the blank paper, "that such flimsy stuff as this should make such strong hawsers; vile hawsers, too. Barber," starting up, "I won't put it in black and white. It were a reflection upon our joint honor. I will take your word, and you shall take mine."

"But your memory may be none of the best, sir. Well for you, on your side, to have it in black and white, just for a memorandum like, you know."

"That, indeed! Yes, and it would help *your* memory, too, wouldn't it, barber? Yours, on your side, being a little weak, too, I dare say. Ah, barber! how ingenious we human beings are; and how kindly we reciprocate each other's little delicacies, don't we? What better proof, now, that we are kind, considerate fellows, with responsive fellow-feelings—eh, barber? But to business. Let me see. What's your name, barber?"

"William Cream, sir."

Pondering a moment, he began to write; and, after some corrections, leaned back, and read aloud the following:

"AGREEMENT
"Between
"FRANK GOODMAN, Philanthropist, and Citizen of the World,
"and
"WILLIAM CREAM, Barber of the Mississippi steamer, Fidèle.

"The first hereby agrees to make good to the last any loss that may come from his trusting mankind, in the way of his vocation, for the residue of the present trip; PROVIDED that William Cream keep out of sight, for the given term, his notification of 'No Trust,' and by no other mode convey any, the least hint or intimation, tending to discourage men from soliciting trust from him, in the way of his vocation, for the time above specified; but, on the contrary, he do, by all proper and reasonable words, gestures, manners, and looks, evince a perfect confidence in all men, especially strangers; otherwise, this agreement to be void.

"Done, in good faith, this 1st day of April, 18—, at a quarter to twelve o'clock, P.M., in the shop of said William Cream, on board the said boat, Fidèle."

"There, barber; will that do?"

"That will do," said the barber, "only now put down your name."

Both signatures being affixed, the question was started by the barber, who should have custody of the instrument; which point, however, he settled for himself, by proposing that both should go together to the captain, and give the document into his hands—the barber hinting that this would be a safe proceeding, because the captain was necessarily a party disinterested, and, what was more, could not, from the nature of the present case, make anything by a breach of trust. All of which was listened to with some surprise and concern.

"Why, barber," said the cosmopolitan, "this don't show the right spirit; for me, I have confidence in the captain purely because he is a man; but he shall have nothing to do with our affair; for if you have no confidence in me, barber, I have in you. There, keep the paper yourself," handing it magnanimously.

"Very good," said the barber, "and now nothing remains but for me to receive the cash."

Though the mention of that word, or any of its singularly numerous equivalents, in serious neighborhood to a requisition upon one's purse, is attended with a more or less noteworthy effect upon the human countenance, producing in many an abrupt fall of it—in others, a writhing and screwing up of the features to a point not undistressing to behold, in some, attended with a blank pallor and fatal consternation—

yet no trace of any of these symptoms was visible upon the countenance of the cosmopolitan, notwithstanding nothing could be more sudden and unexpected than the barber's demand.

"You speak of cash, barber; pray in what connection?"

"In a nearer one, sir," answered the barber, less blandly, "than I thought the man with the sweet voice stood, who wanted me to trust him once for a shave, on the score of being a sort of thirteenth cousin."

"Indeed, and what did you say to him?"

"I said, 'Thank you, sir, but I don't see the connection.' "

"How could you so unsweetly answer one with a sweet voice?"

"Because, I recalled what the son of Sirach says in the True Book: 'An enemy speaketh sweetly with his lips;' and so I did what the son of Sirach advises in such cases: 'I believed not his many words.' "

"What, barber, do you say that such cynical sort of things are in the True Book, by which, of course, you mean the Bible?"

"Yes, and plenty more to the same effect. Read the Book of Proverbs."

"That's strange, now, barber; for I never happen to have met with those passages you cite. Before I go to bed this night, I'll inspect the Bible I saw on the cabin-table, to-day. But mind, you mustn't quote the True Book that way to people coming in here; it would be impliedly a violation of the contract. But you don't know how glad I feel that you have for one while signed off all that sort of thing."

"No, sir; not unless you down with the cash."

"Cash again! What do you mean?"

"Why, in this paper here, you engage, sir, to insure me against a certain loss, and—"

"Certain? Is it so *certain* you are going to lose?"

"Why, that way of taking the word may not be amiss, but I didn't mean it so. I meant a *certain* loss; you understand, a CERTAIN loss; that is to say, a certain loss. Now then, sir, what use your mere writing and saying you will insure me, unless beforehand you place in my hands a money-pledge, sufficient to that end?"

"I see; the material pledge."

"Yes, and I will put it low; say fifty dollars."

"Now what sort of a beginning is this? You, barber, for a given time engage to trust man, to put confidence in men, and, for your first step, make a demand implying no confidence in the very man you engage with. But fifty dollars is nothing, and I would let you have it cheerfully, only I unfortunately happen to have but little change with me just now."

"But you have money in your trunk, though?"

"To be sure. But you see—in fact, barber, you must be consistent. No, I won't let you have the money now; I won't let you violate the inmost spirit of our contract, that way. So good-night, and I will see you again."

"Stay, sir"—humming and hawing—"you have forgotten something."

"Handkerchief?—gloves? No, forgotten nothing. Good-night."

"Stay, sir—the—the shaving."

"Ah, I *did* forget that. But now that it strikes me, I shan't pay you at present. Look at your agreement; you must trust. Tut! against loss you hold the guarantee. Good-night, my dear barber."

With which words he sauntered off, leaving the barber in a maze, staring after.

But it holding true in fascination as in natural philosophy, that nothing can act where it is not, so the barber was not long now in being restored to his self-possession and senses; the first evidence of which perhaps was, that, drawing forth his notification from the drawer, he put it back where it belonged; while, as for the agreement, that he tore up; which he felt the more free to do from the impression that in all human probability he would never again see the person who had drawn it. Whether that impression proved well-founded or not, does not appear. But in after days, telling the night's adventure to his friends, the worthy barber always spoke of his queer customer as the man-charmer—as certain East Indians are called snake-charmers—and all his friends united in thinking him QUITE AN ORIGINAL.

Chapter 44

In which the last three words of the last
chapter are made the text of discourse,
which will be sure of receiving more or less
attention from those readers who do
not skip it

"QUITE AN ORIGINAL:" A phrase, we fancy, rather oftener
used by the young, or the unlearned, or the untraveled,
than by the old, or the well-read, or the man who has made
the grand tour. Certainly, the sense of originality exists at its
highest in an infant, and probably at its lowest in him who
has completed the circle of the sciences.

As for original characters in fiction, a grateful reader will,
on meeting with one, keep the anniversary of that day. True,
we sometimes hear of an author who, at one creation, produces some two or three score such characters; it may be possible. But they can hardly be original in the sense that Hamlet
is, or Don Quixote, or Milton's Satan. That is to say, they are
not, in a thorough sense, original at all. They are novel, or
singular, or striking, or captivating, or all four at once.

More likely, they are what are called odd characters; but
for that, are no more original, than what is called an odd
genius, in his way, is. But, if original, whence came they? Or
where did the novelist pick them up?

Where does any novelist pick up any character? For the
most part, in town, to be sure. Every great town is a kind of
man-show, where the novelist goes for his stock, just as the
agriculturist goes to the cattle-show for his. But in the one
fair, new species of quadrupeds are hardly more rare, than in
the other are new species of characters—that is, original ones.
Their rarity may still the more appear from this, that, while
characters, merely singular, imply but singular forms, so to
speak, original ones, truly so, imply original instincts.

In short, a due conception of what is to be held for this
sort of personage in fiction would make him almost as much
of a prodigy there, as in real history is a new law-giver, a
revolutionizing philosopher, or the founder of a new religion.

In nearly all the original characters, loosely accounted such in works of invention, there is discernible something prevailingly local, or of the age; which circumstance, of itself, would seem to invalidate the claim, judged by the principles here suggested.

Furthermore, if we consider, what is popularly held to entitle characters in fiction to being deemed original, is but something personal—confined to itself. The character sheds not its characteristic on its surroundings, whereas, the original character, essentially such, is like a revolving Drummond light, raying away from itself all round it—everything is lit by it, everything starts up to it (mark how it is with Hamlet), so that, in certain minds, there follows upon the adequate conception of such a character, an effect, in its way, akin to that which in Genesis attends upon the beginning of things.

For much the same reason that there is but one planet to one orbit, so can there be but one such original character to one work of invention. Two would conflict to chaos. In this view, to say that there are more than one to a book, is good presumption there is none at all. But for new, singular, striking, odd, eccentric, and all sorts of entertaining and instructive characters, a good fiction may be full of them. To produce such characters, an author, beside other things, must have seen much, and seen through much: to produce but one original character, he must have had much luck.

There would seem but one point in common between this sort of phenomenon in fiction and all other sorts: it cannot be born in the author's imagination—it being as true in literature as in zoology, that all life is from the egg.

In the endeavor to show, if possible, the impropriety of the phrase, *Quite an Original*, as applied by the barber's friends, we have, at unawares, been led into a dissertation bordering upon the prosy, perhaps upon the smoky. If so, the best use the smoke can be turned to, will be, by retiring under cover of it, in good trim as may be, to the story.

Chapter 45

THE COSMOPOLITAN INCREASES IN SERIOUSNESS

IN THE MIDDLE of the gentlemen's cabin burned a solar lamp, swung from the ceiling, and whose shade of ground glass was all round fancifully variegated, in transparency, with the image of a horned altar, from which flames rose, alternate with the figure of a robed man, his head encircled by a halo. The light of this lamp, after dazzlingly striking on marble, snow-white and round—the slab of a centre-table beneath—on all sides went rippling off with ever-diminishing distinctness, till, like circles from a stone dropped in water, the rays died dimly away in the furthest nook of the place.

Here and there, true to their place, but not to their function, swung other lamps, barren planets, which had either gone out from exhaustion, or been extinguished by such occupants of berths as the light annoyed, or who wanted to sleep, not see.

By a perverse man, in a berth not remote, the remaining lamp would have been extinguished as well, had not a steward forbade, saying that the commands of the captain required it to be kept burning till the natural light of day should come to relieve it. This steward, who, like many in his vocation, was apt to be a little free-spoken at times, had been provoked by the man's pertinacity to remind him, not only of the sad consequences which might, upon occasion, ensue from the cabin being left in darkness, but, also, of the circumstance that, in a place full of strangers, to show one's self anxious to produce darkness there, such an anxiety was, to say the least, not becoming. So the lamp—last survivor of many—burned on, inwardly blessed by those in some berths, and inwardly execrated by those in others.

Keeping his lone vigils beneath his lone lamp, which lighted his book on the table, sat a clean, comely, old man, his head snowy as the marble, and a countenance like that which imagination ascribes to good Simeon, when, having at last beheld the Master of Faith, he blessed him and departed in peace. From his hale look of greenness in winter, and his hands ingrained with the tan, less, apparently, of the present summer, than of accumulated ones past, the old man seemed a well-to-do farmer, happily dismissed, after a thrifty life of activity, from the fields to the fireside—one of those who, at three-score-and-ten, are fresh-hearted as at fifteen; to whom seclusion gives a boon more blessed than knowledge, and at last sends them to heaven untainted by the world, because ignorant of it; just as a countryman putting up at a London inn, and never stirring out of it as a sight-seer, will leave London at last without once being lost in its fog, or soiled by its mud.

Redolent from the barber's shop, as any bridegroom tripping to the bridal chamber might come, and by his look of cheeriness seeming to dispense a sort of morning through the night, in came the cosmopolitan; but marking the old man, and how he was occupied, he toned himself down, and trod softly, and took a seat on the other side of the table, and said nothing. Still, there was a kind of waiting expression about him.

"Sir," said the old man, after looking up puzzled at him a moment, "sir," said he, "one would think this was a coffee-house, and it was war-time, and I had a newspaper here with great news, and the only copy to be had, you sit there looking at me so eager."

"And so you *have* good news there, sir—the very best of good news."

"Too good to be true," here came from one of the curtained berths.

"Hark!" said the cosmopolitan. "Some one talks in his sleep."

"Yes," said the old man, "and you—*you* seem to be talking in a dream. Why speak you, sir, of news, and all that, when you must see this is a book I have here—the Bible, not a newspaper?"

"I know that; and when you are through with it—but not a moment sooner—I will thank you for it. It belongs to the boat, I believe—a present from a society."

"Oh, take it, take it!"

"Nay, sir, I did not mean to touch you at all. I simply stated the fact in explanation of my waiting here—nothing more. Read on, sir, or you will distress me."

This courtesy was not without effect. Removing his spectacles, and saying he had about finished his chapter, the old man kindly presented the volume, which was received with thanks equally kind. After reading for some minutes, until his expression merged from attentiveness into seriousness, and from that into a kind of pain, the cosmopolitan slowly laid down the book, and turning to the old man, who thus far had been watching him with benign curiosity, said: "Can you, my aged friend, resolve me a doubt—a disturbing doubt?"

"There are doubts, sir," replied the old man, with a changed countenance, "there are doubts, sir, which, if man have them, it is not man that can solve them."

"True; but look, now, what my doubt is. I am one who thinks well of man. I love man. I have confidence in man. But what was told me not a half-hour since? I was told that I would find it written—'Believe not his many words—an enemy speaketh sweetly with his lips'—and also I was told that I would find a good deal more to the same effect, and all in this book. I could not think it; and, coming here to look for myself, what do I read? Not only just what was quoted, but also, as was engaged, more to the same purpose, such as this: 'With much communication he will tempt thee; he will smile upon thee, and speak thee fair, and say What wantest thou? If thou be for his profit he will use thee; he will make thee bare, and will not be sorry for it. Observe and take good heed. When thou hearest these things, awake in thy sleep.'"

"Who's that describing the confidence-man?" here came from the berth again.

"Awake in his sleep, sure enough, ain't he?" said the cosmopolitan, again looking off in surprise. "Same voice as before, ain't it? Strange sort of dreamy man, that. Which is his berth, pray?"

"Never mind *him*, sir," said the old man anxiously, "but tell me truly, did you, indeed, read from the book just now?"

"I did," with changed air, "and gall and wormwood it is to me, a truster in man; to me, a philanthropist."

"Why," moved, "you don't mean to say, that what you repeated is really down there? Man and boy, I have read the good book this seventy years, and don't remember seeing anything like that. Let me see it," rising earnestly, and going round to him.

"There it is; and there—and there"—turning over the leaves, and pointing to the sentences one by one; "there—all down in the 'Wisdom of Jesus, the Son of Sirach.' "

"Ah!" cried the old man, brightening up, "now I know. Look," turning the leaves forward and back, till all the Old Testament lay flat on one side, and all the New Testament flat on the other, while in his fingers he supported vertically the portion between, "look, sir, all this to the right is certain truth, and all this to the left is certain truth, but all I hold in my hand here is apocrypha."

"Apocrypha?"

"Yes; and there's the word in black and white," pointing to it. "And what says the word? It says as much as 'not warranted;' for what do college men say of anything of that sort? They say it is apocryphal. The word itself, I've heard from the pulpit, implies something of uncertain credit. So if your disturbance be raised from aught in this apocrypha," again taking up the pages, "in that case, think no more of it, for it's apocrypha."

"What's that about the Apocalypse?" here, a third time, came from the berth.

"He's seeing visions now, ain't he?" said the cosmopolitan, once more looking in the direction of the interruption. "But, sir," resuming, "I cannot tell you how thankful I am for your reminding me about the apocrypha here. For the moment, its being such escaped me. Fact is, when all is bound up together, it's sometimes confusing. The uncanonical part should be bound distinct. And, now that I think of it, how well did those learned doctors who rejected for us this whole book of Sirach. I never read anything so calculated to destroy man's confidence in man. This son of Sirach even says—I saw it but just now: 'Take heed of thy friends;' not, observe, thy seeming friends, thy hypocritical friends, thy false friends, but thy *friends*, thy real friends—that is to say, not the truest friend in the world is to be implicitly trusted. Can Rochefoucault equal that? I should not wonder if his view of human nature, like Machiavelli's, was taken from this Son of Sirach. And to call it wisdom—the Wisdom of the Son of Sirach! Wisdom, indeed! What an ugly thing wisdom must be! Give me the folly that dimples the cheek, say I, rather than the wisdom that curdles the blood. But no, no; it ain't wisdom; it's apocrypha, as you say, sir. For how can that be trustworthy that teaches distrust?"

"I tell you what it is," here cried the same voice as before, only now in less of mockery, "if you two don't know enough to sleep, don't be keeping wiser men awake. And if you want to know what wisdom is, go find it under your blankets."

"Wisdom?" cried another voice with a brogue; "arrah, and is't wisdom the two geese are gabbling about all this while? To bed with ye, ye divils, and don't be after burning your fingers with the likes of wisdom."

"We must talk lower," said the old man; "I fear we have annoyed these good people."

"I should be sorry if wisdom annoyed any one," said the other; "but we will lower our voices, as you say. To resume: taking the thing as I did, can you be surprised at my uneasiness in reading passages so charged with the spirit of distrust?"

"No, sir, I am not surprised," said the old man; then added: "from what you say, I see you are something of my way of thinking—you think that to distrust the creature, is a kind of distrusting of the Creator. Well, my young friend, what is it? This is rather late for you to be about. What do you want of me?"

These questions were put to a boy in the fragment of an old linen coat, bedraggled and yellow, who, coming in from the deck barefooted on the soft carpet, had been unheard. All pointed and fluttering, the rags of the little fellow's red-flannel shirt, mixed with those of his yellow coat, flamed about him like the painted flames in the robes of a victim in *auto-da-fe*. His face, too, wore such a polish of seasoned grime, that his sloe-eyes sparkled from out it like lustrous sparks in fresh coal. He was a juvenile peddler, or *marchand*, as the polite French might have called him, of travelers' conveniences; and, having no allotted sleeping-place, had, in his wanderings about the boat, spied, through glass doors, the two in the cabin; and, late though it was, thought it might never be too much so for turning a penny.

Among other things, he carried a curious affair—a miniature mahogany door, hinged to its frame, and suitably furnished in all respects but one, which will shortly appear. This little door he now meaningly held before the old man, who, after staring at it a while, said: "Go thy ways with thy toys, child."

"Now, may I never get so old and wise as that comes to," laughed the boy through his grime; and, by so doing, disclosing leopard-like teeth, like those of Murillo's wild beggar-boy's.

"The divils are laughing now, are they?" here came the brogue from the berth. "What do the divils find to laugh about in wisdom, begorrah? To bed with ye, ye divils, and no more of ye."

"You see, child, you have disturbed that person," said the old man; "you mustn't laugh any more."

"Ah, now," said the cosmopolitan, "don't, pray, say that; don't let him think that poor Laughter is persecuted for a fool in this world."

"Well," said the old man to the boy, "you must, at any rate, speak very low."

"Yes, that wouldn't be amiss, perhaps," said the cosmopolitan; "but, my fine fellow, you were about saying something to my aged friend here; what was it?"

"Oh," with a lowered voice, coolly opening and shutting his little door, "only this: when I kept a toy-stand at the fair in Cincinnati last month, I sold more than one old man a child's rattle."

"No doubt of it," said the old man. "I myself often buy such things for my little grandchildren."

"But these old men I talk of were old bachelors."

The old man stared at him a moment; then, whispering to the cosmopolitan: "Strange boy, this; sort of simple, ain't he? Don't know much, hey?"

"Not much," said the boy, "or I wouldn't be so ragged."

"Why, child, what sharp ears you have!" exclaimed the old man.

"If they were duller, I would hear less ill of myself," said the boy.

"You seem pretty wise, my lad," said the cosmopolitan; " why don't you sell your wisdom, and buy a coat?"

"Faith," said the boy, "that's what I did to-day, and this is the coat that the price of my wisdom bought. But won't you trade? See, now, it is not the door I want to sell; I only carry the door round for a specimen, like. Look now, sir," standing the thing up on the table, "supposing this little door is your state-room door; well," opening it, "you go in for the night; you close your door behind you—thus. Now, is all safe?"

"I suppose so, child," said the old man.

"Of course it is, my fine fellow," said the cosmopolitan.

"All safe. Well. Now, about two o'clock in the morning, say, a soft-handed gentleman comes softly and tries the knob here—thus; in creeps my soft-handed gentleman; and hey, presto! how comes on the soft cash?"

"I see, I see, child," said the old man; "your fine gentleman is a fine thief, and there's no lock to your little door to keep him out;" with which words he peered at it more closely than before.

"Well, now," again showing his white teeth, " well, now, some of you old folks are knowing 'uns, sure enough; but now comes the great invention," producing a small steel contrivance, very simple but ingenious, and which, being clapped on the inside of the little door, secured it as with a bolt. "There now," admiringly holding it off at arm's-length, "there now, let that soft-handed gentleman come now a' softly trying this little knob here, and let him keep a' trying till he finds his head as soft as his hand. Buy the traveler's patent lock, sir, only twenty-five cents."

"Dear me," cried the old man, "this beats printing. Yes, child, I will have one, and use it this very night."

With the phlegm of an old banker pouching the change, the boy now turned to the other: "Sell you one, sir?"

"Excuse me, my fine fellow, but I never use such blacksmiths' things."

"Those who give the blacksmith most work seldom do," said the boy, tipping him a wink expressive of a degree of indefinite knowingness, not uninteresting to consider in one of his years. But the wink was not marked by the old man, nor, to all appearances, by him for whom it was intended.

"Now then," said the boy, again addressing the old man.

"With your traveler's lock on your door to-night, you will think yourself all safe, won't you?"

"I think I will, child."

"But how about the window?"

"Dear me, the window, child. I never thought of that. I must see to that."

"Never you mind about the window," said the boy, "nor, to be honor bright, about the traveler's lock either, (though I ain't sorry for selling one), do you just buy one of these little jokers," producing a number of suspender-like objects, which he dangled before the old man; "money-belts, sir; only fifty cents."

"Money-belt? never heard of such a thing."

"A sort of pocket-book," said the boy, "only a safer sort. Very good for travelers."

"Oh, a pocket-book. Queer looking pocket-books though, seems to me. Ain't they rather long and narrow for pocket-books?"

"They go round the waist, sir, inside," said the boy; "door open or locked, wide awake on your feet or fast asleep in your chair, impossible to be robbed with a money-belt."

"I see, I see. It *would* be hard to rob one's money-belt. And I was told to-day the Mississippi is a bad river for pick-pockets. How much are they?"

"Only fifty cents, sir."

"I'll take one. There!"

"Thank-ee. And now there's a present for ye," with which, drawing from his breast a batch of little papers, he threw one before the old man, who, looking at it, read *"Counterfeit Detector."*

"Very good thing," said the boy, "I give it to all my customers who trade seventy-five cents' worth; best present can be made them. Sell you a money-belt, sir?" turning to the cosmopolitan.

"Excuse me, my fine fellow, but I never use that sort of thing; my money I carry loose."

"Loose bait ain't bad," said the boy, "look a lie and find the truth; don't care about a Counterfeit Detector, do ye? or is the wind East, d'ye think?"

"Child," said the old man in some concern, "you mustn't

sit up any longer, it affects your mind; there, go away, go to bed."

"If I had some people's brains to lie on, I would," said the boy, "but planks is hard, you know."

"Go, child—go, go!"

"Yes, child,—yes, yes," said the boy, with which roguish parody, by way of congé, he scraped back his hard foot on the woven flowers of the carpet, much as a mischievous steer in May scrapes back his horny hoof in the pasture; and then with a flourish of his hat—which, like the rest of his tatters, was, thanks to hard times, a belonging beyond his years, though not beyond his experience, being a grown man's cast-off beaver—turned, and with the air of a young Caffre, quitted the place.

"That's a strange boy," said the old man, looking after him. "I wonder who's his mother; and whether she knows what late hours he keeps?"

"The probability is," observed the other, "that his mother does not know. But if you remember, sir, you were saying something, when the boy interrupted you with his door."

"So I was.—Let me see," unmindful of his purchases for the moment, "what, now, was it? What was that I was saying? Do *you* remember?"

"Not perfectly, sir; but, if I am not mistaken, it was something like this: you hoped you did not distrust the creature; for that would imply distrust of the Creator."

"Yes, that was something like it," mechanically and unintelligently letting his eye fall now on his purchases.

"Pray, will you put your money in your belt to-night?"

"It's best, ain't it?" with a slight start. "Never too late to be cautious. 'Beware of pick-pockets' is all over the boat."

"Yes, and it must have been the Son of Sirach, or some other morbid cynic, who put them there. But that's not to the purpose. Since you are minded to it, pray, sir, let me help you about the belt. I think that, between us, we can make a secure thing of it."

"Oh no, no, no!" said the old man, not unperturbed, "no, no, I wouldn't trouble you for the world," then, nervously folding up the belt, "and I won't be so impolite as to do it for myself, before you, either. But, now that I think of it," after a pause, carefully taking a little wad from a remote corner of his vest pocket, "here are two bills they gave me at St. Louis, yesterday. No doubt they are all right; but just to pass time, I'll compare them with the Detector here. Blessed boy to make me such a present. Public benefactor, that little boy!"

Laying the Detector square before him on the table, he then, with something of the air of an officer bringing by the collar a brace of culprits to the bar, placed the two bills opposite the Detector, upon which, the examination began, lasting some time, prosecuted with no small research and vigilance, the forefinger of the right hand proving of lawyer-like efficacy in tracing out and pointing the evidence, whichever way it might go.

After watching him a while, the cosmopolitan said in a formal voice, "Well, what say you, Mr. Foreman; guilty, or not guilty?—Not guilty, ain't it?"

"I don't know, I don't know," returned the old man, perplexed, "there's so many marks of all sorts to go by, it makes it a kind of uncertain. Here, now, is this bill," touching one, "it looks to be a three dollar bill on the Vicksburgh Trust and Insurance Banking Company. Well, the Detector says—"

"But why, in this case, care what it says? Trust and Insurance! What more would you have?"

"No; but the Detector says, among fifty other things, that, if a good bill, it must have, thickened here and there into the substance of the paper, little wavy spots of red; and it says they must have a kind of silky feel, being made by the lint of a red silk handkerchief stirred up in the paper-maker's vat—the paper being made to order for the company."

"Well, and is—"

"Stay. But then it adds, that sign is not always to be relied on; for some good bills get so worn, the red marks get rubbed out. And that's the case with my bill here—see how old it is—or else it's a counterfeit, or else—I don't see right—or else—dear, dear me—I don't know what else to think."

"What a peck of trouble that Detector makes for you now; believe me, the bill is good; don't be so distrustful. Proves what I've always thought, that much of the want of confidence, in these days, is owing to these Counterfeit Detectors you see on every desk and counter. Puts people up to suspecting good bills. Throw it away, I beg, if only because of the trouble it breeds you."

"No; it's troublesome, but I think I'll keep it.—Stay, now, here's another sign. It says that, if the bill is good, it must have in one corner, mixed in with the vignette, the figure of a goose, very small, indeed, all but microscopic; and, for added precaution, like the figure of Napoleon outlined by the tree, not observable, even if magnified, unless the attention is directed to it. Now, pore over it as I will, I can't see this goose."

"Can't see the goose? why, I can; and a famous goose it is. There" (reaching over and pointing to a spot in the vignette).

"I don't see it—dear me—I don't see the goose. Is it a real goose?"

"A perfect goose; beautiful goose."

"Dear, dear, I don't see it."

"Then throw that Detector away, I say again; it only makes you purblind; don't you see what a wild-goose chase it has led you? The bill is good. Throw the Detector away."

"No; it ain't so satisfactory as I thought for, but I must examine this other bill."

"As you please, but I can't in conscience assist you any more; pray, then, excuse me."

So, while the old man with much painstakings resumed his work, the cosmopolitan, to allow him every facility, resumed his reading. At length, seeing that he had given up his undertaking as hopeless, and was at leisure again, the cosmopolitan addressed some gravely interesting remarks to him about the book before him, and, presently, becoming more and more grave, said, as he turned the large volume slowly over on the table, and with much difficulty traced the faded remains of the gilt inscription giving the name of the society who had presented it to the boat, "Ah, sir, though every one must be pleased at the thought of the presence in public places of such a book, yet there is something that abates the satisfaction. Look at this volume; on the outside, battered as any old valise in the baggage-room; and inside, white and virgin as the hearts of lilies in bud."

"So it is, so it is," said the old man sadly, his attention for the first directed to the circumstance.

"Nor is this the only time," continued the other, "that I have observed these public Bibles in boats and hotels. All much like this—old without, and new within. True, this aptly typifies that internal freshness, the best mark of truth, however ancient; but then, it speaks not so well as could be wished for the good book's esteem in the minds of the traveling public. I may err, but it seems to me that if more confidence was put in it by the traveling public, it would hardly be so."

With an expression very unlike that with which he had bent over the Detector, the old man sat meditating upon his companion's remarks a while; and, at last, with a rapt look, said: "And yet, of all people, the traveling public most need to put trust in that guardianship which is made known in this book."

"True, true," thoughtfully assented the other.

"And one would think they would want to, and be glad to," continued the old man kindling; "for, in all our wanderings through this vale, how pleasant, not less than obligatory, to feel that we need start at no wild alarms, provide for no wild perils; trusting in that Power which is alike able and willing to protect us when we cannot ourselves."

His manner produced something answering to it in the cosmopolitan, who, leaning over towards him, said sadly: "Though this is a theme on which travelers seldom talk to each other, yet, to you, sir, I will say, that I share something of your sense of security. I have moved much about the world, and still keep at it; nevertheless, though in this land, and especially in these parts of it, some stories are told about steamboats and railroads fitted to make one a little apprehensive, yet, I may say that, neither by land nor by water, am I ever seriously disquieted, however, at times, transiently uneasy; since, with you, sir, I believe in a Committee of Safety, holding silent sessions over all, in an invisible patrol, most alert when we soundest sleep, and whose beat lies as much through forests as towns, along rivers as streets. In short, I never forget that passage of Scripture which says, 'Jehovah shall be thy confidence.' The traveler who has not this trust, what miserable misgivings must be his; or, what vain, short-sighted care must he take of himself."

"Even so," said the old man, lowly.

"There is a chapter," continued the other, again taking the book, "which, as not amiss, I must read you. But this lamp, solar-lamp as it is, begins to burn dimly."

"So it does, so it does," said the old man with changed air, "dear me, it must be very late. I must to bed, to bed! Let me see," rising and looking wistfully all round, first on the stools and settees, and then on the carpet, "let me see, let me see;— is there anything I have forgot,—forgot? Something I a sort of dimly remember. Something, my son—careful man—told me at starting this morning, this very morning. Something about seeing to—something before I got into my berth. What could it be? Something for safety. Oh, my poor old memory!"

"Let me give a little guess, sir. Life-preserver?"

"So it was. He told me not to omit seeing I had a life-preserver in my state-room; said the boat supplied them, too. But where are they? I don't see any. What are they like?"

"They are something like this, sir. I believe," lifting a brown stool with a curved tin compartment underneath; "yes, this, I think, is a life-preserver, sir; and a very good one, I should say, though I don't pretend to know much about such things, never using them myself."

"Why, indeed, now! Who would have thought it? *that* a life-preserver? That's the very stool I was sitting on, ain't it?"

"It is. And that shows that one's life is looked out for, when he ain't looking out for it himself. In fact, any of these stools here will float you, sir, should the boat hit a snag, and go down in the dark. But, since you want one in your room, pray take this one," handing it to him. "I think I can recommend this one; the tin part," rapping it with his knuckles, "seems so perfect—sounds so very hollow."

"Sure it's *quite* perfect, though?" Then, anxiously putting on his spectacles, he scrutinized it pretty closely—"well soldered? quite tight?"

"I should say so, sir; though, indeed, as I said, I never use this sort of thing, myself. Still, I think that in case of a wreck, barring sharp-pointed timbers, you could have confidence in that stool for a special providence."

"Then, good-night, good-night; and Providence have both of us in its good keeping."

"Be sure it will," eying the old man with sympathy, as for the moment he stood, money-belt in hand, and life-preserver under arm, "be sure it will, sir, since in Providence, as in man, you and I equally put trust. But, bless me, we are being left in the dark here. Pah! what a smell, too."

"Ah, my way now," cried the old man, peering before him, " where lies my way to my state-room?"

"I have indifferent eyes, and will show you; but, first, for the good of all lungs, let me extinguish this lamp."

The next moment, the waning light expired, and with it the waning flames of the horned altar, and the waning halo round the robed man's brow; while in the darkness which ensued, the cosmopolitan kindly led the old man away. Something further may follow of this Masquerade.

UNCOLLECTED PROSE

Contents

I. Articles and Reviews

II. Tales

Etchings of a Whaling Cruise

Etchings of a Whaling Cruise, with Notes of a Sojourn on the Island of Zanzibar. To which is appended, a Brief History of the Whale Fishery; its Past and Present Condition. By J. Ross Browne. Illustrated with numerous Engravings on Steel and Wood. Harper & Brothers: 1846. 8vo.

Sailors' Life and Sailors' Yarns. By Captain Ringbolt. New York: C. S. Francis & Co. 1847. 12mo.

F ROM TIME IMMEMORIAL many fine things have been said and sung of the sea. And the days have been, when sailors were considered veritable mermen; and the ocean itself, as the peculiar theatre of the romantic and wonderful. But of late years there have been revealed so many plain, matter-of-fact details connected with nautical life that at the present day the poetry of salt water is very much on the wane. The perusal of Dana's Two Years Before The Mast, for instance, somewhat impairs the relish with which we read Byron's spiritual address to the ocean. And when the noble poet raves about laying his hands upon the ocean's mane (in other words manipulating the crest of a wave) the most vivid image suggested is that of a valetudinarian bather at Rockaway, spluttering and choaking in the surf, with his mouth full of brine.

Mr J. Ross Browne's narrative tends still further to impair the charm with which poesy and fiction have invested the sea. It is a book of unvarnished facts; and with some allowances for the general application of an individual example unquestionably presents a faithful picture of the life led by the 20 thousand seamen employed in the 700 whaling vessels which pursue their game under the American flag. Indeed, what Mr Dana has so admirably done in describing the vicissitudes of the merchant sailor's life, Mr Browne has very creditably achieved with respect to that of the hardy whaleman's. And the book which possesses this merit deserves much in the way of commendation. The personal narrative interwoven with it, also, can not fail to enlist our sympathies for the adventurous author himself. The scenes presented are always graphicly and truthfully sketched, and hence fastidious objections may be made to some of them, on the score of their being too coarsly or harshly drawn. But we take it, that as true unreserved descriptions they are in no respect faulty—and doubtless the author never dreamed of softening down or withholding anything with a view of rendering his sketches the more attractive and pretty. The book is eminently a practical one; and written with the set purpose of accomplishing good by revealing the simple truth. When the brutal tyranny of the Captain of the "Styx" is painted without apology or palliation, it holds up the outrageous abuse to which seamen in our whaling marine are actually subjected, a matter which demands legislation. Mr Browne himself—it seems, was to some extent, the victim of the tyranny of which he complains, and, upon this ground, the personal bitterness in which he at times indulges may be deemed excusable, though it is rather out of place.

As the book professes to embrace a detailed account of all that is interesting in the business of whaling, and, essentially, possesses this merit, one or two curious errors into which the author has unaccountably fallen may, without captiousness, be pointed out.—We are told, for example, of a whale's *roaring* when wounded by the harpoon. We can imagine the veteran Coffins and Colemans and Maceys of old Nantucket elevating their brows at the bare announcement of such a thing. Now the creature in question is as dumb as a shad, or any other of the finny tribes. And no doubt, if Jonah himself could be summoned to the stand, he would cheerfully testify to his not having heard a single syllable, growl, grunt, or bellow engendered in the ventricle cells of the leviathan, during the irksome period of his incarceration therein.

That in some encounters with the sperm whale a low indistinct sound *apparently* issues from the monster is true enough. But all Nantucket and New Bedford are divided as to the causes which produce the phenomenon. Many suppose, however, that it is produced—not by the creature itself—but by the peculiar motion in the water of the line which is attached to the harpoon. For, if upon being struck, the whale "sounds" (descends) as is usually the case, and remains below the surface for any length of time, the rope frequently becomes as stiff as the cord of a harp and the struggles of the animal keep it continually vibrating.

Considering the disenchanting nature of the revelations of

sea life with which we are presented in Mr Browne's book we are inclined to believe that the shipping agents employed in our various cities by the merchants of New Bedford will have to present additional inducements to "enterprising and industrious young Americans of good moral character" in order to persuade them to embark in the fishery. In particular the benevolent old gentleman in Front Street (one of the shipping agents of whom our author discourseth) who so politely accosted Browne and his comrade, upon their entering his office for the purpose of seeking further information touching the rate of promotion in the whaling service—this old gentleman, we say, must hereafter infuse into his address still more of the *suaviter in modo*.

As unaffectedly described by Browne the scene alluded to is irresistably comic. The agent's business, be it understood, consists in decoying "green hands" to send on to the different whaling ports. A conspicuous placard without the office announces to the anxious world, that a few choice vacancies remain to be filled in certain crews of whalemen about to sail upon the most delightful voyages imaginable (only four years long)—To secure a place, of course, instant application should be made.

Our author and his friend attracted by the placard, hurry up a ladder to a dark loft above, where the old man lurks like a spider in the midst of his toils.—But a single glance at the gentlemanly dress and white hands of his visitors impresses the wily agent with the idea that notwithstanding their calling upon him, they may very possibly have heard disagreeable accounts of the nature of whaling. So, after making a bow, and offering a few legs of a chair, he proceeds to disabuse their minds of any unfavorable impressions.—Succeeding in this, he then becomes charmingly facetious and complimentary; assuring the youths that they need not be concerned because of their slender waists and silken muscles; for those who employed him were not so particular about weight as beauty. In short the captains of whaling vessels preferred handsome young fellows who dressed well and conversed genteelly—in short, those who would reflect credit upon the business of tarring down rigging and cutting up blubber. Delighted with the agreeable address of the old gentleman and with many pleasant anticipations of sea-life the visitors listen with increased attention. Whereupon the agent waxes eloquent, and enlarges upon his animating theme in the style parliamentary. "A whaler, gentlemen" he observes "is the home of the unfortunate—the asylum of the oppressed &c &c &c"

Duped Browne! Hapless H———! In the end, they enter into an engagement with the old gentleman, who subsequently sends them on to New Bedford consigned to a mercantile house there. From New Bedford the adventurers at length sail in a small whaling barque bound to the Indian ocean. While yet half dead with sea sickness the unfortunate H——— is sent by the brutal captain to the mast-head, to stand there his allotted two hours on the look out for whale-spouts. He receives a stroke of the sun, which, for a time, takes away his reason and endangers his life. He raves of home and friends, and poor Browne watching by his side, upbraids himself for having been concerned in bringing his companion to such a state.—Ere long the vessel touches at the Azores, where H——— being altogether unfit for duty is left to be sent home by the American consul.

He never recovered from the effects of his hardships; for in the sequel Browne relates that after reaching home himself, he visited his old friend in Ohio, and found him still liable to temporary prostrations directly referable to his sufferings at sea.

With a heavy heart our author after leaving the Azores weathers the Cape of Good Hope and enters upon the Indian ocean. The ship's company—composed mostly of ignorant, half-civilized Portuguese from the Western Islands—are incessantly quarrelling and fighting; the provisions are of the most wretched kind;—their success in the fishery is small; and to crown all, the captain himself is the very incarnation of all that is dastardly, mean, and heartless.

We can not follow Browne through all his adventures. Suffice it to say, that heartily disgusted with his situation he at length, with great difficulty, succeeds in leaving the vessel on the coast of Zanzibar. Here he tarries for some months, and his residence in this remote region (the Eastern coast of Africa, near Madagascar) enables him to make sundry curious observations upon men and things, of which the reader of his work has the benefit. From Zanzibar he ultimately sails for home in a merchant brig; and at last arrives in Boston thoroughly out of conceit of the ocean.

Give ear, now, all ye shore-disdaining, ocean-enamored youths, who labor under the lamentable delusion, that the sea—the "glorious sea" is always and in reality "the blue, the fresh, the ever free!" Give ear to Mr J. Ross Browne, and hearken unto what that experienced young gentleman has to say about the manner in which Barry Cornwall has been humbugging the rising generation on this subject.—Alas! Hereafter we shall never look upon an unsophisticated stripling in flowing "duck" trowsers and a bright blue jacket, loitering away the interval which elapses before sailing on his maiden cruise, without mourning over the hard fate in store for him.—In a ship's forecastle, alas, he will find no Psyche glass in which to survey his picturesque attire. And the business of making his toilet will be comprised in trying to keep as dry and comfortable as the utter absence of umbrellas, wet decks, and leaky forecastles will admit of.—We shudder at all realities of the career they will be entering upon. The long, dark, cold night-watches, which, month after month, they must battle out the best way they can,—the ship pitching and thumping against the bullying waves—every plank dripping—every jacket soaked—and the Captain not at all bland in issuing his order for the poor fellows to mount aloft in the icy sleet and howling tempest.—"Bless me, Captain, go way up there this excessively disagreeable night?"—"Aye up with you, you lubber—*bare*, I say, or look out for squalls"—a figurative expression, conveying a remote allusion to the hasty application of a sea-bludgeon to the head.

Then the whaling part of the business.—My young friends, just fancy yourselves, for the first time in an open boat (so slight that three men might walk off with it) some 12 or 15 miles from your ship and about a hundred times as far from the nearest land, giving chase to one of the oleaginous monsters. "Pull, Pull, you lubberly *hay-makers!*" cries the boat-header jumping up and down in the stern-sheets in a frenzy of professional excitement, while the gasping admirers of Captain Marryat and the sea, tug with might and main at the buckling oars—"Pull, Pull, I say; Break your lazy backs!" Presently the whale is within "darting distance" and you hear the roar of the waters in his wake.—How palpitating the hearts of the frightened oarsmen at this interesting juncture! My young friends, just turn round and snatch a look at that whale—. There he goes, surging through the brine, which ripples about his vast head as if it were the bow of a ship. Believe me, it's quite as terrible as going into battle to a raw recruit.

"Stand up and give it to him!" shrieks the boat-header at the steering-oar to the harpooneer in the bow. The latter drops his oar and snatches his "iron." It flies from his hands—and where are we then, my lovelies?—It's all a mist, a crash,—a horrible blending of sounds and sights, as the agonized whale lashes the water around him into suds and vapor—dashes the boat aside, and at last rushes, madly, through the water towing after him the half-filled craft which rocks from side to side while the disordered crew, clutch at the gunwale to avoid being tossed out. Meanwhile all sorts of horrific edged tools—lances, harpoons and spades—are slipping about; and the imminent line itself—smoking round the logger-head and passing along the entire length of the boat— is almost death to handle, though it grazes your person.

But all this is nothing to what follows. As yet you have but simply *fastened* to the whale: he must be fought and killed. But let imagination supply the rest:—the monster staving the boat with a single sweep of his ponderous flukes;—taking its bows between his jaws (as is frequently the case) and playing with it, as a cat with a mouse. Sometimes he bites it in twain; sometimes crunches it into chips, and strews the sea with them.

—But we forbear. Enough has been said to convince the uninitiated what sort of a vocation whaling in truth is. If further information is desired, Mr Browne's book is purchasable in which they will find the whole matter described in all its interesting details.

After reading the "Etchings of a Whaling Cruise" a perusal of "Sailors' Life and Sailors' Yarns" is in one respect at least like hearing "the other side of the question." For, while

Browne's is a "Voice from the Forecastle" Captain Ringbolt hails us from the quarter deck, the other end of the ship. Browne gives us a sailor's version of sailors' wrongs, and is not altogether free from prejudices acquired during his little experience on ship board; Captain Ringbolt almost denies that the sailor has any wrongs and more than insinuates that sea-captains are not only the best natured fellows in the world but that they have been sorely maligned. Indeed he explicitly charges Mr Dana and Mr Browne with having presented a decidedly one sided view of the matter. And he mournfully exclaims that the Captain of the Pilgrim—poor fellow!—died too soon to vindicate his character from unjust aspersions.

—Now as a class ship owners are seldom disposed partially to judge the captains in their employ. And yet we know of a verity that at least one of the owners of the Pilgrim,—an esteemed citizen of the good old town of Boston—will never venture to dispute that to the extent of his knowledge at least Mr Dana's captain was a most "strict and harsh disciplinarian," which words so applied by a ship owner, mean that the man in question was nothing less than what Mr Dana describes him to have been.—But where is Browne's captain? He is alive and hearty we presume. Let him come forward then and show why he ought not to be regarded in the decidedly unfavorable light in which he is held up to us in the narrative we have noticed? Now for ought we know to the contrary this same Captain of the Styx—who was such a heartless domineering tyrant at sea—may be quite a different character ashore. In truth we think this very probable. For the god Janus never had two more decidedly different faces than your sea captain. Ashore his Nautical Highness has nothing to ruffle him—friends grasp him by the hand and are overjoyed to see him after his long absence—he is invited out and relates his adventures pleasantly and everybody thinks what lucky dogs his sailors must have been to have sailed with such a capital fellow.

—But let poor Jack have a word to say—Why Sir, he will tell you that when they embarked His Nautical Highness left behind him all his "quips and cranks and wanton smiles". Very far indeed is the Captain from cracking any of his jokes with his crew—that would be altogether too condescending. But then there is no reason why he should bestow a curse every time he gives an order—there is no reason why he should never say a word of kindness or sympathy to his men. True; in this respect all sea captains are not alike but still there is enough truth in both Mr Dana's and Mr Browne's statements to justify nearly to the full, the general conclusions to be drawn from what they have said on this subject.—

But Captain Ringbolt's book is very far from being a mere plea for the class to which he belongs.—What he has to say upon the matter is chiefly contained in one brief sketch under the head of Sailors' Rights and Sailors' Wrongs.—The rest of the book is made up of little stories of the sea, simply and pleasantly told and withal entertaining.

Authentic Anecdotes of "Old Zack"

[Reported for YANKEE DOODLE by his special correspondent at the seat of War]

A<small>T THE PRESENT TIME</small> when everything connected with the homespun old hero is perused with unusual interest, and unprincipled paragraphists daily perpetrate the most absurd stories wherewith to titilate public curiosity concerning him, YANKEE DOODLE has thought that a few authentic anecdotes may not be unacceptable to his numerous readers.

They have been collected on the ground from the most reliable and respectable sources, (of course we refer to the anecdotes and not our readers, who every one knows are both respectable and reliable;) and we have the very best reason to believe have never before appeared in print.

Since we are determined to have all the credit of first circulating these anecdotes, be it here known, that YANKEE DOODLE, with his customary enterprise and utter recklessness of all expense where the diversion of his readers is concerned, has sent on a correspondent to the seat of war for the express purpose of getting together and transmitting to us all reliable *on dits* connected with old ZACK: And here we cannot refrain from noticing the flattering reception which our esteemed correspondent received from the venerable hero himself. No sooner did the valiant General hear of his arrival and the object of his visit, than he forthwith bestrided his historic nag and galloped through the camp to meet him, and conduct him to his quarters, where our aforesaid esteemed correspondent is now permanently domiciled as one of the General's family.

Our correspondent moreover informs us that the General was exceedingly delighted at the object of the visit, inasmuch as the fabular anecdotes which he had seen in the papers had greatly scandalized him. "Sir," said he, striking his longitudinal posterior with his clenched hand (a habit of his when greatly excited) "they are making a downright ass of me there at the North—those infernal editors deserve a sound thrashing for hatching such a pack of lies—they do, indeed." Nor was this all that the choleric old hero observed. But as we do not desire further to expose a little weakness of his which the papers have occasionally hinted at, and which he has in common with Gen. JACKSON and other military heroes—namely, that of profane swearing when in a violent passion—we will disclose nothing more on this head. Suffice it to say, that after venting his ire upon the anecdote-making editors of the North the old hero expressed his unbounded satisfaction at the prospect of henceforth having his most trifling actions and sayings faithfully chronicled by a man of purity. He also expressed his intention to further our laudable object in every possible way—immediately gave our correspondent the privilege of his shot box (upon which the General's famous dispatches are written) and agreed to frank all his communications to YANKEE DOODLE.

So eager was the old hero to prevent for the future the circulation of any but authentic anecdotes concerning him, that without solicitation on the part of our esteemed correspondent, he furnished him with a written certificate, to be published in YANKEE DOODLE, asserting our columns to be the only true source where an anxious public can procure a correct insight into his private life and little personal peculiarities.

The certificate, we have caused to be placed in a brass frame cast from a captured Mexican forty-two brass shot. It occupies a conspicuous place in our office, where it may be seen from 9 A.M. till 3 1-2 P.M. every day, Sundays excepted.

The certificate runs thus:

This is to certify that the undersigned hereby authorises Mr. YANKEE DOODLE to publish and circulate such illustrative stories and anecdotes of the undersigned, as may be transmitted to Mr. YANKEE DOODLE by the highly respectable correspondent who has recently been sent into the camp for that purpose.

And the undersigned hereby declares that all other stories and anecdotes which may be hereafter published in any other columns than YANKEE DOODLE's, are base and malignant publications, mostly of no credence, and strongly suspected to be a covert attempt on the part of the enemies of the undersigned to injure his reputation with the people of the United States with a view of defeating his election to the presidency should he run for that office.

MAJOR GENERAL Z. TAYLOR.

CAMP NEAR —— *June 3d, 1847.*

This much by way of introducing the anecdotes, which here follow regularly numbered, and in the order in which they are sent us.

ANECDOTE I

It is well known that upon the battle field the hero of Palo Alto is as cool as a Roman Punch. His surprising self-collectedness and imperturbability in times of the greatest peril, was never more forcibly shown than in a little circumstance at Buena Vista.

A Mexican mortar being in full play upon the front of the American columns, a large shell with the burning fusee fizzing at the aperture weighing hard on 200 cwt: fell directly at the feet of old Zack, who, with his characteristic contempt of danger, was sitting on his horse upon a conspicuous knoll and was surrounded by several of his staff. Thinking it altogether fool-hardy and superogatory to stand still and be blown to pieces, the officers betrayed no delicacy in instantly galloping out of harm's way. But old ZACK moved not a peg. "Don't be alarmed, gentlemen," he observed quietly, shifting his attitude by throwing the other leg on the neck of his horse— "don't be alarmed—them 'are chaps don't bust always. What will you wager now, Major BLISS, that the fusee doesn't go out afore harm's done?"* While the Major at a good distance leveled his long spy glass at the globular apparition, the old hero calmly took out his spectacles, polished their glasses by rubbing them gently against his thigh—clapped them on his

---

*In all cases we give the old man's very words. If they show a want of early attendance at the Grammar School, it must be borne in mind that old ZACK never took a college diploma—was cradled in the backwood camp— and rather glories in the simplicity and unostentation of his speech. "Describe me, Sir," said he to our correspondent,—"describe me, Sir, as I am— no polysyllables—no stuff—it's time they should know me in my true light."

nose—descended, and approaching the shell, bent over and closely scrutinized the fusee. It had just burnt to within a hair's breadth of the inflammable bowels of the shell—and old ZACK taking it between his fore finger and thumb, drew forth the fusee and waving it towards his aghast officers, quietly observed that if any of them had a cigar to smoke he could supply them with a light.

P.S. to *Anecdote, No. I.*—Mr. BARNUM happening to drop in when we opened our communications from our correspondent, we read him the above. He immediately seized pen and ink and wrote to a military acquaintance of his in the army, to institute a diligent search after the above mentioned shell—pack up carefully in cotton and send it on for his Museum with all possible despatch. Thinking, however, that the search might not prove effectual, Mr. BARNUM has given orders for a shell of the proper dimensions to be cast at one of the foundries up town. We feel confident, however, in stating that the latter will not be exhibited for the genuine article, unless the genuine article fails to come to hand.

ANECDOTE II

The Cincinnatus-like simplicity and unaffectedness of old ZACK's habits have frequently been celebrated. But it is not commonly known, perhaps, that he generally does his own washing. Of a pleasant evening, after the war-like toils of the day are closed, the old hero may be seen at the opening of his tent, sitting plump on the ground with a camp-kettle between his legs—and with short sleeves rolled up, creating a loud splashing of his garments in the suds. The old General by the way, wholly excludes hard soap as an unsoldier-like luxury, and uses nothing but the soft; a barrel of which furnishes part of his tent furniture.

The old hero, however, on account of his eye sight, is not very nimble with the needle. Nevertheless, he insists upon doing his own mending, and particularly prides himself upon the neatness and expedition with which he puts a new seat in his ample pants. These nether garments, of course, require

SIMPLICITY OF OLD ZACK'S HABITS.

frequent repairs, owing to the constant practice, and the habit the old hero has of violently slapping his person when excited. At Buena Vista his being a long time in the saddle, united to the ire-provoking and dastardly conduct of the Illinois regiments, came near entirely rending them in pieces and it was late that night before the General retired, as he always makes it a principle not to permit his basket of new clothes to accumulate.

At Monterey, when the deputies from Gen. Ampudia first ushered the old hero at his quarters, they found him sitting cross-legged upon a gun carriage and earnestly engaged in letting out the seams of his coat—a proceeding necessitated by his increasing bulkiness.

Anecdote III

Old ZACK's insensibility to bodily pain is almost equal to his utter indifference to danger. The following little incident will illustrate what we mean. The morning preceding one of his battles, a mischievous young drummer boy came up to the orderly, who, just without the tent, was holding the General's horse ready accoutred for mounting, and offered to relieve him a few moments at the duty. The offer was accepted, and off went the orderly leaving the lad in his place. What now does the young rascal do, but cunningly insert a sharp iron tack, point upwards, into the august saddle of the hero of Palo Alto. Shortly after, the orderly returned to his post, and the General sprang into his saddle and galloped off. He did not dismount for several hours, during all of which time, according to the experience of school boys, the tack must have been within the closest possible vicinity of a rather sensitive part. But, wonderful to relate, the illustrious ZACK never betrayed the slightest consciousness of the presence of what an ordinary man would have deemed no small annoyance. But at evening when he dismounted at the door of his tent, he was most unexpectedly made aware of what must have seemed to him, at the time, a base and pitiful trick of the enemy. The tack caught in the seat of his inexpressibles, and as he sprang to the ground, would not let go, but left the greater part of the garment upon the saddle. Though valiant as Cid, the old hero is as modest as any miss. Instantly muffling up with his coat tails the exposed part, he hurried into his tent, violently and most perfectly enraged at the occurrence.

The outrage was at once imputed to some lurking Mexican spy, concealed in the camp, and as soon as Major BLISS could prepare it, the following proclamation was forthwith made by sound of trumpet:

PROCLAMATION

"The abominable insult offered to the American nation in the diabolical outrage upon the person of the Commanding General calls for the most active measures to discover and condignly punish the author. He is strongly suspected to be one of the Mexican rancheros, observed prowling in the vicinity of the camp yesterday. Any one, whether officer or private, who will apprehend the offender and bring the scoundrel to the General's quarters shall have his name honorably mentioned in the next dispatch to the War Department."

The drummer-boy, however, never was found out. But no sooner did Secretary MARCY receive the dispatch announcing the circumstance to Government, than a generous sympathy prompted him at once to address an unofficial and very friendly letter to the old hero, condoling with him upon the occurrence. He suggested, as a piece of friendly advice, also, that the General had better keep dark about the matter, since he (Secretary MARCY) knew by experience that any thing touching one's inexpressibles was calculated to provoke vulgar mirth. With his customary straight-forwardness, however, Old ZACK announced his resolution not to disguise or suppress the fact—and to the utter consternation of his military family, BARNUM's letter audaciously begging the torn garment for exhibition at his Museum here, was promptly and favorably answered. The public may therefore rely upon soon having a peep at the inexpressibles in which Old ZACK has *so often cased his valiant legs!*

Note.—Yesterday YANKEE DOODLE forwarded to BARNUM the following draught of a placard for the occasion:

"PRODIGIOUS EXCITEMENT!!!!!!
OLD ZACK'S PANTS!!!
GREAT SIGHTS AT THE AMERICAN MUSEUM!!!
OLD ROUGH AND READY!
UP TOWN EMPTIED OF ITS INHABITANTS!
TOM THUMB FLOORED!

The Proprietor of the American Museum has the honor to announce to the American public that at vast expense and trouble he has succeeded in regulating an arrangement whereby the identical sheep-greys worn by Old Rough and Ready at the celebrated engagement of Resaca de la Palma, will be exhibited for three days in a glass case. Also, in a sealed vial, the poisoned Mexican tack taken from the old hero's saddle, and which came near being his death.

Certificates from Major BLISS, GEN. BRAGG, and other distinguished officers of the army will be shown proving the articles genuine.

Take notice: The exhibition will certainly close upon the third day.

Admittance twenty-five cents, &c. &c. &c."

[In lieu of anything of his own our correspondent has furnished us this week the following vivid and powerful description of the personal appearance of Old ZACK, which, from his private note to us, he appears to have procured from a friend in the army, with no little difficulty. We call the attention of our readers to its bold and massive English.]

"GEN. TAYLOR'S PERSONAL APPEARANCE,"
OR OLD ZACK PHYSIOLOGICALLY AND
OTHERWISE CONSIDERED

BY A SURGEON OF THE ARMY IN MEXICO

The hero of Buena Vista, upon the crown of whose caput have descended so many interleaved chaplets of fame, presents in his general exterior personal appearance many of those extraordinary characteristics distinctive of the noble spirit tabernacled within. Of about the common length of ordinary mortals—say about five feet, nine inches, and two barley corns, Long Measure—he rather leans to a squat colossalness of frame and universal spread of figure, particularly on the lower part of the abdominal regions. To counteract a bulging forth of the latter parts, he is said to wear a truss of peculiar conformation. This circumstance, however, is not as yet fully established. Of a thick set and quadratular build, he now inclines to tenuity in the parts lying round about the calf. Originally of great agility of the locomotive apparatus, he now betrays on his partially denuded head a want of energy in the capillary tubes of the hair, as his digestive machinery is liable to frequent suspensions of activity.

His broad and expanded chest shows the hero fully capable of encountering the prodigious fatigues of war, whether in the interminably interlocked everglades of the Floridian southerly terminus of the Republic, or upon the wide-spreading and generally level table-land savannahs of Mexico. His face is a physiognomical phenomenon, which Lavater would have crossed the Atlantic to contemplate. Of soul-awing determination of expression and significant of inflexible and immovable ironness of purpose, it (the external features of the countenance) are softened down and melted into a kindly benevolence which would prepossess a perfect stranger in his favor. His head is large, extremely well developed in the frontal quarter, but not classically elegant in the anterior portion. To employ an expressive, though somewhat rude comparison, it appears as if *squashed* between his shoulders. By close observers, the lobe of the right ear is thought to be depressed more than the corresponding auricular organ, on the opposite lateral part of the caput.

In early adolescence of a beautiful amber or brown color, the hair, through the gradual ravages of time, has assumed a speckled, pepper and salt external appearance. In a most touching manner the thin and scattered locks are parted picturesquely on one side and combed slickly over the brows. The latter are Jupiternian in their awful bushiness—the hairy appendage curling over upon the optic orbits. His frown is Olympian and strikes terror and confusion into the overwhelmed soul of the spectator. The muscular energy of the brows is truly extraordinary. When ever their pupular is under mental excitation, they frequently become knit together in wrinkular pleats like unto the foldular developments under the lateral shoulder of the rhinoceros species of animated nature. His eye is Websternian, though grey. The left organ somewhat affects the dexter side of the socket, while examined by a powerful telescope several minute specks are observable in the pupil of the sinister orbit. But this detracts not from the majesty of its expression: the sun even has its spots. When the hero's soul is lashed into intellectual agitation by the external occurrence of irritating and stimulating circumstance, the eye assumes an inflamed and fiery appearance. The scantiness of the lashes and their short and singed appearance are ascribable, perhaps, to their vicinity to the pupil when thus kindled into fury. When a mental calm, however, pervades the serene soul of the hero, a Saucernian placidity is diffused over the entire visionary orb.

The nostrilian organ, or proboscis, is straight, but neither inclining to the Roman, or Grecian, or, indeed, the Doric or Composite order of nasal architecture. The labial appendages (suspended just under the proboscis) are attenuated—the upper tightly and firmly spread upon the dental parts beneath; and the lower pendant and projecting as represented in the prints. The outline of the caput, generally, is an ovalular ellipsis inclining to the rotund, but having no predisposition to the quadrangular. The obvious cuticle or scarf-skin is wrinkled, freckled, and embrowned—doubtless through age and constant exposure to the ardent rays of the Floridian and Mexicanian sun combined.

The manner of the hero is frank and companionable—and never did mortal leave his society without being constantly impressed with the unavoidable conviction that he had been conversing with a good fellow and a gentleman.

At times he is seen in deep and earnest meditation—the left auricular organ with the head attached thereto, deposited upon the open palm and outspread digits of the manual termination of the arm. At other times he assumes when meditating quite a different posture; the fore finger of the left hand being placed on the dexter side of the proboscis.

In his military discipline, he is firm and unyielding to the last degree of military inflexibility—but is, nevertheless, remarkably lenient to those under him, officers and privates included. Particularly to the youthful portion of his command, whom he treats with all the indulgence of a paternal relative or guardian—often permitting them to lay a-bed late in the morning, when the battle is raging at the fiercest.

In his general toilet he is far from imitating a Brummellian precision and starchedness of cravat. He has no violent predilection for his regimentals and seldom appears in them, which, in fact, is the case with most of his officers, of whom it is even observed, that *"they seldom appear in externals on duty,"*—a habit indicative of superiority to foppish adornments, but might be construed by the fastidious into a want of good taste and decorousness.

Their custom in this respect, however, is defensible upon the ground, that called by Divine Providence to perform their martial functions in the genial and delightful regions of the sunny south, the cumbersome military costume, or, indeed, any dress at all, *"is disagreeable to the physical feelings."*

The hero himself may be usually seen by an ordinary spectator arrayed in a pair of sheep's grey pants, shapeless and inclined to bagging—the latter predisposition being imputed, by a reflecting observer, to the singular fact that the hero never wears the common-place articles called suspenders. His coat is generally of a brownish tinge which in some cases is to be imputed to the original color imparted to the cloth when in the vat of the dyer, and in other cases to an heroic disregard of dust and oleaginous spots on the part of the ungent wearer. His vest usually, though not invariably, is of a darksome hue—resembling the ordinary sable. He wears a long crumpled black silk neck-handkerchief, much knotted and super-twisted, and evidently not put on with any great degree of care. But the carelessness with which it is tied in no respect approaches to the studied artlessness of the Byronic bow. The shirt collar is open, revealing considerable superfluous hair just above the region of the thorax and windpipe, and betokening a disdain of Gouraud's Depillatory. Several individual hairs partake of the greyish tinge of the sparse covering of the head.

The hero sometimes wears a white wool hat, much marked by indentation and irregular depressions and prominences upon the crown. It resembles in most respects the castor of a Mississippi flat-boatman.—His shoes are the common cowhide sandals served out by the Commissary Department to the free use of the army. They are usually stringless and not much polished.

ANECDOTE IV

In the words of the gallant Count HAMILTON, "War is but one half the glory of heroes." So with the valiant ZACK. Years ago, ere 'rose the sun at Palo Alto, or fled the Mexican host at Buena Vista, Old Rough and Ready was every bit as good and true a man, and every whit the hero he is now acknowledged to be. What has he done, but stepped forward to the foot-lights, to receive the applause he deserves? And here let YANKEE DOODLE slip in a sentence, and swear that no lungs are louder, no hands clapped so heartily, and no stick thumped more vehemently than his. Aye! thrice three times three for old ZACK, and, "Damned be he that says Hold, enough." Never mind denting your hats, my lads; toss them into the air!—hurrah! And the ladies, God bless their sweet hearts, how their cambric waves!

It is not our purpose, however, merely to sit perched upon the old hero's shoulder and crow his triumphs; as faithful chroniclers we have something else in view—the circulation of authentic anecdotes, tending to elucidate his character.

And now for something good—nothing less, my countrymen, than the private letters of condolement, hitherto unpublished and unheard of, addressed by old ZACK to SANTA ANNA and other Mexican Generals, upon their successive defeats on the field.

P.S. by YANKEE DOODLE.—It was never intended by their illustrious author that these letters of his should be published. They were written from the dictates of pure and unostentatious benevolence, and solely for the tearful eyes of those to whom they were addressed.

"D—— me, Sir," exclaimed old ZACK, upon our correspondent begging him for copies of the documents in question;—"D—— me, Sir, you can't have 'em! I'll not consent to it—why, you are worse than BARNUM himself, who, yesterday, Major BLISS tells me, wrote on for my private tobacco box, sending a tortoise-shell one as a substitute. No, Sir, those letters can't be published."

"But, my dear Sir, consider the duty you owe to history—to the world—to your own reputation—"

"Well, well—let him have 'em, Major."

And so here they are:

PRIVATE LETTER

ADDRESSED BY MAJOR GENERAL ZACHARY TAYLOR TO GENERAL SANTA ANNA ON THE EVENING SUCCEEDING THE BATTLE OF BUENA VISTA.

NOTE.—The autograph letter presents a remarkable appearance. The characters are almost illegible, and, from certain indications, were most probably traced with the point of a ram-rod on a drum head.

MY DEAR AND MOST AFFLICTED SIR:

Tho' at the call of my country I am your enemy on the field—and tho', as a private gentleman, I have no very elevated notions of your merits, I still consider it my bounden duty, as a fellow creature, to offer you my honest condolence upon this melancholy occasion. You have been beaten, my dear Sir, and tho' I rejoice for my country, I am sincerely sorry for you. But I am most concerned at your inglorious retreat, and at the ridiculous figure you will eventually cut in history.—My dear Sir, I beseech you, for your own sake, as well as mine, that the next time you come to sup on cannon balls, that you will stand up to it like a man, and not bolt two or three and then precipitately leave the table.

I would also respectfully suggest, that a little additional drilling of yourself and troops would not be altogether unprofitable. I would advise, indeed, daily practice at facing bayonets and great guns—so that the next time, you will be able to tell what it is that hurts you.

I regret exceedingly that you should have mistaken our musketry fire for a horizontal falling of hail-stones.

For the future, I am grieved to say that I cannot promise you anything different from what you have already received at my hands. It is my fixed determination to drub you soundly whenever I can, and until you cry *enough*. As for the chance of your ever beating *me*, that, Sir, I cannot hear of. It is out of the question; and I have repeatedly given positive orders to all the troops whom I have the honor to command, not to permit it on any account. My own friendly suggestion to you is, that you had better give up at once and go home and keep quiet. If you do not, but persist in presenting yourself as an object to be repeatedly "*wolloped*," all that I can say is, that "*wolloped*" you shall be to your heart's desire. I wash my hands of all the blood shed at Buena Vista, and remain,

Dear Sir, very respectfully,

And with assurance of high commiseration,

Yours, in the bonds of compassion,

Z. TAYLOR.

The above is the only letter of the batch that has yet come to hand. If the remainder are forwarded to us in time, we shall give them in our next number.

ANECDOTE V

Just before the capitulation of Monterey, Old ZACK had called a council of a few of his chief officers to meet at his quarters, about the time when his dinner is usually served after the deliberations; the old hero with characteristic hospitality invited his fellow soldiers to stay to dinner, which invitation (their quarters not being at that particular time at the Astor House, and a nice smell of hot pie, made out of chickens presented by one desirous of the General's favor, further inducing) was accepted. Just as the hot pie was placed by the General's confidential black servant Sambo, on the table, a round shot struck the table and tin pan, knocking it so as to fall directly on the venerable white head of the brave old hero; in the midst of the confusion caused by this uninvited guest, the hoarse and convulsive laugh of Sambo was heard echoing through the tent, "I 'spect you go now, Massa, lick the Mexicans, you armed *cap a pie*—cause aint you got the hot pie for a cap, ha ha!" On this the General, who hates a pun worse than a Mexican, told Sambo if he dared to make another joke, as bad as that, for the remainder of the campaign, he would send him back to Louisiana.

It is perhaps needless to add that the agent of the individual who is so anxious to secure every relic of General TAYLOR, immediately bought up the damaged tin pan, in which the hot pie had been baked, giving one dozen perfectly new tin pans for the same.

ANECDOTE VI
INFAMOUS PLOT TO OBTAIN POSSESSION OF THE GENERAL

It appears that Sambo who has sold to some sort of agent various articles of dress and furniture belonging to General Taylor; the other day while talking to the old hero, was informed that his principal, who is no other than PETER TAMERLANE B———M, had already possession of one General and hoped soon to get another, and that he need not wonder if he saw his master grinning through the bars of a cage. The next day the General received the following impertinent letter:

DEAR GENERAL:—In case you should resign that post in the armies of your country, which you have filled so nobly, and retire from the fields of warlike powers you have adorned, remember this letter. You have already done enough for your country and for fame; Republics are proverbially ungrateful, and BAJAZET the famous conqueror was exhibited in a cage, remember this. You have been illtreated by the administration, and every press opposed to that administration would justify your resignation. I, then, in the name and behalf of Peter Tamerlane B———, offer you an engagement in a different and highly honorable service. Your salary will be five times the pay of a Major-General in the service of the United States; your rations will be provided for by my principal, you will be associated with all that is curious in nature and art, you will enjoy the society of a General almost as famous as yourself, and more than all you will gratify the lawful desires and advance the happiness of myriads of your countrymen and countrywomen. Can a philanthropist doubt? No, my dear General! I wait with confidence your determination. The easy and only condition will be to surrender yourself entirely to the control and direction of the said Peter Tamerlane B———m, who will treat you no worse than he has the venerable nurse of our beloved Washington and the illustrious General Tom Thumb. Think General, of yourself reclining on the poop of the Chinese Junk, receiving the visits of your friends; adopt this course and you must be elected President; reject it and perhaps—but I forbear to press this matter. I have already sounded Sambo and he appears to have no objection.

Your's on behalf of

P. T. B.

P.S.—We are in treaty for General Antonio Lopez De Santa Anna, and do not know but he will be the better speculation.

It is needless to add that the above insulting missive was torn to a thousand pieces by the indignant old hero, who cautioned Sambo to have no communication with the fellow, who had been so anxious to buy his old clothes, old knives, old forks, old cups, old kettles and old pans, and also to suggest the solemn procession of a ceremonious ride on a Mexican rail, accompanied by the music of the drum solo.

ANECDOTE VII

Nothing has lately occurred to rouse the indignation of old ZACK to such a pitch, as the false and lying version of the celebrated Steamboat story, which has been sent to him in various newspapers from the States. You have of course seen it, and will recollect it describes the General, in the scarcity of births, yielding his own to a sick soldier, and taking his place before the fire in the engine-room, where he was regarded for a long time by the stoker and firemen as some vagabond interloper. He is represented as having passed the better part of the night dozing in the comfortable warmth of its blaze. Now nothing could be more entirely foreign to the restless temper and active habits of the old war horse. The idea of *his* snoozing away a night in front of a Steamboat fire is perfectly ludicrous, nothing could be more grossly absurd. The true state of the case as I have had it from persons who received it directly from the old General's lips, was simply this. There was a sick soldier in the case (one of the Illinoisians, who had caught a severe shot in his neck, on the hard-fought field of Buena Vista,) and to him the General did certainly and most willingly yield up his own comfortable bed. The only embarrassment it occasioned was in the shape of the question, what was he to do with himself for the rest of the night? His first thought was to withdraw to the light of the lamp on the forward deck and spreading himself according to custom on the ground, 'do up' a little mending and patching which his garments at that time happened to require. He found the river air and the fresh breeze from up stream, rather colder than his increasing breadth and fleshiness of constitution would cheerfully endure, and his next thought was of course of the fire. Thither he accordingly repaired, and, always bent on distinguishing himself, the old hero, with the utmost imaginable *sang froid* drew back the door of the oven, with a light spring (surprising in one of his bulkiness) leaped in, and spent the rest of the night in walking about in the flame, and cracking jokes with the firemen or stoker outside, every time his circuit about the oven brought him to the door. At first the stoker was alarmed at what seemed this perilous exposure of the brave old General's person; but when he saw how coolly *he* took it, he entered into the thing—although he kept outside of the fire—with as much spirit as the general himself.

Anecdote VIII

I have procured for you, after many applications and great difficulty, the following communication addressed to yourself, which the General says must be taken as a reply to all letters on the subject, once for all.

DEAR YANKEE DOODLE:—Major Bliss handed to me just now a letter from you. He told me it was upon the Presidency question! I threw it aside at first, with disgust, but the Major told me it was from yourself; I looked at it! I saw that you wish to know my principles! I don't like to commit myself positively; but as a printer, and I'm a sort of a printer myself, having often made a strong impression—you will understand what I say. I shall always endeavor to support the——

D'you understand?
Your's, &c.,
Z. TAYLOR.

ANECDOTE IX

The greatest curiosity is expressed to learn the habits of the old General at table. Constant false reports are flying about the Camp, misrepresenting most grossly his conduct in this respect; when one would think in so plain a matter there could be no opportunity for mistake or mal-information. The errors which are spread about are the more to be wondered at, as witnesses are assuredly not wanting as to the exact state of things: the General's tent being, almost as a matter of course, regularly beset during his meals with lookers on, and the door fairly obstructed with letter-writers note-book in hand, making a minute of every motion of the old hero. What motive these can have for deceiving the public, I cannot imagine unless it be that they are deceived in the first place themselves, mis-apprehending what happens, by reason of the steam, which rises from every dish set before the General, who insists that every thing shall be brought in piping hot. To rectify these deceptions and give you what I have promised from the beginning, authentic and reliable particulars, I have been at some pains for several days past to watch the old General closely, before, at, and immediately after meals. It may be stated as a general truth applicable to the three meals, that the General begins by laying aside his *chapeau* and depositing himself on some sort of settle or other; his present bulk rendering it discomforting and inconvenient to him to partake standing or from on horseback as he used to in the younger and less fleshy period of his life. Seated, he grasps with a firm hold the fork in his left hand and the knife in the right; and in an inappreciably short space of time begins striking right and left in the nearest dish. If the dish should happen (but this is rather a rare chance in camp) to be green peas, the old hero makes indiscriminate play with either hand, tossing the vegetables down his grand old throat pitch-fork fashion at one time, and the next minute sending them home to their destination with shovel-like profusion. His habit is perhaps most marked and striking, and most characteristic of the great strategist he is, when the dish to be disposed of is the common or apple-dumpling. Here he brings into play all the resources of his long experience and practised military skill. It may be premised that the General hates a hot dumpling as he hates the devil; and it is in consequence of this settled feeling that he eyes the smoking pile for several minutes after they are set upon the table before he will touch one of them. His proceedings, even after he has made up his mind to a venture, are extremely cautious and reserved. At first he selects one from the smoking platter, the smallest to start with, and begins tossing it gently, something in the manner of a conjuror with a ball, into the air. Presently he selects a second and sends up after the first, a third joins it and a fourth, and these he keeps in motion juggler-like, for some minutes, when he allows them to descend one by one to the plate, to the last; this he takes upon his fork as it descends, and contemplates in that exposed position with great gravity and steadiness for several minutes; what his object may be in this survey no human being has been able to conjecture. Some suppose that he sees in the spherical piece of pastry, a microcosm or miniature world, and that he is revolving great political events and the possible future destiny of our globe, from the universal spread of republican principles during his coming Presidency. Others have thought that nearer personal considerations affected him, and that at such moments he must be calling to mind his friend, the editor of the New York *Mirror*. It should be observed that he always selects the softest of the dumplings as the subject of these singular contemplations.

With regard to the old General's course after meal, there could be no fouler slander than that which asserts he is accustomed to wipe his mouth on his coat-tail. It is simply untrue, and for a plain reason, he has no coat-tail about him on such occasions, but uniformly and invariably breakfasts, dines and sups in a camp-roundabout or bob. False as are all the other stories in reference to OLD ZACK's private habits, this latter fact is so well known, that I have had innumerable applications during the last three months, from all parts of the Union, for one of the General's old roundabouts. Mr. BARNUM has one which he will exhibit early in September, at his museum, for the satisfaction of the curious. I have also been able to forward one to Secretary MARCY, who, I am told, does the old General the honor to wear it when writing all his official dispatches to him, particularly when he is disposed to put the old hero on a short allowance of troops, the brevity of the garment seeming to harmonize with the nature and character of the communication. From these constant appropriations which require to be replenished, I am sure nothing would be more gratifying to the feelings of old ZACK, than if you would go to BROOKS & SON, corner of Catharine and Cherry Streets, N. Y., and order down to the Camp, a box of their most substantial brown roundabouts, large over the back and free in the arms. Please address Z. TAYLOR, United States Camp, MEXICO.

Mr Parkman's Tour

The California and Oregon Trail; being Sketches of Prairie and Rocky Mountain Life. By
Francis Parkman, Jr. With Illustrations by Darley. Putnam.

MR PARKMAN'S BOOK is the record of some months' adventures in the year 1846 among the Indian tribes scattered between the Western boundary of Missouri and the
Rocky Mountains. Though without literary pretension, it is a
very entertaining work, straightforward and simple throughout, and obviously truthful.

The title will be apt to mislead. There is nothing about
California or Oregon in the book; but though we like it the
better for this, the title is not the less ill-chosen. And here
we must remind all authors of a fact, which sometimes
seems to slip their memory. The christening of books is
very different from the christening of men. Among men,
the object of a name is to individualize; hence, that object
is gained whatever name you bestow, though it be wholly
irrespective of the character of the person named. Not thus
with books; whose names or titles are presumed to express
the contents. And, although during this present gold fever,
patriotic fathers have a perfect right to christen their offspring "Sacramento," or "California"; we deny this privilege
to authors, with respect to their books. For example, a
work on Botany published to day, should not be entitled
"California, or Buds and Flowers"; on the contrary, the
"California" should be dropped. For the correctness of our
judgement in this matter we are willing to appeal to any
sensible man in the community (provided he has no thought
of emigrating to the gold region); nay, we will leave the matter to Mr Parkman himself.—

Possibly, however, it may be urged that the title is correct
after all—"California and the Oregon Trail"—inasmuch, as
the route or "trail" pursued by Mr Parkman towards the
Rocky Mountains would be the one pursued by a traveller
bound overland to the Pacific. Very true. And it would also
be part of the route followed by a traveller bound due West
from Missouri to Pekin or Bombay. But we again appeal to
any sensible man whether the "Pekin and Bombay Trail"

would be a correct title for a book of travels in a region lying East of the Rocky Mountains.

In a brief and appropriate preface Mr Parkman adverts to the representations of the Indian character given by poets and novelists, which he asserts are for the most part mere creations of fancy. He adds that "the Indian is certainly entitled to a high rank among savages, but his good qualities are not those of an Uncas or Outalissi." Now, this is not to be gainsaid. But when in the body of the book we are informed that it is difficult for any white man, after a domestication among the Indians, to hold them much better than brutes; when we are told too, that to such a person, the slaughter of an Indian is indifferent as the slaughter of a buffalo; with all deference, we beg leave to dissent.

It is too often the case, that civilized beings sojourning among savages soon come to regard them with disdain and contempt. But though in many cases this feeling is almost natural, it is not defensible; and it is wholly wrong. Why should we contemn them?—Because we are better than they? Assuredly not; for herein we are rebuked by the story of the Publican and the Pharisee.—Because, then, that in many things we are happier?—But this should be ground for commiseration, not disdain. Xavier and Eliot despised not the savages; and had Newton or Milton dwelt among them, they would not have done so.—When we affect to contemn savages, we should remember that by so doing we asperse our own progenitors; for they were savages also. Who can swear that among the naked British barbarians sent to Rome to be stared at more than 1500 years ago, the ancestor of Bacon might not have been found?—Why, among the very Thugs of India, or the bloody Dyaks of Borneo, exists the germ of all that is intellectually elevated and grand. We are all of us—Anglo-Saxons, Dyaks, and Indians—sprung from one head and made in one image. And if we reject this brotherhood now, we shall be forced to join hands hereafter.—A misfortune is not a fault; and good luck is not meritorious. The savage is born a savage; and the civilized being but inherits his civilization, nothing more. Let us not disdain then, but pity. And wherever we recognize the image of God let us reverence it; though it swing from the gallows.

We have found one fault with the title, and another with the matter of the book; this done, the unpleasantness of fault-finding is done; and gladly we turn.

Mr Parkman's sole object, he tells us, in penetrating into the Land of Moccasons, was to gratify a curiosity he had felt from boyhood:—to inform himself accurately of Indian life. And it may well be expected that with such an object in view, the travels of an educated man, should, when published, impart to others the knowledge he himself sought to attain. And this holds true concerning the book before us. As a record of gentlemanly adventure among our Indian tribes it is by far the most pleasant book which has ever fallen in our way. The style is easy and free, quite flowingly correct. There are no undue sallies of fancy, and no attempts at wit which flash in the pan.

Accompanied by his friend Mr Quincy A. Shaw, our young author sets forth from St Louis, that city of outward-bound caravans for the West, and which is to the praries, what Cairo is to the Desert. At St Louis the friends engaged the services of Delorier, a gay cheerful Canadian, and Henry Chatillon, a hunter, who as guides went out and returned with them.—

In a steamer, crammed with all sorts of adventurers, Spaniards and Indians, Santa-Fe traders and trappers, gamblers and Mormons, the party ascend the Mississippi and Missouri, and at last debark on the banks of the latter stream at a point on the verge of the wilderness. Here they tarry awhile, amused with the strange aspect of things. They visit a man in whose house is a shelf for books, and where they observe a curious illustration of life: they find a holster-pistol standing guard over a copy of Paradise Lost. We presume, then, that on our Western frontier, when a man desires to soar with Milton, he does so with his book in one hand, and a pistol in the other; which last, indeed, might help him in sustaining an "armed neutrality" during the terrible but bloodless battles between Captain Beelzebub and that gallant warrior Michael.

From the banks of the Missouri the adventurers push straight out into the praries; and when they cast off their horses' halters from the post before the log-cabin door, they do as sailors, when they unmoor their cables, and set sail for sea.—They start well provided with horses and mules, rifles and powder, food and medicine, good will and stout hearts.

After encountering certain caravans of Oregon emigrants, the first place of note they arrive at is Fort Laramie, a fortified trading post near a stream tributary to the Platte river.— Here for some days they lounge upon Buffalo robes and eat Buffalo meat, and smoke Indian pipes among mongrel swarms of Canadians and Indians.

We cannot attempt to follow the friends through all their wild rovings. But he who desires to throw himself unreservedly into all the perilous charms of prarie life; to camp out by night in the wilderness, standing guard against prowling Indians and wolves; to ford rivers and creeks; to hunt buffalo, and kill them at full gallop in the saddle, and afterwards banquet on delectable roasted "hump-ribs"; to lodge with Indian warriors in their villages and receive the hospitalities of polite squaws in brass and vermillion; to hear of wars and rumors of wars among the hostile tribes of savages; to listen to the wildest and most romantic little tales of border and wilderness life; in short, he who desires to quit Broadway and the Bowery—though only in fancy—for the region of wampum and calumet, the land of beavers and buffalo— birch canoes and "smoked buckskin shirts" will do well to read Mr Parkman's book. There he will fall in with the veritable grandsons of Daniel Boon; with the Mormons; with war-parties; with Santa Fe traders; with General Kearney; with runaway United States troops; and all manner of outlandish and interesting characters.

There, too, he will make the acquaintance of Henry Chatillon Esq., as gallant a gentleman and hunter-and-trapper as ever shot buffalo. For this Henry Chatillon we feel a fresh and unbounded love. He belongs to a class of men, of whom Kit Carson is the model; a class, unique and not to be transcended in interest by any personages introduced to us by Scott. Long live and hunt Henry Chatillon! May his good rifle never miss fire; and where he roves through the praries, may the buffalo forever abound!

The Reader too will make the acquaintance of Mr Quincy A. Shaw, a high-spirited young gentleman, who always hunted his buffalo, somewhat like Murat charging at the head of cavalry—in wild and ornate attire. He sported richly worked Indian leggins, a red tunic and sash; and let loose among a herd of bison, did execution like our fierce friend Alp in Byron's "Siege of Corinth"—piling the dead round him in semicircles.—Returned from his hunting tour across the Western hemisphere, Mr Shaw, we learn, is now among the wild Bedouins of Arabia.

The book, in brief, is excellent, and has the true wild-game flavor. And amazingly tickled will all their palates be, who are so lucky as to read it. It has two pictorial illustrations by the well-known and talented artist Darley, one of which is exceedingly good.

In conclusion we can not omit mentioning that the book was put together under a most sad and serious disadvantage. Owing to the remote effects of a sickness contracted through the wild experiences of prarie life, the author was obliged to compose his work, throughout, by dictation.

Among numerous fine and dashing descriptive chapters we have only room for the following.

Cooper's New Novel

The Sea Lions; or, The Lost Sealers: a Tale of the Antarctic Ocean. By J. Fenimore Cooper. 2 vols. 12mo. Stringer & Townsend.

The Sea Lions, or The Lost Sealers! An attractive title truly. Nor does this last of Cooper's novels disappoint the promise held forth on the title page.

The story opens on the sea coast of Suffolk County, Long Island; and turns mainly upon the mysterious existence of certain wild islands within the Antarctic Circle, whose precise whereabouts is known but to a choice few, and whose latitude and longitude even the author declares he is not at liberty to make known. For this region, impelled by adverse, if not hostile motives, the two vessels—the Sea Lions—in due time sail, under circumstances full of romance.

After encountering a violent gale, described with a force peculiarly Cooper's, they at last reach the Antarctic seas, finding themselves walled in by "thrilling regions of rock-ribbed ice". Few descriptions of the lonely and the terrible, we imagine, can surpass the grandeur of many of the scenes here depicted. The reader is reminded of the appalling adventures of the United States Exploring Ship in the same part of the world as narrated by Wilkes, and of Scoresby's Greenland narrative.—In these inhospitable regions the hardy crews of the Sea Lions winter,—not snugly at anchor under the lee of a Dutch stove, nor baking and browning over the ovens by which the Muscovite warms himself—but jammed in, masoned up, bolted and barred, and almost hermetically sealed by the ice.—To keep from freezing into chrystal they are fain to turn part of their vessels into fuel.—All this, and much more of the like nature, are told in a style singularly plain, downright and truthful.

At length, after many narrow escapes from ice-bergs, ice-isles, fields and floes of ice, the mariners, at least most of them, make good their return to the North, where the action of the book is crowned by the nuptials of Roswell Gardiner the hero and Mary Pratt the heroine. Roswell we admire for a noble fellow; and Mary we love for a fine example of womanly affection, earnestness, and constancy.—Deacon Pratt, her respected father, is a hard-handed, hard-hearted, psalm-singing old man, with a very stretchy conscience; intent upon getting to heaven, and getting money by the same course of conduct, in defiance of the scriptural maxim to the contrary. There is a good deal of wisdom to be gathered from the story of the Deacon.

Then we have one Stimson, an old Kennebunk boatsteerer, and Professor of Theology, who, wintering on an ice-berg, discourses most unctuously upon various dogmas. This honest old worthy may possibly be recognized for an old acquaintance by the readers of Cooper's novels.—But who would have dreampt of his turning up at the South Pole?—One of the subordinate parts of the book is the timely conversion of Roswell the hero from a too latitudinarian view of Christianity to a more orthodox, and hence a better belief. And as the reader will perceive, the moist rosy hand of our Mary is the reward of his orthodoxy. Somewhat in the pleasant spirit of the Mahometan, this; who rewards all true believers with a houri.

Upon the whole, we warmly recommend The Sea Lions. And even those who more for fashion's sake than any thing else, have of late joined in decrying our National Novelist, will in this last work perhaps recognize one of his happiest.

A Thought on Book-Binding

The Red Rover. By J. Fenimore Cooper. Revised edition. Putnam.

THE SIGHT of the far-famed Red Rover sailing under the sober hued muslin wherewith Mr Putnam equips his lighter sort of craft begets in us a fastidious feeling touching the propriety of such a binding for such a book. Not that we ostentatiously pretend to any elevated degree of artistic taste in this matter;—our remarks are but limited to our egotistical fancies. Egotistically, then, we would have preferred for the "Red Rover" a flaming suit of flame-colored morrocco, as evanescently thin and gauze-like as possible, so that the binding might happily correspond with the sanguinary fugitive title of the book. Still better, perhaps, were it bound in jet black, with a red streak round the borders (pirate fashion)—or, upon third thoughts, omit the streak, and substitute a square of blood-colored bunting on the back, imprinted with the title, so that the flag of the "Red Rover" might be congenially flung to the popular breeze after the buccaneer fashion of Morgan, Black-Beard, and other free and easy, daredevil, accomplished gentlemen of the sea.

While throwing out these cursory suggestions, we gladly acknowledge that the tasteful publisher has attached to the volume, a very felicitous touch of the sea superstitions of pirates. In the mysterious cyphers in book-binders' relievo stamped upon the covers we joyfully recognize a poetical signification and pictorial shadowing forth of the horse-shoe, which in all honest and God-fearing piratical vessels is invariably found nailed to the mast.—By force of contrast this clever device reminds us of the sad lack of invention in most of our bookbinders. Books, gentlemen, are a species of men, and introduced to them you circulate in the "very best society" that this world can furnish, without the intolerable infliction of "dressing" to go into it. In your shabbiest coat and cosiest slippers you may socially chat even with the fastidious Earl of Chesterfield, and lounging under a tree enjoy the divinest intimacy with my late lord of Verulam. Men, then, that they are—living, without vulgarly breathing—never speaking unless spoken to—books should be appropriately apparelled.

Their bindings should indicate and distinguish their various characters. A crowd of illustrations press upon us, but we must dismiss them at present with the simple expression of the hope that our suggestion may not entirely be thrown away.

That we have said thus much concerning the mere outside of the book whose title prefaces this notice, is sufficient evidence of the fact that at the present day we deem any elaborate criticism of Cooper's Red Rover quite unnecessary and uncalled-for. Long ago, and far inland, we read it in our uncritical days, and enjoyed it as much as thousands of the rising generation will when supplied with such an entertaining volume in such agreeable type.

Hawthorne and His Mosses

By a Virginian Spending July in Vermont

A PAPERED CHAMBER in a fine old farm-house—a mile from any other dwelling, and dipped to the eaves in foliage—surrounded by mountains, old woods, and Indian ponds,—this, surely, is the place to write of Hawthorne. Some charm is in this northern air, for love and duty seem both impelling to the task. A man of a deep and noble nature has seized me in this seclusion. His wild, witch voice rings through me; or, in softer cadences, I seem to hear it in the songs of the hill-side birds, that sing in the larch trees at my window.

Would that all excellent books were foundlings, without father or mother, that so it might be, we could glorify them, without including their ostensible authors. Nor would any true man take exception to this;—least of all, he who writes,—"When the Artist rises high enough to achieve the Beautiful, the symbol by which he makes it perceptible to mortal senses becomes of little value in his eyes, while his spirit possesses itself in the enjoyment of the reality."

But more than this. I know not what would be the right name to put on the title-page of an excellent book, but this I feel, that the names of all fine authors are fictitious ones, far more so than that of Junius,—simply standing, as they do, for the mystical, ever-eluding Spirit of all Beauty, which ubiquitously possesses men of genius. Purely imaginative as this fancy may appear, it nevertheless seems to receive some warranty from the fact, that on a personal interview no great author has ever come up to the idea of his reader. But that dust of which our bodies are composed, how can it fitly express the nobler intelligences among us? With reverence be it spoken, that not even in the case of one deemed more than man, not even in our Saviour, did his visible frame betoken anything of the augustness of the nature within. Else, how could those Jewish eyewitnesses fail to see heaven in his glance.

It is curious, how a man may travel along a country road, and yet miss the grandest, or sweetest of prospects, by reason of an intervening hedge, so like all other hedges, as in no way to hint of the wide landscape beyond. So has it been with me concerning the enchanting landscape in the soul of this Hawthorne, this most excellent Man of Mosses. His "Old Manse" has been written now four years, but I never read it till a day or two since. I had seen it in the book-stores—heard of it often—even had it recommended to me by a tasteful friend, as a rare, quiet book, perhaps too deserving of popularity to be popular. But there are so many books called "excellent", and so much unpopular merit, that amid the thick stir of other things, the hint of my tasteful friend was disregarded; and for four years the Mosses on the old Manse never refreshed me with their perennial green. It may be, however, that all this while, the book, like wine, was only improving in flavor and body. At any rate, it so chanced that this long procrastination eventuated in a happy result. At breakfast the other day, a mountain girl, a cousin of mine, who for the last two weeks has every morning helped me to strawberries and raspberries,—which, like the roses and pearls in the fairy-tale, seemed to fall into the saucer from those strawberry-beds her cheeks,—this delightful creature, this charming Cherry says to me—"I see you spend your mornings in the hay-mow; and yesterday I found there 'Dwight's Travels in New England'. Now I have something far better than that,—something more congenial to our summer on these hills. Take these raspberries, and then I will give you some moss."—"Moss!" said I.—"Yes, and you must take it to the barn with you, and good-bye to 'Dwight' ".

With that she left me, and soon returned with a volume, verdantly bound, and garnished with a curious frontispiece in green,—nothing less, than a fragment of real moss cunningly pressed to a fly-leaf.—"Why this," said I spilling my raspberries, "this is the 'Mosses from an Old Manse.' " "Yes" said cousin Cherry "yes, it is that flowery Hawthorne."—"Hawthorne and Mosses" said I "no more: it is morning: it is July in the country: and I am off for the barn".

Stretched on that new mown clover, the hill-side breeze blowing over me through the wide barn door, and soothed by the hum of the bees in the meadows around, how magically stole over me this Mossy Man! and how amply, how bountifully, did he redeem that delicious promise to his guests in the Old Manse, of whom it is written—"Others could give them pleasure, or amusement, or instruction—these could be picked up anywhere—but it was for me to give them rest. Rest, in a life of trouble! What better could be done for weary and world-worn spirits? what better could be done for anybody, who came within our magic circle, than to throw the spell of a magic spirit over him?"—So all that day, half-buried in the new clover, I watched this Hawthorne's "Assyrian dawn, and Paphian sunset and moonrise, from the summit of our Eastern Hill."

The soft ravishments of the man spun me round about in a web of dreams, and when the book was closed, when the spell was over, this wizard "dismissed me with but misty reminiscences, as if I had been dreaming of him".

What a mild moonlight of contemplative humor bathes that Old Manse!—the rich and rare distilment of a spicy and slowly-oozing heart. No rollicking rudeness, no gross fun fed on fat dinners, and bred in the lees of wine,—but a humor so spiritually gentle, so high, so deep, and yet so richly relishable, that it were hardly inappropriate in an angel. It is the very religion of mirth; for nothing so human but it may be advanced to that. The orchard of the Old Manse seems the visible type of the fine mind that has described it. Those twisted, and contorted old trees, "that stretch out their crooked branches, and take such hold of the imagination, that we remember them as humorists, and odd-fellows." And then, as surrounded by these grotesque forms, and hushed in the noon-day repose of this Hawthorne's spell, how aptly might the still fall of his ruddy thoughts into your soul be symbolized by "the thump of a great apple, in the stillest afternoon, falling without a breath of wind, from the mere necessity of perfect ripeness"! For no less ripe than ruddy are the apples of the thoughts and fancies in this sweet Man of Mosses.

"Buds and Bird-voices"—What a delicious thing is that!—"Will the world ever be so decayed, that Spring may not renew its greenness?"—And the "Fire-Worship". Was ever the hearth so glorified into an altar before? The mere title of that piece is better than any common work in fifty folio volumes. How exquisite is this:—"Nor did it lessen the charm of his soft, familiar courtesy and helpfulness, that the mighty spirit, were opportunity offered him, would run riot through the peaceful house, wrap its inmates in his terrible embrace, and leave nothing of them save their whitened bones. This possibility of mad destruction only made his domestic kindness the more beautiful and touching. It was so sweet of him, being endowed with such power, to dwell, day after day, and one long, lonesome night after another, on the dusky hearth, only now and then betraying his wild nature, by thrusting his red tongue out of the chimney-top! True, he had done much mischief in the world, and was pretty certain to do more, but his warm heart atoned for all. He was kindly to the race of man."

But he has still other apples, not quite so ruddy, though full as ripe;—apples, that have been left to wither on the tree, after the pleasant autumn gathering is past. The sketch of "The Old Apple Dealer" is conceived in the subtlest spirit of sadness; he whose "subdued and nerveless boyhood prefigured his abortive prime, which, likewise, contained within itself the prophecy and image of his lean and torpid age". Such touches as are in this piece can not proceed from any common heart. They argue such a depth of tenderness, such a boundless sympathy with all forms of being, such an omnipresent love, that we must needs say, that this Hawthorne is here almost alone in his generation,—at least, in the artistic manifestation of these things. Still more. Such touches as these,—and many, very many similar ones, all through his chapters—furnish clews, whereby we enter a little way into the intricate, profound heart where they originated. And we see, that suffering, some time or other and in some shape or other,—this only can enable any man to depict it in others. All over him, Hawthorne's melancholy rests like an Indian Summer, which though bathing a whole country in one softness, still reveals the distinctive hue of every towering hill, and each far-winding vale.

But it is the least part of genius that attracts admiration. Where Hawthorne is known, he seems to be deemed a pleasant writer, with a pleasant style,—a sequestered, harmless man, from whom any deep and weighty thing would hardly be anticipated:—a man who means no meanings. But there is no man, in whom humor and love, like mountain peaks, soar to such a rapt height, as to receive the irradiations of the upper skies;—there is no man in whom humor and love are developed in that high form called genius; no such man can exist without also possessing, as the indispensable complement of these, a great, deep intellect, which drops down into the universe like a plummet. Or, love and humor are only the eyes, through which such an intellect views this world. The great beauty in such a mind is but the product of its strength. What, to all readers, can be more charming than the piece entitled "Monsieur du Miroir"; and to a reader at all capable of fully fathoming it, what, at the same time, can possess more mystical depth of meaning?—Yes, there he sits, and looks at me,—this "shape of mystery", this "identical Monsieur du Miroir".—"Methinks I should tremble now, were his wizard power of gliding through all impediments in search of me, to place him suddenly before my eyes".

How profound, nay appalling, is the moral evolved by the "Earth's Holocaust"; where—beginning with the hollow follies and affectations of the world,—all vanities and empty theories and forms, are, one after another, and by an admirably graduated, growing comprehensiveness, thrown into the allegorical fire, till, at length, nothing is left but the all-engendering heart of man; which remaining still unconsumed, the great conflagration is nought.

Of a piece with this, is the "Intelligence Office", a wondrous symbolizing of the secret workings in men's souls. There are other sketches, still more charged with ponderous import.

"The Christmas Banquet" and "The Bosom Serpent" would be fine subjects for a curious and elaborate analysis, touching the conjectural parts of the mind that produced them. For spite of all the Indian-summer sunlight on the hither side of Hawthorne's soul, the other side—like the dark half of the physical sphere—is shrouded in a blackness, ten times black. But this darkness but gives more effect to the ever-moving dawn, that forever advances through it, and circumnavigates his world. Whether Hawthorne has simply availed himself of this mystical blackness as a means to the wondrous effects he makes it to produce in his lights and shades; or whether there really lurks in him, perhaps unknown to himself, a touch of Puritanic gloom,—this, I cannot altogether tell. Certain it is, however, that this great power of blackness in him derives its force from its appeals to that Calvinistic sense of Innate Depravity and Original Sin, from whose visitations, in some shape or other, no deeply thinking mind is always and wholly free. For, in certain moods, no man can weigh this world, without throwing in something, somehow like Original Sin, to strike the uneven balance. At all events, perhaps no writer has ever wielded this terrific thought with greater terror than this same harmless Hawthorne. Still more: this black conceit pervades him, through and through. You may be witched by his sunlight,—transported by the bright gildings in the skies he builds over you;—but there is the blackness of darkness beyond; and even his bright gildings but fringe, and play upon the edges of thunder-clouds.—In one word, the world is mistaken in this Nathaniel Hawthorne. He himself must often have smiled at its absurd misconception of him. He is immeasurably deeper than the plummet of the mere critic. For it is not the brain that can test such a man; it is only the heart. You cannot come to know greatness by inspecting it; there is no glimpse to be caught of it, except by intuition; you need not ring it, you but touch it, and you find it is gold.

Now it is that blackness in Hawthorne, of which I have spoken, that so fixes and fascinates me. It may be, nevertheless, that it is too largely developed in him. Perhaps he does not give us a ray of his light for every shade of his dark. But however this may be, this blackness it is that furnishes the infinite obscure of his back-ground,—that back-ground, against which Shakespeare plays his grandest conceits, the things that have made for Shakespeare his loftiest, but most circumscribed renown, as the profoundest of thinkers. For by philosophers Shakespeare is not adored as the great man of tragedy and comedy.—"Off with his head! so much for Buckingham!" this sort of rant, interlined by another hand, brings down the house,—those mistaken souls, who dream of Shakespeare as a mere man of Richard-the-Third humps, and Macbeth daggers. But it is those deep far-away things in him; those occasional flashings-forth of the intuitive Truth in him; those short, quick probings at the very axis of reality;—

these are the things that make Shakespeare, Shakespeare. Through the mouths of the dark characters of Hamlet, Timon, Lear, and Iago, he craftily says, or sometimes insinuates the things, which we feel to be so terrifically true, that it were all but madness for any good man, in his own proper character, to utter, or even hint of them. Tormented into desperation, Lear the frantic King tears off the mask, and speaks the sane madness of vital truth. But, as I before said, it is the least part of genius that attracts admiration. And so, much of the blind, unbridled admiration that has been heaped upon Shakespeare, has been lavished upon the least part of him. And few of his endless commentators and critics seem to have remembered, or even perceived, that the immediate products of a great mind are not so great, as that undeveloped, (and sometimes undevelopable) yet dimly-discernable greatness, to which these immediate products are but the infallible indices. In Shakespeare's tomb lies infinitely more than Shakspeare ever wrote. And if I magnify Shakespeare, it is not so much for what he did do, as for what he did not do, or refrained from doing. For in this world of lies, Truth is forced to fly like a scared white doe in the woodlands; and only by cunning glimpses will she reveal herself, as in Shakespeare and other masters of the great Art of Telling the Truth,—even though it be covertly, and by snatches.

But if this view of the all-popular Shakespeare be seldom taken by his readers, and if very few who extol him, have ever read him deeply, or, perhaps, only have seen him on the tricky stage, (which alone made, and is still making him his mere mob renown)—if few men have time, or patience, or palate, for the spiritual truth as it is in that great genius;—it is, then, no matter of surprise that in a contemporaneous age, Nathaniel Hawthorne is a man, as yet, almost utterly mistaken among men. Here and there, in some quiet arm-chair in the noisy town, or some deep nook among the noiseless mountains, he may be appreciated for something of what he is. But unlike Shakespeare, who was forced to the contrary course by circumstances, Hawthorne (either from simple disinclination, or else from inaptitude) refrains from all the popularizing noise and show of broad farce, and blood-besmeared tragedy; content with the still, rich utterances of a great intellect in repose, and which sends few thoughts into circulation, except they be arterialized at his large warm lungs, and expanded in his honest heart.

Nor need you fix upon that blackness in him, if it suit you not. Nor, indeed, will all readers discern it, for it is, mostly, insinuated to those who may best understand it, and account for it; it is not obtruded upon every one alike.

Some may start to read of Shakespeare and Hawthorne on the same page. They may say, that if an illustration were needed, a lesser light might have sufficed to elucidate this Hawthorne, this small man of yesterday. But I am not, willingly, one of those, who, as touching Shakespeare at least, exemplify the maxim of Rochefoucault, that "we exalt the reputation of some, in order to depress that of others";— who, to teach all noble-souled aspirants that there is no hope for them, pronounce Shakespeare absolutely unapproachable. But Shakespeare has been approached. There are minds that have gone as far as Shakespeare into the universe. And hardly a mortal man, who, at some time or other, has not felt as great thoughts in him as any you will find in Hamlet. We must not inferentially malign mankind for the sake of any one man, whoever he may be. This is too cheap a purchase of contentment for conscious mediocrity to make. Besides, this absolute and unconditional adoration of Shakespeare has grown to be a part of our Anglo Saxon superstitions. The Thirty Nine articles are now Forty. Intolerance has come to exist in this matter. You must believe in Shakespeare's unapproachability, or quit the country. But what sort of a belief is this for an American, a man who is bound to carry republican progressiveness into Literature, as well as into Life? Believe me, my friends, that Shakespeares are this day being born on the banks of the Ohio. And the day will come, when you shall say who reads a book by an Englishman that is a modern? The great mistake seems to be, that even with those Americans who look forward to the coming of a great literary genius among us, they somehow fancy he will come in the costume of Queen Elizabeth's day,—be a writer of dramas founded upon old English history, or the tales of Boccaccio. Whereas, great geniuses are parts of the times; they themselves are the times; and possess a correspondent coloring. It is of a piece with the Jews, who while their Shiloh was meekly walking in their streets, were still praying for his magnificent coming; looking for him in a chariot, who was already among them on an ass. Nor must we forget, that, in his own life-time, Shakespeare was not Shakespeare, but only Master William Shakespeare of the shrewd, thriving, business firm of Condell, Shakespeare & Co., proprietors of the Globe Theatre in London; and by a courtly author, of the name of Greene, was hooted at, as an "upstart crow" beautified "with other birds' feathers." For, mark it well, imitation is often the first charge brought against real originality. Why this is so, there is not space to set forth here. You must have plenty of sea-room to tell the Truth in; especially, when it seems to have an aspect of newness, as America did in 1492, though it was then just as old, and perhaps older than Asia, only those sagacious philosophers, the common sailors, had never seen it before; swearing it was all water and moonshine there.

Now, I do not say that Nathaniel of Salem is a greater than William of Avon, or as great. But the difference between the two men is by no means immeasurable. Not a very great deal more, and Nathaniel were verily William.

This, too, I mean, that if Shakespeare has not been equalled, he is sure to be surpassed, and surpassed by an American born now or yet to be born. For it will never do for us who in most other things out-do as well as out-brag the world, it will not do for us to fold our hands and say, In the highest department advance there is none. Nor will it at all do to say, that the world is getting grey and grizzled now, and has lost that fresh charm which she wore of old, and by virtue of which the great poets of past times made themselves what we esteem them to be. Not so. The world is as young today, as when it was created; and this Vermont morning dew is as wet to my feet, as Eden's dew to Adam's. Nor has Nature been all over ransacked by our progenitors, so that no new charms and mysteries remain for this latter generation to find. Far from it. The trillionth part has not yet been said; and all that has been said, but multiplies the avenues to what remains to be said. It is not so much paucity, as superabundance of material that seems to incapacitate modern authors.

Let America then prize and cherish her writers; yea, let her glorify them. They are not so many in number, as to exhaust her good-will. And while she has good kith and kin of her own, to take to her bosom, let her not lavish her embraces upon the household of an alien. For believe it or not England, after all, is, in many things, an alien to us. China has more bowels of real love for us than she. But even were there no Hawthorne, no Emerson, no Whittier, no Irving, no Bryant, no Dana, no Cooper, no Willis (not the author of the "Dashes", but the author of the "Belfry Pigeon")—were there none of these, and others of like calibre among us, nevertheless, let America first praise mediocrity, even in her own children, before she praises (for everywhere, merit demands acknowledgment from every one) the best excellence in the children of any other land. Let her own authors, I say, have the priority of appreciation. I was much pleased with a hot-headed Carolina cousin of mine, who once said,—"If there were no other American to stand by, in Literature,—why, then, I would stand by Pop Emmons and his 'Fredoniad,' and till a better epic came along, swear it was not very far behind the Iliad." Take away the words, and in spirit he was sound.

Not that American genius needs patronage in order to expand. For that explosive sort of stuff will expand though screwed up in a vice, and burst it, though it were triple steel. It is for the nation's sake, and not for her authors' sake, that I would have America be heedful of the increasing greatness among her writers. For how great the shame, if other nations should be before her, in crowning her heroes of the pen. But this is almost the case now. American authors have received more just and discriminating praise (however loftily and ridiculously given, in certain cases) even from some Englishmen, than from their own countrymen. There are hardly five critics in America; and several of them are asleep. As for patronage, it is the American author who now patronizes his country, and not his country him. And if at times some among them appeal to the people for more recognition, it is not always with selfish motives, but patriotic ones.

It is true, that but few of them as yet have evinced that decided originality which merits great praise. But that graceful writer, who perhaps of all Americans has received the

most plaudits from his own country for his productions,—
that very popular and amiable writer, however good, and self-
reliant in many things, perhaps owes his chief reputation to
the self-acknowledged imitation of a foreign model, and to
the studied avoidance of all topics but smooth ones. But it is
better to fail in originality, than to succeed in imitation. He
who has never failed somewhere, that man can not be great.
Failure is the true test of greatness. And if it be said, that
continual success is a proof that a man wisely knows his powers,—it is only to be added, that, in that case, he knows them
to be small. Let us believe it, then, once for all, that there is
no hope for us in these smooth pleasing writers that know
their powers. Without malice, but to speak the plain fact, they
but furnish an appendix to Goldsmith, and other English authors. And we want no American Goldsmiths; nay, we want
no American Miltons. It were the vilest thing you could say
of a true American author, that he were an American Tomp-
kins. Call him an American, and have done; for you can not
say a nobler thing of him.—But it is not meant that all American writers should studiously cleave to nationality in their
writings; only this, no American writer should write like an
Englishman, or a Frenchman; let him write like a man, for
then he will be sure to write like an American. Let us away
with this Bostonian leaven of literary flunkeyism towards England. If either must play the flunkey in this thing, let
England do it, not us. And the time is not far off when
circumstances may force her to it. While we are rapidly preparing for that political supremacy among the nations, which
prophetically awaits us at the close of the present century; in
a literary point of view, we are deplorably unprepared for it;
and we seem studious to remain so. Hitherto, reasons might
have existed why this should be; but no good reason exists
now. And all that is requisite to amendment in this matter, is
simply this: that, while freely acknowledging all excellence,
everywhere, we should refrain from unduly lauding foreign
writers and, at the same time, duly recognize the meritorious
writers that are our own;—those writers, who breathe that
unshackled, democratic spirit of Christianity in all things,
which now takes the practical lead in this world, though at
the same time led by ourselves—us Americans. Let us boldly

contemn all imitation, though it comes to us graceful and fragrant as the morning; and foster all originality, though, at first, it be crabbed and ugly as our own pine knots. And if any of our authors fail, or seem to fail, then, in the words of my enthusiastic Carolina cousin, let us clap him on the shoulder, and back him against all Europe for his second round. The truth is, that in our point of view, this matter of a national literature has come to such a pass with us, that in some sense we must turn bullies, else the day is lost, or superiority so far beyond us, that we can hardly say it will ever be ours.

And now, my countrymen, as an excellent author, of your own flesh and blood,—an unimitating, and, perhaps, in his way, an inimitable man—whom better can I commend to you, in the first place, than Nathaniel Hawthorne. He is one of the new, and far better generation of your writers. The smell of your beeches and hemlocks is upon him; your own broad praries are in his soul; and if you travel away inland into his deep and noble nature, you will hear the far roar of his Niagara. Give not over to future generations the glad duty of acknowledging him for what he is. Take that joy to your self, in your own generation; and so shall he feel those grateful impulses in him, that may possibly prompt him to the full flower of some still greater achievement in your eyes. And by confessing him, you thereby confess others; you brace the whole brotherhood. For genius, all over the world, stands hand in hand, and one shock of recognition runs the whole circle round.

In treating of Hawthorne, or rather of Hawthorne in his writings (for I never saw the man; and in the chances of a quiet plantation life, remote from his haunts, perhaps never shall) in treating of his works, I say, I have thus far omitted all mention of his "Twice Told Tales", and "Scarlet Letter". Both are excellent; but full of such manifold, strange and diffusive beauties, that time would all but fail me, to point the half of them out. But there are things in those two books, which, had they been written in England a century ago, Nathaniel Hawthorne had utterly displaced many of the bright names we now revere on authority. But I am content to leave Hawthorne to himself, and to the infallible finding of posterity; and however great may be the praise I have bestowed upon him, I feel, that in so doing, I have more served and honored myself, than him. For, at bottom, great excellence is praise enough to itself; but the feeling of a sincere and appreciative love and admiration towards it, this is relieved by utterance; and warm, honest praise ever leaves a pleasant flavor in the mouth; and it is an honorable thing to confess to what is honorable in others.

But I cannot leave my subject yet. No man can read a fine author, and relish him to his very bones, while he reads, without subsequently fancying to himself some ideal image of the man and his mind. And if you rightly look for it, you will almost always find that the author himself has somewhere furnished you with his own picture.—For poets (whether in prose or verse), being painters of Nature, are like their brethren of the pencil, the true portrait-painters, who, in the multitude of likenesses to be sketched, do not invariably omit their own; and in all high instances, they paint them without any vanity, though, at times, with a lurking something, that would take several pages to properly define.

I submit it, then, to those best acquainted with the man personally, whether the following is not Nathaniel Hawthorne;—and to himself, whether something involved in it does not express the temper of his mind,—that lasting temper of all true, candid men—a seeker, not a finder yet:—

"A man now entered, in neglected attire, with the aspect of a thinker, but somewhat too rough-hewn and brawny for a scholar. His face was full of sturdy vigor, with some finer and keener attribute beneath; though harsh at first, it was tempered with the glow of a large, warm heart, which had force enough to heat his powerful intellect through and through. He advanced to the Intelligencer, and looked at him with a glance of such stern sincerity, that perhaps few secrets were beyond its scope.

" 'I seek for Truth', said he."

*   *   *

Twenty four hours have elapsed since writing the foregoing. I have just returned from the hay mow, charged more and more with love and admiration of Hawthorne. For I have just been gleaning through the Mosses, picking up many things here and there that had previously escaped me. And I found that but to glean after this man, is better than to be in at the harvest of others. To be frank (though, perhaps, rather foolish) notwithstanding what I wrote yesterday of these Mosses, I had not then culled them all; but had, nevertheless, been sufficiently sensible of the subtle essence, in them, as to write as I did. To what infinite height of loving wonder and admiration I may yet be borne, when by repeatedly banquetting on these Mosses, I shall have thoroughly incorporated their whole stuff into my being,—that, I can not tell. But already I feel that this Hawthorne has dropped germinous seeds into my soul. He expands and deepens down, the more I contemplate him; and further, and further, shoots his strong New-England roots into the hot soil of my Southern soul.

By careful reference to the "Table of Contents", I now find, that I have gone through all the sketches; but that when I yesterday wrote, I had not at all read two particular pieces, to which I now desire to call special attention,—"A Select Party", and "Young Goodman Brown". Here, be it said to all those whom this poor fugitive scrawl of mine may tempt to the perusal of the "Mosses," that they must on no account suffer themselves to be trifled with, disappointed, or deceived by the triviality of many of the titles to these Sketches. For in more than one instance, the title utterly belies the piece. It is as if rustic demijohns containing the very best and costliest of Falernian and Tokay, were labelled "Cider", "Perry," and "Elderberry wine". The truth seems to be, that like many other geniuses, this Man of Mosses takes great delight in hoodwinking the world,—at least, with respect to himself. Personally, I doubt not, that he rather prefers to be generally esteemed but a so-so sort of author; being willing to reserve the thorough and acute appreciation of what he is, to that party most qualified to judge—that is, to himself. Besides, at the bottom of their natures, men like Hawthorne, in many things, deem the plaudits of the public such strong presumptive evidence of mediocrity in the object of them, that it would in some degree render them doubtful of their own powers, did they hear much and vociferous braying concerning them in the public pastures. True, I have been braying myself (if you please to be witty enough, to have it so) but then I claim to be the first that has so brayed in this particular matter; and therefore, while pleading guilty to the charge still claim all the merit due to originality.

But with whatever motive, playful or profound, Nathaniel Hawthorne has chosen to entitle his pieces in the manner he has, it is certain, that some of them are directly calculated to deceive—egregiously deceive, the superficial skimmer of pages. To be downright and candid once more, let me cheerfully say, that two of these titles did dolefully dupe no less an eagle-eyed reader than myself; and that, too, after I had been impressed with a sense of the great depth and breadth of this American man. "Who in the name of thunder" (as the country-people say in this neighborhood) " who in the name of thunder", would anticipate any marvel in a piece entitled "Young Goodman Brown"? You would of course suppose that it was a simple little tale, intended as a supplement to "Goody Two Shoes". Whereas, it is deep as Dante; nor can you finish it, without addressing the author in his own words—"It is yours to penetrate, in every bosom, the deep mystery of sin". And with Young Goodman, too, in allegorical pursuit of his Puritan wife, you cry out in your anguish,—

> " 'Faith!' shouted Goodman Brown, in a voice of agony and desperation; and the echoes of the forest mocked him, crying—'Faith! Faith!' as if bewildered wretches were seeking her all through the wilderness."

Now this same piece, entitled "Young Goodman Brown", is one of the two that I had not all read yesterday; and I allude to it now, because it is, in itself, such a strong positive illustration of that blackness in Hawthorne, which I had assumed from the mere occasional shadows of it, as revealed in several of the other sketches. But had I previously perused "Young Goodman Brown", I should have been at no pains to draw the conclusion, which I came to, at a time, when I was ignorant that the book contained one such direct and unqualified manifestation of it.

The other piece of the two referred to, is entitled "A Select Party", which, in my first simplicity upon originally taking hold of the book, I fancied must treat of some pumpkin-pie party in Old Salem, or some chowder party on Cape Cod. Whereas, by all the gods of Peedee! it is the sweetest and sublimest thing that has been written since Spencer wrote. Nay, there is nothing in Spencer that surpasses it, perhaps, nothing that equals it. And the test is this: read any canto in "The Faery Queen", and then read "A Select Party", and decide which pleases you the most,—that is, if you are qualified to judge. Do not be frightened at this; for when Spencer was alive, he was thought of very much as Hawthorne is now,— was generally accounted just such a "gentle" harmless man. It may be, that to common eyes, the sublimity of Hawthorne seems lost in his sweetness,—as perhaps in this same "Select Party" of his; for whom, he has builded so august a dome of sunset clouds, and served them on richer plate, than Belshazzar's when he banquetted his lords in Babylon.

But my chief business now, is to point out a particular page in this piece, having reference to an honored guest, who under the name of "The Master Genius" but in the guise of "a young man of poor attire, with no insignia of rank or acknowledged eminence", is introduced to the Man of Fancy, who is the giver of the feast. Now the page having reference to this "Master Genius", so happily expresses much of what I yesterday wrote, touching the coming of the literary Shiloh of America, that I cannot but be charmed by the coincidence; especially, when it shows such a parity of ideas, at least in this one point, between a man like Hawthorne and a man like me.

And here, let me throw out another conceit of mine touching this American Shiloh, or "Master Genius", as Hawthorne calls him. May it not be, that this commanding mind has not been, is not, and never will be, individually developed in any one man? And would it, indeed, appear so unreasonable to suppose, that this great fullness and overflowing may be, or may be destined to be, shared by a plurality of men of genius? Surely, to take the very greatest example on record, Shakespeare cannot be regarded as in himself the concretion of all the genius of his time; nor as so immeasurably beyond Marlow, Webster, Ford, Beaumont, Jonson, that those great men can be said to share none of his power? For one, I conceive that there were dramatists in Elizabeth's day, between whom and Shakespeare the distance was by no means great. Let any-

one, hitherto little acquainted with those neglected old authors, for the first time read them thoroughly, or even read
Charles Lamb's Specimens of them, and he will be amazed at
the wondrous ability of those Anaks of men, and shocked at
this renewed example of the fact, that Fortune has more to
do with fame than merit,—though, without merit, lasting
fame there can be none.

Nevertheless, it would argue too illy of my country were
this maxim to hold good concerning Nathaniel Hawthorne, a
man, who already, in some few minds, has shed "such a light,
as never illuminates the earth, save when a great heart burns
as the household fire of a grand intellect."

The words are his,—in the "Select Party"; and they are a
magnificent setting to a coincident sentiment of my own, but
ramblingly expressed yesterday, in reference to himself. Gainsay it who will, as I now write, I am Posterity speaking by
proxy—and after times will make it more than good, when I
declare—that the American, who up to the present day, has
evinced, in Literature, the largest brain with the largest heart,
that man is Nathaniel Hawthorne. Moreover, that whatever
Nathaniel Hawthorne may hereafter write, "The Mosses from
an Old Manse" will be ultimately accounted his masterpiece.
For there is a sure, though a secret sign in some works which
prove the culmination of the powers (only the developable
ones, however) that produced them. But I am by no means
desirous of the glory of a prophet. I pray Heaven that Hawthorne may *yet* prove me an impostor in this prediction. Especially, as I somehow cling to the strange fancy, that, in all
men, hiddenly reside certain wondrous, occult properties—as
in some plants and minerals—which by some happy but very
rare accident (as bronze was discovered by the melting of the
iron and brass in the burning of Corinth) may chance to be
called forth here on earth; not entirely waiting for their better
discovery in the more congenial, blessed atmosphere of
heaven.

Once more—for it is hard to be finite upon an infinite subject, and all subjects are infinite. By some people, this entire
scrawl of mine may be esteemed altogether unnecessary, inasmuch, "as years ago" (they may say) " we found out the rich
and rare stuff in this Hawthorne, whom you now parade

forth, as if only *yourself* were the discoverer of this Portuguese diamond in our Literature."—But even granting all this; and adding to it, the assumption that the books of Hawthorne have sold by the five-thousand,—what does that signify?— They should be sold by the hundred-thousand; and read by the million; and admired by every one who is capable of admiration.

Fragments from a Writing Desk

No. 1

MY DEAR M——, I can imagine you seated on that dear, delightful, old fashioned sofa; your head supported by its luxurious padding, and with feet perched aloft on the aspiring back of that straight limbed, stiff-necked, quaint old chair, which, as our facetious W—— assured me, was the identical seat in which old Burton composed his Anatomy of Melancholy. I see you reluctantly raise your optics from the huge-clasped quarto which encumbers your lap, to receive the package which the servant hands you, and can almost imagine that I see those beloved features illumined for a moment with an expression of joy, as you read the superscription of your gentle protege. Lay down I beseech you that odious black-lettered volume and let not its musty and withered leaves sully the virgin purity and whiteness of the sheet which is the vehicle of so much good sense, sterling thought, and chaste and elegant sentiment.

You remember how you used to rate me for my hang-dog modesty, my *mauvaise honte*, as my Lord Chesterfield would style it. Well! I have determined that hereafter you shall not have occasion again to inflict upon me those flattering appellations, of "Fool!" "Dolt!" "Sheep!" which in your indignation you used to shower upon me, with a vigor and a facility which excited my wonder, while it provoked my resentment.

And how do you imagine that I rid myself of this annoying hindrance? Why, truly, by coming to the conclusion that in this pretty corpus of mine was lodged every manly grace; that my limbs were modeled in the symmetry of the Phidian Jupiter; my countenance radiant with the beams of wit and intelligence, and my whole person, the envy of the beaux, the idol of the women and the admiration of the tailor. And then my mind! why, sir, I have discovered it to be endowed with the most rare and extraordinary powers, stored with universal knowledge, and embellished with every polite accomplishment.

Pollux! what a comfortable thing is a good opinion of one's self! Why, I walk the Broadway of our village with a certain air, that puts me down at once in the estimation of any intelligent stranger who may chance to meet me, as a *distingue* of the purest water, a blade of the true temper, a blood of the first quality! Lord! how I despise the little sneaking vermin who dodge along the street as though they were so many footmen or errand-boys; who, have never learned to carry the head erect in conscious importance, but hang that noblest of the human members as though it had been boxed by some virago of an Amazon; who shuffle along the walk, with a quick uneasy step, a hasty clownish motion, which by the magnitude of the contrast, set off to advantage my own slow and magisterial gait, which I can at pleasure vary to an easy, abandoned sort of carriage, or, to the more engaging alert and lively walk, to suit the varieties of time, occasion, and company.

And in society, too—how often have I commiserated the poor wretches who stood aloof, in a corner, like a flock of scared sheep; while myself, beautiful as Apollo, dressed in a style which would extort admiration from a Brummell, and belted round with self-esteem as with a girdle, sallied up to the ladies—complimenting one, exchanging a repartee with another; tapping this one under the chin, and clasping this one round the waist; and finally, winding up the operation by kissing round the whole circle to the great edification of the fair, and to the unbounded horror, amazement and ill-suppressed chagrin of the aforesaid sheepish multitude; who with eyes wide open and mouths distended, afforded good subjects on whom to exercise my polished wit, which like the glittering edge of a Damascus sabre "dazzled all it shone upon."

And then, when the folding doors are thrown open, as the lacquey announces supper to be ready, how often have I stepped forward and with a profound obeisance to the ladies, vowing by the bow of Cupid, and appealing to Venus for my sincerity, when I wished I had an hundred arms at their service, escorted them right gallantly and merrily to the banquet; while those poor bashful creatures, like a drove of dumb cattle, strayed into the apartment, stumbling, blushing, stammering and alone.

Verily! by my elegant accomplishments and superior parts; by my graceful address, and above all by my easy self-posses-sion, I have unwittingly provoked to an irreconcilable degree, the resentment of half a score of these village beaux; whom, although I had rather have their esteem, I value too little to dread their malice.

By my halidome! sir, this same village of Lansingburgh con-tains within its pretty limits as fair a set of blushing damsels, as one would wish to look upon on a dreamy summer-day! —When I traverse the broad pavements of my own metropo-lis, my eyes are arrested by beautiful forms flitting hither and thither; and I pause to admire the elegance of their attire, the taste displayed in their embellishments; the richness of the mate-rial; and sometimes, it may be, at the loveliness of the features, which no art can heighten and no negligence conceal.

But here, sir, here—where woman seems to have erected her throne, and established her empire; here, where all feel and acknowledge her sway, she blooms in unborrowed charms; and the eye undazzled by the profusion of extraneous ornament, settles at once upon the loveliest faces, which our clayey natures can assume. The poet has sung:

"When first the Rhodian's mimic art arrayed
  The queen of Beauty in her Cyprian shade,
  The happy master mingled on his piece
  Each look that charm'd him in the fair of Greece.
  To faultless nature true, he stole a grace
  From every finer form and sweeter face;
  And, as he sojourned on the Ægean isles,
  Woo'd all their love and treasur'd all their smiles;
  Then glowed the tints, pure, precious, and refined,
  And mortal charms seemed heavenly when combined."

Now, had this same Apelles flourished in our own enlight-ened day, and more particularly, had he taken up his domicile in this goodly village, I could with ease have presented him with many a Hebe, in whom were united all the requisite graces which make up the beau-ideal of female loveliness. Nor, my dear M., does there reign in all this bright display, that same monotony of feature, form, complexion, which elsewhere is beheld; no, here are all varieties, all the orders of

Beauty's architecture; the Doric, the Ionic, the Corinthian, all are here.

I have in "my mind's eye, Horatio," three (the number of the Graces, you remember) who may stand, each at the head of their respective orders. The one, were she arrayed in sylvan garb, and did she in her hand carry her bow, might with equal justice and propriety stand the picture of Diana herself. Her figure is bold, her stature erect and tall, her presence queenly and commanding, and her complexion is clear and fair as the face of Heaven on a May day, through which sparkles an eye of that indefinable hue, which is beyond comparison the most striking that can garnish the human countenance. The vermillion in her cheeks perpetually wears that ruddy healthful tint, which one is accustomed to behold illumine, but for a moment alas! the face of a city belle when she takes her annual ramble in the country, to revel for a period in the retreats of rustic life.

If to these qualities you superadd, that majesty of carriage, and dignity of mien, which we would fancy the royal mistress of Antony to have possessed; together with that heroic and Grecian cast of countenance which the imagination unconsciously ascribes to the Jewess, Rebecca, when resisting the vile arts of the Templar,—you have in my poor opinion the portraiture of ——.

When I venture to describe the second of this beautiful trinity, I feel my powers of delineation inadequate to the task; but, nevertheless I will try my hand at the matter, although like an unskilful limner, I am fearful I shall but scandalize the charms I endeavor to copy.

Come to my aid, ye guardian spirits of the Fair! Guide my awkward hand, and preserve from mutilation the features ye hover over and protect! Pour down whole floods of sparkling champaigne, my dear M——, until your brain grows giddy with emotion; con over the latter portion of the 1st Canto of Childe Harold, and ransack your intellectual repository for the liveliest visions of the Fairy Land, and you will be in a measure prepared to relish the epicurian banquet *I* shall spread.

The stature of this beautiful mortal (if she be indeed of earth) is of that perfect heighth, which while it is freed from the charge of being low, cannot with propriety be denomi-

nated tall. Her figure is slender almost to fragility but strikingly modeled in spiritual elegance, and is the only form I
ever saw, which could bear the trial of a rigid criticism.

Every man who is gifted with the least particle of imagination, must in some of his reveries have conjured up from the
realms of fancy, a being bright and beautiful beyond every
thing he had ever before apprehended, whose main and distinguishing attribute invariably proves to be a form the indiscribable loveliness of which seems to,

> ——"Sail in liquid light,
> And float on seas of bliss."

The realization of these seraphic visions is seldom permitted
us; but I can truly say that when my eyes for the first time
fell upon this lovely creature, I thought myself transported to
the land of Dreams, where lay embodied, the most brilliant
conceptions of the wildest fancy. Indeed, could the Prome-
thean spark throw life and animation into the Venus de' Me-
dici, it would but present the counterpart of ——.

Her complexion has the delicate tinge of the Brunett, with
a little of the roseate hue of the Circassian; and one would
swear that none but the sunny skies of Spain had shone upon
the infancy of the being, who looks so like her own "dark-
glancing daughters."

The outline of her head, together with the profile of her
countenance are sketched in classick purity, and while the one
indicates refined and elegant sentiment; the other is not more
chaste and regular than the mind which beams from every
feature of the face. Her hair is black as the wing of the raven,
and is parted a la Madonna over a forehead where sits, girt
round with her sister graces the very genius of poetic beauty,
hope and love.

And then her eyes! they open their dark, rich orbs upon
you like the full noon of heaven, and blaze into your very soul
the fires of day! Like the offerings laid upon the sacrificial
altars of the Hebrew, when in an instant the divine spark falling from the propitiated God kindled them in flames; so, a
single glance from that oriental eye as quickly fires your soul,
and leaves your bosom in a perfect conflagration! Odds Cu-
pids and Darts! with one broad sweep of vision in a crowded

ball-room, that splendid creature would lay around her like the two-handed sword of Minotti, hearts on hearts, piled round in semicircles! But it is well for the more rugged sex that this glorious being can vary her proud dominion, and give to the expression of her eye a melting tenderness which dissolves the most frigid heart and heals the wounds she gave before.

If the devout and exemplary Mussulman who dying fast in the faith of his Prophet anticipates reclining on beds of roses, gloriously drunk through all the ages of eternity, is to be waited on by Houris such as these: waft me ye gentle gales beyond this lower world and,

> "Lap me in soft Lydian airs"!

But I am falling into I know not what extravagances, so I will briefly give you a portrait of the last of these three divinities, and will then terminate my tiresome lucubrations.

This last is a Lilliputian beauty; diminutive in stature, fair haired, and with a foot for which Cinderella's slipper would be too large; a countenance sweet and interesting and in her manners eminently refined and engaging. The cast of her physiognomy is singularly mild and amiable, and her whole person is replete with every feminine grace. Her eyes,

> "Effuse the mildness of their azure beam;"

and to her, above all her sex, are applicable the lines of our gentle Coleridge:

> "Maid of my Love, sweet ——!
> In beauty's light you glide along:
> Your eye is like the star of eve,
> And sweet your voice as seraph's song.
> Yet not your heavenly beauty gives
> This heart with passion soft to glow:
> Within your soul a voice there lives!
> It bids you hear the tale of woe.
> When sinking low the sufferer wan
> Beholds no hand outstretched to save,
> Fair as the bosom of the swan
> That rises graceful o'er the wave,

> I've seen your breast with pity heave,
> And therefore love I you sweet ——."

Here my dear M——, closes this catalogue of the Graces, this chapter of Beauties, and I should implore your pardon for trespassing so long on your attention. If you, yourself, in whose breast may possibly be extinguished the amatory flame, should not feel an interest in these three "counterfeit presentments," do not fail to show them to——and solicit her opinion as to their respective merits.

Tender my best acknowledgments to the Major for his prompt attention to my request, and, for yourself, accept the assurance of my undiminished regard; and hoping that the smiles of heaven may continue to illumine your way,

I remain, ever yours,

L. A. V.

No. 2

"Confusion seize the Greek!" exclaimed I, as wrathfully rising from my chair, I flung my ancient Lexicon across the room, and seizing my hat and cane, and throwing on my cloak, I sallied out into the clear air of heaven. The bracing coolness of an April evening calmed my aching temples, and I slowly wended my way to the river side. I had promenaded the bank for about half an hour, when flinging myself upon the grassy turf, I was soon lost in revery, and up to the lips in sentiment.

I had not lain more than five minutes, when a figure effectually concealed in the ample folds of a cloak, glided past me, and hastily dropping something at my feet, disappeared behind the angle of an adjoining house, ere I could recover from my astonishment at so singular an occurrence.—"Certes!" cried I, springing up, "here is a spice of the marvelous!" and stooping down, I picked up an elegant little, rose-coloured, lavender-scented billet-doux, and hurriedly breaking the seal (a heart, transfixed with an arrow) I read by the light of the moon, the following:

"Gentle Sir—
If my fancy has painted you in genuine colours, you will

on the receipt of this, incontinently follow the bearer where she will lead you.

INAMORATA."

"The deuce I will!" exclaimed I, — "But soft!" — And I re-perused this singular document, turned over the billet in my fingers, and examined the hand-writing; which was femi-ninely delicate, and I could have sworn was a woman's. Is it possible, thought I, that the days of romance are revived? — No, "The days of chivalry are over!" says Burke.

As I made this reflection, I looked up, and beheld the same figure which had handed me this questionable missive, beck-oning me forward. I started towards her; but, as I ap-proached, she receded from me, and fled swiftly along the margin of the river at a pace, which, encumbered as I was with my heavy cloak and boots, I was unable to follow; and which filled me with sundry misgivings, as to the nature of the being, who could travel with such amazing celerity. At last perfectly breathless, I fell into a walk; which, my myste-rious fugitive perceiving, she likewise lessened her pace, so as to keep herself still in sight, although at too great a distance to permit me to address her.

Having recovered from my fatigue and regained my breath: I loosened the clasp of my cloak, and inwardly resolving that I would come at the bottom of the mystery, I desperately flung the mantle from my shoulders, and dashing my beaver to the ground, gave chase in good earnest to the tantalizing stranger. No sooner did I from my extravagant actions an-nounce my intention to overtake her, than with a light laugh of derision, she sprang forward at a rate, which in attempting to outstrip, soon left me far in the rear, heartily disconcerted and crest-fallen, and inly cursing the ignus fatuus, that danced so provokingly before me.

At length, like every one else, learning wisdom from expe-rience; I thought my policy lay in silently following the foot-steps of my eccentric guide, and quietly waiting the denouement of this extraordinary adventure. So soon as I re-laxed my speed, and gave evidence of having renounced my more summary mode of procedure; the stranger, regulating her movements by mine, proceeded at a pace which preserved between us a uniform distance, ever and anon, looking back like a wary general to see if I were again inclined to try the mettle of her limbs.

After pursuing our way in this monotonous style for some time; I observed that my conductress rather abated in her precautions, and had not for the last ten or fifteen minutes taken her periodical survey over her shoulder; whereat, plucking up my spirits, which I can assure you, courteous reader, had fallen considerably below zero by the ill-success of my previous efforts,—I again rushed madly forward at the summit of my speed, and having advanced ten or twelve rods unperceived, was flattering myself that I should this time make good my purpose; when, turning suddenly round, as though reminded of her late omission, and descrying me plunging ahead like an infuriated steed, she gave a slightly audible scream of surprise, and once more fled, as though helped forward by invisible wings.

This last failure was too much. I stopped short, and stamping the ground in ungovernable rage, gave vent to my chagrin in a volley of exclamations: in which, perhaps, if narrowly inspected, might have been detected two or three expressions which savored somewhat of the jolly days of the jolly cavaliers. But if a man was ever excusable for swearing; surely, the circumstances of the case were palliative of the crime. What! to be thwarted by a woman? Peradventure, baffled by a girl? Confusion! It was too bad! To be outgeneraled, routed, defeated, by a mere rib of the earth? It was not to be borne! I thought I should never survive the inexpressible mortification of the moment; and in the heighth of my despair, I bethought me of putting a romantic end to my existence upon the very spot which had witnessed my discomfiture.

But when the first transports of my wrath had passed away, and perceiving that the waters of the river, instead of presenting an unruffled calm, as they are wont to do on so interesting an occasion, were discomposed and turbid; and remembering, that beside this, I had no other means of accomplishing my heroic purpose, except the vulgar and inelegant one, of braining myself against the stone wall which traversed the road; I sensibly determined after taking into consideration the aforementioned particulars, together with the fact that I had an unfinished game of chess to win, on which depended no inconsiderable wager, that to commit suicide under such circumstances would be highly inexpedient, and probably be attended with many inconveniencies.—During the time I had consumed in arriving at this most wise and discreet conclusion, my mind had time to recover its former tone, and had become comparatively calm and collected; and I saw my folly in endeavoring to trifle with one, apparently so mysterious and inexplicable.

I now resolved, that whatever might betide, I would patiently await the issue of the affair: and advancing forward in the direction of my guide, who all this time had maintained her ground, stedfastly watching my actions,—we both simultaneously strode forward, and were soon on the same footing as before.

We walked on at an increased pace, and were just passed the suburbs of the town, when my conductress plunging into a neighboring grove, pursued her way with augmented speed, till we arrived at a spot, whose singular and grotesque beauty, even amidst the agitating occurrences of the evening I could not refrain from observing. A circular space of about a dozen acres in extent had been cleared in the very heart of the grove: leaving, however, two parallel rows of lofty trees, which at the distance of about twenty paces, and intersected in the centre by two similar ranges, traversed the whole diameter of the circle. These noble plants shooting their enormous trunks to an amazing heighth, bore their verdant honors far aloft, throwing their gigantic limbs abroad and embracing each other with their rugged arms. This fanciful union of their sturdy boughs formed a magnificent arch, whose grand proportions, swelling upward in proud preeminence, presented to the eye a vaulted roof, which to my perturbed imagination at the time, seemed to have canopied the triumphal feasts of the sylvan god.—This singular prospect burst upon me in all its beauty, as we emerged from the surrounding thicket, and I had unconsciously lingered on the borders of the wood, the better to enjoy so unrivalled a view; when as my eye was following the dusky outline of the grove, I caught the diminutive figure of my guide, who standing at the entrance of the arched-way I have been endeavoring to describe, was making the most extravagant gestures of impatience at my delay.— Reminded at once of the situation, which put me for a time under the control of this capricious mortal, I replied to her summons by immediately throwing myself forward, and we soon entered the Atlantean arbor, in whose umbrageous shades we were completely hid.

Lost in conjecture, during the whole of this eccentric ramble, as to its probable termination—the sombre gloom of these ancestral trees, gave a darkening hue to my imaginings, and I began to repent the inconsiderate haste which had hurried me on, in an expedition, so peculiar and suspicious. In spite of all my efforts to exclude them, the fictions of the nursery poured in upon my recollection, and I felt with Bob Acres in the "Rivals," that "my valor was certainly going." Once, I am almost ashamed to own it to thee, gentle reader, my mind was so haunted with ghostly images, that in an agony of apprehension, I was about to turn and flee, and had actually made some preliminary movements to that effect, when my hand, accidentally straying into my bosom, griped the billet, whose romantic summons had caused this nocturnal adventure. I felt my soul regain her fortitude, and smiling at the absurd conceits which infested my brain, I once more stalked proudly forward, under the overhanging branches of these ancient trees.

Emergent from the shades of this romantic region, we soon beheld an edifice, which seated on a gentle eminence, and embowered amidst surrounding trees, bore the appearance of a country villa; although its plain exterior showed none of those fantastic devices which usually adorn the elegant chateaux. My conductress as we neared this unpretending mansion seemed to redouble her precautions; and although she evinced no positive alarm, yet her quick and startled glances bespoke no small degree of apprehension. Motioning me to conceal myself behind an adjacent tree, she approached the house with rapid but cautious steps; my eyes followed her until she disappeared behind the shadow of the garden wall, and I remained waiting her reappearance with the utmost anxiety.—An interval of several moments had elapsed, when I descried her, swinging open a small postern, and beckoning me to advance. I obeyed the summons, and was soon by her side, not a little amazed at the complacency, which after what had transpired, brooked my immediate vicinity. Dissembling my astonishment, however, and rallying all my powers, I followed with noiseless strides the footsteps of my guide, fully persuaded that this mysterious affair was now about to be brought to an eclaircissement.

The appearance of this spacious habitation was any thing but inviting; it seemed to have been built with a jealous eye to concealment; and its few, but well-defended windows were sufficiently high from the ground, as effectually to baffle the prying curiosity of the inquisitive stranger. Not a single light shone from the narrow casement; but all was harsh, gloomy and forbidding. As my imagination, ever alert on such an occasion, was busily occupied in assigning some fearful motive for such unusual precautions; my leader suddenly halted beneath a lofty window, and making a low call, I perceived slowly descending therefrom, a thick silken chord, attached to an ample basket, which was silently deposited at our feet. Amazed at this apparition, I was about soliciting an explanation: when laying her fingers impressively upon her lips, and placing herself in the basket, my guide motioned me to seat myself beside her. I obeyed; but not without considerable trepidation: and in obedience to the same low call which had procured its descent our curious vehicle, with sundry creakings, rose in air.

To attempt an analysis of my feelings at this moment were impossible. The solemnity of the hour—the romantic nature of my present situation—the singularity of my whole adventure—the profound stillness which prevailed—the solitude of the place, were enough of themselves to strike a panic into the stoutest heart, and to unsettle the strongest nerves. But when to these, was added the thought,—that at the dead of night, and in the company of a being so perfectly inexplicable, I was effecting a clandestine entrance into so remarkable an abode: the kind and sympathising reader will not wonder, when I wished myself safely bestowed in my own snug quarters in ———— street.

Such were the reflections which passed through my mind, during our aerial voyage, throughout which my guide maintained the most rigid silence, only broken at intervals by the occasional creakings of our machine, as it rubbed against the side of the house in its ascent. No sooner had we gained the window, than two brawny arms were extended circling me in their embrace, and ere I was aware of the change of locality, I found myself standing upright in an apartment, dimly illuminated by a solitary taper. My fellow voyager was quickly beside me, and again enjoining silence with her finger, she seized the lamp and bidding me follow, conducted me through a long corridor, till we reached a low door concealed behind some old tapestry, which opening to the touch, disclosed a spectacle as beautiful and enchanting as any described in the Arabian Nights.

The apartment we now entered, was fitted up in a style of Eastern splendor, and its atmosphere was redolent of the most delicious perfumes. The walls were hung round with the most elegant draperies, waving in graceful folds, on which were delineated scenes of Arcadian beauty. The floor was covered with a carpet of the finest texture, in which were wrought with exquisite skill, the most striking events in ancient mythology. Attached to the wall by chords composed of alternate threads of crimson silk and gold, were several magnificent pictures illustrative of the loves of Jupiter and Semele,—Psyche before the tribunal of Venus, and a variety of other scenes, limned all with felicitous grace. Disposed around the room, were luxurious couches, covered with the finest damask, on which were likewise executed after the Italian fashion the early fables of Greece and Rome. Tripods, designed to represent the Graces bearing aloft vases, richly chiseled in the classic taste, were distributed in the angles of the room, and exhaled an intoxicating fragrance.

Chandeliers of the most fanciful description, suspended from the lofty ceiling by rods of silver, shed over this voluptuous scene a soft and tempered light, and imparted to the whole, that dreamy beauty, which must be seen in order to be duly appreciated. Mirrors of unusual magnitude, multiplying in all directions the gorgeous objects, deceived the eye by their reflections, and mocked the vision with long perspective.

But overwhelming as was the display of opulence, it yielded in attraction to the being for whom all this splendour glistened; and the grandeur of the room served only to show to advantage the matchless beauty of its inmate. These superb decorations, though lavished in boundless profusion, were the mere accessories of a creature, whose loveliness was of that spiritual cast that depended upon no adventitious aid, and which as no obscurity could diminish, so, no art could heighten.

When I first obtained a glimpse of this lovely being, she lay reclining upon an ottoman; in one hand holding a lute, and with the other lost in the profusion of her silken tresses, she supported her head.—I could not refrain from recalling the passionate exclamation of Romeo:

> "See how she leans her cheek upon her hand;
> Oh! that I were a glove upon that hand,
> That I might kiss that cheek!"

She was habited in a flowing robe of the purest white, and her hair, escaping from the fillet of roses which had bound it, spread its negligent graces over neck and bosom and shoulder, as though unwilling to reveal the extent of such transcendant charms.—Her zone was of pink satin, on which were broidered figures of Cupid in the act of drawing his bow; while the ample folds of her Turkish sleeve were gathered at the wrist by a bracelet of immense rubies, each of which represented a heart pierced thro' by a golden shaft. Her fingers were decorated with a variety of rings, which as she waved her hand to me as I entered, darted forth a thousand coruscations, and gleamed their brilliant splendors to the sight. Peeping from beneath the envious skirts of her mantle, and almost buried in the downy quishion on which it reposed, lay revealed the prettiest little foot you can imagine; cased in a satin slipper, which clung to the fairy-like member by means of a diamond clasp.

As I entered the apartment, her eyes were downcast, and the expression of her face was mournfully interesting; she had apparently been lost in some melancholy revery. Upon my entrance, however, her countenance brightened, as with a queenly wave of the hand, she motioned my conductress from the room, and left me standing, mute, admiring and bewildered in her presence.

For a moment my brain spun round, and I had not at com-

mand a single one of my faculties. Recovering my self possession however, and with that, my good-breeding, I advanced
en cavalier, and gracefully sinking on one knee, I bowed my
head and exclaimed—"Here do I prostrate myself, thou sweet
Divinity, and kneel at the shrine of thy peerless charms!"—I
hesitated,—blushed, looked up, and beheld bent upon me a
pair of Andalusian eyes, whose melting earnestness of expression pierced me to the soul, and I felt my heart dissolving
away like ice before the equinoctial heats.

Alas! For all the vows of eternal constancy I had sworn to
another!—The silken threads were snapped asunder; the
golden chords had parted! A new dominion was creeping o'er
my soul, and I fell, bound at the feet of my fair enchantress.
A moment of unutterable interest passed, while I met the
gaze of this glorious being with a look as ardent, as burning,
as steadfast as her own.—But it was not in mortal woman to
stand the glance of an eye which had never quailed before a
foe; and whose fierce lightnings were now playing in the wild
expression of a love, that rent my bosom like a whirlwind,
and tore up my past attachments as though they were but of
the growth of yesterday.—The long dark lashes fell! smothered were the fires, whose brightness had kindled my soul in
flames! I seized the passive hand, I lifted it to my lips and
covered it with burning kisses! "Fair mortal!" I exclaimed, "I
feel my passion is requited: but, seal it with thy own sweet
voice, or I shall expire in uncertainty!"

Those lustrous orbs again opened on me all their fires; and
maddened at her silence, I caught her in my arms, and im-
printing one long, long kiss upon her hot and glowing lips, I
cried "Speak! Tell me, thou cruel! Does thy heart send forth
vital fluid like my own? Am I loved,—even wildly, madly as I
love?" She was silent; gracious God! what horrible apprehension crossed my soul?—Frantic with the thought, I held her
from me, and looking in her face, I met the same impassioned
gaze; her lips moved—my senses ached with the intensity
with which I listened,—all was still,—they uttered no sound;
I flung her from me, even though she clung to my vesture, and
with a wild cry of agony I burst from the apartment!—She
was dumb! Great God, she was dumb! DUMB AND DEAF!

L. A. V.

The Happy Failure

THE APPOINTMENT was that I should meet my elderly uncle at the river-side, precisely at nine in the morning. The skiff was to be ready, and the apparatus to be brought down by his grizzled old black man. As yet, the nature of the wonderful experiment remained a mystery to all but the projector.

I was first on the spot. The village was high up the river, and the inland summer sun was already oppressively warm. Presently I saw my uncle advancing beneath the trees, hat off, and wiping his brow; while far behind staggered poor old Yorpy, with what seemed one of the gates of Gaza on his back.

"Come, hurrah, stump along, Yorpy!" cried my uncle, impatiently turning round every now and then.

Upon the black's staggering up to the skiff, I perceived that the great gate of Gaza was transformed into a huge, shabby, oblong box, hermetically sealed. The sphinx-like blankness of the box quadrupled the mystery in my mind.

"Is *this* the wonderful apparatus?" said I, in amazement. "Why, it's nothing but a battered old dry-goods box, nailed up. And is *this* the thing, uncle, that is to make you a million of dollars ere the year be out? What a forlorn-looking, lacklustre, old ash-box it is."

"Put it into the skiff!" roared my uncle to Yorpy, without heeding my boyish disdain. "Put it in, you grizzled-headed cherub—put it in carefully, carefully! If that box bursts, my everlasting fortune collapses."

"Bursts?—collapses?" cried I, in alarm. "It ain't full of combustibles? Quick! let me go to the further end of the boat!"

"Sit still, you simpleton!" cried my uncle again. "Jump in, Yorpy, and hold on to the box like grim death while I shove off. Carefully! carefully! you dunderheaded black! Mind t'other side of the box, I say! Do you mean to destroy the box?"

"Duyvel take te pox!" muttered old Yorpy, who was a sort

of Dutch African. "De pox has been my cuss for de ten long 'ear."

"Now, then, we're off—take an oar, youngster; you, Yorpy, clinch the box fast. Here we go now. Carefully! carefully! You, Yorpy, stop shaking the box! Easy! easy! there's a big snag. Pull now. Hurrah! deep water at last! Now give way, youngster, and away to the island."

"The island!" said I. "There's no island hereabouts."

"There is ten miles above the bridge, though," said my uncle, determinately.

"Ten miles off! Pull that old dry-goods box ten miles up the river in this blazing sun!"

"All that I have to say," said my uncle, firmly, "is that we are bound to Quash Island."

"Mercy, uncle! if I had known of this great long pull of ten mortal miles in this fiery sun, you wouldn't have juggled *me* into the skiff so easy. What's *in* that box?—paving-stones? See how the skiff settles down under it. I won't help pull a box of paving-stones ten miles. What's the use of pulling 'em?"

"Look you, simpleton," quoth my uncle, pausing upon his suspended oar. "Stop rowing, will ye! Now then, if you don't want to share in the glory of my experiment; if you are wholly indifferent to halving its immortal renown; I say, sir, if you care not to be present at the first trial of my Great Hydraulic-Hydrostatic Apparatus for draining swamps and marshes, and converting them, at the rate of one acre the hour, into fields more fertile than those of the Genessee; if you care not, I repeat, to have this proud thing to tell—in far future days, when poor old I shall have been long dead and gone, boy—to your children, and your children's children; in that case, sir, you are free to land forthwith."

"Oh, uncle! I did not mean—"

"No words, sir! Yorpy, take his oar, and help pull him ashore."

"But, my dear uncle; I declare to you that—"

"Not a syllable, sir: you have cast open scorn upon the Great Hydraulic-Hydrostatic Apparatus. Yorpy, put him ashore, Yorpy. It's shallow here again. Jump out, Yorpy, and wade with him ashore."

"Now, my dear, good, kind uncle, do but pardon me this one time, and I will say just nothing about the apparatus."

"Say nothing about it! when it is my express end and aim it shall be famous! Put him ashore, Yorpy."

"Nay uncle, I *will* not give up my oar. I have an oar in this matter, and I mean to keep it. You shall not cheat me out of my share of your glory."

"Ah, now there—that's sensible. You may stay, youngster. Pull again now."

We were all silent for a time, steadily plying our way. At last I ventured to break water once more.

"I am glad, dear uncle, you have revealed to me at last the nature and end of your great experiment. It is the effectual draining of swamps; an attempt, dear uncle, in which, if you do but succeed (as I know you will), you will earn the glory denied to a Roman emperor. He tried to drain the Pontine marsh, but failed."

"The world has shot ahead the length of its own diameter since then," quoth my uncle, proudly. "If that Roman emperor were here, *I*'d show him what can be done in the present enlightened age."

Seeing my good uncle so far mollified now as to be quite self-complacent, I ventured another remark.

"This is a rather severe, hot pull, dear uncle."

"Glory is not to be gained, youngster, without pulling hard for it—against the stream, too, as we do now. The natural tendency of man, in the mass, is to go down with the universal current into oblivion."

"But why pull so far, dear uncle, upon the present occasion? Why pull ten miles for it? You do but propose, as I understand it, to put to the actual test this admirable invention of yours. And could it not be tested almost any where?"

"Simple boy," quoth my uncle, " would you have some malignant spy steal from me the fruits of ten long years of high-hearted, persevering endeavor? Solitary in my scheme, I go to a solitary place to test it. If I fail—for all things are possible—no one out of the family will know it. If I succeed, secure in the secrecy of my invention, I can boldly demand any price for its publication."

"Pardon me, dear uncle; you are wiser than I."

"One would think years and gray hairs should bring wisdom, boy."

"Yorpy there, dear uncle; think you his grizzled locks thatch a brain improved by long life?"

"Am I Yorpy, boy? Keep to your oar!"

Thus padlocked again, I said no further word till the skiff grounded on the shallows, some twenty yards from the deep-wooded isle.

"Hush!" whispered my uncle, intensely; "not a word now!" and he sat perfectly still, slowly sweeping with his glance the whole country around, even to both banks of the here wide-expanded stream.

"Wait till that horseman, yonder, passes!" he whispered again, pointing to a speck moving along a lofty, river-side road, which perilously wound on midway up a long line of broken bluffs and cliffs. "There—he's out of sight now, behind the copse. Quick! Yorpy! Carefully, though! Jump overboard, and shoulder the box, and—Hold!"

We were all mute and motionless again.

"Ain't that a boy, sitting like Zaccheus in yonder tree of the orchard on the other bank? Look, youngster—young eyes are better than old—don't you see him?"

"Dear uncle, I see the orchard, but I can't see any boy."

"He's a spy—I know he is," suddenly said my uncle, disregardful of my answer, and intently gazing, shading his eyes with his flattened hand. "Don't touch the box, Yorpy. Crouch! crouch down, all of ye!"

"Why, uncle—there—see—the boy is only a withered white bough. I see it very plainly now."

"You don't see the tree I mean," quoth my uncle, with a decided air of relief, "but never mind; I defy the boy. Yorpy, jump out, and shoulder the box. And now then, youngster, off with your shoes and stockings, roll up your trowsers legs, and follow me. Carefully, Yorpy, carefully. That's more precious than a box of gold, mind."

"Heavy as de gelt anyhow," growled Yorpy, staggering and splashing in the shallows beneath it.

"There, stop under the bushes there—in among the flags—so—gently, gently—there, put it down just there. Now, youngster, are you ready? Follow—tiptoes, tiptoes!"

"I can't wade in this mud and water on my tiptoes, uncle; and I don't see the need of it either."

"Go ashore, sir—instantly!"

"Why, uncle, I *am* ashore."

"Peace! follow me, and no more."

Crouching in the water in complete secrecy, beneath the bushes and among the tall flags, my uncle now stealthily produced a hammer and wrench from one of his enormous pockets, and presently tapped the box. But the sound alarmed him.

"Yorpy," he whispered, "go you off to the right, behind the bushes, and keep watch. If you see any one coming, whistle softly. Youngster, you do the same to the left."

We obeyed; and presently, after considerable hammering and supplemental tinkering, my uncle's voice was heard in the utter solitude, loudly commanding our return.

Again we obeyed, and now found the cover of the box removed. All eagerness, I peeped in, and saw a surprising multiplicity of convoluted metal pipes and syringes of all sorts and varieties, all sizes and calibres, inextricably interwreathed together in one gigantic coil. It looked like a huge nest of anacondas and adders.

"Now then, Yorpy," said my uncle, all animation, and flushed with the foretaste of glory, "do you stand this side, and be ready to tip when I give the word. And do you, youngster, stand ready to do as much for the other side. Mind, don't budge it the fraction of a barley-corn till I say the word. All depends on a proper adjustment."

"No fear, uncle. I will be careful as a lady's tweezers."

"I s'ant lift de heavy pox," growled old Yorpy, "till de wort pe given; no fear o' dat."

"Oh boy," said my uncle now, upturning his face devotionally, while a really noble gleam irradiated his gray eyes, locks, and wrinkles; "oh boy! this, *this* is the hour which for ten long years has, in the prospect, sustained me through all my pains-taking obscurity. Fame will be the sweeter because it comes at the last; the truer, because it comes to an old man like me, not to a boy like you. Sustainer! I glorify Thee."

He bowed over his venerable head, and—as I live—something like a shower-drop somehow fell from my face into the shallows.

"Tip!"

We tipped.

"A little more!"

We tipped a little more.

"A *leetle* more!"

We tipped a *leetle* more.

"Just a *leetle*, very *leetle* bit more."

With great difficulty we tipped just a *leetle*, very *leetle* more.

All this time my uncle was diligently stooping over, and striving to peep in, up, and under the box where the coiled anacondas and adders lay; but the machine being now fairly immersed, the attempt was wholly vain.

He rose erect, and waded slowly all round the box; his countenance firm and reliant, but not a little troubled and vexed.

It was plain something or other was going wrong. But as I was left in utter ignorance as to the mystery of the contrivance, I could not tell where the difficulty lay, or what was the proper remedy.

Once more, still more slowly, still more vexedly, my uncle waded round the box, the dissatisfaction gradually deepening, but still controlled, and still with hope at the bottom of it.

Nothing could be more sure than that some anticipated effect had, as yet, failed to develop itself. Certain I was, too, that the water-line did not lower about my legs.

"Tip it a *leetle* bit—very *leetle* now."

"Dear uncle, it is tipped already as far as it can be. Don't you see it rests now square on its bottom?"

"You, Yorpy, take your black hoof from under the box!"

This gust of passion on the part of my uncle made the matter seem still more dubious and dark. It was a bad symptom, I thought.

"Surely you *can* tip it just a *leetle* more!"

"Not a hair, uncle."

"Blast and blister the cursed box then!" roared my uncle, in a terrific voice, sudden as a squall. Running at the box, he dashed his bare foot into it, and with astonishing power all but crushed in the side. Then seizing the whole box, he disemboweled it of all its anacondas and adders, and, tearing and wrenching them, flung them right and left over the water.

"Hold, hold, my dear, dear uncle!—do for heaven's sake desist. Don't destroy so, in one frantic moment, all your long calm years of devotion to one darling scheme. Hold, I conjure!"

Moved by my vehement voice and uncontrollable tears, he paused in his work of destruction, and stood steadfastly eying me, or rather blankly staring at me, like one demented.

"It is not yet wholly ruined, dear uncle; come put it together now. You have hammer and wrench; put it together again, and try it once more. While there is life there is hope."

"While there is life hereafter there is *despair*," he howled.

"Do, do now, dear uncle—here, here, put these pieces together; or, if that can't be done without more tools, try a *section* of it—that will do just as well. Try it once; try, uncle."

My persistent persuasiveness told upon him. The stubborn stump of hope, plowed at and uprooted in vain, put forth one last miraculous green sprout.

Steadily and carefully culling out of the wreck some of the more curious-looking fragments, he mysteriously involved them together, and then, clearing out the box, slowly inserted them there, and ranging Yorpy and me as before, bade us tip the box once again.

We did so; and as no perceptible effect yet followed, I was each moment looking for the previous command to tip the box over yet more, when, glancing into my uncle's face, I started aghast. It seemed pinched, shriveled into mouldy whiteness, like a mildewed grape. I dropped the box, and sprang toward him just in time to prevent his fall.

Leaving the woeful box where we had dropped it, Yorpy and I helped the old man into the skiff, and silently pulled from Quash Isle.

How swiftly the current now swept us down! How hardly before had we striven to stem it! I thought of my poor uncle's saying, not an hour gone by, about the universal drift of the mass of humanity toward utter oblivion.

"Boy!" said my uncle at last, lifting his head.

I looked at him earnestly, and was gladdened to see that the terrible blight of his face had almost departed.

"Boy, there's not much left in an old world for an old man to invent."

I said nothing.

"Boy, take my advice, and never try to invent any thing but—happiness."

I said nothing.

"Boy, about ship, and pull back for the box."

"Dear uncle!"

"It will make a good wood-box, boy. And faithful old Yorpy can sell the old iron for tobacco-money."

"Dear massa! dear old massa! dat be very fust time in de ten long 'ear yoo hab mention kindly old Yorpy. I tank yoo, dear old massa; I tank yoo so kindly. Yoo is yourself agin in de ten long 'ear."

"Ay, long ears enough," sighed my uncle; "Esopian ears. But it's all over now. Boy, I'm glad I've failed. I say, boy, failure has made a good old man of me. It was horrible at first, but I'm glad I've failed. Praise be to God for the failure!"

His face kindled with a strange, rapt earnestness. I have never forgotten that look. If the event made my uncle a good old man, as he called it, it made me a wise young one. Example did for me the work of experience.

When some years had gone by, and my dear old uncle began to fail, and, after peaceful days of autumnal content, was gathered gently to his fathers—faithful old Yorpy closing his eyes—as I took my last look at his venerable face, the pale resigned lips seemed to move. I seemed to hear again his deep, fervent cry—"Praise be to God for the failure!"

The Fiddler

So my poem is damned, and immortal fame is not for me! I am nobody forever and ever. Intolerable fate!

Snatching my hat, I dashed down the criticism, and rushed out into Broadway, where enthusiastic throngs were crowding to a circus in a side-street near by, very recently started, and famous for a capital clown.

Presently my old friend Standard rather boisterously accosted me.

"Well met, Helmstone, my boy! Ah! what's the matter? Haven't been committing murder? Ain't flying justice? You look wild!"

"You have seen it, then?" said I, of course referring to the criticism.

"Oh yes; I was there at the morning performance. Great clown, I assure you. But here comes Hautboy. Hautboy—Helmstone."

Without having time or inclination to resent so mortifying a mistake, I was instantly soothed as I gazed on the face of the new acquaintance so unceremoniously introduced. His person was short and full, with a juvenile, animated cast to it. His complexion rurally ruddy; his eye sincere, cheery, and gray. His hair alone betrayed that he was not an overgrown boy. From his hair I set him down as forty or more.

"Come, Standard," he gleefully cried to my friend, "are you not going to the circus? The clown is inimitable, they say. Come; Mr. Helmstone, too—come both; and circus over, we'll take a nice stew and punch at Taylor's."

The sterling content, good-humor, and extraordinary ruddy, sincere expression of this most singular new acquaintance acted upon me like magic. It seemed mere loyalty to human nature to accept an invitation from so unmistakably kind and honest a heart.

During the circus performance I kept my eye more on Hautboy than on the celebrated clown. Hautboy was the sight for me. Such genuine enjoyment as his struck me to the soul with a sense of the reality of the thing called happiness. The jokes of the clown he seemed to roll under his tongue as ripe magnum-bonums. Now the foot, now the hand, was employed to attest his grateful applause. At any hit more than ordinary, he turned upon Standard and me to see if his rare pleasure was shared. In a man of forty I saw a boy of twelve; and this too without the slightest abatement of my respect. Because all was so honest and natural, every expression and attitude so graceful with genuine good-nature, that the marvelous juvenility of Hautboy assumed a sort of divine and immortal air, like that of some forever youthful god of Greece.

But much as I gazed upon Hautboy, and much as I admired his air, yet that desperate mood in which I had first rushed from the house had not so entirely departed as not to molest me with momentary returns. But from these relapses I would rouse myself, and swiftly glance round the broad amphitheatre of eagerly interested and all-applauding human faces. Hark! claps, thumps, deafening huzzas; the vast assembly seemed frantic with acclamation; and what, mused I, has caused all this? Why, the clown only comically grinned with one of his extra grins.

Then I repeated in my mind that sublime passage in my poem, in which Cleothemes the Argive vindicates the justice of the war. Ay, ay, thought I to myself, did I now leap into the ring there, and repeat that identical passage, nay, enact the whole tragic poem before them, would they applaud the poet as they applaud the clown? No! They would hoot me, and call me doting or mad. Then what does this prove? Your infatuation or their insensibility? Perhaps both; but indubitably the first. But why wail? Do you seek admiration from the admirers of a buffoon? Call to mind the saying of the Athenian, who, when the people vociferously applauded in the forum, asked his friend in a whisper, what foolish thing had he said?

Again my eye swept the circus, and fell on the ruddy radiance of the countenance of Hautboy. But its clear honest cheeriness disdained my disdain. My intolerant pride was rebuked. And yet Hautboy dreamed not what magic reproof to a soul like mine sat on his laughing brow. At the very instant I felt the dart of the censure, his eye twinkled, his hand waved, his voice was lifted in jubilant delight at another joke of the inexhaustible clown.

Circus over, we went to Taylor's. Among crowds of others, we sat down to our stews and punches at one of the small marble tables. Hautboy sat opposite to me. Though greatly subdued from its former hilarity, his face still shone with gladness. But added to this was a quality not so prominent before; a certain serene expression of leisurely, deep good sense. Good sense and good humor in him joined hands. As the conversation proceeded between the brisk Standard and him—for I said little or nothing—I was more and more struck with the excellent judgment he evinced. In most of his remarks upon a variety of topics Hautboy seemed intuitively to hit the exact line between enthusiasm and apathy. It was plain that while Hautboy saw the world pretty much as it was, yet he did not theoretically espouse its bright side nor its dark side. Rejecting all solutions, he but acknowledged facts. What was sad in the world he did not superficially gain-say; what was glad in it he did not cynically slur; and all which was to him personally enjoyable, he gratefully took to his heart. It was plain, then—so it seemed at that moment, at least—that his extraordinary cheerfulness did not arise either from deficiency of feeling or thought.

Suddenly remembering an engagement, he took up his hat, bowed pleasantly, and left us.

"Well, Helmstone," said Standard, inaudibly drumming on the slab, "what do you think of your new acquaintance?"

The two last words tingled with a peculiar and novel significance.

"New acquaintance indeed," echoed I. "Standard, I owe you a thousand thanks for introducing me to one of the most singular men I have ever seen. It needed the optical sight of such a man to believe in the possibility of his existence."

"You rather like him, then," said Standard, with ironical dryness.

"I hugely love and admire him, Standard. I wish I were Hautboy."

"Ah? That's a pity now. There's only one Hautboy in the world."

This last remark set me to pondering again, and somehow it revived my dark mood.

"His wonderful cheerfulness, I suppose," said I, sneering

with spleen, "originates not less in a felicitous fortune than in a felicitous temper. His great good sense is apparent; but great good sense may exist without sublime endowments. Nay, I take it, in certain cases, that good sense is simply owing to the absence of those. Much more, cheerfulness. Unpossessed of genius, Hautboy is eternally blessed."

"Ah? You would not think him an extraordinary genius then?"

"Genius? What! such a short, fat fellow a genius! Genius, like Cassius, is lank."

"Ah? But could you not fancy that Hautboy might formerly have had genius, but luckily getting rid of it, at last fatted up?"

"For a genius to get rid of his genius is as impossible as for a man in the galloping consumption to get rid of that."

"Ah? You speak very decidedly."

"Yes, Standard," cried I, increasing in spleen, "your cheery Hautboy, after all, is no pattern, no lesson for you and me. With average abilities; opinions clear, because circumscribed; passions docile, because they are feeble; a temper hilarious, because he was born to it—how can your Hautboy be made a reasonable example to a heady fellow like you, or an ambitious dreamer like me? Nothing tempts him beyond common limit; in himself he has nothing to restrain. By constitution he is exempted from all moral harm. Could ambition but prick him; had he but once heard applause, or endured contempt, a very different man would your Hautboy be. Acquiescent and calm from the cradle to the grave, he obviously slides through the crowd."

"Ah?"

"Why do you say *ah* to me so strangely whenever I speak?"

"Did you ever hear of Master Betty?"

"The great English prodigy, who long ago ousted the Siddons and the Kembles from Drury Lane, and made the whole town run mad with acclamation?"

"The same," said Standard, once more inaudibly drumming on the slab.

I looked at him perplexed. He seemed to be holding the master-key of our theme in mysterious reserve; seemed to be throwing out his Master Betty too, to puzzle me only the more.

"What under heaven can Master Betty, the great genius and prodigy, an English boy twelve years old, have to do with the poor common-place plodder Hautboy, an American of forty?"

"Oh, nothing in the least. I don't imagine that they ever saw each other. Besides, Master Betty must be dead and buried long ere this."

"Then why cross the ocean, and rifle the grave to drag his remains into this living discussion?"

"Absent-mindedness, I suppose. I humbly beg pardon. Proceed with your observations on Hautboy. You think he never had genius, quite too contented and happy, and fat for that—ah? You think him no pattern for men in general? affording no lesson of value to neglected merit, genius ignored, or impotent presumption rebuked?—all of which three amount to much the same thing. You admire his cheerfulness, while scorning his common-place soul. Poor Hautboy, how sad that your very cheerfulness should, by a by-blow, bring you despite!"

"I don't say I scorn him; you are unjust. I simply declare that he is no pattern for me."

A sudden noise at my side attracted my ear. Turning, I saw Hautboy again, who very blithely reseated himself on the chair he had left.

"I was behind time with my engagement," said Hautboy, "so thought I would run back and rejoin you. But come, you have sat long enough here. Let us go to my rooms. It is only a five minutes' walk."

"If you will promise to fiddle for us, we will," said Standard.

Fiddle! thought I—he's a jigembob *fiddler* then? No wonder genius declines to measure its pace to a fiddler's bow. My spleen was very strong on me now.

"I will gladly fiddle you your fill," replied Hautboy to Standard. "Come on."

In a few minutes we found ourselves in the fifth story of a sort of storehouse, in a lateral street to Broadway. It was curiously furnished with all sorts of odd furniture which seemed to have been obtained, piece by piece, at auctions of old-fashioned household stuff. But all was charmingly clean and cosy.

Pressed by Standard, Hautboy forthwith got out his dented old fiddle, and sitting down on a tall rickety stool, played away right merrily at Yankee Doodle and other off-handed, dashing, and disdainfully care-free airs. But common as were the tunes, I was transfixed by something miraculously superior in the style. Sitting there on the old stool, his rusty hat sideways cocked on his head, one foot dangling adrift, he plied the bow of an enchanter. All my moody discontent, every vestige of peevishness fled. My whole splenetic soul capitulated to the magical fiddle.

"Something of an Orpheus, ah?" said Standard, archly nudging me beneath the left rib.

"And I, the charmed Bruin," murmured I.

The fiddle ceased. Once more, with redoubled curiosity, I gazed upon the easy, indifferent Hautboy. But he entirely baffled inquisition.

When, leaving him, Standard and I were in the street once more, I earnestly conjured him to tell me who, in sober truth, this marvelous Hautboy was.

"Why, haven't you seen him? And didn't you yourself lay his whole anatomy open on the marble slab at Taylor's? What more can you possibly learn? Doubtless your own masterly insight has already put you in possession of all."

"You mock me, Standard. There is some mystery here. Tell me, I entreat you, who is Hautboy?"

"An extraordinary genius, Helmstone," said Standard, with sudden ardor, " who in boyhood drained the whole flagon of glory; whose going from city to city was a going from triumph to triumph. One who has been an object of wonder to the wisest, been caressed by the loveliest, received the open homage of thousands on thousands of the rabble. But to-day he walks Broadway and no man knows him. With you and me, the elbow of the hurrying clerk, and the pole of the remorseless omnibus, shove him. He who has a hundred times been crowned with laurels, now wears, as you see, a bunged beaver. Once fortune poured showers of gold into his lap, as showers of laurel leaves upon his brow. To-day, from house to house, he hies, teaching fiddling for a living. Crammed once with fame, he is now hilarious without it. *With* genius and *without* fame, he is happier than a king. More a prodigy now than ever."

"His true name?"

"Let me whisper it in your ear."

"What! Oh Standard, myself, as a child, have shouted myself hoarse applauding that very name in the theatre."

"I have heard your poem was not very handsomely received," said Standard, now suddenly shifting the subject.

"Not a word of that, for heaven's sake!" cried I. "If Cicero, traveling in the East, found sympathetic solace for his grief in beholding the arid overthrow of a once gorgeous city, shall not my petty affair be as nothing, when I behold in Hautboy the vine and the rose climbing the shattered shafts of his tumbled temple of Fame?"

Next day I tore all my manuscripts, bought me a fiddle, and went to take regular lessons of Hautboy.

Cock-A-Doodle-Doo!
Or, The Crowing of the Noble Cock
Beneventano

IN ALL PARTS of the world many high-spirited revolts from rascally despotisms had of late been knocked on the head; many dreadful casualties, by locomotive and steamer, had likewise knocked hundreds of high-spirited travelers on the head (I lost a dear friend in one of them); my own private affairs were also full of despotisms, casualties, and knockings on the head, when early one morning in Spring, being too full of hypoes to sleep, I sallied out to walk on my hill-side pasture.

It was a cool and misty, damp, disagreeable air. The country looked underdone, its raw juices squirting out all round. I buttoned out this squitchy air as well as I could with my lean, double-breasted dress-coat—my over-coat being so long-skirted I only used it in my wagon—and spitefully thrusting my crab-stick into the oozy sod, bent my blue form to the steep ascent of the hill. This toiling posture brought my head pretty well earthward, as if I were in the act of butting it against the world. I marked the fact, but only grinned at it with a ghastly grin.

All round me were tokens of a divided empire. The old grass and the new grass were striving together. In the low wet swales the verdure peeped out in vivid green; beyond, on the mountains, lay light patches of snow, strangely relieved against their russet sides; all the humped hills looked like brindled kine in the shivers. The woods were strewn with dry dead boughs, snapped off by the riotous winds of March, while the young trees skirting the woods were just beginning to show the first yellowish tinge of the nascent spray.

I sat down for a moment on a great rotting log nigh the top of the hill, my back to a heavy grove, my face presented toward a wide sweeping circuit of mountains enclosing a rolling, diversified country. Along the base of one long range of heights ran a lagging, fever-and-agueish river, over which was a duplicate stream of dripping mist, exactly corresponding in every meander with its parent water below. Low down, here and there, shreds of vapor listlessly wandered in the air, like abandoned or helmless nations or ships—or very soaky towels hung on criss-cross clothes-lines to dry. Afar, over a distant village lying in a bay of the plain formed by the mountains, there rested a great flat canopy of haze, like a pall. It was the condensed smoke of the chimneys, with the condensed, exhaled breath of the villagers, prevented from dispersion by the imprisoning hills. It was too heavy and lifeless to mount of itself; so there it lay, between the village and the sky, doubtless hiding many a man with the mumps, and many a queasy child.

My eye ranged over the capacious rolling country, and over the mountains, and over the village, and over a farm-house here and there, and over woods, groves, streams, rocks, fells—and I thought to myself, what a slight mark, after all, does man make on this huge great earth. Yet the earth makes a mark on him. What a horrid accident was that on the Ohio, where my good friend and thirty other good fellows were sloped into eternity at the bidding of a thick-headed engineer, who knew not a valve from a flue. And that crash on the railroad just over yon mountains there, where two infatuate trains ran pell-mell into each other, and climbed and clawed each other's backs; and one locomotive was found fairly shelled, like a chick, inside of a passenger car in the antagonist train; and near a score of noble hearts, a bride and her groom, and an innocent little infant, were all disembarked into the grim hulk of Charon, who ferried them over, all baggageless, to some clinkered iron-foundry country or other. Yet what's the use of complaining? What justice of the peace will right this matter? Yea, what's the use of bothering the very heavens about it? Don't the heavens themselves ordain these things— else they could not happen?

A miserable world! Who would take the trouble to make a fortune in it, when he knows not how long he can keep it, for the thousand villains and asses who have the management of railroads and steamboats, and innumerable other vital things in the world. If they would make me Dictator in North America a while, I'd string them up! and hang, draw, and quarter; fry, roast, and boil; stew, grill, and devil them, like

so many turkey-legs—the rascally numskulls of stokers; I'd
set them to stokering in Tartarus—I would.

Great improvements of the age! What! to call the facilita-
tion of death and murder an improvement! Who wants to
travel so fast? My grandfather did not, and he was no fool.
Hark! here comes that old dragon again—that gigantic
gad-fly of a Moloch—snort! puff! scream!—here he comes
straight-bent through these vernal woods, like the Asiatic
cholera cantering on a camel. Stand aside! here he comes, the
chartered murderer! the death monopolizer! judge, jury, and
hangman all together, whose victims die always without benefit of clergy. For two hundred and fifty miles that iron fiend
goes yelling through the land, crying "More! more! more!"
Would fifty conspiring mountains would fall atop of him!
And, while they were about it, would they would also fall
atop of that smaller dunning fiend, my creditor, who frightens the life out of me more than any locomotive—a lantern-
jawed rascal, who seems to run on a railroad track too, and
duns me even on Sunday, all the way to church and back, and
comes and sits in the same pew with me, and pretending to
be polite and hand me the prayer-book opened at the proper
place, pokes his pesky bill under my nose in the very midst of
my devotions, and so shoves himself between me and salvation; for how can one keep his temper on such occasions?

I can't pay this horrid man; and yet they say money was
never so plentiful—a drug in the market; but blame me if I
can get any of the drug, though there never was a sick man
more in need of that particular sort of medicine. It's a lie;
money ain't plenty—feel of my pocket. Ha! here's a powder
I was going to send to the sick baby in yonder hovel, where
the Irish ditcher lives. That baby has the scarlet fever. They
say the measles are rife in the country too, and the varioloid,
and the chicken-pox, and it's bad for teething children. And
after all, I suppose many of the poor little ones, after going
through all this trouble, snap off short; and so they had the
measles, mumps, croup, scarlet-fever, chicken-pox, cholera-
morbus, summer-complaint, and all else, in vain! Ah! there's
that twinge of the rheumatics in my right shoulder. I got it
one night on the North River, when, in a crowded boat, I
gave up my berth to a sick lady, and staid on deck till morn-

ing in drizzling weather. There's the thanks one gets for charity! Twinge! Shoot away, ye rheumatics! Ye couldn't lay on worse if I were some villain who had murdered the lady instead of befriending her. Dyspepsia too—I am troubled with that.

Hallo! here come the calves, the two-year-olds, just turned out of the barn into the pasture, after six months of cold victuals. What a miserable-looking set, to be sure! A breaking up of a hard winter, that's certain: sharp bones sticking out like elbows; all quilted with a strange stuff dried on their flanks like layers of pancakes. Hair worn quite off too, here and there; and where it ain't pancaked, or worn off, looks like the rubbed sides of mangy old hair-trunks. In fact, they are not six two-year-olds, but six abominable old hair-trunks wandering about here in this pasture.

Hark! By Jove, what's that? See! the very hair-trunks prick their ears at it, and stand and gaze away down into the rolling country yonder. Hark again! How clear! how musical! how prolonged! What a triumphant thanksgiving of a cock-crow! *"Glory be to God in the highest!"* It says those very words as plain as ever cock did in this world. Why, why, I begin to feel a little in sorts again. It ain't so very misty, after all. The sun yonder is beginning to show himself: I feel warmer.

Hark! There again! Did ever such a blessed cock-crow so ring out over the earth before! Clear, shrill, full of pluck, full of fire, full of fun, full of glee. It plainly says—*"Never say die!"* My friends, it is extraordinary is it not?

Unwittingly, I found that I had been addressing the two-year-olds—the calves—in my enthusiasm; which shows how one's true nature will betray itself at times in the most unconscious way. For what a very two-year-old, and calf, I had been to fall into the sulks, on a hill-top too, when a cock down in the lowlands there, without discourse of reason, and quite penniless in the world, and with death hanging over him at any moment from his hungry master, sends up a cry like a very laureate celebrating the glorious victory of New Orleans.

Hark! there it goes again! My friends, that must be a Shanghai; no domestic-born cock could crow in such prodigious exulting strains. Plainly, my friends, a Shanghai of the Emperor of China's breed.

But my friends the hair-trunks, fairly alarmed at last by such clamorously-victorious tones, were now scampering off, with their tails flirting in the air, and capering with their legs in clumsy enough sort of style, sufficiently evincing that they had not freely flourished them for the six months last past.

Hark! there again! Whose cock is that? Who in this region can afford to buy such an extraordinary Shanghai? Bless me— it makes my blood bound—I feel wild. What? jumping on this rotten old log here, to flap my elbows and crow too? And just now in the doleful dumps. And all this from the simple crow of a cock. Marvelous cock! But soft—this fellow now crows most lustily; but it's only morning; let's see how he'll crow about noon, and toward night-fall. Come to think of it, cocks crow mostly in the beginning of the day. Their pluck ain't lasting, after all. Yes, yes; even cocks have to succumb to the universal spell of tribulation: jubilant in the beginning, but down in the mouth at the end.

> . . . . "Of fine mornings,
> We fine lusty cocks begin our crows in gladness;
> But when eve does come we don't crow quite so much,
> For then cometh despondency and madness."

The poet had this very Shanghai in his mind when he wrote that. But stop. There he rings out again, ten times richer, fuller, longer, more obstreperously exulting than before! Why this is equal to hearing the great bell of St. Paul's rung at a coronation! In fact, that bell ought to be taken down, and this Shanghai put in its place. Such a crow would jollify all London, from Mile-End (which is no end) to Primrose Hill (where there ain't any primroses), and scatter the fog.

Well, I have an appetite for my breakfast this morning, if I have not had it for a week before. I meant to have only tea and toast; but I'll have coffee and eggs—no, brown-stout and a beef-steak. I want something hearty. Ah, here comes the down-train: white cars, flashing through the trees like a vein of silver. How cheerfully the steam-pipe chirps! Gay are the passengers. There waves a handkerchief—going down to the city to eat oysters, and see their friends, and drop in at the

circus. Look at the mist yonder; what soft curls and undulations round the hills, and the sun weaving his rays among
them. See the azure smoke of the village, like the azure tester
over a bridal-bed. How bright the country looks there where
the river overflowed the meadows. The old grass has to knock
under to the new. Well, I feel the better for this walk. Home
now, and walk into that steak and crack that bottle of brown-
stout; and by the time that's drank—a quart of stout—by
that time, I shall feel about as stout as Samson. Come to think
of it, that dun may call, though. I'll just visit the woods and
cut a club. I'll club him, by Jove, if he duns me this day.

Hark! there goes Shanghai again. Shanghai says, "Bravo!"
Shanghai says, "Club him!"

Oh, brave cock!

I felt in rare spirits the whole morning. The dun called
about eleven. I had the boy Jake send the dun up. I was reading Tristram Shandy, and could not go down under the circumstances. The lean rascal (a lean farmer, too—think of
that!) entered, and found me seated in an arm-chair, with my
feet on the table, and the second bottle of brown-stout handy,
and the book under eye.

"Sit down," said I; "I'll finish this chapter, and then attend
to you. Fine morning. Ha! ha!—this is a fine joke about my
Uncle Toby and the Widow Wadman! Ha! ha! ha! let me read
this to you."

"I have no time; I've got my noon *chores* to do."

"To the deuce with your *chores*!" said I. "Don't drop your
old tobacco about here, or I'll turn you out."

"Sir!"

"Let me read you this about the Widow Wadman. 'Said the
Widow Wadman—' "

"There's my bill, sir."

"Very good. Just twist it up, will you;—it's about my
smoking-time; and hand a coal, will you, from the hearth
yonder!"

"My bill, sir!" said the rascal, turning pale with rage and
amazement at my unwonted air (formerly I had always
dodged him with a pale face), but too prudent as yet to betray the extremity of his astonishment. "My bill, sir!"—and
he stiffly poked it at me.

"My friend," said I, "what a charming morning! How sweet the country looks! Pray, did you hear that extraordinary cock-crow this morning? Take a glass of my stout!"

"*Yours?* First pay your debts before you offer folks *your* stout!"

"You think, then, that, properly speaking, I have no *stout*," said I, deliberately rising. "I'll undeceive you. I'll show you stout of a superior brand to Barclay and Perkins."

Without more ado, I seized that insolent dun by the slack of his coat—(and, being a lean, shad-bellied wretch, there was plenty of slack to it)—I seized him that way, tied him with a sailor-knot, and, thrusting his bill between his teeth, introduced him to the open country lying round about my place of abode.

"Jake," said I, "you'll find a sack of blue-nosed potatoes lying under the shed. Drag it here, and pelt this pauper away: he's been begging pence of me, and I know he can work, but he's lazy. Pelt him away, Jake!"

Bless my stars, what a crow! Shanghai sent up such a perfect pæan and *laudamus*—such a trumpet-blast of triumph, that my soul fairly snorted in me. Duns!—I could have fought an army of them! Plainly, Shanghai was of the opinion that duns only came into the world to be kicked, hanged, bruised, battered, choked, walloped, hammered, drowned, clubbed!

Returning in-doors, when the exultation of my victory over the dun had a little subsided, I fell to musing over the mysterious Shanghai. I had no idea I would hear him so nigh my house. I wondered from what rich gentleman's yard he crowed. Nor had he cut short his crows so easily as I had supposed he would. This Shanghai crowded till mid-day, at least. Would he keep a-crowing all day? I resolved to learn. Again I ascended the hill. The whole country was now bathed in a rejoicing sunlight. The warm verdure was bursting all round me. Teams were a-field. Birds, newly arrived from the South, were blithely singing in the air. Even the crows cawed with a certain unction, and seemed a shade or two less black than usual.

Hark! there goes the cock! How shall I describe the crow of the Shanghai at noon-tide? His sun-rise crow was a whisper to it. It was the loudest, longest, and most strangely-musical crow that ever amazed mortal man. I had heard plenty of cock-crows before, and many fine ones;—but this one! so smooth and flute-like in its very clamor—so self-possessed in its very rapture of exultation—so vast, mounting, swelling, soaring, as if spurted out from a golden throat, thrown far back. Nor did it sound like the foolish, vain-glorious crow of some young sophomorean cock, who knew not the world, and was beginning life in audacious gay spirits, because in wretched ignorance of what might be to come. It was the crow of a cock who crowed not without advice; the crow of a cock who knew a thing or two; the crow of a cock who had fought the world and got the better of it, and was now resolved to crow, though the earth should heave and the heavens should fall. It was a wise crow; an invincible crow; a philosophic crow; a crow of all crows.

I returned home once more full of reinvigorated spirits, with a dauntless sort of feeling. I thought over my debts and other troubles, and over the unlucky risings of the poor oppressed *peoples* abroad, and over the railroad and steamboat accidents, and over even the loss of my dear friend, with a calm, good-natured rapture of defiance, which astounded myself. I felt as though I could meet Death, and invite him to dinner, and toast the Catacombs with him, in pure overflow of self-reliance and a sense of universal security.

Toward evening I went up to the hill once more to find whether, indeed, the glorious cock would prove game even from the rising of the sun unto the going down thereof. Talk of Vespers or Curfew!—the evening crow of the cock went out of his mighty throat all over the land and inhabited it, like Xerxes from the East with his double-winged host. It was miraculous. Bless me, what a crow! The cock went game to roost that night, depend upon it, victorious over the entire day, and bequeathing the echoes of his thousand crows to night.

After an unwontedly sound, refreshing sleep I rose early, feeling like a carriage-spring—light—elliptical—airy—buoyant as sturgeon-nose—and, like a foot-ball, bounded up the hill. Hark! Shanghai was up before me. The early bird that caught the worm—crowing like a bugle worked by an engine—lusty, loud, all jubilation. From the scattered farm-houses a multitude of other cocks were crowing, and replying to each other's crows. But they were as flageolets to a trombone. Shanghai would suddenly break in, and overwhelm all their crows with his one domineering blast. He seemed to have nothing to do with any other concern. He replied to no other crow, but crowed solely by himself, on his own account, in solitary scorn and independence.

Oh, brave cock!—oh, noble Shanghai!—oh, bird rightly offered up by the invincible Socrates, in testimony of his final victory over life.

As I live, thought I, this blessed day will I go and seek out the Shanghai, and buy him, if I have to clap another mortgage on my land.

I listened attentively now, striving to mark from what direction the crow came. But it so charged and replenished, and made bountiful and overflowing all the air, that it was impossible to say from what precise point the exultation came. All that I could decide upon was this: the crow came from out of the East, and not from out of the West. I then considered with myself how far a cock-crow might be heard. In this still country, shut in, too, by mountains, sounds were audible at great distances. Besides, the undulations of the land, the abuttings of the mountains into the rolling hill and valley below, produced strange echoes, and reverberations, and multiplications, and accumulations of resonance, very remarkable to hear, and very puzzling to think of. Where lurked this valiant Shanghai—this bird of cheerful Socrates—the game-fowl Greek who died unappalled? Where lurked he? Oh, noble cock, where are you? Crow once more, my Bantam! my princely, my imperial Shanghai! my bird of the Emperor of China! Brother of the Sun! Cousin of great Jove! where are you?—one crow more, and tell me your master!

Hark! like a full orchestra of the cocks of all nations, forth burst the crow. But where from? There it is; but where? There was no telling, further than it came from out the East.

After breakfast I took my stick and sallied down the road. There were many gentlemen's seats dotting the neighboring country, and I made no doubt that some of these opulent gentlemen had invested a hundred dollar bill in some royal

Shanghai recently imported in the ship Trade Wind, or the ship White Squall, or the ship Sovereign of the Seas; for it must needs have been a brave ship with a brave name which bore the fortunes of so brave a cock. I resolved to walk the entire country, and find this noble foreigner out; but thought it would not be amiss to inquire on the way at the humblest homesteads, whether, peradventure, they had heard of a lately-imported Shanghai belonging to any of the gentlemen settlers from the city; for it was plain that no poor farmer, no poor man of any sort, could own such an Oriental trophy— such a Great Bell of St. Paul's swung in a cock's throat.

I met an old man, plowing, in a field nigh the road-side fence.

"My friend, have you heard an extraordinary cock-crow of late?"

"Well, well," he drawled, "I don't know—the Widow Crowfoot has a cock—and Squire Squaretoes has a cock— and I have a cock, and they all crow. But I don't know of any on 'em with 'strordinary crows."

"Good-morning to you," said I, shortly; "it's plain that you have not heard the crow of the Emperor of China's chanticleer."

Presently I met another old man mending a tumble-down old rail-fence. The rails were rotten, and at every move of the old man's hand they crumbled into yellow ochre. He had much better let the fence alone, or else get him new rails. And here I must say, that one cause of the sad fact why idiocy more prevails among farmers than any other class of people, is owing to their undertaking the mending of rotten rail-fences in warm, relaxing spring weather. The enterprise is a hopeless one. It is a laborious one. It is a bootless one. It is an enterprise to make the heart break. Vast pains squandered upon a vanity. For how can one make rotten rail-fences stand up on their rotten pins? By what magic put pith into sticks which have lain freezing and baking through sixty consecutive winters and summers? This it is, this wretched endeavor to mend rotten rail-fences with their own rotten rails, which drives many farmers into the asylum.

On the face of the old man in question incipient idiocy was plainly marked. For, about sixty rods before him extended one of the most unhappy and desponding broken-hearted Virginia rail-fences I ever saw in my life. While in a field behind, were a set of young steers, possessed as by devils, continually butting at this forlorn old fence, and breaking through it here and there, causing the old man to drop his work and chase them back within bounds. He would chase them with a piece of rail huge as Goliath's beam, but as light as cork. At the first flourish, it crumbled into powder.

"My friend," said I, addressing this woeful mortal, "have you heard an extraordinary cock-crow of late?"

I might as well have asked him if he had heard the death-tick. He stared at me with a long, bewildered, doleful, and unutterable stare, and without reply resumed his unhappy labors.

What a fool, thought I, to have asked such an uncheerful and uncheerable creature about a cheerful cock!

I walked on. I had now descended the high land where my house stood, and being in a low tract could not hear the crow of the Shanghai, which doubtless overshot me there. Besides, the Shanghai might be at lunch of corn and oats, or taking a nap, and so interrupted his jubilations for a while.

At length, I encountered riding along the road, a portly gentleman—nay, a *pursy* one—of great wealth, who had recently purchased him some noble acres, and built him a noble mansion, with a goodly fowl-house attached, the fame whereof spread through all that country. Thought I, Here now is the owner of the Shanghai.

"Sir," said I, "excuse me, but I am a countryman of yours, and would ask, if so be you own any Shanghais?"

"Oh, yes; I have ten Shanghais."

"Ten!" exclaimed I, in wonder; "and do they all crow?"

"Most lustily; every soul of them; I wouldn't own a cock that wouldn't crow."

"Will you turn back, and show me those Shanghais?"

"With pleasure: I am proud of them. They cost me, in the lump, six hundred dollars."

As I walked by the side of his horse, I was thinking to myself whether possibly I had not mistaken the harmoniously combined crowings of ten Shanghais in a squad, for the supernatural crow of a single Shanghai by himself.

"Sir," said I, "is there one of your Shanghais which far exceeds all the others in the lustiness, musicalness, and inspiring effects of his crow?"

"They crow pretty much alike, I believe," he courteously replied; "I really don't know that I could tell their crow apart."

I began to think that after all my noble chanticleer might not be in the possession of this wealthy gentleman. However, we went into his fowl-yard, and I saw his Shanghais. Let me say that hitherto I had never clapped eye on this species of imported fowl. I had heard what enormous prices were paid for them, and also that they were of an enormous size, and had somehow fancied they must be of a beauty and brilliancy proportioned both to size and price. What was my surprise, then, to see ten carrot-colored monsters, without the smallest pretension to effulgence of plumage. Immediately, I determined that my royal cock was neither among these, nor could possibly be a Shanghai at all; if these gigantic gallows-bird fowl were fair specimens of the true Shanghai.

I walked all day, dining and resting at a farm-house, inspecting various fowl-yards, interrogating various owners of fowls, hearkening to various crows, but discovered not the mysterious chanticleer. Indeed, I had wandered so far and deviously, that I could not hear his crow. I began to suspect that this cock was a mere visitor in the country, who had taken his departure by the eleven o'clock train for the South, and was now crowing and jubilating somewhere on the verdant banks of Long Island Sound.

But next morning, again I heard the inspiring blast, again felt my blood bound in me, again felt superior to all the ills of life, again felt like turning my dun out of doors. But displeased with the reception given him at his last visit, the dun staid away. Doubtless being in a huff; silly fellow that he was to take a harmless joke in earnest.

Several days passed, during which I made sundry excursions in the regions roundabout, but in vain sought the cock. Still, I heard him from the hill, and sometimes from the house, and sometimes in the stillness of the night. If at times I would relapse into my doleful dumps, straightway at the sound of the exultant and defiant crow, my soul, too, would turn chanticleer, and clap her wings, and throw back her throat, and breathe forth a cheerful challenge to all the world of woes.

At last, after some weeks I was necessitated to clap another mortgage on my estate, in order to pay certain debts, and among others the one I owed the dun, who of late had commenced a civil-process against me. The way the process was served was a most insulting one. In a private room I had been enjoying myself in the village-tavern over a bottle of Philadelphia porter, and some Herkimer cheese, and a roll, and having apprised the landlord, who was a friend of mine, that I would settle with him when I received my next remittances, stepped to the peg where I had hung my hat in the bar-room, to get a choice cigar I had left in the hall, when lo! I found the civil-process enveloping the cigar. When I unrolled the cigar, I unrolled the civil-process, and the constable standing by rolled out, with a thick tongue, "Take notice!" and added, in a whisper, "Put that in your pipe and smoke it!"

I turned short round upon the gentlemen then and there present in that bar-room. Said I, "Gentlemen, is this an honorable—nay, is this a lawful way of serving a civil-process? Behold!"

One and all they were of opinion, that it was a highly inelegant act in the constable to take advantage of a gentleman's lunching on cheese and porter, to be so uncivil as to slip a civil-process into his hat. It was ungenerous; it was cruel; for the sudden shock of the thing coming instanter upon the lunch, would impair the proper digestion of the cheese, which is proverbially not so easy of digestion as *blanc-mange*.

Arrived home, I read the process, and felt a twinge of melancholy. Hard world! hard world! Here I am, as good a fellow as ever lived—hospitable—open-hearted—generous to a fault: and the Fates forbid that I should possess the fortune to bless the country with my bounteousness. Nay, while many a stingy curmudgeon rolls in idle gold, I, heart of nobleness as I am, I have civil-processes served on me! I bowed my head, and felt forlorn—unjustly used—abused—unappreciated—in short, miserable.

Hark! like a clarion! yea, like a jolly bolt of thunder with bells to it—came the all-glorious and defiant crow! Ye gods,

how it set me up again! Right on my pins! Yea, verily on
stilts!

Oh, noble cock!

Plain as cock could speak, it said, "Let the world and all
aboard of it go to pot. Do you be jolly, and never say die.
What's the world compared to you? What is it, any how, but
a lump of loam? Do you be jolly!"

Oh, noble cock!

"But my dear and glorious cock," mused I, upon second
thought, "one can't so easily send this world to pot; one can't
so easily be jolly with civil processes in his hat or hand."

Hark! the crow again. Plain as cock could speak, it said:
"Hang the process, and hang the fellow that sent it! If you
have not land or cash, go and thrash the fellow, and tell him
you never mean to pay him. Be jolly!"

Now this was the way—through the imperative intimations of the cock—that I came to clap the added mortgage
on my estate; paid all my debts by fusing them into this one
added bond and mortgage. Thus made at ease again, I renewed my search for the noble cock. But in vain, though I
heard him every day. I began to think there was some sort of
deception in this mysterious thing: some wonderful ventriloquist prowled around my barns, or in my cellar, or on my
roof, and was minded to be gayly mischievous. But no—
what ventriloquist could so crow with such an heroic and celestial crow?

At last, one morning there came to me a certain singular
man, who had sawed and split my wood in March—some
five-and-thirty cords of it—and now he came for his pay. He
was a singular man, I say. He was tall and spare, with a long
saddish face, yet somehow a latently joyous eye, which offered the strangest contrast. His air seemed staid, but unde-
pressed. He wore a long, gray, shabby coat, and a big
battered hat. This man had sawed my wood at so much a
cord. He would stand and saw all day long in a driving snow-
storm, and never wink at it. He never spoke unless spoken to.
He only sawed. Saw, saw, saw—snow, snow, snow. The saw
and the snow went together like two natural things. The first
day this man came, he brought his dinner with him, and volunteered to eat it sitting on his buck in the snow-storm. From

my window, where I was reading Burton's Anatomy of Melancholy, I saw him in the act. I burst out of doors bareheaded. "Good heavens!" cried I; "what are you doing? Come in. *This* your dinner!"

He had a hunk of stale bread and another hunk of salt beef, wrapped in a wet newspaper, and washed his morsels down by melting a handful of fresh snow in his mouth. I took this rash man indoors, planted him by the fire, gave him a dish of hot pork and beans, and a mug of cider.

"Now," said I, "don't you bring any of your damp dinners here. You work by the job, to be sure; but I'll dine you for all that."

He expressed his acknowledgments in a calm, proud, but not ungrateful way, and dispatched his meal with satisfaction to himself, and me also. It afforded me pleasure to perceive that he quaffed down his mug of cider like a man. I honored him. When I addressed him in the way of business at his buck, I did so in a guardedly respectful and deferential manner. Interested in his singular aspect, struck by his wondrous intensity of application at his saw—a most wearisome and disgustful occupation to most people—I often sought to gather from him who he was, what sort of a life he led, where he was born, and so on. But he was mum. He came to saw my wood, and eat my dinners—if I chose to offer them— but not to gabble. At first, I somewhat resented his sullen silence under the circumstances. But better considering it, I honored him the more. I increased the respectfulness and deferentialness of my address toward him. I concluded within myself that this man had experienced hard times; that he had had many sore rubs in the world; that he was of a solemn disposition; that he was of the mind of Solomon; that he lived calmly, decorously, temperately; and though a very poor man, was, nevertheless, a highly respectable one. At times I imagined that he might even be an elder or deacon of some small country church. I thought it would not be a bad plan to run this excellent man for President of the United States. He would prove a great reformer of abuses.

His name was Merrymusk. I had often thought how jolly a name for so unjolly a wight. I inquired of people whether they knew Merrymusk. But it was some time before I learned much about him. He was by birth a Marylander, it appeared, who had long lived in the country round about; a wandering man; until within some ten years ago, a thriftless man, though perfectly innocent of crime; a man who would work hard a month with surprising soberness, and then spend all his wages in one riotous night. In youth he had been a sailor, and run away from his ship at Batavia, where he caught the fever, and came nigh dying. But he rallied, reshipped, landed home, found all his friends dead, and struck for the Northern interior, where he had since tarried. Nine years back he had married a wife, and now had four children. His wife was become a perfect invalid; one child had the white-swelling, and the rest were rickety. He and his family lived in a shanty on a lonely barren patch nigh the railroad-track, where it passed close to the base of a mountain. He had bought a fine cow to have plenty of wholesome milk for his children; but the cow died during an accouchement, and he could not afford to buy another. Still, his family never suffered for lack of food. He worked hard and brought it to them.

Now, as I said before, having long previously sawed my wood, this Merrymusk came for his pay.

"My friend," said I, "do you know of any gentleman hereabouts who owns an extraordinary cock?"

The twinkle glittered quite plain in the wood-sawyer's eye.

"I know of no *gentleman*," he replied, "who has what might well be called an extraordinary cock."

Oh, thought I, this Merrymusk is not the man to enlighten me. I am afraid I shall never discover this extraordinary cock.

Not having the full change to pay Merrymusk, I gave him his due, as nigh as I could make it, and told him that in a day or two I would take a walk and visit his place, and hand him the remainder. Accordingly one fine morning I sallied forth upon the errand. I had much ado finding the best road to the shanty. No one seemed to know where it was exactly. It lay in a very lonely part of the country, a densely-wooded mountain on one side (which I call October Mountain, on account of its bannered aspect in that month), and a thicketed swamp on the other, the railroad cutting the swamp. Straight as a die the railroad cut it; many times a day tantalizing the wretched shanty with the sight of all the beauty, rank, fashion, health, trunks, silver and gold, dry-goods and groceries, brides and grooms, happy wives and husbands, flying by the lonely door—no time to stop—flash! here they are—and there they go!—out of sight at both ends—as if that part of the world were only made to fly over, and not to settle upon. And this was about all the shanty saw of what people call "life."

Though puzzled somewhat, yet I knew the general direction where the shanty lay, and on I trudged. As I advanced, I was surprised to hear the mysterious cock-crow with more and more distinctness. Is it possible, thought I, that any gentleman owning a Shanghai can dwell in such a lonesome, dreary region? Louder and louder, nigher and nigher, sounded the glorious and defiant clarion. Though somehow I may be out of the track to my wood-sawyer's, I said to myself, yet, thank heaven, I seem to be on the way toward that extraordinary cock. I was delighted with this auspicious accident. On I journeyed; while at intervals the crow sounded most invitingly, and jocundly, and superbly; and the last crow was ever nigher than the former one. At last, emerging from a thicket of elders, straight before me I saw the most resplendent creature that ever blessed the sight of man.

A cock, more like a golden eagle than a cock. A cock, more like a Field-Marshal than a cock. A cock, more like Lord Nelson with all his glittering arms on, standing on the Vanguard's quarter-deck going into battle, than a cock. A cock, more like the Emperor Charlemagne in his robes at Aix la Chapelle, than a cock.

Such a cock!

He was of a haughty size, stood haughtily on his haughty legs. His colors were red, gold, and white. The red was on his crest alone, which was a mighty and symmetric crest, like unto Hector's helmet, as delineated on antique shields. His plumage was snowy, traced with gold. He walked in front of the shanty, like a peer of the realm; his crest lifted, his chest heaved out, his embroidered trappings flashing in the light. His pace was wonderful. He looked like some noble foreigner. He looked like some Oriental king in some magnificent Italian Opera.

Merrymusk advanced from the door.

"Pray is not that the Signor Beneventano?"

"Sir?"

"That's the cock," said I, a little embarrassed. The truth was, my enthusiasm had betrayed me into a rather silly inadvertence. I had made a somewhat learned sort of allusion in the presence of an unlearned man. Consequently, upon discovering it by his honest stare, I felt foolish; but carried it off by declaring that *this was the cock.*

Now, during the preceding autumn I had been to the city, and had chanced to be present at a performance of the Italian Opera. In that Opera figured in some royal character a certain Signor Beneventano—a man of a tall, imposing person, clad in rich raiment, like to plumage, and with a most remarkable, majestic, scornful stride. The Signor Beneventano seemed on the point of tumbling over backward with exceeding haughtiness. And, for all the world, the proud pace of the cock seemed the very stage-pace of the Signor Beneventano.

Hark! Suddenly the cock paused, lifted his head still higher, ruffled his plumes, seemed inspired, and sent forth a lusty crow. October Mountain echoed it; other mountains sent it back; still others rebounded it; it overran the country round. Now I plainly perceived how it was I had chanced to hear the gladdening sound on my distant hill.

"Good Heavens! do you own the cock? Is that cock yours?"

"Is it my cock!" said Merrymusk, looking slyly gleeful out of the corner of his long, solemn face.

"Where did you get it?"

"It chipped the shell here. I raised it."

"You?"

Hark! Another crow. It might have raised the ghosts of all the pines and hemlocks ever cut down in that country. Marvelous cock! Having crowed, he strode on again, surrounded by a bevy of admiring hens.

"What will you take for Signor Beneventano?"

"Sir?"

"That magic cock!—what will you take for him?"

"I won't sell him."

"I will give you fifty dollars."

"Pooh!"

"One hundred!"

"Pish!"

"Five hundred!"

"Bah!"

"And you a poor man?"

"No; don't I own that cock, and haven't I refused five hundred dollars for him?"

"True," said I, in profound thought; "that's a fact. You won't sell him, then?"

"No."

"Will you give him?"

"No."

"Will you *keep* him, then!" I shouted, in a rage.

"Yes."

I stood awhile admiring the cock, and wondering at the man. At last I felt a redoubled admiration of the one, and a redoubled deference for the other.

"Won't you step in?" said Merrymusk.

"But won't the cock be prevailed upon to join us?" said I.

"Yes. Trumpet! hither, boy! hither!"

The cock turned round, and strode up to Merrymusk.

"Come!"

The cock followed us into the shanty.

"Crow!"

The roof jarred.

Oh, noble cock!

I turned in silence upon my entertainer. There he sat on an old battered chest, in his old battered gray coat, with patches at his knees and elbows, and a deplorably bunged hat. I glanced round the room. Bare rafters overhead, but solid junks of jerked beef hanging from them. Earth floor, but a heap of potatoes in one corner, and a sack of Indian meal in another. A blanket was strung across the apartment at the further end, from which came a woman's ailing voice and the voices of ailing children. But somehow in the ailing of these voices there seemed no complaint.

"Mrs. Merrymusk and children?"

"Yes."

I looked at the cock. There he stood majestically in the middle of the room. He looked like a Spanish grandee caught in a shower, and standing under some peasant's shed. There was a strange supernatural look of contrast about him. He irradiated the shanty; he glorified its meanness. He glorified the battered chest, and tattered gray coat, and the bunged hat. He glorified the very voices which came in ailing tones from behind the screen.

"Oh, father," cried a little sickly voice, "let Trumpet sound again."

"Crow," cried Merrymusk.

The cock threw himself into a posture.

The roof jarred.

"Does not this disturb Mrs. Merrymusk and the sick children?"

"Crow again, Trumpet."

The roof jarred.

"It does not disturb them, then?"

"Didn't you hear 'em *ask* for it?"

"How is it, that your sick family like this crowing?" said I. "The cock is a glorious cock, with a glorious voice, but not exactly the sort of thing for a sick chamber, one would suppose. Do they really like it?"

"Don't *you* like it? Don't it do *you* good? Ain't it inspiring? don't it impart pluck? give stuff against despair?"

"All true," said I, removing my hat with profound humility before the brave spirit disguised in the base coat.

"But then," said I still, with some misgivings, "so loud, so wonderfully clamorous a crow, methinks might be amiss to invalids, and retard their convalescence."

"Crow your best now, Trumpet!"

I leaped from my chair. The cock frightened me, like some overpowering angel in the Apocalypse. He seemed crowing over the fall of wicked Babylon, or crowing over the triumph of righteous Joshua in the vale of Ajalon. When I regained my composure somewhat, an inquisitive thought occurred to me. I resolved to gratify it.

"Merrymusk, will you present me to your wife and children?"

"Yes. Wife, the gentleman wants to step in."

"He is very welcome," replied a weak voice.

Going behind the curtain, there lay a wasted, but strangely cheerful human face; and that was pretty much all; the body, hid by the counterpane and an old coat, seemed too shrunken to reveal itself through such impediments. At the bedside, sat a pale girl, ministering. In another bed lay three children, side by side: three more pale faces.

"Oh, father, we don't mislike the gentleman, but let us see Trumpet too."

At a word, the cock strode behind the screen, and perched himself on the children's bed. All their wasted eyes gazed at him with a wild and spiritual delight. They seemed to sun themselves in the radiant plumage of the cock.

"Better than a 'pothecary, eh?" said Merrymusk. "This is Dr. Cock himself."

We retired from the sick ones, and I reseated myself again, lost in thought, over this strange household.

"You seem a glorious independent fellow!" said I.

"And I don't think you a fool, and never did. Sir, you are a trump."

"Is there any hope of your wife's recovery?" said I, modestly seeking to turn the conversation.

"Not the least."

"The children?"

"Very little."

"It must be a doleful life, then, for all concerned. This lonely solitude—this shanty—hard work—hard times."

"Haven't I Trumpet? He's the cheerer. He crows through all; crows at the darkest; 'Glory to God in the highest!' continually he crows it."

"Just the import I first ascribed to his crow, Merrymusk, when first I heard it from my hill. I thought some rich nabob owned some costly Shanghai; little weening any such poor man as you owned this lusty cock of a domestic breed."

"*Poor* man like *me*? Why call *me* poor? Don't the cock *I* own glorify this otherwise inglorious, lean, lantern-jawed land? Didn't *my* cock encourage *you*? And *I* give you all this glorification away gratis. I am a great philanthropist. I am a rich man—a very rich man, and a very happy one. Crow, Trumpet."

The roof jarred.

I returned home in a deep mood. I was not wholly at rest concerning the soundness of Merrymusk's views of things, though full of admiration for him. I was thinking on the matter before my door, when I heard the cock crow again. Enough. Merrymusk is right.

Oh, noble cock! oh, noble man!

I did not see Merrymusk for some weeks after this; but hearing the glorious and rejoicing crow, I supposed that all went as usual with him. My own frame of mind remained a rejoicing one. The cock still inspired me. I saw another mortgage piled on my plantation; but only bought another dozen of stout, and a dozen-dozen of Philadelphia porter. Some of my relatives died; I wore no mourning, but for three days drank stout in preference to porter, stout being of the darker color. I heard the cock crow the instant I received the unwelcome tidings.

"Your health in this stout, oh, noble cock!"

I thought I would call on Merrymusk again, not having seen or heard of him for some time now. Approaching the place, there were no signs of motion about the shanty. I felt a strange misgiving. But the cock crew from within doors, and the boding vanished. I knocked at the door. A feeble voice bade me enter. The curtain was no longer drawn; the whole house was a hospital now. Merrymusk lay on a heap of old clothes; wife and children were all in their beds. The cock was perched on an old hogshead hoop, swung from the ridge-pole in the middle of the shanty.

"You are sick, Merrymusk," said I, mournfully.

"No, I am well," he feebly answered.—"Crow, Trumpet."

I shrunk. The strong soul in the feeble body appalled me. But the cock crew.

The roof jarred.

"How is Mrs. Merrymusk?"

"Well."

"And the children?"

"Well. All well."

The last two words he shouted forth in a kind of wild ecstasy of triumph over ill. It was too much. His head fell back. A white napkin seemed dropped upon his face. Merrymusk was dead.

An awful fear seized me.

But the cock crew.

The cock shook his plumage as if each feather were a banner. The cock hung from the shanty roof as erewhile the trophied flags from the dome of St. Paul's. The cock terrified me with exceeding wonder.

I drew nigh the bedsides of the woman and children. They marked my look of strange affright; they knew what had happened.

"My good man is just dead," breathed the woman lowly. "Tell me true?"

"Dead," said I.

The cock crew.

She fell back, without a sigh, and through long-loving sympathy was dead.

The cock crew.

The cock shook sparkles from his golden plumage. The cock seemed in a rapture of benevolent delight. Leaping from the hoop, he strode up majestically to the pile of old clothes, where the wood-sawyer lay, and planted himself, like an armorial supporter, at his side. Then raised one long, musical, triumphant, and final sort of crow, with throat heaved far back, as if he meant the blast to waft the wood-sawyer's soul sheer up to the seventh heavens. Then he strode, king-like, to the woman's bed. Another upturned and exultant crow, mated to the former.

The pallor of the children was changed to radiance. Their faces shone celestially through grime and dirt. They seemed children of emperors and kings, disguised. The cock sprang upon their bed, shook himself, and crowed, and crowed again, and still and still again. He seemed bent upon crowing the souls of the children out of their wasted bodies. He seemed bent upon rejoining instanter this whole family in the upper air. The children seemed to second his endeavors. Far, deep, intense longings for release transfigured them into spirits before my eyes. I saw angels where they lay.

They were dead.

The cock shook his plumage over them. The cock crew. It was now like a Bravo! like a Hurrah! like a Three-times-three! hip! hip! He strode out of the shanty. I followed. He flew upon the apex of the dwelling, spread wide his wings, sounded one supernatural note, and dropped at my feet.

The cock was dead.

If now you visit that hilly region, you will see, nigh the railroad track, just beneath October Mountain, on the other side of the swamp—there you will see a grave-stone, not with skull and cross-bones, but with a lusty cock in act of crowing, chiseled on it, with the words beneath:

> —"Oh! death, where is thy sting?
> Oh! grave, where is thy victory?"

The wood-sawyer and his family, with the Signor Beneventano, lie in that spot; and I buried them, and planted the stone, which was a stone made to order; and never since then have I felt the doleful dumps, but under all circumstances crow late and early with a continual crow.

Cock-a-doodle-doo!—oo!—oo!—oo!—oo!

Poor Man's Pudding and Rich Man's Crumbs

PICTURE FIRST
Poor Man's Pudding

Y OU SEE," said poet Blandmour, enthusiastically—as some forty years ago we walked along the road in a soft, moist snow-fall, toward the end of March—"you see, my friend, that the blessed almoner, Nature, is in all things beneficent; and not only so, but considerate in her charities, as any discreet human philanthropist might be. This snow, now, which seems so unseasonable, is in fact just what a poor husbandman needs. Rightly is this soft March snow, falling just before seed-time, rightly is it called 'Poor Man's Manure.' Distilling from kind heaven upon the soil, by a gentle penetration it nourishes every clod, ridge, and furrow. To the poor farmer it is as good as the rich farmer's farm-yard enrichments. And the poor man has no trouble to spread it, while the rich man has to spread his."

"Perhaps so," said I, without equal enthusiasm, brushing some of the damp flakes from my chest. "It may be as you say, dear Blandmour. But tell me, how is it that the wind drives yonder drifts of 'Poor Man's Manure' off poor Coulter's two-acre patch here, and piles it up yonder on rich Squire Teamster's twenty-acre field?"

"Ah! to be sure—yes—well; Coulter's field, I suppose, is sufficiently moist without further moistenings. Enough is as good as a feast, you know."

"Yes," replied I, "of this sort of damp fare," shaking another shower of the damp flakes from my person. "But tell me, this warm spring-snow may answer very well, as you say; but how is it with the cold snows of the long, long winters here?"

"Why, do you not remember the words of the Psalmist?— 'The Lord giveth snow like wool;' meaning not only that snow is white as wool, but warm, too, as wool. For the only reason, as I take it, that wool is comfortable, is because air is entangled, and therefore warmed among its fibres. Just so, then, take the temperature of a December field when covered with this snow-fleece, and you will no doubt find it several degrees above that of the air. So, you see, the winter's snow *itself* is beneficent; under the pretense of frost—a sort of gruff philanthropist—actually warming the earth, which afterward is to be fertilizingly moistened by these gentle flakes of March."

"I like to hear you talk, dear Blandmour; and, guided by your benevolent heart, can only wish to poor Coulter plenty of this 'Poor Man's Manure.' "

"But that is not all," said Blandmour, eagerly. "Did you never hear of the 'Poor Man's Eye-water?' "

"Never."

"Take this soft March snow, melt it, and bottle it. It keeps pure as alcohol. The very best thing in the world for weak eyes. I have a whole demijohn of it myself. But the poorest man, afflicted in his eyes, can freely help himself to this same all-bountiful remedy. Now, what a kind provision is that!"

"Then 'Poor Man's Manure' is 'Poor Man's Eye-water' too?"

"Exactly. And what could be more economically contrived? One thing answering two ends—ends so very distinct."

"Very distinct, indeed."

"Ah! that is your way. Making sport of earnest. But never mind. We have been talking of snow; but common rain-water—such as falls all the year round—is still more kindly. Not to speak of its known fertilizing quality as to fields, consider it in one of its minor lights. Pray, did you ever hear of a 'Poor Man's Egg?' "

"Never. What is that, now?"

"Why, in making some culinary preparations of meal and flour, where eggs are recommended in the receipt-book, a substitute for the eggs may be had in a cup of cold rain-water, which acts as leaven. And so a cup of cold rain-water thus used is called by housewives a 'Poor Man's Egg.' And many rich men's housekeepers sometimes use it."

"But only when they are out of hen's eggs, I presume, dear Blandmour. But your talk is—I sincerely say it—most agreeable to me. Talk on."

"Then there's 'Poor Man's Plaster' for wounds and other

bodily harms; an alleviative and curative, compounded of simple, natural things; and so, being very cheap, is accessible to the poorest of sufferers. Rich men often use 'Poor Man's Plaster.' "

"But not without the judicious advice of a fee'd physician, dear Blandmour."

"Doubtless, they first consult the physician; but that may be an unnecessary precaution."

"Perhaps so. I do not gainsay it. Go on."

"Well, then, did you ever eat of a 'Poor Man's Pudding?' "

"I never so much as heard of it before."

"Indeed! Well, now you shall eat of one; and you shall eat it, too, as made, unprompted, by a poor man's wife, and you shall eat it at a poor man's table, and in a poor man's house. Come now, and if after this eating, you do not say that a 'Poor Man's Pudding' is as relishable as a rich man's, I will give up the point altogether; which briefly is: that, through kind Nature, the poor, out of their very poverty, extract comfort."

Not to narrate any more of our conversations upon this subject (for we had several—I being at that time the guest of Blandmour in the country, for the benefit of my health), suffice it that, acting upon Blandmour's hint, I introduced myself into Coulter's house on a wet Monday noon (for the snow had thawed), under the innocent pretense of craving a pedestrian's rest and refreshment for an hour or two.

I was greeted, not without much embarrassment—owing, I suppose, to my dress—but still with unaffected and honest kindness. Dame Coulter was just leaving the wash-tub to get ready her one o'clock meal against her good man's return from a deep wood about a mile distant among the hills, where he was chopping by day's-work—seventy-five cents per day and found himself. The washing being done outside the main building, under an infirm-looking old shed, the dame stood upon a half-rotten, soaked board to protect her feet, as well as might be, from the penetrating damp of the bare ground; hence she looked pale and chill. But her paleness had still another and more secret cause—the paleness of a mother to be. A quiet, fathomless heart-trouble, too, couched beneath the mild, resigned blue of her soft and wife-like eye. But she smiled upon me, as apologizing for the unavoidable disorder of a Monday and a washing-day, and, conducting me into the kitchen, set me down in the best seat it had—an old-fashioned chair of an enfeebled constitution.

I thanked her; and sat rubbing my hands before the ineffectual low fire, and—unobservedly as I could—glancing now and then about the room, while the good woman, throwing on more sticks, said she was sorry the room was no warmer. Something more she said, too—not repiningly, however—of the fuel, as old and damp; picked-up sticks in Squire Teamster's forest, where her husband was chopping the sappy logs of the living tree for the Squire's fires. It needed not her remark, whatever it was, to convince me of the inferior quality of the sticks; some being quite mossy and toad-stooled with long lying bedded among the accumulated dead leaves of many autumns. They made a sad hissing, and vain spluttering enough.

"You must rest yourself here till dinner-time, at least," said the dame; " what I have you are heartily welcome to."

I thanked her again, and begged her not to heed my presence in the least, but go on with her usual affairs.

I was struck by the aspect of the room. The house was old, and constitutionally damp. The window-sills had beads of exuded dampness upon them. The shriveled sashes shook in their frames, and the green panes of glass were clouded with the long thaw. On some little errand the dame passed into an adjoining chamber, leaving the door partly open. The floor of that room was carpetless, as the kitchen's was. Nothing but bare necessaries were about me; and those not of the best sort. Not a print on the wall; but an old volume of Doddridge lay on the smoked chimney-shelf.

"You must have walked a long way, sir; you sigh so with weariness."

"No, I am not nigh so weary as yourself, I dare say."

"Oh, but *I* am accustomed to that; *you* are not, I should think," and her soft, sad blue eye ran over my dress. "But I must sweep these shavings away; husband made him a new ax-helve this morning before sunrise, and I have been so busy washing, that I have had no time to clear up. But now they are just the thing I want for the fire. They'd be much better though, were they not so green."

Now if Blandmour were here, thought I to myself, he would call those green shavings "Poor Man's Matches," or "Poor Man's Tinder," or some pleasant name of that sort.

"I do not know," said the good woman, turning round to me again—as she stirred among her pots on the smoky fire— "I do not know how you will like our pudding. It is only rice, milk, and salt boiled together."

"Ah, what they call 'Poor Man's Pudding,' I suppose you mean."

A quick flush, half resentful, passed over her face.

"*We* do not call it so, sir," she said, and was silent.

Upbraiding myself for my inadvertence, I could not but again think to myself what Blandmour would have said, had he heard those words and seen that flush.

At last a slow, heavy footfall was heard; then a scraping at the door, and another voice said, "Come, wife; come, come— I must be back again in a jif—if you say I *must* take all my meals at home, you must be speedy; because the Squire— Good-day, sir," he exclaimed, now first catching sight of me as he entered the room. He turned toward his wife, inquiringly, and stood stock-still, while the moisture oozed from his patched boots to the floor.

"This gentleman stops here awhile to rest and refresh: he will take dinner with us, too. All will be ready now in a trice: so sit down on the bench, husband, and be patient, I pray. You see, sir," she continued, turning to me, "William there wants, of mornings, to carry a cold meal into the woods with him, to save the long one-o'clock walk across the fields to and fro. But I won't let him. A warm dinner is more than pay for the long walk."

"I don't know about that," said William, shaking his head. "I have often debated in my mind whether it really paid. There's not much odds, either way, between a wet walk after hard work, and a wet dinner before it. But I like to oblige a good wife like Martha. And you know, sir, that women will have their whimseys."

"I wish they all had as kind whimseys as your wife has," said I.

"Well, I've heard that some women ain't all maple-sugar; but, content with dear Martha, I don't know much about others."

"You find rare wisdom in the woods," mused I.

"Now, husband, if you ain't too tired, just lend a hand to draw the table out."

"Nay," said I; "let him rest, and let me help."

"No," said William, rising.

"Sit still," said his wife to me.

The table set, in due time we all found ourselves with plates before us.

"You see what we have," said Coulter—"salt pork, rye-bread, and pudding. Let me help you. I got this pork of the Squire; some of his last year's pork, which he let me have on account. It isn't quite so sweet as this year's would be; but I find it hearty enough to work on, and that's all I eat for. Only let the rheumatiz and other sicknesses keep clear of me, and I ask no flavors or favors from any. But you don't eat of the pork!"

"I see," said the wife, gently and gravely, "that the gentleman knows the difference between this year's and last year's pork. But perhaps he will like the pudding."

I summoned up all my self-control, and smilingly assented to the proposition of the pudding, without by my looks casting any reflections upon the pork. But, to tell the truth, it was quite impossible for me (not being ravenous, but only a little hungry at the time) to eat of the latter. It had a yellowish crust all round it, and was rather rankish, I thought, to the taste. I observed, too, that the dame did not eat of it, though she suffered some to be put on her plate, and pretended to be busy with it when Coulter looked that way. But she ate of the rye-bread, and so did I.

"Now, then, for the pudding," said Coulter. "Quick, wife; the Squire sits in his sitting-room window, looking far out across the fields. His time-piece is true."

"He don't play the spy on you, does he?" said I.

"Oh, no!—I don't say that. He's a good-enough man. He gives me work. But he's particular. Wife, help the gentleman. You see, sir, if I lose the Squire's work, what will become of—" and, with a look for which I honored humanity, with sly significance he glanced toward his wife; then, a little changing his voice, instantly continued—"that fine horse I am going to buy."

"I guess," said the dame, with a strange, subdued sort of inefficient pleasantry—"I guess that fine horse you sometimes so merrily dream of will long stay in the Squire's stall. But sometimes his man gives me a Sunday ride."

"A Sunday ride!" said I.

"You see," resumed Coulter, "wife loves to go to church; but the nighest is four miles off, over yon snowy hills. So she can't walk it; and I can't carry her in my arms, though I have carried her up-stairs before now. But, as she says, the Squire's man sometimes gives her a lift on the road; and for this cause it is that I speak of a horse I am going to have one of these fine sunny days. And already, before having it, I have christened it 'Martha.' But what am I about? Come, come, wife! the pudding! Help the gentleman, do! The Squire! the Squire!—think of the Squire! and help round the pudding. There, one—two—three mouthfuls must do me. Good-by, wife. Good-by, sir. I'm off."

And, snatching his soaked hat, the noble Poor Man hurriedly went out into the soak and the mire.

I suppose now, thinks I to myself, that Blandmour would poetically say, He goes to take a Poor Man's saunter.

"You have a fine husband," said I to the woman, as we were now left together.

"William loves me this day as on the wedding-day, sir. Some hasty words, but never a harsh one. I wish I were better and stronger for his sake. And, oh! sir, both for his sake and mine" (and the soft, blue, beautiful eyes turned into two well-springs), "how I wish little William and Martha lived—it is so lonely-like now. William named after him, and Martha for me."

When a companion's heart of itself overflows, the best one can do is to do nothing. I sat looking down on my as yet untasted pudding.

"You should have seen little William, sir. Such a bright, manly boy, only six years old—cold, cold now!"

Plunging my spoon into the pudding, I forced some into my mouth to stop it.

"And little Martha—Oh! sir, she was the beauty! Bitter, bitter! but needs must be borne."

The mouthful of pudding now touched my palate, and touched it with a mouldy, briny taste. The rice, I knew, was of that damaged sort sold cheap; and the salt from the last year's pork barrel.

"Ah, sir, if those little ones yet to enter the world were the same little ones which so sadly have left it; returning friends, not strangers, strangers, always strangers! Yet does a mother soon learn to love them; for certain, sir, they come from where the others have gone. Don't you believe that, sir? Yes, I know all good people must. But, still, still—and I fear it is wicked, and very black-hearted, too—still, strive how I may to cheer me with thinking of little William and Martha in heaven, and with reading Dr. Doddridge there—still, still does dark grief leak in, just like the rain through our roof. I am left so lonesome now; day after day, all the day long, dear William is gone; and all the damp day long grief drizzles and drizzles down on my soul. But I pray to God to forgive me for this; and for the rest, manage it as well as I may."

Bitter and mouldy is the "Poor Man's Pudding," groaned I to myself, half choked with but one little mouthful of it, which would hardly go down.

I could stay no longer to hear of sorrows for which the sincerest sympathies could give no adequate relief; of a fond persuasion, to which there could be furnished no further proof than already was had—a persuasion, too, of that sort which much speaking is sure more or less to mar; of causeless self-upbraidings, which no expostulations could have dispelled. I offered no pay for hospitalities gratuitous and honorable as those of a prince. I knew that such offerings would have been more than declined; charity resented.

The native American poor never lose their delicacy or pride; hence, though unreduced to the physical degradation of the European pauper, they yet suffer more in mind than the poor of any other people in the world. Those peculiar social sensibilities nourished by our own peculiar political principles, while they enhance the true dignity of a prosperous American, do but minister to the added wretchedness of the unfortunate; first, by prohibiting their acceptance of what little random relief charity may offer; and, second, by furnishing them with the keenest appreciation of the smarting distinction between their ideal of universal equality and their grindstone experience of the practical misery and infamy of poverty —a misery and infamy which is, ever has been, and ever will be, precisely the same in India, England, and America.

Under pretense that my journey called me forthwith, I bade the dame good-by; shook her cold hand; looked my last into her blue, resigned eye, and went out into the wet. But cheerless as it was, and damp, damp, damp—the heavy atmosphere charged with all sorts of incipiencies—I yet became conscious, by the suddenness of the contrast, that the house air I had quitted was laden down with that peculiar deleterious quality, the height of which—insufferable to some visitants— will be found in a poor-house ward.

This ill-ventilation in winter of the rooms of the poor—a thing, too, so stubbornly persisted in—is usually charged upon them as their disgraceful neglect of the most simple means to health. But the instinct of the poor is wiser than we think. The air which ventilates, likewise *cools*. And to any shiverer, ill-ventilated warmth is better than well-ventilated cold. Of all the preposterous assumptions of humanity over humanity, nothing exceeds most of the criticisms made on the habits of the poor by the well-housed, well-warmed, and well-fed.

*   *   *

"Blandmour," said I that evening, as after tea I sat on his comfortable sofa, before a blazing fire, with one of his two ruddy little children on my knee, "you are not what may rightly be called a rich man; you have a fair competence; no more. Is it not so? Well then, I do not include *you*, when I say, that if ever a Rich Man speaks prosperously to me of a Poor Man, I shall set it down as— I won't mention the word."

PICTURE SECOND
Rich Man's Crumbs

In the year 1814, during the summer following my first taste of the "Poor Man's Pudding," a sea-voyage was recommended to me by my physician. The Battle of Waterloo having closed the long drama of Napoleon's wars, many strangers were visiting Europe. I arrived in London at the time the victorious princes were there assembled enjoying the Arabian Nights' hospitalities of a grateful and gorgeous aristocracy, and the courtliest of gentlemen and kings—George the Prince Regent.

I had declined all letters but one to my banker. I wandered about for the best reception an adventurous traveler can have —the reception, I mean, which unsolicited chance and accident throw in his venturous way.

But I omit all else to recount one hour's hap under the lead of a very friendly man, whose acquaintance I made in the open street of Cheapside. He wore a uniform, and was some sort of a civic subordinate; I forget exactly what. He was off duty that day. His discourse was chiefly of the noble charities of London. He took me to two or three, and made admiring mention of many more.

"But," said he, as we turned into Cheapside again, "if you are at all curious about such things, let me take you—if it be not too late—to one of the most interesting of all—our Lord Mayor's Charities, sir; nay, the charities not only of a Lord Mayor, but, I may truly say, in this one instance, of emperors, regents, and kings. You remember the event of yesterday?"

"That sad fire on the river-side, you mean, unhousing so many of the poor?"

"No. The grand Guildhall Banquet to the princes. Who can forget it? Sir, the dinner was served on nothing but solid silver and gold plate, worth at the least £200,000—that is, 1,000,000 of your dollars; while the mere expenditure of meats, wines, attendance and upholstery, &c., can not be footed under £25,000 —125,000 dollars of your hard cash."

"But, surely, my friend, you do not call that charity—feeding kings at that rate?"

"No. The feast came first—yesterday; and the charity after— to-day. How else would you have it, where princes are concerned? But I think we shall be quite in time—come; here we are at King Street, and down there is Guildhall. Will you go?"

"Gladly, my good friend. Take me where you will. I come but to roam and see."

Avoiding the main entrance of the hall, which was barred,

he took me through some private way, and we found our-selves in a rear blind-walled place in the open air. I looked round amazed. The spot was grimy as a back-yard in the Five Points. It was packed with a mass of lean, famished, fe-rocious creatures, struggling and fighting for some mysterious precedency, and all holding soiled blue tickets in their hands.

"There is no other way," said my guide; "we can only get in with the crowd. Will you try it? I hope you have not on your drawing-room suit? What do you say? It will be well worth your sight. So noble a charity does not often offer. The one following the annual banquet of Lord Mayor's day—fine a charity as that certainly is—is not to be mentioned with what will be seen to-day. Is it, ay?"

As he spoke, a basement door in the distance was thrown open, and the squalid mass made a rush for the dark vault beyond.

I nodded to my guide, and sideways we joined in with the rest. Ere long we found our retreat cut off by the yelping crowd behind, and I could not but congratulate myself on having a civic, as well as civil guide; one, too, whose uniform made evident his authority.

It was just the same as if I were pressed by a mob of can-nibals on some pagan beach. The beings round me roared with famine. For in this mighty London misery but maddens. In the country it softens. As I gazed on the meagre, murder-ous pack, I thought of the blue eye of the gentle wife of poor Coulter. Some sort of curved, glittering steel thing (not a sword; I know not what it was), before worn in his belt, was now flourished overhead by my guide, menacing the creatures to forbear offering the stranger violence.

As we drove, slow and wedge-like, into the gloomy vault, the howls of the mass reverberated. I seemed seething in the Pit with the Lost. On and on, through the dark and the damp, and then up a stone stairway to a wide portal; when, diffusing, the pestiferous mob poured in bright day between painted walls and beneath a painted dome. I thought of the anarchic sack of Versailles.

A few moments more and I stood bewildered among the beggars in the famous Guildhall.

Where I stood—where the thronged rabble stood, less than twelve hours before sat His Imperial Majesty, Alexander of Russia; His Royal Majesty, Frederic William, King of Prussia; His Royal Highness, George, Prince Regent of England; His world-renowned Grace, the Duke of Wellington; with a mob of magnificoes, made up of conquering field-marshals, earls, counts, and innumerable other nobles of mark.

The walls swept to and fro, like the foliage of a forest with blazonings of conquerors' flags. Naught outside the hall was visible. No windows were within four-and-twenty feet of the floor. Cut off from all other sights, I was hemmed in by one splendid spectacle—splendid, I mean, every where, but as the eye fell toward the floor. *That* was foul as a hovel's—as a kennel's; the naked boards being strewed with the smaller and more wasteful fragments of the feast, while the two long parallel lines, up and down the hall, of now unrobed, shabby, dirty pine-tables were piled with less trampled wrecks. The dyed banners were in keeping with the last night's kings; the floor suited the beggars of to-day. The banners looked down upon the floor as from his balcony Dives upon Lazarus. A line of liveried men kept back with their staves the impatient jam of the mob, who, otherwise, might have instantaneously converted the Charity into a Pillage. Another body of gowned and gilded officials distributed the broken meats— the cold victuals and crumbs of kings. One after another the beggars held up their dirty blue tickets, and were served with the plundered wreck of a pheasant, or the rim of a pasty— like the detached crown of an old hat—the solids and meats stolen out.

"What a noble charity!" whispered my guide. "See that pasty now, snatched by that pale girl; I dare say the Emperor of Russia ate of that last night."

"Very probably," murmured I; "it looks as though some omnivorous Emperor or other had had a finger in that pie."

"And see yon pheasant too—there—*that* one—the boy in the torn shirt has it now—look! The Prince Regent might have dined off that."

The two breasts were gouged ruthlessly out, exposing the bare bones, embellished with the untouched pinions and legs.

"Yes, who knows!" said my guide, "his Royal Highness the Prince Regent might have eaten of that identical pheasant."

"I don't doubt it," murmured I, "he is said to be uncommonly fond of the breast. But where is Napoleon's head in a charger? I should fancy *that* ought to have been the principal dish."

"You are merry. Sir, even Cossacks are charitable here in Guildhall. Look! the famous Platoff, the Hetman himself—(he was here last night with the rest)—no doubt he thrust a lance into yon fat pork-pie there. Look! the old shirtless man has it now. How he licks his chops over it, little thinking of or thanking the good, kind Cossack that left it him! Ah! another—a stouter has grabbed it. It falls; bless my soul!—the dish is quite empty—only a bit of the hacked crust."

"The Cossacks, my friend, are said to be immoderately fond of fat," observed I. "The Hetman was hardly so charitable as you thought."

"A noble charity, upon the whole, for all that. See, even Gog and Magog yonder, at the other end of the hall, fairly laugh out their delight at the scene."

"But don't you think, though," hinted I, "that the sculptor, whoever he was, carved the laugh too much into a grin—a sort of sardonical grin?"

"Well, that's as you take it, sir. But see—now I'd wager a guinea the Lord Mayor's lady dipped her golden spoon into yonder golden-hued jelly. See, the jelly-eyed old body has slipped it, in one broad gulp, down his throat."

"Peace to that jelly!" breathed I.

"What a generous, noble, magnanimous charity this is! unheard of in any country but England, which feeds her very beggars with golden-hued jellies."

"But not three times every day, my friend. And do you really think that jellies are the best sort of relief you can furnish to beggars? Would not plain beef and bread, with something to do, and be paid for, be better?"

"But plain beef and bread were not eaten here. Emperors, and prince-regents, and kings, and field marshals don't often dine on plain beef and bread. So the leavings are according. Tell me, can you expect that the crumbs of kings can be like the crumbs of squirrels?"

"*You!* I mean *you!* stand aside, or else be served and away! Here, take this pasty, and be thankful that you taste of the same dish with her Grace the Duchess of Devonshire. Graceless ragamuffin, do you hear?"

These words were bellowed at me through the din by a red-gowned official nigh the board.

"Surely he does not mean *me*," said I to my guide; "he has not confounded *me* with the rest."

"One is known by the company he keeps," smiled my guide. "See! not only stands your hat awry and bunged on your head, but your coat is fouled and torn. Nay," he cried to the red-gown, "this is an unfortunate friend; a simple spectator, I assure you."

"Ah! is that you, old lad?" responded the red-gown, in familiar recognition of my guide—a personal friend as it seemed; "well, convey your friend out forthwith. Mind the grand crash; it will soon be coming; hark! now! away with him!"

Too late. The last dish had been seized. The yet unglutted mob raised a fierce yell, which wafted the banners like a strong gust, and filled the air with a reek as from sewers. They surged against the tables, broke through all barriers, and billowed over the hall—their bare tossed arms like the dashed ribs of a wreck. It seemed to me as if a sudden impotent fury of fell envy possessed them. That one half-hour's peep at the mere remnants of the glories of the Banquets of Kings; the unsatifying mouthfuls of disembowelled pasties, plundered pheasants, and half-sacked jellies, served to remind them of the intrinsic contempt of the alms. In this sudden mood, or whatever mysterious thing it was that now seized them, these Lazaruses seemed ready to spew up in repentant scorn the contumelious crumbs of Dives.

"This way, this way! stick like a bee to my back," intensely whispered my guide. "My friend there has answered my beck, and thrown open yon private door for us two. Wedge—wedge in—quick—there goes your bunged hat—never stop for your coat-tail—hit that man—strike him down! hold! jam! now! now! wrench along for your life! ha! here we breathe freely; thank God! You faint. Ho!"

"Never mind. This fresh air revives me."

I inhaled a few more breaths of it, and felt ready to proceed.

"And now conduct me, my good friend, by some front passage into Cheapside, forthwith. I must home."

"Not by the side-walk though. Look at your dress. I must get a hack for you."

"Yes, I suppose so," said I, ruefully eying my tatters, and then glancing in envy at the close-bodied coat and flat cap of my guide, which defied all tumblings and tearings.

"There, now, sir," said the honest fellow, as he put me into the hack, and tucked in me and my rags, " when you get back to your own country, you can say you have witnessed the greatest of all England's noble charities. Of course, you will make reasonable allowances for the unavoidable jam. Good-by. Mind, Jehu"—addressing the driver on the box—"this is a *gentleman* you carry. He is just from the Guildhall Charity, which accounts for his appearance. Go on now. London Tavern, Fleet Street, remember, is the place."

*   *   *

"Now, Heaven in its kind mercy save me from the noble charities of London," sighed I, as that night I lay bruised and battered on my bed; "and Heaven save me equally from the 'Poor Man's Pudding' and the 'Rich Man's Crumbs.' "

The Two Temples

(Dedicated to Sheridan Knowles)

TEMPLE FIRST

"THIS IS TOO BAD," said I, "here have I tramped this blessed Sunday morning, all the way from the Battery, three long miles, for this express purpose, prayer-book under arm; here I am, I say, and, after all, I can't get in.

"Too bad. And how disdainful the great, fat-paunched, beadle-faced man looked, when in answer to my humble petition, he said they had no galleries. Just the same as if he'd said, they did n't entertain poor folks. But I'll wager something that had my new coat been done last night, as the false tailor promised, and had I, arrayed therein this bright morning, tickled the fat-paunched, beadle-faced man's palm with a bank-note, then, gallery or no gallery, I would have had a fine seat in this marble-buttressed, stained-glassed, spic-and-span new temple.

"Well, here I am in the porch, very politely bowed out of the nave. I suppose I'm excommunicated; excluded, anyway.—That's a noble string of flashing carriages drawn up along the curb; those champing horses too have a haughty curve to their foam-flaked necks. Property of those 'miserable sinners' inside, I presume. I dont a bit wonder they unreservedly confess to such misery as *that*.—See the gold hat-bands too, and other gorgeous trimmings, on those glossy groups of low-voiced gossippers near by. If I were in England now, I should think those chaps a company of royal dukes, right honorable barons &c. As it is, though, I guess they are only lackeys.—By the way, here I dodge about, as if I wanted to get into their aristocratic circle. In fact, it looks a sort of lackeyish to be idly standing outside a fine temple, cooling your heels, during service.—I had best move back to the Battery again, peeping into my prayer-book as I go.—But hold; dont I see a small door? Just in there, to one side, if I dont mistake, is a very low and very narrow vaulted door. None seem to go that way. Ten to one, that identical door leads up into the tower. And now that I think of it, there is usually in these splendid, new-fashioned Gothic Temples, a curious little window high over the orchestra and everything else, away up among the gilded clouds of the ceiling's frescoes; and that little window, seems to me, if one could but get there, ought to command a glorious bird's-eye view of the entire field of operations below.—I guess I'll try it. No one in the porch now. The beadle-faced man is smoothing down some ladies' cushions, far up the broad aisle, I dare say. Softly now. If the small door ain't locked, I shall have stolen a march upon the beadle-faced man, and secured a humble seat in the sanctuary, in spite of him.—Good! Thanks for this! The door is not locked. Bell-ringer forgot to lock it, no doubt. Now, like any felt-footed grimalkin, up I steal among the leads."

Ascending some fifty stone steps along a very narrow curving stair-way, I found myself on a blank platform forming the second story of the huge square tower.

I seemed inside some magic-lantern. On three sides, three gigantic Gothic windows of richly dyed glass, filled the otherwise meagre place with all sorts of sun-rises and sun-sets, lunar and solar rainbows, falling stars, and other flaming fireworks and pyrotechnics. But after all, it was but a gorgeous dungeon; for I could n't look out, any more than if I had been the occupant of a basement cell in "the Tombs." With some pains, and care not to do any serious harm, I contrived to scratch a minute opening in a great purple star forming the center of the chief compartment of the middle window; when peeping through, as through goggles, I ducked my head in dismay. The beadle-faced man, with no hat on his head, was just in act of driving three ragged little boys into the middle of the street; and how could I help trembling at the apprehension of his discovering a rebellious caitiff like me peering down on him from the tower? For in stealing up here, I had set at nought his high authority. He whom he thought effectually ejected, had burglariously returned. For a moment I was almost ready to bide my chance, and get to the side walk again with all dispatch. But another Jacob's ladder of lofty steps,—wooden ones, this time—allured me to another and still higher flight,—in sole hopes of gaining that one secret window where I might, at distance, take part in the proceedings.

Presently I noticed something which owing to the first marvellous effulgence of the place, had remained unseen till now. Two strong ropes, dropping through holes in the rude ceiling high overhead, fell a sheer length of sixty feet, right through the center of the space, and dropped in coils upon the floor of the huge magic-lantern. Bell-ropes these, thought I, and quaked. For if the beadle-faced man should learn that a grimalkin was somewhere prowling about the edifice, how easy for him to ring the alarm. Hark!—ah, that's only the organ—yes—it's the "Venite, exultemus Domine." Though an insider in one respect, yet am I but an outsider in another. But for all that, I will not be defrauded of my natural rights. Uncovering my head, and taking out my book, I stood erect, midway up the tall Jacob's ladder, as if standing among the congregation; and in spirit, if not in place, participated in those devout exultings. That over, I continued my upward path; and after crossing sundry minor platforms and irregular landings, all the while on a general ascent, at last I was delighted by catching sight of a small round window in the otherwise dead-wall side of the tower, where the tower attached itself to the main building. In front of the window was a rude narrow gallery, used as a bridge to cross from the lower stairs on one side to the upper stairs on the opposite.

As I drew nigh the spot, I well knew from the added clearness with which the sound of worship came to me, that the window did indeed look down upon the entire interior. But I was hardly prepared to find that no pane of glass, stained or unstained, was to stand between me and the far-under aisles and altar. For the purpose of ventilation, doubtless, the opening had been left unsupplied with sash of any sort. But a sheet of fine-woven, gauzy wire-work was in place of that. When, all eagerness, and open book in hand, I first advanced to stand before the window, I involuntarily shrank, as from before the mouth of a furnace, upon suddenly feeling a forceful puff of strange, heated air, blown, as by a blacksmith's bellows, full into my face and lungs. Yes, thought I, this window is doubtless for ventilation. Nor is it quite so comfortable as I fancied it might be. But beggars must not be choosers. The furnace which makes the people below there feel so snug and cosy in their padded pews, is to me, who stand here upon the naked gallery, cause of grievous trouble. Besides, though my face is scorched, my back is frozen. But I wont complain. Thanks for this much, any way,—that by hollowing one hand to my ear, and standing a little sideways out of the more violent rush of the torrid current, I can at least hear the priest sufficiently to make my responses in the proper place. Little dream the good congregation away down there, that they have a faithful clerk away up here. Here too is a fitter place for sincere devotions, where, though I see, I remain unseen. Depend upon it, no Pharisee would have my pew. I like it, and admire it too, because it is so very high. Height, somehow, hath devotion in it. The archangelic anthems are raised in a lofty place. All the good shall go to such an one. Yes, Heaven is high.

As thus I mused, the glorious organ burst, like an earthquake, almost beneath my feet; and I heard the invoking cry—"Govern them and *lift* them up forever!" Then down I gazed upon the standing human mass, far, far below, whose heads, gleaming in the many-colored window-stains, showed like beds of spangled pebbles flashing in a Cuban sun. So at least, I knew they needs would look, if but the wire-woven screen were drawn aside. That wire-woven screen had the effect of casting crape upon all I saw. Only by making allowances for the crape, could I gain a right idea of the scene disclosed.

Surprising, most surprising, too, it was. As said before, the window was a circular one; the part of the tower where I stood was dusky-dark; its height above the congregation-floor could not have been less than ninety or a hundred feet; the whole interior temple was lit by nought but glass dimmed, yet glorified with all imaginable rich and russet hues; the approach to my strange look-out, through perfect solitude, and along rude and dusty ways, enhanced the theatric wonder of the populous spectacle of this sumptuous sanctuary. Book in hand, responses on my tongue, standing in the very posture of devotion, I could not rid my soul of the intrusive thought, that, through some necromancer's glass, I looked down upon some sly enchanter's show.

At length the lessons being read, the chants chanted, the white-robed priest, a noble-looking man, with a form like the incomparable Talma's, gave out from the reading-desk the

hymn before the sermon, and then through a side door vanished from the scene. In good time I saw the same Talma-like
and noble-looking man re-appear through the same side door,
his white apparel wholly changed for black.

By the melodious tone and persuasive gesture of the
speaker, and the all-approving attention of the throng, I knew
the sermon must be eloquent, and well adapted to an opulent
auditory; but owing to the priest's changed position from the
reading-desk, to the pulpit, I could not so distinctly hear him
now as in the previous rites. The text however,—repeated at
the outset, and often after quoted,—I could not but plainly
catch:—"Ye are the salt of the earth."

At length the benediction was pronounced over the mass
of low-inclining foreheads; hushed silence, intense motionlessness followed for a moment, as if the congregation were
one of buried, not of living men; when, suddenly, miraculously, like the general rising at the Resurrection, the whole
host came to their feet, amid a simultaneous roll, like a great
drum-beat from the enrapturing, overpowering organ. Then,
in three freshets,—all gay sprightly nods and becks—the
gilded brooks poured down the gilded aisles.

Time for me too to go, thought I, as snatching one last
look upon the imposing scene, I clasped my book and put it
in my pocket. The best thing I can do just now, is to slide
out unperceived amid the general crowd. Hurrying down the
great length of ladder, I soon found myself at the base of the
last stone step of the final flight; but started aghast—the door
was locked! The bell-ringer, or more probably that forever-
prying suspicious-looking beadle-faced man has done this. He
would not let me in at all at first, and now, with the greatest
inconsistency, he will not let me out. But what is to be done?
Shall I knock on the door? That will never do. It will only
frighten the crowd streaming by, and no one can adequately
respond to my summons, except the beadle-faced man; and if
he see me, he will recognise me, and perhaps roundly rate
me—poor, humble worshiper—before the entire public. No,
I wont knock. But what then?

Long time I thought, and thought, till at last all was
hushed again. Presently a clicking sound admonished me that
the church was being closed. In sudden desperation, I gave a

rap on the door. But too late. It was not heard. I was left alone and solitary in a temple which but a moment before was more populous than many villages.

A strange trepidation of gloom and loneliness gradually stole over me. Hardly conscious of what I did, I reascended the stone steps; higher and higher still, and only paused, when once more I felt the hot-air blast from the wire-woven screen. Snatching another peep down into the vast arena, I started at its hushed desertness. The long ranges of grouped columns down the nave, and clusterings of them into copses about the corners of the transept; together with the subdued, dim-streaming light from the autumnal glasses; all assumed a secluded and deep-wooded air. I seemed gazing from Pisgah into the forests of old Canaan. A Puseyitish painting of a Madonna and child, adorning a lower window, seemed showing to me the sole tenants of this painted wilderness—the true Hagar and her Ishmael.—

With added trepidation I stole softly back to the magic-lantern platform; and revived myself a little by peeping through the scratch, upon the unstained light of open day.— But what is to be done, thought I, again.

I descended to the door; listened there; heard nothing. A third time climbing the stone steps, once more I stood in the magic-lantern, while the full nature of the more than awkwardness of my position came over me.

The first persons who will reënter the temple, mused I, will doubtless be the beadle-faced man, and the bell-ringer. And the first man to come up here, where I am, will be the latter. Now what will be his natural impressions upon first descrying an unknown prowler here? Rather disadvantageous to said prowler's moral character. Explanations will be vain. Circumstances are against me. True, I may hide, till he retires again. But how do I know, that he will then leave the door unlocked? Besides, in a position of affairs like this, it is generally best, I think, to anticipate discovery, and by magnanimously announcing yourself, forestall an inglorious detection. But how announce myself? Already have I knocked, and no response. That moment, my eye, impatiently ranging roundabout, fell upon the bell-ropes. They suggested the usual signal made at dwelling-houses to convey tidings of a stranger's presence. But I was not an outside caller; alas, I was an inside prowler. — But one little touch of that bell-rope, would be sure to bring relief. I have an appointment at three o'clock. The beadle-faced man must naturally reside very close by the church. He well knows the peculiar ring of his own bell. The slightest possible hum would bring him flying to the rescue. Shall I, or shall I not? — But I may alarm the neighborhood. Oh no; the merest tingle, not by any means a loud vociferous peal. Shall I? Better voluntarily bring the beadle-faced man to me, than be involuntarily dragged out from this most suspicious hiding-place. I have to face him, first or last. Better now than later. — Shall I? —

No more. Creeping to the rope, I gave it a cautious twitch. No sound. A little less warily. All was dumb. Still more strongly. Horrors! my hands, instinctively clapped to my ears, only served to condense the appalling din. Some undreamed-of mechanism seemed to have been touched. The bell must have thrice revolved on its thunderous axis, multiplying the astounding reverberation.

My business is effectually done, this time, thought I, all in a tremble. Nothing will serve me now but the reckless confidence of innocence reduced to desperation.

In less than five minutes, I heard a running noise beneath me; the lock of the door clicked, and up rushed the beadle-faced man, the perspiration starting from his cheeks.

"You! Is it *you*? The man I turned away this very morning, skulking here? *You* dare to touch that bell? Scoundrel!"

And ere I could defend myself, seizing me irresistably in his powerful grasp, he tore me along by the collar, and dragging me down the stairs, thrust me into the arms of three policemen, who, attracted by the sudden toll of the bell, had gathered curiously about the porch.

All remonstrances were vain. The beadle-faced man was bigoted against me. Represented as a lawless violator, and a remorseless disturber of the Sunday peace, I was conducted to the Halls of Justice. Next morning, my rather gentlemany appearance procured me a private hearing from the judge. But the beadle-faced man must have made a Sunday night call on him. Spite of my coolest explanations, the circumstances of the case were deemed so exceedingly suspicious, that only after paying a round fine, and receiving a stinging reprimand, was I permitted to go at large, and pardoned for having humbly indulged myself in the luxury of public worship.

TEMPLE SECOND

A stranger in London on Saturday night, and without a copper! What hospitalities may such an one expect? What shall I do with myself this weary night? My landlady wont receive me in her parlor. I owe her money. She looks like flint on me. So in this monstrous rabblement must I crawl about till, say ten o'clock, and then slink home to my unlighted bed.

The case was this: The week following my inglorious expulsion from the transatlantic temple, I had packed up my trunks and damaged character, and repaired to the fraternal, loving town of Philadelphia. There chance threw into my way an interesting young orphan lady and her aunt-duenna; the lady rich as Cleopatra, but not as beautiful; the duenna lovely as Charmian, but not so young. For the lady's health, prolonged travel had been prescribed. Maternally connected in old England, the lady chose London for her primal port. But ere securing their passage, the two were looking round for some young physician, whose disengagement from pressing business, might induce him to accept, on a moderate salary, the post of private Esculapius and knightly companion to the otherwise unprotected fair. The more necessary was this, as not only the voyage to England was intended, but an extensive European tour, to follow.

Enough. I came; I saw; I was made the happy man. We sailed. We landed on the other side; when after two weeks of agonized attendance on the vacillations of the lady, I was very cavalierly dismissed, on the score, that the lady's maternal relations had persuaded her to try, through the winter, the salubrious climate of the foggy Isle of Wight, in preference to the fabulous blue atmosphere of the Ionian Isles. So much for national prejudice.

Nota Bene.—The lady was in a sad decline.—

Having ere sailing been obliged to anticipate nearly a quarter's pay to foot my outfit bills, I was dismally cut adrift in Fleet street without a solitary shilling. By disposing, at certain pawnbrokers, of some of my less indispensable apparel, I had managed to stave off the more slaughterous onsets of my landlady, while diligently looking about for any business that might providentially appear.

So on I drifted amid those indescribable crowds which every seventh night pour and roar through each main artery and block the bye-veins of great London, the Leviathan. Saturday Night it was; and the markets and the shops, and every stall and counter were crushed with the one unceasing tide. A whole Sunday's victualling for three millions of human bodies, was going on. Few of them equally hungry with my own, as through my spent lassitude, the unscrupulous human whirlpools eddied me aside at corners, as any straw is eddied in the Norway Maelstrom. What dire suckings into oblivion must such swirling billows know. Better perish mid myriad sharks in mid Atlantic, than die a penniless stranger in Babylonian London. Forlorn, outcast, without a friend, I staggered on through three millions of my own human kind. The fiendish gas-lights shooting their Tartarean rays across the muddy sticky streets, lit up the pitiless and pitiable scene.

Well, well, if this were but Sunday now, I might conciliate some kind female pew-opener, and rest me in some inn-like chapel, upon some stranger's outside bench. But it is Saturday night. The end of the weary week, and all but the end of weary me.

Disentangling myself at last from those skeins of Pandemonian lanes which snarl one part of the metropolis between Fleet street and Holborn, I found myself at last in a wide and far less noisy street, a short and shopless one, leading up from the Strand, and terminating at its junction with a crosswise avenue. The comparative quietude of the place was inexpressively soothing. It was like emerging upon the green enclosure surrounding some Cathedral church, where sanctity makes all things still. Two lofty brilliant lights attracted me in this tranquil street. Thinking it might prove some moral or religious meeting, I hurried towards the spot; but was surprised to see two tall placards announcing the appearance that night, of the stately Macready in the part of Cardinal Richelieu. Very few loiterers hung about the place, the hour being rather late, and the play-bill hawkers mostly departed, or keeping entirely quiet. This theatre indeed, as I afterwards discovered, was not only one of the best in point of acting, but likewise one of the most decorous in its general management, inside and out. In truth the whole neighborhood, as it seemed to me—issuing from the jam and uproar of those turbulent tides against which, or borne on irresistably by which, I had so long been swimming—the whole neighborhood, I say, of this pleasing street seemed in good keeping with the character imputed to its theatre.

Glad to find one blessed oasis of tranquility, I stood leaning against a column of the porch, and striving to lose my sadness in running over one of the huge placards. No one molested me. A tattered little girl, to be sure, approached, with a hand-bill extended, but marking me more narrowly, retreated; her strange skill in physiognomy at once enabling her to determine that I was penniless. As I read, and read—for the placard, of enormous dimensions, contained minute particulars of each successive scene in the enacted play—gradually a strong desire to witness this celebrated Macready in this his celebrated part stole over me. By one act, I might rest my jaded limbs, and more than jaded spirits. Where else could I go for rest, unless I crawled into my cold and lonely bed far up in an attic of Craven Street, looking down upon the muddy Phlegethon of the Thames. Besides, what I wanted was not merely rest, but cheer; the making one of many pleased and pleasing human faces; the getting into a genial humane assembly of my kind; such as, at its best and highest, is to be found in the unified multitude of a devout congregation. But no such assemblies were accessible that night, even if my unbefriended and rather shabby air would overcome the scruples of those fastidious gentry with red gowns and long gilded staves, who guard the portals of the first-class London tabernacles from all profanation of a poor forlorn and fainting wanderer like me. Not inns, but ecclesiastical hotels, where the pews are the rented chambers.

No use to ponder, thought I, at last; it is Saturday night, not Sunday; and so, a Theatre only can receive me. So powerfully in the end did the longing to get into the edifice come over me, that I almost began to think of pawning my overcoat for admittance. But from this last infatuation I was providentially with-held by a sudden cheery summons, in a voice unmistakably benevolent. I turned, and saw a man who seemed to be some sort of a working-man.

"Take it," said he, holding a plain red ticket towards me, full in the gas-light. "You want to go in; I know you do. Take it. I am suddenly called home. There—hope you'll enjoy yourself. Good-bye."

Blankly, and mechanically, I had suffered the ticket to be thrust into my hand, and now stood quite astonished, bewildered, and for the time, ashamed. The plain fact was, I had received charity; and for the first time in my life. Often in the course of my strange wanderings I had needed charity, but never had asked it, and certainly never, ere this blessed night, had been offered it. And a stranger; and in the very maw of the roaring London too! Next moment my sense of foolish shame departed, and I felt a queer feeling in my left eye, which, as sometimes is the case with people, was the weaker one; probably from being on the same side with the heart.

I glanced round eagerly. But the kind giver was no longer in sight. I looked upon the ticket. I understood. It was one of those checks given to persons inside a theatre when for any cause they desire to step out a moment. Its presentation ensures unquestioned readmittance.

Shall I use it? mused I.—What? It's charity.—But if it be gloriously right to do a charitable deed, can it be ingloriously wrong to receive its benefit?—No one knows you; go boldly in.—Charity.—Why these unvanquishable scruples? All your life, nought but charity sustains you, and all others in the world. Maternal charity nursed you as a babe; paternal charity fed you as a child; friendly charity got you your profession; and to the charity of every man you meet this night in London, are you indebted for your unattempted life. Any knife, any hand of all the millions of knives and hands in London, has you this night at its mercy. You, and all mortals, live but by sufferance of your charitable kind; charitable by omission, not performance.—Stush for your self-upbraidings, and pitiful, poor, shabby pride, you friendless man without a purse.—Go in.

Debate was over. Marking the direction from which the stranger had accosted me, I stepped that way; and soon saw a low-vaulted, inferior-looking door on one side of the edifice. Entering, I wandered on and up, and up and on again, through various doubling stairs and wedge-like, ill-lit passages, whose bare boards much reminded me of my ascent of the Gothic tower on the ocean's far other side. At last I gained a lofty platform, and saw a fixed human countenance facing me from a mysterious window of a sort of sentry-box or closet. Like some saint in a shrine, the countenance was illuminated by two smoky candles. I divined the man. I exhibited my diploma, and he nodded me to a little door beyond; while a sudden burst of orchestral music, admonished me I was now very near my destination, and also revived the memory of the organ-anthems I had heard while on the ladder of the tower at home.

Next moment, the wire-woven gauzy screen of the ventilating window in that same tower, seemed enchantedly reproduced before me. The same hot blast of stifling air once more rushed into my lungs. From the same dizzy altitude, through the same fine-spun, vapory crapey air; far, far down upon just such a packed mass of silent human beings; listening to just such grand harmonies; I stood within the topmost gallery of the temple. But hardly alone and silently as before. This time I had company. Not of the first circles, and certainly not of the dress-circle; but most acceptable, right welcome, cheery company, to otherwise uncompanioned me. Quiet, well-pleased working men, and their glad wives and sisters, with here and there an aproned urchin, with all-absorbed, bright face, vermillioned by the excitement and the heated air, hovering like a painted cherub over the vast human firmament below. The height of the gallery was in truth appalling. The rail was low. I thought of deep-sea-leads, and the mariner in the vessel's chains, drawing up the line, with his long-drawn musical accompaniment. And like beds of glittering coral, through the deep sea of azure smoke, there, far down, I saw the jewelled necks and white sparkling arms of crowds of ladies in the semicirque. But, in the interval of two acts, again the orchestra was heard; some inspiring national anthem now was played. As the volumed sound came undulating up, and broke in showery spray and foam of melody against our gallery rail, my head involuntarily was bowed, my hand instinctively sought my pocket. Only by a second thought, did I check my momentary lunacy and remind myself that this time I had no small morocco book with me, and that this was not the house of prayer.

Quickly was my wandering mind—preternaturally affected by the sudden translation from the desolate street, to this bewildering and blazing spectacle—arrested in its wanderings, by feeling at my elbow a meaning nudge; when turning suddenly, I saw a sort of coffee-pot, and pewter mug hospitably presented to me by a ragged, but good-natured looking boy.

"Thank you," said I, "I wont take any coffee, I guess."

"Coffee?—I guess?—Aint you a Yankee?"

"Aye, boy; true blue."

"Well dad's gone to Yankee-land, a seekin' of his fortin'; so take a penny mug of ale, do, Yankee, for poor dad's sake."

Out from the tilted coffee-pot-looking can, came a coffee-colored stream, and a small mug of humming ale was in my hand.

"I dont want it, boy. The fact is, my boy, I have no penny by me. I happened to leave my purse at my lodgings."

"Never do you mind, Yankee; drink to honest dad."

"With all my heart, you generous boy; here's immortal life to him!"

He stared at my strange burst, smiled merrily, and left me, offering his coffee-pot in all directions, and not in vain.

'Tis not always poverty to be poor, mused I; one may fare well without a penny. A ragged boy may be a prince-like benefactor.

Because that unpurchased penny-worth of ale revived my drooping spirits strangely. Stuff was in that barley-malt; a most sweet bitterness in those blessed hops. God bless the glorious boy!

The more I looked about me in this lofty gallery, the more was I delighted with its occupants. It was not spacious. It was, if anything, rather contracted, being the very cheapest portion of the house, where very limited attendance was expected; embracing merely the very crown of the topmost semicircle; and so, commanding, with a sovereign outlook, and imperial downlook, the whole theatre, with the expanded stage directly opposite, though some hundred feet below. As at the tower, peeping into the transatlantic temple, so stood I here, at the very main-mast-head of all the interior edifice.

Such was the decorum of this special theatre, that nothing objectionable was admitted within its walls. With an unhurt eye of perfect love, I sat serenely in the gallery, gazing upon the pleasing scene, around me and below. Neither did it abate from my satisfaction, to remember, that Mr Macready, the chief actor of the night, was an amiable gentleman, combining the finest qualities of social and Christian respectability, with the highest excellence in his particular profession; for which last he had conscientiously done much, in many ways, to refine, elevate, and chasten.

But now the curtain rises, and the robed Cardinal advances. How marvellous this personal resemblance! He looks every inch to be the self-same, stately priest I saw irradiated by the glow-worm dies of the pictured windows from my high tower-pew. And shining as he does, in the rosy reflexes of these stained walls and gorgeous galleries, the mimic priest down there; he too seems lit by Gothic blazonings.—Hark! The same measured, courtly, noble tone. See! the same imposing attitude. Excellent actor is this Richelieu!

He disappears behind the scenes. He slips, no doubt, into the Green Room. He reappears somewhat changed in his habiliments. Do I dream, or is it genuine memory that recalls some similar thing seen through the woven wires?

The curtain falls. Starting to their feet, the enraptured thousands sound their responses, deafeningly; unmistakably sincere. Right from the undoubted heart. I have no duplicate in my memory of this. In earnestness of response, this second temple stands unmatched. And hath mere mimicry done this? What is it then to act a part?

But now the music surges up again, and borne by that rolling billow, I, and all the gladdened crowd, are harmoniously attended to the street.

I went home to my lonely lodging, and slept not much that night, for thinking of the First Temple and the Second

Temple; and how that, a stranger in a strange land, I found sterling charity in the one; and at home, in my own land, was thrust out from the other.

The Paradise of Bachelors and the Tartarus of Maids

I. THE PARADISE OF BACHELORS

IT LIES not far from Temple-Bar.

Going to it, by the usual way, is like stealing from a heated plain into some cool, deep glen, shady among harboring hills.

Sick with the din and soiled with the mud of Fleet Street— where the Benedick tradesmen are hurrying by, with ledger-lines ruled along their brows, thinking upon rise of bread and fall of babies—you adroitly turn a mystic corner—not a street—glide down a dim, monastic way, flanked by dark, sedate, and solemn piles, and still wending on, give the whole care-worn world the slip, and, disentangled, stand beneath the quiet cloisters of the Paradise of Bachelors.

Sweet are the oases in Sahara; charming the isle-groves of August prairies; delectable pure faith amidst a thousand perfidies: but sweeter, still more charming, most delectable, the dreamy Paradise of Bachelors, found in the stony heart of stunning London.

In mild meditation pace the cloisters; take your pleasure, sip your leisure, in the garden waterward; go linger in the ancient library; go worship in the sculptured chapel: but little have you seen, just nothing do you know, not the sweet kernel have you tasted, till you dine among the banded Bachelors, and see their convivial eyes and glasses sparkle. Not dine in bustling commons, during term-time, in the hall; but tranquilly, by private hint, at a private table; some fine Templar's hospitably invited guest.

Templar? That's a romantic name. Let me see. Brian de Bois Guilbert was a Templar, I believe. Do we understand you to insinuate that those famous Templars still survive in modern London? May the ring of their armed heels be heard, and the rattle of their shields, as in mailed prayer the monk-knights kneel before the consecrated Host? Surely a monk-knight were a curious sight picking his way along the Strand, his gleaming corselet and snowy surcoat spattered by an omnibus. Long-bearded, too, according to his order's rule; his face fuzzy as a pard's; how would the grim ghost look among the crop-haired, close-shaven citizens? We know indeed—sad history recounts it—that a moral blight tainted at last this sacred Brotherhood. Though no sworded foe might outskill them in the fence, yet the worm of luxury crawled beneath their guard, gnawing the core of knightly troth, nibbling the monastic vow, till at last the monk's austerity relaxed to was-sailing, and the sworn knights-bachelors grew to be but hyp-ocrites and rakes.

But for all this, quite unprepared were we to learn that Knights-Templars (if at all in being) were so entirely secular-ized as to be reduced from carving out immortal fame in glorious battling for the Holy Land, to the carving of roast-mutton at a dinner-board. Like Anacreon, do these degener-ate Templars now think it sweeter far to fall in banquet than in war? Or, indeed, how can there be any survival of that famous order? Templars in modern London! Templars in their red-cross mantles smoking cigars at the Divan! Templars crowded in a railway train, till, stacked with steel helmet, spear, and shield, the whole train looks like one elongated locomotive!

No. The genuine Templar is long since departed. Go view the wondrous tombs in the Temple Church; see there the rig-idly-haughty forms stretched out, with crossed arms upon their stilly hearts, in everlasting and undreaming rest. Like the years before the flood, the bold Knights-Templars are no more. Nevertheless, the name remains, and the nominal soci-ety, and the ancient grounds, and some of the ancient edifices. But the iron heel is changed to a boot of patent-leather; the long two-handed sword to a one-handed quill; the monk-giver of gratuitous ghostly counsel now counsels for a fee; the defender of the sarcophagus (if in good practice with his weapon) now has more than one case to defend; the vowed opener and clearer of all highways leading to the Holy Sep-ulchre, now has it in particular charge to check, to clog, to hinder, and embarrass all the courts and avenues of Law; the knight-combatant of the Saracen, breasting spear-points at Acre, now fights law-points in Westminster Hall. The helmet is a wig. Struck by Time's enchanter's wand, the Templar is to-day a Lawyer.

But, like many others tumbled from proud glory's height —like the apple, hard on the bough but mellow on the ground —the Templar's fall has but made him all the finer fellow.

I dare say those old warrior-priests were but gruff and grouty at the best; cased in Birmingham hardware, how could their crimped arms give yours or mine a hearty shake? Their proud, ambitious, monkish souls clasped shut, like horn-book missals; their very faces clapped in bomb-shells; what sort of genial men were these? But best of comrades, most affable of hosts, capital diner is the modern Templar. His wit and wine are both of sparkling brands.

The church and cloisters, courts and vaults, lanes and passages, banquet-halls, refectories, libraries, terraces, gardens, broad walks, domicils, and dessert-rooms, covering a very large space of ground, and all grouped in central neighborhood, and quite sequestered from the old city's surrounding din; and every thing about the place being kept in most bachelor-like particularity, no part of London offers to a quiet wight so agreeable a refuge.

The Temple is, indeed, a city by itself. A city with all the best appurtenances, as the above enumeration shows. A city with a park to it, and flower-beds, and a river-side—the Thames flowing by as openly, in one part, as by Eden's primal garden flowed the mild Euphrates. In what is now the Temple Garden the old Crusaders used to exercise their steeds and lances; the modern Templars now lounge on the benches beneath the trees, and, switching their patent-leather boots, in gay discourse exercise at repartee.

Long lines of stately portraits in the banquet-halls, show what great men of mark—famous nobles, judges, and Lord Chancellors—have in their time been Templars. But all Templars are not known to universal fame; though, if the having warm hearts and warmer welcomes, full minds and fuller cellars, and giving good advice and glorious dinners, spiced with rare divertisements of fun and fancy, merit immortal mention, set down, ye muses, the names of R. F. C. and his imperial brother.

Though to be a Templar, in the one true sense, you must needs be a lawyer, or a student at the law, and be ceremoniously enrolled as member of the order, yet as many such, though Templars, do not reside within the Temple's precincts, though they may have their offices there, just so, on the other hand, there are many residents of the hoary old domicils who are not admitted Templars. If being, say, a lounging gentleman and bachelor, or a quiet, unmarried, literary man, charmed with the soft seclusion of the spot, you much desire to pitch your shady tent among the rest in this serene encampment, then you must make some special friend among the order, and procure him to rent, in his name but at your charge, whatever vacant chamber you may find to suit.

Thus, I suppose, did Dr. Johnson, that nominal Benedick and widower but virtual bachelor, when for a space he resided here. So, too, did that undoubted bachelor and rare good soul, Charles Lamb. And hundreds more, of sterling spirits, Brethren of the Order of Celibacy, from time to time have dined, and slept, and tabernacled here. Indeed, the place is all a honeycomb of offices and domicils. Like any cheese, it is quite perforated through and through in all directions with the snug cells of bachelors. Dear, delightful spot! Ah! when I bethink me of the sweet hours there passed, enjoying such genial hospitalities beneath those time-honored roofs, my heart only finds due utterance through poetry; and, with a sigh, I softly sing, "Carry me back to old Virginny!"

Such then, at large, is the Paradise of Bachelors. And such I found it one pleasant afternoon in the smiling month of May, when, sallying from my hotel in Trafalgar Square, I went to keep my dinner-appointment with that fine Barrister, Bachelor, and Bencher, R. F. C. (he *is* the first and second, and *should be* the third; I hereby nominate him), whose card I kept fast pinched between my gloved forefinger and thumb, and every now and then snatched still another look at the pleasant address inscribed beneath the name, "No. —, Elm Court, Temple."

At the core he was a right bluff, care-free, right comfortable, and most companionable Englishman. If on a first acquaintance he seemed reserved, quite icy in his air—patience;

this Champagne will thaw. And if it never do, better frozen Champagne than liquid vinegar.

There were nine gentlemen, all bachelors, at the dinner. One was from "No. —, King's Bench Walk, Temple;" a second, third, and fourth, and fifth, from various courts or passages christened with some similarly rich resounding syllables. It was indeed a sort of Senate of the Bachelors, sent to this dinner from widely-scattered districts, to represent the general celibacy of the Temple. Nay it was, by representation, a Grand Parliament of the best Bachelors in universal London; several of those present being from distant quarters of the town, noted immemorial seats of lawyers and unmarried men—Lincoln's Inn, Furnival's Inn; and one gentleman, upon whom I looked with a sort of collateral awe, hailed from the spot where Lord Verulam once abode a bachelor—Gray's Inn.

The apartment was well up toward heaven. I know not how many strange old stairs I climbed to get to it. But a good dinner, with famous company, should be well earned. No doubt our host had his dining-room so high with a view to secure the prior exercise necessary to the due relishing and digesting of it.

The furniture was wonderfully unpretending, old, and snug. No new shining mahogany, sticky with undried varnish; no uncomfortably luxurious ottomans, and sofas too fine to use, vexed you in this sedate apartment. It is a thing which every sensible American should learn from every sensible Englishman, that glare and glitter, gimcracks and gewgaws, are not indispensable to domestic solacement. The American Benedick snatches, down-town, a tough chop in a gilded show-box; the English bachelor leisurely dines at home on that incomparable South Down of his, off a plain deal board.

The ceiling of the room was low. Who wants to dine under the dome of St. Peter's? High ceilings! If that is your demand, and the higher the better, and you be so very tall, then go dine out with the topping giraffe in the open air.

In good time the nine gentlemen sat down to nine covers, and soon were fairly under way.

If I remember right, ox-tail soup inaugurated the affair. Of a rich russet hue, its agreeable flavor dissipated my first con-founding of its main ingredient with teamster's gads and the raw-hides of ushers. (By way of interlude, we here drank a little claret.) Neptune's was the next tribute rendered—turbot coming second; snow-white, flaky, and just gelatinous enough, not too turtleish in its unctuousness.

(At this point we refreshed ourselves with a glass of sherry.) After these light skirmishers had vanished, the heavy artillery of the feast marched in, led by that well-known En-glish generalissimo, roast beef. For aids-de-camp we had a saddle of mutton, a fat turkey, a chicken-pie, and endless other savory things; while for avant-couriers came nine silver flagons of humming ale. This heavy ordnance having de-parted on the track of the light skirmishers, a picked brigade of game-fowl encamped upon the board, their camp-fires lit by the ruddiest of decanters.

Tarts and puddings followed, with innumerable niceties; then cheese and crackers. (By way of ceremony, simply, only to keep up good old fashions, we here each drank a glass of good old port.)

The cloth was now removed; and like Blucher's army com-ing in at the death on the field of Waterloo, in marched a fresh detachment of bottles, dusty with their hurried march.

All these manœuvrings of the forces were superintended by a surprising old field-marshal (I can not school myself to call him by the inglorious name of waiter), with snowy hair and napkin, and a head like Socrates. Amidst all the hilarity of the feast, intent on important business, he disdained to smile. Venerable man!

I have above endeavored to give some slight schedule of the general plan of operations. But any one knows that a good, genial dinner is a sort of pell-mell, indiscriminate affair, quite baffling to detail in all particulars. Thus, I spoke of tak-ing a glass of claret, and a glass of sherry, and a glass of port, and a mug of ale—all at certain specific periods and times. But those were merely the state bumpers, so to speak. Innu-merable impromptu glasses were drained between the periods of those grand imposing ones.

The nine bachelors seemed to have the most tender concern for each other's health. All the time, in flowing wine, they

most earnestly expressed their sincerest wishes for the entire
well-being and lasting hygiene of the gentlemen on the right
and on the left. I noticed that when one of these kind bachelors desired a little more wine (just for his stomach's sake, like
Timothy), he would not help himself to it unless some other
bachelor would join him. It seemed held something indeli-
cate, selfish, and unfraternal, to be seen taking a lonely, un-
participated glass. Meantime, as the wine ran apace, the spirits
of the company grew more and more to perfect genialness
and unconstraint. They related all sorts of pleasant stories.
Choice experiences in their private lives were now brought
out, like choice brands of Moselle or Rhenish, only kept for
particular company. One told us how mellowly he lived when
a student at Oxford; with various spicy anecdotes of most
frank-hearted noble lords, his liberal companions. Another
bachelor, a gray-headed man, with a sunny face, who, by his
own account, embraced every opportunity of leisure to cross
over into the Low Countries, on sudden tours of inspection
of the fine old Flemish architecture there—this learned,
white-haired, sunny-faced old bachelor, excelled in his descriptions of the elaborate splendors of those old guild-halls,
town-halls, and stadthold-houses, to be seen in the land of
the ancient Flemings. A third was a great frequenter of the
British Museum, and knew all about scores of wonderful antiquities, of Oriental manuscripts, and costly books without a
duplicate. A fourth had lately returned from a trip to Old
Granada, and, of course, was full of Saracenic scenery. A fifth
had a funny case in law to tell. A sixth was erudite in wines.
A seventh had a strange characteristic anecdote of the private
life of the Iron Duke, never printed, and never before announced in any public or private company. An eighth had
lately been amusing his evenings, now and then, with trans-
lating a comic poem of Pulci's. He quoted for us the more
amusing passages.

And so the evening slipped along, the hours told, not by a
water-clock, like King Alfred's, but a wine-chronometer.
Meantime the table seemed a sort of Epsom Heath; a regular
ring, where the decanters galloped round. For fear one decanter should not with sufficient speed reach his destination,
another was sent express after him to hurry him; and then a

third to hurry the second; and so on with a fourth and fifth. And throughout all this nothing loud, nothing unmannerly, nothing turbulent. I am quite sure, from the scrupulous gravity and austerity of his air, that had Socrates, the field-marshal, perceived aught of indecorum in the company he served, he would have forthwith departed without giving warning. I afterward learned that, during the repast, an invalid bachelor in an adjoining chamber enjoyed his first sound refreshing slumber in three long, weary weeks.

It was the very perfection of quiet absorption of good living, good drinking, good feeling, and good talk. We were a band of brothers. Comfort—fraternal, household comfort, was the grand trait of the affair. Also, you could plainly see that these easy-hearted men had no wives or children to give an anxious thought. Almost all of them were travelers, too; for bachelors alone can travel freely, and without any twinges of their consciences touching desertion of the fire-side.

The thing called pain, the bugbear styled trouble—those two legends seemed preposterous to their bachelor imaginations. How could men of liberal sense, ripe scholarship in the world, and capacious philosophical and convivial understandings—how could they suffer themselves to be imposed upon by such monkish fables? Pain! Trouble! As well talk of Catholic miracles. No such thing.—Pass the sherry, Sir.—Pooh, pooh! Can't be!—The port, Sir, if you please. Nonsense; don't tell me so.—The decanter stops with you, Sir, I believe.

And so it went.

Not long after the cloth was drawn our host glanced significantly upon Socrates, who, solemnly stepping to a stand, returned with an immense convolved horn, a regular Jericho horn, mounted with polished silver, and otherwise chased and curiously enriched; not omitting two life-like goat's heads, with four more horns of solid silver, projecting from opposite sides of the mouth of the noble main horn.

Not having heard that our host was a performer on the bugle, I was surprised to see him lift this horn from the table, as if he were about to blow an inspiring blast. But I was relieved from this, and set quite right as touching the purposes of the horn, by his now inserting his thumb and forefinger into its mouth; whereupon a slight aroma was stirred up, and my nostrils were greeted with the smell of some choice Rappee. It was a mull of snuff. It went the rounds. Capital idea this, thought I, of taking snuff about this juncture. This goodly fashion must be introduced among my countrymen at home, further ruminated I.

The remarkable decorum of the nine bachelors—a decorum not to be affected by any quantity of wine—a decorum unassailable by any degree of mirthfulness—this was again set in a forcible light to me, by now observing that, though they took snuff very freely, yet not a man so far violated the proprieties, or so far molested the invalid bachelor in the adjoining room as to indulge himself in a sneeze. The snuff was snuffed silently, as if it had been some fine innoxious powder brushed off the wings of butterflies.

But fine though they be, bachelors' dinners, like bachelors' lives, can not endure forever. The time came for breaking up. One by one the bachelors took their hats, and two by two, and arm-in-arm they descended, still conversing, to the flagging of the court; some going to their neighboring chambers to turn over the Decameron ere retiring for the night; some to smoke a cigar, promenading in the garden on the cool river-side; some to make for the street, call a hack, and be driven snugly to their distant lodgings.

I was the last lingerer.

"Well," said my smiling host, "what do you think of the Temple here, and the sort of life we bachelors make out to live in it?"

"Sir," said I, with a burst of admiring candor—"Sir, this is the very Paradise of Bachelors!"

II. The Tartarus of Maids

It lies not far from Woedolor Mountain in New England. Turning to the east, right out from among bright farms and sunny meadows, nodding in early June with odorous grasses, you enter ascendingly among bleak hills. These gradually close in upon a dusky pass, which, from the violent Gulf Stream of air unceasingly driving between its cloven walls of haggard rock, as well as from the tradition of a crazy spinster's hut having long ago stood somewhere hereabouts, is called the Mad Maid's Bellows'-pipe.

Winding along at the bottom of the gorge is a dangerously narrow wheel-road, occupying the bed of a former torrent. Following this road to its highest point, you stand as within a Dantean gateway. From the steepness of the walls here, their strangely ebon hue, and the sudden contraction of the gorge, this particular point is called the Black Notch. The ravine now expandingly descends into a great, purple, hopper-shaped hollow, far sunk among many Plutonian, shaggy-wooded mountains. By the country people this hollow is called the Devil's Dungeon. Sounds of torrents fall on all sides upon the ear. These rapid waters unite at last in one turbid brick-colored stream, boiling through a flume among enormous boulders. They call this strange-colored torrent Blood River. Gaining a dark precipice it wheels suddenly to the west, and makes one maniac spring of sixty feet into the arms of a stunted wood of gray-haired pines, between which it thence eddies on its further way down to the invisible lowlands.

Conspicuously crowning a rocky bluff high to one side, at the cataract's verge, is the ruin of an old saw-mill, built in those primitive times when vast pines and hemlocks superabounded throughout the neighboring region. The black-mossed bulk of those immense, rough-hewn, and spike-knotted logs, here and there tumbled all together, in long abandonment and decay, or left in solitary, perilous projection over the cataract's gloomy brink, impart to this rude wooden ruin not only much of the aspect of one of rough-quarried stone, but also a sort of feudal, Rhineland, and Thurmberg look, derived from the pinnacled wildness of the neighboring scenery.

Not far from the bottom of the Dungeon stands a large white-washed building, relieved, like some great white sepulchre, against the sullen background of mountain-side firs, and other hardy evergreens, inaccessibly rising in grim terraces for some two thousand feet.

The building is a paper-mill.

Having embarked on a large scale in the seedsman's business (so extensively and broadcast, indeed, that at length my seeds were distributed through all the Eastern and Northern States, and even fell into the far soil of Missouri and the Carolinas), the demand for paper at my place became so great, that the expenditure soon amounted to a most important item in the general account. It need hardly be hinted how paper comes into use with seedsmen, as envelopes. These are mostly made of yellowish paper, folded square; and when filled, are all but flat, and being stamped, and superscribed with the nature of the seeds contained, assume not a little the appearance of business-letters ready for the mail. Of these small envelopes I used an incredible quantity—several hundreds of thousands in a year. For a time I had purchased my paper from the wholesale dealers in a neighboring town. For economy's sake, and partly for the adventure of the trip, I now resolved to cross the mountains, some sixty miles, and order my future paper at the Devil's Dungeon paper-mill.

The sleighing being uncommonly fine toward the end of January, and promising to hold so for no small period, in spite of the bitter cold I started one gray Friday noon in my pung, well fitted with buffalo and wolf robes; and, spending one night on the road, next noon came in sight of Woedolor Mountain.

The far summit fairly smoked with frost; white vapors curled up from its white-wooded top, as from a chimney. The intense congelation made the whole country look like one petrifaction. The steel shoes of my pung craunched and gritted over the vitreous, chippy snow, as if it had been broken glass. The forests here and there skirting the route, feeling the same all-stiffening influence, their inmost fibres penetrated with the cold, strangely groaned—not in the swaying branches merely, but likewise in the vertical trunk—as the fitful gusts remorselessly swept through them. Brittle with excessive frost, many colossal tough-grained maples, snapped in twain like pipe-stems, cumbered the unfeeling earth.

Flaked all over with frozen sweat, white as a milky ram, his nostrils at each breath sending forth two horn-shaped shoots of heated respiration, Black, my good horse, but six years old, started at a sudden turn, where, right across the track—not ten minutes fallen—an old distorted hemlock lay, darkly undulatory as an anaconda.

Gaining the Bellows'-pipe, the violent blast, dead from behind, all but shoved my high-backed pung up-hill. The gust shrieked through the shivered pass, as if laden with lost spirits bound to the unhappy world. Ere gaining the summit, Black, my horse, as if exasperated by the cutting wind, slung out with his strong hind legs, tore the light pung straight up-hill, and sweeping grazingly through the narrow notch, sped downward madly past the ruined saw-mill. Into the Devil's Dungeon horse and cataract rushed together.

With might and main, quitting my seat and robes, and standing backward, with one foot braced against the dashboard, I rasped and churned the bit, and stopped him just in time to avoid collision, at a turn, with the bleak nozzle of a rock, couchant like a lion in the way—a road-side rock.

At first I could not discover the paper-mill.

The whole hollow gleamed with the white, except, here and there, where a pinnacle of granite showed one wind-swept angle bare. The mountains stood pinned in shrouds—a pass of Alpine corpses. Where stands the mill? Suddenly a whirling, humming sound broke upon my ear. I looked, and there, like an arrested avalanche, lay the large whitewashed factory. It was subordinately surrounded by a cluster of other and smaller buildings, some of which, from their cheap, blank air, great length, gregarious windows, and comfortless expression, no doubt were boarding-houses of the operatives. A snow-white hamlet amidst the snows. Various rude, irregular squares and courts resulted from the somewhat picturesque clusterings of these buildings, owing to the broken, rocky nature of the ground, which forbade all method in their relative arrangement. Several narrow lanes and alleys, too, partly blocked with snow fallen from the roof, cut up the hamlet in all directions.

When, turning from the traveled highway, jingling with bells of numerous farmers—who, availing themselves of the fine sleighing, were dragging their wood to market—and frequently diversified with swift cutters dashing from inn to inn of the scattered villages—when, I say, turning from that bustling main-road, I by degrees wound into the Mad Maid's Bellows'-pipe, and saw the grim Black Notch beyond, then something latent, as well as something obvious in the time and scene, strangely brought back to my mind my first sight of dark and grimy Temple-Bar. And when Black, my horse, went darting through the Notch, perilously grazing its rocky wall, I remembered being in a runaway London omnibus, which in much the same sort of style, though by no means at an equal rate, dashed through the ancient arch of Wren. Though the two objects did by no means completely correspond, yet this partial inadequacy but served to tinge the similitude not less with the vividness than the disorder of a dream. So that, when upon reining up at the protruding rock I at last caught sight of the quaint groupings of the factory-buildings, and with the traveled highway and the Notch behind, found myself all alone, silently and privily stealing through deep-cloven passages into this sequestered spot, and saw the long, high-gabled main factory edifice, with a rude tower—for hoisting heavy boxes—at one end, standing among its crowded outbuildings and boarding-houses, as the Temple Church amidst the surrounding offices and dormitories, and when the marvelous retirement of this mysterious mountain nook fastened its whole spell upon me, then, what memory lacked, all tributary imagination furnished, and I said to myself, "This is the very counterpart of the Paradise of Bachelors, but snowed upon, and frost-painted to a sepulchre."

Dismounting, and warily picking my way down the dangerous declivity—horse and man both sliding now and then upon the icy ledges—at length I drove, or the blast drove me, into the largest square, before one side of the main edifice. Piercingly and shrilly the shotted blast blew by the corner; and redly and demoniacally boiled Blood River at one side. A long wood-pile, of many scores of cords, all glittering in mail of crusted ice, stood crosswise in the square. A row of horse-posts, their north sides plastered with adhesive snow, flanked the factory wall. The bleak frost packed and paved the square as with some ringing metal.

The inverted similitude recurred—"The sweet, tranquil Temple garden, with the Thames bordering its green beds," strangely meditated I.

But where are the gay bachelors?

Then, as I and my horse stood shivering in the wind-spray, a girl ran from a neighboring dormitory door, and throwing her thin apron over her bare head, made for the opposite building.

"One moment, my girl; is there no shed hereabouts which I may drive into?"

Pausing, she turned upon me a face pale with work, and blue with cold; an eye supernatural with unrelated misery.

"Nay," faltered I, "I mistook you. Go on; I want nothing."

Leading my horse close to the door from which she had come, I knocked. Another pale, blue girl appeared, shivering in the doorway as, to prevent the blast, she jealously held the door ajar.

"Nay, I mistake again. In God's name shut the door. But hold, is there no man about?"

That moment a dark-complexioned well-wrapped person-age passed, making for the factory door, and spying him com-ing, the girl rapidly closed the other one.

"Is there no horse-shed here, Sir?"

"Yonder, to the wood-shed," he replied, and disappeared inside the factory.

With much ado I managed to wedge in horse and pung between the scattered piles of wood all sawn and split. Then, blanketing my horse, and piling my buffalo on the blanket's top, and tucking in its edges well around the breast-band and breeching, so that the wind might not strip him bare, I tied him fast, and ran lamely for the factory door, stiff with frost, and cumbered with my driver's dread-naught.

Immediately I found myself standing in a spacious place, intolerably lighted by long rows of windows, focusing inward the snowy scene without.

At rows of blank-looking counters sat rows of blank-look-ing girls, with blank, white folders in their blank hands, all blankly folding blank paper.

In one corner stood some huge frame of ponderous iron, with a vertical thing like a piston periodically rising and fall-ing upon a heavy wooden block. Before it—its tame minis-ter—stood a tall girl, feeding the iron animal with half-quires of rose-hued note paper, which, at every downward dab of the piston-like machine, received in the corner the impress of a wreath of roses. I looked from the rosy paper to the pallid cheek, but said nothing.

Seated before a long apparatus, strung with long, slender strings like any harp, another girl was feeding it with foolscap sheets, which, so soon as they curiously traveled from her on the cords, were withdrawn at the opposite end of the machine by a second girl. They came to the first girl blank; they went to the second girl ruled.

I looked upon the first girl's brow, and saw it was young and fair; I looked upon the second girl's brow, and saw it was ruled and wrinkled. Then, as I still looked, the two—for some small variety to the monotony—changed places; and where had stood the young, fair brow, now stood the ruled and wrinkled one.

Perched high upon a narrow platform, and still higher upon a high stool crowning it, sat another figure serving some other iron animal; while below the platform sat her mate in some sort of reciprocal attendance.

Not a syllable was breathed. Nothing was heard but the low, steady, overruling hum of the iron animals. The human voice was banished from the spot. Machinery—that vaunted slave of humanity—here stood menially served by human beings, who served mutely and cringingly as the slave serves the Sultan. The girls did not so much seem accessory wheels to the general machinery as mere cogs to the wheels.

All this scene around me was instantaneously taken in at one sweeping glance—even before I had proceeded to unwind the heavy fur tippet from around my neck. But as soon as this fell from me the dark-complexioned man, standing close by, raised a sudden cry, and seizing my arm, dragged me out into the open air, and without pausing for a word instantly caught up some congealed snow and began rubbing both my cheeks.

"Two white spots like the whites of your eyes," he said; "man, your cheeks are frozen."

"That may well be," muttered I; " 'tis some wonder the frost of the Devil's Dungeon strikes in no deeper. Rub away."

Soon a horrible, tearing pain caught at my reviving cheeks. Two gaunt blood-hounds, one on each side, seemed mumbling them. I seemed Actæon.

Presently, when all was over, I re-entered the factory, made known my business, concluded it satisfactorily, and then begged to be conducted throughout the place to view it.

"Cupid is the boy for that," said the dark-complexioned man. "Cupid!" and by this odd fancy-name calling a dimpled, red-cheeked, spirited-looking, forward little fellow, who was rather impudently, I thought, gliding about among the passive-looking girls—like a gold fish through hueless waves—yet doing nothing in particular that I could see, the man bade him lead the stranger through the edifice.

"Come first and see the water-wheel," said this lively lad, with the air of boyishly-brisk importance.

Quitting the folding-room, we crossed some damp, cold boards, and stood beneath a great wet shed, incessantly showering with foam, like the green barnacled bow of some East Indiaman in a gale. Round and round here went the enormous revolutions of the dark colossal water-wheel, grim with its one immutable purpose.

"This sets our whole machinery a-going, Sir; in every part of all these buildings; where the girls work and all."

I looked, and saw that the turbid waters of Blood River had not changed their hue by coming under the use of man.

"You make only blank paper; no printing of any sort, I suppose? All blank paper, don't you?"

"Certainly; what else should a paper-factory make?"

The lad here looked at me as if suspicious of my common-sense.

"Oh, to be sure!" said I, confused and stammering; "it only struck me as so strange that red waters should turn out pale chee—paper, I mean."

He took me up a wet and rickety stair to a great light room, furnished with no visible thing but rude, manger-like receptacles running all round its sides; and up to these mangers, like so many mares haltered to the rack, stood rows of girls. Before each was vertically thrust up a long, glittering scythe, immovably fixed at bottom to the manger-edge. The curve of the scythe, and its having no snath to it, made it look exactly like a sword. To and fro, across the sharp edge, the girls forever dragged long strips of rags, washed white, picked from baskets at one side; thus ripping asunder every seam, and converting the tatters almost into lint. The air swam with the fine, poisonous particles, which from all sides darted, sub-tilely, as motes in sun-beams, into the lungs.

"This is the rag-room," coughed the boy.

"You find it rather stifling here," coughed I, in answer; "but the girls don't cough."

"Oh, they are used to it."

"Where do you get such hosts of rags?" picking up a handful from a basket.

"Some from the country round about; some from far over sea—Leghorn and London."

" 'Tis not unlikely, then," murmured I, "that among these heaps of rags there may be some old shirts, gathered from the dormitories of the Paradise of Bachelors. But the buttons are all dropped off. Pray, my lad, do you ever find any bachelor's buttons hereabouts?"

"None grow in this part of the country. The Devil's Dungeon is no place for flowers."

"Oh! you mean the *flowers* so called—the Bachelor's Buttons?"

"And was not that what you asked about? Or did you mean the gold bosom-buttons of our boss, Old Bach, as our whispering girls all call him?"

"The man, then, I saw below is a bachelor, is he?"

"Oh, yes, he's a Bach."

"The edges of those swords, they are turned outward from the girls, if I see right; but their rags and fingers fly so, I can not distinctly see."

"Turned outward."

Yes, murmured I to myself; I see it now; turned outward; and each erected sword is so borne, edge-outward, before each girl. If my reading fails me not, just so, of old, con-demned state-prisoners went from the hall of judgment to their doom: an officer before, bearing a sword, its edge turned outward, in significance of their fatal sentence. So, through consumptive pallors of this blank, raggy life, go these white girls to death.

"Those scythes look very sharp," again turning toward the boy.

"Yes; they have to keep them so. Look!"

That moment two of the girls, dropping their rags, plied

each a whet-stone up and down the sword-blade. My unaccustomed blood curdled at the sharp shriek of the tormented steel.

Their own executioners; themselves whetting the very swords that slay them; meditated I.

"What makes those girls so sheet-white, my lad?"

"Why"—with a roguish twinkle, pure ignorant drollery, not knowing heartlessness—"I suppose the handling of such white bits of sheets all the time makes them so sheety."

"Let us leave the rag-room now, my lad."

More tragical and more inscrutably mysterious than any mystic sight, human or machine, throughout the factory, was the strange innocence of cruel-heartedness in this usage-hardened boy.

"And now," said he, cheerily, "I suppose you want to see our great machine, which cost us twelve thousand dollars only last autumn. That's the machine that makes the paper, too. This way, Sir."

Following him, I crossed a large, bespattered place, with two great round vats in it, full of a white, wet, woolly-looking stuff, not unlike the albuminous part of an egg, soft-boiled.

"There," said Cupid, tapping the vats carelessly, "these are the first beginnings of the paper; this white pulp you see. Look how it swims bubbling round and round, moved by the paddle here. From hence it pours from both vats into that one common channel yonder, and so goes, mixed up and leisurely, to the great machine. And now for that."

He led me into a room, stifling with a strange, blood-like, abdominal heat, as if here, true enough, were being finally developed the germinous particles lately seen.

Before me, rolled out like some long Eastern manuscript, lay stretched one continuous length of iron frame-work—multitudinous and mystical, with all sorts of rollers, wheels, and cylinders, in slowly-measured and unceasing motion.

"Here first comes the pulp now," said Cupid, pointing to the nighest end of the machine. "See; first it pours out and spreads itself upon this wide, sloping board; and then—look—slides, thin and quivering beneath the first roller there. Follow on now, and see it as it slides from under that to the next cylinder. There; see how it has become just a very little less pulpy now. One step more, and it grows still more to some slight consistence. Still another cylinder, and it is so knitted—though as yet mere dragon-fly wing—that it forms an air-bridge here, like a suspended cobweb, between two more separated rollers; and flowing over the last one, and under again, and doubling about there out of sight for a minute among all those mixed cylinders you indistinctly see, it reappears here, looking now at last a little less like pulp and more like paper, but still quite delicate and defective yet awhile. But—a little further onward, Sir, if you please—here now, at this further point, it puts on something of a real look, as if it might turn out to be something you might possibly handle in the end. But it's not yet done, Sir. Good way to travel yet, and plenty more of cylinders must roll it."

"Bless my soul!" said I, amazed at the elongation, interminable convolutions, and deliberate slowness of the machine; "it must take a long time for the pulp to pass from end to end, and come out paper."

"Oh! not so long," smiled the precocious lad, with a superior and patronizing air; "only nine minutes. But look; you may try it for yourself. Have you a bit of paper? Ah! here's a bit on the floor. Now mark that with any word you please, and let me dab it on here, and we'll see how long before it comes out at the other end."

"Well, let me see," said I, taking out my pencil; "come, I'll mark it with your name."

Bidding me take out my watch, Cupid adroitly dropped the inscribed slip on an exposed part of the incipient mass.

Instantly my eye marked the second-hand on my dial-plate.

Slowly I followed the slip, inch by inch; sometimes pausing for full half a minute as it disappeared beneath inscrutable groups of the lower cylinders, but only gradually to emerge again; and so, on, and on, and on—inch by inch; now in open sight, sliding along like a freckle on the quivering sheet; and then again wholly vanished; and so, on, and on, and on—inch by inch; all the time the main sheet growing more and more to final firmness—when, suddenly, I saw a sort of paper-fall, not wholly unlike a water-fall; a scissory sound smote my ear, as of some cord being snapped; and down dropped an unfolded sheet of perfect foolscap, with my "Cupid" half faded out of it, and still moist and warm.

My travels were at an end, for here was the end of the machine.

"Well, how long was it?" said Cupid.

"Nine minutes to a second," replied I, watch in hand.

"I told you so."

For a moment a curious emotion filled me, not wholly unlike that which one might experience at the fulfillment of some mysterious prophecy. But how absurd, thought I again; the thing is a mere machine, the essence of which is unvarying punctuality and precision.

Previously absorbed by the wheels and cylinders, my attention was now directed to a sad-looking woman standing by.

"That is rather an elderly person so silently tending the machine-end here. She would not seem wholly used to it either."

"Oh," knowingly whispered Cupid, through the din, "she only came last week. She was a nurse formerly. But the business is poor in these parts, and she's left it. But look at the paper she is piling there."

"Ay, foolscap," handling the piles of moist, warm sheets, which continually were being delivered into the woman's waiting hands. "Don't you turn out any thing but foolscap at this machine?"

"Oh, sometimes, but not often, we turn out finer work—cream-laid and royal sheets, we call them. But foolscap being in chief demand, we turn out foolscap most."

It was very curious. Looking at that blank paper continually dropping, dropping, dropping, my mind ran on in wonderings of those strange uses to which those thousand sheets eventually would be put. All sorts of writings would be writ on those now vacant things—sermons, lawyers' briefs, physicians' prescriptions, love-letters, marriage certificates, bills of divorce, registers of births, death-warrants, and so on, without end. Then, recurring back to them as they here lay all blank, I could not but bethink me of that celebrated comparison of John Locke, who, in demonstration of his theory that man had no innate ideas, compared the human mind at birth to a sheet of blank paper; something destined to be scribbled on, but what sort of characters no soul might tell.

Pacing slowly to and fro along the involved machine, still humming with its play, I was struck as well by the inevitability as the evolvement-power in all its motions.

"Does that thin cobweb there," said I, pointing to the sheet in its more imperfect stage, "does that never tear or break? It is marvelous fragile, and yet this machine it passes through is so mighty."

"It never is known to tear a hair's point."

"Does it never stop—get clogged?"

"No. It *must* go. The machinery makes it go just *so*; just that very way, and at that very pace you there plainly *see* it go. The pulp can't help going."

Something of awe now stole over me, as I gazed upon this inflexible iron animal. Always, more or less, machinery of this ponderous, elaborate sort strikes, in some moods, strange dread into the human heart, as some living, panting Behemoth might. But what made the thing I saw so specially terrible to me was the metallic necessity, the unbudging fatality which governed it. Though, here and there, I could not follow the thin, gauzy vail of pulp in the course of its more mysterious or entirely invisible advance, yet it was indubitable that, at those points where it eluded me, it still marched on in unvarying docility to the autocratic cunning of the machine. A fascination fastened on me. I stood spell-bound and wandering in my soul. Before my eyes—there, passing in slow procession along the wheeling cylinders, I seemed to see, glued to the pallid incipience of the pulp, the yet more pallid faces of all the pallid girls I had eyed that heavy day. Slowly, mournfully, beseechingly, yet unresistingly, they gleamed along, their agony dimly outlined on the imperfect paper, like the print of the tormented face on the handkerchief of Saint Veronica.

"Halloa! the heat of the room is too much for you," cried Cupid, staring at me.

"No—I am rather chill, if any thing."

"Come out, Sir—out—out," and, with the protecting air of a careful father, the precocious lad hurried me outside.

In a few moments, feeling revived a little, I went into the folding-room—the first room I had entered, and where the desk for transacting business stood, surrounded by the blank counters and blank girls engaged at them.

"Cupid here has led me a strange tour," said I to the dark-complexioned man before mentioned, whom I had ere this discovered not only to be an old bachelor, but also the principal proprietor. "Yours is a most wonderful factory. Your great machine is a miracle of inscrutable intricacy."

"Yes, all our visitors think it so. But we don't have many. We are in a very out-of-the-way corner here. Few inhabitants, too. Most of our girls come from far-off villages."

"The girls," echoed I, glancing round at their silent forms. "Why is it, Sir, that in most factories, female operatives, of whatever age, are indiscriminately called girls, never women?"

"Oh! as to that—why, I suppose, the fact of their being generally unmarried—that's the reason, I should think. But it never struck me before. For our factory here, we will not have married women; they are apt to be off-and-on too much. We want none but steady workers: twelve hours to the day, day after day, through the three hundred and sixty-five days, excepting Sundays, Thanksgiving, and Fast-days. That's our rule. And so, having no married women, what females we have are rightly enough called girls."

"Then these are all maids," said I, while some pained homage to their pale virginity made me involuntarily bow.

"All maids."

Again the strange emotion filled me.

"Your cheeks look whitish yet, Sir," said the man, gazing at me narrowly. "You must be careful going home. Do they pain you at all now? It's a bad sign, if they do."

"No doubt, Sir," answered I, " when once I have got out of the Devil's Dungeon, I shall feel them mending."

"Ah, yes; the winter air in valleys, or gorges, or any sunken place, is far colder and more bitter than elsewhere. You would hardly believe it now, but it is colder here than at the top of Woedolor Mountain."

"I dare say it is, Sir. But time presses me; I must depart."

With that, remuffling myself in dread-naught and tippet, thrusting my hands into my huge seal-skin mittens, I sallied out into the nipping air, and found poor Black, my horse, all cringing and doubled up with the cold.

Soon, wrapped in furs and meditations, I ascended from the Devil's Dungeon.

At the Black Notch I paused, and once more bethought me of Temple-Bar. Then, shooting through the pass, all alone with inscrutable nature, I exclaimed—Oh! Paradise of Bachelors! and oh! Tartarus of Maids!

Jimmy Rose

A TIME AGO, no matter how long precisely, I, an old man, removed from the country to the city, having become unexpected heir to a great old house in a narrow street of one of the lower wards, once the haunt of style and fashion, full of gay parlors and bridal chambers; but now, for the most part, transformed into counting-rooms and warehouses. There bales and boxes usurp the place of sofas; day-books and ledgers are spread where once the delicious breakfast toast was buttered. In those old wards the glorious old soft-warfle days are over.

Nevertheless, in this old house of mine, so strangely spared, some monument of departed days survived. Nor was this the only one. Amidst the warehouse ranges some few other dwellings likewise stood. The street's transmutation was not yet complete. Like those old English friars and nuns, long haunting the ruins of their retreats after they had been de-spoiled, so some few strange old gentlemen and ladies still lingered in the neighborhood, and would not, could not, might not quit it. And I thought that when, one spring, emerging from my white-blossoming orchard, my own white hairs and white ivory-headed cane were added to their loiter-ing census, that those poor old souls insanely fancied the ward was looking up—the tide of fashion setting back again.

For many years the old house had been unoccupied by an owner; those into whose hands it from time to time had passed having let it out to various shifting tenants; decayed old towns-people, mysterious recluses, or transient, ambigu-ous-looking foreigners.

While from certain cheap furbishings to which the exterior had been subjected, such as removing a fine old pulpit-like porch crowning the summit of six lofty steps, and set off with a broad-brimmed sounding-board overshadowing the whole, as well as replacing the original heavy window-shutters (each pierced with a crescent in the upper panel to admit an Ori-ental and moony light into the otherwise shut-up rooms of a sultry morning in July) with frippery Venetian blinds; while, I repeat, the front of the house hereby presented an incon-

gruous aspect, as if the graft of modernness had not taken in
its ancient stock; still, however it might fare without, within
little or nothing had been altered. The cellars were full of
great grim, arched bins of blackened brick, looking like the
ancient tombs of Templars, while overhead were shown the
first-floor timbers, huge, square, and massive, all red oak, and
through long eld, of a rich and Indian color. So large were
those timbers, and so thickly ranked, that to walk in those
capacious cellars was much like walking along a line-of-battle
ship's gun-deck.

All the rooms in each story remained just as they stood
ninety years ago, with all their heavy-moulded, wooden cornices, paneled wainscots, and carved and inaccessible mantles
of queer horticultural and zoological devices. Dim with longevity, the very covering of the walls still preserved the patterns of the times of Louis XVI. In the largest parlor (the
drawing-room, my daughters called it, in distinction from
two smaller parlors, though I did not think the distinction
indispensable) the paper hangings were in the most gaudy
style. Instantly we knew such paper could only have come
from Paris—genuine Versailles paper—the sort of paper that
might have hung in Marie Antoinette's boudoir. It was of
great diamond lozenges, divided by massive festoons of roses
(onions, Biddy the girl said they were, but my wife soon
changed Biddy's mind on that head); and in those lozenges,
one and all, as in an overarbored garden-cage, sat a grand
series of gorgeous illustrations of the natural history of the
most imposing Parisian-looking birds; parrots, macaws, and
peacocks, but mostly peacocks. Real Prince Esterhazies of
birds; all rubies, diamonds, and Orders of the Golden Fleece.
But, alas! the north side of this old apartment presented a
strange look; half mossy and half mildew; something as ancient forest trees on their north sides, to which particular side
the moss most clings, and where, they say, internal decay first
strikes. In short, the original resplendence of the peacocks had
been sadly dimmed on that north side of the room, owing to
a small leak in the eaves, from which the rain had slowly trickled its way down the wall, clean down to the first floor. This
leak the irreverent tenants, at that period occupying the premises, did not see fit to stop, or rather, did not think it worth

their while, seeing that they only kept their fuel and dried their clothes in the parlor of the peacocks. Hence many of the once glowing birds seemed as if they had their princely plumage bedraggled in a dusty shower. Most mournfully their starry trains were blurred. Yet so patiently and so pleasantly, nay, here and there so ruddily did they seem to bide their bitter doom, so much of real elegance still lingered in their shapes, and so full, too, seemed they of a sweet engaging pensiveness, meditating all day long, for years and years, among their faded bowers, that though my family repeatedly adjured me (especially my wife, who, I fear, was too young for me) to destroy the whole hen-roost, as Biddy called it, and cover the walls with a beautiful, nice, genteel, cream-colored paper, despite all entreaties, I could not be prevailed upon, however submissive in other things.

But chiefly would I permit no violation of the old parlor of the peacocks or room of roses (I call it by both names), on account of its long association in my mind with one of the original proprietors of the mansion—the gentle Jimmy Rose.

Poor Jimmy Rose!

He was among my earliest acquaintances. It is not many years since he died; and I and two other tottering old fellows took hack, and in sole procession followed him to his grave.

Jimmy was born a man of moderate fortune. In his prime he had an uncommonly handsome person; large and manly, with bright eyes of blue, brown curling hair, and cheeks that seemed painted with carmine; but it was health's genuine bloom, deepened by the joy of life. He was by nature a great ladies' man, and like most deep adorers of the sex, never tied up his freedom of general worship by making one willful sacrifice of himself at the altar.

Adding to his fortune by a large and princely business, something like that of the great Florentine trader, Cosmo the Magnificent, he was enabled to entertain on a grand scale. For a long time his dinners, suppers, and balls, were not to be surpassed by any given in the party-giving city of New York. His uncommon cheeriness; the splendor of his dress; his sparkling wit; radiant chandeliers; infinite fund of small-talk; French furniture; glowing welcomes to his guests; his bounteous heart and board; his noble graces and his glorious wine; what wonder if all these drew crowds to Jimmy's hospitable abode? In the winter assemblies he figured first on the manager's list. James Rose, Esq., too, was the man to be found foremost in all presentations of plate to highly successful actors at the Park, or of swords and guns to highly successful generals in the field. Often, also, was he chosen to present the gift on account of his fine gift of finely saying fine things.

"Sir," said he, in a great drawing-room in Broadway, as he extended toward General G—— a brace of pistols set with turquois. "Sir," said Jimmy with a Castilian flourish and a rosy smile, "there would have been more turquois here set, had the names of your glorious victories left room."

Ah, Jimmy, Jimmy! Thou didst excel in compliments. But it was inwrought with thy inmost texture to be affluent in all things which give pleasure. And who shall reproach thee with borrowed wit on this occasion, though borrowed indeed it was? Plagiarize otherwise as they may, not often are the men of this world plagiarists in praise.

But times changed. Time, true plagiarist of the seasons.

Sudden and terrible reverses in business were made mortal by mad prodigality on all hands. When his affairs came to be scrutinized, it was found that Jimmy could not pay more than fifteen shillings in the pound. And yet in time the deficiency might have been made up—of course, leaving Jimmy penniless—had it not been that in one winter gale two vessels of his from China perished off Sandy Hook; perished at the threshold of their port.

Jimmy was a ruined man.

It was years ago. At that period I resided in the country, but happened to be in the city on one of my annual visits. It was but four or five days since seeing Jimmy at his house the centre of all eyes, and hearing him at the close of the entertainment toasted by a brocaded lady, in these well-remembered words: "Our noble host; the bloom on his cheek, may it last long as the bloom in his heart!" And they, the sweet ladies and gentlemen there, they drank that toast so gayly and frankly off; and Jimmy, such a kind, proud, grateful tear stood in his honest eye, angelically glancing round at the sparkling faces, and equally sparkling, and equally feeling, decanters.

Ah! poor, poor Jimmy—God guard us all—poor Jimmy Rose!

Well, it was but four or five days after this that I heard a clap of thunder—no, a clap of bad news. I was crossing the Bowling Green in a snow-storm not far from Jimmy's house on the Battery, when I saw a gentleman come sauntering along, whom I remembered at Jimmy's table as having been the first to spring to his feet in eager response to the lady's toast. Not more brimming the wine in his lifted glass than the moisture in his eye on that happy occasion.

Well, this good gentleman came sailing across the Bowling Green, swinging a silver-headed ratan; seeing me, he paused, "Ah, lad, that was rare wine Jimmy gave us the other night. Sha'n't get any more, though. Heard the news? Jimmy's burst. Clean smash, I assure you. Come along down to the Coffee-house and I'll tell you more. And if you say so, we'll arrange over a bottle of claret for a sleighing party to Cato's to-night. Come along."

"Thank you," said I, "I—I—I am engaged."

Straight as an arrow I went to Jimmy's. Upon inquiring for him, the man at the door told me that his master was not in; nor did he know where he was; nor had his master been in the house for forty-eight hours.

Walking up Broadway again, I questioned passing acquaintances; but though each man verified the report, no man could tell where Jimmy was, and no one seemed to care, until I encountered a merchant, who hinted that probably Jimmy, having scraped up from the wreck a snug lump of coin, had prudently betaken himself off to parts unknown. The next man I saw, a great nabob he was too, foamed at the mouth when I mentioned Jimmy's name. "Rascal; regular scamp, Sir, is Jimmy Rose! But there are keen fellows after him." I afterward heard that this indignant gentleman had lost the sum of seventy-five dollars and seventy-five cents indirectly through Jimmy's failure. And yet I dare say the share of the dinners he had eaten at Jimmy's might more than have balanced that sum, considering that he was something of a wine-bibber, and such wines as Jimmy imported cost a plum or two. Indeed, now that I bethink me, I recall how I had more than once observed this same middle-aged gentleman, and how that toward the close of one of Jimmy's dinners he would sit at the table pretending to be earnestly talking with beaming Jimmy, but all the while, with a half furtive sort of tremulous eagerness and hastiness, pour down glass after glass of noble wine, as if now, while Jimmy's bounteous sun was at meridian, was the time to make his selfish hay.

At last I met a person famed for his peculiar knowledge of whatever was secret or withdrawn in the histories and habits of noted people. When I inquired of this person where Jimmy could possibly be, he took me close to Trinity Church rail, out of the jostling of the crowd, and whispered me, that Jimmy had the evening before entered an old house of his (Jimmy's), in C——— Street, which old house had been for a time untenanted. The inference seemed to be that perhaps Jimmy might be lurking there now. So getting the precise locality, I bent my steps in that direction, and at last halted before the house containing the room of roses. The shutters were closed, and cobwebs were spun in their crescents. The whole place had a dreary, deserted air. The snow lay unswept, drifted in one billowy heap against the porch, no footprint tracking it. Whoever was within, surely that lonely man was an abandoned one. Few or no people were in the street; for even at that period the fashion of the street had departed from it, while trade had not as yet occupied what its rival had renounced.

Looking up and down the sidewalk a moment, I softly knocked at the door. No response. I knocked again, and louder. No one came. I knocked and rung both; still without effect. In despair I was going to quit the spot, when, as a last resource, I gave a prolonged summons, with my utmost strength, upon the heavy knocker, and then again stood still; while from various strange old windows up and down the street, various strange old heads were thrust out in wonder at so clamorous a stranger. As if now frightened from its silence, a hollow, husky voice addressed me through the keyhole.

"Who are you?" it said.

"A friend."

"Then shall you not come in," replied the voice, more hollowly than before.

"Great Heaven! this is not Jimmy Rose?" thought I, starting. This is the wrong house. I have been misdirected. But still, to make all sure, I spoke again.

"Is James Rose within there?"

No reply.

Once more I spoke:

"I am William Ford; let me in."

"Oh, I can not, I can not! I am afraid of every one."

It *was* Jimmy Rose!

"Let me in, Rose; let me in, man. I am your friend."

"I will not. I can trust no man now."

"Let me in, Rose; trust at least one, in me."

"Quit the spot, or—"

With that I heard a rattling against the huge lock, not made by any key, as if some small tube were being thrust into the keyhole. Horrified, I fled fast as feet could carry me.

I was a young man then, and Jimmy was not more than forty. It was five-and-twenty years ere I saw him again. And what a change. He whom I expected to behold—if behold at all—dry, shrunken, meagre, cadaverously fierce with misery and misanthropy—amazement! the old Parisian roses bloomed in his cheeks. And yet poor as any rat; poor in the last dregs of poverty; a pauper beyond alms-house pauperism; a promenading pauper in a thin, thread-bare, careful coat; a pauper with wealth of polished words; a courteous, smiling, shivering gentleman.

Ah, poor, poor Jimmy—God guard us all—poor Jimmy Rose!

Though at the first onset of his calamity, when creditors, once fast friends, pursued him as carrion for jails; though then, to avoid their hunt, as well as the human eye, he had gone and denned in the old abandoned house; and there, in his loneliness, had been driven half mad, yet time and tide had soothed him down to sanity. Perhaps at bottom Jimmy was too thoroughly good and kind to be made from any cause a man-hater. And doubtless it at last seemed irreligious to Jimmy even to shun mankind.

Sometimes sweet sense of duty will entice one to bitter doom. For what could be more bitter than now, in abject need, to be seen of those—nay, crawl and visit them in an humble sort, and be tolerated as an old eccentric, wandering in their parlors—who once had known him richest of the rich, and gayest of the gay? Yet this Jimmy did. Without rudely breaking him right down to it, fate slowly bent him more and more to the lowest deep. From an unknown quarter he received an income of some seventy dollars, more or less. The principal he would never touch, but, by various modes of eking it out, managed to live on the interest. He lived in an attic, where he supplied himself with food. He took but one regular repast a day—meal and milk—and nothing more, unless procured at others' tables. Often about the tea-hour he would drop in upon some old acquaintance, clad in his neat, forlorn frock coat, with worn velvet sewed upon the edges of the cuffs, and a similar device upon the hems of his pantaloons, to hide that dire look of having been grated off by rats. On Sunday he made a point of always dining at some fine house or other.

It is evident that no man could with impunity be allowed to lead this life unless regarded as one who, free from vice, was by fortune brought so low that the plummet of pity alone could reach him. Not much merit redounded to his entertainers because they did not thrust the starving gentleman forth when he came for his poor alms of tea and toast. Some merit had been theirs had they clubbed together and provided him, at small cost enough, with a sufficient income to make him, in point of necessaries, independent of the daily dole of charity; charity not sent to him either, but charity for which he had to trudge round to their doors.

But the most touching thing of all were those roses in his cheeks; those ruddy roses in his nipping winter. How they bloomed; whether meal and milk, and tea and toast could keep them flourishing; whether now he painted them; by what strange magic they were made to blossom so; no son of man might tell. But there they bloomed. And besides the roses, Jimmy was rich in smiles. He smiled ever. The lordly door which received him to his eleemosynary teas, knew no such smiling guest as Jimmy. In his prosperous days the smile of Jimmy was famous far and wide. It should have been trebly famous now.

Wherever he went to tea, he had all of the news of the town to tell. By frequenting the reading-rooms, as one privileged through harmlessness, he kept himself informed of European affairs and the last literature, foreign and domestic. And of this, when encouragement was given, he would largely talk. But encouragement was not always given. At certain houses, and not a few, Jimmy would drop in about ten minutes before the tea-hour, and drop out again about ten minutes after it; well knowing that his further presence was not indispensable to the contentment or felicity of his host.

How forlorn it was to see him so heartily drinking the generous tea, cup after cup, and eating the flavorous bread and butter, piece after piece, when, owing to the lateness of the dinner hour with the rest, and the abundance of that one grand meal with them, no one besides Jimmy touched the bread and butter, or exceeded a single cup of Souchong. And knowing all this very well, poor Jimmy would try to hide his hunger, and yet gratify it too, by striving hard to carry on a sprightly conversation with his hostess, and throwing in the eagerest mouthfuls with a sort of absent-minded air, as if he ate merely for custom's sake, and not starvation's.

Poor, poor Jimmy—God guard us all—poor Jimmy Rose!

Neither did Jimmy give up his courtly ways. Whenever there were ladies at the table, sure were they of some fine word; though, indeed, toward the close of Jimmy's life, the young ladies rather thought his compliments somewhat musty, smacking of cocked hats and small clothes—nay, of old pawnbrokers' shoulder-lace and sword belts. For there still lingered in Jimmy's address a subdued sort of martial air; he having in his palmy days been, among other things, a general of the State militia. There seems a fatality in these militia generalships. Alas! I can recall more than two or three gentlemen who from militia generals become paupers. I am afraid to think why this is so. Is it that this military leaning in a man of an unmilitary heart—that is, a gentle, peaceable heart—is an indication of some weak love of vain display? But ten to one it is not so. At any rate, it is unhandsome, if not unchristian, in the happy, too much to moralize on those who are not so.

So numerous were the houses that Jimmy visited, or so cautious was he in timing his less welcome calls, that at certain mansions he only dropped in about once a year or so. And annually upon seeing at that house the blooming Miss Frances or Miss Arabella, he would profoundly bow in his forlorn old coat, and with his soft, white hand take hers in gallant wise, saying, "Ah, Miss Arabella, these jewels here are bright upon these fingers; but brighter would they look were it not for those still brighter diamonds of your eyes!"

Though in thy own need thou hadst no pence to give the poor, thou, Jimmy, still hadst alms to give the rich. For not the beggar chattering at the corner pines more after bread than the vain heart after compliment. The rich in their craving glut, as the poor in their craving want, we have with us always. So, I suppose, thought Jimmy Rose.

But all women are not vain, or if a little grain that way inclined, more than redeem it all with goodness. Such was the sweet girl that closed poor Jimmy's eyes. The only daughter of an opulent alderman, she knew Jimmy well, and saw to him in his declining days. During his last sickness, with her own hands she carried him jellies and blanc-mange; made tea for him in his attic, and turned the poor old gentleman in his bed. And well hadst thou deserved it, Jimmy, at that fair creature's hands; well merited to have thy old eyes closed by woman's fairy fingers, who through life, in riches and in poverty, was still woman's sworn champion and devotee.

I hardly know that I should mention here one little incident connected with this young lady's ministrations, and poor Jimmy's reception of them. But it is harm to neither; I will tell it.

Chancing to be in town, and hearing of Jimmy's illness, I went to see him. And there in his lone attic I found the lovely ministrant. Withdrawing upon seeing another visitor, she left me alone with him. She had brought some little delicacies, and also several books, of such a sort as are sent by serious-minded well-wishers to invalids in a serious crisis. Now whether it was repugnance at being considered next door to death, or whether it was but the natural peevishness brought on by the general misery of his state; however it was, as the gentle girl withdrew, Jimmy, with what small remains of strength were his, pitched the books into the furthest corner, murmuring, "Why will she bring me this sad old stuff? Does she take me for a pauper? Thinks she to salve a gentleman's heart with Poor Man's Plaster?"

Poor, poor Jimmy—God guard us all—poor Jimmy Rose!

Well, well, I am an old man, and I suppose these tears I drop are dribblets from my dotage. But Heaven be praised, Jimmy needs no man's pity now.

Jimmy Rose is dead!

Meantime, as I sit within the parlor of the peacocks—that chamber from which his husky voice had come ere threatening me with the pistol—I still must meditate upon his strange example, whereof the marvel is, how after that gay, dashing, nobleman's career, he could be content to crawl through life, and peep about among the marbles and mahoganies for contumelious tea and toast, where once like a very Warwick he had feasted the huzzaing world with Burgundy and venison.

And every time I look at the wilted resplendence of those proud peacocks on the wall, I bethink me of the withering change in Jimmy's once resplendent pride of state. But still again, every time I gaze upon those festoons of perpetual roses, mid which the faded peacocks hang, I bethink me of those undying roses which bloomed in ruined Jimmy's cheek.

Transplanted to another soil, all the unkind past forgot, God grant that Jimmy's roses may immortally survive!

The 'Gees

IN RELATING to my friends various passages of my sea-goings, I have at times had occasion to allude to that singular people the 'Gees, sometimes as casual acquaintances, sometimes as shipmates. Such allusions have been quite natural and easy. For instance, I have said *The two 'Gees*, just as another would say *The two Dutchmen*, or *The two Indians*. In fact, being myself so familiar with 'Gees, it seemed as if all the rest of the world must be. But not so. My auditors have opened their eyes as much as to say, "What under the sun is a 'Gee?" To enlighten them I have repeatedly had to interrupt myself, and not without detriment to my stories. To remedy which inconvenience, a friend hinted the advisability of writing out some account of the 'Gees, and having it published. Such as they are, the following memoranda spring from that happy suggestion:

The word *'Gee* (*g* hard) is an abbreviation, by seamen, of *Portuguee*, the corrupt form of *Portuguese*. As the name is a curtailment, so the race is a residuum. Some three centuries ago certain Portuguese convicts were sent as a colony to Fogo, one of the Cape de Verds, off the northwest coast of Africa, an island previously stocked with an aboriginal race of negroes, ranking pretty high in incivility, but rather low in stature and morals. In course of time, from the amalgamated generation all the likelier sort were drafted off as food for powder, and the ancestors of the since called 'Gees were left as the *caput mortuum*, or melancholy remainder.

Of all men seamen have strong prejudices, particularly in the matter of race. They are bigots here. But when a creature of inferior race lives among them, an inferior tar, there seems no bound to their disdain. Now, as ere long will be hinted, the 'Gee, though of an aquatic nature, does not, as regards higher qualifications, make the best of sailors. In short, by seamen the abbreviation 'Gee was hit upon in pure contumely; the degree of which may be partially inferred from this, that with them the primitive word Portuguee itself is a reproach; so that 'Gee, being a subtle distillation from that word, stands, in point of relative intensity to it, as attar of roses does to rose-water. At times, when some crusty old sea-dog has his spleen more than usually excited against some luckless blunderer of Fogo his shipmate, it is marvelous the prolongation of taunt into which he will spin out the one little exclamatory monosyllable Ge-e-e-e-e!

The Isle of Fogo, that is, "Fire Isle," was so called from its volcano, which, after throwing up an infinite deal of stones and ashes, finally threw up business altogether, from its broadcast bounteousness having become bankrupt. But thanks to the volcano's prodigality in its time, the soil of Fogo is such as may be found of a dusty day on a road newly Macadamized. Cut off from farms and gardens, the staple food of the inhabitants is fish, at catching which they are expert. But none the less do they relish ship-biscuit, which, indeed, by most islanders, barbarous or semi-barbarous, is held a sort of lozenge.

In his best estate the 'Gee is rather small (he admits it), but, with some exceptions, hardy; capable of enduring extreme hard work, hard fare, or hard usage, as the case may be. In fact, upon a scientific view, there would seem a natural adaptability in the 'Gee to hard times generally. A theory not uncorroborated by his experiences; and furthermore, that kindly care of Nature in fitting him for them, something as for his hard rubs with a hardened world Fox the Quaker fitted himself, namely, in a tough leather suit from top to toe. In other words, the 'Gee is by no means of that exquisitely delicate sensibility expressed by the figurative adjective thin-skinned. His physicals and spirituals are in singular contrast. The 'Gee has a great appetite, but little imagination; a large eyeball, but small insight. Biscuit he crunches, but sentiment he eschews.

His complexion is hybrid; his hair ditto; his mouth disproportionally large, as compared with his stomach; his neck short; but his head round, compact, and betokening a solid understanding.

Like the negro, the 'Gee has a peculiar savor, but a different one—a sort of wild, marine, gamy savor, as in the sea-bird called haglet. Like venison, his flesh is firm but lean.

His teeth are what are called butter-teeth, strong, durable, square, and yellow. Among captains at a loss for better discourse during dull, rainy weather in the horse-latitudes, much debate has been had whether his teeth are intended for carnivorous or herbivorous purposes, or both conjoined. But as on his isle the 'Gee eats neither flesh nor grass, this inquiry would seem superfluous.

The native dress of the 'Gee is, like his name, compendious. His head being by nature well thatched, he wears no hat. Wont to wade much in the surf, he wears no shoes. He has a serviceably hard heel, a kick from which is by the judicious held almost as dangerous as one from a wild zebra.

Though for a long time back no stranger to the seafaring people of Portugal, the 'Gee, until a comparatively recent period, remained almost undreamed of by seafaring Americans. It is now some forty years since he first became known to certain masters of our Nantucket ships, who commenced the practice of touching at Fogo, on the outward passage, there to fill up vacancies among their crews arising from the short supply of men at home. By degrees the custom became pretty general, till now the 'Gee is found aboard of almost one whaler out of three. One reason why they are in request is this: An unsophisticated 'Gee coming on board a foreign ship never asks for wages. He comes for biscuit. He does not know what other wages mean, unless cuffs and buffets be wages, of which sort he receives a liberal allowance, paid with great punctuality, besides perquisites of punches thrown in now and then. But for all this, some persons there are, and not unduly biassed by partiality to him either, who still insist that the 'Gee never gets his due.

His docile services being thus cheaply to be had, some captains will go the length of maintaining that 'Gee sailors are preferable, indeed every way, physically and intellectually, superior to American sailors—such captains complaining, and justly, that American sailors, if not decently treated, are apt to give serious trouble.

But even by their most ardent admirers it is not deemed prudent to sail a ship with none but 'Gees, at least if they chance to be all green hands, a green 'Gee being of all green things the greenest. Besides, owing to the clumsiness of their feet ere improved by practice in the rigging, green 'Gees are wont, in no inconsiderable numbers, to fall overboard the first dark, squally night; insomuch that when unreasonable owners insist with a captain against his will upon a green 'Gee crew fore and aft, he will ship twice as many 'Gees as he would have shipped of Americans, so as to provide for all contingencies.

The 'Gees are always ready to be shipped. Any day one may go to their isle, and on the showing of a coin of biscuit over the rail, may load down to the water's edge with them.

But though any number of 'Gees are ever ready to be shipped, still it is by no means well to take them as they come. There is a choice even in 'Gees.

Of course the 'Gee has his private nature as well as his public coat. To know 'Gees—to be a sound judge of 'Gees—one must study them, just as to know and be a judge of horses one must study horses. Simple as for the most part are both horse and 'Gee, in neither case can knowledge of the creature come by intuition. How unwise, then, in those ignorant young captains who, on their first voyage, will go and ship their 'Gees at Fogo without any preparatory information, or even so much as taking convenient advice from a 'Gee jockey. By a 'Gee jockey is meant a man well versed in 'Gees. Many a young captain has been thrown and badly hurt by a 'Gee of his own choosing. For notwithstanding the general docility of the 'Gee when green, it may be otherwise with him when ripe. Discreet captains won't have such a 'Gee. "Away with that ripe 'Gee!" they cry; "that smart 'Gee; that knowing 'Gee! Green 'Gees for me!"

For the benefit of inexperienced captains about to visit Fogo, the following may be given as the best way to test a 'Gee: Get square before him, at, say three paces, so that the eye, like a shot, may rake the 'Gee fore and aft, at one glance taking in his whole make and build—how he looks about the head, whether he carry it well; his ears, are they over-lengthy? How fares it in the withers? His legs, does the 'Gee stand strongly on them? His knees, any Belshazzar symptoms there? How stands it in the region of the brisket? etc., etc.

Thus far for bone and bottom. For the rest, draw close to, and put the centre of the pupil of your eye—put it, as it were, right into the 'Gee's eye; even as an eye-stone, gently, but firmly slip it in there, and then note what speck or beam of viciousness, if any, will be floated out.

All this and much more must be done; and yet after all, the
best judge may be deceived. But on no account should the
skipper negotiate for his 'Gee with any middle-man, himself a
'Gee. Because such an one must be a knowing 'Gee, who will
be sure to advise the green 'Gee what things to hide and what
to display, to hit the skipper's fancy; which, of course, the
knowing 'Gee supposes to lean toward as much physical and
moral excellence as possible. The rashness of trusting to one
of these middle-men was forcibly shown in the case of the
'Gee who by his countrymen was recommended to a New
Bedford captain as one of the most agile 'Gees in Fogo. There
he stood straight and stout, in a flowing pair of man-of-war's-
man's trowsers, uncommonly well filled out. True, he did not
step around much at the time. But that was diffidence. Good.
They shipped him. But at the first taking in of sail the 'Gee
hung fire. Come to look, both trowser-legs were full of ele-
phantiasis. It was a long sperm-whaling voyage. Useless as so
much lumber, at every port prohibited from being dumped
ashore, that elephantine 'Gee, ever crunching biscuit, for
three weary years was trundled round the globe.

Grown wise by several similar experiences, old Captain Hosea Kean, of Nantucket, in shipping a 'Gee, at present man-
ages matters thus: He lands at Fogo in the night; by secret
means gains information where the likeliest 'Gee wanting to
ship lodges; whereupon with a strong party he surprises all
the friends and acquaintances of that 'Gee; putting them under guard with pistols at their heads; then creeps cautiously
toward the 'Gee, now lying wholly at unawares in his hut,
quite relaxed from all possibility of displaying aught deceptive
in his appearance. Thus silently, thus suddenly, thus unan-
nounced, Captain Kean bursts upon his 'Gee, so to speak, in
the very bosom of his family. By this means, more than once,
unexpected revelations have been made. A 'Gee, noised
abroad for a Hercules in strength and an Apollo Belvidere for
beauty, of a sudden is discovered all in a wretched heap; forlornly adroop as upon crutches, his legs looking as if broken
at the cart-wheel. Solitude is the house of candor, according
to Captain Kean. In the stall, not the street, he says, resides
the real nag.

The innate disdain of regularly bred seamen toward 'Gees

receives an added edge from this. The 'Gees undersell them, working for biscuit where the sailors demand dollars. Hence, any thing said by sailors to the prejudice of 'Gees should be received with caution. Especially that jeer of theirs, that the monkey-jacket was originally so called from the circumstance that that rude sort of shaggy garment was first known in Fogo. They often call a monkey-jacket a 'Gee-jacket. However this may be, there is no call to which the 'Gee will with more alacrity respond than the word "Man!"

Is there any hard work to be done, and the 'Gees stand round in sulks? "Here, my men!" cries the mate. How they jump. But ten to one when the work is done, it is plain 'Gee again. "Here, 'Gee! you 'Ge-e-e-e!" In fact, it is not unsurmised, that only when extraordinary stimulus is needed, only when an extra strain is to be got out of them, are these hapless 'Gees ennobled with the human name.

As yet, the intellect of the 'Gee has been little cultivated. No well-attested educational experiment has been tried upon him. It is said, however, that in the last century a young 'Gee was by a visionary Portuguese naval officer sent to Salamanca University. Also, among the Quakers of Nantucket, there has been talk of sending five comely 'Gees, aged sixteen, to Dartmouth College; that venerable institution, as is well known, having been originally founded partly with the object of finishing off wild Indians in the classics and higher mathematics. Two qualities of the 'Gee which, with his docility, may be justly regarded as furnishing a hopeful basis for his intellectual training, are his excellent memory, and still more excellent credulity.

The above account may, perhaps, among the ethnologists, raise some curiosity to see a 'Gee. But to see a 'Gee there is no need to go all the way to Fogo, no more than to see a Chinaman to go all the way to China. 'Gees are occasionally to be encountered in our sea-ports, but more particularly in Nantucket and New Bedford. But these 'Gees are not the 'Gees of Fogo. That is, they are no longer green 'Gees. They are sophisticated 'Gees, and hence liable to be taken for naturalized citizens badly sunburnt. Many a Chinaman, in new coat and pantaloons, his long queue coiled out of sight in one of Genin's hats, has promenaded Broadway, and been taken merely for an eccentric Georgia planter. The same with 'Gees; a stranger need have a sharp eye to know a 'Gee, even if he see him.

Thus much for a general sketchy view of the 'Gee. For further and fuller information apply to any sharp-witted American whaling captain, but more especially to the before-mentioned old Captain Hosea Kean, of Nantucket, whose address at present is "Pacific Ocean."

I and My Chimney

I AND MY CHIMNEY, two grey-headed old smokers, reside in the country. We are, I may say, old settlers here; particularly my old chimney, which settles more and more every day.

Though I always say, *I and my chimney*, as Cardinal Wolsey used to say, *I and my King*, yet this egotistic way of speaking, wherein I take precedence of my chimney, is hardly borne out by the facts; in everything, except the above phrase, my chimney taking precedence of me.

Within thirty feet of the turf-sided road, my chimney—a huge, corpulent old Harry VIII. of a chimney—rises full in front of me and all my possessions. Standing well up a hillside, my chimney, like Lord Rosse's monster telescope, swung vertical to hit the meridian moon, is the first object to greet the approaching traveler's eye, nor is it the last which the sun salutes. My chimney, too, is before me in receiving the first-fruits of the seasons. The snow is on its head ere on my hat; and every spring, as in a hollow beech tree, the first swallows build their nests in it.

But it is within doors that the preëminence of my chimney is most manifest. When in the rear room, set apart for that object, I stand to receive my guests (who, by the way call more, I suspect, to see my chimney than me), I then stand, not so much before, as, strictly speaking, behind my chimney, which is, indeed, the true host. Not that I demur. In the presence of my betters, I hope I know my place.

From this habitual precedence of my chimney over me, some even think that I have got into a sad rearward way altogether; in short, from standing behind my old-fashioned chimney so much, I have got to be quite behind the age too, as well as running behind-hand in everything else. But to tell the truth, I never was a very forward old fellow, nor what my farming neighbors call a forehanded one. Indeed, those rumors about my behindhandedness are so far correct, that I have an odd sauntering way with me sometimes of going about with my hands behind my back. As for my belonging to the rear-guard in general, certain it is, I bring up the rear of my chimney—which, by the way, is this moment before me—and that, too, both in fancy and fact. In brief, my chimney is my superior; my superior by I know not how many heads and shoulders; my superior, too, in that humbly bowing over with shovel and tongs, I much minister to it; yet never does it minister, or incline over to me; but, if any thing, in its settlings, rather leans the other way.

My chimney is grand seignior here—the one great domineering object, not more of the landscape, than of the house; all the rest of which house, in each architectural arrangement, as may shortly appear, is, in the most marked manner, accommodated, not to my wants, but to my chimney's, which, among other things, has the centre of the house to himself, leaving but the odd holes and corners to me.

But I and my chimney must explain; and as we are both rather obese, we may have to expatiate.

In those houses which are strictly double houses—that is, where the hall is in the middle—the fire-places usually are on opposite sides; so that while one member of the household is warming himself at a fire built into a recess of the north wall, say another member, the former's own brother, perhaps, may be holding his feet to the blaze before a hearth in the south wall—the two thus fairly sitting back to back. Is this well? Be it put to any man who has a proper fraternal feeling. Has it not a sort of sulky appearance? But very probably this style of chimney building originated with some architect afflicted with a quarrelsome family.

Then again, almost every modern fire-place has its separate flue—separate throughout, from hearth to chimney-top. At least such an arrangement is deemed desirable. Does not this look egotistical, selfish? But still more, all these separate flues, instead of having independent masonry establishments of their own, or instead of being grouped together in one federal stock in the middle of the house—instead of this, I say, each flue is surreptitiously honeycombed into the walls; so that these last are here and there, or indeed almost anywhere, treacherously hollow, and, in consequence, more or less weak. Of course, the main reason of this style of chimney building is to economize room. In cities, where lots are sold by the inch, small space is to spare for a chimney constructed on magnanimous principles; and, as with most thin men, who are generally tall, so with such houses, what is lacking in breadth must be made up in height. This remark holds true even with regard to many very stylish abodes, built by the most stylish of gentlemen. And yet, when that stylish gentleman, Louis le Grand of France, would build a palace for his lady friend, Madame de Maintenon, he built it but one story high—in fact in the cottage style. But then how uncommonly quadrangular, spacious, and broad—horizontal acres, not vertical ones. Such is the palace, which, in all its one-storied magnificence of Languedoc marble, in the garden of Versailles, still remains to this day. Any man can buy a square foot of land and plant a liberty-pole on it; but it takes a king to set apart whole acres for a grand Trianon.

But nowadays it is different; and furthermore, what originated in a necessity has been mounted into a vaunt. In towns there is large rivalry in building tall houses. If one gentleman builds his house four stories high, and another gentleman comes next door and builds five stories high, then the former, not to be looked down upon that way, immediately sends for his architect and claps a fifth and a sixth story on top of his previous four. And, not till the gentleman has achieved his aspiration, not till he has stolen over the way by twilight and observed how his sixth story soars beyond his neighbor's fifth—not till then does he retire to his rest with satisfaction.

Such folks, it seems to me, need mountains for neighbors, to take this emulous conceit of soaring out of them.

If, considering that mine is a very wide house, and by no means lofty, aught in the above may appear like interested pleading, as if I did but fold myself about in the cloak of a general proposition, cunningly to tickle my individual vanity beneath it, such misconception must vanish upon my frankly conceding, that land adjoining my alder swamp was sold last month for ten dollars an acre, and thought a rash purchase at that; so that for wide houses hereabouts there is plenty of room, and cheap. Indeed so cheap—dirt cheap—is the soil, that our elms thrust out their roots in it, and hang their great boughs over it, in the most lavish and reckless way. Almost all our crops, too, are sown broadcast, even peas and turnips. A farmer among us, who should go about his twenty-acre field, poking his finger into it here and there, and dropping down a mustard seed, would be thought a penurious, narrow-minded husbandman. The dandelions in the river-meadows, and the forget-me-nots along the mountain roads, you see at once they are put to no economy in space. Some seasons, too, our rye comes up, here and there a spear, sole and single like a church-spire. It doesn't care to crowd itself where it knows there is such a deal of room. The world is wide, the world is all before us, says the rye. Weeds, too, it is amazing how they spread. No such thing as arresting them—some of our pastures being a sort of Alsatia for the weeds. As for the grass, every spring it is like Kossuth's rising of what he calls the peoples. Mountains, too, a regular camp-meeting of them. For the same reason, the same all-sufficiency of room, our shadows march and countermarch, going through their various drills and masterly evolutions, like the old imperial guard on the Champs de Mars. As for the hills, especially where the roads cross them, the supervisors of our various towns have given notice to all concerned, that they can come and dig them down and cart them off, and never a cent to pay, no more than for the privilege of picking blackberries. The stranger who is buried here, what liberal-hearted landed proprietor among us grudges him his six feet of rocky pasture?

Nevertheless, cheap, after all, as our land is, and much as it is trodden under foot, I, for one, am proud of it for what it bears; and chiefly for its three great lions—the Great Oak, Ogg Mountain, and my chimney.

Most houses, here, are but one and a half stories high; few exceed two. That in which I and my chimney dwell, is in width nearly twice its height, from sill to eaves—which accounts for the magnitude of its main content—besides, showing that in this house, as in this country at large, there is abundance of space, and to spare, for both of us.

The frame of the old house is of wood—which but the more sets forth the solidity of the chimney, which is of brick. And as the great wrought nails, binding the clapboards, are unknown in these degenerate days, so are the huge bricks in the chimney walls. The architect of the chimney must have had the pyramid of Cheops before him; for, after that famous structure, it seems modeled, only its rate of decrease towards the summit is considerably less, and it is truncated. From the exact middle of the mansion it soars from the cellar, right up through each successive floor, till, four feet square, it breaks water from the ridge-pole of the roof, like an anvil-headed whale, through the crest of a billow. Most people, though, liken it, in that part, to a razeed observatory, masoned up.

The reason for its peculiar appearance above the roof touches upon rather delicate ground. How shall I reveal that, forasmuch as many years ago the original gable roof of the old house had become very leaky, a temporary proprietor hired a band of woodmen, with their huge, cross-cut saws, and went to sawing the old gable roof clean off. Off it went, with all its birds' nests, and dormer windows. It was replaced with a modern roof, more fit for a railway wood-house than an old country gentleman's abode. This operation—razeeing the structure some fifteen feet—was, in effect upon the chimney, something like the falling of the great spring tides. It left uncommon low water all about the chimney—to abate which appearance, the same person now proceeds to slice fifteen feet off the chimney itself, actually beheading my royal old chimney—a regicidal act, which, were it not for the palliating fact, that he was a poulterer by trade, and, therefore, hardened to such neck-wringings, should send that former proprietor down to posterity in the same cart with Cromwell.

Owing to its pyramidal shape, the reduction of the chimney inordinately widened its razeed summit. Inordinately, I say, but only in the estimation of such as have no eye to the picturesque. What care I, if, unaware that my chimney, as a free citizen of this free land, stands upon an independent basis of its own, people passing it, wonder how such a brick-kiln, as they call it, is supported upon mere joists and rafters? What care I? I will give a traveler a cup of switchel, if he want it; but am I bound to supply him with a sweet taste? Men of cultivated minds see, in my old house and chimney, a goodly old elephant-and-castle.

All feeling hearts will sympathize with me in what I am now about to add. The surgical operation, above referred to, necessarily brought into the open air a part of the chimney previously under cover, and intended to remain so, and, therefore, not built of what are called weather-bricks. In consequence, the chimney, though of a vigorous constitution, suffered not a little, from so naked an exposure; and, unable to acclimate itself, ere long began to fail—showing blotchy symptoms akin to those in measles. Whereupon travelers, passing my way, would wag their heads, laughing: "See that wax nose—how it melts off!" But what cared I? The same travelers would travel across the sea to view Kenilworth peeling away, and for a very good reason: that of all artists of the picturesque, decay wears the palm—I would say, the ivy. In fact, I've often thought that the proper place for my old chimney is ivied old England.

In vain my wife—with what probable ulterior intent will, ere long, appear—solemnly warned me, that unless something were done, and speedily, we should be burnt to the ground, owing to the holes crumbling through the aforesaid blotchy parts, where the chimney joined the roof. "Wife," said I, "far better that my house should burn down, than that my chimney should be pulled down, though but a few feet. They call it a wax nose; very good; not for me to tweak the nose of my superior." But at last the man who has a mortgage on the house dropped me a note, reminding me that, if my chimney was allowed to stand in that invalid condition, my policy of insurance would be void. This was a sort of hint not to be neglected. All the world over, the picturesque yields to the pocketesque. The mortgagor cared not, but the mortgagee did.

So another operation was performed. The wax nose was taken off, and a new one fitted on. Unfortunately for the expression—being put up by a squint-eyed mason, who, at the time, had a bad stitch in the same side—the new nose stands a little awry, in the same direction.

Of one thing, however, I am proud. The horizontal dimensions of the new part are unreduced.

Large as the chimney appears upon the roof, that is nothing to its spaciousness below. At its base in the cellar, it is precisely twelve feet square; and hence covers precisely one hundred and forty-four superficial feet. What an appropriation of terra firma for a chimney, and what a huge load for this earth! In fact, it was only because I and my chimney formed no part of his ancient burden, that that stout peddler,

Atlas of old, was enabled to stand up so bravely under his pack. The dimensions given may, perhaps, seem fabulous. But, like those stones at Gilgal, which Joshua set up for a memorial of having passed over Jordan, does not my chimney remain, even unto this day?

Very often I go down into my cellar, and attentively survey that vast square of masonry. I stand long, and ponder over, and wonder at it. It has a druidical look, away down in the umbrageous cellar there, whose numerous vaulted passages, and far glens of gloom, resemble the dark, damp depths of primeval woods. So strongly did this conceit steal over me, so deeply was I penetrated with wonder at the chimney, that one day—when I was a little out of my mind, I now think—getting a spade from the garden, I set to work, digging round the foundation, especially at the corners thereof, obscurely prompted by dreams of striking upon some old, earthen-worn memorial of that by-gone day, when, into all this gloom, the light of heaven entered, as the masons laid the foundation-stones, peradventure sweltering under an August sun, or pelted by a March storm. Plying my blunted spade, how vexed was I by that ungracious interruption of a neighbor, who, calling to see me upon some business, and being informed that I was below, said I need not be troubled to come up, but he would go down to me; and so, without ceremony, and without my having been forewarned, suddenly discovered me, digging in my cellar.

"Gold digging, sir?"

"Nay, sir," answered I, starting, "I was merely—ahem!—merely—I say I was merely digging—round my chimney."

"Ah, loosening the soil, to make it grow. Your chimney, sir, you regard as too small, I suppose; needing further development, especially at the top?"

"Sir!" said I, throwing down the spade, "do not be personal. I and my chimney—"

"Personal?"

"Sir, I look upon this chimney less as a pile of masonry than as a personage. It is the king of the house. I am but a suffered and inferior subject."

In fact, I would permit no gibes to be cast at either myself or my chimney; and never again did my visitor refer to it in my hearing, without coupling some compliment with the mention. It well deserves a respectful consideration. There it stands, solitary and alone—not a council of ten flues, but, like his sacred majesty of Russia, a unit of an autocrat.

Even to me, its dimensions, at times, seem incredible. It does not look so big—no, not even in the cellar. By the mere eye, its magnitude can be but imperfectly comprehended, because only one side can be received at one time; and said side can only present twelve feet, linear measure. But then, each other side also is twelve feet long; and the whole obviously forms a square; and twelve times twelve is one hundred and forty-four. And so, an adequate conception of the magnitude of this chimney is only to be got at by a sort of process in the higher mathematics, by a method somewhat akin to those whereby the surprising distances of fixed stars are computed.

It need hardly be said, that the walls of my house are entirely free from fire-places. These all congregate in the middle—in the one grand central chimney, upon all four sides of which are hearths—two tiers of hearths—so that when, in the various chambers, my family and guests are warming themselves of a cold winter's night, just before retiring, then, though at the time they may not be thinking so, all their faces mutually look towards each other, yea, all their feet point to one centre; and, when they go to sleep in their beds, they all sleep round one warm chimney, like so many Iroquois Indians, in the woods, round their one heap of embers. And just as the Indians' fire serves, not only to keep them comfortable, but also to keep off wolves, and other savage monsters, so my chimney, by its obvious smoke at top, keeps off prowling burglars from the towns—for what burglar or murderer would dare break into an abode from whose chimney issues such a continual smoke—betokening that if the inmates are not stirring, at least fires are, and in case of an alarm, candles may readily be lighted, to say nothing of muskets.

But stately as is the chimney—yea, grand high altar as it is, right worthy for the celebration of high mass before the Pope of Rome, and all his cardinals—yet what is there perfect in this world? Caius Julius Cæsar, had he not been so inordinately great, they say that Brutus, Cassius, Antony, and the rest, had been greater. My chimney, were it not so mighty in its magnitude, my chambers had been larger. How often has my wife ruefully told me, that my chimney, like the English aristocracy, casts a contracting shade all round it. She avers that endless domestic inconveniences arise—more particularly from the chimney's stubborn central locality. The grand objection with her is, that it stands midway in the place where a fine entrance-hall ought to be. In truth, there is no hall whatever to the house—nothing but a sort of square landing-place, as you enter from the wide front door. A roomy enough landing-place, I admit, but not attaining to the dignity of a hall. Now, as the front door is precisely in the middle of the front of the house, inwards it faces the chimney. In fact, the opposite wall of the landing-place is formed solely by the chimney; and hence—owing to the gradual tapering of the chimney—is a little less than twelve feet in width. Climbing the chimney in this part, is the principal staircase—which, by three abrupt turns, and three minor landing-places, mounts to the second floor, where, over the front door, runs a sort of narrow gallery, something less than twelve feet long, leading to chambers on either hand. This gallery, of course, is railed; and so, looking down upon the stairs, and all those landing-places together, with the main one at bottom, resembles not a little a balcony for musicians, in some jolly old abode, in times Elizabethan. Shall I tell a weakness? I cherish the cobwebs there, and many a time arrest Biddy in the act of brushing them with her broom, and have many a quarrel with my wife and daughters about it.

Now the ceiling, so to speak, of the place where you enter the house, that ceiling is, in fact, the ceiling of the second floor, not the first. The two floors are made one here; so that ascending this turning stairs, you seem going up into a kind of soaring tower, or light-house. At the second landing, midway up the chimney, is a mysterious door, entering to a mysterious closet; and here I keep mysterious cordials, of a choice, mysterious flavor, made so by the constant nurturing and subtle ripening of the chimney's gentle heat, distilled through that warm mass of masonry. Better for wines is it than voyages to the Indies; my chimney itself a tropic. A chair by my chimney in a November day is as good for an invalid as a long season spent in Cuba. Often I think how grapes might ripen against my chimney. How my wife's geraniums bud there! Bud in December. Her eggs, too—can't keep them near the chimney, on account of hatching. Ah, a warm heart has my chimney.

How often my wife was at me about that projected grand entrance-hall of hers, which was to be knocked clean through the chimney, from one end of the house to the other, and astonish all guests by its generous amplitude. "But, wife," said I, "the chimney—consider the chimney: if you demolish the foundation, what is to support the superstructure?" "Oh, that will rest on the second floor." The truth is, women know next to nothing about the realities of architecture. However, my wife still talked of running her entries and partitions. She spent many long nights elaborating her plans; in imagination building her boasted hall through the chimney, as though its high mightiness were a mere spear of sorrel-top. At last, I gently reminded her that, little as she might fancy it, the chimney was a fact—a sober, substantial fact, which, in all her plannings, it would be well to take into full consideration. But this was not of much avail.

And here, respectfully craving her permission, I must say a few words about this enterprising wife of mine. Though in years nearly old as myself, in spirit she is young as my little sorrel mare, Trigger, that threw me last fall. What is extraordinary, though she comes of a rheumatic family, she is straight as a pine, never has any aches; while for me with the sciatica, I am sometimes as crippled up as any old apple tree. But she has not so much as a toothache. As for her hearing—let me enter the house in my dusty boots, and she away up in the attic. And for her sight—Biddy, the housemaid, tells other people's housemaids, that her mistress will spy a spot on the dresser straight through the pewter platter, put up on purpose to hide it. Her faculties are alert as her limbs and her senses. No danger of my spouse dying of torpor. The longest night in the year I've known her lie awake, planning her campaign for the morrow. She is a natural projector. The maxim, "Whatever is, is right," is not hers. Her maxim is, Whatever is, is wrong; and what is more, must be altered; and what is still more, must be altered right away. Dreadful maxim for the wife of a dozy old dreamer like me, who dote on seventh days as days of rest, and out of a sabbatical horror of industry, will, on a week day, go out of my road a quarter of a mile, to avoid the sight of a man at work.

That matches are made in heaven, may be, but my wife would have been just the wife for Peter the Great, or Peter the Piper. How she would have set in order that huge littered empire of the one, and with indefatigable painstaking picked the peck of pickled peppers for the other.

But the most wonderful thing is, my wife never thinks of her end. Her youthful incredulity, as to the plain theory, and still plainer fact of death, hardly seems Christian. Advanced in years, as she knows she must be, my wife seems to think that she is to teem on, and be inexhaustible forever. She doesn't believe in old age. At that strange promise in the plain of Mamre, my old wife, unlike old Abraham's, would not have jeeringly laughed within herself.

Judge how to me, who, sitting in the comfortable shadow of my chimney, smoking my comfortable pipe, with ashes not unwelcome at my feet, and ashes not unwelcome all but in my mouth; and who am thus in a comfortable sort of not unwelcome, though, indeed, ashy enough way, reminded of the ultimate exhaustion even of the most fiery life; judge how to me this unwarrantable vitality in my wife must come, sometimes, it is true, with a moral and a calm, but oftener with a breeze and a ruffle.

If the doctrine be true, that in wedlock contraries attract, by how cogent a fatality must I have been drawn to my wife! While spicily impatient of present and past, like a glass of ginger-beer she overflows with her schemes; and, with like energy as she puts down her foot, puts down her preserves and her pickles, and lives with them in a continual future; or ever full of expectations both from time and space, is ever restless for newspapers, and ravenous for letters. Content with the years that are gone, taking no thought for the morrow, and looking for no new thing from any person or quarter whatever, I have not a single scheme or expectation on earth, save in unequal resistance of the undue encroachment of hers.

Old myself, I take to oldness in things; for that cause

mainly loving old Montaigne, and old cheese, and old wine;
and eschewing young people, hot rolls, new books, and early
potatoes, and very fond of my old claw-footed chair, and old
club-footed Deacon White, my neighbor, and that still nigher
old neighbor, my betwisted old grape-vine, that of a summer
evening leans in his elbow for cosy company at my window-
sill, while I, within doors, lean over mine to meet his; and
above all, high above all, am fond of my high-mantled old
chimney. But she, out of that infatuate juvenility of hers,
takes to nothing but newness; for that cause mainly, loving
new cider in autumn, and in spring, as if she were own
daughter of Nebuchadnezzar, fairly raving after all sorts of
salads and spinages, and more particularly green cucumbers
(though all the time nature rebukes such unsuitable young
hankerings in so elderly a person, by never permitting such
things to agree with her), and has an itch after recently-dis-
covered fine prospects (so no grave-yard be in the background), and also after Swedenborgianism, and the Spirit
Rapping philosophy, with other new views, alike in things
natural and unnatural; and immortally hopeful, is forever
making new flower-beds even on the north side of the house,
where the bleak mountain wind would scarce allow the wiry
weed called hard-hack to gain a thorough footing; and on the
road-side sets out mere pipe-stems of young elms; though
there is no hope of any shade from them, except over the
ruins of her great granddaughter's grave-stones; and won't
wear caps, but plaits her gray hair; and takes the Ladies' Magazine for the fashions; and always buys her new almanac a
month before the new year; and rises at dawn; and to the
warmest sunset turns a cold shoulder; and still goes on at odd
hours with her new course of history, and her French, and
her music; and likes young company; and offers to ride young
colts; and sets out young suckers in the orchard; and has a
spite against my elbowed old grape-vine, and my club-footed
old neighbor, and my claw-footed old chair, and above all,
high above all, would fain persecute, unto death, my high-
mantled old chimney. By what perverse magic, I a thousand
times think, does such a very autumnal old lady have such a
very vernal young soul? When I would remonstrate at times,
she spins round on me with, "Oh, don't you grumble, old

man (she always calls me old man), it's I, young I, that keep you from stagnating." Well, I suppose it is so. Yea, after all, these things are well ordered. My wife, as one of her poor relations, good soul, intimates, is the salt of the earth, and none the less the salt of my sea, which otherwise were unwholesome. She is its monsoon, too, blowing a brisk gale over it, in the one steady direction of my chimney.

Not insensible of her superior energies, my wife has frequently made me propositions to take upon herself all the responsibilities of my affairs. She is desirous that, domestically, I should abdicate; that, renouncing further rule, like the venerable Charles V., I should retire into some sort of monastery. But indeed, the chimney excepted, I have little authority to lay down. By my wife's ingenious application of the principle that certain things belong of right to female jurisdiction, I find myself, through my easy compliances, insensibly stripped by degrees of one masculine prerogative after another. In a dream I go about my fields, a sort of lazy, happy-go-lucky, good-for-nothing, loafing, old Lear. Only by some sudden revelation am I reminded who is over me; as year before last, one day seeing in one corner of the premises fresh deposits of mysterious boards and timbers, the oddity of the incident at length begat serious meditation. "Wife," said I, " whose boards and timbers are those I see near the orchard there? Do you know any thing about them, wife? Who put them there? You know I do not like the neighbors to use my land that way; they should ask permission first."

She regarded me with a pitying smile.

"Why, old man, don't you know I am building a new barn? Didn't you know that, old man?"

This is the poor old lady that was accusing me of tyrannizing over her.

To return now to the chimney. Upon being assured of the futility of her proposed hall, so long as the obstacle remained, for a time my wife was for a modified project. But I could never exactly comprehend it. As far as I could see through it, it seemed to involve the general idea of a sort of irregular archway, or elbowed tunnel, which was to penetrate the chimney at some convenient point under the staircase, and carefully avoiding dangerous contact with the fire-places, and particularly steering clear of the great interior flue, was to conduct the enterprising traveler from the front door all the way into the dining-room in the remote rear of the mansion. Doubtless it was a bold stroke of genius, that plan of hers, and so was Nero's when he schemed his grand canal through the Isthmus of Corinth. Nor will I take oath, that, had her project been accomplished, then, by help of lights hung at judicious intervals through the tunnel, some Belzoni or other might not have succeeded in future ages in penetrating through the masonry, and actually emerging into the dining-room, and once there, it would have been inhospitable treatment of such a traveler to have denied him a recruiting meal.

But my bustling wife did not restrict her objections, nor in the end confine her proposed alterations to the first floor. Her ambition was of the mounting order. She ascended with her schemes to the second floor, and so to the attic. Perhaps there was some small ground for her discontent with things as they were. The truth is, there was no regular passage-way up stairs or down, unless we again except that little orchestra-gallery before mentioned. And all this was owing to the chimney, which my gamesome spouse seemed despitefully to regard as the bully of the house. On all its four sides, nearly all the chambers sidled up to the chimney for the benefit of a fire-place. The chimney would not go to them; they must needs go to it. The consequence was, almost every room, like a philosophical system, was in itself an entry, or passage-way to other rooms, and systems of rooms—a whole suite of entries, in fact. Going through the house, you seem to be forever going somewhere, and getting nowhere. It is like losing one's self in the woods; round and round the chimney you go, and if you arrive at all, it is just where you started, and so you begin again, and again get nowhere. Indeed—though I say it not in the way of fault-finding at all—never was there so labyrinthine an abode. Guests will tarry with me several weeks and every now and then, be anew astonished at some unforeseen apartment.

The puzzling nature of the mansion, resulting from the chimney, is peculiarly noticeable in the dining-room, which has no less than nine doors, opening in all directions, and into all sorts of places. A stranger for the first time entering this

dining-room, and naturally taking no special heed at what
door he entered, will, upon rising to depart, commit the
strangest blunders. Such, for instance, as opening the first
door that comes handy, and finding himself stealing up stairs
by the back passage. Shutting that door, he will proceed to
another, and be aghast at the cellar yawning at his feet. Trying
a third, he surprises the housemaid at her work. In the end,
no more relying on his own unaided efforts, he procures a
trusty guide in some passing person, and in good time successfully emerges. Perhaps as curious a blunder as any, was
that of a certain stylish young gentleman, a great exquisite, in
whose judicious eyes my daughter Anna had found especial
favor. He called upon the young lady one evening, and found
her alone in the dining-room at her needle-work. He stayed
rather late; and after abundance of superfine discourse, all the
while retaining his hat and cane, made his profuse adieus, and
with repeated graceful bows proceeded to depart, after the
fashion of courtiers from the Queen, and by so doing, opening a door at random, with one hand placed behind, very
effectually succeeded in backing himself into a dark pantry,
where he carefully shut himself up, wondering there was no
light in the entry. After several strange noises as of a cat
among the crockery, he reappeared through the same door,
looking uncommonly crest-fallen, and, with a deeply embarrassed air, requested my daughter to designate at which of the
nine he should find exit. When the mischievous Anna told me
the story, she said it was surprising how unaffected and matter-of-fact the young gentleman's manner was after his reappearance. He was more candid than ever, to be sure; having
inadvertently thrust his white kids into an open drawer of
Havana sugar, under the impression, probably, that being
what they call "a sweet fellow," his route might possibly lie
in that direction.

Another inconvenience resulting from the chimney is, the
bewilderment of a guest in gaining his chamber, many strange
doors lying between him and it. To direct him by finger-posts
would look rather queer; and just as queer in him to be
knocking at every door on his route, like London's city guest,
the king, at Temple Bar.

Now, of all these things and many, many more, my family

continually complained. At last my wife came out with her sweeping proposition—in toto to abolish the chimney.

"What!" said I, "abolish the chimney? To take out the backbone of anything, wife, is a hazardous affair. Spines out of backs, and chimneys out of houses, are not to be taken like frosted lead-pipes from the ground. Besides," added I, "the chimney is the one grand permanence of this abode. If undisturbed by innovators, then in future ages, when all the house shall have crumbled from it, this chimney will still survive— a Bunker Hill monument. No, no, wife, I can't abolish my back-bone."

So said I then. But who is sure of himself, especially an old man, with both wife and daughters ever at his elbow and ear? In time, I was persuaded to think a little better of it; in short, to take the matter into preliminary consideration. At length it came to pass that a master-mason—a rough sort of architect—one Mr. Scribe, was summoned to a conference. I formally introduced him to my chimney. A previous introduction from my wife had introduced him to myself. He had been not a little employed by that lady, in preparing plans and estimates for some of her extensive operations in drainage. Having, with much ado, extorted from my spouse the promise that she would leave us to an unmolested survey, I began by leading Mr. Scribe down to the root of the matter, in the cellar. Lamp in hand, I descended; for though up stairs it was noon, below it was night.

We seemed in the pyramids; and I, with one hand holding my lamp over head, and with the other pointing out, in the obscurity, the hoar mass of the chimney, seemed some Arab guide, showing the cobwebbed mausoleum of the great god Apis.

"This is a most remarkable structure, sir," said the master-mason, after long contemplating it in silence, "a most remarkable structure, sir."

"Yes," said I complacently, "every one says so."

"But large as it appears above the roof, I would not have inferred the magnitude of this foundation, sir," eyeing it critically.

Then taking out his rule, he measured it.

"Twelve feet square; one hundred and forty-four square

feet! sir, this house would appear to have been built simply for the accommodation of your chimney."

"Yes, my chimney and me. Tell me candidly, now," I added, " would you have such a famous chimney abolished?"

"I wouldn't have it in a house of mine, sir, for a gift," was the reply. "It's a losing affair altogether, sir. Do you know, sir, that in retaining this chimney, you are losing, not only one hundred and forty-four square feet of good ground, but likewise a considerable interest upon a considerable principal?"

"How?"

"Look, sir," said he, taking a bit of red chalk from his pocket, and figuring against a whitewashed wall, "twenty times eight is so and so; then forty-two times thirty-nine is so and so—aint it, sir? Well, add those together, and subtract this here, then that makes so and so," still chalking away.

To be brief, after no small ciphering, Mr. Scribe informed me that my chimney contained, I am ashamed to say how many thousand and odd valuable bricks.

"No more," said I fidgeting. "Pray now, let us have a look above."

In that upper zone we made two more circumnavigations for the first and second floors. That done, we stood together at the foot of the stairway by the front door; my hand upon the knob, and Mr. Scribe hat in hand.

"Well, sir," said he, a sort of feeling his way, and, to help himself, fumbling with his hat, " well, sir, I think it can be done."

"What, pray, Mr. Scribe; *what* can be done?"

"Your chimney, sir; it can without rashness be removed, I think."

"*I* will think of it, too, Mr. Scribe," said I, turning the knob, and bowing him towards the open space without, "I will *think* of it, sir; it demands consideration; much obliged to ye; good morning, Mr. Scribe."

"It is all arranged, then," cried my wife with great glee, bursting from the nighest room.

"When will they begin?" demanded my daughter Julia.

"To-morrow?" asked Anna.

"Patience, patience, my dears," said I, "such a big chimney is not to be abolished in a minute."

Next morning it began again.

"You remember the chimney," said my wife.

"Wife," said I, "it is never out of my house, and never out of my mind."

"But when is Mr. Scribe to begin to pull it down?" asked Anna.

"Not to-day, Anna," said I.

"*When*, then?" demanded Julia, in alarm.

Now, if this chimney of mine was, for size, a sort of belfry, for ding-donging at me about it, my wife and daughters were a sort of bells, always chiming together, or taking up each other's melodies at every pause, my wife the key-clapper of all. A very sweet ringing, and pealing, and chiming, I confess; but then, the most silvery of bells may, sometimes, dismally toll, as well as merrily play. And as touching the subject in question, it became so now. Perceiving a strange relapse of opposition in me, wife and daughters began a soft and dirge-like, melancholy tolling over it.

At length my wife, getting much excited, declared to me, with pointed finger, that so long as that chimney stood, she should regard it as the monument of what she called my broken pledge. But finding this did not answer, the next day, she gave me to understand that either she or the chimney must quit the house.

Finding matters coming to such a pass, I and my pipe philosophized over them awhile, and finally concluded between us, that little as our hearts went with the plan, yet for peace' sake, I might write out the chimney's death-warrant, and, while my hand was in, scratch a note to Mr. Scribe.

Considering that I, and my chimney, and my pipe, from having been so much together, were three great cronies, the facility with which my pipe consented to a project so fatal to the goodliest of our trio; or rather, the way in which I and my pipe, in secret, conspired together, as it were, against our unsuspicious old comrade—this may seem rather strange, if not suggestive of sad reflections upon us two. But, indeed, we, sons of clay, that is my pipe and I, are no whit better than the rest. Far from us, indeed, to have volunteered the betrayal of our crony. We are of a peaceable nature, too. But that love of peace it was which made us false to a mutual friend, as soon as his cause demanded a vigorous vindication. But I rejoice to add, that better and braver thoughts soon returned, as will now briefly be set forth.

To my note, Mr. Scribe replied in person.

Once more we made a survey, mainly now with a view to a pecuniary estimate.

"I will do it for five hundred dollars," said Mr. Scribe at last, again hat in hand.

"Very well, Mr. Scribe, I will think of it," replied I, again bowing him to the door.

Not unvexed by this, for the second time, unexpected response, again he withdrew, and from my wife and daughters again burst the old exclamations.

The truth is, resolve how I would, at the last pinch I and my chimney could not be parted.

"So Holofernes will have his way, never mind whose heart breaks for it," said my wife next morning, at breakfast, in that half-didactic, half-reproachful way of hers, which is harder to bear than her most energetic assault. Holofernes, too, is with her a pet name for any fell domestic despot. So, whenever, against her most ambitious innovations, those which saw me quite across the grain, I, as in the present instance, stand with however little steadfastness on the defence, she is sure to call me Holofernes, and ten to one takes the first opportunity to read aloud, with a suppressed emphasis, of an evening, the first newspaper paragraph about some tyrannic day-laborer, who, after being for many years the Caligula of his family, ends by beating his long-suffering spouse to death, with a garret door wrenched off its hinges, and then, pitching his little innocents out of the window, suicidally turns inward towards the broken wall scored with the butcher's and baker's bills, and so rushes headlong to his dreadful account.

Nevertheless, for a few days, not a little to my surprise, I heard no further reproaches. An intense calm pervaded my wife, but beneath which, as in the sea, there was no knowing what portentous movements might be going on. She frequently went abroad, and in a direction which I thought not unsuspicious; namely, in the direction of New Petra, a griffin-like house of wood and stucco, in the highest style of ornamental art, graced with four chimneys in the form of erect dragons spouting smoke from their nostrils; the elegant modern residence of Mr. Scribe, which he had built for the purpose of a standing advertisement, not more of his taste as an architect, than his solidity as a master-mason.

At last, smoking my pipe one morning, I heard a rap at the door, and my wife, with an air unusually quiet for her, brought me a note. As I have no correspondents except Solomon, with whom, in his sentiments, at least, I entirely correspond, the note occasioned me some little surprise, which was not diminished upon reading the following:—

"New Petra, April 1st.

"Sir:—During my last examination of your chimney, possibly you may have noted that I frequently applied my rule to it in a manner apparently unnecessary. Possibly also, at the same time, you might have observed in me more or less of perplexity, to which, however, I refrained from giving any verbal expression.

"I now feel it obligatory upon me to inform you of what was then but a dim suspicion, and as such would have been unwise to give utterance to, but which now, from various subsequent calculations assuming no little probability, it may be important that you should not remain in further ignorance of.

"It is my solemn duty to warn you, sir, that there is architectural cause to conjecture that somewhere concealed in your chimney is a reserved space, hermetically closed, in short, a secret chamber, or rather closet. How long it has been there, it is for me impossible to say. What it contains is hid, with itself, in darkness. But probably a secret closet would not have been contrived except for some extraordinary object, whether for the concealment of treasure, or what other purpose, may be left to those better acquainted with the history of the house to guess.

"But enough: in making this disclosure, sir, my conscience is eased. Whatever step you choose to take upon it, is of course a matter of indifference to me; though, I confess, as respects the character of the closet, I cannot but share in a natural curiosity.

"Trusting that you may be guided aright, in determining whether it is Christian-like knowingly to reside in a house, hidden in which is a secret closet,

"I remain,

"With much respect,

"Yours very humbly,

"HIRAM SCRIBE."

My first thought upon reading this note was, not of the alleged mystery of manner to which, at the outset, it alluded—for none such had I at all observed in the master mason during his surveys—but of my late kinsman, Captain Julian Dacres, long a ship-master and merchant in the Indian trade, who, about thirty years ago, and at the ripe age of ninety, died a bachelor, and in this very house, which he had built. He was supposed to have retired into this country with a large fortune. But to the general surprise, after being at great cost in building himself this mansion, he settled down into a sedate, reserved, and inexpensive old age, which by the neighbors was thought all the better for his heirs: but lo! upon opening the will, his property was found to consist but of the house and grounds, and some ten thousand dollars in stocks; but the place, being found heavily mortgaged, was in consequence sold. Gossip had its day, and left the grass quietly to creep over the captain's grave, where he still slumbers in a privacy as unmolested as if the billows of the Indian Ocean, instead of the billows of inland verdure, rolled over him. Still, I remembered long ago, hearing strange solutions whispered by the country people for the mystery involving his will, and, by reflex, himself; and that, too, as well in conscience as purse. But people who could circulate the report (which they did), that Captain Julian Dacres had, in his day, been a Borneo pirate, surely were not worthy of credence in their collateral notions. It is queer what wild whimsies of rumors will, like toadstools, spring up about any eccentric stranger, who, settling down among a rustic population, keeps quietly to himself. With some, inoffensiveness would seem a prime cause of offense. But what chiefly had led me to scout at these rumors, particularly as referring to concealed treasure, was the circumstance, that the stranger (the same who razeed the roof and the chimney) into whose hands the estate had passed on my kinsman's death, was of that sort of character, that had there been the least ground for those reports, he would speedily have tested them, by tearing down and rummaging the walls.

Nevertheless, the note of Mr. Scribe, so strangely recalling the memory of my kinsman, very naturally chimed in with what had been mysterious, or at least unexplained, about him; vague flashings of ingots united in my mind with vague gleamings of skulls. But the first cool thought soon dismissed such chimeras; and, with a calm smile, I turned towards my wife, who, meantime, had been sitting near by, impatient enough, I dare say, to know who could have taken it into his head to write me a letter.

"Well, old man," said she, "who is it from, and what is it about?"

"Read it, wife," said I, handing it.

Read it she did, and then—such an explosion! I will not pretend to describe her emotions, or repeat her expressions. Enough that my daughters were quickly called in to share the excitement. Although they had never before dreamed of such a revelation as Mr. Scribe's; yet upon the first suggestion they instinctively saw the extreme likelihood of it. In corroboration, they cited first my kinsman, and second, my chimney; alleging that the profound mystery involving the former, and the equally profound masonry involving the latter, though both acknowledged facts, were alike preposterous on any other supposition than the secret closet.

But all this time I was quietly thinking to myself: Could it be hidden from me that my credulity in this instance would operate very favorably to a certain plan of theirs? How to get to the secret closet, or how to have any certainty about it at all, without making such fell work with the chimney as to render its set destruction superfluous? That my wife wished to get rid of the chimney, it needed no reflection to show; and that Mr. Scribe, for all his pretended disinterestedness, was not opposed to pocketing five hundred dollars by the operation, seemed equally evident. That my wife had, in secret, laid heads together with Mr. Scribe, I at present refrain from affirming. But when I consider her enmity against my chimney, and the steadiness with which at the last she is wont to carry out her schemes, if by hook or by crook she can, especially after having been once baffled, why, I scarcely knew at what step of hers to be surprised.

Of one thing only was I resolved, that I and my chimney should not budge.

In vain all protests. Next morning I went out into the road, where I had noticed a diabolical-looking old gander, that, for its doughty exploits in the way of scratching into forbidden inclosures, had been rewarded by its master with a portentous, four-pronged, wooden decoration, in the shape of a collar of the Order of the Garotte. This gander I cornered, and rummaging out its stiffest quill, plucked it, took it home, and making a stiff pen, inscribed the following stiff note:

"CHIMNEY SIDE, April 2.

"Mr. SCRIBE.

"Sir:—For your conjecture, we return you our joint thanks and compliments, and beg leave to assure you, that

"We shall remain,
"Very faithfully,
"The same,
"I and my Chimney."

Of course, for this epistle we had to endure some pretty sharp raps. But having at last explicitly understood from me that Mr. Scribe's note had not altered my mind one jot, my wife, to move me, among other things said, that if she remembered aright, there was a statute placing the keeping in private houses of secret closets on the same unlawful footing with the keeping of gunpowder. But it had no effect.

A few days after, my spouse changed her key.

It was nearly midnight, and all were in bed but ourselves, who sat up, one in each chimney-corner; she, needles in hand, indefatigably knitting a sock; I, pipe in mouth, indolently weaving my vapors.

It was one of the first of the chill nights in autumn. There was a fire on the hearth, burning low. The air without was torpid and heavy; the wood, by an oversight, of the sort called soggy.

"Do look at the chimney," she began; "can't you see that something must be in it?"

"Yes, wife. Truly there is smoke in the chimney, as in Mr. Scribe's note."

"Smoke? Yes, indeed, and in my eyes, too. How you two wicked old sinners do smoke!—this wicked old chimney and you."

"Wife," said I, "I and my chimney like to have a quiet smoke together, it is true, but we don't like to be called names."

"Now, dear old man," said she, softening down, and a little shifting the subject, "when you think of that old kinsman of yours, you *know* there must be a secret closet in this chimney."

"Secret ash-hole, wife, why don't you have it? Yes, I dare say there is a secret ash-hole in the chimney; for where do all the ashes go to that we drop down the queer hole yonder?"

"I know where they go to; I've been there almost as many times as the cat."

"What devil, wife, prompted you to crawl into the ash-hole! Don't you know that St. Dunstan's devil emerged from the ash-hole? You will get your death one of these days, exploring all about as you do. But supposing there be a secret closet, what then?"

"What, then? why what should be in a secret closet but ———"

"Dry bones, wife," broke in I with a puff, while the sociable old chimney broke in with another.

"There again! Oh, how this wretched old chimney smokes," wiping her eyes with her handkerchief. "I've no doubt the reason it smokes so is, because that secret closet interferes with the flue. Do see, too, how the jams here keep settling; and it's down hill all the way from the door to this hearth. This horrid old chimney will fall on our heads yet; depend upon it, old man."

"Yes, wife, I do depend on it; yes, indeed, I place every dependence on my chimney. As for its settling, I like it. I, too, am settling, you know, in my gait. I and my chimney are settling together, and shall keep settling, too, till, as in a great feather-bed, we shall both have settled away clean out of sight. But this secret oven; I mean, secret closet of yours, wife; where exactly do you suppose that secret closet is?"

"That is for Mr. Scribe to say."

"But suppose he cannot say exactly; what, then?"

"Why then he can prove, I am sure, that it must be somewhere or other in this horrid old chimney."

"And if he can't prove that; what, then?"

"Why then, old man," with a stately air, "I shall say little more about it."

"Agreed, wife," returned I, knocking my pipe-bowl against the jam, "and now, to-morrow, I will a third time send for Mr. Scribe. Wife, the sciatica takes me; be so good as to put this pipe on the mantel."

"If you get the step ladder for me, I will. This shocking old chimney, this abominable old-fashioned old chimney's mantels are so high, I can't reach them."

No opportunity, however trivial, was overlooked for a subordinate fling at the pile.

Here, by way of introduction, it should be mentioned, that besides the fire-places all round it, the chimney was, in the most hap-hazard way, excavated on each floor for certain curious out-of-the-way cupboards and closets, of all sorts and sizes, clinging here and there, like nests in the crotches of some old oak. On the second floor these closets were by far the most irregular and numerous. And yet this should hardly have been so, since the theory of the chimney was, that it pyramidically diminished as it ascended. The abridgment of its square on the roof was obvious enough; and it was supposed that the reduction must be methodically graduated from bottom to top.

"Mr. Scribe," said I when, the next day, with an eager aspect, that individual again came, "my object in sending for you this morning is, not to arrange for the demolition of my chimney, nor to have any particular conversation about it, but simply to allow you every reasonable facility for verifying, if you can, the conjecture communicated in your note."

Though in secret not a little crestfallen, it may be, by my phlegmatic reception, so different from what he had looked for; with much apparent alacrity he commenced the survey;

throwing open the cupboards on the first floor, and peering into the closets on the second; measuring one within, and then comparing that measurement with the measurement without. Removing the fire-boards, he would gaze up the flues. But no sign of the hidden work yet.

Now, on the second floor the rooms were the most rambling conceivable. They, as it were, dovetailed into each other. They were of all shapes; not one mathematically square room among them all—a peculiarity which by the master-mason had not been unobserved. With a significant, not to say portentous expression, he took a circuit of the chimney, measuring the area of each room around it; then going down stairs, and out of doors, he measured the entire ground area; then compared the sum total of all the areas of all the rooms on the second floor with the ground area; then, returning to me in no small excitement, announced that there was a difference of no less than two hundred and odd square feet—room enough, in all conscience, for a secret closet.

"But, Mr. Scribe," said I stroking my chin, "have you allowed for the walls, both main and sectional? They take up some space, you know."

"Ah, I had forgotten that," tapping his forehead; "but," still ciphering on his paper, "that will not make up the deficiency."

"But, Mr. Scribe, have you allowed for the recesses of so many fire-places on a floor, and for the fire-walls, and the flues; in short, Mr. Scribe, have you allowed for the legitimate chimney itself—some one hundred and forty-four square feet or thereabouts, Mr. Scribe?"

"How unaccountable. That slipped my mind, too."

"Did it, indeed, Mr. Scribe?"

He faltered a little, and burst forth with, "But we must not allow one hundred and forty-four square feet for the legitimate chimney. My position is, that within those undue limits the secret closet is contained."

I eyed him in silence a moment; then spoke:

"Your survey is concluded, Mr. Scribe; be so good now as to lay your finger upon the exact part of the chimney wall where you believe this secret closet to be; or would a witch-hazel wand assist you, Mr. Scribe?"

"No, sir, but a crow-bar would," he, with temper, rejoined.

Here, now, thought I to myself, the cat leaps out of the bag. I looked at him with a calm glance, under which he seemed somewhat uneasy. More than ever now I suspected a plot. I remembered what my wife had said about abiding by the decision of Mr. Scribe. In a bland way, I resolved to buy up the decision of Mr. Scribe.

"Sir," said I, "really, I am much obliged to you for this survey. It has quite set my mind at rest. And no doubt you, too, Mr. Scribe, must feel much relieved. Sir," I added, "you have made three visits to the chimney. With a business man, time is money. Here are fifty dollars, Mr. Scribe. Nay, take it. You have earned it. Your opinion is worth it. And by the way,"—as he modestly received the money—"have you any objections to give me a—a—little certificate—something, say, like a steam-boat certificate, certifying that you, a competent surveyor, have surveyed my chimney, and found no reason to believe any unsoundness; in short, any—any secret closet in it. Would you be so kind, Mr. Scribe?"

"But, but, sir," stammered he with honest hesitation.

"Here, here are pen and paper," said I, with entire assurance.

Enough.

That evening I had the certificate framed and hung over the dining-room fire-place, trusting that the continual sight of it would forever put at rest at once the dreams and stratagems of my household.

But, no. Inveterately bent upon the extirpation of that noble old chimney, still to this day my wife goes about it, with my daughter Anna's geological hammer, tapping the wall all over, and then holding her ear against it, as I have seen the physicians of life insurance companies tap a man's chest, and then incline over for the echo. Sometimes of nights she almost frightens one, going about on this phantom errand, and still following the sepulchral response of the chimney, round and round, as if it were leading her to the threshold of the secret closet.

"How hollow it sounds," she will hollowly cry. "Yes, I declare," with an emphatic tap, "there is a secret closet here. Here, in this very spot. Hark! How hollow!"

"Psha! wife, of course it is hollow. Who ever heard of a solid chimney?"

But nothing avails. And my daughters take after, not me, but their mother.

Sometimes all three abandon the theory of the secret closet, and return to the genuine ground of attack—the unsightliness of so cumbrous a pile, with comments upon the great addition of room to be gained by its demolition, and the fine effect of the projected grand hall, and the convenience resulting from the collateral running in one direction and another of their various partitions. Not more ruthlessly did the Three Powers partition away poor Poland, than my wife and daughters would fain partition away my chimney.

But seeing that, despite all, I and my chimney still smoke our pipes, my wife reoccupies the ground of the secret closet, enlarging upon what wonders are there, and what a shame it is, not to seek it out and explore it.

"Wife," said I, upon one of these occasions, "why speak more of that secret closet, when there before you hangs contrary testimony of a master mason, elected by yourself to decide. Besides, even if there were a secret closet, secret it should remain, and secret it shall. Yes, wife, here for once I must say my say. Infinite sad mischief has resulted from the profane bursting open of secret recesses. Though standing in the heart of this house, though hitherto we have all nestled about it, unsuspicious of aught hidden within, this chimney may or may not have a secret closet. But if it have, it is my kinsman's. To break into that wall, would be to break into his breast. And that wall-breaking wish of Momus I account the wish of a church-robbing gossip and knave. Yes, wife, a vile eaves-dropping varlet was Momus."

"Moses?—Mumps? Stuff with your mumps and your Moses!"

The truth is, my wife, like all the rest of the world, cares not a fig for my philosophical jabber. In dearth of other philosophical companionship, I and my chimney have to smoke and philosophize together. And sitting up so late as we do at it, a mighty smoke it is that we two smoky old philosophers make.

But my spouse, who likes the smoke of my tobacco as little

as she does that of the soot, carries on her war against both. I live in continual dread lest, like the golden bowl, the pipes of me and my chimney shall yet be broken. To stay that mad project of my wife's, naught answers. Or, rather, she herself is incessantly answering, incessantly besetting me with her terrible alacrity for improvement, which is a softer name for destruction. Scarce a day I do not find her with her tape-measure, measuring for her grand hall, while Anna holds a yard-stick on one side, and Julia looks approvingly on from the other. Mysterious intimations appear in the nearest village paper, signed "Claude," to the effect that a certain structure, standing on a certain hill, is a sad blemish to an otherwise lovely landscape. Anonymous letters arrive, threatening me with I know not what, unless I remove my chimney. Is it my wife, too, or who, that sets up the neighbors to badgering me on the same subject, and hinting to me that my chimney, like a huge elm, absorbs all moisture from my garden? At night, also, my wife will start as from sleep, professing to hear ghostly noises from the secret closet. Assailed on all sides, and in all ways, small peace have I and my chimney.

Were it not for the baggage, we would together pack up, and remove from the country.

What narrow escapes have been ours! Once I found in a drawer a whole portfolio of plans and estimates. Another time, upon returning after a day's absence, I discovered my wife standing before the chimney in earnest conversation with a person whom I at once recognized as a meddlesome architectural reformer, who, because he had no gift for putting up anything, was ever intent upon pulling down; in various parts of the country having prevailed upon half-witted old folks to destroy their old-fashioned houses, particularly the chimneys.

But worst of all was, that time I unexpectedly returned at early morning from a visit to the city, and upon approaching the house, narrowly escaped three brickbats which fell, from high aloft, at my feet. Glancing up, what was my horror to see three savages, in blue jean overalls, in the very act of commencing the long-threatened attack. Aye, indeed, thinking of those three brickbats, I and my chimney have had narrow escapes.

It is now some seven years since I have stirred from home. My city friends all wonder why I don't come to see them, as in former times. They think I am getting sour and unsocial. Some say that I have become a sort of mossy old misanthrope, while all the time the fact is, I am simply standing guard over my mossy old chimney; for it is resolved between me and my chimney, that I and my chimney will never surrender.

The Apple-Tree Table
Or, Original Spiritual Manifestations

WHEN I FIRST saw the table, dingy and dusty, in the
furthest corner of the old hopper-shaped garret, and
set out with broken, be-crusted old purple vials and flasks,
and a ghostly, dismantled old quarto, it seemed just such a
necromantic little old table as might have belonged to Friar
Bacon. Two plain features it had, significant of conjurations
and charms—the circle and tripod; the slab being round, supported by a twisted little pillar, which, about a foot from the
bottom, sprawled out into three crooked legs, terminating
in three cloven feet. A very satanic-looking little old table,
indeed.

In order to convey a better idea of it, some account may as
well be given of the place it came from. A very old garret of
a very old house in an old-fashioned quarter of one of the
oldest towns in America. This garret had been closed for
years. It was thought to be haunted; a rumor, I confess,
which, however absurd (in my opinion), I did not, at the
time of purchasing, very vehemently contradict; since, not improbably, it tended to place the property the more conveniently within my means.

It was, therefore, from no dread of the reputed goblins
aloft, that, for five years after first taking up my residence in
the house, I never entered the garret. There was no special
inducement. The roof was well slated, and thoroughly tight.
The company that insured the house, waived all visitation of
the garret; why, then, should the owner be over-anxious
about it?—particularly, as he had no use for it, the house
having ample room below. Then the key of the stair-door
leading to it was lost. The lock was a huge, old-fashioned
one. To open it, a smith would have to be called; an unnecessary trouble, I thought. Besides, though I had taken some
care to keep my two daughters in ignorance of the rumor
above-mentioned, still, they had, by some means, got an inkling of it, and were well enough pleased to see the entrance
to the haunted ground closed. It might have remained so for
a still longer time, had it not been for my accidentally discov-

ering, in a corner of our glen-like, old, terraced garden, a large and curious key, very old and rusty, which I, at once, concluded must belong to the garret-door—a supposition which, upon trial, proved correct. Now, the possession of a key to anything, at once provokes a desire to unlock and explore; and this, too, from a mere instinct of gratification, irrespective of any particular benefit to accrue.

Behold me, then, turning the rusty old key, and going up, alone, into the haunted garret.

It embraced the entire area of the mansion. Its ceiling was formed by the roof, showing the rafters and boards on which the slates were laid. The roof shedding the water four ways from a high point in the centre, the space beneath was much like that of a general's marquee—only midway broken by a labyrinth of timbers, for braces, from which waved innumerable cobwebs, that, of a summer's noon, shone like Bagdad tissues and gauzes. On every hand, some strange insect was seen, flying, or running, or creeping, on rafter and floor.

Under the apex of the roof was a rude, narrow, decrepit step-ladder, something like a Gothic pulpit-stairway, leading to a pulpit-like platform, from which a still narrower ladder— a sort of Jacob's ladder—led some ways higher to the lofty scuttle. The slide of this scuttle was about two feet square, all in one piece, furnishing a massive frame for a single small pane of glass, inserted into it like a bull's-eye. The light of the garret came from this sole source, filtrated through a dense curtain of cobwebs. Indeed, the whole stairs, and platform, and ladder, were festooned, and carpeted, and canopied with cobwebs; which, in funereal accumulations, hung, too, from the groined, murky ceiling, like the Carolina moss in the cypress forest. In these cobwebs, swung, as in aerial catacombs, myriads of all tribes of mummied insects.

Climbing the stairs to the platform, and pausing there, to recover my breath, a curious scene was presented. The sun was about half-way up. Piercing the little sky-light, it slopingly bored a rainbowed tunnel clear across the darkness of the garret. Here, millions of butterfly moles were swarming. Against the sky-light itself, with a cymbal-like buzzing, thousands of insects clustered in a golden mob.

Wishing to shed a clearer light through the place, I sought

to withdraw the scuttle-slide. But no sign of latch or hasp was visible. Only after long peering, did I discover a little padlock, imbedded, like an oyster at the bottom of the sea, amid matted masses of weedy webs, chrysalides, and insectivorous eggs. Brushing these away, I found it locked. With a crooked nail, I tried to pick the lock, when scores of small ants and flies, half-torpid, crawled forth from the key-hole, and, feeling the warmth of the sun in the pane, began frisking around me. Others appeared. Presently, I was overrun by them. As if incensed at this invasion of their retreat, countless bands darted up from below, beating about my head, like hornets. At last, with a sudden jerk, I burst open the scuttle. And ah! what a change. As from the gloom of the grave and the companionship of worms, man shall at last rapturously rise into the living greenness and glory immortal, so, from my cobwebbed old garret, I thrust forth my head into the balmy air, and found myself hailed by the verdant tops of great trees, growing in the little garden below—trees, whose leaves soared high above my topmost slate.

Refreshed by this outlook, I turned inward to behold the garret, now unwontedly lit up. Such humped masses of obsolete furniture. An old escritoir, from whose pigeon-holes sprang mice, and from whose secret drawers came subterranean squeakings, as from chipmuncks' holes in the woods; and broken-down old chairs, with strange carvings, which seemed fit to seat a conclave of conjurors. And a rusty, iron-bound chest, lidless, and packed full of mildewed old documents; one of which, with a faded red ink-blot at the end, looked as if it might have been the original bond that Doctor Faust gave to Mephistopheles. And, finally, in the least lighted corner of all, where was a profuse litter of indescribable old rubbish—among which was a broken telescope, and a celestial globe staved in—stood the little old table, one hoofed foot, like that of an Evil One, dimly revealed through the cobwebs. What a thick dust, half paste, had settled upon the old vials and flasks; how their once liquid contents had caked, and how strangely looked the mouldy old book in the middle—Cotton Mather's "Magnalia."

Table and book I removed below, and had the dislocations of the one and the tatters of the other repaired. I resolved to surround this sad little hermit of a table, so long banished from genial neighborhood, with all the kindly influences of warm urns, warm fires, and warm hearts; little dreaming what all this warm nursing would hatch.

I was pleased by the discovery, that the table was not of the ordinary mahogany, but of apple-tree wood, which age had darkened nearly to walnut. It struck me as being quite an appropriate piece of furniture for our cedar-parlor—so called, from its being, after the old fashion, wainscoted with that wood. The table's round slab, or *orb*, was so contrived as to be readily changed from a horizontal to a perpendicular position; so that, when not in use, it could be snugly placed in a corner. For myself, wife, and two daughters, I thought it would make a nice little breakfast and tea-table. It was just the thing for a whist table, too. And I also pleased myself with the idea, that it would make a famous reading-table.

In these fancies, my wife, for one, took little interest. She disrelished the idea of so unfashionable and indigent-looking a stranger as the table intruding into the polished society of more prosperous furniture. But when, after seeking its fortune at the cabinet-maker's, the table came home, varnished over, bright as a guinea, no one exceeded my wife in a gracious reception of it. It was advanced to an honorable position in the cedar-parlor.

But, as for my daughter Julia, she never got over her strange emotions upon first accidentally encountering the table. Unfortunately, it was just as I was in the act of bringing it down from the garret. Holding it by the slab, I was carrying it before me, one cobwebbed hoof thrust out, which weird object, at a turn of the stairs, suddenly touched my girl, as she was ascending; whereupon, turning, and seeing no living creature—for I was quite hidden behind my shield—seeing nothing, indeed, but the apparition of the Evil One's foot, as it seemed, she cried out, and there is no knowing what might have followed, had I not immediately spoken.

From the impression thus produced, my poor girl, of a very nervous temperament, was long recovering. Superstitiously grieved at my violating the forbidden solitude above, she associated in her mind the cloven-footed table with the reputed goblins there. She besought me to give up the idea of domesticating the table. Nor did her sister fail to add her entreaties. Between my girls there was a constitutional sympathy. But my matter-of-fact wife had now declared in the table's favor. She was not wanting in firmness and energy. To her, the prejudices of Julia and Anna were simply ridiculous. It was her maternal duty, she thought, to drive such weakness away. By degrees, the girls, at breakfast and tea, were induced to sit down with us at the table. Continual proximity was not without effect. By and by, they would sit pretty tranquilly, though Julia, as much as possible, avoided glancing at the hoofed feet, and, when at this I smiled, she would look at me seriously—as much as to say, Ah, papa, you, too, may yet do the same. She prophecied that, in connection with the table, something strange would yet happen. But I would only smile the more, while my wife indignantly chided.

Meantime, I took particular satisfaction in my table, as a night reading-table. At a ladies' fair, I bought me a beautifully worked reading-cushion, and, with elbow leaning thereon, and hand shading my eyes from the light, spent many a long hour—nobody by, but the queer old book I had brought down from the garret.

All went well, till the incident now about to be given—an incident, be it remembered, which, like every other in this narration, happened long before the time of the "Fox girls."

It was late on a Saturday night in December. In the little old cedar-parlor, before the little old apple-tree table, I was sitting up, as usual, alone. I had made more than one effort to get up and go to bed; but I could not. I was, in fact, under a sort of fascination. Somehow, too, certain reasonable opinions of mine seemed not so reasonable as before. I felt nervous. The truth was, that though, in my previous night-readings, Cotton Mather had but amused me, upon this particular night he terrified me. A thousand times I had laughed at such stories. Old wives' fables, I thought, however entertaining. But now, how different. They began to put on the aspect of reality. Now, for the first time it struck me that this was no romantic Mrs. Radcliffe, who had written the "Magnalia;" but a practical, hard-working, earnest, upright man, a learned doctor, too, as well as a good Christian and orthodox clergyman. What possible motive could such a man have to deceive? His style had all the plainness and unpoetic boldness of truth. In the most straightforward way, he laid before me detailed accounts of New England witchcraft, each important item corroborated by respectable townsfolk, and, of not a few of the most surprising, he himself had been eye-witness. Cotton Mather testified whereof he had seen. But, is it possible? I asked myself. Then I remembered that Dr. Johnson, the matter-of-fact compiler of a dictionary, had been a believer in ghosts, besides many other sound, worthy men. Yielding to the fascination, I read deeper and deeper into the night. At last, I found myself starting at the least chance sound, and yet wishing that it were not so very still.

A tumbler of warm punch stood by my side, with which beverage, in a moderate way, I was accustomed to treat myself every Saturday night; a habit, however, against which my good wife had long remonstrated; predicting that, unless I gave it up, I would yet die a miserable sot. Indeed, I may here mention that, on the Sunday mornings following my Saturday nights, I had to be exceedingly cautious how I gave way to the slightest impatience at any accidental annoyance; because such impatience was sure to be quoted against me as evidence of the melancholy consequences of over-night indulgence. As for my wife, she, never sipping punch, could yield to any little passing peevishness as much as she pleased.

But, upon the night in question, I found myself wishing that, instead of my usual mild mixture, I had concocted some potent draught. I felt the need of stimulus. I wanted something to hearten me against Cotton Mather—doleful, ghostly, ghastly Cotton Mather. I grew more and more nervous. Nothing but fascination kept me from fleeing the room. The candles burnt low, with long snuffs, and huge winding-sheets. But I durst not raise the snuffers to them. It would make too much noise. And yet, previously, I had been wishing for noise. I read on and on. My hair began to have a sensation. My eyes felt strained; they pained me. I was conscious of it. I knew I was injuring them. I knew I should rue this abuse of them next day; but I read on and on. I could not help it. The skinny hand was on me.

All at once———Hark!

My hair felt like growing grass.

A faint sort of inward rapping or rasping—a strange, inexplicable sound, mixed with a slight kind of wood-pecking or ticking.

Tick! Tick!

Yes, it was a faint sort of ticking.

I looked up at my great Strasbourg clock in one corner. It was not that. The clock had stopped.

Tick! Tick!

Was it my watch?

According to her usual practice at night, my wife had, upon retiring, carried my watch off to our chamber to hang it up on its nail.

I listened with all my ears.

Tick! Tick!

Was it a death-tick in the wainscot?

With a tremulous step I went all round the room, holding my ear to the wainscot.

No; it came not from the wainscot.

Tick! Tick!

I shook myself. I was ashamed of my fright.

Tick! Tick!

It grew in precision and audibleness. I retreated from the wainscot. It seemed advancing to meet me.

I looked round and round, but saw nothing, only one cloven foot of the little apple-tree table.

Bless me, said I to myself, with a sudden revulsion, it must be very late; ain't that my wife calling me? Yes, yes; I must go to bed. I suppose all is locked up. No need to go the rounds.

The fascination had departed, though the fear had increased. With trembling hands, putting Cotton Mather out of sight, I soon found myself, candle-stick in hand, in my chamber, with a peculiar rearward feeling, such as some truant dog may feel. In my eagerness to get well into the chamber, I stumbled against a chair.

"Do try and make less noise, my dear," said my wife from the bed. "You have been taking too much of that punch, I fear. That sad habit grows on you. Ah, that I should ever see you thus staggering at night into your chamber."

"Wife, wife," hoarsely whispered I, "there is—is something tick—ticking in the cedar-parlor."

"Poor old man—quite out of his mind—I knew it would be so. Come to bed; come and sleep it off."

"Wife, wife!"

"Do, do come to bed. I forgive you. I won't remind you of it to-morrow. But you must give up the punch-drinking, my dear. It quite gets the better of you."

"Don't exasperate me," I cried now, truly beside myself; "I will quit the house!"

"No, no! not in that state. Come to bed, my dear. I won't say another word."

The next morning, upon waking, my wife said nothing about the past night's affair, and, feeling no little embarrassment myself, especially at having been thrown into such a panic, I also was silent. Consequently, my wife must still have ascribed my singular conduct to a mind disordered, not by ghosts, but by punch. For my own part, as I lay in bed watching the sun in the panes, I began to think that much midnight reading of Cotton Mather was not good for man; that it had a morbid influence upon the nerves, and gave rise to hallucinations. I resolved to put Cotton Mather permanently aside. That done, I had no fear of any return of the ticking. Indeed, I began to think that what seemed the ticking in the room, was nothing but a sort of buzzing in my ear.

As is her wont, my wife having preceded me in rising, I made a deliberate and agreeable toilet. Aware that most disorders of the mind have their origin in the state of the body, I made vigorous use of the flesh-brush, and bathed my head with New England rum, a specific once recommended to me as good for buzzing in the ear. Wrapped in my dressing gown, with cravat nicely adjusted, and finger-nails neatly trimmed, I complacently descended to the little cedar-parlor to breakfast.

What was my amazement to find my wife on her knees, rummaging about the carpet nigh the little apple-tree table, on which the morning meal was laid, while my daughters, Julia and Anna, were running about the apartment distracted.

"Oh, papa, papa!" cried Julia, hurrying up to me, "I knew it would be so. The table, the table!"

"Spirits! spirits!" cried Anna, standing far away from it, with pointed finger.

"Silence!" cried my wife. "How can I hear it, if you make such a noise? Be still. Come here, husband; was this the ticking you spoke of? Why don't you move? Was this it? Here, kneel down and listen to it. Tick, tick, tick!—don't you hear it now?"

"I do, I do," cried I, while my daughters besought us both to come away from the spot.

Tick, tick, tick!

Right from under the snowy cloth, and the cheerful urn, and the smoking milk-toast, the unaccountable ticking was heard.

"Ain't there a fire in the next room, Julia," said I, "let us breakfast there, my dear," turning to my wife—"let us go—leave the table—tell Biddy to remove the things."

And so saying I was moving towards the door in high self-possession, when my wife interrupted me.

"Before I quit this room, I will see into this ticking," she said with energy. "It is something that can be found out, depend upon it. I don't believe in spirits, especially at breakfast-time. Biddy! Biddy! Here, carry these things back to the kitchen," handing the urn. Then, sweeping off the cloth, the little table lay bare to the eye.

"It's the table, the table!" cried Julia.

"Nonsense," said my wife. "Who ever heard of a ticking table? It's on the floor. Biddy! Julia! Anna! move everything out of the room—table and all. Where are the tack-hammers?"

"Heavens, mamma—you are not going to take up the carpet?" screamed Julia.

"Here's the hammers, marm," said Biddy, advancing tremblingly.

"Hand them to me, then," cried my wife; for poor Biddy was, at long gun-distance, holding them out as if her mistress had the plague.

"Now, husband, do you take up that side of the carpet, and I will this." Down on her knees she then dropped, while I followed suit.

The carpet being removed, and the ear applied to the naked floor, not the slightest ticking could be heard.

"The table—after all, it is the table," cried my wife. "Biddy, bring it back."

"Oh no, marm, not I, please, marm," sobbed Biddy.

"Foolish creature!—Husband, do you bring it."

"My dear," said I, " we have plenty of other tables; why be so particular?"

"Where is that table?" cried my wife, contemptuously, regardless of my gentle remonstrance.

"In the wood-house, marm. I put it away as far as ever I could, marm," sobbed Biddy.

"Shall I go to the wood-house for it, or will you?" said my wife, addressing me in a frightful, business-like manner.

Immediately I darted out of the door, and found the little apple-tree table, upside down, in one of my chip-bins. I hurriedly returned with it, and once more my wife examined it attentively. Tick, tick, tick! Yes, it was the table.

"Please, marm," said Biddy, now entering the room, with hat and shawl—"please, marm, will you pay me my wages?"

"Take your hat and shawl off directly," said my wife; "set this table again."

"Set it," roared I, in a passion, "set it, or I'll go for the police."

"Heavens! heavens!" cried my daughters, in one breath. "What will become of us!—Spirits! Spirits!"

"Will you set the table?" cried I, advancing upon Biddy.

"I will, I will—yes, marm—yes, master—I will, I will. Spirits!—Holy Vargin!"

"Now, husband," said my wife, "I am convinced that, whatever it is that causes this ticking, neither the ticking nor the table can hurt us; for we are all good Christians, I hope. I am determined to find out the cause of it, too, which time and patience will bring to light. I shall breakfast on no other table but this, so long as we live in this house. So, sit down, now that all things are ready again, and let us quietly breakfast. My dears," turning to Julia and Anna, "go to your room, and return composed. Let me have no more of this childishness."

Upon occasion my wife was mistress in her house.

During the meal, in vain was conversation started again and again; in vain my wife said something brisk to infuse into others an animation akin to her own. Julia and Anna, with heads bowed over their tea-cups, were still listening for the tick. I confess, too, that their example was catching. But, for the time, nothing was heard. Either the ticking had died quite away, or else, slight as it was, the increasing uproar of the street, with the general hum of day, so contrasted with the repose of night and early morning, smothered the sound. At the lurking inquietude of her companions, my wife was indignant; the more so, as she seemed to glory in her own exemption from panic. When breakfast was cleared away she took my watch, and, placing it on the table, addressed the supposed spirits in it, with a jocosely defiant air: "There, tick away, let us see who can tick loudest!"

All that day, while abroad, I thought of the mysterious table. Could Cotton Mather speak true? Were there spirits? And would spirits haunt a tea-table? Would the Evil One dare show his cloven foot in the bosom of an innocent family? I shuddered when I thought that I myself, against the solemn warnings of my daughters, had willfully introduced the cloven foot there. Yea, three cloven feet. But, towards noon, this sort of feeling began to wear off. The continual rubbing against so many practical people in the street, brushed such chimeras away from me. I remembered that I had not acquitted myself very intrepidly either on the previous night or in the morning. I resolved to regain the good opinion of my wife.

To evince my hardihood the more signally, when tea was dismissed, and the three rubbers of whist had been played, and no ticking had been heard—which the more encouraged me—I took my pipe, and, saying that bed-time had arrived for the rest, drew my chair towards the fire, and, removing my slippers, placed my feet on the fender, looking as calm and composed as old Democritus in the tombs of Abdera, when one midnight the mischievous little boys of the town tried to frighten that sturdy philosopher with spurious ghosts.

And I thought to myself, that the worthy old gentleman had set a good example to all times in his conduct on that occasion. For, when at the dead hour, intent on his studies, he heard the strange sounds, he did not so much as move his eyes from his page, only simply said: "Boys, little boys, go

home. This is no place for you. You will catch cold here."
The philosophy of which words lies here: that they imply the
foregone conclusion, that any possible investigation of any
possible spiritual phenomena was absurd; that upon the first
face of such things, the mind of a sane man instinctively affirmed them a humbug, unworthy the least attention; more
especially if such phenomena appear in tombs, since tombs
are peculiarly the place of silence, lifelessness, and solitude;
for which cause, by the way, the old man, as upon the occasion in question, made the tombs of Abdera his place of
study.

Presently I was alone, and all was hushed. I laid down my
pipe, not feeling exactly tranquil enough now thoroughly to
enjoy it. Taking up one of the newspapers, I began, in a nervous, hurried sort of way, to read by the light of a candle
placed on a small stand drawn close to the fire. As for the
apple-tree table, having lately concluded that it was rather too
low for a reading-table, I thought best not to use it as such
that night. But it stood not very distant in the middle of the
room.

Try as I would, I could not succeed much at reading.
Somehow I seemed all ear and no eye; a condition of intense
auricular suspense. But ere long it was broken.

Tick! tick! tick!

Though it was not the first time I had heard that sound;
nay, though I had made it my particular business on this occasion to wait for that sound, nevertheless, when it came, it
seemed unexpected, as if a cannon had boomed through the
window.

Tick! tick! tick!

I sat stock still for a time, thoroughly to master, if possible,
my first discomposure. Then rising, I looked pretty steadily at
the table; went up to it pretty steadily; took hold of it pretty
steadily; but let it go pretty quickly; then paced up and down,
stopping every moment or two, with ear pricked to listen.
Meantime, within me, the contest between panic and philosophy remained not wholly decided.

Tick! tick! tick!

With appalling distinctness the ticking now rose on the
night.

My pulse fluttered—my heart beat. I hardly know what might not have followed, had not Democritus just then come to the rescue. For shame, said I to myself, what is the use of so fine an example of philosophy, if it cannot be followed? Straightway I resolved to imitate it, even to the old sage's occupation and attitude.

Resuming my chair and paper, with back presented to the table, I remained thus for a time, as if buried in study; when, the ticking still continuing, I drawled out, in as indifferent and dryly jocose a way as I could; "Come, come, Tick, my boy, fun enough for to-night."

Tick! tick! tick!

There seemed a sort of jeering defiance in the ticking now. It seemed to exult over the poor affected part I was playing. But much as the taunt stung me, it only stung me into persistence. I resolved not to abate one whit in my mode of address.

"Come, come, you make more and more noise. Tick, my boy; too much of a joke—time to have done."

No sooner said than the ticking ceased. Never was responsive obedience more exact. For the life of me, I could not help turning round upon the table, as one would upon some reasonable being, when————could I believe my senses? I saw something moving, or wriggling, or squirming upon the slab of the table. It shone like a glow-worm. Unconsciously, I grasped the poker that stood at hand. But bethinking me how absurd to attack a glow-worm with a poker, I put it down. How long I sat spell-bound and staring there, with my body presented one way and my face another, I cannot say; but at length I rose, and, buttoning my coat up and down, made a sudden intrepid forced march full upon the table. And there, near the centre of the slab, as I live, I saw an irregular little hole, or, rather, short nibbled sort of crack, from which (like a butterfly escaping its chrysalis) the sparkling object, whatever it might be, was struggling. Its motion was the motion of life. I stood becharmed. Are there, indeed, spirits, thought I; and is this one? No; I must be dreaming. I turned my glance off to the red fire on the hearth, then back to the pale lustre on the table. What I saw was no optical illusion, but a real marvel. The tremor was increasing, when, once again,

Democritus befriended me. Supernatural coruscation as it appeared, I strove to look at the strange object in a purely scientific way. Thus viewed, it appeared some new sort of small shining beetle or bug, and, I thought, not without something of a hum to it, too.

I still watched it, and with still increasing self-possession. Sparkling and wriggling, it still continued its throes. In another moment it was just on the point of escaping its prison. A thought struck me. Running for a tumbler, I clapped it over the insect just in time to secure it.

After watching it a while longer under the tumbler, I left all as it was, and, tolerably composed, retired.

Now, for the soul of me, I could not, at that time, comprehend the phenomenon. A live bug come out of a dead table? A fire-fly bug come out of a piece of ancient lumber, for one knows not how many years stored away in an old garret? Was ever such a thing heard of, or even dreamed of? How got the bug there? Never mind. I bethought me of Democritus, and resolved to keep cool. At all events, the mystery of the ticking was explained. It was simply the sound of the gnawing and filing, and tapping of the bug, in eating its way out. It was satisfactory to think, that there was an end forever to the ticking. I resolved not to let the occasion pass without reaping some credit from it.

"Wife," said I, next morning, "you will not be troubled with any more ticking in our table. I have put a stop to all that."

"Indeed, husband," said she, with some incredulity.

"Yes, wife," returned I, perhaps a little vain-gloriously. "I have put a quietus upon that ticking. Depend upon it, the ticking will trouble you no more."

In vain she besought me to explain myself. I would not gratify her; being willing to balance any previous trepidation I might have betrayed, by leaving room now for the imputation of some heroic feat whereby I had silenced the ticking. It was a sort of innocent deceit by implication, quite harmless, and, I thought, of utility.

But when I went to breakfast, I saw my wife kneeling at the table again, and my girls looking ten times more frightened than ever.

"Why did you tell me that boastful tale," said my wife, indignantly. "You might have known how easily it would be found out. See this crack, too; and here is the ticking again, plainer than ever."

"Impossible," I exclaimed; but upon applying my ear, sure enough, tick! tick! tick! The ticking was there.

Recovering myself the best way I might, I demanded the bug.

"Bug?" screamed Julia. "Good heavens, papa!"

"I hope, sir, you have been bringing no bugs into this house," said my wife, severely.

"The bug, the bug!" I cried; "the bug under the tumbler."

"Bugs in tumblers!" cried the girls; "not *our* tumblers, papa? You have not been putting bugs into our tumblers? Oh, what does—what *does* it all mean?"

"Do you see this hole, this crack here?" said I, putting my finger on the spot.

"That I do," said my wife, with high displeasure. "And how did it come there? What have you been doing to the table?"

"Do you see this crack?" repeated I, intensely.

"Yes, yes," said Julia; "that was what frightened me so; it looks so like witch-work."

"Spirits! spirits!" cried Anna.

"Silence!" said my wife. "Go on, sir, and tell us what you know of the crack."

"Wife and daughters," said I, solemnly, "out of that crack, or hole, while I was sitting all alone here last night, a wonderful———"

Here, involuntarily, I paused, fascinated by the expectant attitudes and bursting eyes of Julia and Anna.

"What, what?" cried Julia.

"A bug, Julia."

"A bug?" cried my wife. "A bug come out of this table? And what did you do with it?"

"Clapped it under a tumbler."

"Biddy! Biddy!" cried my wife, going to the door. "Did you see a tumbler here on this table when you swept the room?"

"Sure I did, marm, and a 'bomnable bug under it."

"And what did you do with it?" demanded I.

"Put the bug in the fire, sir, and rinsed out the tumbler ever so many times, marm."

"Where is that tumbler?" cried Anna. "I hope you scratched it—marked it some way. I'll never drink out of that tumbler; never put it before me, Biddy. A bug—a bug! Oh, Julia! oh, mamma! I feel it crawling all over me, even now. Haunted table!"

"Spirits! spirits!" cried Julia.

"My daughters," said their mother, with authority in her eyes, "go to your chamber till you can behave more like reasonable creatures. Is it a bug—a bug that can frighten you out of what little wits you ever had? Leave the room. I am astonished. I am pained by such childish conduct."

"Now tell me," said she, addressing me, as soon as they had withdrawn, "now tell me truly, did a bug really come out of this crack in the table?"

"Wife, it is even so."

"Did you see it come out?"

"I did."

She looked earnestly at the crack, leaning over it.

"Are you sure?" said she, looking up, but still bent over.

"Sure, sure."

She was silent. I began to think that the mystery of the thing began to tell even upon her. Yes, thought I, I shall presently see my wife shaking and shuddering, and, who knows, calling in some old dominie to exorcise the table, and drive out the spirits.

"I'll tell you what we'll do," said she suddenly, and not without excitement.

"What, wife?" said I, all eagerness, expecting some mystical proposition; " what, wife?"

"We will rub this table all over with that celebrated 'roach powder' I've heard of."

"Good gracious! Then you don't think it's spirits?"

"Spirits?"

The emphasis of scornful incredulity was worthy of Democritus himself.

"But this ticking—this ticking?" said I.

"I'll whip that out of it."

"Come, come wife," said I, "you are going too far the other way, now. Neither roach powder nor whipping will cure this table. It's a queer table, wife; there's no blinking it."

"I'll have it rubbed, though," she replied, " well rubbed;" and calling Biddy, she bade her get wax and brush, and give the table a vigorous manipulation. That done, the cloth was again laid, and we sat down to our morning meal; but my daughters did not make their appearance. Julia and Anna took no breakfast that day.

When the cloth was removed, in a business-like way, my wife went to work with a dark colored cement, and hermetically closed the little hole in the table.

My daughters looking pale, I insisted upon taking them out for a walk that morning, when the following conversation ensued:

"My worst presentiments about that table are being verified, papa," said Julia; "not for nothing was that intimation of the cloven foot on my shoulder."

"Nonsense," said I. "Let us go into Mrs. Brown's, and have an ice-cream."

The spirit of Democritus was stronger on me now. By a curious coincidence, it strengthened with the strength of the sunlight.

"But is it not miraculous," said Anna, "how a bug should come out of a table?"

"Not at all, my daughter. It is a very common thing for bugs to come out of wood. You yourself must have seen them coming out of the ends of the billets on the hearth."

"Ah, but that wood is almost fresh from the woodland. But the table is at least a hundred years old."

"What of that?" said I, gayly. "Have not live toads been found in the hearts of dead rocks, as old as creation?"

"Say what you will, papa, I feel it is spirits," said Julia. "Do, do now, my dear papa, have that haunted table removed from the house."

"Nonsense," said I.

By another curious coincidence, the more they felt frightened, the more I felt brave.

Evening came.

"This ticking," said my wife; "do you think that another bug will come of this continued ticking?"

Curiously enough, that had not occurred to me before. I had not thought of there being twins of bugs. But now, who knew; there might be even triplets.

I resolved to take precautions, and, if there was to be a second bug, infallibly secure it. During the evening, the ticking was again heard. About ten o'clock I clapped a tumbler over the spot, as near as I could judge of it by my ear. Then we all retired, and locking the door of the cedar-parlor, I put the key in my pocket.

In the morning, nothing was to be seen, but the ticking was heard. The trepidation of my daughters returned. They wanted to call in the neighbors. But to this my wife was vigorously opposed. We should be the laughing-stock of the whole town. So it was agreed that nothing should be disclosed. Biddy received strict charges; and, to make sure, was not allowed that week to go to confession, lest she should tell the priest.

I stayed home all that day, every hour or two bending over the table, both eye and ear. Towards night, I thought the ticking grew more distinct, and seemed divided from my ear by a thinner and thinner partition of the wood. I thought, too, that I perceived a faint heaving up, or bulging of the wood, in the place where I had placed the tumbler. To put an end to the suspense, my wife proposed taking a knife and cutting into the wood there; but I had a less impatient plan; namely, that she and I should sit up with the table that night, as, from present symptoms, the bug would probably make its appearance before morning. For myself, I was curious to see the first advent of the thing—the first dazzle of the chick as it chipped the shell.

The idea struck my wife not unfavorably. She insisted that both Julia and Anna should be of the party, in order that the evidence of their senses should disabuse their minds of all nursery nonsense. For that spirits should tick, and that spirits should take unto themselves the form of bugs, was, to my wife, the most foolish of all foolish imaginations. True, she could not account for the thing; but she had all confidence that it could be, and would yet be, somehow explained, and that to her entire satisfaction. Without knowing it herself, my wife was a female Democritus. For my own part, my present feelings were of a mixed sort. In a strange and not unpleasing way, I gently oscillated between Democritus and Cotton Mather. But to my wife and daughters I assumed to be pure Democritus—a jeerer at all tea-table spirits whatever.

So, laying in a good supply of candles and crackers, all four of us sat up with the table, and at the same time sat round it. For a while my wife and I carried on an animated conversation. But my daughters were silent. Then my wife and I would have had a rubber of whist, but my daughters could not be prevailed upon to join. So we played whist with two dummies, literally; my wife won the rubber, and, fatigued with victory, put away the cards.

Half past eleven o'clock. No sign of the bug. The candles began to burn dim. My wife was just in the act of snuffing them, when a sudden, violent, hollow, resounding, rumbling, thumping was heard.

Julia and Anna sprang to their feet.

"All well!" cried a voice from the street. It was the watchman, first ringing down his club on the pavement, and then following it up with this highly satisfactory verbal announcement.

"All well! Do you hear that, my girls?" said I, gayly.

Indeed it was astonishing how brave as Bruce I felt in company with three women, and two of them half frightened out of their wits.

I rose for my pipe, and took a philosophic smoke.

Democritus forever, thought I.

In profound silence, I sat smoking, when lo!—pop! pop! pop!—right under the table, a terrible popping.

This time we all four sprang up, and my pipe was broken.

"Good heavens! what's that?"

"Spirits! spirits!" cried Julia.

"Oh, oh, oh!" cried Anna.

"Shame," said my wife, "it's that new bottled cider, in the cellar, going off. I told Biddy to wire the bottles to-day."

I shall here transcribe from memoranda, kept during part of the night.

"One o'clock. No sign of the bug. Ticking continues. Wife getting sleepy.

"Two o'clock. No sign of the bug. Ticking intermittent. Wife fast asleep.

"Three o'clock. No sign of the bug. Ticking pretty steady. Julia and Anna getting sleepy.

"Four o'clock. No sign of the bug. Ticking regular, but not spirited. Wife, Julia, and Anna, all fast asleep in their chairs.

"Five o'clock. No sign of the bug. Ticking faint. Myself feeling drowsy. The rest still asleep."

So far the journal.

—Rap! rap! rap!

A terrific, portentous rapping against a door.

Startled from our dreams, we started to our feet.

Rap! rap! rap!

Julia and Anna shrieked.

I cowered in the corner.

"You fools!" cried my wife, "it's the baker with the bread."

Six o'clock.

She went to throw back the shutters, but ere it was done, a cry came from Julia. There, half in and half out of its crack, there wriggled the bug, flashing in the room's general dimness, like a fiery opal.

Had this bug had a tiny sword by its side—a Damascus sword—and a tiny necklace round its neck—a diamond necklace—and a tiny gun in its claw—a brass gun—and a tiny manuscript in his mouth—a Chaldee manuscript—Julia and Anna could not have stood more charmed.

In truth, it was a beautiful bug—a Jew jeweler's bug—a bug like a sparkle of a glorious sunset.

Julia and Anna had never dreamed of such a bug. To them, bug had been a word synonymous with hideousness. But this was a seraphical bug; or, rather, all it had of the bug was the B, for it was beautiful as a butterfly.

Julia and Anna gazed and gazed. They were no more alarmed. They were delighted.

"But how got this strange, pretty creature into the table?" cried Julia.

"Spirits can get anywhere," replied Anna.

"Pshaw!" said my wife.

"Do you hear any more ticking?" said I.

They all applied their ears, but heard nothing.

"Well, then, wife and daughters, now that it is all over, this very morning I will go and make inquiries about it."

"Oh, do, papa," cried Julia, "do go and consult Madame Pazzi, the conjuress."

"Better go and consult Professor Johnson, the naturalist," said my wife.

"Bravo, Mrs. Democritus!" said I, "Professor Johnson is the man."

By good fortune I found the professor in. Informing him briefly of the incident, he manifested a cool, collected sort of interest, and gravely accompanied me home. The table was produced, the two openings pointed out, the bug displayed, and the details of the affair set forth; my wife and daughters being present.

"And now, Professor," said I, " what do you think of it?"

Putting on his spectacles, the learned professor looked hard at the table, and gently scraped with his pen-knife into the holes, but said nothing.

"Is it not an unusual thing, this?" anxiously asked Anna.

"Very unusual, Miss."

At which Julia and Anna exchanged significant glances.

"But is it not wonderful, very wonderful?" demanded Julia.

"Very wonderful, Miss."

My daughters exchanged still more significant glances, and Julia, emboldened, again spoke.

"And must you not admit, sir, that it is the work of—of—of sp———?"

"Spirits? No," was the crusty rejoinder.

"My daughters," said I, mildly, "you should remember that this is not Madame Pazzi, the conjuress, you put your questions to, but the eminent naturalist, Professor Johnson. And now, professor," I added, "be pleased to explain. Enlighten our ignorance."

Without repeating all that the learned gentleman said—for, indeed, though lucid, he was a little prosy—let the following summary of his explication suffice.

The incident was not wholly without example. The wood of the table was apple-tree, a sort of tree much fancied by various insects. The bugs had come from eggs laid inside the bark of the living tree in the orchard. By careful examination of the position of the hole from which the last bug had emerged, in relation to the cortical layers of the slab, and then allowing for the inch and a half along the grain, ere the bug had eaten its way entirely out, and then computing the whole number of cortical layers in the slab, with a reasonable conjecture for the number cut off from the outside, it appeared that the egg must have been laid in the tree some ninety years, more or less, before the tree could have been felled. But between the felling of the tree and the present time, how long might that be? It was a very old-fashioned table. Allow eighty years for the age of the table, which would make one hundred and fifty years that the bug had laid in the egg. Such, at least, was Professor Johnson's computation.

"Now, Julia," said I, "after that scientific statement of the case (though, I confess, I don't exactly understand it), where are your spirits? It is very wonderful as it is, but where are your spirits?"

"Where, indeed?" said my wife.

"Why, now, she did not *really* associate this purely natural phenomenon with any crude, spiritual hypothesis, did she?" observed the learned professor, with a slight sneer.

"Say what you will," said Julia, holding up, in the covered tumbler, the glorious, lustrous, flashing, live opal, "say what you will, if this beauteous creature be not a spirit, it yet teaches a spiritual lesson. For if, after one hundred and fifty years' entombment, a mere insect comes forth at last into light, itself an effulgence, shall there be no glorified resurrection for the spirit of man? Spirits! spirits!" she exclaimed, with rapture, "I still believe in spirits, only now I believe in them with delight, when before I but thought of them with terror."

The mysterious insect did not long enjoy its radiant life; it expired the next day. But my girls have preserved it. Embalmed in a silver vinaigrette, it lies on the little apple-tree table in the pier of the cedar-parlor.

And whatever lady doubts this story, my daughters will be happy to show her both the bug and the table, and point out to her, in the repaired slab of the latter, the two sealing-wax drops designating the exact place of the two holes made by the two bugs, something in the same way in which are marked the spots where the cannon balls struck Brattle street church.

BILLY BUDD, SAILOR

(An Inside Narrative)

DEDICATED
TO
JACK CHASE
ENGLISHMAN

Wherever that great heart may now be
Here on Earth or harbored in Paradise

Captain of the Maintop
in the year 1843
in the U.S. Frigate
United States

I

IN THE TIME before steamships, or then more frequently than now, a stroller along the docks of any considerable seaport would occasionally have his attention arrested by a group of bronzed mariners, man-of-war's men or merchant sailors in holiday attire, ashore on liberty. In certain instances they would flank, or like a bodyguard quite surround, some superior figure of their own class, moving along with them like Aldebaran among the lesser lights of his constellation. That signal object was the "Handsome Sailor" of the less prosaic time alike of the military and merchant navies. With no perceptible trace of the vainglorious about him, rather with the offhand unaffectedness of natural regality, he seemed to accept the spontaneous homage of his shipmates.

A somewhat remarkable instance recurs to me. In Liverpool, now half a century ago, I saw under the shadow of the great dingy street-wall of Prince's Dock (an obstruction long since removed) a common sailor so intensely black that he must needs have been a native African of the unadulterate blood of Ham—a symmetric figure much above the average height. The two ends of a gay silk handkerchief thrown loose about the neck danced upon the displayed ebony of his chest, in his ears were big hoops of gold, and a Highland bonnet with a tartan band set off his shapely head. It was a hot noon in July; and his face, lustrous with perspiration, beamed with barbaric good humor. In jovial sallies right and left, his white teeth flashing into view, he rollicked along, the center of a company of his shipmates. These were made up of such an assortment of tribes and complexions as would have well fitted them to be marched up by Anacharsis Cloots before the bar of the first French Assembly as Representatives of the Human Race. At each spontaneous tribute rendered by the wayfarers to this black pagod of a fellow—the tribute of a pause and stare, and less frequently an exclamation—the motley retinue showed that they took that sort of pride in the evoker of it which the Assyrian priests doubtless showed for their grand sculptured Bull when the faithful prostrated themselves.

To return. If in some cases a bit of a nautical Murat in setting forth his person ashore, the Handsome Sailor of the period in question evinced nothing of the dandified Billy-be-Dam, an amusing character all but extinct now, but occasionally to be encountered, and in a form yet more amusing than the original, at the tiller of the boats on the tempestuous Erie Canal or, more likely, vaporing in the groggeries along the towpath. Invariably a proficient in his perilous calling, he was also more or less of a mighty boxer or wrestler. It was strength and beauty. Tales of his prowess were recited. Ashore he was the champion; afloat the spokesman; on every suitable occasion always foremost. Close-reefing topsails in a gale, there he was, astride the weather yardarm-end, foot in the Flemish horse as stirrup, both hands tugging at the earing as at a bridle, in very much the attitude of young Alexander curbing the fiery Bucephalus. A superb figure, tossed up as by the horns of Taurus against the thunderous sky, cheerily hallooing to the strenuous file along the spar.

The moral nature was seldom out of keeping with the physical make. Indeed, except as toned by the former, the comeliness and power, always attractive in masculine conjunction, hardly could have drawn the sort of honest homage the Handsome Sailor in some examples received from his less gifted associates.

Such a cynosure, at least in aspect, and something such too in nature, though with important variations made apparent as the story proceeds, was welkin-eyed Billy Budd—or Baby Budd, as more familiarly, under circumstances hereafter to be given, he at last came to be called—aged twenty-one, a foretopman of the British fleet toward the close of the last decade of the eighteenth century. It was not very long prior to the time of the narration that follows that he had entered the King's service, having been impressed on the Narrow Seas from a homeward-bound English merchantman into a seventy-four outward bound, H.M.S. *Bellipotent*; which ship, as was not unusual in those hurried days, having been obliged to put to sea short of her proper complement of men. Plump upon Billy at first sight in the gangway the boarding officer, Lieutenant Ratcliffe, pounced, even before the merchantman's crew was formally mustered on the quarter-deck for his deliberate inspection. And him only he elected. For whether it was because the other men when ranged before him showed to ill advantage after Billy, or whether he had some scruples in view of the merchantman's being rather short-handed, however it might be, the officer contented himself with his first spontaneous choice. To the surprise of the ship's company, though much to the lieutenant's satisfaction, Billy made no demur. But, indeed, any demur would have been as idle as the protest of a goldfinch popped into a cage.

Noting this uncomplaining acquiescence, all but cheerful, one might say, the shipmaster turned a surprised glance of silent reproach at the sailor. The shipmaster was one of those worthy mortals found in every vocation, even the humbler ones—the sort of person whom everybody agrees in calling "a respectable man." And—nor so strange to report as it may appear to be—though a ploughman of the troubled waters, lifelong contending with the intractable elements, there was nothing this honest soul at heart loved better than simple peace and quiet. For the rest, he was fifty or thereabouts, a little inclined to corpulence, a prepossessing face, unwhiskered, and of an agreeable color—a rather full face, humanely intelligent in expression. On a fair day with a fair wind and all going well, a certain musical chime in his voice seemed to be the veritable unobstructed outcome of the innermost man. He had much prudence, much conscientiousness, and there were occasions when these virtues were the cause of over-much disquietude in him. On a passage, so long as his craft was in any proximity to land, no sleep for Captain Graveling. He took to heart those serious responsibilities not so heavily borne by some shipmasters.

Now while Billy Budd was down in the forecastle getting his kit together, the *Bellipotent's* lieutenant, burly and bluff, nowise disconcerted by Captain Graveling's omitting to proffer the customary hospitalities on an occasion so unwelcome to him, an omission simply caused by preoccupation of thought, unceremoniously invited himself into the cabin, and also to a flask from the spirit locker, a receptacle which his experienced eye instantly discovered. In fact he was one of those sea dogs in whom all the hardship and peril of naval life in the great prolonged wars of his time never impaired the natural instinct for sensuous enjoyment. His duty he always faithfully did; but duty is sometimes a dry obligation, and he was for irrigating its aridity, whensoever possible, with a fertilizing decoction of strong waters. For the cabin's proprietor there was nothing left but to play the part of the enforced host with whatever grace and alacrity were practicable. As necessary adjuncts to the flask, he silently placed tumbler and water jug before the irrepressible guest. But excusing himself from partaking just then, he dismally watched the unembarrassed officer deliberately diluting his grog a little, then tossing it off in three swallows, pushing the empty tumbler away, yet not so far as to be beyond easy reach, at the same time settling himself in his seat and smacking his lips with high satisfaction, looking straight at the host.

These proceedings over, the master broke the silence; and there lurked a rueful reproach in the tone of his voice: "Lieutenant, you are going to take my best man from me, the jewel of 'em."

"Yes, I know," rejoined the other, immediately drawing back the tumbler preliminary to a replenishing. "Yes, I know. Sorry."

"Beg pardon, but you don't understand, Lieutenant. See here, now. Before I shipped that young fellow, my forecastle was a rat-pit of quarrels. It was black times, I tell you, aboard the *Rights* here. I was worried to that degree my pipe had no comfort for me. But Billy came; and it was like a Catholic priest striking peace in an Irish shindy. Not that he preached to them or said or did anything in particular; but a virtue went out of him, sugaring the sour ones. They took to him like hornets to treacle; all but the buffer of the gang, the big shaggy chap with the fire-red whiskers. He indeed, out of envy, perhaps, of the newcomer, and thinking such a "sweet and pleasant fellow," as he mockingly designated him to the others, could hardly have the spirit of a gamecock, must needs bestir himself in trying to get up an ugly row with him. Billy forebore with him and reasoned with him in a pleasant way—he is something like myself, Lieutenant, to whom aught like a quarrel is hateful—but nothing served. So, in the second dogwatch one day, the Red Whiskers in presence of the others, under pretense of showing Billy just whence a sirloin steak was cut—for the fellow had once been a butcher—insultingly gave him a dig under the ribs. Quick as lightning Billy let fly his arm. I dare say he never meant to do quite as much as he did, but anyhow he gave the burly fool a terrible drubbing. It took about half a minute, I should think. And, lord bless you, the lubber was astonished at the celerity. And will you believe it, Lieutenant, the Red Whiskers now really loves Billy—loves him, or is the biggest hypocrite that ever I heard of. But they all love him. Some of 'em do his washing, darn his old trousers for him; the carpenter is at odd times making a pretty little chest of drawers for him. Anybody will do anything for Billy Budd; and it's the happy family here. But now, Lieutenant, if that young fellow goes—I know how it will be aboard the *Rights*. Not again very soon shall I, coming up from dinner, lean over the capstan smoking a quiet pipe—no, not very soon again, I think. Ay, Lieutenant, you are going to take away the jewel of 'em; you are going to take away my peacemaker!" And with that the good soul had really some ado in checking a rising sob.

"Well," said the lieutenant, who had listened with amused interest to all this and now was waxing merry with his tipple; " well, blessed are the peacemakers, especially the fighting peacemakers. And such are the seventy-four beauties some of which you see poking their noses out of the portholes of yonder warship lying to for me," pointing through the cabin window at the *Bellipotent*. "But courage! Don't look so downhearted, man. Why, I pledge you in advance the royal approbation. Rest assured that His Majesty will be delighted to know that in a time when his hardtack is not sought for by sailors with such avidity as should be, a time also when some shipmasters privily resent the borrowing from them a tar or two for the service; His Majesty, I say, will be delighted to learn that *one* shipmaster at least cheerfully surrenders to the King the flower of his flock, a sailor who with equal loyalty makes no dissent.—But where's my beauty? Ah," looking through the cabin's open door, "here he comes; and, by Jove, lugging along his chest—Apollo with his portmanteau!—My man," stepping out to him, "you can't take that big box aboard a warship. The boxes there are mostly shot boxes. Put your duds in a bag, lad. Boot and saddle for the cavalryman, bag and hammock for the man-of-war's man."

The transfer from chest to bag was made. And, after seeing his man into the cutter and then following him down, the lieutenant pushed off from the *Rights-of-Man*. That was the merchant ship's name, though by her master and crew abbreviated in sailor fashion into the *Rights*. The hardheaded Dundee owner was a staunch admirer of Thomas Paine, whose book in rejoinder to Burke's arraignment of the French Revolution had then been published for some time and had gone everywhere. In christening his vessel after the title of Paine's volume the man of Dundee was something like his contemporary ship-owner, Stephen Girard of Philadelphia, whose sympathies, alike with his native land and its liberal philosophers, he evinced by naming his ships after Voltaire, Diderot, and so forth.

But now, when the boat swept under the merchantman's stern, and officer and oarsmen were noting—some bitterly and others with a grin—the name emblazoned there; just then it was that the new recruit jumped up from the bow where the coxswain had directed him to sit, and waving hat to his silent shipmates sorrowfully looking over at him from the taffrail, bade the lads a genial good-bye. Then, making a salutation as to the ship herself, "And good-bye to you too, old *Rights-of-Man*."

"Down, sir!" roared the lieutenant, instantly assuming all the rigor of his rank, though with difficulty repressing a smile.

To be sure, Billy's action was a terrible breach of naval decorum. But in that decorum he had never been instructed; in consideration of which the lieutenant would hardly have been so energetic in reproof but for the concluding farewell to the ship. This he rather took as meant to convey a covert sally on the new recruit's part, a sly slur at impressment in general, and that of himself in especial. And yet, more likely, if satire it was in effect, it was hardly so by intention, for Billy, though happily endowed with the gaiety of high health, youth, and a free heart, was yet by no means of a satirical turn. The will to it and the sinister dexterity were alike wanting. To deal in double meanings and insinuations of any sort was quite foreign to his nature.

As to his enforced enlistment, that he seemed to take pretty much as he was wont to take any vicissitude of weather. Like the animals, though no philosopher, he was, without knowing it, practically a fatalist. And it may be that he rather liked this adventurous turn in his affairs, which promised an opening into novel scenes and martial excitements.

Aboard the *Bellipotent* our merchant sailor was forthwith rated as an able seaman and assigned to the starboard watch of the foretop. He was soon at home in the service, not at all disliked for his unpretentious good looks and a sort of genial happy-go-lucky air. No merrier man in his mess: in marked contrast to certain other individuals included like himself among the impressed portion of the ship's company; for these when not actively employed were sometimes, and more particularly in the last dogwatch when the drawing near of twilight induced revery, apt to fall into a saddish mood which in some partook of sullenness. But they were not so young as our foretopman, and no few of them must have known a hearth of some sort, others may have had wives and children left, too probably, in uncertain circumstances, and hardly any but must have had acknowledged kith and kin, while for Billy, as will shortly be seen, his entire family was practically invested in himself.

2

THOUGH our new-made foretopman was well received in the top and on the gun decks, hardly here was he that cynosure he had previously been among those minor ship's companies of the merchant marine, with which companies only had he hitherto consorted.

He was young; and despite his all but fully developed frame, in aspect looked even younger than he really was, owing to a lingering adolescent expression in the as yet smooth face all but feminine in purity of natural complexion but where, thanks to his seagoing, the lily was quite suppressed and the rose had some ado visibly to flush through the tan.

To one essentially such a novice in the complexities of factitious life, the abrupt transition from his former and simpler sphere to the ampler and more knowing world of a great warship; this might well have abashed him had there been any conceit or vanity in his composition. Among her miscellaneous multitude, the *Bellipotent* mustered several individuals who however inferior in grade were of no common natural stamp, sailors more signally susceptive of that air which continuous martial discipline and repeated presence in battle can in some degree impart even to the average man. As the Handsome Sailor, Billy Budd's position aboard the seventy-four was something analogous to that of a rustic beauty transplanted from the provinces and brought into competition with the highborn dames of the court. But this change of circumstances he scarce noted. As little did he observe that something about him provoked an ambiguous smile in one or two harder faces among the bluejackets. Nor less unaware was he of the peculiar favorable effect his person and demeanor had upon the more intelligent gentlemen of the quarter-deck. Nor could this well have been otherwise. Cast in a mold peculiar to the finest physical examples of those Englishmen in whom the Saxon strain would seem not at all to partake of any Norman or other admixture, he showed in face that humane look of reposeful good nature which the Greek sculptor in some instances gave to his heroic strong man, Hercules. But this again was subtly modified by another and pervasive quality. The ear, small and shapely, the arch of the foot, the curve in mouth and nostril, even the indurated hand dyed to the orange-tawny of the toucan's bill, a hand telling alike of the halyards and tar bucket; but, above all, something in the mobile expression, and every chance attitude and movement, something suggestive of a mother eminently favored by Love and the Graces; all this strangely indicated a lineage in direct contradiction to his lot. The mysteriousness here became less mysterious through a matter of fact elicited when Billy at the capstan was being formally mustered into the service. Asked by the officer, a small, brisk little gentleman as it chanced, among other questions, his place of birth, he replied, "Please, sir, I don't know."

"Don't know where you were born? Who was your father?"

"God knows, sir."

Struck by the straightforward simplicity of these replies, the officer next asked, "Do you know anything about your beginning?"

"No, sir. But I have heard that I was found in a pretty silk-lined basket hanging one morning from the knocker of a good man's door in Bristol."

"*Found*, say you? Well," throwing back his head and looking up and down the new recruit; " well, it turns out to have been a pretty good find. Hope they'll find some more like you, my man; the fleet sadly needs them."

Yes, Billy Budd was a foundling, a presumable by-blow, and, evidently, no ignoble one. Noble descent was as evident in him as in a blood horse.

For the rest, with little or no sharpness of faculty or any trace of the wisdom of the serpent, nor yet quite a dove, he possessed that kind and degree of intelligence going along with the unconventional rectitude of a sound human creature, one to whom not yet has been proffered the questionable apple of knowledge. He was illiterate; he could not read, but he could sing, and like the illiterate nightingale was sometimes the composer of his own song.

Of self-consciousness he seemed to have little or none, or about as much as we may reasonably impute to a dog of Saint Bernard's breed.

Habitually living with the elements and knowing little more of the land than as a beach, or, rather, that portion of the terraqueous globe providentially set apart for dance-houses, doxies, and tapsters, in short what sailors call a "fiddler's green," his simple nature remained unsophisticated by those moral obliquities which are not in every case incompatible with that manufacturable thing known as respectability. But are sailors, frequenters of fiddlers' greens, without vices? No; but less often than with landsmen do their vices, so called, partake of crookedness of heart, seeming less to proceed from viciousness than exuberance of vitality after long constraint: frank manifestations in accordance with natural

law. By his original constitution aided by the co-operating
influences of his lot, Billy in many respects was little more
than a sort of upright barbarian, much such perhaps as Adam
presumably might have been ere the urbane Serpent wriggled
himself into his company.

And here be it submitted that apparently going to corroborate the doctrine of man's Fall, a doctrine now popularly
ignored, it is observable that where certain virtues pristine
and unadulterate peculiarly characterize anybody in the external uniform of civilization, they will upon scrutiny seem not
to be derived from custom or convention, but rather to be
out of keeping with these, as if indeed exceptionally transmitted from a period prior to Cain's city and citified man. The
character marked by such qualities has to an unvitiated taste
an untampered-with flavor like that of berries, while the man
thoroughly civilized, even in a fair specimen of the breed, has
to the same moral palate a questionable smack as of a compounded wine. To any stray inheritor of these primitive qualities found, like Caspar Hauser, wandering dazed in any
Christian capital of our time, the good-natured poet's famous
invocation, near two thousand years ago, of the good rustic
out of his latitude in the Rome of the Caesars, still appropriately holds:

> Honest and poor, faithful in word and thought,
> What hath thee, Fabian, to the city brought?

Though our Handsome Sailor had as much of masculine
beauty as one can expect anywhere to see; nevertheless, like
the beautiful woman in one of Hawthorne's minor tales, there
was just one thing amiss in him. No visible blemish indeed,
as with the lady; no, but an occasional liability to a vocal
defect. Though in the hour of elemental uproar or peril he
was everything that a sailor should be, yet under sudden
provocation of strong heart-feeling his voice, otherwise singularly musical, as if expressive of the harmony within, was
apt to develop an organic hesitancy, in fact more or less of a
stutter or even worse. In this particular Billy was a striking
instance that the arch interferer, the envious marplot of Eden,
still has more or less to do with every human consignment to

this planet of Earth. In every case, one way or another he is
sure to slip in his little card, as much as to remind us—I too
have a hand here.

The avowal of such an imperfection in the Handsome
Sailor should be evidence not alone that he is not presented
as a conventional hero, but also that the story in which he is
the main figure is no romance.

3

AT THE TIME of Billy Budd's arbitrary enlistment into the
Bellipotent that ship was on her way to join the Mediterranean fleet. No long time elapsed before the junction was
effected. As one of that fleet the seventy-four participated in
its movements, though at times on account of her superior
sailing qualities, in the absence of frigates, dispatched on separate duty as a scout and at times on less temporary service.
But with all this the story has little concernment, restricted as
it is to the inner life of one particular ship and the career of
an individual sailor.

It was the summer of 1797. In the April of that year had
occurred the commotion at Spithead followed in May by a
second and yet more serious outbreak in the fleet at the Nore.
The latter is known, and without exaggeration in the epithet,
as "the Great Mutiny." It was indeed a demonstration more
menacing to England than the contemporary manifestoes and
conquering and proselyting armies of the French Directory.
To the British Empire the Nore Mutiny was what a strike in
the fire brigade would be to London threatened by general
arson. In a crisis when the kingdom might well have anticipated the famous signal that some years later published along
the naval line of battle what it was that upon occasion England expected of Englishmen; *that* was the time when at the
mastheads of the three-deckers and seventy-fours moored in
her own roadstead—a fleet the right arm of a Power then all
but the sole free conservative one of the Old World—the
bluejackets, to be numbered by thousands, ran up with huz-

zas the British colors with the union and cross wiped out; by that cancellation transmuting the flag of founded law and freedom defined, into the enemy's red meteor of unbridled and unbounded revolt. Reasonable discontent growing out of practical grievances in the fleet had been ignited into irrational combustion as by live cinders blown across the Channel from France in flames.

The event converted into irony for a time those spirited strains of Dibdin—as a song-writer no mean auxiliary to the English government at that European conjuncture—strains celebrating, among other things, the patriotic devotion of the British tar: "And as for my life, 'tis the King's!"

Such an episode in the Island's grand naval story her naval historians naturally abridge, one of them (William James) candidly acknowledging that fain would he pass it over did not "impartiality forbid fastidiousness." And yet his mention is less a narration than a reference, having to do hardly at all with details. Nor are these readily to be found in the libraries. Like some other events in every age befalling states everywhere, including America, the Great Mutiny was of such character that national pride along with views of policy would fain shade it off into the historical background. Such events cannot be ignored, but there is a considerate way of historically treating them. If a well-constituted individual refrains from blazoning aught amiss or calamitous in his family, a nation in the like circumstance may without reproach be equally discreet.

Though after parleyings between government and the ringleaders, and concessions by the former as to some glaring abuses, the first uprising—that at Spithead—with difficulty was put down, or matters for the time pacified; yet at the Nore the unforeseen renewal of insurrection on a yet larger scale, and emphasized in the conferences that ensued by demands deemed by the authorities not only inadmissible but aggressively insolent, indicated—if the Red Flag did not sufficiently do so—what was the spirit animating the men. Final suppression, however, there was; but only made possible perhaps by the unswerving loyalty of the marine corps and a voluntary resumption of loyalty among influential sections of the crews.

To some extent the Nore Mutiny may be regarded as analogous to the distempering irruption of contagious fever in a
frame constitutionally sound, and which anon throws it off.

At all events, of these thousands of mutineers were some of
the tars who not so very long afterwards—whether wholly
prompted thereto by patriotism, or pugnacious instinct, or by
both—helped to win a coronet for Nelson at the Nile, and
the naval crown of crowns for him at Trafalgar. To the mutineers, those battles and especially Trafalgar were a plenary
absolution and a grand one. For all that goes to make up
scenic naval display and heroic magnificence in arms, those
battles, especially Trafalgar, stand unmatched in human
annals.

4

IN THIS MATTER of writing, resolve as one may to keep to
the main road, some bypaths have an enticement not
readily to be withstood. I am going to err into such a by-
path. If the reader will keep me company I shall be glad. At
the least, we can promise ourselves that pleasure which is
wickedly said to be in sinning, for a literary sin the divergence will be.

Very likely it is no new remark that the inventions of our
time have at last brought about a change in sea warfare in
degree corresponding to the revolution in all warfare effected
by the original introduction from China into Europe of gunpowder. The first European firearm, a clumsy contrivance,
was, as is well known, scouted by no few of the knights as a
base implement, good enough peradventure for weavers too
craven to stand up crossing steel with steel in frank fight. But
as ashore knightly valor, though shorn of its blazonry, did not
cease with the knights, neither on the seas—though nowadays in encounters there a certain kind of displayed gallantry
be fallen out of date as hardly applicable under changed circumstances—did the nobler qualities of such naval magnates
as Don John of Austria, Doria, Van Tromp, Jean Bart, the

long line of British admirals, and the American Decaturs of 1812 become obsolete with their wooden walls.

Nevertheless, to anybody who can hold the Present at its worth without being inappreciative of the Past, it may be forgiven, if to such an one the solitary old hulk at Portsmouth, Nelson's *Victory*, seems to float there, not alone as the decaying monument of a fame incorruptible, but also as a poetic reproach, softened by its picturesqueness, to the *Monitors* and yet mightier hulls of the European ironclads. And this not altogether because such craft are unsightly, unavoidably lacking the symmetry and grand lines of the old battleships, but equally for other reasons.

There are some, perhaps, who while not altogether inaccessible to that poetic reproach just alluded to, may yet on behalf of the new order be disposed to parry it; and this to the extent of iconoclasm, if need be. For example, prompted by the sight of the star inserted in the *Victory*'s quarter-deck designating the spot where the Great Sailor fell, these martial utilitarians may suggest considerations implying that Nelson's ornate publication of his person in battle was not only unnecessary, but not military, nay, savored of foolhardiness and vanity. They may add, too, that at Trafalgar it was in effect nothing less than a challenge to death; and death came; and that but for his bravado the victorious admiral might possibly have survived the battle, and so, instead of having his sagacious dying injunctions overruled by his immediate successor in command, he himself when the contest was decided might have brought his shattered fleet to anchor, a proceeding which might have averted the deplorable loss of life by shipwreck in the elemental tempest that followed the martial one.

Well, should we set aside the more than disputable point whether for various reasons it was possible to anchor the fleet, then plausibly enough the Benthamites of war may urge the above. But the *might-have-been* is but boggy ground to build on. And, certainly, in foresight as to the larger issue of an encounter, and anxious preparations for it—buoying the deadly way and mapping it out, as at Copenhagen—few commanders have been so painstakingly circumspect as this same reckless declarer of his person in fight.

Personal prudence, even when dictated by quite other than selfish considerations, surely is no special virtue in a military man; while an excessive love of glory, impassioning a less burning impulse, the honest sense of duty, is the first. If the name *Wellington* is not so much of a trumpet to the blood as the simpler name *Nelson*, the reason for this may perhaps be inferred from the above. Alfred in his funeral ode on the victor of Waterloo ventures not to call him the greatest soldier of all time, though in the same ode he invokes Nelson as "the greatest sailor since our world began."

At Trafalgar Nelson on the brink of opening the fight sat down and wrote his last brief will and testament. If under the presentiment of the most magnificent of all victories to be crowned by his own glorious death, a sort of priestly motive led him to dress his person in the jewelled vouchers of his own shining deeds; if thus to have adorned himself for the altar and the sacrifice were indeed vainglory, then affectation and fustian is each more heroic line in the great epics and dramas, since in such lines the poet but embodies in verse those exaltations of sentiment that a nature like Nelson, the opportunity being given, vitalizes into acts.

5

YES, the outbreak at the Nore was put down. But not every grievance was redressed. If the contractors, for example, were no longer permitted to ply some practices peculiar to their tribe everywhere, such as providing shoddy cloth, rations not sound, or false in the measure; not the less impressment, for one thing, went on. By custom sanctioned for centuries, and judicially maintained by a Lord Chancellor as late as Mansfield, that mode of manning the fleet, a mode now fallen into a sort of abeyance but never formally renounced, it was not practicable to give up in those years. Its abrogation would have crippled the indispensable fleet, one wholly under canvas, no steam power, its innumerable sails and thousands of cannon, everything in short, worked by muscle alone; a fleet the more insatiate in demand for men, because then multiplying its ships of all grades against contingencies present and to come of the convulsed Continent.

Discontent foreran the Two Mutinies, and more or less it lurkingly survived them. Hence it was not unreasonable to apprehend some return of trouble sporadic or general. One instance of such apprehensions: In the same year with this story, Nelson, then Rear Admiral Sir Horatio, being with the fleet off the Spanish coast, was directed by the admiral in command to shift his pennant from the *Captain* to the *Theseus*; and for this reason: that the latter ship having newly arrived on the station from home, where it had taken part in the Great Mutiny, danger was apprehended from the temper of the men; and it was thought that an officer like Nelson was the one, not indeed to terrorize the crew into base subjection, but to win them, by force of his mere presence and heroic personality, back to an allegiance if not as enthusiastic as his own yet as true.

So it was that for a time, on more than one quarter-deck, anxiety did exist. At sea, precautionary vigilance was strained against relapse. At short notice an engagement might come on. When it did, the lieutenants assigned to batteries felt it incumbent on them, in some instances, to stand with drawn swords behind the men working the guns.

6

B UT ON BOARD the seventy-four in which Billy now swung his hammock, very little in the manner of the men and nothing obvious in the demeanor of the officers would have suggested to an ordinary observer that the Great Mutiny was a recent event. In their general bearing and conduct the commissioned officers of a warship naturally take their tone from the commander, that is if he have that ascendancy of character that ought to be his.

Captain the Honorable Edward Fairfax Vere, to give his

full title, was a bachelor of forty or thereabouts, a sailor of distinction even in a time prolific of renowned seamen. Though allied to the higher nobility, his advancement had not been altogether owing to influences connected with that circumstance. He had seen much service, been in various engagements, always acquitting himself as an officer mindful of the welfare of his men, but never tolerating an infraction of discipline; thoroughly versed in the science of his profession, and intrepid to the verge of temerity, though never injudiciously so. For his gallantry in the West Indian waters as flag lieutenant under Rodney in that admiral's crowning victory over De Grasse, he was made a post captain.

Ashore, in the garb of a civilian, scarce anyone would have taken him for a sailor, more especially that he never garnished unprofessional talk with nautical terms, and grave in his bearing, evinced little appreciation of mere humor. It was not out of keeping with these traits that on a passage when nothing demanded his paramount action, he was the most undemonstrative of men. Any landsman observing this gentleman not conspicuous by his stature and wearing no pronounced insignia, emerging from his cabin to the open deck, and noting the silent deference of the officers retiring to leeward, might have taken him for the King's guest, a civilian aboard the King's ship, some highly honorable discreet envoy on his way to an important post. But in fact this unobtrusiveness of demeanor may have proceeded from a certain unaffected modesty of manhood sometimes accompanying a resolute nature, a modesty evinced at all times not calling for pronounced action, which shown in any rank of life suggests a virtue aristocratic in kind. As with some others engaged in various departments of the world's more heroic activities, Captain Vere though practical enough upon occasion would at times betray a certain dreaminess of mood. Standing alone on the weather side of the quarter-deck, one hand holding by the rigging, he would absently gaze off at the blank sea. At the presentation to him then of some minor matter interrupting the current of his thoughts, he would show more or less irascibility; but instantly he would control it.

In the navy he was popularly known by the appellation "Starry Vere." How such a designation happened to fall upon one who whatever his sterling qualities was without any brilliant ones, was in this wise: A favorite kinsman, Lord Denton, a freehearted fellow, had been the first to meet and congratulate him upon his return to England from his West Indian cruise; and but the day previous turning over a copy of Andrew Marvell's poems had lighted, not for the first time, however, upon the lines entitled "Appleton House," the name of one of the seats of their common ancestor, a hero in the German wars of the seventeenth century, in which poem occur the lines:

> This 'tis to have been from the first
> In a domestic heaven nursed,
> Under the discipline severe
> Of Fairfax and the starry Vere.

And so, upon embracing his cousin fresh from Rodney's great victory wherein he had played so gallant a part, brimming over with just family pride in the sailor of their house, he exuberantly exclaimed, "Give ye joy, Ed; give ye joy, my starry Vere!" This got currency, and the novel prefix serving in familiar parlance readily to distinguish the *Bellipotent*'s captain from another Vere his senior, a distant relative, an officer of like rank in the navy, it remained permanently attached to the surname.

7

IN VIEW of the part that the commander of the *Bellipotent* plays in scenes shortly to follow, it may be well to fill out that sketch of him outlined in the previous chapter.

Aside from his qualities as a sea officer Captain Vere was an exceptional character. Unlike no few of England's renowned sailors, long and arduous service with signal devotion to it had not resulted in absorbing and *salting* the entire man. He had a marked leaning toward everything intellectual. He loved books, never going to sea without a newly replenished library, compact but of the best. The isolated leisure, in some cases so wearisome, falling at intervals to commanders even during a war cruise, never was tedious to Captain Vere. With nothing of that literary taste which less heeds the thing conveyed than the vehicle, his bias was toward those books to which every serious mind of superior order occupying any active post of authority in the world naturally inclines: books treating of actual men and events no matter of what era—history, biography, and unconventional writers like Montaigne, who, free from cant and convention, honestly and in the spirit of common sense philosophize upon realities. In this line of reading he found confirmation of his own more reserved thoughts—confirmation which he had vainly sought in social converse, so that as touching most fundamental topics, there had got to be established in him some positive convictions which he forefelt would abide in him essentially unmodified so long as his intelligent part remained unimpaired. In view of the troubled period in which his lot was cast, this was well for him. His settled convictions were as a dike against those invading waters of novel opinion social, political, and otherwise, which carried away as in a torrent no few minds in those days, minds by nature not inferior to his own. While other members of that aristocracy to which by birth he belonged were incensed at the innovators mainly because their theories were inimical to the privileged classes, Captain Vere disinterestedly opposed them not alone because they seemed to him insusceptible of embodiment in lasting institutions, but at war with the peace of the world and the true welfare of mankind.

With minds less stored than his and less earnest, some officers of his rank, with whom at times he would necessarily consort, found him lacking in the companionable quality, a dry and bookish gentleman, as they deemed. Upon any chance withdrawal from their company one would be apt to say to another something like this: "Vere is a noble fellow, Starry Vere. 'Spite the gazettes, Sir Horatio" (meaning him who became Lord Nelson) "is at bottom scarce a better seaman or fighter. But between you and me now, don't you think there is a queer streak of the pedantic running through him? Yes, like the King's yarn in a coil of navy rope?"

Some apparent ground there was for this sort of confidential criticism; since not only did the captain's discourse never fall into the jocosely familiar, but in illustrating of any point touching the stirring personages and events of the time he would be as apt to cite some historic character or incident of antiquity as he would be to cite from the moderns. He seemed unmindful of the circumstance that to his bluff company such remote allusions, however pertinent they might really be, were altogether alien to men whose reading was mainly confined to the journals. But considerateness in such matters is not easy to natures constituted like Captain Vere's. Their honesty prescribes to them directness, sometimes far-reaching like that of a migratory fowl that in its flight never heeds when it crosses a frontier.

8

THE LIEUTENANTS and other commissioned gentlemen forming Captain Vere's staff it is not necessary here to particularize, nor needs it to make any mention of any of the warrant officers. But among the petty officers was one who, having much to do with the story, may as well be forthwith introduced. His portrait I essay, but shall never hit it. This was John Claggart, the master-at-arms. But that sea title may to landsmen seem somewhat equivocal. Originally, doubtless, that petty officer's function was the instruction of the men in the use of arms, sword or cutlass. But very long ago, owing to the advance in gunnery making hand-to-hand encounters less frequent and giving to niter and sulphur the pre-eminence over steel, that function ceased; the master-at-arms of a great warship becoming a sort of chief of police charged among other matters with the duty of preserving order on the populous lower gun decks.

Claggart was a man about five-and-thirty, somewhat spare and tall, yet of no ill figure upon the whole. His hand was

too small and shapely to have been accustomed to hard toil.
The face was a notable one, the features all except the chin
cleanly cut as those on a Greek medallion; yet the chin, beardless as Tecumseh's, had something of strange protuberant
broadness in its make that recalled the prints of the Reverend
Dr. Titus Oates, the historic deponent with the clerical drawl
in the time of Charles II and the fraud of the alleged Popish
Plot. It served Claggart in his office that his eye could cast a
tutoring glance. His brow was of the sort phrenologically
associated with more than average intellect; silken jet curls
partly clustering over it, making a foil to the pallor below, a
pallor tinged with a faint shade of amber akin to the hue of
time-tinted marbles of old. This complexion, singularly contrasting with the red or deeply bronzed visages of the sailors,
and in part the result of his official seclusion from the sunlight, though it was not exactly displeasing, nevertheless
seemed to hint of something defective or abnormal in the
constitution and blood. But his general aspect and manner
were so suggestive of an education and career incongruous
with his naval function that when not actively engaged in it
he looked like a man of high quality, social and moral, who
for reasons of his own was keeping incog. Nothing was
known of his former life. It might be that he was an Englishman; and yet there lurked a bit of accent in his speech suggesting that possibly he was not such by birth, but through
naturalization in early childhood. Among certain grizzled sea
gossips of the gun decks and forecastle went a rumor perdue
that the master-at-arms was a *chevalier* who had volunteered
into the King's navy by way of compounding for some mysterious swindle whereof he had been arraigned at the King's
Bench. The fact that nobody could substantiate this report
was, of course, nothing against its secret currency. Such a rumor once started on the gun decks in reference to almost anyone below the rank of a commissioned officer would, during
the period assigned to this narrative, have seemed not altogether wanting in credibility to the tarry old wiseacres of a
man-of-war crew. And indeed a man of Claggart's accomplishments, without prior nautical experience entering the
navy at mature life, as he did, and necessarily allotted at the
start to the lowest grade in it; a man too who never made

allusion to his previous life ashore; these were circumstances which in the dearth of exact knowledge as to his true antecedents opened to the invidious a vague field for unfavorable surmise.

But the sailors' dogwatch gossip concerning him derived a vague plausibility from the fact that now for some period the British navy could so little afford to be squeamish in the matter of keeping up the muster rolls, that not only were press gangs notoriously abroad both afloat and ashore, but there was little or no secret about another matter, namely, that the London police were at liberty to capture any able-bodied suspect, any questionable fellow at large, and summarily ship him to the dockyard or fleet. Furthermore, even among voluntary enlistments there were instances where the motive thereto partook neither of patriotic impulse nor yet of a random desire to experience a bit of sea life and martial adventure. Insolvent debtors of minor grade, together with the promiscuous lame ducks of morality, found in the navy a convenient and secure refuge, secure because, once enlisted aboard a King's ship, they were as much in sanctuary as the transgressor of the Middle Ages harboring himself under the shadow of the altar. Such sanctioned irregularities, which for obvious reasons the government would hardly think to parade at the time and which consequently, and as affecting the least influential class of mankind, have all but dropped into oblivion, lend color to something for the truth whereof I do not vouch, and hence have some scruple in stating; something I remember having seen in print though the book I cannot recall; but the same thing was personally communicated to me now more than forty years ago by an old pensioner in a cocked hat with whom I had a most interesting talk on the terrace at Greenwich, a Baltimore Negro, a Trafalgar man. It was to this effect: In the case of a warship short of hands whose speedy sailing was imperative, the deficient quota, in lack of any other way of making it good, would be eked out by drafts culled direct from the jails. For reasons previously suggested it would not perhaps be easy at the present day directly to prove or disprove the allegation. But allowed as a verity, how significant would it be of England's straits at the time confronted by those wars which like a flight of harpies rose shrieking from the din and dust of the fallen Bastille. That era appears measurably clear to us who look back at it, and but read of it. But to the grandfathers of us graybeards, the more thoughtful of them, the genius of it presented an aspect like that of Camoëns' Spirit of the Cape, an eclipsing menace mysterious and prodigious. Not America was exempt from apprehension. At the height of Napoleon's unexampled conquests, there were Americans who had fought at Bunker Hill who looked forward to the possibility that the Atlantic might prove no barrier against the ultimate schemes of this French portentous upstart from the revolutionary chaos who seemed in act of fulfilling judgment prefigured in the Apocalypse.

But the less credence was to be given to the gun-deck talk touching Claggart, seeing that no man holding his office in a man-of-war can ever hope to be popular with the crew. Besides, in derogatory comments upon anyone against whom they have a grudge, or for any reason or no reason mislike, sailors are much like landsmen: they are apt to exaggerate or romance it.

About as much was really known to the *Bellipotent's* tars of the master-at-arms' career before entering the service as an astronomer knows about a comet's travels prior to its first observable appearance in the sky. The verdict of the sea quidnuncs has been cited only by way of showing what sort of moral impression the man made upon rude uncultivated natures whose conceptions of human wickedness were necessarily of the narrowest, limited to ideas of vulgar rascality—a thief among the swinging hammocks during a night watch, or the man-brokers and land-sharks of the seaports.

It was no gossip, however, but fact that though, as before hinted, Claggart upon his entrance into the navy was, as a novice, assigned to the least honorable section of a man-of-war's crew, embracing the drudgery, he did not long remain there. The superior capacity he immediately evinced, his constitutional sobriety, an ingratiating deference to superiors, together with a peculiar ferreting genius manifested on a singular occasion; all this, capped by a certain austere patriotism, abruptly advanced him to the position of master-at-arms.

Of this maritime chief of police the ship's corporals, so called, were the immediate subordinates, and compliant ones; and this, as is to be noted in some business departments ashore, almost to a degree inconsistent with entire moral volition. His place put various converging wires of underground influence under the chief's control, capable when astutely worked through his understrappers of operating to the mysterious discomfort, if nothing worse, of any of the sea commonalty.

9

LIFE IN THE FORETOP well agreed with Billy Budd. There, when not actually engaged on the yards yet higher aloft, the topmen, who as such had been picked out for youth and activity, constituted an aerial club lounging at ease against the smaller stun'sails rolled up into cushions, spinning yarns like the lazy gods, and frequently amused with what was going on in the busy world of the decks below. No wonder then that a young fellow of Billy's disposition was well content in such society. Giving no cause of offense to anybody, he was always alert at a call. So in the merchant service it had been with him. But now such a punctiliousness in duty was shown that his topmates would sometimes good-naturedly laugh at him for it. This heightened alacrity had its cause, namely, the impression made upon him by the first formal gangway-punishment he had ever witnessed, which befell the day following his impressment. It had been incurred by a little fellow, young, a novice afterguardsman absent from his assigned post when the ship was being put about; a dereliction resulting in a rather serious hitch to that maneuver, one demanding instantaneous promptitude in letting go and making fast. When Billy saw the culprit's naked back under the scourge, gridironed with red welts and worse, when he marked the dire expression in the liberated man's face as with his woolen shift flung over him by the executioner he rushed forward from the spot to bury himself in the crowd, Billy was horrified. He resolved that never through remissness would he make himself liable to such a visitation or do or omit aught that might merit even verbal reproof. What then was his surprise and concern when ultimately he found himself getting into petty trouble occasionally about such matters as the stowage of his bag or something amiss in his hammock, matters under the police oversight of the ship's corporals of the lower decks, and which brought down on him a vague threat from one of them.

So heedful in all things as he was, how could this be? He could not understand it, and it more than vexed him. When he spoke to his young topmates about it they were either lightly incredulous or found something comical in his unconcealed anxiety. "Is it your bag, Billy?" said one. "Well, sew yourself up in it, bully boy, and then you'll be sure to know if anybody meddles with it."

Now there was a veteran aboard who because his years began to disqualify him for more active work had been recently assigned duty as mainmastman in his watch, looking to the gear belayed at the rail roundabout that great spar near the deck. At off-times the foretopman had picked up some acquaintance with him, and now in his trouble it occurred to him that he might be the sort of person to go to for wise counsel. He was an old Dansker long anglicized in the service, of few words, many wrinkles, and some honorable scars. His wizened face, time-tinted and weather-stained to the complexion of an antique parchment, was here and there peppered blue by the chance explosion of a gun cartridge in action.

He was an *Agamemnon* man, some two years prior to the time of this story having served under Nelson when still captain in that ship immortal in naval memory, which dismantled and in part broken up to her bare ribs is seen a grand skeleton in Haden's etching. As one of a boarding party from the *Agamemnon* he had received a cut slantwise along one temple and cheek leaving a long pale scar like a streak of dawn's light falling athwart the dark visage. It was on account of that scar and the affair in which it was known that he had received it, as well as from his blue-peppered complexion, that the Dansker went among the *Bellipotent*'s crew by the name of "Board-Her-in-the-Smoke."

Now the first time that his small weasel eyes happened to light on Billy Budd, a certain grim internal merriment set all his ancient wrinkles into antic play. Was it that his eccentric unsentimental old sapience, primitive in its kind, saw or thought it saw something which in contrast with the warship's environment looked oddly incongruous in the Handsome Sailor? But after slyly studying him at intervals, the old Merlin's equivocal merriment was modified; for now when the twain would meet, it would start in his face a quizzing sort of look, but it would be but momentary and sometimes replaced by an expression of speculative query as to what might eventually befall a nature like that, dropped into a world not without some mantraps and against whose subtleties simple courage lacking experience and address, and without any touch of defensive ugliness, is of little avail; and where such innocence as man is capable of does yet in a moral emergency not always sharpen the faculties or enlighten the will.

However it was, the Dansker in his ascetic way rather took to Billy. Nor was this only because of a certain philosophic interest in such a character. There was another cause. While the old man's eccentricities, sometimes bordering on the ursine, repelled the juniors, Billy, undeterred thereby, revering him as a salt hero, would make advances, never passing the old *Agamemnon* man without a salutation marked by that respect which is seldom lost on the aged, however crabbed at times or whatever their station in life.

There was a vein of dry humor, or what not, in the mastman; and, whether in freak of patriarchal irony touching Billy's youth and athletic frame, or for some other and more recondite reason, from the first in addressing him he always substituted *Baby* for Billy, the Dansker in fact being the originator of the name by which the foretopman eventually became known aboard ship.

Well then, in his mysterious little difficulty going in quest of the wrinkled one, Billy found him off duty in a dogwatch ruminating by himself, seated on a shot box of the upper gun deck, now and then surveying with a somewhat cynical regard certain of the more swaggering promenaders there. Billy recounted his trouble, again wondering how it all happened.

The salt seer attentively listened, accompanying the foretopman's recital with queer twitchings of his wrinkles and problematical little sparkles of his small ferret eyes. Making an end of his story, the foretopman asked, "And now, Dansker, do tell me what you think of it."

The old man, shoving up the front of his tarpaulin and deliberately rubbing the long slant scar at the point where it entered the thin hair, laconically said, "Baby Budd, *Jemmy Legs*" (meaning the master-at-arms) "is down on you."

"*Jemmy Legs!*" ejaculated Billy, his welkin eyes expanding. "What for? Why, he calls me 'the sweet and pleasant young fellow,' they tell me."

"Does he so?" grinned the grizzled one; then said, "Ay, Baby lad, a sweet voice has Jemmy Legs."

"No, not always. But to me he has. I seldom pass him but there comes a pleasant word."

"And that's because he's down upon you, Baby Budd."

Such reiteration, along with the manner of it, incomprehensible to a novice, disturbed Billy almost as much as the mystery for which he had sought explanation. Something less unpleasingly oracular he tried to extract; but the old sea Chiron, thinking perhaps that for the nonce he had sufficiently instructed his young Achilles, pursued his lips, gathered all his wrinkles together, and would commit himself to nothing further.

Years, and those experiences which befall certain shrewder men subordinated lifelong to the will of superiors, all this had developed in the Dansker the pithy guarded cynicism that was his leading characteristic.

10

THE NEXT DAY an incident served to confirm Billy Budd in his incredulity as to the Dansker's strange summing up of the case submitted. The ship at noon, going large before the wind, was rolling on her course, and he below at dinner and engaged in some sportful talk with the members of his mess, chanced in a sudden lurch to spill the entire contents of his soup pan upon the new-scrubbed deck. Claggart, the master-at-arms, official rattan in hand, happened to be passing along the battery in a bay of which the mess was lodged, and the greasy liquid streamed just across his path. Stepping over it, he was proceeding on his way without comment, since the matter was nothing to take notice of under the circumstances, when he happened to observe who it was that had done the spilling. His countenance changed. Pausing, he was about to ejaculate something hasty at the sailor, but checked himself, and pointing down to the streaming soup, playfully tapped him from behind with his rattan, saying in a low musical voice peculiar to him at times, "Handsomely done, my lad! And handsome is as handsome did it, too!" And with that passed on. Not noted by Billy as not coming within his view was the involuntary smile, or rather grimace, that accompanied Claggart's equivocal words. Aridly it drew down the thin corners of his shapely mouth. But everybody taking his remark as meant for humorous, and at which therefore as coming from a superior they were bound to laugh " with counterfeited glee," acted accordingly; and Billy, tickled, it may be, by the allusion to his being the Handsome Sailor, merrily joined in; then addressing his messmates exclaimed, "There now, who says that Jemmy Legs is down on me!"

"And who said he was, Beauty?" demanded one Donald with some surprise. Whereat the foretopman looked a little foolish, recalling that it was only one person, Board-Her-in-the-Smoke, who had suggested what to him was the smoky idea that this master-at-arms was in any peculiar way hostile to him. Meantime that functionary, resuming his path, must have momentarily worn some expression less guarded than that of the bitter smile, usurping the face from the heart—some distorting expression perhaps, for a drummer-boy heedlessly frolicking along from the opposite direction and chancing to come into light collision with his person was strangely disconcerted by his aspect. Nor was the impression lessened when the official, impetuously giving him a sharp cut with the rattan, vehemently exclaimed, "Look where you go!"

11

WHAT WAS the matter with the master-at-arms? And, be the matter what it might, how could it have direct relation to Billy Budd, with whom prior to the affair of the spilled soup he had never come into any special contact official or otherwise? What indeed could the trouble have to do with one so little inclined to give offense as the merchant-ship's "peacemaker," even him who in Claggart's own phrase was "the sweet and pleasant young fellow"? Yes, why should Jemmy Legs, to borrow the Dansker's expression, be "down" on the Handsome Sailor? But, at heart and not for nothing, as the late chance encounter may indicate to the discerning, down on him, secretly down on him, he assuredly was.

Now to invent something touching the more private career of Claggart, something involving Billy Budd, of which something the latter should be wholly ignorant, some romantic incident implying that Claggart's knowledge of the young bluejacket began at some period anterior to catching sight of him on board the seventy-four—all this, not so difficult to do, might avail in a way more or less interesting to account for whatever of enigma may appear to lurk in the case. But in fact there was nothing of the sort. And yet the cause necessarily to be assumed as the sole one assignable is in its very realism as much charged with that prime element of Radcliffian romance, the mysterious, as any that the ingenuity of the author of *The Mysteries of Udolpho* could devise. For what can more partake of the mysterious than an antipathy spontaneous and profound such as is evoked in certain exceptional mortals by the mere aspect of some other mortal, however harmless he may be, if not called forth by this very harmlessness itself?

Now there can exist no irritating juxtaposition of dissimilar personalities comparable to that which is possible aboard a great warship fully manned and at sea. There, every day among all ranks, almost every man comes into more or less of contact with almost every other man. Wholly there to avoid even the sight of an aggravating object one must needs give it Jonah's toss or jump overboard himself. Imagine how all this might eventually operate on some peculiar human creature the direct reverse of a saint!

But for the adequate comprehending of Claggart by a normal nature these hints are insufficient. To pass from a normal nature to him one must cross "the deadly space between." And this is best done by indirection.

Long ago an honest scholar, my senior, said to me in reference to one who like himself is now no more, a man so unimpeachably respectable that against him nothing was ever openly said though among the few something was whispered, "Yes, X—— is a nut not to be cracked by the tap of a lady's fan. You are aware that I am the adherent of no organized religion, much less of any philosophy built into a system. Well, for all that, I think that to try and get into X——, enter his labyrinth and get out again, without a clue derived from some source other than what is known as 'knowledge of the world'—that were hardly possible, at least for me."

"Why," said I, "X——, however singular a study to some, is yet human, and knowledge of the world assuredly implies the knowledge of human nature, and in most of its varieties."

"Yes, but a superficial knowledge of it, serving ordinary purposes. But for anything deeper, I am not certain whether to know the world and to know human nature be not two distinct branches of knowledge, which while they may coexist in the same heart, yet either may exist with little or nothing of the other. Nay, in an average man of the world, his constant rubbing with it blunts that finer spiritual insight indispensable to the understanding of the essential in certain exceptional characters, whether evil ones or good. In a matter of some importance I have seen a girl wind an old lawyer about her little finger. Nor was it the dotage of senile love. Nothing of the sort. But he knew law better than he knew the girl's heart. Coke and Blackstone hardly shed so much light into obscure spiritual places as the Hebrew prophets. And who were they? Mostly recluses."

At the time, my inexperience was such that I did not quite see the drift of all this. It may be that I see it now. And, indeed, if that lexicon which is based on Holy Writ were any longer popular, one might with less difficulty define and denominate certain phenomenal men. As it is, one must turn to some authority not liable to the charge of being tinctured with the biblical element.

In a list of definitions included in the authentic translation of Plato, a list attributed to him, occurs this: "Natural Depravity: a depravity according to nature," a definition which, though savoring of Calvinism, by no means involves Calvin's dogma as to total mankind. Evidently its intent makes it applicable but to individuals. Not many are the examples of this depravity which the gallows and jail supply. At any rate, for notable instances, since these have no vulgar alloy of the brute in them, but invariably are dominated by intellectuality, one must go elsewhere. Civilization, especially if of the austerer sort, is auspicious to it. It folds itself in the mantle of respectability. It has its certain negative virtues serving as silent auxiliaries. It never allows wine to get within its guard. It is not going too far to say that it is without vices or small sins. There is a phenomenal pride in it that excludes them. It is never mercenary or avaricious. In short, the depravity here meant partakes nothing of the sordid or sensual. It is serious, but free from acerbity. Though no flatterer of mankind it never speaks ill of it.

But the thing which in eminent instances signalizes so exceptional a nature is this: Though the man's even temper and discreet bearing would seem to intimate a mind peculiarly subject to the law of reason, not the less in heart he would seem to riot in complete exemption from that law, having apparently little to do with reason further than to employ it as an ambidexter implement for effecting the irrational. That is to say: Toward the accomplishment of an aim which in wantonness of atrocity would seem to partake of the insane, he will direct a cool judgment sagacious and sound. These men are madmen, and of the most dangerous sort, for their lunacy is not continuous, but occasional, evoked by some special object; it is protectively secretive, which is as much as to say it is self-contained, so that when, moreover, most active it is to the average mind not distinguishable from sanity, and for the reason above suggested: that whatever its aims may be—and the aim is never declared—the method and the outward proceeding are always perfectly rational.

Now something such an one was Claggart, in whom was

the mania of an evil nature, not engendered by vicious training or corrupting books or licentious living, but born with
him and innate, in short "a depravity according to nature."

Dark sayings are these, some will say. But why? Is it because they somewhat savor of Holy Writ in its phrase "mystery of iniquity"? If they do, such savor was far enough from
being intended, for little will it commend these pages to many
a reader of today.

The point of the present story turning on the hidden nature
of the master-at-arms has necessitated this chapter. With an
added hint or two in connection with the incident at the
mess, the resumed narrative must be left to vindicate, as it
may, its own credibility.

1 2

THAT CLAGGART'S FIGURE was not amiss, and his face,
save the chin, well molded, has already been said. Of
these favorable points he seemed not insensible, for he was
not only neat but careful in his dress. But the form of Billy
Budd was heroic; and if his face was without the intellectual
look of the pallid Claggart's, not the less was it lit, like his,
from within, though from a different source. The bonfire in
his heart made luminous the rose-tan in his cheek.

In view of the marked contrast between the persons of the
twain, it is more than probable that when the master-at-arms
in the scene last given applied to the sailor the proverb
"Handsome is as handsome does," he there let escape an
ironic inkling, not caught by the young sailors who heard it,
as to what it was that had first moved him against Billy,
namely, his significant personal beauty.

Now envy and antipathy, passions irreconcilable in reason,
nevertheless in fact may spring conjoined like Chang and Eng
in one birth. Is Envy then such a monster? Well, though many
an arraigned mortal has in hopes of mitigated penalty pleaded
guilty to horrible actions, did ever anybody seriously confess
to envy? Something there is in it universally felt to be more

shameful than even felonious crime. And not only does everybody disown it, but the better sort are inclined to incredulity when it is in earnest imputed to an intelligent man. But since its lodgment is in the heart not the brain, no degree of intellect supplies a guarantee against it. But Claggart's was no vulgar form of the passion. Nor, as directed toward Billy Budd, did it partake of that streak of apprehensive jealousy that marred Saul's visage perturbedly brooding on the comely young David. Claggart's envy struck deeper. If askance he eyed the good looks, cheery health, and frank enjoyment of young life in Billy Budd, it was because these went along with a nature that, as Claggart magnetically felt, had in its simplicity never willed malice or experienced the reactionary bite of that serpent. To him, the spirit lodged within Billy, and looking out from his welkin eyes as from windows, that ineffability it was which made the dimple in his dyed cheek, suppled his joints, and dancing in his yellow curls made him pre-eminently the Handsome Sailor. One person excepted, the master-at-arms was perhaps the only man in the ship intellectually capable of adequately appreciating the moral phenomenon presented in Billy Budd. And the insight but intensified his passion, which assuming various secret forms within him, at times assumed that of cynic disdain, disdain of innocence— to be nothing more than innocent! Yet in an aesthetic way he saw the charm of it, the courageous free-and-easy temper of it, and fain would have shared it, but he despaired of it.

With no power to annul the elemental evil in him, though readily enough he could hide it; apprehending the good, but powerless to be it; a nature like Claggart's, surcharged with energy as such natures almost invariably are, what recourse is left to it but to recoil upon itself and, like the scorpion for which the Creator alone is responsible, act out to the end the part allotted it.

13

PASSION, and passion in its profoundest, is not a thing demanding a palatial stage whereon to play its part.

Down among the groundlings, among the beggars and rakers of the garbage, profound passion is enacted. And the circumstances that provoke it, however trivial or mean, are no measure of its power. In the present instance the stage is a scrubbed gun deck, and one of the external provocations a man-of-war's man's spilled soup.

Now when the master-at-arms noticed whence came that greasy fluid streaming before his feet, he must have taken it—to some extent wilfully, perhaps—not for the mere accident it assuredly was, but for the sly escape of a spontaneous feeling on Billy's part more or less answering to the antipathy on his own. In effect a foolish demonstration, he must have thought, and very harmless, like the futile kick of a heifer, which yet were the heifer a shod stallion would not be so harmless. Even so was it that into the gall of Claggart's envy he infused the vitriol of his contempt. But the incident confirmed to him certain telltale reports purveyed to his ear by "Squeak," one of his more cunning corporals, a grizzled little man, so nicknamed by the sailors on account of his squeaky voice and sharp visage ferreting about the dark corners of the lower decks after interlopers, satirically suggesting to them the idea of a rat in a cellar.

From his chief's employing him as an implicit tool in laying little traps for the worriment of the foretopman—for it was from the master-at-arms that the petty persecutions heretofore adverted to had proceeded—the corporal, having naturally enough concluded that his master could have no love for the sailor, made it his business, faithful understrapper that he was, to foment the ill blood by perverting to his chief certain innocent frolics of the good-natured foretopman, besides inventing for his mouth sundry contumelious epithets he claimed to have overheard him let fall. The master-at-arms never suspected the veracity of these reports, more especially as to the epithets, for he well knew how secretly unpopular may become a master-at-arms, at least a master-at-arms of those days, zealous in his function, and how the bluejackets shoot at him in private their raillery and wit; the nickname by which he goes among them (Jemmy Legs) implying under the form of merriment their cherished disrespect and dislike. But in view of the greediness of hate for pabulum it hardly needed a purveyor to feed Claggart's passion.

An uncommon prudence is habitual with the subtler depravity, for it has everything to hide. And in case of an injury but suspected, its secretiveness voluntarily cuts it off from enlightenment or disillusion; and, not unreluctantly, action is taken upon surmise as upon certainty. And the retaliation is apt to be in monstrous disproportion to the supposed offense; for when in anybody was revenge in its exactions aught else but an inordinate usurer? But how with Claggart's conscience? For though consciences are unlike as foreheads, every intelligence, not excluding the scriptural devils who "believe and tremble," has one. But Claggart's conscience being but the lawyer to his will, made ogres of trifles, probably arguing that the motive imputed to Billy in spilling the soup just when he did, together with the epithets alleged, these, if nothing more, made a strong case against him; nay, justified animosity into a sort of retributive righteousness. The Pharisee is the Guy Fawkes prowling in the hid chambers underlying some natures like Claggart's. And they can really form no conception of an unreciprocated malice. Probably the master-at-arms' clandestine persecution of Billy was started to try the temper of the man; but it had not developed any quality in him that enmity could make official use of or even pervert into plausible self-justification; so that the occurrence at the mess, petty if it were, was a welcome one to that peculiar conscience assigned to be the private mentor of Claggart; and, for the rest, not improbably it put him upon new experiments.

14

NOT MANY DAYS after the last incident narrated, something befell Billy Budd that more graveled him than aught that had previously occurred.

It was a warm night for the latitude; and the foretopman, whose watch at the time was properly below, was dozing on the uppermost deck whither he had ascended from his hot hammock, one of hundreds suspended so closely wedged together over a lower gun deck that there was little or no swing to them. He lay as in the shadow of a hillside, stretched under the lee of the booms, a piled ridge of spare spars amidships between foremast and mainmast among which the ship's largest boat, the launch, was stowed. Alongside of three other slumberers from below, he lay near that end of the booms which approaches the foremast; his station aloft on duty as a foretopman being just over the deck-station of the forecastlemen, entitling him according to usage to make himself more or less at home in that neighborhood.

Presently he was stirred into semiconsciousness by somebody, who must have previously sounded the sleep of the others, touching his shoulder, and then, as the foretopman raised his head, breathing into his ear in a quick whisper, "Slip into the lee forechains, Billy; there is something in the wind. Don't speak. Quick, I will meet you there," and disappearing.

Now Billy, like sundry other essentially good-natured ones, had some of the weaknesses inseparable from essential good nature; and among these was a reluctance, almost an incapacity of plumply saying *no* to an abrupt proposition not obviously absurd on the face of it, nor obviously unfriendly, nor iniquitous. And being of warm blood, he had not the phlegm tacitly to negative any proposition by unresponsive inaction. Like his sense of fear, his apprehension as to aught outside of the honest and natural was seldom very quick. Besides, upon the present occasion, the drowse from his sleep still hung upon him.

However it was, he mechanically rose and, sleepily wondering what could be in the wind, betook himself to the designated place, a narrow platform, one of six, outside of the high bulwarks and screened by the great deadeyes and multiple columned lanyards of the shrouds and backstays; and, in a great warship of that time, of dimensions commensurate to the hull's magnitude; a tarry balcony in short, overhanging the sea, and so secluded that one mariner of the *Bellipotent*, a Nonconformist old tar of a serious turn, made it even in daytime his private oratory.

In this retired nook the stranger soon joined Billy Budd. There was no moon as yet; a haze obscured the starlight. He could not distinctly see the stranger's face. Yet from something in the outline and carriage, Billy took him, and correctly, for one of the afterguard.

"Hist! Billy," said the man, in the same quick cautionary whisper as before. "You were impressed, weren't you? Well, so was I"; and he paused, as to mark the effect. But Billy, not knowing exactly what to make of this, said nothing. Then the other: "We are not the only impressed ones, Billy. There's a gang of us.—Couldn't you—help—at a pinch?"

"What do you mean?" demanded Billy, here thoroughly shaking off his drowse.

"Hist, hist!" the hurried whisper now growing husky. "See here," and the man held up two small objects faintly twinkling in the night-light; "see, they are yours, Billy, if you'll only——"

But Billy broke in, and in his resentful eagerness to deliver himself his vocal infirmity somewhat intruded. "D—d—damme, I don't know what you are d—d—driving at, or what you mean, but you had better g—g—go where you belong!" For the moment the fellow, as confounded, did not stir; and Billy, springing to his feet, said, "If you d—don't start, I'll t—t—toss you back over the r—rail!" There was no mistaking this, and the mysterious emissary decamped, disappearing in the direction of the mainmast in the shadow of the booms.

"Hallo, what's the matter?" here came growling from a forecastleman awakened from his deck-doze by Billy's raised voice. And as the foretopman reappeared and was recognized by him: "Ah, Beauty, is it you? Well, something must have been the matter, for you st—st—stuttered."

"Oh," rejoined Billy, now mastering the impediment, "I found an afterguardsman in our part of the ship here, and I bid him be off where he belongs."

"And is that all you did about it, Foretopman?" gruffly demanded another, an irascible old fellow of brick-colored visage and hair who was known to his associate forecastlemen as "Red Pepper." "Such sneaks I should like to marry to the gunner's daughter!"—by that expression meaning that he would like to subject them to disciplinary castigation over a gun.

However, Billy's rendering of the matter satisfactorily accounted to these inquirers for the brief commotion, since of all the sections of a ship's company the forecastlemen, veterans for the most part and bigoted in their sea prejudices, are the most jealous in resenting territorial encroachments, especially on the part of any of the afterguard, of whom they have but a sorry opinion—chiefly landsmen, never going aloft except to reef or furl the mainsail, and in no wise competent to handle a marlinspike or turn in a deadeye, say.

15

THIS INCIDENT sorely puzzled Billy Budd. It was an entirely new experience, the first time in his life that he had ever been personally approached in underhand intriguing fashion. Prior to this encounter he had known nothing of the afterguardsman, the two men being stationed wide apart, one forward and aloft during his watch, the other on deck and aft.

What could it mean? And could they really be guineas, those two glittering objects the interloper had held up to his (Billy's) eyes? Where could the fellow get guineas? Why, even spare buttons are not so plentiful at sea. The more he turned the matter over, the more he was nonplussed, and made uneasy and discomfited. In his disgustful recoil from an overture which, though he but ill comprehended, he instinctively knew must involve evil of some sort, Billy Budd was like a young horse fresh from the pasture suddenly inhaling a vile whiff from some chemical factory, and by repeated snortings trying to get it out of his nostrils and lungs. This frame of mind barred all desire of holding further parley with the fellow, even were it but for the purpose of gaining some enlightenment as to his design in approaching him. And yet he was not without natural curiosity to see how such a visitor in the dark would look in broad day.

He espied him the following afternoon in his first dog-watch below, one of the smokers on that forward part of the upper gun deck allotted to the pipe. He recognized him by his general cut and build more than by his round freckled face and glassy eyes of pale blue, veiled with lashes all but white. And yet Billy was a bit uncertain whether indeed it were he— yonder chap about his own age chatting and laughing in free-hearted way, leaning against a gun; a genial young fellow enough to look at, and something of a rattlebrain, to all appearance. Rather chubby too for a sailor, even an after-guardsman. In short, the last man in the world, one would think, to be overburdened with thoughts, especially those perilous thoughts that must needs belong to a conspirator in any serious project, or even to the underlying of such a conspirator.

Although Billy was not aware of it, the fellow, with a side-long watchful glance, had perceived Billy first, and then noting that Billy was looking at him, thereupon nodded a familiar sort of friendly recognition as to an old acquaintance, without interrupting the talk he was engaged in with the group of smokers. A day or two afterwards, chancing in the evening promenade on a gun deck to pass Billy, he offered a flying word of good-fellowship, as it were, which by its un-expectedness, and equivocalness under the circumstances, so embarrassed Billy that he knew not how to respond to it, and let it go unnoticed.

Billy was now left more at a loss than before. The ineffec-tual speculations into which he was led were so disturbingly alien to him that he did his best to smother them. It never entered his mind that here was a matter which, from its ex-treme questionableness, it was his duty as a loyal bluejacket to report in the proper quarter. And, probably, had such a step been suggested to him, he would have been deterred from taking it by the thought, one of novice magnanimity, that it would savor overmuch of the dirty work of a telltale. He kept the thing to himself. Yet upon one occasion he could not forbear a little disburdening himself to the old Dansker, tempted thereto perhaps by the influence of a balmy night when the ship lay becalmed; the twain, silent for the most part, sitting together on deck, their heads propped against the bulwarks. But it was only a partial and anonymous account that Billy gave, the unfounded scruples above referred to preventing full disclosure to anybody. Upon hearing Billy's version, the sage Dansker seemed to divine more than he was told; and after a little meditation, during which his wrinkles were pursed as into a point, quite effacing for the time that quizzing expression his face sometimes wore: "Didn't I say so, Baby Budd?"

"Say what?" demanded Billy.

"Why, *Jemmy Legs* is *down* on you."

"And what," rejoined Billy in amazement, "has *Jemmy Legs* to do with that cracked afterguardsman?"

"Ho, it was an afterguardsman, then. A cat's-paw, a cat's-paw!" And with that exclamation, whether it had reference to a light puff of air just then coming over the calm sea, or a subtler relation to the afterguardsman, there is no telling, the old Merlin gave a twisting wrench with his black teeth at his plug of tobacco, vouchsafing no reply to Billy's impetuous question, though now repeated, for it was his wont to relapse into grim silence when interrogated in skeptical sort as to any of his sententious oracles, not always very clear ones, rather partaking of that obscurity which invests most Delphic deliverances from any quarter.

Long experience had very likely brought this old man to that bitter prudence which never interferes in aught and never gives advice.

16

YES, despite the Dansker's pithy insistence as to the master-at-arms being at the bottom of these strange experiences of Billy on board the *Bellipotent*, the young sailor was ready to ascribe them to almost anybody but the man who, to use Billy's own expression, "always had a pleasant word for him." This is to be wondered at. Yet not so much to be wondered at. In certain matters, some sailors even in mature life remain unsophisticated enough. But a young seafarer of the disposition of our athletic foretopman is much of a child-man. And yet a child's utter innocence is but its blank ignorance, and the innocence more or less wanes as intelligence waxes. But in Billy Budd intelligence, such as it was, had advanced while yet his simple-mindedness remained for the most part unaffected. Experience is a teacher indeed; yet did Billy's years make his experience small. Besides, he had none of that intuitive knowledge of the bad which in natures not good or incompletely so foreruns experience, and therefore may pertain, as in some instances it too clearly does pertain, even to youth.

And what could Billy know of man except of man as a mere sailor? And the old-fashioned sailor, the veritable man before the mast, the sailor from boyhood up, he, though indeed of the same species as a landsman, is in some respects singularly distinct from him. The sailor is frankness, the landsman is finesse. Life is not a game with the sailor, demanding the long head—no intricate game of chess where few moves are made in straightforwardness and ends are attained by indirection, an oblique, tedious, barren game hardly worth that poor candle burnt out in playing it.

Yes, as a class, sailors are in character a juvenile race. Even their deviations are marked by juvenility, this more especially holding true with the sailors of Billy's time. Then too, certain things which apply to all sailors do more pointedly operate here and there upon the junior one. Every sailor, too, is accustomed to obey orders without debating them; his life afloat is externally ruled for him; he is not brought into that promiscuous commerce with mankind where unobstructed free agency on equal terms—equal superficially, at least—soon teaches one that unless upon occasion he exercise a distrust keen in proportion to the fairness of the appearance, some foul turn may be served him. A ruled undemonstrative distrustfulness is so habitual, not with businessmen so much as with men who know their kind in less shallow relations than business, namely, certain men of the world, that they come at last to employ it all but unconsciously; and some of them would very likely feel real surprise at being charged with it as one of their general characteristics.

17

B
UT AFTER the little matter at the mess Billy Budd no
more found himself in strange trouble at times about his
hammock or his clothes bag or what not. As to that smile
that occasionally sunned him, and the pleasant passing word,
these were, if not more frequent, yet if anything more pronounced than before.

But for all that, there were certain other demonstrations
now. When Claggart's unobserved glance happened to light
on belted Billy rolling along the upper gun deck in the leisure
of the second dogwatch, exchanging passing broadsides of
fun with other young promenaders in the crowd, that glance
would follow the cheerful sea Hyperion with a settled meditative and melancholy expression, his eyes strangely suffused
with incipient feverish tears. Then would Claggart look like
the man of sorrows. Yes, and sometimes the melancholy
expression would have in it a touch of soft yearning, as if
Claggart could even have loved Billy but for fate and ban. But
this was an evanescence, and quickly repented of, as it were,
by an immitigable look, pinching and shriveling the visage
into the momentary semblance of a wrinkled walnut. But
sometimes catching sight in advance of the foretopman coming in his direction, he would, upon their nearing, step aside
a little to let him pass, dwelling upon Billy for the moment
with the glittering dental satire of a Guise. But upon any
abrupt unforeseen encounter a red light would flash forth
from his eye like a spark from an anvil in a dusk smithy. That
quick, fierce light was a strange one, darted from orbs which
in repose were of a color nearest approaching a deeper violet,
the softest of shades.

Though some of these caprices of the pit could not but be
observed by their object, yet were they beyond the construing
of such a nature. And the thews of Billy were hardly compatible with that sort of sensitive spiritual organization which in
some cases instinctively conveys to ignorant innocence an admonition of the proximity of the malign. He thought the
master-at-arms acted in a manner rather queer at times. That
was all. But the occasional frank air and pleasant word went

for what they purported to be, the young sailor never having heard as yet of the "too fair-spoken man."

Had the foretopman been conscious of having done or said anything to provoke the ill will of the official, it would have been different with him, and his sight might have been purged if not sharpened. As it was, innocence was his blinder.

So was it with him in yet another matter. Two minor officers, the armorer and captain of the hold, with whom he had never exchanged a word, his position in the ship not bringing him into contact with them, these men now for the first began to cast upon Billy, when they chanced to encounter him, that peculiar glance which evidences that the man from whom it comes has been some way tampered with, and to the prejudice of him upon whom the glance lights. Never did it occur to Billy as a thing to be noted or a thing suspicious, though he well knew the fact, that the armorer and captain of the hold, with the ship's yeoman, apothecary, and others of that grade, were by naval usage messmates of the master-at-arms, men with ears convenient to his confidential tongue.

But the general popularity that came from our Handsome Sailor's manly forwardness upon occasion and irresistible good nature, indicating no mental superiority tending to excite an invidious feeling, this good will on the part of most of his shipmates made him the less to concern himself about such mute aspects toward him as those whereto allusion has just been made, aspects he could not so fathom as to infer their whole import.

As to the afterguardsman, though Billy for reasons already given necessarily saw little of him, yet when the two did happen to meet, invariably came the fellow's offhand cheerful recognition, sometimes accompanied by a passing pleasant word or two. Whatever that equivocal young person's original design may really have been, or the design of which he might have been the deputy, certain it was from his manner upon these occasions that he had wholly dropped it.

It was as if his precocity of crookedness (and every vulgar villain is precocious) had for once deceived him, and the man he had sought to entrap as a simpleton had through his very simplicity ignominiously baffled him.

But shrewd ones may opine that it was hardly possible for

Billy to refrain from going up to the afterguardsman and bluntly demanding to know his purpose in the initial interview so abruptly closed in the forechains. Shrewd ones may also think it but natural in Billy to set about sounding some of the other impressed men of the ship in order to discover what basis, if any, there was for the emissary's obscure suggestions as to plotting disaffection aboard. Yes, shrewd ones may so think. But something more, or rather something else than mere shrewdness is perhaps needful for the due understanding of such a character as Billy Budd's.

As to Claggart, the monomania in the man—if that indeed it were—as involuntarily disclosed by starts in the manifestations detailed, yet in general covered over by his self-contained and rational demeanor; this, like a subterranean fire, was eating its way deeper and deeper in him. Something decisive must come of it.

18

AFTER THE mysterious interview in the forechains, the one so abruptly ended there by Billy, nothing especially germane to the story occurred until the events now about to be narrated.

Elsewhere it has been said that in the lack of frigates (of course better sailers than line-of-battle ships) in the English squadron up the Straits at that period, the *Bellipotent 74* was occasionally employed not only as an available substitute for a scout, but at times on detached service of more important kind. This was not alone because of her sailing qualities, not common in a ship of her rate, but quite as much, probably, that the character of her commander, it was thought, specially adapted him for any duty where under unforeseen difficulties a prompt initiative might have to be taken in some matter demanding knowledge and ability in addition to those qualities implied in good seamanship. It was on an expedition of the latter sort, a somewhat distant one, and when the *Bellipotent* was almost at her furthest remove from the fleet, that in the latter part of an afternoon watch she unexpectedly came in sight of a ship of the enemy. It proved to be a frigate. The latter, perceiving through the glass that the weight of men and metal would be heavily against her, invoking her light heels crowded sail to get away. After a chase urged almost against hope and lasting until about the middle of the first dogwatch, she signally succeeded in effecting her escape.

Not long after the pursuit had been given up, and ere the excitement incident thereto had altogether waned away, the master-at-arms, ascending from his cavernous sphere, made his appearance cap in hand by the mainmast respectfully waiting the notice of Captain Vere, then solitary walking the weather side of the quarter-deck, doubtless somewhat chafed at the failure of the pursuit. The spot where Claggart stood was the place allotted to men of lesser grades seeking some more particular interview either with the officer of the deck or the captain himself. But from the latter it was not often that a sailor or petty officer of those days would seek a hearing; only some exceptional cause would, according to established custom, have warranted that.

Presently, just as the commander, absorbed in his reflections, was on the point of turning aft in his promenade, he became sensible of Claggart's presence, and saw the doffed cap held in deferential expectancy. Here be it said that Captain Vere's personal knowledge of this petty officer had only begun at the time of the ship's last sailing from home, Claggart then for the first, in transfer from a ship detained for repairs, supplying on board the *Bellipotent* the place of a previous master-at-arms disabled and ashore.

No sooner did the commander observe who it was that now deferentially stood awaiting his notice than a peculiar expression came over him. It was not unlike that which uncontrollably will flit across the countenance of one at unawares encountering a person who, though known to him indeed, has hardly been long enough known for thorough knowledge, but something in whose aspect nevertheless now for the first provokes a vaguely repellent distaste. But coming to a stand and resuming much of his wonted official manner, save that a sort of impatience lurked in the intonation of the opening word, he said "Well? What is it, Master-at-arms?"

With the air of a subordinate grieved at the necessity of being a messenger of ill tidings, and while conscientiously determined to be frank yet equally resolved upon shunning overstatement, Claggart at this invitation, or rather summons to disburden, spoke up. What he said, conveyed in the language of no uneducated man, was to the effect following, if not altogether in these words, namely, that during the chase and preparations for the possible encounter he had seen enough to convince him that at least one sailor aboard was a dangerous character in a ship mustering some who not only had taken a guilty part in the late serious troubles, but others also who, like the man in question, had entered His Majesty's service under another form than enlistment.

At this point Captain Vere with some impatience interrupted him: "Be direct, man; say *impressed men*."

Claggart made a gesture of subservience, and proceeded. Quite lately he (Claggart) had begun to suspect that on the gun decks some sort of movement prompted by the sailor in question was covertly going on, but he had not thought himself warranted in reporting the suspicion so long as it remained indistinct. But from what he had that afternoon observed in the man referred to, the suspicion of something clandestine going on had advanced to a point less removed from certainty. He deeply felt, he added, the serious responsibility assumed in making a report involving such possible consequences to the individual mainly concerned, besides tending to augment those natural anxieties which every naval commander must feel in view of extraordinary outbreaks so recent as those which, he sorrowfully said it, it needed not to name.

Now at the first broaching of the matter Captain Vere, taken by surprise, could not wholly dissemble his disquietude. But as Claggart went on, the former's aspect changed into restiveness under something in the testifier's manner in giving his testimony. However, he refrained from interrupting him. And Claggart, continuing, concluded with this: "God forbid, your honor, that the *Bellipotent*'s should be the experience of the ——"

"Never mind that!" here peremptorily broke in the superior, his face altering with anger, instinctively divining the ship that the other was about to name, one in which the Nore Mutiny had assumed a singularly tragical character that for a time jeopardized the life of its commander. Under the circumstances he was indignant at the purposed allusion. When the commissioned officers themselves were on all occasions very heedful how they referred to the recent events in the fleet, for a petty officer unnecessarily to allude to them in the presence of his captain, this struck him as a most immodest presumption. Besides, to his quick sense of self-respect it even looked under the circumstances something like an attempt to alarm him. Nor at first was he without some surprise that one who so far as he had hitherto come under his notice had shown considerable tact in his function should in this particular evince such lack of it.

But these thoughts and kindred dubious ones flitting across his mind were suddenly replaced by an intuitional surmise which, though as yet obscure in form, served practically to affect his reception of the ill tidings. Certain it is that, long versed in everything pertaining to the complicated gun-deck life, which like every other form of life has its secret mines and dubious side, the side popularly disclaimed, Captain Vere did not permit himself to be unduly disturbed by the general tenor of his subordinate's report.

Furthermore, if in view of recent events prompt action should be taken at the first palpable sign of recurring insubordination, for all that, not judicious would it be, he thought, to keep the idea of lingering disaffection alive by undue forwardness in crediting an informer, even if his own subordinate and charged among other things with police surveillance of the crew. This feeling would not perhaps have so prevailed with him were it not that upon a prior occasion the patriotic zeal officially evinced by Claggart had somewhat irritated him as appearing rather supersensible and strained. Furthermore, something even in the official's self-possessed and somewhat ostentatious manner in making his specifications strangely reminded him of a bandsman, a perjurous witness in a capital case before a court-martial ashore of which when a lieutenant he (Captain Vere) had been a member.

Now the peremptory check given to Claggart in the matter of the arrested allusion was quickly followed up by this: "You say that there is at least one dangerous man aboard. Name him."

"William Budd, a foretopman, your honor."

"William Budd!" repeated Captain Vere with unfeigned astonishment. "And mean you the man that Lieutenant Ratcliffe took from the merchantman not very long ago, the young fellow who seems to be so popular with the men— Billy, the Handsome Sailor, as they call him?"

"The same, your honor; but for all his youth and good looks, a deep one. Not for nothing does he insinuate himself into the good will of his shipmates, since at the least they will at a pinch say—all hands will—a good word for him, and at all hazards. Did Lieutenant Ratcliffe happen to tell your honor of that adroit fling of Budd's, jumping up in the cutter's bow under the merchantman's stern when he was being taken off? It is even masked by that sort of good-humored air that at heart he resents his impressment. You have but noted his fair cheek. A mantrap may be under the ruddy-tipped daisies."

Now the Handsome Sailor as a signal figure among the crew had naturally enough attracted the captain's attention from the first. Though in general not very demonstrative to his officers, he had congratulated Lieutenant Ratcliffe upon his good fortune in lighting on such a fine specimen of the *genus homo*, who in the nude might have posed for a statue of young Adam before the Fall. As to Billy's adieu to the ship *Rights-of-Man*, which the boarding lieutenant had indeed reported to him, but, in a deferential way, more as a good story than aught else, Captain Vere, though mistakenly understanding it as a satiric sally, had but thought so much the better of the impressed man for it; as a military sailor, admiring the spirit that could take an arbitrary enlistment so merrily and sensibly. The foretopman's conduct, too, so far as it had fallen under the captain's notice, had confirmed the first happy augury, while the new recruit's qualities as a "sailor-man" seemed to be such that he had thought of recommending him to the executive officer for promotion to a place that would more frequently bring him under his own observation, namely, the captaincy of the mizzentop, replacing there in the starboard watch a man not so young whom partly for that reason he deemed less fitted for the post. Be it parenthesized here that since the mizzentopmen have not to handle such breadths of heavy canvas as the lower sails on the mainmast and foremast, a young man if of the right stuff not only seems best adapted to duty there, but in fact is generally selected for the captaincy of that top, and the company under him are light hands and often but striplings. In sum, Captain Vere had from the beginning deemed Billy Budd to be what in the naval parlance of the time was called a "King's bargain": that is to say, for His Britannic Majesty's navy a capital investment at small outlay or none at all.

After a brief pause, during which the reminiscences above mentioned passed vividly through his mind and he weighed the import of Claggart's last suggestion conveyed in the phrase "mantrap under the daisies," and the more he weighed it the less reliance he felt in the informer's good faith, suddenly he turned upon him and in a low voice demanded: "Do you come to me, Master-at-arms, with so foggy a tale? As to Budd, cite me an act or spoken word of his confirmatory of what you in general charge against him. Stay," drawing nearer to him; "heed what you speak. Just now, and in a case like this, there is a yardarm-end for the false witness."

"Ah, your honor!" sighed Claggart, mildly shaking his shapely head as in sad deprecation of such unmerited severity of tone. Then, bridling—erecting himself as in virtuous self-assertion—he circumstantially alleged certain words and acts which collectively, if credited, led to presumptions mortally inculpating Budd. And for some of these averments, he added, substantiating proof was not far.

With gray eyes impatient and distrustful essaying to fathom to the bottom Claggart's calm violet ones, Captain Vere again heard him out; then for the moment stood ruminating. The mood he evinced, Claggart—himself for the time liberated from the other's scrutiny—steadily regarded with a look difficult to render: a look curious of the operation of his tactics, a look such as might have been that of the spokesman of the envious children of Jacob deceptively imposing upon the troubled patriarch the blood-dyed coat of young Joseph.

Though something exceptional in the moral quality of Captain Vere made him, in earnest encounter with a fellow man, a veritable touchstone of that man's essential nature, yet now as to Claggart and what was really going on in him his feeling partook less of intuitional conviction than of strong suspicion clogged by strange dubieties. The perplexity he evinced proceeded less from aught touching the man informed against— as Claggart doubtless opined—than from considerations how best to act in regard to the informer. At first, indeed, he was naturally for summoning that substantiation of his allegations which Claggart said was at hand. But such a proceeding would result in the matter at once getting abroad, which in the present stage of it, he thought, might undesirably affect the ship's company. If Claggart was a false witness—that closed the affair. And therefore, before trying the accusation, he would first practically test the accuser; and he thought this could be done in a quiet, undemonstrative way.

The measure he determined upon involved a shifting of the scene, a transfer to a place less exposed to observation than the broad quarter-deck. For although the few gun-room officers there at the time had, in due observance of naval etiquette, withdrawn to leeward the moment Captain Vere had begun his promenade on the deck's weather side; and though during the colloquy with Claggart they of course ventured not to diminish the distance; and though throughout the interview Captain Vere's voice was far from high, and Claggart's silvery and low; and the wind in the cordage and the wash of the sea helped the more to put them beyond earshot; nevertheless, the interview's continuance already had attracted observation from some topmen aloft and other sailors in the waist or further forward.

Having determined upon his measures, Captain Vere forthwith took action. Abruptly turning to Claggart, he asked, "Master-at-arms, is it now Budd's watch aloft?"

"No, your honor."

Whereupon, "Mr. Wilkes!" summoning the nearest midshipman. "Tell Albert to come to me." Albert was the captain's hammock-boy, a sort of sea valet in whose discretion and fidelity his master had much confidence. The lad appeared.

"You know Budd, the foretopman?"

"I do, sir."

"Go find him. It is his watch off. Manage to tell him out of earshot that he is wanted aft. Contrive it that he speaks to nobody. Keep him in talk yourself. And not till you get well aft here, not till then let him know that the place where he is wanted is my cabin. You understand. Go.—Master-at-arms, show yourself on the decks below, and when you think it time for Albert to be coming with his man, stand by quietly to follow the sailor in."

19

Now when the foretopman found himself in the cabin, closeted there, as it were, with the captain and Claggart, he was surprised enough. But it was a surprise unaccompanied by apprehension or distrust. To an immature nature essentially honest and humane, forewarning intimations of subtler danger from one's kind come tardily if at all. The only thing that took shape in the young sailor's mind was this: Yes, the captain, I have always thought, looks kindly upon me. Wonder if he's going to make me his coxswain. I should like that. And may be now he is going to ask the master-at-arms about me.

"Shut the door there, sentry," said the commander; "stand without, and let nobody come in.—Now, Master-at-arms, tell this man to his face what you told of him to me," and stood prepared to scrutinize the mutually confronting visages.

With the measured step and calm collected air of an asylum physician approaching in the public hall some patient beginning to show indications of a coming paroxysm, Claggart deliberately advanced within short range of Billy and, mesmerically looking him in the eye, briefly recapitulated the accusation.

Not at first did Billy take it in. When he did, the rose-tan of his cheek looked struck as by white leprosy. He stood like one impaled and gagged. Meanwhile the accuser's eyes, removing not as yet from the blue dilated ones, underwent a phenomenal change, their wonted rich violet color blurring into a muddy purple. Those lights of human intelligence, losing human expression, were gelidly protruding like the alien eyes of certain uncatalogued creatures of the deep. The first mesmeristic glance was one of serpent fascination; the last was as the paralyzing lurch of the torpedo fish.

"Speak, man!" said Captain Vere to the transfixed one, struck by his aspect even more than by Claggart's. "Speak! Defend yourself!" Which appeal caused but a strange dumb gesturing and gurgling in Billy; amazement at such an accusation so suddenly sprung on inexperienced nonage; this, and, it may be, horror of the accuser's eyes, serving to bring out his lurking defect and in this instance for the time intensifying it into a convulsed tongue-tie; while the intent head and entire form straining forward in an agony of ineffectual eagerness to obey the injunction to speak and defend himself, gave an expression to the face like that of a condemned vestal priestess in the moment of being buried alive, and in the first struggle against suffocation.

Though at the time Captain Vere was quite ignorant of Billy's liability to vocal impediment, he now immediately divined it, since vividly Billy's aspect recalled to him that of a bright young schoolmate of his whom he had once seen struck by much the same startling impotence in the act of eagerly rising in the class to be foremost in response to a testing question put to it by the master. Going close up to the young sailor, and laying a soothing hand on his shoulder, he said, "There is no hurry, my boy. Take your time, take your time." Contrary to the effect intended, these words so fatherly in tone, doubtless touching Billy's heart to the quick, prompted yet more violent efforts at utterance—efforts soon ending for the time in confirming the paralysis, and bringing to his face an expression which was as a crucifixion to behold. The next instant, quick as the flame from a discharged cannon at night, his right arm shot out, and Claggart dropped to the deck. Whether intentionally or but owing to the young athlete's superior height, the blow had taken effect full upon the forehead, so shapely and intellectual-looking a feature in the master-at-arms; so that the body fell over lengthwise, like a heavy plank tilted from erectness. A gasp or two, and he lay motionless.

"Fated boy," breathed Captain Vere in tone so low as to be almost a whisper, " what have you done! But here, help me."

The twain raised the felled one from the loins up into a sitting position. The spare form flexibly acquiesced, but inertly. It was like handling a dead snake. They lowered it back. Regaining erectness, Captain Vere with one hand covering his face stood to all appearance as impassive as the object at his feet. Was he absorbed in taking in all the bearings of the event and what was best not only now at once to be done, but also in the sequel? Slowly he uncovered his face; and the effect was as if the moon emerging from eclipse should reappear with quite another aspect than that which had gone into hiding. The father in him, manifested towards Billy thus far in the scene, was replaced by the military disciplinarian. In his official tone he bade the foretopman retire to a stateroom aft (pointing it out), and there remain till thence summoned. This order Billy in silence mechanically obeyed. Then going to the cabin door where it opened on the quarter-deck, Captain Vere said to the sentry without, "Tell somebody to send Albert here." When the lad appeared, his master so contrived it that he should not catch sight of the prone one. "Albert," he said to him, "tell the surgeon I wish to see him. You need not come back till called."

When the surgeon entered—a self-poised character of that grave sense and experience that hardly anything could take him aback—Captain Vere advanced to meet him, thus unconsciously intercepting his view of Claggart, and, interrupting the other's wonted ceremonious salutation, said, "Nay. Tell me how it is with yonder man," directing his attention to the prostrate one.

The surgeon looked, and for all his self-command somewhat started at the abrupt revelation. On Claggart's always pallid complexion, thick black blood was now oozing from nostril and ear. To the gazer's professional eye it was unmistakably no living man that he saw.

"Is it so, then?" said Captain Vere, intently watching him. "I thought it. But verify it." Whereupon the customary tests confirmed the surgeon's first glance, who now, looking up in unfeigned concern, cast a look of intense inquisitiveness upon his superior. But Captain Vere, with one hand to his brow, was standing motionless. Suddenly, catching the surgeon's arm convulsively, he exclaimed, pointing down to the body, "It is the divine judgment on Ananias! Look!"

Disturbed by the excited manner he had never before observed in the *Bellipotent*'s captain, and as yet wholly ignorant of the affair, the prudent surgeon nevertheless held his peace, only again looking an earnest interrogatory as to what it was that had resulted in such a tragedy.

But Captain Vere was now again motionless, standing absorbed in thought. Again starting, he vehemently exclaimed, "Struck dead by an angel of God! Yet the angel must hang!"

At these passionate interjections, mere incoherences to the listener as yet unapprised of the antecedents, the surgeon was profoundly discomposed. But now, as recollecting himself, Captain Vere in less passionate tone briefly related the circumstances leading up to the event. "But come; we must dispatch," he added. "Help me to remove him" (meaning the body) "to yonder compartment," designating one opposite that where the foretopman remained immured. Anew disturbed by a request that, as implying a desire for secrecy, seemed unaccountably strange to him, there was nothing for the subordinate to do but comply.

"Go now," said Captain Vere with something of his wonted manner. "Go now. I presently shall call a drumhead court. Tell the lieutenants what has happened, and tell Mr. Mordant" (meaning the captain of marines), "and charge them to keep the matter to themselves."

2 0

FULL OF DISQUIETUDE and misgiving, the surgeon left the cabin. Was Captain Vere suddenly affected in his mind, or was it but a transient excitement, brought about by so strange and extraordinary a tragedy? As to the drumhead court, it struck the surgeon as impolitic, if nothing more. The thing to do, he thought, was to place Billy Budd in confinement, and in a way dictated by usage, and postpone further

action in so extraordinary a case to such time as they should
rejoin the squadron, and then refer it to the admiral. He recalled the unwonted agitation of Captain Vere and his excited
exclamations, so at variance with his normal manner. Was he
unhinged?

But assuming that he is, it is not so susceptible of proof.
What then can the surgeon do? No more trying situation is
conceivable than that of an officer subordinate under a captain whom he suspects to be not mad, indeed, but yet not
quite unaffected in his intellects. To argue his order to him
would be insolence. To resist him would be mutiny.

In obedience to Captain Vere, he communicated what had
happened to the lieutenants and captain of marines, saying
nothing as to the captain's state. They fully shared his own
surprise and concern. Like him too, they seemed to think that
such a matter should be referred to the admiral.

2 1

WHO IN THE RAINBOW can draw the line where the violet tint ends and the orange tint begins? Distinctly we
see the difference of the colors, but where exactly does the
one first blendingly enter into the other? So with sanity and
insanity. In pronounced cases there is no question about
them. But in some supposed cases, in various degrees supposedly less pronounced, to draw the exact line of demarcation
few will undertake, though for a fee becoming considerate
some professional experts will. There is nothing namable but
that some men will, or undertake to, do it for pay.

Whether Captain Vere, as the surgeon professionally and
privately surmised, was really the sudden victim of any degree
of aberration, every one must determine for himself by such
light as this narrative may afford.

That the unhappy event which has been narrated could not
have happened at a worse juncture was but too true. For it
was close on the heel of the suppressed insurrections, an after-
time very critical to naval authority, demanding from every

English sea commander two qualities not readily interfusable—prudence and rigor. Moreover, there was something crucial in the case.

In the jugglery of circumstances preceding and attending the event on board the *Bellipotent*, and in the light of that martial code whereby it was formally to be judged, innocence and guilt personified in Claggart and Budd in effect changed places. In a legal view the apparent victim of the tragedy was he who had sought to victimize a man blameless; and the indisputable deed of the latter, navally regarded, constituted the most heinous of military crimes. Yet more. The essential right and wrong involved in the matter, the clearer that might be, so much the worse for the responsibility of a loyal sea commander, inasmuch as he was not authorized to determine the matter on that primitive basis.

Small wonder then that the *Bellipotent*'s captain, though in general a man of rapid decision, felt that circumspectness not less than promptitude was necessary. Until he could decide upon his course, and in each detail; and not only so, but until the concluding measure was upon the point of being enacted, he deemed it advisable, in view of all the circumstances, to guard as much as possible against publicity. Here he may or may not have erred. Certain it is, however, that subsequently in the confidential talk of more than one or two gun rooms and cabins he was not a little criticized by some officers, a fact imputed by his friends and vehemently by his cousin Jack Denton to professional jealousy of Starry Vere. Some imaginative ground for invidious comment there was. The maintenance of secrecy in the matter, the confining all knowledge of it for a time to the place where the homicide occurred, the quarter-deck cabin; in these particulars lurked some resemblance to the policy adopted in those tragedies of the palace which have occurred more than once in the capital founded by Peter the Barbarian.

The case indeed was such that fain would the *Bellipotent*'s captain have deferred taking any action whatever respecting it further than to keep the foretopman a close prisoner till the ship rejoined the squadron and then submitting the matter to the judgment of his admiral.

But a true military officer is in one particular like a true monk. Not with more of self-abnegation will the latter keep his vows of monastic obedience than the former his vows of allegiance to martial duty.

Feeling that unless quick action was taken on it, the deed of the foretopman, so soon as it should be known on the gun decks, would tend to awaken any slumbering embers of the Nore among the crew, a sense of the urgency of the case overruled in Captain Vere every other consideration. But though a conscientious disciplinarian, he was no lover of authority for mere authority's sake. Very far was he from embracing opportunities for monopolizing to himself the perils of moral responsibility, none at least that could properly be referred to an official superior or shared with him by his official equals or even subordinates. So thinking, he was glad it would not be at variance with usage to turn the matter over to a summary court of his own officers, reserving to himself, as the one on whom the ultimate accountability would rest, the right of maintaining a supervision of it, or formally or informally interposing at need. Accordingly a drumhead court was summarily convened, he electing the individuals composing it: the first lieutenant, the captain of marines, and the sailing master.

In associating an officer of marines with the sea lieutenant and the sailing master in a case having to do with a sailor, the commander perhaps deviated from general custom. He was prompted thereto by the circumstance that he took that soldier to be a judicious person, thoughtful, and not altogether incapable of grappling with a difficult case unprecedented in his prior experience. Yet even as to him he was not without some latent misgiving, for withal he was an extremely good-natured man, an enjoyer of his dinner, a sound sleeper, and inclined to obesity—a man who though he would always maintain his manhood in battle might not prove altogether reliable in a moral dilemma involving aught of the tragic. As to the first lieutenant and the sailing master, Captain Vere could not but be aware that though honest natures, of approved gallantry upon occasion, their intelligence was mostly confined to the matter of active seamanship and the fighting demands of their profession.

The court was held in the same cabin where the unfortunate affair had taken place. This cabin, the commander's, embraced the entire area under the poop deck. Aft, and on either side, was a small stateroom, the one now temporarily a jail and the other a dead-house, and a yet smaller compartment, leaving a space between expanding forward into a goodly oblong of length coinciding with the ship's beam. A skylight of moderate dimension was overhead, and at each end of the oblong space were two sashed porthole windows easily convertible back into embrasures for short carronades.

All being quickly in readiness, Billy Budd was arraigned, Captain Vere necessarily appearing as the sole witness in the case, and as such temporarily sinking his rank, though singularly maintaining it in a matter apparently trivial, namely, that he testified from the ship's weather side, with that object having caused the court to sit on the lee side. Concisely he narrated all that had led up to the catastrophe, omitting nothing in Claggart's accusation and deposing as to the manner in which the prisoner had received it. At this testimony the three officers glanced with no little surprise at Billy Budd, the last man they would have suspected either of the mutinous design alleged by Claggart or the undeniable deed he himself had done. The first lieutenant, taking judicial primacy and turning toward the prisoner, said, "Captain Vere has spoken. Is it or is it not as Captain Vere says?"

In response came syllables not so much impeded in the utterance as might have been anticipated. They were these: "Captain Vere tells the truth. It is just as Captain Vere says, but it is not as the master-at-arms said. I have eaten the King's bread and I am true to the King."

"I believe you, my man," said the witness, his voice indicating a suppressed emotion not otherwise betrayed.

"God will bless you for that, your honor!" not without stammering said Billy, and all but broke down. But immediately he was recalled to self-control by another question, to which with the same emotional difficulty of utterance he said, "No, there was no malice between us. I never bore malice against the master-at-arms. I am sorry that he is dead. I did not mean to kill him. Could I have used my tongue I would not have struck him. But he foully lied to my face and in presence of my captain, and I had to say something, and I could only say it with a blow, God help me!"

In the impulsive aboveboard manner of the frank one the court saw confirmed all that was implied in words that just previously had perplexed them, coming as they did from the testifier to the tragedy and promptly following Billy's impassioned disclaimer of mutinous intent—Captain Vere's words, "I believe you, my man."

Next it was asked of him whether he knew of or suspected aught savoring of incipient trouble (meaning mutiny, though the explicit term was avoided) going on in any section of the ship's company.

The reply lingered. This was naturally imputed by the court to the same vocal embarrassment which had retarded or obstructed previous answers. But in main it was otherwise here, the question immediately recalling to Billy's mind the interview with the afterguardsman in the forechains. But an innate repugnance to playing a part at all approaching that of an informer against one's own shipmates—the same erring sense of uninstructed honor which had stood in the way of his reporting the matter at the time, though as a loyal man-of-war's man it was incumbent on him, and failure so to do, if charged against him and proven, would have subjected him to the heaviest of penalties; this, with the blind feeling now his that nothing really was being hatched, prevailed with him. When the answer came it was a negative.

"One question more," said the officer of marines, now first speaking and with a troubled earnestness. "You tell us that what the master-at-arms said against you was a lie. Now why should he have so lied, so maliciously lied, since you declare there was no malice between you?"

At that question, unintentionally touching on a spiritual sphere wholly obscure to Billy's thoughts, he was nonplussed, evincing a confusion indeed that some observers, such as can readily be imagined, would have construed into involuntary evidence of hidden guilt. Nevertheless, he strove some way to answer, but all at once relinquished the vain endeavor, at the same time turning an appealing glance towards Captain Vere as deeming him his best helper and friend. Captain Vere, who had been seated for a time, rose to his feet, addressing the interrogator. "The question you put to him comes naturally enough. But how can he rightly answer it?—or anybody else, unless indeed it be he who lies within there," designating the compartment where lay the corpse. "But the prone one there will not rise to our summons. In effect, though, as it seems to me, the point you make is hardly material. Quite aside from any conceivable motive actuating the master-at-arms, and irrespective of the provocation to the blow, a martial court must needs in the present case confine its attention to the blow's consequence, which consequence justly is to be deemed not otherwise than as the striker's deed."

This utterance, the full significance of which it was not at all likely that Billy took in, nevertheless caused him to turn a wistful interrogative look toward the speaker, a look in its dumb expressiveness not unlike that which a dog of generous breed might turn upon his master, seeking in his face some elucidation of a previous gesture ambiguous to the canine intelligence. Nor was the same utterance without marked effect upon the three officers, more especially the soldier. Couched in it seemed to them a meaning unanticipated, involving a prejudgment on the speaker's part. It served to augment a mental disturbance previously evident enough.

The soldier once more spoke, in a tone of suggestive dubiety addressing at once his associates and Captain Vere: "Nobody is present—none of the ship's company, I mean—who might shed lateral light, if any is to be had, upon what remains mysterious in this matter."

"That is thoughtfully put," said Captain Vere; "I see your drift. Ay, there is a mystery; but, to use a scriptural phrase, it is a 'mystery of iniquity,' a matter for psychologic theologians to discuss. But what has a military court to do with it? Not to add that for us any possible investigation of it is cut off by the lasting tongue-tie of—him—in yonder," again designating the mortuary stateroom. "The prisoner's deed—with that alone we have to do."

To this, and particularly the closing reiteration, the marine soldier, knowing not how aptly to reply, sadly abstained from saying aught. The first lieutenant, who at the outset had not unnaturally assumed primacy in the court, now overrulingly instructed by a glance from Captain Vere, a glance more effective than words, resumed that primacy. Turning to the prisoner, "Budd," he said, and scarce in equable tones, "Budd, if you have aught further to say for yourself, say it now."

Upon this the young sailor turned another quick glance toward Captain Vere; then, as taking a hint from that aspect, a hint confirming his own instinct that silence was now best, replied to the lieutenant, "I have said all, sir."

The marine—the same who had been the sentinel without the cabin door at the time that the foretopman, followed by the master-at-arms, entered it—he, standing by the sailor throughout these judicial proceedings, was now directed to take him back to the after compartment originally assigned to the prisoner and his custodian. As the twain disappeared from view, the three officers, as partially liberated from some inward constraint associated with Billy's mere presence, simultaneously stirred in their seats. They exchanged looks of troubled indecision, yet feeling that decide they must and without long delay. For Captain Vere, he for the time stood—unconsciously with his back toward them, apparently in one of his absent fits—gazing out from a sashed porthole to windward upon the monotonous blank of the twilight sea. But the court's silence continuing, broken only at moments by brief consultations, in low earnest tones, this served to arouse him and energize him. Turning, he to-and-fro paced the cabin athwart; in the returning ascent to windward climbing the slant deck in the ship's lee roll, without knowing it symbolizing thus in his action a mind resolute to surmount difficulties even if against primitive instincts strong as the wind and the sea. Presently he came to a stand before the three. After scanning their faces he stood less as mustering his thoughts for expression than as one inly deliberating how best to put them to well-meaning men not intellectually mature, men with whom it was necessary to demonstrate certain principles that were axioms to himself. Similar impatience as to talking is perhaps one reason that deters some minds from addressing any popular assemblies.

When speak he did, something, both in the substance of what he said and his manner of saying it, showed the influence of unshared studies modifying and tempering the practical training of an active career. This, along with his phraseology, now and then was suggestive of the grounds whereon rested that imputation of a certain pedantry socially alleged against him by certain naval men of wholly practical cast, captains who nevertheless would frankly concede that His Majesty's navy mustered no more efficient officer of their grade than Starry Vere.

What he said was to this effect: "Hitherto I have been but the witness, little more; and I should hardly think now to take another tone, that of your coadjutor for the time, did I not perceive in you—at the crisis too—a troubled hesitancy, proceeding, I doubt not, from the clash of military duty with moral scruple—scruple vitalized by compassion. For the compassion, how can I otherwise than share it? But, mindful of paramount obligations, I strive against scruples that may tend to enervate decision. Not, gentlemen, that I hide from myself that the case is an exceptional one. Speculatively regarded, it well might be referred to a jury of casuists. But for us here, acting not as casuists or moralists, it is a case practical, and under martial law practically to be dealt with.

"But your scruples: do they move as in a dusk? Challenge them. Make them advance and declare themselves. Come now; do they import something like this: If, mindless of palliating circumstances, we are bound to regard the death of the master-at-arms as the prisoner's deed, then does that deed constitute a capital crime whereof the penalty is a mortal one. But in natural justice is nothing but the prisoner's overt act to be considered? How can we adjudge to summary and shameful death a fellow creature innocent before God, and whom we feel to be so?—Does that state it aright? You sign sad assent. Well, I too feel that, the full force of that. It is Nature. But do these buttons that we wear attest that our allegiance is to Nature? No, to the King. Though the ocean, which is inviolate Nature primeval, though this be the element where we move and have our being as sailors, yet as the King's officers lies our duty in a sphere correspondingly natural? So little is that true, that in receiving our commissions we in the most important regards ceased to be natural free agents. When war is declared are we the commissioned fighters previously consulted? We fight at command. If our judgments approve the war, that is but coincidence. So in other particulars. So now. For suppose condemnation to follow these present proceedings. Would it be so much we ourselves that would condemn as it would be martial law operating through us? For that law and the rigor of it, we are not responsible. Our vowed responsibility is in this: That however pitilessly that law may operate in any instances, we nevertheless adhere to it and administer it.

"But the exceptional in the matter moves the hearts within you. Even so too is mine moved. But let not warm hearts betray heads that should be cool. Ashore in a criminal case, will an upright judge allow himself off the bench to be waylaid by some tender kinswoman of the accused seeking to touch him with her tearful plea? Well, the heart here, sometimes the feminine in man, is as that piteous woman, and hard though it be, she must here be ruled out."

He paused, earnestly studying them for a moment; then resumed.

"But something in your aspect seems to urge that it is not solely the heart that moves in you, but also the conscience, the private conscience. But tell me whether or not, occupying the position we do, private conscience should not yield to that imperial one formulated in the code under which alone we officially proceed?"

Here the three men moved in their seats, less convinced than agitated by the course of an argument troubling but the more the spontaneous conflict within.

Perceiving which, the speaker paused for a moment; then abruptly changing his tone, went on.

"To steady us a bit, let us recur to the facts.—In wartime at sea a man-of-war's man strikes his superior in grade, and the blow kills. Apart from its effect the blow itself is, according to the Articles of War, a capital crime. Furthermore ——"

"Ay, sir," emotionally broke in the officer of marines, "in one sense it was. But surely Budd purposed neither mutiny nor homicide."

"Surely not, my good man. And before a court less arbitrary and more merciful than a martial one, that plea would largely extenuate. At the Last Assizes it shall acquit. But how here? We proceed under the law of the Mutiny Act. In feature no child can resemble his father more than that Act resembles in spirit the thing from which it derives—War. In His Majesty's service—in this ship, indeed—there are Englishmen forced to fight for the King against their will. Against their conscience, for aught we know. Though as their fellow creatures some of us may appreciate their position, yet as navy officers what reck we of it? Still less recks the enemy. Our impressed men he would fain cut down in the same swath with our volunteers. As regards the enemy's naval conscripts, some of whom may even share our own abhorrence of the regicidal French Directory, it is the same on our side. War looks but to the frontage, the appearance. And the Mutiny Act, War's child, takes after the father. Budd's intent or nonintent is nothing to the purpose.

"But while, put to it by those anxieties in you which I cannot but respect, I only repeat myself—while thus strangely we prolong proceedings that should be summary—the enemy may be sighted and an engagement result. We must do; and one of two things must we do—condemn or let go."

"Can we not convict and yet mitigate the penalty?" asked the sailing master, here speaking, and falteringly, for the first.

"Gentlemen, were that clearly lawful for us under the circumstances, consider the consequences of such clemency. The people" (meaning the ship's company) "have native sense; most of them are familiar with our naval usage and tradition; and how would they take it? Even could you explain to them—which our official position forbids—they, long molded by arbitrary discipline, have not that kind of intelligent responsiveness that might qualify them to comprehend and discriminate. No, to the people the foretopman's deed, however it be worded in the announcement, will be plain homicide committed in a flagrant act of mutiny. What penalty for that should follow, they know. But it does not follow. *Why?* they will ruminate. You know what sailors are. Will they not revert to the recent outbreak at the Nore? Ay. They know the well-founded alarm—the panic it struck throughout England. Your clement sentence they would account pusillanimous. They would think that we flinch, that we are afraid of them—afraid of practicing a lawful rigor singularly demanded at this juncture, lest it should provoke new troubles. What shame to us such a conjecture on their part, and how deadly to discipline. You see then, whither, prompted by duty and the law, I steadfastly drive. But I beseech you, my friends, do not take me amiss. I feel as you do for this unfortunate boy. But did he know our hearts, I take him to be of that generous nature that he would feel even for us on whom in this military necessity so heavy a compulsion is laid."

With that, crossing the deck he resumed his place by the sashed porthole, tacitly leaving the three to come to a decision. On the cabin's opposite side the troubled court sat silent. Loyal lieges, plain and practical, though at bottom they dissented from some points Captain Vere had put to them, they were without the faculty, hardly had the inclination, to gainsay one whom they felt to be an earnest man, one too not less their superior in mind than in naval rank. But it is not improbable that even such of his words as were not without influence over them, less came home to them than his closing appeal to their instinct as sea officers: in the forethought he threw out as to the practical consequences to discipline, considering the unconfirmed tone of the fleet at the time, should a man-of-war's man's violent killing at sea of a superior in grade be allowed to pass for aught else than a capital crime demanding prompt infliction of the penalty.

Not unlikely they were brought to something more or less akin to that harassed frame of mind which in the year 1842 actuated the commander of the U.S. brig-of-war *Somers* to resolve, under the so-called Articles of War, Articles modeled upon the English Mutiny Act, to resolve upon the execution at sea of a midshipman and two sailors as mutineers designing the seizure of the brig. Which resolution was carried out though in a time of peace and within not many days' sail of home. An act vindicated by a naval court of inquiry subsequently convened ashore. History, and here cited without comment. True, the circumstances on board the *Somers* were different from those on board the *Bellipotent*. But the urgency felt, well-warranted or otherwise, was much the same.

Says a writer whom few know, "Forty years after a battle it is easy for a noncombatant to reason about how it ought to have been fought. It is another thing personally and under

fire to have to direct the fighting while involved in the ob-
scuring smoke of it. Much so with respect to other emergencies involving considerations both practical and moral, and
when it is imperative promptly to act. The greater the fog the
more it imperils the steamer, and speed is put on though at
the hazard of running somebody down. Little ween the snug
card players in the cabin of the responsibilities of the sleepless
man on the bridge."

In brief, Billy Budd was formally convicted and sentenced
to be hung at the yardarm in the early morning watch, it
being now night. Otherwise, as is customary in such cases,
the sentence would forthwith have been carried out. In war-
time on the field or in the fleet, a mortal punishment decreed
by a drumhead court—on the field sometimes decreed by but
a nod from the general—follows without delay on the heel
of conviction, without appeal.

22

IT WAS CAPTAIN VERE himself who of his own motion communicated the finding of the court to the prisoner, for that
purpose going to the compartment where he was in custody
and bidding the marine there to withdraw for the time.

Beyond the communication of the sentence, what took
place at this interview was never known. But in view of the
character of the twain briefly closeted in that stateroom, each
radically sharing in the rarer qualities of our nature—so rare
indeed as to be all but incredible to average minds however
much cultivated—some conjectures may be ventured.

It would have been in consonance with the spirit of Captain Vere should he on this occasion have concealed nothing
from the condemned one—should he indeed have frankly
disclosed to him the part he himself had played in bringing
about the decision, at the same time revealing his actuating
motives. On Billy's side it is not improbable that such a
confession would have been received in much the same spirit
that prompted it. Not without a sort of joy, indeed, he might

have appreciated the brave opinion of him implied in his captain's making such a confidant of him. Nor, as to the sentence
itself, could he have been insensible that it was imparted to
him as to one not afraid to die. Even more may have been.
Captain Vere in end may have developed the passion sometimes latent under an exterior stoical or indifferent. He was
old enough to have been Billy's father. The austere devotee
of military duty, letting himself melt back into what remains
primeval in our formalized humanity, may in end have caught
Billy to his heart, even as Abraham may have caught young
Isaac on the brink of resolutely offering him up in obedience
to the exacting behest. But there is no telling the sacrament,
seldom if in any case revealed to the gadding world, wherever
under circumstances at all akin to those here attempted to be
set forth two of great Nature's nobler order embrace. There
is privacy at the time, inviolable to the survivor; and holy
oblivion, the sequel to each diviner magnanimity, providentially covers all at last.

The first to encounter Captain Vere in act of leaving the
compartment was the senior lieutenant. The face he beheld,
for the moment one expressive of the agony of the strong,
was to that officer, though a man of fifty, a startling revelation. That the condemned one suffered less than he who
mainly had effected the condemnation was apparently indicated by the former's exclamation in the scene soon perforce
to be touched upon.

23

Of a series of incidents within a brief term rapidly following each other, the adequate narration may take up
a term less brief, especially if explanation or comment here
and there seem requisite to the better understanding of such
incidents. Between the entrance into the cabin of him who
never left it alive, and him who when he did leave it left it as
one condemned to die; between this and the closeted interview just given, less than an hour and a half had elapsed. It

was an interval long enough, however, to awaken speculations among no few of the ship's company as to what it was
that could be detaining in the cabin the master-at-arms and
the sailor; for a rumor that both of them had been seen to
enter it and neither of them had been seen to emerge, this
rumor had got abroad upon the gun decks and in the tops,
the people of a great warship being in one respect like villagers, taking microscopic note of every outward movement or
non-movement going on. When therefore, in weather not at
all tempestuous, all hands were called in the second dogwatch, a summons under such circumstances not usual in
those hours, the crew were not wholly unprepared for some
announcement extraordinary, one having connection too with
the continued absence of the two men from their wonted
haunts.

There was a moderate sea at the time; and the moon, newly
risen and near to being at its full, silvered the white spar deck
wherever not blotted by the clear-cut shadows horizontally
thrown of fixtures and moving men. On either side the
quarter-deck the marine guard under arms was drawn up; and
Captain Vere, standing in his place surrounded by all the
wardroom officers, addressed his men. In so doing, his manner showed neither more nor less than that properly pertaining to his supreme position aboard his own ship. In clear
terms and concise he told them what had taken place in the
cabin: that the master-at-arms was dead, that he who had
killed him had been already tried by a summary court and
condemned to death, and that the execution would take place
in the early morning watch. The word *mutiny* was not named
in what he said. He refrained too from making the occasion
an opportunity for any preachment as to the maintenance of
discipline, thinking perhaps that under existing circumstances
in the navy the consequence of violating discipline should be
made to speak for itself.

Their captain's announcement was listened to by the
throng of standing sailors in a dumbness like that of a seated
congregation of believers in hell listening to the clergyman's
announcement of his Calvinistic text.

At the close, however, a confused murmur went up. It began to wax. All but instantly, then, at a sign, it was pierced

and suppressed by shrill whistles of the boatswain and his mates. The word was given to about ship.

To be prepared for burial Claggart's body was delivered to certain petty officers of his mess. And here, not to clog the sequel with lateral matters, it may be added that at a suitable hour, the master-at-arms was committed to the sea with every funeral honor properly belonging to his naval grade.

In this proceeding as in every public one growing out of the tragedy strict adherence to usage was observed. Nor in any point could it have been at all deviated from, either with respect to Claggart or Billy Budd, without begetting undesirable speculations in the ship's company, sailors, and more particularly men-of-war's men, being of all men the greatest sticklers for usage. For similar cause, all communication between Captain Vere and the condemned one ended with the closeted interview already given, the latter being now surrendered to the ordinary routine preliminary to the end. His transfer under guard from the captain's quarters was effected without unusual precautions—at least no visible ones. If possible, not to let the men so much as surmise that their officers anticipate aught amiss from them is the tacit rule in a military ship. And the more that some sort of trouble should really be apprehended, the more do the officers keep that apprehension to themselves, though not the less unostentatious vigilance may be augmented. In the present instance, the sentry placed over the prisoner had strict orders to let no one have communication with him but the chaplain. And certain unobtrusive measures were taken absolutely to insure this point.

24

In a seventy-four of the old order the deck known as the upper gun deck was the one covered over by the spar deck, which last, though not without its armament, was for the most part exposed to the weather. In general it was at all hours free from hammocks; those of the crew swinging on the lower gun deck and berth deck, the latter being not only

a dormitory but also the place for the stowing of the sailors'
bags, and on both sides lined with the large chests or movable
pantries of the many messes of the men.

On the starboard side of the *Bellipotent*'s upper gun deck,
behold Billy Budd under sentry lying prone in irons in one of
the bays formed by the regular spacing of the guns comprising the batteries on either side. All these pieces were of
the heavier caliber of that period. Mounted on lumbering
wooden carriages, they were hampered with cumbersome harness of breeching and strong side-tackles for running them
out. Guns and carriages, together with the long rammers and
shorter linstocks lodged in loops overhead—all these, as customary, were painted black; and the heavy hempen breech-
ings, tarred to the same tint, wore the like livery of the
undertakers. In contrast with the funereal hue of these surroundings, the prone sailor's exterior apparel, white jumper
and white duck trousers, each more or less soiled, dimly glimmered in the obscure light of the bay like a patch of discolored snow in early April lingering at some upland cave's black
mouth. In effect he is already in his shroud, or the garments
that shall serve him in lieu of one. Over him but scarce illuminating him, two battle lanterns swing from two massive
beams of the deck above. Fed with the oil supplied by the
war contractors (whose gains, honest or otherwise, are in
every land an anticipated portion of the harvest of death),
with flickering splashes of dirty yellow light they pollute the
pale moonshine all but ineffectually struggling in obstructed
flecks through the open ports from which the tampioned cannon protrude. Other lanterns at intervals serve but to bring
out somewhat the obscurer bays which, like small confession-
als or side-chapels in a cathedral, branch from the long dim-
vistaed broad aisle between the two batteries of that covered
tier.

Such was the deck where now lay the Handsome Sailor.
Through the rose-tan of his complexion no pallor could have
shown. It would have taken days of sequestration from the
winds and the sun to have brought about the effacement of
that. But the skeleton in the cheekbone at the point of its
angle was just beginning delicately to be defined under the
warm-tinted skin. In fervid hearts self-contained, some brief

experiences devour our human tissue as secret fire in a ship's hold consumes cotton in the bale.

But now lying between the two guns, as nipped in the vice of fate, Billy's agony, mainly proceeding from a generous young heart's virgin experience of the diabolical incarnate and effective in some men—the tension of that agony was over now. It survived not the something healing in the closeted interview with Captain Vere. Without movement, he lay as in a trance, that adolescent expression previously noted as his taking on something akin to the look of a slumbering child in the cradle when the warm hearth-glow of the still chamber at night plays on the dimples that at whiles mysteriously form in the cheek, silently coming and going there. For now and then in the gyved one's trance a serene happy light born of some wandering reminiscence or dream would diffuse itself over his face, and then wane away only anew to return.

The chaplain, coming to see him and finding him thus, and perceiving no sign that he was conscious of his presence, attentively regarded him for a space, then slipping aside, withdrew for the time, peradventure feeling that even he, the minister of Christ though receiving his stipend from Mars, had no consolation to proffer which could result in a peace transcending that which he beheld. But in the small hours he came again. And the prisoner, now awake to his surroundings, noticed his approach, and civilly, all but cheerfully, welcomed him. But it was to little purpose that in the interview following, the good man sought to bring Billy Budd to some godly understanding that he must die, and at dawn. True, Billy himself freely referred to his death as a thing close at hand; but it was something in the way that children will refer to death in general, who yet among their other sports will play a funeral with hearse and mourners.

Not that like children Billy was incapable of conceiving what death really is. No, but he was wholly without irrational fear of it, a fear more prevalent in highly civilized communities than those so-called barbarous ones which in all respects stand nearer to unadulterate Nature. And, as elsewhere said, a barbarian Billy radically was—as much so, for all the costume, as his countrymen the British captives, living trophies, made to march in the Roman triumph of Germanicus. Quite as much so as those later barbarians, young men probably, and picked specimens among the earlier British converts to Christianity, at least nominally such, taken to Rome (as today converts from lesser isles of the sea may be taken to London), of whom the Pope of that time, admiring the strangeness of their personal beauty so unlike the Italian stamp, their clear ruddy complexion and curled flaxen locks, exclaimed, "Angles" (meaning *English*, the modern derivative), "Angles, do you call them? And is it because they look so like angels?" Had it been later in time, one would think that the Pope had in mind Fra Angelico's seraphs, some of whom, plucking apples in gardens of the Hesperides, have the faint rosebud complexion of the more beautiful English girls.

If in vain the good chaplain sought to impress the young barbarian with ideas of death akin to those conveyed in the skull, dial, and crossbones on old tombstones, equally futile to all appearance were his efforts to bring home to him the thought of salvation and a Savior. Billy listened, but less out of awe or reverence, perhaps, than from a certain natural politeness, doubtless at bottom regarding all that in much the same way that most mariners of his class take any discourse abstract or out of the common tone of the workaday world. And this sailor way of taking clerical discourse is not wholly unlike the way in which the primer of Christianity, full of transcendent miracles, was received long ago on tropic isles by any superior *savage*, so called—a Tahitian, say, of Captain Cook's time or shortly after that time. Out of natural courtesy he received, but did not appropriate. It was like a gift placed in the palm of an outreached hand upon which the fingers do not close.

But the *Bellipotent's* chaplain was a discreet man possessing the good sense of a good heart. So he insisted not in his vocation here. At the instance of Captain Vere, a lieutenant had apprised him of pretty much everything as to Billy; and since he felt that innocence was even a better thing than religion wherewith to go to Judgment, he reluctantly withdrew; but in his emotion not without first performing an act strange enough in an Englishman, and under the circumstances yet more so in any regular priest. Stooping over, he kissed on the fair cheek his fellow man, a felon in martial law, one whom though on the confines of death he felt he could never convert to a dogma; nor for all that did he fear for his future.

Marvel not that having been made acquainted with the young sailor's essential innocence the worthy man lifted not a finger to avert the doom of such a martyr to martial discipline. So to do would not only have been as idle as invoking the desert, but would also have been an audacious transgression of the bounds of his function, one as exactly prescribed to him by military law as that of the boatswain or any other naval officer. Bluntly put, a chaplain is the minister of the Prince of Peace serving in the host of the God of War—Mars. As such, he is as incongruous as a musket would be on the altar at Christmas. Why, then, is he there? Because he indirectly subserves the purpose attested by the cannon; because too he lends the sanction of the religion of the meek to that which practically is the abrogation of everything but brute Force.

25

THE NIGHT so luminous on the spar deck, but otherwise on the cavernous ones below, levels so like the tiered galleries in a coal mine—the luminous night passed away. But like the prophet in the chariot disappearing in heaven and dropping his mantle to Elisha, the withdrawing night transferred its pale robe to the breaking day. A meek, shy light appeared in the East, where stretched a diaphanous fleece of white furrowed vapor. That light slowly waxed. Suddenly *eight bells* was struck aft, responded to by one louder metallic stroke from forward. It was four o'clock in the morning. Instantly the silver whistles were heard summoning all hands to witness punishment. Up through the great hatchways rimmed with racks of heavy shot the watch below came pouring, overspreading with the watch already on deck the space between the mainmast and foremast including that occupied by the capacious launch and the black booms tiered on either side of it, boat and booms making a summit of observation for the powder-boys and younger tars. A different group comprising one watch of topmen leaned over the rail of that sea balcony, no small one in a seventy-four, looking down on the crowd below. Man or boy, none spake but in whisper, and few spake at all. Captain Vere—as before, the central figure among the assembled commissioned officers—stood nigh the break of the poop deck facing forward. Just below him on the quarter-deck the marines in full equipment were drawn up much as at the scene of the promulgated sentence.

At sea in the old time, the execution by halter of a military sailor was generally from the foreyard. In the present instance, for special reasons the mainyard was assigned. Under an arm of that yard the prisoner was presently brought up, the chaplain attending him. It was noted at the time, and remarked upon afterwards, that in this final scene the good man evinced little or nothing of the perfunctory. Brief speech indeed he had with the condemned one, but the genuine Gospel was less on his tongue than in his aspect and manner towards him. The final preparations personal to the latter being speedily brought to an end by two boatswain's mates, the consummation impended. Billy stood facing aft. At the penultimate moment, his words, his only ones, words wholly unobstructed in the utterance, were these: "God bless Captain Vere!" Syllables so unanticipated coming from one with the ignominious hemp about his neck—a conventional felon's benediction directed aft towards the quarters of honor; syllables too delivered in the clear melody of a singing bird on the point of launching from the twig—had a phenomenal effect, not unenhanced by the rare personal beauty of the young sailor, spiritualized now through late experiences so poignantly profound.

Without volition, as it were, as if indeed the ship's populace were but the vehicles of some vocal current electric, with one voice from alow and aloft came a resonant sympathetic echo: "God bless Captain Vere!" And yet at that instant Billy alone must have been in their hearts, even as in their eyes.

At the pronounced words and the spontaneous echo that voluminously rebounded them, Captain Vere, either through stoic self-control or a sort of momentary paralysis induced by emotional shock, stood erectly rigid as a musket in the ship-armorer's rack.

The hull, deliberately recovering from the periodic roll to leeward, was just regaining an even keel when the last signal, a preconcerted dumb one, was given. At the same moment it chanced that the vapory fleece hanging low in the East was shot through with a soft glory as of the fleece of the Lamb of God seen in mystical vision, and simultaneously therewith, watched by the wedged mass of upturned faces, Billy ascended; and, ascending, took the full rose of the dawn.

In the pinioned figure arrived at the yard-end, to the wonder of all no motion was apparent, none save that created by the slow roll of the hull in moderate weather, so majestic in a great ship ponderously cannoned.

26

WHEN SOME DAYS afterwards, in reference to the singularity just mentioned, the pursuer, a rather ruddy, rotund person more accurate as an accountant than profound as a philosopher, said at mess to the surgeon, "What testimony to the force lodged in will power," the latter, saturnine, spare, and tall, one in whom a discreet causticity went along with a manner less genial than polite, replied, "Your pardon, Mr. Purser. In a hanging scientifically conducted—and under special orders I myself directed how Budd's was to be effected—any movement following the completed suspension and originating in the body suspended, such movement indicates mechanical spasm in the muscular system. Hence the absence of that is no more attributable to will power, as you call it, than to horsepower—begging your pardon."

"But this muscular spasm you speak of, is not that in a degree more or less invariable in these cases?"

"Assuredly so, Mr. Purser."

"How then, my good sir, do you account for its absence in this instance?"

"Mr. Purser, it is clear that your sense of the singularity in this matter equals not mine. You account for it by what you call will power—a term not yet included in the lexicon of science. For me, I do not, with my present knowledge, pretend to account for it at all. Even should we assume the hypothesis that at the first touch of the halyards the action of Budd's heart, intensified by extraordinary emotion at its climax, abruptly stopped—much like a watch when in carelessly winding it up you strain at the finish, thus snapping the chain—even under that hypothesis how account for the phenomenon that followed?"

"You admit, then, that the absence of spasmodic movement was phenomenal."

"It was phenomenal, Mr. Purser, in the sense that it was an appearance the cause of which is not immediately to be assigned."

"But tell me, my dear sir," pertinaciously continued the other, " was the man's death effected by the halter, or was it a species of euthanasia?"

"*Euthanasia*, Mr. Purser, is something like your *will power*: I doubt its authenticity as a scientific term—begging your pardon again. It is at once imaginative and metaphysical—in short, Greek.—But," abruptly changing his tone, "there is a case in the sick bay that I do not care to leave to my assistants. Beg your pardon, but excuse me." And rising from the mess he formally withdrew.

27

THE SILENCE at the moment of execution and for a moment or two continuing thereafter, a silence but emphasized by the regular wash of the sea against the hull or the flutter of a sail caused by the helmsman's eyes being tempted astray, this emphasized silence was gradually disturbed by a sound not easily to be verbally rendered. Whoever has heard the freshet-wave of a torrent suddenly swelled by pouring showers in tropical mountains, showers not shared by the plain; whoever has heard the first muffled murmur of its slop-

ing advance through precipitous woods may form some conception of the sound now heard. The seeming remoteness of
its source was because of its murmurous indistinctness, since
it came from close by, even from the men massed on the
ship's open deck. Being inarticulate, it was dubious in significance further than it seemed to indicate some capricious revulsion of thought or feeling such as mobs ashore are liable
to, in the present instance possibly implying a sullen revoca-
tion on the men's part of their involuntary echoing of Billy's
benediction. But ere the murmur had time to wax into clamor
it was met by a strategic command, the more telling that it
came with abrupt unexpectedness: "Pipe down the starboard
watch, Boatswain, and see that they go."

Shrill as the shriek of the sea hawk, the silver whistles of
the boatswain and his mates pierced that ominous low sound,
dissipating it; and yielding to the mechanism of discipline the
throng was thinned by one-half. For the remainder, most of
them were set to temporary employments connected with
trimming the yards and so forth, business readily to be got
up to serve occasion by any officer of the deck.

Now each proceeding that follows a mortal sentence pronounced at sea by a drumhead court is characterized by
promptitude not perceptibly merging into hurry, though bordering that. The hammock, the one which had been Billy's
bed when alive, having already been ballasted with shot and
otherwise prepared to serve for his canvas coffin, the last offices of the sea undertakers, the sailmaker's mates, were now
speedily completed. When everything was in readiness a second call for all hands, made necessary by the strategic movement before mentioned, was sounded, now to witness burial.

The details of this closing formality it needs not to give.
But when the tilted plank let slide its freight into the sea, a
second strange human murmur was heard, blended now with
another inarticulate sound proceeding from certain larger sea-
fowl who, their attention having been attracted by the peculiar commotion in the water resulting from the heavy sloped
dive of the shotted hammock into the sea, flew screaming to
the spot. So near the hull did they come, that the stridor or
bony creak of their gaunt double-jointed pinions was audible.
As the ship under light airs passed on, leaving the burial spot

astern, they still kept circling it low down with the moving shadow of their outstretched wings and the croaked requiem of their cries.

Upon sailors as superstitious as those of the age preceding ours, men-of-war's men too who had just beheld the prodigy of repose in the form suspended in air, and now foundering in the deeps; to such mariners the action of the seafowl, though dictated by mere animal greed for prey, was big with no prosaic significance. An uncertain movement began among them, in which some encroachment was made. It was tolerated but for a moment. For suddenly the drum beat to quarters, which familiar sound happening at least twice every day, had upon the present occasion a signal peremptoriness in it. True martial discipline long continued superinduces in average man a sort of impulse whose operation at the official word of command much resembles in its promptitude the effect of an instinct.

The drumbeat dissolved the multitude, distributing most of them along the batteries of the two covered gun decks. There, as wonted, the guns' crews stood by their respective cannon erect and silent. In due course the first officer, sword under arm and standing in his place on the quarter-deck, formally received the successive reports of the sworded lieutenants commanding the sections of batteries below; the last of which reports being made, the summed report he delivered with the customary salute to the commander. All this occupied time, which in the present case was the object in beating to quarters at an hour prior to the customary one. That such variance from usage was authorized by an officer like Captain Vere, a martinet as some deemed him, was evidence of the necessity for unusual action implied in what he deemed to be temporarily the mood of his men. "With mankind," he would say, "forms, measured forms, are everything; and that is the import couched in the story of Orpheus with his lyre spellbinding the wild denizens of the wood." And this he once applied to the disruption of forms going on across the Channel and the consequences thereof.

At this unwonted muster at quarters, all proceeded as at the regular hour. The band on the quarter-deck played a sacred air, after which the chaplain went through the customary morning service. That done, the drum beat the retreat; and toned by music and religious rites subserving the discipline and purposes of war, the men in their wonted orderly manner dispersed to the places allotted them when not at the guns.

And now it was full day. The fleece of low-hanging vapor had vanished, licked up by the sun that late had so glorified it. And the circumambient air in the clearness of its serenity was like smooth white marble in the polished block not yet removed from the marble-dealer's yard.

28

THE SYMMETRY of form attainable in pure fiction cannot so readily be achieved in a narration essentially having less to do with fable than with fact. Truth uncompromisingly told will always have its ragged edges; hence the conclusion of such a narration is apt to be less finished than an architectural finial.

How it fared with the Handsome Sailor during the year of the Great Mutiny has been faithfully given. But though properly the story ends with his life, something in way of sequel will not be amiss. Three brief chapters will suffice.

In the general rechristening under the Directory of the craft originally forming the navy of the French monarchy, the *St. Louis* line-of-battle ship was named the *Athée* (the *Atheist*). Such a name, like some other substituted ones in the Revolutionary fleet, while proclaiming the infidel audacity of the ruling power, was yet, though not so intended to be, the aptest name, if one consider it, ever given to a warship; far more so indeed than the *Devastation*, the *Erebus* (the *Hell*), and similar names bestowed upon fighting ships.

On the return passage to the English fleet from the detached cruise during which occurred the events already recorded, the *Bellipotent* fell in with the *Athée*. An engagement ensued, during which Captain Vere, in the act of putting his ship alongside the enemy with a view of throwing his boarders across her bulwarks, was hit by a musket ball from a porthole of the enemy's main cabin. More than disabled, he dropped to the deck and was carried below to the same cockpit where some of his men already lay. The senior lieutenant took command. Under him the enemy was finally captured, and though much crippled was by rare good fortune successfully taken into Gibraltar, an English port not very distant from the scene of the fight. There, Captain Vere with the rest of the wounded was put ashore. He lingered for some days, but the end came. Unhappily he was cut off too early for the Nile and Trafalgar. The spirit that 'spite its philosophic austerity may yet have indulged in the most secret of all passions, ambition, never attained to the fulness of fame.

Not long before death, while lying under the influence of that magical drug which, soothing the physical frame, mysteriously operates on the subtler element in man, he was heard to murmur words inexplicable to his attendant: "Billy Budd, Billy Budd." That these were not the accents of remorse would seem clear from what the attendant said to the *Bellipotent*'s senior officer of marines, who, as the most reluctant to condemn of the members of the drumhead court, too well knew, though here he kept the knowledge to himself, who Billy Budd was.

29

SOME FEW WEEKS after the execution, among other matters under the head of "News from the Mediterranean," there appeared in a naval chronicle of the time, an authorized weekly publication, an account of the affair. It was doubtless for the most part written in good faith, though the medium, partly rumor, through which the facts must have reached the writer served to deflect and in part falsify them. The account was as follows:

"On the tenth of the last month a deplorable occurrence took place on board H.M.S. *Bellipotent*. John Claggart, the ship's master-at-arms, discovering that some sort of plot was incipient among an inferior section of the ship's company, and that the ringleader was one William Budd; he, Claggart, in the act of arraigning the man before the captain, was vindictively stabbed to the heart by the suddenly drawn sheath knife of Budd.

"The deed and the implement employed sufficiently suggest that though mustered into the service under an English name the assassin was no Englishman, but one of those aliens adopting English cognomens whom the present extraordinary necessities of the service have caused to be admitted into it in considerable numbers.

"The enormity of the crime and the extreme depravity of the criminal appear the greater in view of the character of the victim, a middle-aged man respectable and discreet, belonging to that minor official grade, the petty officers, upon whom, as none know better than the commissioned gentlemen, the efficiency of His Majesty's navy so largely depends. His function was a responsible one, at once onerous and thankless; and his fidelity in it the greater because of his strong patriotic impulse. In this instance as in so many other instances in these days, the character of this unfortunate man signally refutes, if refutation were needed, that peevish saying attributed to the late Dr. Johnson, that patriotism is the last refuge of a scoundrel.

"The criminal paid the penalty of his crime. The promptitude of the punishment has proved salutary. Nothing amiss is now apprehended aboard H.M.S. *Bellipotent*."

The above, appearing in a publication now long ago superannuated and forgotten, is all that hitherto has stood in human record to attest what manner of men respectively were John Claggart and Billy Budd.

30

EVERYTHING is for a term venerated in navies. Any tangible object associated with some striking incident of the service is converted into a monument. The spar from which the foretopman was suspended was for some few years kept trace of by the bluejackets. Their knowledges followed it from ship to dockyard and again from dockyard to ship, still pursuing it even when at last reduced to a mere dockyard boom. To them a chip of it was as a piece of the Cross. Ignorant though they were of the secret facts of the tragedy, and not thinking but that the penalty was somehow unavoidably inflicted from the naval point of view, for all that, they instinctively felt that Billy was a sort of man as incapable of mutiny as of wilful murder. They recalled the fresh young image of the Handsome Sailor, that face never deformed by a sneer or subtler vile freak of the heart within. This impression of him was doubtless deepened by the fact that he was gone, and in a measure mysteriously gone. On the gun decks of the *Bellipotent* the general estimate of his nature and its unconscious simplicity eventually found rude utterance from another foretopman, one of his own watch, gifted, as some sailors are, with an artless *poetic* temperament. The tarry hand made some lines which, after circulating among the shipboard crews for a while, finally got rudely printed at Portsmouth as a ballad. The title given to it was the sailor's.

BILLY IN THE DARBIES

Good of the chaplain to enter Lone Bay
And down on his marrowbones here and pray
For the likes just o' me, Billy Budd.—But, look:
Through the port comes the moonshine astray!
It tips the guard's cutlass and silvers this nook;
But 'twill die in the dawning of Billy's last day.
A jewel-block they'll make of me tomorrow,
Pendant pearl from the yardarm-end
Like the eardrop I gave to Bristol Molly—
O, 'tis me, not the sentence they'll suspend.
Ay, ay, all is up; and I must up too,
Early in the morning, aloft from alow.
On an empty stomach now never it would do.
They'll give me a nibble—bit o' biscuit ere I go.
Sure, a messmate will reach me the last parting cup;
But, turning heads away from the hoist and the belay,
Heaven knows who will have the running of me up!

No pipe to those halyards.—But aren't it all sham?
A blur's in my eyes; it is dreaming that I am.
A hatchet to my hawser? All adrift to go?
The drum roll to grog, and Billy never know?
But Donald he has promised to stand by the plank;
So I'll shake a friendly hand ere I sink.
But—no! It is dead then I'll be, come to think.
I remember Taff the Welshman when he sank.
And his cheek it was like the budding pink.
But me they'll lash in hammock, drop me deep.
Fathoms down, fathoms down, how I'll dream fast asleep.
I feel it stealing now. Sentry, are you there?
Just ease these darbies at the wrist,
And roll me over fair!
I am sleepy, and the oozy weeds about me twist.

Chronology

1819　　　Herman Melville born August 1, New York City, third child (second son) of Allan Melvill, importer and merchant of Scottish descent, and Maria Gansevoort, daughter of General Peter Gansevoort, a hero of the American Revolution and member of a prominent Albany family.

1825–29　Attends New-York Male High School.

1829–30　Attends Columbia Grammar School, New York, beginning September 1829.

1830　　　Father fails in business, and family moves to Albany in October.

1830–31　Attends Albany Academy, October 1830 to October 1831.

1832　　　Father dies, January 28, in debt.

1832–34　Works as clerk at the New York State Bank in Albany.

1834–35　Works on his uncle Thomas's farm near Pittsfield, Mass.

1835–37　Works in Albany as bookkeeper and clerk in his brother's fur business. Attends Albany Classical School in 1835; returns to Albany Academy, September 1, 1836, to March 1, 1837.

1837　　　Brother's business fails, April. Teaches in Sikes District School near Pittsfield for the fall term. Returns to Albany at the end of the year.

1838　　　Moves with family to nearby Lansingburgh in the spring. Returns briefly to his uncle's farm in the autumn. Back in Lansingburgh in November, studies surveying at the Lansingburgh Academy.

1839　　　Two sketches, "Fragments from a Writing Desk," published pseudonymously in *Democratic Press, and Lansingburgh Advertiser*, May. Sails from New York to Liverpool and back as crew member on the trading ship *St. Lawrence*, June 5 to October 1.

1437

1839–40   Teaches school in Greenbush, N.Y., and briefly (late May 1840) in Brunswick, N.Y.

1840   Visits his uncle Thomas in Galena, Ill., in the summer, accompanied by his friend, Eli Fly, and probably travels on a Mississippi River steamer during the visit. In autumn searches for a job in New York.

1841–42   Sails from New Bedford harbor, January 3, 1841, on the maiden voyage of the whaling ship *Acushnet*, bound for the South Seas. On July 9, 1842, deserts the *Acushnet* with Richard Tobias Greene at Nuku Hiva in the Marquesas.

1842   After a month in the Taipi valley, sails August 9 on the Australian whaling ship *Lucy Ann*; at Tahiti, is sent ashore with others as mutineer; escapes with John B. Troy in October; the two explore Tahiti and Eimeo and work on a potato farm.

1842–43   Sails on the Nantucket whaling ship *Charles and Henry* from November 7, 1842, through April 27, 1843; is discharged at Lahaina in the Hawaiian Islands, May 2, and takes various jobs in Honolulu.

1843–44   Enlists in the United States Navy in Honolulu; sails August 19, 1843, aboard the frigate *United States*, on which his superior and friend is John J. Chase; arrives in Boston October 3, 1844—having been away nearly four years—and is discharged October 14. Returns to Lansingburgh.

1845   Works on manuscript of a book based on his adventures in the Marquesas; it is rejected by Harper & Brothers in New York but is accepted by John Murray in London, through the efforts of his brother Gansevoort, secretary of the American Legation there.

1846   *Narrative of a Four Months' Residence among the Natives of a Valley of the Marquesas Islands* published by John Murray in London, February 26; published by Wiley & Putnam in New York, under the title *Typee*, about March 20. A "Revised Edition" published in New York in August.

1847   *Omoo* published by Murray in London, March 30, and by
            Harper & Brothers in New York, about May 1. Marries
            Elizabeth Shaw, daughter of Chief Justice Lemuel Shaw
            of the Massachusetts Supreme Court, August 4, and moves
            to Manhattan.

1847–50   Publishes anonymous reviews (including "Hawthorne and
            His Mosses," August 1850) and satirical pieces, the former
            in the *Literary World*, edited by his friend Evert A. Duyc-
            kinck, and the latter in *Yankee Doodle*, edited by a member
            of Duyckinck's circle, Cornelius Mathews.

1849   A son, Malcolm, born February 16. *Mardi* published by
            Richard Bentley in London, March 16, and by Harper in
            New York, April 14. *Redburn* published by Bentley in
            London, September 29, and by Harper in New York,
            November 14.

1849–50   Makes a trip to London (to visit publishers) and the con-
            tinent, October 11, 1849, to February 1, 1850.

1850   *White-Jacket* published by Bentley in London, January 23,
            and by Harper in New York, March 21. Meets Nathaniel
            Hawthorne at a picnic near Pittsfield, Mass., August 5,
            and they become friends. Borrowing money from his
            father-in-law, Melville purchases a farm (which he names
            "Arrowhead") near Pittsfield, September 14, and his family
            is in residence there by early October.

1851   *Moby-Dick* published by Bentley in London, October 18
            (under the title *The Whale*), and by Harper in New York,
            November 14. A second son, Stanwix, born October 22.

1852   *Pierre* published by Harper in New York, August 6, and
            by Sampson Low in London in November.

1853   Melville's family and friends, concerned about his health,
            attempt unsuccessfully during the spring to secure a con-
            sulship for him. A daughter, Elizabeth, born May 22.
            From about this time, and through the next quarter cen-
            tury, his wife's family worries about her life with Melville,
            involving financial insecurity and his recurrent depression.

1853–56   Publishes fourteen tales and sketches in *Putnam's Monthly Magazine* and *Harper's New Monthly Magazine*.

1855   *Israel Potter* published by G. P. Putnam in New York in early March (having been serialized in *Putnam's Monthly Magazine*, July 1854–March 1855) and—without authorization—by George Routledge in London in May. A second daughter, Frances, born March 2.

1856   *The Piazza Tales*, consisting of five of the *Putnam's* pieces and a newly written title piece, published by Dix & Edwards in New York in late May and distributed in England by Sampson Low.

1856–57   Takes a trip (financed by his father-in-law) for his health, sailing for Glasgow October 11, 1856; visits Hawthorne in Liverpool; then tours the Holy Land, Greece, and Italy; returns to Liverpool and, on May 5, 1857, begins the voyage back to New York, arriving May 20.

1857   *The Confidence-Man* published by Dix & Edwards in New York, April 1, and by Longman, Brown, Green, Longmans, & Roberts in London in early April.

1857–60   Goes on the lecture circuit for three seasons, lecturing the first season on "Statues in Rome," the second on "The South Seas," and the third on "Traveling."

1860   Embarks May 28 for San Francisco on the clipper ship *Meteor* as a guest of the captain, his brother Thomas; returns via Panama, arriving in New York on November 12.

1861   Travels to Washington in March to attempt to secure a consular appointment. Father-in-law dies. Family spends the winter in New York.

1863   Leaves Pittsfield permanently in October, trading Arrowhead for his brother Allan's New York house at 104 East 26th Street.

1864   Visits his cousin Col. Henry Gansevoort in an army camp on the Virginia front, April.

1866   Publishes some Civil War poems in *Harper's*. A collection of his war poems, *Battle-Pieces and Aspects of the War*, published by Harper, August 23. Appointed a deputy inspector of customs at the port of New York, December 5.

1867   In the spring, Melville's wife's family (some of whom regard him as insane) discuss with her minister the possibility of a legal separation between her and Melville. Their son Malcolm dies by his own pistol, September 11.

1876   The long poem *Clarel* published (at his uncle Peter Gansevoort's expense) by Putnam in early June.

1878   Melville's wife inherits money from the estate of her aunt, Martha Marett.

1885   Resigns position as customs inspector, December 31.

1886   Son Stanwix dies in San Francisco, February 23.

1887   Receives his last royalty statement from the Harper firm, March 4, there having been no printings of his books since 1876; some copies of *Typee*, *Mardi*, *Redburn*, *Pierre*, and *Battle-Pieces* are still in stock, but *Omoo*, *White-Jacket*, and *Moby-Dick* are out of print. (The total sales of these eight books during Melville's lifetime amounted to about 35,000 copies in the United States and 16,000 in Britain; his lifetime earnings from all his books came to about $5900 from the United States and $4500 from Britain.)

1888   *John Marr and Other Sailors* privately printed at the De Vinne Press in an edition of twenty-five copies.

1891   *Timoleon* privately printed at the Caxton Press in May in an edition of twenty-five copies. Dies September 28, leaving a number of poems and *Billy Budd, Sailor* in manuscript.

Note on the Texts

The texts presented in this volume, with the exception of *Billy Budd, Sailor*, are those of the Northwestern-Newberry Edition of *The Writings of Herman Melville*, edited by Harrison Hayford, Hershel Parker, and G. Thomas Tanselle and published by the Northwestern University Press and The Newberry Library (*Pierre* in 1971, *Israel Potter* in 1983, *The Confidence-Man* in 1984, and *The Piazza Tales and Other Prose Pieces, 1839–1860* forthcoming). Those texts were prepared according to the standards established by—and they have received the official approval of—the Center for Editions of American Authors of the Modern Language Association of America. (See its *Statement of Editorial Principles and Procedures*, revised edition, 1972.) The text of *Billy Budd, Sailor* is that edited by Harrison Hayford and Merton M. Sealts, Jr., and published by the University of Chicago Press in 1962.

The textual problems addressed in the Northwestern-Newberry Edition are relatively simple, although they differ somewhat from book to book and among the uncollected shorter pieces, depending upon whether there is more than one authoritative text of a given work. When there is only one text authorized by Melville, the main editorial problem, after the correction of obvious errors (whether by author, copyist, or typesetter), concerns wording that cannot be what Melville intended because it makes no sense or insufficient sense. Such wording must be emended, whenever possible, with wording that is more likely what Melville intended (and that could have been misread as the word originally printed). When there are two authoritative texts, it is also necessary to discriminate authorial from nonauthorial readings among the variants in the later of the two—to determine, that is, whether each of these variants is more likely Melville's own revision or a change made in the publisher's office or by the typesetter. The conservative policy followed by the Northwestern-Newberry editors in such cases is to keep the earlier reading unless there is compelling reason to believe that the later variant is Melville's.

For none of the four books in this volume is the manuscript Melville supplied to the publisher preserved (though twenty-six manuscript fragments, all discarded worksheets, do survive for *The Confidence-Man*), nor does a separate English edition offer (as was the case with Melville's earlier books) an additional text with possible authorial variants. Only *The Confidence-Man* had a separate English edition, and that edition was set from the American with no opportunity for Melville to make changes. *Pierre* and *Israel Potter* were published in England using imported American sheets issued with the imprint of Sampson Low, Son & Co., who also distributed in England the American edition of *The Piazza Tales*, on whose title page its firm name was included. Moreover, none of these four books had a later edition during Melville's lifetime (apart from the unauthorized Routledge 1855 London edition of *Israel Potter*). The basic text adopted by the Northwestern-Newberry editors is the one nearest Melville's manuscript: for *Pierre* and *The Confidence-Man* the first edition of each; for *Israel Potter* and *The Piazza Tales* (one piece excepted) the component texts as they first appeared in the numbers of *Putnam's Monthly Magazine*. The one exception is "The Piazza," which Melville wrote as the book's title piece and for which the basic text adopted, in the absence of a manuscript, is its original appearance in *The Piazza Tales* volume.

The first edition of *Pierre* was set from the manuscript Melville supplied (largely as copied by his sister Augusta and perhaps his wife) to Harper & Brothers, New York, who published it in the late summer of 1852 (on August 6, according to a contemporary record, although the first reviews appeared a week or so earlier). The textual problems here are simply the detection and correction of corrupt readings. Some are readily found and emended, but acute reading is required to recognize others, which once seen may or may not be easy to emend (see the note for 251.43).

The manuscript for *The Confidence-Man* was also supplied by Melville to his American publisher in fair copy prepared by his sister (and possibly his wife). The English edition was set from corrected proofs of the American; though differing at about one hundred points in wording and at scores in spelling, punctuation, and capitalization, it contains no

changes made by Melville himself. The American edition
(New York: Dix, Edwards, & Co., 1857) appeared, with unaccountable appropriateness, on April 1, and the English
(Longman, Brown, Green, Longmans, & Roberts, 1857) two
or three days later. The Northwestern-Newberry editors have
corrected sixty-four obvious errors and made seventy-four
other emendations, including such corrections of corrupt
readings as "fraternal" for "paternal" (868.24) and "life. As
elsewhere" for "life as elsewhere." (914.4–5). For other examples see the notes for 914.6, 918.30, 930.34, 1005.20, 1091.10,
and 1103.7. Questionable or plainly corrupt readings for which
no satisfactory emendations were found include "myth"
(841.28), the repetition of "Piazza, Covent Garden" (987.25–
26), "touch" (1100.38), and "this beats printing" (1105.29).

Israel Potter has two authoritative texts, the one first serialized in nine numbers of *Putnam's Magazine* (July 1854–March
1855), set from manuscripts Melville supplied, and the later
book text, set from the magazine sheets. The book edition
(New York: G. P. Putnam & Co., 1855) was published in the
spring and was followed by two more impressions during 1855
with no significant variants. Comparison of the book text
with that of the magazine installments shows one major omission (see note 605.11) and scores of minor changes, including
needed corrections; but none of these appear to have been
made by Melville. Apart from the deletion of the magazine
subtitle "A FOURTH OF JULY STORY," which was most likely
the publisher's addition in the first place, the one major authorial change was Melville's addition of the dedication to the
Bunker Hill Monument, with its reference to the "tattered
copy" of Israel Potter's autobiographical story from which he
said—or rather admitted—"the present account has been
drawn." Actually, this primary source book, *Life and Remarkable Adventures of Israel R. Potter* (Providence, 1824), as well
as four others that Melville did not acknowledge, enabled the
Northwestern-Newberry editors to locate and correct several
errors in the basic *Putnam's Magazine* text that were worse
than any caught and corrected by the Putnam editor and
typesetters who produced the book text. These works are
cited and examples given in the notes to this volume. A final
source of later corrections by Melville (adopted by the North-

western-Newberry editors)—rather curious ones in light of more serious ones he passed over—is a copy of *Israel Potter* in the Harvard Melville Collection; in it he penciled the change from "illy" to "ill" four times (at 456.17, 471.22, 490.2, and 561.21), changed "birth" to "berth" (531.12), and twice corrected "boquets" to "bouquets" (501.19 and 501.29).

In *The Piazza Tales*, the textual problems are more complex not only because there are two authoritative texts of each piece (except "The Piazza")—that of *Putnam's Magazine*, set from Melville's manuscript, and that of the book—but also because Melville himself revised the magazine texts, as he evidently had not done for *Israel Potter*. In letters to Dix & Edwards (Jan. 7 and 19, 1856) he requested copies of the magazines so he could "do my share of the work without delay"; and in sending the revised copies he reported, "I have prepared for republication the Articles agreed upon. . . . Aside from ordinary corrections, some few other improvements have been made, and a desirable note or two added." In another letter, when returning proofs (March 24, 1857), he complained, "There seems to have been a surprising profusion of commas in these proofs. I have struck them out pretty much; but hope that someone who understands punctuation better than I do, will give the final hand to it." Comparison of the two texts shows that nothing was done to eliminate the "profusion of commas," and it is clear that Melville did not have control of the many changes in punctuation, spelling, and capitalization that appear in the book; but an editor may be tempted, in light of the earlier letters, to accept most of the many verbal revisions as Melville's own—as constituting the "some few improvements" he made. The Northwestern-Newberry editors, however, conservatively hold to the magazine versions, their basic texts, unless the changes in wording are convincingly authorial rather than the sort of "improvement" that a house editor might make or changes a compositor might unconsciously blunder into. Too many seem to be "softenings" of earlier wording—apparently made by someone at Dix & Edwards to avoid offense to readers. One of these, involving the disappearance of the grub-man's name, Mr. Cutlets, in "Bartleby the Scrivener," is discussed in the note for 670.9.

Melville's uncollected prose in this volume is divided into two parts, one of tales and the other of articles and reviews, and is arranged chronologically by order of composition (reconstructed, as close as is possible so far, by Merton M. Sealts, Jr., for the Northwestern-Newberry Edition). The uncollected tales—apart from "The Two Temples" and *Billy Budd, Sailor*—do not survive in manuscript and were not reprinted by Melville. The authoritative texts are therefore the first printings: "Fragments from a Writing Desk" in the *Democratic Press, and Lansingburgh Advertiser* (May 4, and May 18, 1839); "The Happy Failure" in *Harper's New Monthly Magazine* (July 1854); "The Fiddler" in *Harper's* (Sept. 1854); "Cock-A-Doodle-Doo!" in *Harper's* (Dec. 1853); "Poor Man's Pudding and Rich Man's Crumbs" in *Harper's* (June 1854); "The Paradise of Bachelors and the Tartarus of Maids" in *Harper's* (Apr. 1855); "Jimmy Rose" in *Harper's* (Nov. 1855); "The 'Gees" in *Harper's* (Mar. 1856); "I and My Chimney" in *Putnam's Monthly Magazine* (Mar. 1856); and "The Apple-Tree Table" in *Putnam's* (May 1856). Neither is there a manuscript or other authoritative text for the article "Authentic Anecdotes of 'Old Zack,' " except the text printed in *Yankee Doodle,* II (July 24, July 31, Aug. 7, Aug. 14, Aug. 21, Aug. 28, and Sept. 11, 1847), pp. 152, 165, 167, 172, 188, 199, 202, and 229. The editorial work in each of these pieces, then, is of the same kind as in *Pierre* and *The Confidence-Man*: correcting obvious errors and identifying, and emending if possible, any corrupt readings.

The manuscript for "The Two Temples," which Melville submitted (in his sister Augusta's copyist hand) to *Putnam's*, was rejected and remained unpublished during his lifetime. It is now in the Melville Collection of the Houghton Library of Harvard University, and is the basic text for the Northwestern-Newberry edition. For all five of the reviews the basic texts are the printer's copy manuscripts preserved (in the Duyckinck Collection of the New York Public Library) among the papers of Evert A. and George L. Duyckinck, in whose New York *Literary World* they were published: "Etchings of a Whaling Cruise" on March 6, 1847; "Mr Parkman's Tour" on March 31, 1849; "Cooper's New Novel" on April 28, 1849; "A Thought on Book-Binding" on March 16, 1850; and

"Hawthorne and His Mosses" on August 17 and August 24, 1850. In no instance did the editors adopt, as Melville's own revision, the variants in the *Literary World* texts. Many are simply misreadings of the manuscript, as well as deliberate editorial and compositorial alterations. Most notorious is the flattening misreading "same madness" for "sane madness" in "Hawthorne and His Mosses"—one at which Mrs. Hawthorne reported Melville's vexation. Each of the manuscripts also contains some misreadings by the copyist (such as the evident misreading of "fraternal" as "paternal" by Melville's sister Augusta) and various errors of Melville's own. The manuscript of "Hawthorne and His Mosses" reveals Evert A. Duyckinck's patent editorial interference with the text as Melville originally wrote it (and as his wife copied it), as well as Melville's own revisions, some of them made evidently under Duyckinck's suasion.

The *Billy Budd* manuscript, left unfinished as a semi-final draft at Melville's death, has not yet been prepared by the Northwestern-Newberry editors according to the principles they follow in editing Melville's other works. The text presented in this volume, therefore, is the "reading text" edited by Hayford and Sealts, who have made the most thorough analysis of the manuscript to date. The first publication of *Billy Budd* was an edition prepared by Raymond Weaver in 1924 (revised by him in 1928). Weaver prepared a "reading text" that was as near as he could make it to what he judged Melville would have wanted a publisher to print, but not following in every detail what is in the manuscript. Weaver found that in many details Melville's intention cannot be ascertained because of "the state of the manuscript." F. Barron Freeman prepared a "literal text" in 1948, attempting, not always successfully, to report in every detail exactly what Melville put on the paper, including the revisions, in a way that would account for all the writing of any sort that appears in the manuscript. It was an edition for the scholar, not a finished narrative for the general reader. Freeman's and Weaver's texts each suffered the limitations of its chosen method, and each had its individual shortcomings and errors. Because no single text can accommodate both Weaver's and Freeman's objectives, Hayford and Sealts prepared two separate texts:

one a "genetic text," the other a "reading text" based on it. The divergences between the principles followed by Hayford and Sealts in their "reading text" (as stated in their "Textual Notes," pp. 213 ff.) and those established in the completed volumes of the Northwestern-Newberry Edition are minor as to treatment of *wording*; thus differences in the wording of the eventual Northwestern-Newberry edition are likely to result merely from normal and necessary judgmental differences in the application of principles to individual problems. There will be greater divergence in the treatment of the spelling and punctuation. The Northwestern-Newberry editors do not follow the policy Hayford and Sealts adopted: "His [Melville's] inconsistent spelling, capitalization, hyphenation, paragraphing, and punctuation . . . have here been standardized—within the limits imposed by his own characteristic syntax—in accordance with present-day usage."

The standards for American English continue to fluctuate and in some ways were conspicuously different in earlier periods from what they are now. In nineteenth-century writings, for example, a word might be spelled in more than one way, even in the same work, and such variations might be carried into print. Commas were sometimes used expressively to suggest the movements of voice, and capitals were sometimes meant to give significances to a word beyond those it might have in its uncapitalized form. Since modernization would remove such effects, this volume (that is, all its text except *Billy Budd*) preserves the spelling, punctuation, capitalization, and wording of the Northwestern-Newberry Edition, which strives to be as faithful to Melville's usage as surviving evidence permits. It also contains the original tables of contents despite their inconsistencies with the chapter headings found in the body of the texts.

The texts in this volume follow exactly the Northwestern-Newberry texts of *Pierre* (first printing), *Israel Potter* (first printing), *The Piazza Tales and Other Prose Pieces, 1839–1860* (page proofs), and *The Confidence-Man* (first printing), with four exceptions: in *Pierre*, "nor" replaces "not" at 104.4, "nether" replaces "nearer" at 127.28, and the sentence "And he . . . groping." is properly placed in the paragraph at

420.10; and in *The Confidence-Man*, "throwing" replaces "thowing" at 866.8. (These corrections will be made in future printings of the Northwestern-Newberry texts.) The text of *Billy Budd, Sailor* follows exactly that of the University of Chicago Press edition (seventh printing). The present edition is concerned only with representing the *texts* of these editions; it does not attempt to reproduce features of the typographic design—such as the display capitalization of chapter openings. In this volume the reader has the results of the most detailed scholarly efforts thus far made to establish the texts of *Pierre, Israel Potter, The Piazza Tales, The Confidence-Man*, Melville's uncollected tales, articles, and reviews, and his last and never quite finished work, *Billy Budd, Sailor*.

Notes

For more detailed notes, references to other studies, and further biographical background than is provided in the Chronology, see the relevant volumes of the Northwestern-Newberry edition; for *Pierre* see also Henry A. Murray's edition (New York: Hendricks House, 1949); for *The Confidence-Man* see the editions of Elizabeth S. Foster (New York: Hendrick House, 1954), H. Bruce Franklin (Indianapolis: Bobbs-Merrill, 1967), and Hershel Parker (New York: Norton, 1971); and for *Billy Budd*, see the edition of Harrison Hayford and Merton M. Sealts, Jr., (Chicago: The University of Chicago Press, 1962). For further information on biography and sources, see Leon Howard, *Herman Melville, A Biography* (Berkeley and Los Angeles: University of California Press, 1951) and Tom Quirk, *Melville's Confidence-Man: From Knave to Knight* (Columbia: University of Missouri Press, 1982). In the notes below, the reference numbers denote page and line of the present volume (the line count includes chapter headings). Notes printed at the foot of the page of the text are Melville's own. No note is made for material included in a standard desk-reference book.

PIERRE

3.2   *Greylock's*]   The highest mountain in Massachusetts, it dominates the north view from Melville's Arrowhead piazza and from the study in which he wrote *Moby-Dick*, *Pierre*, and other works in this volume.

15.12   Bridgewater Canal]   Between Liverpool and Manchester.

16.34   regular armies]   Such tenant-landlord conflicts occurred in New York in 1839–46.

20.9   *Nemo . . . ipse.*]   "No one against God but God himself." Quoted in Goethe's *Autobiography, Truth and Poetry*, which Melville bought in London in 1849.

36.8–9   *"Love . . . boy,"*]   Song by J. A. Wade.

52.22–23   sweet . . . belly]   Cf. Revelation 10:9.

75.33   faintly,]   Perhaps the comma misrepresents what Melville meant: not "exclaimed faintly" but "faintly starting."

84.26   Ehrenbreitstein]   A fortress near Coblenz.

104.3–5   "Ah! . . . one!"]   Canto 25, Cary's translation. The first edition of *Pierre* had "not double" for "nor double," an error corrected here but overlooked by the Northwestern-Newberry editors.

107.14   sea of trouble]   Cf. Shakespeare, *Hamlet*, II, i, 59.

121.30   sins of the father]   Cf. Exodus 20:5.

123.14–15   And . . . adulteress?"]   "And Jesus said unto her, Neither do I condemn thee: go, and sin no more." John 8:11.

124.10–11   serpent and dove]   Cf. Matthew 10:16.

134.3   sapphire throne]   Ezekiel 1:26.

157.11   remarkable stone]   The original for this stone was a similar one, still to be seen near Pittsfield, Massachusetts, known as Balance Rock.

162.5   Montaignized]   Melville marked this passage in *Hamlet* (in his copy now at Harvard): "there is nothing either good or bad but thinking makes it so"—and wrote in the margin, "Here is forcibly shown the great Montaigneism of Hamlet."

166.31   hollow of His hand]   See Isaiah 40:12.

168.9–12   angelic . . . world.]   Matthew 19:14.

178.32   Saya]   Melville saw this skirt-and-hood female costume when he visited Lima in 1843 and refers to it in several works.

199.16–17   Inferno . . . Hamlet]   Canto 3, Cary's translation; *Hamlet*, I, v, 189.

200.3   Carrisbrook well]   At Carisbrooke Castle, Isle of Wight; famous for its 160-foot depth, in which a dropped pebble echoes impressively.

243.9   long tongs]   The legend is that St. Dunstan, when tempted by the Devil in the form of a pretty girl, pinched the Devil's nose with red-hot tongs.

248.31–32   My . . . world?]   Cf. John 18:36. "My kingdom is not of this world."

249.7   earthly . . . God]   I Corinthians 3:19.

249.41   Ephesian matron]   In the *Satyricon* of Petronius Arbiter a sentry, supposed to be guarding a body, seduces this newly widowed matron grieving in her husband's tomb. The sentry pleases her so much that when the body he was guarding is stolen, she saves his life by offering him her husband's body as a substitute for the stolen one.

251.43   all good,]   The first edition has "at all," but the Northwestern-Newberry editors point out that Plinlimmon doesn't mean becoming "at all good" but "all good."

281.21–22   Lock-and-Sin hospitals]   In London, for the treatment of venereal diseases.

305.15–18   he . . . hath]   See Matthew 25:29.

337.26–27   birthright . . . pottage]   Genesis 25:33–34.

350.13–14   Fairmount, Croton, and Cochituate]   The quite new reservoirs for Philadelphia, New York, and Boston.

353.6–7   brass . . . cymbal!"]   I Corinthians 13:1.

354.24   Piko]   Pico Alto, the highest mountain on the island of Pico in the Azores.

401.18   leaden Titan]   Melville saw this sculpture by Balthazar Marsy when he visited Versailles in December 1849.

407.17   The Cenci of Guido]   This supposed portrait of Beatrice Cenci, attributed to Guido Reni, was fashionably admired after Shelley's *Cenci* (1819) popularized the story of her (supposed) incestuous victimization by her father, whom she murdered. Melville went to see it when in Rome in 1857 and owned an engraving of it. Hawthorne, too, brings it into *The Marble Faun* (1862).

ISRAEL POTTER

425.18   reprint]   Only chapters 2–6 are a close rewriting of *Life and Remarkable Adventures of Israel R. Potter* (Providence, 1824), ghostwritten and published by Henry Trumbull. Later chapters, dealing with Benjamin Franklin (7–11), Squire Woodcock (12–13), John Paul Jones at sea (14–20), and Ethan Allen (21–22), are improvised from other sources, following hints from Potter's book. The last four chapters (23–26) draw only a few basic facts from it. The Northwestern-Newberry edition includes a photofacsimile of the original *Life*, keyed line-by-line to Melville's text, and discusses his use of it and other sources. When or how Melville acquired the *Life* is not known, but entries in his London journal show that he had a copy in 1849, and that he bought an old London map and explored the city in case he might "serve up the Revolutionary narrative of the beggar"—a writing job he postponed until 1854.

429.10   Berkshire, Mass.]   Both the title page and first sentence of Potter's *Life* name his birthplace as Cranston, Rhode Island.

431.16   Saddleback]   Mt. Greylock. See the dedication to *Pierre* (p. 3) and note 3.2.

435.19   poling]   The Northwestern-Newberry editors emend the misreading "pulling" (which occurs in both the magazine and book texts) from Potter's *Life*, which makes clear that the canoe was propelled by a pole.

439.25–26   regiment . . . Patterson] Melville shifted Potter's regiment from Rhode Island to the Berkshires. This and other details are taken from *A History of the County of Berkshire, Massachusetts* (1829), edited by David Dudley Field. Melville's own annotated copy of this work is preserved.

439.32   Putnam] Major-General Israel Putnam, whose command—"Don't fire till you see the whites of their eyes"—became proverbial; see 440.14

441.10   Sicinius Dentatus] "The Roman Achilles," legendary hero of the plebians.

442.36   what ship?"] The Northwestern-Newberry editors supply this question, not present in the magazine and book texts, from Potter's *Life*, where it is both asked and answered.

449.29   nineteen] This reading is adopted by the Northwestern-Newberry editors from Potter's *Life* to correct the magazine and book reading "ten" for the width in feet of the "great ditch" Israel jumped.

456.17   Ill] In a copy of *Israel Potter* (now at Harvard) Melville corrected the form "Illy" to "Ill" here and at 471.22, 490.2, and 561.21. The Northwestern-Newberry editors adopt his corrections. In the same copy Melville corrected "wild" to "mild" at 486.33, a reading also adopted in the Northwestern-Newberry edition.

459.2   conversation . . . monarch.] In his *Life*, Potter says that he did remove his hat and was ordered by the king to replace it.

462.3–5   FRIENDS . . . PURLEY."] Potter's *Life* reports this episode, naming these friends of America as Woodcock, Bridges, and Horne Tooke, the last of whom began the book referred to (1786) while imprisoned for his pro-American activities. See the further reference to Tooke, 517.34.

468.23   Doctor Franklin] Melville goes beyond Potter's single paragraph in the *Life* about his meeting with Franklin and draws material for his portrait from *The Works of Benjamin Franklin*, ed. Jared Sparks (1836–40). For the Latin Quarter and "mysteries" of the lodging-house (chapters 8 and 9), he drew on his own recollections and 1849 Paris journal entries.

489.27   Paul Jones] This Revolutionary hero is not mentioned in Potter's *Life*. The materials for treatment of Jones's character and naval exploits (chapters 15–19) are drawn from two books: Roberts C. Sands's compilation, *Life and Correspondence of John Paul Jones* (1830), and James Fenimore Cooper's *History of the Navy of the United States*, revised edition (1840).

501.4   a little closet] This entire episode was not present in Potter's *Life*. In the *Life*, Potter was courier to Franklin a second time, was then prevented by the war from a third crossing to France, where he was to have received Franklin's help in returning to America, and soon after went to London, not to sea.

518.11–13   clergyman . . . dean]   The trio referred to are: William Tooke, translator of Lucian (1820); Laurence Sterne, author of *Tristram Shandy* (1760); and Jonathan Swift, author of *Gulliver's Travels* (1726) and Dean of St. Paul's Cathedral, Dublin.

545.7   Earl of Selkirk]   This historical episode is drawn from materials in Sands's *Life and Correspondence of John Paul Jones*, including the letters to Lord and Lady Selkirk (whom Jones in fact did not encounter personally).

555.3   THREE MONTHS]   Actually it was one year and three months since the expedition sailed from Groix in August 1779.

556.36–37   *Bon Homme Richard*]   Sands says the famous ship was so named at Jones's request.

559.35   Rev. Mr. Shirra's]   The anecdote is from Sands, who spells the name "Shirra." The magazine and book spelling, "Shirrer," may reflect Melville's New England pronunciation, as do other misspellings in his works (e.g. "Happar" for "Hapaa" in *Typee*).

561.3   THE BATTLE]   The historical facts are mostly from Sands and Cooper (see note 489.27).

567.15   Ere long,]   In the magazine and book publication, "CHAPTER XIX. CONTINUED" begins here. Because the Northwestern-Newberry editors think this division of chapter 19 was made by a Putnam editor and not by Melville, they disregard it and include the contents in chapter 19. Similarly, they drop the magazine and book division of chapter 23 into two parts at 601.21, the second part numbered "XXIV"; thus the magazine and book chapters XXV, XXVI, and XXVII become chapters 24, 25, and 26 in the Northwestern-Newberry edition.

569.22   chess-player]   Invented by Wolfgang von Kempelen (1734–1804) and exhibited in the United States from 1826 by Johann Maelzel, this supposed mechanical chess-player concealed a human player. See Edgar Allan Poe's discussion in "Maelzel's Chess-Player."

569.31   Apollyon]   In Revelation 9:11, "the angel of the bottomless pit"; in *Pilgrim's Progress*, he is encountered by Christian.

579.11   " 'Cease . . . growling!' "]   One of Charles Dibdin's many late-eighteenth-century sea songs.

585.15   straight streets]   The streets of Boston are proverbially crooked.

587.13   a martial man]   The material here is mostly drawn from Allen's own *A Narrative of Colonel Ethan Allen's Captivity* (1779).

587.23   four]   The number "three," which appears in the magazine and book texts, does not agree with "four of the soldiers" just above. The Northwestern-Newberry editors emend it to "four" because four soldiers would be the more likely number for the job and because the "three officers" involved may have caused the confusion.

590.24–25   Jehovah . . . Congress]   Allen's famous demand for the surrender of Fort Ticonderoga (1775) is echoed: "In the name of the great Jehovah and the Continental Congress."

594.7   a curious combination]   That is, of a strong man (Hercules), jokester (Joe Miller), perfect knight (Bayard), and champion pugilist (Tom Hyer).

594.37   General Prescott]   The magazine and book texts read "Colonel McCloud," but since in Melville's source (Allen's *Narrative*) General Prescott mistreats Allen while Captain McCloud protects him, the Northwestern-Newberry editors correct the misidentification as unintended by Melville.

595.21–22   Abbé Bellegarde]   Author of *Politeness of Manners and Behaviour in Fashionable Society, From the French* (1817), Melville's copy of which survives.

596.34–35   Sergeant Singles]   In Potter's *Life*, Israel is recognized by this old friend in a London prison, and he is not the husband of Israel's faithless early sweetheart.

603.2   CITY OF DIS]   Melville's 1849 London journal records his own landing in England on Guy Fawkes Day and later notes that "While on one of the Bridges, the thought struck me again that a fine thing might be written about a Blue Monday in November London—a city of Dis (Dante's)—clouds of smoke—the damned &c. . . ."

605.11   Milton . . . Hinnom]   Milton's and Shelley's works were on the Index of Prohibited Books. This paragraph, which had appeared in the magazine text, was cut from the book text, probably by a Putnam editor who feared that readers might be offended by its tenor. Melville had promised in a letter to G. P. Putnam, "I engage that the story shall contain nothing of any sort to shock the fastidious. There will be very little reflective writing in it; nothing weighty. It is adventure."

606.2   FORTY-FIVE YEARS]   Melville uses Potter's *Life* only sketchily in this chapter, omitting some squalid details but inventing others as well as Israel's hallucinations (609–10).

608.6   "Facilis . . . Averni."]   "Easy is the descent of Avernus." Virgil, *Æneid*, VI, 126. Avernus is the mouth of Hades.

613.4   Fourth-of-July]   Not in Potter's *Life*, which records only the fact that he landed in New York in 1823.

THE PIAZZA TALES

621.2–3   "With . . . Fidele—"]   Shakespeare, *Cymbeline*, IV, ii, 218–19.

621.5   farm-house . . . piazza] This sketch fancifully describes Melville's own farmhouse residence, Arrowhead, with its great central chimney, its Berkshire setting, and the piazza he added in 1851.

621.18   Hearth Stone Hills] Melville's own name for the Hoosac Mountains.

622.20   reclining majesty] Hamlet's father. *Hamlet*, I, v, 59 ff.

623.11   1848] Alluding to the European revolutions of that year and to their repression.

625.1   Adullam cave] I Samuel 22:1–2.

625.25   Potosi mine] Silver mine in Bolivia.

626.9   Lucifer and Michael] In Milton, *Paradise Lost.*

629.26   Una] In Spenser's *The Faerie Queene*, Book I.

630.13   Marianna] See the "dejected Mariana" at the "moated grange" in Shakespeare's *Measure for Measure*, III, i, 227 ff, and Tennyson's "Mariana" and "Mariana in the South."

634.17   Memnon-like] See *Pierre*, 157.10–160.13.

635.1–2   *Bartleby . . . Wall-Street*] Although in the book publication this tale was titled simply "Bartleby," the Northwestern-Newberry editors restore the full title carried by the *Putnam's Magazine* text.

636.12–19   Master . . . Constitution] The new New York Constitution of 1846 abolished various privileges of the wealthy, including this office.

639.28   the Tombs] The central prison of New York City, built in 1839, was styled after a specific Egyptian tomb, and named accordingly.

651.38   Marius . . . Carthage!] Gaius Marius (157–86 B.C.), Roman general and consul, engaged in civil wars against Sulla. In 88 B.C., defeated and driven from Rome to refuge in Africa, he landed at Carthage (destroyed 146 B.C. by Roman armies) and finds bitter consolation in the sight of the once-great city in ruins.

661.7–8   Adams . . . Colt] John C. Colt was convicted of the Broadway office murder of Samuel Adams (1841). On the day scheduled for his hanging he was married and committed suicide in the Tombs.

661.25–26   "A new commandment . . . another."] John 13:34.

662.15–16   "Edwards . . . Necessity."] The works named, by Jonathan Edwards (1754) and Joseph Priestley (1778), both argue, on different grounds, that man's will is not free.

670.9   Mr. Cutlets;] The Northwestern-Newberry editors follow the *Putnam's Magazine* version of this scene. The book version was revised (pos-

sibly by an editor) to omit the name "Mr. Cutlets" from the lawyer's introduction and to alter the grub-man's invitation from "May Mrs. Cutlets and I
have the pleasure of your company to dinner, sir, in Mrs. Cutlets' private
room?" to "What will you have for dinner today?"

670.27   Monroe Edwards] This "gentleman forger" was confined in the
Tombs, where he "furnished his cell elegantly, like a little parlor." After his
conviction in 1842, he was sent to Sing-Sing prison, where he died.

670.35   in quest of Bartleby;] A single, spoiled fair-copy page of the
manuscript, in the hand of Melville's sister Augusta, has an earlier and briefer
version of the lawyer's second visit. In it he finds Bartleby dead in his cell,
not in the yard, with a tombstone that does not appear in the published
version.

671.23   "With kings and counsellors,"] Job 3:14.

673.2–6   1799 . . . Chili.] This story is adapted freely from chapter eighteen of Captain Amasa Delano's *A Narrative of Voyages and Travels* (1817). The
date is moved back from 1805 to 1799 and the island of Santa Maria is relo-
cated from the coast of central Chile near Concepción to "down towards its
southern extremity." The names of both ships are changed (from *Perseverance*
to *Bachelor's Delight* and from *Tryal* to *San Dominick*), the time span lengthened considerably, the legal deposition abridged and altered, the number of
blacks multiplied, and names and roles are switched. Some major changes are
pointed out in the notes that follow. The Northwestern-Newberry edition
reproduces Delano's original chapter, keyed to Melville's text, and cites dis-
cussions of Melville's treatment.

676.15   "*Sequid vuestro jefe,*"] This command does not appear in Delano's
Narrative.

676.18   "SAN DOMINICK,"] The proper form is "San Domingo."

680.15   Babo] In Delano's *Narrative*, Muri is Benito's servant and Babo
is his father's name.

686.35   hawse-hole . . . cabin-window] Sailors' proverbial way of saying
he came aboard as an inexperienced officer rather than having worked his
way up from a common sailor.

688.17–18   Bachelor's Delight] For Delano's ship *Perseverance*, Melville
substituted the name of William Cowley's ship.

704.29–30   Mungo Park] This name in the magazine text was changed
by someone to "Ledyard," but neither name fits the sentence. Park (1771–
1806), the famous explorer in Africa, did not write the "noble account" Melville has in mind, while John Ledyard (1751–89) wrote about women in Asia,
not Africa, where he had not traveled. The Northwestern-Newberry editors
keep the original reading since no satisfactory emendation is possible.

709.22–23   a white bone] Sailors' idiom for the foam at the ship's bow.

716.27   Fletcher] Byron's valet, William Fletcher, was white. Melville might have been thinking of a black servant of Edward Trelawny who took some journeys with Byron.

730.35–36   Jew . . . betray?] Judas Iscariot, at the last supper. Matthew 26:20–25.

736.9   pirate] Not mentioned by Delano, and cut from the book version.

738.12   Preston Pans] A battle (1745) in which the English were defeated by Scottish Highlanders championing the Stuart pretender.

739.22   Audience] Judicial district.

739.33   beside . . . hardware] Melville added this phrase in the book text to account for the cases of hatchets and the hatchet-polishing in his story, which were not in Delano's account.

754.39   "The negro."] In Spanish, not only "the black," but also "blackness."

756.3   Acroceraunian] The Greek region was famous for thunderstorms.

757.4   Olympus] "Old Greylock" in the *Putnam's Magazine* text.

758.17   "My] In the book text, this speech begins, "How very dull you are."

758.22–24   Criggan . . . Assembly-room] The place seems fictitious, but a famous large elm in Pittsfield was seamed by lightning strokes (1841), and the assembly hall of a Pittsfield church was memorably struck (1835).

762.33–34   "Begone . . . worm."] These lines were left out of *The Piazza Tales* text, more likely by oversight or editorial interference than by Melville's own revision.

764.2   SALVATOR R. TARNMOOR] This pseudonym appeared on all three installments of "The Encantadas" in *Putnam's Magazine* but not in the book text. The name is kept here because Melville may have written the sketches in the distinctive persona the name suggests, as Washington Irving did with "Geoffrey Crayon" and Samuel Clemens did with "Mark Twain." Attributions to "L. A. V." (1179.15 and 1187.40), the "special correspondent" (1125.2), and "A Virginian" (1154.2) are also kept.

764.5–22   "That . . . howl."] These two epigraphs, and all seven of those for the other nine sketches, are from Spenser's *The Faerie Queene*. The text used is based on John Upton's 1758 edition, possibly that of Robert Anderson, 1792–93. From this text the Northwestern-Newberry editors correct various transcriptional errors (made by Melville, his copyist, or the typesetter) that appeared in *Putnam's Magazine* and *The Piazza Tales*; but they leave changes Melville may have made intentionally. The epigraphic lines for Sketch First are from II. XII. xi. 1–9, and II. XII. xii. 7–9.

765.22   Lazarus]   Luke 16:24

765.27   Babylon]   Jeremiah 51:37.

767.28   Apples of Sodom]   The Dead Sea apples, lovely but full of ashes, are mentioned by several writers in antiquity (not biblical).

768.2   Asphaltum]   Figuratively, a "Dead Sea" (Asphaltites) region.

768.28–29   memory . . . fancy]   Melville touched at the Galapagos Islands twice on the *Acushnet*, in 1841 and 1842, and he at least passed them on both the *Charles and Henry* and the frigate *United States* in 1843.

768.39   ****]   The Northwestern-Newberry editors emend the number and position of the asterisks, which were five superscript spaced-out ones in both of the original texts; presumably Melville meant them to stand for the four letters of "mori" in the common tag "Memento mori" ("remember you must die").

769.3–17   "Most . . . lye."]   *The Faerie Queene*, II. XII. xxiii. 1–5 (with minor changes), II. XII. xxvi. 1–3, 6, 8, 9.

772.26–773.8   "Forthy . . . were."]   *The Faerie Queene*, with minor variations: II. XII. viii. 1–6; II. XII. xxxiii. 1–4; II. XII. xxxiii. 8–9; II. XII. xxxv. 6–9; II. XII. xxxvi. 1–2. The reading "For they" in both original texts is emended to "Forthy" (meaning "Therefore"); and the *Putnam's Magazine* reading "vase" is emended (as in *The Piazza Tales*) to "base" (772.33).

773.12–13   Newport one]   An old stone mill in Rhode Island, an object of popular wonder, was argued by some to be a Norse relic.

776.25–26   on . . . saw]   This passage, omitted in the book version, is kept by the Northwestern-Newberry editors because it seems needed to make clear the place of the paragraph in the whole account of that morning's experience.

777.17   PISGAH]   The mountain whence Moses viewed the Promised Land; Deuteronomy 3:17 and 34:1–4.

777.18–19   —"That . . . shows:"——]   Melville's slight adaptation of *The Faerie Queene*, I. X. liii. 1 and I. X. lv. 1.

779.4–780.5   Prior . . . solitudes.]   The information here comes from James Burney's *A Chronological History of the Discoveries in the South Sea* (1803–17).

780.29   a familiar diagram]   No diagram was supplied by the typesetter in the space left for it in *Putnam's Magazine*. In *The Piazza Tales*, an ⊓ was supplied, whose downturned position neither matches the ⊐-shaped island's westward opening as shown on the maps of Porter and Colnett which Melville saw, nor fits his description given at 781.13. The Northwestern-Newberry editors consequently turn the letter as Melville must have intended it, to open left.

782.33   Stuart]   He was "luckless" because as James II he was deposed (1688) and defeated at the battle of the Boyne (1690).

783.8   that . . . Buccaneer]   Cowley.

783.26   Wood's Isle]   Apparently the same island as Hood's, though Melville treats them as separate ones.

783.34–37   "Looking . . . flight."]   From Spenser's "Visions of the World's Vanities," ix. 1–4.

787.27   nails]   Melville's source passage in Colnett's *Voyage* has "nails," though both original texts have "sails." Melville's wife restored "nails" in her copy of *The Piazza Tales*.

788.10–20   ——————So . . . toyle.]   *The Faerie Queene*, II. IX. xiii. 1–7, and Spenser's "Prosopopoia," lines 155–58, both with slight changes.

792.13   Alsatia]   The London district of Whitefriars, once a sanctuary for debtors and criminals.

793.2   CHOLA WIDOW]   This woman's story was adapted from contemporary news accounts.

793.3–18   "At last . . . dead."]   *The Faerie Queene*, II. XII. xxvii. 5–9; Thomas Chatterton's *Ælla: A Tragycal Enterlude* ("The Mynstreelles Songe"); William Collins' "Dirge in Cymbeline" (the last was not present in *Putnam's Magazine* but was added in *The Piazza Tales*).

806.3–6   The last . . . cross.]   After this sketch was published in *Putnam's Magazine*, Charles F. Briggs, the editor, wrote to Melville apologizing for "making a slight alteration" in this paragraph—just what he did not say. "That I did not injure the idea, or mutilate the touching figure you introduced, by the slight excision I made, I received good evidence of, in a letter from James [Russell] Lowell, who said that the figure of the cross in the ass' neck, brought tears into his eyes, and he thought it the finest touch of genius he had seen in prose." Melville marked a similar passage in Wordsworth's "Peter Bell" and had seen the South American breed of ass which is conspicuously marked with such a cross.

806.9–20   "That . . . abouts."]   *The Faerie Queene*, I. IX. xxxv. 1–9, I. IX. xxxvi. 1–3, with slight changes.

808.30   "This . . . mother;"]   From Shakespeare's *The Tempest*, I, ii. Melville has Oberlus quote line 332 exactly, in a speech by the deformed Caliban, son of the witch Sycorax.

815.11–14   "And . . . been."]   *The Faerie Queene*, I. IX. xxxiv. 1–4, with "knotty" (presumably Melville's change) for Spenser's "rocky."

818.7–9   grave: "Here . . . death."]   The quotation marks, not present in the two original texts, are supplied (set off with a colon rather than a period) by the Northwestern-Newberry editors to make clear that Melville intended this to be read as the lieutenant's epitaph, not as an authorial comment. He adapted it from Porter's *Journal*, adding "attaining his majority in death." Porter placed the duel on "Charles Island" not "Chatham." The following epitaph seems to be Melville's own refashioning of a formulaic one common in old cemeteries.

819.24–29   Babel's . . . Shinar]   Genesis 11:1–9.

821.3   Shadrach]   One of the three youths thrown into the fiery furnace. Daniel 3:12–20.

823.30   Haman]   Haman built a high gallows for Mordecai, but was hanged on it himself. Esther 5:14 and 7:10.

826.25   Sisera's . . . Del Fonca's]   Deborah prophesied the death of Sisera, whom Jael killed by driving a tent nail into his temples. Judges 4:4–21. Del Fonca is invented by Melville.

827.24   Shiloh]   A revelation. Shiloh is where the Lord appeared to Samuel. Cf. I Samuel 3:21.

830.20   Talus]   In Greek mythology, a man made of brass who guards the island of Crete. In Spenser's *The Faerie Queene* (V. I. xii), an iron man with an iron flail.

THE CONFIDENCE-MAN

841.34–35   Meason . . . Harpe]   Samuel Meason, John Murrel (or Murrell), and the Harpe brothers were among notorious early swindlers and murderers of the Southwest; their exploits were recounted in popular works of the kind being sold on the *Fidèle*.

842.12   "Charity . . . evil."]   The words written on the slate are from I Corinthians 13.

846.31   Ving-King-Ching]   Presumably a humorous reference to the Grand Canal of China.

851.23   the comedy]   Shakespeare, *A Midsummer Night's Dream*, II, ii, 115.

856.16   Jeremy Diddler]   A petty swindler in the British farce *Raising the Wind* (1803), by James Kenny.

859.18   Werter's Charlotte]   In Goethe's *Sorrows of Young Werther*, Werther (or Werter) falls in love with Charlotte when he sees her slicing bread, which in Thackeray's verse parody becomes "cutting bread and butter."

863.1–2   descent . . . fate."]   A paraphrase of *Paradise Lost*, II, 14–17: "From this descent/Celestial vertues more dread then from no fall, / And trust themselves to fear no second fate. . . ."

867.21–22   Scripture saying]   Paraphrased from Sirach (Ecclesiasticus) 19:25.

867.39–40   Auburn and Greenwood]   In Cambridge, Massachusetts, and Brooklyn, New York.

877.32   him.]   The Northwestern-Newberry editors supply this word (not in either the American or the English edition) to make sense of the defective idiom.

878.22   Hebrew governor]   The Roman governor of Judea, Pontius Pilate (Matthew 27:24).

884.32–33   confidence . . . mountains.]   I Corinthians 13:2.

884.39   millenial promise]   Revelation 20:1–6.

891.38   Good-Enough-Morgan]   In 1836 Thurlow Weed was reported as saying about a corpse doubtfully identified as that of William Morgan, a supposed victim of the Masons, that it was "a good enough Morgan" until after the election.

893.19–22   "My . . . bosom—]   Francis Bacon, in the dedication of his *Essays* (1625) wrote: "My essays . . . come home to men's business, and bosoms."

894.16   Arimanius]   The Northwestern-Newberry editors correct the misspelling "Ariamius" in the first edition for the name of the Zoroastrian evil principle.

902.1   meal and bran]   *Cymbeline*, IV, ii, 27.

903.11   Thrasea]   A republican Roman senator, victim of Nero, as cited by Pliny (Book VIII, Epistle 22).

910.2–3   secure Malakoff]   This Russian fortress in the Crimean War was still resisting siege in the summer of 1855 when Melville began this book; it fell in September.

914.6   man's experience]   The American and English editions' reading, "no one man," is corrected to "no one man's experience" by the Northwestern-Newberry editors, from Melville's working drafts.

914.39   fearfully . . . made.]   Psalms 139.14.

918.30   I wish my friend]   The American and English editions have commas around "my friend" so the speaker addresses the miser thus, but this seems contrary to the sense of the passage and the Northwestern-Newberry editors omit the commas.

922.21   Calvin Edson]   A "living skeleton," one of the freaks exhibited in P. T. Barnum's American Museum.

923.31–32   'Medea . . . Æson?']   Shakespeare, *The Merchant of Venice*, V, i, 12–14.

925.36 'Nature in Disease.'] By Jacob Bigelow, M.D. (1854).

928.28 Iapis in Virgil] The name Iapis is corrected by the Northwestern-Newberry editors from the American and English editions misreading "Japus"; the quotation is from Dryden's translation of the *Aeneid*, Book XII, 632–33 (with "power" for "hands").

930.21 haunted Cock Lane] London street where manifestations of ghosts were exposed by Dr. Johnson and others (1732). Melville visited it in 1849 and alludes to it in *Moby-Dick* and elsewhere, apparently supposing Johnson believed in the ghosts.

930.34 bead] The American and English editions have "lead," which is corrected by the Northwestern-Newberry editors.

935.13–14 as Hamlet says,] *Hamlet*, V, i, 227; the speech paraphrased is Horatio's.

939.3 Molino . . . Palma?] American victories (1846 and 1847) in the Mexican War.

939.4 *Tombs*] See note 639.28.

954.3 Peter the Wild Boy] A child discovered in the Hanover woods in 1725 and brought to England by George I. Many writers took a philosophical interest in him.

961.2–3 Tusculan disputations] Book of philosophical conversations (45 B.C.) by Cicero.

966.29 'the child . . . man;'] From Wordsworth's "My Heart Leaps Up."

967.25 'A . . . sea!'—] The first line of Allen Cunningham's poem of that name (1825).

970.35 we respectfully ask,] This reading, in both the American and English editions, is retained by the Northwestern-Newberry editors, although they point out that perhaps it should be punctuated as an aside to Pitch rather than as part of what is supposedly spoken to a prospective employer. A number of such punctuation problems apparently arose from Melville's habit of instructing his copyist to leave out most punctuation and his own oversights in filling it in later.

973.14 founder of La Trappe] Probably Abbot de Rancé (1626–1700), not the founder but the reformer of that Cistercian abbey.

978.19 Apemantus' dog] The hypothetical dog of Timon's companion, presumably as cynical as his master, in Shakespeare's *Timon of Athens* and Plutarch's life of Antony.

981.8 Signor Marzetti] Joseph Marzetti played the part of an Ethiopian ape in a skit popular in New York in the late 1840s.

981.24–26   *fortiter . . . modo*]   "Strongly in deed, gently in method."

989.9   Colonel John Moredock]   Melville adapted the ensuing account from James Hall's *Sketches of History, Life, and Manners, in the West* (1835), and possibly from other works by Hall that also treat the subject. Hall's book is the only source from which Melville is known to have rewritten passages wholesale for *The Confidence-Man*, as he had often done for his earlier works. Melville's version intensifies the treachery of the Indians and the Indian-haters.

995.20   Hairy Orson]   In the medieval French romance, Orson was carried off and reared by a bear and became a wild man, while his brother became a courtier.

996.35   Moyamensing]   Philadelphia County prison.

996.36–37   treaty-breaker . . . Austrian]   In 1849, Austria broke promises it had made to mollify the revolutionary movement in 1848.

996.37   Palmer]   Dr. William Palmer, a notorious British poisoner arrested in December 1855, tried in May, and hanged in June 1856—dates which offer clues to the time of composition of this chapter.

1003.5   ENGLISH MORALIST]   Dr. Johnson, quoted by Hester L. Piozzi in her *Anecdotes of the Late Samuel Johnson* (1786), which also records his reaction to the Lisbon earthquake, cited at 1009.1–2.

1005.1   voice . . . garden.]   Genesis 3:8–10.

1005.20   number]   The nonsensical American and English reading "murder" was first emended by Parker to "number"—a word that in Melville's hand could easily be misread as "murder" and that corresponds to the word "party" in his source passage from Hall (see note 989.9).

1011.8–9   "Let . . . Sansovine."]   From Leigh Hunt's *Bacchus in Tuscany* (1825), with "Let us drink" for "And drink."

1015.38   smile . . . villain]   *Hamlet*, I, v, 107 ff.

1016.14–21   Aristotle . . . Phalaris]   Neither allusion is correct; the remark about humor is not in Aristotle's *Politics* and no such punning execution is recorded of Phalaris.

1020.4–25   'PRAISE . . . pain.' "]   The paragraph paraphrases Proverbs 23:29–31.

1024.11–12   'sell . . . poor?']   Matthew 19:21.

1072.37   Death . . . horse]   Revelation 6:8.

1082.9–12   "All . . . parts."]   Shakespeare, *As You Like It*, II, vii, 139–42.

1083.27–30   just . . . tombs.]   Genesis 19:5, Matthew 8:28, and Mark 5:2.

1084.29–30   Thersites . . . Agamemnon] In Shakespeare's *Troilus and Cressida*.

1089.12   Philanthropos . . . mankind.] This reverses Timon's line, "I am misanthropos, and hate mankind. . . ." in *Timon of Athens*, IV, iii, 52.

1089.23   traveler] The American and English texts read "barber"; but since the three kings of Cologne were patron saints of travelers, not of barbers, the Northwestern-Newberry editors correct the misreading, which probably resulted from Melville's unclear handwriting.

1091.10   bald] The reading of the American and English texts—"bold"—is emended by the Northwestern-Newberry editors to "bald" to restore the clearly intended sense.

1095.15   'An enemy . . . lips;'] Sirach (Ecclesiasticus) 12:16.

1101.23–27   'With . . . sleep.'] Sirach (Ecclesiasticus) 13:11–13.

1103.7   only now . . . mockery,] The American and English texts read "only more . . ." which the Northwestern-Newberry editors emend to "now" as the simplest way to make sense of the passage.

1110.39–40   'Jehovah . . . confidence.'] Proverbs 3:26.

UNCOLLECTED PROSE

1119.13   *suaviter in modo*.] See note 981.24–26.

1121.10   Barry Cornwall] Author of "The Sea," quoted in the previous sentence.

1121.16   Psyche glass] A full-length mirror in a tilting frame.

1123.39   "quips . . . smiles".] Adapted from Milton's "L'Allegro," lines 27–28: "Quips and cranks and wanton wiles,/Nods, and becks, and wreathed smiles."

1127.15   Buena Vista] The site of Taylor's major victory over Santa Anna, February 22–23, 1847.

1131.27   MARCY) . . . experience] William L. Marcy, Secretary of War, had been the subject of newspaper humor in an episode involving his trousers ("inexpressibles").

1136.19–20   "Damned . . . enough."] Cf. Shakespeare, *Macbeth*, V, vii, 34: "Damned be him that first cries 'Hold, enough! ' "

1146.8   Uncas or Outalissi.] Indians in James Fenimore Cooper's *Leatherstocking Tales* and Thomas Campbell's *Gertrude of Wyoming*.

1146.21   Publican . . . Pharisee.] Luke 18:9–14.

1147.35   "armed neutrality"] The association of northern European states in 1780 and 1800 were known by this name. Cf. Sir Walter Scott, *The Life of Napoleon Buonaparte*, IV, (1827), 253.

1149.19   the following:] The review concludes with this extract:

We had scarcely gone a mile when an imposing spectacle presented itself. From the river bank on the right, away over the swelling prairie on the left, and in front as far as we could see, extended one vast host of buffalo. The outskirts of the herd were within a quarter of a mile. In many parts they were crowded so densely together that in the distance their rounded backs presented a surface of uniform blackness; but elsewhere they were more scattered, and from amid the multitude rose little columns of dust where the buffalo were rolling on the ground. Here and there a great confusion was perceptible, where a battle was going forward among the bulls. We could distinctly see them rushing against each other, and hear the clattering of their horns and their hoarse bellowing. Shaw was riding at some distance in advance, with Henry Chatillon: I saw him stop and draw the leather covering from his gun. Indeed, with such a sight before us, but one thing could be thought of. That morning I had used pistols in the chase. I had now a mind to try the virtue of a gun. Delorier had one, and I rode up to the side of the cart; there he sat under the white covering, biting his pipe between his teeth and grinning with excitement.

"Lend me your gun, Delorier," said I.

"Oui, Monsieur, oui," said Delorier, tugging with might and main to stop the mule, which seemed obstinately bent on going forward. Then everything but his moccasins disappeared as he crawled into the cart and pulled at the gun to extricate it.

"Is it loaded?" I asked.

"Oui, bien chargé, you'll kill, mon bourgeois; yes, you'll kill—c'est un bon fusil."

I handed him my rifle and rode forward to Shaw.

"Are you ready?" he asked.

"Come on," said I.

"Keep down that hollow," said Henry, "and then they won't see you till you get close to them."

The hollow was a kind of ravine very wide and shallow; it ran obliquely towards the buffalo, and we rode at a canter along the bottom until it became too shallow; when we bent close to our horses' necks, and then finding that it could no longer conceal us, came out of it and rode directly towards the herd. It was within gunshot; before its outskirts, numerous grizzly old bulls were scattered, holding guard over their females. They glared at us in anger and astonishment, walked towards us a few yards, and then turning slowly round retreated at a trot which afterwards broke into a clumsy gallop. In an instant the main body caught the alarm. The buffalo began to crowd away from the point towards which we were approaching, and a gap was opened in the side of the herd. We entered it, still restraining our excited horses. Every instant the tumult was thickening. The buffalo, pressing together in large bodies, crowded away from us on every hand. In front and on either side we could see dark columns and masses, half hidden by clouds of dust, rushing along in terror and confusion, and hear the tramp and clattering of ten thousand hoofs. That countless multitude of powerful brutes, ignorant of their own strength, were flying in a panic from the approach of two feeble horsemen. To remain quiet longer was impossible.

"Take that band on the left," said Shaw; "I'll take these in front."

He sprang off, and I saw no more of him. A heavy Indian whip was fastened by a band to my wrist; I swung it into the air and lashed my horse's flank with all the strength of my arm. Away she darted, stretching close to the ground. I could see nothing but a cloud of dust before me, but I knew that it concealed a band of many hundreds of buffalo. In a moment I was in the midst of the cloud, half suffocated by the dust and stunned by the trampling of the flying herd; but I was drunk with the chase and cared for nothing but the buffalo. Very soon a long, dark mass became visible, looming through the dust; then I could distinguish each bulky carcase, the hoofs flying out beneath, the short tails held rigidly erect. In a moment I was so close that I could have touched them with my gun. Suddenly, to my utter amazement, the hoofs were jerked upwards, the tails flourished in the air, and amid a cloud of dust the buffalo seemed to sink into the earth before me. One vivid impression of that instant remains upon my mind. I remember looking down upon the backs of several buffalo dimly visible through the dust. We had run unawares upon a ravine. At that moment I was not the most accurate judge of depth and width, but when I passed it on my return, I found it about twelve feet deep, and not quite twice as wide at the bottom. It was impossible to stop; I would have done so gladly if I could; so, half sliding, half plunging, down went the little mare. I believe she came down on her knees in the loose sand at the bottom; I was pitched forward violently against her neck and nearly thrown over her head among the buffalo, who amid dust and confusion came tumbling in all around. The mare was on her feet in an instant, and scrambling like a cat up the opposite side. I thought for a moment that she would have fallen back and crushed me, but with a violent effort she clambered out and gained the hard prairie above. Glancing back I saw the huge head of a bull clinging as it were by the forefeet at the edge of the dusty gulf. At length I was fairly among the buffalo. They were less densely crowded than before, and I could see nothing but bulls, who always run at the rear of a herd. As I passed amid them they would lower their heads, and turning as they ran, attempt to gore my horse; but as they were already at full speed there was no force in their onset, and as Pauline ran faster than they, they were always thrown behind her in the effort. I soon began to distinguish cows amid the throng. One just in front of me seemed to my liking, and I pushed close to her side. Dropping the reins I fired, holding the muzzle of the gun within a foot of her shoulder. Quick as lightning she sprang at Pauline; the little mare dodged the attack, and I lost sight of the wounded animal amid the tumultuous crowd. Immediately after, I selected another, and urging forward Pauline, shot into her both pistols in succession. For awhile I kept her in view, but in attempting to load my gun, lost sight of her also in the confusion. Believing her to be mortally wounded, and unable to keep up with the herd, I checked my horse. The crowd rushed onward. The dust and tumult passed away, and on the prairie, far behind the rest, I saw a solitary buffalo galloping heavily. In a moment I and my victim were running side by side. My firearms were all empty, and I had in my pouch nothing but rifle bullets, too large for the pistols and too small for the gun. I loaded the latter, however, but as often as I levelled it to fire, the little bullets would roll out of the muzzle and the gun returned only a faint report like a squib, as the powder harmlessly exploded. I galloped in front of the buffalo and attempted to turn her back; but her eyes glared, her mane bristled, and lowering her head, she rushed at me with astonishing fierceness and activity. Again and again I rode before her, and again and again she repeated her furious charge. But little Pauline was in her element. She dodged her enemy at every rush, until at length the buffalo stood still, exhausted with her own efforts; she panted, and her tongue hung lolling from her jaws.

Riding to a little distance, I alighted, thinking to gather a handful of dry grass to serve the purpose of wadding, and load the gun at my leisure. No sooner were my feet on the ground than the buffalo came bounding in such a rage towards me that I jumped back again into the saddle with all possible dispatch. After waiting a few minutes more, I made an attempt to ride up and stab her with my knife; but the experiment proved such as no wise man would repeat. At length, bethinking me of the fringes at the seams of my buckskin pantaloons, I jerked off a few of them, and reloading the gun, forced them down the barrel to keep the bullet in its place; then approaching, I shot the wounded buffalo through the heart. Sinking on her knees, she rolled over lifeless on the prairie. To my astonishment, I found that instead of a fat cow I had been slaughtering a stout yearling bull. No longer wondering at the fierceness he had shown, I opened his throat, and cutting out his tongue, tied it at the back of my saddle. My mistake was one which a more experienced eye than mine might easily make in the dust and confusion of such a chase.

Then for the first time I had leisure to look at the scene around me. The prairie in front was darkened with the retreating multitude, and on the other hand the buffalo came filing up in endless unbroken columns from the low plains upon the river. The Arkansas was three or four miles distant. I turned and moved slowly towards it. A long time passed before, far down in the distance, I distinguished the white covering of the cart and the little black specks of horsemen before and behind it. Drawing near, I recognised Shaw's elegant tunic, the red flannel shirt conspicuous far off. I overtook the party, and asked him what success he had met with. He had assailed a fat cow, shot her with two bullets, and mortally wounded her. But neither of us were prepared for the chase that afternoon, and Shaw, like myself, had no spare bullets in his pouch; so he abandoned the disabled animal to Henry Chatillon, who followed, dispatched her with his rifle, and loaded his horse with her meat.

We encamped close to the river. The night was dark, and as we lay down, we could hear mingled with the howlings of wolves the hoarse bellowing of the buffalo, like the ocean beating upon a distant coast.

1150.17–18   "thrilling . . . ice".]   From *Measure for Measure*, III, i, 123, with "rock-ribbed" for "thick-ribbed."

1151.1   father]   Actually, Deacon Pratt is Mary's uncle, not her father.

1151.7   Stimson]   Besides other small errors, Melville's manuscript has several ear-spellings (corrected in the *Literary World* printing and by the Northwestern-Newberry editors): "Stimpson," "Antartic" (1150.16), "grandure" (1150.19) and "nuptuals" (1150.35).

1152.36   lord of Verulam.]   Francis Bacon.

1154.1   *Hawthorne and His Mosses*]   Some of the following notes call attention to textual matters from the manuscript, which survives, not in original draft but in Melville's wife's fair copy for the editor of *The Literary World*, with many revisions in Melville's own hand. Some of these revisions are rejected by the Northwestern-Newberry editors because they seem so clearly to be changes that the editor, Evert Duyckinck, persuaded Melville to make to tone down his more extreme views as he had originally expressed them.

1154.2   BY A VIRGINIAN]   This fictional ascription and several later references to the Virginian were added by Melville to his wife's fair-copy manuscript of the essay. Also fictional was the declaration (1165.29) that its writer had never met Hawthorne.

1154.17–20   "When . . . reality."]   The last sentence of Hawthorne's "The Artist of the Beautiful" (with "artist" capitalized and the verbs changed from past to present tense).

1155.23   'Dwight's . . . England'.]   Four-volume work (1822) by Timothy Dwight, president of Yale.

1156.2–8   "Others . . . him?"]   Adapted from "The Old Manse," omitting about one hundred words between "spirits? what."

1156.10–11   "Assyrian . . . Hill."]   Adapted from "The Old Manse," where Hawthorne paraphrased it from Emerson's *Nature*.

1156.14–15   "dismissed . . . him".]   Adapted (with pronouns changed) from "The Old Manse."

1156.16   mild]   Earlier editions all give the misreading "wild."

1156.25–27   "that . . . odd-fellows."]   From "The Old Manse" (with "that" for "they").

1156.31–33   "the . . . ripeness"!]   From "The Old Manse" with altered word order; Hawthorne's sentence begins, "In the stillest afternoon, if I listened, the thump of a great apple was audible, falling . . ." and continues to the end as Melville quotes it.

1156.36–37   "Will . . . greenness?"]   From "Buds and Bird-Voices."

1159.34–35   "Off . . . Buckingham!"]   Colley Cibber supplied the quoted line in his adaptation of *Richard III* (1700), following IV, iii, 57.

1160.8   sane madness]   Printed as "same madness" in *The Literary World*; Melville complained to Mrs. Hawthorne about this "provoking mistake."

1161.13–14   "we . . . others";]   Melville's source for this wording is unlocated. In the 1706 London edition of *Moral Reflections and Maxims*, No. 198 reads, "We raise the reputation of some, to pull down that of others. . . ."

1161.26   Thirty Nine articles]   The articles of the faith of the Church of England (1551, 1563).

1161.31   that . . . born]   Melville's revision to "that men not very much inferior to Shakespeare are this day being born" is rejected by the Northwestern-Newberry editors as an instance of toning down done under the influence of the editor, Evert Duyckinck.

1162.23–27   equalled . . . none.]   Melville had toned down this passage severely in a revision not accepted by the Northwestern-Newberry editors: ". . . if Shakespeare has not been equalled, give the world time, & he is sure to be surpassed, in one hemisphere or the other."

1163.7–9   no . . . Pigeon"]   Melville originally wrote "no Hawthornes Emersons Whittiers Danas Coopers"; he revised it to the reading adopted by the Northwestern-Newberry editors; the *Literary World* editor, Duyckinck, revised it further on the manuscript in heavy ink, tactfully lining out the individual names and rewording the passage in more general terms. Melville's reference to Nathaniel Parker Willis shows he thought more of him as a poet than as a prose writer.

1163.11–21   praise . . . sound.]   Melville heavily revised the original fair-copy version of these lines, to bring in the "hot-headed Carolina cousin" as the speaker of the lines about Pop Emmons, which had first been the essay writer's own.

1163.18   'Fredoniad,']   *The Fredoniad; or Independence Preserved. An Epick Poem on the Late War of 1812*, by Richard Emmons, M.D., 4 vols., Boston, 1827.

1164.24   Bostonian]   The Northwestern-Newberry editors restore this adjective, canceled by Melville on the fair copy, evidently to satisfy Duyckinck.

1164.26–27   And . . . it.]   This sentence, canceled by Melville on the fair copy, is also restored by the Northwestern-Newberry editors.

1166.25–34   "A . . . he."]   From "The Intelligence Office."

1168.20–21   "It . . . sin".]   Adapted from "Young Goodman Brown." The passage following is quoted exactly.

1169.14   sunset clouds,]   From the first paragraph of "A Select Party," as is the ensuing feast figure.

1170.3   Specimens]   *Specimens of English Dramatic Poets, Who Lived about the Time of Shakespeare.* Melville owned the 1845 New York edition.

1175.22–31   "When . . . combined."]   Thomas Campbell, "The Pleasures of Hope," II, 73–82.

1176.3   "my . . . Horatio,"]   *Hamlet*, I, ii, 185.

1176.19–23   mistress . . . Templar,]   The references are to Cleopatra and to Sir Brian de Bois-Guilbert in Sir Walter Scott's *Ivanhoe*.

1177.22–23   "dark-glancing daughters."]   Byron, *Childe Harold's Pilgrimage*, I, lix, 7.

1178.2   Minotti]   Though he performs sword feats in Byron's *The Siege of Corinth*, he has no such sword.

1178.13   "Lap . . . airs"!]   Milton, "L'Allegro," line 136.

1178.26–1179.2   "Maid . . . sweet ——."]   Coleridge, "Genevieve," omitting her name from the first and last lines.

1179.7–8   "counterfeit presentments,"]   *Hamlet*, III, iv, 55.

1180.9   "The . . . over!"]   Paraphrased from *Reflections on the Revolution in France*: "But the age of chivalry is gone."

1186.12–14   "See . . . cheek!"]   Shakespeare, *Romeo and Juliet*, II, i, 23–25, with "kiss" for "touch."

1188.13   gates of Gaza]   See Judges 16:3.

1190.16   Roman emperor.]   Trajan.

1191.20   Zaccheus]   Luke 19:4.

1197.30–32   Athenian . . . said?]   From Plutarch's *Life of Phocion*.

1199.10   Cassius]   In Shakespeare, *Julius Caesar*, I, ii, 193, he has "a lean and hungry look."

1207.18–21   "Of . . . madness."]   Parody of Wordsworth's "Resolution and Independence," stanza 7, lines 6–7: "We Poets in our youth begin in gladness;/But thereof come in the end despondency and madness."

1226.6–7   —"Oh . . . victory?"]   I Corinthians 15:55.

1237.4   Five Points.]   Notorious slum district of New York City.

1238.20   Dives . . . Lazarus.]   Luke 16:19–31.

1239.19   Gog and Magog]   Two statues of Albian giants, in the Guildhall.

1243.23   "the Tombs."]   See note 639.28.

1246.12   "Ye . . . earth."]   Matthew 5:13.

1249.17   Charmian,]   Cleopatra's attendant in Shakespeare's *Antony and Cleopatra*.

1259.39   R. F. C.]   Robert Francis Cooke of 4 Elm Court, The Temple, who entertained Melville there at a dinner in December 1849; Melville in his journal called it "the Paradise of Bachelors."

1263.4   wine . . . stomach's sake.]   I Timothy 5:23.

1263.30   Iron Duke,]   Arthur Wellesley, Duke of Wellington (1769–1852), victor at Waterloo.

1277.33   face]   That of Jesus, to whom Veronica gave her handkerchief on the way to Calvary.

1294.34   Belshazzar]   Daniel 5:6: ". . . the joints of his loins were loosed, and his knees smote against one another."

1296.40   Genin's]   John Nicholas Genin (1819–78), hatter and merchant in New York City, had a shop next to Barnum's American Museum, and shared with him a genius for publicity.

1298.7   *I . . . King*]   Cf. Shakespeare, *Henry VIII*, III, ii, 313–16.

1301.11   Alsatia]   See note 792.13.

1302.6   razeed]   Shortened, as a ship is cut down to fewer decks.

1304.3   Gilgal]   Joshua 4:8–9.

1305.3   council of ten]   The autocratic Council of Ten ruled medieval Venice.

1308.15   strange promise]   I.e., God's promise that the aged Sarah should bear a son to Abraham (Genesis 18:10–12).

1309.12   Nebuchadnezzar]   ". . . he was driven from men, and did eat grass as oxen . . ." (Daniel 4:33).

1311.9   might not]   The Northwestern-Newberry editors supply "not" (lacking in *Putnam's*) as required by the intended sense.

1317.8–9   Solomon . . . sentiments]   I.e., in Ecclesiastes, then still attributed to Solomon.

1321.21   St. Dunstan's devil]   See note 243.9.

1325.11–12   Three Powers]   In the eighteenth century, Austria, Russia, and Prussia repeatedly partitioned Poland and in 1846 agreed to Austrian occupation of Cracow.

1326.2–3   bowl . . . broken.]   Ecclesiastes 12:6.

1328.7–8   Friar Bacon]   The philosopher Roger Bacon (1214?–1294), popularly regarded as a necromancer.

1332.24   "Fox girls."]   Margaret Fox (1833–93) and her sisters started the vogue of "spirit rappings."

1333.7   Dr. Johnson]   See note 930.21.

1350.3–4   Brattle . . . church]   During the Revolution, Brattle Street church in Boston was occupied by the British and hit by a cannon-ball shot from the American camp in Cambridge.

BILLY BUDD, SAILOR

1351.1   BILLY BUDD, SAILOR]   Editors Hayford and Sealts adopt this title as the later of the two manuscript versions. The superseded earlier version (adopted in the editions of Raymond Weaver and F. Barron Freeman) was: "*Billy Budd / Foretopman /* What befell him / in the year of the / Great Mutiny / &c." Other editors have adopted combinations of the two.

1352.3   JACK CHASE]   The dedication shows Melville's lasting admiration for this shipmate whom he celebrates in *White-Jacket*, the book he based on his own service aboard the frigate *United States*, 1843–44.

1353.15–16   Liverpool]   Visited by Melville on his first voyage (1839), described in *Redburn*.

1354.6–7   tempestuous Erie Canal]   The "terrible storms" on "the raging Can-all" were a sailor joke.

1354.35   *Bellipotent*]   Until late in the writing of the book, the ship's name was the *Indomitable*, which occurs often in the manuscript and was adopted by editors before Hayford and Sealts determined that Melville's final choice was *Bellipotent*.

1356.31   buffer]   Boxer or fighter (slang).

1359.10   able seaman]   The highest of the three ratings of sailors; the other two are "ordinary seaman" and "boy."

1360.29–37   But . . . lot.]   Hayford and Sealts show that this passage grew out of the earliest paragraphs Melville wrote for *Billy Budd* as a simple headnote to the ballad "Billy in the Darbies."

1361.19   wisdom of the serpent]   Matthew 10:16. See also *Pierre*, 124.10–11, and *Israel Potter*, 477.14–15.

1362.13   Cain's city]   Genesis 4:16–17.

1362.24–25   Honest . . . brought?]   Martial, *Epigrams*, I, iv, 1–2, Cowley translation.

1362.28   beautiful woman]   Georgiana in "The Birthmark."

1363.12   seventy-four]   The *Bellipotent*, mounting seventy-four guns, was a line-of-battle ship, larger than frigates with thirty-two to thirty-six, though smaller than the "three-deckers" mentioned with ninety or more.

1363.20–21   Spithead . . . Nore.]   Spithead is a roadstead in the Channel between Portsmouth and the Isle of Wight; the Nore is a sandbank at the mouth of the Thames. Melville's statements about historical and naval matters in the story are correct in general though occasionally inaccurate in particulars. Some of these inaccuracies are corrected by Hayford and Sealts; see the Note on the Texts.

1363.29–31   famous . . . expected]   "England expects every man to do his duty!" is the version of Nelson's flag signal at Trafalgar given in Robert Southey's *Life of Nelson*, Melville's copy of which survives.

1364.9   Dibdin]   His "Poor Jack" is the song quoted below, one of many allusions in Melville's works (e.g., *White-Jacket*, chap. 90).

1364.14   (William James)]   Author of *The Naval History of Great Britain* (6 vols., 1860), from which Melville took notes on a surviving library slip, including the phrase quoted below. In a lapse in the manuscript, corrected by Hayford and Sealts, Melville has "G. P. R" (the initials of the novelist, whom he had met in 1851) at this point, instead of "William."

1364.19–20   events . . . America]   In earlier works Melville had himself exposed various national abuses. His manuscript here has an undeveloped note, which reads, "Do we publish no medicines past the lines"—an allusion to the Civil War blockade of medicines by the Union.

1365.16   bypaths]   Melville had set aside this chapter of the manuscript for further work. It was one of only three (4, 12, 26) he had given a title: "Concerning the greatest sailor since the world began"—from Tennyson's "Ode on the Death of the Duke of Wellington," to which he alludes below. Melville's marked copy of Southey's *Life of Nelson* shows that he relied on it for facts and went beyond it in his own interpretations, for example, Nelson's "priestly motive" in wearing his decorations at Trafalgar, which Southey had said was "as usual."

1366.5   Portsmouth]   Melville visited the *Victory* there in 1849.

1368.7–8   One instance]   Taken from Southey's *Life of Nelson*. Hayford and Sealts correct Melville's manuscript error at 1368.9, where he calls Nelson in 1797 "then Vice-Admiral," and another error at 1377.30–31, referring to Nelson in 1795 as "but Sir Horatio," which is corrected to "still captain."

1375.5   Spirit of the Cape]   Admastor, in Camoëns' *The Lusiads*.

1380.21   " with counterfeited glee,"]   As the students dutifully laugh at the schoolmaster's jokes in Oliver Goldsmith's "The Deserted Village" (line 201).

1381.38 Jonah's toss] Jonah 1:15.

1382.5 "the deadly space between."] From Thomas Campbell's "The Battle of the Baltic."

1382.7 honest scholar] Melville occasionally invented spokesmen or documents, as here. In *Moby-Dick*, chapter 2, it is an "old writer—of whose works I possess the only copy extant"; in "The Bell-Tower," the epigraphs "from a private MS."; and in *Billy Budd* there is also the "writer whom few know" at 1417.38.

1383.3 authentic translation] Hayford and Sealts identify this as the Bohn edition of Plato's works (6 vols., 1848–64), in which "the list of definitions" is included and "Natural Depravity" is defined as "a badness by nature, and a sinning in that, which is according to nature" (VI, 143).

1384.3 nature."] In the Weaver and Freeman editions a paragraph follows here, which Hayford and Sealts determined does not belong in the final text. The paragraph gives Melville's brief early treatment of topics he later developed into the drumhead court sequence (chapter 21):

> by the way can it be the phenomenon, disowned or at least not acknowledged/conceded that in some criminal cases puzzles the courts? For this cause have our juries at times not only to endure the prolonged contentions of lawyers with their fees but also the yet more perplexing strife of the medical experts with theirs? But why leave it to them? why not subpoena as well the clerical proficients? Their vocation bringing them into peculiar contact with so many human beings, and sometimes in their least guarded hour, in interviews very much more confidential than those of physician and patient; this would seem to qualify them to know something about those intricacies involved in the question of moral responsibility; whether in a given case, say, the crime proceeded from mania in the brain or rabies of the heart. As to any differences among themselves these clerical proficients might develop on the stand, these could hardly be greater than the direct practical contradictions exchanged between the remunerated medical experts.

1384.4 Dark sayings] Psalms 78:2.

1384.5–6 "mystery of iniquity"] II Thessalonians 2:7.

1384.14 12] One of only three chapters for which Melville's incomplete manuscript supplied a draft title: "Pale ire, envy and despair," from *Paradise Lost*, IV, 115, where it describes Satan's passions when about to attack Adam and Eve. Melville omitted a comma after "pale," indicating he took it as an adjective. In an earlier draft he wrote, " 'Pale ire, envy, and despair' is Miltonic. Behind these frescoed walls of flesh it is the closeted skeleton. . . ."

1385.8 Saul's visage] I Samuel 16:18 and 18:8 ff.

1387.4–5 injury but suspected,] References to Shakespeare's *Othello* occur several times in this passage; besides this phrase there are "monstrous disproportion," "an inordinate usurer," "lawyer to his will," and "ogres of trifles."

1387.12   scriptural devils]   James 2:19.

1394.16   man of sorrows]   That is, Christ; cf. Isaiah 53:3.

1395.2   "too fair-spoken man."]   A proverbial expression; cf. Proverbs 26:24–25.

1401.37   envious children]   Genesis 37:31–32.

1405.31–1407.31   The surgeon . . . afford.]   In a late revision Melville replaced five and a half pages of the manuscript with the eight pencil-drafted ones of this passage. The earlier version (in ink, before the pencil revisions) is given here, with its variant spellings, for comparison. The last three pages (with pencil revisions), forming a separate chapter, were mistakenly printed as a preface in all editions before that of Hayford and Sealts.

At catching sight of the dark blood now oozing from nostril and ear, and strikingly in contrast with Claggart's always bleached complexion, the Surgeon from this as well as other indications at once inferred what it was that lay plank-like before him. Yes, the young mute's blow, an athlete's, a blow electrically energized by the spasm of his heart, unintentionally had had upon its object the instantanious operation of the divine judgement on Annannias.

Captain Vere intently watching the Surgeon's face, asked, "Is it so then? I thought it. But verify it." And the customary tests were made, confirming the Surgeon's first glance.

At Captain Vere's motion, the Surgeon assisted him removing the body to the compartment aft opposite to that where the foretopman remained for the time self-immured. This being done, the officer was in brief terms enlightened as to the circumstances which had resulted in the trajedy.

"Go now" said Captain Vere in conclusion; "before taking action I must have a few moments to mature the line of conduct I shall adopt. The case is without precedent, and it could not have happened at a worse time either for me or the striker of the blow." Too well the thoughtful officer knew what his superior meant. As the former withdrew he could not help thinking how worse than futile the utmost discretion sometimes proves in a world subject to unforseeable fatalities; the prudent method adopted by Captain Vere to obviate publicity and trouble having resulted in an event that necessitated the former, and, under existing circumstances in the navy indefinitely magnified the latter.

[Chapter division mark]

The year 1797, the year of this narrative, belongs to a period which as every thinker now feels, involved a crisis for Christendom not exceeded in its undetermined momentousness at the time by any other recorded era.

The opening proposition made by the Spirit of that Age, involved [*earlier*: was one hailed by the noblest men of it. Even the dry tinder of a Wordsworth took fire.] the rectification of the Old World's hereditary wrongs. In France to some extent this was bloodily effected. But what then? Straightway the Revolution itself became a wrongdoer, more oppressive than the Kings. Under Napoleon it enthroned upstart kings, and initiated that prolonged agony of general war that ended in Waterloo. Nor during those years could the wisest have forseen that the outcome of all would be what apparently it has turned out to be, a political advance along nearly the whole line for Europeans.

Now, as elsewhere hinted, it was something caught from the Revolutionary Spirit that at Spithead emboldened the man-of-war's men to rise against real abuses, and afterwards at the Nore to make inordinate aggressive demands, successful resistance to which was confirmed only when the ring-leaders were hung for an admonitory spectacle to the anchored fleet. Yet in a way analagous to the operation of the Revolution at large the Great Mutiny, tho' by Englishmen naturally deemed monstrous at the time, doubtless gave the first latent prompting to those progressive reforms in the British navy which for its sailors makes it a service so much more humane than it was in the time of Nelson.

1406.3   Ananias]   Acts 5:3–5; see also note at 1405.31–1407.31.

1408.34   Peter the Barbarian]   Peter the Great of Russia (1672–1725), who founded St. Petersburg in 1703.

1409.15   usage]   Specific statutes required the captain to refer the case to the admiral; Melville suggests, however, that naval usage of the time would have sanctioned his conduct.

1417.27   *Somers*]   In this controversial case Commander Alexander Slidell Mackenzie, with a council of officers including Melville's cousin, Lieutenant Guert Gansevoort, found "in the necessities" of the situation, not in the Articles of War, justification for hanging the mutiny's instigator, Acting Midshipman Philip Spencer, along with the boatswain's mate, Samuel Cromwell, and a seaman, Elisha Small. (Melville's manuscript statement that the incident involved "a midshipman and two petty officers" is emended by Hayford and Sealts to "a midshipman and two sailors.") Hayford and Sealts show from manuscript evidence that Melville brought the elements of resemblance to this case into the story late in its composition.

1420.37–38   clergyman's announcement]   Melville penciled "Jonathan Edwards" in the margin of the manuscript.

1424.5   the Pope]   The anecdote concerns Pope Gregory the Great, but before he became Pope in 590.

1425.4   essential innocence]   Melville wrote at the foot of the manuscript page: "an irruption of heretic thought hard to suppress"—probably referring to some thought of his own on two omitted ensuing pages.

1425.12–13   musket . . . altar]   Melville jotted a note here for an addition
he did not make: "that musket of Beecher &c"—probably referring to the
twenty-five rifles, known as "Beecher's Bibles," given by the Reverend Henry
Ward Beecher's church to Free-Soil Kansas settlers.

1425.22–23   prophet . . . Elisha]   II Kings 2:11–13.

1431.23   *Athée*]   Melville left a blank space in the manuscript for this ship's
name, with the penciled notation "Athéiste," which his wife copied into the
blank space. Evidently he meant to check the correct French form, which
Hayford and Sealts supply along with its parenthetical translation, as Melville
supplied "(the *Hell*)" just below. Earlier he had named the ship the *Directory*.

1432.10   Nile and Trafalgar]   Nelson's victories over the French in 1798
and 1805.

1433.30   Billy Budd.]   At an earlier stage, Melville had switched the ballad
to come before this chapter (29), which ended the story, with a penciled coda
he later canceled: "Here ends a story not unwarranted by what sometimes
happens in this [*one undeciphered word*] world of ours—Innocence and infamy, spiritual depravity and fair repute."

1434.21   BILLY IN THE DARBIES]   A prose headnote to this ballad has
been shown by Hayford and Sealts to have been the origin for the story of
Billy Budd, developed by Melville through several phases, though never quite
finished, during the years of his retirement (1885–91).

LIBRARY OF CONGRESS CATALOGING IN PUBLICATION DATA

Melville, Herman, 1819–1891.

Pierre, Israel Potter, The piazza tales, The confidence-man, uncollected prose, Billy Budd, Sailor.

(The Library of America; 24)
"Harrison Hayford wrote the notes and selected the texts for this volume"—Prelim. p. v.

I. Hayford, Harrison, 1916-   . II. Title: Pierre. III. Title: Israel Potter. IV. Title: The Piazza Tales. V. Title: The Confidence-Man. VI. Title: Billy Budd, Sailor. VII. Series.

PS2382 1984   813′.3   84-11249

ISBN 0-940450-24-0

This book is set in 10 point Linotron Galliard, a face designed for photocomposition by Matthew Carter and based on the sixteenth-century face Granjon. The paper is Olin Nyalite and conforms to guidelines adopted by the Committee on Book Longevity of the Council on Library Resources. The binding material is Brillianta, a 100% rayon cloth made by Van Heek-Scholco Textielfabrieken, Holland. Composition by Haddon Craftsmen, Inc. and The Clarinda Company. Printing and binding by R. R. Donnelley & Sons Company. Designed by Bruce Campbell.